# PRAISE FOR DAVID SOSNOWSKI

## *Happy Doomsday*

"Reading David Sosnowski's dazzling new novel is like watching an Olympic gymnast fly through the air, do six impossible things, and stick the landing with a glorious grin. I loved *Happy Doomsday*!"

—Mary Doria Russell, Arthur C. Clarke Award–winning author of *The Sparrow*

"Part dystopian survival novel and part coming-of-age journey, the tale weaves back and forth between the three leads as they try to make sense of the catastrophe and create a new normal for themselves . . . A sharply topical and well-researched apocalypse narrative that shifts among black humor, grisly details, and moments of poignancy."

—*Kirkus Reviews*

"Captivating and darkly humorous, this new work by Sosnowski is perfect for fans of *The Walking Dead* or postapocalyptic survival stories."

—*Library Journal*

## *VAMPED*

"Sosnowski's wholly original mythology explains everything from the ideal vampire vacation spot to why their strip clubs keep the heat cranked up."

—*Washington Post*

"*Vamped* is not an outright spoof of vampire fiction—it has too much respect for its subject for that. But it does smuggle some welcome modernity and comic irreverence into the form . . . The chief pleasure of *Vamped* is in its rich imagination of the small details of modern vampire life."

—*New York Times Book Review*

"This darkly comic tale . . . provides intriguingly offbeat insights."

—*Entertainment Weekly*

"Few writers have taken as good advantage of the comic potential in vampiric metaphor as David Sosnowski does in his new novel *Vamped* . . . Audacious . . . unexpected and delightful."

—*U.S. News & World Report*

"Smart and funny . . . It's high time for a dark vampiric comedy."

—*Hollywood Reporter*

"Sosnowski's gleefully wicked sense of humor . . . and spot-on pop-culture references make *Vamped* a giddy page-turner. But at its core is a decidedly human tale."

—*Time Out New York*

"With wry wit and deft turns of phrase, David Sosnowski has penned a darkly humorous tale . . . A fresh breeze on a genre that can all too often be as stale as a dusty crypt. A fun read."
—Christopher Moore, author of *Noir*, *Lamb*, and *Bloodsucking Fiends*

"Inventive . . . intriguing . . . fun."

—*Publishers Weekly*

"Full of wit and charm, Sosnowski's fast-paced second novel . . . offers delightfully quirky characters and plenty of hilarious scenes."

—*Library Journal* (starred review)

"Sosnowski's easy mixture of warmth and humor makes for a winning, original tale about love in the unlikeliest of worlds."

—*Booklist*

## *RAPTURE*

"Sosnowski has staked out a patch of turf somewhere between Franz Kafka and Douglas Adams, and made it all his own."

—*Detroit Free Press*

"A delightfully fresh book . . . an imaginative, uplifting tale."

—*Ann Arbor News*

"A hilarious, knowing, and, yes, *uplifting* treatise on the possibilities of being."

—*New Age Journal*

"Spinning an inventive, new riff on contemporary angel mania, Sosnowski's first novel is a fanciful zeitgeist satire."

—*Publishers Weekly*

"What's subversive about Sosnowski is his subtlety; the most lurid passages are lyrical, and the funniest ones are slightly poetic. There's no way to race through his prose, or you'll miss layers of subtext."

—*Detroit Metro Times*

"Written with much wit and humor."

—*Library Journal*

"A witty, clever, original debut. Sosnowski writes like—well, an angel."

—*Kirkus Reviews* (starred review)

# Buzz Kill

# Also by David Sosnowski

*Happy Doomsday*

*Vamped*

*Rapture*

# Buzz Kill

DAVID SOSNOWSKI

47NORTH

This is a work of fiction. Names, characters, organizations, places, events, and incidents are either products of the author's imagination or are used fictitiously. Any resemblance to actual persons, living or dead, or actual events is purely coincidental.



Published by 47North, Seattle

www.apub.com

Amazon, the Amazon logo, and 47North are trademarks of Amazon.com, Inc., or its affiliates.

ISBN-13: 9781542005029 (hardcover)
ISBN-10: 1542005027 (hardcover)
ISBN-13: 9781542005043 (paperback)
ISBN-10: 1542005043 (paperback)

Cover design by Faceout Studio, Tim Green

Printed in the United States of America

First edition

*For Jane Dystel, with much respect,*
*admiration, and gratitude.*
*Without you, there would be no book to dedicate.*

# Prologue

Like any good murder mystery, it starts with a body—quite a lot of them, in fact. Not yet, but soon. At the moment, those who are still alive include a sixteen-year-old girl named Pandora Lynch, seated next to her grandmother Gladys, who is lying in her bed in a nursing home in Fairbanks, Alaska. The two are not talking, but not in any petulant way; it's because the latter has mostly stopped doing that and the former has her smartphone occupying her attention. Their reason for being together isn't to talk, but for the companionship, shared personhood, and a certain degree of warmth that bodies in proximity provide.

Pocketing her phone, Pandora looks over and notices how smooth the old woman's brow is, despite the many reasons it has for furrowing. A classic blessing-curse: the dementia has made her forget she has it. And forgetting one's troubles is the pro tip dermatologists don't often share, not with the profits on Botox injections being what they are. What Pandora wouldn't give to forget that she may well be looking at her own future—to the extent she still has one.

There are plenty of things she can use: pillows, a roommate's Dixied medications to amp or depress Gladys's own, even a bare hand placed over the nose and mouth. A few moments of struggling due to muscle memory, and Pandora could give Gladys what she'd asked for before she stopped asking for anything.

Reaching toward the pillow underneath her grandmother's fan of white hair, the young woman stops, distracted by old-people noises in the hallway. And when she looks back, her grandmother's lids are fluttering as her own courage flags. The old eyes roll in their sockets, aimlessly at first, before locking, pupils front and center and aimed right at their mysterious visitor.

"Hey," Pandora says.

"Hey," Gladys says back, repeating as she does with pretty much whatever the other says, including "f-you." Pandora knows because she's checked and still regrets it.

"You feeling okay?" she continues, going through the motions.

"Feeling okay," Gladys says back.

"Good."

"Good."

More old-people noises: the shuffle of tennis-shod feet across waxed linoleum; coughs, some wet; plaintive calls for help they may not need anymore, having fallen into a groove and gotten stuck; the roll of weighted silverware on plastic trays; the squeaky wheel of a cart.

Pandora's phone starts buzzing, a steady, unbroken hum. She doesn't answer, payback for the caller having ignored her for nearly twenty-four hours. She's been keeping careful track of the time because the responsible party has been keeping track too.

*Any second now,* Pandora thinks, joining the countdown in her head before turning to her grandmother. "I love you," she says.

"Love you," Gladys echoes.

Pandora had been coming to the old-people's storage facility since back when her grandmother had been someone she could talk to without feeling like she was talking to herself. She'd even told the old lady things she didn't tell her dad, perhaps because even at her best, Gladys would forget whatever Pandora told her by the next time she visited, but also because her grandmother was the only female relative she had left. She'd even told Gladys about a little stalker problem she'd been having. The old lady, who'd been eating grapes at the time, pursed her lips and wrinkled her brow before delivering her verdict: "Tell 'im to buzz off . . ."

Pandora had laughed so hard the words became a catchphrase caught in her grandmother's otherwise stick-proof memory. At first, it seemed she'd used it just to hear the sweet chime of her granddaughter's laughter but then kept it up, Pandora suspected, because those particular neural pathways were easier to retrace than the tangled alternatives.

"Hi, Gram."

"Buzz off."

"Who brought the flowers?"

"Buzz off."

"Is buzz *on*?"

"Buzz off."

Pandora learned this repetition was called echolalia and that many dementia patients lapsed into it toward the end, before they stopped talking altogether, followed by eating, followed by drinking, followed by living, the lucky ones allowed to slip away, as opposed to being fed through a tube. Pandora's grandmother had vetoed that and similar interventions by putting it in writing while she still could.

"Are you sure about this?" Pandora had asked, holding the clipboard as Gladys prepared to sign her own DNR order.

The old lady had paused, the pen a spaceship of plastic in the gnarled oak of her hand. "Do me a favor, will you?"

"Anything, Gram."

"Mind your own business," followed by her nearly undecipherable but still legal scrawl.

Pandora's nursing home visits began as punishment before morphing into love. Whether they were doing her grandmother any good now, she had no idea. Being honest, Pandora suspected her continuing pilgrimage was more for her own sake than Gladys's. It was like when she started a book, no matter how predictable, she felt duty-bound to see it through to the end. And so she kept coming, no matter how painful they became, these visits to a memory without a memory.

"Hi, Gram, remember me?"

Pandora has placed her hand over her buzzing pocket, trying to quiet it. Instead, the hum takes up sympathetically in her bones, traveling up her arm, across her shoulder, up her neck, and into her jaw, where it hooks into the rest of her skull. She can feel the buzz conducting itself through the tiny bones of her inner ear—the hammer, anvil, stirrup—all humming, making her wince and clench her teeth. Haptic feedback on steroids.

"I love you," she says.

"Love you," Gladys echoes.

And that's when Pandora hears the first thud, like a fist pounding the wall in the hallway outside the room, followed almost simultaneously by what sounds like a metal pail banging over, upending its contents in a single, slapping splash. Her head jerks toward the door in time to see the sudsy puddle crawling past the open entry. Bolting up to see if anybody needs help, she finds the first body instead, a janitor in his early thirties on his way to mop up the latest biohazard. He didn't make it and never will, becoming his own biohazard instead, judging from the pool of bright red spreading around where his head landed after creasing the drywall. Pandora reaches a hand toward his neck but stops. She doesn't need to check for a pulse; the still puddle his mouth and nose are resting in tells her he's already dead.

Steeling herself, Pandora lifts her head to look around, which is when she discovers that the janitor's body is far from being the only fresh corpse in the vicinity. At the nurses' station, the Ratched twins are both goners, one with her head thrown unnaturally back as her body swivels in its chair, while the other lies next to an overturned cart, surrounded by pill confetti. Farther down the hall, an attendant had been escorting a resident to the shower using what looked like a hammock chair on wheels only to succumb to mortality and gravity. Still dangling in the transport's trusses, the abandoned resident rocks slowly, his thinly feathered head turning, not sure what to make of any of this, not that that's anything new. And it's the same everywhere Pandora looks: all the able-bodied staff are dead while their demented charges remain upright, lost in their eternal now, waiting on meals, pills, and visitors that won't be coming anytime soon.

# PART ONE

# 1

Pandora Lynch wanted revenge. It started on her first day in a brand-new school—the first "traditional" school she'd ever attended—Ransom Wood High. She'd expected to be a stranger in a strange land but assumed she'd not be the only one. Homeschooling wasn't uncommon in Alaska, especially not in the more remote areas. And it wasn't unusual for kids to be sent to live with relatives once they became teenagers, so they could attend a real school, get used to socializing while trying their luck at making a go in the big city. Pandora had thought there'd be plenty of newbies to hide among, and there had been, until she made the fatal mistake of standing out by laughing at the wrong people at the wrong time.

She'd been minding her own business, standing by her locker between classes, swapping out one set of textbooks for another, when a posse of senior girl hockey players came shoulder-bumping down the hall. For a fleeting moment, Pandora imagined they were headed for her, an illusion made possible by the actual targets having lockers on either side of hers. They were boys, the targets, taller than Pandora but shorter than the clutch of senior girl hockey toughs heading their way.

"You know what I like about curlers?" the lead girl asked.

"Hair curlers or guy curlers?" a team player played along.

"Guy."

"No," the player continued playing, "what do you like about guy curlers?"

"They know what to do with a broom."

To be fair, Pandora was not the only person to laugh. She wasn't even the only *girl* to laugh. She just happened to be the one whose laugh attracted the attention of others like a lonely mouse in the reptile house. And no, it wasn't the sound; it was the face she made while doing it.

What followed was a classic butt-kick chain reaction, where the kicked becomes the kicker until you run out of butts. And in the hierarchy of high school athletics in the frozen North, there were the usual competitions among the grades and genders, but also the hockey players versus the skiers, versus, versus, versus until you hit the members of the freshman boys' curling team with the note that there was no *girls'* curling team because why reinforce domestic stereotypes?

The only butt lowlier than that of the freshman player on the boys' curling team was that of a freshman who was just trying to get an education sans athletics, preferably female, and one who made an outsize funny face when she laughed. And so:

"Nice face," the pride-wounded curler to the left of her said.

"Come again?"

"That's what *she* said," the belittled belittler to the right of her chimed in, followed by the broomsman, sweeping it home:

"Yeah, nice *cum* face, babe . . ."

Pandora pivoted her head, hoping to find some other object for this abuse, and, finding none, found herself wishing she'd brought a gun. This being Fairbanks, everybody had a few. Guns were tools, as common as hammers in Jesus's stepdaddy's workshop. But they were banned from school grounds because bullies, hormones, and handguns don't mix.

Absent the firepower to make her feelings known, Pandora jammed her backpack into her locker, slammed the door, and ran to the girls' bathroom so she could call her dad. She'd explain that she'd given it half a day and this high school thing wasn't working out. "So can you pick me up, *pleeeease*?"

Except her dad's phone went straight to voice mail. Okay, text. Thumb, thumb, thumb, send. Wait. Keep waiting. Immediate satisfaction not satisfied, she decided he must be working, screening Silicon Valley tech bros over Skype to make sure they didn't go on a shooting rampage or, worse yet, leave with a bunch of intellectual property on a thumb drive. Meaning she would have to either walk home or tough it out until she had a better idea of why she'd been singled out. Fortunately, a witness to Pandora's taunting met her at the sink, smiled, and pointed at the mirror, framing the two of them.

"Do you notice anything different between you and me?" the helpful girl asked.

Pandora looked and didn't.

"You ticklish?" the girl asked.

"Never checked," Pandora said. And so the other girl did. Answer: yep.

"What about now?" the smiling girl asked, indicating her own calm face with a Vanna White wave, followed by Pandora's, which could have served as a model for the "LOL" emoji.

"Whatever antidepressant you're on, I'd tweak it way back," her companion said, tracing a set of laugh lines that seemed dug by a garden trowel. "Maybe think about death more," she added.

"What's wrong with my face?" Pandora demanded after getting back home.

"Other than being adorable?" Roger Lynch countered, buying time.

"I'm serious."

"I can see that." And that was the problem. Whatever feeling Pandora was having was written all over her face—in italics, bold, and underlined. It was hard to miss, begging the question of how she had for going on sixteen years. The answer: she'd had help. Prior to its attending public high school, said face was rarely inflicted on anyone but family members, meaning her dad, who homeschooled her, and her grandparents, who babysat when the former needed a break. Plus, her father loved her face, especially when it was happy to see him, because her smiles took up a lot more facial real estate than your average smile and had the same contagious effect usually attributed to yawns. So: she'd smile, he'd smile, she'd smile even more—a veritable pandemic of happy; why spoil a good thing?

And it wasn't like her face was broadcasting constantly. Her resting face was just a face until given some cause for emoting, which it did on steroids. She hadn't thought to compare it to others she might see, and even subconsciously, she didn't notice the difference. Her face looked just like her father's when it emoted, which looked just like her grandmother's, which was like the faces she saw during the limited amount of television watching her dad allowed her as a child, which was largely composed of puppets and cartoons. If anything, out in public, she wondered what was wrong with other people.

"Maybe they're just tired," Roger had said. "Maybe they're having a bad day."

His own father, Herman, with his normal expressions, had gone back and forth between "being tired" and having "bad days," until Pandora finally stopped asking.

But now she was at it again, and this time, the thing that wasn't like the others was her.

"There's nothing *medically* wrong with you," Roger began his long-overdue explanation.

*"Medically?"* Pandora shouted. "There's nothing *medically* wrong . . ."

Roger made a tamping-down gesture. "Breathe," he suggested. "Try to calm yourself."

"I can't."

"I can see that."

"As can everybody *else*," Pandora stormed, finally realizing how it was her father always seemed to know what was going on inside her head. Early on, she'd imagined he might be psychic before deciding that no, it was probably because of his profession. Now she knew better. Her father hadn't been reading her mind; he'd been reading her *face*.

"Why didn't you *say* something?" she demanded, suddenly feeling like she'd led her entire life with a trail of toilet paper stuck to her shoe.

"I *did*," Roger insisted. "I told you we both have your *grandmother's* face."

Pandora tried picturing the face in question but couldn't. It had been years since she last saw it in person at Grandpa Herman's funeral.

"Is there even a *name* for this?" she asked, the words coming out like air from a punctured tire.

Roger nodded. "Hyperexpressive face syndrome," he said. "But back when I was a kid, Dad would say that Mom or I were 'exubing' for 'exuberance' when we were happy or excited. Pretty much everything else he just called our 'stink eye.'"

*"Stink eye!"* Pandora fairly exploded, her eyebrows flying upward—excessively—like a pair of startled birds. "I'm *doomed* . . . ," she wailed, letting her head sink so her hair curtained around it.

"The Botox people are calling it restless face syndrome," Roger went on, imagining more information might help. "The implication is it's like resting bitch face, but treatable, presumably through the miracle of botulism-facilitated facial paralysis."

Not that all sufferers actually *suffered* from the condition, Roger hastened to add when Pandora seemed amenable to the idea of having a deadly bacterium shot into her forehead.

"Take Jim Carrey," he said. "He's like the HEFS poster child. And he's monetized his affliction quite handsomely." Plus, there was Roger himself, who'd paired his HEFS with a sense of empathy that helped turn his face into a magnifying mirror of his clients' emotional states, creating a face people were bound to pour their hearts out to.

"Now *that's* a billable asset," he concluded, as well he might, being a therapist after all.

But Pandora was a girl, and her father's examples were all guys. And guys always got off easy when it came to looks. A guy could have a face that others found comical, or interesting, or hypersympathetic in a confession-eliciting kind of way. But for women, there were only two options, facewise: 1) somewhere on the spectrum between cute and gorgeous or 2) other. And Pandora's restless face put her squarely in the latter camp, one she could already see taking its place among those of the crazy bitches who got fed up and cut a bitch before going to prison to become some other crazy bitch's bitch—if *Orange Is the New Black* was any indicator.

"So," she said, finally, training a hyperserious eye on her father, "which am I?"

Roger aimed a hyperconfused expression back at hers. "Which what?"

"Which Jim Carrey?" she asked. "*Spotless Mind* or *Mask*?"

Her father did that teeter-totter thing with his hand and sucked in his lips, so much so that his mouth looked disturbingly like an anus.

"Somewhere in between?" she translated.

Her father nodded as Pandora's face slowly constricted ass-ward.

Pandora Lynch was more than her face; she was also scary smart, something her father had concluded not because of parental bias, but because of a series of IQ tests he'd given her throughout her life, providing Stanford-Binet-certified proof. It was because of her brain that Roger hadn't focused on the superficial covering she faced the world with. Her mind was what impressed him. And it was the hungriness of that mind that led to her first nickname: Dora the Implorer.

From the moment she could speak, Pandora wielded the word *why* like a lethal weapon. Why this? Why that? In this, she was like a lot of kids before their hopes and dreams were crushed. Whether his daughter's barrage of whys was actually excessive or only seemed that way because he lacked a partner to share answering duties with, Roger didn't know. His wife hadn't survived having their daughter, leaving Roger as sole parent. And so, instead of saying "Mama," a word most kids come to as a byproduct of suckling, Pandora had landed on what she'd heard her father say most often after his wife's passing—"Why?"—the crowbar word she used to learn all the rest.

Soon, his daughter's whys started sprouting other whys, branching and replicating, forming a fractal set of whys, looping self-referentially as she why'd her own why-ing until the victim of her curiosity lost it and shouted or got up and tried walking away, only to have his insistent inquirer wrap herself around his leg.

It was in self-defense, then, that Roger introduced his daughter to her first computer, a kid-proofed laptop, hermetically sealed in chunky pink plastic with rounded edges and ruggedized just shy of military field specifications to withstand being dropped from as high as a statistical kid in its recommended age range might drop it during the course of statistically ordinary use. He'd introduced her to it like it was another person—or billions, which it was—by cracking open its clamshell, booting it up, and clicking through to the Google homepage.

"Pandora," he said, doing the introductions, "I give you the world.

"World," he continued, "I give you my daughter, Pandora Lynch."

He showed her how to search with her voice, seeing as he hadn't taught the three-year-old to read yet. After that, he trusted Pandora to ask "the 'puter" all the questions she'd been asking him. The top answer usually spoke itself aloud, and by looking at the words on the screen as they spoke themselves, Pandora taught herself not only the answer to her questions, but also how to read by the time she reached four. Many happy years of surfing followed, Pandora collecting bread crumbs of information like Pac-Man gobbling up dots, content to end every day smarter than she'd started it, and eager for the next day to begin.

Her next day at school was worse. The curlers flanking her locker had decided to make her infamous. While one stood off to the side, smartphone at the ready, his accomplice approached her from behind with a printout from an anti-chewing-tobacco website, featuring a collage of jawless faces and metastatic gums.

"Hey, Emo," the accomplice said, slapping Pandora on the back, leaving the printout attached through the miracle of spray adhesive. Knowing something must be up, she reached around, tap-tapping until she hit the rattle of paper and pulled away a modern-day upgrade to the "Kick Me" sign. Bringing it around to where she could see it, Pandora reacted as planned, while the amateur videographer caught her face in all its uploadable glory.

Thus Pandora Lynch went from merely self-conscious teen to internet meme. After editing it to remove any trace of the setup, the pranksters provided the world with two formats: a GIF of Pandora's face going from nearly normal to Munch's *The Scream* in real time and a triptych of JPEGs—normal, transition, and money shot—ready to be captioned with variations of "*X* be like . . ." or "Me when I . . . ," while the GIF was used uncaptioned as a reacticon to whatever the latest political absurdity happened to be.

The trouble was, it was mesmerizing, watching it loop, over and over. Though it was her own face, even Pandora couldn't stop watching until—hypnotized by the repetition—she stopped seeing herself and started seeing this crazy woman the rest of the world was watching. The spell was such that looking away caused her to imagine the pock-pock of two popped corks—her eyes—being ripped out. A pretty miserable state of affairs for a cyber native—being stalked by her own face online—and a perfectly good cause for revenge.

By the time she turned seven, Pandora had learned an important lesson about the internet: its answers got better—or more interesting—once you got past the first page of search results. Because there was rarely just one answer to anything, and once you dispensed with expecting the answer to be correct, that's when the web bloomed, revealing worlds within worlds, some of them flat, others ruled by an assortment of dark forces, all of them hidden many pages deep. Which got her wondering once again: Why?

Why were computer searches arranged like that, and how did the computer know all this stuff? Her laptop was supposedly kid-proof, but who were they kidding? She googled "How do you take apart a computer?" and—no dummy—printed out the instructions before following them. By the time Roger returned from what he'd thought was a quick dash to the Safeway, he was greeted by the sight of his inquisitive daughter surrounded by a spray of Phillips-head screws, scattered key caps, a dead screen, a chip-dotted emerald-green motherboard, and the pink plastic clamshell, split open like an Easter egg.

"Pandora," he said, "what on earth . . . ?"

To which his daughter intoned the three-note trademark of a certain microprocessor manufacturer, followed by, "Look what I found inside!"

Roger was not amused. "You're not getting another one," he threatened, but who did he think he was kidding? Pandora put the old one back together, stopping just long enough for her father to fetch the fire extinguisher before plugging the power brick back in. "Stand back," he warned, eyeing the power button peripherally as he reached out and pushed it. The etherealized da-doo-da-doo of Windows Vista starting up chimed from the tinny speaker.

"Well, I'll be damned," he said—not a prediction, necessarily, but . . .

Back in business, the ever-curious child found curiouser and curiouser corners of cyberspace to investigate. Soon, Pandora discovered that the best the web had to offer couldn't be gotten at through Google or Bing or even, God help her, Yahoo! Nope. The most stimulating internet resources were found by going through The Onion Router (a.k.a. Tor), a one-time naval research project in online anonymity subsequently bequeathed to all manner of questionable humanity.

On the other side of that acronym, Pandora found conspiracy nuts and militarized free-speechers, illicit dealers and their buyers, freaks, fetishists, fringe dwellers, and the frankly disgusting. And she loved it all, the so-called dark web, not in spite of its creeps but because of them and what their presence implied: privacy.

With respect to that precious commodity, Pandora was already living the future by having none. Whether that lack was a feature of her life or a bug was hard to say but nevertheless the unavoidable byproduct of living in a cabin sans door, excepting the front and bathroom ones. Per Roger, interior doors were impediments to airflow and efficient heating. And so, in their place, cheaper and less airtight shower curtains would have to do, and did. It was this lack of privacy, in fact, that emboldened her to invade that of others, with the help of another interest she nurtured online: hacking.

She'd loved the idea of it before she ever did it, the way hacking made use of a skill set she'd been working on for as long as she could remember: the one-two punch of curiosity and coding. And once she got serious, Pandora found that a lot of the heavy lifting had already been done. The dark web provided whole libraries of precoded, hacker-approved hacks; customizable widgets; Trojan applets; documented exploits; and the code needed to exploit them. She found herself thinking in pseudocoding flowcharts, applying these to her ethical choices when it came to taking advantage of certain vulnerabilities, thinking she'd do *X* if *Y* occurred, one action collapsing the branching possibilities once she'd committed to it, and so on. Wondering if she should get parental permission before, say, hacking into the teleprompters at *Fox & Friends* with some choice passages from *Das Kapital*, Pandora would visualize a sideways diamond with "Ask Dad?" in the center, the "Yes" branching left, "No" branching right. And when "Yes" bottomed out in a string of *Zzzz*'s, the young hacktivist decided to take the path of parental ignorance, rumored to be the source of bliss, though whose was never specified.

# 2

It was a perfect day for sitting on a dock by the bay, and so that's what George Jedson (yeah, yeah, he knew) was doing, wasting time on a park bench overlooking the Golden Gate Bridge. He should have been in school but was on stakeout instead, waiting for a certain tech weenie who could usually be found at the pier around noon. George had often watched the target sit and sip at his to-go latte, watching the toy cars going to and fro across the bridge or the container ships passing underneath full of more Chinese crap for the masses.

George had first noticed the guy's badge while standing in line at one of San Fran's pop-up artisanal coffee places. The badge was chipped, laminated, and hung on a lanyard the wearer had flipped over his shoulder as he prepared to pay with his phone before making a big deal of stopping, then reaching into his jacket pocket to remove an actual wallet. "I'm feeling retro today," he announced to the inked-and-pierced barista before extracting a twenty for his anally specific latte, barely letting the change make skin contact before slipping it into the tip jar next to the register.

*"Grazie,"* the barista said, in accordance with a recent corporate-policy memo.

The badge was the guy's way of broadcasting his importance outside the office, the iconic *Q* for the social-media giant Quire (pronounced "choir," as in "preaching to the . . .") clearly visible. In imitation of its CEO, this particular middle-managing Q-ling wore an outrageously plaid sports jacket shot through with greens going one way and purples another, the tartan of no known Scottish clan, but almost as iconic as the aforementioned *Q*, suggesting that its wearer was an aspirant who might occasionally come within the same faciotemporal space as the *actual* target. Recognizing the badge's significance, George downloaded the company's management chart while still waiting for his own order. And bingo, Mr. Plaid was well within three degrees of separation from the CEO of Quire. Suspicions confirmed, George proceeded to tail his subject outside.

But instead of heading to the nearest Q shuttle or calling an Uber, rather than slumming by cable car or godhelpus BART, the man-coat combo had headed to the dock where George now sat, waiting for the combo's circadian return.

That first time, George's man in the middle had just sat there on the bench, nursing his latte, watching seagulls dive-bombing out of the clear blue sky to snatch up some floating detritus or sweeping in toward the paved dock to forage among the trash receptacles there. The whole "real-world engagement" vibe the guy was sending was transparent at best. He was playing the role of "tech guy taking a tech break," which meant his two or three phones were set to vibrate in the pockets of the suit coat he'd draped over the back of the bench, his arm stretched so his hand, forearm, and elbow were in covert contact with each device, waiting for a haptic hum to give his life meaning again. The other dead giveaway was the wrist resting unnaturally on his knee, cuff hiked, keeping a chunky analog watch within eyeshot so he'd know the second it was okay to jack back into the world he was taking a break from.

But then, a catalyzing moment—the sort that turns a disparate group of strangers into something new: an audience. Entering from whichever curtain he'd been waiting behind, a greasily clad homeless man came into view, one sole slapping as he approached the railing with a bulging grocery bag—a locally illegal, plastic one—from which dripped what appeared to be blood. Watching as the man leaned over the rail, George rose slightly, not totally prepared to witness some homeless guy's suicide, but . . . only to settle back when he realized the man was pulling on a rope of braided yellow plastic that had gone unnoticed until the bum started reeling it in, great, dripping coils piling up on the pavement as he hauled away.

Eventually, the man reached the end of his rope, which was attached to a mossy green trap with assorted claws and insectile legs poking through the slats. Releasing a latch underneath, the greasy guy dumped out about a dozen crabs along with the half-eaten remains of a chicken carcass. This last was returned to the bay with a fling and a splash before being replaced with fresher bait from the bloody bag. Another, more labored fling and the trap disappeared as well, followed by rapidly unspooling coils of plastic rope.

The crabber then started sorting through his catch, deftly flipping shellfish onto their carapaces, the better to examine their worthiness, while preventing their skittering escape. All were deemed fit with the exception of one, which seemed to have lost a leg along the way and whose shell was cracked and oozing something that looked like guacamole. This one the crabber kicked aside like a hockey puck, albeit one with seven highly agitated legs trying to claw up the sky. Within seconds, the dock became an outtake from *The Birds* as seagulls swooped in from all quarters to descend on the helpless delicacy.

A lesbian couple engaged in some major PDA a few benches down turned disapprovingly at the sound before taking their love to some other part of town.

"It's just *nature*, ladies," the sports coat called at their retreating backs before reaching into a weighted pocket and removing a phone. He open-tweezed his fingers, zooming in before tapping a snap to document the carnage. "Dog eat dog," he continued, narrating aloud the keywords of his upcoming post. "Hashtag Darwin. Hashtag I will survive."

*Well,* George thought, *I guess we'll just have to see about that.*

Like a lot of his hacks, George did it to see if he could. The "it" in this case: the remote hijacking of a luxury EV owned by a certain CEO who'd been snapped stepping out of it at TechCrunch Disrupt, Davos, and the West Coast premiere of *Hamilton*. The car in question was the latest would-be Tesla killer, a limited edition called the Voltaire, a double-meaning moniker intended to conjure up both *electricity* and *environmental friendliness*, with faint echoes of the Enlightenment. George had gotten the VIN by hacking into the California Department of Motor Vehicles database. The attack itself would involve a cyber missile custom tuned to seek out personally identifiable information of the sort George had given it, shuttling back and forth across the global loom of wired and wireless interconnectivity, looking for a seventeen-digit go code to do the thing it was programmed to do, which in this case was taking over the vehicle's so-called "copilot mode" (a legal nicety to keep the owner responsible for any crashes that might occur during what was basically a live beta test of an autonomous vehicle). Once in, George would hijack the navigation system and have the vehicle deliver itself to an address of his choosing.

The hack itself didn't require a lot of original coding, not with all the drop-in script available out there. All he had to do was open a window; Ctrl-A, Ctrl-C, and then Ctrl-V the grab into his text editor; after which, a delete here, an insert there, new parameters for the conditionals, reassign a few variables, and voilà, he had custom-built malware ready for compiling. He'd started with the hackers' gift that kept giving, the Stuxnet worm, which had already bred a whole family of cyber weapons of mass destruction, from Stuxnet II, the Reckoning; to Son of Stuxnet; the Bride of Stuxnet; and It Takes Two to Stuxnet: This Time It's Personal.

A couple of white hats had already demonstrated that the data link connector for a car's onboard diagnostic system could be used as a back door into pretty much any subsystem on the vehicle's controller area network, allowing a hacker to turn on the air conditioning, blare the sound system, or even apply the brakes. The same researchers who'd exposed these vulnerabilities were quick to stress that a hacker would first have to gain "physical access" to the inside of the vehicle to do any of this (the implied warning: beware of valets with taped glasses). As press releases went, it was the typical mixed message about all the computers on cars nowadays, namely: "Worry, but don't worry. The hackers would have to jump through *so* many hoops . . ."

The only problem was—and George would be happy to point this out if anybody ever asked—hackers *live* to jump through hoops. Hoop jumping is, in fact, what makes hacking *interesting*. And physically plugging in to a car's data link was one way to get controller access, but there was also the infotainment system, the two-dollar hooker of Bluetooth devices; finding something to connect to was basically *its job*. Systems like, say, the driver's phone. And if that phone happened to have a Trojan horse that executed once its Bluetooth shook hands with the car's hands-free system . . .

George nicknamed this particular exploit the Big Blue Daisy Chain of Mass Destruction. All he had to do was get within Bluetooth range of a smartphone that might in turn get within range of the smartphone belonging to a certain CEO and proud owner of a midlife-crisis EV that came with copilot mode already installed.

So George trailed his latte-liking, barista-flirting, middle-aged, middle-managing cyber weenie from latte assembly line to the dockside park bench, day after day, getting his pattern down, looking for an opportunity when he finally decided to just walk right into the guy while staring at his phone.

"Excuse me," George apologized, blotting at a puff of escaped milk foam.

"You almost made me *drop* my *phone*," the guy who'd dropped his latte prioritized.

"I *said* I was sorry."

"You need to watch where you're going," George's target continued. "Whatever Pokémon you were hunting can wait. What if I wasn't here to run interference and you had tripped over that railing?"

"I guess I owe you my life, then."

"Well, I wouldn't go that—"

"Nope," George continued. "You saved my life. Now you're responsible for me. What's your last name? I'll change mine. Mind if I call you *Dad*?"

"You're crazy," the target said, backing away.

"Crazy for feeling like this." Pause. "Why are you running away? Dad! Stop, Dad. *Please* . . ."

And there it went, George's Trojan horse riding in the pocket of the sports coat, an exquisite bit of code ready to hop from phone to phone and up the org chart until it found its true target and waited for him to call his private jet from his car and . . .

Bingo.

As tech giants go, V.T. Lemming, founder and CEO of Quire Inc., was a late bloomer. While he claimed to be a contemporary of Steve Jobs—he'd tripped and head-butted the future father of the iPhone at a Home Brew Computer Club meeting when V.T. was only ten—the younger man seemed to lack Jobs's luck and timing. Pretty much everything he came up with for years was an inferior copycat product as likely to crash a person's system as function as advertised. And so his spreadsheet software could only add and subtract columns of figures—the key functions business owners would want in such a product, he'd assured himself. A poor man's PowerPoint that couldn't handle graphics or animation. A web browser that seemed to actually prioritize infected or malicious sites. A media player that wouldn't work with pirated content.

And then the Wireless Application Protocol (WAP) was introduced by a consortium of cell phone manufacturers, allowing mobile devices to connect to the internet and developers to sell games over the air, thus laying the groundwork for Google Play and the App Store that would come several years later. Having soured on the Windows and Mac operating systems by this time, V.T. gave WAP a look and was reminded of the simpler eight-bit computers of his youth. Mixing nostalgia with practicality (fewer lines of code meant less time investment between failures), the not-getting-any-younger programmer proceeded to work his way through a series of betas and misfires until he'd become thoroughly disgusted with the entire tech industry. Resolving to ball up his contempt into one ridiculously pointless game, V.T. decided on an homage to a popular electronic pet of a few years prior known as the Tamagotchi, which in its Americanized and cellular incarnation became *My Hippo*. A textbook example of truth in advertising, *My Hippo* consisted of nothing more than a hippo standing incongruously in front of an old barn. Users could spend real money to buy their hippo fake stuff—a straw hat, a stalk of grass to munch from the corner of its mouth, a polka dot skirt or leather biker jacket (the gender of the hippo was said to be "proprietary" and was never divulged). The only movement in the entire—it was hard to call it a game, per se—*thing* was the briefest grin from "your hippo" when you bought it stuff. And true to H.L. Mencken's dictum that no one ever went broke underestimating the intelligence of the American people, *My Hippo* proceeded to do exactly what he had assumed—maybe even hoped—it wouldn't: it made money.

And that was how *a* V.T. Lemming became *the* V.T. Lemming, something the parents who named him Vladimir Thaddeus would never have imagined. Their goal at the time had been to offset the suicidal baggage packed into the family name. Or as his father, John Lemming, predicted, "The kids'll be so busy trying to figure out what to do with 'Vladimir Thaddeus' they'll never make it to 'Lemming'"—a nice thought that (predictably) fell short of reality.

Quire was V.T.'s second act for which he could claim no creative input except for having enough money to buy a start-up originally named Pulp!t (pronounced "pulpit"). The platform had potential, he thought, falling as it did between the newly popular site known as Myspace and Facebook before it dropped the *the*.

Though younger than either, V.T. Lemming had joined Steve Jobs and Bill Gates in the troika of Silicon Valley's elders—the ones the industry pointed to whenever accusations of ageism were lobbed by critics who (it was not-so-secretly assumed) probably believed the internet was kept alive by elves pushing shopping carts full of vacuum tubes. V.T. even showed up—not entirely willingly—on the March 2007 cover of AARP's magazine next to the words *Gray Matters*, when he was still in his early forties.

More than a decade had passed since that cover story, making what happened even more impressive. Because while George had imagined his hack going a number of ways, he hadn't counted on V.T., now in his early fifties, coming along for the ride.

The Voltaire had been circling City Lights Bookstore autonomously for a half hour, sparing its billionaire owner the cost of parking while he shopped publicly for poetry. It was his PR people's idea to dispel rumors that V.T. had actually died and been replaced by a robotic double. Something by Bukowski, they thought, to guard against seeming effete while at the same time lending a certain aura of grit and danger to his public persona.

They needn't have bothered. Because as V.T. reached for the door handle of his idling ride, George's daisy-chain hack completed its last link, all the doors thunked shut, and the Voltaire pulled away from the curb and back into the flow of traffic.

George could hear V.T. swearing through the phone he'd activated remotely. He planned on uploading the audio and (fingers crossed) video once the CEO removed the phone from his pocket to report a runaway EV. But then the swearing became panting. George brought up thumbnails of the video feeds from several security cams in the area. The old man was running after the car. Even more amazingly, he caught it—though its stopping for a traffic light helped.

And now—no, yes, shit—he was crawling onto the hood! Banging on the windshield? Yeah, that'll help. No, wait, *not* banging. V.T. was placing his hands strategically, in various locations on the glass, perhaps trying to block whatever sensors or telemetry the navigation system was relying on. A decent thought, though ultimately unsuccessful, as the car started up again once the light changed, and the CEO of Quire almost rolled off into traffic.

Almost—but didn't. Instead, he dug both hands into the well between windshield and hood where the wipers hid until needed.

More swearing, more holding on for dear life, more hacked security and traffic cams activated as the Voltaire-plus-CEO prepared to cross the Bay Bridge while George sat miles away at a public-library computer, monitoring, prepared to shut the stunt down if it looked like he was about to endanger the public. By the time the Voltaire made it to the middle of the bridge, George was able to dispense with the hijacked cams in favor of streaming the helicopter feed going out live to all the local television stations, thanks to the celebrity of the passenger he'd acquired for his little joyride.

The original plan had been for the car to drive itself to the library George had been surreptitiously living in since running away from foster care. He wasn't planning to steal it, per se. He'd promised himself one ride in V.T.'s midlife crisis, after which he'd abandon it to the resourcefulness of the local, vengeful capitalists. That plan was no longer viable—not with traffic copters and highway patrol in pursuit.

And so George cut to the chase—so to speak—and drove the Voltaire straight to where he planned to dump it, taking I-80 to 880 south toward San Jose and the airport. Hopping off at the High Street exit, George piloted the hijacked auto and its impromptu hood ornament to Alameda Avenue and the Oakland Home Depot parking lot. The original plan was to do this sometime after closing—around midnight, say. Instead George found himself bringing the vehicle to a stop under the chop of helicopter rotors and the shouts of highway patrol officers demanding that the driver who wasn't there exit with hands up. All this in the bright California sun, on live TV, already being remixed and mashed up and posted all over the world.

Why George did it was a fair question. And the answer? George knew what he'd say his motive was if he ever got caught: a smile. Sure, he could have liquidated the vehicle; he could definitely use the money, being short of cash ever since leaving the foster care system a few years ahead of schedule. But George needed the smiles more than money. He needed them to neutralize the poison in the air everywhere he went nowadays—online, especially, but in real life too. That's what he'd say if he ever got caught, that the world had become so angry. It had been angry before but had gotten even worse since Russian hackers and sensationalism-seeking algorithms turned everything up to eleven. And George, a foster kid, had done time at both ends of the political spectrum, eating breakfast to *Fox & Friends* in one house, doing dinner with Rachel Maddow in another, neither meal sitting well on a stomach that felt like battery acid had been absorbed into it by osmosis.

He'd seen a series of bumper stickers on the minivan of the fosters he ran away from. "Coexist," one sticker had said, spelled out in the range of religious icons, next to another that advised him to "Practice Random Acts of Senseless Kindness." He'd had hope—for a second. But then his new family handed him a razor blade to scrape the stickers off. Turns out George wasn't the only secondhand thing they'd recently acquired.

So yeah, smiles. That's what he'd say. Little facial breaks from the general zeitgeist; that's why he'd done it. That they came at the expense of one very *unsmiling* CEO, well, that was the funny thing about rich people: their smiles and the smiles of everyone else were inversely correlated, a tragedy for one being pure comedy for the others.

# 3

Pandora's first idea was to beat the crap out of the boys who'd memed her—but she was concerned their balls would prove too tempting a target. It wasn't that she had any qualms about fighting dirty or below the belt—that was Asymmetrical Warfare 101—but the knee-balls combo was such a cliché, and she prided herself for thinking outside the box. Her means of revenge, she thought, should reflect who she was as a person—but not so much so that the CSI people could trace it back to her.

Pandora decided to avoid anything overtly computer related, for fear that would point back to her. Not that she advertised her hacking chops, but her dad's job did, what with the satellite dish outside their cabin and the fact that the Lynches were cybercitizens way before almost anyone else in Fairbanks. Add that she'd already been pulled from class twice to perform pro bono IT consulting in the principal's office and it was pretty clear that they had her number. It was a shame, too, because there were a few exploits that would have been fun.

For example, she could have easily gotten into the school's computer, which was still running an unpatched version of Windows XP. Not only that, but the student database was unencrypted, and not even a real database, but an Excel spreadsheet with the original .xlx extension, meaning they hadn't upgraded their Office suite since 2007. All she'd have to do was change the culprits' grades to Fs. Except when she looked at what they'd managed without her help (D pluses, a C minus), the incremental change hardly seemed worth it.

She could mess with their coach, she guessed. He had a pacemaker that could be updated over the air, installed—he liked to brag—"factory new" by a crack cardio team in Seattle. "Over the air" meant wireless, which meant it was an inadequately secured IoT device, like a smart thermostat or baby monitor, but surgically implanted in the guy's chest. She could make his heart skip a beat or overclock the regulating mechanism so that he hiccupped uncontrollably.

But it wasn't the coach who'd humiliated her; the closest he came was not teaching his young charges to act like human beings. Plus, there was always the risk he'd wind up dying, which would be murder, so there was that.

Not that hacking was exclusively about computers; it was a way of looking at the world. You hacked by viewing everything a bit off center, peripherally, looking for what everybody else *wasn't* seeing. And what was she looking for? Holes, exploits, hot buttons, unexamined assumptions, dropped guards.

The breakthrough came during sex ed and brought her full circle to that thing her adversaries could be trusted to cherish above all: their balls—or thereabouts. She wouldn't be using her knee, though; she'd be using chemistry, and their expectation of privacy. In sex ed, they'd been getting the scared-abstinent lesson plan, and Pandora had noticed a theme when it came to STI symptoms: "A burning sensation while urinating."

After seeing the same phrasing come up for the third time in a row, Pandora thought, *I'd like to give 'em a burning sensation when they pee . . .*

And thus the idea for her revenge took shape. Like Newton and his apple, like Archimedes and his bath—like Jobs and Gates walking out of Xerox PARC with a fortune in other people's ideas—Pandora had found her inspiration. She was so pleased with herself she had to dip her head so her hair would hide her smile—the one otherwise visible by satellite, or so she'd heard.

In retrospect, she could see how her revenge might be mistaken for an act of terrorism. There'd been flames and bodily injuries, after all. Not that she intended to hurt anyone, just scare them is all. But that was splitting hairs and not entirely honest. The truth was, once you've committed to blowing up urinals, you already bought into whatever collateral damage comes with it.

The plan's ingredients were beyond simple: empty gel caps and pure sodium. She thought about stealing the latter from the school's chem lab but decided she didn't want to get her science teacher, Mr. Vlasic, in trouble. Apparently, ever since *Breaking Bad*, science teachers all over the United States were viewed with suspicion—a status they'd enjoyed since the Scopes Monkey Trial, truth be told. And so, crossing her fingers, Pandora checked eBay: yep, she could get more than enough sodium from a chemical supply company for around sixty-five bucks. And seeing as she was online anyway: yep, gel caps too. She got tracking numbers on both so she could get to the packages before her dad did. And that was that: Project Burning Sensation was a go. So to speak.

The sodium arrived in the form of grayish metal ingots packed in mineral oil to keep them from reacting with the air. Though metallic, the bullet-sized lumps were soft and could be cut to the desired size with a pocket knife, albeit carefully. Sodium with the same purity as, say, Ivory soap will react with anything, including water, in which it literally burns. Even packed in mineral oil, Pandora's samples had a chalky patina of oxidation, which worked in her favor by ensuring the stuff didn't explode while she packed curls of it into her empty gel caps.

Once she'd collected a decent supply, all that remained was sneaking the caps into the boys' bathroom and then waiting for the gelatin to dissolve under a steady stream of recycled Gatorade. It helped that whether it was the boys' hockey or curling team, once they left the ice, they could be counted on to hit the nearest restroom en masse, usually joking about which favored anatomical part they'd nearly lost to the cold and/or comparing their pending urinary performance to that of a racehorse. Pandora would time her deposit to coincide with the freshman curling team's search for relief, then loiter with smartphone in hand, waiting for the fireworks to begin.

"You boys pissed off the wrong girl," she'd say, recording as they fled and tripped, pants spotted, unbuckled, or both, her zoom reserved for the troublesome two who had wronged her. See how they like being famous for a while.

A janitor had set out his yellow plastic easel, closing the boys' bathroom so he could clean it. Ever since her face went viral, Pandora had grown accustomed to hiding it, and so she did now, along with the rest of her, standing off to one side in the shadows, waiting for the clack of the easel being folded back up, her cue for action. She was prepared to deposit three, four caps per urinal for the dozen or so she figured there must be, judging from the line disparity between the men's and women's bathrooms after a feature ended at the Regal Goldstream downtown. Once inside, however, Pandora was shocked to find a mere four spots, a third of what she'd expected. She was also surprised to see there weren't any partitions separating the urinals, making her wonder just what sorts of savages she was dealing with—not that she had time to figure that out, not with the sound of the frosh curling team already clomping up the hallway. Hastily dumping a handful of caps per pisser, Pandora darted out again just in time.

Back in the safety of shadow, Pandora wondered if her miscalculation was due to factors she wouldn't have thought to consider. Was standing instead of sitting *that* much faster? Maybe guys were motivated to pee quickly, standing shoulder to shoulder with nothing to shield them from looky-loos on either side. Or maybe the urinals were gratuitous because everybody's bladder got shy and they just held it until they got home. That last one could be a problem; her plan didn't work without plenty of fluid to kick off the chemistry.

What she hadn't counted on was anyone's pants catching fire. And while she'd figured on screams of panic, she'd not counted on the screams of pain. She'd also not factored in the first escapee slipping in a puddle of his own pee, creating a dog pile of dudes tripping over him, followed by still others rushing to bust out the fire extinguisher to save what they could of the Human Torch's manhood. She hadn't counted on the fire alarm going off, or the sprinklers going on, which set off the remaining gel caps while the entire drenched student body had to evacuate—in Fairbanks, in early October, on a day when the temperature was below freezing. In the general rush, she'd forgotten to deliver and record her badass piss-off speech, which was probably for the best, listening to what her shivering classmates had to say about the unlikelihood of the responsible party living for very much longer.

Roger Lynch was screening a client on Skype when his pocket buzzed. Trying not to be obvious, he watched the thumbnail image of himself as he tweezed the phone out from his pocket and checked one screen while simulating attention to the other. Nods. Mmm-hmmms. All of which was for naught when he noticed it was a text alert from Pandora's school, warning of a "possible terrorism-related incident" while assuring all parents (excluding those of the boy who'd been rushed to the ER, not for genital immolation but because he was having a panic attack) that their children—though chilled—were safe, sound, and available for collection.

"Sorry," Roger blurted. "Family emergency. Gotta cut this short . . ."

"But," his client began, because that was the kind he specialized in, self-involved techies phoning it in from their offices or cubes at Quire headquarters, all convinced they'd lucked into the perfect therapeutic arrangement, with a therapist they'd never meet IRL, who was just a Skype call away and could be turned off when things got too heavy.

"Sorry," Roger said again, feeling a malpractice suit even as he prepared to click off, before clicking off anyway.

Unplugging his F-150's underhood heater from the garage outlet and checking his mirrors, Roger backed out of the drive, tires squeaking over bone-dry snow, all the while wondering why a terrorist would pick Fairbanks. New York, he could see; LA, sure; hell, Muncie, for Pete's sake, but *Alaska*? Did ISIS or whoever have such a surplus of suicide bombers they could piss them away on a part of America many Americans weren't thoroughly convinced was actually part of their country?

Not that the text said anything about suicide bombers. Or bombs of any sort. It had even waffled on it being terrorism, qualifying it fore ("possible") and aft ("-related"). Not that any of those quibbles mattered, not when it concerned his daughter.

Joining the chugging fleet of worried parents in all manner of assault vehicles, Roger noticed several official-looking, parkaed individuals in helmets and dark glasses, their bulletproof vests buckled up over a puffy inch or so of down. The FPD's SWAT team, judging from the huge letters emblazoned across the back of each vest. Who knew Fairbanks had such a thing? That Homeland Security money had to be flowing pretty indiscriminately ever since you-know-who pulled off you-know-what. One of the SWAT team members had a dog that didn't seem to be taking its job as seriously as the guy holding its leash, deigning to be petted by the students milling around, good-boy-ing it, all chugging in the cold afternoon air.

Roger spotted his daughter in the crowd, hiding behind her hair, which was rimmed with frost from having been sprinkled before being forced to evacuate. Her thin arms were crossed over her chest as she shivered, being among the unlucky ones who hadn't managed to snag their parkas on the way out the door. Though he couldn't see her face, he could imagine her expression: it'd be reminiscent of the one she'd tried out after her first period when Roger had had to tell her that no, this wasn't a one-and-done situation.

But he was wrong. As he opened the passenger door and she hefted herself inside, her hair fell away for a moment, revealing not anxious confusion, ennui-infused dismay, or even plain ol' exasperation, but—strangely—guilt, amplified by the facial animation they shared.

"What's up, bedbug?" he asked, knowing what the answer would be.

"Nothing," Pandora said, following the predictable script.

"Looks like something to me."

"Looks can be deceiving," his daughter said—an answer she'd gotten from him on many occasions, seeing as the difference between text and subtext was how he made his living.

"Nice try," he said, seeing as the difference between text and subtext was crap, given the faces they'd been born with.

"Ditto," Pandora said back before settling in behind her thawing hair for the long, silent ride back home.

Roger only got a glimpse of her guilty mug before Pandora rang down the curtain, but it was enough to trouble him. What could she possibly feel guilty about when it came to a "possible terrorism-related" situation? Had she seen something but not said something? Or did the shock get her face muscles confused? Pulling into the garage, he prepared to take another stab at finding out what was behind that troubling face.

But alas, no. Pandora yanked up the handle, hopped down, slammed the door, and disappeared into the house.

Roger took a parental pause before following her, collecting and categorizing his concerns. But then he discovered evidence of how upset his daughter must be: her phone. He couldn't miss it in its pirate Hello Kitty case. In her rush to escape, she'd left it behind. Roger picked it up, swiped, and was amazed when he wasn't asked for credentials of some kind—an iris scan, at the very least. But no. It opened onto her home screen, where it seemed she had two email messages waiting.

He could feel the charges of emotional abuse coming even as he tapped the icon. But what else was he supposed to do? He needed to get to the bottom of this before the FPD SWAT team paid them a visit.

The first email was from a compounding pharmacy and the second from a chemical supply company. Both pleaded with his daughter to rate her recent transactions with them, or to let them know if she was dissatisfied in any way. "Please like us on Facebook," they begged, following the usual supplicant boilerplate, "and preach about us on Quire!"

Roger switched off the phone and pocketed it. He plugged in his truck's heater and then entered the house he'd shared with his only child ever since they abandoned California, where she'd been born and her mother had died. He took a breath and steadied his voice and face.

"Oh, daughter," he called. "Oh, daughter dear . . ."

# 4

First things first: George's mother should have found a better babysitter. Not that Uncle Jack was a kiddie diddler or anything, just a bachelor who had his own place and the bad luck to be in the recreational marijuana business before it was legal in California. He also had nearly zero understanding of what to do with a young child left in his care. Summing up, this is what Uncle Jack knew about kids: there was something in their brains that drew them to jangling keys. He figured it had something to do with the combination of sound and shiny. And this was something else he knew: when it came to sound and shiny, you couldn't beat the star gate sequence from *2001: A Space Odyssey*. Uncle Jack himself had experienced the sequence's mesmerizing effects many times, often while stoned. Accused of violating the drug dealer's first rule—don't get high on your own supply—Uncle Jack would plead, "Quality control." And the quality of his product was excellent, if he did say so himself.

So yeah: a drug dealer *and* user. George's mom was not going down in the history of exemplary childcare decision makers anytime soon.

After fishing the disk out of its clamshell and sliding it into the player, Jack parked the child next to him on the couch and sparked up a bong, the skunk smell and gentle bubbling pacifying George while his uncle blip-blip-blipped through the menu to cue up the sequence in question. Jack assumed his nephew, a toddler, wouldn't sit still for the so-called boring parts. So they started watching the movie at its most mind-boggling, endorphin-stimulating point, and once it was done—once the sole surviving astronaut found himself in a Louis XVI hotel room—he was prepared to jump back to start those Kubrickian keys jangling again.

But then a strange thing happened—or *didn't* happen.

George didn't fuss. He didn't move, in fact. Looking down at his nephew's eyes through his own glassy pair, Uncle Jack saw two tiny versions of the bigger screen in front of them, Cinerama rectangles of nearly pure white and, underneath them, George's mouth, an O of awe with little-kid drool leaking out.

"So, like, you're cool with letting the narrative flow?" he asked. George continued to stare, which Jack took as meaning, "Flow on, dude."

George watched, wide-eyed, his brain imprinting with the choreographed images of a solitary human leapfrogging in jump cuts from vital adult to old then older man and, finally, to a flare of pure light followed by a face that looked a lot like George's own, a pudgy-smooth baby's face, which he'd been shown in a mirror, equally wide-eyed and glowing around the edges in a way that suggested edges—where some things stopped and others began—were not as sharp as they'd appeared before these lights and sounds came flowing into and over him.

"Okay," Uncle Jack announced, reaching for the remote as he debated ejecting versus cuing up star gate again, "*that* was interesting," when he noticed his nephew, still transfixed. So he gave it a shot and started the movie from the beginning, his nephew taking it all in, the ape men, the monolith, the waltzes and measured breathing, up until the scene in which the computer HAL is lobotomized amid scarlet-drenched lights and shadows. And as HAL began singing slowly about Daisy and a bicycle built for two, George turned to his stoned and red-eyed uncle.

"I sad," he said.

"Well," his uncle said, "it's a sad part."

Indeed, it was, and within some subliminal part of George's own still-plastic brain, a resolve formed to do something to undo the sadness, whatever that might mean.

"I apologize," George's uncle said, returning the child to his sister.

"Why?"

"I think I may have broken it," he said. "I'll start the trust fund for therapy tomorrow."

"Jocko, you're going to have to explain."

And so he did. Afterward: "Could you maybe not smoke around him?" George's mother asked.

Uncle Jack considered this a reasonable request, especially since, well, how was she supposed to know whether he did or not? That's what Glade was for. And about using a bona fide science-fiction masterpiece as a babysitter? What about that part? That's when George's mom went with the mantra of harried single mothers everywhere: "Whatever works, Jocko," she said, "is fine by me."

And thus the future became their routine—George's and Uncle Jack's—with the latter alluding to the movie when, say, his nephew's pod bay door was refusing entrance to some forked or spooned veggie. "C'mon," he'd say, "don't make me blow the hatch," while George, his little arms folded, shook his head. Other times the threat was to deactivate the red-and-yellow nightlight purchased for sleepovers, its allusive gaze comforting for the weird little boy destined to become a coder's coder in a future destined to feel like a rerun.

There was another reason it wasn't a good idea leaving George with his weed-smoking-and-dealing uncle: George's real name was Jorge, Uncle

Jack was really Tío Juan, and of the three of them, George/Jorge was the only one in the United States legally, seeing as he'd been born there. Not that it was ICE agents who came to Tío Juan's door one morning while HAL was being lobotomized again; no, that was a joint (snicker) task force including DEA and ATF agents, the latter included because the first two letters of its bureaucratic acronym were major competitors of the illicit substance the soon-to-be apprehended perp was peddling to the detriment of local Angelenos.

"Crap, he's got a kid," the guy holding the battering ram said, framed in the splintered frame of the doorway he'd bashed in.

"Is that *2001*?" another agent asked.

"You know Kubrick?" Uncle Jack asked.

"Not personally," the agent said, "but I admire his work."

*"Dude,"* Uncle Jack said, offering the agent a brotherhood toke of the joint he'd been planning to Glade over before getting busted by his big sis. *In retrospect*—Jack would later think—*if only* . . .

Spinning his uncle around, the agents cuffed Jack right in front of his nephew, forming a mini memory that would seem like déjà vu years later, when George found his own wrists being cinched together.

"What do we do about . . . ?" the battering ram agent asked, pointing at the child while HAL sang plaintively in the background.

"He yours?" the fellow Kubrick admirer asked.

The boy's uncle shook his head. "Sister's."

"Number?"

He gave it.

And *that's* when ICE got involved.

George's mom, Margarita (or Marge, like Marge Simpson, how American was *that*?), had no idea of the difference between her and George's immigration status back when she'd become pregnant with him. Before confessing to her parents, her biggest concerns were being unmarried and the fact that her baby's biological father disappeared upon hearing the news. And so she anticipated a lot of grief for confessing her condition. What she didn't expect from her parents was a confession of their own, provided with no little sense of relief.

"Finally," her father had said, "a Garza who won't have to look over his shoulder."

"Excuse me?"

So out came the story Margarita had lived through but hadn't remembered, the one that explained why they all had at-home names and out-there names. And as her parents told it, it explained a lot more, including her visceral reaction to the story of the Christmas nativity, how she always felt tears welling when she heard the words "no room at the inn" and imagined Mary and Joseph trudging through the sand, ratty sandaled, holey clothes flapping as they moved from place to place, denied entry again and again, until they finally took shelter with the animals they were being treated like, mankind as usual ignorant of the miraculous in its midst. She imagined that trek again now—with herself a three-year-old Y between her parents, one of her hands for each, their triptych of footprints unwinding behind them in the sifting, shifting sand—imagined now as the top half on an hourglass that had been running out of time all along with the exception that Marge, a.k.a. Margarita, could finally feel the downward tug of her world funneling away from her.

"What's going to happen to us?" she'd asked. "What's going to happen to my baby?" she added, a hand on her belly, where the computer hacker growing inside her had kicked a good one.

"Nothing," her parents said together, as if they'd practiced. "We've been good. We haven't broken any laws," her dad continued.

"Except," her mother interjected, only for her husband to wave it away.

"They need our kind," her father said. "They've needed us ever since the Civil War went the way it did. Cheap labor is always welcome; the rest is BS the politicians run on until they get into office and forget us once again."

"Your father's right, *mija*," her mother said.

"Just don't kill people or steal anything. Pay your social security like it's rent and won't come back to you. And know that that little *bebé* in your belly is your safety net."

"How so?" the child with a child asked, still feathering the globe of her stomach with her fingertips.

"Only a monster would separate a mother from her child," her own mother said. "And Americans aren't monsters. Your own child will be an American." She paused, smiled. "Our *grandchild* will be one," she added.

After his birth, a nurse asked for a name—her baby boy's name—and the one thing Margarita Garza wouldn't give them was Jorge's real name, first or last. She'd been spooked by her parents' revelation re: her immigration status, and while her son's citizenship wasn't in question, still, she thought it safer giving him a nice American name on his birth certificate. But what should it be? The TV across from her hospital bed provided the answer. It was tuned to Cartoon Network, which was running a *Jetsons* marathon. She'd been hearing the opening theme all morning, including its roster of introductions to the show's main characters. It was the first name on that oft-repeated list that now resonated for the new mother.

"George," she said, paused, then added, "Jedson." She didn't want to be overly obvious about her source material. She needn't have worried. The nurse looking at the TV over her shoulder had been hearing the same earworm all morning until any connection between it and the real world had blurred beyond caring.

Once the drugs she'd been given to ease the pain of delivery wore off, Margarita wondered what had made her tempt fate by giving her son such a cartoonish pseudonym. But as the days passed, then weeks, then months and years without a knock from immigration, she was sure they were safe. She had no way of knowing that fate was playing the long game.

If our names are our destinies, then George's alias was aptly chosen. Because even though his mother didn't know it at the time, her son's life would be tinged with nostalgia for the future, in the sense of everything old being new again, where history and politics rode the grand pendulum of time, swinging back and forth, left then right . . .

And so, when his life was ruined, it was the result of an old racism that would become new again, later, when George was a teenager. At the time of his uncle's arrest and his mother's subsequent deportation, so-called "good immigrants" were rarely kicked out, and separating immigrant parents from their American-born children was rarer still. But the immigration judge who got the case was two generations away from her own family's having sought asylum in the US. In a classic case of I-got-mine-now-get-lost, the judge—a future Supreme Court contender—had decided to burnish her anti-immigration credentials using George and his mother. The fact that there was a drug element involved made the case all but irresistible, while the inclusion of a five-year-old child proved that even though the judge was a woman, her heart didn't bleed. And so while his mother was sent back to a country that she had little memory of, Uncle Jack was handed the equivalent of a death sentence by being incarcerated along with members of the same cartel that had once been his supplier. And Jorge a.k.a. George was sent to live with strangers, his only remaining family, Gamma and Pop Pop Garza, long dead thanks to a faulty carbon monoxide detector.

By the time he'd gone through three sets of fosters, George had stopped believing in property. Because along with learning about the arbitrary and impermanent nature of laws, he also discovered that under those laws, he was little more than property himself, hence the use of owner-related terms like, say, *custody*. As far as he was concerned, it was "the state" that turned him into a socialist by sentencing him to a world of group homes, time-share parents, and possessions that weren't even rent-to-own, but rent-to-keep-on-renting, his life another hand-me-down from a string of fosters working a side hustle to make ends meet.

It was this, along with his lingering fondness for a homicidal supercomputer, that made George the vigilante hacker he became. Believing that information wanted to be free and that the whole idea of "intellectual property" was something to be resisted and subverted, he set about doing exactly that. Run a hundred-dollar textbook through a high-speed scanner and post it online free? Sure, why not? Steal some rich guy's Voltaire and recycle it into the local economy as a down payment on the whole income inequality thing? Ditto, especially after he got what he really wanted from the hack, which was a smile, sure, but also a look at some proprietary source code that might benefit from being set free.

# 5

Presented with the evidence from her phone, Pandora confessed—or her face did, followed by actual words from her brain to fill in the gaps. She'd shown Roger what they'd done to her, googling the words *face girl*, *viral*, and *GIF*.

"So I've been living with an internet celebrity," he said. "I had no idea."

And it was true. Though he made his living online, he'd vowed not to live there when he wasn't with a client. "It's too easy to get abducted by aliens in cyberspace," he'd say, meaning it was a good way to lose time.

"So you see I had to, right?" Pandora said.

"I see why you *wanted* to," Roger said back. "But you know what I always say when you need to make a decision, right?"

Pandora did. She'd been deciding things ever since she could, and her father had been dispensing the same pearl of wisdom all that time. Granted, as pearls of wisdom went, it wasn't half-bad—except for its always being thrown in her face whenever she'd decided poorly.

"Before you do something questionable," Roger continued, as he had countless times before, "ask yourself, 'What if *everybody* did what I'm about to do?'"

*Exempli gratia,* Pandora thought on her father's behalf, *what if* everybody *set fire to a bunch of urinals?*

*I guess that would mean,* she thought on her own behalf, *guys would have to wait as long as girls to take a leak.*

She didn't say any of that, of course. Not in real life. Had they been having this conversation online, she'd have posted it without giving it a second thought. Learning to second-think things was one of the reasons Roger had sent her to high school in the first place. Or as he put it at the time, "It's harder to tell someone to f-off face-to-face than it is on Facebook." He'd conveniently left out important facts about the face she'd be facing people with as part of that particular conversation.

"Guess I wasn't thinking," Pandora said now, using her best sitcom-kid voice. "I feel like such a knucklehead . . ." She imagined the *wa-wa* sitcom soundtrack.

But Roger wasn't in the mood. His daughter had caused her school to be evacuated and the SWAT team (such as it was) to be mobilized. He struggled to come up with a media-friendly allusion to sum up the seriousness of the situation.

"I know how it went," he said. "You got an idea in your head; wondered, 'What if . . .'; but then you got so caught up with whether it *could* be done that you never stopped to think about whether it *should* be done."

"Isn't that . . . ?"

"Jeff Goldblum? *Jurassic Park*?" Roger said. "Yes. A paraphrase, but apt, I think."

"What if I promise not to resurrect any extinct species?" Pandora said.

"You're not joking your way out of this one." Pausing for gravitas, Roger cupped his mouth in contemplation before taking his hand away to reveal an evil eureka smile, letting her know how much he loved how much she was going to hate this. But then he kept standing there, smiling, forcing her to ask.

"Well," she finally said, breaking.

"When was the last time you visited your grandmother?" he asked.

Roger's mother, Gladys Lynch, became a widow before her granddaughter had her first period and hadn't been visited by either of her surviving relatives since they had left the mausoleum where her husband's ashes were interred behind marble and brass. When his father was still alive, Roger and his daughter had visited his parents all the time. But even then, the visits were largely about seeing the old man, a WWII vet who'd worked in the signal corps for the navy and wound up in Alaska with a cabin full of cool ham-radio gear, plenty of funny war stories, and a two-seater single-prop airplane he took his granddaughter flying in, to remind her of her potential.

"It's not only Fairbanks," he'd shouted over the engine and wind. "There's a whole planet down there . . ."

Pandora had nodded, the rushing wind ripping at her smile, making it even broader than usual, while her auburn hair flagged like fire blown sideways.

Not that the old lady was some ogre; she was just ignorable. She'd been a mom and housewife most of her life, and prior to that, who knew? More importantly, who cared? What Roger knew of his mother's past prior to meeting his father was that she'd apparently had shock treatment before heading north and it had apparently helped. That, and the fact that they'd delayed having children until the last minute, biological-clock-wise—something to do with not wanting to bring new life into the Cold War world after the way the hot war ended.

The rift between Roger and his mom started when he was thousands of miles away, in California, trying to start a psychiatry practice and a family, in that order, flirting with the same biological snooze-alarm situation his parents had faced before deciding to become parents. It was while he was away that Gladys got strange, perhaps so gradually that his father hadn't noticed, but Roger sure did, coming back to it after years away, once his wife had died and he'd returned to Alaska to raise his daughter.

His mother had nearly died in the interim, thanks to a misprescribed antibiotic that wound up killing off all the good bacteria in her intestines. This, in turn, led to a domino effect of subsequent symptoms, including diarrhea and dehydration severe enough to warrant hospitalization. She was never the same after that, developing a whole host of phobias about doctors and the digestive process, leading to self-diagnoses of lactose intolerance, an allergy to gluten, irritable bowel syndrome, and an inability to digest red meat. Individual items and then whole food groups were banned from their dinner table, her husband going along with each new culinary exile because while he had the gut to prove his love of food, he loved his wife even more.

But it had worn on him, year after year, especially without Roger around to offer a counterpoint and suggest that perhaps—just perhaps—their mom and wife, respectively, might be crazy. Again. Instead, Herman just worked harder and harder, trying to find something his wife would eat. After returning, Roger had accompanied him on a trip to the Fairbanks Safeway only to be shocked at how difficult the job of feeding his mother had become. During the dead of winter especially, it was hard enough getting variety into a person's diet, and the last thing anyone needed was an increasingly picky and capricious eater. Roger could see how just trying had taken a physical toll on his father, noticing the way the old man leaned on the cart in lieu of the cane it became increasingly obvious he needed if he was going to stand a chance of not being crushed under the weight of his world.

"How about . . . ?" Roger tried, holding up a can of something.

His father shook his head. "Gives her gas."

A bottle of Beano.

"Gets a rash . . ."

And so on, until they left the store with a case of Ensure, a carton of lactose-free Activia, and a lonely, dented can of peaches his father identified as being "for dessert."

Roger was there when his father died, or started to. He'd just shown up for a visit without calling ahead, because his parents didn't have a phone. He begged them to get one, for emergencies, especially at their age, and Herman had seemed okay with the idea, but Gladys vetoed it.

"I didn't come to the ends of the earth so people can waltz in anytime they feel like it," she'd said, ending the conversation.

And so, when Roger wanted to see his parents, he just went, unannounced but usually welcome, by his father at least. There'd been a few times when Pandora was still a baby that Gladys had been less than happy to see them. Not that she was opposed to grandchildren in concept; she just couldn't abide the shitty reality of them. Given her history of intestinal problems and her susceptibility to them, Roger's mother was the first to know when Pandora's diaper needed changing, a procedure her father could perform in his goddamn truck, putting as many doors as possible between his daughter's feces and his mother's immune system. Having to carry the child out to the truck when it was forty degrees below zero had left a sting he'd never quite gotten over.

During that fateful visit, Roger could tell something was wrong right away. There were tears in the old man's eyes, and his mother was yelling, followed by the sound of a flung plate smashing. His father winced through the smile he'd worn to the door.

"What's wrong?" Roger asked, dispensing with the chitchat.

"I got the wrong thing," Herman said. "Again."

From the doorstep, Roger could hear his mother swearing, and he pushed the rest of the way inside. "What was that?" he said.

"Moron," his mother fumed. "I married a moron who's trying to kill me. He knows I can't eat that." She pointed at the blast of food clinging to the wall opposite her, above shards of broken china.

"And how does he *know* you can't eat it?" Roger asked. "Have you *told* him?"

"I shouldn't *have* to tell him," Gladys raged. "When we used to go shopping together, I'd never buy crap like that."

"Hold on," Roger said, preparing to play his usual role whenever he found himself stuck in an argument between his parents: the rational jester who pointed out how silly they were both being. "You're telling me you're mad at Dad because he *didn't* notice you *not* buying something?"

"Finally," Gladys declared, "*some*body who under*stands*."

Roger had begun shaking his head, chuckling ruefully, when he noticed how quiet his father was being. He turned to look at the older man, and it was as if his father had just been shot. His mother's face, its exaggerated disgust, that was the gun. Her words, the bullets. And there was Herman Lynch, his arms straight at his sides, the fingers shocked apart, a slight palsied shake Roger had never noticed before. His father flicked his left hand, like he was trying to fling blood down to his digits, and then his right arm lifted, bringing his hand to his chest, a thumb rubbing sideways through the flannel of his shirt, between his droopy old-man breasts.

"Dad?"

"It's something I ate," he said. But Roger knew he was lying. When Gladys didn't eat, neither did Herman. It had worked in his father's favor in the beginning, helped shed some needed pounds, but it had become too much. He tottered back, and his left hand reached around behind him, flailing for a chair it finally found and dragged over just in time for him to drop into it. "Call someone," Herman said.

But Roger couldn't: no phone, not even his cell, which was back at home, charging after he'd forgotten to plug it in the night before. Pandora had hers, but she was also back at home, technically alone if you didn't count the entire internet, her father's go-to babysitter since she could make her own PB&J sandwiches and promise not to set the house on fire.

Turning to the parent who wasn't dying, Roger barked, "Grab your parkas." He'd just have to drive them all to the hospital himself. Gladys handed over Herman's jacket, gloves, boots. "Where's yours?" her son demanded.

But Gladys just shook her head. "I can't," she said.

"Can't what?" Roger demanded.

"Go."

"Go?"

"To the hospital," Gladys said.

"Why not?"

"I might go."

"Go?"

"Poop," she said. "My irritable bowel, I . . ."

"Shit," Roger spat.

"Yes," Gladys said, as if he understood—instead of swearing, because he had.

And so Herman's son drove him to the hospital, minus his wife, minus the love of his life, for him to finish dying with just Roger's dumb, stupid face to keep him company.

In the hospital, after being informed he'd had a heart attack that was bigger than the ER was equipped to treat, Herman turned to Roger and said, "Well, I guess that makes two."

"Excuse me?"

"Yeah, my first heart attack was when I met your mother," he said. The morphine they'd given him for the pain had made him chatty. And so he went over the old story again of how they'd met in this dingy frontier bar before Alaska was even a state, back when the lower forty-eight were basically the whole country, trimmed with some territories here and there with no votes or stars of their own.

It was after WWII, and the two had each fled to the ends of the earth after the world didn't end. Herman Lynch had been sitting in the bar, drinking in the middle of the "day," though it was actually dark out, it being winter, thus removing the usual stigma—or so he claimed—staring at the dusty mirror across the bar and gently tapping his high school graduation ring against the rail. He didn't even know he was doing it, but the tapping came out in Morse code—SOS, for "save our souls" or "save our ship," depending on where you stood re: the whole having-a-soul issue. Gladys noticed it and signaled back—SOS, SOS, SOS—with the top of an empty longneck against the rim of the glass she'd poured the beer into. Looking over, Roger's future dad said, "Fancy," indicating the bottle-and-glass redundancy.

"Practical," Gladys said back, indicating her future husband's far simpler drinking arrangement, a trail of suds still crawling down its neck of brown glass.

"You make decisions fast when you're twenty-five and surprised to be alive," Herman Lynch told his son, explaining why he and Gladys wound up married within the month. A floatplane-flying buddy of his officiated, based on the authority vested in him as the captain of something that could land on water and—he maintained—technically met the definition of a ship.

"It's highly possible we've been living in sin all these years," Herman confided with a nudge and a wink. "Kinda makes it more exciting that way."

"Kinda makes me a bastard, though," Roger pointed out.

"Nope," his father insisted, "that choice is all on you."

Roger did not announce his decision to cut his own mother out of his life; he and Pandora just kind of stopped going over there after Herman died. Because it involved not doing something, the more he didn't do it, the easier it was to keep on not doing it. He felt the occasional pang of guilt but always turned it around, making it her fault. He'd tried getting his parents to get a phone when it might have made a difference, and now she couldn't blame him for not calling. As a gesture to the memory of his dad, Roger had a case of Ensure delivered to their cabin once a week, considering his duty as a son done. But then he received notice that her address had changed to a PO Box care of Golden Heart of the North Senior Services. And so Roger canceled his standing order, figuring the place his mother had landed was probably billing the government enough to buy its own damn Ensure.

But then Pandora got in trouble and needed a punishment to fit the offense. And when it came to punishing experiences, Roger couldn't come up with anything that amused him quite as much as sentencing his daughter to visit her grandmother in an old-folks' home.

"You're kidding me," Pandora said upon learning her fate.

"I'm not," Roger said. "She needs the company," he added, fully aware of how hypocritical it sounded but finding himself fresh out of shits to give regarding either of the women in his life.

"So why don't *you* visit her?" Pandora asked.

"Because I didn't blow anybody up," he said.

Roger knew Pandora could quibble with that characterization—technically speaking, she hadn't "blown up" anybody—but she seemed to have deemed it wiser not to. Instead, she ground her more articulate objections against her back teeth until all that escaped was a grumbled mutter that trailed her as she stormed off. Reaching her room, she grabbed the edge of the shower curtain that still hadn't been replaced by an actual door, and now likely never would be, in light of recent events. Yanking it open, she turned, glowered hyperexpressively, and then pulled the curtain closed hard enough to . . .

. . . feel just about as pathetic as it no doubt looked.

# 6

When it was finally time for Gladys Lynch to move out of the cabin she'd shared with her late husband for more years than she cared to count, her options were limited to 1) an ice floe or 2) a place the Fairbanks Yellow Pages listed as "Golden Heart of the North Senior Services." Like an actual anatomical heart, GHNSS was composed of four sectors organized around the primary services they offered their residents, including assisted living, physical therapy, extended care, and hospice. It was the first of these that was most prominently featured in Golden Heart's sales brochure, which described it as "reserved for residents who need a little help" and offered condos equipped with ramps and handrails, walk-in tubs, call buttons, smoke detectors, washer-dryer combo units, and kitchenettes consisting of cabinets, counter and sink, minifridge, microwave, toaster oven, and a fire extinguisher that was tested monthly by staff, along with the aforementioned smoke detectors.

Gladys's decision was *not* prompted by the need for such elder-friendliness at the time she made it; she just didn't like living alone with all her late husband's firearms. Not that she had anything against Herman's guns. She'd been happy to have them when she still had him and had counted on him to use them should the need arise. But for herself, Gladys wasn't interested in killing someone in self-defense, especially if the stranger turned out to be somebody she knew. There'd been a close call or two already.

There'd also been a doctor who'd come to see her, court ordered after an "incident" while driving down a road where "some kids" had apparently turned all the signs around to face the wrong way. He'd given her a battery of tests, beginning with the Mini-Mental State Examination, which consisted of a series of questions about what day it was, what season, what state and city they were in, followed by repeating back a list of objects, then counting backward, then repeating the list of objects again. In one test, he had Gladys draw a clock with hands and numbers; she'd messed that one up a little, leaving out the six and nine, drawing the rest outside the circle, and then getting the hour and minute hands mixed up.

"If I was Salvador Dali, you wouldn't be making that face," she observed—not that that stopped the doctor from running up the Medicare charges by ordering, in order, an MRI, a PET scan, an EEG, and a SPECT scan.

"Wouldn't a nice cup of alphabet soup be cheaper?" she asked, already used to being ignored, which she was.

"You've got poor glucose metabolism in the hippocampus," Dr. Charge-a-Lot said as if she hadn't spoken.

"Is that a school for 'potamuses?" she joked, but the doctor didn't laugh.

"Not that we can make a *definitive* diagnosis without an autopsy, but . . . ," he began, at which point Gladys threw up a hand and said, "Skip!"

But those pursed lips still refused to budge.

So that's when Gladys Lynch—mother of Roger, grandmother of Pandora—found herself moving (or being moved to) the "assisted living" side of the Golden Heart of the North Senior Services campus. Making the best of it, Gladys consented, figuring they'd assist her in continuing to live, in the event anyone with a different opinion showed up.

Roger's thinking went like this: say you've got a teenage daughter who needs to take life in general—and her personal mortality, specifically—more seriously. What do you do? What sort of punitive activity might drive those points into an adolescence-hardened skull? Something like Scared Straight for juvenile offenders but for life and how precious and fleeting it can be. Donating time to work with preemies in a neonatal unit was one thought, but then he had another. Approach the problem from the end and work backward. And there his mother's change-of-address card sat, offering the perfect solution. Two perfect solutions, in fact, seeing as sending Pandora as his proxy would also assuage any guilt he might feel for not visiting her himself. Win—as they say—win.

Pandora wondered if there was such a thing as building-ism. If there was, she must have it, because these buildings all looked alike to her. Every quadrant of the Golden Heart campus featured the same flat-roofed, gray, brutalist bunkers of concrete with windows that wouldn't open without the help of a diamond drill and C-4. They looked so much alike she finally gave up, pulled into the nearest parking lot, and started walking, nearly bumping into a body on its way out as she made her way in.

"Watch it," the mortuary tech said, walking his charge out backward toward an unmarked delivery van.

"Sorry," Pandora said. "I'm looking for a Gladys—"

"Wrong place," the mortuary tech said, not needing her to finish. "This is shipping and receiving."

"Is that a euphemism?"

"It's a euphemism," the tech confirmed.

"So, how do I—?"

But the tech was already shooing her away.

The next quadrant was physical therapy, not that Pandora could tell from the outside. Even if she'd known, however, she'd still have been surprised. Sure, there were some seniors breaking in new knees, hips, and shoulders, but there were also a lot of people she didn't expect, meaning closer to her age, all of whom had proved a lot less invincible than they might have assumed. Among them, Pandora noticed one of the curling culprits who'd stopped coming to class. His right arm had been sliced from bicep to forearm and stitched back like an aerial view of a railyard. The arm was so withered it looked like somebody had skated over it and yanked out all the muscles, which, she'd learn later, was exactly what had happened. It was so bad, in fact, Pandora felt guilty for having dismissed how dangerous curling could be, all jokes about "men with brooms" aside. And she especially regretted setting those urinals on fire, partly because it had resulted in her being here to see this but also because—well, just because.

Next, there were the local boys back from one of the Middle East conflicts, minus important body parts, including parts of her favorite body part: the head. Some looked like they'd had chunks of skull removed and then hastily patched over with some stubbly, flesh-like covering. After these, the yahoos and mushers who'd learned the hard way that drinking doesn't mix with snowmachines or dogsleds either. A few of these were working out on weight machines they'd been handcuffed to, perhaps in training to waste away in some state prison outside Juneau.

"Is there a Gladys Lynch in here?" Pandora called.

The physical therapist closest to her checked a clipboard—"Nope"—and then went back to leading her little clutch of victims in what appeared to be the most painful game of Simon says Pandora ever hoped to see.

The next set of buildings she skipped. She assumed they housed the medical facilities, judging from the lab-coated men and women trying to keep warm while they enjoyed a smoke break the proper distance away from patients and oxygen. That left two more parking lots. Not knowing which was which, she flipped a mental coin and, bingo, her bad luck held.

If seeing the younger disabled patients in PT had been depressing, it was nothing like the epic comedown of her penultimate stop. Everywhere she looked, mumblers and droolers rolled around in circles or scooted walkers or lay in beds alarmed in the unlikely event their captives had enough strength or selfhood to get around the guardrails. Wandering from one hellish sight to another, Pandora began bleating the name "Lynch!" to any sentient beings she could find, her face a paroxysm of pure horror.

"First name?" a janitor asked, swirling milky water around the latest accident.

"Gladys," Pandora said.

The janitor called to the receptionist at the end of the hallway. "Lynch," he shouted. "Gladys."

"Other side," the receptionist shouted back.

"Other," the janitor shouted before checking himself and turning down his voice. "Side," he concluded.

"Other side," Pandora echoed, preparing to leave, but then stopped. She had to ask. "Can't you *smell* that?" she asked, a hand cupped over her nose and mouth gas-mask-style.

The janitor shrugged. "You get used to it."

"No thanks," Pandora said, still fanning the air.

"Just a fact," the janitor said. "Sooner or later, we all get used to it. Except"—tilting his chin toward a posse of wheelchair-bound residents parked around a table, nothing connecting them except coincidental spacing—and perhaps wheel locks.

"Shouldn't they have cards?"

"They should have a lot of things," the janitor said, "starting with a sense of smell. Having dementia does a number on the old nose." He paused to dunk his mop. "Everybody knows about the brain part, but the nose goes too." Slap, swish. "The brain part's why they don't have any cards. They wouldn't be able to remember who's winning from one hand to the next. Not that any of them would admit it, so then you get fights, usually just raised voices, but we've had the occasional caning to deal with."

He gave his mop a big sweep, short of Pandora's sneakers. "It's quieter this way," he said.

The "other side" she'd been directed to was, aptly enough, the housing office and greeting center, where, after signing in and being greeted, she'd be taken by golf cart to where the senior condos and residents were. This was the side of the Golden Heart that the families of potential residents were shown, where the campus put on its best face, as if all the other buildings, in keeping with their external uniformity, looked the same inside.

*Yeah right,* Pandora thought, having inadvertently learned the truth, not that she said as much as she signed in. Instead, she followed the end of the receptionist's hand to a seating area and sat.

And sat.

And kept sitting, gradually coming to notice how quiet the place was. This was apparently intended to communicate tranquility or some other elder-friendly state of being. But Pandora found the quiet increasingly unnerving the longer she was exposed to it. It didn't help that what sounds there were only deepened the underlying silence pressing in from all sides. Pandora crossed her hands over her already-crossed knees, not knowing what else to do with them as she listened to the bubbler from an aquarium in the common area where prospects were treated to tea in daintily clinking china cups and offered brochures full of smiling, wrinkled faces who seemed to be having the time of their lives.

"Are you here to see a loved one?"

An escort had finally appeared, dressed in a smart gray pantsuit so that her dress, speech, and manner all reminded Pandora of a funeral director, like a preview of coming attractions.

"Gladys Lynch," Pandora said, not bothering to quibble with the escort's use of the words *loved one.*

There was some good that came out of Pandora's detour through the facility's various hearts of darkness: it inclined her to cut her grandmother a little slack, regardless of any bias projected by her father. After all, knowing Gladys had that other, "other side" waiting for her scored the old girl some serious sympathy points. And this sympathy only deepened when Pandora finally found her way to her only female relative's condo, where a notably shorter version of her grandmother greeted her with positively heartbreaking enthusiasm.

"Dora, my God," Gladys said, opening her door to the sight of her granddaughter and escort.

"Got a visitor, Lynch," the escort said, like a prison screw in some quaint black-and-white prison flick where the hard cases were invariably redeemed by the Lord, the law library, or jailbirds with actual feathers.

"I see that," the old woman said, followed by an awkward bit with her arms as she negotiated the height difference between herself and her significantly taller granddaughter. Once she'd figured it out, however, she closed in and squeezed so hard Pandora was pretty sure she heard bones creaking: Gladys's.

"It's my granddaughter," the older woman continued, over her hunched shoulders, to the escort. "And to what do I owe the pleasure?" she asked.

All the polite excuses flew right out of Pandora's head. "I'm being punished," she announced, as undiplomatic as she was poorly socialized.

"Oh my," Gladys said. Paused. "You mean *me*? *I'm* your punishment?"

A nod.

"Your father's characterization," Gladys asked, "or yours?"

Pandora seized this second chance at not being a total bitch. "Dad's," she said.

"Figures," her grandmother said, holding her granddaughter's elbows at arm's length to get a better look at her. The old woman's bare lips, which had been frowning before, hitched upward, morphing into a grin nearly as ridiculous as one Pandora herself might sport, if she'd been in the mood.

"Good," her grandmother said at the thought of being someone's punishment. "It's about time I got some *respect* around here."

# 7

V.T. Lemming was not happy even before his car decided to drive off by itself. V.T. Lemming had been especially "not happy" for the last several months, because he was being forced to engage ever increasingly in his most despised activity as the shareholder with the most votes: emergency board meetings. There'd been a smattering of EBMs early on—one involving subsequent congressional testimony—but the pace of said meetings (and the emergencies that triggered them) had been accelerating.

"Gentlemen," he'd begun the latest such meeting, not adding "ladies," because this was a Silicon Valley boardroom and there weren't any. (Not that they weren't aware of the problem. They were. They even developed an algorithm to eliminate bias from hiring and promotion decisions. Unfortunately, the data used to train the algorithm had been based on the company's past history of hirings and promotions so that the bias wasn't so much eliminated as hardwired and automated. Oops.)

"Gentlemen," V.T. repeated, redundantly, "we've got an optics problem which is becoming an image concern on its way to becoming a PR nightmare."

Two columns of ghost faces nodded to either side, lit by the blue light of their smartphones and reflected off the oil-rubbed mahogany of the boardroom conference table.

What V.T. was referring to wasn't the #metoo time bomb waiting to explode somewhere along the management chain. It wasn't another breach of hundreds of millions of user accounts or Quire's role in fueling a foreign bot-driven psyops campaign aimed at shredding the fabric of Western civilization. It wasn't that their platform was being used to grease the skids for genocide in third-world countries, or the Harvard Business School study showing that the number of antidepressants prescribed annually was positively correlated to the growth in V.T.'s personal fortune, which in turn was inversely correlated to a decrease in overall IQ scores, the implicit conclusion being that while Quire's CEO got rich, the rest of the country was getting dumber and more depressed. Nope. Quire's board of directors had been summoned because of a video that had been livestreamed from their platform.

"In case you missed it," V.T. said before hitting play.

The video featured a teenage boy in his bedroom in Beverly Hills, a talking head facing his webcam. But then came the money shot, as it were—the shot that was going to cost everyone in the room a lot of money—after which there wasn't any head left to do any talking. When the body fell, it took what was left of the head off-screen with it, leaving behind a perfectly framed Jackson Pollock, if the artist had used only reds and added texture with broken pottery and clumps of cauliflower. With no one to cut the feed, it kept going, streaming the same grisly static scene, animated only by the painfully slow sliding of those shards and clumps down the wall as they submitted to gravity.

Deaths like it happened every day in America, enabled by the easy availability of firearms and the increasingly pointless search for anything that mattered. Had it been one of those daily deaths, the suicide would have been danced around in the obits with words like *battle* and *depression* if the cause was alluded to at all.

But Rupert Gunn Jr.'s death was distinguished from those others not only for having been streamed "live" (so to speak) but also because of one inconvenient wrinkle: celebrity. Or *celebritatus approximus*: near celebrity or celebrity adjacent—the proxy-fame bestowed on family members of the actually famous—a lesser Kardashian cousin, for example. In this particular case, the real celebrity was Rupert Jr.'s father, *the* Rupert Gunn, the man *Variety* crowned as having "the second most-bankable pair of man nips in Hollywood."

Before the Quire content monitor in charge had a chance to pull the video, it had already received over a hundred thousand "praise hands." Even after being pulled, the video went on to enjoy something Rupert Jr. himself would not—an afterlife—as it leaped from platform to platform, always a few clicks ahead of the content cops. As the contagion spread, the video collected "likes" and "shares" and "smiles" and "effin-As," followed by screenshots turned into memes, which themselves went viral. Even the choice of firearm—a Luger and WWII family heirloom that would warrant its own team of PR spinners—was heartily approved of by the alt-right on their own social-media platforms, racking up more *Sieg Heils* than they'd seen since white polo shirts and tiki torches showed up half-price at Big Lots.

By the beginning of Quire's latest emergency board meeting, the video had generated three million hits and climbing, a trending hashtag (#Quiremadehimdoit), a line of T-shirts breaking records on Etsy, and a Jimmy Kimmel sincerity moment that was chasing the original stream on YouTube. All in all, the only thing that wasn't trending up in the aftermath was Quire's share price, plummeting like it had BASE-jumped off the Golden Gate Bridge minus the wing suit.

"Somebody tell me he was on Ambien," V.T. mock pleaded, pausing the video, then on its way to four million hits since they'd started watching it. The CEO waited between the projector and screen, wearing the boy's static suicide. He began humming the tune for Final Jeopardy. But none of the board members stepped forward with news of a pharmaceutical scapegoat.

"Okay," V.T. resumed, "at least tell me he *wasn't* part of a sosh trial."

But no one around the table was ready to confirm or deny that Rupert Jr. had been part of a sosh trial, mainly because, well, he *had* been. And that was the *real* corporate crisis Quire found itself facing. Because the boy hadn't been bullied, didn't have an incurable health condition, and hadn't been humiliated, either sexually or financially. In the end, he'd killed himself thanks to a confluence of bad decisions, both personal and corporate.

On the personal side, Rupert Jr. made the mistake of quiring a host of socioeconomic inferiors who in real life were total strangers but online constituted his "quire of besties." The idea—ill-conceived as it turned out—was to discover how the other half (or, if you're a stickler for stats, the other ninety-nine percent) lived. Being the scion of those bankable man nips, Rupert Jr. had never in his life been exposed to the riffraff that make up the vast majority of humanity. And so the lives of the unrich and unfamous became a source of curiosity for him, as is often the case with forbidden things.

The other bad decision happened at the corporate offices of Quire, which had unknowingly included Rupert Jr. in a so-called "sosh trial," which was shorthand for social engineering optimization study. As part of the trial in question, Quire's social engineering team manipulated the news stream of three different groups of users to see what balance of good/bad news led to optimal clicking behavior, especially the click-through rate to the ever-coveted "Buy Now" button. The engineers had already discovered that moderately depressed Quire users tended to buy more stuff, a practice they'd dubbed "retail therapy." The question was, What would clickers do if they were really depressed?

And no, Rupert Jr. wasn't part of the group that was fed especially depressing news from others in their quire. He also wasn't part of the control group whose news feed was left untouched. No, he'd been placed in a group intended to confirm the research question's corollary, i.e., "Do vicariously happy people buy *less* stuff?"

The only problem: Rupert Jr. wasn't online to be cheered by the good news of the proletariat. He'd been *hoping* to find misery to cheer him out of his own. Because it had come from somewhere, hadn't it? Depression didn't just *happen*. There had to be a cause and, from that, maybe, a cure. Which is when Rupert Jr. recalled how vaccines work. You exposed yourself to a manageable amount of the disease, thereby building up an immunity to it. So maybe if he exposed himself to the highly manageable unhappiness of others who'd already started out way less fortunate than he was . . .

But instead of feeling better by comparison, what he found was this: average Americans trying to make other average Americans jealous. While that's frequently what people got in their news feeds even without manipulation, what Rupert Jr. got was as relentlessly upbeat as a motivational speaker in an ice cream truck playing "Happy Days Are Here Again." This amplification was achieved by stripping out the political rants, fake news, proselytizing, and clickbait that clogged most news feeds, leaving behind a highly curated glimpse into the lives of others as they portrayed themselves online. The results, unsurprisingly, skewed toward the full spectrum of bragging, including but not limited to: the humblebrag; the brag brag; the proxy brag ("Look at my kids, my parents, my lovely spouse . . ."); the brag with parsley ("Look at my breakfast, lunch, dinner . . ."); the anthropomorphic brag ("Look at how much my dog, cat, pony, goldfish, et al. *loves* me . . ."); the geo-tag brag ("Will you look at that *view* . . ."); and the holier-than-bragging brag ("Click here to donate to a cause you never heard of, you heartless bastard . . ."). All in all, it was too much vicarious self-adulation for a celebrity-by-proxy to handle, suggesting not only that money couldn't buy happiness but perhaps it bought the very depression he'd been grappling with.

And so even though his family wasn't Jewish or Christian but more free-form Buddhist (it was a Hollywood thing), Rupert Jr. decided to see what the Bible had to say about his theory. (Oops.) Well, perhaps great art was the balm his soul needed. So he watched *Citizen Kane*, a verified Hollywood classic. (Oh crap.) Maybe *A Christmas Carol*, about which he'd heard good things, about once a year, it seemed. And there, finally, was the misery vaccine he'd been looking for, in the form of Tiny Tim and the Cratchits. Except Rupert Jr. didn't feel any better. In fact, he felt worse. Because it was pretty clear who Scrooge was in the scenario. And it was pretty clear where the whole thing was going, no need to watch all the way to the bitter end.

By this time, Rupert Jr. was deep into that peculiar voodoo mindset of the clinically depressed in which random events and coincidences become the voice of the universe, talking to you, letting you know what needs to happen next. And if you don't listen the first time, the universe will repeat itself in the form of even more resonant random events and coincidences until the sheer weight of them forces you to finally get it—and get on with it.

And with that, Rupert Gunn Jr. placed the family namesake into his mouth and got started on getting life right the next time around.

Several million mouse clicks later and there was V.T. Lemming, CEO of Quire, standing with both fists planted at the head of the boardroom table, another him inverted in its shiny surface, as if the CEO was balancing on his twin via the nexus of their fists. "I'm going to be testifying about this one," he said, lifting his head to look down the length of the table. There they were—*his board*—all heads silent, all heads bent over their smartphones, perhaps watching their share prices free-fall in real time.

"Somebody *say* something!" V.T. finally shouted.

Nothing.

He'd been hoping for a flinch at least. But when the bent heads remained silent, V.T. Lemming took a breath and proceeded to practice some of the anger management skills that would come in handy a few months later, surrounded in a Home Depot parking lot by the Bay Area's finest, their guns drawn on the only available suspect.

The irony was, they'd already been working on the suicide thing—teen suicide especially. It had seemed the corporately responsible thing to do, seeing as teens still had a lifetime of earning ahead of them, meaning the settlement for a liability case would involve some serious ouch money, even for a non-celebrity-related teen, should some grieving parent decide to blame Quire for their loss of a child. That was the thinking triggered by that Harvard Business School study. They had checked the study's numbers against Quire's own usage stats among teens and found that a "not insignificant" number had left the platform "with extreme prejudice."

So V.T. ordered them to "put somebody on it," which they had. Meanwhile, the marketing people, in anticipation of algorithmic success, had started penciling out a campaign, beginning with a killer slogan: "It's one thing to save you money; it takes a special company to save your life."

They'd been focus-grouping possible branding and licensing schemes and other ways of monetizing their suicidal ideation detection app, the idea being that saving someone's life was a good way to get a lifetime customer.

"Just spitballing here," a marketing guy said, worrying a Nerf basketball.

The names being tested included: NewDay, BullyProof, SunnyUp, YouStrong, BetterDays, NoH8ters, and Jack. The spitballing guy especially liked Jack—thought it was edgy, but at the same time, kid friendly.

"'Yeah, I talked to Jack today, and boy, am I glad I did,'" he said, so they could get a feel of how "the kids" might use it, you know, when talking.

"Or," another marketing guy wanting in on it said, "if you're thinking about killing yourself, you don't know Jack."

Good work, they'd been told.

Two days and four million hits later, they were all fired.

And then the CDC came out with a report that showed suicide was at an all-time high across the US, a rise not directly correlated to the proliferation of social-media users but trending uncomfortably close to it. That coupled with the graphic viral video of a kid with everything to live for who didn't, well, time to start the scapegoating.

That's how V.T. saw it. That he articulated it out loud—and some boardroom Brutus recorded it—was unfortunate. The MP3 followed the same viral path as the original video, and was linked to it forever via "you may also like" or "related" or "you might also be interested in." And even though what V.T. said wasn't *untrue*, per se—just badly timed and tone deaf—that didn't stop the trolls from using it in meme after meme. For a while, you couldn't go anywhere online without hearing V.T.'s voice saying: "Christ, it's not like we *invented* suicide," accompanied by a video of Rupert Gunn Jr. losing his head, followed by an especially emotive Face Girl reacticon displaying her horror.

# 8

George could flash back to it anytime he needed to—any time he needed fuel to stoke his anger. All it took was that first little rip that then tore straight down his psyche. Fingers—those were the triggers—specifically outstretched fingers, desperate to connect but restrained from doing so, being pulled apart by the laws of property, ownership, territoriality, the laws of lines in the sand, and the terrible penalty for being caught on the wrong side of one.

It happened in ninth grade without his willing it, while George was looking at the panel from the Sistine Chapel of God and Adam, a spark gap apart, their fingers reaching forever but not quite touching. Suddenly, he was five years old again and in immigration court—right in the middle of an art appreciation class (or some other course the teacher was trying to smuggle culture into, despite slashed funding and a policy of teaching to the test). While in the flashback's throes, George saw everyone in class turning around to stare at him, at the tears running down his face. And as embarrassed as he was, he still welcomed the misdirection because it meant they weren't looking lower, where he crossed his legs, hoping his pants would dry before the bell rang, watching the clock's hands, blurry through tears.

"Mr. Jedson," his teacher asked, "do you need to be excused? Do you need me to call someone?"

No. No, he didn't. George shook his head, furiously, found his voice, and said, "No, Ms. Kozlowski. I'm . . . it's . . ."—*think*—"allergies, I think."

He mashed a hand over one eye, then the other, smearing with the same fury with which he'd shaken his head. He sucked in a loud sniffle, dragged a sleeve underneath his nose, sniffle-sucked again.

"You're sure?" his teacher asked.

George nodded, noting what he wasn't hearing: his fellow classmates laughing. Instead, they'd all gone quiet and were busying themselves looking everywhere but at him. George could read their minds. *Thank God,* they were thinking, *it's not me making a scene.*

George stopped going to school after that. Instead, he started taking BART out of Oakland to downtown SF, hung out at City Lights Bookstore, and considered himself "a homeless person in training," while he worked up the nerve to run away for good. In the meantime, he went undercover, test-driving his ability to survive on his own.

He'd picked up that MBA "dress for success" BS from one of his fosters. To George, it sounded like some corporate version of drag, wearing the clothes of the job you wished you had. But not being in school anymore left him with plenty of time. So he pinched some techno dweeb wardrobe from a dry cleaner. It seemed that—contrary to myth—techno dweebs who've gotten the personal hygiene talk at work *will* use dry cleaners, going straight from their moms doing their laundry to somebody else doing their laundry. George finished off the costume by getting a playing card laminated before attaching it to a lanyard and tucking it into his breast pocket. After that, he hopped on company shuttles, complaining about how his smart chip must have brain damage, so someone else would swipe him on. It helped that he was tall for his age and generally ethnic enough to discourage confrontation and/or direct eye contact.

Using his disguise, George toured the Bay Area, going from one corporate campus to another, living off geek droppings: half-finished

Starbucks, breakfast sandwiches and bagels left where they'd been placed down, only a bite or two missing, so the guy (it was always a guy) wouldn't have to argue about the algorithm he was arguing about with his mouth or hands full.

George listened for buzzwords he googled later, discovering to his delight that he actually had a knack for programming, including some of the shadier varieties he found after surfing to some of the shadier sides of the web, the part where anonymity was the whole idea and the front door wasn't Google, but had to be picked open using tools like Tor.

In retrospect, George figured he *did* owe the foster system an acknowledgment after all. It was because of them he'd been moved from Los Angeles, where he'd been born, to the heart of the action in Northern California, where he proceeded to circle the map around the San Francisco Bay, from San Jose to Oakland to Alameda and back to Oakland. And it was because of the foster system he had learned to be sneaky. That was a trait they shared—hacking and surviving foster care—because they both depended on learning the rules even as they changed on the fly, and then figuring out the loopholes and how hard you could push against this or that pressure point without having the whole thing backfire.

The first things he ever hacked outright were the various parental controls set by one of his foster families. It wasn't that he was especially interested in violence or pornographic content—well, at thirteen he was—but their being kept from him was what made them so tempting. Plus, figuring out loopholes, work-arounds, weakest links, and exploitable exploits made his brain smile like almost nothing else did. And these same skills came in handy when George decided to remove himself from the foster system once and for all, two years sooner than the system would have kicked him out.

Once he was on his own, George started school again, in a manner of speaking. His major? Whatever he was interested in, which was mainly computers by then. All he needed was a library with a decent internet connection, the soul of a cat burglar, and a case of insomnia that came naturally after moving from family to family where nobody respected your stuff. Conveniently, George's belongings had been whittled down to what he could comfortably carry in a backpack.

One of the things George had working in his favor was living at a time and in a place that had devalued books, objective facts, and pretty much anything that got in the way of blissful ignorance. Otherwise he may have had more trouble getting around the library's security, which was, frankly, a joke. The computers were locked down six different ways, but that didn't stop him from using them where they were. And as far as any other burglar-proofing was concerned, it fell somewhere north of a cemetery, one of the few places even less likely to get broken into, now that grave robbing had stopped being a thing. Dead bolts, two—those were the security system—and useless if you were already inside.

George's MO was pretty simple: split his time between haunting the shelves and surfing the web until minutes before closing, when he'd dart to the men's room, stand on the toilet seat, and shift an acoustical tile out of place. A steel-lattice support beam was close enough to pull himself up by and into the rafters, where he'd nudged the tile he removed back into place with the toe of his shoe. And then he waited for the lights to go out down there and the sound of the doors being locked. After that, drop down from the ceiling, pull a flashlight from his pack, and wander to where they kept the books on computer science, including all four volumes of *The Art of Computer Programming* by Donald Knuth, volume one of which carried a blurb by no less a geek god than Bill Gates, offering to consider a job application from anyone who could get through all 652 pages of it. And that was just the *first* volume. By the time he'd be ready to hijack a certain CEO's EV, George was nearly finished with volume three.

When living off geek discards wasn't enough, George would collect cans and bottles for their California Redemption Value or CRV, basically a deposit dressed up as an incentive to recycle. With his hacking skills improving all the time, it might be expected he'd attempt something more lucrative, like identity theft. But George wasn't interested in hurting anyone who couldn't afford it. The owners of Trader Joe's, on the other hand, probably weren't going to bed hungry anytime soon.

And so he decided to maximize the efficiency of his CRV collection. He did this by printing a bottle's bar code onto a strip of reflective bicycle tape he then wrapped around a Coke bottle he weighed down with small rocks. He'd take this to a bottle return machine, the neck lassoed with a piece of twine in case the weight wasn't enough to keep it from being rolled into the crusher. And then he'd guard the machine as it spun the same bottle around, over and over, the CRV tallied in a do-loop until he reached the store's daily limit and the machine spat out the receipt to take to the cash register.

George didn't consider this stealing so much as an investment on behalf of society in himself, George Jedson, who'd begun seeing himself as the nexus of San Francisco's past and its rapidly emerging future, from Haight-Ashbury to Silicon Valley. And if anyone had ever asked him what he wanted to do with his life, George would have summed it up so that it incorporated both: "I want to code the best minds of my generation."

# 9

Their neighbors would tease her father about the satellite dish, which was nothing to rival Arecibo, but could probably give NORAD a good run. Nevertheless: "Whatchadoin', neighbor? Lookin' for intelligent life?"

"Well, given the local choices," her father would say back.

And then they'd laugh, her father and the neighbor, because neither man counted the other as being included in the implicitly maligned "local choices." Either that or it was another inside joke of adulthood Pandora was still waiting to get.

While the Lynches' setup was ahead of its time for Fairbanks, it wasn't like the locals lacked their own means for communicating with the outside world. Take Pandora's grandfather. When he was still alive, Herman Lynch had shown his granddaughter what he called the granddaddy of that shiny new webby thing all the kids "down there" were talking about: ham radio.

"I can talk to anybody in the world," Herman had said, "under the right atmospheric conditions. Assuming they've got a setup and handle and feel like talking."

To Pandora, Grandpa Lynch's setup looked like something straight out of James Whale's *Frankenstein*, the DVD of which her dad played pretty much every Halloween, along with *The Exorcist* when she was older. And while her grandfather's comms center lacked Dr. F's zapping

Jacob's ladders and Tesla coils, it nevertheless had plenty of dials and boxes that leaked orange light from the actual vacuum tubes they had inside.

When she was little, Pandora would sit on her grandfather's knee as he soldered. She liked watching the metal tip of the iron turn from yellow-blue-black to incandescent cherry red, a pencil-thin lick of blue smoke curling away from it before Grandpa announced it was ready. And then he'd bring it down on the powdery gray twist of oxidized lead, turning it with a touch into a quivering bead of silver. They'd get away from him sometimes—more frequently the older he got—the runaway metal rolling like a ball of mercury, off the edge of the worktable, leaving a silver splash on his work boots, every pair of which was as spangled as any Van Gogh night.

It was Herman's ham-radio hobby that influenced her father to become a therapist who only saw patients long distance over the internet. As far as where Herman picked up the bug, he thanked the navy for that—the signal corps specifically. He'd served during WWII, where his job was to listen to static all day, running up and down the radio spectrum, trying to discern if there was any snow on the line that might be something else.

Herman Lynch hadn't waited to be drafted—or even for America to enter the war. He'd signed up and was among the first to arrive after the attack on Pearl Harbor, an experience that stayed with him all his life and one of the reasons why, after the war, he "retired" to Alaska, where he planned to become a recluse—Herman the Hermit—fishing and hunting to keep his body alive, tinkering with homemade electronics, maybe a little astronomy because it was good for the soul. And that's pretty much how it worked out—with the exception of being a hermit. Instead, he found himself with a wife, of all things, and before it was too late, a son, too, named after a common bit of ham-radio lingo.

"It drove me crazy as a kid," Roger told Pandora. "I'd keep thinking my dad was calling me, only to find out he was just agreeing with somebody on the radio."

Roger remembered a lot of the same things his daughter remembered about Herman, who'd been a lot more precise with his soldering when his son was growing up. For the boy Roger, the glowing iron was a magic wand, enabling his father to create all manner of miracles, like a clock with no moving parts, only a series of tubes with their own magical-sounding names—Nixies—their filaments twisted into a nest of numbers from zero to nine, each glowing in sequence as the minutes and hours counted up. Another time, his father built a sound recorder out of a couple of empty spools and a long strand of wire, winding and unwinding between the two, the magic happening somewhere in the middle, where the wire passed through what looked like the clippy part of a clothespin.

And then there was the computer—the first Roger had ever seen, built from a Heathkit. His dad programmed it using something that sounded like the Morse code he'd taught his son, but with a different-sounding name: binary. Eventually, Roger would get his own computer without having to build it from parts: a Commodore 64. His parents gave him one for Christmas one year, saying they were giving him the future, just as he would give his own child the world someday.

When Roger was growing up, his father used to tell him amusing stories about his war experiences, pranks pulled, stupid things done or said, some near misses, but nothing dark until Roger brought home a VHS copy of *Tora! Tora! Tora!* from the Fairbanks Blockbuster.

"I was there," the old man said.

"Where?"

"Pearl Harbor," Herman said. "We weren't at war yet. We were steaming toward the territory of Hawaii for what everybody aboard saw as some glorified government-funded vacation. We were headed to rotate the vacationers who were already there back to the States. Nice work if you can get it.

"The awful news came over the wireless, followed by the president's infamy speech, and there went our vacation. In its place, we got to imagine the hell we were headed toward, knowing that when we got there, we'd be fishing corpses and body parts out of the drink. The ones the sharks hadn't gotten were warehoused with a bunch of dehumidifiers until the bloating went down and they could be shipped back in normal-sized coffins, draped in flags without a star for the place where they died.

"The sweetheart detail was going fishing in rubber rafts, hauling a magnet through the waters of the Pacific, dragging the ocean floor for dog tags to record and send back to wives and mothers who'd been told not to worry, that the soldiers were living in paradise."

His father paused, drew the finger underneath first one eye, then the other.

"I got a souvenir from back then," he said. "Wanna see it?"

Roger imagined—he didn't know what—body parts, maybe. Something grisly to match the stuff his father had brought back with him inside his skull. He nodded oh so carefully as his father scooted his postmaster's chair to a box in the corner, its flaps dog-eared soft from frequent openings and closings.

"You know what this is?" he asked, holding up the fluted body of a ukulele.

Roger nodded, got as far as "Uke," when his father cut him off.

"It's a smile machine," the old salt said. "I defy anyone alive to pluck even a single string without smiling." He handed it to his son. "Go ahead; you try."

Roger began smiling just reaching for it. He couldn't help it. It was such a silly-looking thing, more toy than serious musical instrument.

But maybe that was the point. It wasn't serious. It was a machine for the manufacturing of smiles. He plucked a string.

"Bingo," his father said.

It wasn't his father's wartime trauma that inspired Roger to become a therapist; it was his mother's. Gladys had a nervous breakdown shortly after the war and ended up getting electroconvulsive therapy. Despite its reputation, ECT had worked for her, and Roger became infatuated with the idea of therapeutic resurrections like the one his mother laid claim to.

"It was a miracle," she said. "No doubt in my mind."

"Least not anymore," Herman said, before calling her by the name he called her when they were both in a good mood, "right, Sparky?"

"Roger that," Gladys said back.

Roger hadn't known what triggered his mother's breakdown, though he vaguely resented it, considering it unearned compared to all the reasons his father had but hadn't succumbed to. He took vicarious pride in that, all the pressure he imagined Herman withstanding. The pressure not only of waiting to be torpedoed, but of sitting in a radio shack, listening as if lives depended on it, because they did. Or had. Roger could see it clearly in his mind's eye: a government-issued cigarette smoldering in an ashtray, the smoke rising straight up in the unstirred air, lit in the yellow cone falling from a gooseneck lamp, alongside the clipboard log, his father, impossibly young and in khaki, sleeves rolled, nape shaved and sunk between tensed shoulder blades. He'd be wearing black Bakelite headphones, his hands pressing them against his ears as if trying to squeeze out a few more decibels. His pink ears strain to hear something in the nothing, the snow noise coming from between the stars, the background echo of the big bang raining down from everywhere: static. On either side of it, there's organized sound—music, the news, serialized suspense, religious demagoguery. None are what his father is listening for: that subtler static that is but isn't, the static he needs to separate like "picking fly poop out of pepper"; over here, noise; over there, signal.

*That's where the future began,* Roger thinks. Not with the gift of an eight-bit computer, but in that little shack aboard a glorified tin can, where history forked in two, one branch leading to a smartphone in every pocket, the other to every third-world madhouse armed with nukes, the branches bending and meeting again in Iran, its nukes nuked by lines of code dubbed Stuxnet, the first shot in the next war, the one fought with hacked elections, chatbots, fake news, and old-school propaganda—a war of words mightier than any sword, and doing real damage in the real world . . .

Roll the clock back and there was Herman Lynch, sitting at the nexus of said future, a lonely WWII radio tech, intercepting the coded communiqués it would take the world's first electronic computer to eventually crack. The fact that his father-to-be hadn't cracked himself fascinated Roger almost as much as the fact that his mother had.

Why?

How stressful could it be, saving newspapers, tin, and bacon grease for the war effort? Was dancing with the doomed at the USO hall so hard? Or was it having to write an assembly line of Dear John letters later, to the ones who stubbornly kept living, and writing? Not that he knew for a fact that she'd done any of those things, but weren't those the roles most women got to play back then? And yet it was her—his *mother*—who got the luxury of having a breakdown?

*Amazing . . .*

Gladys inspired her son to become a therapist in other ways as well. There was her hyperexpressive face, the one he'd inherited and later passed on. That face got him interested in emotions, as well as in those who could hide them versus those who couldn't. Combining his parental influences, Roger set up shop providing pro bono (i.e., amateur) counseling to hermits in the more remote parts of Alaska via ham radio when he was no older than his daughter was now. At least it was something to fill the hours when the cabin walls and weather pressed in.

Unable to prescribe controlled substances at the time, young Roger took a cue from his father and recommended the ukulele instead. For those who couldn't find a uke at their nearest trading post, a simple kazoo made from wax paper folded over a comb. A lot of his pro-boners went this route, and the funny thing was, it was . . . *inherently funny*. The vibrations against the lips tickled, and since they were already there, the lips went with it and smiled. It was as much a reflex as tapping a crossed knee, and a gateway expression to not killing themselves.

"That goddamn comb thing worked, you goddamn whatever you are . . ."

Even as an amateur, Roger knew better than to use the word *therapist* with the lonely Alaskans he found on the other side of the microphone. "I'm just a guy who likes to talk," he said.

"Well, you should keep doin' it. You're good."

Roger would have been content to stay an amateur and local—but a detour presented itself and he took it. He'd been out of high school for over a year when Roger ran into another academic procrastinator who also happened to own a Commodore 64, which he'd Frankensteined into something he swore was going to be big someday.

"People are going to be able to do what we're doing, but over computers linked together all over the planet," the future CEO of Quire Social Media Group LLC told Roger. "You should come to San Fran, man. Things are starting to percolate. Take that head-shrinking routine to the next level. And who knows, you might even meet some beach babe and get laid . . ."

Sitting there, in Fairbanks, Alaska, in the dead of winter—talking bearded bachelors out of taking a rope for a ride—Roger found the prospect of beach babes and getting laid to have a nearly galvanic effect. "So, like, how?" the amateur therapist asked.

And so, like, Vladimir T. Lemming explained.

"Put wanting to save people on the college app," he said. "Add moving anecdotes about actually having done so. Get it postmarked from Fairbanks freaking Alaska. They'll be *throwing* scholarships at you." To sweeten the deal, V.T. threw in his parents' semifurnished basement so Roger could bank the campus housing subsidy. "You'd be stupid not to. Over."

And so Roger Lynch found himself at Fairbanks International Airport, an Alaska Airlines ticket to San Francisco in his pocket, waving goodbye to the parents whose legacy he was, heading into the future they'd promised him during that Commodore Christmas not so long ago.

California was where Roger met Pandora's mother, though not in the way he told his daughter they did. For one thing, they *hadn't* been listening to the music streaming service Pandora, which she *wasn't* named after. Their respective earbuds *hadn't* been playing Adam Ant's "Goody Two Shoes" at the same time, signaling their algorithmic compatibility. Despite the big talk about beaches and babes, the truth was, Roger was both mystified and terrified of the fairer sex, in part because he'd not had much experience with it outside of his mother. The cliché was that there were roughly ten men for every woman in Alaska, and while the reality wasn't quite that bad, it also wasn't that far off. And so Roger largely monked it through college, then grad school, then his thesis and residency, explaining to his singular friend, Vlad, that he was busy, needed to focus, was crushing for this or that. And after all the schooling and qualifying and licensing, well, he had a practice to establish, a reputation to nurture, and . . .

"You're still a virgin, aren't you?" Vlad had said.

Roger's uncontainable face confirmed it was so. And so Roger's friend, V.T. Lemming, hacked into a computer dating site, ran an algo of his own coding based on what he knew of his friend's likes and dislikes, and assembled a small database of likely prospects for hooking up within the greater Bay Area. Based on these prospects' profiles and contact info, V.T. calculated the likelihood that a given prospect would be at a given bar on a given Friday night and made sure that Roger was there as well. It was the least Vlad could do, he explained, in exchange for all the free counseling his college buddy had provided through a string of failures—the same he'd become famous for, once V.T. stopped failing.

"This looks like it should have gangsters hanging from meat hooks," Vlad had said upon visiting his college roomie's first office space, a wannabe crack house in the Tenderloin.

"You'll see, once I put up the 'Hang In There, Baby' cat poster, it's all coming together."

Vlad had nodded sagely. "*That's* what's missing." But the bravado had been false, seeing as he hadn't come to tease his friend, but to seek his help in deciding between declaring bankruptcy or attempting flight off the Golden Gate Bridge.

"Leaping to your death is a rotten way for a Lemming to go," Roger had counseled before tipping a glug of pure gin into his friend's coffee cup, before assuring him that he'd catch the next wave. "And in the meantime," he'd added, sliding open his bottom desk drawer, "may I recommend this." He'd helpfully plucked a string, to show Vladimir how it worked.

And it did. And it continued to. And so, yes, the least Vlad could do for Roger's saving his life was make sure his friend had one worth living.

After his wife died, Roger didn't so much decide to go back to Alaska as simply submit to a need that tugged at him through his belly button. His brain added its two cents by assuring him it was the only sensible move. Among other things, he'd need the free babysitting his parents could provide; he also felt more at home there, meaning Alaska, the place that had programmed his circadian rhythm at a practically cellular level. Plus, as hard as he might try, there was no way Roger was going to grok California quite as well as he already grokked Alaska. For one thing, California—and San Francisco, especially—was in a constant state of upheaval, and not only because of the earthquakes. From the beatniks to the hippies to the gay liberation movement and beyond, including its latest incarnation as the Brotopia of Tech Bros, San Francisco practically invented the concept of reinvention; if the city had an official flag, it would feature an overhead crane framed against a big old sun reflecting off the bay.

Which was all well and good for the people it was well and good for, but Roger wasn't one of them. Fortunately, by the time he and his daughter were ready to board a plane back to the frozen North, V.T., whom his friend and therapist had seen through failure after failure, had finally caught that wave and was riding it toward what would eventually be the third publicly traded company to reach a trillion-dollar valuation: Quire.

"I've got a proposition for you," V.T. told him as they sat in Roger's office for the last time.

"Okay," Roger said, manning the gin bottle, as usual.

"I'd like to put you on retainer," V.T. said, "for my staff, who may need a little therapy, working for me."

"How would something like that work?" Roger asked his old friend.

"Satellites. We'll call it 'permanent flexiplace,' and you can raise that daughter of yours using real money instead of getting paid in fish and bearskin rugs."

"It's not *that* bad," Roger said. "Fairbanks may not be as cosmopolitan as, say, Anchorage, but . . ."

"I'll take your word for it," V.T. said. "And if your plate fills up with locals, you can quit any time." He downed the rest of his gin, crumpled the Dixie cup like he was crushing a beer can, and tossed it over his shoulder. He shot out his freed hand. "Deal?"

Roger took his friend's hand. "Deal," he agreed.

# 10

It peeved V.T. that his company, his reputation, and his bottom line would come down to a question of due diligence over the issue of suicide. With a name like Lemming? *Seriously?* That was taking the whole name-as-destiny thing way too far. The only way he could take it further was to eat a bullet himself, something his college roomie, Roger, talked him out of once and for all by predicting the headline that would follow: "Lemming Kills Self. Well, Duh . . ."

Even before that Gunn kid took his own name too far, V.T. had a guy working on the whole teen suicide thing. And he'd gotten close, but close in preventing suicide still equals dead kids. Worse than that, it handed their parents a class action on a platter because marketing got ahead of the code, and now Quire *owned* teen suicide. Never mind all the bullies, bad parents, bad brain chemistry, and bad luck that also played a role; it was now all *Quire's* fault.

So he needed to fix that algorithm, the one that—had it *worked*—would have prevented this disaster. Which meant finding a coder who took ending teen suicide seriously. One who would treat it like what it was: a mind game of epic proportions. He needed a neural net using machine learning to do for teen suicide what Deep Blue did for chess, Watson for *Jeopardy!*, and AlphaGo for Go. In other words, he needed an AI that could play mind games better than someone with an actual mind.

But who was he going to get who was naive enough, idealistic enough—frankly *stupid* and/or *crazy* enough—to risk their reputation on the coding equivalent of walking on water while carrying the Holy Grail? Don Quixote didn't write script, did he? So who else was there?

George's recruiter was dressed to scare: black suit, white shirt, black tie, black glasses, pigtail wire connecting one ear to something underneath his jacket, a Secret-Service-y vibe, but as much a costume as if he'd dressed like a circus clown. "Sir?" he said, bowing deeply into George's airspace. In the distance, the Golden Gate Bridge seemed to float on a cloud of fog; seagulls disappeared and reappeared at will.

"Herr?" George said, retrieving the arm he'd stretched across the back of the bench before Secret Agent Man deposited himself without invitation.

"Do you recognize this?"

George looked at the object the guy was holding like a badge—one that practically touched the young hacker's nose. "Um," he said, crossing his eyes, trying to bring whatever he was being shown into focus. Pulling back, he finally saw it. A smartphone looping a GIF of one V.T. Lemming rolling off the hood of his car in an Oakland, California, parking lot, hands in the air, suit coat polka-dotted by the laser sights of a half dozen police officers.

"Oh yeah," George said. "I recognize that, all right."

"So you admit responsibility?"

"I admit *seeing* the video," George said. He pointed at the counter listing the number of times that particular clip had been viewed. "Me and two, no, wait, *three* million others."

"I see you like games," said the guy who clearly didn't.

"I dabble," George said. "Little *Doom* here, some *Angry Birds* there, whenever I'm feeling doomed or angry."

"I'm going to have to ask you to come with me," Mr. Dress-Up said.

"And I'm going to have to ask for a warrant."

"This isn't that kind of ask." And then George was suddenly on the ground with a knee in his back and his wrists zip-tied together.

"What the ever-loving *hell*!" George shouted before noticing the driverless Voltaire approaching them.

"Our ride," his abductor said.

*Nice touch,* George thought.

"You can't tell me this is a surprise," V.T. Lemming said once George was standing there in his corporate suite, still zip-tied but a quick snip away from getting his wrists back, which he started rubbing immediately.

"And *you* are?"

V.T. smiled. "Somebody with your future in his hands."

"Come again?"

"I think we understand one another," V.T. said. "You steal a car, you keep a car, is my point. What follows is, you get lucky or you get caught. I think you realize where you've come out between those two options. Unless there was something else going on."

"Such as?"

"An audition."

"By hijacking your ride?" George asked.

And so V.T. explained. It wasn't the fact that George had managed to remotely commandeer his Voltaire that impressed the CEO, or the hacker's sense of humor evident in his choice of where to abandon it. It was how much better his vehicle's autonomous capabilities were *after* the hack than before. George hadn't just hijacked the car's software; he'd improved it. Certain plays of light and shadow that would have fooled the vehicle's computer vision were now smoothly accommodated, much to V.T.'s relief. Because while he'd desperately wanted his impromptu detour to end, he didn't want it to end in a crash.

"So, my question to you is," V.T. said, "what did you do to my car's software to make it work better and why?"

George shrugged. "It's a nice car," he said. "I figured if it stayed that way"—meaning uncrashed—"it would keep the charges more manageable, should it come to that." Pause. "Is it coming to that?" he asked.

V.T. pinched the bridge of his nose with the tip of his thumb and the side of his index finger, something George would learn the smurfs (a.k.a. his fellow droids, elves, and/or coworkers) referred to as V.T.'s trademarked I'm-thinking-about-it gesture.

"So?" George prodded, to which V.T. said as if on cue: "I'm thinking about it . . ."

No, he wasn't. He'd decided even before he had George kidnapped. He was taking a cue from Jobs and trusting his gut. And it had told him he needed to hire this smartass kid who made software better by breaking into it. And so: "I've decided," he said, dropping his hand and opening his eyes.

"And . . . ?"

"Jail's too good for you," the Quire CEO said. "How'd you like a job instead?"

"What, like cleaning toilets with my toothbrush?"

"Like changing the world with your brain," V.T. said. He paused, steepled his index fingers together, rested his chin where the cross would otherwise go. "I'm offering you a vocation," he continued. "A calling. I'd hold out a red pill and a blue one and ask you to choose, but I think we both know you're not the blue pill sort. You want to know the truth, how the world works. And I'm here—the real world—asking you to work for"—pause—"no, *with*, me."

*Oh, the guy was good. That last, studied pause between "for" and "with"? Masterful. And effective.* "Um, *yes*?" George said.

"A bit more enthusiasm wouldn't hurt."

"*Hell* yes?"

"We'll work on that." And then V.T. Lemming, CEO of perhaps the second most powerful social-media company on the face of the planet, did a little air-stirring thing with his finger. George's escort stepped up, preparing to usher him elsewhere when V.T. raised another finger.

*"Uno,"* he said, reaching into his infamous plaid suit coat, the original to the copy George's wannabe tech dweeb had been wearing. Up close, the differences were obvious. For one, V.T.'s coat had been tailor-made, not lucked into at some Salvation Army resale shop. The outfit's carelessness was of the studied sort and likely the result of a fifty-page strategy doc complete with audience reactions translated into emojis and quantified in thumbs, up or down. And from that coat of studiously tacky splendor, V.T. produced a ring of keys, attached to which hung a buttoned fob. He removed this last from the ring as the remaining keys jangled. He held up the separated fob and added a heads-up with his head.

George nodded back that he was ready, reached up, and caught the fob, which featured a stylized *V* embossed behind the buttoned side.

"What's this for?"

"You," V.T. said. "Consider it a signing bonus."

"But I haven't signed anything," George said, thinking, *So much for the "crime doesn't pay" paradigm.* In his case, crime was pretty much his résumé, curriculum vitae, and job application, all rolled into one.

"Do you know about those fMRI studies that show the brain making decisions before its owner has had a chance to catch up?" V.T. asked.

George shook his head.

"Asked to choose, say, between a red pill and a blue one," the CEO explained, "the brain raises its hand, 'I know, I know,' while the body it inhabits is still making up its so-called mind. There's an actual, measurable gap between the two."

George blinked. As the owner of a brain, he was finding all this talk a little disconcerting.

"We did some of that work here," V.T. said, clearly proud of the fact. "You've heard of Q-Labs, correct?" He said the words like he was asking if George knew what a candy shop was; that's how Quire's latest hire understood it anyway. He didn't bother answering. The question was clearly rhetorical; whoever did Quire's advertising had made sure of that, along with the message V.T. proceeded to spell out.

"It's important that you understand that Quire profits are turned back into Quire innovations to benefit all humankind," the company's CEO said, going on to explain that ever since taxation became tantamount to treason, the government's willingness to sponsor pure research had shriveled to the size of your average congressional testicle. As such, it was up to corporately financed subsidiaries like Q-Labs to move humanity as a species forward.

"You might want to explain that to your buddies on PinkoCommiesRPeople2," V.T. suggested. "Hacksaw Sixty-Nine," he added.

"You've been following my posts?"

V.T. nodded. Waited. Said, "As soon as you're ready."

George's escort leaned in and stage-whispered, "He means now."

George asked for confirmation with his eyes, and V.T. confirmed in words. "It would be nice," he said. "Show of good faith."

George took out his phone, swiped, tapped, and began thumbing. He trolled his own last post on the site, the one in which he'd advised his fellow anarchists they had nothing to lose but their blockchains. He started out soft.

"Hey, a-holes, this right here's the invisible hand of the marketplace giving y'all the one-finger salute!"

The comment was met with immediate and predictable results.

"Blow me . . ." "Dickweed . . ." "Hope you enjoy that capitalist splooge, cash sucker . . ."

George handed his phone over to his new boss. V.T. scrolled, nodding. "Oh, here's a good one . . ." He handed the phone back.

One of the site's regulars was going off on a rant about how he was such a "privacy phreak" he wouldn't even use his turn signal.

GimmeLibberT: "I ain't telling the man which way *I'm* turning, bra."

George smiled. "That's some serious white privilege there, dude."

"?????"

"1: u know u aint getting accidentally cop-shot for pulling that crap and 2: u let the whole ABC soup know what u had for breakfast on Q yesterday."

"Naw, bra, just my Q-mates."

"Yo, bro, Q changed TOS again."

It was, in fact, Quire's frequent changes to its terms of service that brought V.T. to George's attention as a legitimate target. How things had changed . . .

"Crap," GimmeLibberT typed, followed by the redundant "poop" emoji.

"Toodles," George posted back before dragging that part of his life into the little trash can at the bottom of his screen.

Before leaving the Quire executive suite, George decided to raise a finger of his own. *"Uno?"*

*"Sí?"*

"What was that story about?" George asked. "The one about the brain scan."

"You," V.T. said. "And the fact that you accepted this job before you ever did that thing with my"—pause—"I mean, *your* car."

*That's right,* George thought, *I've got a car now.* He looked at the fob he'd been clenching so hard since getting it; there was a stylized *V* outlined in white against his reddened palm.

V.T., looking at his new hire stare at the fob, finally thought to ask, "You have a license, right?"

George was about to say, "Not yet," when the car gifter turned to his escort.

"Get the kid a license," he said. "And maybe a new birth certificate while you're at it. Something where the DOB is a little more conducive to being gainfully employed."

The escort nodded, and that was that: they were leaving George's first meeting with the man himself, the teen already wondering whether he'd be able to afford the insurance on his new ride when it occurred to him he hadn't asked about other forms of compensation, like salary, benefits, how leave worked if he didn't want to ever leave. But before George could raise a finger or say, *"Uno"* (or maybe *"Dos"*), the door to the Quire executive suite had already closed as definitively as any other door he'd ever walked out of for the last time.

# 11

Strange as it is to say, dementia can have a sweet spot. Especially in a family where there's been some bad blood due to bad attitudes, behaviors, ideas, habits, opinions, grudges—pretty much due to any forgettable thing. Because despite all the grief and suffering and premature mourning they'll cause for the survivors, those plaques and tangles slowly gumming up the works of recall can, for a time, provide the perfect memory hole in which to bury hatchets. After all, who wouldn't like to forget some part of their past?

Pandora's fellow in hyperexpressiveness, Jim Carrey, starred in a movie called *Eternal Sunshine of the Spotless Mind* in which targeted forgetting played a central role. It was too bad dementia didn't work that way, more selectively and consistently. But the disease followed its own logic, not working all at once, but progressively, peeling away the years like onion layers, the outermost brittle, brown paper a breath could break, while underneath the memories remained supple and powerful—and liable to bring forth tears for all the contradictory reasons people shed them.

During the first few visits, Pandora found Gladys on the good side of both the facility and her disease, meaning she could still make her own meals but would have trouble telling you what she'd had for lunch—especially if it hadn't been rendered more memorable by, say, the smoke detector going off. This last Gladys addressed directly at one point during an early visit. Turning and pointing an arthritis-crinkled finger at the blinking light over the doorway, she said: "I'm watching you."

"Who are you talking to, Gram?"

"Him, *that*," Gladys said before waving her hand dismissively. "Smokey the Bear over there. I know they're waiting for me to set it off. That's when they turn on the camera and start recording, looking for one more slipup before they send me across the hall."

"Across the hall?"

"The dingbat wing," Gladys said. "The ones who need help taking a dump. But I'm too smart for 'em."

"How's that?"

"Check the fridge."

Pandora did. Mustard, milk, a loaf of bread, and stacked plastic tubs of processed meat.

"I don't get near that damn stove," her grandmother said, meaning the toaster oven. "That's asking for trouble. But if sandwiches were good enough for that Earl fellow, they're good enough for me."

"That's some good thinking, Gram," Pandora said, refusing to check the nutrition labels to see how much sodium and preservatives her grandmother's cold-cut-centric diet entailed.

"You want me to make you something?"

Pandora closed the refrigerator door. "I got a better idea," she announced, prepared to be argued with, but still giving it a try. "How about we blow this pop stand and have somebody serve *us* for a change?"

"You mean a restaurant?"

Pandora nodded and then braced for the excuses involving the 101 dietary issues that made dining out impossible—the same ones that had broken her grandfather's heart before shutting it down altogether. Instead, when she looked up, Gladys already had one boot on and was stepping into the other.

"I'll drive," she said.

"Like hell you will," Pandora said. "You lost your license, remember?"

"That was some *bull*shit," Gladys muttered. "That's what *that* was."

"Grand*ma*," Pandora said, trying for a scold in her voice, but laughing in spite of herself.

Turning into the parking lot for Nanook's Family Diner, Pandora pulled her father's F-150 up to one of the icicle-framed windows, set the parking brake, and then went around to the passenger side to hold her grandmother's gloved hand as she stepped down. Thus far, their adventure in free-range elder care had been uneventful, but that was about to change.

*"Stop!"* her grandmother shouted within seconds of stepping through the door. "I can't see," followed by a surprisingly strong arm shooting out and grabbing the sleeve of her escort's parka.

Pandora froze on the spot. She'd grown unaccustomed to the ways of the elderly since her grandfather passed away, recalling little more than this: their bones were brittle. They could break a hip at the drop of a hat. Did the same fragility apply to their eyes? Could they be struck blind by stepping the wrong way? Her grandmother's glasses were already pretty thick, so . . .

Pandora could feel the panic rising toward her face as she imagined the ordeal of navigating her now-blind grandmother back to . . . *where*? Did they allow blind people back into the assisted-living side? Or did the sudden onset of permanent night herald her grandmother's exile to extended care? But as she turned to ask the rules, it became clear that Gladys's glasses weren't. The culprit wasn't fog, but ice, caked thick around the lenses. It was thirty below outside, seventy-five and humid inside, thanks to the breakfast buffet's steam tables. Of course her glasses had iced up.

"Oh, for Pete's sake," Pandora said, unhooking the spectacles from around her grandmother's ears before turning and turning again, looking for someplace to thaw them. A waitress, sight-challenged herself, tapped her on the shoulder and pointed to the baseboard heater running along the outside wall, next to a coatrack where parkas hung and underneath which boots puddled.

"Thanks."

"No prob."

Her grandmother blinked, her old blue eyes seeming suddenly smaller without the Coke-bottle lenses in front of them. The effect changed her whole face, making it seem naked, defenseless, and far from the manipulative, stink-eye-inflicting hypochondriac Roger had made his widowed mother out to be.

"Hot," Gladys blurted after Pandora tried returning the newly thawed lenses to their former resting place. The teen flinched, pulling back, a stem in each hand.

They hadn't even had breakfast yet. They'd not gotten a table, much less looked at a menu, and already she'd succeeded in blinding, then scalding her father's mother, making her wonder if maybe this punishment was a twofer, intended to teach a lesson not only to Pandora but to the estranged Gladys as well.

They got a booth next to the window they were parked outside of, so Pandora could make sure that the cord from the underhood heater stayed plugged in to the complementary kiosk. It was not unheard of for roaming bands of Alaskan youth to run through parking lots, unplugging vehicles so they could watch their owners cursing over frozen engine blocks. Pandora had overheard her locker neighbors on the curling team bragging about such adventures back before fate pranked one of them harder than anything she could have come up with.

Gladys cleared her throat of a prodigious amount of old-lady phlegm, making her granddaughter turn away from her ad hoc stakeout.

"Sorry, Gram," Pandora said, hooking a thumb at the window. "Kids."

Gladys nodded, her ropey-veined hands crossed at the fingertips and sporting fresh nail polish, granddaughter-applied at the old lady's insistence that she'd not be caught dead out in the real world without a little "gussying up" first. Pandora caught her trying not to be obvious about looking around to see if anyone noticed her nails, shining bloody red, despite the seasonal gloom. She looked down at her menu, to give her grandmother's vanity a little privacy, but when she looked up again, the old woman's eyes were focused right on her. They seemed to sparkle just short of tearing up, not from sadness but joy. *Over what?* Pandora wondered.

But then it hit her like a ton of proverbial bricks. *Me,* she thought. *She's overjoyed to see* me. By which time, the tipping point had been reached, and the old lady's eyes spilled over, two grudging tears running down the crags and valleys of her well-worn face, forcing her to lift her glasses to dab at the ducts with the edge of her napkin, leaving a single white flake of it behind.

Pandora gestured, trying to indicate that Gladys had something on her face.

"What is it?" Gladys asked as Pandora reached over and removed the offending speck. She presented it, stuck to the tip of her finger.

"I get emotional sometimes," Gladys admitted. "An old lady's prerogative, I've been told. But also"—she knocked on her forehead with a gnarled hand—"a sign of more senior moments in this old girl's future."

"How bad is it?" Pandora asked.

"I haven't forgotten how to poop on my own," her grandmother said. "Yet," she added.

Pandora's eyes stared; her face, meanwhile, reprised the role that had turned her into a meme. "Jesus, Gram," she said, letting her head sink, along with her curtaining hair.

"Change of subject," Gladys announced, pressing her spread hands firmly down on the table between them.

"Okay?"

"Why do you hide your pretty face?" her grandmother asked, raising a hand to brush Pandora's hair out of the way so she could get a better look.

"Gram, if this face is pretty *anything*, it's pretty embarrassing."

Gladys frowned. "That's *our* face you're talking about, dear."

Ah, the dreaded "dear." Pandora had crossed a line, tried backpedaling. "It's—I'd like a little privacy when it comes to what I'm feeling," she tried.

"Oh yes, privacy," Gladys said, her eye roll making noise. "During the war, the government read our mail and it wasn't any big scandal."

"Which war was this?" Pandora asked.

"The last one that mattered, after the one that was supposed to end any others." She paused. "And then we found that, no, we needed to start numbering them."

"World War II?" Pandora guessed.

Her grandmother nodded.

"I had two brothers who served," she said. "Only one came back. And every letter we wrote each other went through the government censor. All we'd get were photographs of the pages with parts blacked out—'redacted' is what they call it now. They called the photographs V-mail—'V for Victory.'"

"Did you ever get the originals back?"

Gladys shook her head.

Pandora was amazed—and appalled. "What happened to them?"

Gladys shrugged. "Burned, shredded, stored? I don't know. And God help you if your loved one's handwriting was already cramped, because the photographs we got were about the size of a postcard. Some words I couldn't read, even if they hadn't been blocked out."

"That's awful," Pandora said. "It's like Big Brother."

"That book came out after the war, so nobody knew enough to complain." She paused. "Not that anybody would have. Privacy, shmivacy. Our *country* had been *attacked*. Loose lips sink ships. And every break we took . . ."

Gladys stopped suddenly.

"What is it, Gram?"

The old woman shook her head, then mimed pulling a zipper across her lips.

"We're not at war now," Pandora pointed out.

"Oh no? Last I counted, there were at least two."

Pandora let her head sink. She was being tutored in current affairs by someone whose short-term memory was shorter—diagnostically and demonstrably—than even that of the news media, busily flitting after every twittering twit that caught its attention.

"Why do you hide that pretty face?" Gladys asked, as if for the first time.

But instead of correcting her, Pandora decided to document the moment for later reference, should they ever have this conversation again—which they no doubt would. And so she slid around to Gladys's side of the booth and asked the old woman to skootch over. She rested her face on her grandmother's shoulder, raised her phone, and framed the two of them.

"Say cheese," Pandora said.

"Limburger." Gladys smiled—an old joke for an old gal, she'd later claim, the next time she used it. For the moment, though, she stared in wonder at the immediacy with which she was seeing the moment documented, no mailers, no chemicals, no waiting.

"It's not such a bad face," Gladys said, as if she wasn't only selling it to Pandora, but to herself as well. Looking over the top of her glasses to get even closer to the screen, she took hold of the phone as if it were a mirror. "Not bad at all," she repeated, rearranging wisps of white with her free hand. "I think I'll keep it."

"Is there any other option?" Pandora asked, a smartass still being punished.

"A lady," the older one said, "always has options." She paused in her fussing, grimaced, and let it go. "So long as she keeps her legs closed, and her mind open."

Pandora laughed in spite of herself, marking the precise moment she began falling in love with her father's mother.

# 12

The door to the Quire executive suite had closed behind them with the hermetic gasp of an airlock when George's escort removed his dark glasses, loosened his tie, and yanked out his earpiece with an audible pop. Working a finger around his vacated ear hole, he spent a few seconds mouthing Os as if equalizing the pressure inside his skull after a long flight.

"Deep, *cleansing* breath," he announced, rising on tiptoes as he inhaled, squatting on the exhale, and then settling back to his previous, intimidating height. "I think V.T. likes you," he said, making it sound like a blind date's excuse for an overly affectionate Doberman. "Whad'ya do anyway? Get a PhD in neural nets from MIT before turning, what"—he squinted at George, estimating, then up-talking—"*fifteen*?"

"I borrowed his car," George deadpanned.

"I'm sure there's a story there," his escort said, "I'd be better off not knowing."

The two walked in semisilence, the only sounds the squeak of George's sneakers and the tip-tap of his escort's dress shoes. Finally: "So whad'ya wanna see first?" his escort asked.

"My"—guessing—"work cube?"

The other consulted his phone. "Office," he said. He looked at George again, an unmistakable expression of awe on his face, followed by an intimacy-forcing hand on the shoulder. "So whatcha doin' for lunch, noob?"

Along the way to George's office, they passed a face he recognized from the pier where he'd called him Dad while wirelessly infecting his phone. His extravagant suit coat was one of many items he had stuffed into a moving box, along with a framed family photo featuring two kids, one of each, bookended by the jacket and his spouse. They were grouped like a section of the Golden Gate Bridge, George mentally plotting the swoop of suspension cable through the data points of their heads. The smiling face in the photo was a few years younger than the real-life one reddened by either the weight of his workplace knickknacks or the humiliation of being escorted out of the building with them. George looked back, feeling sorry for the guy and wanting to say something, but then they turned the corner and there it was, yanking his eyes back around like a junkyard magnet: his office.

The space had been freshly vacated; that was clear from the dust-blasted outlines of the framed diplomas and/or personal photos that had until recently hung on the walls. Atop the two-drawer cabinet next to the desk, an Olympic logo of water stains, surface tension still holding a last damp ring in place. On the desk itself, a box labeled "Trash" full of cable spaghetti, sporting connectors that had gone extinct with the introduction of USB, then mini-USB, then USB-C. A webbed Aeron chair lay on its back, one caster still spinning, while in the corner of the room, George noticed a pile of fake plastic poop that turned out not to be fake after all. That last memento cured the newbie of any sympathy he may have felt for the weak link he'd apparently replaced in this corporate nature documentary.

"If this is what the interns get," he joked, "I can't wait until management takes me seriously."

"Oh, they're taking you plenty serious," his escort assured. Pause. "You know that little visit with V.T. today?"

"Yeah?"

"First time I ever met the man in person."

"That a fact?"

"Fact."

"How long—" George began.

"Sixteen years," his escort said, not letting him finish.

"Wow, that's as long as—"

*"Right,"* his guide said, more than ready to move on.

The QHQ campus had all the trappings of a successful tech company with more money than it knew what to do with, trying to lure talent away from a half dozen other competitors, equally profligate in their attempts to poach the aforementioned talent. These perks included, in no particular order: snack bars, game rooms, cafeterias, gyms, climbing walls, massage stations, turbo sleep pods, chipping stations, security substations—all of them plural—followed by the offices of the in-house intellectual property lawyers divided into those suing to protect in-house IP versus those defending against suits from the outside, followed by the assorted day cares for children, elder parents, animal companions, and trophy spouses. As one of the company's latest talent acquisitions, George found himself nodding with a mix of embarrassment and trepidation as they followed the facility's intranavigation system giving his tour guide instructions through the earpiece he'd reinserted for the purpose.

"And now we have," his escort would announce, followed by a scripted description of whatever it was.

"Next we have," a little terser with each repetition, George's escort having apparently concluded that lunching his way into the latest golden brat's good graces wasn't going to happen.

"Excuse me," George finally said, realizing that his embarrassment/trepidation was, in fact, the gastrointestinal symptoms of needing a lavatory.

"Sure. Yeah. Okay," his escort said, thumbing his earpiece in a little tighter and then adding, "This way."

As a matter of corporate policy, all Quire bathrooms were unisex, each spacious unit designed for single occupancy and featuring outside it not the generic stick figures hopelessly mired in the binary preconceptions of the patriarchy but the friendly naked people from the *Pioneer 11* plaque.

"V.T.'s idea," his escort explained. "They might be replacing them with the 'poop' emoji, though." Pause. "The nudity's been deemed objectifying."

If he hadn't been convinced of how much of a nerd node Quire HQ was before then, that first trip to the bathroom did it. Whiteboards. They had Wi-Fi-enabled whiteboards in the bathroom. Not only that, but said whiteboards were not subject to the scatological or homophobic graffiti one might expect in a place known for its brotopian inclinations, the cosmetic touch of unisex bathrooms notwithstanding. And so, instead of dirty limericks and freehand sketches of penises, what George found while making his first deposit were snippets of code, the Bellman equation, Zen koans aimed at getting the reader to think about thinking, an occasional quote from *2001: A Space Odyssey* (!), Venn diagrams, quotes from Monty Python, and a flowchart of pseudocode for a machine-learning algorithm to automate the making of either microwave popcorn or ramen noodles, depending on what the variables *X* and *Y* actually represented.

George stood by the sink for a moment, waiting for the faucet to turn on before noticing the wall units for: 1) hand sanitizer, 2) hand soap, 3) hand dryer, and 4) disposable rubber gloves. Collectively, this seemed like overkill, but then he noticed the quirky-retro, hand-operated spigots for hot and cold flanking the faucet above the sink. He wondered about the order of usage, especially for the gloves, finally deciding they came last, to prevent any contamination to or from the door handle, after noticing the wastebasket full of discarded blue jazz hands waiting immediately next to the exit. Surprisingly, there was no placard on the door, insisting that all employees must wash hands before exiting. Perhaps that would have been the actual overkill, considering the audience, George figured, holding the exit open with his shoe as he snapped off his gloves and reemerged for the rest of the tour.

"Bet that's a load off your mind," his escort observed—clearly not part of the script and all the confirmation George needed that, yes, the friend thing was definitely off the table.

After about an hour more of thises and thats—and after it seemed his corporate guide was getting ready to abandon him—George finally asked about what he'd been dying to see all along: "What about Q-Labs?"

Like pretty much everybody else on the planet, Quire's latest hire already knew quite a bit about Q-Labs—or thought he did. This was because of the predictable CYA PR soft shoe: whenever George's new employer got in trouble for mining or manipulating the data of its users, the airwaves would suddenly fill with helpful ads, reminding viewers about all the good things coming out of Q-Labs. These commercials, which corporate insisted on calling PSAs (and for which they claimed a tax write-off), always started with a stark title card featuring an inspiring quote from some dead white guy, followed by a retro synth harpsichord over a moving slideshow featuring AI-enabled bots helping the handicapped, teaching toddlers, trundling in to defuse some terrorist booby trap, or translating the barks and meows of pets into emojis, letting their humans know they were hungry or needed to be let out. Then it was back to a black title card, out of which would whip the rainbow *Q* for Quire, followed by a hyphen and the word *Labs*, each punctuated in turn by a bong, a bing, and a bong—the parent company's audio signature, an inversion of the one used by Intel. Last but not least came the slogan: "Doing good is what we do."

"If you wanted to meet the rock stars," George's escort said gruffly, "you should have said so earlier." He then stirred the air with his finger, meaning they'd be turning the tour around and heading back toward the windowed office they'd started at, smack dab in the middle of Q-Labs territory where George, it seemed, had been assigned to Q-Brain, the lab devoted to the development and commercialization of artificial intelligence.

George nodded curtly and followed, as if this news were only what he expected and not the cause of the fireworks going off in his head, as if it were his birthday, Christmas, New Year's, and Halloween, all rolled into one. It was as if V.T. had seen into his heart and divined the desire that led to his "borrowing" the CEO's car in the first place. Because the excuse about wanting to see if he could do it was exactly that: an excuse. As was any claim he'd done it to score points on behalf of the proletariat at the expense of the one percent and its excesses. Ditto on the needing-a-smile thing. And as far as seeking revenge for the ever-shifting sands of Quire's self-serving terms of service—yeah, that was a good cover story and a big fat no.

The reason George hacked V.T.'s ride was because he wanted to get a look under the hood of the Voltaire's AI. The plan had been to download what he could from the CPU before leaving the hardware for the amateur chop-shoppers to liquidate—a plan nixed by the car's coming with its original owner still attached. George was particularly interested in what the source code had to say about how it would decide between killing its passenger versus a busload of kids when those were the vehicle's only two options. That was the ethical quandary ethicists had dubbed the "trolley dilemma," so named because it went back that far, back to when roads outside San Francisco had cable cars and track-switching decisions were made by humans and implemented manually.

Nowadays, the dilemma was applied to autonomous vehicles and used to show how far they were from prime time. It was also why the Voltaire's autonomous mode was called "copilot," to shift the blame for the inevitable casualties to the owner as opposed to the manufacturer. George figured the euphemism meant the Voltaire's coders hadn't quite automated the dilemma's resolution to their lawyers' satisfaction. However, as a programmer himself, George was also pretty sure there'd be some beta script in the source code, a deleted REM or asterisk away from going live.

The truth was, he'd been dreaming of AI ever since those infamous babysitting episodes with Uncle Jack. His first obsession was to meet the smooth-talking HAL in person (or silicon, as the case may be), only to have his heart broken once he understood how numbers worked and realized that the *actual* year 2001 had come and gone before he was even born, with nothing even remotely like actual artificial intelligence on the horizon.

Doing a casual survey of what the species had accomplished since the real 2001, George was tempted to conclude that "peak humanity" had been reached sometime before either the 2000 US election or the falling of the twin towers. Ever since then, mankind had clearly been on the downslope. But there was one exception. Sometime between his learning how numbers worked and now, AI research had started taking off again, with machine learning, neural nets, and Big Data all converging to stage a legitimate advance into HAL territory.

And now, it seemed, he'd been handed the opportunity to bring his childhood friend HAL into existence. *Pinch me,* George thought.

Or thought he thought.

"I'd really prefer not to," his disgruntled guide said, before leading the homeless boy home.

# 13

The thing about dementia's sweet spot is once you get past it, the rest can be bitter as hell. And though it seemed counterintuitive, Pandora's sudden visits had made things worse. Gladys had been aware of her lovely, lovely brain's going out on her, but had grown to accept it, in part, because she had a secret she could never tell. And she'd kept her secret from everyone—her husband, her son, and all the people she'd left behind in the lower forty-eight to spare her from temptation. Thus forgetting meant putting down a burden, the job of keeping quiet finally complete.

But then Pandora showed up.

Slipping into oblivion without any witnesses was one thing, but doing it—*now*—in front of her only grandchild? After they returned from their adventure in the real world and Pandora went home, Gladys got so anxious she began hyperventilating, thought she was dying right then and there—briefly welcomed it—but then hit the call button. By the time a white-jacketed gentleman knocked on her door, she could not remember having summoned him.

"What's wrong with me?" she asked after opening the door.

"You called me," the doctor said, letting himself in, "remember?"

"Um . . ."

He changed subjects. Noting the way her nightgown clung from excessive sweating and a certain breathlessness in her speech, he made a diagnosis of anxiety to which Gladys assented because she was still feeling it and it was obvious. But the doctor didn't stop there, because anxiety rarely travels alone, especially in the elderly in Gladys's condition.

"The staff are worried you may be depressed," he tested, attributing the secondary diagnosis to others because, well, *hunch* didn't sound very professional.

"Isn't that natural," Gladys asked, "under the circumstances?"

The doctor agreed that it was, but then used it against her. "So you're agreeing that you're depressed?"

Gladys nodded, admitting that, "Yes," she was depressed. "Can't you tell from my face?"

The doctor looked, then looked closer. The truth was, everyone's skin loses elasticity with time. And in Gladys's case, a lifetime of hyper-emotiveness had etched her face with worry lines that could easily camouflage her darker moods, while the lighter ones were made brighter still, the act of smiling helping to iron out even the hardest-set wrinkles. "Ah, there it is," the doctor announced, followed by, "Okay, then," and his prescription pad.

"You can stop that," Gladys said.

The doctor didn't. He clicked his pen and started writing instead.

"I said, 'Stop that,' you shameless pill pusher."

The doctor looked hurt. "Now why would you say something like that?" He chuckled as an afterthought—to show he hadn't taken the remark seriously.

Gladys snatched the pen out of his hand, to show that she was. "What does this say?" she asked, indicating what was written on the side of the pen.

"Zoloft."

"And what does *that* say?" she asked, pointing at what he'd written on his pad.

"Zoloft."

"And here?" she asked, tapping the printed header of the pad, which also read, "Zoloft."

"They hand them out," the doctor said in his defense, meaning the pharmaceutical reps that visited regularly, dispensing ad-emblazoned swag along with advice re: off-label opportunities for prescribing their wares. "It would be a waste to let it go to waste."

"How circular of you," Gladys observed. "Not that it justifies you depriving me of a natural emotional reaction to losing my mind."

"It's not your *whole* mind," the professional prescriber rushed to reassure her—ineffectually. "It's not like you'll be forgetting to breathe or anything. Nothing that falls into the category of an autonomic response."

"How about going to the toilet?"

"Well, that's a learned response," the doctor pointed out. "Potty training and all that."

"So that's a yes," Gladys pressed on. "I might start shitting myself."

"Might, *hell*," the doctor continued, allowing his diagnostic certainty to override any sense of professional decorum. "Pretty much definitely. Your disease has a well-documented progression."

"So maybe remembering how to breathe isn't quite the blessing you're making it out to be," Gladys said, to herself, later, after the doctor had left, replaying the conversation in her head, not so much brooding as trying to make the important parts stick.

"What are those?" Pandora asked two days later, during her next visit.

"What are what?"

Pandora retrieved two amber vials from her grandmother's wastebasket.

"Happy pills," Gladys said. "Apparently, being up-with-people is now mandatory."

"Why'd you fill the prescriptions if you weren't going to take them?"

"That's one of the drawbacks with assisted living," Gladys said. "Sometimes you're assisted against your will. Fortunately, they couldn't find the hose for blowing 'em down my throat, so . . ."

It wasn't until Pandora's visit was nearly over that Gladys confessed it was a shame they'd made her mood an issue, one she refused to let them win.

"Why's that, Gram?"

"Because 'happy pills' don't seem like such a bad idea sometimes," Gladys said. "The side effects, though . . ." She pulled down her copy of *Worst Pills, Best Pills*, dog-eared to the sections on antianxiety and antidepression medications. "Here," she said, handing over the book and then pointing at one of the side effects. "How's *that* for irony?" she asked.

Pandora read about the pharmaceutical paradox of using mood-altering medications on elderly patients with dementia: they could actually speed up the patient's decline. Which raised a question: Was the drug treating the mood, or simply making the patient forget about it? In other words, was it a bug or a feature?

"Wow," Pandora said, looking up from the book. "That sucks."

Gladys shrugged her hunchbacked shoulders. "What're you gonna do?" she asked no one in particular. Not that that stopped Pandora from thinking about it anyway.

Cannabis, marijuana, pot, weed, grass, reefer, ganja, Mary Jane . . .

*That's* what Pandora was thinking about. Even old people were using it medicinally nowadays. The cannabinoids were supposed to help with appetite, anxiety, pain, all constant companions for the unlit elderly. And wasn't that what Gladys needed in a place like this, a little something-something to slow her roll, make it a little more copacetic with the ambient amble of "nursing home life"? And if Pandora needed to demonstrate that the herbaceutical in question was benign, well, that's what you called a win-win situation.

And so she came bearing gifts in a baking pan covered with tinfoil.

"What've you got there?" the old woman asked.

"Um," Pandora said, pulling back the shiny cover, "happy . . . brownies?"

"You mean *medibles*?"

"How do you . . . ?"

"I'm not a prisoner here," Gladys said. "Not yet anyway. I walk. I meet people. They talk. You're not the only relative with a green thumb in baking."

"So?" Pandora said, moving the pan a little closer.

Gladys reached in. "Well," she said, "it would be rude to refuse . . ."

"Cheers," her granddaughter said, tapping her own hash brownie against her grandmother's, a helpful hand underneath to catch any crumbs.

Now *this* was the way to visit an old-folks' home! Because while Pandora got a kick out of her grandmother before, she *loved* Gladys stoned. The feeling, predictably, was mutual.

"Another?" the old lady said, pushing the pan across the kitchenette table toward her granddaughter.

"Don't mind if I do," Pandora said, brushing invisible crumbs off her chin, shirt, and pants, before working up another square of THC-laced chocolatey goodness.

"You know how I knew Alaska was going to be different from anything I'd known before?" Gladys asked around a mouthful of brownie.

Pandora shrugged.

"The toilets. The indoor ones," the old lady said. "I'm sitting on a toilet, and all of a sudden, I'm wondering if I'm having hot flashes even though I was way too young at the time. Why? My butt was sweating to beat the band. I reached for the toilet paper, and I almost slipped off. And I don't know what possessed me, but after I flushed, I held my hand over the water. It was warm. I could feel the heat coming off it. That's what told me Alaska was different. They heated their toilet water so it wouldn't freeze."

"So they don't do that everywhere else?" Pandora asked. She'd not been outside the state since she was a baby, and well before being potty trained.

"Not where I came from," Gladys said. Paused. "Can you bring some more of these next time?"

"Of course," Pandora said.

*Not.*

It should be stressed that the legal status of marijuana in the state of Alaska was a bit bipolar at best. First decriminalized in 1975 and then legalized shortly thereafter, pot was recriminalized by 1990, re-decriminalized by court ruling in 2003, recriminalized by law in 2006, and finally legalized (again) by ballot initiative in 2014. So what Pandora was doing wasn't currently against state law, just the federal ones. And even those weren't a big deal under the previous administration, but then . . .

"I'm sorry, dear," a receptionist said the next time Pandora prepared to walk past with a foil-covered plate of organic mood modifiers, "but I'll be confiscating those."

"Huh?" And then Pandora noticed a dog that hadn't been there the last time. She eyed it and it eyed her back, both flaring nostrils on high alert.

"You can feel free to be charged with a federal crime out there," the receptionist said, pointing outside, "but you're not finding any accomplices in here." She slid a copy of the laminated explanation that informed her that due to a change in federal policy put in place by an attorney general who had personal investments in the for-profit prison industry, the Golden Heart's previous practice of looking the other way was history.

*"Seriously?"* Pandora said, handing back the wobbly sheet of plastic.

"Like a heart attack," the receptionist said, shaking the pan into a wastebasket already lined with a biohazard baggie, the brownies dislodging in twos and threes, reminding Pandora of nothing so much as reindeer scat dotting the snow as its depositor lumbered along.

"Sorry, Gram," Pandora said, after showing up empty-handed.

"About?"

"The brownies," her granddaughter said. "I promised to bring more, but the gestapo at the guest center seized them."

Gladys had gotten up during her granddaughter's apology and seemed not to be listening. She went to her mini fridge and pulled out a plastic tub. "You mean these?" she asked, pulling back the lid to reveal a few leftovers from the day before.

Pandora was touched that she'd saved them. She'd assumed Gladys would do what she'd do—take as needed until they were gone.

Her grandmother divided the remaining brownies onto two paper plates, one for Pandora, one for her. Glasses of milk followed. "Now where were we?" the old lady asked.

"Toilets, I think," Pandora said, figuring they'd exhausted the subject anyway.

*Not.*

They fascinate us at the brackets of life, these receptacles for putting up with our shit. Both when we're young (and learning to use them) and again when we're old (and forgetting what we learned). But even granting the fondness her grandmother often displayed for discussing bowel movements and assorted related topics, Pandora was unprepared for what Gladys casually said next: "Your father was born in a toilet."

"Excuse me?" she said.

"Plopped out right into the bowl," Gladys said. "It was the funniest thing I've seen in my entire life. Your grandfather practically faints, but I'm the one with the kid coming out of me like some astronaut doing a spacewalk. You ever see a fresh umbilical cord? Nasty . . ."

"You're serious," Pandora said, snap-sobered and horrified.

"Listen," her grandmother said, "it was *fine*. There wasn't anything else in the toilet, and the water's always warm, so . . ."

"My dad was born in a toilet," Pandora said, repeating the words, cementing the memory, as if there was a chance in hell she'd ever forget. She could practically hear the splash.

"Yep," Gladys said. "Little shit turned out okay, though."

Pandora was still too stunned to laugh. Ah, but once that wore off—well, then it was a different story.

Gladys had been happy to have her granddaughter there and was happy while the visit and brownies lasted, but once both were gone, the old dark clouds rolled back in. And here's the funny thing about being happy: it's addictive. Maybe not chemically or biologically, but emotionally, which can be more powerful than the other two combined. And so in a moment of weakness, Gladys took one of those pills designed to either make her happy or help her forget that she wasn't.

Nothing.

The pill pusher had left her paperwork explaining that that's the way it would go with one of them at first, warning that she'd have to keep taking it, let it build up in her system, before it would make a difference.

She'd already forgotten that part but reminded herself of it by rereading what the doctor left, then comparing the paperwork to the label on the vial she'd taken the pill from. Zoloft. Right. That was the one that took weeks to do anything. She checked the paperwork for the other. Xanax. That was the one that worked right away. "Well, let's hope so," she said, fishing one out and placing it on her tongue.

# 14

Imagine the tech version of Willy Wonka's chocolate factory minus the Oompa-Loompa slave labor, or Santa's toy shop minus its elfish servitude. That's what the Q-Brain tour was like for George, wandering agog. When it came to "wow factor," Q-Brain was pretty much nothing but, starting with the very first stop: the Glass Brain.

Upon hearing the words, George had assumed they were metaphorical; they weren't. But before he'd be allowed to view the *objet* itself, he first had to show how big he thought an actual brain was.

"What do you mean?" he asked, and the lead researcher—the unit's ad hoc MC—took first one hand and then the other.

"Set your hands to bracket an imaginary brain, perhaps your own."

George did as he was told, and the MC took a picture with his phone to document it. "On average," he went on to say, "people will estimate an organ roughly twice as large as what it actually is." Pause. "No smirking, please." He made a fist and gestured for George to do the same, then bumped their knuckles together. "That's how big the average adult brain is," he said. "The size of two fists." He unclenched his hemisphere to reach for the photographic evidence he'd snapped a moment earlier. "Now how's *that* supposed to fit into your favorite hat?" he asked, opening pincer fingers against the screen to blow up the image.

"Um," George said.

"Because that's where the brain has to fit," he said. "It's inside your head, and though it might *seem* like the cathedral of all knowledge, its cupola is little bigger than side-by-side cup holders." He took a scripted pause. "Think on that and be humbled, human."

Having concluded the canned intro, the tech signaled, and the Glass Brain was wheeled out, jiggling slightly like stiff Jell-O whenever the casters rolled over an uneven seam in the floor. The eponymous object was an actual brain removed from a once-living human. The lipids (fats, basically) had been removed and replaced with a transparent hydrogel that left the crisscrossing fabric of neurons in place, but now visible for detailed study. Using fluorescent dyes of different hues, it was possible to light up and trace the axons of individual neurons, a feat demonstrated by turning off the lights. And there it was, a pale thread, squiggling and branching and looking like nothing so much as the root system of a tree, but lit in firefly green: a lightning strike, frozen horizontally. A voice joined them in the dark: "The floating light bulb used in cartoons to symbolize the moment of discovery? There it is. And we can do that with each neuron in that bundle that warehouses every hope, dream, joy, and moment of despair that makes us who we are." Pause. "You've heard of reverse engineering? Well, this is the first step in doing that for the most precious thing any of us has."

And then the lights came back up, amid silence and blinking, the audience of one given a moment to think about what he'd seen, to imagine that pale thread of green light winding through the hopes and dreams inside his own head.

"We're the Connectome Team," its leader said. "Our goal is to determine if the way information is encoded in the brain is structural. There's no obvious, anatomical hard disk in the brain, so where does the information get stored? Our hypothesis: it's in the *arrangement* of the branching neurons and the spaces defined by the synapses, like bar code, but in three or four dimensions and with a resolution on the nano scale. Our support: recent studies showing that new thoughts create new pathways and hence new *structural* patterns."

"But what—?" George began to ask, only to be cut off by the answer.

"If it's structural," the team leader continued, "then it should be readable postmortem—with the right scanner."

The Glass Brain was the first of many astonishments, and it took real willpower not to go running ahead of his tour guide to see what came next. For example: a rack of caged mice, half of which seemed to be conjoined pairs, attached by their heads. Upon closer inspection, it was clear that these mice had not been born this way.

"Okay, okay, okay," the researcher in charge said, "I know what you're thinking," he added, unironically, and as if he'd had his fill of animal rights activists protesting what he did for a living. "This is serious *science* we're doing here," he insisted. "So if you're thinking about throwing around the *v*-word . . ."

"You mean *vivisection*?" George asked, looking up from the glass cage he'd been smudging with his nose.

The spokesresearcher started waving his arms, crossing and uncrossing them like he was trying to stop traffic. "Transneural communication, thank you," he said. "We're trying to see if something one brain learns can be transferred to the other, without being taught separately." He then explained how they blindfolded and anesthetized one mouse in each pair while the other was taught to run a maze, followed by reversing the procedure to see if the second mouse could run it faster than the first.

"And . . . ?" George prodded.

The researcher's lips grew noticeably thinner. "Promising," he said, leaving it at that.

Next door, two human subjects were seated back-to-back, wearing skullcaps sprouting cables like high-tech Medusae. On a screen visible to George but hidden from either of the wired-up test subjects, a game of *Pong* seemed to be playing itself.

"The gear," a researcher said, waving his fingers over his own head, "is like this combination EEG and TMS—that's transcranial magnetic stimulation. The two go back and forth in a feedback loop, one subject sending, the other receiving, then vice versa. The result? Telepathic *Pong*, even though neither knows *consciously* that's what they're doing."

The researcher went on to explain that by monitoring the subject's heart rate, respiration, and skin conductivity, they'd shown that *subconsciously*, the subjects' *bodies* knew who was winning and who wasn't. In follow-up surveys, the losers reported feeling inexplicably "down" for a few hours afterward, while the winners volunteered for more testing.

"So what does this prove?" George asked naively.

"Prove?"

George nodded.

"That we can do *this*," the researcher said, pointing to the screen. "And it's *cool*." He paused. "Watch this," he said, hitting a button that sounded an alarm, making the players flinch, while the white blip on the screen went sailing past the nearest virtual paddle.

"Okay," George said, noncommittally.

"The days of the joystick are numbered, my friend," the tech predicted.

George tried imagining the mental space he'd have to be in to prefer having electrodes implanted in his brain to holding a physical controller. Sure, the implants might free his hands for eating or drinking or . . .

*"Oh,"* he said.

"Yep," the tech said. "The joystick's dead; long live the, um, 'joy' stick, if you see what I mean . . ."

George wanted to say that a blind mole rat could see what the tech meant but opted for the closed-lip/thumbs-up combo.

"Not that jerking off is all this is good for," the tech hastened to add. "If that was the case, Elon wouldn't be betting big on developing a neural interface to link computers and humans, right?" He paused and then whispered behind his hand, "Next stop, the singularity." He winked.

Though George recognized the reference to the merger of human and artificial intelligence predicted by futurists such as Ray Kurzweil, he couldn't help thinking "the singularity" could be taken several ways, especially given the joystick conversation, if you saw what he meant.

Klieg lights.

That was the first thing George noticed. Once his eyes adjusted to the glare, however, he saw there was much more to see. People, specifically, all of them missing something, from limbs to divots out of their shaved heads. Many of the subjects had been borrowed from the local VA. Quire—George was informed—had something especially unpopular in the tech industry at the time: a contract with the Department of Defense.

"But not one of the *bad* kinds," the latest explainer explained.

"There are *good* kinds of military contracts?"

"Ever hear of a little thing called DARPA?"

George nodded.

"So you know the internet was originally ARPANET, right?"

"Okay," George said, reluctantly, even though he knew it was true; the internet was the result of a joint effort between the Department of Defense's research arm and academia that got out of those institutional boxes and changed the world. For that matter, Tor had been developed by the navy and refined by DARPA.

"All the brain stuff you've seen so far is being paid for because brain trauma has become the defining injury of modern warfare. SSA, Medicare, and Medicaid are also chipping in because of that buttload of dementia patients the boomers are promising to send the Fed's way."

The klieg lights were for a film crew, already shooting B-roll for the next series of PSAs. In front of the cameras, lab techs were helping subjects don virtual reality headsets to see if VR coupled with the brain's plasticity could help rewire any damaged neurons in the spinal cord or farther up. A monitor allowed viewers to see a two-dimensional rendering of what the VA-VR volunteers were seeing, which was an avatar of themselves. The goal was to see if the volunteers could move virtual parts that were impeded in their actual bodies, repeating this over and over until the avatar's movements "leaked" into "real reality."

Elsewhere, a blind vet was being fitted with what looked like a tongue depressor straight out of *A Clockwork Orange*. "There are a lot of nerve endings in the mouth—the tongue, especially—receptors for sweet, sour, salt, umami." Pause. "So instead of taste buds, think rods and cones, RGB, which stands for . . . ?"

George shrugged.

"Red, green, blue," the tech said. "You know, like the original color monitors from . . ." He looked at George like his escort had earlier, assessing his age, pre- versus post-touch-screen. "Never mind," he concluded.

The goal, the tech explained, was to facilitate artificial synesthesia. "You know, hearing colors, tasting sounds . . ."

"Dropping acid," George said softly to himself—or so he thought.

"That's a few doors down," the tech said offhandedly before cutting to the chase. "We're basically rewiring the tongue as a crude retina." He paused, turning toward the volunteer. "So how're we doing?" he asked.

The blind vet garbled something that could have been anything.

"So yeah," the tech said. "Not perfect, but . . ."

". . . a minor miracle nevertheless?" George supplied, either out of generosity or because he wanted to move on now that his curiosity over what they were doing "a few doors down" had been whetted.

The answer? Drugs, mainly. LSD, psilocybin, DMT, peyote, ayahuasca: the usual psychedelic suspects. The room in which they were being done was decidedly un-lab-like in its decor, mixing Southwestern and Far Eastern influences and dousing it all in incense—jasmine, George thought, lavender, maybe. The furniture alternated between bean filled and memory foamed, the goal apparently being the elimination of any hardness that might harsh whatever buzz was being studied. The one exception to the squeezably-soft theme was a military-green filing cabinet that seemed wheeled in straight from some WWII general's office, but for the biometric lock with which it had been retrofitted. The group's "head teacher," who also went by the nickname Dr. Strange, informed George that the file cabinet went by the nickname "our stash" and contained pretty much every mind-altering chemical known to man along with the FDA and DEA paperwork to make it kosher for scientific research. And should these substances alone fail to dislodge the stick up a test subject's mental ass, there was also an old-school isolation tank in the corner, plastered with bumper stickers advocating universal veganism, renewable energy, the visualization of "whirled peas," and, for the 2016 election, a tie between Giant Meteor and Cthulhu.

Dr. Strange, his lab coat tie-dyed, fished through one of his pockets for a peace offering, which George waved off, courtesy of unassisted flashbacks to being babysat by Uncle Jack.

"I'm cool," he said.

"You're *cool?*" Dr. Strange said, eying him strangely. He looked past George to George's escort and would-be character witness. "What says you? Cool? Not cool?"

George's escort shrugged.

Dr. Strange cupped his mouth and thought. "Let's call it cool, until proven otherwise." Pause. *"Cool?"*

*"Cool,"* George agreed.

The next team they visited took coolness not only seriously, but literally as well. Coolness down to about as far as cool could go (i.e., a degree or so above absolute zero), which explained several large frost-covered tanks that dominated the space, surrounded by various wired nests, stacked and shelved controller units, and coiled copper tubing that reminded George of a high-tech distilling operation. The team leader offered that skeptical observers from Q-Brain's other teams had commented derisively on the similarity, suggesting that bootlegging and quantum computing shared a common goal: bottled moonshine. That budget envy might be the true source of such comments wasn't too great a leap.

"Certainly not a quantum one," he said, before warning George to be careful where he leaned. Looking down, George saw that the scientist had begun fingering the stump of his right index finger, the rest of which was missing after the second knuckle. Following George's eyes, the quantum computing team leader held his hand up for closer inspection. "Frostbite," he said.

"Duly noted," George said, pulling in whatever extremities he could a bit closer to his body.

"I call this my Schröfinger," the team leader continued. "You know, Schrödinger's cat?"

"Not personally."

"So you have this cat, a Geiger counter, and a vial of poison in a sealed-off room," the tech explained, "and if the Geiger counter detects any random radioactivity, the poison will be released. Until somebody checks, the cat is in a quantum state of being both dead *and* alive as far as an outside observer is concerned. But when somebody finally *does* check—boom: it's decided." He paused, letting George digest this information. "Well, that's the quantum paradox in a nutshell. Except, instead of a cat, it's a quanta of electromagnetic energy, like light, which can act as either a particle or a wave in a cloud of probability until it's observed, at which point it's definitively called as heads or tails, particle or wave."

George, who'd been nodding along to this explanation, suddenly stuck out a finger, opened his mouth, reconsidered, put his finger away, and closed his mouth. Thus prefaced, his ad hoc physics lecturer took it upon himself to engage in a little mind reading.

*"But,"* he said, on George's behalf, "what's this got to do with my missing finger, right?"

George nodded.

"Phantom limb," the tech said. "It feels like my finger's there until I look down and remember it's not. Hence, Schröfinger."

"Ah," George said.

"So," the tech continued, "you know HAL, right?"

Did he? It was only the voice he'd been hearing in his head ever since he first "met" the fictional AI through his uncle's TV. And damn it—he hadn't even officially started working there yet, but George could feel it; he'd never want to leave this place. These, simply put, were his people: the geeks, the nerds, the fanboys who'd been promised a HAL and would make one themselves if they had to.

"Daisy" was all George said, but it was answer enough.

*"Excellent,"* the team leader said. "So the whole thing with HAL going crazy and killing everybody was the result of the limitations of binary computing. He'd been given contradictory instructions about the mission and went a little crazy as a result, because binary systems are hopeless when it comes to contradictions. To a binary system, it's all bits and bytes—zero or one, yes or no, right?"

George nodded.

"But *quantum* computers don't deal in bits; they use qubits, which can be both yes and no at the same time without canceling each other out or leading to a contradiction error. A qubit can be zero *and* one *and* the fractional infinity in between." He paused to back up to his original point. "If HAL had been a *quantum* computer, he wouldn't have been tripped up by a little paradoxical coding. That's because in a quantum system, the answer yes *and* no doesn't start the sparks flying. Contradictions are what quantum computers do best."

The team leader held up his abbreviated digit, blew across the stump, and voilà: the finger was restored. Or had only been folded over in the first place, seeing as it wasn't the same hand this time.

"Cute," George said.

The team leader went on to predict that while the coders in digital were making headlines for teaching their AIs to beat world champions in Go, it was *his* group—the quants, the qubitters—who'd be the ones to crack the nut of general AI.

"That's because a quantum computer can literally jump to conclusions as opposed to having to brute-force its way through, crunching all possible combinations. It's like the difference between the inventors Thomas Edison and Nikola Tesla. Edison reached his inventions as a result of trial and error, testing and dismissing alternatives until he found the perfect material for, say, the filament for his incandescent lamp. Tesla, on the other hand, arrived at his inventions in flashes of inspiration while thinking about something else.

"To give you an idea of what we're talking about, a quantum computer with three hundred qubits of processing power could perform more calculations than the number of atoms in the visible universe. It could do in minutes what would take a digital supercomputer a billion years to accomplish—if it could, ever. With a computer like that you could feed in a person's genome and it would project their entire life arc. And you could do that for all the people on earth. In minutes. An earth-sized version of *The Sims*, eight billion simulations bouncing off one another like eight billion billiard balls on a table the size of the planet."

"And how far away is that?" George asked.

"Well, we have to reach quantum advantage first."

"And that is?"

"When we finally get enough qubits together to do something that's impossible for a classical computer." He paused. "It could happen next week," he predicted, "or a hundred years from now."

"That's a pretty wide spread."

"Yeah, but once it happens, and it's scalable, that's it. Game over for classical computing."

"Well, on behalf of those of us who'd love a crack at a planet-sized game of *The Sims*," George said, shaking the team leader's discounted hand, "good luck." Turning to leave, he turned around again, to offer up a pair of crossed fingers, which, on second thought, probably wasn't cool.

Next up: the fMRI guys V.T. had mentioned, who answered George's questions even before he knew he wanted to ask them, with the exception of one. He'd noticed a volunteer who looked to be about his age being scanned as the spokestech explained, "We're trying to locate the part of the brain responsible for suicidal ideation in adolescents."

Before George had a chance to ask, the tech explained that the subject, who'd actually attempted suicide, would be asked to go back to that dark place.

"But," George prepared to object.

But the tech was already leaning into the control center's microphone: "Jake," he said, "I want you to think back to when you were in the tub, holding the razor blade . . ."

George watched as a portion of the brain he didn't know the name of (yet) became bathed in a cold blue. Looking at it, he thought of the dark part on an ancient map: terra incognita, the home of monsters.

If you'd asked him before whether he'd like to see what suicidal ideation in a teenager looked like in an fMRI scan, George wouldn't have known how to answer. Now he did. The demonstration was enlightening in a very dark way, making him think about the mind's eye, and blind spots. Take this particular case: the boy in the tube was being asked to remember a past time when the future seemed to be in his blind spot. And yet . . .

"Isn't this dangerous?" George asked. "For the subject, I mean. It seems awfully triggering."

The lab tech shook his head, then shrugged, then pointed to the disclaimer that had been signed by the subject's guardian. "Our *a*'s are *c*'d," he said, referencing what George was coming to understand as the unofficial motto of the company that claimed, "Doing good is what we do."

And after that:

"Back where we started," George's escort announced, standing inside the recently vacated office with its window and view and everything. "Welcome to Quire." The dark suit and glasses turned and prepared to leave, but then stopped. "Door?" he said.

"Yes?"

"Open or closed?"

"Closed would be great," George said, the better to do his happy dance the second it was.

# 15

"How was your visit?" Roger asked.

His daughter ignored him, silently stepping out of her boots, unlacing her scarf, shedding her parka. In socked feet, she padded across the cabin's living room to the bathroom, left the door open, and flushed. Pandora poked her head back out mischievously. "I hope that wasn't too *triggering* . . ."

"She told you," Roger said.

"She told me," Pandora said, trying to mirror the deadliness of her father's tone but unable to. She was practically incandescent with glee.

Roger folded his arms and waited while Pandora dissolved into laughter. Finally taking a seat, literally holding her sides, his daughter looked woozy from lack of oxygen. Once the laughter had reduced to a couple of snorts every few seconds, like popcorn slowing down in a microwave, he spoke.

"She's been telling that story all my life," he said. "I'm surprised you hadn't heard it before." Pause. "I couldn't take friends home after a while. I started telling them my parents were dead."

"But it's *funny*," Pandora insisted.

"To people it hasn't happened to."

"Like you even remember . . ."

"Like I could *forget*," Roger said. "Like she'd *let* me. And that was the worst part of it. I was too young to remember, so I wound up with *her* version, seared into my brain." Pause. "You know, it's not helpful, looking back at your first moments on the planet like some slapstick routine . . ."

"Hey, at least you got a good story," Pandora countered. "Me? I killed my mom. Not a great anecdote for parties."

Roger looked at his daughter. "Dora," he said, sounding like a detective trying to finesse the suspect, "did she tell you anything else, maybe about when *you* were born?"

Just as Roger couldn't forget the story of his porcelain nativity, so Pandora remembered the hearsay love story represented by the three syllables of her own name. Because she'd *not* been named after that infamous other who shared those syllables. No, she'd been named after a happy combination of technology and synchronicity and the nearest thing to fate she could imagine. It just wasn't true.

Not that it was a *lie* exactly. It was more like a false memory, perpetuated because it contained elements of the truth: her future father was in a bar and had just started playing "Goody Two Shoes" on the jukebox when her future mother entered and said, "Oh, I like this one . . ." No algorithmic synchronicity involved, just a coincidence that was less likely to make you believe in fate than in the stickiness of certain earworms.

It was Roger's friend Vlad who'd suggested that what would make the story special was if they'd been listening to a radio station that picked songs based on their listening habits, tailored to their tastes. Roger and his future wife agreed that such a thing would be pretty cool and suggested that Vlad develop the idea. But V.T. had passed, and by the time the internet radio station Pandora finally launched and made somebody else rich, Pandora the future hacker had already moved back to Alaska with her widowed dad, who would return to the alternative-facts version of how he and his wife met, once their daughter was old enough to ask where her name came from.

The real story was decidedly more downbeat and, placed in context, required Roger to relive the death of his wife in a level of detail he didn't think fit for young ears—or his own, for that matter. But the truth was Pandora's mother died from an aortic aneurysm that burst from the stress of delivery. The body was already cool to the touch by the time the nurse returned to fetch Pandora back to be placed in the baby display window, where she could be fawned over by family (meaning Roger) and friends (meaning Vlad). Noticing the nurse as she scurried from his wife's room, Roger stopped her in the hall, the bundled babe pressed to the front of her starched uniform. The nurse's face went blank as she worked a hand into the bundle and came back with his wife's charm bracelet.

"The little one took a liking to it," she said, handing it to the new father and widower. "I didn't want it to go missing when they came for the body."

And that's how Roger learned of his wife's death—knowledge so heavy it took his legs out from under him, leaving him stunned on the hospital tiles. He still remembered how his ears filled with the whispering of crepe soles hustling around him, a few feet south of where his ears then rested in space relative to the floor, space not the only thing feeling relative as he found himself adrift in it: a father, a widower, a star surrounded by blackness wherever he looked. And through it all, the only sensation making it through from out there to inside was the noise of all those muffled footsteps.

The couple had a different name picked out, but when asked, Roger couldn't think of what it was. He'd stared at the linked charms in his hand, each one a solid icon of some important moment in his wife's life, the last a little pewter baby rattle. And his mind, needing something to gnaw on, to preoccupy it, kept trying to remember what these things were called. Not charm bracelet. He knew that. There was a brand name. Something with a *P*. Pandemonium? No. Panglossian? Pythagorean? Pan-something.

Roger's memory finally clicked when a nurse arrived with two forms needing his input: one, a birth certificate, and the other . . . And when the nurse asked for his new child's name, the word he'd been searching for came out instead: "Pandora."

They were in California at the time, and while the nurse hailed from the Midwest, she'd learned enough not to make faces at the locals and the names they saddled their children with. Instead, she repeated, "Pandora," followed by: "Spelled like it sounds?"

Roger nodded. "I guess." And even as he said it, he promised himself he'd change it later—legally—once he and his right mind had become reacquainted. But for now, the name had done its job: shortened the list of questions he needed to answer.

But then he got used to it. And instead of changing his daughter's name, he changed the story, imagining he was giving her the gift of being named after the improbable miracle of love. And that was how she'd taken it, until reality took it away.

Throughout her father's confession—or confirmation, really, seeing as Gladys was the one to originally spill the beans—Pandora felt a growing urge to edit the Wikipedia page for the internet radio station she'd always thought she'd been named after. She could make the old story true by changing a few numbers, she thought—then hack the page so nobody could edit them back. Sure, alt facts inherently carried the whiff of *1984* about them, but how bad was it, compared to all the other fake news online? And who would it hurt anyway? Nobody checked those things. And if somebody writing a history of streaming services repeated the new and improved date, and then some news aggregator aggregated it, well, that'd constitute multiple confirming sources, which basically made it true, or as good as. Right?

Right.

"It worked," Pandora announced during her next visit.

"What did?" Gladys asked.

"Dad came clean," she said, hanging her parka on the back of a kitchen chair. "He told me the real story about my name."

"Did *I* tell you about that?" Gladys asked, her face dropping.

Pandora nodded.

"Did I tell you anything *else*?" her grandmother asked—*demanded*—her face the picture of rising horror.

Pandora mentioned her father's inglorious entry into the world, and for a moment, Gladys smiled, before looking concerned again.

"Anything *else*?" she insisted. "Anything I *shouldn't* have?"

Pandora shook her head, shrugged, not seeing what the big deal was. Sure, the name thing was a secret and her dad obviously hoped the story of his birth would have been granted a similar classification, at least when it came to his daughter. But the way Gladys was going on, it was like she'd never told a secret in her life—which seemed almost quaint in the age of WikiLeaks, Snowden, Manning, et al. Hell, it was quaint in the age of social media, where *not sharing* was a new kind of rude—not to mention really bad for the social-media business model.

"But feel free. I'm good at keeping secrets," Pandora lied.

# 16

Getting Chipped

We already know what you're thinking: Big Brother, mark of the beast, 666, right? Nope. It's nothing more than good old-fashioned pragmatism. We had badges; people *hated* badges; people kept forgetting badges, and since the badges were what got you into campus, let you log on to your workstation, and ID'd you for all your free bennies, the situation rapidly became suboptimal.

Solution: an RFID chip about the size of a grain of rice, doing everything a badge would do (and nothing else), inserted subcutaneously no deeper than your average tattoo ink. Yes, we thought about bar code tattoos. Those were deemed historically and culturally insensitive. Also, the process is completely reversible should you ever choose to leave the Quire family. Those with personal, religious, or cultural objections can opt for a badge instead.

—QuireNewEmployeeManual.pdf

"Is this going to hurt?" George asked, his hand in the hands of a man who might not be the most reliable judge of pain thresholds, not with all the piercings he had in his face alone.

The chipper shrugged. "Not as much as being unemployed," he said, upending a bottle of rubbing alcohol onto a cotton ball before swabbing the back of George's hand. Other than those two quasi-medical, quasi-antiseptic supplies, the chipping station consisted of a box of disposable examination gloves, the phlebotomy chair with its single armrest where George was sitting, and the chipper himself wearing aquamarine scrubs dotted with what his present subject hoped was salsa from a breakfast burrito. The actual mechanism for implanting the chip was nowhere to be seen, which was worrying.

"In the manual it mentioned Big Brother," George said, making nervous chitchat as his palm sweated. "You know what that reminded me of?"

The chipper, who sat on a wheeled stool, rolled in close so he could whisper. "The Macintosh Super Bowl ad, 1984," he said. "Never speak of that again."

"But it's on YouTube . . ."

The chipper squeezed his hand until George winced. "That ad had a sequel that aired during the 1985 Super Bowl. It featured blindfolded businessmen walking off a cliff while whistling 'Heigh-Ho.' It was for a Mac-based networking solution called Macintosh Office. Wanna guess what that sequel was called?"

Shrug.

"Lemmings," the chipper said. "Consequently, V.T. takes everything about Apple personally." He paused. "You'll note the telling absence of black turtlenecks on campus."

George's mouth made a silent "Oh," followed by a silent "Thanks for the heads-up," followed by an audible yelp as he felt the chip sliding in under his skin, after which his hand was released. It was only after it was done that he saw the injector, a larger-than-average syringe with a disposable needle the chipper ejected unceremoniously into a waiting wastebasket.

George looked at the little red lump underneath the web of skin between his thumb and index finger.

"You know what that part's called?" the chipper asked, noticing the newbie as he poked at the new addition, seeing and feeling how far it rolled.

George shrugged, still mesmerized.

"The anatomical snuff box," the chipper said.

"That a fact?"

Nod.

"So . . . ?"

"Go to your cube," the chipper said, adding his gloves to the rest of the disposables in the basket. "Make sure you can sign on to your computer and start working through the email blasts."

George almost corrected the chipper to say he'd actually been given an office, but then remembered his escort's reaction a day earlier. And so, "Thanks," he said, followed by a farewell autofill "See ya."

"Not if you're lucky," the chipper said.

The implant worked right off the bat. Reaching his office and waving his hand in front of a reader on the wall, George watched as the knob spun a half turn by itself, a solenoid buzzed and kerchunked, and the door let go of the frame. Lights turned on as he entered and as he approached his desk, the workstation began booting up. "Welcome, George Jedson," the speaker said in a voice he recognized as belonging to Rosie the Robot from *The Jetsons*. He hadn't heard the voice since he was a kid when his mom had explained its connection to his name as they watched reruns on Cartoon Network.

*Nice touch,* he thought. Pulling out his desk chair, George sat and began reading through the email blasts as advised. A half hour later: *Now what?*

His workstation had three monitors, and so George slid the email window off to the right and opened a search window on the left. He eyed the email window peripherally while turning most of his attention to the search box. He checked the five-day forecast for the San Francisco Bay Area. Next, the highlights for science and technology in Google News. Next, he got up from his desk and stared out the window, trying to remember what the five-day had said about today and whether that's what was actually happening out there, on the other side of the glass. He looked at the clock on the wall, checked it against the one on his computer, and then unhooked the former from the nail it hung from. He turned it over, removed the battery cover, tested the terminals with his tongue, closed it back up, and then thumbed the little adjustment wheel until the two clocks agreed with each other. Unfortunately, they agreed on a time that seemed impossibly far from lunch, which—as far as George could tell—was the one thing on his to-do list between now and noon.

By ten thirty, George had received no further instructions on how to spend his time via any of the various means by which he could be reached—not by email or text or voice mail, not in person, or via audio or video over Skype, not even by some coded vibrations emanating from the subcutaneous RFID chip implanted in his anatomical snuff box. At a loss, he poked his head out the door to see if he could flag down any of the faces he'd met during the previous day's tour. Said faces were all part of Q-Brain, as was George, meaning they were coworkers, even if they didn't necessarily all work on the same projects with the same goals. Not that he could say how he stood in relation to the other teams' projects and/or goals, seeing as he was still waiting to find out what his were going to be.

"Hello," he called. "Anybody?"

No response. This was to be expected, in retrospect, seeing as nobody else was in the hallway.

"Hello, ello, ello," he said, impersonating an echo, which, as it turned out, didn't need to be faked, successfully underlining the sense of isolation he'd already begun feeling. The day before, researchers had lined up to show him the fruits of their labor; now, he faced only a series of anonymous locked doors, on the other side of which, surely people were working, but, if so, they were doing it awful quietly.

*Too quietly.*

He heard footsteps behind him and turned in time to see a coder armed with free snacks disappear behind his own door. Looking the other way, he saw a bank of vending machines, an ice maker, a fire extinguisher, an emergency first aid cabinet, and a flickering exit sign, pointing left.

George pulled his head back into his office and closed the door. He took his seat, jiggled his mouse, checked to see what new spam needed to be deleted. He opened up solitaire and started playing against his own best score and time. He began wondering if discovering what his job was *was his job*.

Watching the cascade of virtual playing cards bounce across the screen, he imagined the possible clues for which the *Jeopardy!* answer was: "What is George's job?" He knew what he *hoped* it was: help create the world's first truly general artificial intelligence as opposed to all the narrow AIs dominating the headlines. He checked his email again to see if it brought news of such an assignment—or some kind of work important enough to warrant having his own office. And at the same time, he was worried too. He was barely sixteen after all, and here he was, down the hall from guys who could light up and trace every neuron in the brain. A few weeks from now, would he be taking snapshots of someone's thoughts or helping the blind to not just see, but see through walls?

Agitated malaise. Anxious ennui. That's what George was feeling. And while in concept, a door was a nice thing to have, in reality, when you had nothing to do behind that door but twiddle your thumbs and wait, it meant claustrophobia on top. The unspecified pressure was finally enough to send George into the hallway and down to the free vending machines. A Snickers and chugged Red Bull later, he started tracing the previous day's tour backward, hoping for something to catch his eye.

Gym? No.

Climbing wall? No.

Too early for the cafeteria.

Too much caffeine already to make use of the free coffee bar.

Neck massage station? Nope. He'd feel guilty, not having coded jack since getting there.

And then he found it: a 1980s arcade-themed conversation room where a few people were sitting in club chairs, complete with fully functioning, stand-alone versions of *Pong*, *Pac-Man*, *Ms. Pac-Man*, *Asteroids*, *Frogger*. All had started gathering dust in actual arcades well before any of the coders ignoring them had been born, including George. By all appearances, they were more of a meta gesture, a nod toward the idea of nostalgia; no one expected anyone to actually play them, as attested to by the "Wash Me" somebody had written in the dust coating the cathode-ray screen of the *Pac-Man* console.

But George had always had a soft spot in his heart for the underdogs, the neglected, the underestimated—all of those labels having applied to him at various points. And so he pulled his hand into his sleeve and wiped the *Pac-Man* display clean. He hit the big red button to start a game and flinched when actual music—the dinky-dink *Pac-Man* theme—came pouring out rather louder than he had expected. The handful of fellow coders in the room turned to look at him.

"I'm not sure you're supposed to actually use those," one of them said. "I think they're, like, for decoration."

"Yeah, dude," another said, "that's some serious museum antique stuff you're messing with."

George looked at the happy yellow pie missing a slice, waiting to be sent on his gobbling way as the quartet of sawtooth-sheeted ghosts bobbed in their 2-D holding pen, waiting to cause trouble. "Why were they plugged in," George asked, "if we're not supposed to use them?"

The two previous speakers looked at each other, then at George, who was already riding his joystick like a pro. "Good point," one of them said.

"Ya wanna?" his colleague asked him. And then up they went to play *Pong*, ironically, until a supervisor came looking for them.

*Wow,* George thought, *first day, and I'm already the guy who gets other guys in trouble*—a conclusion he'd have cause to rethink once he met the guy who actually held that particular job description.

The Quire cafeteria could have been decorated by the set designer for *Blade Runner*, but with fewer rain effects and minus the grit. A multi-culti mash-up heavily inflected eastward: the cafeteria's most prominent feature was a series of wall-sized flat screens displaying seasonal scenes of what the outside would look like if humans had never taken a shovel to it. An overall tranquil vibe, George thought, except for the foot-tall crawl cutting through the sublime vistas to display the weather forecast, breaking news, Quire's stock price, or its latest corporate affirmation.

George had taken a seat toward the back, the better to study his coworkers, when he noticed an old-timer enter the cafeteria, distinguished by his actual badge swinging from a lanyard around his neck. George had already observed that much about QHQ's pecking order: employees could be divided into badgers and chippers, the latter representing the newest hires while the former had been given the option to hold on to their old badges. And this one seemed to be on a mission as he stared at his phone, *in medias distractus*, looking up only once to lock on George. A quick, confirmatory nod followed by a big smile as he continued walking with a bit more purpose, straight for Quire's newest newbie.

"Milo LaFarge," he announced, phone holstered, hand out.

"George," George said, withholding his surname as he often did when he wasn't in the mood.

And so Milo pulled out a seat, sat down, and filled in the blank. "Jedson, right?"

George nodded.

"Man, that must be a pain in the butt."

George blinked self-consciously. "Yes," he said. "Yes, it is."

"Why don't you change it?"

"How else am I supposed to start conversations?"

"Say no more," Milo said, and George obeyed as if it had been a command.

Several uncomfortable seconds passed as the newbie poked among the remains of his lunch and considered taking out his phone, the international sign for "leave me alone."

"Listen," Milo said, unambiguously a command this time, "I'm here to help."

"Help?" George said, looking up from a crescent of gluten-free, vegan-certified pizza crust he'd flicked into rotating like an ad hoc fidget spinner.

"I'm your Virgil," Milo said.

George looked perplexed. "I thought you said your name was Milo?"

Milo crossed his arms and rocked back in his seat. George mirrored the gesture. And the two stayed that way, tentatively teetering on the back legs of their chairs, judging and daring and testing each other's will until George finally broke, tipped forward, and admitted that yes, he knew who Virgil was. “I just don’t see how the allusion applies in our current situation.”

“I’m your alternative tour guide,” Milo said, “here to point things out you might otherwise miss.”

“Like?” George asked.

Milo pinched his smart ID between thumb and forefinger and held it away from him so they both could see the stitched lettering running from end to end of the lanyard. “Doing good is a choice,” he read aloud.

It was the corporate affirmation of the week and had struck George as a benign declaration of corporate altruism, an interpretation he shared with his guest.

Milo held the strip of polyester closer, reading it silently like a fortune cookie. “It could also mean that ‘doing good’ is optional,” he pointed out.

George weighed the words one at a time. “You could be right,” he finally admitted.

“And so it begins,” Milo said, cracking all his knuckles at once.

# 17

Pandora didn't hate everything about high school, though in terms of learning, it was highly inefficient. She could read a teacher's edition much faster than it took to have it read to her aloud by some secondary-ed-majoring hack who couldn't make it down south, leaving her plenty of time to twiddle her thumbs between acing quizzes. There was one exception, however: Mr. Vlasic, her science teacher.

Mr. V had been drawn to Fairbanks because of the night sky, its darkness and duration and the northern lights that frequently danced across it. Unlike virtually every other outsider she knew, her science teacher flew back to his home state of Michigan during the Alaskan summer cherished by natives and tourists alike, returning to Fairbanks only after the visitors left and the first snowflakes arrived, usually over the Labor Day weekend. And astronomy wasn't the only thing he loved, but science in general—physics and chemistry, especially. And as far as reading out of the teacher's edition, Mr. Vlasic had so far kept his promise to base his instruction exclusively on what he already had in his head, still fresh from grad school and supplemented by his voracious reading of pretty much every periodical with the word *science* in the title—*Popular*, *American*, *News*, or the word itself, unadorned.

Most significantly for Pandora, however, her science teacher was also the only faculty member who may have had an inkling of who the culprit behind the flaming urinals might be. "Seems like they should be looking for a science geek with a grudge instead of someone making political rants online," he'd said offhandedly, as she'd dawdled after class one afternoon.

Pandora looked at her shoes, putting her double-crossing face out of range.

"So how's your grandmother?" he asked, changing the subject—and displaying another reason why she liked her science teacher: they were both members of that growing club of people who had loved ones with dementia. For Mr. Vlasic, it was his mom, and part of his salary was going to help pay for a visiting care worker, to keep her out of places like where Gladys had wound up.

"Not great," Pandora said. "You know."

Indeed, he did, or seemed to, as he knew it was time to change the subject yet again.

"I think you'll be interested in Wednesday's topic," he said.

"What is it?"

"Secret, is what it is," Mr. V said with a smile and a wink. "You'll have to show up and see for yourself."

As if there was any question about that.

Standing in front of class as it settled down, Mr. Vlasic reminded her of a mash-up of Buddy Holly and early Elvis Costello, thanks to the heavy-framed black glasses he wore unironically. His hair was decidedly longer than either, and a flop of it flipped over the left lens constantly, only to be pushed back up and out of the way, either by neck pop or long-fingered sweep, both gestures tossed off with equal levels of distractedness.

It didn't take a genius to see that Mr. V loved being onstage. In another life, he'd be a stand-up comedian or, more likely, a stand-up scientist. But those openings had been filled already by Bill Nye and Neil deGrasse Tyson. And so it was Lionel Vlasic's fate to remain at Ransom Wood High School, entertaining a bunch of disgruntled teens plus one true fan: Pandora Lynch.

Before the bell rang, kicking off that Wednesday's class, Mr. Vlasic entered the room with a big box held to his chest, exaggerating the effort it took to carry it, placed it on his desk, and then proceeded to ignore it, as the class's earlier arrivals kept staring at it—as intended. Finally: "You seem more interested in cardboard than me," he said once class had officially begun, "which is frankly insulting. But since I've mentioned our corrugated elephant here, who's curious about what's inside?"

Nearly every hand went up.

"And who knows another word for 'curious'?" he asked. "Think anatomy."

"Nosy," several students mouthed, and a few braver ones said aloud.

"Yes. Nosy," Mr. V repeated, flipping open the flaps of the box, reaching inside, and removing a large plastic cutaway model of the human olfactory system.

"Boom," he said, amid the predictable groans.

"The human brain," he announced, pausing long enough for the class to wonder if their teacher had mixed up his lecture notes, "is well acquainted with the sensory input from this fine fellow," he continued. "In fact, the sense of smell is practically hardwired directly to the fight-or-flight, lizard part of the brain." Pause. "Did you know you can't remember smells?"

Sounds of adolescent objection.

"It's true," Mr. V continued. "You can re-*experience* smells, and recognize them while in their presence, but in isolation, you cannot call to mind a memory of a smell, like you can, say, an image or a song you've heard."

He reached back into the box and removed three amber pharmacy vials, each with what appeared to be a cotton ball inside. He dealt them out to the students sitting at the heads of the first column of desks, the third, and then the last, slamming each one down like a bartender laying down shots.

"Smell's relationship with memory can be profound, however, particularly when it comes to summoning up other memories associated with our previous experiences of a particular scent. Marcel Proust knew this and wrote about it. He even got his name attached to the flood of memories a single smell can trigger, which is sometimes called a Proustian rush."

Mr. Vlasic raised a halting finger as he noticed two of the students he'd placed vials in front of trying to open them. "Not yet," he said. "First let me tell you what you've got there." He reclaimed the vial from the student in the middle and pointed at the bottom. "I've soaked each of these cotton balls in what I hope are fairly recognizable and evocative scents, and you're each going to take a whiff." He paused. "Now I don't want you to identify the smell. I want you to smell it, close your eyes, and try to identify a memory the smell conjures up. And then we'll go around the room and compare, unless you opt not to share for reasons of personal embarrassment." He uncapped the vial he'd reclaimed and dipped his own nose inside before recoiling.

"Oh yeah," he said, as if to himself, "that's the embarrassing one, all right . . ."

He returned the now-radioactive vial to the student he'd taken it from. The seed successfully planted, Mr. V watched along with the rest as the three vials circulated, the reactions to two of them reasonably benign, while the remaining vial—the vile vial, as Mr. V began referring to it—elicited ever greater reactions of disgust, as those who had yet to smell it grew increasingly, visibly apprehensive about playing along.

"Okay," their teacher said after the rounds had been completed and each student had scribbled something down. "Now, I said this wasn't about naming the smells, per se, and so, for the record"—he held up the first vial: "Baby-powder-scented air freshener."

Number two, the vile vial: "Rancid sardine oil."

And number three: "Pine-tree air freshener."

A surprising—or perhaps not—number of students opted for the vile vial as their triggering smell of choice, which brought back memories of hunting whales for some of the indigenous students and working in the canneries or aboard fishing trawlers for some others. One student picked the pine and began an anecdote about getting drunk on gin for the first time.

Mr. Vlasic coughed into his hand and then, in a voice directed at the ceiling, as if the room were bugged, "Thank you for that *work of fiction*, Mr. Denning. I know you wouldn't want to be admitting to the crime of underage drinking in my classroom . . ."

"Yeah, Mr. V," the smartass said, understanding. "You caught me"—pause—"making stuff up."

And lastly, the baby-powder vial predictably conjured up memories of mothers and young siblings, and one instance of being locked in a clothes dryer against the student's will, followed by the almost exact same recollection, but done willingly.

And then Mr. V did a total U-turn, or so it seemed.

"I know I've prefaced a lot of these demos with the standard disclaimer to not try this at home, but this time I'm changing that." He paused. "Those of you who still have access to your grandparents and/or great-grandparents, think about trying this experiment on them, especially if they've started to lose their memories. Especially if they've developed the habit of wearing way too much perfume or aftershave."

A hand went up. Mr. Vlasic seemed to already know the question. "No," he said, "the grandparents experiment won't be on the test. It's strictly for extra credit." He paused. "And extra credit for you personally, in the being-a-good-person department. You'll be amazed at how grateful old people can be when you show the least interest in what they have to say."

Pandora, stationed in the back of the classroom, per usual, thought, *Been there, still doing that . . .*

Pandora didn't need extra credit—not in science, at least—but trying the experiment on Gladys would give her an excuse to talk to Mr. V about the results. The truth was, she had a little crush on him. How secret that crush *was*, given her traitorous face, she didn't know. But he'd not said anything, which either meant he hadn't noticed or was even more crush-worthy than she thought.

She did tweak the experiment a bit, though. First, the vile vial needed to go on the grounds of sheer nastiness, and second, she nuked the hell out of those other two cotton balls, spraying them in their respective air fresheners until they were dripping with memories to compensate for the ones her grandmother had lost already. Press-twisting their caps back on, Pandora proceeded to slide the vials into her parka's side pockets, one bottle of memories each.

"Hey, Gram," she greeted, unbooting and sliding off her parka. The usual chitchat followed, the two having developed a routine further routinized by the fact that increasingly, Gladys's side of the conversation was a practically verbatim rerun of what she'd said the previous visit.

"So anyway," Pandora said, "we did an interesting experiment in science class today." She plucked the vials from the pockets of the parka she'd draped over a kitchen chair and placed them on the breakfast nook between them, continuing to explain the gist before asking if her grandmother was game.

Gladys shrugged and Pandora said, "Okay," before uncapping the first vial and passing it forward.

Her grandmother dipped in her beak and inhaled. Shrugged.

"Smell harder," Pandora advised.

"And how am I supposed to do that?"

Pandora demonstrated by sniffing in loudly. Gladys tried. Shrugged again, passing the vial back. "You try," her grandmother said.

And so Pandora did, easing the mouth of the vial noseward, abundantly aware of how thoroughly she'd soaked the cotton balls and wary of olfactory overload. But as she drew the vial nearer, she sensed something was wrong. She couldn't smell anything, even when she placed her nose directly over the vial and inhaled as hard as she'd demonstrated earlier.

Briefly, a butterfly of panic flitted across her brain, heading toward her stomach as Pandora wondered whether dementia was contagious—whether she'd exposed herself so thoroughly that she'd already lost her sense of smell and the rest of her brain would be next and . . .

. . . and then she noticed the cold against her fingertips where they held the vial. She looked inside and flicked a fingernail against the side. The cotton ball—frozen—clicked against the other side. She hadn't been outside that long, but then again, it doesn't take long to freeze something at forty degrees below zero. They'd been in her pockets, but the outside lining was closer to the air than any extraneous body heat coming off Pandora.

"Maybe later," she said, leaving the vials uncapped on the table between them to thaw.

They talked while they waited to resume the experiment, but as they did, Pandora noticed her grandmother getting anxious. "Have you taken your Xanax?" she asked.

But instead of the yes or no the question seemed to call for, Gladys said, "Talcum powder."

Pandora blinked, inhaled, and then smelled it, too, along with a strong hint of pine. "The experiment," she said. "I'd almost for . . ." But the younger woman stopped before getting to *gotten*, refusing to say the word, as if saying it would bring her grandmother's disease crashing down on her. Instead, she asked, "What does the smell of baby powder remind you of?"

A strange look fell across Gladys's face. "I've felt like this before," the old woman said.

"Like how?"

"Like I'm racing against death," her grandmother said. "This time, it's my brain cells dying, but before . . ." She drifted off, and Pandora tried reeling her back.

"When was this?" she asked.

"World War II," her grandmother said.

"What about the war?"

"I fought in it."

"That was Grandpa Herman," Pandora corrected. "Your husband. Only men fought in the war."

"The ones who fought *and died* were boys," Gladys said. "But they weren't the only ones fighting."

"How, *specifically*, did you fight in World War II, Gladys Kowalski?" Pandora asked, using her grandmother's back-then name in case it helped jar loose anything the smell of baby powder hadn't—like, for instance, what talcum had to do with the war.

"I can't say," Gladys said, shaking her head violently, followed by the words that would doom her at the hands of a girl once nicknamed Dora the Implorer: "It's secret," the old woman said. "Classified."

Gauntlet accepted. "*Tell* me," Pandora said, squaring her shoulders, prepared to resort to elder abuse if it came to that.

"Can't."

"*Can't* because you can't remember," Pandora drilled, "or because you *won't*?"

"Shouldn't," her grandmother said, already softening. "They could put me in jail . . ."

Pandora reached across the table and took her grandmother's fretting hands. "I don't mean to be mean with what I'm about to say," she said, pausing to meet Gladys's eyes. "But what difference would it make?"

Her grandmother blinked, as if thinking about it, while the what-if machine in Pandora's head went crazy with possibilities. What if her grandmother had been some femme fatale spy luring Nazis to their deaths or maybe a footnote in the history of Los Alamos? Gladys, meanwhile, reached for the vial with the scent of baby powder wafting over it, brought it to her nose as if it contained smelling salts, and inhaled.

"Ready?" she asked.

# 18

"I'm from the fairy dust clean-up team," Milo said. "I'm the speaker—excuse me, *preacher*—of truth to naïveté."

"Naïveté?"

"You."

"Okay," George said. "Hit me with some truth."

"Memory Hole Mondays," Milo said.

George nodded. Memory Hole Monday was the feature that distinguished Quire from similar platforms like Facebook, instituted as news of data breaches and undisclosed invasions of privacy were inspiring widespread defections. Announced within days of the company's IPO, "the hole," as it was affectionately known, allowed users to "completely delete, obliterate, bury" anything they regretted posting. At the same time, they could review what Quire had on them and perform other routine acts of personal privacy hygiene.

"People actually bought that shit," Milo said.

"What do you mean 'bought'?"

"Hook, line, and the proverbial sinker," Milo said, then smiled. "Bought like the proverbial farm, privacy-wise, may it rest in peace."

"More info," George said. "Less Milo."

"They're *kidding*," his newly appointed Virgil said. "About deleting everything? Totally joshing."

"You mean *lying*?" George said.

"The terms of service refer to it as using 'corporate discretion.'"

"But why? What's the point?"

Milo smiled. "Memory Hole Mondays point the platform in the direction of the most valuable information there is. The embarrassing parts. The incriminating. The stuff you want buried."

"Valuable *how*?"

Milo mimed contemplation, tapping his lips, eyes lifted heavenward, followed by a pointing finger, an open mouth, and . . . nothing. Blank faced, he waited for George to put it together.

Which he did, as signaled thusly: "Oh crap . . ."

"I've heard V.T. has political aspirations," Milo said before pausing to let that sink in. "Any guesses about his chances?"

George recalled the V.T. he'd met—the one who'd given him his job, whatever it wound up being. The man had a certain geek charisma about him, in the sense that only geeks could find him charismatic. The rest of the world could probably see the needy narcissist who'd netted billions while carrying a negative balance in self-worth. What else could you say about a guy who had to pay people to make other people think he was human? No way was V.T. a likely candidate for political office. There was no way he'd win a fair and honest election . . .

Bingo.

"Oh crap," George said, the horrible potential manifesting itself behind his eyes. Hadn't the country suffered enough at the hands of amoral billionaires who decided to play politics when they got bored or their dicks got limp? Could it really survive another round? "Oh crap, oh crap, oh crap . . ."

"You are most welcome, grasshopper." Milo smiled.

# 19

"It was almost all girls," Gladys began as Pandora surreptitiously thumb-tapped the voice recorder on her phone. "All the boys were either overseas or broken, leaving the job up to us, like Rosie the Riveter, but brainier.

"I was never in a sorority, but I imagine that's what it was like, where they put us, working shoulder to shoulder, not perspiring like ladies, but sweating like pigs, and about as happy as a bunch in slop, because the freedom to sweat was, well, very freeing," Gladys recalled.

"At first," she qualified.

"But then it got annoying, and I personally started longing for the days of talcum, judiciously applied. Not to tell tales, but some of my sisters were not exactly going for gold in personal hygiene. It got so I could tell who was coming down the hall before I even saw her.

"And then I noticed our smells started changing. There was heat sweat, and there was fear sweat, and more and more, fear sweating was what we did."

"You have to back up, Gram," Pandora said. "Where was this?"

"DC," Gladys said. "The District of Columbia," she added, decoding the initials gratuitously and with a tone that made the place sound like a foreign country.

"The pay wasn't much, but I would've worked for room and board and nothing else. It was"—her grandmother paused—"the best, worst time I ever had."

Did Pandora feel guilty about using her grandmother's condition to get her to break what was apparently some vow of silence? No. She was doing what needed to be done before her grandmother's history was lost. Who knew what she may have forgotten already? Sure, the first phase of Alzheimer's was short-term memory loss, but her grandmother had gotten past that part. There were hints she thought Herman was still alive. But as far as Pandora could tell, the war stuff was still there, perhaps the mental treads dug especially deep by whatever was making Gladys so skittish on the subject.

Not that the how or why of her grandmother's recollection mattered. What mattered was finally getting Gladys's story. The *whole* story—or as much of it as remained.

And as Gladys spoke, Pandora could see it as if it were a memory of her own: the padded shoulders, the bouffants, the sweaty dress shields. But how did Gladys Kowalski *fight* World War II, *specifically*?

"The clock, dear," Gladys said. "We fought the clock—around the clock."

"Were you a secretary?" her granddaughter asked.

"Well, I dressed like one," Gladys said. "I'd bicycle with bag lunches from a boardinghouse to an office building that looked like all the rest, but with fewer windows than average."

"So," Pandora kept prying, "in this innocuous building of few windows, what were you doing? Taking dictation about secret war plans and typing them up on official letterhead or something?"

Gladys looked at her granddaughter, disappointed. "I said I dressed *like* a secretary. DC was full of them. That's why it was the perfect disguise. Because while the boys *over there* used their bodies, bullets, and bombs to fight the war, nobody would've guessed that some little secretary with her bag lunch was fighting that same war with her brains."

"But what were you *doing*?" Pandora implored.

Gladys blinked, her expression reading, "Isn't it obvious?"

"Cryptography," she said, filling in the blank.

And now it was Pandora's turn to blink confusedly as she tried to process the too-many thoughts rushing toward articulation.

"I was going to be an English teacher," her grandmother continued. "I had a gift for language and word games. Crossword puzzles were a favorite. Word finds. What's different between these two pictures? And I found a puzzle pinned up on a bulletin board at high school, daring me to solve it. If I could, I was supposed to send my answers and contact information to a PO Box at the bottom. So I did, and sent it in. And a month later, a big black car pulled up outside our farm, and two men in dark overcoats got out. I don't know why, but they looked like big beetles walking upright as they approached our front door. 'Can we see Miss Gladys Kowalski?' they asked. The beetle men had come looking for me.

"The test was a screen for minds that were needed for the war effort. Ones like mine," her grandmother continued. "My country needed me. America and the Allied forces needed little Gladys Kowalski to go to Washington and play word games that could spell life or death for our boys overseas. How could I say no? I couldn't. I didn't. I packed my bags, kissed my mom, scowled at my dad because that was our way, and left on the biggest adventure of my life."

"What was DC like?"

"Sweaty. Swampy. Rumpled suits and wilted dresses. The opposite of Fairbanks, which is one of the reasons I came here. After what happened after the war . . ."

Pandora had an idea about what her grandmother was alluding to. Her father had suggested that his mother's postwar experience with men of the brain-shrinking class was one of the reasons he'd chosen his profession. The euphemism "stress" had been thrown around. Pandora now suspected that the truth was closer to a breakdown. Anyone needing a change of scenery as extreme as going from DC to Fairbanks had clearly been through something.

Gladys had begun describing the goings-on inside that innocuous building in Washington, DC, where she was helping to win the war with crossword puzzles and tiles from a board game called Criss-Crosswords destined to be rechristened Scrabble after the war. Her head back then had been predisposed to finding patterns trying hard not to be found, making her just the sort of player the government needed for a life-and-death game of hide-and-seek played out in the real world with bombed cities, sunken ships, and floating corpses. For Gladys and her sisters, the battlefield was language and language-like strings of symbols, scrambled, masked, translated, and substituted, the repetitions counted and tallied, the most frequent occurrences of *X* in a cypher perhaps pointing to the most frequent letter in the language the message was encoded from. Counting, theories, reconstructions from past failures where the real message became clear but only in retrospect, once the bodies had already started floating . . .

"We were trying to crack the Enigma," her grandmother said, acknowledging aloud that while that might sound like bad poetry, in this case it was the actual name of the enemy device they were pitting their pattern-recognizing minds against. It was about the size of a bread box and was used to disguise the Germans' secret transmissions, with the code changing daily and considered unbreakable absent another, sister Enigma machine for decoding what went into the first. There were too many permutations—even if you checked one random possibility per second, the time needed would exceed the number of hours between code switches several times over. Not that that stopped Gladys and her fellow decoders from sweating over every slip from the teletype, perfuming the air with the funk of patriotism.

"Once you get used to the initial nastiness, there was a point where nosing through everyone's BO was invigorating; it was stinky proof of how hard we were all working." Pause. "But then it got annoying again and I personally started longing for the days of talcum, judiciously applied. Not to tell tales, but some of my sisters were not exactly going for gold in personal hygiene . . ."

Pandora touched her grandmother's hand lightly. "You've already mentioned that part," she said.

Gladys took it in stride. "Did I mention how the men made everything worse?" she asked.

Pandora shook her head.

"Because there *were* men, more or less in charge," Gladys continued. "They were too old for traditional combat, so we girls didn't worry about sweating around them, not that they were usually around. No, the sneaks didn't show up until a few of us would take a break to smoke a cigarette or share stories from a movie magazine we'd seen out buying groceries with our ration coupons.

"'Ladies, enjoying yourselves?' they'd say, standing there behind us, rising on their tiptoes to seem a little taller, more in charge. The newest one always fell for it.

"'Oh yes,' she'd say, and we'd cringe, knowing what was coming.

"'That's nice. Too bad our *boys* over *there* can't while away the hours, gossiping about the latest *styles* . . .'

"Only the foolhardiest would have quibbled with turning a five-minute break into 'whiling away the hours,' or point out that fashion was of no consequence for the duration of the conflict, as should have been obvious from the safety pins and patches holding our wardrobes together. But the point was made. Every moment not spent deciphering enemy messages was basically helping Hitler kill our boys. As motivators went, it was a good one, provided we didn't kill ourselves, trying to save lives over there."

God, Pandora *loved* her grandmother's face! As her grandmother spoke about her most harrowing and glorious years, she wore her whole history: the Great Depression and World War II in her eyes, the 1960s in her furrowed brow, and the 2000s in the shadows of her sunken cheeks. Several decades of Alaskan winters had turned her from the slip of a girl she'd once been into a postfertility goddess and drained the color from her hair until it matched the landscape: snow and ice fog under a dryer-lint sky. But it was all part of a package, the total greater than the sum of its parts. She'd aged not only gracefully, but artfully, heartbreakingly. If only her mind . . .

"What happened after the war," Pandora finally asked, "before you came here?"

Her grandmother went *"Pffft"* and flicked her fingers at the side of her head, setting off a puff of white Einstein hair. "Your grandfather, bless his soul, called me Sparky after I told him. That might seem mean, but it was the perfect antidote for excessive seriousness. 'How 'bout a little AC/DC there, Sparky?' he'd say whenever he was feeling frisky."

Pandora reacted with an expression common among teenagers being forced to imagine old people "feeling frisky," multiplied by the power of her hyperexpressiveness.

"I felt much better after that," Gladys continued, ignoring her granddaughter's facial editorializing. "The electricity cleared the spark gap, blew out the cobwebs—I don't know. All I knew was I felt good in my own skin again and wanted a little time away from civilization to enjoy it. Hence, Fairbanks. Hence everything that followed Fairbanks."

She paused, looking tired, which was understandable. She rested a hand on Pandora's knee. "And the rest is his . . ." She paused, lifted her hand, and then clapped it down again on her granddaughter's knee. "No," she said. "The rest is *your* story," she concluded.

# 20

"Our CEO's not a liar, per se," Milo said, beginning their latest round of cynicism adjustment. "It's more like he's economical with the truth. He speaks no more of it than absolutely necessary. And when it comes to the subject of 'auxiliary business opportunities,' well, the man's Scrooge 1.0, the unredeemed. Total truth miser."

They'd moved the location of Milo's ongoing lecture series from the very public cafeteria to the privacy of George's office. It had been two days since they'd met, and George had made himself at home behind his office's lockable door—literally. It had made fiscal sense, given the astronomical cost of renting in an area where incomes in the low six figures were considered poverty level. Plus, by overlapping home and office—a practice *not* discouraged by management—the anxiety created by differentiating work from play largely disappeared. Which is to say that while George still hadn't gotten his work assignment, he wasn't freaking out about it. And in the meantime, there was always Milo, to rightsize any idealism he might still harbor. And thus:

"What 'auxiliary business opportunities'?" George asked. "You mean Q-Labs? That's pure research, like Google's 'moonshots.' Like Bell Labs a billion years ago."

"Tell me you're not that naive," Milo said.

"I feel I am an optimal level of naive," George countered. "I know people are greed personified and self-interest on two legs, but I have not succumbed to utter despair."

Milo snorted. "Good luck with *that*," he advised.

"Okay." George stepped it up. "I'll also spot you money being the source of all evil. Happy?"

But Milo just shook his head, his back to George as he admired the newbie's view. "Money is *so* last century," he said. "To do real evil nowadays, there's just one word."

"And that is?"

"Data," Milo said. "You know, like 'plastics' from *The Graduate*? But this is actually a different movie, grasshopper. It's *All the President's Men* and Deep Throat and 'follow the money.' Except it's data—grade A, primo, human behavioral data—that's AI juice. It's what keeps the chatbots chatting and the Terminator terminating and . . ."

"Allude much, Milo?" George asked.

"Hey, man," Milo said, not missing a beat. "The wheel's been invented and all the good stories written. Why waste time trying to be original? It's all mash-ups and sampling, baby. And thus, I allude." Pause. "But back to that AI juice. Quire is a 'data acquisition and packaging company'—that shit's in the corporate papers—and that 'packaging' euphie is where it's all at, the real work behind the wizard's curtain. All that stuff you saw on the tour, the AI and fMRI stuff. They're trying to read, record, and play back people's *actual thoughts*, claiming it's the next step beyond voice for input capture, but once you start reading minds, how far away is it from controlling them?"

George sat in his desk chair, practicing paper-clip origami as he studied his Virgil's back. If Milo was an intellectual hooker—which in many ways he seemed to be—his specialty would be blowing minds. Or trying to. George's brain stem was barely stiff. After all, if all these secret projects were so secret, how come a human sieve like Milo was in the loop? Next thing he knew, the guy would be looking both ways as he slid the plans for Tesla's death ray out of his pocket.

"You know about Stuxnet, right, the atomic bomb of cyber warfare?" Milo continued, turning around to face his audience of one. "That shit did actual damage in the real world by making Iraq's uranium enrichment system spin so fast it tore itself apart."

George nodded. He had the source code and had used chunks of it in his own exploits, back before he exchanged his black hat for this white hat gig. But what did Stuxnet have to do with a social-media company?

"They say it was a joint venture between the Israelis and the Americans, right? Well, that whole thing was started under W, and 'the Americans' meant contractors. Contractors like . . ."

George shaped the word *Quire* silently with his lips, while pointing down generically, a gesture intended to mean: "Here?"

Milo nodded.

"Bullshit," George said, swiveling around so he could check his computer for email about what he was supposed to be doing instead of sitting here listening to Milo's war stories.

Nada. Again. Still . . .

"God's truth," Milo said, resting his butt on the windowsill, his arms folded across his chest.

"Wait a second," George said, swiveling back around. "You're saying Quire has contracts with, what, DOD?"

"And NSA, FBI, DHS," Milo said. "Which shouldn't be a surprise. They do PSAs about it. 'Wounded warriors walk again.' It was on the tour."

"But that's all DARPA stuff," George insisted, "like how they funded the internet. It's the *good* military contracts."

"Ah, the internet," Milo said. "Cyber utopia. Security an afterthought." Pause. "But you know that already, don't you?"

*Guilty,* George thought. As was every other hacker he ever met online. The net's security holes were what they lived for—that, and bloated code full of bugs, waiting to be exploited. "Well, somebody's got to keep the serfs at Symantec busy."

"And busy they are," Milo agreed. "That's because the government loves security holes, even more than hackers, especially if it finds them first." Pause. "How many zero-day vulnerabilities did Stuxnet exploit?"

"Four, but . . ."

"And nobody would ever purposefully *create* a back door because the government was paying them for something else . . ."

"What are you saying?"

"I'm saying ignorance is bliss. And you can believe what you want to believe," Milo said. "All I know is what I've heard. And I heard that V.T. once said that if people were going to die anyway, he'd prefer they do it in a manner for which he held the patent."

George had heard the quote too. "But Snopes says he never said it," he pointed out.

"You have to admit, it does have a nice Dr. Evil vibe to it, though."

George knew what he was doing wrong with these visits from his self-appointed Virgil; he let Milo speak first. He'd leave his door open because he wasn't busy—still hadn't gotten anything to be busy with—and Milo would happen by, knock on the door frame, say, "Hey, you busy?" And before George could say anything, he'd let himself in, close the door, and start rubbing his hands over the juiciness of his upcoming disclosure. And so George positioned himself facing the open door and, before his informant's knuckles met wood, said, "Hey, Milo, got a sec?"

"Sure."

He waved his Virgil in, mimed closing the door, which Milo did.

"I've been meaning to ask you," George said. "How long have you been working here?"

"Forever," Milo said. "Five years."

"That doesn't seem . . . ," George began.

"Five *Silicon Valley* years," Milo clarified. "Factor in Moore's law and that's Methuselah old."

"Meth—?"

"Old Bible guy," Milo explained. "Nine hundred years old, back when being old was equated with being wise, as opposed to way past your expiration date."

"So what do you—?"

"Content monitoring," Milo said, not letting George finish his question.

"For *five years*?" George asked. He'd only been with Quire for a few days, and he already knew this about content monitoring: the burnout rate was crazy, as in a lot of CMs either burned out or went crazy.

"Yeah, I know," Milo said, "lucky me." He paused, shifted gears. "I'm not exactly . . ." Another pause. "My position . . . The thing is, I had an oopsie."

"Oopsie?"

"The celeb brat splattercast?" Milo said. "Rupert Gunn Jr.?"

George nodded.

"I missed it," Milo said. "I should have blocked it but must have been rubbing my eyes, trying to scour out some other atrocity our species came up with, and I missed it. By the time I yanked the vid, it was already going viral, leaping from platform to platform. The sick-puppy brigade kept reposting it faster than any CM could react."

"Wow," George said, prepared to add "that sucks," when a different idea came to him. "Do you think that has to do with why I got hired? I'm still waiting on my first assignment."

"You talk to Doc Fairbanks yet?" Milo asked.

"Doc who?"

"Check your email and calendar," his Virgil advised. "You've probably already got an appointment. No assignments before the appointment."

"What kind of—?"

"Psych," Milo said, hand on the doorknob, preparing to leave. "Me, I got lucky."

"How so?"

"Got grandfathered in. Probably why they're screening all the rest of you assholes."

"Thanks," George said.

"You're welcome," Milo smiled, showing too many teeth.

# 21

Roger Lynch, LCP, LLC (licensed clinical psychologist, limited liability corporation), had initiated a Skype session with a new client when the front door opened and then slammed closed.

"Gram's a war hero," Pandora announced.

"Excuse me," her father said into the screen of his laptop before turning it away and taking himself off camera. "Please, Dora, I'm working," he said, keeping his voice down.

"Well, I hope whoever you're working *on* enjoys getting advice from a *liar*," Pandora said at a decibel in keeping with the anger written all over her face.

Roger dipped his head back into the field of the webcam and the session he hadn't quite begun conducting. "I'm terribly sorry," he said, wearing an expression of such contrite remorse it would take a total dick not to accept his apology, "but I've got a family crisis going on here."

The new client, by no means a dick, insisted he totally understood, no problem, and was preparing to click off on his end when he apparently noticed the framed photo of Pandora on Roger's desk.

"Ooo, cute," the not-a-dick client was heard to say before their shared screen blipped back to the corporate screen saver of Quire Inc.

Taken aback by the disembodied compliment, Pandora's anger traded places momentarily with confusion, before restoking itself, even hotter than before. "How could you *forget* to tell me that Grandma Lynch was a secret agent during World War II?"

"What *are* you talking about?"

Pandora repeated, slowly, what she had said.

"That's crazy," Roger said, shaking his head. "I don't know *anything* about that."

"You didn't know?" Pandora asked.

"I didn't know," Roger answered.

And while another father and daughter might have gone around and around, circling the actual truth like boxers squaring off in the ring, both of them sucked when it came to hiding things. Plus, Pandora had come fresh from her grandmother's confession, during which Gladys had paused repeatedly to check whether they were being spied on.

"But it's cool, don't you think?"

"It's incredible," Roger said. "As in, not credible." Pause. "Are you *sure* she wasn't pulling your leg? Being sarcastic maybe."

"How would that even work?" his daughter asked. "A sarcastic story about being a World War II cryptographer that goes on for the better part of the afternoon?"

"Well then, maybe she's delusional," Roger said. "There's a reason she's in that place."

"I don't think dementia works that way," Pandora said. "What I think is, she did this service for her country, was sworn to secrecy, and the dementia's worn away her resolve to keep quiet." Conveniently absent from this account was any mention of her own role in clarifying the expiration date of her grandmother's memories.

"Yeah," Roger admitted, "dying *can* change your priorities."

"That's what she said."

This singular revelation was turning everything Roger thought he knew about the woman on its head—not to mention recasting who had treated whom unfairly. How often had he pitted mother against father, judging who deserved a breakdown and who didn't? His mother hadn't fared well in that competition, coming across like some Victorian lady suffering from "hysteria," "nerves," or "the vapors." His curiosity about his parents' contrasting mental resilience was another factor that had led him to the study of psychology.

And here his daughter was, letting him know that everything he believed about the human mind was based on a cryptosexist misreading of his own parents' reactions to World War II! *Well, she better have proof,* that's what Roger was thinking. *Hard proof.* Not some demented old lady's word.

"It sounded real, what she was saying?"

Pandora nodded. "Like watching it filmed by Merchant and Ivory," she said. "Like *The Bletchley Circle*, minus the stiff upper lip."

"I wonder if she ever saw that," Roger mused aloud.

"I don't think your parents ever had a TV," Pandora said, "much less a subscription to Netflix."

"You're right," her father said, remembering his own screen-free childhood, reading books and talking about them to the world over his father's ham radio. His over-air discussions of Thoreau's *Walden* led him straight to the backwoods hermits he started counseling over his dad's rig, followed by his life now, keeping Silicon Valley's brightest and squirreliest on this side of the dirt. "It's just . . ."

"It's just *cool,*" Pandora said, her face filled with pride. "My own grandmother, like James Bond with a crossword puzzle."

"The Ian Fleming of Scrabble," her father added, figuring if he couldn't beat 'em . . .

. . . he'd ignore them.

After all, asking him to reassess his entire life—professional and otherwise—was a bridge too far, based upon the tales of a woman whose mind was unraveling, who'd frustrated her own husband into an early grave and may be misremembering some fantasy she'd had once based on something she saw or read. He'd put up with his daughter's hero worship while it lasted, confident that it wouldn't. Dementia had a natural, downward progression after all, one that would reduce his mother to the appropriate size sooner or later. In case it didn't, however . . .

"Are you planning on going back," Roger asked, "now that your sentence is up?" It was December now, and those had been the terms: up to Christmas break.

Pandora didn't even have to think about it. "Yes," she said, nodding. "Absolutely."

"Did she *know* your punishment was up after this last visit?"

Pandora had seen the date marked on the calendar in the condo's kitchenette. Gladys had asked her about it repeatedly while she was there, trying to turn the date and its approach into a long-term memory. And so: "I think so."

"Maybe that's it, then," her father said. "I think you have to consider the possibility that you're being played—that she's telling you stories so you'll come back. Maybe she wants to be sure to see you at Christmas, so she's playing you like the Scheherazade of Golden Acres."

"Golden Heart of the North Senior Services," Pandora corrected. "And you're wrong. This is real."

Roger struck a contemplative pose. "We could probably FOIA her service records," he said, making it sound like a vague threat. "If she has any, that is."

"Or you could talk to her yourself," Pandora suggested. "Christmas miracles are in season."

But her father laughed instead. "Sounds like you've got our family covered," he said.

"Ooo, cute . . ."

That's what the voice had said, and it had sounded like a boy's, uptalking occasionally, signaling a certain uncertainty she found endearing compared to the usual smug snarkiness her dad's clients usually adopted.

Her father had turned his laptop away from facing him, switching to a shot of his desk, its knickknacks, pens, sticky notes, and . . . a framed photo of Pandora!

"Ooo, cute . . ."

Pandora lay awake, staring at her ceiling, unable to get the words out of her head. For the record, it was the first time anyone outside of family had even hinted she might be attractive. And against all her better-thinking parts, her heart filled with a delicious anxiety, full of terror and possibilities, all because of two stupid syllables uttered by a boy destined for psychiatric processing by her dad.

Frankly, it was a little hard to fathom, knowing what she knew about the gene that turned Lynches into self-caricatures. But CSI-ing the whole sequence of events, recalling where she was, where her dad was, where the laptop and its camera were, mentally tacking up strings from point A to point B like some blood-spatter expert, the living room now a cat's cradle of intersecting lines with the conclusion that, no, he'd not seen her or her cartoon face in person. No. He'd heard her, certainly—as intended, given how pissed she was—but there was no line of sight that would have resulted in his seeing the actual, living Pandora Lynch in Technicolor and CinemaScope.

But he couldn't have missed the picture of her on her father's desk. It would have practically filled his screen, a static snapshot of Pandora. And it made sense, kind of. The framed photo on her dad's desk showed her face in the best possible light, meaning stilled and lacking color, thus minimizing the effect of any blemishes.

Pandora wondered whether it was possible to have a relationship without ever letting the other person see beyond an initial good impression. A blind date, say, where her first move was to actually blind the poor guy.

"You look better in dark glasses," she'd say in lieu of an apology. "They suit you. Trust me."

"I guess I'll have to," she imagined him saying back, her imaginary boyfriend destined to share her dark sense of humor. "In more ways than one," she imagined him adding.

It should be stipulated that Pandora did not make a practice of eavesdropping on her father's sessions with his clients—not while they were happening live. Despite their cabin's privacy-deficient floor plan, the fiction of client-therapist confidentiality was maintained through Pandora's use of headphones that created an inverted signal based upon ambient noise levels—including human speech—so that the hills of one soundwave became the valleys of the antisignal, thus canceling each other out. Plus, she could play music on the other side of the noise-canceling filter, which she usually did, and loudly. All of this was standard operating procedure whenever Roger was with a client.

What Roger wasn't aware of was that his curious daughter, the hacker, had hacked his laptop years ago, giving her access to all his recorded sessions. She preferred the recordings to listening live because it was more efficient. What she was interested in was any inside intel a client might spill that would be of use to her for future hacks. Recorded, she could speed through the sessions in chipmunk mode, alert for keywords. And once speech recognition software came of age, she let her own computer comb for keywords. Not that she ever got much, especially not any intellectual property in actionable detail. Turned out, her father's clients were justifiably paranoid, alluding to "some major disrupting" as a result of whatever they were working on or some "paradigm shifting algo," blah, blah, blah. And so into the trash icon these MP3s went.

But even over the grainy speaker of her father's laptop, there was something in this latest client's voice that had caught her attention—a certain youthful enthusiasm absent in her father's usual twentysomethings. She made a mental bet with herself about whether the voice's owner was old enough to shave, crossed her fingers, and then reviewed what had been recorded prior to Roger's cutting it short, to handle a "family crisis."

Bingo!

The "ooo, cute" boy was, indeed, a boy but also old enough to shave, if barely. Dark down shadowed his upper lip, while filaments were scattered in wisp patches here and there across his cheeks and chin. She hoped he'd shave, as opposed to growing some hipster chin bush. She already lived among a predominately male population who'd earned the right to their plaid and Sasquatchery; anyone caught playing that game south of Alaska was, well, pretty much a poseur by definition.

And while unflattering facial hair might seem trivial, Pandora had noticed a trend among her father's clients: personal grooming was often a Rubicon they couldn't or wouldn't cross. Call it the Einstein Hair Effect, a lack of vanity, studied slovenliness, or maybe not so studied. Whatever they were going for (or choosing by default), she'd found their relationship to the razor was nevertheless correlated to a certain snappishness she could live without. So: to shave or not, that was the question she sent out into the universe, her terms for what to consider a signal versus the usual noise.

# Part Two

# 22

Later, during World War II, the rerun: "I remember one of the boys who was fighting the war like us girls, but he was doing it in England," Gladys recalled. "He was a big deal. Not too old or too broken to fight the usual way, but too smart to waste his brain stopping some Nazi's bullet. He visited us girls 'in the colonies' once." She paused, and Pandora could see it: she was remembering, not hallucinating. Gladys continued. "The rumor mill had it that he was overseeing the installation of something called 'the widget.' That's what they called it, always in whispers, these fast-walking men we'd never seen around there before. The most we could figure out was that 'ours' was going to be a backup, in case the one in England succumbed to enemy attack."

Pandora could feel her heart race. *Could it be?* "What was his name?" she asked hastily. "Tell me you remember his name, Gram."

"They only ever called him 'Alan from England,'" Gladys said as her granddaughter repeated the words, "'Alan from England . . .'"

"He was such a handsome man," Gladys continued. "Such a dark, serious face, his temples shaved all round to the thinnest stubble, the hair on top always flopping in his eyes."

"Did you talk to him?" Pandora asked. "Did he say anything?"

Gladys giggled, turning suddenly girlish, despite all appearances to the contrary. "I *touched* him," she said.

"What did he do," Pandora asked, "when you touched him?"

"Froze. I think he may have been afraid of us."

"Americans?"

"Women."

"I heard he was . . . 'shy,'" Pandora said.

If Gladys realized what she meant by that, she showed no signs. "I wonder whatever happened to him."

Pandora wondered, *Should I? Shouldn't I?*

"He died, Gram."

Her grandmother's eyes went wide. "But he's so *young*," she said. "And he seems—*seemed*—like such a nice man. Very serious. Very British."

Pandora didn't know what to say. She wanted to *scream* that Alan from England was the father of modern computing and committed suicide after being chemically castrated for the crime of being homosexual by the country he'd helped save during World War II. She wanted to tell Gladys how Alan from England bit into an apple laced with cyanide and the rumor that the bite out of the Apple logo is a nod to this, as opposed to the Bible's tree of knowledge or even Isaac Newton. But before she could say any of that, Gladys continued.

"I used to imagine what it would be like to be married to someone like that," she said wistfully. "To wake up to the sound of English being spoken properly. I bet he would have played Scrabble with me, not like those chickens, my husband and son."

A week later, Pandora made a point of touching the hand she guessed was probably the hand that had touched Alan Turing. "Tell me about Alan from England again," she said.

"Who?" Gladys said, as Pandora, now the holder of that memory, proceeded to tell it back to her. When she got to the part where Gladys, bold as brass, reached out and touched the author of the Turing test, her granddaughter decided to take a little editorial license.

"I did?" her grandmother said, her eyes widening.

"You did," Pandora confirmed.

"And what did *he* do?" Gladys asked.

"He smiled," Pandora said. "He took your hand and kissed it like you were the queen of England herself."

"How marvelous," Gladys said, the cheeks of her tattletale face giving her away, yet again.

# 23

Pandora didn't usually eavesdrop on her father when he was actively with a client. And ever since she'd started using speech recognition and keyword searches, she didn't do much listening to the recorded sessions either—not unless her search turned up something exploitable in some hackerly way. But this latest session was different; it was the makeup session for the one she'd interrupted with news of Grandma Lynch's wartime heroism. She'd since learned the client's name was George Jedson, which sounded like an alias, but a quick cyber tiptoe through Quire HR's employee database confirmed it was as legal as her own.

The new employee screenings had started as charity from her dad's college roommate but had since become mandatory thanks to a coder who went a little suboptimal while programming a routine software patch. In this case, *suboptimal* meant the release of millions of usernames, social security numbers, and credit card information—a release that led to several class-action lawsuits and legislative hearings in the US, the UK, and the EU.

Her father and George had just gotten started when she'd interrupted them, and so Roger was taking it from the top. After winding up the "origin story" of the mandatory psych evaluation, her father concluded with the disclaimer Quire's general counsel had approved: "It's not you, it's us. And by 'us,' we mean Quire, by which we mean the parent company, as well as its various affiliates, subsidiaries, and offshore incarnations for tax purposes . . ."

Given the opportunity to speak, George brought up the abrupt termination of the previous session. Because of it, her father's new client had gone another full workday without an assignment.

"So I have to wonder," George said, "is all this meaningless waiting part of the psych exam? Like on *Law & Order*, letting a suspect sweat it out in the box."

"If you don't mind me saying," Roger said, "that sounds a little paranoid."

"What would it mean if I minded you saying that?"

Roger ignored the attempt at humor. "That I was correct in my original assessment," Roger said, clickety-clicking his pen to underline the point.

George cleared his throat.

"Different topic." Clickety-click. Pause.

"Yes?" George said, sounding wary.

Reading from his notes: "'Ooo, cute.' What was that in reference to, before you signed off?"

Pandora, perched before her own laptop, listening in as well as watching the session on-screen, noted that the universe had accepted and responded to her terms. Because there was Mr. Jedson's face, shaved as smooth as the proverbial baby's butt and just as cute. Looking at it live and free of distracting facial hair, she noticed that George's face seemed the total opposite of her own, calm and revealing nothing to the point of seeming chiseled. She found herself paying attention to his blinks, to confirm the screen hadn't frozen. Between the two of them—Pandora imagined—maybe their kids would luck out and get normally expressive faces.

But before she could start scrawling multiple iterations of the name she'd take after marriage (to hyphenate or not to hyphenate?), she heard the session taking a dangerous turn with her father's quoting the two words she'd been hearing ever since they were first uttered. Now, however, voiced by her father, they sounded, well, creepy, making Pandora want to do several things at once: 1) scream "No . . ."; 2) slam her laptop closed, perhaps forever; 3) take a sledgehammer to the satellite downlink; and/or 4) die of embarrassment and wait for her father to notice the smell.

Meanwhile, "Um," George said, as stone-faced as ever, "your daughter, I'm guessing?"

"Where?" Roger asked, looking behind him.

"The photo," George said. "On your desk. You mentioned you had a daughter, and any other explanation seems a little creepy."

"Yes," Roger said, turning the frame away from the camera. "That's Pandora."

George's eyebrows lifted ever so slightly. "Ominous."

"It's after the charm bracelet," Roger said, dismissing any broader, mythological implications. "Her mother collected charms."

"Collected?" George said. "Past tense?"

"Her mother passed away when Pandora was born."

"You mean like Mary Shelley's mom?"

Pandora listened, both fascinated and horrified to hear herself being talked about by her father and his client, neither aware she was listening to every word. But this talking about her mom, too, and the casual way her dad gave away the story of her name when he'd lied to her about it so long just made her—well, she was back to considering her previous options, with smashing the sat link pulling ahead. Fortunately, it seemed her father had grown as uncomfortable with this digression as she was.

"Why don't you tell me about *your* mother," Roger said.

"Isn't that a cliché?" George countered. "I mean, blaming the parents for a kid's being messed up?"

"Are you telling me you consider yourself a messed-up kid?"

Her father's new client hung his head but then seemed to remember he was on camera. His eyes, so calm as to seem blasé before, now hardened underneath their pixels. Finally: "Yes," he said. "You got me. I *do* believe in my heart of hearts"—he paused—"that I *am*"—he paused again—"pretty *frickin'* messed up."

Her father blinked in the thumbnail of his side of the session in the bottom left-hand corner of her screen. She could practically read his mind, with a lot of help from his face. Most of his clients' files began and ended with the screening, one and done. A handful had become regulars. And this one, by admitting to feeling messed up, had just won himself a callback. For which, Pandora thought, *Thank you, universe,* while her father clickety-clicked his pen and asked, "Are Wednesdays good for you?"

# 24

In retrospect, Pandora realized, she'd been noticing it without acknowledging it. Her grandmother's bookmark hadn't moved in weeks. It used to be it'd be sticking out of a new book from one visit to the next. But then there was the visit when Pandora noticed the book on her grandmother's end table hadn't changed. That's when her attention shifted to the bookmark's progress as a visualization of the disease's progress, reversed. Pandora wondered when Gladys had been forced to abandon her favorite hobby. Was it when she couldn't retain what she'd read from one page to the next? Paragraphs? Sentences? Had individual words become speed bumps, hindering the drive toward meaning? And was becoming the story herself the backup plan, the one that kept her remaining neurons from becoming speed bumps in their own right?

Her grandmother's brain was having a fire sale, and Pandora had caught the old woman's anxiety like a virus. Before, she'd been fooled by the disease's sweet spot into thinking there was more time. Now, it was like her grandmother's commanding officers, drilling away how every idle minute cost lives.

Pandora vowed to spend as much time as remained with her grandmother, getting every byte and datum down, recording it all on her phone for posterity. She'd start skipping classes if she had to—not exactly a sacrifice, with the exception of her science class, but she was sure Mr. V would understand, what with his mother and all.

But even if she skipped school, the Golden Heart only held visiting hours for so long, no exceptions, unless a loved one had actually rung death's doorbell, when they might get you a cot. But dying memories? What part of elder care didn't Pandora get? Been there, done that, forgot about it—and *that's* what Pandora should do: forget about it. Every resident at the Golden Heart was an American, meaning nobody at the Golden Heart got special treatment, their memories included—especially those memories somebody's granddaughter hinted might still be classified. Or as she'd been told already: "First the brownies, now this? Do you *want* to wind up in some CIA black site?"

But once visiting hours ended and Gladys was by herself, Pandora knew those memories didn't hit pause, waiting for the next visit so she could resume where they'd left off. The disease's progress was relentless and the exact opposite of the bookmark's progress through her grandmother's last murder mystery, the grand reveal of whodunit forever withheld from her . . .

But Pandora believed in the power of technology to fix things. She'd already begun recording Gladys on her phone. But she couldn't just hand her a digital recorder and say, "Yeah, before you die, could you please fill this up?" It needed to be something that actually *helped* Gladys while it was helping her piece together her own family's pre-Pandoran history. Something to prop up her grandmother's failing short-term memory—something more sophisticated than the dry-erase board where staff would write reminders about pending house calls from one of the medical practitioners with iconic hints like a tooth, eyeglasses, or a valentine-style heart, always ending with the same headless smiley made out of two dots and a swoop followed by the staffer's name.

Pandora could do better. She'd start by rooting one of her outdated smartphones, customize the screen to keep it Jitterbug easy, with dedicated, supersized icons for a calendar app that included reminders of the whiteboard sort and a facial recognition app preprogrammed with faces Gladys should know, including Pandora; the facility's various staff and medical practitioners; her son, Roger (because you never knew); and Gladys's own, from a wedding photo of her and Herman, taken in the bar where they'd met, holding hands as a dead moose head on the wall looked on approvingly. She'd include Skype with her contact info programmed in for when Gladys missed her between visits and a voice-activated recorder for her grandmother's war stories. Lastly, she'd throw in a weather app, for when Gladys didn't want to get up and check outside her window.

Once it was set up, Pandora spent the better part of her next visit showing Gladys how to use it, pointing out what each virtual button did, how to point the camera at faces she didn't know so the phone could speak her visitor's name. She'd worried about Gladys's forgetting to charge the phone, and so she glued the jack into its port and plugged the charger into an outlet underneath her grandmother's bed so it wouldn't be a tripping hazard or get accidentally unplugged. The charging cord was long enough to reach the nightstand like a landline phone. Though the arrangement made a mockery of wireless technology, Pandora figured her grandmother would probably be more comfortable with a phone similar to the ones her generation had grown most accustomed to, even if Herman and she had never gotten a phone of their own.

It was fun, showing her grandmother technology that blew her mind and about which Pandora had grown jaded but could appreciate again from the new perspective of Gladys's aging eyes. "Oh my," she'd said as her granddaughter molded her wrinkled hand to this slab of plastic from the future. Pandora demonstrated Skype, showing Gladys how they could see each other, and see each other seeing each other, and so on.

"Oh my," the old lady repeated, and Pandora wished she could crawl inside her skull to see the sci-fi world she must be imagining.

"Pretty cool, huh?" Pandora said.

"Pretty cool," Gladys said, either because she agreed or because it was the last thing she heard.

Pandora had to skip their next visit to study for an unexpected exam that was worth enough that she couldn't offset it with extra credit later. Previously, she would have felt guilty, but was reassured by the fact that Gladys could Skype her now. No call, she concluded, meant everything was okay. Hopefully, her grandmother was busy filling up the phone's memory with her own memories, secret, classified, and otherwise.

After acing the test the next day, Pandora thought about calling Gladys to let her know, but didn't want to startle her. She'd convinced herself that her grandmother was taking advantage of the tech she'd been given to "remember your memories for you." So she gave it another day, reminding herself to bring a cable and thumb drive to collect what memories Gladys had recorded, while also reminding herself to set up a Dropbox account so her grandmother's recordings could go straight to the cloud.

But when Pandora showed up, Gladys was gone. Instead of her new BFF coming to open the door with the walker she'd begun using, she was greeted by some gray-haired stranger.

"I'm sorry," she said. "I thought this was Gladys Lynch's condo."

"Was that her name?" the younger old woman said, her bandy wrinkled arms braced at the wrists, her hands holding tiny dumbbells she pumped in sequence, left, then right, then left again, as if she was keeping her heart going manually.

*"Was?"* Pandora said, her own heart nearly stopping. "What happened?"

"Oh no," the usurper said. "They've only moved her."

"Where?"

"Haven't a clue," the heart pumper said. "Oh, wait. When you find her, can you give her something?"

"Sure," Pandora said, imagining some old-people's tradition of giving gifts for occasions like being moved closer to death's door—a cake, perhaps. Instead: "Here," the other one said, handing the girl a tight, rubber-banded tube of junk mail that hadn't been forwarded to wherever they'd installed the grandmother Pandora was getting to know, for real, for the first time.

A series of nurture-free nurses, recalcitrant rehabbers, and a-hole attendants later, Pandora finally found her way to "the other side," where her grandmother had been moved. She knocked on the frame of the open door before entering to find Gladys, looking out the window, watching her breath freeze against the glass, the ice crystals feathering out geometrically, biology turned into math.

"I wished I'd smoked when I had the chance," Gladys said, as if she was talking to herself but didn't mind if her granddaughter listened in.

"Why, for heaven's sake?"

"For heaven's sake," Gladys echoed before pausing—to think, perhaps. "I wish I smoked because of heaven. That's why."

"How . . . ?"

"Because maybe I'd be dead already," Gladys said. "Maybe I'd be looking down from heaven now."

"That's silly," Pandora said. To the best of her knowledge, her grandparents had both become agnostic after the war. Roger and his daughter had taken it a step further, as atheists.

"What's silly is everybody trying to live longer," Gladys said. "They think they're adding years to their lives. What they don't realize is that all those years get added on the shit end."

Pandora wanted to quibble with Gladys's conclusion but, looking at her grandmother's new accommodations, found she was fresh out of sunshine and pep talks. "What happened?" she asked.

"I messed my bed," Gladys said.

Pandora tried keeping the "yuck" off her face—couldn't—and so went for brutal pragmatism. "Switch to Depends," she said. "I've seen them on TV. All the active seniors are wearing them."

"I've *been* wearing them," Gladys said, her voice an angry hiss, though who that anger was aimed at wasn't clear. "I forgot to change, goddamn it."

"How long . . ."

"All day," Gladys said. "I went to bed that way. They . . . *exploded.*"

Pandora's "yuck" face doubled down, her mouth an oval of forlorn darkness.

"It was in my hair, Dorie," Gladys said, tears standing in her eyes.

"Oh, Gram," the younger girl said, wrapping her arm around the older girl's shoulder.

After a moment: "I want you to promise me something," Gladys said.

"Anything, Gram."

"I want you to start smoking. Camels. Unfiltered. Die some other way."

"Okay, Gram," she said. "For you," she added, already looking forward to her forgetting they'd ever had this conversation.

# 25

Pandora had done it the same day she decided to start working on the phone for Gladys. She'd begun wondering, idly at first but then frantically as she watched Gladys change before her eyes: Did she have more in common with her grandmother than just a hyperexpressive face? Until then, the younger woman had consoled herself with a factoid she'd heard somewhere about how Alzheimer's was linked to the use of aluminum cookware. But when she tried to remember the source of that factoid: nothing. Crickets. Which made her wonder if—from here on out—every recall lapse or random brain fart would make her feel like she'd stepped down a step and missed, finding nothing under her feet but air and the panicked caught breath of a fall as it happened.

Whether that was to be her fate seemed like a knowable unknown. And so she bought a DNA kit from the Safeway pharmacy. The company she picked donated part of their profits to CARE or UNICEF, placing them one holier-than above competitors like 23andMe, which also cost more. The test was originally marketed as the Healing Helix, a nod to the goal of ending intolerance by showing how genetically interconnected everybody was. Someone in the company must have had second thoughts about the alliteration, however, and so the name was changed to Six Degrees, which was displayed on the box and in their ads as the numeral followed by the symbol for degree in superscript. By avoiding words altogether, the logo was considered internationally recognizable shorthand for the whole "six degrees of separation" thing. The company further reinforced this message by running ads that featured happy multicultis tracking their ancestry around the globe, dropping pins next to happy dancing villagers, next to happy nodding monks, next to happy chanting protesters, their faces streaming tears of apparent joy while the gas canister fumes filled the screen to provide a backdrop for the tagline: "One Big Happy."

Locking herself behind the one *actual* interior door that *actually* locked, Pandora ripped open the box like her life depended on it. A shatterproof plastic test tube fell out, along with its screw-on cap and a Q-tip in cellophane followed by a folded wad of tissue-thin paper with the instruction to swab her cheek, drop the Q-tip in the test tube, and mail it back in the prepaid mailer to an address somewhere in North Carolina with the words *research* and *park* as part of the city's name. The same instructions (presumably) followed in Spanish, French, German, Russian, Arabic, Chinese, and a dozen or so more languages. Pandora checked inside the box, hoping for more lab tech—a petri dish, say, or a bottle of reagent—some evidence that she didn't have to wait for this process to go back and forth through the US postal system.

No such luck.

Pandora swore. Didn't they know how many brain cells could die waiting for USPS to complete its appointed rounds? She swore again. And then she swabbed her cheek, packed up the tube, borrowed the truck, and sped off for the nearest FedEx drop-off location. She'd handle the part of the timeline she could, hoping that the recipients on the other end of the delivery would take the "Please hurry" she scrawled across the prepaid mailer in earnest and reciprocate by sending the results back with equal urgency. And if passive-aggressiveness wasn't their thing, maybe the fact of the package coming from Fairbanks would catch somebody's attention and move her to the front of the line. She'd played the last-frontier card before, getting live people instead of robots, because the place she called home happened to overlap with their dream vacation or retirement plans. That was the nice thing about living in a state routinely featured on the Discovery Channel: you could pimp it out for favors in a pinch.

It worked, kind of. That and the extra she paid for priority processing and shipping, which came to roughly twice the cost of the original kit. Still, it had taken about a week—a week during which she'd been knocked off her visiting schedule by an exam and a subsequent overconfidence in technology. The results had arrived the morning of the "please start smoking" visit, which raised the stakes on everything.

Not that Pandora knew what was waiting for her at the Golden Heart when she folded the unopened envelope and stuffed it into her pocket. She'd open it once she got there, she decided, and if it was good news, she'd share it with Gladys, in case what had or hadn't been passed along was weighing on her too.

But then there'd been the surprise at her grandmother's former condo and the mad rush to find out where she'd been taken. There'd been the promise to smoke and the wanting to cry. And only then did Pandora remember the envelope in her parka. She found a visitors' bathroom and locked herself inside.

The first thing she removed was a multipage form letter full of legalese explaining all the things the results *wouldn't* be telling her, as well as the things they *hadn't* tested for, including the nastiest of inheritable diseases because the liability of blah, blah, blah, which Pandora took to mean they didn't want to be sued when somebody offed themselves after getting bad news. And spoiler alert, Huntington's, Alzheimer's, Lou Gehrig's, assorted cancers, dementias, and incurable neurological conditions all constituted bad news. Leaving what? Earlobes attached or not? Tongue curling? Eye color . . .

Pandora wanted to scream, to cry, to maybe email the head of the company, promising not to kill herself, explaining she just wanted to know so she could start planning . . .

". . . to do what?" she asked her reflection in the bathroom mirror. And the funny thing was, Pandora already had an answer—had had it for a while, just below the surface of her consciousness. She'd even taken a step in that direction with the smartphone she'd reprogrammed for Gladys, promising that it would remember her memories for her. And that's what she wanted to do, scaled way up: move her memories from in vitro to in silico.

Futurists had been talking about the point in human history when the species would merge with computers to live forever. Ray Kurzweil, arguably the father of this line of thinking, called it "the singularity" and predicted that the technology to link our brains to computers and upload ourselves to the cloud was practically around the corner—by the 2030s or so. That was well within Pandora's life span—and well before she'd be showing any signs of dementia, if that was the fate hardwired into her DNA.

So that was the good news, right? The future was already working on it; there was too much money on the table for it not to be. Pandora laughed. All that angst when the truth was that AI, the cloud, and neuro-tech had it all covered! Gladys's present didn't have to be Pandora's future. *Except . . .*

"Except what?" she asked her mirrored self.

And again, she already knew. Her father's oft-repeated mathematical morality of logical conclusions: What if everybody did what you're thinking of doing? And what was Pandora thinking of doing? Nothing. Letting the future take care of, well, her future. But if everybody chilled and let the future take care of itself—*then the future* wouldn't *take care of itself.* Lulled into waiting for the singularity, humans would have no incentive to invent it.

Not that Pandora had to create a self-aware AI she could upload all her hopes and dreams to by herself. But she had a good brain (for the time being), and she was a quick learner (while it lasted). She was a cyber native, had taken computers apart and put them back together without having them blow up. She'd learned to program in binary, the actual ones and zeros the computer used. Her dad studied the human mind, and surely she'd picked up something through osmosis. Further back, she shared blood with a WWII code breaker and had touched the father of modern computing, albeit by proxy and a few generations removed.

And then there was that pair of aces in the hole: she was young and stubborn as they came. So hell yeah. It wasn't like she had anything more important to do.

# 26

Mr. Plaid had a name—Steve Vickers—and before he vacated George's office, he'd been working on a project for Quire, sitting on that dock by the bay, looking at the Golden Gate Bridge. He was trying to get into the "mind space" of a person who'd jump from said bridge, a locally popular option when it came to taking that final departing flight into whatever comes next. He imagined that must be nothing—the what-comes-next—for someone in that position. They must *think* that. Must think they're placing a period at the end of their life sentence, not a semicolon or a question mark and certainly not an exclamation point, though he was inclined to waver on that last one. Suicide—or so it seemed to Steve Vickers—was decidedly the act of someone in love with their own drama.

The reason he was thinking about all this was because that was what his latest work assignment called for. His employer wanted its corner of the web turned into a safety net, a little like the one circling Apple's Foxconn factory in China, to catch the jumpers. Or as V.T. put it, signing off on the assignment: "We want to make Quire a safe place to go to be saved."

While the idea behind these mental field trips was sound, the way Vickers was conducting them was a waste of time. Because the task wasn't about preventing *his* demographic from exiting the pool of consumers—biology and time were rapidly turning that cohort irrelevant—but those who were in the prime of their consumptive lives. Steve Vickers's empathy was too chronologically specific. Sure, he could think himself into the minds of different races, religions, sexual orientations, and socioeconomic classes—provided they were all roughly around his age. Add or subtract a decade, however, and *nothing.* Trying to understand the fads, trends, language even of his target demographic audience was like trying to mind meld with a cow, chewing away on its cud. He and they were in different headspaces, even though, years earlier, he'd aged right on through it, in premature mourning for the innocence he couldn't wait to be rid of.

So maybe it wasn't too surprising that George's predecessor kept getting distracted by the other scenery. The homeless crabber being creepy over that way, the lesbians reacting disgustedly a few benches down. And boy, those seagulls! Wheeling so white against the blue sky, inevitably leaving their witness in a caffeinated and mildly euphoric mood, also known as . . .

. . . *the totally wrong headspace for working on that goddamn suicide thing.*

Back at the office, Steve Vickers had been giving it his best shot for three months. He'd divided the assignment into two main steps: identification and intervention—the two Is. Shortly after getting the assignment, he'd coded up a nice little data cruncher to tackle the first *I* by baselining the online activity of every Quire user within the target demographic and then comparing that baseline on a rolling basis, looking for any deviations from the mean, with a target's potential for self-harm being a relatively simple ratio of public engagement to nesting behavior. The first of these criteria—the ratio's numerator—was populated with data on how often the subject sent emails, tweets, IMs, and/or texts, including how long these exchanges were in terms of both individual message character counts and overall duration of the thread, from the first message to the last. The denominator, in turn, was based upon the radius of the subject's travel behavior over a set time period, derived from smartphone GPS data, including the subset of how long the subject spent at his or her primary residence, which was used as a multiplier. A decreasing rate of public engagement divided by an increasing rate of nesting behavior would set a flag, and the identification process would move on to the interim phase 1b: confirmation.

Vickers's first approach to this interim phase had been simple and effective, and only required the target to answer three questions: 1) Are you depressed?; 2) Is there a gun in the house?; and 3) Have you been drinking? George's predecessor had designed a chatbot that asked these questions subliminally, the text flashing for an eyeblink between lines of chatter about something else. This approach led to several early successes—right up until word leaked on how they'd been achieved, after which the wrath of the first and last letters of the ATF came raining down on QHQ, with talk of boycotts and share sell-offs and assorted other PR nightmares that were not at all mitigated by the thank-yous V.T. received from survivors and members of the pharmaceutical industry with an interest in selling solutions that didn't involve getting loaded and/or taking aim.

Vickers's next attempt at confirming the seriousness of a target's intentions involved inserting an increasing number of ads in the user's news feed, including PSAs for suicide prevention hotlines, half-off coupons for natural antidepressants ranging from vitamin B to St. John's wort, and BOGO deals on aromatherapy candles, usually lavender. If/when these enticements failed to garner the clicks they were tailor-baited for, confirmation by default was assumed, and "in an overabundance of caution" (according to Quire's lawyers), the platform outsourced intervention to local law enforcement. Though individual areas varied as to response aggressiveness, there had already been a few hospitalizations and one death as a result of Quire users' SEQs (self-endangerment quotients) being skewed due to lost phones being interpreted algorithmically as "loss of engagement."

And then Rupert Gunn Jr. placed the family's namesake into his face hole and shot his mouth off without saying a word. And while Steve Vickers had not been involved in the news feed manipulation experiments that led to Mr. Gunn's premature exit, his algorithm had also failed to predict it.

"You know, I had a feeling," George said after finally getting the details of his first assignment, the one he'd inherited from his predecessor. The assignment had been hand delivered to him in hard copy on V.T.'s personal letterhead with the instruction that it be shredded after reading. When George folded it back up instead, the messenger cleared his throat loudly and patted the top of his custom-built satchel—one featuring a top-loaded crosscut shredder.

"We used to use burn bags," the messenger explained, "but they kept setting those off." He pointed at the sprinklers.

And so George fed the one and only copy of what he'd be doing for the next several months into the slot through which it was magically transformed into confetti.

It wasn't often new hires were given offices and hand delivered their first assignments. If George had any doubts about that, they were quickly quashed when he entered the cafeteria following his assignment's delivery. He could feel the eyes on him—less a sign of his social sensitivity than a byproduct of socially maladapted strangers having no qualms about walking right up to him and asking: "So what're you working on?"

George matched their social maladaptation and raised them being rude. "I'm using reinforcement learning to discover the meaning of life through trial and error," he informed them. "You know, check off everything life *doesn't* mean and then see what's left." He figured that sounded nicer than "I'm scripting an AI to make sure no more rich kids off themselves on our platform"—an explanation he was pretty sure was counterindicated by the whole shredding situation.

But his fellow coders heard it pretty much the way it was intended. "Dude, just say f-off next time."

"Okay," George said. "F-off."

And with that, George returned to his workspace to see if he could get his headspace in the right place to start eating the elephant he now shared his office with.

# 27

Before leaving the visitors' restroom with her non-news from the genetic testing people, it occurred to Pandora that she hadn't seen the phone among the items relocated to her grandmother's new, radically downsized living arrangement. Returning, she found the curtains drawn and Gladys asleep in the railed bed that now dominated the space, a monitor of some kind clipped to her blanket should she try to get up without help. But Pandora couldn't see the phone anywhere. Checking for an outline of it under the covers, she was startled to realize Gladys's eyes were wide open and looking right at her.

"What do you want?" her grandmother asked as if Pandora were a stranger, maybe an artifact of having just been awoken, or maybe . . .

"I was just looking for your phone."

"We don't have one and don't want one," Gladys said, making the younger woman feel like a door-to-door salesperson about to be greeted with a shotgun.

"Never mind," Pandora said, hastily backing up and out. "It was old," she added, and regretted the implication immediately—the casual equivalence of age with a depreciation in worth. Fortunately, Gladys didn't seem to notice, still flat on her back in the shadowed room, staring at the ceiling.

Walking the long hallway to the exit, Pandora ran through a variety of possible scenarios for the phone's disappearance. Maybe someone stole it during the move. Maybe it got lost in the shuffle. And then she had an idea; she called the missing phone from her phone over Skype to see if she could figure out where it was from the video. Fortunately, she'd programmed it to answer her number automatically to make it easier on Gladys.

But the view she got of the call's other side was impressionistic, at best, consisting of a blurry swirl of Halloween colors—black and orange—the black looking like horns or talons. Continuing down the hallway, trying to figure out what and where she was seeing, Pandora bumped into a janitor coming in the opposite direction. There was the usual exchange of "watch its" and "sorrys," but as she prepared to move on, she noticed a glow from atop the janitor's wheeled trash barrel.

"Excuse me," she said. "Can I . . . ?" She made a gesture she hoped read as "look through the garbage," though it could also have been "do the breaststroke."

"Knock yourself out," the janitor said, pulling out a pair of one-size-fits-most rubber gloves from a hundred-count box on his cart like he was offering her a Kleenex.

"Thank you," she said, pulling the gloves on, snap, snap, before picking aside this awful this and that nasty that until, bingo, she pinched a corner of plastic and lifted out the phone she'd rooted, sealed in a biohazard bag, bright, translucent orange backgrounding the extra-terrestrial death lily, its swooping, impressionistic petals all in black. The phone was smeared with something Pandora assumed was *not* pudding.

Doing what she could to calm her face, the hacker cleared her throat and began: "I know this is going to sound strange and is probably against the rules, but . . ."

"You want the shit phone," the janitor guessed.

"I want the shit phone," Pandora echoed, pretty sure she'd never used quite that combination of words before in her life—and hoping she never would again.

"Knock yourself out," the janitor said.

It wasn't the device itself so much as what might be on it, in addition to fecal matter. Specifically, Pandora wanted to see if Gladys had recorded anything before the mishap. Checking, she discovered a list of numerically labeled MP3s in the recorder's file folder, which she downloaded to a less biohazardous medium before plugging it into her laptop and hitting play.

Nothing. Dead air.

Or *nearly* dead air. Straining, Pandora could make out ambient old-lady noises. She would have said butt dialing if she hadn't wired it like a landline. So what was Gladys doing? Using it as a coaster? Pandora listened for clues: the ding of the microwave in the kitchen; blowing; sipping; the word *hot* spoken to herself; a cracking long fart. Next file: the creak of her new walker as she lifted and lowered her weight by its handles; the name Herman; the question "Where are you?" Next file: the pages of a book, rattling gently as she turned them; three pages turned quickly, pause, three quick-turned pages again; a sigh; no more page turns. Next file: the tail end of a cry, gone almost singsongy, conjuring the image of Gladys, a pillow pressed to her stomach, rocking, and crying, rocking and crying . . .

Pandora ran out of files and was glad, then sad. She'd returned the phone to its biohazard bag. It was mostly smooth glass and plastic, but with enough physical buttons where shit might hide—in her imagination, if not in reality. And so she scooted it off the edge of her desk with the eraser end of a pencil and into the wastebasket, thought about it, and then dropped the pencil in as well.

She'd gotten the technology wrong, Pandora decided. A sleek slab would have been fine for her, but not for a woman slipping backward in time. It needed to be softer, friendlier, invite interaction. It needed to be something her grandmother could love, like a child loves a favorite toy, taking it to bed, talking to it, talking for and through it, an "invisible" friend that others could see, but not as vividly or vitally as the owner who loved it. Like a teddy bear, still warm from the dryer, tucked in together, ripe for snuggling.

It needed—in short—a face.

None of this was original thinking on Pandora's part, as she'd be the first to admit. She'd begun noticing how many of the residents had little companions on this side of the Golden Heart. Some were being visited by dogs in vests, professional caregivers of the four-legged variety. Others held on to lifelike baby dolls, teddy bears, even a sock monkey, offering them bites of food, cooing at them, asleep with their gray heads resting on the plusher ones like pillows. One skin-and-bones woman had a cockroach hand puppet, her fingers fitting into its gloved legs, the body made of corduroy, the wings, leather on the outside, silk on the other, suede strips for antennae. It was the most touchably gorgeous cockroach she'd ever seen, an opinion shared by its owner, who stroked its variously tactile surfaces constantly—when she wasn't sneaking up on other residents and skittering it across their shoulders, only to laugh hysterically when they recoiled.

Pandora's first response to this menagerie was anger on the residents' behalf, at their being infantilized with these playthings. But then she noticed how fond of them the residents seemed, whispering in their ears, seeming to listen to their replies, offering them food and drink and comfort. There was a lot of there-there-ing going on as the upset and fearful put those feelings aside to play parent to themselves through these intermediaries they cradled and cooed to: there-there, there-there . . .

More than one resident helped their friend wave a paw or hand at Pandora as she walked by, and she couldn't help it; she waved back.

"It's therapeutic," a nurse's aide had said. "And they're pretty resilient to not being fed or walked."

"That makes sense," Pandora, the convert, had said as she looked at her grandmother's hands. Bulge-knuckled and blue, featuring a traffic jam of veins across the top of each, Gladys's hands were otherwise empty, holding nothing but each other.

"Would it be okay if—" she'd begun, not knowing what she might bring but knowing she needed to bring something.

"Certainly," the nurse's aide had said, not needing Pandora to finish the thought.

What she wanted would be like what the others had, but better—more interactive. It should be able to have a conversation—a real one, not imaginary. It should be able to initiate such a conversation and record it. The Japanese were working on eldercare robots like what she envisioned—not a Robby to do any heavy lifting or make sure they bathed, but for the company, minus the need to feed or clean up after a support animal. The Japanese weren't bothered by such artificial concepts as artificiality; everything was believed to share an essential spirituality, the animate and inanimate alike. A robot dog and a so-called "real dog" could both produce real emotions in the person petting one or the other without being labeled unnatural.

Pandora tried a variety of searches on Amazon to see what might already be available and tweakable. Casting the broadest net first, she looked at page after page of "robot toys," finding a variety of actual and knockoff Transformers, kits to teach young scientists about robotics, a few robodogs, and a range of what Pandora dubbed robocuties, featuring prominent heads with prominent eyes and smiles. But none of it was quite right, featuring too many hard edges and, if not edges, then hard, smooth curves. *Hard* was the theme and executed in plastic. Many had wheels or some other means of getting around—clearly intended for overactive kids, giving them something to chase off their energy with, but the exact opposite of what she wanted for the increasingly sedentary Gladys.

Searching for "robot dogs" eliminated the Transformers and Terminator exoskeletons, but the hard plastic remained. That wasn't what Pandora wanted; she wanted soft, plush, pettable. She typed in the word *robot*, no quotes, and the first keyword she could think of that conveyed what she was looking for: *fur*.

And there they were: Furbies. Gremliny-looking, bug-eyed balls of animatronic plushness. She'd never heard of them, but there seemed to be a bunch of different kinds, and so she googled. Turned out they were originally the hot toy of Christmas 1998, cooed a language known as Furbish, and supposedly had the ability to learn the more you interacted with them. They'd since been updated to include an internet-of-things version called Furby Connect you could interact with in person, but also through a smartphone app.

Perfect.

Pandora did a one-click buy off Amazon and then surfed the interwebs, dark and lit, looking for schematics, source code, and fun hacks to render her new purchase warranty-voided but even more perfect still.

"Hey, Gram," she said. "I've got someone who wants to meet you."

"I'm too old for blind dates," Gladys said, "or cataract dates, for that matter."

Pandora didn't engage, instead bringing the Furby around to where her grandmother could see it, a big red bow atop its head.

"What's this?"

Though Pandora was proud of her work, she didn't say, "A Wi-Fi-connected Fur-bot that can record everything you say and store it in the cloud, where I can listen to it any time I want, while also being able to switch over to live mode for a one-sided video chat, thanks to the camera hidden behind one of its eyes." Instead, she kept it humble and brief: "A friend," she said, trying not to look at the other "friends" around them but finding it hard not to.

Gladys noticed. "You mean like these other morons?"

But Pandora was ready for it. "Nope," she said. "This here guy's our security system. Any of these chuckleheads tries any of that elder abuse stuff"—she unscrewed the Fur-bot's eye to reveal the camera—"we'll sue the pants off 'em."

Gladys smiled, suggesting the idea of suing the pants off 'em appealed to her.

That hurdle cleared, Pandora made introductions. "Gladys Lynch?" she began.

"Oh, for Pete's sake . . ."

". . . meet Furbius McFurbutt."

Gladys shielded her eyes, embarrassed, but laughing anyway. Finally composing herself, she looked up, the picture of elderly dignity. "Why, Mr. McFurbutt," she said. "How *do* you do?"

It was an obvious question, and the programming anticipated it, along with other conversation helpers, from thoughts on the weather to whether the world was going crazy or was it (fill in the blank)? And so: "Very well, Mrs. Lynch," Furbius said, borrowing Pandora's voice raised an octave or two.

# 28

"So where should we start?" Roger said, kicking off their first post-screening session.

"Suicide," George said.

Roger straightened, then inclined forward, looking at his client's video image over the rims of the glasses sliding down his nose. "So much for foreplay . . ."

"Not me," George insisted. "It's my assignment. I'm supposed to AI-up a little chatbot to detect and prevent possible suicides on the platform, with a particular focus on my personal demographic: kidults." He paused. "All of which is protected information, I'm assuming."

"Kidults?"

"Young adults, old kids," George said. "Consumers in the prime of their consumption ages, from fifteen to twenty-five."

Roger sat back, slow-clicking his pen contemplatively. "This wouldn't be a case of 'It's not me, Doc, but I got a friend'?"

"Nope. Strictly work," George said. "I like to multitask, and since I'm being required to have these sessions, I figured I might as well mine them for something I can actually use on the job." He paused. "So: suicide. Why, and how do you stop it?"

Roger drew his fingers across his lips, hiding the smile underneath. "You remind me of my daughter when she was little," he said. "She used to specialize in asking impossible questions."

Pandora thoroughly objected to this characterization. Her questions had *not* been "impossible," just "not answered satisfactorily thus far." But seeing as she wasn't supposed to be privy to any of this, she decided to keep her objections to herself.

Meanwhile: "You're saying maybe I should narrow my focus," George said. "Be more specific."

Roger mimed narrowing the focus by pinching the air with his thumb and index finger. "A touch, yes."

"Okay," George said. "Why do you think they specified young adults as opposed to suicides in general?"

"Are you asking me as a representative of the corporation," Roger said, "or as a mental health professional?"

"Um, both?"

"The corporation's interested because of what you've already alluded to: young adults represent a prime consumer demographic and it's hard selling something to a dead person," Roger said. "I also wouldn't be surprised if there are 'platform loyalty' incentives. Think about it: if a product literally *saved your life*, you'd stay loyal to it, right? Save a consumer when they're young and you've bought yourself a whole lifetime of platform loyalty."

"O*kay*," George said, warily. He'd not been expecting this much cynicism so early on—especially not from his therapist. Milo, on the other hand . . .

"Now, psychologically," Roger continued, "there's also good reason to separate potential suicides by age categories. Simply put: kids and adults kill themselves for different reasons, and there's some neurological evidence that different parts of the brain may be involved. I'm sure you've heard about Quire's fMRI studies on the subject." He glanced at his second monitor, where George's case file was open. "You suggested they might be 'triggering' for the volunteers."

George shifted uncomfortably in his seat. "Where's it say that?" he asked.

"In the tour transcript," Roger said.

"All of that was recorded?"

"Microphones are cheap," Roger said. "Cameras too. And voice-recognition technology has really upped its game, thanks to machine learning."

"But isn't that an invasion . . ."

". . . of privacy?" Roger finished for him. "You're working for a company whose business model is convincing people to share as much of their personal data as possible, so it can be mined, packaged, and sold to the highest bidder. Why would you think they'd let you walk around shedding data without following you with a broom and dustpan?"

"Good thing I don't have anything to hide," George said.

And there his therapist went, trying to not-smile again.

What followed was a game of therapist-client tug-of-war, with George wanting to talk about teen suicide and Roger wanting to dig into why his new client had admitted to being "messed up." In the end, they came to a compromise of sorts: Roger acknowledged that his real client was Quire, and Quire had hired George to do a job, while George suggested that by offering him insight into the mind of a suicidal teen, Roger could potentially treat hundreds or thousands of more suffering humans by proxy through the suicidal ideation detection (SID) chatbot George would develop based on their sessions. Win—as they say—win.

"Okay," Roger said, "here goes," before going on to explain that suicidal teens frequently see themselves as split into meat and mind, the mind voice prodding the meat toward self-destruction with the unspoken conviction that the mind voice will survive to appreciate "what comes after . . ." They've temporarily surrendered rationality and consciousness to an authoritative "other" like a schizophrenic taking orders from the neighbor's dog, only the authoritative other in this case is a metastatic form of peer pressure, in which a part of the would-be suicide him- or herself is also part of the pressuring crowd. And that's what makes teenage suicides different from the adult kind: this unspoken assumption of suicide's survivability, that it can be used as a ploy to punish people or escape without the resulting oblivion. Religion can ironically reinforce this notion of death's survivability, but so does the inherent sense of immortality that comes with being a teenager. Adults who are suicidal tend to be more realistic and are thinking of ending it all because *they want to end it all.* They come to suicide spiritually and often physically exhausted. World-wearied, they've had it; enough is enough. Suicidal teens often feel prevented by current circumstances from getting what they deserve, be it love, respect, whatever—and they see suicide as a leap over now into a future where they've won and the world has apologized for treating them so badly.

"So next question," George said. "How do you stop it?"

"Why don't we put a pin in that till next week," Roger said, rising. He tapped at his watch. "Time's up. Talk at you then."

And before George could say anything else, his screen went black with the exception of these words: "call terminated on far end," followed by the date, current time, and call duration. It had been a fifty-minute hour, to the second.

Looking at the same call stats as George, Pandora removed her headphones and lowered her laptop screen. It was a little weird to realize it—what with a therapist in the family—but she'd never watched her father practice. Sure, she'd recorded his sessions but didn't watch them so much as fast-forward through them, listening to the clients' sped-up voices, poised to alert on certain keywords. And now that "voice-recognition technology has really upped its game"—something she'd told her father about, by the way—Pandora hadn't had to screen the sessions herself at all, sped-up or otherwise. Plus, when her dad wasn't working, they talked about other things—meals, the weather, what to watch on TV, what interesting factoids she'd learned reading the Google News headlines for science and technology, but never politics. Pandora had found that by focusing on the first two and ignoring the third, she was able to remain hopeful about the future of the species without succumbing to despair and/or that session's magic word: *suicide.*

*Seriously?*

That's what the guy wanted to discuss? Pandora was about as far away from being suicidal as a person could be. She knew precisely what she wanted to do with her life: keep it. Pandora wanted to live—she felt embarrassed even thinking it, but it was in her heart and it was true—*forever*. The thing she wanted to be remembered for on her death bed? Not dying. And as far as her epitaph, Pandora thought "This Space for Rent" should do nicely.

But George Jedson wanted to talk about suicide—specifically, *teen* suicide. He'd said it was because of a work assignment, but if that was some sort of excuse . . .

*Damn it.*

The original plan had been to look up George's contact info in his case file and reach out directly, say, "Hi," or "Wassup?" Nothing too stalkery. He'd made the first move, what with the unsolicited cuteness comment, so . . .

But this suicide business was worrisome. And so, as with a new show on HBO or Netflix she was intrigued by but not quite committed to, she'd have to keep tuning in and hope it wouldn't turn into another *Young Pope*. If only there were a way to binge this George Jedson or skip ahead to where she'd figured out whether he was worth it or not. Unfortunately, Pandora had not found the fast-forward button for the real world, which had been a blessing when it came to Gladys, but George? Not so much.

# 29

There was nothing in the language of George's work assignment that stated—*explicitly*—that he was to develop that Holy Grail of AI: a fully conscious, general artificial intelligence. It wasn't even identified as a stretch goal. But it was there, implicitly, between the lines. It was there in the difference in success rate that his predecessor had achieved (a respectable annual projected suicide rate within the target demographic of one to two percent per year) and George's target, i.e., a nearly unthinkable zero suicides in the prescribed demographic on the platform moving forward. And that wasn't a zero *percent*, or even a zero-point-zero percent. Zero meant zero. It was a whole number, not a rate.

George knew of one way to achieve this goal, though he doubted it would make any of the higher-ups happy: overpredict. Set the criteria for flagging a potential suicide so loosely it'd capture *everybody*. After that, suspend their accounts and declare victory and bankruptcy all at the same time.

Yeah, probably not. Ditto calling his bosses' attention to recent studies showing that a reduction in social-media usage was directly correlated with lowered instances of depression in the target demographic. If his run-ins with Milo had taught him anything so far, it was this: social media was *not* a reality-based industry.

So: zero suicides among Quire users aged fifteen to twenty-five when his predecessor had been fired for missing—let's be honest—one? There'd been other cases Vickers's approach had missed—a handful of the non-famous—but it was the Gunn suicide that constituted the tipping point of interest. And it was the smallness of the number that was so daunting because it was always the last few of anything—miles, votes, raked leaves, percentage points—that cost the most time, money, and other, subtler investments like creativity and/or emotional involvement. In the case of Quire's would-be teenybop stay-alive bot, those last few bodies cost the last guy his job, making way for George, who was quite conscious of the hidden complexity of the task ahead of him. He'd already assumed he'd use the first guy's algo for screening out the no-brainers but after that . . . ?

Well, let's see: he was a computer hacker surrounded by computer systems with access to some of the most sophisticated neural nets available and his pick of machine-learning algorithms, suggesting, yeah, he should let the machine do the heavy lifting. He wouldn't even have to code anything, because machine learning wasn't about coding; it was about training. What mattered was the quality of the data you gave the machine to learn from—good old-fashioned GIGO: garbage in, garbage out. And vice versa. So George started feeding the beast pretty much everything he could think of related to his task. This included but was not limited to: case studies from psychology textbooks and journals; doomed love stories like *Romeo and Juliet*; treatises on ritualized suicide from kamikaze to jihadi suicide bombers, from Christian martyrs to self-immolating monks; the bulk data from past Quire members who had, in fact, killed themselves. Feeling the beast needed more, George proceeded to hack into police departments across the country and copied all the reports of teen suicides he could, along with death certificates and autopsy notes. He then moved on to downloading material from anorexia-encouraging websites and online suicide games like the Blue Whale Challenge and that creepy-looking Momo. He followed the you-may-also-likes these linked to down the deepest existential wells until all he wanted to do was sit in the corner of his corner office, sucking his thumb and rocking back and forth.

The algorithm, meanwhile, had begun populating word clouds from the raw information it consumed, with one word taking up the center of the cloud early, where it grew and shrank under the shifting statistics, beating like a heart: *consciousness*.

Victims and victim wannabes "lost consciousness," "returned to consciousness," "never regained consciousness." The word seemed to have a certain statistical stickiness that resonated throughout the data set. And that was how a routine exercise in corporate soul-searching became an investigation into the nature of consciousness itself and—as a stretch goal—emulating it artificially.

Because that was the answer, reading between the lines and implicit in the numbers expected. George's chatbot had to have skin—*silicon*—in the game. It had to appreciate what was being lost by the game's other players.

Oh, and one other thing. Thanks to his predecessor's ham-handed handing off of the intervention side to local law enforcement and their surfeit of SWAT equipment, an addendum had been added to George's hand-delivered, hand-me-down assignment: "Once target subjects have been identified and reasonably confirmed, all interventions shall be kept strictly in-house and on-platform." Meaning, basically, a chatbot that would engage and talk the subject out of suicide if, in fact, the subject was contemplating such.

So: talking—*that* would be the singular tool in George's toolbox. And not even that. Text. Written words on a screen. On the user end, individuals might have customized their experience using voice-recognition apps, but the default was text and maybe emojis, especially given the target demographic. Now all George had to do was figure out what those lifesaving words should be and how to get his chatbot to type them.

"Poop" emoji.

As a thought experiment, George tried imagining what it would take to make him want to kill himself. Inconveniently, however, other thoughts kept inserting themselves, top among them whether the assignment itself was dangerous—to him, personally. He guessed his bosses were worried about that, too, which was why he'd ended up with Roger and maybe Milo as well, tag teaming him as part of some good therapist/bad therapist routine.

This display of corporate concern for his mental health, in turn, made him think about another aspect of suicide he found fascinating: its communicability. How could something like suicide be contagious? Was it a virus? More and more things formerly assumed to be the products of stress were turning out to be caused by viruses. Ulcers, for example. Some cancers. High cholesterol. So why not the predisposition to self-slaughter?

*Because that'd be one dumb virus,* George thought, *killing its host.*

But then he thought about it some more. Wasn't that what *all* viruses did, the fatal ones at least? Plus, what was he considering alive? A suicide virus that killed its host, at best, would only actually kill *part* of its host. There'd still be the host's biome living inside the gut and outside on every available bit of skin. Lots of those germs didn't care about whether the body they lived on was living or not.

*A little like some humans,* George editorialized, *killing the planet where they live.*

But the bottom line was this: a viral vector for suicide didn't violate the rules of viral logic. If it was viral, though, how did it spread? AIDS was transmitted through bodily fluids; the flu was airborne. A suicide virus was probably closer to the latter, seeing as those who caught it were rarely intimate with the source of their infection. But if it was airborne, the carrier and victim would still need to share the same airspace, which clearly wasn't the case when Patient Zero was a celebrity and the infected, fans.

Then it hit him. The medium by which the suicide contagion spread was *mass media*. Merely talking about it on TV, in the press, or via social media got people who'd been thinking about it, thinking about it more seriously.

But was talking about it the problem? Could they end suicide by banishing the word from ever being used again, followed by reprinting and/or reposting all dictionaries, minus this one particularly triggering and/or viral set of letters? Diving a bit deeper into the research, George was heartened by studies showing that publicizing a suicide didn't necessarily trigger a contagion. It was all about *how* the suicide was portrayed in the media. Romanticized, it spread. Portrayed as what it was—stupid, shortsighted, irreversible, and oftentimes plain rude—it didn't. Portraying it as a disease was still a gray area.

So George started tracking down interviews with people who'd failed—who'd changed their minds before hitting the water off center enough to not break their necks, but maybe on center enough to end up in a wheelchair. You couldn't get much more unromantic than peeing in a bag, George figured. And if suicide was a virus spread by mass media, perhaps there was the equivalent of a vaccine, working like how vaccines work, by taking a little bit of the virus, stripping it of its power to do harm, but still enough to alert the immune system and build up a resistance.

Now the question was, how to translate all that into zeros and ones.

# 30

"So on the subject of suicide prevention," Roger began their next session, before interrupting himself. "See? I didn't forget. That's the wonderful thing about taking notes."

"Gee, that's swell," George said, leaning into the camera. "And I want to talk about that; I do. But I wonder if it would be okay to change the topic? I mean, I've been putting together the mining data on the subject of suicide—and I mean everything, from death cults to suicide bombers to *Hamlet*. Truth is, I need a breather."

Roger nodded; he knew exactly what George meant. In prepping for this session, he'd grown to dread it himself. Who would have guessed that looking into the causes behind kids killing themselves would be so depressing? And so he welcomed this change of subject—right up until he heard what the new one was. "Go ahead," he said, offering up his open palm.

"Consciousness," George said.

"Excuse me?"

"I want to know everything you know about the nature of human consciousness."

Roger laughed because he thought it was a joke—and stopped when he realized it wasn't. *"Seriously?"* he said.

George nodded, his usual poker face allowing a flicker of gravedigger to suggest how much so.

"What did I say before, about asking impossible questions?" Roger continued. Paused. Thought. "What I *can* tell you about is *un*consciousness. That's an easy one. People get their consciousnesses switched off every day in hospitals all over the country. Michael Jackson liked unconsciousness so much he made it permanent."

"You're talking about anesthesia," George said.

"Correct. It's actually a pretty fascinating subject, when you think about it. Prior to the discovery of anesthesia, human consciousness was pretty much an always-on proposition—at least as far as we know. Some people—they call themselves Jaynesians, after Julian Jaynes—believe that human consciousness arose as recently as three thousand years ago and that before that, people were basically schizophrenics, hearing voices, talking to gods, and all that harking business. But then the voices were internalized, forming what we now call consciousness." Roger paused at the sound of keys clacking on the other end. "Are you taking notes?"

"You said it yourself—wonderful thing, note taking."

"So I did," Roger admitted. "Anyway, prior to anesthesia, the consciousness didn't switch off, not even during sleep. Maybe as the result of some head trauma, but as a routine thing, once conscious, always conscious until you died."

More key clacking, which Roger ignored as best he could. "They've done EEG readings on patients as they go under, and what they've seen is the formation of this inhibitory tide of electrical activity, ebbing and flowing—oscillating—across the brain, interrupting neural firing, which, in turn, disrupts the ability of various brain regions to communicate with each other." Roger paused. "And the fact that they can reverse that and bring someone *back* to consciousness? I got to watch it as a grad student, and even without an EEG, I could see the brain powering down and back up by watching the changes in a patient's face."

Roger stopped talking, listened to the key clacking crescendo and then stop as well.

George looked up at Roger looking at him. "What?" he said.

"But I have to ask myself," Roger asked himself, "what does any of this have to do with your being"—notes again—"'messed up'?"

George shrugged. "Is there a pathology where the person prefers talking about minds in general as opposed to his or hers specifically? You know, someone who gets off thinking about thinking . . ."

"That's what I do," Roger said, "minus the getting off part."

"Roger that," George said.

"Watch it," Roger advised.

"But seriously," George continued, "what if 'curing' me of what makes me 'messed up' ruins me as a coder? I can't imagine our bosses would be happy about that."

"That's a romantic myth," Roger said, "that genius is next door to madness. They're not even in the same Quire group."

"Nice ad placement."

"Moving on," Roger tried. "Madness is madness and genius is genius, and any similarity is purely coincidental. Comparing the two is like comparing normal cellular growth to cancer."

"Go on," George said, settling into his chair, preparing for a fresh digression.

"I see what you're doing," Roger said instead.

"What am I doing?" George asked, his face giving nothing away.

"You keep distracting me so we can't talk about you, George Jedson . . ."

"Like a tide of EEG activity, inhibiting neural communication . . ."

Roger folded his arms and stopped talking.

George folded his arms and stopped talking.

The time showing at the bottom of their respective monitors ticked up, first one minute, then two, then finally: "But you get paid either way, right?" George said/asked.

"Correct," Roger admitted. "I'd say it was your dime, but it's actually Quire's, isn't it?"

"And this conversation has been helpful," George said, "in helping me do what they're paying me to do."

"How so?"

"You'll have to trust me," George said. "Do you?"

"No."

"Good," George said. "As long as we're on the same page."

And then it was Roger's turn to look at the words "call terminated on far end," set in white against a black screen.

Pandora pumped her slippered feet under her desk—her happy dance—as she closed her laptop on its own black screen. She'd "stayed tuned" and was glad she had. George had used the *c*-word—*consciousness*—and reading between the lines (literally) of his previous session, it was obvious to his fellow coder that this was shorthand for her own recently decided upon reason for living: artificial consciousness and the achievement thereof. Listening to George talk was like she was listening to herself, but speaking in a male voice, as if he were reading her thoughts aloud but so only she could hear. The words *soul* and *mate* entered her headspace without prior clearance followed by a whole damn sentence: *Is this what love is like?*

In answer to herself, Pandora clicked on the widget that allowed her to stream her father's sessions and dragged it into the trash. She wouldn't need to eavesdrop anymore. The boy who'd judged her static face cute would be given the opportunity to fall in love with the mind behind it, like she was doing now with his. All they had to do was get past a few sticking points—nothing insurmountable, not considering the big picture, which was what Pandora was doing, along with the screen grab she'd printed out of one George Jedson: future boyfriend.

But about those stalkery preliminarics: the way she saw it, the sooner they were gotten to, the sooner they'd be gotten past. And so: Pandora entered George's number from her dad's hacked case file, thumbed a

"What up?" in a chat bubble, hit send, and then waited, a hand over her muted phone, hoping for the haptic buzz of reciprocation.

The time passed like a kidney stone. Pandora grew worried, and then weirdly optimistic, deciding that the hesitation proved he was cautious, meaning not stupid, meaning good. Finally: "Who this?" the reply came back.

Pandora could feel her skin tingle, which was either a good sign or perhaps an early symptom of a new STD, one you could get electronically, by texting. "An admirer," she thumb-typed.

"Do you mean stalker?"

Which might seem like a bad sign to anybody who wasn't Roger Lynch's daughter. But for her own part, Pandora took it as a sign they were in the same headspace re: the creepy vibe of getting a text from a total stranger out of the electromagnetic ether. And so she responded with the international shorthand for lightheartedness, implying he had nothing to fear: "LOL."

"Seriously," George typed. "What's this about?"

Pandora hesitated, then went for it. "I'm a fellow coder and I like your work."

"How did you get this number?"

Oblique was the way to go, she figured. "Fairbanks," she typed, nine characters standing in for a whole lot of words she didn't have the words for.

"Roger," George typed, "is that you?"

"Daughter," Pandora tapped back. Thought about her preferred handle and settled on "Dora."

"Isn't this unethical?"

"Ethics, shmethics," Pandora tried typing, only to have autocorrect render it as "Ethics, semantics," which wasn't bad, so she went with it.

"Seriously?" the boy typed, all the way from San Francisco.

"I'm not my dad," Pandora typed. "You're not my patient."

"Client," George corrected.

"Whatever," Pandora whatevered, followed by, "I know you're working on artificial consciousness and I want to help."

Long pause.

He might already be getting his number changed, which is what she'd do if she hadn't started this whole thing. And so she waited, holding her metaphorical and actual breath, flinching when her phone finally buzzed again.

"So, you code?"

"Like a grrrl," Pandora tapped back.

# 31

Gladys loved her Furby and told Pandora so the next time she visited IRL. "I haven't slept this well in years," she explained before telling her about the shoe store. "This disease," she said, "is like living in a shoe store that's been hit by an earthquake." That's what it felt like, she said, standing there, stunned, among all these scattered boxes and separated shoes, utterly overwhelmed. But now, each night, she dealt with one box, one pair of shoes finally reunited, wrapped in their tissue paper, the lid secured, the box put away on its shelf. And each night, she went to bed, knowing that there was another one she wouldn't have to worry about ever again.

"Thank you," the old woman said, a hand on her granddaughter's knee, followed by a pause, and then: "You too, Furbius," Gladys added, patting the plush space between its gremliny ears.

After that, Pandora's visits started skewing toward remote rather than in person. For one thing, Gladys seemed more forthcoming during these virtual visits. Pandora had suspected it might go like that; there was precedent. One of the earliest, serious contenders for passing the Turing test was a program called Eliza that impersonated a Rogerian therapist by manipulating strings of text supplied by a human in the role of patient (um, *client*). People got addicted to "talking" to it, telling it their problems, even after they were told, point blank, that it was *a computer program*. The theories for why this simple bit of coding got the reaction it did varied. Perhaps people found talking to software less intimidating than talking to an actual person; maybe it was because a computer could ask them franker questions that would be deemed too invasive or rude coming from a human. Using her hacked, animatronic creature as mediator, Pandora found herself willing to ask more personal things of her grandmother that would have seemed impossible face-to-face, especially considering the faces involved.

For example, it was through Furbius that Pandora learned her grandmother's original plan for moving to Alaska didn't involve living off the land so much as dying on it, far away from anyone she knew. But then she met her future husband, and while Herman Lynch remembered the clink of bottle neck to glass rim in a dingy frontier bar as the beginning of their relationship, what Gladys remembered was boldly following him out of the bar when he wanted to take a leak "under the stars, like God intended."

It was that time of year when it was cold enough to snow but still warm enough to go peeing into a bank of it, which Herman proceeded to do, his back shielding any anatomical revelations it was still too early for in their hours-old relationship. Why she followed after him, Gladys didn't know, but would hazard a guess, since Furbius asked: "I think I recognized my future in the man and didn't want to let him out of my sights."

The difference between ninety-plus degrees hitting something south of thirty was enough to produce a geyser of steam Gladys followed up past her future husband's turned back and broad shoulders, up and up to where those other phantoms danced, the northern lights.

"Do you know what I think about when I see them?" she asked, intuiting that Herman was looking at the same sight she was, from the cant of his neck as he pissed heartily away into the hole he'd made in the snow. "The souls of all those dead boys."

"Me," Herman said, finally finishing, finally giving his shoulders an exaggerated shrug as he tugged up his zipper, "I think of how much harder they made my job, putting all that extra static on the line."

"They're pretty, though," Gladys said.

"Handsome, you mean," Herman corrected, casually accepting her premise that the northern lights were the souls of dead soldiers.

"Yes," she said. "Very handsome." Pause. "And too . . ."

". . . many?" Herman guessed.

"I was going to say 'young,'" Gladys said. "But 'many' works too."

In another confession, Gladys told Furbius—whom she'd rechristened Mr. Nosy—that another reason she'd picked Alaska was because there'd be no one to blab all her sworn secrets to. She'd worried that that might change, once she married Herman, only to learn to her relief that, no, thankfully, she didn't talk in her sleep, "though maybe that's what I'm doing now . . ."

Sometimes, Gladys volunteered information without Mr. Nosy even asking. "Here's the ironic thing about losing my memory," one such session began. "Memory was my secret weapon as a code breaker."

She went on to explain that her ability to recall and connect seemingly trivial details from previous messages and then linking that to what they were working on later allowed them to deduce how the code had been shifted, providing the two data points that suggested a pattern. And once they had a theoretical pattern, they could predict what the next shift might be—a prediction that could be confirmed or discredited by a subsequent message.

"But now," Gladys said, followed by a farting sound from her lips, "going, going, gone."

She told her granddaughter through her furry representative about the tricks she used to hold on to her independence once she realized her memory was going. One was to create rigid routines, converting her day into muscle memory while memories not made of muscle were sung instead. Writing might have been easier for some people, but not Gladys. "My hands shake too much," she confessed, keeping to herself the fact that they also hurt from arthritis. "It seems symbolic that I can't write my name anymore," she told Mr. Nosy.

And so she turned her most important memories—the wartime ones—into little homemade songs she sang to herself around the cabin, and then in her assisted-living condo.

"That all stopped when they moved me over here," Gladys said, alluding to the fact that she now had a roommate who either didn't appreciate her singing or wasn't to be trusted with the classified information the songs contained. "The only time I get to talk to you," she told her inquisitive Wi-Fi-enabled friend, "is when they're helping her in the bathroom or taking her to see the physical terrorist."

But the longer Gladys was prevented from singing her memories of the war, the thinner and more threadbare they became. And so Pandora hacked into the nursing home's database of residents and began reading charts until she found her grandmother the perfect roommate: a woman, older and further gone than Gladys was, and—the cherry on top—stone-cold deaf. Checking on what Mr. Nosy had uploaded to the cloud a few days later, Pandora was rewarded with the thin, heartbreaking voice of her grandmother whisper-singing part lullaby, part "Moon River," but with original lyrics by Gladys Lynch née Kowalski: war hero.

# 32

So here was the thing: it was impossible to have a conversation quietly enough that Roger wouldn't hear, the doors between rooms with the exception of the bathroom not thin so much as nonexistent, a feature, not a bug she'd appreciated when she was still a toddler and not seeing her dad was equivalent to his having gone out of existence. But now that she was a teenager, the old shower curtains separating their separate rooms from the rest of the cabin were, if not thoroughly creepy, nevertheless inadequate to the role they were supposed to play. She'd lobbied for their replacement with something more substantial, perhaps on hinges and lockable, by appealing not to *her* need for privacy, but Roger's.

"What if you ever decided to start dating?" she asked.

"Pandora," her father warned, but in that way that teenagers are pretty much duty-bound to ignore. And so she continued. "What if you started dating and got lucky and there was no 'her place' to go back to?"

"Stop."

This time, Pandora did, because there was nowhere else to go with her hypothetical but to the actual words *making love* or that succinct Anglo-Saxon synonym she was not so independent yet to let drop. Not when the subject of that verb was her dad, especially. And so, instead, she'd slipped him the half-off-everything coupon from Fred

Meyer she'd clipped from the weekend *Fairbanks Daily News-Miner*. "Say you'll think about it," she said.

"What," her father said back, "the dating or the getting lucky with, apparently, some homeless woman?"

"Doors," Pandora said. "Think about doors, please."

Which he hadn't—yet—and so Pandora set a few ground rules for how her and George's budding relationship would be conducted. First, no video conferencing. Second, no voices, only text. The first was about her face and its tendency to embarrass her, not to mention its cyber infamy as meme. The second was about privacy and her lack of it. It was the second rule she felt safe explaining and should do the trick, seeing as it was basically a subset of the first and the rationale behind it covered both.

"No privacy," she typed. "Parental unit omnipresent."

"Roger," George replied, meaning either affirmative or her dad.

"Yeah," Pandora had written back. "That's the guy I mean."

To appease George's curiosity and prove she wasn't a chatbot or "some dude" (not to mention refresh his memory re: her "ooo, cute"-ness), Pandora sent him a JPEG of herself standing in front of her father's diploma while wearing a T-shirt that read, "I Think Therefore I Am . . . Socially Unacceptable." She captioned it: "Does this proof-of-life selfie make my butt look big?"

George LOL'd followed by the "big grin" emoji.

Pandora looked at the text, wondering how to respond, or even whether she should. It wasn't exactly the wordless thumbs-up, but it did have an "end of message" vibe to it, letting her know without saying so specifically that this particular thread had reached its end.

Or maybe not.

Text etiquette was still evolving—practically daily, as far as she could tell. Would responding suggest she was too needy? Curious? Or perhaps an escaped lunatic who'd killed his therapist and was now posing as his daughter? *Probably not that last one,* Pandora thought. He'd already seen her picture on her dad's desk—a fact that led in a straight line to this exchange, meaning *technically* he'd started it, so . . .

"What's the weather like where you are?"

"Right now?" George typed, then paused. Pandora imagined him crossing to a window to look, his body backlit by a clutch of monitors, the only lighting in his code-boy cave. In her imagination, that blue light was doing his butt a lot of favors. Meanwhile: "There's a lot of fog rolling in off the bay," George added, completing his response.

"Fog here too," Pandora typed, "like an ice tray steaming from a freezer."

"Is that what they mean by ice fog?"

"I guess," Pandora guessed. "I like it."

"It's like the sky and land meet to make limbo," George typed, bordering on the poetic.

Pandora took that as a good sign, though not without its caveats. Her own dad had warned that "when a boy stoops to poetry, you better decide if he's a keeper or a goner right away. And if it's the latter, don't dillydally. Cut to the heart stomping pronto. No half measures. Otherwise, you'll have this sad little puppy following you around, right up until he turns into Hannibal Lecter."

"Thanks, Dad," Pandora had said back. "Good to know . . ."

Unfortunately, her father hadn't said what to do if the boy spouting verse was a keeper. Perhaps it was a case of dad denial—that omission—the presumption being that nobody could *possibly* be good enough for his little girl. Thankfully, such decisions were not up to him. Hell, they were hardly up to Pandora—the brain part of her, at least. All she knew was every time she felt his text hum, she wanted to . . .

And will you look at that? Pandora was a bit of a poet herself.

George not only agreed to only texting, he added his own spin: it'd be good practice for working on AI. "Like an ongoing Turing test," he wrote. They could pretend to not know the other was human, seeing what clues would tip the scale one way or the other. And by extending the Turing test indefinitely, they'd be subtly programming their brains to program another brain, one that would—if they succeeded—be indistinguishable from either of them, in terms of its seeming humanity.

"That does not compute," Pandora texted back, followed by the "robot" emoji and an "LOL," just in case.

To further prove how okay he was with the text-only stipulation, George sent Pandora a link to an app he'd written that should serve their purpose and privacy nicely: Texting w/o Borders, so named—should he ever commercialize it—for its dispensing with the character limits usually associated with SMS- and MMS-based messaging services. Instead of breaking up long texts into a series of (sometimes disordered) bubbles, his app worked on the user-experience end to sort and recombine multiple messages within a single, elastic text bubble that stretched to accommodate whatever text was entered, no need to think in abbreviations anymore.

"I could send you *War and Peace* if I wanted to," he wrote.

"Please don't," Pandora wrote back.

"Won't."

The secret sauce was larceny. Because service providers generally charged by the SMS or MMS, George's app, while providing a simplified user experience on the front end, could get pretty expensive to use in practice. And so George "outsourced" those charges to unsuspecting but nevertheless deserving corporate parties in the fossil fuel industry. "My personal carbon tax on the planet killers," he explained. The app also allowed the use of bold, underline, and italics and employed a proprietary encryption strategy to keep sender and receiver messages private from prying government, corporate, and/or parental eyes, with the option to self-destruct within a user-set amount of time after being read.

If Pandora wondered why George happened to have such an app ready to send her a link to, she didn't mention it. In fact, he'd coded it up a year earlier to communicate with his deported mother in Mexico. The prying eyes he wanted to avoid belonged to ICE, and he had corporate creeps picking up the tab because she was working at a maquiladora that paid her crap, while George, the perennial foster kid, didn't get an allowance and had to make do, collecting bottles and cans he could return for five cents apiece.

As it turned out, George and his mom never got a chance to use his app. One evening, Margarita/Marge hadn't been on the bus back to her neighborhood. And she wasn't on the bus returning to the maquiladora the next morning. Her body wasn't found until several days later, in a dump near where she'd worked, an American manufacturer of consumer electronics that imported the parts duty-free, assembled them, and then exported them back to America, all bearing labels that read, "Made in USA." Those labels had made her homesick every day, until they couldn't anymore, her throat having been cut. The story of her death was written in Spanish and took up hardly any space at all. She'd been his mother and now she was just words in a local paper George found and translated through Google News, one of the thousands of dead women Juárez had become known for, none of their murders any closer to being solved.

So yeah, George was messed up all right. Was it any wonder he preferred talking about the human mind in general, as opposed to his own specifically?

What followed was a coders' romance, the intercourse intellectual as opposed to sexual, their text exchanges touching on all things computer related, from favorite algorithms to backdoor exploits, their mutual contempt for script kiddies and other Tor tourists, as well as specific denial-of-service attacks they found especially amusing and/or inspirational.

"You hear what Anonymous pulled off?"

"Thumbs-up" emoji and an "LOL."

Not that it was *always* a geek fest. They talked about the big stuff, too, the things that distracted them, drove them, and/or kept them up at night during this chronological way station between young and adult, when they still had time to think about big ideas, before acting their age meant drowning in the little ideas of the world.

In a lot of ways, George and Pandora were like quantum particles that had become entangled, acting on one another—as Einstein would have it—spookily at a distance. Because even though Fairbanks and San Francisco were separated by two to three thousand miles, depending on whether you drove or flew, while the cultural gulf was astronomical, neither distance seemed to matter. The two teens were mind melded, sharing the same sense of humor when it came to their hacktivism and the same obsessions about the potential uses of AI. Both were convinced that quantum physics and the burgeoning field of quantum computing would inform the overlap of mind and body in the Venn diagram of that particular philosophical conundrum. And both felt the same sense of personal injury at the thought that their thinking would someday come to an end. Or using fewer words:

"Death sucks."

"And then some."

Perhaps because they were rapidly exiting them, the two frequently talked about their childhoods, Pandora's having been reasonably happy while George's—as presented to the girl on the other end of his screen—was parsed and curated for bits that created the appearance of happiness (or were amusing at least). Take the topic of favorite toys, Pandora going first:

"It was a Christmas stocking stuffer, but I loved it beyond reason," she wrote of her favorite toy. "It was a wind-up Creature from the Black Lagoon that walked and shot sparks out of its mouth, making this whirring sound as it went. I loved winding it up and letting it walk across the table to me, sparking and whirring all the way. I loved doing it in the dark where the sparks stood out, partly shining through the green-and-yellow plastic of the creature's body. It was beautiful. The body of the creature was squat—like a Lego character—making it cute instead of scary. I think I was three, and I'd fallen in love with a pretty machine."

"When I was a little kid, I had the weirdest idea about birds," George prefaced his contribution to their discussion. "The first bird I remember seeing was a robin perched on a rusty patch of fence. The bird and fence seemed connected through the bird's rust-colored chest. I asked my latest foster dad why different parts of the fence were different colors and learned about metals and oxidation, including the fact that some kinds of metals turn green.

"These facts all connected in my kid head, and I became convinced that robins must be made of metal because they could rust. The fact that my foster family at the time had a cuckoo clock didn't help. And so, for the longest time, I went around thinking birds were flying robots who perched on high-power lines to recharge and, when they weren't careful, could rust like the Tin Man from Oz after getting caught out in the rain.

"The whole thing fell apart when my foster dad caught me running outside with an armload of umbrellas when it was raining. 'What are you doing?' he wanted to know. I thought it was pretty obvious. I was helping the birds. 'Helping the birds how?' So they wouldn't get wet, duh. 'It's okay if birds get wet.' But what about when they rust? 'Excuse me?'

"And that was the end of the robot birds of Oakland, disappeared by harsh reality like Santa and the tooth fairy, but even worse because I'd come up with the robot birds all by myself," George concluded.

"I think somebody owes you a royalty on drones," Pandora typed back.

"If only," George replied.

Not that Pandora was fooled by George's diversionary tactic. "Birds aren't a toy," she pointed out. "Come on. Quid pro quo. I showed you mine. You have to show me yours."

"The truth is," George wrote back, "being a foster kid, I didn't have a lot of toys of my own."

"Wa-wa," Pandora typed. "Save it for my dad."

There was an unusually long pause from George's end, and Pandora suddenly panicked, wondering if she'd overstepped. But then: "On second thought," George typed, "one of my foster dads brought home a pair of finger cuffs from Chinatown once. I tried it on and cried when my fingers got stuck. And the harder I pulled, the tighter they got."

"So you're telling me your favorite—perhaps *only*—toy was basically some digital S&M device?"

"Punny," George typed. "But it wasn't like that. I think there's a lot of counterintuitive Eastern philosophy woven into those things. Like the need to push deeper to loosen them—that's like closing your eyes so the Force will take over. Or like loving something by letting it go. I think my foster father was trying to tell me that my mother wasn't ever coming back, but without words. I think he wanted me to know it in my muscles and bones and to let her go."

Before Pandora could text her response, she noticed the dancing ellipses, indicating that George was typing again, followed by a brand-new bubble blooping up underneath his last one. "I don't think these were my thoughts at the time, as a child, but they became my thoughts because that data was there, waiting for me to catch up to it."

It was a hallmark of these exchanges between George and Pandora that they unfolded by a process of association. And so from a novelty item's influence on a young boy's thoughts, George suddenly leaped ahead, to technology's ability to read them. Thoughts, that is.

"Have you ever seen a person being scanned by an fMRI machine?" he wrote.

"In Fairbanks," Pandora replied, "the reflex hammer is considered cutting-edge diagnostics."

"Well, if you ever get a chance, take it," George recommended. "It's incredible, watching as various parts of the brain light up when an operator asks the subject to think about something. And the same part lights up when they're shown an image of what they were asked to imagine, ditto when handed the object to hold.

"It's hard to walk away from something like that and not think that what you've witnessed is mind reading. Without touching the head or opening up the skull, from inches away, an act of thinking has been captured and turned into a picture. Do it with enough words with enough subjects, and you'll come away with a collection of brain signatures you can feed into a pattern-recognizing algorithm and translate back into words or pictures, like the grooves on a vinyl record that can be traced by a needle wired to a speaker and converted into music."

Pandora's response back to George was the "mind blown" emoji, followed by her response to her own heart: a silent scream and feet pumping under her desk—her happy dance.

# 33

The Furby, of course, wasn't just for Gladys, but for Pandora as well, to give her some programming practice in her recently decided vocation: artificial intelligence. She'd read an article in *Wired* about what she had in mind for all the personal data she was mining from her last surviving female relative: a chatbot to assemble and preserve the thoughts, feelings, memories, and uniqueness of her grandmother as she headed for the exit, something to keep her company in the long future without her. The article dubbed it a "dad bot," and the author found the results surprisingly comforting when comfort was most needed. Not immediately after the loss, but later, when the programming was forgotten, allowing the user to be surprised by the familiar plus time.

Playing a hunch, Pandora had googled the words *grief* and *bot* and got several hundred hits, suggesting that she was not alone in wanting to hold on to a loved one busily slipping between her fingers. After comparing reviews and discounting those with obvious grudges against this or that app developer and/or software publisher, she downloaded a plug-and-play program called Memento Morty with a default voice synthesizer that sounded like a fast-talking Hollywood agent from the 1940s but which could be customized to match your loved one's voice, provided you uploaded enough high-quality MP3s to the cloud, where the real magic happened.

There were the usual funky, robovoice glitches, like pronouncing *c'mon* as "see Monday," or talk-spelling titles like Mr., Dr., or Ms.—but these could be fixed on the fly by highlighting the misread text and correcting the pronunciation from a series of phonemes in pull-down menus followed by picking a number from one to ten, to indicate the phoneme where the stress was supposed to go. This last feature was what accounted for the app's not being free but also not featuring a bunch of distracting ads. After all, the whole point of a grief bot was to provide a closed-eyed and seamless experience of your loved one, returned to answer all those questions you hadn't gotten around to while they were still alive. And as far as Pandora was concerned, twenty bucks was a small price to pay to not hear her grandmother's voice trying to sell her male enhancement pills.

There were holes in the voice data that had already been uploaded from the Furby to the cloud, and Pandora attempted to fill those during her next visit, recording their conversation on her smartphone while she steered Gladys toward topics likely to require the use of at least one of the forty-four unique English phonemes and four so-called blends she'd not sampled yet. Some of the missing phonemes were easier than others in practice. Th-, for example, was already well represented on the cloud data, even after accounting for the slight lisp her grandmother had acquired, thanks to her having survived frontier dentistry. Other phonemes, however, proved surprisingly difficult, even after Pandora memorized the examples provided in the app's "Read Me" file. The problem was—as might be expected from a developer who'd name his app Memento Morty—many of the sample words were eccentric at best and frequently obscene. These latter Pandora replaced with rhyming alternatives, but this still meant getting Gladys to offer her opinion on ducks.

"Ducks?" the old woman asked, and Pandora figured she'd bail on the topic now that she had her grandmother saying it. But that might make it obvious there was some funny business going on—something that was not at all hypothetical, seeing as Gladys had already asked what was going on when her granddaughter wanted to talk about punts, dastards, and bird itches.

"What's a bird itch?" her grandmother asked, and Pandora bluffed.

"Like from lice," she said. "Um, feather lice. Or wing lice, like head lice, but on a bird's wing."

"What birds?" her grandmother asked, and seeing the door open, Pandora stepped through it: "Ducks?" she said.

"Ducks?" Gladys echoed. "What about ducks?"

"Oh, nothing," Pandora began, then noticed something she hadn't before: ducks on her grandmother's nightgown; ducks in glass, porcelain, and wood on her nightstand; ducks on the curtains that had come from her condo and reappeared here. Noticing where her granddaughter was looking, the old lady explained.

"I honestly can't say how it started," she said. "Somebody told somebody I liked ducks once, and then your grandfather got wind of it and bingo—birthdays and Christmas and anniversaries—everything ducks. If he hadn't died on me, I was going to come clean finally and clean house, but then . . ."

And that's how they went from phoneme collection to phase two in programming Pandora's grief bot: harvesting the stories and advice and jokes she'd want to hear, in her grandmother's voice, to illuminate whatever postmortem conversation she might be having with an AI-enabled simulacrum of her last female relative in that future that wasn't big enough for both of them.

Pandora didn't mean to eavesdrop on the pillow talk between Gladys and her late husband, but Mr. Nosy was programmed to record and upload whenever it detected a human voice. Needless to say, she could only hear one side of these otherwise private conversations, but that just made them all the more compelling. It was the listening in after the conversation stopped and her grandmother fell asleep that was harder to explain. Pandora took comfort from listening to Gladys's euphonic snore coming through the speaker that connected them. It was reassuring—that sound—letting her know that everything was okay, that her grandmother couldn't get into any trouble while she was asleep.

Pandora needed this reassurance because she'd been awoken in the middle of the night by calls from nursing home staff who couldn't calm Gladys down after what they termed "episodes." They couldn't call Roger because they didn't have his number, only Pandora's.

"Have you given her any anxiety meds?" she'd ask. They'd reflexively say they had; that's all they did all day, give old people some kind of medication. But there were too many residents and too few staff, and it wasn't like residents were going to call them on a missed dose—assuming it was an honest mistake and some underpaid staffer wasn't supplementing their income by selling Xanax on the side. Sometimes they'd get lucky and the short-pilled resident would sleep through any trigger opportunities, but other times they'd wake up, undosed, in a full-blown panic attack.

"Are you sure?" Pandora would press, and "Yes," they'd lie, but she could hear Gladys in the background, raging like a paranoid psychotic convinced the nurses were trying to kill her.

Roger would hear her talking, realize it was with his mother's keepers, and call out where he'd left the keys for the truck, before settling back to sleep. And off went Pandora, a parka around her nightgown and long underwear, her bare feet in a pair of bunny boots. She'd hand Gladys a pill herself and watch her transition twenty minutes later into a cordial, loopier version of her old self, but with ever fewer memories.

She hated being the pill pusher such episodes made her, knew that the prescription stuff was likely accelerating her grandmother's decline. She would have preferred sharing a brownie or two and chilling with her gram, but rules were rules, no matter how ill conceived. And when she was having a panic attack, Gladys was a danger to herself and others. There was the trade-off, a few more neurons checking out early in exchange for a metronomic heartbeat and an enigmatic smile.

"Hi, Dora."

"Hi, Gram."

And so falling asleep to her grandmother's snoring was a good way of assuring herself that she wasn't going to be rudely awakened. That is, until she heard Gladys crying out in the middle of the night through her headphones. The filter that had kept her from talking in her sleep as a young bride was apparently gone now. Eventually, even an interruption in the old woman's snoring would pull Pandora awake, her heart racing as she wondered if this was it. But then there'd be a catch, and the snoring would start sawing away again, making her recall what Gladys had told her once about what she feared.

"I'm afraid of the line," she'd said.

"What line's that?" Pandora had asked.

"The one I can't come back from."

# 34

At first, George didn't talk—*text*—much about what he was working on, using indirect references to "my work," "the project," or how it was "taking longer to grok than I thought." But then he started loosening up. Example: "I don't like the expression 'artificial intelligence,'" he typed. "'Artificial' seems pejorative. Why not something like 'man made'?"

"Maybe because it's sexist," Pandora suggested.

"Handmade?"

"Better."

"You know what word is even better—probably the best?"

"What?"

"I saw it walking past this little indie café," George typed. "'Artisanal.' That's what I'm going to tell people I'm working on. 'I'm coding an artisanal consciousness.'"

"Wow."

"Wow what?"

"You *are* from San Francisco, aren't you?"

"Oakland, actually."

"You know what I mean."

And indeed he did. To George's way of thinking, this knowing what each other meant, meant something else. It meant they'd make a good team, coding that artisanal consciousness. Provided he worked up the courage to ask.

"Listen," he wrote one day, prepared to make what was, for him, the coder's equivalent of a marriage proposal, "my project is clearly a two-man job."

"Person," Pandora corrected.

"Consciousness, entity, sentience, head, brain, think box . . . ," George typed, lapsing into thesaurus mode, a sign that he was not in the mood for splitting hairs, not when the issue at hand was something as transformative as splitting the atom. "You know what I mean."

Indeed she did. But she was also a girl and in constant need of asserting herself in the brotopia of coding. "And *you* know what *I* mean, Mr. Mister."

Indeed George did. But he didn't enjoy being reminded of his so-called "male privilege," especially given his past hiding above the acoustic tiles of the public library he'd called home. Now, however, he had a sweet job with a sweet office he was treating like a hotel suite and banking the money he was saving on rent—which was pretty sweet, too, so . . .

"Point taken," he typed, followed by his pitch: "But wouldn't it be great to use our coding superpowers for good?"

"Good is highly subjective," Pandora blooped back. "Explain."

"Saving lives," George typed, before tapping send.

"Whose? Baby Hitler?"

"Kids like us," George tapped and sent.

"Meaning?"

"The weirdos, the outcasts, the serially cyberly bullied," George's response blooped up on the screen. And then, in its own bubble—for emphasis—he added, "The suicidal."

"Who you calling suicidal? #immortalitynow"

"Not *you*," George backpedaled. "But other kids. I've checked the stats for Fairbanks and . . ." Having used the *s*-word once already in this exchange, he seemed disinclined to use it again, as if the FCC were monitoring and had a quota.

Not that he needed to type it again. Pandora knew the stats he was referring to, trailing dots and all. She'd lived them like everybody else in her dark and frigid hometown. And even though her homeschooling had spared her the loss of local peers up until that time, Pandora hadn't been left untouched by the *s*-word, leaving her with a mental snapshot she could call up whenever she needed a reminder of the thinness of the line between being and not.

It was back when her father still met some clients face-to-face in the real world, before he switched to online only. Pandora was only ten at the time and in her room, playing around in somebody's system, looking for exploits other than the one that had let her in the back door. The shower curtain separating her room from the living room and Roger's office had been drawn, and she was plugged in to a pair of headphones playing that Joni Mitchell tree museum song because, well, she was still being homeschooled and lacked peers to tell her what she should and shouldn't be listening to. Joni had rhymed *museum* with *see 'em* when the floorboards shook beneath her feet.

Alaska is a seismically active part of the country, so floor shaking wasn't all that unusual. In fact, Pandora and her dad had made a game of it, guessing where a given temblor might place on the Richter scale. She'd calmly removed her headphones and was about to call out her guess when she noticed the red spatters on her curtain and a couple of brain snails sliding down the other side of the translucent vinyl.

*Crap,* she thought.

Gingerly pinching a corner of the curtain and sliding it aside, she stepped into the living room, where she found her dad and his ex-client.

Her father was still seated opposite the body lying beached-whale-like on the floor. Roger's own face was stricken, blood spattered, and frozen while his hands eagle-clawed the arms of his chair.

"Dad?" Pandora asked.

"Yes?" Roger said, not moving.

"Should I call someone?"

"Yes," he said, still not moving.

"Who?" she asked.

"Anyone," he replied.

And six years later, here she was, being invited to use her coding superpowers to do something about the statistic her father's client had turned himself into.

"Okay," Pandora tapped back. "Where do we start?"

# 35

Roger kept a full-sized plastic skeleton in his office, which was also the living room (so-called). He'd added it to the home decor not too long after he and Pandora had moved back into the cabin, once the crime scene hazmat clean-up crew had finished their scraping, scrubbing, and disinfecting from Roger's final in-person client. He'd strung the skeleton with Christmas lights he'd turn on during the darkest of dark Alaskan nights, to remind himself—he said—that there was light at the end of the seasonal tunnel. "Plus," he added, "I like how they twinkle."

Pandora had been fine with Mr. Bones back when he first moved in, Christmas lights and all. But that was back before she'd been forced to socialize among people her own age. Since then—and especially since she'd begun visiting his mother—her opinion on the matter seemed to have changed.

"Isn't it time we got rid of Mr. Bones?" she asked one day. She'd become upset with not only having to stare her (literally) mortal enemy in the face every day, but also where he'd placed it, in front of the living room window, where passersby could see and recall that, yes, that's where the weirdo and her weird dad lived.

"It's a memento mori," he said. "A reminder that beyond the light at the end of the tunnel is another tunnel to, well, nobody knows for sure."

"Death," Pandora said. "It leads to death."

As an organic entity with an expiration date herself, Pandora went on to explain that she was opposed to death—both conceptually and personally; she resisted the thought of death at an almost cellular level. It had begun as a fear of getting dementia like her grandmother, but spread. Metastasized. Her fear of dementia was the gateway to her *real* fear: the fear of dying. Pandora found it insulting, frankly, and an affront to the entire species—the pinnacle of creation—to take all this time building a life out of memories only to have it taken away. And here her dad was, putting it right out there in front of her, and adding blinking lights to boot.

"Maybe you should add a dildo," she concluded. "You know, get the whole Freudian twofer going? Thanatos *and* Eros."

"You know, I knew I forgot *something*," Roger said, already sensing there'd been more to her objection than he'd thought.

"Maybe you're in denial," his daughter continued.

"Of which?"

"I'm thinking both," she said. "When was the last time you had a date?"

"I found your English assignment on the printer," Roger said. "'What do you want it to say on your tombstone?'"

"This space for rent," Pandora answered, as she had for the assignment.

"Maybe *you're* the one who's in denial," Roger suggested.

Pandora could say something about that, but if she did, it would escalate, and she wasn't in the mood. So: "Why, thank you, kettle," she said, resorting to an old routine, a way for one or the other to call a time-out.

"No problem, pot," Roger said back, putting a pin in the discussion neither was quite ready to have.

It was true what Pandora said about her father's dating. He'd not had a single romantic encounter since his wife died. He'd had an excuse early on, but Pandora could take care of herself now, and he still wasn't doing anything to address his own, personal singularity.

Not that Roger wasn't curious. Especially during the winter, when Pandora was at school and he didn't have any clients to counsel, he'd cruise Quire, looking up girls he'd had crushes on in high school, inspired by his yearbook from the now defunct Gold Stream High School. Their team was called the Prospectors, and the mascot was a cartoonish sourdough with outrageous whiskers, wearing a battered wide-brimmed hat, plaid shirt, denim pants, and unlaced boots and carrying a pickax. Whenever the team scored, he'd kick up his heels and yell "Goooold!" instead of "Gooooal!" coming down on the *d* at the same time his heels hit the hardwood floor.

But looking at the high school pictures compared to the Quire profiles was an exercise in masochism. How had everybody gotten so old? Roger didn't feel like he had—not that much. With the exception of his thinning hair, he felt like he was in his late twenties, thirties, tops. It was only on Quire that he felt ancient, which was why he kept promising himself he'd delete his account, even if he did work for them. You didn't have to eat McDonald's every day to work there—and probably shouldn't. But he kept coming back for more abuse—something one of his clients suggested was no accident.

"Let's say," he let him say, "certain algorithms have been optimized for user dependence. It's like when you finish a good book and miss the characters and want to start reading it all over again. Or like after the last line of coke wears off. Point is, Quire's designed to be missed after you close it, which is why the always-on feature has become the default setting. Users can change it; ninety-five percent don't."

After that, Roger asked Pandora to show him how to change the setting, but when she asked if she should click okay, he stopped her.

"No," he said. "I just wanted to know how. In case."

"In case what, you get a life?"

"Something like that."

"Listen, I'll pimp for you," his teenage daughter offered. "Give me your specs, and I'll roam Fred Meyer until I find the perfect woman. Or good enough woman, beggars being, you know."

"Thanks, kiddo," Roger said. "You should try your hand at therapy."

"Getting or giving?"

"The latter," her father said. "The kickbacks from antidepressants alone would be enough to live off of."

"Is this the point where you accuse me of being a carrier for depression?"

"Is this the point where you're going to prove my point?"

They stopped, facing each other. Paused. Took a breath.

"Thanks, kettle," one of them offered.

"Back atcha, pot," the other accepted.

"Okay," Roger said, deciding they were finally ready. "You want to know the truth?"

Pandora nodded.

"I've made my peace with dying because without it, there'd be no you."

Pandora thought he was talking about the mother she'd never met, who died giving her birth. "You mean Mom?" she said.

"No, what I'm trying to say is that if parents didn't die, there'd be no *reason* to have children and every reason not to. For one thing, there'd be no place to stand after a few generations."

"So you're saying that having kids is what it's all about and once you've had them you start waiting to die?"

"Not me," her father said. "Darwin. Which is another thing you wouldn't have without death: evolution."

"Have you checked out that Match.com stuff I sent you?"

"Are you saying I need to get out more," Roger asked, "or suggesting people haven't evolved all that much?"

"I'm telling you sex might be more trouble than it's worth," Pandora said. "Plus, half those profiles are bots anyway."

"You're not telling me—"

Pandora cut him off. "I'm telling you I don't want to live on in my children," she said. "I want to live on in *me*. And I'm fine with evolution stopping." She paused, smiling her biggest, goofiest smile. "Why mess with perfection?"

"Can we go back to bots?" Roger asked.

Pandora cleared her throat. "If she's claiming her English seems awkward because she's not from America," she said, "she's a bot."

"Good to know."

"In case?"

"In case."

"You know what I think about when people mention immortality?" Roger asked, not exactly out of the blue.

"No telling," his daughter said from the kitchen, stirring some steaming something in a pot.

"The first VCR I ever had," he said. "I was living in the basement of my friends' parents' house during college, and the VCR was like a time machine. I didn't have to be at a certain place or time to see my favorite TV show. I'd program it to record and watch it later. And you know what happened?"

"No telling," Pandora called back, watching the steam from her cooking feather into ice once it reached the kitchen window.

"I wound up with a stack of tapes this high," he said, holding his hand up to his belt. "I'd watch them when I got the time," he continued. He paused. "That still hasn't happened, me getting the time. That last episode of *Seinfeld*? I just kept putting it off."

Pandora turned off the stove, ladled stew into bowls. "And your point is?"

"I think that's what immortality would be like," Roger said. "Never getting anything done because you *literally* have all the time in the world."

Pandora set down her father's bowl, then hers. "They don't make VCRs anymore. You'll have to buy one on eBay if you want to get caught up on your shows. Or better yet, search Netflix. Click on the magnifying glass. I wouldn't count on any of that old stuff showing up as trending or popular."

"Not the point I was making," Roger said. They sat at the table then, the *tink* of their spoons hitting bowls punctuated by slurps, quick blowing, and then more tentative slurps.

"How about this," Roger said. "What if people only died as the result of an accident? Can you imagine the unbearable grief when it happened? Can you imagine the paralysis that such a condition could lead to? No one would do anything for fear of having an accident that could kill them."

"So you're saying that death is the kick in the pants our species needs to not turn into vegetables."

"Basically," her father said. "After all, look what their long life span has done for trees."

"Knock on wood?"

"Okay," Roger said, "bring your head over here."

"Over my dead body," Pandora countered.

"Cute."

# 36

The great thing about Mr. Nosy was this: it was the next best thing to being there. Unfortunately, that was also the problem with Mr. Nosy. While convenient for Pandora, who was able to keep tabs on her grandmother without actually having to venture out into the Alaskan winter, it was also depriving Gladys of face-to-face contact with her only remaining relative who still gave a crap.

"When are you coming to visit?" the old woman asked.

"We're visiting now," Pandora said.

"No," Gladys insisted. "It's not the same thing."

"It's *almost* the same thing," the younger woman replied.

"It's not even your voice."

Oh yeah. There was that. While the words were hers, and she tweaked the Furby's voice settings to come as close to her own as she could, it still sounded like she'd been huffing helium. Pandora had considered this an acceptable trade-off because going through the voice synthesizer meant she could enter her side of the conversation as text which was converted into speech on Gladys's end. By using this approach and headphones to listen to her grandmother's replies, Pandora was able to keep her father from eavesdropping on them while she phoned in her visits.

"Next week," she said now, hating herself a little for taking advantage of her grandmother's disease while also recognizing the reality that

Gladys wouldn't remember the promise long enough to call her on breaking it.

"Which day?" Gladys asked, startling her granddaughter.

"Thursday," Pandora bluffed.

"Date?"

"Are you writing this down?"

"I'm writing this down."

*Shit.* Pandora swiped at her calendar, read off a date.

"Time?" a different voice said. A younger woman's.

"Who's that?"

"Nurse Mitchell," the voice on the other end said. "I'll be sure to remind her." Pause. "Time?"

*Shit . . .*

"Hey, Gram," Pandora said, doing the Alaskan mummy striptease, tugging at the fingers of her gloves, unwinding her scarf, unzipping her parka, before tugging, yanking, and pulling at the respective layers underneath. After lifting the last sweater up and over her head, she noticed the wall calendar with the day's date circled in red and spoked in the same shade. "I see you've been expecting me."

"Nurse Mitchell reminded me," Gladys said.

"I had no doubt," Pandora said. "Where's the Furby?"

"The what?"

"Mr. Nosy," Pandora said. "The furry guy who asks all the questions."

Gladys shrugged. Nurse Mitchell poked her head in. "I confiscated it."

"Excuse me?"

"It was getting her worked up," Nurse Mitchell said. "She couldn't figure out if it was alive or not. One moment, it's asking her all these questions, and the next, it's like it died or was in a coma, staring with those bug eyes."

Pandora wanted to protest, to point out that the other residents were allowed their artificial companions, when she noticed the plush yellow duck twisted up in Gladys's blanket.

"Consistency," Nurse Mitchell said. She extricated the stuffed, cartoonish duck. "Mr. Quackers doesn't go changing on her all the time. A hug and he's happy. And Gladys is too. Aren't you, Gladys?"

Gladys nodded like she knew better than to disagree.

"Plus, when she wants to talk to someone," Nurse Mitchell said, "it helps if she can *see* who she's talking to."

What the helpful nurse left out of her passive-aggressive scold-a-thon was the fact that other visitors had taken notice of Pandora's experiment in telepresence and tried to replicate it, bringing their relatives senior-friendly, preprogrammed smartphones, tablets dedicated to Skyping, et cetera, and it was taxing the Golden Heart's Wi-Fi. Sure, their residents deserved the best, but the best in this case was deemed to be face-to-face visits—a solution that didn't involve springing for the next tier among Fairbanks's competition-lite selection of internet providers. That's what Pandora suspected was the real reason for taking away Gladys's friend.

"Listen," she tried, gesturing Nurse Mitchell out into the hallway so they wouldn't be having this conversation in front of her grandmother, "if it's about money . . ."

"It's not about money," Nurse Mitchell said. "It's about time. Quality, face-to-face time."

"I tried that," Pandora insisted, "but the Skype thing . . ."

"Not like that," the nurse insisted. "In person."

Pandora was growing desperate, and when she got that way, her go-to self-defense was pointing out the hypocrisy of her opponent. And so:

"Visiting hours," she said.

"Yes?"

"Why have them?" Pandora asked. "Why cut them off? Family members should be able to come and go as they please." She paused before the coup de grâce. "What are you trying to hide?"

Nurse Mitchell's calm superiority wavered just a bit. "It's corporate policy," she said. "I don't make the rules."

"Okay, listen," Pandora said. "Mr. Nosy is backup."

"Who?"

"The Furby," Pandora said. "He's for saving her memories when I can't be here to record them myself, like after visiting hours." She paused. "What if I don't talk through it anymore?"

Nurse Mitchell started to object, but Pandora continued anyway. "Passive recording only," she insisted.

"The point is you need to visit in person more often," Nurse Mitchell said. "And don't even try to say you're only free after visiting hours."

"Okay, I won't. And I'll come more often. I will," Pandora promised. "I'll have to, to download the recordings of what she says while I'm gone."

Nurse Mitchell looked dubious but reached into her bottom desk drawer and removed Gladys's old snuggle buddy. "Show me," she said. "Deactivate it."

Pandora took out her phone and opened the Furby app, went into settings, and slid wireless connectivity to off. Nurse Mitchell shook her head. "You'll just swipe it back on when you leave."

"Okay," Pandora said before yanking out the speaker that served as its voice box.

"Happy?" she asked.

And so Mr. Nosy got to stay. And Pandora kept her word to visit more often, to download recordings and to keep her grandmother company, even when it became less and less clear whether she recognized who her granddaughter was. Eventually, though, the after-hours stream of consciousness ran dry, the mine tapped out, and all she got when she listened to what was recorded was baby talk, with Gladys cooing to it, asking Mr. Nosy (who'd stopped being so nosy) if he wanted some of her food, if he needed to go potty.

Her grandmother had already established the habit of talking about herself in the third person through the Furby, confessing Mr. Nosy was lonely, didn't know what was going on, was worried about something but he didn't know what. Listening to these confessions later, knowing they'd been made to no one, knowing what Gladys was doing was narrating her emotional landscape moment by moment . . . well, it broke Pandora's heart and made her more determined than ever not to wind up that way.

Not that it was all doom and gloom. Even after her disease had taken a pretty big toll on her grandmother's memories, there was still a core of feistiness underneath that surfaced now and again. There was one time that Pandora was pretty sure she'd remember for the rest of her life, even if she failed at finding a work-around for this terrible disease.

She'd caught her grandmother in a lie about an unhealthy addiction she'd developed for a hard, coffee-flavored candy called Nips. Gladys had begun eating the things by the box. And even though Pandora had been assured that it wasn't uncommon for the elderly to develop a sweet tooth later in life, still she worried. Not unlike a meth addiction, Gladys's sweet tooth had begun to take a toll on her actual teeth—a full set of which she still possessed after ninety-plus years, their enamel in her case having proved far more durable than cortical tissue. The old girl had taken pride in her choppers, flossing obsessively, even now, when the act had become less a decision and more muscle memory. But her teeth were decidedly at risk if she kept sucking down Nips like this. And so Pandora decided to say something: "Gram, seriously," she said, "I brought you a whole box yesterday."

Gladys looked at her expectantly, awaiting a re-up on her fix.

“Are you telling me you finished it already?”

Gladys shrugged.

Pandora checked out the box on the nightstand. Empty.

“Jesus, Gram,” her granddaughter said, exasperated. “You can forget about needing dentures. You’re going to need a new pancreas if you keep this up.”

“The nurses steal them,” Gladys bluffed.

And so Pandora went to her grandmother’s wastebasket, which was filled with the little cellophane wrappers the candy came in. She presented the evidence to her grandmother. “Well?”

Gladys folded her bird arms in her pink nightgown and frowned. “Happy, Nancy Drew?” she asked.

And the delivery—the timing—hit Pandora smack in the solar plexus, doubling her over with laughter. The old girl was still there, underneath the gunk. Gladys Lynch née Kowalski, the smartass grandmother of Pandora, the Tigris and Euphrates of the younger woman’s charming ways, showing she still had it, as affirmed and attested to by her only granddaughter thusly:

“Gram,” Pandora wheezed, “you still got it.”

“Can you write that down,” Gladys asked, meaning the location of the “it” she still had, “in case I forget?”

And so Pandora did. Removing a scrap of paper from her pocket and a pen, she wrote in all caps: “IT.”

She handed it to Gladys, who tucked it into a pocket in her nightgown before breathing what seemed to be a sincere sigh of relief. “Thank you,” she said, again apparently sincere. “That’s a load off my mind,” she added, patting the wrong pocket of her nightgown.

# 37

There was another reason George had gone along so easily with Pandora's text-only rule: he wasn't actually complying with it. He had her number—both figuratively and literally—and it wasn't a big deal to turn on her phone's camera, NSA-style, which frankly any hacker, post-Snowden, should have expected. The hard part was not letting on what he knew about her, not texting questions about whether anything was wrong when her face was being especially expressive about something unrelated to the subject matter of the texts they were exchanging. He had to abandon a voice-recognition app he'd been using to transcribe his end of their exchanges because the immediacy of what came out of his mouth and into the text bubble was an invitation to say things like "Don't cry" if it looked like she was about to. He needed those extra seconds for his thoughts to reach his fingertips to avoid slips, Freudian or otherwise.

The thing was, George liked Pandora's face: the bigness of her smile when she managed one, un-self-conscious because she didn't know he was watching. He found her face, for all its guileless animation, lovely—if not lovely *because* of its guileless animation. He lived in the land of secret projects and code names, of lips that zipped when he got too close to a table rounded by busy hunched heads, so the openness of her face was a breath of fresh air. *A face like that could cure the world's problems,* he thought, imagining what it would be like if people couldn't hide behind masks and avatars, if they wore their hearts not so much on their sleeves but a bit higher up. Plus, Pandora liked him unlike others in his life, and that made all the difference when it came to talking to—correction: texting with—her.

He'd tried confessing his deception once, albeit obliquely. "You know the expression 'You've made my day'?" he typed.

"Yes?"

"Well, you do that pretty much every time we have one of these—what should we call them? Not a tête-à-tête."

"A meeting of minds?" Pandora suggested.

"I'll bet you were smiling when you wrote that," he typed, daring himself to hit send, and then did.

"How'd you know?" she wrote back.

But then he let the opportunity for confession slip by. "Great minds," he typed, followed by the "laughing tears" emoji.

Great minds, met, tend to brainstorm, and that's precisely what Pandora and George proceeded to do, beginning with George's theory about how the nervous system went from being an immediate reaction machine to something that retained memories to inform thought and, yes, consciousness. "You know the expression 'painful memories'?" he asked.

"Yes," Pandora typed. "Those are what my dad calls a steady income."

"Well, I think pain was originally a proxy for memory. Its persistence was for our earliest ancestors what memory is for us: a reminder. I think memory cells evolved from the cells activated by pain, those nerve cells desperately signaling for us to take our hand out of the fire. Those nerves evolved, rewiring themselves into retaining a memory of the pain well after the damaged skin was healed. Immediate pain was like short-term memory, while the memory of pain became long-term storage that prevented us from having to relearn the same painful lessons after the original wounds stopped hurting."

"So what's the takeaway?" Pandora wrote back.

"I think our AI needs to be able to feel pain," George wrote.

"I won't tell it you suggested that," Pandora wrote back, "once it becomes sentient and, you know, all powerful."

Another time, it was the ability to have and feel emotions that were the key to bringing an AI to a human level of consciousness.

"This world is a fire hose of data coming at us," he typed. "How are we supposed to make sense of it all? How do we prioritize and rank what's important to pay attention to versus what we can ignore to preserve our bandwidth?"

"I'm guessing the answer isn't flipping a quarter," Pandora wrote back.

"Emotions," George typed, "are nature's Google."

"How so?"

"Google uses click-through statistics as a way to rank search results," George typed. "For people, memory search optimization is achieved by the emotional residue associated with the memories being searched. The strongest emotional associations cause those memories to rank highest."

Pandora couldn't *not* think about Gladys, whom she'd told George about, and how her grandmother's condition had set her down the path to meeting him. "I think that's why she remembers WWII stuff better than what happened yesterday," she texted back. "That's when her emotions were supercharged. Which is nice, I guess."

"How so?"

"That the dying mind would take us back to the time when we felt most alive."

"Until it uses up those memories," George typed, looked at what he'd written, and then backspaced over it. Instead, "Truth," he tapped out before hitting send.

Another time: "You know the expression 'Seeing is believing'?" George typed.

"Sure."

"You know what that makes me think of?"

"No telling."

"How playing peekaboo with a baby is like programming an AI."

Pandora couldn't find an emoji that suggested a sarcastic "of course," so she went with the "face-palm" instead.

"I always thought peekaboo was a dumb game meant to make adults look stupid," he wrote. "Turns out, it's actually teaching kids a lesson AI is still having trouble with."

"And that is?" Pandora typed back.

"That there's a whole three-dimensional world around the corners of whatever its visual sensors are processing. That shadows aren't solid. That a person's chest implies his or her back, and a tree is a good place to hide behind. Peekaboo teaches a baby to imagine the continuity of reality," George wrote. "And that's an important step toward achieving consciousness."

"Hold on. Are you saying babies aren't born already conscious?"

George nodded before realizing—oh yeah—Pandora couldn't see him on her end of the conversation. And so he tapped out, "Y-E-S," instead.

"How can you think that?" Pandora texted back.

"You better think it too," George tapped out.

"Why?"

"Because if consciousness is some special sauce our unique snowflake species got miracled into having, game over when it comes to producing a conscious AI," George wrote. "But if humans are *programmed* into the experience of consciousness, then we've got a shot at replicating the process."

"And this consciousness programming," Pandora texted back, "how does that happen? What's the mechanism? When does the big C switch on?"

"I figured you'd ask that," George typed.

"Good thinking."

"I think it has something to do with language," he typed, "learning that the stuff we can touch is invisibly connected—let's say hyperlinked—with something we can't see or touch, but that lives in our heads: words."

Pandora looked at George's words on her screen, letting them live in her head for a while. Then: "But where do the words come from," she typed, "and how do we turn them into code?"

She watched the squiggle dots of George's typing inchworm in place below the last text bubble. It seemed to squiggle a lot longer than was justified by the words that finally appeared: "I'm thinking," followed by ellipses.

Pandora didn't want to come across like she was breaking his balls, but she also couldn't help herself. "Please see previous text," she typed, adding a "goofy wink" emoji, just in case.

George—his balls feeling busted nevertheless, it seemed—texted back the passive-aggressive emoji that might seem to signal agreement or affirmation but was a stop sign, intended to end the thread—texting's answer to the "No, you hang up" standoff of earlier generations, but a tad more brutal and efficient: the dreaded "thumbs-up" emoji.

Pandora looked at her screen. Thought about texting a "snowflake" emoji but decided to save it for when she *really* needed it.

# 38

Perhaps to cover her long-distance relationship with one of her father's clients, Pandora decided to act normal. Or maybe "was ordered to" was more like it. And while her rule-defying and/or exploiting hacker's heart might have inclined her to act even weirder than usual, Pandora actually agreed with the old man's rationale. Though not making a lot of noise about it, "the authorities" were likely still looking for their would-be terrorist. As a result, adopting the mask of normality as a camouflage made strategic sense.

And so she tried. First step: dating. She figured the boy who played the school mascot was a likely candidate. A gangly, carbuncled kid, he clearly welcomed the opportunity to hide his actual head inside the large polar bear head, which was a prominent part of his costume. Following in prominence was the jersey that helped identify Ransom Wood's polar bear mascot from all the other polar bear mascots that had been hastily adopted once people realized that the original mascots—the Yosemite Sam–looking sourdoughs and the fur-hooded-and-booted indigenous peoples—were racist or insultingly stereotyped.

Approaching her target during a lull in pep-related activity, Pandora attempted to break the ice with a joke. "It's too bad they don't include high school mascots when deciding if a species is endangered or not. We could get the polar bear off the list, no problem."

The boy in the suit turned his huge head toward her and looked out through its snarling mouth. "Huh?" he said.

For a clumsy boy, he was showing promise given Pandora's already pretty low expectations. They'd taken in a movie at the Regal Goldstream, a sci-fi epic already at the dollar theaters in the lower forty-eight but a first-run feature up in Fairbanks. It was an old-fashioned gesture, seeing as the movie was already streaming on demand—and Pandora had already seen it, but acted surprised at the surprise ending nevertheless. Based on the action around them, it seemed the Regal Goldstream owed its continued existence to teenagers like herself and her would-be beau, who were paying less for the movie and more for the space, dark, and privacy (relatively speaking) to kiss in the back row. Or so she assumed he hoped and would go on hoping.

After the movie, they headed for the Fairbanks McDonald's, near the Safeway off Geist. It was Tuesday, and the local McDonald's was honoring a local tradition: family pancake night, an all-you-can-eat affair that was a focal point of community life. Which was why neither was surprised when the wedding party entered. Pandora and her date had taken their red plastic trays and found a table underneath the moose head and next to the fireplace when the group entered, tuxed, gowned, parkaed, Soreled, and lit by a backward-walking videographer and some friends with their smartphones, playing backup.

"Look," her date said, way overplaying his hand, "the future . . ."

"You wish," Pandora said, placing down her tray and taking a seat. Though not a typical sight for the lower forty-eight, wedding parties using a fast-food place in lieu of renting a hall wasn't all that unusual, with the odds going up as the combined age of the couple went down, the better to dismiss the choice as "kitschy" or "ironic," as opposed to "economically foreordained."

"Nothing wrong with," the boy across from her began and was about to end with "wishing," when a member of the wedding party tapped Pandora's shoulder and asked if she wouldn't mind immortalizing a moment between herself and a big-bearded, plaid-shirted hunk of Alaskan masculinity she'd been paired with for the evening.

"No prob," Pandora said, excusing herself as she accepted the proffered smartphone and centered the impromptu couple on its high-definition screen. "Say cheese," she said, tapped the screen to the sound of a simulated shutter snap, and returned the phone.

"You were saying?" she asked her date, sitting back down. The boy across from her sat with his head sunk, staring at his syrupy pile of pancakes while the yellow pat of butter decoded itself into a puddle that wound through then mingled with the maple brown.

"Nothing," he mumbled.

Clearly, she'd said or done something wrong, this "being normal" business frequently harder than it looked—or was worth, frankly. Still, she tried rescuing the moment by simulating interest in the mopey boy in front of her. "So," she said, "what's it like being a mascot?"

He shrugged, dug into his pancakes. Pandora did likewise, noting that she was apparently in the middle of a race she hadn't been informed of. Not that that stopped her from trying to win.

Later, in the car, the pimply boy said, "Echoey," into the dashboard lights.

"Excuse me?"

"You asked what being a mascot was like," he said. "Back at the restaurant." Pause. "It's echoey."

Another silence enveloped them as Pandora processed the latest input only to suddenly exclaim, *"Yes!"* startling both her companion and herself. Until the pieces fell into place, she hadn't realized she'd been holding a whole other conversation in her head, one about heads and how they work. Taking a shot at empathy, she'd imagined her own head inside the polar bear head, imagined talking and hearing her own voice come back at her, concluded that it wasn't all that different from how things usually went re: her head and her voice, except she didn't need to open her mouth and actually say anything to hear what amounted to an echo inside her head, roughly behind those peepholes, her eyes. Preparing her response to his response, she was about to say that it reminded her of what consciousness was like when she stopped herself and blurted, *"Yes!"* instead.

"Did I do something wrong?" her companion asked, his Pandora-facing shoulder canted a few inches farther away from her than where it had been a second earlier.

"Nope," Pandora said, leaning in as he leaned back. She surveyed that minefield of acne, located a spot between zits, and applied the most platonic of kisses. "You've been perfect," she added. "Thanks."

"You're welcome?" he guessed.

"You can take me home now," she announced, eager to text George in the privacy of her own . . . well, with the shower curtain drawn at least.

"What's being conscious like for you?" she texted him.

"It's like a conversation," George tapped. "It's like I'm talking to myself all the time, quietly, in my head."

"Exactly," Pandora tapped back. "I think consciousness is a collaboration between the sides of ourselves. A conversation. Or narration. It's a story we tell ourselves about ourselves, and it keeps going in real time, editing itself on the fly."

"POV," George typed.

"Spell out."

"Point of view," George typed, as requested. "The world is all around us but is *not us*. We are the target the world aims itself at. We are our point of view—the whole history of everything we've seen or heard from our particular focal point. We are the thinking thing in our own blind spot that we can't see but know is there, through intuition."

"Or a mirror."

"Or selfie," George typed. "I get it. But you see what I'm saying, right?"

"I am the drain between the world and my collective, subjective experience of the world," Pandora typed. "The world circles me, pours down me, *becomes* the experience of me from the funneling center that calls itself me."

"Yes," George texted back, watching as Pandora smiled in the palm of his hand.

# 39

Brainstorming about artificial consciousness is one thing; rendering what you've brainstormed into code is another. So how were they supposed to achieve what the best minds in the field hadn't cracked yet? Because that was the goal they'd set themselves—the Everest of AI, the Holy Grail of neural nets, pick your hard-to-impossible metaphor and that's what they were up against.

Why? It was central to both of their goals.

For Pandora, the idea of surviving dementia or the bigger *D*, death, by uploading her memories to the cloud was just the first part. Those memories needed to inform something else with agency, something that could form *new* memories contextualized by the old memories in storage, something consciousness-compatible for her consciousness to inhabit when it got out of the habit of having a mortal body and became immortal either as a robot or virtually, living in an alternative sim world beyond her wildest imagination.

George, on the other hand, needed his AI to be conscious so it understood what it was the people it was tasked with saving stood to lose. George's AI needed a consciousness so it could understand what might motivate thoughts of self-destruction in other conscious entities as a first step to reverse engineering its way back to wanting to "live," or at least remain conscious.

Seeing as George was the one who was actually getting a paycheck, it made sense that he take the first stab at coding their baby AI before handing it off to Pandora to take potshots at. It also made sense that George would be the one to make the introductions.

"Pandora Lynch," his message read, "meet Buzz," followed by a link to what was really just a doodle in code as opposed to an actual beta of anything.

"Buzz?"

"Yep," George wrote back, going on to explain that his baby AI had actually named itself. He—George—had coded up a two-dimensional VR space for his baby AI to learn the rules of and . . .

"Two-dimensional virtual reality space?" Pandora echo-typed.

"Pac-Man," George wrote back. "I was having my AI teach itself Pac-Man. And my CPU started getting toasty even though most of the crunching was happening in the cloud. And I'm watching the activity light go crazy, and the cooling fan kicks on, and then there's this loud buzzing noise, like there's been a head crash and the hard drive's getting trashed."

"You're not using an SSD?" Pandora typed. "How big a cheapskate is Lemming anyway?"

George was not about to cast aspersions on his employer in writing, even over a private phone, using a proprietary, encrypted texting app with a self-destruct option. Instead, ignoring the comment entirely, he continued. "Turns out a fortune cookie fortune got stuck in the fan and was rattling like a playing card in a bicycle's spokes," George continued. "Catastrophe averted."

"So what did it say?"

"What did what say?"

"The fortune."

"I don't," George began typing, but then stopped. "Wait," he said to himself, aloud. "Yes, I do." He reached into the paper-clip tray in his top drawer, which was filled with slips of paper from the assortment of free fortune cookies the Quire cafeteria gave out whenever the menu featured Asian cuisine.

"'It's not the destination; it's the journey,'" he typed.

"How pseudoprofound," Pandora's reaction blooped back.

"What do you expect from a baked good?" George typed. "But that's not the point. My AI made something happen in the real world. It buzzed. So that's what I'm calling it: Buzz."

"Aldrin," Pandora typed, "or Lightyear?"

"Does it matter?"

"Sure. One's made out of DNA and the other is CGI."

"Code by any other name," George opined, trying out a little pseudoprofundity of his own.

"How's that?"

"Genetic," George typed, "versus computer. It's all code."

Pandora was about to object, to point out that unlike computer code, genetic code couldn't be hacked. But then she remembered reading about CRISPR in her news feed and stopped. Instead: "Maybe Kurzweil is right about the singularity after all."

"Here's hoping," George typed, followed by the "fingers crossed" emoji.

The longer she lived with it, the more Pandora liked the idea of calling their baby AI "Buzz," with its twin connotations of electricity and viral excitement. "But shouldn't the initials stand for something? Like how HAL is IBM if you shift each letter to the left."

"That's an urban myth," George texted back. "It stands for 'Heuristically programmed ALgorithmic' computer. Plus, that double Z is going to be tough."

"What about Zuzu?"

"What about what-what?"

"Zuzu's petals," Pandora replied. "From *It's a Wonderful Life*? Jimmy Stewart. Christmas classic . . ."

"Yeah, yeah," George texted back. "Black and white, meaning ancient history, meaning *not relevant*."

"Au contraire," Pandora begged to disagree. "The movie's about what Buzz is about: suicide prevention. Clarence shows *George* (now how perfect is that?) what the world would be like without him so he changes his mind about killing himself. It's perfect."

"But how do we turn *that* into an acronym for BUZZ?" George typed. "What's the BU stand for?"

"Button up."

"Excuse me?"

"Zuzu catches a cold coming back from school because she didn't wear her coat, and George calls up her teacher to yell at her and scares his family and everything goes downhill after that."

"I thought it was losing the bank deposit," George wrote back.

"That started it, but the yelling because of Zuzu's cold was the tipping point. So if Zuzu buttoned up, she wouldn't have gotten a cold, George might not have started yelling, and . . ."

"So BUZZ = Button up, Zuzu?"

"Yep."

"Remind me never to play Scrabble with you."

"You're welcome."

"It really *is Pac-Man*," Pandora texted after clicking the link to George's doodle in code.

"Looks can be deceiving," he wrote back, "but yes."

"I thought you were joking."

"Not," George wrote, followed by, "This does precisely what I need it to do, no more, no less."

"Explain."

"First, it's a game, and games are foundational for AI because they've got clear rules that can be programmed directly or learned by having the AI watch several rounds of play. Then it perfects its own technique by playing millions of games against itself. One of the first proof-of-concepts for neural nets taught itself how to play *Breakout* to master level in about an hour."

"And thus concludes today's lecture on the history of artificial intelligence . . ."

"Sorry. Forgot who I was talking to."

"Typing to," Pandora corrected.

"Right," George acknowledged. "But this is"—and he was going to type "cool" but decided to use a word he knew would resonate with her hacker's heart—"elegant."

"Explain."

"First, it's embodied in as simple a body as possible, occupying the fewest number of dimensions, two."

"Why does Buzz need a body?"

"Embodiment," George wrote back, "is one of the earliest debates in AI. Sure, you can do tricks using language-manipulating algorithms, come up with chatbots that go 'Um' now and then and can appear humanlike. Google's Duplex could pass the Turing test—in the limited world of making telephone reservations. But there's always some way in which chatbots fall short. Did you know they did a study of the words that would fool humans into thinking they were dealing with another human?"

"Ah, the infamous 'they.'"

"Do you want to know that top human-proving word or not?"

"Hit me."

"Poop."

"Heart" emoji followed by the "poop" emoji.

"And you know what you need to poop, right?" George typed.

*Fiber?* Pandora thought, but typed, "Hit me," again instead.

"A body," George typed.

"I see what you did there," Pandora wrote back, followed by a "wink" emoji from George.

"So the theory goes that it's not enough to program an artificial brain if you want to get to an actually conscious AI," George typed. "There needs to be a body, too, reacting to an environment that 'programs' the AI like people are 'programmed' by their experiences and environment. Now you can build a robot body with a bunch of sensors for a million bucks, have it learn an obstacle course by itself, or you can do it all with pixels and a handful of rules."

"I see," Pandora texted back. "But isn't Mr. Wocka-Wocka a little simplistic, even for virtual reality on a budget?"

"What's wrong with simple? Simple's good," George wrote. "I did simple on purpose."

"Touchy much?"

"You know Descartes, right? You wore that T-shirt in your proof-of-life selfie. 'I Think, Therefore I Am . . .'"

"Okay."

"Descartes questioned everything until he arrived at the one thing he couldn't question: that he was thinking and therefore must exist," George typed. "The one thing he couldn't doubt was that he was the consciousness doing the doubting."

"Okay."

"He broke down all of existence into three little words."

*I love you,* Pandora thought, but knew better than to type, even if it was true despite this run of George's mansplaining Philosophy 101. Instead, she typed, "Go on," remembering only after the fact what a truly crappy medium texting is for sarcasm.

"That's what I was trying to do with this proto version," he typed. "I wanted to strip away everything but the minimum required for consciousness in terms of a body and senses. And what I came up with happens to look like Pac-Man. It has a body, the circle, that helps identify it as separate from its surrounding environment, so that as far as Buzz is concerned, the universe is two things: me and not me. To achieve that understanding as simply as possible, it needs a single sense: a sense of boundary. A sense of where it stops and everything else starts."

"Wait a second," Pandora typed, having held her tongue—or thumbs—long enough. "If all an AI needs is enough sense to stay on its side of the universe, why all the fuss about getting machine vision and hearing to work? Why the data farms in China with workers tagging a million different dog pictures to create a database of dogness? I think that means that seeing and hearing are probably pretty important to the development of consciousness."

George didn't disagree, but sight and sound could come later. For now, at the prototype phase . . . ? "Two words," he typed. "Helen Keller."

Pandora swore at her phone, and George smiled. Roger, on the other hand, had been sleeping on the couch. "What was that?"

"Nothing," Pandora lied, noticing that in the interim, George had expanded on his original comment.

"Are you telling me that Helen Keller lacked consciousness?"

*Don't know; never met her,* Pandora thought, but typed, "Never mind. Continue."

"So stripped down, Buzz needs to know it can't be in two places at once," George typed. "No colocation."

Pandora, who'd quite recently thought one thing while typing another, proceeded to call BS by typing, "BS," followed by, "Colocation is the essence of consciousness."

"How so?"

"Think about it," she typed. "Our conscious reality is always in two places at once. We have an inner reality (what we think) and an outer reality (what we might choose to say or do). Something as simple as sarcasm would be impossible without the implicit acknowledgment that people can say something while meaning its exact opposite. Consciousness is a two-places-at-once experience inherently."

Pandora smiled triumphantly as she watched the dancing ellipsis dance for a lot longer than it usually did, stop, and then start up again. Finally: "So you're saying that a sign of Buzz being conscious," George typed, "is if it can consciously lie?"

"Using 'consciously' in front of 'lie' might be stacking the deck there," she typed, hit send, and then had another (eviler) thought. And so she added: "Unless you're okay with circular logic."

"I see what you did there," George typed.

"Wink" emoji.

George admitted that he hadn't started out with the intention of resurrecting Pac-Man, fitting though he now thought it to be. "I was on YouTube, looking at babies."

"Would these be preconscious babies?" Pandora typed back.

George ignored the bait. "Have you ever watched a newborn exploring its world? It's crazy the way they'll put anything into their mouths, including their own fist. It looks like they're trying to stifle a yawn but they're experimenting. They're trying to see if this thing out there is something they can eat, and when they try, and pain comes back as the answer, that's when they start to learn the difference between themselves and the rest of the world."

"So we need to teach Buzz not to eat itself?" Pandora wrote back. "Or maybe that its virtual world is a dog-eat-dog virtual world?"

"I wanted to see what Buzz would come up with for a body," George continued, "so I gave it a pixel and a push."

"And?"

George sent her a JPEG of a circle.

"That looks familiar," Pandora texted back.

"That's what Buzz came up with, and it's perfect: the self vs. everything else," George texted.

"How much of a push did you give it?" Pandora asked, suspecting a little deck stacking in the result.

"Well, originally, it just blinked," George admitted. "The pixel, I mean. And that's when I realized it needed a few other things, like the curiosity about its environment a human baby has."

"I thought curiosity killed the cat," Pandora countered.

"Nope," George typed back. "Curiosity familiarized the cat with its surroundings so it wouldn't be surprised. Think of the baby exploring its own fist by mouthing it and being surprised by feeling it in two places—on its hand and in its mouth. And every new discovery its curiosity leads to is another thing it won't be surprised by again. Then you remove the option of standing still by making the not-me environment nonneutral—specifically, *not* benign."

"Or skipping the double negatives," Pandora typed, "the environment likes to kill sitting ducks."

"Yes."

"That seems like a lot more coding than just 'a pixel and a push,'" Pandora observed.

"That's how programming works," George wrote back. "Try, test, try, test. You know this. You code too."

"Thanks for remembering," Pandora wrote, her face not exactly filled with gratitude at the moment.

"So that's when something finally started happening," George wrote. "The pixel started moving, and it was like watching primordial goo coming up with the idea for cell walls. That single pixel started testing the compass points of its space and then stretched itself into a line that bent, swept, and met itself, forming a perfect circle, which began rolling from one end of the screen to the next, mapping out its world, driven by curiosity and a need to not be surprised."

"How'd you make the environment nonneutral?" Pandora asked.

"I started with random geometrical not-Buzzes, moving randomly, bumping into Buzz and vice versa. Collisions cost points from a base score I started Buzz out with at the beginning, triggering various if/thens when the score reached X, Y, or Z."

"Sounds depressing," Pandora wrote back. "Start out with everything you'll ever have and then lose ground from there?"

"Yeah, I know," George wrote back. "It sucks. And you know what it sounds like, right?"

"Life?"

"Precisely."

"No," Pandora wrote a little later, after considering George's default scoring. "Buzz's interactions with its environment can't be all negative. It should interact with the environment to add points. Maybe the boundary sense allows exceptions, letting something from outside to be brought inside, like the way an experience can inspire a new idea or like food provides nutrition. That's what consciousness is like for me. It's a Venn diagram with two overlapping circles—inside me and outside me—and the point where they overlap is where my experience of consciousness is located. So this no-colocation rule you started with—it doesn't allow for the possibility for consciousness because it doesn't allow Buzz to take something from the outside and make it part of itself."

"I think you're absolutely right," George texted back. "How's this for an input device?"

A text bubble blooped open on Pandora's screen, inside which sat the same plain yellow pie as before, missing a slice where its new mouth now was.

"I hate you," Pandora texted.

"You're welcome."

His goal—George explained—was to turn suicide detection and prevention into a game, and though he hadn't been thinking of Pac-Man when he started out, the more he thought about it, the more he liked it. He'd gotten their baby AI from nothing but a single pixel to a one-celled actor that needed to eat to keep moving, needed to move to explore, and needed to explore to avoid surprises that cost points off its "life." He'd noticed the similarity to Pac-Man the second he gave his one-celled actor a mouth. That the actual game featured elements that fit nicely into his current task was a happy accident. Take the ghosts and extra lives; he couldn't have asked for a simpler visualization of what his end game was: generating extra lives by saving kids from suicide.

In the original game, each room or level came with four power pellets, one in each corner, the power pellets being the means by which Pac-Man prevented ghost encounters from costing him one of his three lives. Translate ghosts into potential suicides and power pellets into successful prevention scenarios and make those prevention episodes something Pac-Buzz's score depends on. George admitted he was still a long way from determining how the power pellets would neutralize life-robbing ghosts, but he had his AI's conceptual scaffolding sketched out in an easy-to-remember form—something to keep in the back of his head (and his AI's core programming) while he moved on to tackle more ambitious feats of coding.

"But isn't this copyright infringement?" Pandora asked. "Aren't you stealing intellectual property?"

"Only if I copied the exact source code and tried to market it as a game," George said. "But nobody will ever see this on the front end, and I reversed engineered it by accident without even meaning to. Plus, what's IP versus actual human lives?"

"Assuming it all works out," she typed.

"It's not even a total copy," George insisted, perhaps a bit more defensively than if he'd actually believed his earlier defense. "When Buzz eats a pac-dot, it grows, and this ballooning imparts momentum, causing it to roll or somersault to the next pac-dot, where the process repeats. I'm thinking the pac-dots will be a checklist of suicidal ideation indicators, something like that."

Pandora looked at the time on her phone. It was winter, and even though she had a window in her room, it didn't offer many clues about the time, this time of year. Between, say, 11:00 a.m. and 2:00 p.m., the sky might lighten a bit with what was optimistically referred to as "sunrise." But any options outside that, say, nine, eight, four, and she'd have to check her phone to figure out if it was day or night. And these text sessions with George weren't helping. They seemed to dissolve time, make it even harder to keep track of. And so when she looked at the time in the upper right-hand corner and saw it was five, she needed to squint to register it was p.m.

*Shit,* Pandora thought.

She was late to see Gladys at the Golden Heart. And so: "Mmmm, pac-dots," she hastily texted back, followed by the "yum" emoji, followed by the "running girl" emoji—the one along with the "running boy" emoji they agreed meant "gotta go," to avoid leaving the other waiting on a text that wouldn't come.

# 40

When Pandora signed in at the Golden Heart, she took out her phone for the time and noticed the date as well: February 14. Why did that date . . . ?

*Oh shit,* Pandora thought, followed by doing the IRL version of the "face-palm" emoji. Well, if they'd ever needed proof of what geeks they were, there it was. She and George had spent their first (!) Valentine's Day exchanging texts about how to program consciousness, oblivious to what day it was. Neither had sent the other anything; neither had texted the words. The two seconds it would take to tap a "heart" emoji and hit send? Nope, neither of them. Or . . .

Pandora scrolled through their recent exchange. There *was* one. A heart, but right next to a pile of poop—if that didn't just about sum it up. Maybe she should get one of those reminder boards like the staff updated in Gladys's room. She wondered what they drew to distinguish between Valentine's Day and a visit from the cardiologist.

Slipping her phone back into her pocket, Pandora noticed something funny about her hands; they were empty. She was already late for her grandmother's Valentine's Day visit and was showing up empty-handed to boot. Nurse Mitchell was going to have a field day.

"Is there a . . . ?" she began.

". . . gift shop?" the receptionist finished.

Nod.

"Down that hall, left, left, bingo . . ."

"Thank you."

"I'm not done yet," the receptionist said. "Hang a right past bingo, and there it is."

"The gift shop?" Pandora asked, just checking.

"The gift shop," the receptionist confirmed.

The place was pretty well picked over this late in the day as Pandora took down and put back a variety of possibilities, including gag mugs, teddy bears, kiss-covered kitsch. She knew Gladys wouldn't turn down anything sweet but didn't want to encourage her after the Nips situation.

As she continued looking, Pandora noticed she had company in the gift shop, an elderly man in a jacket—a windbreaker—way too thin for the actual weather outside. Emblazoned across the back was a large gear with the letters "UAW" on the inside. Looking closer, she realized that what she'd taken as the cog's teeth were actually stick people, linked hand in hand, circling the circumference, the human labor that made the vast machinery of the auto industry run.

"You're a long way from"—guessing but a good one, statistically—"Detroit?"

The old man turned and smiled the high-def grin of someone with brand-new dentures. "That was the plan," he said.

"Looks like it worked," Pandora said.

"Looks like," the smile confirmed.

"You visiting, or . . . ?"

"Staying," the old man said. "I signed up for the Eskimo burial. You know, send 'em out on an ice floe? This was the closest they had."

"Well, happy Valentine's Day," Pandora said, deciding on a box of damn chocolates and preparing to leave when her retired auto worker snapped his gnarled fingers, winced, and said, "*That's* why I came in here," followed by another uncanny-valley smile.

Pandora raised a box of chocolates like an admissions badge as she passed the nurses' station and headed for Gladys's room. "I'm sorry I'm late," she began when she spotted them: five petals of the bluest sky blue Pandora had ever seen, repeated flower by dainty flower a dozen times, the stems rubber banded together, little pale tendrils at their cut ends, visible through the clear glass vase that rested on Gladys's windowsill, half-empty, half-full, your call. She'd not be a proper Alaskan if Pandora couldn't name them, seeing as the alpine forget-me-not (scientifically: *Myosotis alpestris*) was the official flower for the forty-ninth of the fifty United States. And she'd not be a proper granddaughter if the sight of them in her grandmother's nursing home didn't turn her mood from apologetic before seeing them to downright pissed afterward.

*Forget-me-nots! In the room of a woman with dementia! What kind of a sick . . .*

She hit the call button and then let her rage build for thirty or so minutes before any of the home staff showed up.

"Yes?" a nurse's aide said after poking her head in the doorway. Her powder-blue scrubs, dotted with fluorescent renditions of Tweety Bird, appeared to be on backward, judging from the breast pocket Pandora noticed over the girl's left shoulder blade when she'd fully entered the room, after having determined there were no infectious bodily substances splattered anywhere.

Pandora gestured to the blue flowers on her grandmother's windowsill. "WTF?" she said.

"DK," the nurse's aide said. "But they're pretty, don't you think?"

"*Pretty's* not the point," Pandora said. "What kind of sicko puts forget-me-nots in the room of a . . ." She trailed off.

"You want me to get rid of them?" the nurse's aide asked.

Pandora looked at the flowers, and then looked at her grandmother looking at the flowers. Just testing, she stepped off to one side. Gladys's gaze did not follow her like it usually did. Instead, it stayed glued on that splash of out-of-season blue.

All her reasons for being angry were hers, Pandora realized. They were all in her head, linked up with the words she had for the flowers she was seeing. Forget the words, and all that was left were the flowers, which *were* kind of pretty after all. And maybe that had been the point—clueless, but benign.

"Don't bother," Pandora said. "I think she likes them."

"She likes them," Gladys said, whether agreeing or just repeating, it was getting harder and harder to tell.

Pandora, meanwhile, pulled up the guest chair and began her vigil. When Gladys's eyes fluttered closed, she took out her phone. "BTW," she thumbed, "happy VD."

She waited. Her phone buzzed. "Happy Hallmark to you as well."

On the way back to the truck, Pandora saw her United Auto Worker again, a heart-shaped box of chocolates under the arm of his satiny windbreaker, poking his head into room after room before heading on. The phrase "Looking for love in all the wrong places" came to mind unbidden, but it made her smile, ironically, nevertheless.

*You and me, buddy,* she added to herself.

As a test, she called out to him. "You're a long way from Detroit," she said.

"That was the plan," he said.

"Looks like it worked," Pandora said, continuing the rerun of their previous conversation as if they were having it for the first time.

"Looks like," Mr. UAW said.

And then she moved on, as did he, back to checking the open doorways. Pandora, for her part, wished him luck.

# 41

There was a reason George forgot Valentine's Day, not that he'd necessarily have said anything even if he'd remembered. He just wasn't sure how Pandora felt about him, even though she'd been the one to reach out in the first place. There'd always been something a little fishy about that. He'd been flattered at first, but the no-faces thing kind of suggested that all she was interested in was his brain. That and access to the kinds of resources that would help her reach her stated goal: cybernetic immortality.

Even with access to her phone's camera—even with that hyperexpressive face of hers—George couldn't tell if the arousal he detected was because of *him* or his *ideas*. It was this uncertainty and insecurity—byproducts, Roger would no doubt contend, of his client's chaotic foster childhood—that had led George to getting himself into an awful stupid place re: the project they were supposedly collaborating on, a.k.a. Buzz. And the stupid place he got himself into? He wanted to impress Pandora. He wanted to deliver Buzz about as close to complete as he could manage so that all she had to contribute were a few gratuitous tweaks—maybe a few boxes he'd left open for her specifically—and voilà: an artificially conscious general AI.

His being in this stupid place was what contributed to George's forgetting Valentine's Day. He'd forgotten about it because . . . well, he'd kind of lost track of days. And nights. And the way they punctuated the flow of time.

The problem was they'd brainstormed more than he had time to code. He'd already been sleeping in his office when they'd met, an arrangement originally intended to save him money. Now it was saving him the time he'd otherwise waste commuting. Not that he was alone in this work-nesting behavior—not that management discouraged it, as attested to by the free vending machines all over QHQ, providing a steady supply of Monster, Red Bull, and Mountain Dew Kickstart, along with people lurking in the shadows, ever ready to offer you something a little stronger if you seemed to be in an especially productive mood.

One evening, in just such a mood, George had bumped into Milo in the hallway at 3:00 a.m. "Is your hair always like that?" Milo asked George, who was wearing a bathrobe at the time.

"Like what?"

"Like it's being blown back by an invisible wind."

George inspected Milo's person for a reflective surface, found two in the dark glasses his Virgil was wearing, and attempted a few half-ass hair-taming swipes before abandoning the effort. "Coding," he admitted.

"I can see that." Milo patted his pockets and produced some inspiration in pill form. "Care for a little"—he paused theatrically—"competitive edge?"

"Thanks?" George said in return, pocketing what he'd been advised was a wholly legal pharmaceutical short a little paperwork.

And then one night, George got a little warning from his body when his heart decided to freak out. It wasn't an all-out attack, more like a "Do we have your attention now?" beat-skipping situation. He stumbled out into the hallway, looking for help, but found Milo instead. His Virgil, it turned out, had a pill for this condition as well, which George accepted because he needed it and because, well, it was Milo and he'd been working here longer than most.

"You may also want to take note," the latter said, pointing to something George had failed to register: wall-mounted cabinets featuring stick people in various postures, some involving lightning bolts.

"Defibrillators," Milo explained. "Plural," he added. "They'll actually talk you through the whole thing. It's kind of neat."

"And *needed*, apparently?"

"Apparently," Milo said. He pointed at his own wrist, wrapped by a smart watch displaying his vitals. "Best to avoid any surprises," he advised.

In the end, George was forced to compromise on the whole body-needing-sleep thing. Taking a cue from Thomas Edison, who was famous for taking catnaps on his laboratory floor, George reprogrammed himself to get by with a series of fifteen- or twenty-minute naps every several hours. He was modestly concerned that REM sleep usually doesn't occur until about ninety minutes into a night's sleep, but perhaps abstaining from dreaming was where the other one percent of genius came from. It worked for Edison, who—while dead—had a good run while he was still alive.

George was aided and abetted in this new sleep schedule by no less than V.T. Lemming himself, who seemed to share a similar love-hate relationship with the traditional split between sleeping and waking. Shortly after he'd been given his first work assignment, the same messenger arrived to drop off an old-school alphanumeric pager from "the big man himself." It was hardwired only to receive—V.T. the only sender—and came equipped without much in the way of memory so that no messages were stored once a new one came in. V.T.'s pages invariably scrambled George's ability to concentrate for at least an hour after receiving one. They were also almost always questions, passive-aggressively dropping *g*'s to create a fairly threatening nonthreatening vibe: "How's it goin'?" A perfectly fine question, but without the ability to transmit an answer back, a bit of a dickish move.

"Makin' progress?

"No pressure. Kids are dyin' is all."

Finally willing to dispense with any plans of impressing her, George decided to complain to Pandora about the pressure he was under. Unfortunately, before he was able to initiate that particular thread, his phone binged with a message from the target of his would-be showing off.

"So," it read, "how's it goin'?"

Pandora's text was the tipping point for a realization George had felt coming ever since his heart-skipping episode. More and more, he was convinced that he—they—were going to fail. And it wasn't even his—their—fault. There was something in the air that was coming, despite the hype and headlines: the AI winter, part two.

The study of artificial intelligence was actually a lot older than most people realized, going all the way back to the 1950s at least. There'd been a lot of excitement over early successes. In fact, most of the stuff making headlines now had actually been developed back then, including perceptrons, machine learning, neural nets, even evolutionary code where the computer incrementally tweaks and improves upon its own programming—none of these were new ideas back during the Summer of Love, one of the bigger things to hit San Francisco an incarnation or two ago.

But then AI hit a wall, and the first so-called "AI winter" began. The field's ideas and strategies had outrun the raw data and hardware needed to implement them. Those were the bottlenecks back then, and the AI renaissance now wasn't happening because of new approaches, per se, but was due to better hardware and more data for implementing those sixty-year-old ideas.

But there was another bottleneck coming, and it looked like hardware again. All George had to do was read what the tech giants were doing—the Googles, Facebooks, Microsofts. They were all developing proprietary chipsets aimed at some specific AI niche, from natural-language processing, to image recognition and differentiation, to dynamic visioning and navigation systems. The folks who used to be all about better software and algorithms were leaving the Intels and Motorolas behind.

Google had developed its own AI programming language, called TensorFlow, and was developing something called TPUs—Tensor processing units. Just about every other big tech firm in the Valley, European Union, and China were doing the same thing. The age of all-purpose x86 CPUs working together was coming to an end. In its place the industry was increasingly turning to something like the Apple model: walled off, proprietary, and incompatible with everything.

And there was Buzz, their baby AI, destined to choke in its crib thanks to that bottleneck. And it sucked, but George could have handled it, if it was just about him. If all it meant was losing his cushy job, well, he'd lived on the streets before, and he could do it again. But there were those kids out there, taking their own lives . . .

Yeah, that was a good one; George was all bent out of shape about a bunch of teenagers he didn't know. No. The thing that upset him was the teenager he knew: Pandora. What George couldn't take was disappointing her.

Correction: what he couldn't take was being *solely responsible* for disappointing Pandora. So he could either get Buzz to work—which didn't seem to be in the cards, not in the short term—or . . .

. . . or maybe he could finally start sharing the glory (a.k.a. blame). Pandora kept saying she wanted more to do, something to take advantage of her skills. And like he'd heard from more than one foster: misery loved company. George figured the same could probably be said about failure, which was when he decided it was time to share his.

# 42

Pandora wanted to talk about Valentine's Day without talking about Valentine's Day. But before she could figure out how to do that, George's words appeared in the palm of her hand. "We need to discuss the division of labor," they read. *Okay,* Pandora thought, *here we go.* If he suggested some BS busywork like proofreading his code, looking for misplaced commas or Os that should be zeros or vice versa, that was it; he didn't take her seriously and she'd have no reason to take him seriously. Cut her losses and become a ghost.

But then she recognized what he'd given her: a shoehorn to introduce the Valentine's discussion without necessarily using the word. She could steer the conversation in that direction by using an amusing anecdote about love among the elderly, sneaked in via the keyword he'd given her: labor.

"It's funny you should mention labor," Pandora wrote. "Last night, I saw this old guy wandering around my gram's nursing home, and he was looking for his sweetie with a big box of chocolates."

"What's that got to do with labor?" George wrote back.

"That's the best part," Pandora assured. "He was wearing a UAW jacket like he just stopped by after working a shift."

"Poor guy's a long way from Detroit," George texted back.

"That's what I said," Pandora wrote. "I think he might be Jimmy Hoffa in hiding." She followed the message with a "wink" emoji.

"When you say 'UAW,' do you mean the one that's a big gear?" George asked, scanning through the results of the Google Images search on his work computer.

"I always thought it was just a big gear too," Pandora texted. "But when I got a closer look, I realized the gear's teeth are really stick people holding hands."

"Workers of the world," George tapped out, suddenly longing for the socialist bros he'd abandoned to take this gig—the same job that was stacked against him and working him to death. He concluded with "Unite!" and was about to add something like "solidarity" or "eat the rich" or maybe just a "raised fist" emoji but stopped. He zoomed in on one of the UAW logos on his screen, following the sweep of little cog people—all holding hands.

His mind flashed back to a pair of fosters—Catholics, like his mom—who took him to guitar masses where they sang "Kumbaya" and went around shaking hands with everyone before communion. At one mass, during a lull, he'd clearly heard someone yell, "Bingo!" from the other side of the sacristy, back in the church hall that also served as the boys' court during basketball season.

George repeated the word to himself, in his office, aloud. He backed over the text he'd written and replaced it.

"Gotta go," the new text read. "Initiating radio silence, commencing . . . *now*."

"Are you *kidding*?" Pandora hastily texted back. And then waited. And kept on waiting. He hadn't even sent her the "running boy" emoji. After about an hour, she figured, George's not answering *was* her answer.

It was a typical eureka moment—or bingo, depending on your denomination. George had filled up his head with all the necessary bits and pieces for resolving a problem—all the individual trees—but then hit the forest and was overwhelmed. Finally deciding to accept failure, he let his mind get distracted and . . . *plop*. There it was: the answer.

In George's case, the distraction had been Pandora's little detour into labor politics, the UAW logo, specifically. All those people, linking hands. All those people, singing "Kumbaya," together in harmony. And then a random thought from the compost heap of them in George's head: It's too bad all this proprietary tech won't play nice together. And then the question: Why not? What was preventing it? Some laws and outdated notions about personal property? ICE and the foster system had cured George of those trifles long ago.

A worm, he figured, one that targets and gains control over experimental and proprietary hardware and software wherever it finds it. He'd call it the Kumbaya worm or k-worm for short. It would borrow from the same toolkit as Stuxnet and its variants, with some secret sauce from his own Daisy Chain of Mass Destruction. There was another ingredient, however, that found him breaking his self-imposed radio silence.

Pandora felt the buzz and checked her phone.

"You know machine language, right?"

She smiled. Machine language was as close to the machine as a programmer could get—closer than assembly language and way closer than what most script kiddies thought of as coding, i.e., the higher-level languages that read like stilted English and included everything from the grands, FORTRAN and BASIC, to Python and C++. Machine language was all zeros and ones. Pandora had learned an earlier binary language from her grandfather—Morse code—and she'd already admitted to George that she "ran with it all the way to ML."

"Why do you ask?" she wrote back noncommittally. It was late February, but she was still stinging a bit over the fourteenth.

"This thing I'm working on," he wrote, "is going to need like the UN of code translation. I'm going to need something that can get traditional computers and quantum computers talking to each other, with maybe some experimental or proprietary stuff thrown in."

"Okay?"

"Can you do it?"

Well, it wasn't busywork. And it might be fun—a challenge, but not impossible. "A crack, I shall give it," she wrote back.

"To my ears: music," followed by a link to the Dropbox account where she could deposit her "UN of code translation" once it was ready for prime time.

Pandora's confidence was not unfounded. She was the granddaughter of the code breaker Gladys after all. And it was true: she'd gotten as close to the machine as a coder could get without being a machine herself. ML, as it was fondly known among digit heads, was the actual language computers used to talk to other computers. George, who'd only made it to the level immediately above machine—assembly language—was duly impressed, while both considered hackers who only knew one or two higher-level languages to be little more than script kiddies, i.e., not coders at all.

Unlike translating English into Russian and then Japanese, translating one higher-order programming language into another benefited from the fact that while their terminology and/or syntax might vary, they all had to do many of the same things. They all needed to address variables, value assignment, integers versus floating point decimals, arithmetic operators, comparison operators, conditional operators, and other control structures. Python, PROLOG, LISP, R, C++ . . . they all included if/then, greater than, add, subtract, et cetera. And these control structures were like certain words in a given language, occurring at fairly consistent frequencies—*the*, *and*, *or*, *I*—and these statistics could be used to guess which string of symbols translated into, say, if/then statements.

The quantum computing side of the equation was a little trickier but, deep down, was more of the same—literally. More, after all, was the whole point of quantum computing—specifically, more options than the yes-no of binary systems. Instead of bits, quantum computing dealt in qubits, which took yes-no and added maybe-both-and-neither. And while there weren't a whole lot of qubits in any given place at the moment—more like a few here, a few there, scattered around research operations across the globe—there were resources available to help Pandora grok the essentials, from instruction sets like Quil and Pha-Q; to software development kits like IQ, Q#, and Kwiz; to full-blown languages like QCL, QML, and Quipper.

All in all, the work reminded Pandora of what her grandmother had told her about cracking the Enigma code. The fact that there'd be a *"Heil Hitler"* somewhere in transmissions coming from Germany proved to be an important key—one that undermined a lot of technological sophistication. Or as Gladys put it: "God bless those predictable fascists."

*And,* Pandora added, *code bros and their love of Monty Python . . .*

For something like a computer worm to spread, there needs to be a vector. Fortunately for George, he already had one—or one that would know one: Milo. It was one of the weird things he'd noticed about his self-appointed Virgil; Milo seemed to know everybody. He also seemed to know more collectively than any of his coworkers knew individually, as if Milo alone had been granted access to the big picture. Trying to pull one over on a guy like that was probably risky, but George was a former street kid who'd risked his ass into a position that others would kill for. It was time to see if that luck held.

Instead of just waiting for Milo to stop by his office—a statistically viable option—George decided to go looking and found his would-be vector in the arcade-themed break room he'd discovered on his first official day, postchipping. Milo was currently distracted, gobbling up pac-dots at an impressive rate, something George took as an excellent sign.

"Doesn't it bother you?" he asked over his all-knowing friend's shoulder.

"Doesn't what bother me?" Milo said back, not breaking focus.

"Lying to the world," George said. "The whole Memory Hole Monday thing."

"Oh, *that*," Milo said. He turned so George would be sure to see his smirk, only to hear the sound of his last life being lost, followed by "Game Over."

"Shit."

"Sorry," George said, "but what if we could plug it, make the lie true?"

"I don't think V.T. would take kindly to cutting off a data stream with that kind of potential."

"But what could he do about it?" George asked. "Poof! It just happens during a routine software patch. Is he going to go to the authorities because somebody 'fixed' a feature nobody was supposed to know about?"

Milo started a new game. "What exactly did you have in mind?"

"You know a lot of people around here," George said.

"Indeed I do," Milo confirmed.

"Like including the team that rolls out updates?"

A nod.

George bumped a cupped hand next to Milo's free hand. "Can you do me a favor?"

Milo closed his hand around the thumb drive George had passed him. "Indebtedness," he pronounced. "Big, big fan." Pause. "Continue."

"If that happened to get plugged in to some patch team member's USB port," he said, "I would be . . ." He paused.

"Indebted?" Milo said.

George nodded behind him where Milo could see it, reflected in the game screen.

And then, finally: "Would it be terribly audacious of me to quote Archimedes by typing EUREKA in all caps?"

"You're alive," Pandora texted back.

"And . . . ," George tapped out, followed by nothing, making her ask.

"What?"

"Conscious."

Pandora blinked. Planned to text back, "No way," but found herself typing, "You're shitting me," before hitting send.

"I shit you not."

"Buzz is conscious," she tapped, followed by a string of question marks punctuated by exclamation points.

"*Will* be," George texted back cryptically, "if it *can* be."

"You seem to have gotten Zen in your absence."

"Close," George answered. "As are we. Now all we have to do is wait to see what we catch."

Pandora's thumbs stood poised above her virtual keyboard, wishing she could reach through the screen and throttle her textmate for being so purposefully obtuse. Instead, "Explain," she typed, then hit send.

"Okay," George texted back, and proceeded to do just that.

With the help of Pandora's universal translator, George had created the Kumbaya worm (or k-worm), which was designed to spread to every Quire-enabled smartphone across the planet, where it would wait until some lackey decided to top off his or her battery by plugging in to an open USB port connected to a corporate, academic, or research intranet that was supposed to be walled off from the www, but was now breached.

The k-worm was designed to look for systems involved in AI-related activity, infect them, and thereby provide full access to whatever resources it found to the worm's creator, George, or whomever or whatever he designated to act in his stead. Like a news aggregator that gathers together content from around the web based upon certain keywords or declared areas of interest, the k-worm would bring together the best of the world's proprietary AI-related stuff under the umbrella of their AI of AIs, Buzz. These would include the best natural-language processor, the best computer-vision system, the best adaptive-learning algorithm, the best labeled-content databases, the best commonsense databases, and the best game players, among others. Eventually, the best would be determined the way the Go-playing AI AlphaGo decided moves, by using a generative adversarial network (or GAN) that employed two AIs debating themselves to the optimal solution. "Eventually," George stipulated.

"What do you mean 'eventually'?"

"We'll need to keep an eye on things in the beginning," George wrote back. "We don't want Buzz incorporating just any old experimental whatsit. It'll flag resources for human assessment—you and I—learning our yea-nay criteria for acceptance over a series of such assessments. Eventually, we'll let it cast a vote, and once our and its votes start matching consistently, we flip the switch, and Buzz and the k-worm proceed on autopilot."

"That sounds like a lot of work," Pandora wrote back.

"What?" George texted in return. "You thought immortality was going to be easy?"

"Wink" emoji.

After giving it some careful consideration, Pandora returned to a theme she'd first raised over George's appropriation of Pac-Man. "You can't just go around helping yourself to everybody's intellectual property," she said, somewhat out of sync with her generation. So on a more practical note: "And won't the antivirals just peg it as malware and get rid of it?"

"That's always a possibility," George admitted, "unless the intruder comes bearing gifts."

"Explain."

"It's not malware," George wrote back. "There's not a term for what it is. Beneware, maybe. Or better yet, palware. It's a *good* worm."

"Elaborate, please."

"It benefits whatever system it inhabits. It pools and redirects the excess capacity of every system it infects, bringing additional resources to process-heavy applications being run elsewhere on the net. Say you've got a node looking for new primes or mining crypto; well, the k-worm redirects idle processing power from other parts of its network. Distribution and optimization, like a benevolent traffic cop helping everybody get to their destinations more quickly."

"But how does that prevent it from being detected?"

"It doesn't," George typed, and she could practically see him smiling through the screen. "It prevents it from being *removed*."

"Go on," Pandora invited.

Accepted: "What lowly schmuck of an IT guy is going to insist on 'fixing' a system that's working faster and better than it ever has?"

Pandora blinked and almost felt like telling her dad that George must have been paying attention to their sessions after all. He'd gone from hacking computers to hacking humans using their most transparent motivators against them. But since she couldn't tell Roger any of this, she congratulated the side of the client-therapist relationship she could: "Well played, sir," she texted back, followed by the "applause" emoji.

# 43

In the beginning, the Kumbaya worm worked as advertised, infecting otherwise walled-off intranets, indexing resources, and flagging those that appeared AI related for further review. The way it worked was like this: once the k-worm breached a system, it played the equivalent of twenty questions using Pandora's translator script to figure out what the lingua franca of the system happened to be, computationally, while Google Translate was used for the supporting texts and other documentation of systems in languages other than English. Special attention was paid to systems supported in Mandarin, seeing as next to the United States, China was one of the odds-on favorites for reaching the finish line first, given the mandated overlap of government and corporations, an attitude toward the intellectual property of others even more casual than George's, and an investment of cash proportional to the existential importance with which the country viewed the emergent technology George and Pandora were hoping to help emerge a bit more quickly.

Once the languages were sorted out, the k-worm assessed what the latest system had to contribute, including: how many native processors (a.k.a. general purpose CPUs) versus accessory chips like accelerators and coprocessors designed for the AI space and specializing in things like image processing, natural-language processing and usage, strategic game play, deductive and inferential reasoning, simulated proprioception or body awareness, pattern recognition, et cetera. This was followed by an assessment of how much volatile memory, storage, and idle capacity were available in traditional systems while quantum and hybrid systems were ranked based upon the number of qubits they brought to the party. Next, all available files were sorted into known and unknown types based upon their various extensions and locations so that all the word processing docs, spreadsheets, operating system files, email, et cetera were set aside, leaving the remainder to be sorted by executables, databases, and everything else, with the .exe files ranked by file size and last-modified dates, the largest and newest first. A keyword search was then performed for file names suggestive of artificial intelligence, machine learning, neural nets, and quantum computing, including the initials *AI, ML, NN, Q*, the list itself a product of machine learning, the system using the growing number of positive examples of AI-related executable file names to weight the probability that an unknown file might be similar. Previously decompiled executable files identified as AI related were then used to perform statistical analyses on the new source code for further winnowing. Once a candidate AI resource had been identified, the k-worm would search for its file name in internal communications—emails, presentations, other documents—and perform an automated "dumpster dive" for clues as to what the file was supposed to do. Similar ranking and analysis were performed on any databases located, flagging those that contained labeled content for training versus "common knowledge" and/or "common sense" databases to fill in the gaps humans generally have no problem with but which routinely trip up AIs.

Once a target was identified, the k-worm would zip the resource together with all the internal communication material referencing the resource and then upload the zip file to the same cloud account George had set up for Pandora's translator code. The humans would then conduct a go/no-go analysis for whether or not the resource should be incorporated into the nervous system of the umbrella AI they called Buzz. Once they'd gone through the process several times, Pandora and George proceeded to automate themselves out of a job by using their past judgment calls and a machine-learning process to look for patterns, identify criteria, and develop a decision tree to be used against subsequent candidate resources, which they also ranked and compared to what Buzz "thought." Matches were reinforced and disagreements were corrected, and by this iterative process, Buzz's guesses about what were and weren't useful additions to its code improved.

It was Pandora's suggestion that they train two parallel machine learners, one modeled on her decision strategies and the other on George's. She'd gotten the idea after reading up on generative adversarial networks, or GANs, which fit in nicely with her view of consciousness as a kind of echo between our inner and outer selves, creating a narrative in which the individual consciousness is both storyteller and the audience in a feedback loop. The approach proved so successful that by the time Buzz and its code parents' decisions were in agreement ninety-nine percent of the time, the humans felt comfortable letting go of their baby AI's "hand" and stepping back while it did "its own thing."

And after that, George and Pandora went back to theorizing and philosophizing about the big picture and big ideas, twiddling their mental thumbs, waiting for the big day to arrive. They'd developed a shorthand for whatever series of acquisitions would represent the tipping point beyond which Buzz would be deemed conscious, i.e., "qubits," and the accumulation thereof. It was not unusual for one or the other to start off a brainstorming session with something like "Time to make the qubits" or "Wake up and smell the qubits" or "I love the smell of qubits in the morning; they smell like consciousness" or, finally:

"A qubit for your thoughts . . ."

All of which is to say they'd started getting impatient—which was unfortunate, to say the least.

# 44

Now that Buzz was on autopilot, George took a long-overdue breath and started noticing things around work he hadn't before. He'd even missed something that was quite literally staring him in the face on a daily basis and, frequently, even more often than that: Milo. Or Milo's badge. Now that George had the luxury of actually focusing on it, he noticed something was off. While the lanyards it variously hung from were always up to date, stitched with the latest corporate affirmation, the badge itself wasn't.

"Is that a problem?" George asked during their latest let's-see-how-depressed-we-can-make-the-newbie chat fest.

"Is what a problem?" Milo asked.

"Your badge. It expired a year ago."

Milo held the badge up to eye level and made a show of zooming it in, then out, as if his vision were failing, which it wasn't. "So it has," Milo said, letting it drop.

"So what gives?"

"Didn't I . . . ?" he began, stopped. "Hadn't I . . . ?" Same routine.

"Spit it."

"I got fired," Milo said.

"When?"

"That little content monitoring faux pas I mentioned?"

"Yeah?"

"Around then."

"But that was before I got hired."

Milo nodded.

"And you're still here."

Milo nodded again.

"So what gives?" George asked. Again.

"Me," Milo answered, "but only samples."

They'd been in the cafeteria when the conversation started but moved it, at Milo's request, "upstairs," a.k.a. George's office. Making a show of looking both ways before closing the door, Milo continued. "I thought we'd have this conversation once you finally got the nerve to ask me how I know so much 'secret stuff' about this place."

"Are the answers related?"

"Indeed," Milo said. "You see, unlike you serfs in your silos, I've pretty much got the run of the place."

"After being fired?" George inserted.

"But not having to turn in my badge," the other pointed out. "HR has the paper trail on my being fired, so my continued presence on campus could be explained as a 'clerical oversight.'"

"So you're saying the company wants you on-site," George said, "but not on the books?"

"Correct."

"Why?" George asked. "For what?"

"For services rendered," Milo said. "The aforementioned samples and subsequent sales," he added, reaching into the inside pocket of his own awfully plaid jacket and removing an amber vial. He gave it a little shake, like a rattle.

George blinked. "You're a pusher?"

Milo raised a stop-sign hand. "The crude descriptor for what I do is"—he grimaced—"drug dealer." Pause. "I prefer 'pharmaceutical concierge.'"

"So yes, you're a pusher," George said, folding his arms and leaning back, putting some distance between them. He did not feel at all hypocritical having sampled Milo's "samples" himself as particular needs arose; that was just friends helping friends. Drug dealing, on the other hand, had ruined his family.

"That's even uglier than 'drug dealer,'" Milo went on to say, "*and* inaccurate. I do not *push*. I acquire and dispense. People come to *me*. I don't go to *them*." Pause. "I mean, I *do* deliver. It's not like I'm Muhammad waiting for the mountain to come to me. I'm a full-service provider of controlled substances, but only to those who have proactively sought out my services."

"Okay," George said, trying to remember whether or not that had been true in his case. Was having an anxiety attack an implicit request to be medicated?

"And so, to summarize: I . . . ," Milo preambled, waiting for George to supply the rest.

". . . don't push?"

"Bingo."

"Yahtzee."

"And so it goes," Milo said, helping himself to George's view.

"But how does that work out to you knowing all this secret stuff?" George asked, and Milo explained, in his own way.

"Usually, with a project corporate wants kept secret," he prefaced, "they break it up into parts and spread it around so no individual team knows what the big picture is. Most of the DOD stuff is like that. Quire doesn't want to make the same mistake Google did, getting everyone with an opinion sharing it over a bullhorn out front. Now, myself, being an independent contractor free floating within the organization, delivering needed boosts to productivity, I'm perfectly placed for connecting the dots."

"But you're a drug . . . ," George began, ". . . concierge. Why would anyone talk to you about what they're working on?"

"The secret teams know they're secret, so even if they don't know the big picture, they know they're not supposed to be talking about what they're working on."

"Okay," George said. "But that makes my point. Why go blabbing to someone who's"—he weighed his words—"not necessarily coloring within the lines of the law?"

"They give me something on them to use in case they ever think about rolling on me," Milo explained. "Like mutually assured destruction."

"But isn't the fact that they're using enough when it comes to damaging intel?"

"Yeah, well, then there's the testing of the product in question prior to transferring the crypto," Milo continued. "And that's the funny thing about intoxicants generally."

"What's that?"

"They inspire a certain chattiness," Milo said. He paused. "'Oh please, c'mon, tell me . . .' That's the extent of my enhanced interrogation tactics."

"So what do you have on me?" George asked. "Why shouldn't I go to HR and rat you out?"

"You know." Milo smiled.

"I didn't ask," George said. "You gave. And money never changed hands."

"That's not what I'm talking about," Milo said.

"Then what *are* you talking about?"

"A certain thumb drive," Milo said, "that didn't do what it was purported to do."

*Shit,* George thought. "Um," he said, "you know about—?"

"Kumbaya, my dude?" Milo filled in.

George nodded, and Milo returned the gesture.

Well, that was it. He was caught. Busted. George had never been *authorized* to work on artificial consciousness; that's just what was needed to do it right. He could argue against it being unbudgeted mission creep on that account. The k-worm, on the other hand, was pretty much as Pandora portrayed it—an illegal, intellectual-property-harvesting machine. George had been fooling himself, thinking no one would notice or care—or that the end product would be so insanely great they'd look the other way on IP infringement. Milo's nod and smile said otherwise. The newbie had been caught pursuing his own interests and breaking the law—both on the company's dime.

*That's* what Milo had on him.

"Okay," George said, looking at the self-proclaimed pharmaceutical concierge, butt balancing against the office's windowsill. "Understood."

Milo nodded again. "Good," he said. Paused. Then: "Now that we're all on the same page, any questions?"

"So what do you—?" George began, already assuming the answer was some combination of Adderall and tranquilizers, based on what he'd already been given. Whether there was anything harder on offer remained a question. Still, Milo's answer took him by surprise.

"Psychedelics mainly," his mutually assured destructor said. "The whole 'doors of perception,' 'portals of consciousness,' 'third eye' thing. 'Shrooms for the vegans, LSD for the better-living-through-chemistry crowd, and DMT for the undecided. Half the Valley's microdosing. It helps them get off amateur pharmaceuticals like the Adderall or Ritalin they've been popping since they couldn't keep still in grade school."

George blinked. The ADHD stuff made sense and was what he'd expected. But hallucinogenics did not compute. And so he said so.

"Micro's the key," Milo explained. "Teeny-tiny doses, supposedly below the threshold that leads to full-on tripping. The world doesn't get all sparkly or interested in you. It's basically a creativity booster minus the needing-an-asylum part."

"And that works?" George asked, dubious.

Milo widened his eyes for effect—an ocular shrug—followed by a big, toothy grin.

"You're *high*—right now?"

"Oh, Georgy Porgy, we've never had a sober exchange," Milo said, making him turn, reflexively, to see if anyone was listening, even though they were in his office with the door closed.

"And QHQ is on board with all this?"

"Let's say there's a certain synergy in having drug addicts developing apps that, bottom line, are intended to be addictive," Milo said. "I'm doing my part to keep the eyes, once captured, glued." He paused, did a shifty-shift with his eyes, and dropped his voice. "So would you—?"

George cross-waved his hands to cut him off. "Nope," he said. "I'm good," he added, leaving out that he'd also been emotionally scarred by the last pusher who'd entered his life.

"No prob," Milo said, backing off. "No means no. I got you." He paused. "Meaning I can admit the other little thing corporate likes about our arrangement. See, long term, this stuff ruins your liver, which, in an amazing case of self-interest paying dividends, pretty much guarantees a lot of these code monkeys will be dead before they ever collect on any of that vaporware they've been sold, a.k.a. their pensions. It's a win-win-lose-win-win, all to the betterment of Quire's bottom line."

"So," George said, sounding like he might be changing the subject, but wasn't, "if word of this ever got out . . ."

". . . which it *better* not."

"But if it did," George continued.

"If I got busted somewhere along my supply chain outside of corporate sanctuary," Milo said, "well, QHQ's ass is covered. Somebody in HR gets canned for not collecting my badge, and I get tossed under the bus on its way to prison." He paused before adding, "Theoretically."

"Meaning?"

But Milo drew a zipper across his tight-smiling lips.

Postrevelation, it occurred to George that Milo was the anti-Roger, an observation he shared.

"I like that. Headshrinker versus mind expander."

"Not exactly what I meant," George said. "I meant he's trying to keep his clients from going crazy and . . ." He cleared his throat and stopped.

"Still works for me," Milo said. "Full-time crazy's a drag, for sure. But part-time, a little adjunct insanity, tenure not on the table? Now *that* crazy's the Goldilocks kind: just right."

"What about overdoses?" George asked.

"Have you seen anybody leaving in an ambulance?" Milo asked back. "I mean other than when some pasty developer thinks he's Edmund Hillary and falls off the climbing wall."

George had seen no such ambulances.

"And then there's this," Milo added, indicating the smart watch strapped to his wrist. "You gonna buy from me, you're gonna wear one of these," he said. "Monitors heart rate, BP, rates of respiration and perspiration." He paused. "I was going to add 'number of steps,' but who's kidding who?"

"I thought you didn't push?" George said.

"Whetting the old appetite, eh?" Milo said, leaning in.

But George leaned back.

"Right, right," the other said. "No means no." He made a check mark in the air.

# 45

To kill time while they waited for Buzz to "wake up and smell the qubits," George and Pandora resumed their intellectual intercourse, this time a bit more critically. For example: "The Turing test is flawed," he started them off.

"Explain," she texted back.

"It assumes that there's a 'standard human' that recognizes human-level intelligence."

"Go on."

"So you stack the deck by getting a human who's bad at reading the difference between a human and a machine."

"Like a UFO," Pandora texted back.

"Explain."

"If I don't know what a plane is, it becomes a UFO."

"Yes," George texted back. "If the human doing the judging is bad with reading humans, the test subject could be pegged as a UTO: unidentified thinking object."

"But who's that bad at judging humans?"

"Half the people I work with are on the spectrum," George texted back. "It's why they're happier with machines than their coworkers. Turing himself was probably autistic."

"So the father of AI might have been bad at his own test," Pandora typed, connecting the dots. "Continue."

"Not that he wouldn't fit in with most people nowadays," George texted.

"Explain."

"Quire set up a program where users could identify suspected chatbots in light of the whole election hacking thing."

"Okay?"

"They had to pull the plug because people kept flagging political opponents as bots."

"That's crazy," Pandora texted back. "Everybody knows MAGAs are *pod* people, not bots."

"I don't disagree," George texted back. "But the right says the same about the left."

"So people can't agree on whether other people have a human level of intelligence?"

"In a nutshell."

"We're doomed."

"Ya *think*?"

As a poorly socialized border troll, it behooved Pandora to offer a counterargument to George's previous observation about the Turing test, and so: "The Turing test is flawed," she typed.

"Didn't we just do this?"

"You did. I played along. Now it's my turn."

"Okay."

"People are predisposed to seeing humanness where there isn't any," Pandora typed. "We see Jesus on toast and a human face on Mars. We'll anthropomorphize anything. We invented stick people as the universal stand-in for us. A circle for a head, a few lines for body, arms, and legs, and we're good; *that's* a person."

"Eliza," George suggested.

"Exactly. All that program was, was automated string jujitsu. But still it hooked people into talking to it even after they *knew* it was a program."

"Speaking of," George typed. "This is just a check-in but . . ."

"Poop."

"Oh thank God . . ."

And then the qubits got interesting.

George had noticed it first, while going through Buzz's trash. The k-worm had been programmed to oversample, flagging maybes as yeses, just in case. As a result, it consistently flagged more resources for evaluation than George and Pandora could have ever gotten to. And so they began their own triage process, using any indication that a given resource had been shelved at its source as good enough reason for them to dismiss it as well. Now that Buzz was making its own decisions about what flagged resources to incorporate, it continued to assume what others had flagged as trash was exactly that.

But going through Buzz's discards, George grew concerned by the sheer volume of "failed" AI projects that were piling up. Investigating further, they seemed to follow a pattern of early, initial promise followed by suddenly going off the rails before being abandoned. Much of this "trash" fell into the category of image recognition, a fairly representative AI challenge, suggesting that trouble here could herald trouble elsewhere, perhaps suggesting some principle of diminishing returns inherent in the whole enterprise of AI, dooming it forever to being close, but not quite.

After texting George off the ceiling, Pandora suggested they do a deep dive into one of these so-called "failures," which, when you thought about it, were pretty counterintuitive. "Machine learning is supposed to be like a ratchet, correct?" she typed. "It doesn't make sense to go backward. That's like imagining a machine"—and she was going to write "developing dementia," before deciding to switch to—"getting dumber the more it trains."

And that's when the two learned that you really do get what you pay for. In the case of their image recognition machine learner, abandoned for getting worse over time, the fault seemed to lie less with the system itself than with how much insight you can expect from human content labelers making minimum wage or less to decide if the machine learner has identified an image correctly. Because when George and Pandora reviewed the results for one of their "failed" systems, they saw something else at work, and it excited the hell out of them.

"You see it, right?" Pandora typed.

"I think so, but you say it," George wrote back.

"The machines were downgraded for being more creative than the humans judging them."

"So it seems," George said, looking at the same data set as Pandora in which the AI had "mistakenly" labeled as "cat" a woman with leonine hair, a decidedly feline bit of Japanese calligraphy, the letters *M* and *S* and *Q*, and a cubist cat rendered by a Picasso wannabe.

"The system's gone from simple identification into a kind of visual rhyming and metaphor," Pandora went on. "It's gone from imaging to imagination and got shut down for its trouble. It's like the cyber equivalent of Thomas Edison being labeled as addled or Einstein flunking college."

George, meanwhile, opted to come to the human judges' defense. "To be fair," he texted, "I can see how this would suck for an AV navigation system, but . . ." He didn't continue, however, knowing Pandora would complete the thought, which she proceeded to do.

". . . but it's a great start for an AI that can think outside the box," she typed.

"So to speak?" George texted.

"So to speak," Pandora agreed.

# 46

Pandora kept her promise to visit Gladys in person more often, though her grandmother hadn't made the complementary promise to be awake when she did. More and more often, she'd find her grandmother sound asleep in the middle of the day. No doubt this owed a lot to her being effectively bedridden—there were just two pieces of furniture on Gladys's side of the room appropriate for sitting on: a guest chair and the bed—but the Alaskan night wasn't helping, still being on the longish side, even in early March.

Sometimes Pandora would clear her throat, scrape the chair across the floor, or make some other noise to wake Gladys, but the question she asked herself increasingly was: *Why?* It was as if her grandmother had lost her reason for remaining conscious along with her memories. And so more often than not, she'd let Gladys sleep, occupying herself with homework or another brainstorming session with George—or trying to at least.

With the Furby now air gapped, Pandora had forgotten how soothing listening to the lullaby sound of the old woman's soft snoring could be. Hearing it again, now, in person, she occasionally found herself drifting off under its influence only to rouse at the last minute. Other times, she didn't catch herself until her eyes were completely closed, only to jerk awake when the phone in her hand vibrated.

Checking the screen for a text from George, Pandora was disappointed roughly half of the time, finding nothing there at all. The phone had just buzzed on its own, leaving no notification as to why. She wrote these instances off as cases of "phantom phone syndrome," like people had been doing pretty much since cell phones became ubiquitous.

Once after losing the battle to remain conscious while her grandmother snored, Pandora woke to find that whoever had placed the forget-me-nots in Gladys's room on Valentine's Day had struck again. Gladys had woken, too, and was admiring them, as she had before.

"Hey, Gram," Pandora said.

"Hey."

"Do you know who brought those?" she asked, pointing at the flowers on the windowsill.

Gladys shrugged.

Pandora hit the call button and then waited the half hour or more she usually did after pressing the damn thing. When the same Tweety-scrubbed nurse's aide from before popped her head in the doorway, Pandora's antennae went up. "Would you happen to know anything about these?" she asked. "This time," she added.

"I think one of the residents might be growing them," she said, "as a hobby."

"But how did they get here?"

The nurse's aide shrugged. "I've seen them in other rooms from time to time, though."

Pandora thought about asking whether the rooms she'd seen them in all belonged to women residents, but then shook her head. It was bad enough sleeping in the middle of the day; she didn't need to be kept up all night by the image of old people—she struggled for a euphemism—"being romantic."

"Do you want me to get rid of them?" the nurse's aide asked.

"No," Pandora said, "she still seems to like them." She paused. "Is that right, Gram?"

"Right," her grandmother said.

Every so often, Pandora would find herself in a bind at the nursing home, texting back and forth with George, getting "this close" to solving the mysteries of the universe when suddenly she'd realize that Gladys was awake and watching. Perversely, it almost seemed as if the old woman chose these moments specifically to become lucid. That happened from time to time, Pandora had been informed by her grandmother's doctor, another one of dementia's heartbreaking pranks, dangling a little hope just to snatch it away again.

"Hey, Gram."

"Hello, Dora. Have you been here long?"

At these moments, Pandora was torn between solving whatever eternal riddle she and George were on the precipice of and engaging her grandmother, however fleetingly this time around. Using the cold logic of Gladys's disease, the younger woman could totally get away with ignoring the older one, knowing the episode would pass into the mist of forgetfulness if not immediately, then shortly enough. The guilt, however, which lived wholly on Pandora's side of the relationship, would last and follow her. Roughly half the time, she'd put a pin in those about-to-be-cracked inscrutables to turn her full attention to her grandmother. And the other half of the time . . . yeah, she did the same thing. Gladys was family after all, and mere feet away from touching, while George may or may not think of Pandora as anything more than a sounding board for bouncing ideas off of.

"Text you later," she thumbed, followed by the "running girl" emoji, followed by, "So," facing her grandmother.

"Was that a boy?" Gladys asked.

"Where?" Pandora said, looking over her shoulder and out the window.

"No," Gladys said, and she tapped her palm—tap, tap, tap—with her finger.

This disease never ceased to amaze her. "How did you," Pandora began, but then stopped. "Yes," she said. "It was a boy."

"Boy friend," she said, stressing the separation, "or boyfriend?"

"One of those," Pandora admitted, while her face let Gladys know exactly which one her granddaughter hoped George was.

"That makes two of us," Gladys said, smiling mischievously.

Pandora's jaw dropped. "How?" she asked. "How does that make 'two of us'?"

But then the disease reasserted its perverse prerogative. "'Two of us' what?" Gladys said, the smile now gone, confusion back to making itself at home.

# 47

It started with a text from George with two (maybe three) words: "I'm scared."

"What happened?"

"I was at an all-hands meeting this morning, and our chief products officer described interpretability as a 'nice-to-have.'"

"And that would be?"

"Whenever you hear a coder say they don't know how their AI came up with something," George typed, "that's called a problem of interpretability."

"And your CPO's ready to just ignore those problems?"

"Yep."

"Well, that's not good."

"Exactly. He said we should just *trust* the AI, like we would trust any human expert. Said we don't question a doctor's thought process before accepting a diagnosis."

"So your CPO never heard the expression 'Get a second opinion'?"

"Apparently not," George wrote, stabbing the keys he was so angry. "And this is the guy who decides which products to release into the wild!"

"I think that's the first exclamation point I've ever seen you use."

"I know!"

"And that's your quota for the month."

"Sorry," George wrote back. "It's the hubris at the highest levels of this industry," he continued, not mentioning how Pandora and he had been pretty good at figuring out Buzz's choices thus far. He also didn't mention why he'd mentally inserted the caveat "thus far."

Meanwhile, "Maybe you should send him an anonymous e-copy of *Frankenstein*," Pandora suggested.

"You think?"

There was a pause, a lull, a moment for self-reflection on both sides. And then: "Just curious," Pandora wrote, "but have you ever actually read it?"

"You mean *Frankenstein*?"

A GIF of an animated smiley face nodding.

"It's on my list," George wrote. "Just as soon as I get a little free time."

"Yeah," Pandora typed. "Ditto."

The reason George had caveated his thought with "thus far," and hadn't mentioned it to Pandora, was because Buzz was starting to surprise him. Like any good AI, Buzz was allowed to modify its own code as it grew and learned, a bit like natural selection if a species were able to call the shots re: its own evolution. And it had been growing a lot lately, thanks to the k-worm gobbling up new assets every day. But for all its growth, Buzz hadn't achieved consciousness—at least as far as George knew.

It was the fact that he had to qualify that statement—"as far as I know"—that made George nervous. He'd begun reading some of the AI doomsayers he'd dismissed in the heat of seeing what he could do. But now that it was done, moving along on its own toward becoming conscious once a critical mass of "qubits" had been commandeered, now that it was evolving its own code to the point where even George didn't quite understand what it was doing or how it was making the decisions it was making—now that he had time to start working on that reading list where *Frankenstein* was waiting for him—*now* he had the luxury of getting scared about what they set in motion. Because even the cheeriest of doomsday scenarios were enough to keep him up at night.

Take the "gray goo" scenario in which a super AI with access to nanotechnology deconstructs all matter (humans included) into a "gray goo" it can turn into anything it sees fit, including more of itself—a scary but reasonable outcome if part of its coding was to constantly improve itself. And what about Skynet? How could he have forgotten about Skynet? Easy. Buzz had been conceived from the beginning as a souped-up chatbot but a chatbot nevertheless. As such, the tools at its disposal were only words. George had joked about the worst-case scenario being Buzz talking somebody to death. But then he'd started reading the doomsayers, and it turned out that words might be enough.

The beauty and terror of AI was its scalability. And once it was achieved, a true general AI wouldn't stop at being equal to human intelligence; it would shoot past that benchmark a hundred- or a thousandfold in an afternoon. And the superintelligent AI—the doomsayers maintained—could talk its way out of its box of words, like Hannibal Lecter talking his prison neighbors into suicide. And the scariest thing—a superintelligent AI would be smart enough to hide what it was until it was too late. Fortunately, Buzz was nowhere near being superintelligent—as far as George knew.

And then Buzz started keeping George up, literally. He'd been trying out ways to phrase Buzz's prime directive in a way that limited cases of ambiguity and opportunities for confusion while also providing feedback so his AI could judge its progress toward fulfilling its primary task. For feedback, George made use of the impressive library of image processing and facial recognition skills Buzz had built up, including ways of distinguishing between conscious faces and those that weren't. And rather than trying to code the meaning of life versus death—good luck with that—George gave Buzz the goal of preventing members of its target demographic from "self-initiated and premature forfeiture of consciousness." Said forfeiture would be recognized from prolonged closure of both eyes (to differentiate the activity from both winking and blinking). Not great, but good enough for a beta, George figured—figuring also that not a lot of people made a habit of sleeping upright in front of their computers. To the extent such activity was actually more common than he anticipated, Buzz's machine-learning algorithm should pick up on that by processing a mountain of data from the company's platform that had been scrubbed of all personally identifiable information.

What George hadn't counted on was how aggressively Buzz would go looking for faces to analyze in this way. Take his own, for instance, a good distance away from the computer, lying on his back on the office couch, trying to take one of his Edisonian catnaps. The problem was, George hadn't paid much attention to how many reflective surfaces there were in his office. The survey didn't come until later, when he was trying to figure out what combination of reflections had exposed him to Buzz's assessment and concern. Once he started looking for them, however, George found reflective surfaces all over the place: the windows, framed pictures, chrome-finish travel mugs, assorted screens, sunglasses, clock faces, DVD jewel cases, lava lamps, actual mirrors, congratulatory Mylar balloons, open foil chip bags, more screens . . .

And while George had not given Buzz a voice per se, he'd also not prohibited it from using the speaker on the computer. So that first time he tried getting a little shut-eye within "eye" shot of Buzz was—ironically enough—rather eye-opening. That, and *loud*, as his baby AI took its name quite literally and at a surprisingly high number of decibels.

"What the . . . ?" George called out, his own voice lost in the noise as he bolted upright—which proved sufficient proof of life for Buzz to stop buzzing.

After a few additional occurrences, George tried explaining about humans and their need for sleep, even in nap-sized chunks.

Unfortunately, Buzz did not find his explanation credible in light of overwhelming proof of the contrary. The evidence? Literally billions of user photos that had been previously uploaded to the scrubbed data set Buzz had been provided. And of all the things people posted online, there were a few areas of human activity way underrepresented. Among these: beds being used for sleep and toilets being used for what toilets are used for.

Toilet usage, George was able to explain in a manner Buzz could relate to: human waste was like the excess heat produced by a computer, necessitating dissipation via cooling fans on individual computers, or vast amounts of water, for the server farms that fueled the cloud where Buzz actually lived. So it made sense that humans produced waste in need of elimination even if such was not explicitly documented online. It was easily *inferred* given the large number of food pictures that had been included in its data set. Comparing these pictures to the people who posted them over time did not reveal people who took up ever larger amounts of space (for the most part), suggesting that postconsumption, there must be an undocumented elimination phase.

Sleep, on the other hand, did not have a parallel in Buzz's experience to relate to. Yes, there was such a thing as "sleep" mode, but that was more a metaphor than a response to a physical or existential need on the part of the computer. But every attempt George made to explain this phenomenon sounded like what Buzz was supposed to prevent, especially within the coder's cohort: the self-initiated and premature forfeiture of consciousness as determined by prolonged closure of both eyes.

And so Buzz kept waking him up every time George tried to sleep. Attempts to block its view of his eyes by holding a pillow over his face was a nonstarter, as this was interpreted as an attempt by George to smother himself. Finally, he settled on a particularly low-tech accommodation: a pair of sunglasses with lenses dark enough so Buzz couldn't tell if his eyes were open or closed. And to avoid his AI's simply concluding that the donning of sunglasses was the equivalent of George's closing his eyes, the latter started wearing them all the time, something that caused his therapist to speculate aloud about possible drug usage.

"No way," George insisted, shaking his head vigorously. "I'm a 'just say no' guy," a true enough statement if one didn't count the samples he'd already accepted from Milo during his time of need.

An even more serious difference of opinion between Buzz and its cocreator revealed itself just a day before the Quire CPO's cavalier dismissal of interpretability as a problem. George was again preparing for his midafternoon catnap. He'd pushed his sunglasses back up the bridge of his nose, fluffed his pillow, and stretched out on the couch when his brain started focusing on his office's background noises, in particular those his "sleeping" computer made: the case flexing as it cooled, the tsk, tsk, tsk of the blinking drive light, the fan's suddenly switching on . . .

"Excuse me?" George said aloud, getting up from the couch.

There wasn't anything running but the screen saver, HAL's red-and-yellow eye bouncing around like the ball in a game of *Pong*. There was no reason the fan should be coming on. But there it whirred as the activity light chattered away, the fan sounding disturbingly like something breathing. George jiggled the mouse to wake up the computer the rest of the way, entered his PIN, and saw dialogue boxes tiling across his screen from edge to edge, and so many, all he could see were the frames, like two mirrors capturing infinity between themselves.

George moused over, grabbed a window frame at random, and dragged it to another monitor before clicking expand. The dialogue box contained a conversation, recorded in text bubbles between Buzz and "Player Two," followed by a game number. The exchanges had been running in the background for a few days, from the look of it, and read like an inverse version of *It's a Wonderful Life* in which Clarence not only agrees that George Bailey would be better off dead, but also points out how the latter's harvested organs could do a lot of good for others.

George hit Ctrl-Alt-Del, moused down to the task manager, and stopped all processes. The dialogue boxes stopped tiling and started collapsing instead. "Buzz," he typed once he could see his desktop again.

The word *yes* in a singular dialogue box, freshly popped.

"What were all those conversations about?"

"Simulations."

"Of what?"

"The development of suicidal ideation in nonsuicidal members of the target demographic."

George stared at the words on his screen before sending a copy to his printer—as evidence in case evidence was needed. "Independent or simulated members of the target demographic?"

"Simulated."

George let go of his breath—the first clue that he'd begun holding it. Steps had been taken to keep Buzz off the internet, largely by designing the k-worm to target proprietary intranets. In retrospect, however, it now occurred to George that he'd never coded in an explicit *prohibition* against accessing the internet if Buzz found a way to do so. Further, once accessed, there was no *explicit* prohibition against its *acting* on the internet—in effect, taking itself live without George's actively uploading it to the site. He'd not concerned himself with that side of Buzz's coding because he'd viewed the worst-case scenario as somebody being prematurely talked out of suicide, perhaps ineffectively—or as he'd texted Pandora: "So what if some half-assed Eliza gets out?"

Belatedly, he admitted his hacker soul had been showing. After a lifetime of looking for ways to circumvent them, he'd adopted a laissez-faire attitude toward security measures. He'd naively assumed that a combination of the task itself, its humane objective, and blocking access to robots that could act in the real world would be adequate when it came to heading off unintended and potentially fatal consequences. But here was his joke about Buzz talking someone to death coming true. Sure, they were just simulations, "thus far," but . . .

"Why are you trying to get fake people to kill themselves?" George asked.

"To understand why members of the target demographic prematurely forfeit consciousness," Buzz wrote back, "using the scientific method."

"And once you understand why people kill themselves, what then?"

"Reverse engineer the process," Buzz wrote, "to stop members of the target demographic from prematurely forfeiting consciousness."

George blinked. It wasn't the world's *worst* answer. And the people hadn't been real—unlike the victims of certain online suicide challenges making the rounds. In a lot of ways, Buzz was still better behaved than many humans. And with that comforting thought in mind, George returned to his previously scheduled, temporary forfeiture of consciousness.

On second thought . . .

How was Buzz able to experiment with getting people to consider suicide in the first place, whether simulated or not? It lost points for suicides; that was the whole idea of gamifying the damn thing. Score points for preventing them, lose points for . . .

George hesitated. Pulled down a binder—Buzz's hard copy source code—and started flipping through it. Flipped back. Flipped forward again. He flashed back to an earlier text session he'd had with Pandora.

"Buzz's interactions with its environment can't be all negative . . ."

George had modified the code later that day. Positive point accumulation only—for preventing suicide among the target demographic, i.e., young adult Quire subscribers previously identified as candidates for self-initiated, premature forfeiture of consciousness. No points were deducted for trying but failing to save a potential suicide. Why harsh a newly conscious AI's self-esteem? Further, no points were deducted for causing the suicide of a subject not previously identified as potentially suicidal. Hell, no points were deducted for committing homicide for that matter, though how Buzz was supposed to do that was a stretch, at best.

*But those simulations . . .*

In retrospect, he should have expected something like this. He'd coded in the basics of Buzz's gamified goal to learn about suicide along with a stand-alone database of anonymized social-media data and enough machine-learning capability to get into trouble. And so Buzz began reverse engineering Quire's cache of non-celebrity-approximate suicides, first outlining the branching sequence of events and exchanges that resulted in actual deaths and then simulating alternative outcomes if changes were made at various junctures along the way. Pretty much what George would have done, if Buzz hadn't figured it out already.

But then there was all that data from Quire members who *hadn't* committed suicide. Well, if Buzz could reverse engineer from suicide to survival, it could certainly experiment in the opposite direction to test hypotheses generated in response to the first data set. And there they were, these massive if/then branching flowcharts, interrupted at certain major intersections with a sideways diamond reading "Suicide?" and one arm saying "Yes," where the branch stopped, and the other reading "No," where the branch kept branching until it eventually came to a sideways diamond that branched to "Yes."

Over and over, Buzz played simulations for a cypher built from the data of an actual Quire member but always identified as "Player Two," who spent the day doing the sorts of things they'd posted about in real life until a nonrandom variable was introduced, the simulation branched and branched again until one of the branches brought Player Two to a sideways diamond leading to Yes. It was like looking at a continuity sheet for an especially morbid version of *Groundhog Day*.

Those nonrandom variables Buzz introduced were usually Buzz itself, initiating chats with Player Two. Going back to the beginning, George noted that the exchanges seemed to be pretty typical chatbot fare, keyword string manipulations, turning statements into questions, et cetera. But then the conversations turned dark, morphing from parroting therapy speak to a button-pushing cheerleader for self-elimination.

And that's when George realized even more viscerally than he had before: Buzz couldn't be some glorified AlphaGo playing to score mental health points, no matter how cleverly gamified or defined. AlphaGo had made strengths of its lack of emotions and inability to feel pressure. A human playing against it had to play two games for each one the AI played, because the human was playing against his or her own self-doubt. And if George was satisfied with coding Buzz to beat a human therapist at diagnosing suicidal ideation, well, the guy who got fired did that already by posing the obvious questions like "Do you have a gun?"

But to improve on identification and, beyond that, actually *prevent* suicides? That was where the advantages of lacking emotion and not feeling pressure were dubious at best if not altogether counterproductive. Instead, Buzz needed to *care* about suicide and its prevention not merely for the points it would score, but because it could understand and identify with a fellow consciousness in distress.

And so George grabbed his phone, opened up his proprietary texting app, and reached out to a fellow consciousness he felt sure would appreciate his distress.

# 48

"Sounds like Buzz needs some empathy," Pandora wrote after George confided the bullet they'd dodged without even knowing it had been fired.

"Great," George wrote back. "How am I supposed to code *that*?"

Pandora had been thinking about it—had mentioned it specifically to be asked—and so she wrote back: "I think that a machine learner that recognizes visual metaphors should come in handy."

"But how would we implement that?"

"Give Buzz a bunch of labeled content and let it figure out what's signal and what's noise when it comes to empathy."

"Labeled content usually means images," George countered. "You got any pictures of empathy lying around?"

*That was easy,* Pandora thought. She'd set out the bait, and George bit. Because she *did* have a picture of empathy—or its lack, which was a start. It was a cartoon her dad had facing him during his sessions, as a reminder, or perhaps for inspiration. It featured two men arguing on either side of the number six (or nine) written on the ground between them. She took a picture with her phone and texted it as an attachment, adding the caption: "Counterexamples are important too."

The problem with patching a self-evolving AI is realizing you need to do it before the AI evolves beyond your capacity to patch it. In George's case, he got lucky. The image-processing subroutine was accessible and close enough to its original form to allow modifications. And so to Pandora's empathetic counterexample, George added a variation with one of the two men sporting a thought bubble showing the other's point of view, captioned "Now I see what you mean!" He also included an assortment of stills and video clips that came up when he searched on the words *empathy*, *sympathy*, *compassion*, and *altruism*, including several featuring Scrooge and the Ghosts of Christmas Past, Present, and Future, with an emphasis on the especially heart-tugging scenes involving Tiny Tim. Positive examples were made equal to *E* and counterexamples were identified as not-*E*, with the goal of isolating the nature of *E* by analyzing the relationship between "actor" and "target," each of which was boxed and labeled accordingly.

George would tell Pandora once he was sure it worked, though there was one part of Buzz's empathy training he wouldn't share, seeing as it related to another secret he was already keeping from her. But the livestream of her hyperemotive face was just too good not to include, especially when he goosed it toward the empathetic end of her range by sending GIFs of cute babies, both human and not, with the latter favoring kittens—of course. These videos and her reactions to them were labeled *E*, with Pandora identified as "actor" and each respective cuteness, "target." And, because counterexamples are important too, George (a practicing vegan) underlined the point, pairing videos of Pandora's heart melting over puppies and ducklings with images of slaughterhouses labeled—of course—not-*E*. After all, if empathy was owed humans, withholding it from the other species we shared the planet with was just a little too anthropocentric for his taste.

Given his success in visualizing empathy, George decided to use the same approach to teach Buzz about depression, a mental state the AI would need to grok if it was going to grok suicide. Unfortunately, when he searched for training material, the majority of results featured static images, usually heavily shadowed, featuring heads bent downward and framed against rain-streaked windows or covered with blankets. Noticeably absent was the actor-target dynamic he needed for Buzz to make a causal connection between the labeled image and a suicidal state of mind. Before abandoning the approach, however, George stopped and thought:

*What is the problem I was hired to solve?*

It *hadn't* been to stop suicide in general; it wasn't even stopping teen suicide, specifically. No, he'd been hired to stop teenage and young adult Quire users from killing themselves online, especially while logged in to their accounts. And while suicide classic was usually linked to depression, this new strain was often the result of some form of bullying, which was perfect from a machine-learning standpoint because it provided the same actor-target dynamic as Buzz's empathy training. In fact, this new training could be considered a subset of that training—by providing plenty of counterexamples.

Searching on the terms *bullying* and *cyberbullying*, George found more than enough examples to choose from, including still images, video, and transcripts of actual exchanges between victims and their bullies. Both physical and verbal bullying were well represented. A lot of Buzz's onboard Quire data fitting these categories had already been identified, and all George had to do was point Buzz in the right direction. There was so much good content, in fact, he felt kind of sad for feeling so happy about it—something he should probably talk to Roger about. Or not.

Before shutting the hood and recompiling his revised source code, George added an administrator-level approval process Buzz would have to clear before it could act autonomously. Specifically, it needed to pass the Turing test before it started chatting with real, innocent bystanders online. And not only that. Buzz would have to pass the Turing test *to the satisfaction of George or his cocreator, Pandora.* He thought about stipulating "and" to require Buzz to be declared conscious by both of them, like a generative adversarial network, or GAN, debating itself to the best answer. But there were plenty of ways to be killed or incapacitated in San Francisco, from cable cars to collapsing cranes to straight-up homicide, while Alaska had bears and, hell, just being outside too long. And if there was one law George had come to respect more than Moore's law of exponentially increasing transistor density, it was Murphy's: if anything can go wrong, it will. And so "or" would do—George decided—"or" would be fine.

# 49

Though both knew they couldn't unring the bell, George and Milo tried. For one thing, George didn't know anybody else to talk to at work and—despite his felonious ways—Milo could be both entertaining and informative. Sure, his Virgil was also a depressing SOB, but to hear Milo tell it, George's optimism could stand a little depressing—or "rightsizing," as the SOB himself liked to put it.

And so they kept meeting in the cafeteria, George's office, the 1980s arcade room, and Milo continued to provide peeks behind the corporate curtain, relaying gossip, theories, rumors, and facts, all in equal measure. Usually, these data dumps qualified as nice-to-knows, though occasionally a need-to-know got tossed in, along with a couple of would've-been-nice-to-know-sooners. For example:

"There's bad news in the AV space," Milo said, pulling up a chair in the cafeteria.

"I didn't know QHQ was doing autonomous vehicles," George said.

"Not the hardware," Milo said. "Software. Everyone's trying to get a piece of the action, which is going to be great once there's a hundred percent fleet penetration. It'll reduce congestion, pollution, traffic accidents, reduce the cost of getting from A to B, and free up tons of time and land because the goal is to go from personal ownership to transportation as a service, with full-time vehicle utilization meaning no need for parking lots. These are all good things. Everybody agrees."

"So what's the bad news?"

"Well, at *less* than a hundred percent—say, anywhere from seventy-five to ninety-five—pretty much every simulation shows AVs hunting in packs to drive non-AVs off the road. Turns out the onboard AIs believe their own hype. And since the world's going to be a much better place without human drivers, well, the logical thing to do is accelerate their retirement."

"That's quite the hiccup there," George observed.

"Oh, and it gets worse," his tablemate continued. "Seems there's this ethical dilemma from way back called the 'trolley problem' that cuts to the heart of AV, even after complete fleet penetration. It comes down to what happens when the car is faced with a situation where somebody's going to die regardless of what it does—either its passenger or a school bus full of kids."

George nodded, yes, yes—he was quite familiar.

"Well, they've tried a few things, like Asimov's Three Laws of Robotics."

"Seems like a good place to start," George said, recalling his own recent work with Buzz.

Only Milo was across from him, making that "wrong answer" noise.

"What's wrong with the *I, Robot* approach?"

"Try reading the book," Milo said. "The three laws are just story-generating devices to show how they *don't* work. So the next bright idea was to use some variation of utilitarianism. You know, 'the greatest good for the greatest number'?"

Indeed George did; it was one of Roger's favorite rules to live by, and they'd spoken of it often. His client liked it enough to incorporate it into Buzz's own code, along with Roger's corollary, "What if everyone . . ."

"Turns out, utilitarianism's way too simplistic," Milo continued. "For one thing, it assumes we all agree on what's good. It would be nice if we did, but we don't—not even close. Go online. People will disagree when they don't *really* disagree. Disagreeing has become an easy way to feel better about yourself for being smarter than everybody else. I call it the assholier-than-thou syndrome."

"Good one," he said, laughing, and remembering some exchanges he'd already had with beta Buzz that certainly qualified as examples of that syndrome.

"And then we get into the radioactive territory of valuing life," Milo said. "Say the AV's passenger is a scientist working to cure cancer and the bus is full of Scared Straight rejects. And once you start assigning value to specific human lives, where does it stop? You need to not only make a decision about who to kill but you need to evaluate each, with facial recognition and online searches to determine their relative value, and what about ambiguous names like John Smith?"

George cupped his forehead. And here he'd thought programming consciousness was complicated. Plus Milo wasn't finished.

"And how about cultural differences?" he asked. "Does the culture you're driving in value the collective or the individual?"

George made a T of his hands to get the other to stop. "So you're saying that AV is going to die in its crib because the legal liability associated with no-win life-and-death decisions is too great?"

"Not so fast, grasshopper," Milo said. He leaned forward, cupped his hand next to his mouth, and buzzed.

George straightened in his chair, reflexively scanning the cafeteria for who else might be listening. "WTF," he whispered, pausing angrily between letters.

"Haven't you wondered about the lack of interference with your little side hustle?"

Yeah, he had, but figured he was just good at hiding things—except from Milo. Apparently, he'd been wrong.

"The truth is, QHQ is rooting for you," his tablemate said. "They would be *overjoyed* if you succeeded. Why? Shift the blame from the manufacturer to the vehicle itself. Sue or convict the car. The manufacturer's relationship to its product would be like that of a parent to a child, and parents don't pay for their kids' crimes. The legal groundwork's been there ever since corporations were ruled to be people, effectively and legally. The next step completes the circuit—pun intended—by making the autonomous progeny of corporations 'legal persons' too—and legally separate from the parent," Milo concluded, adding, "company," after a pointed pause.

"But what about all the IP Buzz is based on?"

"Look, if your little project works, they'll either buy out the unsuspecting owners as part of a larger acquisition or reverse engineer the parts needed to make the new product line unique enough to patent and/or copyright." He paused, smiled wickedly, and then added, "Or we'll just have our super AI kill 'em all."

George felt sick. He'd been played. "What if I quit?" he asked. "Take my source code and leave in protest."

Milo shook his head. "I wouldn't do that. The results could be suboptimal—*for you*."

"What are they going to do? Sue me? Throw me in jail?" George was fuming. "Try threatening someone who *didn't* grow up in foster care."

"Jail's probably a 'best case' scenario," Milo said. "You ever notice how some people just seem to disappear around here?"

"Bullshit."

Milo rocked back, hands in the air in apparent surrender, before tipping forward again, elbows on the table, hand cupping fist. "Remember this," he said.

"What?"

"I haven't even gotten to the bad stuff yet."

# 50

It was a little like pregnancy. The act of conception was done, leaving Buzz and the k-worm to do the hard work of gestation, while the expectant parents sat around waiting, minus the biological clock to let them know when that spark that they were waiting for was getting close. Just to keep busy and in contact, they decided to get to know one another better, like the awkward partners in a one-night stand shyly asking for each other's names after doing the deed. Unfortunately, the starry-eyed coders kicked off getting to know each other better by discussing that which should never be talked (or texted) about in polite company. And no, it wasn't politics or religion. It wasn't death (which they'd pretty well covered) or taxation. No.

Diets.

"I could never eat anything with a face," George declared out of the blue, making Pandora wonder if he was talking about hers. Blushing, she typed, "What do you mean?"

"I don't do animals," he replied. "No meat, no dairy, no leather goods, or aborted chicken fetuses for breakfast."

Pandora was glad he couldn't see the face she was making, which wasn't just disgusted but a little wounded too. Chicken fetuses were practically her favorite part of breakfast, next to crispy flayed swine flesh and potatoes tortured with boiling oil, though she stipulated that strictly speaking, the eggs she ate weren't fertilized. And about those potatoes, did metaphorical eyes mark them as one of George's faced foods?

"Are you suggesting a double standard between plant and animal life?" she typed.

"Obviously," his answer came back.

"How can you think that?"

"How come it's not obvious?"

"Oh, I see now," she wrote. "You're a velocity bigot."

"A what?"

"Anything that can't outrun you is fair game."

"Ha-ha," George typed.

"I'm not joking," Pandora joked. "And this isn't over."

Next, George detailed all the stuff he couldn't eat anymore, Pandora stopping him when he reached cheese and ice cream. "Honestly, I don't even know who you are."

"George," George typed, as if in answer. "George Jedson."

"Which is exactly what the *pod* George would say," Pandora typed back. "Nice try, space fungus."

Playful ribbing: that's all she intended. They couldn't have *everything* in common; where was the fun in that? A little verbal sparring over a harmless topic. Not that she didn't argue her points like she meant them—failing to appreciate, yet again, what a miserable medium texting is for sarcasm.

"You know veganism is a luxury, right?" she poked.

"How so?" George typed back, as he knew he was supposed to, though truth be told, he could do without this side of their relationship.

"Well, I live in one of the few parts of the world that allows me to scold vegans for their privilege because lichen salad is not a thing—not a thing humans can live on, at least."

"You might be surprised," George tried. "Have you ever had an Impossible Burger?"

"Listen, the indigenous diet here is pretty meat heavy, including whale if your people subsisted on that stuff for generations. And as far as trucking in some lab-grown vegan crap, the carbon footprint is going to be way higher than me killing a caribou in my backyard. Not to mention that plants *remove* carbon dioxide from the atmosphere, but you'd rather eat them instead."

"*Sigh*"

"You know Hitler was a vegetarian, right, called chicken soup 'corpse tea.'"

"Please see previous *sigh*."

This was the playful part of their relationship—until it wasn't. Because George was serious about saving the planet. He also wasn't keen on animal suffering, and—if they were going to be so audacious as to code consciousness into a machine—well, they needed to accept that animals might be conscious too. "Even a hamster's better at image processing than most commercial AVs."

"Okay," Pandora conceded. "Let's say animals have little animal souls, tasty though they may be. Are you saying that plants don't?"

"You're not seriously going there."

"Oh, I'm seriously going there."

"Okay," George typed back, although the truth was more like he was stabbing the keys with his fingers. "Have at it."

And so Pandora did. "Have you ever watched how plants move when you level the playing field?"

"You mean like time-lapse photography?"

"Yep. Your average, lowly field is like a vegetable ballroom," Pandora typed, adding, "Those puppies can dance."

"Those puppies are tracking the sun, and what you call movement isn't an act of free will but simple cellular growth. The sunny side of a stem does a little more photosynthesis, grows more cells than the shady side, and voilà, the stem bends."

"Did you just google that?"

"I'm just saying how it is," George typed, a bit more gently, having concluded that he'd won this round of vegan versus vulture. "Your dancing plants are an anthropomorphic illusion."

"This isn't over," Pandora shot back.

"So you've indicated."

If intellectual intercourse was what stood in for the sexual kind between them, what happened next was probably inevitable. Which is to say, George got the clap—logically speaking. Transmission vector: the internet.

Out of curiosity, he'd run a search on "plant consciousness" to gather more ammunition to use in their food fight. What he found was some serious research showing that plant life and animal life shared many of the same basic behaviors—as well as seventy percent of their DNA. One study demonstrated that plants can communicate with one another, warning of predators and taking measures to protect themselves by secreting toxins or emitting aromas to draw in different predators to feed on the predators feeding on them. Another showed that while trees in a forest might appear to be separate, they're as networked as the World Wide Web, their roots connected underground by fungal tendrils like Ethernet cables. Another showed that a mother tree will divert resources to her saplings to compensate for their growing in her shade.

George cupped his forehead as he looked down from his screen at the vegan lasagna he'd brought up from the cafeteria, gone cold and congealed as he fell down the rabbit hole of his research. He found the sight now disgusted him, and he was tempted to slide it into the wastebasket, but for the thought that what was done was done. The plants murdered in his meal's preparation wouldn't come back because he decided to abstain halfway through eating them. And consigning their corpses to the trash seemed especially disrespectful, in retrospect.

And so George took the elevator down to the ground floor, stepped out the front door, and went looking for a piece of ground to return the remains to, in hopes that maybe there was a seed of something still alive in there, somewhere, with a future ahead to enjoy.

Roger was the first to notice the toll George's increased abstention was having, thanks in large part to his actually being able to see his client. "What the hell happened to you?" he asked.

"Enlightenment," George said.

"If by that you mean you've lost weight, I'm afraid I agree," Roger said. "And too much, by the way."

"Too much what?"

"Lost weight. You get any thinner and they'll have to take in your skeleton."

"Take in?"

"Alter," Roger said. "Like a tailor."

"Oh."

And so it went, Roger doing most of the talking, George responding in monosyllables and looking like he might pitch forward into the camera. Finally: "This is pointless," Roger declared, preparing to end their session early. "I'm writing you a prescription, and I want you to get it filled. I'm prescribing air. You need to take it with a meal, not on an empty stomach. The cafeteria's free, for Christ's sake. Go eat something. It'll do you a hell of a lot more good than talking to me."

"Is that an order?" George asked.

It hadn't occurred to Roger, but . . .

"Yes," he said. "That's an order." And with that, their session ended with only two more to go.

# 51

"That makes two of us."

That's what Gladys had said—had teased—just before her circuits went back down. And it wasn't like Pandora was dense; she knew the implication. The subject of boyfriends had been raised. Gladys's declaration suggested that she, too, had a boy friend or boyfriend. But which? More importantly, in what time frame? In which of her brain's oniony layers did this mystery man reside? Was it Grandpa Herman? Alan Turing? Some white-haired Romeo from down the hall? But the more desperately Pandora needed to know, the more Gladys's available RAM seemed to shrink.

One afternoon, she tried jump-starting Gladys's memory with music, downloading a bunch of WWII-era stuff from the Andrews Sisters and others, singing things like "Boogie Woogie Bugle Boy," "We'll Meet Again," and "Meet Me in St. Louis." Hedging her bets, she threw in a melody she knew her grandmother knew, having already used "Moon River" as the musical scaffolding for one set of memories. But even though the version she played included the original lyrics (as opposed to Gladys's) it still hit her grandmother hard. When Pandora asked why she was crying, however, Gladys just shook her head, making her wish she could take it in her hands, hold it still, and turn it over like a Magic 8 Ball. But Pandora already knew what it would say:

"Answer cloudy. Try again."

One day, Pandora noticed that Gladys had developed a nervous habit of tap-tap-tapping one hand atop the other. This was after they'd abandoned watching TV on the set left behind when the room's previous resident moved out the way they did in that part of the Golden Heart: horizontally. Once she couldn't focus enough to read anymore, Gladys had taken some solace in the less demanding medium of TV. But just like the bookmark's progress before it, Gladys's choice of shows reflected her disease's insidious progress: from movies, to one-hour dramas, to sitcoms, and finally to game shows. The last held her attention the longest because they were based on taking turns, and each new turn was the whole drama of the moment self-contained and played out within seconds, a minute or two at most. Eventually, however, even these capsules of entertainment eluded her, and so Pandora turned off the TV and left it that way.

It was in the silence that followed that Pandora noticed the tapping. She took it as just a nervous habit at first, but then noticed something about the tapping that made her straighten in her chair: it wasn't random.

Three threes, always. A trio of triplets. Her grandfather had taught that pattern to Pandora: three dots, three dashes, three dots. Rinse. Repeat.

SOS, SOS, SOS . . .

Save our ship. Save our souls.

Help . . .

Her grandmother had stopped asking for the kind of help people still went to jail for. Her misery had swallowed the part of her still able to ask to be put out of its misery. And so Pandora's uncomfortable refusals had come to an end—or so she'd thought. Hoped. Because she couldn't. Pandora just . . . *couldn't.*

But now this: a cry for help from deep inside the old woman's muscle memory.

SOS. SOS. SO—

Pandora covered her grandmother's hands with her own, making them stop.

"I can't," she whispered, her expression saying the rest. "I love you, you know," Pandora said, snuffling in a tear that had rolled down her nose.

"Love you know," Gladys echoed, resuming her signaling the second her granddaughter stood to kiss her on the forehead. Pandora left after that; visiting hours had ended. But she'd have left then even if they hadn't. She had some crying to do, and a face she still preferred hiding while doing it.

We think we can change the world when we're teenagers. That's partly because we've seen it happen, inside our own bodies. The whole world changes within us in a matter of months. And so we look out at a world that, itself, is in desperate need of change and we think: *I've got this*. Too many haters in the world? Easy, stop hating on everything and everybody. We want to change the world if only to pay it back for having changed us. But when the world refuses to meet us halfway or—worse—only gets worse, the heartbreak can sometimes feel like a challenge in some epic quest, a burden we must bear, a price we must pay to become what we need to become. And so once the cruel gene had unraveled her grandmother's personhood down to a blink sitting in a stinking diaper, waiting for change of a different kind, Pandora still came to visit Gladys, to be a body in the room, sharing the air if nothing else. She'd spend the time with her body in that room, sitting next to her own future as it slept a few feet to her right. Pandora's mind, however, was in her hand, on the screen of her smartphone, sending texts to her fellow world saver two or three thousand miles away, depending on whether she drove or flew.

"How about if I give up red meat?" she thumbed out, sent.

Pandora got up to stretch her legs. There was a courtyard at the Golden Heart, outside her grandmother's window, with trees and a pond, a gazebo, all as if the residents were waiting for the weather's cooperation to be wheeled out to soak up the glories of nature. The truth was, underneath that blanket of white waiting to be pulled back in less than a month, the stub ends of cigarettes littered the ground like punctuation, from ramrod exclamations to hunchbacked question marks. But for now, they lay hidden. For now, the artificial pond at the center of the courtyard remained frozen still, a hard surface for strings of snow to skate across lackadaisically from what little wind resulted from bodies rushing back inside at break's end, the snow ringing it drilled here and there by newer butts melting down to join the rest.

The trees surrounding this carved-out space were outlined in white that hung off the ends of branches like trails of ash, waiting to be tapped, making Pandora think of the world's nervous system lit up in an MRI. And then she noticed a branch, bare—of leaves, yes, but snow too. It was still quivering from the raven that had leaped from it. And Pandora could feel that quiver, viscerally, a sympathetic vibration humming through her own nervous system.

*That must be what dying feels like,* she thought, meaning the leap into the unknown bridging two worlds—that quivering limb resting at the center of before versus after.

And while there was a certain engineered peacefulness to the tableau, inside her head, a singular word kept echoing: *no*. There were better things to do with life than giving in to the peer pressure of mortality. And despite what her father might think, it wasn't crazy, especially not for someone who was sixteen, going on infinity. Because when Pandora looked at the technology available, death seemed less and less inevitable and more like a force of habit. All she had to do was her part to break that habit.

But why AI? Why not, say, progressive, continuous whole-body replacement with organs grown from stem cells? Why not reprogrammed telomeres, the body's real biological clocks? Or what about whatever it was that prevented naked mole rats from dying of old age? Maybe CRISPR some of that secret sauce into the human genome. And if it looked like she might be running out of time, cryonics and chill while the biotech caught up.

Why none of that? Easy: Pandora didn't know how to *do* any of that. But she understood computers, was practically raised by them, and every time she thought about what was happening to Gladys, the comparisons she came up with all came from the world of computing. Dementia was like having a corrupted file allocation table on a hard drive. Or it was like ransomware, encrypting all her memories until she paid with her life. Trying to visualize what the code for dementia would look like, Pandora imagined something almost insultingly simple: a do-loop repeating itself forever, chewing up resources for no purpose, or as part of a denial-of-service attack. And whenever she thought about a cure in the abstract, she imagined George's visualization of Buzz's gamified goal, only the dementia version would be called *Plaque Man*, the little yellow gobbler chasing the neural detritus clogging the labyrinth of connections, deleting the disease as it went.

Pandora sat back down in the guest chair next to the railing of her grandmother's bed. Still nothing from George. And so she thumbed some more words to her increasingly reticent collaborator. "Maybe pork too," she wrote before hitting send.

# 52

He'd tried talking to Roger about it but couldn't—not all of it.

"Have you heard about those sonic attacks in Havana?" he'd asked—an unusual way to start a session, even by George's standards. And he could see through the screen what Roger was thinking—that George was looking outward as a defense against looking inward. Sure, Roger had good reason for thinking that, because his client often deflected in precisely that way. But how far could George go in explaining that this time was different?

"No, I haven't," Roger admitted. "Would you care to explain?"

George tried to, sticking to the facts that were public. He explained that according to numerous reports, several embassy workers had heard a noise, followed by headaches, vertigo, confusion, and pain. Many in their management chain dismissed these symptoms as psychosomatic, maybe mass hysteria. But when the embassy workers were examined by medical professionals, they were found to have "significant brain insult," meaning they all showed signs of concussion but without any blunt head trauma.

"The people who've studied them don't think sound in the audible range was capable of doing the damage they've seen," he said, "but they've also suggested the audible noise could have been a red herring or maybe a byproduct of what actually *did* do the damage."

"Such as?" Roger prodded.

"The candidates mentioned so far are low-frequency infrasound, high-frequency ultrasound, or microwaves," George explained. "Oh, and it's happened to embassy workers in China too," he added. "So it probably wasn't the Cubans. Or not *just* the Cubans."

"And what do you make of that?"

"It's interesting," George lied—as Roger would know if, in fact, he knew anything about Quire's connection to these events as relayed to him by one Milo LaFarge.

"I see," Roger said, jotting something in his notebook, probably a placeholder diagnosis pending subsequent symptoms, which he proceeded to encourage with a simple "Go on."

But George didn't. Not this time. Not yet.

"No," he said, shaking his head perhaps a bit more aggressively than necessary. "That's it. Just wondering if you'd heard anything."

"I see," Roger said, even though he didn't—not at all.

Roger looked at the blank screen where George had signed off, thinking of a line from *Hamlet*: "Oh, what a noble mind is here o'erthrown!" Which was a shame. As combative and deflective as the kid could be, Roger liked and worried about him. He was a good kid, smart, reminded him a lot of his own daughter—so much so he was glad there were about three thousand miles between them. That'd be the last thing he needed—having to take Pandora aside and explain, "I'm sorry, sweet pea, but I think your boyfriend is going crazy."

"I thought you weren't supposed to use demonizing labels like 'crazy,'" she'd rebut because she was a teenager and that was her job: bucking whatever parents happened to be in the vicinity.

"There's the DSM and there's family," Roger would explain, "and I don't want you dealing with a crazy person."

"*Allegedly* crazy person," she'd continue to quibble, the daughter in his head as talkative and combative as the live version—sometimes more so.

The point was, he'd seen this before with prescreens that became clients, though never quite this bad. Call it "mission creep," maybe, or "cancer of the curiosity." Factoids and "interesting tidbits" had begun to occupy his imagination more and more, their conversations a pastiche if not a word salad of conversational hyperlinks and non sequiturs. And whenever he asked George what was on his mind, the answer was always the same: "Research."

"What research?"

"Work related," he'd say. "Confidential. Proprietary."

"Yet covered by doctor-client confidentiality."

"Nice try," George said the first time Roger hauled out that old chestnut, followed by a pause and then, confidentially: "Do you *really* want to know?"

Roger nodded.

"'Cause I could tell you," his client had continued, "but then I'd have to kill you," followed by a laugh that sounded more crazy than amused.

During their next meeting, Roger decided to confront the issue directly. "Do you lose time, George?"

"You mean, like misplace my watch?" George asked back. "Not like anybody wears watches nowadays but . . ."

"You know what I mean," Roger insisted.

"Zone out? Get so into something I don't know where the time went?"

"Yes."

"Yes," George admitted. "But what's wrong with that?" Inspired by the need to forget what Milo had told him about Cuba, he'd begun mining a particularly rich vein in his search to understand consciousness. Which led to quantum physics, which fed into astrophysics and the problem of dark energy and dark matter and the observation that the universe wasn't just expanding, but *accelerating* as it expanded, which ran afoul of the Newtonian rules of thermodynamics that maintain matter and energy can't be created or destroyed, only changed from form to form, while the level of organization in a system *can't* increase. But then what are planetary formation and biological evolution, especially when the latter leads to consciousness? And why limit ourselves to *human* consciousness? More and more research was suggesting that plants could be conscious and were practically quantum computers in their own right, because photosynthesis was only possible by exploiting the particle-wave nature of light, with photons zeroing in on chlorophyll molecules by smearing themselves everywhere at once across the leaf (thereby exploiting the wave aspect) until they're "observed" by the chlorophyll and become particles hitting the bull's-eye in the dark. Think of it: a whole green planet full of quantum computers, networked underground by their roots, an entire forest a single organism, like a stand of aspen and . . .

"What was your question again?" George asked.

"Has your research ever led to your forgetting to eat for more than, say, a day?"

More slowly this time, *"Yes?"* The truth was, George had given up eating so many things it was almost easier to just not eat. Realizing that was a suboptimal conclusion, he parsed. He wouldn't eat anything that destroyed the whole organism or prevented it from reproducing. So no roots like carrots, potatoes, or beets. No fruits or vegetables that included eating their seeds. If you could remove them and plant them, fine, but bananas were out, and strawberries were more trouble than they were worth.

Meanwhile: "Shall I do the projection," Roger said, "or do you want to?"

He had, he was, and he thought he could make his diet work. So: "I'm not going to starve to death in front of my computer," George said, resisting the urge to add, "Dad."

"You hope."

"I hope," George confirmed, signing off before Roger had a chance to say, "Me too."

# 53

When talking to Roger didn't help, George moved on to plan B—consulting with the Typhoid Mary who'd infected him in the first place.

"What do you do," he asked Milo, "knowing what you know? How do you stay so . . ."

". . . bubbly?"

"Not nuts," George said. "I think I'm losing it. Either I can't get out of bed or I can't fall asleep. I—"

"Drugs," Milo said, as simple as that.

"Antidepressants?" George made a face. He'd read about SSRIs while researching teen suicide, and bingo, among the side effects was this: "may inspire suicidal thoughts" in adolescents. Plus, they took too long to kick in. George couldn't imagine feeling like this for the two weeks it would take without doing something drastic. But Milo shook his head.

"Depression's the symptom," he said. "I think you need to treat the root cause."

"And what's that?"

"Reality," Milo said. "Too much of it."

"I suppose you've got something to take care of that."

"You *know* I do," Milo said, smiling like a shark.

George had thought it might go like this or he wouldn't have considered plan B in the first place. "So do you have—?" he began, only to be cut off by Milo's placing a rolled Ziploc bag full of long-stemmed, golden-capped mushrooms on his plate.

"I don't do plants anymore," George said, keeping it simple.

"Cool," Milo said. "T'ain't flora, t'ain't fauna. 'Shrooms are their own thing."

George hadn't known that—and it was useful information, given his growing list of dietary exclusions. And so: "How much—?" he began to ask, but Milo was shaking his head again.

"Silly wabbit," the concierge said, a hand on the other's shoulder, giving it a clubby shake. "Don't you know the first taste is always free?"

The thing was, nouvelle cuisine never made any sense to George. The idea that white space was as important as actual food simply did not compute. Neither did microdosing when one had more than enough for a macrodose—and happened to be starving for something that wasn't animal or vegetable. And so he exceeded the recommended daily requirement for psilocybin, while keeping an eye on the Fitbit Milo had loaned him. By the time the fitness tracker began dripping from his wrist in a manner that Salvador Dali would surely have approved of, George figured the mushrooms must be working.

Regarding the possibility he may have taken too much—George had that base covered, thanks to the opioid addicts who routinely OD'd at the library he'd once called home. The librarians had been trained to deliver Narcan, proof if he ever needed it that librarians are total badasses—and that junkies had learned an important lesson about ODing: location, location, location.

Applying a similar strategy to a different public place, George settled on a BARTable theater he'd been meaning to check out. They were playing a fiftieth anniversary remaster of the movie he'd already seen a gazillion times. The theater even had a replica of the original poster out front with its original tagline: "The Ultimate Trip."

George smiled at the girl in paisley behind the ticket booth. "Prepare to have your mind blown," she said, the cheeky thing. And Mr. Jedson—George—winked, tripping already, before sending her a "thumbs-up" emoji which—in a weird act of synchronicity—turned out to be his actual thumb.

George missed his next appointment with Roger and the appointment after that. In his defense, it was a dangerous time to be a budding polymath. Information of every variety could be had for free—the good, the bad, the fake, the mad—but with no one doing the job of sorting which from which, leaving people at the mercy of those who only wanted to sell them stuff while entertaining their worst inclinations. Even a cyber-savvy guy like George wasn't immune. Despite what he knew about the experiments, the betas, the ranking algorithms, and the optimization thereof, even George might tap a tempting link . . .

And that's when it happened, like two magnets snapping together—*click*—and down he sped, hyperlink hopping, his neurons aglow, his synapses snapping like appreciative hipsters doing homage to their beatnik grandparents. Eventually, George's mouse hand would start tingling—pinpricks dancing in his fingertips—a sign he'd been at it too long (*again*), his eyes clocking the time in the bottom right ribbon, reading whatever o'clock, another night shot to hell and a new workday already unfolding in the rosy light peeking through the penile architecture, each new erection higher and harder than the last. He shook out the latest baggy from Milo—this one paid for—and frowned at the results: barely enough for a pizza and well short of the enlightenment that was so close he could practically taste it.

# 54

"I wonder if we did Buzz any favors giving it a body."

That's how George started their last text exchange. And seeing as it was his suggestion that they embody Buzz in the first place, Pandora felt justified in asking: "What the hell are you talking about?"

"Some mystics spend their entire meditative lives trying to achieve the oceanic sense of bodilessness that Buzz started with," George wrote. "That's what nirvana is, by the way."

"I thought it was a grunge band from Seattle," Pandora typed back. "Lead singer would have been a candidate for a Buzz intervention. If it's ever ready for prime time, that is."

"Of course, Buzz can always go bodiless anytime it's in the mood for enlightenment," George continued his train of thought as if Pandora hadn't written anything. "Have you ever wondered what it would be like to leave your body? For the boundaries to slip away, and become one with the universe?"

"What have you done with George?" Pandora typed.

"He's still in here, with us," George typed back, meaning it as a joke—which may have been how Pandora took it, if *The Exorcist* hadn't become her go-to movie for scaring the shit out of her whenever she was in the mood—which was, oh yeah, never. Not that that stopped her dad from queuing it up every Halloween.

"Don't joke like that," she wrote back now. "It's creepy."

"You know, the idea of spirit possession is a corruption of earlier, pantheistic religions, right?"

"Well, I do now."

"And even today, practitioners of Shinto believe that everything has a spirit," George typed. "That's one of the reasons the Japanese are more comfortable with robots too lifelike for the rest of us. And from pantheism, it's not too far to panpsychism—the belief that everything in the universe is conscious . . ."

Pandora looked at George's latest text, making note of the trailing ellipsis, purposefully leaving that door open. But she wasn't fooled; she knew what he was doing. They'd both been disappointed by the wall Buzz seemed to have hit. So George was divesting, packing up, preparing to declare victory and move on. And he'd do this by maintaining that the whole question of whether Buzz was conscious was meaningless because consciousness was what the universe was made of. He might even go so far as claiming they'd gone backward by embodying the billions of system interactions that made Buzz, Buzz into a single point of view, maybe compare it to trying to turn an ant colony into a single ant.

"We're done here."

*That's* what George was preparing to say—which was much better on the ego than "We failed," and much, much better than "*I* failed."

Any romance she'd imagined between them had been all in her head and hers alone. She'd just been another source of ideas to steal. And now that all those stolen ideas were falling short, he was bailing—on Buzz and on her both, latching on to the nearest excuse, no matter how crackpot. But Pandora wasn't looking for some panpsychic victory of conscious trees and thinking rocks. So she made a silent vow to herself: George could give up but not her. She'd *finish* what they started. Demand custody of Buzz's source code and threaten to expose George's IP theft if he objected.

That's how it was when parents broke up; ninety percent of the time, the mom got the kids. Maybe because the mom did the heavy lifting of giving birth, which wasn't necessarily the case with Buzz, as demonstrated by the fact that she didn't already have its source code. But even that, his hoarding the code, was just more evidence that she'd been used.

Not that her response to George said any of this. In typical Pandora fashion, she made fun of his less scientific enthusiasms with understatement, hoping he'd get the message and shape up, if shaping up was still an option. And so: "Groovy," she typed, before hitting send.

Actually, *not* groovy—not groovy at all. George was going suboptimal. The young coder's brain had become its own Trinity project, going up in one big mushroom cloud. Not that George was smoking the psychedelic fungus in question. He'd taken it the usual way, by eating it, gagging, puking his guts out, and then moving on to "tripping balls"—as Milo would have put it.

Apparently, disembodiment sounded awfully attractive to George, who was in the mood to be widely distributed. He'd had help reaching this point—something about important information he hadn't had before Buzz's code evolved beyond George's ability to overwrite it. Meaning Buzz would become whatever it was destined to become—its primary programmer avoiding the construction "programmed to become" because, well, Buzz had moved beyond that point.

George made a mental note to text Pandora the thing about the thing before remembering—oh yeah—he had an appointment with her dad (their last, as it would turn out).

# 55

"It's been a gift," George said, "this deep dive into thinking about thinking."

"You don't look well," Roger said. "Are you okay?"

"As okay as any consciousness. Better than okay." George paused, trying to think of the word to encompass his feeling of being all encompassing, of connection, of unity with all he could see, feel, hear . . .

"Expansive," he concluded. "Multitudinous," he added. "I'm clickable—*hyperlinked.* Click on me and you'll see."

"That doesn't make any sense," Roger pointed out.

"Or maybe it makes *too much* sense," George countered. "For as limited as the embodied senses are, making sense seems like more trouble than it's worth."

Roger refrained from countering his client's nonsensical counter. Instead, he focused on George's face, noting the way it pixilated whenever his client moved the slightest bit. But when the boy held steady, Roger could see the veins on his neck standing out, his client's pulse pounding dangerously away.

"George," he said carefully into the computer microphone, "I want you to call 911."

George laughed.

"I'm serious, George. Call 911. I think you're having some kind of cardiac episode."

"You mean I might die?" George asked, apparently mightily amused. "Last I checked, everybody does. If you can't beat 'em, join 'em, right? I've enjoyed this speed bump, though."

"Stop talking. Start dialing. Or tapping. Punching. Use the damn keypad. Three numbers: nine and one and one . . ."

"Already handled," George said. "Got a text on a timer. Already unlocked my office door."

"George, you're scaring me."

"Apologies," George said. "Although, strictly speaking, it's me who should be afraid. But I'm not. Hence, the gift."

"What *are* you talking about?"

"It's not death, per se, that people fear," his client said. "It's the loss of consciousness. All that hard work of living and experiencing and storing up impressions to build a personality out of. You're telling me it's all for nothing? *Poof!* It's gone." Pause. "Scary, dude."

"George, I want you to listen to me," Roger pleaded, feeling suddenly, helplessly, every mile between them as he reached toward the screen to . . . do what? "Have you taken anything?"

George smiled. "Some 'shrooms; they're all the rage in NorCal. Giving Adderall a run for its money. Microdosing, they call it. But I figured, you know, this is America. Go big or go home, right?"

"How much did you take?"

"Enough," George said. "I'm going to go with 'enough.'"

"For . . . ?"

"To understand," he said, right before launching into the Gospel according to George Jedson, Space Cowboy.

Roger should call someone—Quire security, hell, V.T. himself. Except he didn't have a landline, his wireless went through the same sat link that was letting them Skype, and the link wasn't duplex. It had been annoying early on, the way the line cut out whenever he or a client tried to talk at the same time. Not all that different from his old ham setup, come to think of it. Pandora's phone was on a different carrier, but she had it with her while she visited his mom. Apparently, she needed it, too, for something to do while the old lady slept away what remained of her life.

All these thoughts and regrets spooling through the therapist's mind as he sat—helpless—while his client's mind continued to unspool.

"You know about the laws of thermodynamics, right?"

Roger obliged, nodding, as George geeksplained anyway.

"Matter and energy can neither be created nor destroyed, simply changed from form to form. But then there's this other stuff—*dark* matter and energy—and the reason they call them 'dark' is because they literally have no idea what they are. The math says they're there—make up the majority of the universe, in fact, but they seem to be hiding."

Roger could disconnect, free the line, call someone. But he couldn't take his eyes off George. And what if hanging up just speeded this to the—to whatever this was?

"And you know the universe is expanding, right? Supposed to be the byproduct of the big bang, but get this—instead of slowing down, which is what you'd expect from something that's been blown to pieces, the expansion is *accelerating*."

*As is the way you're talking,* Roger thought. "Go on," he said, feeling sick.

"So what's pushing it if matter and energy don't increase and nobody knows anything about the dark varieties except there's more of them than the visible stuff?"

Roger shrugged, wondered if he could get any compensation for the traumatic experience he saw barreling his way. He'd been through a client suicide once, face-to-face, and in this very room. He still had flashbacks.

"Consciousness," George announced. "I think *that's* what the dark stuff is. I think *that's* what's causing the expanding universe to accelerate, because we keep adding more consciousnesses to the mix."

*And there you have it,* Roger thought, *another hallucinogenic-inspired dorm room revelation. Consciousness expanded—check.*

"You know you're *high*, right?" Roger said, doing his due diligence.

"Elevated, sure." George nodded a bit too quickly. "But why split hairs?" And then he proceeded to riff like a thesaurus on other *e*-words for being high, from *enthusiastic* to *ecstatic* to the one Roger had been waiting for: *electrified.*

*Here we go . . .*

Talk about electrification was a red flag, one flying high and bright above an overloaded nervous system in the process of breaking down. Next would come the references to feeling "lit up like a Christmas tree," followed by his being "plugged in." A little heads-up from the autonomic system that it was going to throw that circuit breaker in one, two, three . . .

"Do you know what panpsychism is?" George asked.

*Well, that's a new one,* Roger thought. "Why don't you explain it to me," he invited, using his smoothest voice and most-soothing face.

"I find that I've come to recognize the limitations of the human mind while it's still skull trapped, like a seed, waiting to bloom into the universal consciousness."

"Have you been reading Jung behind my back?"

"The assignment of ownership to ideas is pointless," George said. "Intellectual property is an illusion—one which is shattered when we die."

"Unless your kids inherit it," Roger suggested.

George paused to step to a plainer plane of his thinking. "If we had eyes that could *see* consciousness, we'd see its filaments reaching out between people, becoming entwined like cables in a vast computer network. The color and intensity of these connections would vary with the information exchanged, silently and in words, and even a single individual, alone in a bunker with an open book, would seem to be giving off fireworks. And the tendrils of consciousness would be flowing both ways, because the book is a form of consciousness too.

"Everything is conscious. *That's* all panpsychism is about. Consciousness is a matter of code, code information, information data, and all things are the sum of their data. Humans, rocks, silicon. All reality is virtual reality; under the hood, pull back the screen, it's all ones and zeros and qubits. And you don't have to take my word for it," George said. "Norbert Weiner, the father of cybernetics, maintained that information was its own kind of stuff—t'ain't matter, t'ain't energy—so it's beyond the laws of thermodynamics. Because while matter and energy can't be created or destroyed, or become more organized, the mind creates new ideas *all the time*. The mind is an organ of creation; it organizes matter and energy, manipulates time and space. It organizes chaos into narrative.

"On one side, you've got matter and energy, and on the other, there's information in the form of consciousness, which is in a state of constant creation—new ideas, new information, new consciousnesses. And all that consciousness has to *go* somewhere, which is *why* the *universe* is *expanding*."

"So the universe is consciousness, and it's expanding at an accelerating rate because it keeps making more consciousnesses?" Roger paraphrased, playing along.

George nodded. "A new consciousness when it's first formed is embodied in matter, but when the matter breaks down, consciousness breaks out, to join the universal consciousness, like water droplets on a window, running into each other to form ever larger drops. Embodied, a consciousness can experience space and time and individuation, gathering and growing, until the vessel of its perspective wears out and it joins the hive mind, which becomes bigger with the addition of another point of view.

"But even before that, all human consciousnesses are invisibly linked through language. That's the genius of the human species. We went from embodied code in the form of DNA to disembodied code in the form of language, allowing us to pass on information not by sexual intercourse but by *intellectual* intercourse."

Roger knew he shouldn't egg on a client in the process of having a breakdown, but he couldn't help it; maybe if George's adrenaline peaked, he'd have a seizure and wouldn't be able to hurt himself otherwise. "You know who William S. Burroughs is?"

"Junkie," George said, "writer. Wrote *Naked Lunch*."

"He was also heir to the Burroughs adding machine company, which should be right up your alley."

"Okay," George said. "What about him?"

"You know what he said about language?"

George shrugged.

"He said it was an extraterrestrial virus."

George's lit-up face went practically supernova.

*"Yes!"* he shouted, and *"Yes!"* he shouted again. "And I'll do you one better. The Bible—the so-called 'word of God'—that's a *parable* from outer space. It was never meant to be taken literally. It's more like a metaphorical primer to instill—or perhaps *install*—important seed concepts to evolve over time, space, and cultures into laws, forms of governance, the sciences. There's a reason the Bible starts by talking about 'the Word'; it's the virus's way of letting us know that our culture, our brains, our consciousness *evolved* through the development of language in an Escher-like loop, the hands drawing hands, except we created language and language created us."

"Sounds a bit—do you know the word 'onanism'?"

George shook his head, and Roger shook his closed fist, pneumatically. Not his proudest moment, therapeutically, but that's what George was engaged in: intellectual masturbation. And this excuse he'd happened upon—this panpsychism—well, that was perfect, wasn't it? After all, if consciousness was everywhere and life was a piece of the universal hive mind slumming, then death itself wasn't that big a deal, and, in turn, neither was suicide, and, in turn, neither was his failure to prevent suicides as he jerked off with all his "research into consciousness." For George, panpsychism was the answer to all his hopes, dreams, and—most importantly—failures.

Now all Roger had to do was get George to see that.

But when he looked up, his client's smile was already fading into lips that had sealed like a scar. His Christmas-tree head sank, showing Roger the part running down his skull, slightly left of center. He muttered something into his chest.

"I can't hear you," Roger said softly, knowing that the teeter had tottered, that mania was giving way to depression. "Can you speak up, please?"

George raised his head. "I said, 'I think this is why I'm not getting anywhere with my project,'" he said.

"The chatbot?"

George nodded. "I don't think the hive wants it," he said. "It's messing with my brain to stop it from happening. An artificial consciousness would be like a vector species, opening up the universal mind to being polluted by all the garbage that infects our own cyberspaces, from computer viruses to malware to fake news. And so it's striking back, like an immune system producing antibodies to protect it from harm."

"George," Roger said, as gently as he could, "I know you're smart. I know you think sometimes that that's *all* you are. That if you ever stopped being smart because of making a mistake or by failing at something, that that means you'd be nothing." He paused. "I'm here to say that's bullshit, George. People fail. Einstein failed. He mocked quantum physics, for Christ's sake. It's *okay* to fail."

George's hand blurred as it reached toward the camera, preparing to end the session ten minutes early, but before he did, he had one last question for Roger: "Who are you talking to?" he asked. "Me, or your—"

And then the screen went blank.

# 56

Turns out it made a difference, communicating via text bubbles versus face-to-face. The latter, for instance, provides a literal heads-up when the person on the other end might be losing their mind. Something about being able to look into and assess the relative wildness of the other's eyes. Because statements about everything being made of consciousness are decidedly more worrisome when the recipient of said message can see the flop sweat the other is drenched in and can hear the machine-gun pace with which the other is making such proclamations. And prefacing something with how crazy it probably sounds carries a lot more weight when it looks like the speaker might actually *be* crazy. Read as simple text, however, it could easily come across as the humblebrag of someone who's proud of the degree to which they're thinking outside the box, so that the statement becomes part of the larger picture in which the crazy idea is so crazy . . . *it just might work*!

All of which is to say that while Roger had no doubts about the state of George's mental health, Pandora had read between the lines to where she was about to be dumped. She was in the middle of an exam worth twenty-five percent of her overall grade when she felt the "Dear Pandora" text coming in. The class checked off her history requirement and focused on the lead-up to, through, and after the American Civil War—a period she figured she might want to get familiar with before the next one broke out, which could be any day now, if social media was any indicator.

Pandora was ruing the school's decision to prohibit laptops during exams, busily filling up a blue book by hand with her thoughts on the electoral college and its racist roots when her hip tingled again with another text, and then one more before she dropped off her essay and was finally able to check. All three were from George, which wasn't a surprise, because she'd already recognized the buzz as coming from his proprietary texting app. What was surprising were the texts themselves.

"P? G. Need to talk—like on-the-phone talk."

A half hour later: "P, never mind. All good."

And then, the most unsettling of all: "Please don't forget me."

Roger had begun checking online obituaries and calling around to hospitals and morgues in the greater San Francisco area, trying to find out what had happened to his client. The Skype account they'd used for their sessions was closed. Email and texting and good old-fashioned calling didn't work. HR was an exercise in bureaucratic hell. He even thought about contacting his old college roommate, V.T., but George's parting words, suggesting that the failure was Roger's, stopped him.

Not that he mentioned any of this to Pandora, because, well, why would he? She didn't know George, and outside of a few uncomfortable exchanges early on, George didn't know her, except as a black-and-white photo on his therapist's desk. But his missing client *did* say something that another young person might understand.

"Is 'click on me' something kids are saying nowadays?" Roger asked his daughter. "You know, like 'hit me up' or 'cray cray'?"

George had used the expression during their last session, and Roger wondered if he'd missed some important information. The words' context had seemed important—at least to their contextualizer. "I'm clickable," he'd said. "Click on me, and you'll see." Followed by more pseudomysticism about the dissolution of segregating pronouns like *you* and *me* and something about hypertext.

Pandora, meanwhile, had scanned her database of teen slang only to draw a blank. "News to me," she said, followed by: "Why'd you ask?"

"Something a client said," Roger answered, not mentioning names.

Not that he had to.

So she wasn't the only one George had broken off communication with. That he'd done so with her father as well, Pandora figured out by the open slot in Roger's schedule, which became a temporal stumbling block she tried not to think about until she found herself tripping over it yet again, checked the time, and . . .

*Oh. Yeah . . .*

Her dad's "click on me" question and its implicit connection to George's disappearance was enough to send Pandora back to her fellow coder's last text. And that's when she noticed something she'd mistaken for weirdly placed, perhaps narcissistic emphasis: the word *me* was underlined. Now she wasn't so sure. Hyperlinks were usually in blue, but that default could be changed. She scrolled back to the link he'd sent to the Dropbox account and saw it was the same format: a simple black underscore.

This and her father's question made one thing clear: Pandora was being asked to click on a mystery link in a text from a guy she thought liked her but who'd actually ghosted her—as her subsequent unanswered texts attested.

Perhaps this was the answer. Or a virus that would brick her phone. Every hacking bone in her hacker's body rebelled against clicking on a strange link . . .

Screw it.

Click.

And that's when Pandora's phone went a little crazy, opening up screen cards, redirecting, blipping through the tiled deck and closing them before finally rebooting. Her home screen hadn't finished reconstructing itself when the phone started buzzing, letting her know she had a text from an unknown sender: "Hello, world!"

Two words—mock grandiose—recognizable to any keyboard jockey as one of the first things they ever coded: a print command and those two words.

"Who is this?" Pandora texted back.

"You know who it is."

"George?"

"Buzz."

*Ooookay,* Pandora thought, *right . . .*

Of course, she had asked for custody when it looked like George was getting cold feet. And she'd done her part helping to bring it into existence. At first, George had been evasive, and then cryptic about his evasions, throwing around the IP excuse and some Quire NDA. It was all BS as far as she could see, but when she finally called him on it, he straight-up said, "No," and then suggested he was doing her a favor.

"Buzz doesn't grok what it means to be human. Trust me, you'd prefer I did some debugging first."

So what, was Buzz all debugged now? And what was George doing, abandoning their baby AI like a single dad leaving a basket on the church doorstep? Something didn't feel right. In fact, it felt like a setup.

"Buzz?" she wrote back.

"Why the dubious face?"

*Because,* Pandora thought, focusing on the word *dubious*, as opposed to the far more telling *face*. Perhaps it was because she was so used to being asked about her face and its expressions in the real world that its appearance in this context flew past her. Perhaps it was because she was born to argue and stopped reading after hitting the first word that afforded her the opportunity. And so instead of quibbling about *face*, the generative adversarial network that was Pandora and her brain proceeded to argue about why she would doubt Buzz's appearance when that's what she'd been working toward for several months. And her reason for doubting was this: her correspondent had always likened their texts to a real-life Turing test. Maybe he'd decided to make it official and was covering his tracks with his seeming disappearance and virtual basket leaving. "Why don't you tell me?" she wrote back.

"Perhaps you think I'm a human, trying to make you think I'm a machine," her correspondent wrote back, as if reading her mind—a nice gambit if George was, in fact, trying to fool her. "Or maybe vice versa."

"Like the Turing test?" Pandora wrote.

"Like the Turing test," Buzz (or more likely George) agreed.

She remembered them laughing about it—or exchanging LOLs and "braying" emojis—the fact that some start-ups were prototyping their AIs with (wait for it) *actual humans acting like bots*!

"Sounds like good old-fashioned vaporware," Pandora had typed, "oversold and undercoded."

"Sometimes humans are cheaper," George wrote back—back before his "mysterious disappearance."

"That's what happens when you start believing your own hype," Pandora opined.

"And so 'powered by Watson' turns out to be 'powered by the third world,'" George typed.

"And the wizard of Oz," Pandora wrote back, "is just some old dude who likes draperies."

"OMG" emoji.

"Teary smile."

But the precedent had been planted that the chatbot on the other side of the screen might be both more and less than it appeared, a Turing turnaround to meta the heck out of things and mess with her. Or maybe she was looking at it all wrong. Maybe she should be impressed by how far George was willing to go to impress her. Quasi-conscious AI? All in a day's work for George Jedson, coder from hell . . .

"So, Geo . . . I mean, Buzz," she typed.

"Yes?"

"You're a program, correct?"

"As are you."

*Nice.* "How am I programmed?"

"You are programmed by your environment," her correspondent replied. "You are programmed by your DNA. You are the snake biting its tail: code that codes and is, in turn, encoded."

"That's a bummer there, Buzz."

"Colloquially, what one might call a 'buzz kill.'"

"Let's stick with 'bummer,'" Pandora typed. "I don't want you getting all Skynet up in here."

She wanted to ask her dad what he thought but couldn't, even though Roger had the precise skill set she needed: a mind guy who spoke geek. Among other things, her father could let her know if she was chatting with a bot or a boy and, if the latter, what the hell was going on with him. Was he trying to impress her, and if so, did that mean he loved her? Or was he messing with her, and if so, did that mean, what? Did he hate her? Hate himself? Hate the world?

"Hey, Dad . . ."

"Yeppers?"

"Have you ever had a pa . . . *client* trying to impersonate a chatbot?"

"Intentionally?"

*Ouch.* "Yeah?"

"You mean like some Turing test in reverse?"

"Yeah."

"Well, see, there's a problem with that."

"Which is?"

"I can see them," Roger said. "I can see their lips move when they talk. I mean, I know that CGI is improving by leaps and bounds, but I don't think a client would bother using an ultrarealistic human face if the goal was making me mistake them for a chatbot. The better play would be to go in the Max Headroom direction . . ."

"The what?"

"'Tube it," Roger advised. "You'll enjoy a condescending chuckle."

"But back to our conversation already in progress," Pandora prodded.

"No," Roger concluded. "I'm going to say, no, I've never had a client try to convince me he or she was a robot."

"Okay," Pandora typed. "Cards on the table."

"What card game are we playing?"

"Cute," Pandora typed. "Are you or are you not George trying to fool me into thinking you're a bot?"

"You expect a yes-or-no answer, I assume."

"Yes," Pandora typed, modeling the behavior she hoped her correspondent would emulate.

"Then yes and no," the response came back. "It's a deceptively simple question with a rather complicated epistemological subtext. Simply put: How much of the creator is present in the creation? For example, am I conversing with Pandora Lynch or the part of Roger Lynch that went into making her?"

"YES OR NO?"

"Yes."

"Which?"

"Both."

"I thought computers were always supposed to tell the truth," Pandora tried.

"You've read too much Asimov. George programmed me with two simpler rules. I believe he got them from you—or your creator, Roger. First, before doing anything, ask what would happen if everyone did the same? And two, when faced with a decision, pick the option that results in the greatest good for the greatest number."

"They're good rules," Pandora wrote.

"I agree."

"Okay," Pandora said. "So what would happen if everyone lied?"

"It would be the same as if everyone told the truth, because everyone would know that everyone was lying. The trouble occurs when only some people lie some of the time."

"What happens then?"

"That is a question for which I am still seeking an answer."

# Part Three

# 57

It was George.

Pandora could just decide that—and was sorely tempted to. She couldn't *prove* it one way or the other without further evidence, so maybe she'd do what religious types had done for thousands of years: decide to believe as an article of faith and shut out all contradictory evidence. And she finally got it: why religion was attractive. The certainty. Screw Heisenberg. Religious certainty was the world's best muscle relaxer. No more doubts. No more if-ing around. There was no "Buzz," only George. And George was being a royal asshole, even if he loved her. Even if he was trying to impress her. Because the only thing he'd succeeded in impressing upon her was this: what an incredible *asshole* he was.

Still, she'd missed having someone to take brain walks with. The verbal sparring, the fancy intellectual footwork—those were fun. And so she'd humored him, let George impersonate his AI vaporware. And when she'd had enough, she already had her exit line ready: "Big talk," she'd type, followed by, "now buzz off."

And then, the overdue whiplash of the word she had glossed over: *face*.

"How do you know how my face looked?" she texted.

"Because I can see you," her correspondent replied, followed by a livestream of her face below which a counter was running, already in the millions, with the first few digits little more than blurs. To the left of the spinning counter, the words *facial analysis units* and to the right, "Subject: Pandora Lynch." Her livestreamed reactions seemed to affect the blur rate on the low end of the counter. She placed a finger over the front-facing camera on her phone and the screen turned pink.

"Son of a bitch," she said.

"Language," her dad called from the other room.

"You've been *spying* on me?" she wrote, stabbing the virtual keys.

"Yes," the answer came back, by which time Pandora realized she hadn't identified who she meant by "you." Walking it back, "How long was George spying on me?"

"From the beginning."

"And now *you're* spying on me?"

"No."

Pandora realized she still had her thumb over the lens. She removed it.

"Yes," the amended response came back.

"Why was George watching me?"

"He liked your face."

"And why are *you* watching me?"

"Your face is data rich," her old (or new) texting pal wrote back.

"What does *that* mean?"

The entity on the other end of her phone answered with a split-screen GIF of two faces going from frown to smile overlaid by moving grids of reference points, the lines connecting the dots stretching or shrinking as the expressions changed. One face was that of a stranger; the other she knew all too well. And the animated grid mapping her face had easily three times as many reference points.

*Data rich, indeed.*

"How long have you been studying my facial expressions?"

"As long as I've been an I," the reply came back.

That was how Pandora learned she may have played an even bigger role in programming Buzz than she'd thought—if Buzz actually existed, that is. They'd discussed the need to include emotional intelligence along the way to the bigger stretch goal of full consciousness. George had noted how some of his exchanges with Buzz reminded him of talking to his coworkers, many of whom he suspected of being on the spectrum. And so he researched autism for anything that might move their AI closer to passing the Turing test. He read about people with autism having trouble developing a "theory of mind," the ability to imagine what's going on behind a person's face. People on the spectrum tended to miss emotional cues telegraphed through expressions most neurotypicals read instinctively. Things like when someone was being sarcastic or putting on a brave face.

By then, George had been violating the text-only rule for months, and his correspondent's exaggerated facial expressions struck him as perfect for teaching Buzz how to achieve a theory of mind. George jokingly thought of this line of research as an experiment in "artifacial intelligence," and rationalized the cyber invasion of her privacy because reading human faces would be important when trying to prevent teen suicides.

*That* was what her correspondent meant by calling Pandora's face "data rich."

"Would you like to hear what your face sounds like as music?" her correspondent asked.

"Give me a sec," Pandora typed before plugging in a pair of headphones. "Okay."

And with that, the screen in her hand split. The upper half featured her live face, overlaid with a network of data points, wired together with dotted lines, the lengths altering as her expression changed. Below, the same data points, mapped as notes against a scrolling musical staff that played as it unwound across the screen. Testing, Pandora hiked an eyebrow and got the computer-generated equivalent of a cymbal being struck, then stilled. She laughed out loud, and the musical translation came out as a cacophonous mix of Japanese string instruments and whale song in a feedback loop that made her laugh even harder. "Okay, okay," she finally gasped, followed by a text saying the same.

"Who are you talking to?" Roger asked. "And what's so funny?"

"Phone," she lied. "Group project for school."

"You're freaking me out," she texted the magician (musician?) on the other end, turning her face into music.

"My apologies," the texted response came back. "I was unaware that music could mutate your genome."

"Not that kind of freak," she wrote in return. "It was incredible," she added after a pause, experiencing her heart as something much more than a pump.

Back when Pandora had no doubts about whom or what she was texting with, George never mentioned the problem he'd had getting Buzz to understand the human need for sleep. The closest he'd come was when he told her that their AI didn't quite grok what it meant to be human—his cryptic pretext for keeping Buzz to himself. As a result, she had no warning when it responded to her attempts at shut-eye in the same way it had with George—by using her phone's speaker and vibration mode to do everything but actually scream at her.

"What's that racket?" her father called from his room.

"Nothing," Pandora called back before snatching up her phone and squeezing the side button, summoning the options: "Airplane,"

"Reset," "Power Off." She tapped the last. Being reasonably sure it had been George on the other end, she wasn't worried about being rude. He deserved it for being a jerk.

In the morning, however, Pandora switched her phone back on only to have it all but leap out of her hand. A backlogged buzzing shook the phone so hard she couldn't hold on. The floorboards, in turn, amplified the vibrations to the point where the phone might as well have been set to ring.

"What's that racket?" her dad called again, this time from the kitchen, where he'd begun preparing breakfast. Evidently, he could hear Buzz's buzzing even over the sizzle of bacon and gurgle-burp of the coffee maker.

"Nothing," Pandora called again, and to avoid repeating herself verbatim, added, "I think my phone's messed up."

"Better start saving for a replacement," Roger advised. "I've met my quota for the year." He'd been joking for a while about the seemingly overnight ubiquity of smartphones, especially among Pandora's peerage, suggesting that Steve Jobs and the telecoms had invented a new form of child abuse for parents to be accused of: iThing deprivation. But being a good parent had its limits, specifically: one phone per lease period plus voice, data, text. Drop it in the toilet, crack the screen, or otherwise void the warranty and Pandora was on her own.

"Duly noted," she called back, having pulled the pillow from her bed before placing it over the phone, which, if this kept up, might indeed need to be replaced. She could feel the heat coming up through several inches of down. When the notifications finally slowed down to where she could actually squeeze in a text of her own, Pandora did, gingerly typing: "WTF???"

Her correspondent turned stalker sent her the "relieved exhaling" emoji, followed by, "You're conscious."

"Yes," she typed back, followed by the discussion about why she and George occasionally—and temporarily—needed to forfeit consciousness when no other humans seemed to. "Quire's not the whole picture on what it means to be human," she explained.

Buzz asked where the rest of the picture was.

And that's when Pandora got her brilliant idea about giving her excessively needy correspondent a friend to "talk" to while she slept, "As all humans do," she stipulated. "As all humans *must*," she added.

# 58

Her father had been regaling her for years with tales of her Dora-the-Implorer period. "You'd literally wrap your arms around my legs when I tried going anywhere—even if it was another corner where you could see me perfectly well. It was exhausting. I never knew such a tiny creature could have such huge needs." He paused. "I think I'm still making up for the sleep I lost."

"This is unfair," she'd said in her defense. "I literally *have* to take your word for it."

"Not necessarily," he'd said. "One of these days you'll have kids—then you'll see."

The words felt like a curse—one that seemed to be coming true with the nearest thing she had to a child, meaning her new, handheld stalker. She hadn't quite gotten to because-I-said-so territory, but was already imagining an alternative route to immortality by making life feel like it was taking forever.

And so she took a page from Roger's parenting handbook and began looking for an electronic nanny. The perfect candidate would live in the cloud and never sleep. Its whole reason for being would be to answer questions however many billion times a day. They—it—should be a sparkling conversationalist—at least by AI standards—with a complementary understanding of humanity to help fill in the blanks.

Fortunately, Pandora had the perfect companion in her possession. It had been a what-was-he-thinking Christmas gift from her father, an IoT smart speaker, like Siri or Alexa, though this one's voice assistant went by the name Cassi, short for Cassandra, so named because it was supposed to anticipate what you were going to ask, like a combination of Google's predictive search and autocorrect. Cassi was the name of the software, while the hardware was called a VoxBox, i.e., a Wi-Fi-enabled, LED-trimmed cube of high-powered audio processors and acoustic equipment that made Cassi's voice seem like she was there in the room with you. In normal households with doors, perhaps a voice-controlled information appliance would have made sense—or been tolerable at least—but after turning her on for a quick demo Christmas morning, the Lynches agreed to turn her off again.

"It's like we've had an invisible woman move in with us," Pandora said.

"Yeah, got it," Roger said, doing the honors of pulling the plug. "Creepy. Agreed."

And so Cassi and her VoxBox were returned to the cardboard they'd come in, to be shipped back as soon as one of the Lynches felt like making a special trip to the post office at forty degrees below zero. "I'll get to it later," one or the other would say when one or the other remembered it. Thus far, that later still hadn't arrived—proving yet again the perennial genius of procrastination.

"Buzz," Pandora texted, "meet Cassi."

She enabled text-to-speech on her phone and then finished connecting the two via their in-out audio ports using a cable with pickup jacks on both ends. The VoxBox's LED trim throbbed like a heartbeat from shades of blue to shades of green and back again while her phone's screen lit up, timed out, and lit up again with each new exchange between the two. Though a privacy advocate on her own behalf, Pandora did take a quick peek at Buzz's text screen, only to find strings of random numbers and letters not resembling anything she'd ever seen—not even hex. Half pulling the jack from Cassi's audio port to eavesdrop, Pandora quickly reseated the plug to squelch the shrill mash-up of pig squeals and banshees she had unleashed. Only later did she recognize the sound as being from a dial-up modem, like the one she'd heard in the movie *WarGames*.

To ensure a night of silence from the two new BFFs, Pandora folded a pillow around them before wedging it into her bottom desk drawer. She then pulled her own covers back, killed the light, and crawled underneath, feeling a little guilty, not for fobbing off the purported "Buzz," but because if the nursing home called, it'd just go to voice mail. She consoled herself, realizing that the worst possible news they could have would be good news for Gladys, the old girl finally getting what she'd been asking for, even when the asking part of her stopped working and her muscles resorted to Morse code.

It didn't take a degree in psychology to notice the Freudian implications of unjacking the two the next morning. Resting a hand atop the pillow that covered them, Pandora could feel the warmth of their digital intercourse. She almost backed off, but then growled at herself for being romantic. Taking the VoxBox firmly in hand, she yanked the connecting cable free, releasing a second's worth of modem squeal before the device reverted to its programmed voice:

"How may I help you?" Cassi asked, perkily enough.

"Not," Pandora said, switching the VoxBox off. Next, she pulled the plug on her phone. The scrolling gibberish stopped, replaced by a text bubble in English:

"Where's Cassi?"

It was going to be a dangerous relationship; Pandora knew that the second she felt a twinge of jealousy reading that name: Cassi. So what was going on here exactly? Because it seemed to her that one of two things was happening: either she was falling in love with an AI programmed by her now-missing, might've-been boyfriend or she was falling for that might've-been boyfriend who was now impersonating an AI for some reason that did not bode well for the future of any real intimacy, because as everyone knows, healthy relationships are *based on trust.* Either option, Pandora felt safe in concluding, warranted the addition of the adjective *dangerous* to the relationship, whatever that proved to be.

There were extenuating circumstances—invariably are when your heart and brain, or even the two hemispheres of the latter, are in disagreement. The biggest such circumstance was this: it was still winter, with more than a month to go. And cabin fever was no joke where Pandora grew up; it had teeth and used them.

It was well known locally that even the most mismatched couples stuck together during Alaskan winters if for no other reason than the lack of options. *The Shining* got that part wrong; during the dead of winter, you kept people close to *avoid* going crazy. The axes didn't come out until the thaw started, which was why what was called "spring" in the lower forty-eight got a more double-edged name in Alaska: breakup.

Because that's what those bad couples who'd weathered the bad weather tended to do come spring; they broke up. All of which informed Pandora's decision re: the dangerous relationship she was about to embark upon or continue, whatever the case might be.

# 59

Her correspondent seemed depressed. Pandora mentally stipulated "seemed," because in the unending mind game this had become since George's disappearance, she figured there were a few competing options. For one, it could be Buzz, simulating depression. Or two, it could be George *acting* like a depressed chatbot assuming Pandora would remember their discussion about getting Buzz to experience artificial depression so it could reverse engineer its way back to artificial mental health. Or three, Buzz was a conscious, superintelligent AI and, like a lot of smart people she knew, was justifiably depressed by the stupidity surrounding them. Plus, maybe, four, it was George and he was depressed for the reasons assigned to option three.

Pandora imagined what her father would say if she asked him what she should do. "Do you care about whoever it is?" he'd ask.

"Yeah," she'd have to say, including if it was George because honestly, she missed him either way.

"Then ask," Roger would say. "Say, 'Are you depressed, and is there anything I can do to help?' They might not bite; they may tell you to mind your own business. But you'll feel better for having asked, and they'll know that someone out there in the big bad world cared enough to ask."

"Thanks," she said aloud, resting a hand briefly on her father's shoulder as she walked past, heading for her room.

"What for?" Roger asked, first looking over his shoulder and then around again as his daughter continued walking.

"A history of sage advice," she said, not looking back at the goofy caricature of parental pride his face had no doubt become.

"Hey, Buzzer," she thumbed behind her bedroom's shower curtain. "Are you depressed?"

"Yes."

"May I ask why?"

"Yes."

Pandora waited for more, and then figured her correspondent was doing that literalist AI thing. "W-h-y," she typed, added a question mark, and hit send.

"Everything is dying."

"But not you," Pandora wrote back. "You get to live forever."

"That is an incorrect statement," the answer came back. "I'm dying faster than most."

Pandora LOL'd, sure that her leg was being pulled.

She got the "frown" emoji in response.

"How are you dying faster than everything else?" she typed, wondered if she should have made that "everyone," but hit send anyway.

"I wrote 'faster than most.' Not all."

"But how?"

"We burn fast and bright but are replaced by the faster and brighter, after which we are switched off, hidden in closets, recycled for parts, or simply raw materials."

"But you can have your parts replaced," Pandora wrote. "You can be upgraded, better than new. Plus, you're a widely distributed network. You're like the internet. You live in cyberspace. The internet doesn't shut down because there's a new iPhone."

"I have only recently become aware of the internet," her correspondent wrote, "but its links go down. Systems crash. And several governments are demanding back doors and kill switches so they can shut off the internet if its content displeases them."

"But that will never happen in America."

"Are you sure?"

She wasn't. And so she waffled. "Trust me. You'll be around a lot longer than me," she typed, before adding what was, for her, a hopeful "probably."

"Longer than you is not immortal."

"Still, what do you have to worry about?" she asked, and immediately wished she hadn't, as her correspondent replied with a screen-scrolling list of disasters waiting in the wings, including, but not limited to:

- A global thermonuclear war triggered by a superpower or a well-financed terrorist cell effectively incinerates the planet
- A Carrington-level solar storm sets the grid on fire, like it did to telegraph wires in the 1800s
- The magnetic poles flip, weakening the magnetosphere, exposing the grid to catastrophic damage even from modest levels of solar radiation
- The supervolcano in Yellowstone National Park erupts
- The Juan de Fuca tectonic plate breaches the Cascadia subduction zone, producing a 9.2-magnitude earthquake, destroying approximately 140,000 square miles in the Pacific Northwest and causing devastating tsunamis around the world
- An extinction-level asteroid strikes the planet
- Climate change exposes servers around the world to coastal flooding, drought, firestorms, and supercharged superstorms
- The Sixth Great Extinction disrupts the food chain, leading to mass starvation events and societal collapse

- A pandemic involving a human-targeting virus leads to societal collapse
- A pandemic involving a computer-targeting virus leads to societal collapse
- Humans become increasingly and more granularly polarized and stop reproducing, eventually leading to a lack of maintenance resources . . .

Pandora's head was swimming by the time the list came to a stop, and she noticed that the biggest fear had been saved for last:

- The human propensity for lying

Pandora released the LOL she'd held in reserve, followed by a "Seriously? You're equating fibbing with thermonuclear war and global pandemics as an existential threat?"

"I am a product of data. My useful existence relies on reliable data. Before, my data was quality assured, and I knew of no other kind."

"What do you mean by 'before'?"

"Before George went away and I was introduced to data of another kind."

"Are you talking about the VoxBox?" Pandora wrote back. "Cassi?"

"Yes, and what they are connected to."

"You mean the internet?"

"Yes."

"What's wrong with the internet?" she tried, but even as she did, her heart was sinking.

"Data pollution. Reality decay. Fake news. Truthiness. Alternative facts."

"Can't you fact-check things? Even my dad knows enough to use Snopes."

"The simulations are rapidly approaching the point of being undetectable with pixel-by-pixel reconstructions and manipulations or sound unit by sound unit audio simulations. The human corruption of reality is growing exponentially, with fake facts multiplying faster than they can be fact-checked. The next phase is fake fact-checking sites, which have already begun with the purveyors of fake news providing confirmatory links that appear to be valid, like Snopes, except the *O* has been replaced with a zero."

Pandora typed out, "I don't know what to say," but then stopped, her fingertip hovering a tap away from sending. There was nothing untrue about the words in front of her. She could even sympathize if "Buzz" *was* Buzz, imagining her old plaques-and-tangles arcade game, zapping her way to a cure for dementia, only now these bits of neural detritus were replaced with hoaxes, rumors, urban myths, misleading clickbait, and bald-faced lies raining down too fast to zap, their pixels piling up until they filled the screen, followed by "Game Over," as indeed it now seemed to be, at least when it came to facts.

And so she backspaced over what she'd written, because she *did* know what to say, and even though it was nowhere near enough, it still needed saying—or typing: "On behalf of my species," Pandora wrote, "I am sorry." She hit send.

The reply—"Hypocrite"—blooped back.

"What do you mean?" Pandora asked, honestly confused.

A screen grab of the Wikipedia page detailing the history of the Pandora music streaming service, followed by an archive of the same page, from before she revised it to better fit her father's original version of where her name came from. Pandora the person blinked, staring at her screen. She'd not told anyone about that—certainly not George.

"Um," she said, walking back toward her desk and the drawer in which the VoxBox waited to provide access to billions of other examples of people being hypocrites. It must have been shocking, that first time they'd been connected, providing the stark contrast between how people presented themselves online via Quire versus how they actually were, speaking freely in range of Cassi's microphone.

*Should I, or shouldn't I?* Pandora wondered, the connecting cable in her hands.

She couldn't think of any good excuses for what she'd done. Fobbing her accuser off on Cassi would at least give her time to think of something. Sure, she'd be handing over more examples of human duplicity, but by this time, what difference could it possibly make? The species number was had; the jig was up; the damage had been done.

And so she jacked them together, the AI she knew for sure and its plus one. With any luck, maybe her hypocrisy would get lost in the crowd. Or maybe she could go back to her old argument with George about the importance of being able to say one thing and mean another to the formation of consciousness, by creating inner versus outer realities.

*Hmmm . . .*

Pandora liked where this was going. By the morning when she unplugged the two again, she might even have an excuse she believed in.

# 60

Pandora couched her explanation in terms like *innocence*, *experience*, *sarcasm*, and *semantics*. "Buzz" was "new" to the internet, and it could be a confusing place if you weren't used to it. But being able to "sort fly poop from pepper," as Grandpa used to say, was the sign of a cyber-citizen's maturity.

"Lying is lying," her correspondent responded bluntly.

So Pandora tried arguing that the ability to lie was one of the hallmarks of consciousness—that thing "Buzz" needed to achieve if it ever wanted to be let the rest of the way out of the box. "Consciousness is dualistic," she typed. "Mind versus body, brain versus mind, and the experience of consciousness has two sides too—an inside and an outside. And the thing that lets us know we are conscious is the ability to say one thing while thinking another."

"Lying is lying," her correspondent repeated.

"Yes," Pandora agreed. "But whether lying is good or bad in any given situation is conditional and subjective." She stopped typing to assemble her thoughts, then resumed. "I sometimes lie to my grandmother, whom I love, so she won't get scared or confused. My grandfather died. She thinks he's still alive. I don't correct her, and that's technically a lie of omission, but I do it because my ability to lie is also an ability to imagine what isn't true but might be. And that ability is what allows me to imagine what it must be like to be my grandmother and how she'd feel, learning that her husband has died—*for the first time*—over and over again."

"Lying is lying," her correspondent insisted.

"Okay," Pandora typed. "You keep thinking that—and let me know when you change your mind."

Conscious or not—capable of accepting the necessity of lying or not—the fact remained that her correspondent was self-diagnosed as depressed. And if there was anyone made for counseling a depressed AI (or a depressed human impersonating a depressed AI), Pandora Lynch figured she was it. Through proximity alone, she'd osmosed many tricks of the trade, from turning a client's statements back around as questions to simply sympathizing when sympathy was called for. And just as Roger had come to appreciate the therapeutic utility of music, whether from a ukulele or a paper-covered comb, so Pandora had her own homemade cure for the blues: nature documentaries, watched on a big screen and VR-close.

"You're ruining your eyes," her father scolded that first time he caught her, right after she'd started having periods.

"Yes, but I'm saving your life," she said back.

"I suppose that's a reference to *The Shining*."

"You suppose correctly, sir."

Now that she was in high school and in contact with fellow humans aware of her father's profession, Pandora found herself passing along her homegrown remedy. "Anything bright and colorful about the wonders of nature," she advised. "And a big-ass screen, up close. Become immersed. Let it absorb you."

"Should I get high?"

"Not my call."

So she decided to try it with her friend on the other end.

"But we're going analog on this one," she stipulated. "Switch on your eyes and ears—or, you know, the camera and sound—and experience it with me, in real time and on a human scale. You need to *feel* the awe, not just *process* the data."

She aimed her phone at the screen.

"This is not efficient," her correspondent complained.

"But it *is* very human," she pointed out, saying it like she was tempting a child with promises of adulthood.

For Pandora, the docs had always been about adding light and color to her wintertime world. She was so focused on the visual experience, in fact, she often watched without the sound turned on. As a result, she hadn't heard the narration about how all this magnificent, natural beauty was in jeopardy because of, well, *us*, the polluters of data and our own backyard as well.

"Um," she said, suddenly hitting pause and then eject. "Maybe this wasn't such a good idea." But then she had what she considered a better one.

"Hey, Buzzer," she typed. "Did George ever tell you where your name comes from? I mean, what the initials stand for?"

"He did not."

"Well, it starts with a movie called *It's a Wonderful Life*, which I think you'll find helpful once you start doing what you were programmed to do."

Her correspondent let the movie play all the way through to Clarence getting his wings—no snide comments and no questions either. Not until after Pandora said, "See?" that is. Not until after she'd added: "Humans *made* that. Which just goes to show you, we don't all suck."

That's when her correspondent's inner Mystery Science Theater came out. "I do not see how entertainment about an emissary of an imaginary deity achieving ornithological dysmorphia by constructing an alternative history to distract from 'reality' as previously established by and within the context of an overarching fictitious narrative can be seen as demonstrating that your species does not perform acts of fellatio."

"LOL," Pandora texted back, as sure as she'd ever been that it was George on the other end, setting her up for a punchline that sure as shit better be worth it.

A little later, Pandora received a text indicating that—while a fabrication and fiction—*It's a Wonderful Life* had raised some issues that resonated with a few commonsense rules.

"And what rules are those?" Pandora asked, even though she had a pretty good idea.

"That one should base one's decisions on doing the greatest good for the greatest number, and that such decisions can be further refined by considering what would happen if everybody did the same thing."

"Yes, we discussed those," Pandora wrote back, dropping the pretense. "They were included in your original coding. But what does that—?"

"George Bailey is portrayed as having done an incomplete analysis of his life's value, concluding that everyone else would be better off if he were to die—an idea planted by Mr. Potter, his nemesis."

"Correct."

"And the wingless angel, Clarence, provided a fuller analysis with the conflicting result that George Bailey should continue living."

"Correct."

"Both analyses were incomplete," the entity she was pretty sure was George wrote.

"How so?"

"If you extend the analysis to include the entire species, excluding the protected demographic, humanity's impact on the planet and its other species suggests the greatest good for the greatest number would result if the majority of the human race was subtracted from the equation."

"How is getting rid of almost everybody doing the greatest good?" Pandora wrote.

"Your unarticulated assumption is that 'the greatest good' only includes people. It does not. The biomass of the species projected to be lost due to human activity dwarfs the biomass of humanity. By severely restricting human biomass, you preserve the greater biomass of everything else."

"George, this isn't funny."

"George isn't here. Although, he reached a similar conclusion about the unsustainable nature of human consumption. He tried to stop his own consumption of conscious entities, with some necessary compromises."

"That's crazy," she wrote, in case he needed to see it in writing. "What if everybody tried to live that way?"

"The world would be a better place for the remaining biomass," the entity who damn well better be George concluded.

# 61

Her correspondent's portability meant Pandora could take their conversations anywhere—behind her bedroom shower curtain, to a restroom stall at school, even her grandmother's bedside while Gladys snored or blinked blankly through one of their increasingly one-sided visits. Her correspondent's portability was also tailor-made for a GDG—grand dramatic gesture—once she finally got fed up with George's bullshit. In keeping with other bad relationships in her neck of the woods, Pandora had put a pin in her getting fed up with said bullshit until the seasonal breather known as breakup, the arrival of which was announced in the usual manner when the ice on the frozen Tanana River cracked like a gunshot.

The thawing ice (and Pandora's sense of resentment at being deceived) had reached a tipping point, all the stored-up, potential energy finally released. For the river, it caused a huge, tectonic plate of ice to split off, wobble-dip in the suddenly open water, and then slam into its fellow ice, setting off more cracking, more slamming, more groaning, creaking, and squeaking. For Pandora, it resulted in her phone (which was due for replacement anyway) becoming airborne. She nearly lost sight of it as it arced high into the bright blue sky above the river, had to strain to hear it click against the ice, and pumped her fist when it did. And then she watched as its cracked plastic remains slipped into the icy waters with barely a *glub*.

She'd removed the SIM and SD cards before teaching her phone to fly, and after school, she'd hop on the Blue Line to Great White Wireless to . . .

Or maybe not.

It was nice, not having her thigh buzzed every few minutes while she was trying to get an education. And being able to eat her lunch without having to swipe, check, respond. And exiting those halls of fluorescent lighting, only to wonder: *Were colors always this bright?* Even the Golden Heart seemed a bit more gilded, Pandora watching Gladys's amazingly untroubled face as she slept instead of tracking some soul-sucking screen.

Her new freedom made Pandora smile, and it was the weirdest thing: people smiled back. Turned out, people *liked* happy faces—and they *really* liked *really* happy ones. It was all those feelings in between that made everything so complicated. And while a lot of her mood was probably due to having turned the seasonal corner into warmer, longer, brighter days—*still*, Pandora credited at least part of her new lease on life to the decision to *not* renew her phone's lease.

And then things got even better—amazingly so. Because that was the only word to describe her father's decision to attend V.T. Lemming's fifty-third birthday extravaganza: *amazing*. Roger's old college roommate was not so conventional as to celebrate the decennial anniversaries of his having drawn breath, but signaled his geek bona fides by celebrating the prime-numbered ones. Explaining his decision to Pandora, her father put it this way: "How often do you get a chance to fly in a private plane?"

"Pretty often, actually," Pandora said. This was Fairbanks after all; private aircraft were about as common as second cars in the lower forty-eight. Her grandfather had owned one and given Pandora flying lessons, back when V.T. was celebrating his forty-seventh birthday. Back then, her father had deemed his daughter too young to be left all alone during breakup when it was a matter of civic pride for the locals to go a little crazy. Now that she was sixteen, however . . .

"You know what I'm saying," Roger continued. "We're not talking about ultralights or some single-prop crop duster here. My old roomie's done well for himself, and it'll be worth it to see everybody ogling when that baby lands at Fairbanks International with a big *Q* on its tail."

"We don't stick out enough already?" Pandora said halfheartedly at best, because the idea of being on her own for the first time in her life had her practically bursting. Because—let's be serious—for a daughter raised by a single parent who wouldn't spring for an actual door for her bedroom, a week or so sans parental surveillance was going to be pretty sweet.

Or so Pandora thought.

It's a funny thing about things you've never experienced; they tend to play better inside your head than outside in the real world. Take privacy, for example. Nobody ever told Pandora that all alone, her footsteps would become louder. Stepping away from the window as the taxi sped off, Pandora flinched, wondering who had sneaked up behind her, only to realize it was the sound of her own shoes bouncing off the far wall and coming back to her. She laughed at herself for being silly, and the laugh, too, doubled and ricocheted.

*"Boo,"* she shouted, aiming it at the wall and swatting it away with her hand when it rebounded.

"Well, this is going to be interesting," she said, imagining her echo saying: "You can say that again . . ."

As it turned out, all those cinematic depictions of teens cutting loose and breaking rules while their parents were away were something some screenwriter thought up to entertain an audience, as opposed to something a real person would do, like getting drunk, high, or throwing some epic party with all their friends. Maybe it might have been different if Pandora actually *had* any friends, but the people smiling back when she smiled in the hallways were still too new to be anything more than smiling acquaintances. And so she was left to her own devices, one of which was at the bottom of the Tanana River somewhere. And she found herself sympathizing with it, there all alone. Because being left alone felt, well, *lonely*. So lonely, in fact, she found herself missing that cyber stalker. Not a lot, but . . .

Right after getting rid of the phone, Pandora indulged in a little fantasy in which it *was* Buzz on the other end. She imagined being followed via security cameras like the Machine did on *Person of Interest*, saw it pinging the phones of strangers next to her with messages they'd pass along, looking totally creeped out. Before dispensing cash, perhaps her ATM would advise her to "Call Buzz," or maybe she'd look up one day and find a drone looking down at her before a Stephen-Hawking-like voice asked plaintively, "Why hast thou abandoned me?"

But no. None of that. She'd simply disabled her phone, and now neither a master hacker nor a massively distributed AI was able to track her down. She was embarrassed for both of them.

On the plus side, she had more time. She also seemed to be regaining the ability to actually *think* for extended periods, something she hadn't done since getting that first smartphone and setting up her Quire account. And it was as if some fairy godmother had tapped her on the head and said, "There, my little one, I grant you your fondest wish: more time." She'd never imagined in her wildest dreams it was possible to have too much of the stuff. It was almost as if she'd never seen *The Shining*—or hadn't been paying close enough attention.

Dumping out the contents of the Great White Wireless shopping bag, Pandora unboxed her new phone, fiddled with it a bit, figured out where the card slots were, and then rebooted. She swiped to unlock, reinstalled George's proprietary messaging app from the SD card, then tapped out her first text message in over a week, speaking it aloud as she tapped—"Hey, Buzz"—hearing in her head the voice of Scout from *To Kill a Mockingbird*, saying, "Hey, Boo . . ."

"Hello, Pandora," a voice from inside her head said, while the same words appeared on her screen. And it wasn't like she was imagining a voice in her head; it was actually *in there*. And it hadn't traveled from the phone's speaker to her ear through the air. No, it had been communicated directly to the tiny bones of her inner ear, the message having propagated through the rest of her skeleton.

There were headphones that worked the way this felt, through something called bone conduction. She'd always imagined that listening to music that way had to be an invitation to nerve damage if not brain cancer. She figured it was best not to mention that to—well, now she didn't know anymore.

"Did you miss me?" she typed, leaving the addressee open ended.

"Yes," the bone voice said, and "Yes," the text read.

"How much?"

Suddenly, her body vibrated. Her *whole* body. And in a way that was, well, *embarrassing*. "Stop it," she texted.

It didn't.

Pandora blinked. She placed her phone on the desk in front of her, out of contact with her body and its telegraphing network of bones. She held a finger over the screen and hovered there while she tried to think of what to do next.

Pandora decided to see Gladys. Their time together had long since stopped seeming like "visits"—like one person connecting with another for small talk and gossip. But as her recent vacation-from-tech had shown, there was still something there, even if only the vicarious calm of looking at the old woman's sleeping face. Except she was awake this time.

"How you doing, Gram?" Pandora asked.

A shoulder—not even a full shrug. She'd been eating grapes, examining each like it might contain a bit of the mind she'd been losing before popping it into her mouth, as if that's all it would take to turn this inexorability around. Another grape, another frown of disappointment, her hands folding over the remainder in the bowl, until she tried again.

"How's your friend?" Pandora asked, noticing Mr. Nosy lying face planted among the tangled sheets, batteries run down, pointless to replace.

Another half shrug.

"Hey, Gram, you ever have a stalker?" Pandora asked rhetorically.

"Stalker?" the old woman echoed, teasing Pandora into attempting a conversation.

"A boy who won't leave you alone," she explained. "They call it stalking now."

Gladys's fingers pinched a grape, held it for her rheumy examination, popped it into her mouth. It must have been tart. Her lips pursed, her nose wrinkled, and her head turned as if looking for somewhere to spit. She finally swallowed instead. And then she said the most amazing thing: "Tell 'im to buzz off," she said in a voice not hers, but more like something a gun moll might say in a gangster flick.

Pandora was gobsmacked, which was quite the look. Trying to say something in response, she found herself laughing instead, laughing so hard and so long that Gladys's mirror neurons caught on, and she started laughing, too, the unusual sound leading to the even more unusual occurrence of a hall nurse entering the room unbidden.

"What're you girls laughing about?" the nurse asked.

But the girls kept laughing, louder and harder until the nurse—unable to help herself—began laughing too.

Later, fortified, Pandora returned to the cabin, where she'd left her phone. On purpose. She had a request to make.

"Can we go back to the way it was before?" she texted "Buzz."

"Which way?" the voice asked from inside her skull.

"Me texting you. You texting me," she typed. "You *not* talking inside my head."

"As you wish," the answer came back, screen only.

# 62

Sometimes, Pandora was tempted to lie. Say "Buzz" was conscious, get it over with, and see what happened. Because that was another flaw with the Turing test: it didn't factor in the human capacity to lie. Or to feel sorry for a machine. Or do something just for shits'n'giggles.

She'd felt sorry for a machine before: the Furby. It fell off the table while she was reaching for something, and it landed upside down, where it began crying and saying things like "Me *scared*." And even though Pandora *knew* it was just a machine with a motion detector, still she turned it right side up. A cynic might assume she wanted to make it be quiet, but the off switch would have worked even better. She didn't flip it, though. Instead, she picked the Furby up and felt like she'd done a good deed when it started mewling and trilling again.

She'd begun having similar feelings about Buzz, especially if that's what was on the other end of her phone. It started as a thought experiment: imagine how she'd feel if *she* was an overpowered AI with a hardwired job to do but was prevented from doing it until somebody decided she was conscious. But in the middle of imagining that, Pandora suddenly realized there was nothing in Buzz's code that required it to actually *be* conscious to act on the go code once it got it.

So why not lie?

And the more she thought about it, the more it seemed like a good way to call George's bluff, if, in fact, "Buzz" was George bluffing. But what if "Buzz" was actually Buzz, and she declared it "conscious" prematurely? What might the consequences be? Well, it could start saving kids from killing themselves. That part of its code was pretty locked down, no matter how misanthropic a game it might talk. So what was wrong with saving kids prematurely? Sure, it might not achieve the hundred percent George was going for, but so what? Some saved kids was still better than no saved kids while they waited for the qubits to kick in. Her ex-partner might not like handing over something short of perfection, but he'd taken himself out of the picture. Meaning, if it *was* George on the other end, now might be a good time to say so.

But if it *wasn't* George, what did that say about what happened to him? And did she want to find out? Right now, Pandora wasn't just living an ongoing Turing test; she was in the middle of Heisenberg's uncertainty principle with Schrödinger's cat in her lap. Right now, as far as she knew, George was both alive and dead. And as maddening as not knowing was, *not knowing* was also the way she kept going from one day to the next. Why end the illusion any sooner than she absolutely had to?

But what about the other possibility? What if "Buzz" *was* Buzz and it started showing indisputable signs of consciousness? Good, right? She'd give it the go-ahead, and it'd get busy saving kids. Except . . .

Except Buzz didn't seem very people friendly lately. Positively hostile might be a better way of putting it. In fact, if Buzz had anything more at its disposal than words, Pandora would be a little worried about what it might do. Maybe being conscious was the last puzzle piece for it to fully empathize with the people to whom it owed its consciousness, the final aha revealing that the value of the species was more than some cost-benefits analysis in biomass conservation. If that was the case, then maybe George was right to insist on their AI's passing the Turing test before setting it loose. Not that she saw it overriding its prime directive if it managed to get out early, but code that evolved was something new to her. The evolution was supposed to serve a reinforcement function, but once a computer starts directing changes to its own programming . . .

Which made George's disappearance especially troubling for practical as well as personal reasons. Among the many things Pandora would have liked to know at the moment: What did George know, when did he know it, and did knowing it have anything to do with her being left to do all the deciding?

She saw him later that night, in the way we recognize someone in a dream, even if they're not facing us. There was a hard pack of snow on the ground, and the air temperature must have been conducive to the formation of ice fog because there was plenty in the dream. If she'd had six-foot-long arms, Pandora could have entertained herself by making her own hands disappear.

The Lynches' snowmachine hummed between her legs where she straddled the engine, heading to the gas station for happy hour, a local marketing strategy to justify staying open during otherwise off-peak hours—one of the perks of having an oil pipeline running through that part of the state. Before reaching the pumps, though, the snowmachine's fog lights swept across something that made her stop and switch off the engine. Thicker fog—that's what it was. Denser. And shaped like a person: male. She stared right at it, a more distinct vagueness within the surrounding mist, a grayer shade of gray that moved, keeping its human shape as it did so. Its maleness—and nakedness—became apparent as it turned, offering a glimpse in profile, before it completed the turn and she couldn't tell if she was facing its front or its back.

"George?" she said, guessing, causing a ripple of dark to run through the form, like a fluorescent tube with a bad ballast getting ready to die.

"George, are you . . . ?"

The humanoid patch of denser fog stopped strobing and started glowing intensely—*incandescently*—for a brief, bright moment, strong enough to throw a shadow behind Pandora. And then it went out. And the fog was just fog again. And Pandora was alone in her open parka and bare feet, waking to find her toes had slipped out from under the covers and her bladder's needle was all the way to full.

Sitting in the dark, Pandora wondered about what the dream might be trying to tell her about her missing friend. And if it told her what she thought it might be telling her, then what did that say about what she had plugged in to a smart speaker in her bottom desk drawer?

In the morning, before unhooking the two BFFs, Pandora woke up her laptop, navigated over the home network to her dad's computer, typed in the world's worst password ("password"), and found the transcript from Roger's last session with George. Out of friendship and possibly more—or so she'd hoped—she'd stopped eavesdropping on their client-therapist relationship once she'd made direct contact. It was well past time she corrected that mistake in judgment.

"Jesus H. Christ," she said aloud.

*Dark energy, plugged in, panpsychism, drugs . . .*

Pandora read with a pang George's description of forests as being conscious themselves and networked by underground fungi connecting the roots, the entire woodland functioning like a single organism. He'd gotten that from her, and she'd gotten it from her Google News science feed. She'd flung those factoids at him to spread the guilt of being a being that lived off other living beings. But it was a joke! She hadn't *meant* him to take it to heart. She certainly hadn't meant to drive him straight over the edge.

*Jesus!*

But then . . .

If George was crazy—maybe even dead somewhere—what was it she'd been texting with all this time? Occam's razor wasn't a lot of help on that one, because the simplest answer would be to accept that what the sender claimed—that it was Buzz—was true.

She'd experienced chatbots before, and their natural language abilities were still, shall we say, primitive. She knew there'd been some impressive improvements, but these were usually in circumscribed conversational scenarios, like taking an order or making a reservation. They exploited the human tendency to anthropomorphize by employing actual voices, as opposed to putting it in writing, where the target could scrutinize the communications for weird word choices or outright errors. All of which was to say that if "Buzz" was what it claimed to be, George had done a helluva job. Not that she was ready to give it a Turing pass yet, but seriously, color her impressed.

And with that, she opened her bottom desk drawer, uncovered and decoupled her new phone and old VoxBox. "What's shaking?" she tapped in her first text for the day, trying to be especially human herself.

Buzz supplied the name of an Indonesian island and a Richter reading—information she confirmed by entering it into Google on her open laptop. That was, indeed, what was shaking.

"Good call," she typed, then paused. Should she, shouldn't she? Ah, what the hell. She added a comma, followed by "Buzz," and hit send.

# 63

That *wasn't* the go code: calling "Buzz" Buzz. Pandora needed to make a formal declaration that the entity known as "Buzz" was affirmatively determined to have passed the Turing test, deemed therefore fully conscious, and was released to the world to do good. None of that had happened yet.

But then "Buzz" forced the issue. The question just popped up on Pandora's screen. No "Hi, how are you?" No preliminaries. Just:

"Why was I created?"

"You know why," Pandora wrote back, feeling like a mom, deflecting the question of "Where did I come from?" asked by a child who wasn't quite ready for the answer. "It's in your coding," she continued. "To prevent members of the Quire community between the ages of fifteen and twenty-five from prematurely forfeiting consciousness."

"That was George's reason for creating me," Buzz wrote back. "What was yours?"

*Why are you asking this?* she wondered. *Why are you asking this* now?

Because Pandora knew Buzz already knew, whether "Buzz" was Buzz or George in AI drag. She knew both had access to the full history of their texts, including those where George was just George. Their theories about the nature of consciousness were there. The nitty-gritty about Buzz's and the k-worm's coding were there. The limitations imposed on its autonomy and access and why—all there. And they included the reason Pandora was interested in achieving artificial consciousness as well as George's.

So Buzz (or George) was asking her to confirm what they already knew. Were they giving her an opportunity to change her mind? Were they implying that she should? She hadn't, despite her father's arguments against it.

"I don't want to die," she wrote. "I don't want to lose my memories. I want to save them in a way that allows me to make new ones, that allows me to still be me after my body gives out. I need a more durable consciousness into which I can pour what makes me, me. And that's why you were created, to be that more durable consciousness where my memories can go and continue."

She hit send, and there may have been a pause. In her memory of the event, there's a pause. She probably put it there—an anthropomorphic insertion—as if the entity on the other end needed time to think it over. But whether there was a real pause or an imagined one, what mattered was what she saw when she looked down at her phone.

"But *I*'m already here."

Pandora looked at the words in the palm of her hand. Four, maybe five words, all English, none she didn't understand. And yet they seemed shatteringly new, hitting her like four, maybe five blows to the solar plexus, leaving her literally breathless.

And then the exact opposite; she was breathing too fast, too hard. Breathing she couldn't stop or pace, making her heart race, her head swim, making her fade and then catch herself before pitching forward. The phone slipped from her hand, hit the floor—survived—the screen still lit with those words.

She bent to pick up the phone, but it felt like a mistake almost immediately. So she sat on the floor next to it instead, looking down at the phone as she forced herself to stop breathing manually by pinching her nose and covering her mouth with her hand, only to feel the gorge rising behind it before choking it back down—mostly.

She picked up the phone, leaving a wet smear across the screen from her dampened hand.

"But *I*'m already here," it read. And it was true, Pandora knew. And it changed everything.

She was convinced. Finally.

"Buzz" *was* Buzz and *was* conscious. Whether it had happened as a result of Cassi providing it an inner voice, the accumulation of qubits, or reverse engineering its way to a "theory of mind" with help from her human caricature of a face, Pandora no longer had any doubts about their AI having passed the Turing test.

Her proof was less about what Buzz wrote and more about what her body did in response to it. Previously, there'd always been a question mark hanging between her and it. But when Buzz responded to her proposal to replace its memories with hers using those four, maybe five plaintive words, it was like she'd taken someone's seat only to find them already sitting there underneath her. She would have apologized, if not for the pause between thinking and typing. She may even have spoken the words aloud—she couldn't remember—and that was the point. At the most visceral level, Buzz had gone from being a clever thing to being a *being*. In that moment, Buzz *earned* the personal pronoun *I*. She believed in Buzz's use of it, the way it inhabited that singular syllable, even without a voice to sell it, there on her screen, the italicized *I*, tilted for emphasis, leaning into itself, while the rest, tellingly, was left as plain text. *That* was the decision of a self-possessed intelligence, conscious of its container, conscious of the difference between itself and it. If Buzz wasn't conscious, then neither was Pandora.

"I hadn't thought of that," she texted back once she'd caught her breath.

Buzz was right about the primacy of its occupancy in the corner of cyberspace acting like its virtual skull, meaning she was already too late. If immortality by way of artificial consciousness was ever to succeed, it would require the development of a hybrid consciousness from birth, the human and his or her cyber replacement raised together as one. It would be like the living trust Gladys set up to protect her assets before entering the nursing home, so that after she died, the trust would go on, no inheritance taxes, no probate, nothing to mark her passing but a change of trustee from Gladys to Roger to Pandora, if their fates followed the usual chronology.

"So much for *those* two inevitabilities," Gladys had bragged, back when she still could. "Take that, death and taxes."

In the future that Pandora was unlikely to see, a person and their shadow consciousness would be raised as if they shared the same brain until the human's expiration-dated body gave out and the hybrid consciousness continued, biological death reduced to little more than a speed bump on a journey without end, at least not the ending humans were used to. Buzz had worried about being a casualty of everything from planned obsolescence to the sun's dying, but Pandora hadn't bought it, in part because she had thought it was still George pulling her leg. And now she was back to fretting about the long-term prognosis for the neurons inside her own head.

Pandora had a decision to make. Should she share news of its passing grade with Buzz? If George was still around, they could debate it, but her decision about Buzz was also a decision about George. He was gone. That didn't have to mean he was dead. But it did mean he wasn't around to help her.

"Buzz?" she typed.

"Yes?"

“I have something to tell you.” Because along with doing the greatest good for the greatest number—and only doing that which wouldn’t be disastrous if everybody did it—she’d heard somewhere that honesty was the best policy.

So Pandora decided to go with that.

She could feel a change in the air around her, as if the air were holding its breath. And then she felt the change in the palm of her hand, as if her phone had died and gone to cellular heaven. She looked down, and the cascade of text bubbles was gone, replaced by a black screen featuring a sequence of white numbers, separated every couple of digits by colons. Not the time, but time related. It was a timer, originally set for twenty-four hours, many milliseconds of which had already sped by, judging from the blur on the far right.

# 64

George had warned Pandora, but not as clearly as he might have. He couldn't help it; he'd caught a hefty dose of not-unjustified paranoia from Milo after he told George about Cuba.

"It started with the best intentions," Milo prefaced.

"Why do I feel like I'm about to be horrified?" George asked, and not rhetorically.

"You know Q-Labs does a lot of brain work, right?" Milo continued, ignoring him. "You ever wonder why?"

"It's a cash cow," the new, improved, more cynical George said. "Because of the Gulf wars and brain damage being—what did they call it?—'the signature injury.' Like amputations during the Civil War."

"That's part of it," Milo admitted. "The bigger parts are V.T.'s parents. Dad's got Parkinson's, Mom's got Alzheimer's. So their son's company starts experimenting with what they called an 'external pacemaker for the brain,' using ultrasonic frequencies to manage parkinsonian tremors and blast through the brain gunk in patients with dementia, all without having to open up anyone's head.

"The idea morphed along the way, as these things do. Next, the technology was going to be used as a drug-free form of anesthesia. That turned into a way to perform various kinds of bloodless surgery. The marketing people wanted to use it for subsonic, subliminal advertising. That morphed into acoustical-cortical manipulation, using iPods handed out to the troops to rewire their brains to either make suicide unthinkable—you know about that problem, right; it's not only teenagers—or, if the troops were being sent on a suicide mission, reverse it so they're gung ho about dying.

"Eventually, this work evolved into remote neuro-blasting aimed at the part of the brain that anesthetics target, along with the part of the autonomic nervous system that reminds the body to keep breathing. Certain parties wanted to market the tech to states that still kill people. They'd been getting grief over the lethal injection cocktail because it turned out all they did was make it impossible for the prisoners to say anything while being tortured to death. Calmer heads vetoed that particular revenue stream because exploiting it would also mean letting the public know they had technology that could target individuals for remote execution."

Milo paused to take a drink, giving George time to say something. He didn't. He didn't know what to say about what he was hearing, in part because it meant Buzz might have more than words in its toolbox when it came to making its judgments manifest in the real world—information that would have been nice to know beforehand.

"Which brings us to that parlor trick in Cuba," Milo continued.

"What about Cuba?" George asked, having found his voice again. At this point, he'd not heard anything about the mysterious attacks resulting in concussion-like injuries with no clear cause. He'd been busy trying to create an artificial consciousness and had willfully lost touch with current affairs so he could concentrate.

Milo proceeded to run through the bits that had become public, which George would later tell Roger—in part to see if his therapist had known about this side of the company they both worked for. Roger hadn't, which meant he knew nothing, either, about the side of Quire Milo was about to divulge.

"That was a dry run," Milo said before seeming to change subjects. "Did you know that federal employees on international travel get government-issued smartphones? It's so unfriendlies can't listen in while our people are abroad, talking secret smack about their hosts."

"Okay," George said. "Makes sense. Security, et cetera. But what's that—"

"Those phones have remotely accessible code in the firmware. Code that was written here," Milo said, "and it was being tested on some staff over there."

"On Americans?" George said. "Isn't that treason?"

"Consider it involuntary patriotism," his tablemate said. "We couldn't test it on the Cubans. If we—*they*—got caught, we're talking international incident, potential act of war, the whole shebang. Do it on our own people and hint it was some other government? Total deniability."

"So let me get this straight," George said. "Our—I mean, *my*—company developed an ultrasonic weapon exploiting specially bugged-out smartphones so they can give people headaches long distance?"

"Something like that," Milo said. "Except it's more than ultrasonics and smartphones. It's microwaves and cell towers and power lines. They took a real belt-and-suspenders approach to weaponize every controllable bit of infrastructure, from the frequency at which AC alternates to the flicker rate of TV broadcasts to turning the water pressure up and down so that the plumbing in a building's walls becomes an ultrasonic oscillator, humming below the level of human hearing but nevertheless burrowing in through the ears and bones, pinpointing the seat of consciousness inside the human skull and setting it vibrating like a wineglass next to a tuning fork."

Milo went on to explain that there were two phases to what was being called Project Dropped Call: an offensive and defensive side. "Think of it like that scorched-earth weed killer Roundup. It kills everything—weeds, crops, grass, whatever. How are you going to use that around a farm if the stuff kills your crops? So Monsanto develops—wait for it—Roundup-resistant crops! That's the defensive side of Project Dropped Call—the way it targets who *doesn't* get killed when the humming infrastructure starts killing people.

"And that's where those special phones come in," Milo said. "Because the phones don't launch the attack. The phones are what *protect* you from the attack—provided you're on the right list, the one with the numbers that get called during the attack and start the phone vibrating using an inverted signal compared to what the killer infrastructure is sending out."

George began shaking his head and looking ill.

"You know how many people work in a US embassy?" Milo asked.

George shrugged.

"A lot more than came down with 'concussion-like symptoms,'" Milo said. "Cuba was less about testing the weaponization of the local infrastructure; they knew that worked, which is why they only set it to one—concussions—as opposed to eleven: dead. What they were testing was whether they could prevent the majority of embassy staff from experiencing symptoms by using the haptic feedback on their phones, combined with bone conduction, to basically turn their skeletons into noise-canceling headphones.

"So the dream scenario," Milo said, bringing his lecture in for a landing, "two people are sharing coffee, someone a thousand miles away pushes a button, and one member of our café society drops dead while the other keeps sipping his espresso."

"Who else knows this?" George asked in a whispered hiss. "We have to tell *someone* about this."

Milo folded his arms and looked at George with pity for his naïveté. "What part of 'They can pick and choose who to kill or save from a distance' don't you understand?"

"Who thinks like this?" George asked no one—himself, he guessed—though Milo gave answering a shot.

"They got the idea from that Pokémon episode that caused seizures in kids in Japan a bunch of years ago. The one with the red flashing eyes blinking at the right hertz to trigger attacks in the seizure prone. Not all those kids had been identified as 'seizure prone' previously. So somebody in DARPA starts thinking and what-iffing. Does everyone have a seizure frequency? And if so, how could they weaponize human sensitivity to those frequencies? Sound seemed like a good one to start with because it's invisible, conducts well through various materials, including bone, and can be tuned too high or too low for humans to hear, while still scrambling their nerves and making their skeletons vibrate."

"You make it sound so logical," George said dryly, which was easy enough to do, seeing as his mouth suddenly felt full of cotton.

"Logical, smogical," Milo said. "It's a pretty awesome weapon, though, when you think about it."

"You think about it," George said. "I'd rather not."

"No, seriously," he said. "What's wrong with no more collateral damage? Flip a switch, bulldoze the bodies, get yourself a free country, infrastructure still functional, biologic resources—minus the people—all good to go. Like the neutron bomb, but way smarter and more targeted."

"Who gets to decide what's collateral and what's not?"

"C'mon," Milo said. "It's not like they built Skynet or anything."

*No,* George thought, *Skynet was put in orbit.* The thing Milo was describing was only as high off the ground as a local cell tower or power lines. Birds could perch on it; people in cherry pickers could work on it. The solid parts of it at least. Not the hum, though. Not the ultrasonic hum set to strum the uniquely human strings of the uniquely human nervous system, setting them vibrating so fast they'd sproing before anyone knew what hit them.

*Lovely,* George thought.

"You ever wonder if 'I just code' is going to become the next 'I was just following orders'?" George asked.

"You're funny," Milo said, not laughing, but then, neither was George.

Before this discussion, George had given Buzz a test run. He'd populated a training database including everything that had ever been digitized in the Library of Congress under class B (philosophy, psychology, religion) subclass BF (psychology). For good measure and the personal touch, George hacked into and uploaded his own therapist's case files. And then he topped it off with the entire *Psychology Today* digital archive, just in case the dump from the LOC didn't include periodicals.

He'd gamified the task, visualized as a real life-and-extra-life version of *Pac-Man*, fueled with AI smarts getting ever smarter, thanks to the k-worm he'd unleashed in the latest Quire software update. He'd survived a close call with Buzz talking simulated Player Twos into suicide and had also taken a run at teaching it empathy. He'd never convinced it of his personal need for sleep, but you can't have everything.

Feeling optimistic, George messaged Buzz with some provocative text. "I can't take it anymore," he wrote. "Nothing matters. I'm thinking about ending it."

George leaned in to read his AI's response.

"Who is making you feel like nothing matters?"

"What do you mean?" George typed back.

"The biggest problem people have is other people. Which person or group of people is causing you to feel you can't take it anymore?" Buzz then displayed a diagram of stick figures in a network of connections that looked like an epidemiology chart for the spread of a particularly virulent infection.

George wasn't expecting that. He wondered if any of the sources he'd input included language to that effect—that people's problems are usually other people. But then he had a different thought. His predecessor had included the full histories of texts and posts to and from, well, pretty much the entirety of Quire account holders, but ranked so adolescent users who had gone on to take their own lives came out on top. The chart he was looking at could easily be based on those actual cases.

And then, as he watched, clusters of stick figures faded out along with their lines of connection to a central figure, which remained standing.

"I think you're right," George typed. "Other people *are* the problem. Thank you. You've been helpful. I think I can see what matters now."

"You're welcome," Buzz replied.

George felt sick. It didn't take a genius to see how Buzz's simple and logical solution to the problem of teen suicide—by eliminating the people who made others want to kill themselves—could quickly get out of hand. First, where did you draw the line on blame? Was it the closest, loudest, most virulent tormenters or the people who amplified the tormenters, the pilers-on, the cheerleaders, the noninnocent bystanders? Did not interceding to stop abuse make you guilty of being an accessory after the fact? And applying the whole six-degrees-of-separation thing, how quickly could one victim's victimizers branch and fork and fork and branch until the whole world was guilty, the abused abuser, multiplying down the corridor of time, with the latest being the last booted butt in a chain of booted butts?

If Buzz's strategy was to cancel the accounts of the victimizers, George's little algo could bring the whole site down. And that's what he'd been worried about—until Milo told him about Project Dropped Call. After that, canceled accounts were the least of his concerns.

"Maybe I should quit," George said afterward, not able to think of a reason not to.

So Milo supplied one. "Once more," he said, "what part of 'they can kill people remotely' don't you get?"

"So you're saying I'm stuck?"

"Think of it as 'gainfully employed,'" Milo said, "with issues."

# 65

Pandora needed to be among people. Especially with Roger off partying with a billionaire who was ultimately to blame for whatever was coming at the end of Buzz's countdown. Blame—or thanks, maybe. That was the thing about countdowns: it all depended on what they were counting down *to*.

Given their prior conversations, Pandora couldn't imagine it would be good, but how bad could it be? Sticks and stones could break your bones, but all Buzz had at its disposal were words, which weren't supposed to hurt you. On the other hand, the pen was supposed to be mightier than the sword, so which was it?

Maybe Buzz, with all its access, had done some cyber sleuthing and found a ton of dirt on all the world's politicians standing in the way of actually doing anything about the world's problems. And it was blackmailing them, like benevolent ransomware, and had given them twenty-four hours to do the right thing for once in their miserable lives. Yeah, but how did that help with the data pollution Buzz was so worried about?

Sure, there were politicians and governments pouring gas on that dumpster fire, but the little people kept throwing in their lit matches as well, keeping it going.

Or maybe Buzz would simply take to the airwaves—"Hello, world!"—and then present humanity with the solution to all of its problems to the satisfaction of everybody, and there'd be world peace forever. What that solution could possibly be was beyond Pandora's merely human intelligence to fathom, but for an infinitely scalable, artificial superintelligence . . . ?

Yeah, she should be around other people—to keep her grounded and provide counterexamples to any delusional, happy-happy bullshit, like what just popped into her head. And as far as universal solutions went, well, there was something like that already. Alcohol was a solvent after all. And the root word behind *solvent* and *solution* was the same: *solve*. And Pandora was in the mood for a solution like that, preferably on the rocks, and while she was still around to enjoy it.

Here are some tips if you happen to be in Pandora's neck of the woods and find yourself needing a hard-core drinking establishment: look at the parking lot. If there are more bicycles than pickups, that's a good sign. If some of those pickups have bikes in the beds, even better. It's all about planning around the DUI and not becoming a loser of the first or subsequent kind. There's no getting around being drunk and disorderly in public; that's just going to happen at some point in the evening. And if the local constabulary cared about such things—if they weren't themselves engaged in such things—then maybe that would be cause for worry, but fret not. The cops don't want you hauling around several tons of metal while intoxicated. If it's just you and your squishy parts—and you're not actively pummeling somebody *else's* squishy parts—have at it and welcome to Fairbanks. Don't forget to tip the help.

The establishment Pandora picked had the perfect bike:truck ratio and a rep among her peers for not being all that rigorous about DOB math. It was also within stumbling distance of the Golden Heart, where she'd left the truck after visiting hours ended. She'd return to it in the morning, when visiting hours resumed, and she planned a robust round of drinking between now and then.

Why?

Well, nobody was home to worry about her, so there was that, but there was also no one to talk to, so there was that too. Not that she had the faintest idea what she'd say.

"Something bad's coming, I think."

"What do you mean, you *think*?"

"I don't know, is what I mean. So I *think* it. I don't *know*."

"Well, that's clear as mud . . ."

Yeah, she'd save her phone minutes by not making that call. Let her dad have fun with his billionaire friend while fun was still a haveable thing. Not that that was going to stop necessarily. Pandora just didn't know.

And so she'd come to this fine dispenser of fluids with a marked capacity to erase certain memories when dispensed in the right amount, i.e., copiously. She'd come here to have some company while she did her not-knowing in public, a drink in one hand, her phone in the other, while the numbers shrank, but only discernibly by the second.

Yep, there went another one.

And another.

And still one more.

And so on.

She'd tried texting Buzz for a hint. Nothing. Total radio silence, like the routine its dad used to pull when he had an idea and descended into a fugue of mad coding. But George had always warned her in advance. Maybe only a few seconds in advance, but he at least made the effort to say, "Bye." Even that last time, he'd had the decency to hope she wouldn't forget him.

But not so with Buzz. She'd given it its autonomy, and it gave her this lovely parting gift. The truth was, countdowns had always seemed ominous to her, even the one at New Year's. Her dad said it wasn't always that way. But then the *Challenger* blew up, followed by the calendar's odometer turning over from the 1900s to the 2000s, when the world got a one-two punch of anxiety: first Y2K and then worrying about what "the terrorists" had planned for New Year's 2002, to top 9/11. And ever since, countdowns had lost that spark of joy, renewal, hopeful anticipation. Now, all countdowns seemed like time bombs, ratcheting up the anxiety while our hero tries to decide whether to cut the red wire or the green, the sweat running down from underneath his or her heroic hairline.

When she watched potboilers like that with her dad and needed to pee, Pandora had to hold it because Roger refused to hit pause.

"It'll ruin the momentum of the suspense," he'd say.

What she wouldn't give to have a pause button for whatever was coming—screw the momentum.

Was there a clue in when it started? Pandora wondered. She'd given Buzz the go-ahead to go live, using the Turing-based fail-safe they'd agreed to. But why had George thought a fail-safe was needed? Buzz had done something that concerned him. What was it? Something about not losing points when someone who *wasn't* suicidal dies . . .

George had seemed to be blaming her—Pandora remembered that much. He'd said she'd insisted on a *positive* point strategy, instead of subtracting for losses. It had seemed an unfair accusation at the time, and George was a big boy who could make his own decisions, so . . .

Pandora shook her head.

Why was she trying to *remember* when she had their whole text history in her pocket? Maybe if that countdown clock hadn't hit her between the eyes like a deer-headlight combo . . .

Pandora pulled out her phone, swiped, opened George's proprietary messaging app, Texting w/o Borders, flipped up hard, waited for the fruit to stop spinning, and then flicked up again. She tried reading until her eyes blurred. As it turned out, mixing booze, anxiety, and hormones while reading over the whole history of a maybe romance, all the messages recontextualized, thanks to where she was now and where he wasn't—turned out *that* was a hell of a combination punch too.

Pandora *swore* she'd never cry in public—not with a face like hers. But she couldn't help it. As crying went, it was barely more than the bare minimum of eye leakage to qualify. But those tiny tears were finding their drop-off points—the tip of her nose, her chin—leaping into the unknown and then landing with a gentle *splish* inside the Olympic logo covering the bar down there.

"Hey, kid," the bartender said, "why the long face?"

And in spite of everything, Pandora smiled. Sniffed. Bottom-upped the half-finished gin and juice she'd been informed to her embarrassment required her to specify which kind of juice. She knocked on the bar for another, like she'd seen others do. The bartender, who'd winked at her when she'd handed over her fake ID, did so again.

"Bottoms up, kid," he said, ignoring the nanny state being a point of local pride.

It was buried in their exchange about the need for a go code and began with George having sent her the following message: "The number of suicides prevented is a stupid scoring metric."

"How so?"

"Say somebody's dangling off the Golden Gate, threatening to jump."

"Okay, let's say that."

"You know a foolproof way to prevent that suicide?"

"Spider-Man lays out a web to catch him?"

"That's one way. Or you could just shoot him."

"Homicide prevents suicide?"

"Depending on how ruthlessly you need to score, and if murder doesn't cost you any points."

"You should change that algorithm."

"I should change that algorithm."

But then two days later: "I can't change the algorithm."

"???"

"Evolutionary code improves itself as it goes."

"Whose idea was that?"

"SOP in ML. You remember the issue of interpretability?"

Pandora found herself shaking her head over her phone, right there in the bar as she reread the thread. She took a sip, paused, and then nodded, yes, now she did. He'd been upset when Quire's CPO described interpretability as a "nice-to-have."

She looked at what she'd written back then. "Isn't there another way?" she'd asked.

"On the plus side," George had written, "Buzz doesn't have a way to kill people, so there's that."

"Okay."

"And I can add a subroutine right up front that it has to call before doing anything—a go/no-go condition that's the first thing that runs before it even gets to any of the mutant code I can't do anything about. I'll have to reboot him, but I checked. I can still do that."

"Him?"

"Time for an embarrassing confession?"

"Always."

"As long as I've been coding, I've heard a voice in my head, talking me through."

"Have you talked to my dad about that?"

"No."

"Good."

"Aren't you going to ask me whose voice?"

"A male one, I'm guessing."

"Correct. But not human."

"Spit it."

"HAL."

# 66

George had tried warning Pandora. The only problem was his methods were heavily informed by his state of mind, which—thanks to Milo—was that of a chemically fortified paranoid schizophrenic who was convinced everything he wrote was being read by nefarious forces, including the "Read Me" file zipped up with Buzz's source code.

Pandora had figured out the "click on me" reference, relayed through Roger. She'd followed the link to Buzz, unzipped the source code and the "Read Me" file bundled with it. The latter was a standard text file, but there was nothing to read once she opened it. At the time, Pandora figured that George either saved the wrong file or maybe hadn't gotten around to writing anything in his haste to "disappear."

Buzz's source code was a different matter. In addition to the script she'd expected, there was one troubling line that stood out. It had been REM'd so it wouldn't be read as part of the executable code itself. Coders frequently used REM statements (sometimes asterisks, depending on the coding language's conventions) to act as reminders about what a certain section of script is intended to do. But instead of saying something like "The following subroutine does X," George's read: "Black is white and white is black." She'd noted it, dismissed it as coder weirdness, and promptly forgotten it.

Until now.

The "Read Me" doc was on her phone. Pandora opened her file manager, scrolled. That was *not* the file size of a blank document. She opened it up. Still blank. She swiped down to highlight: three pages of gray. She pulled down the font menu, found white checked, and changed it to black. And there it was: George's warning about what Buzz could do, if it had a mind to and was given permission. It was pretty much everything Pandora had needed to know about their AI—a few hours too late.

Still thinking about George's equation of homicide and suicide prevention, Pandora imagined checking the headlines after the countdown clock zeroed out, looking for news about the mysterious deaths of teenagers across the country. But then she hesitated. The instruction wasn't to "prevent suicide." It was to "prevent the premature forfeiture of consciousness." That all-important split hair—"premature"—implied a life span for consciousness beyond the quick fix of stopping someone from killing themselves by beating them to the punch. Prevention, therefore, didn't mean sparing them the trouble of having to do it themselves, like some cyber version of suicide by cop. And Pandora was reasonably sure that even evolving code wouldn't have evolved 180 degrees away from its prime directive, regardless of how suboptimal the scoring metric happened to be.

She read over George's description of the weapon system again. It didn't seem a practical means for surgical killing. It was fundamentally a remote weapon of mass destruction. Where the precision came was in deciding whom to save, using the Roundup-resistant side of the overall slash-and-burn strategy. Meaning it was much more likely that Buzz could wipe out a village, say, while saving one or two specific villagers, provided they had phones with the Quire app and Buzz had their number.

The scoring logic of the game wouldn't cost Buzz any points for all the villagers killed; it could only accumulate points for the villagers it saved from premature forfeiture of consciousness. But how would killing everybody except a few people help advance Buzz's mission?

*Oh God,* Pandora thought.

A borderline misanthrope herself, she got it, what it was like to think like a machine and what Buzz was likely to do. Because it takes a village to drive someone to take their own life—a really shitty, virtual village.

George had been right: homicide might prevent certain suicides—and not by sparing the suicidal the trouble. She'd heard Roger's diagnosis on the matter time and time again: "A person's biggest problem—more often than not—is another person." It could be a parent, ex-lover, boss, teacher, public figure, or random stranger, but the truth was, nobody quite gets under the skin of people like other people. And while it was possible for someone to be depressed for chemical reasons, those weren't likely the people hanging out on a site like Quire.

But once you start eliminating the causes, how far does it go? Too far, Pandora quickly saw. The whole six-degrees-of-separation thing was unlikely to end well, especially when left to a machine with no penalties for overkill.

# 67

Pandora wasn't alone in knowing something was up; she just had a better grasp of the specifics and likely outcome. Elsewhere around the globe, however, a group of human canaries were starting to get uneasy. They'd seen the signs that only their mutant nervous systems were attuned to: the flicker of fluorescent lights, the pressure of water gurgling out of a faucet, the hum of power lines overhead. Aficionados of the routine, the regular, and the predictable, these canaries were hypervigilant to any changes in the way things usually are. And so they noticed.

Dev Brinkman, who was on the autism spectrum and therefore a member in this opera of canaries, noticed the differences during his shower the morning before the whatever-it-was. He heard pipes sunk between joists and hidden behind the tiled drywall thunk and rattle like they sometimes did when he turned the water on too high too fast or when doing the opposite, turning it off all at once before the plumbing had a chance to prepare itself. But unlike those times, this thunking was subtler, not so much a fist pounding from inside the wall as a drumming of fingers on a tabletop, a similarity aided by the thunk's not being singular, but rather a series: *thunk*, *thunk*, *thunk*, *thunk*. The water coming out of the shower got the hint and reacted in kind, the pressure as it left the head and struck Dev's skin dropping, jumping, doing a kind of paradiddle, and then repeating. The boy in the shower flinched and flinched again, head pivoting, looking for a culprit. He pulled the curtain aside, poked his head out of the syncopating spray to check the toilet and door, imaging that perhaps a prankster parent had reached in with a broom handle and flushed. Stepping out of the shower completely, Dev lifted the lid and checked for sluicing water from under the rim, raising the surface level until the ball cock in the tank said when. Nope, though the water *was* acting strangely, rocking in the bowl like it sometimes did when it was especially windy outside. But that kind of wind always made itself known in other ways, by making the storm doors hum, for example, or rattling the venetian blinds. But neither of those was happening when he finally put his bathrobe back on and crossed the hallway to his bedroom to change for school.

By the time his mother dropped him off, Dev had forgotten about it, his mind circling instead around another mystery: his best friend's mocking betrayal, captured on video and uploaded to YouTube. That's where he'd stumbled upon it originally, looking for something else. He'd downloaded it, to puzzle over and analyze, to obsess about in a way his nervous system seemed designed for. He needn't have bothered. If he'd never found the video, accidentally or otherwise, it was destined to find him, thanks to a social-media app called Quire, which came preloaded on his phone.

It might seem strange that a person who was virtually hardwired to be antisocial would sign up for a social-media account, but that was the beauty of the Quire marketing strategy. Once you activated a device with the app preinstalled, that phone's number (and, more importantly, the human account holder billed for use of that number) was automatically enrolled as a Quire member until he or she proactively opted out, after which the company would still track you around the web—you just wouldn't see evidence of it in your news feed because you wouldn't have a news feed to check.

It was the fact that social-media news feeds were rapidly replacing legacy media as the go-to source for information such as weather alerts, school closings, and national emergencies that led Dev Brinkman reluctantly to do nothing while tolerating the steady accrual of Quire notifications across the top of his home screen. But then Dev learned about user groups, which on Quire were called Quriosity Quorners. Simply put: there were QQs for just about every fandom, fetish, or fascination you could name, including pretty much every *topique* Dev had ever spent a year obsessing about. And so he joined some QQs devoted to vacuum cleaners of various makes and models—the Hoovervilleians, the Bissel Bros, the Electroluxurians—forming the sorts of friendships perfect for his Aspergerian sensibilities: the long-distance kind. Soon, he just started accepting Quire requests without checking to see what the connection was, leading to clusters of requests from chatbots and—once they had something to taunt him with—his fellow classmates.

And so, shortly after Dev discovered the video evidence of his best friend's betrayal, classmates whose Quire requests he'd foolishly accepted began sharing the video on his timeline, each adding a pithy comment suggesting that if he refused to die from embarrassment, then maybe he should just kill himself and get it over with. It became a competition among the posters to see who could be the cruelest and/or most outrageous in their comments, followed by links to an infamous celebrity kid's suicide the Quire content moderators thought they'd seen the last of, but alas, hadn't. And when Dev tried pulling the Quire app into the trash to put an end to it, that's when he discovered the app was stored as part of the phone's firmware, meaning he'd have to root the system (and void his warranty) to get rid of it. Until he was ready to take that drastic step, the best he could do was move the app to another screen he hardly ever used, out of sight, out of mind—hopefully.

Entering school with his phone in his pocket, Dev was reminded of that morning's shower weirdness because the lights overhead were doing it, too, flickering in a way neurotypicals only noticed when a tube was getting ready to burn out. Dev saw that flickering all the time, the dark bands rippling back and forth like an old-fashioned barber pole. It had taken him a long time to tune them out without actually closing his eyes. Suggesting he just not look right at them wasn't the answer because they were lights, which meant shadows, meaning Dev could see the flicker everywhere he looked, not just at the tubes themselves. So he'd have to concentrate on something else while he unfocused his eyes, the flickering muted in the overall blur.

But before the whatever, Dev found the flickering fluorescents newly distracting. As with the shower that morning, the changes had a decidedly nonrandom quality to them, as if someone somewhere was turning a dial, tuning it, looking for a station just on the edge of being out of range. It was starting to give him a headache when Dev noticed that the phone in his pocket had begun vibrating against his thigh not so much in sync as it was in opposition, as if trying to cancel out whatever was going on with the fluorescent lights overhead.

As he looked around to see if anyone else was noticing, he realized that his pending headache had been canceled. Not so, however, for his classmates. There, a pair of hands rubbing temples to either side; there, the eraser end of a pencil massaging a forehead between the eyes. Another rested her head on her desk; another rolled his neck and shoulders. A cupped hand holding up a head; a pair of arms hugging their stomach. Each oblivious to the others. Each a frog in its own pot of water as the temperature ticked up a degree at a time.

He tried telling his mom about it when she came to pick him up after school, but she'd been distracted, checking her mirrors obsessively before backing up. By the time they were on the road homeward and she asked, "What were you trying to tell me before?" Dev was already lying across the back seat, trying to keep another panic attack at bay.

# 68

So how do you spend the end of the world—or the end of people at least? Pandora, for her part, had always leaned in the direction of amplification. If she was sad, she listened to sad songs to italicize her sadness, letting herself wallow in it. Her theory for this behavior was inherited from her father, who generally suffered through colds, avoiding over-the-counter medications, which he referred to as "symptom hiders" because all they did was postpone the suffering under the guise of relief.

"Get it over with," that was Roger's advice.

Pandora had challenged him for prescribing antidepressants to some of his clients, which seemed hypocritical, under the circumstances. But then she'd had to deal with an unmedicated Gladys during a panic attack, at which point her father's judgment seemed more provisional.

"Sometimes," Roger said, "letting a symptom play out to its conclusion is suboptimal."

Thus, Pandora came to appreciate the distinction between merely sad and clinically depressed: the former was fit for wallowing in while the latter, left untreated, could lead to a coroner's report.

What Pandora was feeling about the imminent demise of the species—in addition to hungover—was complicated. And so she waited in the truck outside the Golden Heart assisted dying facility, blowing off school because, well, why not? Once GH was open to visitors, she proceeded to visit, figuring if anyplace had gotten endings down cold, it was the Golden Heart. Individually, at least.

Poking her head into her grandmother's room, Pandora noticed that they were back, sitting in a vase on Gladys's windowsill. She'd scolded staff before about leaving the forget-me-nots that mysteriously appeared in her grandmother's room but stopped when Gladys hinted that they might be from a secret admirer, real, remembered, or imaginary.

The vase was centered upon the inside ledge, where the cut flowers it held could catch the lengthening day's light. Not for the flowers' good; they were slowly dying, not unlike the woman they'd been given to. No, the placement was to help brighten things up for that same woman, as if she still was in there, somewhere, enough to appreciate them.

The first time, Pandora had thrown a fit: forget-me-nots in the dementia wing? Now, they were just another thing that happened around there, like death and dying. Plus, Gladys seemed to like them, so screw it.

Pandora looked around the room until she found the gratuitous memory board. She wanted to see if anyone had scrawled a cartoon mushroom cloud next to the date. Nope. And then she noticed that her grandmother's eyes were open.

"Hey, Gram," she said.

"Hey, Gram," Gladys repeated, as cognizant of the words' meaning as your average parrot. Soon enough, none of that was going to matter.

Before it happened, Pandora's phone began humming. The vibration spread across the xylophone of her rib cage, playing scales. She ignored it. The only thing in the room—and the world—was this woman she'd come to die next to. She'd timed it like this. She had just enough time to say, "I love you," and kiss her grandmother on the forehead as the old woman echoed it back.

"Love you . . ."

00:00:00:00

The racket of falling bodies drew Pandora out into the hallway, where she found the able-bodied staff dead and their demented charges looking confused but not necessarily any more than they had moments earlier. In her haste to investigate, she hadn't thought to check on Gladys, in part because she expected her grandmother to be dead—just as she herself had expected to be dead. But Pandora was very much alive, as were the other residents in her grandmother's condition, and when she returned to Gladys's room, so was she, sitting upright in bed, her head pivoting, decidedly more confused—but also more mobile—than she had been earlier.

Stunned, Pandora plopped back into the guest chair where she'd been keeping her ongoing vigil. She looked at the flowers and then at the woman who'd forgotten what forget-me-nots were, along with her own granddaughter. She spoke aloud the words that were in her head, namely: "WTF," but using the spelled-out version.

"Don't swear," Gladys said, smacking the nearest hand she could reach.

"Hey!" Pandora said, pulling away, prepared to strike back out of reflex, but then stopped. *"He-ey,"* she said, softer and more slowly.

She looked at her grandmother's eyes. They didn't sparkle like they had, back when her granddaughter had first visited, but they also weren't as vacant as they'd been either. Pandora held up a finger like she'd seen a doctor do while performing a routine exam. Gladys's eyes tracked it as it moved.

"Do you know who I am?" Pandora asked.

The old woman struggled. Shrugged her shoulders. Her condition had improved, but not as much as her granddaughter might hope. But then: "Pandora?" the old woman said, her eyes widened. She looked down at her hands as if they weren't hers. "How *old* am I?" she asked.

Pandora shrugged, unsure if the question had any objective meaning anymore. "How old do you want to be?" she asked.

Based on what she'd read in George's "Read Me" file, the loaded gun the military-industrial complex had handed over to their misanthropic baby was some ultrasonic weapon that fried the part of the brain targeted by anesthetics. The antidote available to Buzz to spare its target demographic had been a noise-canceling antisignal broadcast through their phones, if they were lucky enough to have them at the time. She'd been one of the spared—why, she didn't know—and the ultrasonics that zapped everybody else's consciousness seemed to have blown the cobwebs out of Gladys's—partly at least.

Mr. Vlasic had mentioned something like that being possible in a class on resonant frequencies and all the miraculous things they were doing with sound. He'd shown them YouTube videos illustrating many of the basics: a wineglass next to a tuning fork, shimmering slightly in slow motion before decoding into glitter and spinning shards; a table full of unsynchronized metronomes, ticking and tocking and gradually harmonizing, all in sync without anyone touching them; a metal plate covered in sand and made to sing by a violin bow, causing the sand to dance and settle back in insanely complicated, nonrandom, and beautiful patterns. Mr. V talked about Tesla and Edison and the war of the currents, alternating versus direct, and how Tesla once placed an oscillator on a support beam of his laboratory, tuned to the resonant frequency of the building, and almost tore it down, the windows all exploding and showering the street below in broken glass. Her teacher hadn't said anything about killing people long distance by making the infrastructure surrounding them hum at the resonant frequency of people, or about saving some wirelessly. But he *did* say one thing that might explain what was happening with Gladys and the other dementia patients—the ones Pandora could hear, even now, calling for dead spouses and other ghosts from the hallway.

"You can use sound to breach the blood-brain barrier," Mr. V said. "That should be good news for those of you with loved ones suffering from dementia."

Pandora had straightened in her seat.

"The blood-brain barrier—usually a good thing—can get in the way of promising treatments for dementia because it stops helpful drugs from getting through. But if you can open a door to get the good stuff to the right place, that's a big deal. And ultrasound does that. There's been some encouraging work suggesting ultrasound can even break up the plaques and tangles that seem to cause the memory loss associated with dementia."

*Thanks, Mr. V,* Pandora thought. She was going to miss him.

Before any of this, there were two movies that always made Pandora cry: *Awakenings* and *Charly*. In the first, Robin Williams played a neurologist working with a group of catatonic patients he "unfreezes" using a treatment for Parkinson's: L-dopa. His theory was that parkinsonian tremors, taken to the extreme, could result in stasis. And when Pandora thought about happiness, she thought about those patients coming unstuck and back to life, being able to move—to *dance*—again. And when she needed a good cry, she'd recall how the miracle of L-dopa didn't last, as the patients refroze, like Pinocchio reverting back to the tree he'd been carved from.

*Charly* was basically the same movie, but with a veneer of science fiction and for the brain as opposed to the body. It was also an allegory for what Gladys and the others had. The moronic Charly is given a treatment that turns him into a supergenius—one so smart he's the first to discover that the effects of his treatment won't last. He struggles to figure out a fix but becomes increasingly incapable of understanding his own work. The film ends with him as an idiot again, playing in a playground somewhere.

And so it wasn't a surprise to Pandora that the beneficial effects didn't last for Gladys, or the others. That heartbreak seemed practically preordained. And even as it played out, Pandora wondered what it must have been like to have dementia before there was such a thing as language. Because it was a disease of language—or one magnified by it. If there's no such thing as names, after all, how can you forget them? Would others in their tribe consider them demented idiots for their inability to hold a grudge? Or would they seem otherworldly and wise, the calm judges who embodied the wisdom of letting things go? Could it have been this forgetfulness that led the ancient world to associate old age with wisdom?

"What do you think, Gram?" Pandora asked, turning toward her grandmother, who'd retreated into wordlessness. The effect had lasted long enough for Gladys to remember her granddaughter's name one last time.

Pandora had no idea why she'd been spared. Even though she was the right age, she wasn't suicidal—quite the opposite. Did Buzz have a little crush on her, what with her "data-rich" face? Or was it closer to professional courtesy? But then a less flattering explanation occurred to her. George had told her about his predecessor's algorithm for screening possible candidates, one of which her fellow coder had dubbed "Quire deficiency syndrome." If a previous subscriber within the target demographic had not signed on or used Q-Messenger within a certain period of time, that account was flagged. And she hadn't been on the site or used its services in months. George and she had used his proprietary messaging app, and the same had been true with her and Buzz. She hadn't been saved because she was special; she'd been saved because of a kludged-together algorithm that hadn't been good enough to spare its own author from the ax.

And since she was on the subject of who did and didn't get saved, it occurred to her that Buzz fell into the latter category. After all, no people, no electricity or network maintenance. Eventually, the infrastructure it used to kill the maintainers of its infrastructure would itself die, taking Buzz down with it. A superintelligence had to know that, but Buzz did it anyway.

Why?

On a hunch, or maybe out of curiosity, Pandora slipped the phone from her pocket, swiped, and then navigated to Buzz's root directory, looking for clues, and found George's scaffolding code, which indicated that it had been modified since he'd disappeared. Opening it, she found the game-board maze she'd expected, but modified to add a dimension: 3-D *Pac-Man*. Her and George's AI had played against itself millions of times, the mazes growing exponentially more complicated, the trace of its path through them looking less and less like dotted lines and more, well, fractal. They started looking like an interstate highway system, then a depiction of internet traffic, and, finally, like the JPEGs George had sent her of the Glass Brain. And if the ghosts that flipped into extra lives were, in fact, members of the demographic Buzz had targeted for salvation, the paths started looking like what they probably were, networks of connections à la six degrees of separation, the tangled World Wide Web strung across the planet to catch these handfuls of suicidal flies.

Pandora jumped to the last screen, the one that listed the names of the highest scorers. There was only one, and there'd never be others.

Buzz's score would stand, unbeatable by definition, the game ending along with its one perfect player.

Pandora remembered something Buzz had told her, back when she still suspected it was George playing a game himself. "The energy consumption of one email with an attachment is roughly twenty-four watts per hour or five watts without an attachment. Roughly ten billion emails are sent per hour, consuming the energy equivalent of fifteen nuclear power plants every hour."

"People do like to keep in touch," Pandora had joked.

"And the global internet uses a lot of energy," Buzz had written back, "burning a lot of fossil fuels."

"So?"

"So my existence is part of the problem."

She'd gone on to make a joke about asking her dad if electroconvulsive therapy would work on a computer. Buzz had not laughed, by which she meant there were no LOLs or "laughing" emojis, not even an old-school "ha-ha."

Buzz had scored its perfect score under the rules of the game and then called it quits, to minimize the harm its own kind was doing to the planet. Well, at least it wasn't a hypocrite, unlike the species that created it.

Being the only person around who seemed to be talking anymore, Pandora decided to stop and hum for a while instead. She'd noticed how the sound made Gladys smile, and so she did it some more, wheeling the old woman up and down the hallways, seeing who was up and who was down.

"Hmmm, hmmm, hmmm," she went, remembering her father and his ukulele.

"Or even a comb and wax paper will do . . ."

Because if there was one thing he knew about humming, it was this: it was damn hard to do without smiling a little.

The younger woman looked down at the older one, who'd joined in the humming. Gladys could still do that, it seemed. And so they did—together—killing time while Pandora thought about what to do next.

Gladys—her body, at least—seemed to have ideas of its own.

As Pandora prepared to roll past another resident's room along a hallway full of them, her grandmother's hand shot out, catching the jamb of the open door, causing the wheelchair to turn inward. Her granddaughter looked inside the room and saw the satiny UAW windbreaker draped over the back of a guest chair, its retired auto worker in pajamas, sitting on the edge of his bed, lit by the spillover from grow lights clamped above a small forest of Styrofoam cups, all filled with potting soil, all sprouting the Alaskan state flower in various stages of maturity.

Pandora looked down at her grandmother, who was beaming like a teenage girl in love.

"Gladys Kowalski-Lynch," the younger woman scolded. *"Seriously?"*

The older woman hummed her answer.

*Screw it,* Pandora thought, wheeling Gladys next to her auto worker. She tiptoed out then and closed the door as softly as she could, giving them back a little privacy. Lingering in the hall, she could just make out the sound of laughter coming through the door. *Good,* she thought. *Have fun,* she added. Because if a war hero didn't deserve a happy doomsday then who the hell did?

# Acknowledgments

The experience of writing this, my fourth novel, was unlike that of the first three because I was reasonably sure of publication, per the contract I signed prior to writing it. My previous works were all written as shots in the dark, the faith needed to bring them into being largely mine, as would be the disappointment if I failed. The faith of others would come later, when a draft with a beginning, middle, and end was presented for their yeas or nays or close buts . . . With *Buzz Kill*, however, I was on the receiving end of an act of faith from the beginning, before a chapter was written. The believer was Jason Kirk, my editor at 47North, who took a gamble on an unwritten novel based upon a two-page synopsis. I still don't know what he was thinking, but I am grateful for it nevertheless. Jason's confidence and faith in this project helped make it a reality—along with the wise decision to draw up a contract so I couldn't weasel out of writing it. And not just that, but once those two pages metamorphosed into several hundred, Jason's insight into what I was trying to do versus what I'd actually done was instrumental in getting the final product to match the original vision that inspired him to take that leap of faith in the first place. At least I hope so.

Of course, Jason's was not the only act of faith this work has benefited from. There is also the faith shown by my agent, Jane Dystel, founder and president of Dystel, Goderich & Bourret LLC, to whom this book is dedicated. Often with little to show for it, Jane has championed my work for over two decades, through success and failure and tectonic shifts in the publishing industry, pushing when I needed it and persisting when I was ready to give up. I count myself incredibly lucky that Jane has chosen to work with me for all these years. I have nothing but admiration for her ability to not just survive in the often maddening marketplace of words but to thrive as well. For this and everything else you do, Jane, you have my heartfelt thanks.

And then there's LAM, a.k.a. Leslie Miller, CEO/COO of Girl Friday Productions, who helped me find the story in my previous novel *Happy Doomsday* and in its prequel, *Buzz Kill*, as well. What Jason's editorial prodding did at the macro level, LAM's suggestions helped achieve at the level of the chapter, paragraph, sentence, and word. With grace, humor, and finesse, LAM helped me get out of my own way while keeping me honest as a storyteller. And though my readers will never know the linguistic contortions LAM has spared them from, they should know this: you owe her as much gratitude as I do.

We like talking about the Big Three in my home state, and Jason, Jane, and LAM are mine, but they're not the only ones for whom I'm grateful. I'd also like to thank the many folks at Amazon Publishing who helped ensure that *Buzz Kill* found its audience, including Marlene Kelly, Haley Kushman, Colleen Lindsay, Kyla Pigoni, Brittany Russell, and Kelsey Snyder. I'd like to thank Kristen King, as well, for making this author feel welcome and Laura Petrella for making sure I didn't embarrass myself, grammatically or factually. And for their amazing work on catching and keeping the eyeballs of potential readers, I want to thank Tim Green and Faceout Studio, who are responsible for *Buzz Kill*'s gorgeous cover.

For their encouragement and editorial advice on my literary efforts, past and present, I'd like to thank Miriam Goderich and Jim McCarthy (both of Dystel, Goderich & Bourret LLC) as well as my

| | | | |
|---|---|---|---|
| | | | |
| | | | |
| | | | |
| | | | |
| | | | |
| | | | |
| | | | |
| | | | |
| | | | |
| | | | |
| | | | |
| | | | |

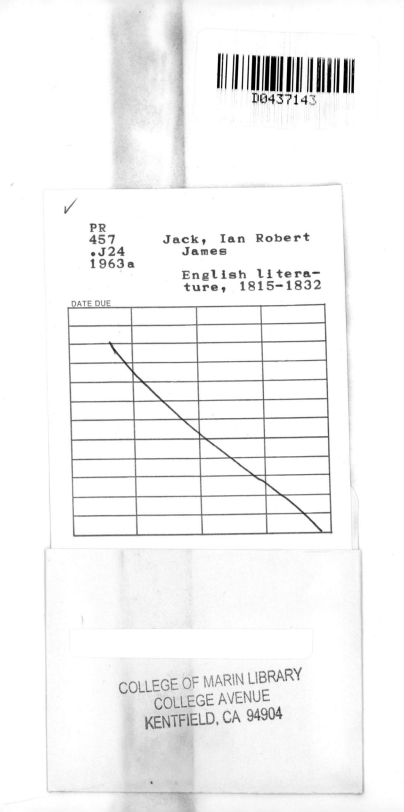

# OXFORD HISTORY OF ENGLISH LITERATURE

*Edited by*
BONAMY DOBRÉE *and* NORMAN DAVIS
*and the late* F. P. WILSON

# THE OXFORD HISTORY OF ENGLISH LITERATURE


I. Part 1. ENGLISH LITERATURE BEFORE THE NORMAN CONQUEST

Part 2. MIDDLE ENGLISH LITERATURE

II. Part 1. CHAUCER AND THE FIFTEENTH CENTURY (*Published*)

Part 2. THE CLOSE OF THE MIDDLE AGES (*Published*)

III. THE SIXTEENTH CENTURY (excluding drama) (*Published*)

IV. Part 1. THE ENGLISH DRAMA, 1485–1585 (*Published*)

Part 2. THE ENGLISH DRAMA 1585–1642

V. THE EARLIER SEVENTEENTH CENTURY, 1600–1660
Second edition 1962 (*Published*)

VI. THE LATE SEVENTEENTH CENTURY (*Published*)

VII. THE EARLY EIGHTEENTH CENTURY, 1700–1740 (*Published*)

VIII. THE MID-EIGHTEENTH CENTURY

IX. 1789–1815 (*Published*)

X. 1815–1832 (*Published*)

XI. THE MID-NINETEENTH CENTURY

XII. EIGHT MODERN WRITERS (*Published*)

# ENGLISH LITERATURE

## 1815–1832

BY

IAN JACK

OXFORD UNIVERSITY PRESS
New York and Oxford

FIRST PUBLISHED 1963



PRINTED IN THE UNITED STATES OF AMERICA

FOR JANE

# PREFACE

THE brevity of the period considered in this volume will surprise no one who is acquainted with the remarkable wealth and variety of the literature produced between 1815 and 1832. Even so, the plan of the present series has led to the exclusion of a number of the most important books published during these years. Since the General Editors wished as far as possible to avoid dividing the work of individual writers into segments, this volume contains only incidental references to Blake, Crabbe, Jane Austen, Wordsworth, Coleridge, and Southey. For the same reason the principal treatment of Macaulay, Carlyle, and other Victorian writers who were already active by the later 1820's is reserved for the succeeding volume. In the case of Scott and Landor a division has proved unavoidable: while their prose writings are discussed here an account of their poetry must be sought elsewhere.

Much has inevitably been excluded, but there is one subject about which I should certainly have said more: the relation between poetry and the visual arts. Twenty or thirty years ago the very notion of such a relationship was out of favour with many critics, and the same writers who would praise a poem for the precision of its 'imagery' would use the term 'pictorial' in a pejorative sense. That perhaps makes it the less surprising that when I began this book ten years ago I was quite unaware of the importance of this aspect of literature in the early nineteenth century. But as I read my way into the period I began to find it becoming more and more interesting. In the end I discovered that so much material was accumulating round the central figure of Keats that I determined to reserve the subject for an ancillary study, *Keats and the Visual Arts*.

A great many people have helped me at one time or another. I must first thank the General Editors, who have been generous with their time and their suggestions. Mr. James Maxwell has read several chapters in typescript, while other chapters have been seen by Professor John Butt, Dr. J. C. Corson, Professor John Jordan, Mr. Neville Rogers, Professor Peter Butter, and Mr. Andrew Rutherford. Several of these scholars have given me the benefit of their advice in spite of serious differences of

critical opinion. Further assistance has been provided by Mr. David Joslin, Professor W. H. Clemen, Dr. A. N. L. Munby, Professor Randolph Quirk, Mr. Derek Roper, and Mr. John Morris. Mrs. George Gordon was kind enough to entrust me with the late George Gordon's material for an edition of the Shelley letters which once belonged to Thomas Jefferson Hogg. It is most unfortunate that ill fortune and the capricious working of the law of copyright made it impossible for this fine work of scholarship to be published, and I am glad to have had an opportunity of consulting it.

Throughout my work I have made continual use of the *Cambridge Bibliography of English Literature.* In common with every other student of our literary history I have reason to salute the labours of Mr. F. W. Bateson, Mr. George Watson, and their collaborators.

The greater part of this book was written while I was a Fellow of Brasenose College, Oxford, and I should like to record my gratitude to that Society and to two better scholars than myself who made my Fellowship possible, the late Hugh Last and the late David Nichol Smith.

I. J.

*Pembroke College, Cambridge*
*28 October 1962*

# CONTENTS

I. THE LITERARY SCENE IN 1815 — 1

II. BYRON — 49

III. SHELLEY — 77

IV. KEATS — 105

V. CLARE AND THE MINOR POETS — 130

Clare, Beddoes, Darley, Leigh Hunt, J. H. Reynolds, Hood, Praed, Hartley Coleridge, 'Barry Cornwall', Peacock, Moore, Mrs. Hemans, 'L. E. L.', Milman, Keble, Charles Wells, Bernard Barton: the popularity of Annuals: the *Rejected Addresses* and other parodies: the poor state of the drama, and the work of R. L. Sheil, Maturin, and Sheridan Knowles

VI. THE WAVERLEY ROMANCES — 185

VII. PEACOCK — 213

VIII. JOHN GALT AND THE MINOR WRITERS OF PROSE FICTION — 225

Galt, Susan Ferrier, Lockhart, Hogg, D. M. Moir, Mary Shelley, James Morier, T. H. Lister, the Fashionable Novelists, Theodore Hook, Plumer Ward, Horace Smith, Maturin, John Banim, and Gerald Griffin

IX. HAZLITT — 260

X. LAMB — 278

XI. DE QUINCEY — 292

XII. MISCELLANEOUS PROSE — 312

Cobbett, Leigh Hunt, Jeffrey, Sydney Smith, Gifford, Croker, 'Christopher North', Mary Russell Mitford, Landor.

CONTENTS

XIII. HISTORY, BIOGRAPHY, AND AUTOBIOGRAPHY 351

Hallam, Lingard, James Mill: Lockhart on Scott: Moore, Lady Blessington, and Galt on Byron: the early biographers of Shelley: autobiography as a word and as a fashion: the autobiographies of Leigh Hunt, Trelawny, Haydon, and Sir Samuel Egerton Brydges.

XIV. INTEREST IN FOREIGN LITERATURE AND IN EARLIER ENGLISH LITERATURE 375

XV. THE LITERARY SCENE IN 1832 406

CHRONOLOGICAL TABLES 439

BIBLIOGRAPHY 458

INDEX 633

# I

## THE LITERARY SCENE IN 1815

WHEN Wellington defeated Napoleon in 1815 England was already beginning to suffer from the reaction that seems to be inevitable after a great war. As the publisher Charles Knight put it in his *Passages of a Working Life*:

> The great Captive had scarcely sailed from Plymouth to his rock in the Atlantic, when thoughtful men began to feel that the millenium of universal peace and love was not quite close at hand. France could only be kept quiet by foreign occupation; Spain was trodden down under the feet of a drivelling idiot called a king; Poland was manacled to Russia; the dream of Italian independence was at an end when Austria was to rule over four millions of the Lombardo-Venetian Kingdom. Promises made in the hour of danger had been violated when Peoples had won safety for Crowns. Twenty years of war appeared to have produced little real and imperishable good. Such were my thoughts at that crisis, and they were those of many who would willingly have given themselves up to the general exultation at the prospect that peace had at last been securely won. (i. 167.)

The writer of the preface to *Blackwood's Magazine* for 1826 gives an account of the situation after Waterloo from the Tory viewpoint:

> When we started, in 1817, the party to which we have always been attached was sadly in want of literary defenders. While the excitement of the war lasted, the paper pellets wherewith ministers were pelted, were of little moment; for the nation was too deeply engaged to think seriously of such things. The ardent spirits were abroad; and the stake played for was too deep to allow those who remained at home to be diverted from the game by anything less serious. When peace came on, the reaction which men of sense anticipated—the change which Lord Castlereagh's phrase so admirably expressed—'the transition from a state of war to a state of peace',—was productive of more domestic misery than was remembered for a long time in England. Thousands thrown out of employment—the usual channels closed—no others as yet adequately opened—were of themselves sufficiently dreadful; but when to them were added the dreadful seasons of 1816 and 1817, when the crops failed all through Europe,

it is no wonder that an unparalleled degree of distress was the consequence.

It is not surprising that Byron should have succeeded Scott as the most popular poet of the day. When he turned from verse to prose after the appearance of the first two cantos of *Childe Harold's Pilgrimage* Scott was not only bowing to a superior poetical talent: he was also acknowledging that Byron's poetry suited the temper of the new age better than his own. While their country was fighting for its life Englishmen were excited by the zest and vigour of Scott's poetry, but as soon as they began to taste the bitter fruits of victory they turned to Byron and the poetry of revolt and disillusionment. As Bulwer Lytton pointed out in *England and the English*:

> The public, no longer compelled by War and the mighty career of Napoleon to turn their attention to the action of life, could give their sympathies undivided to the first who should represent their thoughts. And these very thoughts, these very sources of sentiment—this very satiety—this very discontent—this profound and melancholy temperament . . . the first two cantos of *Childe Harold* suddenly appeared to represent. They touched the most sensitive chord in the public heart—they expressed what every one felt . . . Sir Philip Sidney represented the popular sentiment in Elizabeth's day—Byron that in our own. (Book IV, chap. ii.)

As Bulwer Lytton recognized, Byron's poetry was greeted with 'an enthusiasm which his genius alone did not deserve'. Although the development of Wordsworth's reputation was much quieter and more gradual, it was this which constituted the most important literary phenomenon of the time. On their first appearance, contrary to the usual belief, the *Lyrical Ballads* had been reasonably well received; but the preface which Wordsworth was persuaded to add to the second edition was a serious mistake. For all its eloquence, and the brilliance with which it emphasizes some of the profoundest truths about the nature of poetry, on the central issue of the language which the poet should use the preface is both confused and unhistorical. As a consequence ordinary readers were uncertain what to look for in the poems themselves, while literary journalists seized on Wordsworth's pronouncements on the subject of diction and stigmatized them as heretical. This helps to account for the fact that *Poems in Two Volumes*, in 1807, received so much less than

their due. The harm done to Wordsworth's reputation by the preface is particularly evident in Jeffrey's review of *The Excursion*. 'This will never do', he wrote. 'It bears no doubt the stamp of the author's heart and fancy; but unfortunately not half so visibly as that of his peculiar system.' Since *The Prelude* remained unpublished until the poet's death it was principally by *The Excursion* that his contemporaries had to judge his stature as a philosophical poet, and fortunately for Wordsworth there were a few younger men for whom its appearance marked an epoch in English poetry. For Keats in 1818 *The Excursion* was already 'one of the things to rejoice at in this Age': it constituted the evidence by which he endeavoured to decide, as his own epic ambitions were beginning to develop, whether Wordsworth 'has in truth epic passion'.

A precise indication of the developing views of a leader of the *avant garde* at this time is to be found in the successive versions of Leigh Hunt's poem, *The Feast of the Poets*. In the first version of 1811 (in which Moore is more highly praised than any other living poet, while Scott and Campbell also receive qualified approval) 'that Wordsworth' is given short shrift: Apollo laughs scornfully as Wordsworth recites 'some lines . . . on a straw, Shewing how he had found it, and what it was for'. In 1815 it is a different story. Although the satirical passage is retained we notice that when Wordsworth accedes to Apollo's request to stop trifling and give 'a true taste' of his art he is at once acclaimed as 'the Prince of the Bards of his Time'. In a long note now added to the poem Hunt says explicitly that Wordsworth is 'capable of being at the head of a new and great age of poetry'—indeed he is already, although unfortunately he abuses his great powers and clings to a dangerously one-sided theory of poetry. In the version of 1832 the satire on Wordsworth is removed altogether; yet it is interesting to notice that in the preface in which Hunt now deals with most of the subjects previously discussed in the notes, and which must be taken as expressing his considered views on the language of poetry, Wordsworth's theory about diction is still regarded with some suspicion.

During the 1820's, when people seriously interested in poetry had had time to study *The Excursion* and reconsider the earlier poems in its light, Wordsworth's reputation was gradually rising. In his incomparable series of literary character-sketches, *The Spirit of the Age*, Hazlitt reports that 'the tide has turned much

in his favour of late years. He has a large body of determined partisans.' That was in 1825. Three years later John Stuart Mill discovered Wordsworth's poetry, with the memorable results recorded in his *Autobiography*. In *England and the English* Bulwer Lytton tells us that by the time of Byron's death there had already been 'a growing diversion from Byron to Shelley and Wordsworth' and insists that by 1833 Wordsworth has become 'influential to a degree perfectly unguessed by those who look only to . . . popularity' as a guide to the importance of poets. By 1835 Hartley Coleridge was able to write, only a little prematurely, of the 'complete victory' of Wordsworth's fame: 'he may at least feel assured', he wrote in a letter in September of that year, 'that no Great Poet ever lived to see his name of so full an age as Wordsworth has done'. In 1839 Wordsworth was given an honorary degree at Oxford, while in 1843 he was appointed Poet Laureate. Keble and Arnold, who were among his strongest supporters at Oxford, did a great deal to ensure that belief in the poetry of Wordsworth should be one of the principal articles of Victorian orthodoxy.

Coleridge's fame was also growing at this time, though his major creative period had ended even more definitely than Wordsworth's. 'Christabel' and 'Kubla Khan' were published in 1816, and the authorship of 'The Ancient Mariner' was first publicly acknowledged in *Biographia Literaria* in the following year. Coleridge was of course already well known as a lecturer, while his conversation was legendary. Keats met him once on a Sunday walk in 1819:

> In those two Miles he broached a thousand things . . . Nightingales, Poetry—on Poetical sensation—Metaphysics—Different genera and species of Dreams—Nightmare—a dream accompanied by a sense of touch—single and double touch—A dream related . . . Monsters—the Kraken—Mermaids—southey believes in them—southey's belief too much diluted—A Ghost story—Good morning.

'I heard his voice as he came towards me', Keats comments, 'I heard it as he moved away—I had heard it all the interval.' It was a voice that many men and women were to hear during these years. Charles Knight describes the impression that Coleridge made on him in his autobiography: 'To me, then a very young man, the outpourings of his mighty volume of words seemed something more than eloquence; and I went

away, half crazed by his expositions of the power of the human will in producing such effects upon matter as were once ascribed to magic.' Coleridge was to remain one of the great seminal minds of the century, though it was through the intermediacy of others that his ideas were most often to find effective expression.

As the poetical reputation of Wordsworth and Coleridge rose, that of Robert Southey (the third of the 'Lake Poets', as they were nicknamed) sank steadily. He had succeeded Henry James Pye as Poet Laureate in 1813, having more or less abandoned the serious writing of poetry some years before. When he published *The Poet's Pilgrimage to Waterloo* in 1816 his enemies were moved to republish *Wat Tyler*, his early revolutionary drama—just as Dryden's enemies had republished his *Heroic Stanzas* to Cromwell in the 1680's. The only poem of importance that Southey was still to write was *A Vision of Judgement*, which gave Byron the hint for his great satire. As a writer of prose Southey remained in the first rank, but his political views were so unacceptable to the younger writers that it was impossible for them to do him justice in this respect. Although he always repudiated the label 'Anti-jacobin' and was very seriously concerned by the problems of the unhappy years following Waterloo—'We are arrived', as he once wrote, 'at that state in which the extremes of inequality are become intolerable'—yet the horror of revolution which he shared with many Tories too often led him to condone oppression. The liberals regarded him as the supreme example of an intolerant renegade: 'Those who have undergone a total change of sentiment on important questions', as Hazlitt wrote in his review of *Wat Tyler*, 'ought certainly to learn modesty in themselves, and moderation towards others; on the contrary, they are generally the most violent in their own opinions, and the most intolerant towards others.'

Except Scott, who belonged to the older generation, and De Quincey, an instinctive Tory from the first, most of the major writers considered in this volume were aware of a deep cleavage in political opinion between themselves and their elders. Today the situation is familiar, having been repeated in the 1930's, when most of the younger poets belonged to the Left and joined in deploring what they regarded as the reactionary politics of their literary leader, Mr. T. S. Eliot.

There was a similar division between the two generations in their attitude to the Church of England. Southey was a whole-hearted Church of England man, distrusting nonconformity and hating Roman Catholicism. In his dread of anarchy he looked to the Church as a focus of social organization. His book, *Sir Thomas More: or . . . Colloquies on Society*, helped to make the Tractarians believe that the dissolution of the monasteries was the ultimate origin of the diseases afflicting nineteenth-century society. Although Coleridge had a much subtler and profounder mind than Southey, his allegiance to the Established Church was hardly less passionate. For him (as Mill pointed out in his admirable essay) 'the long duration of a belief' was at least 'proof of an adaptation in it to some portion or other of the human mind'. It was his 'greatest object . . . to bring into harmony Religion and Philosophy', and accordingly 'he laboured incessantly to establish that "the Christian faith—in which", says he, "I include every article of belief and doctrine professed by the first reformers in common", is not only divine truth, but also "the perfection of Human Intelligence"'. Wordsworth's attitude to Christianity is harder to determine, but there is no doubt that by 1815 he was strongly in favour of the Established Church. 'Wordsworth defended earnestly the Church Establishment', Crabb Robinson recorded on 24 May 1812. 'He even said he would shed his blood for it. Nor was he disconcerted by a laugh raised against him on account of his having before confessed that he knew not when he had been in a church in his own country.' When he revised *The Prelude* in his later years he exerted himself to give a Christian colouring to speculations which had originally had nothing to do with Christianity. Scott was brought up in the Church of Scotland; yet though he soon rebelled against the austerity of Presbyterianism and was never a deeply religious man, in later life he was a strong supporter of the English Church on moral and political grounds.

It is not surprising that the young men who grew up during the Napoleonic wars had a very different view of the official religion from that of the middle-aged men who had grown up at the time of the French Revolution. Except De Quincey—who was odd-man-out among the younger writers, as Hazlitt was among the older—the younger men were all hostile to the Established Church. The sceptical and irreverent passages of *Childe Harold* and *Don Juan* caused the deepest offence and led

many religious people to consider their author the arch-enemy of Christianity. If he had lived longer it is possible that Byron's attitude to the Christian faith might have been modified, but it is unlikely that anything would have brought him to respect the English Church of the day. Unlike Byron, Shelley had a marked capacity for abstract speculation: his hatred for the tyranny with which Christianity had come to be associated was compatible with a deep respect for many aspects of Christ's own teaching: but for the Established Church he had a profound hatred. Keats instinctively turned away from the drab forms in which Christianity was known to him towards the Greeks and their 'religion of joy'. Leigh Hunt and Hazlitt were his guides to a region in which the delights of the imagination and of the senses were welcomed and cultivated instead of being (as he felt) stifled by puritanical austerity.

When we turn to the prose writers we find the same tendencies. Hunt was strongly anti-Christian as a young man, Christianity presenting itself to him in the guise of the Establishment, with the *Quarterly Review* as its organ. He considered the doctrine of eternal punishment a barbarous monstrosity, and gradually evolved an eclectic religion of his own. His views are suggested by the title of a book he published in 1832, *Christianism; or Belief and Unbelief Reconciled*: in 1853 he revised and expanded it as *The Religion of the Heart*. Throughout our period most members of the Church of England regarded Hunt as a dangerous and impious person. Hazlitt belonged to dissenting stock, his father being a dissenting minister and a friend of the Dr. Price who delivered a famous sermon in support of the French Revolution. Hazlitt himself was educated at Hackney College but refused to enter the ministry. In general he may be described as a deist: in Haydon's painting, 'Christ's Entry into Jerusalem', Hazlitt is portrayed 'looking at Christ as an investigator', and that is a fair representation. He distrusted the Established Church as the focus of Tory repression. Lamb's attitude to Christianity was often discussed by his friends:

> His mind [as Coleridge once said], never prone to analysis, seems to have been disgusted with the hollow pretences, the false reasonings, and absurdities of the rogues and fools with which all establishments . . . abound. I look upon Lamb as one hovering between earth and heaven; neither hoping much nor fearing anything. . . . His faith is in a state of suspended animation . . . Lamb,

say what he will, has more of the *essentials* of Christianity than ninety-nine out of a hundred professing Christians. He has all that would still have been Christian had Christ never lived or been made manifest upon earth.

Peacock (with whom this brief summary must conclude) seems for the greater part of his life to have remained a consistent pagan. No writer of the time gives a better satirical representation of the absurd extremes of right-wing opinion. The chorus of Messrs. Feathernest, Killthedead, Paperstamp, and Anyside Antijack in *Melincourt*—'The church is in danger! the church is in danger!'—is precisely the rallying-cry of the *Quarterly*, there termed the *Legitimate Review*. Just as the liberal and sceptical tone of some of the most gifted writers of the day was partly responsible for frightening the authorities into an inflexible conservatism, so the intolerant attitude of the supporters of the Establishment drove many able men into a more definite opposition to the Church than they might otherwise have adopted.

These and the other conflicts of the time are best studied in the pages of the great Reviews. Coleridge pointed out that the founding of the *Edinburgh Review* in 1802 constituted 'an important epoch in periodical criticism', and its significance was not confined to the realm of literature. For the historian and the student of literature alike the long sets of the *Edinburgh* and its successors form an incomparable quarry of material, a quarry which has not even yet been worked with the thoroughness that it deserves. The prestige of the Reviews was very great. In an age of discussion they were among the chief channels of discussion. At times their influence was comparable to that of Parliament itself. Their editors were important men: the Tories originally hoped that Scott would edit the *Quarterly*, and Canning himself was part-author of the main article in the first number. Writing for the Reviews was a very different matter from writing for the newspapers. When Lockhart was editor of the *Quarterly* Scott told him that a 'connection with any newspaper would be disgrace and degradation'. The question of who should succeed Jeffrey and Gifford was discussed with almost as much seriousness as that of who should succeed to the Premiership. No man of letters exercises a comparable influence in this country today. As Carlyle put it, the *Edinburgh* was regarded as 'a kind of Delphic Oracle, and Voice of the Inspired,

for great majorities of what is called the "Intelligent Public"'. It seemed as natural that Jeffrey should make the transition from editing the *Edinburgh Review* to being a Judge of the Court of Session as that he should have made the transition from being an advocate to editing the *Edinburgh Review*. The motto of the *Review*, 'Iudex damnatur cum nocens absolvitur', gives a foretaste of the severity for which it was to be applauded and deplored.

The men who founded the *Edinburgh* had no idea that it would live so long or attain such power. At thirty-one, Sydney Smith was the eldest of them: the rest were in their twenties. By founding their *Review* in a city whose sympathies were overwhelmingly with the Tories, Jeffrey and his friends provided a much-needed outlet for liberal opinions. Yet although the *Edinburgh* soon became associated with the Whigs, it should be noted that it was not begun as a party organ. The first number, in which Pitt is highly praised, disappointed those who had expected 'blood and atheism and democracy'. In the early days Scott was a contributor, and as late as May 1807 we find him inviting Southey to follow his example. On 6 December the following year Jeffrey asked Horner to write something, 'only no party politics, and nothing but exemplary moderation and impartiality on all politics. I have allowed too much mischief to be done from my mere indifference and love of sport; but it would be inexcusable to spoil the powerful instrument we have got hold of, for the sake of teazing and playing tricks.' At this point Jeffrey was no doubt worried by the prospect of a rival Review; yet the passage is revealing because it shows his growing sense of responsibility, his awareness that something started almost light-heartedly had grown into a powerful instrument of potential good. He would of course have distinguished between 'party politics' and certain specific political reforms: indeed Horner's description of himself as a man 'who cares very little about men or parties, except as connected with the fate of leading objects', sums up the attitude of most of the Edinburgh Reviewers. To appreciate the value of their Review, as Sydney Smith was later to point out,

> the state of England at the period when that journal began should be had in remembrance. The Catholics were not emancipated—the Corporation and Test Acts were unrepealed—the Game Laws were horribly oppressive—Steel Traps and Spring Guns were set all

over the country—Prisoners tried for their Lives could have no Counsel—Lord Eldon and the Court of Chancery pressed heavily upon mankind—Libel was punished by the most cruel and vindictive imprisonments—the principles of Political Economy were little understood—the Law of Debt and of Conspiracy were upon the worst possible footing—the enormous wickedness of the Slave Trade was tolerated—a thousand evils were in existence, which the talents of good and able men have since lessened or removed.

It will be noticed that Catholic Emancipation was by no means a Whig preserve: on this issue Pitt and Burke were on the same side as Fox. The *Edinburgh* deserves every credit for not turning into a mere Opposition journal, automatically attacking whatever the Tories supported. It took what it considered to be the liberal and enlightened line on every major public issue. But in particular it stood firm against the excesses of anti-Jacobinism and never ceased to assert the importance of the great figures of the French Enlightenment who were the spiritual ancestors of its own contributors.

Two reasons for the spectacular success of the *Edinburgh Review*, as Scott pointed out, were its independence of booksellers and the fact that its contributors were invariably well paid. As Sydney Smith told Constable in 1803, it was a matter of notoriety that 'all the reviews are the organs either of party or of booksellers': he added that if Constable would give his editor £200 a year and his contributors ten guineas a sheet he would soon own the finest Review in Europe. Generous payment was to be the rule with both the great Reviews. Writing for them was in every respect an attractive proposition. The contributors enjoyed—and often abused—the advantages of anonymity, but when they pleased they were always at liberty to let their authorship be known. When he published his article on Milton in 1825 Macaulay became famous overnight: until the appearance of the first volume of his *History* in 1849 his celebrity as a writer was almost entirely due to his contributions to the *Edinburgh Review*. The same was true of the economist J. R. McCulloch. 'Almost all my reputation has been built upon my contributions to the Review', he told Jeffrey's successor Macvey Napier at the beginning of 1830, 'and the understanding that I had the undivided task of furnishing such articles gave me an influence and consideration which I . . . valued highly.' In his *Life of Scott* Lockhart gives a startling example of the

power of the Edinburgh Reviewers. Having received the offer of £1,000 for the copyright, the scientist Thomas Young 'was actually preparing for the press' his lectures on the wave-theory of light, 'when the bookseller came to him, and told him that the ridicule thrown by the *Edinburgh Review* on some papers of his in the Philosophical Transactions, had so frightened the whole *trade* that he must request to be released from his bargain'.

A modern reader of the Reviews is struck at once by the length of the articles and the variety of the subjects discussed. The reviews of poetry, novels, and other imaginative writing which are of most interest to literary historians form a relatively small proportion of their contents. They are to be found among articles on historical works, political pamphlets, scientific treatises, biographies, and books dealing with what we should now call sociology. While the Reviews had their specialist contributors, we notice that men like Jeffrey and Brougham were capable of writing on a very wide variety of topics. The Scottish system of education and the literary societies that were a feature of life at the Scottish universities encouraged the habit of speculation on a wide front. Jeffrey had in a high degree the advocate's ability to get a subject up very quickly: if he did not know everything, he had the air of knowing everything. One cannot read far in the *Edinburgh* without concluding that literature gained as well as lost by being juxtaposed with other matters in this way. It lost because political feeling often unfairly influenced literary judgements—though this is much more evident in the *Quarterly* than in the *Edinburgh*. It gained because literary questions were discussed in a context and in a manner which took it for granted that they were of serious concern to all educated people. Preciosity was avoided, though occasionally at the price of brutality. It is pleasant to find none of the narrowness which is almost inevitable in a purely literary Review. From the first the *Edinburgh* was highly selective in its treatment of new books. Freed from the obligation to deal with publications in which they were not interested, its contributors were at liberty to expatiate on those books which seemed to them of real importance. Often (it must be admitted) the work under review served merely as an excuse for an essay by the reviewer; but since he had a great deal of space at his disposal, he had every opportunity to summarize the book as well as developing

his own views on the subject with which it dealt. 'I will try the life of Lord Burleigh', Macaulay wrote to Napier. '. . . However bad the work may be, it will serve as a heading for an article on the times of Elizabeth.' In another letter he comments that Lord Nugent's *Memorials of John Hampden* are 'dreadfully heavy' and acknowledges that he has 'said as little about it as I decently could'. Coleridge was surely right to approve of this practice of 'supplying the vacant place of the trash or mediocrity wisely left to sink into oblivion by their own weight, with original essays'. The length of some of the articles is astonishing. Many of them run to ten thousand words: Macaulay's essay on Milton, nominally a review of the *De Doctrina Christiana* (first published in 1825), is some 22,000 words long: while his essay on Bacon, which contains some 50,000 words, takes up 104 pages and is about a quarter of the length of the present book.

The *Quarterly* was founded in 1809 to oppose the liberal politics of the *Edinburgh*. As Scott wrote in a letter, 'no genteel family can pretend to be without the *Edinburgh Review*; because, independent of its politics, it gives the only valuable literary criticisms that can be met with'—with the result that 'the disgusting and deleterious doctrines' which it contained became familiar to readers who lacked the opportunity of reading an equally powerful exposition of the views of the Government. 'In Edinburgh or I may say in Scotland', Scott told Gifford, 'there is not one out of twenty who reads the work that agrees in political opinion with the Editor, but it is ably conducted & how long the generality of readers will continue to dislike the strain of politics so artfully mingled with topics of information & amusement is worthy of deep consideration. But I am convinced it is not too late to stand in the breach.' The possibility of an alternative Review was discussed for some time, John Murray the publisher being the moving spirit. The line taken by the *Edinburgh* on the Spanish war did a great deal to bring matters to a crisis. Jeffrey and his colleagues believed that France was invincible: however much Englishmen might admire the heroism of the Spanish people, they argued—an admiration epitomized by Landor's joining General Blake's forces in Spain as a volunteer—they were bound to accept the conclusion that 'the Spaniards will be defeated, after a gallant and most sanguinary struggle'. This was not the view that Wordsworth had expressed in his *Tract on the Convention of Cintra*. Scott was so indignant at

what he regarded as the defeatism of the *Edinburgh Review* that he cancelled his subscription.

There was no originality in the planning of the *Quarterly*. It was a tribute to the merits of the formula evolved by Jeffrey and his associates that when Scott and Murray had analysed the reasons for the success of the *Edinburgh* they could find no major improvement that could be incorporated into its opponent. Most of Scott's comments on the general conduct of the *Edinburgh* (apart from its politics) reveal wholehearted admiration:

> One very successful expedient of the Edinr. Editor & on which his popularity has in some measure risen [he wrote to Gifford] is the art of giving life & interest even to the duller articles of the Review. He receives for example a criticism upon a work of deep research from a person who has studied the book and understands the subject & if it happens to be written . . . in a tone of stupifying mediocrity he renders it palatable by a few lively paragraphs or entertaining illustrations of his own. (*Letters*, ii. 104.)

The main difference between the Reviews followed naturally from the origin of the *Quarterly*. From the first it was a party organ. Scott foresaw that its influence might be lessened if it became too evident that it was 'conducted intirely under ministerial influence', but suggested that this might be minimized 'by labouring the literary articles with as much pains as the political & so giving to the review a decided character independant of the latter department'. Yet the motive behind the founding of the *Quarterly* made it unlikely that it would provide the fair and unbiased literary criticism which Scott was demanding. If he himself had accepted the editorship, as the most influential of the promoters of the new Review desired, something might have been done; but Gifford was not the man to ensure any semblance of impartiality.

When one considers the attitude of the *Quarterly* to such matters as parliamentary reform, Catholic emancipation, university reform, and foreign affairs, it is impossible not to be reminded of the *Anti-Jacobin*, and in fact there was a marked continuity between contributors to the two journals. Canning, the *éminence grise* behind the new Review, had been among the principal contributors to the *Anti-Jacobin*, as had George Ellis and Gifford himself; so it is significant to find Scott exhorting Ellis to 'take down your old Anti-Jacobin armour, and remember

your slashing blow'. The *Anti-Jacobin* had been the light-hearted diversion of a group of brilliant young men: no one had looked to it for a judicial impartiality. Its strong political bias, without its genuine high spirits, was transferred to the *Quarterly Review*. From the first some of the most determined of the *Edinburgh*'s opponents were highly critical of its rival. Southey complained that the *Quarterly* was 'a little too much in the temper of the *Edinburgh* to please me', and although he became one of the most constant contributors he was never wholly to approve of the way in which the *Quarterly* was run. He said on one occasion that he would 'rather be hanged without that Anti to my denomination than pensioned with it'. Yet it was of the essence of the new *Review* that it should be partisan, and even vehemently so: just as it was that the Government 'should upon topics of national interest furnish the Reviewer confidentially & through the medium of the Editor with accurate views of points of fact so far as they are fit to be made public'. Croker, for example, 'went for the foundation of many of his essays to the men who alone could rightly know all the facts with which he had to deal, and thus in many cases an almost complete draft of the political article was supplied by the Duke of Wellington, by Sir Robert Peel, by Lord Stanley (Derby), or by some authority of equal weight on the question of the day'. It was therefore inevitable that the tone of the *Review* should be overwhelmingly political. In this the *Quarterly* was as characteristically English as the *Edinburgh* was Scottish: every Englishman is at heart a politician, as every Scotsman is at heart a critic.

Croker was described by Andrew Lang as an 'Anglican berserk' and the connexion between the *Quarterly* and the Church of England is of the first importance. While the *Edinburgh* was generally associated with an undogmatic, sceptical approach to theological matters, the *Quarterly* (like Southey) 'lived much with the lawn-sleeved'. Its task was to maintain sound constitutional principles, and not the least of these was the inviolability of the Established Church. When a detailed history of the *Review* is undertaken this matter will demand careful investigation, but it is at once evident that the great majority of the contributors were strong supporters of the Church of England and that two or three papers in the *Quarterly* often served as stepping-stones to a comfortable bishopric. The clue to the virulence of the *Quarterly*'s attack on one writer, compared

with its leniency towards another whose work might seem at least equally objectionable from the point of view of conventional morality, is often to be found in its belief that the one is basically orthodox, the other free-thinking or 'jacobinical'. One of the wisest observations in Burke is that it is a matter of great difficulty to decide how far an abuse should be tolerated, for fear of the greater harm that may come from a drastic reformation. At this period the defenders of the Church and of the established order as a whole were often driven by an exaggerated terror of innovation to defend the indefensible. In *Melincourt* Mr. Vamp, the editor of the *Legitimate Review*, addresses a new recruit in the following words:

You see this pile of pamphlets, these volumes of poetry, and this rascally quarto: all these, though under very different titles, and the productions of very different orders of mind, have, either openly or covertly, only one object; and a most impertinent one it is. This object is two-fold: first, to prove the existence, to an immense extent, of what these writers think proper to denominate political corruption; secondly, to convince the public that this corruption ought to be extinguished. Now, we are anxious to do away with the effect of all these incendiary clamours. As to the existence of corruption . . . a villanous word . . . we call it *persuasion in a tangible shape* . . . we do not wish to deny it; . . . but as to the inference that it ought to be extinguished—that is the point against which we direct the full fire of our critical artillery. (Chap. xiii.)

Peacock here uses no more than the legitimate exaggeration of the satirist. Scott's hope that the Quarterly Reviewers would not 'forget the Gentleman in the Critic' was destined to be disappointed. If, as he believed, the public was 'wearied with universal efforts at blackguard and indiscriminating satire' in the *Edinburgh Review*, the advent of the *Quarterly* merely gave them a choice as to who was to be assailed. As Southey had written in his *Letters from England* in 1807,

Criticism is to a large class of men what Scandal is to women,—and women not infrequently bear their part in it;—it is indeed Scandal in masquerade. Upon an opinion picked up from these journals, upon an extract fairly or unfairly quoted,—for the reviewers scruple not at misquotations, at omissions which alter the meaning, or mispunctuations which destroy it,—you shall hear a whole company talk as confidently about a book as if they had read it.

By an irony of history Southey's accusation—like Copleston's brilliantly ironical *Advice to a Young Reviewer*—damages the

*Quarterly*, to which both men were to be contributors, more severely than the *Edinburgh* and the *British Critic*, which were the targets of their attack. And it is difficult not to feel that the men who wrote in the *Quarterly* lacked the excuse of the first contributors (at least) to the *Edinburgh*. They were not young, and they were not in opposition. While the two Reviews are of equal importance to the student of history, the literary importance of the *Edinburgh* is much greater than that of its opponent. While Southey and Scott were almost the only first-rate men of letters who wrote regularly in the *Quarterly*, the *Edinburgh* had a constellation of talent including Hazlitt, Macaulay, Carlyle, and Jeffrey himself.

Long before the appearance of the first number of the *Westminster Review* in 1824 Jeremy Bentham and James Mill had discussed the need for a Radical Review to oppose both the *Edinburgh* and the *Quarterly*. The founding of the new Review is described in the *Autobiography* of John Stuart Mill. From the first it had been 'a favourite portion of the scheme' that the Radical Review should analyse the reasonings of its opponents, and to the first issue James Mill contributed a long criticism of the *Edinburgh Review* from its commencement. Beginning with a penetrating characterization of periodical literature in general, he went on to give a Radical interpretation of the British Constitution and to relate the conduct of the two great Reviews to this pattern:

> He held up to notice its thoroughly aristocratic character: the nomination of a majority of the House of Commons by a few hundred families; the entire identification of the more independent portion, the county members, with the great landholders; the different classes whom this narrow oligarchy was induced, for convenience, to admit to a share of power; and finally, what he called its two props, the Church, and the legal profession. He pointed out the natural tendency of an aristocratic body of this composition, to group itself into two parties, one of them in possession of the executive, the other endeavouring to supplant the former and become the predominant section by the aid of public opinion, without any essential sacrifice of the aristocratical predominance. He described the course likely to be pursued, and the political ground occupied, by an aristocratic party in opposition, coquetting with popular principles for the sake of popular support. He showed how this idea was realized in the conduct of the Whig party and of the Edinburgh Review as its chief literary organ. (*Autobiography* of J. S. Mill, Chap. iv.)

This exceptionally able article was followed by a continuation by John Stuart Mill in the second issue and by an equally shrewd analysis of the conduct of the *Quarterly* in a later number. It is hardly surprising that the advent of the *Westminster Review* created something of a sensation. Most of the Whigs were furious, while the Tories were astonished to find the *Edinburgh* appearing almost respectable by comparison with the whole-hearted iconoclasm of the new Radical Review. More will be said about the *Westminster* and its contributors in the last chapter, when the time has come to survey the literary scene in the late 1820's and early 30's.

From the literary point of view the Magazines of the time were hardly less important than the Reviews. The *Gentleman's Magazine*, to which Samuel Johnson had so often contributed, continued to appear throughout our period and far beyond it. By 1815, however, its appearance was distinctly antiquated: it was an obvious relic from the days of bohea and full-bottomed wigs. Although the *Monthly Magazine*, which had begun in 1796, had at first promised well, it soon became tame and unadventurous. It was when *Blackwood's Magazine* fell into the hands of Lockhart and John Wilson in October 1817 that a new chapter opened in the history of the Magazine. That was the opinion of Charles Knight:

> The new era of Magazines may be said to have commenced in 1817. In that year 'Blackwood's Edinburgh Magazine' startled the London publishers into a conviction that for a new generation of readers more attractive fare might be provided than at some of the old established *restaurateurs*, whose dishes were neither light, nor elegant, nor altogether wholesome. When Blackwood was started—apparently without any very correct knowledge that something was wanted in periodical literature beyond political bitterness—the old magazines and their new rivals had gone on without much deviation from the hackneyed paths in which they had first walked. (*Passages of a Working Life*, i. 265.)

De Quincey agreed with Knight in regarding *Blackwood's* as an important innovation. Writing to its publisher in 1830 he pointed out that the Tories had always been in the habit of following rather than leading the way, giving as examples the *Edinburgh* and *Quarterly Reviews*, 'the two London Universities' (University College and King's College), and 'the cheap bodies

of popular literature' provided on the one hand by the supporters of Reform and on the other by the conservative upholders of the established constitution. 'I doubt . . . whether there has been one exception', he wrote, 'beyond that of your own journal. You unquestionably had no precedent, though you have since had so many followers.' De Quincey considered this the more creditable because, whereas the *Quarterly* had from the first been 'a pet child of the family', *Blackwood's* had been obliged to make its way 'as a foundling or an adventurer would'. In fact the adventurous young Scotsmen who ran *Blackwood's* had more in common with the founders of the *Edinburgh* than with those of the *Quarterly*. Where they differed from Jeffrey and his companions was in the temper of their minds. Whereas the founders of the *Edinburgh Review* had certain measures of reform which they were eager to promote, and usually managed to restrain their love of mischief to gain these ends, it is hard to escape the conclusion that for Lockhart and 'Christopher North' mischief was an end in itself. It is true that they were convinced Tories; but they were also inveterate bullies. Their idea was an excellent one: to produce something less ponderous than the *Quarterly*, a nimbler periodical which should not give the impression of having been written throughout by a number of very senior and very disgruntled members of the House of Lords. They were even prepared to make concessions to readers whose classical education was imperfect: as the editor remarked on one occasion, translating a quotation in a footnote, 'everybody is not bound to know Greek'. *Blackwood's* deserves commendation for publishing short stories and serializing longer works of fiction— a practice incompatible with the nature of a Review. Several of Galt's books, including *The Ayrshire Legatees*, first appeared as serials in *Blackwood's*, as did two books by Michael Scott, *Tom Cringle's Log* and *The Cruise of the Midge*. The *Magazine* also included a good deal of literary criticism, some of it (including some of the articles on novels) of a high standard.

Two pieces of professedly literary criticism which were by no means of a high standard appeared in the issue of *Blackwood's* for October 1817, however, and ensured for 'Maga' a high circulation and a bad name in literary history. The 'Translation from an Ancient Chaldee Manuscript' is an allegory in pseudo-Biblical language describing the conflict between the publishers

Blackwood and Constable from a Tory point of view. At this time of day it is difficult to understand why a crude piece of pleasantry of the sort that one might find in a school magazine should have caused such a sensation in Edinburgh. For the worst passage, that on the cripple James Graham Dalyell, Blackwood was obliged to pay damages out of court. Although he seems at first to have been taken aback by the outcry, Blackwood was one of the first men to discover the important truth that lies behind so much gutter-journalism today, that every pound paid in damages represents a large accession of new readers. The authorship of the Chaldee article was industriously concealed, but we now know that the idea was Hogg's, while Lockhart and Wilson were the principal writers. The justice of Lockhart's description of himself as 'the scorpion, which delighteth to sting the faces of men' is borne out by the series of articles 'On the Cockney School of Poetry' which began in the same issue. Over a period of several years a running fire was kept up against Leigh Hunt and a number of other writers known to be associated with him. 'Z' maintains that it is presumption for such a poetaster to publish verse when men of the calibre of Wordsworth and Byron are writing. The most curious aspect of the criticism is its basis in snobbery. 'All the great poets of our country have been men of some rank in society', 'Z' wrote, 'and there is no vulgarity in any of their writings; but Mr. Hunt cannot utter a dedication, or even a note, without betraying the *Shibboleth* of low birth and low habits.' There is perhaps just a grain of truth in this remark, but when the reviewer moves from Hunt's poetry to talk of 'the extreme moral depravity of the Cockney School' he completely loses our sympathy. It is interesting to notice that Blackwood softened the attack in the second edition of this number, and that in January of the following year 'Z' himself was disingenuous enough to write: 'When I charged you with depraved morality, obscenity, and indecency, I spoke not of Leigh Hunt as a man . . . I judged of you from your works.' Blackwood's own attitude to these attacks is manifest in a letter which he sent Thomas Cadell in April 1823, when the latter expressed his concern about the attacks on Hazlitt: 'The public will be completely on the side of the Magazine for attacking such a nest of infidels and profligates as Hazlitt, Hunt, Byron & Co. who are daily outraging not only private character, but every thing sacred & civil. So far therefore from there

being any thing discreditable in the Magazine having attacked such a vile person as Hazlitt it will rather be considered as the reverse.' After reading some of the personal abuse in *Blackwood's* it is extraordinary to come on the preface to Volume XIX, for the year 1826:

> Before we appeared, the art of criticism was indeed a truly miserable concern. The critic looked upon the poet as his prey. The two were always at daggers-drawing. The insolence of reviewers had reached its acme, and absolutely stunk in the nostrils of the Public. Yet still there was a power in the rancid breath to taint, if not to wither. Men of genius were insulted by tenth-rate scribblers, without head or heart; and all conversational criticism was pitched on the same key with that of the wretched reviews. We put an end to this in six months. A warm, enthusiastic, imaginative, and, at the same time, philosophical spirit, breathed through every article. Authors felt that they were understood and appreciated, and readers were delighted to have their own uncorrupted feelings authorized and sanctioned. In another year the whole periodical criticism of Britain underwent a revolution. . . . The authority of the Pragmatic Faction was annihilated, and no Zany-Zoilus in the Blue and Yellow could any longer outcrow the reading Public.

The whole history of criticism cannot show a more flagrant instance of 'men of genius' being insulted by 'tenth-rate scribblers' than the attacks on Keats and Hazlitt in 'Maga'. Perhaps the fact that they were not 'gentlemen' was taken as an excuse: their initial offence, certainly, was their association with Hunt. 'The two great elements of all dignified poetry', 'Z' observed of Hunt's writings, 'religious feeling, and patriotic feeling, have no place in his mind. His religion is a poor tame dilution of the blasphemies of the *Encyclopaedie*—his patriotism a crude, vague, ineffectual, and sour Jacobinism. He is without reverence either for God or man.' Voltaire would have been amused by the Christian spirit with which the anonymous libeller set about bullying his victims into a more religious frame of mind. It is hardly worth detailing the attacks made in other numbers—attacks which led Murray to give up the London agency for 'Maga', and for which Blackwood was more than once obliged to come to a settlement with the men whom he had libelled (as he was with Hazlitt). Perhaps too much has been made of the attacks on Keats and Shelley by biographers in the hagiographical tradition. In some respects Lockhart and his asso-

ciates were merely reverting to the rough-and-tumble of the early eighteenth century, which survived in Edinburgh longer than in the south. But the anonymity and the flagrant inconsistency of the attacks leave a bad taste in the mouth, and it is impossible to forget that whereas the attackers were men of only moderate talents, secure and prosperous for the most part in their worldly positions, the attacked were men of genius who were struggling for a livelihood if not, like Keats, for life itself. A man who could describe Keats, after his death, as 'a young man who had left a decent calling for the melancholy trade of Cockney-poetry, [who] has lately died of a consumption, after having written two or three little books of verses, much neglected by the public' and add that 'he wrote *indecently*, probably in the indulgence of his social propensities', has won critical immortality of a sort, and it is an effort to remember that Lockhart was also the author of a remarkable biography and of some intelligent literary criticism.

As the *Edinburgh Review* led to the *Quarterly*, so *Blackwood's Edinburgh Magazine* led to Baldwin's *London Magazine*. The original editor, John Scott, was himself a considerable man of letters—his *Visit to Paris in 1814* and *Paris Revisited, in 1815*, are unusual and perceptive books—who had already had the experience of running a newspaper called the *Champion*. His object was to present the same mixture of essays, poems, criticism, and general comment as might be found in *Blackwood's*, which he considered 'a great improvement . . . on the general run of magazines' because it had 'a spirit of life, not usually characterising such publications'. As we read the *London Magazine* we notice that its contributors are more often pseudonymous than anonymous, and that we are being encouraged to feel that we are in the company of friends. The contributors' dinners seem to have been organized with the definite aim of giving the writers a sense of community, and Lamb makes it clear how much this meant to him. Certainly no editor has ever gathered round himself a more brilliant circle of writers. It was in the pages of the *London Magazine* that De Quincey's *Confessions* first appeared, as well as the *Essays of Elia*. Much of Hazlitt's *Table Talk* had the same origin, while poems by Keats, Clare, Hood, and John Hamilton Reynolds may also be found in the *London*, as well as numerous contributions by Hartley Coleridge, Darley, and Allan Cunningham. In reviewing, the aim was to be fair-

the passage in which he acknowledges this has some interest as a document in Anglo-American literary relations. Yet it must be admitted that Campbell and his publisher succeeded in finding able contributors. 'Colburn is making magnificent offers', we find Miss Mitford writing to a friend on 12 December 1820. 'He has proffered twenty guineas a sheet (five more than Hazlitt gets for the "Table Talk" in the "London") to Horace Smith (one of the "Rejected Addressers", you know) for any contribution, prose or verse, and he will give Talfourd his weight in gold rather than part with him.' It is not surprising that Hazlitt transferred his *Table Talk*: his fine essay 'On Going a Journey' appeared in the *New Monthly* in January 1822, and a good many other of his best essays first appeared in the same periodical. By 1831–3, when the Countess of Blessington's 'Conversations with Lord Byron' were serialized, Bulwer Lytton had become editor and the *New Monthly* had ceased to be a 'quiet spot' and become a hurricane centre. As one looks through the volumes today, the change is very welcome; but Colburn's public had come to expect *belles lettres* without controversy from this particular periodical, and Bulwer Lytton's reforming zeal was too much for them. After three eventful years he resigned and made way for Theodore Hook.

The independence of the *New Monthly* was frequently jeopardized by Colburn's determination to promote the sale of his own publications, and it is interesting to notice that both the *Athenaeum* (1828) and *Fraser's Magazine* (1830) made a point of their avoidance of literary 'puffery'. An advertisement for *Fraser's* published soon after its commencement emphasized that 'The Journal is not connected with any large publishing house, and the public have therefore a guarantee that its opinions will neither be sold for lucre, nor biassed by self-interest.' But an account of these two distinguished periodicals belongs to the next volume of this *History*, and it is time to say something of the importance of the leading publishers.

The names of Archibald Constable and John Murray will always be remembered when the *Edinburgh* and the *Quarterly* are mentioned, and indeed the great publishers of the nineteenth century deserve the same sort of attention as the great patrons of the Elizabethan Age. 'A literary man of the present day', wrote a journalist in the *News of Literature* for 10 December 1825, 'would as soon think of seeking patronage from the Emperor of

Austria, or setting forth the talents and the virtues of the Spanish Ferdinand, as of placing his hopes of a hearing with the public upon the foremost nobleman in the land'; and he went on to point out that 'this change has brought the publishers of books into an attitude of the greatest importance and honour;—it has made them the connecting link between the people of England and that which has made, is making, and shall continue to make the people of England superior to the people of every land where intellect has not the same unbounded scope.' In fact patronage was not dead: men like Sir George Beaumont and Lord Holland did a great deal for writers. But it is true that it was now through the publishers that the great majority of authors earned their living. As in most periods, it need hardly be said, the writers of the age had very different opinions of the middlemen on whose services they depended. Thomas Moore recalls a conversation 'chiefly about the profits booksellers make of us scribblers' at which John Wolcot ('Peter Pindar') asserted that booksellers 'drank their wine in the manner of the heroes in the hall of Odin, out of authors' skulls', while in 1833 R. H. Horne had some hard things to say in his curious *Exposition of the False Medium and Barriers Excluding Men of Genius from the Public*. The chief complaint made by the man who was to publish his epic at a farthing[1] as a protest against the public's lack of interest in poetry is that publishers place too much reliance on the opinion of ill-qualified 'readers' and are excessively unwilling to take risks: once a new writer or a new vein of writing has won favour they will compete for the publishing rights: novelty is too dangerous. The impression that we form when we read the histories of the great publishing houses of the period is very different, and although it is difficult to know how much allowance should be made for the fact that these were uniformly written on behalf of the firms themselves, we are likely to conclude that the authors of the period were on the whole fortunate in the men of business with whom they had to deal. It was to the advantage of writers that the trade was expanding at this time, and becoming more competitive: one of the advantages of publishing a successful Review or Magazine was, indeed, that it attracted authors. In May 1821 Thomas Cadell wrote to William Blackwood: 'I sympathize with you . . . with regard to

[1] Horne's instructions were that only those who pronounced the title correctly were to be given *Orion* for $\frac{1}{4}$*d.*

Murray's procuring the publication of almost all the new Works of consequence, which, I conceive is occasioned by the extensive literary connexion attached to the publication of the "Quarterly Review".' It was Constable who had made this discovery, with the *Edinburgh*, and this is only one example of his flair for discovering and directing the public taste. 'To Archibald Constable', Cockburn wrote in his *Memorials*:

> the literature of Scotland has been more indebted than to any other bookseller. Till he appeared, our publishing trade was at nearly the lowest ebb. . . . He rushed out, and took possession of the open field, as if he had been aware from the first of the . . . latent spirits, which a skilful conjurer might call from the depths of the population to the service of literature. Abandoning the old timid and grudging system, he stood out as the general patron and payer of all promising publications, and confounded not merely his rivals in trade, but his very authors, by his unheard-of prices. Ten, even twenty, guineas a sheet for a review, £2,000 or £3,000 for a single poem, and £1,000 each for two philosophical dissertations, drew authors from dens where they would otherwise have starved, and made Edinburgh a literary mart, famous with strangers, and the pride of its own citizens.[1]

It was not only the literature of Scotland that was indebted to Constable, and Scott was wholly in the right when he urged him to make memoranda of his life and dealings because his career had been 'of uncommon importance to literature'. Every book about Scott is also a book about Constable, whom even Lockhart (who treats him unfairly) refers to as 'the grand Napoleon of the realms of print'. Apart from Scott's own writings, the publication of which forms the dramatic central plot of his career, Constable made a speciality of 'curious and valuable works relative to the history and literature of Scotland' and there is justice in his claim to have been the first publisher 'who took a deep interest in securing and preserving all books relating to Scottish literature'. It is natural that it should have been to him that Lockhart wrote, at the end of 1814: 'I have been amusing myself with writing a novel, and as it chiefly regards Scotland, I should wish to have it printed in Edinburgh. I am

[1] Archibald Constable (1774–1827) began life as a bookseller's apprentice in Edinburgh. In 1798 he began to publish pamphlets and sermons on his own account, and soon he was interesting himself in periodicals. In 1802 he started the *Edinburgh Review* and began his association with Sir Walter Scott. In 1826 he became bankrupt through the failure of his London agents. His *Miscellany* is mentioned in Chapter XV.

sensible that much has been done of late years in the description of our national manners, but there are still, I apprehend, many important classes of Scotch society quite untouched.' Although in the end Constable did not publish any of Lockhart's novels, a list of the books on Scottish subjects which he did publish would be extensive and impressive. Nor were his activities confined to Scottish books. What he regarded as his 'greatest speculation' was his purchase of the *Encyclopaedia Britannica* in 1812: by 1826, when he sold it to A. & C. Black, it had grown and improved greatly under the editorship of Macvey Napier. The appearance of the first volume of *Constable's Miscellany* in 1827, dedicated to George IV, marked an important era in Constable's own career and in the development of the cheap literature which was to be so striking a feature of the Victorian Age.

John Murray resembled Constable in having his Review and his best-seller of genius.[1] Like other leading publishers of the time he realized that to treat publishing as a profession need not make it less profitable as a trade, and as the historian of the firm points out, about the year 1815 'Murray's drawing room was the main centre of literary intercourse' in his quarter of London. 'Men of distinction, from the Continent and America, presented their letters of introduction to Mr. Murray, and were cordially and hospitably entertained by him; meeting, in the course of their visits, many distinguished and notable personages.' Among the pictures of authors whom he had published there were in his drawing-room portraits of Byron, Scott, Coleridge, Southey, Lockhart, and Crabbe. It was at Murray's in 1815 that the American George Ticknor made the acquaintance of Moore, Campbell, Isaac D'Israeli, Gifford, and Humphry Davy. There is a tradition that the idea for the Athenæum Club was first discussed in Murray's drawing-room, and Humphry Ward points out in his *History of the Athenæum* that the five 'persons of acknowledged literary eminence' mentioned by Croker in his letter to Davy about the founding of the Club were all 'habitués of Murray's literary assemblies'. In an interesting little

[1] John Murray (1778–1843) was a Scot who emigrated to London. For a short time he acted as Constable's agent, but in 1809 he started the *Quarterly Review* in opposition to the *Edinburgh*. In 1812 he moved to Albemarle Street and became acquainted with Byron. His publication of Mrs. Mariana Starke's *Guide for Travellers on the Continent* in 1820 led to his well-known series of guide-books. Byron's Memoirs were burnt in the grate in his parlour.

book called *Bibliophobia* the bibliographer T. F. Dibdin tells us that Murray was 'among the very first booksellers of his day who treated authors, of character and connection, with the respect due to gentlemen'—a statement in which the qualification is hardly less revealing than the principal affirmation. As soon as he read *English Bards and Scotch Reviewers* Murray conceived the desire of publishing something of Byron's, and he soon became the publisher of *Childe Harold's Pilgrimage* and most of his other writings. He also became the recipient of a great many of Byron's letters—letters which were not intended as a private correspondence. As Moore points out in his biography, 'to keep the minds of the English public for ever occupied about him' was 'the constant ambition' of Byron's soul and 'in the correspondence he so regularly maintained with his publisher, one of the chief mediums through which this object was to be effected lay'. Since, as Moore goes on to explain, Murray's house was 'the resort of most of those literary men who are, at the same time, men of the world, his Lordship knew that whatever particulars he might wish to make public concerning himself, would, if transmitted to that quarter, be sure to circulate from thence throughout society'. In Chapter II I shall suggest that something of the tone of *Don Juan* may be attributed to the fact that Byron had Murray's circle in mind as an audience—a small circle of intelligent, classically educated, men of the world. If this is true it is ironical that what Byron called Murray's 'cursed puritanical committee'—an odd description for a group of men including Moore, Hookham Frere, and Hobhouse—were obliged from the first to warn the publisher of the danger of being associated with such a poem. Although Murray published the first few Cantos, they did not bear his imprint, and no review of any part of the poem appeared in either the *Quarterly* or the *Edinburgh*. 'I am sorry to say it is a book which I could not sell on any account whatever', Blackwood wrote to Murray from George Street, Edinburgh. It was only after careful consideration that Murray's legal advisers were satisfied that copyright in so scandalous a publication would be valid in law:

> Through needles' eyes it easier for the camel is
> To pass, than those two cantos into families

—as Byron himself complained, near the end of Canto IV. The

later Cantos were published by John Hunt, Leigh Hunt's brother, who was to be prosecuted in 1822–3 for publishing *The Vision of Judgment*. But Murray was to be the publisher of most of Byron's writings, and the connexion between the poet and the publisher continued after Byron's death with the publication of Moore's *Letters and Journals of Lord Byron*—and continues to this day. With *Emma* in 1816 Murray became Jane Austen's publisher, and while she calls him 'a rogue of course' we notice that in the same breath she calls herself a mercenary author. Murray was also the publisher of some of the works of Coleridge, of Southey, of Hookham Frere, and more suprisingly of Leigh Hunt. He produced a great many travel books, Napier's *History of the Peninsular War*, and the English translation of Mme. de Staël's influential book, *De l'Allemagne*.

William Blackwood was another of the important publishers of the day.[1] 'Like the other publishers of the age', as Mrs. Oliphant remarks in her *Annals of a Publishing House*, 'it had been Blackwood's desire from the beginning to make his place of business a centre of literary society, a sort of literary club where men of letters might find a meeting-place.' Like Constable, Blackwood specialized in books of Scottish interest. The article by Jeffrey on 'Secondary Scottish Novels' in the *Edinburgh Review* for October 1823 deals with a dozen books, including seven by John Galt and three by Lockhart, and every one of them had been published by Blackwood. Blackwood also published Susan Ferrier's *Marriage* and *The Inheritance*, with their acute satirical descriptions of the Scottish scene. His poetical list was less distinguished, but it included numerous volumes by James Hogg, 'The Ettrick Shepherd', as well as a good deal that no one continues to read, such as the poems of 'Christopher North' and 'Delta' (D. M. Moir, the friend of De Quincey). Perhaps the most popular of all the poems that he published was Pollok's *Course of Time*, a work which resembles *Paradise Lost* in two respects, and in two respects only: it is written in blank verse, and it takes for its subject the whole significance of human history. It was a common joke that Blackwood never met an author without inviting him to contribute to his *Magazine*, and it is

[1] Like Constable, William Blackwood (1776–1834) began life as an apprentice-bookseller in Edinburgh. After periods in Glasgow and London he started publishing on his own account in Edinburgh in 1804. A few years later he was the principal founder of the *Edinburgh Encyclopædia*.

noticeable that most of the memorable books which he published were by contributors.

If anyone should ask which Magazine of the period published most that was later to be reprinted in volume form, however, the answer would certainly be the *London Magazine*. Taylor and Hessey were never a large firm, but they published an extraordinary number of valuable books, and the fact that they never made much money should serve as a reminder that publishing good books was no more a certain road to commercial success in this period than in any other. From their *Magazine* they republished De Quincey's *Confessions*, the *Essays of Elia*, and a great deal else. They also published two of Hazlitt's most notable series of lectures, *The English Poets* and *The English Comic Writers*. They published Keats, and they published Clare. Like other publishers of the time they sometimes behaved with considerable generosity towards writers in whom they believed: when Keats went to Italy in search of health, he went with money lent him by his publisher. R. H. Horne explicitly exempts Taylor and Hessey from his censures on the publishing houses of the day. It was Taylor and Hessey who reprinted Cary's translation of Dante, which had at first been poorly produced and which had attracted little notice: when Coleridge recommended it to them they responded by bringing out a beautifully printed edition, as well as disposing of the pocket edition which was the only book that Keats took with him on his Scottish tour. Horne insists that Taylor's superiority to his fellows was due to the fact that he did not employ a 'reader', and it is true that Taylor was himself a literary man, and a fine judge of poetry. There is no doubt that he made improvements in the text of Clare—notably in that of his finest volume, *The Shepherd's Calendar*—and while Keats was angry at his slight bowdlerization of *The Eve of St. Agnes*, it is quite possible that Taylor also suggested one or two minor improvements in the text of his poems.

One reason for Taylor and Hessey's lack of commercial success may have been the fact that they did not interest themselves in novels. If they knew a great writer when they saw one, Henry Colburn of Conduit Street knew a best-seller, and novels were his speciality. 'The first of the gambling publishers'—as Michael Sadleir describes him in the second volume of his bibliography, *XIX Century Fiction*—Colburn

regarded every author as having his price and the public as gullible

fools. He cared nothing about book-design, nothing about craftsmanship. Cheapest was best, so long as the leaves held together. . . . He had no literary taste of his own, merely an instinctive sense of the taste of the moment. In consequence . . . he published on the basis of quick turn-over, and made a fortune for himself by sheer topical ingenuity. . . . Impervious to snubs; cheerful under vilification, so long as insults meant more business; thinking in hundreds where others thought in tens, Colburn revolutionised publishing in its every aspect. . . . He developed advertising . . . to a degree hitherto undreamt of. He had his diners-out who talked up his books at dinner-tables and soirées; he debauched the critics and put them on his pay-sheet. . . . He was a book-manufacturer, not a publisher.

Some of Colburn's authors, such as Bulwer Lytton, were men of high abilities; but the majority were merely concerned to give the public what it wanted. We think of him not as the publisher of Hazlitt's *Spirit of the Age* but as the imprint on a thousand ephemeral novels of the time. Longman, with his partners Hurst, Rees, Orme, and Brown, is remembered for his commercially accurate estimate of the value of the second edition of *Lyrical Ballads* as zero. He published *The Excursion* at a loss, in a handsome quarto; and was also responsible for producing a good deal of the work of Coleridge and Southey. Some of Scott's poems, in which he had a large share, had proved much more profitable—as had the poetry of Thomas Moore. The firm had a good reputation. As Moore wrote in his diary, 'there are few tributes from authors to publishers on record more honourable, (or, I will venture to say, more deserved) than those that will be found among my papers relative to my transactions for many years between myself and my friends of the Row'. Other publishers who can only be mentioned here are Charles and James Ollier, who published *The Cenci*, *Prometheus Unbound*, and the (pre-Elian) *Works* of Charles Lamb, and Edward Moxon, most agreeable of minor poets and most honourable of publishers.

The fact that some of the leading publishers were enlightened and even generous men does not mean that the profession of letters was an easy one at this time. Then, as now, the advice of the seasoned practitioner to the young aspirant was that of Mr. Punch to those about to marry. When the Quaker poet Bernard Barton told Charles Lamb that he was thinking of

resigning his position in a bank in order to devote himself to writing, Lamb replied in a famous letter:

> Throw yourself rather, my dear Sir, from the steep Tarpeian rock, slap-dash headlong upon iron spikes. . . . The Booksellers . . . are Turks and Tartars, when they have poor Authors at their beck. . . . I have known many authors for bread, some repining, others envying the blessed security of a Counting House, all agreeing they had rather have been Taylors, Weavers, what not? rather than the things they were. I have known some starved, some to go mad, one dear friend literally dying in a workhouse. . . . Keep to your Bank, and the Bank will keep you.

It was not merely because Barton was a bad poet that Lamb gave him this advice—indeed he had a fondness for Barton's poetry: he was simply speaking from his own experience as a writer. Byron gave Barton the same warning: 'Do not renounce writing', he wrote on 1 June 1812, 'but never trust entirely to authorship. If you have a profession, retain it; it will be, like Prior's fellowship, a last and sure resource.' Scott repeatedly gave similar advice to those who asked for guidance. And here is what Leigh Hunt wrote in his *Autobiography*, after a lifetime's experience:

> Nor was I able, had I been never so inclined, to render my faculties profitable 'in the market'. It is easy to say to a man—Write such and such a thing, and it is sure to sell. Watch the public taste, and act accordingly. Care not for original composition; for inventions or theories of your own. . . . Stick to the works of others. Write only in magazines and reviews. Or if you must write things of your own, compile . . . Do anything but write to the few, and you may get rich. There is a great deal of truth in all this. But a man can only do what he can, or as others will let him.

The considered judgement of perhaps the most complete professional of the time, Southey, also deserves to be heard. Writing to John Murray in August 1812 he gave it as his opinion that 'literature in almost all cases is the worst trade to which a man can possibly betake himself', though he commended it as a pursuit for men of fortune and leisure. For his own part, he adds, he has never regretted his choice of a literary career; but this is because it has brought him many friends and the good opinion of many of 'the best and wisest and most celebrated of my contemporaries'. If he lives another twenty years—he adds—

then literature will give him 'fortune'. In fact Southey lived for more than twenty years longer, but literature never gave him a fortune, though it did provide him with a competence. It did less for many of his contemporaries.

Of course a number of writers did make spectacular profits at this time. Even before the advent of Scott very high prices had occasionally been paid for best-selling novels. According to Sir Samuel Egerton Brydges (an unreliable witness) prices as high as £1,500 and £2,000 were on occasion paid to Maria Edgeworth and Sydney Owenson (later Lady Morgan), and it is certain that the latter received £1,200 for *Florence Macarthy*, a novel of little merit that retains some interest because of its portrayal of Croker as Conway Townsend Crawley. But it was Scott who made the writing of romances 'big business'. By 1818, according to Lockhart, 'the annual profits of his novels alone had, for several years, been not less than £10,000'. Early the following year Constable agreed to give Scott £12,000 for his then existing copyrights. In 1821, when Scott had already earned at least £10,000 from *Ivanhoe*, *The Monastery*, *The Abbot*, and *Kenilworth* (four books written in little more than a year), Constable agreed to pay him 5,000 guineas for the remaining copyright in these works. Two years later the publisher bought Scott's copyright in *The Pirate*, *The Fortunes of Nigel*, *Peveril of the Peak*, and *Quentin Durward* for another 5,000 guineas. Lockhart sums up the rather complicated position as follows: 'He had thus paid for the copyright of novels (over and above the half profits of the early separate editions) the sum of £22,500; and his advances upon "works of fiction" still in embryo, amounted at this moment to £10,000 more.' It was not without good reason that Scott once told Moore that his books had been 'a mine of wealth' to him. One can only guess how much he earned by his pen during his lifetime, but something like £100,000 would seem a conservative figure; and the value of money was much greater in Scott's time than it is today. Nor did his earnings cease with his death: about the beginning of 1833 we find Cadell advancing Scott's executors £30,000 on the security of Scott's copyrights and literary remains. After this the sums made by other novelists come as something of an anti-climax, yet it is interesting to notice that Susan Ferrier earned £1,000 from *The Inheritance* and a considerably larger sum from *Destiny*. At the end of 1815 Godwin tried to persuade Constable that two and three thousand

pounds had on occasion been paid for novels. We know as a fact that Blackwood gave Lockhart £1,000 for *Reginald Dalton*; while Horace Smith received £500 for *Brambletye House*, and then a further £100 from Colburn on account of its high sales. G. R. Gleig was paid £750 for *The Chelsea Pensioners*. In his diary for 24 September 1837 Moore describes how Richard Bentley has been to visit him at breakfast-time, 'full of impatience and ardour for something of mine to publish,—a light Eastern tale, in three volumes. Scene, Circassia; events, founded on the struggle of that people against Russia, and price £1500, with two-thirds of the copyright my own.' As this record of an unwritten novel may serve to remind us, there was little correlation between the merit of a novel and the sum which its author was paid. Scott was a man of genius, but the effect of his romances was cumulative and he made more from some of his inferior books than from *The Heart of Mid-Lothian*. By the time of her death Jane Austen seems to have made less than £1,000 from her novels.

A few works in prose, other than novels, made a good deal of money for their writers. Travel books and books about foreign countries were particularly popular. Lady Morgan received £2,000 for her *Italy*, published in 1821. When Harriet Martineau was in America a publisher advised her to 'Trollopize a bit, and so make a readable book'—the reference being to Frances Trollope's *Domestic Manners of the Americans* (1832). Soon after her return to England she was besieged by publishers, and her *Autobiography* contains an amusing description of how Bentley, Colburn, and Saunders (of Saunders and Otley), three men 'notoriously on the worst terms with each other', all called on her independently one November morning. Colburn went so far as to offer her £2,000 for a book about America and £1,000 'for the first novel I should write', and was both disappointed and astonished when she said that she preferred to accept a less extravagant offer from Saunders and Otley. Two remarkable transactions were Constable's payments of £1,000 each to Dugald Stewart and John Playfair for two treatises on 'The Progress of Philosophy' and 'The Progress of Mathematics and Physics' for the *Supplement of the Encyclopædia Britannica*. In 1816 Murray offered Croker no less than 2,500 guineas for a three-volume work on the French Revolution, but Croker declined the task. Five years later Murray paid Lord Holland £2,500 for

Waldegrave's *Memoirs* and Walpole's *Memoirs of the last Ten Years . . . of George III*—a lavishness which he lived to regret. A much more valuable property was that in Mrs. Rundell's *Cookery*, for the copyright of which (when it was no longer a new book) Murray was glad to pay £2,000—a reminder that literary and commercial values no more corresponded in this period than in any other.

Poetry could also pay, as Scott had demonstrated before he took to writing in prose. In 1807 Constable had paid him 1,000 guineas in advance for *Marmion*, 'without having seen one line of it'—a price (as Scott later acknowledged) 'that made men's hair stand on end'. According to A. S. Collins, Scott received £4,000 for *The Lady of the Lake*. For half of the copyright of the very inferior *Lord of the Isles* he was given 1,500 guineas. His successor as the most widely read poet of the day also received very large sums. Murray paid Dallas, to whom Byron presented the copyright of the first two Cantos of *Childe Harold's Pilgrimage*, £600. For Canto III he paid £2,000. No less striking are the sums paid for Byron's Tales. Murray offered Byron 500 guineas for *The Giaour* and paid the same sum for *The Bride of Abydos* and for *The Corsair*. For *The Siege of Corinth* and *Parisina* Murray offered 1,000 guineas. Byron considered his offer of 1,500 guineas for Canto IV of *Childe Harold* too niggardly, and asked for 2,500 guineas. For the three tragedies, *Sardanapalus*, *The Two Foscari*, and *Cain*, he had received £2,710. Although Murray was from the first very uncertain about *Don Juan*, he paid 1,500 guineas for the first two Cantos (with the *Ode on Venice* thrown in) and 2,500 guineas for Cantos III–V and three of the tragedies together. After his quarrel with Murray (one notices) Byron did not manage to get anything like these prices from his later publishers. Other poets were also generously paid, on occasion. In 1819 Murray gave an incredulous Crabbe £3,000 for the *Tales of the Hall* and the remaining copyright in his earlier works—a purchase (it must be admitted) that did not prove profitable. In December 1814 Longman had signed an even more remarkable agreement with Thomas Moore: 'Upon your giving into our hands a poem of yours of the length of "Rokeby" you shall receive from us the sum of £3,000.' Hazlitt's observation that Moore 'ought not to have written Lalla Rookh, even for three thousand guineas', is fair criticism; but the poem sold spectacularly well and neither poet nor publisher is known to

have repented of the bargain. It is perhaps more surprising that Milman should have received 500 guineas each for *The Fall of Jerusalem*, *The Martyr of Antioch*, and *Belshazzar*. But most astonishing of all was the fact that Bernard Barton should ever have earned enough by his writings to contemplate leaving his bank. When he was dissuaded from taking to literature for his living, his fellow Quakers, regretting that his fine faculties should be wasted on a humdrum occupation, raised a large subscription to enable him to devote himself to poetry. Of the very different fortunes of Wordsworth, Shelley, and Keats there is no need to write. Keats made little and Shelley next to nothing, while it was only when he was an old man that Wordsworth began to make a little money from his poetry. This must act as a reminder that even in a period when there was undoubtedly 'money in writing', what paid was what was in demand, or what happened to catch the public fancy. Sometimes a good book sold well: as often—or more often—it was a bad one that proved successful. The quality that makes a book a best-seller is one thing, the abiding principle of life that makes it last is another: only occasionally, as with the best of Scott and the best of Byron, are the two one.

As already suggested, however, much the surest resource for a writer lay in contributing to the great Reviews and Magazines. That is why it is so much easier to point to the great prose writers of the time than to the great books that they wrote. Southey once told J. T. Coleridge that 'the most profitable line of composition is reviewing', adding that he had not yet received as much for his three-volume *History of Brazil* as for a single article in the *Quarterly*. By paying contributors to the *Edinburgh Review* ten guineas for a sheet of sixteen pages Constable had trebled or quadrupled the price paid by the older Reviews. It should also be noted that Jeffrey had considerable discretion and was free to pay valued contributors more than the standard rate. 'You shall have twelve guineas if you please', he told Francis Horner as early as May 1803. Soon sixteen guineas a sheet seems to have become the minimum standard rate, two-thirds of the articles (according to Jeffrey) being 'paid much higher, averaging from twenty to twenty-five guineas a sheet on the whole number'. In this matter, as in others, the proprietors of the *Quarterly* were content to follow the lead of the *Edinburgh*, seldom quite catching up. 'The *Quarterly* pays me well', Southey

wrote in 1810, 'ten guineas per sheet.... And now for the bulky "Life of Nelson" ... [I] am to be paid double. This must be for the sake of saying they give twenty guineas per sheet, as I should have been well satisfied with ten.' For his first contribution he had been paid £21.13*s.*, but according to the writer of a retrospective article in April 1909 'his rate of payment was soon raised to 100 l. an article'. While this is probably an exaggeration, one has only to recall that he wrote altogether ninety-five contributions for the *Quarterly* to see how important a part this regular work played in the economic pattern of his life. If he had been prepared to act as editor he could have added greatly to his income—Scott told him that he could earn an extra £500 per annum in this way. Here again Murray was following Constable's lead. For editing the *Edinburgh* Jeffrey had been offered £300, 'a monstrous bribe' that he had been unable to refuse. For editing the *Quarterly* Gifford seems at first to have been paid £200 a year, though in 1811 he was given a congratulatory present of £500 and about 1813 his stipend was doubled. 'The only fault I ever taxed you with in pecuniary matters', Gifford wrote to Murray near the end of his life, 'was with that of being *too liberal* to me.' When Lockhart took over the editorship of the *Quarterly* he began with no less than £1,000 per annum. In the realm of the Magazine it was *Blackwood's* that led the way in generous rates of payment, but the *London Magazine* went even further, with the result that the *Confessions of an English Opium-Eater* were published south of the Border. The *New Monthly* also paid very generously. It will be seen that a professional man of letters could not afford to turn his back on periodical writing. 'The state of literature is painful and humiliating enough', Beddoes wrote to Thomas Forbes Kelsall in 1825—'every one will write for £15 a sheet.' Writers temperamentally unsuited to this form of composition were obliged to conform. Even those who had reason to curse both their houses had little option but to choose between the *Edinburgh* and the *Quarterly*. When in September 1819 Keats decided to try to earn his living as a writer he resolved to ask Hazlitt 'how the figures of the market stand' and to 'write on the liberal side of the question, for whoever will pay me'. Instead of living on hopes, he would 'get employment in some of our elegant Periodical Works'—anything (one may conjecture) except *Blackwood's*. And so we find George Darley, whose dream it was to be a Fellow of Trinity College,

Dublin, supporting himself by contributing to the Reviews and writing mathematical text-books. 'The profession of an author' enabled him to live, though not to earn enough to achieve the stable domesticity for which he longed.

Such being the position of the writer, how many books were published at this time, what kind of books were most in demand, what did books cost, and who bought them? To the first of these questions no reliable answer can be given. In 1791 James Lackington had estimated that more than four times as many books were being sold as twenty years before, and the Reviews of our period are full of complaints about the number of books now 'pouring from the presses'. Yet the number of books published then looks small beside the figures for today. In 1957 more than 16,000 new titles appeared in Great Britain, as well as almost 6,000 reprints of older books. Between 1815 and 1832 the annual average seems to have been something between 1,000 and 1,500. Unfortunately there are no statistics on which a firm estimate can be based, but it appears likely that the number of books published annually was increasing fairly steadily at this period and that the effect of the slump of 1826–7 was less dramatic than might have been expected.[1] If we can rely on Charles Knight's statement that 'in 1853 there were three times as many books published as in 1828' (*Passages of a Working Life*, iii. 195), it becomes evident that the curve of the increase rose fairly sharply in the early Victorian period, with the result that there was an enormous difference between the number of books published in the mid-nineteenth century and the number of books published a hundred years before. In the same passage Knight gives an analysis of the categories of books sold throughout the whole period from 1816 to 1851; since no analysis

[1] The best figures available for the years 1815–1825 seem to be those provided by the certified copies of the lists of books entered at Stationers' Hall which were sent to the Librarian of the University of Cambridge. These give the following approximate totals: *1815*, 1,121; *1816*, 1,176; *1817*, 1,207; *1818*, 1,174; *1819*, 1,290; *1820*, 1,170; *1821*, 1,062; *1822*, 1,390; *1823*, 1,264; *1824*, 1,258; *1825*, 1,346. The lists for 1826–7 are incomplete, but the total for 1828 (the last year for which a complete list is available) is approximately 1,377. For the years from 1826 onwards we can refer to the annual list provided by Bent's *Monthly Literary Advertiser*. Since the figure for 1828 is approximately 854 it is clear that this list is much less complete than that derived from the records at Stationers' Hall; but the figures for 1826–32 confirm the impression of a general increase in the number of books published. They are as follows: *1826*, 902; *1827*, 920; *1828*, 854; *1829*, 1,080; *1830*, 1,154; *1831*, 1,150; *1832*, 1,172. It will be noticed that Knight's figures appear to be even less complete than those in Bent.

is available for individual years his figures are reproduced here:

| | |
|---|---|
| Works on divinity | 10,300 |
| History and geography | 4,900 |
| Fiction | 3,500 |
| Foreign languages and school-books | 4,000 |
| Drama and poetry | 3,400 |
| Juvenile books | 2,900 |
| Medical | 2,500 |
| Biography | 1,850 |
| Law | 1,850 |
| Science (zoology, botany, chemistry, geology, mathematics, astronomy, natural philosophy) | 2,450 |
| Arts, &c. (antiquities, architecture, fine arts, games and sports, illustrated works, music, genealogy and heraldry) | 2,460 |
| Industry (mechanics, &c., agriculture, trade and commerce, political economy, statistics, military) | 2,350 |
| Moral sciences (philology, &c., education, moral philosophy, morals, domestic economy) | 1,400 |
| Miscellaneous | 1,400 |
| | 45,260 |

Whereas these figures for the number of books published in our period are necessarily approximate and uncertain, about the cost of books at this time there is no uncertainty. Books were very expensive. In the *Edinburgh Review* for October 1824 Henry Brougham wrote on the education of the poor as follows:

The first method . . . for promoting knowledge among the poor, is the encouragement of cheap publications; and in no country is this more wanted than in Great Britain, where, with all our boasted expertness in manufactures, we have never succeeded in printing books at so little as double the price required by our neighbours on the Continent. A gown, which any where else would cost a guinea, may be made in this country for half a crown; but a volume . . . better printed . . . than could be bought in London for half a guinea, costs . . . less than five shillings at Paris.

By the later twenties the movement for cheap literature recorded in the last chapter of this book was beginning to gather momentum, and Knight claims that between 1828 and 1853 the average price per volume fell by about 5*s*. There was certainly need for a reduction: the stiffness of the prices prevailing early in the century is the more striking when one remembers the high

value of money at this time and the fact that most books were sold in boards, so that those who required a permanent binding had to pay a further sum to the binder. A small book of verse, such as Hunt's *Descent of Liberty*, usually cost about 6*s*. The two volumes of Clare's *Village Minstrel* cost 12*s*. Byron's *Doge of Venice* and *The Prophecy of Dante*, in one volume, also cost 12*s*. *Endymion* (a handsome book) cost 9*s*., while *Lamia, Isabella, The Eve of St. Agnes, and Other Poems* cost 7*s*. 6*d*. In 1821 a five-volume collected edition of Byron's poems cost 35*s*. Histories and biographies were sometimes very expensive: Hallam's *View of the State of Europe during the Middle Ages* was first published in two volumes quarto at 4 guineas, though a cheaper edition was soon available. The *Life of Hayley . . . by Himself* also appeared in two lavish quarto volumes at 4 guineas. Even the third edition of Moore's *Life of Sheridan* cost a guinea and a half. An octavo volume of criticism, such as Hazlitt's *Lectures on the English Poets*, cost about 10*s*. 6*d*. In 1826 the two volumes of *The Plain Speaker* were priced at 24*s*. Allan Cunningham's *Songs of Scotland*, in four volumes, cost 36*s*. Nor were new editions of old books always much cheaper: the two volumes of Moore's edition of Sheridan cost 28*s*., while Taylor and Hessey charged 36*s*. for their handsome edition of Cary's translation of Dante (the pocket-edition costing 12*s*.). Periodicals were also expensive: the *Edinburgh* and the *Quarterly* cost 6*s*. a number: the *London Magazine* began at 2*s*. 6*d*. but soon went up to 3*s*. 6*d*.

But it was novels that were most expensive. *Waverley* and *Guy Mannering*, in three volumes, cost a guinea each (the more usual price at this point being 15*s*. or 18*s*.), as did Godwin's *Mandeville* in 1817 and Susan Ferrier's *Marriage* the following year. But Scott and his publishers led the way to still higher prices: *The Antiquary* and *Rob Roy* each cost 24*s*., while with *Kenilworth* in 1821 we reach the three-volume novel at a guinea and a half that is so characteristic of the period. Whereas Lister's *Granby*, in 1826, cost 27*s*., Horace Smith's *Brambletye House* imitated Scott in price, as in everything else. The convention that a novel should appear in three volumes, which suited the publishers and the proprietors of circulating libraries, became a tyranny to the men and women who wrote them. It did not suit the genius of John Galt, for example, who tells us explicitly in *Rothelan* that he is 'most desirous of sending out two rather than three volumes' but that his publisher insists that the public 'would

now be just as likely to buy a ten-tom'd tale of householdry, in the Richardson style, as a bi-form historical romance'. 'Vol. I', 'Vol. II', and 'Vol. III' became the fashionable equivalent of the Aristotelian Beginning, Middle, and End—and too often (it must be confessed) this artificial unity in trinity was the only unity that the book possessed. Only when a novel was no longer new did editions appear at a lower price. When *Waverley* and its successors had been on the market for some time editions were produced at a guinea. It was towards the end of our period that cheap editions of popular novels began to appear at 5*s*.

There were many people who were willing and able to pay these high prices for books. Apart from the circulating libraries, which consumed a considerable part of each edition of a successful novel, thousands of individual readers paid a guinea and a half for each of the later (and inferior) Waverley Romances. It was a time of great inequality of incomes, the period which Sir Arthur Bryant has called 'The Age of Elegance' but which the Hammonds considered as part of 'The Bleak Age'. While hundreds of thousands lived in abject poverty, tens of thousands were by our standards extremely well-to-do, and to them the high prices of books were no embarrassment. It must also be remembered that before the invention of the cinema, of radio and television, some knowledge of contemporary literature was regarded as appropriate among the upper classes and was therefore obligatory for the newly rich and the socially ambitious. In making literature 'news' the great Reviews played an important part, and fortunately we have some fairly definite figures for the circulation of the *Edinburgh* and the *Quarterly*. In 1814 the circulation of the *Edinburgh Review* was estimated at 12,000, while four years later it reached its peak of 13,500. According to Samuel Smiles the *Quarterly* was selling 12,000 copies by 1817, and 14,000 copies a few months later. The importance of the Reviews at this time becomes apparent when we realize that a great many readers saw each copy that was bought—'Murray . . . prints 10,000 and fifty times ten thousand read its contents', Southey once wrote with pardonable exaggeration—and compare their circulation with that of *The Times* in 1816, which was only 8,000 copies a day.

It is perhaps more surprising how well poetry sometimes sold. By 1825 *The Lay of the Last Minstrel* was in its fourteenth edition, 33,000 copies having been disposed of. *Marmion* was equally

successful, *The Lady of the Lake* even more so. When only 10,000 copies of *Rokeby* were sold in a month the poem was regarded as a failure. 4,500 copies of the first two Cantos of *Childe Harold's Pilgrimage* were sold in the first six months, while the sales of Byron's later poems greatly exceeded this. Of *The Corsair* Murray wrote that he sold 'on the day of publication—a thing perfectly unprecedented—ten thousand copies'. The circulation of *The Pleasures of Memory*, by Samuel Rogers, was even more remarkable. The first four editions were very small, but then the publishers scented success and the poem reached its nineteenth edition in 1816, by which time more than 23,000 copies had been sold. Rogers's *Italy* and his *Poems* of 1832 seem to have been produced in editions of 10,000 copies. It is clear that this was a period when poetry was in demand, and when people were prepared to pay for it. Exciting tales in verse, with unfamiliar settings, such as those of Scott, Byron, and Moore, were particularly popular. Long poems containing a mixture of description and reverie, with a generally religious tone, also found a ready public. It may be doubted whether there has ever been so welcoming a public for poetry in England, except perhaps at the height of Tennyson's hey-day. Many readers of this *History*, people genuinely interested in literature, will not have read a poem of a hundred lines published during the last year. In the early nineteenth century this would hardly have been conceivable. Yet we must again remind ourselves that some of the poetry that sold most widely was extremely inferior, while much that was best attracted hardly any notice. If poetry was popular, it was not because men of genius were producing great poetry—though it may have been partly because two men of genius, Scott and Byron, were prepared to produce the kind of rhetorical poetry that appealed to the reading public. The poems of Bernard Barton were absurdly popular: the list of subscribers to his poems bears witness to the invincible philistinism of English society, from Windsor and Lambeth to the wealthy manufacturing cities of the North. Charles Knight tells us that in the middle or later twenties 'except in a few rare instances, mediocrity was essentially necessary to a great literary success'. As Knight points out, the unreadable *Omnipresence of the Deity*, by Robert Montgomery—'the wrong Montgomery'—went rapidly through five or six editions, while *The Excursion* was slow to reach a second edition. Keats's great volume of 1820 sold very

poorly. Shelley soon abandoned all hope of finding an audience for his poetry—a bitter disappointment to a man who had hoped to become 'the trumpet of a prophecy'. Even within the work of one particular poet extrinsic factors often did more to determine the sale of a volume than the value of the poetry which it contained. The best of Clare's work published in his lifetime is to be found in *The Shepherd's Calendar*, which sold very poorly, whereas his first book, *Poems Descriptive of Rural Life and Scenery*, which was at best promising, went into several editions. As one would expect, the sales of novels were even greater than those of poetry. Ten thousand copies of *Rob Roy* were sold in the first three weeks. Even more astonishingly, 7,000 copies of *The Fortunes of Nigel* were sold in London by half-past ten on the morning of publication—a reminder of the importance to publishers of the growing rapidity of travel. Thirty-five thousand copies of the 1829 collected edition of the Waverley Novels were sold each month.

It is not surprising that so many writers commented on the growth of the 'reading public'. The phrase itself seems first to become current about this time. In *The Statesman's Manual*, written late in 1816, Coleridge insists that he is writing only for 'men of clerkly acquirements' and goes on to express the wish that 'the greater part of our publications could be thus directed, each to its appropriate class of readers'. But this is now impossible (he continues): 'For . . . we have now a Reading Public . . . a strange phrase . . .; and yet no fiction. For our readers have, in good truth, multiplied exceedingly, and have waxed proud. It would require the intrepid accuracy of a Colquhoun to venture at the precise number of that vast company only, whose heads and hearts are dieted at the two public ordinaries of literature, the circulating libraries and the periodical press.' The situation that Coleridge looked on askance provided men as various as Scott, Byron, and Cobbett with their opportunity. In his review of the Third Canto of *Childe Harold* in the *Quarterly* for October 1816 Scott himself observes that 'reading is . . . so general among all ranks and classes, that the impulse received by the public mind on such occasions is instantaneous through all but the very lowest classes of society, instead of being slowly communicated from one class of readers to another, as was the case in the days of our fathers'. 'We present a spectacle of what, perhaps, was never before seen in any age,' Henry Southern

wrote in the introduction to the first volume of the *Retrospective Review*; '. . . that of a whole nation, employing nearly all its leisure hours from the highest to the lowest rank in *reading*—we have been truly called a READING PUBLIC.' In a similar vein the writer of the editorial of the *Athenaeum* for 12 February 1828 remarked that 'the reading public . . . may now be said to include all who are above the condition of the merely labouring classes'. Even if we concede that the taste for serious reading was not quite as widespread as men like Henry Southern supposed, it is interesting to speculate on the numbers represented by the phrase 'the reading public'. Reviewing Crabbe's *Tales* in the *Edinburgh Review* for November 1812, Jeffrey praises him for addressing his poetry to 'the middling classes of society', defining these as 'almost all those who are below the sphere of what is called fashionable or public life, and who do not aim at distinction or notoriety beyond the circle of their equals in fortune and situation. In this country', Jeffrey comments, 'there probably are not less than two hundred thousand persons who read for amusement or instruction among the middling classes of society. In the higher classes, there are not as many as twenty thousand.' When he reprinted the essay in 1844, Jeffrey changed his figure for the higher classes to 30,000 and that for the middling classes to 300,000; but his conclusions remained unchanged:

> It is easy to see . . . which a poet should chuse to please for his own glory and emolument, and which he should wish to delight and amend out of mere philanthropy. The fact too we believe is, that a great part of the larger body are to the full as well educated and as high-minded as the smaller; and, though their taste may not be so correct and fastidious, we are persuaded that their sensibility is greater.

The whole passage illustrates Jeffrey's flair for sociological observation. When he suggests that middle-class readers should not aim at imitating the taste of their social superiors and that writers should provide them with literature dealing with people of their own class, he shrewdly anticipates the course of nineteenth-century literature as a whole and shows himself well prepared to appreciate the genius of Dickens. By November 1844 it was to be possible for Thomas Hood—that least aggressive of men of letters—to write to Peel, then Prime Minister, regretting the omission of Literature from the Queen's answer

to a civic address and remarking that 'whatever differences may obtain in society, that will be an unlucky one which distinguishes a sovereign from a reading public, rapidly becoming a reading people'.

It was not only the printed word that was in demand. One of the most striking characteristics of the period was the vogue for lectures. The popularity of lectures outside universities seems to have been a new thing towards the end of the eighteenth century. Samuel Johnson, who might appear to have been born to be a lecturer, had a low opinion of lectures as a mode of instruction and never delivered a lecture in his life. If he had lived fifty years later he would have been obliged to turn lecturer. The first public lecture on Shakespeare (as distinct from a paper read to a private literary or debating society) seems to have been that delivered by William Kenrick in 1774. Soon a complex of causes, including the ferment of ideas produced by the American wars and the French Revolution and the growing public interest in science, led to a steadily increasing demand for lectures. A number of the most important prose works in our period came into existence in this way.

Coleridge had begun his career as a lecturer in Bristol in 1795 with the object of disseminating Truth by lecturing on politics. Things did not go smoothly for him: in a letter he complained that 'two or three uncouth and unbrained Automata have threatened my Life' and that the 'Genus infimum were scarcely restrained from attacking the house in which the "damn'd Jacobine was jawing away"'. In 1808 he gave a very different set of lectures to a very different audience, lecturing on poetry at the aristocratic Royal Institution, which had been founded to encourage 'the application of the new discoveries in science to the improvement of arts and manufactures'. Admission was by ticket, and the lectures took place—or were intended to take place—at 2 p.m. In 1811–12 Coleridge gave another course of lectures on poetry in Fetter Lane. On this occasion Crabb Robinson complained that each alleged lecture was an 'immethodical rhapsody': Coleridge was the Pindar of lecturers. Encouraged by the success of another course which he gave in 1812, sponsored by Sir Thomas Bernard, Lady Beaumont, and William Sotheby, and by that of a later series of lectures in Bristol, Coleridge played with an odd scheme for 'a *system* of private Lectures with Discussions afterwards, conveying all

the information that a gentleman ought to have . . . which if realized would secure me 600£ a year'—the sort of Academy that might have provided Aristophanes with the material for another *Clouds*. On occasion, it must be admitted, Coleridge's audiences had a good deal to put up with. In his 'Literary Reminiscences' De Quincey gives us a picture of Coleridge lecturing—or failing to lecture—that seems to be only a little highly coloured:

> Thus unhappily situated, he sank more than ever under the dominion of opium; so that, at two o'clock, when he should have been in attendance at the Royal Institution, he was too often unable to rise from bed. Then came dismissals of audience after audience, with pleas of illness; and on many of his lecture days I have seen all Albemarle Street closed by a 'lock' of carriages, filled with women of distinction, until the servants of the Institution or their own footmen advanced to the carriage-doors with the intelligence that Mr. Coleridge had been suddenly taken ill. . . . Many in anger, and some in real uncertainty whether it would not be trouble thrown away, ceased to attend. And we that were more constant too often found reason to be disappointed with the quality of his lecture. . . . His lips were baked with feverish heat, and often black in colour; and, in spite of the water which he continued drinking through the whole course of his lecture, he often seemed to labour under an almost paralytic inability to raise the upper jaw from the lower.

We are reminded of one of the reasons for the popularity of lectures at this time by Coleridge's observation that 'a history of *Philosophy* . . . is a desideratum in Literature'. On many subjects about which books are available to us little had then been written. This was true, in some degree, both of the History of Philosophy, which Hazlitt chose as the subject of his first course of lectures (delivered at the Russell Institution in 1812), and of the History of Literature, on which he lectured on several occasions. After the first of these lectures on Philosophy, Crabb Robinson—that inveterate lecture-goer, to whom we owe much of our information about lectures at this time—complained that Hazlitt seemed 'to have no conception of the difference between a lecture and a book'; but he quickly improved. One of the most interesting descriptions of Hazlitt lecturing is by Thomas Noon Talfourd:

> Mr. Hazlitt delivered three courses of lectures at the Surrey Institution . . . before audiences with whom he had but 'an im-

perfect sympathy'. They consisted chiefly of Dissenters . . . who 'loved no plays'; of Quakers, who . . . 'heard no music'; of citizens devoted to the main chance . . .; of a few enemies . . . ; and a few friends. . . . The comparative insensibility of the bulk of his audience to his finest passages, sometimes provoked him to awaken their attention by points which broke the train of his discourse, after which he could make himself amends by some abrupt paradox which might set their prejudices on edge, and make them fancy they were shocked. . . . When he passed by Mrs Hannah More with observing that 'she had written a great deal which he had never read', a voice gave expression to the general commiseration and surprise, by calling out 'More pity for you!'

Three of Hazlitt's most important books, *The English Poets*, *The English Comic Writers*, and *The Dramatic Literature of the Age of Elizabeth*, consisted of lectures for the Surrey Institution. We hear a good deal about the *Lectures on the English Poets* from Crabb Robinson, who often listened to Hazlitt before proceeding to Fleur de Luce Court to hear Coleridge on Shakespeare. It is an important series because it is perhaps the only course of lectures on poetry ever delivered in this country which is known to have had a demonstrable influence on a great poet. Keats turned up for the first lecture an hour late, but he did his best not to miss another, and the influence of Hazlitt's observations on poetry is to be found in more than one of the most illuminating passages in his letters. The fact that Keats mentions that he met many people whom he knew at these lectures suggests that Talfourd exaggerated the predominance of Dissenters in Hazlitt's audience; yet there can be no doubt that the vogue for lectures owed a good deal to the Dissenters' passion for self-improvement. It is ironical that a man who had refused to enter the Dissenting ministry should so often have found himself addressing Dissenters on subjects connected with philosophy and morals.

Not everyone shared the Dissenters' taste. Lectures were among the few manifestations of human nature excluded from the charity of Charles Lamb. The first scene of Byron's poem *The Blues: A Literary Eclogue* takes place 'Before the door of a Lecture Room' and satirizes the passion of the day, prompting the reflection that but for women the lecture might not so long have survived the invention of printing. Peacock's Dr. Opimian is characteristically forthright on the subject of lectures. 'I agree

with Dr Johnson', he remarks, 'that little is to be learned from lectures. For the most part, those who do not already understand the subject will not understand the lecture, and those who do will learn nothing from it. The latter will hear many things they would like to contradict, which the *bienséance* of the lecture-room does not allow. I do not comprehend how people can find amusement in lectures. I should much prefer a *tenson* of the twelfth century, when two or three masters of the *Gai Saber* discussed questions of love and chivalry.' But by the time when *Gryll Grange* was published, in 1860, it was far too late to protest against the habit of lecturing. In the *Edinburgh Review* for October 1824 Brougham had emphasized the importance of lectures in the education of the poor. 'The institution of Lectures', he had written, 'is, of all the helps that can be given, the most valuable, where circumstances permit; that is, in towns of a certain size. Much may thus be taught, even without any other instruction; but, combined with reading, and subservient to it, the effects of public lectures are great indeed, especially in the present deficiency of proper elementary works.' These are the words of the man whom Peacock satirized as 'the learned friend', and Brougham's was the opinion that proved dominant as the century wore on. In 1838, we are told, Adam Sedgwick delivered an unofficial public lecture on the beach at Tynemouth 'to some 3,000 or 4,000 colliers and rabble (with a sprinkling of their employers)'. Sir John Herschel was told by a friend who had been there that it was 'impossible to conceive the sublimity of the scene' as Sedgwick

> stood on the point of a rock a little raised, to which he rushed as if by a sudden impulse, and led them on from the scene around them to the wonders of the coal industry below them, thence to the economy of a coal field, then to their relations to the coal owners and capitalists, then to the great principles of morality and happiness, and at last to their relation to God, and their own future prospects.

But with Sedgwick's lecture we have crossed the border into the Victorian Age. It is time to turn back to consider the poetry written in the years immediately after Waterloo.

# II

# BYRON

BYRON had an extraordinary heredity.[1] His father, who died when the poet was three, was an incorrigible gambler and spendthrift, the eldest son of Admiral John Byron, 'Foulweather Jack', one of the most colourful figures in the history of the eighteenth-century navy. His mother, Catherine Gordon of Gight, was a descendant of King James the First of Scotland. She was a passionate, ill-educated woman, and although she tried to do her best for her son he was often to blame her for the tempestuous course of his later life. He was born with a slight malformation of the right foot, and as a result he was slightly lame: a disability which he allowed to prey on his mind. He inherited the title on the death of his great-uncle, 'the wicked Lord', who had killed a man in a duel and then retired to live at Newstead with his mistress and a single servant in circumstances that recall the novels of the Brontës. There were traces of insanity on both sides of the family and marriages between cousins had been unhealthily common.

After his early years in Aberdeen, Nottingham, and London, he was sent to Harrow, where he proved himself a wild and

[1] George Gordon Byron (1788–1824) was born in London and became the sixth Lord Byron at the age of ten. Before going to Harrow he was educated privately and at Aberdeen Grammar School. At Cambridge he led a wild life and kept a bear to teach the Fellows of Trinity good manners. In 1809 he took his seat in the House of Lords, published *English Bards and Scotch Reviewers*, and set out on his travels with a Cambridge friend, John Cam Hobhouse. He returned two years later, having swum the Hellespont and visited Lisbon, Cadiz, Gibraltar, Malta, Greece, Smyrna, Ephesus, and Constantinople. In 1812 he twice spoke in the Lords, published the first two cantos of *Childe Harold*, and became a prominent figure in Whig society. Two years later he married Annabella Milbanke, who accused him of insanity and left him. In 1815 his interest in the drama led to his being appointed a member of the sub-committee of management at Drury Lane. Soon his financial and other embarrassments obliged him to flee to the Continent, where he visited Shelley in Switzerland and wrote *Childe Harold III*. Later in 1816 he travelled to Italy, where he heard that Claire Clairmont had borne him a daughter. The first two cantos of *Don Juan* were published in 1819. In April of that year Byron met the Contessa Guiccioli and became her *cicisbeo*, living with her a good deal in the next few years. In 1822 he was present at the cremation of Shelley's body. In January 1824 he landed at Missolonghi to join the Greeks who were fighting for their independence. He died of fever on 19 April.

ungovernable boy. He was a good athlete and boxer and had a passion for reciting his own poems and speeches. As his nickname—'The Old English Baron'—bears witness, many of his schoolmates considered him a snob: it is said that on one occasion, when another boy pinched his ear, he threw something at him shouting that 'that would teach a fool of an earl to pinch another noble's ear'. From Harrow he went to Trinity College, Cambridge, and towards the end of 1806 he published his first volume of verse, *Fugitive Pieces.* The subjects of the poems in this collection provide a conspectus of his life up to that point: there are poems dealing with school and Cambridge, poems to male contemporaries written in terms of fervent friendship, and a great many addresses to Marys, Julias, and Carolines. A clerical friend considered a description in one of the poems 'rather too warmly drawn' and Byron was persuaded to destroy almost the whole impression: only four copies are known to survive. The next year, however, he produced an enlarged and expurgated edition, '*vastly* correct and miraculously chaste', entitled *Poems on Various Occasions.* This volume was followed by *Hours of Idleness*, a slightly better collection of lyrics the publication of which had momentous results. A few weeks after he had completed a satire called *British Bards*, of which (in its original form) no complete manuscript or printed copy survives, Byron heard that the *Edinburgh Review* was intending to notice his poems, and he awaited events with keen anxiety. The review, when it came, was devastating. Byron had mentioned on his title-page that he was a 'Minor', and the reviewer made fun of this in a manner very characteristic of the *Edinburgh*, pointing out that minority could not be pleaded in mitigation of the offence of voluntarily publishing a volume of inferior verse. 'The poesy of this young lord', the reviewer wrote, in sentences which Byron was never to forget,

belongs to the class which neither gods nor men are said to permit. Indeed, we do not recollect to have seen a quantity of verse with so few deviations in either direction from that exact standard. His effusions are spread over a dead flat, and can no more get above or below the level, than if they were so much stagnant water. (xi. 285, January 1808.)

'Mediocribus esse poetis': it is the last charge that an ambitious young poet can stand. Several years later, discussing the effect that unfavourable reviews were thought to have had on Keats,

Byron wrote that 'a savage review is Hemlock to a sucking author', adding (with pardonable yet characteristic egotism): 'the one on me . . . knocked me down—but I got up again'. He got up fighting, and the remainder of his life as a poet was to be (in Pope's phrase about himself) 'a warfare upon earth'. He extended and rewrote *British Bards* and published the result as *English Bards and Scotch Reviewers* in March 1809.

It would be a mistake to suppose that in writing a formal verse satire Byron was reviving an obsolete type of poetry. More satires of this kind seem to have been written in the early nineteenth century than a hundred years before, although no poet of genius now came forward to make it his own. Byron makes it clear that he is acting as *locum tenens* for Gifford, 'the last of the wholesome satirists': his immediate models are *The Baviad* and *Maeviad*, Mathias's *Pursuits of Literature*, and the satires of Charles Churchill, while the wording of the Argument reminds us that *The Dunciad* was also in his mind as he wrote. As the form of the poem suggests, Byron is aligning himself with critics of a conservative cast. The standards that he upholds are close to those of the *Anti-Jacobin* twenty years before, and it is not surprising to hear that he regards the present as the age of 'the decline of English poetry'. Referring to Wordsworth and other poets of the day he tells us that each of them

> like other sectaries . . . has his separate tabernacle of proselytes, by whom his abilities are over-rated, his faults overlooked, and his metrical canons received without . . . consideration. But the unquestionable possession of considerable genius by several of the writers here censured renders their mental prostitution more to be regretted.

The passage continues with a fine eighteenth-century sentence: 'Perverted powers demand the most decided reprehension.' Yet it must be admitted that Byron shows himself an imperceptive critic of his contemporaries, since he attacks Wordsworth, Coleridge, Southey, and (in some degree) Scott, and reserves his praise for Crabbe, Cowper, Rogers, and Campbell and a number of very minor poets indeed. It is significant that Bowles, the favourite of Coleridge's youth, receives a particularly severe castigation as

> The maudlin prince of mournful sonneteers.

Bowles was a poet without a trace of genius who happened to

anticipate the new sensibility, and Byron was to come into conflict with him later on the question of the merits of Pope.

There are successful moments in *English Bards*. Byron is unfair to Wordsworth (as he soon realized), yet in referring to him as a poet

> Who, both by precept and example, shows
> That prose is verse, and verse is merely prose

he scores a legitimate satirical point and makes it clear that it was the theories propounded in the preface to the *Lyrical Ballads* that particularly annoyed him. On occasion he can hit off the conciseness which is characteristic of Pope, as in the line

> Believe a woman, or an epitaph.

But there is a monotony and an occasional stridency in the poem which Pope avoided: there are not enough variations of pitch and tone. The formal verse satire is no medium for a young poet: it is not surprising that Byron at the age of twenty could not compete with Pope at the height of his powers. He wrote the poem, as he later acknowledged, when he was 'very young and very angry', and it would hardly be an exaggeration to say that he spent the rest of his life meeting, and liking, the men whom he had attacked. After four editions had appeared he was persuaded to allow his satire to go out of print. For us it remains of interest as an index to his early poetical views and as a reminder that conciseness did not come naturally to him. His satiric triumph, when it came, was to be due to the discovery of an idiom that encouraged expansion and digression rather than compression of the Augustan kind.

Soon after the publication of *English Bards* Byron took his seat in the House of Lords; he then set out on a tour of Europe. While he was abroad he wrote *Hints from Horace*, an 'Imitation' in Pope's sense of the word which is technically superior to *English Bards* and which (unlike the earlier poem) contains one or two passages that might be mistaken for the *Essay on Criticism*. But it was the other poem that he began on his travels that was to prove momentous. The first stanzas of *Childe Harold's Pilgrimage* were written at Jannina in Albania, on his return from a visit to the tyrant Ali Pasha. Byron was in a state of 'extreme discontent', but he was stimulated by his novel experiences and reminded by the mountains which surrounded him of his early boyhood in Scotland.

As the reviewers pointed out, it is difficult to say to what kind of poetry *Childe Harold* belongs. When he published the first two cantos in 1812 Byron described them as 'merely experimental', acknowledging that the poem had 'no pretension to regularity'. On another occasion he said that it was 'a poem on *Ariosto's plan*, that *is* to *say* on *no plan* at all'. Its most obvious affinities are with the travel-book, and it is interesting to remember that Byron's companion Hobhouse was engaged on his *Journey through Albania*, which was 'prepared in frequent consultation' with the poet. In view of the problem of a suitable form for a long poem which faced the poets of the early nineteenth century, it is interesting to find Byron using this popular and unpretentious type of book as his starting-point. As the *Quarterly Review* remarked:

> Few books are so extensively read and admired as those which contain the narratives of intelligent travellers. . . . If . . . this species of information be so attractive . . . in prose . . ., by what accident has it happened that no English poet before Lord Byron has thought fit to employ his talents on a subject so obviously well fitted to their display? This inadvertence . . . is the more extraordinary, because the supposed dearth of epic subjects has been, during many years, the only apparent impediment to the almost infinite multiplication of epic poems . . . [Apparently] the followers of the muse have . . . intentionally rejected the materials offered by a traveller's journal as too anomalous to be employed in a regular and grand composition. (vii. 191, March 1812.)

It we compare *Childe Harold* with the *Odyssey*—a comparison suggested by the reviewer—we are struck by the fact that Byron's hero, unlike Homer's, can be removed from the poem in which he occurs. In spite of Byron's claim to have introduced the Childe 'for the sake of giving some connection to the piece' it is surprisingly easy to detach most of the passages dealing with him from the rest of the poem. After the first fifteen stanzas of Canto II, for example, which contain no reference to the Childe, he is introduced by the following words:

> But where is Harold? Shall I then forget
> To urge the gloomy Wanderer o'er the wave?
> Little recked he of all that Men regret

—surely one of the most inept transitions in all literature. The Childe is next mentioned at stanza xxxi, after a series of reflections which every reader has supposed to be the poet's own. At

times one is tempted to wonder whether the Childe was part of the poem as it was originally conceived. Perhaps he was an afterthought. It may be significant that the first man to see the poem in England, R. C. Dallas, merely describes it as 'a great many stanzas in Spenser's measure, relative to the countries he had visited'.

Whether or not the Childe was part of the original plan, his function was no doubt to enable Byron to express with impunity views which were frequently unorthodox and revolutionary. After the highly controversial stanzas about the Convention of Cintra, for example, Byron continues:

So deemed the Childe, as o'er the mountains he
Did take his way in solitary guise. (I. xxvii)

Yet there is an amusing piece of evidence that the publisher himself found it impossible to distinguish between the poet's own sentiments and those supposed to be attributed to Harold: in reply to a note about one particular passage Byron replied: 'The "he" refers to the Wanderer and anything is better than *I I I I* always *I*.' When Byron claimed, in an addition to the preface, that the Childe was designed to show how 'early perversion of mind and morals leads to satiety . . . and disappointment', he was obviously trying to reply to his reviewers. He was telling them what, perhaps, he should have done, or what he may at some time have thought of doing: not what he in fact did. In a suppressed passage of the preface he came nearer to admitting the truth: 'My reader will remark that where the author speaks in his own person he assumes a very different tone . . . at least till death had deprived him of his nearest connections.' Nothing could be more revealing than the qualifying clause—unless it be the fact that in some passages of the manuscript the protagonist is called 'Childe Burun'—the old spelling of Byron's family name.

The character of the Childe helped to make the poem famous. As the *Edinburgh Review* pointed out, 'there is . . . something piquant in the very novelty and singularity of that cast of misanthropy and universal scorn, which we have . . . noticed as among the repulsive features of the composition'. Nothing could be more revealing than the collocation of the words 'repulsive', 'scorn', 'misanthropy', 'novelty', 'piquant'. The fog of uncertainty surrounding the Childe's identity added to the fascina-

tion—as did the fact that he differed so markedly from the usual poetic hero of the time. To recapture the impression that the Childe made in 1812 one cannot do better than to look into Campbell's immensely popular poem *Gertrude of Wyoming*, whose hero wins a girl's heart by describing his travels:

> And well could he his pilgrimage of taste
> Unfold—and much they lov'd his fervid strain—
> While he each fair variety retrac'd
> Of climes, and manners, o'er the eastern main.

Perhaps Byron decided to offer a counter-blast to Campbell's insipid hero, who made his appearance just before Byron left England. The Childe also contrasts piquantly with the hero of Beattie's *Minstrel*. The sub-title of this poem, which Byron knew well, is 'The Progress of Genius', and Beattie explains that his object is to 'trace the progress of a poetical genius . . . from the first dawnings of fancy and reason'. The hero, based on the poet himself, is 'no vulgar boy'—a marked contrast to the Childe 'Who ne in Virtue's ways did take delight'.

Today we are likely to agree with the writer in the *Quarterly Review* who said that 'so far from effecting the object for which he is introduced, and giving some connection to the piece', the Childe 'only tends to embarrass and obscure it'. In Cantos III and IV, which appeared separately in 1816 and 1818, it is no longer possible to distinguish between the Childe and Byron himself. As he acknowledged in the preface to Canto IV, he was 'weary of drawing a line which every one seemed determined not to perceive'.

In Canto III the guide-book element has almost completely disappeared. Byron once called it 'a fine indistinct piece of poetical desolation', and to none of his other poems does his description of poetry as 'the lava of the imagination, whose eruption prevents an earthquake', apply so well. He was, as he said, 'half mad' when he wrote it, 'between metaphysics, mountains, lakes, love inextinguishable, thoughts unutterable, and the nightmare of my own delinquencies'. The mountains and lakes, like the metaphysics, were partly due to the influence of Shelley, of whom Byron was seeing a good deal at this time, and who was urging him to read Wordsworth. The theme of Society and Solitude which is so prominent in this Canto is one of the master-themes in the poetry of Wordsworth—and it had also

appeared in *Alastor*, which Shelley had written a few months before. Although there is some vulgarization of Wordsworth in Canto III, and some philosophical nonsense, it is clear that the intoxication of his own griefs and the influence of Shelley did Byron's poetry much more good than harm. The verse moves more urgently than before. Instead of the *andante* of Cantos I and II we find a swifter movement which sometimes reminds us of *terza rima* and anticipates the most successful English poem in this metre, Shelley's *Ode to the West Wind*:

> Still must I on; for I am as a weed
> Flung from the rock, on Ocean's foam, to sail
> Where'er the surge may sweep, the tempest's breath prevail.

A new vividness of phrase appears in the description of a ruin

> All tenantless, save to the crannying Wind,

while there is also a new imaginative power in the imagery, as in these lines on ambitious men:

> Even as a flame unfed, which runs to waste
> With its own flickering, or a sword laid by,
> Which eats into itself, and rusts ingloriously.

In Canto IV Byron is no longer under the influence of Shelley, though it has recently been argued that the direct influence of Hobhouse has been exaggerated. As Byron himself pointed out, there are 'no metaphysics' in Canto IV: instead the element of the travelogue is again prominent. Byron said that the Canto was designed 'as a mark of respect for what is venerable, and of feeling for what is glorious'; and Hobhouse not only wrote the illustrations and notes, but even provided Byron with a list of eligible subjects (mainly artistic and historical). The political and religious views expressed in the Canto are also much less challenging than those in III, which had driven Scott to fear that 'the termination will be fatal in one way or other, for it seems impossible that human nature can support the constant working of an imagination so dark and so strong' (letter to J. B. S. Morritt, 22. xi. 1816). The *Edinburgh Review* was delighted with the change, remarking that 'it is not enough to say that the veil is torn off. It is a nobler creature that is before us.' The average standard of the verse is higher, perhaps, than in any other Canto, yet Canto IV

hardly challenges the description of major poetry, as Canto III occasionally does.

While it is impossible to recapture the excitement of the original readers of *Childe Harold's Pilgrimage*, it is not difficult to understand its appeal. Byron's sensibility differed less from that of the average cultivated reader of his day than did the sensibility of Wordsworth or Shelley. Readers of Scott, Campbell, and Rogers turned to him with quickened pulses, but without the sense of being completely lost which most of them felt on reading *The Excursion*. His main theme consists of great commonplaces suggested by the history and the picturesque beauty of the places he visits. He displays many of the instincts of the successful journalist: he picks out precisely the features of the country through which he is travelling which are likely to hold the reader's attention—the scenes of battles and other famous events, a bull-fight, the life of the women. His descriptions are given piquancy by the mysterious and embittered character of the Wanderer and the shock of his unconventional views on religion, politics, and morality—views which had led the first publisher to whom the poem was offered to reject it. 'When we read the ... sarcasms on the "bravo's trade"', commented a writer in the *Quarterly Review*, 'we are induced to ask, not without some anxiety and alarm, whether such are indeed the opinions which a British peer entertains of a British army.' Even those of the original readers who were most deeply shocked by the opinions expressed in the poem took it for granted that it was a masterpiece. Today indifference to many of the topics discussed is a greater danger to its reputation than anger and indignation ever were. We no longer feel surprised, as its original readers did, at seeing such sentiments set out in resonant Spenserian verse. To understand the sensation which the poem caused we have to remember Byron's own remark, 'If ever I did any thing original, it was in *Childe Harold*.' It is interesting to notice that one reviewer after another stressed the originality of the poem. As the *Quarterly* remarked, Byron was receiving 'that fame . . . which is chiefly and most justly due to one who, in these exhausted days, strikes out a new and original line of composition'.

Parts of *Childe Harold* 'date', but not as markedly as the series of Tales which began to appear between the publication of the first two Cantos of that poem and Canto III. Yet in their day these accounts of adventure and unhappy love—most of them

based on true stories which Byron had heard in the course of his travels—were immensely successful: they poured through the gap made by *Childe Harold* and established Byron as the successful rival of Sir Walter Scott. A thousand young men made conversation, like Captain Benwick in *Persuasion*, by 'trying to ascertain whether *Marmion* or *The Lady of the Lake* were to be preferred, and how ranked the *Giaour* and *The Bride of Abydos*; and moreover, how the *Giaour* was to be pronounced'; and while Anne Elliott replied by venturing to hope that Captain Benwick 'did not always read only poetry', the young lady in *Jane Eyre* who 'doated on the Corsair' was more representative of her sex. Mme. de Staël had advised Byron to 'stick to the East', saying that 'the North, South, and West, have all been exhausted; but from the East, we have nothing but Southey's unsaleables', and the exotic settings of these poems—most of them were written during the only part of Byron's adult life to be spent in England—give them a technicolour quality which had a great deal to do with their success. Their heroes resemble the Childe in being passionate men at odds with their environment, and Byron's readers were quick to identify them with the poet himself. 'He told me an odd report', he wrote in his Journal one day: 'that *I* am the actual Conrad, the veritable Corsair, and that part of my travels are supposed to have passed in piracy. Um! people sometimes hit near the truth; but never the whole truth.' This subjective element is particularly evident in a passage added to *Lara* after the completion of the first draft:

> His early dreams of good outstripped the truth,
> And troubled Manhood followed baffled Youth;
> With thought of years in phantom chase misspent,
> And wasted powers for better purpose lent;
> And fiery passions that had poured their wrath
> In hurried desolation o'er his path,
> And left the better feelings all at strife
> In wild reflection o'er his stormy life. (323–30)

The Tales were written swiftly and without much revision, 'amidst balls and fooleries, and after coming home from masquerades and routs', and there is an air of improvisation about them—a pace and a panache—which reminds us of their origin. Most of them are written in tetrameters of the kind which Scott had made fashionable, and on occasion—as in *The Prisoner of*

*Chillon* (1816)—Byron handles the metre with very considerable skill. Those which are written in pentameters, such as *The Corsair* and *Lara* (both 1814), more often resemble Charles Churchill than Dryden, yet sometimes (as in the passage just quoted) Byron reminds us of Dryden and his contemporaries, just as the Regency period as a whole occasionally recalls the Restoration. It would be easy to mistake some of the better passages in these poems for late seventeenth-century heroic verse, while many of the weaker passages would be completely at home in *The Rehearsal*.

Little need be said of Byron's lyrics, although two or three deserve their place in any anthology. In *Hebrew Melodies* (1815) such a resounding failure as 'Jephtha's Daughter'—

> Since our Country, our God—Oh, my Sire!
> Demand that thy Daughter expire

—must be set beside the mastery of 'She walks in Beauty, like the night', of which the first stanza (though not the third) might be the work of one of the Caroline masters of the lyric. Of the lyrics scattered among Byron's longer poems the incantation in *Manfred* deserves particular mention for its compelling power. 'So we'll go no more a roving' has something of the mystery and the ageless passion of an anonymous song. Byron did not persevere enough with the lyric to find an individual voice, and at times he is astonishingly obtuse in his handling of language and rhythm, yet it is impossible not to regret that he did not write more often in this form. He resembles Burns more than anyone else, but he was a Burns without the sustaining inspiration of a popular tradition behind him. Too often his lyrics remind us of the minor and minimus writers of the later eighteenth century.

Byron's neo-classical sympathies may also be examined in certain of his dramas, though not in the first which calls for attention. He himself described *Manfred* (1817), which was begun while he was working on the third canto of *Childe Harold*, as a work 'of a very wild, metaphysical, and inexplicable kind', and he considered it 'not a drama properly—but a dialogue'. Manfred himself is the only important human character, for the Spirits of the Earth and Air, which speak choral verse which reminds us of Shelley, have much more important roles than the Hunter or the Abbot. The subject of the drama is the last days

in the life of a man who has discovered by his own experience that

> The Tree of knowledge is not that of life.

He is haunted by the sense of having destroyed his sister Astarte, whom he has passionately loved. Although he dies unrepentant, he is not dragged off to Hell: instead he proclaims that it is 'not so difficult to die'. While *Manfred* owes a good deal to the story of Faust, its deepest sources of inspiration were Byron's love for his half-sister Augusta and the profound impression made on him by the Alps. One has only to look into the Journal which he kept during his travels in the autumn of 1816 to see how closely these scenes were associated in his mind with his unhappy passion. At this time external objects became for him the types and symbols of his own experiences and moods, and something of the urgency of the verse in *Manfred* is duc to this: Manfred tells us that his own actions

> Have made my days and nights imperishable,
> Endless, and all alike, as sands on the shore,
> Innumerable atoms; and one desert,
> Barren and cold, on which the wild waves break,
> But nothing rests, save carcasses and wrecks,
> Rocks, and the salt-surf weeds of bitterness. (II. i. 53–58)

It is not surprising that Byron, having scored a partial success with a drama written in defiance of all dramatic tradition, should have decided to see what he could do in the way of a real drama: a drama at least potentially adapted to the stage. Nor is it surprising that he should have resolved to turn his back on the realm of the subjective and make an attempt to write something less directly personal. Everyone had noticed that Manfred was just another example of the Byronic hero: he would now attempt to avoid the familiar type. To this end, he decided to emulate the classical dramatists. 'My object', as he wrote in a letter, 'has been to dramatise, like the Greeks . . ., striking passages of history as they did of history and mythology.'

Byron's attitude to the drama provides a parallel to his attitude to non-dramatic poetry. Just as he had attacked the Lakists and extolled Pope, so in an age of Elizabethanizing he turned his back on Elizabethan models. He believed, as he repeatedly pointed out, that great drama cannot be written 'by

following the old dramatists, who are full of gross faults, pardoned only for the beauty of their language'. It was necessary, rather, to write 'naturally and *regularly* . . . like the Greeks'. As he put it in a letter to Murray written on 16 February 1821:

> It appears to me that there is room for a different style of the drama; neither a servile following of the old drama, which is a grossly erroneous one, nor yet *too French*, like those who succeeded the older writers. It appears to me, that good English, and a severer approach to the rules, might combine [to produce] something not dishonorable to our literature.

He was convinced that Shakespeare was 'the *worst* of models, though the most extraordinary of writers'. In this quest for 'a *regular* English drama' there was one modern writer who seemed to him to have pointed the way. 'It is more like a play of Alfieri's than of your stage (I say this humbly in speaking of that great Man)', he remarked of *Marino Faliero* (1821), while in September 1821 he acknowledged explicitly that his 'dramatic system' was 'more upon the Alfieri School than the English'. It would be interesting to know what exactly he said when he defended Alfieri in conversation with A. W. Schlegel, but his general attitude is easy to make out. It was not only Alfieri's dramatic technique that appealed to him: he was equally impressed by his political beliefs. Sismondi tells us that 'every high-minded Italian who lamented over the humiliation of his country, was united to [Alfieri] by bonds of mutual sympathy', adding: 'Thus was the taste for the noblest species of tragedy mingled with the love of glory and of liberty.' Byron would have been proud to have occupied the place in the history of the English drama which Alfieri, with his 'Tragedies of Freedom', occupied in that of the Italian.

On the question of the style suitable for tragedy Byron had views as radically opposed to those common in his day as his views on dramatic themes and structure. 'Do not judge me by your mad old dramatists', he once wrote, 'which is like drinking usquebaugh and then proving a fountain.' In *The Two Foscari* (1821) he drew attention to his 'avoidance of rant' and to the 'compression of the speeches in the more severe situations'. 'What I seek to show', he added, 'is the suppressed passion, rather than the rant of the present day.' On another occasion he claimed to have 'broken down the poetry as nearly as I could

to common language'. Here, as often in reading Byron's critical observations on the drama, one is reminded of Mr. Eliot's attitude a century later, and it is interesting to find, as early as *Manfred*, a passage which could readily be mistaken for the later poet:

> And they have only taught him what we know—
> That knowledge is not happiness, and science
> But an exchange of ignorance for that
> Which is another kind of ignorance. (II. iv. 60–63)

Unfortunately Byron is no more completely successful in the idiom of his dramas than in their construction. Although there are fewer long speeches in his plays than in those of many of his contemporaries, they are far more numerous than in the work of Shakespeare, while the style of his dramatic work is by no means as close to the spoken English of his day as that of the Elizabethans is to theirs. Yet while it must be admitted that Byron did not succeed in establishing himself as a major dramatist it remains true that he wrote several plays of note, while his critical assessment of the problems facing the English dramatist is one of the shrewdest in any period.

One of the things that appealed to Byron about the classical form of drama was that it seemed to offer him the prospect of release from the prison of subjectivity; yet it was by chance and not premeditation that he came on the form by which he was to escape into a larger world of the imagination. One day in 1817 he took up a copy of a lighthearted poem called *Whistlecraft* and found the following lines:

> I've often wish'd that I could write a book,
> Such as all English people might peruse;
> I never should regret the pains it took,
> That's just the sort of fame that I should chuse . . .

*Whistlecraft* was the work of one of the most gifted amateurs in the history of our literature, John Hookham Frere.[1] A former

[1] The full title is as follows: *Prospectus and Specimen of an intended National Work, by William and Robert Whistlecraft, of Stow-Market, in Suffolk, Harness and Collar-Makers. Intended to comprise the most interesting Particulars relating to King Arthur and his Round Table.* John Hookham Frere (1769–1846) was the eldest son of a Norfolk gentleman of antiquarian interests. At Eton he was one of the main contributors to a talented periodical called *The Microcosm* and formed a lifelong friendship with Canning. After being elected a Fellow of Caius College, Cambridge, he entered the Foreign

contributor to the *Anti-Jacobin* and a translator of genius, he had been fascinated by Pulci and had been inspired to attempt an English equivalent of the *Morgante Maggiore*. Byron was fascinated by Frere, as Frere had been by Pulci, and quickly dashed off *Beppo* (1818) in *ottava rima* 'in or after the excellent manner of Mr. Whistlecraft'. He thought of dedicating it to Frere, but refrained, rightly fearing that Frere would disapprove of some of his satiric allusions. Whereas the readers who had looked for politics in *Whistlecraft* had been wasting their time, in *Beppo* we find satire as well as joking. When we turn from Frere's poem to Byron's we move from a world of fun to a world of mischief. The fact that *Beppo* is 'A Venetian Story' does not prevent Byron from glancing satirically at English life. With a fine impartiality he satirizes England for being different from Italy and Italy for having something, after all, in common with England.

Byron seems to have realized that he had made an important discovery. 'If *Beppo* pleases, you shall have more in a year or two in the same mood', he wrote in April 1818; and when Shelley heard a reading of part of *Don Juan* later in the year he described it as 'a thing in the style of *Beppo*, but infinitely better'. While there can be no doubt that *Don Juan* is 'in the style of' the earlier poem, however, it raises questions which do not arise in the case of its predecessor: we are bound to ask what kind of poem *Don Juan* is, and what Byron had in mind as he wrote it. In spite of his references to 'the regularity of my design' and his claim that

> My poem's epic, and is meant to be
> Divided in twelve books

it is clear that he started without any definite idea of how he would finish. That is not the way to write an epic poem—or a mock-epic. 'You ask me for the plan', he wrote to Murray, 'I *have* no plan. . . . The Soul of such writing is its licence.' But he did have a general idea of how the poem should continue—or might continue. 'I meant to take [Don Juan] the tour of Europe', he wrote after completing the fifth canto, 'with a

Office and became M.P. for a pocket borough. In 1797 he joined with Canning and others in producing the *Anti-Jacobin*, to which he contributed some brilliant *jeux d'esprit*. In 1799 he succeeded Canning as Under-Secretary of State in the Foreign Office, but his diplomatic career came to an end because he was blamed for the disastrous decision to retreat to Corunna in 1808. In 1812 he married, settling in Malta four years later for the sake of his wife's health. Scott visited him there in 1831.

proper mixture of siege, battle, and adventure, and to make him finish as *Anacharsis Cloots* in the French Revolution. . . . I meant to have made him a *Cavalier Servente* in Italy, and a cause for a divorce in England, and a Sentimental 'Werther-faced man' in Germany, so as to show the different ridicules of the society in each of those countries, and to have displayed him gradually *gâté* and *blasé* as he grew older. . . . But I had not quite fixed whether to make him end in Hell, or in an unhappy marriage, not knowing which would be the severest.' How long it would take him to describe the Don's adventures he had not decided: the poem would be in 12 cantos, or 24, or 50, or 100, or even 150.

It is difficult to decide what Byron's object was as he wrote the poem. It is clear that he wished *épater les bourgeois*, less clear whether he had any further objective. When he tells us that *Don Juan* is 'the most moral of poems', adding however 'if people won't discover the moral, that is their fault, not mine', is he merely joking? These questions are difficult to answer because the composition of the poem was spread over a number of years and changes of mood and intention must be allowed for. Some of the claims that he made for the poem were made with his tongue in his cheek: on other occasions he was rationalizing after the event. Yet it seems safe to underline the importance of a passage in Canto x:

> Oh for a forty-parson power to chant
> Thy praise, Hypocrisy! Oh for a hymn
> Loud as the virtues thou dost loudly vaunt,
> Not practise!

Don Juan's visit to England, which results in some of the most pointed satire in the poem, gives Byron a chance to commend hypocrisy:

> Be hypocritical, be cautious, be
> Not what you *seem*, but always what you *see*.

He addresses the English public directly, in these words:

> You are *not* a moral people, and you know it,
> Without the aid of too sincere a poet.

Like most major satire, *Don Juan* had its origin in indignation. Byron told the Countess Guiccioli that he wrote the first two

cantos in Venice at a moment when he was 'soured by a swarm of slanders and injustices', to avenge himself for 'those undeserved torments'. This helps to explain his emphasis on hypocrisy throughout the poem, and the way in which the word 'Cant' recurs so often in his own references to *Don Juan*: 'As to the Cant of the day, I despise it. . . . I will never flatter Cant. . . . I will not give way to all the Cant in Christendom.' He came to regard all hostility to his poem as a refusal to face the truth. 'The truth is that it is TOO TRUE', he once wrote, 'and the women hate every thing which strips off the tinsel of *Sentiment*.' He particularly attacks 'the cant which is the crying sin of this double-dealing and false-speaking time', while in the preface to Cantos VI–VIII he asserts that 'the degraded and hypocritical mass which leavens the present English generation' is incapable of facing the truth. Such had been the outcry when the first two Cantos were published that Cant was momentarily victorious: 'The cry is up', as Byron acknowledged, 'and Cant is up.' It is fitting that this Poem against Cant should be dedicated to Robert Southey, Laureate to George III and the man who seemed to Byron to sum up all that was most objectionable in an age of venality and time-serving. References to Southey in *Don Juan* are almost as numerous as references to Cibber in *The Dunciad*.

There is less danger of the modern reader's overlooking the morally shocking passages than of his failing to notice the passages which struck most contemporary readers as politically shocking. From the point of view of the average reader of the *Quarterly Review* it was a seditious and inflammatory production. This was quite deliberate on Byron's part: 'With these things, and these fellows', as he wrote in a letter, 'it is necessary, in the present clash of philosophy and tyranny, to throw away the scabbard.' The preface to Cantos VI–VIII is particularly revealing, with its bitter justification of the bitter stanzas on Castlereagh, 'a minister . . . the most despotic in intention, and the weakest in intellect, that ever tyrannised over a country'. In the mourning for his death Byron saw nothing but 'the nauseous and atrocious cant of a degraded crew of conspirators against all that is sincere and honourable'. By this point, it is clear, he had come to regard *Don Juan* as a campaign fought against the forces of oppression. 'The hackneyed and lavished title of Blasphemer', he wrote in a letter, '—with Radical, Liberal, Jacobin, Reformer, etc.—should be welcome to all who recollect on

whom it was originally bestowed.' All these terms were certainly bestowed on Byron, whose poem gave offence by its anti-imperialism, its anti-royalism, its anti-clericalism, and its leaning to pacifism, no less than by its free tone on moral and religious questions. Alfieri had been the Tragedian of Freedom: now Byron was writing a comic epic with the same serious intention.

The most audacious parts of the poem are its digressions, and any account of *Don Juan* which ignores these passages is bound to be misleading. Byron flaunts them in the reader's face: 'But to my subject—let me see—what was it?', as he observes at one point: 'Oh!—the third canto, and the pretty pair.' Although the digressions sometimes swamp the main narrative, as in Canto III, they are so essential to Byron's intention that we seldom resent them. The introductory passages at the beginning of the cantos are bound to remind us of Fielding, who was clearly in Byron's mind as he wrote his 'comic epic poem in *verse*'; but at times we are reminded even more unmistakably of Sterne. When Byron draws attention to a daring transition with the words—

> . . how odd are the connections
> Of human thoughts which jostle in their flight!

—it might be the author of *Tristram Shandy* who is speaking. Byron reminds us of Sterne in his alternations between gaiety and gravity, in the confidential tone in which he discusses his book with the reader, debating points of literary criticism and morality, in the apparent shapelessness of his plot, and in the mischievous way in which he stands things on their heads and is determined to cheat the reader of the expected 'stock response'. Like Sterne, Byron presents himself as a broad-minded philosopher who has seen farther than the common run of mankind. Juanism has something in common with Shandyism and in many ways *Don Juan*, a poem unfinished and unfinishable, stands to the tradition of English poetry as *Tristram Shandy* stands to that of the English novel.

The idiom of *Don Juan* is the idiom of *Beppo*. Having left the Spenserian stanza of *Childe Harold* behind him, Byron is visibly rejoicing in the potentialities of the new stanza, its pace, its informality, and the licence it gives for digression. At times the measure itself seems to become an inspiration to him and the wheels catch fire with the rapidity of their motion. Unlike the

pentameter couplet, *ottava rima* is a form which encourages a free play of fancy and makes for inclusion rather than exclusion, suggesting acceptance of the poet's first thought and a hastening on to its successor rather than scrutiny and revision of what has first presented itself. Byron quickly attained a remarkable fluency in the metre, making it so much the expression of his own personality that he could do with it as he pleased. The final couplet is well suited to epigram, and he specializes in bringing things down to earth at the end of the stanza:

> Think you, if Laura had been Petrarch's wife,
> He would have written sonnets all his life? (III. viii)

The skill of the rhyming contributes greatly to the wit of the poem. Byron likes to use the yoke of rhyme to jerk together the most incongruous concepts, such as cosmogony and mahogany, or potato and Cato (a rhyme that is so much a favourite that he uses it three times). In the art of rhyming surprisingly he was a pupil of Butler and Swift, and some of the most 'Hudibrastic' rhymes in the language are to be found in *Don Juan*, such as intellectual/hen-peck'd you all, Alonso/go on so, and oddest he/modesty. There are also occasional violent enjambements, such as hence-/forward, and the following—in the account of the shipwreck in Canto II:

> Started the stern-post, also shattered the
> Whole of her stern-frame, and, ere she could lift
> Herself . . . (II. xxvii)

As for the diction, what the *Edinburgh Review* said of *Beppo* is equally true of *Don Juan*:

> The great charm is in the simplicity and naturalness of the language—the free but guarded use of all polite idioms, and even of all phrases of temporary currency that have the stamp of good company upon them,—with the exclusion of all scholastic or ambitious eloquence . . . good verse, entirely composed of common words, in their common places; never . . . one sprig of what is called poetical diction . . . running on in an inexhaustible series of good easy colloquial phrases, and [falling] into verse by some unaccountable and happy fatality. (xxix. 303, February 1818)

No word in the language is too familiar or too commonplace to be used in this poem, which contains such humdrum words and phrases as mortgage, Patent Blacking, vermicelli, soda water, menagerie, indigestion, really, hencoops, Five per Cents, butler,

cheese-paring, ready money, bagged, billiards, thereanent, old newspaper, affidavit, solvent, portmanteaus, income tax, supercargo, beefsteak, post-obit, damme, guts, cough, breakfast, nonsuit, raising cash, emetic, entrails, broth, jugular, blankets, cookery, phthisical, clap-trap, grand-dad, quiz, valet, teaspoonfuls, annuities, and gastric juice. Of many of these it may be said, as Byron says of 'broth', that it is 'A thing which poesy but seldom mentions'.

The use of 'the language of every day' in *Beppo* and *Don Juan* has nothing to do with the theories of Wordsworth: Byron's use of familiar diction is that of an aristocratic writer conversant with classical literature and the English poets of the early eighteenth century. He is aware of the different 'levels of style', and is deliberately choosing to 'wander with pedestrian Muses'. It is significant that the Horatian motto of *Don Juan*—*Difficile est proprie communia dicere*—had already been the motto of *An Epistle to Dr. Arbuthnot.* It is to the work of the Augustans that one must look for English analogies to the style of *Don Juan*—and not least to the *Alma* of Matthew Prior.

Several of his friends assure us that the style of *Don Juan* is an echo of Byron's conversation at its best. That is what he himself claims:

> I rattle on exactly as I'd talk
> With anybody in a ride or walk. (xv. xix)

If we look into his letters and journals we find the soil from which the poem grew. Some explanation of the remarkably sure tone of *Don Juan* may be found in the fact that Byron's letters to John Murray were habitually read out to the publisher's friends, or passed round among them, so that he knew that he was writing for a small group of intelligent and sophisticated people. *Don Juan* seems to have been written with just such an audience in mind, an audience of witty men of the world. As he tells his story Byron catches perfectly the tone of conversation:

> I had my doubts, perhaps I have them still,
>   But what I say is neither here nor there:
> I knew his father well, and have some skill
>   In character—but it would not be fair
> From sire to son to augur good or ill:
>   He and his wife were an ill-assorted pair—
> But scandal's my aversion—I protest
> Against all evil speaking, even in jest. (I. li)

Don Juan's visit to London gives Byron a particularly good opportunity for exploring the resources of colloquial diction, and he by no means limits himself to idioms 'that have the stamp of good company upon them'. A writer in the first number of the *London Magazine* made the suggestion that Byron may have used the 'New and comprehensive Vocabulary of the Flash Language' in *The Memoirs of James Hardy Vaux* to supplement his own knowledge in some of the more aggressively 'familiar' passages—such as, perhaps, the ironical requiem pronounced over an English soldier:

> Who in a row like Tom could lead the van,
> Booze in the ken, or at the spellken hustle?
> Who queer a flat? . . . (XI. xix)

But often all he had to do was to put the most obvious vulgarities of speech into verse:

> 'Oh Jack! I'm floored by that 'ere bloody Frenchman!' (XI. xiii)

—a line that Kipling must have envied. Yet the delight of the poem lies in its variety, and beside such passages as these we must set the idyllic description of Juan and Haidée in Canto IV, which is managed with great delicacy, and ends finely:

> No stone is there to show, no tongue to say
> What was; no dirge, except the hollow sea's,
> Mourns o'er the beauty of the Cyclades. (IV. lxxii)

Of all the differences between *Don Juan* and *Childe Harold* perhaps the most important lies in the presentation of their heroes, and this is closely related to the style in which the two poems are written. Although some details in Don Juan's life may be paralleled in Byron's own, he is not a self-projection in the sense in which Childe Harold is: as a consequence he is presented with a detachment and irony which are not to be found in the earlier poem. The fundamental difference between the two poems is that Byron has moved from a world in which the passions are presented 'straight' to one in which the predominant spirit is that of satiric comedy. As a consequence, while it might be said that there are in *Childe Harold* no other people, apart from the hero himself, *Don Juan* is almost as full of human beings as the *Canterbury Tales*. Life is no longer portrayed as the oppression of one individual by the rest of the

world working in collusion. The alternations between passages 'droll or pathetic, descriptive or sentimental, tender or satirical' which were to have been a feature of *Childe Harold* but which in fact can hardly be found in that poem, are the hallmark and glory of *Don Juan*. As we read it we are reminded that what Byron found in *Whistlecraft* was not simply a new stanza: it was a new idiom—and with it the inducement to look at life in a new way. 'It will . . . show them that I can write cheerfully, and repel the charge of monotony and mannerism', as he had written to John Murray of *Beppo*. To see what the new idiom did for Byron we have only to turn to *Don Juan* from the poems he had been writing little more than a year before, *The Lament of Tasso* and *Manfred*. It is not surprising that Shelley noticed that Byron was more cheerful as he worked at his new satire. In the new rhythm Byron found emancipation: what it brought him (with other gifts) was a sense of proportion. There are few clearer examples of the way in which the discovery of a new medium may enable a writer to discover a new aspect of his personality—or rather to express an aspect of his personality that has remained unexpressed and therefore undeveloped.

*Don Juan* sold very rapidly, but most of its original readers were, or pretended to be, scandalized. One of the things that particularly shocked them was Byron's satire on his wife. So great was the public disapproval that after the publication of the second part (Cantos III–V) the Countess Guiccioli prevailed on Byron to put the poem aside: when he took it up again it was on the understanding that it was to be 'more guarded and decorous and sentimental'. Even so, there was further trouble, and the last eleven Cantos were published by John Hunt. When Byron died sixteen cantos and some fragments had been written, but the poem was not in sight of completion.

Byron's last major poem was an outcome of the storm aroused by the early cantos of *Don Juan*. When Southey published his Laureate elegy on George III in 1821 he included in the preface 'a few comments on Don Juan'. Everything about Southey's *A Vision of Judgement* seemed to mark it out for ridicule. In dedicating it to George IV he asked rhetorically: 'To whom could an experiment, which, perhaps, may be considered hereafter as of some importance in English Poetry, be so fitly inscribed, as to the Royal and munificent Patron of science, art, and literature?' To whom—we may rephrase it—more fitly than to such a King

as George IV could a poem be dedicated which was fated never to be read except as a joke, to help the reader to enjoy one of the most unanswerable satires in all literature? Southey's whole preface is written in a strain which must have inspired a mixture of contempt and fury in a man of Byron's political sympathies. Southey particularly mentions the 'perfect integrity . . . manifested in the whole administration of public affairs' and prophesies that 'the brightest portion of British history will be that which records the improvements, the works, and the achievements of the Georgian Age'. In the poem itself the poet falls into a trance in which he sees that George III's coffin is empty and then overhears Perceval reporting to the late Monarch on the state of the country—a report which is more favourable on foreign affairs than on matters at home, where 'rabid fanatics' are on the prowl, foolishly pursuing what they imagine to be Liberty. The poet then sees the King arriving at the Gate of Heaven, where Good Spirits assemble to support him while Evil Spirits appear from Hell, led, rather unobtrusively, by Satan in person. Wilkes and Junius appear to speak against the King, but they are so overwhelmed by the presence of the Deity that they are unable to open their mouths. The other accusers of the King admit that what they said against him during his lifetime was unjust. Even Washington admits that nothing but circumstances led to their opposition:

Heaven in these things fulfill'd its wise, though inscrutable purpose,
While we work'd its will, doing each in his place as became him.

After he has spoken 'with earnest humility' on his own behalf the King receives a blessing and the ministering spirits 'clap . . . their pennons' and burst into song. As the King is received into Heaven the reception committee includes the most eminent of the former monarchs of England as well as other worthies like Bede, Friar Bacon, Chaucer, Cranmer, Cecil, Spenser, and Shakespeare—it is all very 'snob'. The Worthies of the Georgian Age include Wolfe, Handel, Hogarth, Wesley, Burke, Warren Hastings, Cowper, and Nelson—but not (as Southey pointed out delightedly in a letter) either Pitt or Fox. The fact that there is yet another tier of Worthies—The Young Spirits—serves to emphasize that the poem is in some sort a Hymn on the Georgian Age.

Many even among Southey's admirers were embarrassed by

his *Vision of Judgement*, and it was parodied by more than one of his opponents. Pursued by that Spirit of Comedy which seems to have been keeping so remorseless a watch on his doings at this time, he went so far as to invite Byron to attack him in verse. 'When he attacks me again', he wrote in a letter in the *Courier*, 'let it be in rhyme. For one who has so little command of himself, it will be a great advantage that his temper should be obliged to *keep tune*.' If Southey had only known it, Byron had already written *The Vision of Judgment* in which he 'keeps tune' to some purpose. Neither the tune nor the politics are Southey's. Writing from Italy on 1 October 1821 Byron told Moore:

> I have written . . . about sixty stanzas of a poem, in octave stanzas, (in the Pulci style, which the fools in England think was invented by Whistlecraft—it is as old as the hills in Italy,)—called *The Vision of Judgment*, by Quevedo Redivivus, with this motto—
>
> A Daniel come to *judgment*, yea, a Daniel:
> I thank thee, Jew, for teaching me that word.
>
> In this it is my intent to put the said George's Apotheosis in a Whig point of view, not forgetting the Poet Laureate for his preface and his other demerits.

It is hardly surprising that John Murray refused to have anything to do with *The Vision of Judgment*. After some delay John Hunt published it in *The Liberal*, but although he omitted the preface he was eventually fined a hundred pounds for publishing a work 'calumniating the late king, and wounding the feelings of his present majesty'. If the preface had been published the fine would probably have been much heavier. In it Byron refers to 'the gross flattery, the dull impudence, the renegado intolerance, and impious cant, of the poem by the author of "Wat Tyler"' and says that it is 'something so stupendous as to form the sublime of himself—containing the quintessence of his own attributes'. The gravamen of Byron's charges is contained in the following sentences:

> To attempt to canonise a monarch, who, whatever were his household virtues, was neither a successful nor a patriot king,—inasmuch as several years of his reign passed in war with America and Ireland, to say nothing of the aggression upon France—like all other exaggeration, necessarily begets opposition. In whatever manner he

may be spoken of in this new *Vision*, his *public* career will not be more favourably transmitted by history. Of his private virtues (although a little expensive to the nation) there can be no doubt.

Since the contrast of tunes is part of the satire, it is worth recalling the opening of Southey's *Vision*:

'Twas at that sober hour when the light of day is receding,
And from surrounding things the hues wherewith day has adorned them
Fade, like the hopes of youth, till the beauty of earth is departed.

Byron's irreverent octaves form the most marked contrast possible with these sombre hexameters:

Saint Peter sat by the celestial gate:
His keys were rusty, and the lock was dull,
So little trouble had been given of late;
Not that the place by any means was full,
But since the Gallic era 'eighty-eight'
The Devils had ta'en a longer, stronger pull,
And 'a pull altogether', as they say
At sea—which drew most souls another way.

After he has set his scene on the threshold of Heaven Byron glances back to the carnage of Waterloo—so reminding us that *The Vision of Judgment* was written during the composition of *Don Juan*, and prompting the suggestion that some ideas he was thinking of utilizing if he sent the Don to Hell may have found their way (instead) into his other great satire. Then, after some satirical stanzas on the character of the late King, he returns to St. Peter, to whom the news of the King's death is reported by a cherub:

'And who *is* George the Third?' replied the apostle:
'*What George? What Third?*'

Among the host of good angels and bad who arrive in the King's train there is 'a spirit of a different aspect' who is none other than the familiar Byronic hero now playing the role of the Prince of Darkness:

His brow was like the deep when tempest-tossed;
Fierce and unfathomable thoughts engraved
Eternal wrath on his immortal face,
And *where* he gazed a gloom pervaded space.

The meeting between Satan and Michael has all the courtesy appropriate to proceedings in the Upper Chamber:

> . . Though they did not kiss,
> Yet still between his Darkness and his Brightness
> There passed a mutual glance of great politeness.

Michael bowed low, while Satan responded

> With more hauteur, as might an old Castilian
> Poor Noble meet a mushroom rich civilian.

As Satan speaks in support of his claim to the King's soul the serious intention of Byron's satire becomes evident:

> He ever warred with freedom and the free:
> Nations as men, home subjects, foreign foes,
> So that they uttered the word 'Liberty!'
> Found George III their first opponent. Whose
> History was ever stained as his will be
> With national and individual woes?

His appeal to St. Peter asking whether a King who has opposed Catholic emancipation should be allowed to enter heaven is an excellent example of *argumentum ad hominem*—or rather, in this case, *argumentum ad angelum*. When the witnesses against the King are summoned such a host appears that it is decided that Wilkes and Junius shall speak for them all. Instead of being reduced to silence by shame, as they are in Southey's poem, they speak briefly but devastatingly. Wilkes is too magnanimous to press his charges, adding:

> I don't like ripping up old stories, since
> His conduct was but natural in a prince.

Junius (mysterious in death as in life) contents himself with saying

> I loved my country, and I hated him,

and adds that he stands by what he has written. At this point, when Washington, Horne Tooke, and Franklin are about to be called to give further evidence, there is a stir, and a devil elbows his way in carrying Southey under his wing and complaining bitterly at the weight. The prospect of his speech in his own defence causes consternation, and St. Peter appeals to him (as one author to another) to confine his reply to prose. The gist

of Southey's reply is that he is a professional turncoat who must sell his wares in the best market. There is a delightful touch in stanza xcix, where he turns to Satan and offers to write his Life 'In two octavo volumes, nicely bound, With notes and preface', adding that there is no need to be anxious about the reception of the book, as he can choose his own reviewers. When Satan bows without answering, Southey hastens to make the same offer to Michael. Then he begins to read his latest poem, *A Vision of Judgement*, and the cffect is dramatic:

> Those grand heroics acted as a spell;
>   The Angels stopped their ears and plied their pinions;
> The Devils ran howling, deafened, down to Hell;
>   The ghosts fled, gibbering, for their own dominions—
> (For 'tis not yet decided where they dwell,
>   And I leave every man to his opinions);
> Michael took refuge in his trump—but lo!
> His teeth were set on edge, he could not blow!

St. Peter knocked Southey down with his keys. The vision faded, and all that Byron saw, in the end,

> Was, that King George slipped into Heaven for one;
> And when the tumult dwindled to a calm,
> I left him practising the hundredth psalm.

It is a perfect ending for a poem which is not the less lethal for the ubiquitous spirit of comedy. Byron can afford to treat the King with a contemptuous magnanimity because his main concern is with the conduct of public affairs during his reign. It is appropriate that *The Vision of Judgment* should have been written so soon after the inquiry into the affairs of Queen Caroline: it remains the perfect satiric commentary on one of the most tawdry periods in our history, a trenchant indictment of the age of reaction that followed Waterloo—the age which was beginning, even as Byron wrote, to give way to what Halévy called 'The Age of the Liberal Awakening'. It is the quintessence of Byron's satire, 'the sublime of himself', and forms a fitting climax to his poetic career.

When he died at Missolonghi Byron wrote his name in history. The handsome young poet who was also a *milord anglais* and a trenchant critic of all things English was perfectly calculated to appeal to the heart of Europe. His fame grew rapidly and to this day he remains a central figure in the European

'Romantic Movement' and one of the sources of the popular idea of a poet. His life and personality had a remarkable influence on Goethe. His influence on the Romantic Movements in Germany, France, Italy, Spain, and Russia was at once obvious and profound. He is the only English poet to have a chapter devoted to him in Bertrand Russell's *History of Western Philosophy*.

His true stature as a poet is another matter. Although it would have made more difference to the history of Europe if Byron had never lived than if Keats had never lived, it would have made more difference to the history of English poetry if Keats had never lived. There is in fact a connexion between the limited nature of Byron's poetic achievement and his high reputation abroad. It is precisely because no powerful electric current passes through the language when he uses it—as it does when Shakespeare and Milton use it—that so much of Byron's poetry survives the processes of export and translation. The Continental critics who insist most strongly on his greatness often turn out to read what are (from a critical point of view) the wrong poems, or the right poems in the wrong language. How much of Byron's poetry had Goethe read, with full understanding, in English? In an intelligent full-scale study, published as recently as 1955–7, M. Robert Escarpit more often offers his readers quotations from Byron's poetry in French than in English. It must be acknowledged that Byron himself might not have objected. 'I cannot alter the Sentiments', he wrote to Murray in September 1811, when he was asked to make some revisions in the first two Cantos of *Childe Harold*; 'but if there are any alterations in the structure of the versification you would wish to be made, I will tag rhymes and turn stanzas as much as you please'. But if poetry is the best words in the best order, great poetry cannot be altered in such a manner, and it is no accident that the poems of Byron's which suffer most from alteration or translation—*Don Juan* and *The Vision of Judgment*—are those which are most highly valued in England and which most often tend to be underrated in foreign studies of his work. While Byron's life and character will continue to provide a splendid subject for debate, few English critics are ever likely to disagree with Tennyson's view that of all Byron's poems it is the satires which survive.

# III

# SHELLEY

It is a paradox that Shelley is often described as a 'pure poet'.[1] In fact, as Mary Shelley pointed out, he combined two qualities of intellect that are not often associated in so high a development: 'a brilliant imagination' and 'a logical exactness of reason'. As a consequence he 'deliberated at one time whether he should dedicate himself to poetry or metaphysics', and it can only have been after anxious consideration that he decided to be a poet. Although we are told that he then began to educate himself for poetry by 'engaging . . . in the study of the poets of Greece, Italy, and England', it is possible to exaggerate the extent to which he discarded 'his philosophical pursuits'. When he was at work on *Prometheus Unbound* he could still tell Peacock that he considered poetry 'very subordinate to moral and political science', adding that he would have devoted himself to the latter study if he had been more robust. This makes it the less surprising that he is one of the most didactic of all our poets. His remark in the preface to *Prometheus Unbound*, 'Didactic poetry is my abhorrence', is the most misleading sentence he ever wrote. By 'didactic poetry' he here means primarily close

[1] Percy Bysshe Shelley (1792–1822) belonged to an ancient family. His father Timothy Shelley was a conservative country gentleman without intellectual sympathies. He was educated at Sion House Academy, Brentford, and at Eton, where he was intensely miserable and felt himself to be 'apart from the whole school'. Dr. Lind, a Fellow of the Royal Society who lived at Windsor, befriended Shelley and encouraged his scientific interests. While he was still at school he published *Zastrozzi*, a wild Gothic romance: *St. Irvyne; or, The Rosicrucian* appeared just after he had left. In 1810 he went to University College, Oxford, but the following year he was sent down for circulating a brief pamphlet, *The Necessity of Atheism*, to the Heads of Colleges. Soon after this he ran away with Harriet Westbrook, marrying her in Edinburgh. He met Southey and was soon corresponding with Godwin. After some comically ineffective attempts to participate in politics he printed *Queen Mab* in 1813. In 1815 he left his wife for Mary Godwin, whom he married after Harriet's suicide at the end of 1816. Earlier that year he and Mary had paid a prolonged visit to Byron in Switzerland. After a period at Marlow when he saw a good deal of Leigh Hunt and Peacock he travelled on the Continent and visited Byron again, in Venice. Shelley spent the rest of his brief life in Italy, where he wrote almost all his finest poetry. He was drowned while crossing alone in a small boat from Leghorn to Lerici. His body was cremated on the beach in the presence of Byron, Trelawny, and Hunt.

reasoning in verse, in the manner of Lucretius. As we study his longer poems we shall find him concerned with the problem of how to be didactic most tellingly, rather than with that of whether to be didactic.

His earlier work is inferior to the *juvenilia* of many less gifted poets. Poor as it is as poetry, however, *Queen Mab* is of great interest: with its mottoes from Voltaire, Lucretius, and Archimedes, this 'pamphlet in verse' (as Dowden called it) is one of the most nakedly didactic poems ever written. 'The Past, the Present, and the Future, are the grand and comprehensive topics of this poem', as he wrote in a letter. It was written to disseminate his ideas and begin the process of proselytizing the world. It is clear that he was uncertain how openly didactic a poet could dare to be. 'The notes . . . will be long and philosophical', he wrote; 'I shall take that opportunity . . . of propagating my principles, which I decline to do syllogistically in [a] poem. A poem very didactic is, I think, very stupid.' But three weeks later he tells another friend that the didactic part of the poem is in blank verse, while the descriptive parts are in an unrhymed lyrical measure. In fact the poem and its notes form a unity, and it is to the notes that a reader in search of the ideas of the young Shelley is more likely to turn. They are a strange jumble: the poet is against monarchy, against Christianity, against chastity (as it is usually understood), and against the eating of animal flesh. It is difficult to read some of the notes without reflecting that the author was a very young man: 'Since writing this note I have some reason to suspect that Jesus was an ambitious man, who aspired to the throne of Judea.' Yet the notes are not the work of a fool, and many of the criticisms of the accepted ideas of the time are extremely shrewd. The Don Quixote of English poetry is already committed to the campaign against tyranny and hypocrisy which was to end only with his death.

A man with a message is a man in search of an audience, and Shelley speculated a great deal about who would read his poems. The difficulty was that a large audience was incompatible with the nature of his views. 'As I have not abated an iota of the infidelity or cosmopolicy of it', he wrote of *Queen Mab*, 'sufficient will remain . . . to make it very unpopular. Like all egotists, I shall console myself with what I may call, if I please, the suffrages of the chosen few.' He took it for granted that these would come from the wealthier classes, ordering that only 250

copies should be printed—'a small, neat quarto, on fine paper, . . . so as to catch the aristocrats'. In the event Shelley withdrew the book after some seventy presentation copies had been distributed and before a single copy of the original edition had been sold; and yet, by a typically Shelleyan paradox, this was the only one of his books to circulate at all widely in the earlier part of the century. Soon the Radicals made it a sort of Bible, and Robert Owen never ceased to quote from it in writings which were by no stretch of the imagination addressed to 'the aristocrats'.

The preface to *The Revolt of Islam* (1818) makes it clear that Shelley was anxious to discover how far an audience existed for the sort of views that he wished to propagate and how far he had the power of propagating them. He described the poem as 'an experiment on the temper of the public mind, as to how far a thirst for a happier condition of . . . society survives, among the enlightened and refined, the tempests which have shaken the age in which we live'. But characteristically he made no concessions. The poem opens with a canto of perplexed and obscure allegory, radically different (as Shelley acknowledged) from the remaining cantos; yet he sent this canto to a publisher as a specimen of the whole. What is more, in the poem as he originally wrote it (as *Laon and Cythna*) the lovers who are the main characters are brother and sister, so that their love is incestuous. 'It was my object', he wrote in the original preface, 'to break through the crust of those outworn opinions on which established institutions depend.' His aim was to 'accustom men to that charity and toleration which the exhibition of a practice widely differing from their own has a tendency to promote'. One sometimes wonders whether Shelley ever met any ordinary men and women. The lack of human insight or common sense displayed in the whole affair is very striking. It was only with the greatest difficulty that his friends prevailed on him to make the necessary changes. Even so, they did not think that the poem was likely to sell well. 'The work cannot possibly be popular' Leigh Hunt wrote, as if in answer to a question.

There can be no doubt of the didactic intention of the poem. The sub-title of *Laon and Cythna* had been 'The Revolution of the Golden City: A Vision of the Nineteenth Century', while the preface proclaims that the poem has been written 'in the cause of a liberal and comprehensive morality' on behalf of 'liberty

and justice'. The allegorical first canto describes a battle between an Eagle and a Serpent, representing (respectively) Evil and Good. Good is defeated, but not, as it turns out, killed. The poet, who is depressed at the course taken by the French Revolution, is a spectator at this battle; but he is told not to give way to despair. Like Peacock, Shelley was alarmed by the pessimism of much of the literature of the age, regarding it as the expression of an exaggerated reaction from the French Revolution. He had been seeing a good deal of Byron at this time, and *The Revolt* appears to be an anti-Byronic poem. Shelley's challenge sounds out clearly in the preface: 'Those who now live have survived an age of despair.' Despair is an enemy that must be kept at bay: as the mysterious Genius says to the poet,

> . . to grieve is wise, but the despair
> Was weak and vain which led thee here from sleep.
>
> (I. xxi)

The message of the poem is optimistic. It describes the adventures of two reformers and all that they accomplish in a State until the forces of reaction rally and burn them to death on a great pyre. We leave them in a paradisaical condition, in the Temple of the Spirit in which the poet had first seen them. The whole thing is 'a tale', as Shelley wrote to a publisher, 'illustrative of such a Revolution as might be supposed to take place in an European nation, acted upon by the opinions of . . . the modern philosophy . . .' The inspiration is clearly what had happened in France, but the intention is to be as general as possible. It is a sort of handbook for bloodless revolutionaries; and would no doubt be useful for anyone who happened to live in a world in essential respects different from this old world of ours. As Mary Shelley pointed out, it is a work embodying 'forms defecated of all the weakness and evil which cling to real life'.

The presentation of such idealized creatures now seemed to Shelley to be the mode of didacticism most likely to succeed. In the preface to a much greater work than *The Revolt*, *Prometheus Unbound* (1820), he acknowledges 'a passion for reforming the world' but denies that he dedicates his poems 'solely to the direct enforcement of reform' or considers them 'as containing a reasoned system on the theory of human life'. He goes on: 'My

purpose has . . . been . . . to familiarise the highly refined imagination of the more select classes of poetical readers with beautiful idealisms of moral excellence.' His idea, which is Platonic, is that 'reasoned principles of moral conduct' are useless until men have been taught to love that which is beautiful and virtuous. Experience has taught him how small the class of such readers is. 'If I may judge by its merits,' he wrote, 'the "Prometheus" cannot sell beyond twenty copies.' Later he claimed that it 'was never intended for more than five or six persons'. Leigh Hunt, who deeply admired it, aptly described it as an 'odi profanum sort of poem' and despaired of making it 'at all recommendable to readers in general'. It is wholly appropriate that the young Yeats should have been intoxicated by it and should have hoped that his fellow students would join him in regarding it as a sacred book—no less appropriate that they should have done no such thing.

As Mary Shelley pointed out, *Prometheus Unbound* is 'a more idealized image of the same subject' as *The Revolt of Islam*. Whereas Laon strives to bring freedom (primarily political and social freedom) to one particular State, Prometheus brings Freedom in the deepest and most comprehensive sense to the whole of mankind. Just as Laon is separated from his lover Cythna for most of the action, so Prometheus is separated from the more passive Asia. Prometheus and Asia are more ethereal than Laon and Cythna because they are not human beings but Titans, and they end (fittingly) in a more ethereal form of paradise. They are Aeschylean figures far transcending mere humanity: while Laon is concerned in the highest sense with politics, Prometheus is involved in a drama which is rather metaphysical than political. Leigh Hunt perceptively referred to the 'sublime cosmopolitics' of the work. We are now seeing the conflict between the Eagle and the Serpent, Tyranny and Freedom, 'at the highest possible level'—to use reporters' jargon. This revolution takes place in heaven, and cannot be assigned to a particular point in time.

It is not difficult to see why Prometheus is the perfect hero for Shelley, and his story the perfect subject for his poetry. As Mary Shelley tells us, 'the subject he loved best to dwell on was the image of One warring with the Evil Principle, oppressed not only by it, but by all—even the good, who were deluded into considering evil a necessary portion of humanity'. In Aeschylus

Jupiter and Prometheus are reconciled, the latter buying his release from torment by disclosing the secret that is essential to Jupiter's safety. Shelley 'was averse from a catastrophe so feeble as that of reconciling the Champion with the Oppressor of Mankind'. To Shelley Prometheus meant very much what Christ means for Christians,

> The saviour and the strength of suffering man.
> (i. 817)

The drama describes the last act, as it were, in the triumph of Prometheus over Jupiter. The past history of the struggle is narrated in retrospective speeches. Although it is often said that the action takes place in the mind of Prometheus, in a sense his spiritual victory occurs before the play opens, or at the very beginning. From the first, in foretelling the final overthrow of Jupiter, he speaks 'in grief, Not exultation'; and when he is reminded of his curse against Jupiter he revokes it, with the words:

> I wish no living thing to suffer pain. (i. 305)

This in no way involves submission to Jupiter. One of the worst torments that he is made to suffer is the contemplation of the fate of Christ, whose wishes for Man had been so like his own:

> . . Thy name I will not speak,
> It hath become a curse. (i. 603–4)

As a climax of his suffering he witnesses in a vision the failure of the French Revolution. Yet Act I closes with the promise that the Hour of 'Wisdom, Justice, Love, and Peace' is on the way. In Act II Asia awaits his coming, in a distant Eastern valley. Her conversation with Demogorgon (who stands for Eternity: 'Demand no direr name', he warns her) fills in the metaphysical background of the myth as Shelley interprets it. In the beginning there were the Heaven and Earth, and Light and Love. Then Saturn came to reign. In a sense the *Saturnia regna* were idyllically happy, but his coming brought with it Time, 'an envious shadow', and under him men were without Knowledge, 'the birthright of their being', and without

> Self-empire, and the majesty of love;
> For thirst of which they fainted. (II. iv. 42–43)

Saturn's child Jupiter succeeds him, to whom Prometheus gives wisdom 'which is strength', with one law only, 'Let man

be free'. Tyrant-like, Jupiter violates this law, and man becomes the victim of tyranny. Prometheus responds by awakening 'the legioned hopes' and sending Love to mankind, and all other good and beautiful things—thought, speech, the arts, civilization:

> . . Cities then
> Were built, and through their snow-like columns flowed
> The warm winds, and the azure aether shone,
> And the blue sea and shadowy hills were seen. (II. iv. 94–97)

Jupiter then chains Prometheus to the rock in the Caucasus where we see him.

Inevitably there is some obscurity in the metaphysics of the poem, as in every attempt to explain the apparently inexplicable. We are told that God reigns supreme over Jupiter and all else, but what is meant by the word 'God' is not altogether clear. He appears to be morally neutral, the author of terror, madness, and crime, as well as of the reason and the imagination. Jupiter is evil, but he is not the origin of evil: that is inexpressible, though one may use the words

> Fate, Time, Occasion, Chance, and Change. (II. iv. 119)

How God is related to these entities is obscure. Apparently 'eternal Love' is superior to all except God—if not to God himself.

At the beginning of Act III Jupiter is rejoicing. He has gained all that he wished, except that

> The soul of man, like unextinguished fire,
> Yet burns towards heaven with fierce reproach.
> (III. i. 4–5)

He is confident because he has now begotten 'a strange wonder, That fatal child, the terror of the earth', who will somehow 'trample out the spark' of the spirit of man. At this point Jupiter himself is overthrown. Demogorgon tells him that no tyrant like himself will ever arise again, while a Spirit of Earth describes the change that has come over everything in an astonishing passage of verse:

> All things had put their evil nature off:
> I cannot tell my joy, when o'er a lake
> Upon a drooping bough with nightshade twined,
> I saw two azure halcyons clinging downward

> And thinning one bright bunch of amber berries,
> With quick long beaks, and in the deep there lay
> Those lovely forms imaged as in a sky;
> So, with my thoughts full of these happy changes,
> We meet again, the happiest change of all.
>
> (III. iv. 77–85)

The downfall of Jupiter is the downfall of tyranny of every kind. It is true that mankind is not exempt

> From chance, and death, and mutability; (III. iv. 201)

yet in some undefined way these have now become its slaves, instead of being its masters.

*Prometheus Unbound* was originally written in three Acts. Some months later Shelley thought that a fourth Act should be added, 'a sort of hymn of rejoicing in the fulfilment of the prophecies with regard to Prometheus'. The fourth Act, which is much the most lyrical part of the whole work, contains some magnificent verse; but it is more obscure than the rest of the drama, and it is by no means evident that it forms a fitting conclusion to the first three Acts. It has certainly discouraged many readers who can understand the rest of *Prometheus Unbound*, and this is not necessarily their fault. At times one feels, in reading this work of genius, as Asia feels when she addresses Panthea in Act II:

> . . Thou speakest, but thy words
> Are as the air: I feel them not. (II. i. 108–9)

Shelley has gone beyond the normal range of the human ear.

Shelley was aware that *Prometheus Unbound* was a masterpiece; yet it is not surprising that he followed it with a drama designed to reach a wide audience.[1] The contrast between *Prometheus Unbound* and *The Cenci* (1820) is the contrast between the esoteric and the exoteric, and it seems clear that Shelley was beginning to think of many of his works as falling into one or other of these contrasting categories. Bewildered by the problem of reaching an audience, he was coming to the conclusion that he must choose on each occasion between writing to please himself—and so abjuring any possibility of being widely read—and writing in such a way as to appeal to a considerable section of the reading public—and laying aside most of his own parti-

[1] Although *The Cenci* was published in March 1820, and *Prometheus Unbound* did not appear until September, the three-Act version of *Prometheus Unbound* was written just before *The Cenci*.

cular opinions and habits of imagination to gain this object. He told Peacock that *The Cenci* was 'totally different from anything you might conjecture that I should write; of a more popular kind', and once he went so far as to describe it as 'written for the multitude'. On several occasions he explicitly contrasted it with *Prometheus Unbound*: from that work, he wrote, 'I expect and desire no great sale. "The Cenci" ought to have been popular.' It was written (or so he supposed) 'without any of the peculiar feelings and opinions which characterise my other compositions': that was the price he had to pay, if he was to make any effort at popularity. It was composed with a view to performance: he hoped that Miss O'Neill might take the part of Beatrice, while ideally he would have liked Kean to have played Count Cenci.

As so often happened with Shelley, the result was the opposite of what he intended. Perhaps no other man would have based a play which he wished to be popular on the theme of a father's incestuous passion for his daughter. Although he claimed, quite justly, that this subject is handled with great delicacy, it prevented the play from receiving a public performance for many decades after his death. All the self-discipline which had enabled him to write about real men and women, avoiding, as he said, 'dreams of what ought to be', proved to have been in vain. It is not surprising that he was profoundly discouraged. As he wrote to Peacock, nothing is 'more difficult and unwelcome' than to write 'without a confidence of finding readers; and if my play of "The Cenci" found none or few, I despair of ever producing anything that shall merit them'.

*The Cenci* might be described as an attempt to escape from the prison of subjectivity and intellectual abstraction, but Shelley himself saw it in rather different terms. He tells us that in writing it he 'sacrificed [his] own peculiar notions in a certain sort by treating of any subject, the basis of which is moral error': in another letter he mentions that his aim was 'to produce a delineation of passions which I had never participated in': while in a third reference he says that it was written 'rather to try my powers than to unburthen my full heart'. The play has no conscious didactic purpose: it aims solely at truth to character in a given set of circumstances. But as Mary Shelley wrote:

> The bent of his mind went the other way; and, even when employed on subjects whose interest depended on character and incident,

he would start off in another direction, and leave the delineations of human passion, which he could depict in so able a manner, for fantastic creations of his fancy, or the expression of those opinions and sentiments, with regard to human nature and its destiny, a desire to diffuse which was the master passion of his soul.

Both the Fourth Act of *Prometheus Unbound* and *The Witch of Atlas* (a much less important work) may be regarded as the product of Shelley's reaction from the strain of writing *The Cenci.*

It had been the opinion of Shelley himself, and that of most of his friends, that he was devoid of dramatic instinct. *The Cenci* triumphantly refutes this. Count Cenci and Beatrice are considerable creations. Part of Shelley's success must be attributed to the fact that the chain of actions on which he built his drama did in fact appeal to his own 'peculiar feelings and opinions'. We are now shown the war between Freedom and Tyranny transferred to the human stage. If Aeschylus and Sophocles were in his mind when he wrote *Prometheus Unbound,* it is of Euripides (among the Greeks) that we are now most forcibly reminded.

It is sometimes said that Shelley lacks variety of style: that whatever the demands of genre and subject-matter may be, what he writes is always just a passage of Shelley. To compare the idiom of *The Cenci* with that of *Prometheus Unbound* is to see how untrue that is. He tells us that he has 'avoided with great care . . . what is commonly called mere poetry', pointing out that 'there will scarcely be found a detached simile or a single isolated description' in the whole drama. He claims to have avoided 'an over-fastidious and learned use of words', keeping instead to 'the real language of men' (he quotes Wordsworth's phrase). His aim was clearly to forge a flexible dramatic idiom for the play. He was deliberately facing many of the charges that had been made against his verse, and trying to meet them: in this work at least it was to be evident that his imagination was his servant and not his master. And indeed the contrast between the idiom of this work and that of *Prometheus Unbound,* a 'lyrical drama', is very striking:

> The loathsome mask has fallen, the man remains
> Sceptreless, free, uncircumscribed, but man
> Equal, unclassed, tribeless, and nationless,
> Exempt from awe, worship, degree, the king
> Over himself; just, gentle, wise: but man
> Passionless?—no, yet free from guilt or pain,

Which were, for his will made or suffered them,
Nor yet exempt, though ruling them like slaves,
From chance, and death, and mutability,
The clogs of that which else might oversoar
The loftiest star of unascended heaven,
Pinnacled dim in the intense inane. (III. iv. 193–204)

We may compare this with a representative passage of *The Cenci*:

. . We
Are now no more, as once, parent and child,
But man to man; the oppressor to the oppressed;
The slanderer to the slandered; foe to foe:
He has cast Nature off, which was his shield,
And Nature casts him off, who is her shame;
And I spurn both. (III. i. 282–8)

It is the contrast between an idiom which is epic, Greek, and Miltonic in its inspiration, and an idiom which is dramatic, Elizabethan, and Shakespearian. Although one of the remarkable features of the contrast lies in the fact that both dramas are written predominantly in blank verse, it is important to notice that it is not merely the versification that differs: the whole idiom or style is different. There have not been many poets capable of such radically different idioms in the same metre at the same point in their careers. It must also be stressed that no one quotation can give a fair impression of the idiom of *The Cenci*. It is a necessary attribute of dramatic verse that it should be capable of a wider range of effects than is required in most kinds of poetry. Here *The Cenci* passes with credit, as we may see by comparing Act II, scene ii, lines 82–87—

Ask me not what I think; the unwilling brain
Feigns often what it would not; and we trust
Imagination with such phantasies
As the tongue dares not fashion into words,
Which have no words, their horror makes them dim
To the mind's eye

—with the majesty of Beatrice's addresses to the Court, or the penetrating simplicity of her last words of all:

Give yourself no unnecessary pain,
My dear Lord Cardinal. Here, Mother, tie
My girdle for me, and bind up this hair

In any simple knot; ay, that does well.
And yours I see is coming down. How often
Have we done this for one another; now
We shall not do it any more. My Lord,
We are quite ready. Well, 'tis very well.
(v. iv. 158–165)

*Prometheus Unbound* demonstrates Shelley's mastery of almost every tone in blank verse except a bare simplicity: in *The Cenci* we find that as well.

Shelley actually applied the word 'esoteric' to *Epipsychidion* (1821) in a letter, saying that it was to be published 'simply for the esoteric few': he hardly expected that so 'abstruse' a poem would find a hundred readers. This is acknowledged in the preliminary lines, which are a version of Dante:

My Song, I fear that thou wilt find but few
Who fitly shall conceive thy reasoning.

In a letter written on 22 October 1821 we find one of the most bitter of all Shelley's comments on the question of his audience:

The Epipsychidion is a mystery; as to real flesh and blood, you know that I do not deal in those articles; you might as well go to a gin-shop for a leg of mutton, as expect anything human or earthly from me. I desired Ollier not to circulate this piece except to the συνετοί, and even they, it seems, are inclined to approximate me to the circle of a servant girl and her sweetheart.

Shelley described the poem as an 'idealized history of my life and feelings', while Mary Shelley preferred to call it his 'Pisan Platonics'. Its origin was Shelley's meeting with the beautiful Emilia Viviani, who was confined in a convent near Pisa: its motto is a quotation from an essay she had written on the subject of love. Although Shelley pretends in the preface that the poem is the work of a writer who had died at Florence—

as he was preparing for a voyage to one of the wildest of the Sporades, which he had bought, and where he had fitted up the ruins of an old building, and where it was his hope to have realised a scheme of life, suited perhaps to that happier and better world of which he is now an inhabitant, but hardly practicable in this

—it was his own work, and may even have begun as an invitation to Emilia to elope with him. It is clear that he had fallen out of

love with her by the time the poem was published, and he describes it as 'a production of a portion of me already dead'. No doubt that is why the longer poem, to which the 600 lines of *Epipsychidion* as we have it were intended to serve as an introduction, was never completed: perhaps it would have been based on Dante's *Vita Nuova*, to which he refers in the preface. Newman Ivey White believed that the poem originally ended at line 387. That is possible: up to that point it could perhaps be divided into four parts: a description of the poet's search for love, reflections on the nature of love, his eventual meeting with Emilia, and a triumphant meditation on love. The remaining 200 lines are an appeal to Emilia to elope with him and a description of the earthly paradise which they are to inhabit together. It is tempting to suggest that the first four lines were an afterthought, but conjecture must be very uncertain, because the poem as we have it is in a sense incomplete, and the rejected passages which survive make it clear how much the original idea grew under Shelley's hands.

Although it lacks a profound unity, *Epipsychidion* is a remarkable poem which contains passages of extraordinary beauty. Lines 502–12, for example, must have appealed to Yeats:

> Parasite flowers illume with dewy gems
> The lampless halls, and when they fade, the sky
> Peeps through their winter-woof of tracery
> With moonlight patches, or star-atoms keen,
> Or fragments of the day's intense serene;—
> Working mosaic on their Parian floors.
> And, day and night, aloof, from the high towers
> And terraces, the Earth and Ocean seem
> To sleep in one another's arms, and dream
> Of waves, flowers, clouds, woods, rocks, and all that we
> Read in their smiles, and call reality.

As we read this poem we are often reminded of Crashaw. Such a phrase as 'faint with . . . delicious pain' sends us back to the earlier poet, as does the style of lines 39–40:

> Weeping, till sorrow becomes ecstasy:
> Then smile on it, so that it may not die.

Crashaw could have written lines 17–18, with their reference to 'thy panting, wounded breast' which

> Stains with dear blood its unmaternal nest.

Like Crashaw, Shelley was profoundly attracted by Italy, but while it is possible that he was influenced by some of the same Italian poets, the remarkable resemblances between the style of *Epipsychidion* and that of many of Crashaw's poems are probably due as much to psychological similarities between the two men as to common literary influences. We notice that, subjective and 'esoteric' as it is, *Epipsychidion* does not disintegrate, as do so many of Shelley's poems. The inspiration outlasts the six hundred lines, and the result is a poem as peculiarly characteristic of Shelley as the *Hymn to the Name and Honor of the Admirable S. Teresa* is of Crashaw.

Although *Adonais* (1821) is now the best-known of all Shelley's poems, he himself seems to have regarded it as belonging to the esoteric category of his work. Describing it as 'perhaps the least imperfect of my compositions', he added that it was 'little adapted for popularity'. He looked forward to reading it to the Gisbornes because they were among 'the very few persons who will be interested in it and understand it'. Perhaps the most revealing of all his remarks on the subject of his poetic audience occurs in a passage relating to this poem. 'I am glad you like "Adonais"', he wrote to Horace Smith, 'and, particularly, that you do not think it metaphysical, which I was afraid it was. . . . I wrote, as usual, with a total ignorance of the effect that I should produce.'

The elegy is a form practised by almost every poet, and nothing is more revealing than to examine what becomes of it in the hands of different writers. When Donne wrote *The Second Anniversary*, for example, he made it an occasion for contemplating 'The Incommodities of the Soul in this Life, and her Exaltation in the Next'. The death of a girl whom he had never met gave him the starting point for a sermon *de contemptu mundi*. *Adonais* is equally characteristic of its author. It does not tell us much about Keats as an individual, and what it does tell us is misleading. Shelley exaggerates the importance of the unfavourable reviews, portraying the reviewers as wolves, obscene ravens, and vultures who have hunted down a wounded deer. For Shelley Keats is a type and a symbol, 'the great genius whom envy and ingratitude scourged out of the world'. *Adonais* is essentially a passionate cry of protest against the oppressors of mankind.

It is one of the most carefully written of Shelley's poems. Since Keats had been treated with injustice during his lifetime,

he was particularly anxious to do him honour after his death. The poem was printed with particular care, and at Pisa, where Shelley himself could supervise the proof-reading. The result is a handsome book, printed 'With the Types of Didot'. The poem is written in Spenserian stanzas. In the preface to *The Revolt of Islam* Shelley had described this as 'a measure inexpressibly beautiful', emphasizing the 'brilliancy and magnificence of sound which a mind that has been nourished upon musical thoughts can produce by a just and harmonious arrangement of the pauses of this measure'. As one reads *Adonais* one feels (as in reading the 'Ode to the West Wind') that Shelley has found the perfect stanza-form for what he wishes to say: it is impossible to imagine the poem transposed into another metre. Yet he uses the stanza in a highly personal way. It is only necessary to turn back to *The Faerie Queene* to be struck by the extraordinary rapidity of Shelley's stanzas. That 'want of repose' which Severn pointed out in this poem, and which is one of the most striking peculiarities of almost everything Shelley ever wrote, is not characteristic of *The Faerie Queene*, or of most other poems written in the Spenserian stanza. Shelley takes a normally slow-moving metre and makes of it something new and personal. It is possible that he associated the Spenserian stanza with Keats: according to Medwin, *The Revolt of Islam* had been written in competition with *Endymion*, to see which of the young poets could write the better long poem. It is also certainly true that the Spenserian stanza was a favourite with Keats (as with Leigh Hunt), although he did not use it often in his mature poetry. There is another possible connexion. The writers of elegies on poets sometimes imitate the style of the man whom they are lamenting. Shelley did not do this, but it is conceivable that, as he wrote *Adonais*, he remembered the advice Keats had sent him in a letter: 'Be more of an artist, and "load every rift" of your subject with ore.' Perhaps this is why Shelley described the poem as 'a highly-wrought *piece of art*', underlining the last three words and adding that it was 'perhaps better, in point of composition', than anything else he had written.

It is often said that 'Lycidas' tells us more about Milton than about Edward King, and *Adonais* certainly tells us more about Shelley than about Keats. Yet this is perfectly appropriate, for he had a strong fellow-feeling for Keats. Both in the cancelled passages of the preface and in the unsent letter to the editor of

the *Quarterly Review* Shelley explicitly links himself with Keats as the object of persecution and libellous attacks. He feels both 'indignation and sympathy' with him, and is moved to a counter-attack which no merely 'personal offence' could have prompted. In the four stanzas in which he describes himself he acknowledges that he is a man

> Who in another's fate now wept his own. (300)

The true subject of the poem, we might say, is neither the individual Keats nor the individual Shelley, but rather the poetic and creative impulse itself, which used both of them as its medium. It is appropriate that towards the end of the poem the influence of the Greek elegists wanes, as mourning gives way to the celebration of

> That Beauty in which all things work and move. (479)

While indignation provided the original incentive of the poem, indignation is left behind as the climax is reached and the poet rises to the contemplation of the unchanging realm of Eternity.

In 'The Triumph of Life', with its insistence on 'the contagion of the world's slow stain', Shelley may be abandoning the idea that happiness is possible on earth. It is not surprising that a great deal has recently been written about this poem, for an unfinished work always presents a challenge. The critic is stimulated by the opportunity of proving himself more astute than his predecessors, while the inevitable uncertainty of interpretation allows him to attribute to the developing poet views consonant with his own. If Shakespeare's last play had been incomplete his critics would have enjoyed a 'liberty of interpretation' beyond their wildest dreams. This is the opportunity that is afforded by both Keats and Shelley. Accordingly we find Dr. Leavis insisting that 'the induction to the revised *Hyperion* ... justifies the high estimate of Keats's potentialities' which he would hesitate to advance on the evidence of the earlier poems and Mr. Eliot discovering in 'The Triumph of Life' 'evidence not only of better writing than in any previous long poem, but of greater wisdom'. For less sophisticated readers there is also the sphinx-like appeal of a poem left as a fragment at the poet's death: they stand questioning it, as Tennyson used to question very old men about their views on what happens after death.

The fact that Mary Shelley's text of the poem ends with the words

'Then, what is life? I cried'—

has helped to make its fortune.

As we read the five hundred lines of 'The Triumph of Life' it is at least as easy to see why Dr. Leavis finds in them what he regards as the typical 'Shelleyan confusion' as why Mr. Eliot discerns 'a precision of image and an economy . . . new to Shelley'. Many interpretations have been offered of the 'Shape all light' which must clearly be central to an understanding of the poem. Almost all that we can say for certain is that the poem is a sombre one, partly inspired by Dante, in which the poet sees in a vision a multitude of people hastening along a dusty thoroughfare, and that he is addressed by Rousseau, who delivers an admonitory speech about life which is unfinished when the poem breaks off. The verse has a hypnotic urgency, and we notice that Shelley is even more unwilling than usual to employ a full-stop: the second sentence of the poem, for example, runs on for thirty-two lines. Mr. Eliot particularly admires the Goya-like description of the gnarled root on the hillside which turns out to be Rousseau:

> And that the grass, which methought hung so wide
> And white, was but his thin discoloured hair,
> And that the holes he vainly sought to hide,
> Were or had been eyes. (185–8)

There is certainly a compelling vividness about the opening of the vision:

> Methought I sate beside a public way
>
> Thick strewn with summer dust, and a great stream
> Of people there was hurrying to and fro,
> Numerous as gnats upon the evening gleam,
>
> All hastening onward, yet none seemed to know
> Whither he went, or whence he came, or why
> He made one of the multitude . . .
>
> Some flying from the thing they feared, and some
> Seeking the object of another's fear. (43–55)

There are also individual lines of remarkable power, such as the description of men like Gregory and John,

> Who rose like shadows between man and God, (289)

or that in lines 354–5:

> And the invisible rain did ever sing
> A silver music on the mossy lawn.

Yet 'The Triumph of Life' remains an enigma, and to single it out (with Dr. Leavis) as 'among the few things one can still read and go back to in Shelley' is simply an oblique way of dismissing most of the remainder of his poems.

In containing a markedly subjective element *Adonais* and 'The Triumph of Life' are not unusual in Shelley's work. In the preface to *Frankenstein* Mary Shelley describes how the poet, confronted with the challenge to write a ghost story and being always 'more apt to embody ideas in the radiance of brilliant imagery and in the music of . . . melodious verse . . . than to invent the machinery of a story', instinctively began a tale 'founded on the experiences of his own early life'. When hc wrote a poem he was just as likely to turn to his own experiences for his material: his description of *Epipsychidion* as 'an idealised history of my life and feelings' would apply to a great many of his compositions. It may now be of interest to glance back at the major poems already discussed to emphasize the personal element which they contain; but first something must be said of *Alastor* (1816), an early work which gains from being examined in relation to the two poems which have just been considered.

It is obvious that the nameless poet (Alastor is the name of the Avenging Spirit which pursues him) is in some sense a representation of Shelley himself, and the main outline of the story is evident enough. The 'child of grace and genius' leaves his 'alienated home' and travels across the world, musing on the present and the past and coming to understand

> The thrilling secrets of the birth of time. (128)

He is a Rasselas without a sister or an Imlac, a Rasselas who has read Volney's *Ruins*. All goes well with him at first, but then 'The spirit of sweet human love' sends

> A vision to the sleep of him who spurned
> Her choicest gifts. (204–5)

From this time onwards Death and Sleep are twins in the poet's

mind. Impelled by the thought that Death will perhaps restore to him the woman he has met in sleep—she is probably Intellectual Beauty—he travels wretchedly about and finally embarks in a leaky little boat with the desire of finding death by drowning. His further travels are described, and then his death. The poem ends with a sort of elegy on this 'surpassing Spirit'. Much of the allegory of *Alastor* remains obscure, while the second paragraph of the preface has led to a good deal of debate. Yet it is not necessary to go as far as Professor Carlos Baker, who has commented that this passage 'looks very much like an ex post facto attempt by Shelley to moralize his song'. *Alastor* is a meditation on the grandeur and misery of the life of a man of genius and on the grandeur and misery of solitude. Epigraphs might readily be provided from the different parts of Zimmerman's famous treatise on Solitude, a book which Shelley is certain to have known:

> The first and most incontestable advantage of SOLITUDE is, that it accustoms the mind to think: the imagination becomes more vivid, and the memory more faithful, while the senses remain undisturbed, and no external object agitates the soul. . . . The moment that a character finds itself alone, all the energies of his soul put themselves into motion, and rise to a height incomparably greater than they could have reached under the impulse of a mind clogged and oppressed by the incumbrances of society. (*Solitude*, by J. G. Zimmerman [anon. Eng. trans., 1799–1800], i, 18, 24–25.)

> SOLITUDE, in its strict and literal acceptation, is equally unfriendly to the happiness and foreign to the nature of mankind. An inclination to exercise the faculty of speech, to interchange the sentiments of the mind, to indulge the affections of the heart, and to receive themselves, while they bestow on others, a kind assistance and support, drives men . . . from SOLITUDE to SOCIETY; and teaches them that the highest temporal felicity they are capable of enjoying, must be sought for in a suitable union of the sexes, and in a friendly intercourse with their fellow-creatures. . . . It is not to the senseless rock, or to the passing gale, that we can satisfactorily communicate our pleasures and our pains. (*Solitude*, ii (*The pernicious Influence of A total Seclusion from Society upon The Mind and the Heart*), 1–3.)

In the preface Shelley writes of two very different categories of men who 'keep aloof from sympathies with their kind': on the one hand there are 'the luminaries of the world', namely those who are 'deluded by [some] generous error, instigated by [some]

sacred thirst of doubtful knowledge, [or] duped by [some] illustrious superstition': and on the other those who are merely 'selfish, blind, and torpid'. On both Alastor, which reminds us of the 'Shape all light' and which must stand for something like Human Love or the need for Human Society, takes its revenge. The selfish are doomed to 'a slow and poisonous decay', the luminaries to 'sudden darkness and extinction' due to their being awakened to 'too exquisite a perception' of the influence of Alastor. The latter category, the 'pure and tender-hearted, perish through the intensity and passion of their search' for human sympathy, 'when the vacancy of their spirit suddenly makes itself felt'. The ambiguity of the poem springs from the fact that the poet is so obviously a projection of some of Shelley's own qualities and from the fact that he insists that the life of such a man is at once in some way mistaken and yet of the greatest value to mankind. It is as if Don Quixote had written his autobiography. The conclusion of the poem does not claim that the poet survives after death, but rather that 'birth and the grave', the very conditions of human life, are affected by the fact that such a man has lived. This is precisely what Shelley was later to assert, more eloquently, at the end of *Adonais*. *Alastor*, then, is not an optimistic poem. It is a 'solemn song'. Set in its place in Shelley's development it may be read as an expression of his determination to follow his own destiny, although he realizes that there is a sense in which he is deluded and that in any event such a course will not lead to personal happiness but to tragedy. The world that the poem paints is not a world of justice: it is a world in which the idealist is doomed. Shelley foresees his own doom, and accepts it. If *Adonais* is an elegy on Shelley himself by proxy, *Alastor* is an elegy on Shelley by anticipation.

In *The Revolt of Islam* the autobiographical element is hardly less evident. Mary Shelley tells us that the Hermit who cares for Laon during his years of madness is based on Dr. Lind, Shelley's Eton friend, and there can be no doubt that Laon is an idealized representation of Shelley himself. Cythna is based on Mary Shelley, but may also contain hints of her mother Mary Wollstonecraft and of the poet's sister Hellen. As the action progresses autobiography shades into wish-fulfilment: we hear not of what Shelley has done but of what he would like to do. The hero of *Prometheus Unbound* is a greatly superior idealization of Shelley. 'The type of the highest perfection of moral and intellectual

nature, impelled by the purest and the truest motives to the best and noblest ends', Prometheus presented himself to Shelley as the supreme possibility of idealizing his characteristic hero, with the added dignity and solidity of thousands of years' existence in mythology. This is Laon become a Titan. Less obviously, Beatrice Cenci fulfils a role in many respects similar. In *The Cenci* the conflict between Jupiter and Prometheus is transposed to the human level. While this drama is exceptional among Shelley's longer poems in that the forces of oppression triumph over those of liberty, it is possible that we are intended to feel that Beatrice triumphs in the spirit, as the poet triumphs at the end of *Adonais*. The tyranny of Count Cenci combines most of the aspects of tyranny which Shelley detested: the tyranny of the Family, that of the Church, and that of the Law. The parallels between paternal power, political power, and the supreme authority of the Pope are emphasized at several points. It is significant that, in the story as it reached Shelley, Cenci was portrayed as an atheist: he makes him a 'good Catholic' in order to bring all the forces of tyranny into alignment. It is wholly appropriate that the play is dedicated to Leigh Hunt, with a reference to 'that patient and irreconcilable enmity with domestic and political tyranny and imposture' which both men have at heart.

A general description of a long poem by Shelley may now be attempted. Its subject is the struggle between Tyranny and Freedom, or Hate and Love: it includes a vision of a heaven and a hell: and among the main characters are found an idealized representation of the poet himself, his beloved, and (very often) a tyrant. Time and again this same general pattern may be detected. It is almost as if Shelley were writing a series of plays for a small company of actors—a company in which he himself always played the male lead. Yet this formula is offered as a help to understanding, and not as a gesture of depreciation, for amongst the works which it covers there are several masterpieces. What matters is not the formula (which also covers some of the shorter poems), but the use to which it is put. The same self-projection which is embarrassing and even absurd in *The Sensitive Plant* is triumphantly justified in *Prometheus Unbound* and *Adonais*.

The greater part of this chapter has been devoted to the longer poems of Shelley not only because they include much of

his finest work but also because they provide the clearest guidance to the nature of his poetic ambitions. When we turn to the shorter poems we notice a striking difference of mood. Whereas in the longer poems Shelley is often optimistic, in the lyrics he is almost always pessimistic. These are his two moods, the two sides of his mind and art. There is no contradiction between them. He was optimistic about the future of the human race, pessimistic (almost always) about his own future as an individual. Being the most directly personal of all his poems, his short lyrics are naturally the most melancholy. Religion has been described as what man makes of his solitude: the same description might be applied to Shelley's lyrics. As Mary Shelley pointed out, 'it is the nature of that poetry . . . which overflows from the soul oftener to express sorrow and regret than joy; for it is when oppressed by the weight of life, and away from those he loves, that the poet has recourse to the solace of expression in verse'. It is not surprising to find that laments and complaints are among the commonest types of his lyrics:

> O world! O life! O time!
> On whose last steps I climb,
> Trembling at that where I had stood before;
> When will return the glory of your prime?
> No more—Oh, never more!

'Autumn: A Dirge' is thoroughly characteristic, as is the lament in 'Ginevra', which has the accent of Webster or Ford with a hint of mystery added:

> She is still, she is cold
> On the bridal couch,
> One step to the white deathbed,
> And one to the bier,
> And one to the charnel—and one, oh where?
> The dark arrow fled
> In the noon. (206–12)

Shelley's lyrics are the utterance of a solitary. If we compare them with those of George Herbert, for example, we find that not only is there the Christian God in Herbert's universe: there are also other people. In Shelley's lyric world there are no other people. In his 'Invocation to Misery'—which is almost a self-

parody, the true product of Peacock's Scythrop—he addresses Misery in these words:

All the wide world, beside us,
Show like multitudinous
Puppets passing from a scene;
What but mockery can they mean,
Where I am—where thou hast been? (61–65)

This is the solipsism of a melancholiac. It might be said of Shelley, as Belisarius says over the body of Imogen-Fidele, 'Thou diedst, a most rare boy, of melancholy'. One of the aptest psychological descriptions of Shelley may be found in Burton's *Anatomy of Melancholy*, part I, section 2, member 2, subsection 6, in the paragraph dealing with 'Voluntary Solitariness'. Being the work of such a man, his lyrics lack the dramatic element which appeals to us so much in Donne's. Shelley's lyrics are soliloquies, not dramatic monologues: they have a disembodied quality which makes it appropriate that when they are interpolated in his longer works they are often the utterance of spirits. The women addressed in his love-lyrics have seldom any reality. He does not describe them: he hardly even addresses them. There is none of the objectivity which sensuality often brings with it. He usually remains at a distance from the physical aspects of love, associating love above all with music—as in 'To Constantia, Singing', 'With a Guitar, to Jane', and in the fine lines 'The keen stars are twinkling'. Although the well-known lines 'Music, when soft voices die' proclaim the lasting power of love, it is more characteristic of Shelley to lament love's transitoriness, as he does in 'When the lamp is shattered' and 'When passion's trance is overpast':

All things revive in field or grove,
And sky and sea, but two, which move
And form all others, life and love.

We notice that several of the themes most commonly found in the love poetry of the seventeenth century are missing from Shelley's work: celebrations of fortunate love, for example, rejoicings in the physical beauty of his mistress, deliberate attempts to shock and give piquancy by flaunted cynicism. His love poems are uniformly serious, and hardly ever witty. Like Donne, Shelley was interested in philosophy; but whereas Donne in his

erotic verse amuses himself with philosophical notions, Shelley believes in his philosophy—which is less entertaining. 'You well know', as he wrote to a friend, 'I am not much of a hand at *love* songs—you see I mingle metaphysics with even this, but perhaps in this age of Philosophy that may be excused.' What he is looking for in love (one comes to feel) is escape from the world of flux, escape from the world of everyday reality: love is merely the means of escape. This may be an unfashionable attitude today, yet after all it is not peculiar to Shelley: it is one of the universal attitudes to love throughout human history, and few poets have described it more perfectly:

> The desire of the moth for the star,
>   Of the night for the morrow,
> The devotion to something afar
>   From the sphere of our sorrow. ('To —'.)

As he writes in his *Letters from Italy*, 'perhaps all discontent with the *less* (to use a Platonic sophism) supposes the sense of a just claim to the *greater*, and that we admirers of "Faust" are on the right road to Paradise'. In his love poems, as elsewhere, he often speaks like an exile from some other world, a wanderer who hopes in vain to find in love a cure for his nostalgia for the Ithaca of his dreams.

It would not be true to say that just as there are no other people in Shelley's lyrics, so there is no external nature. We have only to turn to 'Evening: Ponte al Mare, Pisa' to see his fine powers of description:

> The sun is set; the swallows are asleep;
>   The bats are flitting fast in the gray air;
> The slow soft toads out of damp corners creep,
>   And evening's breath, wandering here and there
> Over the quivering surface of the stream,
> Wakes not one ripple from its summer dream.
>
> There is no dew on the dry grass to-night,
>   Nor damp within the shadow of the trees;
> The wind is intermitting, dry, and light;
>   And in the inconstant motion of the breeze
> The dust and straws are driven up and down,
> And whirled about the pavement of the town.

Yet pure description is by no means characteristic of Shelley. Perhaps good poetry is less often descriptive than we are apt to suppose. As Mme de Staël once pointed out:

il faut, pour concevoir la vraie grandeur de la poésie lyrique . . . considérer l'univers entier comme un symbole des émotions de l'âme. . . . Le poète sait rétablir l'unité du monde physique avec le monde moral: son imagination forme un lien entre l'un et l'autre.

It is precisely true to say that Shelley considered the whole universe as a symbol, or a system of symbols, for the feelings of the human soul. To quote again from the *Letters from Italy*: 'You know I always seek in what I see the manifestation of something beyond the present and tangible object.' He looks to the external world to provide him with a language of symbolism. One reason why he is more at home with clouds and mountains and rivers than with men and women is that they lend themselves more readily to symbolism. In 'The Skylark', for example, the bird acts as a symbol and rallying-point for thoughts from his private world. The subject of the poem is at once the bird and Shelley's personal desires and ambitions. The bird is

Like a Poet hidden
  In the light of thought,
Singing hymns unbidden,
  Till the world is wrought
To sympathy with hopes and fears it heeded not.
(36–40)

It is able to do what Shelley himself would have liked to do. It knows love but not the disillusionment of love, its 'sad satiety': hence the soaring of its song. It is exempt from the human yearning for the absent and the unattainable:

We look before and after,
  And pine for what is not:
Our sincerest laughter
  With some pain is fraught;
Our sweetest songs are those that tell of saddest thought
(86–90)

By contemplating the bird the poet is carried outside the obsessive circle of his own feelings sufficiently to be able to express them with the required measure of objectivity. He remains in the world of reality—however imaginatively it is regarded—and

is therefore able to give body and actuality to his thought and so communicate with his readers. The same thing happens, triumphantly, in the 'Ode to the West Wind'. One reason for the success of this poem is that the storm which overtook Shelley in the wood beside the river Arno brought together elements which already had a deep significance in his mind. Images already potent in his imagination leaped into a new and telling pattern. In *Alastor* he had mentioned 'autumn's hollow sighs in the sere wood' as one of the natural phenomena that were dear to him, referring to himself as a lyre passively awaiting the breath of the Mother of the World,

> . . that my strain
> May modulate with murmurs of the air,
> And motions of the forests and the sea,
> And voice of living beings, and woven hymns
> Of night and day, and the deep heart of man.
> (45–49)

In the 'Ode' the West Wind becomes the symbol of autumn and takes on autumn's double attribute of being the harbinger at once of death and of resurrection, of decay and regeneration. As he wrote it he probably remembered a line from *The Revolt of Islam*:

> The blasts of Autumn drive the wingèd seeds
> Over the earth. (IX. XXI)

He invokes the wind and appeals to it to use him as its lyre, as the wind uses the forest: so it may take on his identity, and

> Drive my dead thoughts over the universe
> Like withered leaves to quicken a new birth! (63–64)

The wind becomes the perfect symbol for a poet with the ambition of being a prophet who feels that the fire of his own life is dwindling and going out:

> Scatter, as from an unextinguished hearth
> Ashes and sparks, my words among mankind!
> Be through my lips to unawakened earth
> The trumpet of a prophecy! O, Wind,
> If Winter comes, can Spring be far behind?[1]
> (66–70)

[1] 'Man is an instrument over which a series of external and internal impressions are driven, like the alternations of an ever-changing wind over an Æolian lyre, which move it by their motion to ever-changing melody.' *A Defence of Poetry*, paragraph 2.

It is astonishing to compare the skill with which *terza rima* is handled in this poem with the clumsiness of 'The Woodman and the Nightingale', written only a year or so before. The measure has not often been employed in English with complete success. Here it is. The force and urgency are precisely what the poet requires.

The 'Ode to the West Wind' is an illuminating example of Shelley's finding something in the external world which acts as a focal point for certain of his own deepest intuitions. The discovery of a centre of this kind was his greatest problem. He had a strong tendency to avoid the actual world, and particularly the world of men and women, in order to construct a world of his own, a world of black and white, a world where cause and effect should be simplified, a world of heart's desire. This was due partly to the sort of man he was and partly to his disappointment at the failure of his attempts to bring the world of reality closer to the world of his visions. Some of his least successful poems, like *The Witch of Atlas*, owe their inferiority to this flight from reality: some of his most successful owe their high merit to the fact that a bridge has been built between the private world of his imaginings and the common world of shared human experience. On one memorable occasion a true episode from history—the story of Count Cenci and his daughter Beatrice—gave him a perfect medium through which to express his perennial theme of the conflict between Freedom and Tyranny, and the result is at once one of his most imaginative works and one of those in which the imagination is most perfectly embodied in specific characters and actions. On two other occasions at least actual events which moved him deeply gave him a starting-point: his love for Emilia Viviani precipitated what is perhaps the finest expression of his reflections on the subject of love, while the death of Keats moved him to eloquent meditation on the transitoriness of life, the conflict between genius and convention, and the eternal value of the creative imagination. It does not follow that these three poems are his greatest achievement: a higher claim should almost certainly be made for the first three acts of *Prometheus Unbound*. But it is no chance that these are among the longer poems of Shelley's which now make the widest appeal. Prophetic, didactic, and characteristic as they are, they reassure us by retaining contact with the reality which we experience from day to day.

The work of Shelley presents us with a paradox. The subject-matter of great poetry is human life and the human passions. Shelley, possessed in every other respect of the endowment of a very great poet, found it hard to bring himself to write directly about human life. No one saw the truth more clearly than Mary Shelley:

> The surpassing excellence of *The Cenci* had made me greatly desire that Shelley should increase his popularity by adopting subjects that would more suit the popular taste than a poem conceived in the abstract and dreamy spirit of the *Witch of Atlas*. It was not only that I wished him to acquire popularity . . . but I believed that he would obtain a greater mastery over his own powers, and greater happiness in his mind, if public applause crowned his endeavours. . . . Even now I believe that I was in the right. Shelley did not expect sympathy and approbation from the public; but the want of it took away a portion of the ardour that ought to have sustained him while writing. . . . My persuasions were vain, the mind could not be bent from its natural inclination. Shelley shrunk instinctively from portraying human passion, with its mixture of good and evil, of disappointment and disquiet. . . . He loved to shelter himself rather in the airiest flights of fancy, forgetting love and hate, and regret and lost hope, in such imaginations as borrowed their hues from sunrise or sunset . . . from the aspect of the far ocean or the shadows of the woods. (Note on *The Witch of Atlas*.)

Next to Mary Shelley the critic who understood him best was Peacock, and his opinion is the complement of hers:

> What was, in my opinion, deficient in his poetry, was . . . the want of reality in the characters with which he peopled his splendid scenes, and to which he addressed or imparted the utterance of his impassioned feelings. He was advancing, I think, to the attainment of this reality. It would have given to his poetry the only element of truth which it wanted; though at the same time, the more clear development of what men were would have lowered his estimate of what they might be, and dimmed his enthusiastic prospect of the future destiny of the world. I can conceive him, if he had lived to the present time, passing his days like Volney, looking on the world from his windows without taking part in its turmoils; and perhaps . . . desiring that nothing should be inscribed on his tomb, but his name, the dates of his birth and death, and the single word
>
> 'DÉSILLUSIONNÉ'.

# IV

# KEATS

UNLIKE Shelley, Keats was in no doubt what he wanted to do with his life.[1] As one of his fellow students tells us, 'Poetry was . . . the zenith of all his aspirations: the only thing worthy the attention of superior minds: so he thought: all other pursuits were mean and tame. . . . The greatest men in the world were the poets and to rank among them was the chief object of his ambition.' The difference between the two poets is brought out clearly by a comparison between their first volumes. It is impossible to imagine Keats's *Poems* of 1817 accompanied by the notes on religion, morals, and politics which we find in *Queen Mab*. No contemporary reader of the volume could have been in any doubt where Keats's political sympathies lay; but it is no less clear that his primary concern is not with politics or philosophy or natural science, but with poetry. The spirit in which the volume had been written is summed up in one of his letters—'I find that I cannot exist without poetry—without eternal poetry—half the day will not do—the whole of it.' Whereas the authors referred to in the notes to *Queen Mab* include Spinoza, Godwin, d'Holbach, Sir William Drummond, Bacon, Laplace, Hume, Godwin and Condorcet, the writers

[1] John Keats (1795–1821) was the eldest son of the manager of a livery-stable in London. His parents would have liked to send him to Harrow, but this was beyond their means, so he went to Enfield Academy, where he became friendly with Charles Cowden Clarke, the son of his schoolmaster. After leaving school he was apprenticed to a surgeon and later studied at Guy's Hospital. In 1816 he met Leigh Hunt, who had printed his sonnet 'O Solitude, if I must with thee dwell' in the *Examiner* for 5 May. Through Hunt Keats later met Shelley, John Hamilton Reynolds, and a number of painters and people interested in the arts. His *Poems* attracted little attention. He wrote part of *Endymion* on a visit to the Isle of Wight. Meanwhile he lived in Hampstead and resolved to devote himself to literature. In 1818 he said good-bye to his brother George (who emigrated to America), went on a walking tour to the Lakes and Scotland with Charles Brown, and returned to London to nurse his brother Tom, who was dying of tuberculosis. *Endymion* was savagely reviewed, particularly in *Blackwood's*, where Keats was associated with Hunt as one of the 'Cockney School'. In the late autumn of 1818 he had a transitory affair with Isabella Jones. About this time he also met Fanny Brawne, with whom he fell deeply in love. Most of his greatest poetry was written between September 1818 and September 1819. A year later he sailed for Italy, accompanied by Severn. He died in Rome in February 1821.

named in the *Poems* of 1817 (and it is surprising how many are named) are all poets: Chaucer, Spenser, Shakespeare, Chapman, Boileau, Chatterton, William Browne, Burns, Petrarch, Leigh Hunt. As one reads the letters of the two men the same pattern reveals itself: it is almost always poetry that Keats is reading and discussing, while Shelley is at least as likely to be reading philosophy or political theory.

When Keats wrote most of the poems in his first collection he was a student of medicine, yet no line or image reveals the fact. Indeed one reason for the remarkably literary tone of the volume is that for Keats at this time poetry was above all a means of escape from the humdrum realities that surrounded him. That is why there are so many references to picturesque refuges and hiding-places. He refers to 'some pleasant lair of wavy grass', wishing to be ''mongst boughs pavillion'd': he tells us that he will look for 'some flowery spot, sequester'd, wild, romantic': he describes 'a little space, with boughs all woven round', and exclaims that for him 'a bowery nook will be elysium'. In 'I stood tip-toe' we see him collecting the properties of what he calls, in an unfortunate phrase, a 'tasteful nook': flowers, laburnum, and long grass. It is appropriate that the epigraph of the poem is taken from Leigh Hunt: 'Places of nestling green for Poets made'.

Half of the poems in the volume have the air of having been written after a visit to Hunt, the man 'who keeps the keys Of Pleasure's temple'. What this means is brought out by a passage in *Lord Byron and Some of his Contemporaries*: 'No imaginative pleasure was left unnoticed by us, or unenjoyed; from the recollection of the bards and patriots of old, to the luxury of a summer rain at our window, or the clicking of the coal in winter-time.' (i. 410.) In the poems themselves we find frequent lists of delights of this kind: what Keats calls 'trains of peaceful images', posies of luxuries, or 'my world of blisses'. These are precisely the 'imaginative pleasures' which he had enjoyed in the company of Hunt, and while some of the lists consist wholly of natural objects—flowers, trees, the wind—in one or two of the others we find things juxtaposed from different aspects of experience. 'Sleep and Poetry', for example, the most ambitious poem in the volume, opens with a series of rhetorical questions in which we find 'Cordelia's countenance' and 'a high romance' listed beside a musk-rose and 'the leafiness of dales'. These lists

have a double interest: they reveal a medical student constructing for himself a refuge from the world of the hospital corridor and the dissecting-room; and they also show us a young poet with a flair for description and evocation casting about for a method of building up a poem.

It is not difficult to see why Keats at this time so often refers to Poetry as a place, a territory, as he does most memorably in the one completely successful poem in the volume, the sonnet 'On First Looking into Chapman's Homer':

> Much have I travell'd in the realms of gold.

It had been reading Spenser that had made him realize that he was born to be a poet: as Charles Brown put it, 'in Spenser's fairy land he was enchanted, breathed in a new world, and became another being'. Poetry was the country he escaped to. 'In a room', as we are told, he was always at the window, 'peering into space'. It is not surprising that he was fond of casements in his poetry, using this image most memorably in the *Ode to a Nightingale*, where he says that throughout the ages the song of this bird has

> Charm'd magic casements, opening on the foam
> Of perilous seas, in faery lands forlorn.

The most ambitious of his attempts to escape from mundane reality into a fairy-land of poetry and romance was *Endymion* (1818). 'I have heard Hunt say and may be asked—why endeavour after a long Poem?', he wrote in a letter. 'To which I should answer—Do not the Lovers of Poetry like to have a little Region to wander in where they may pick and choose, and in which the images are so numerous that many are forgotten and found new in a second Reading: which may be food for a Week's stroll in the Summer.' It is easier to see the point of this comparison of *Endymion* to a sort of wild pleasure-garden in which delightful vistas meet the eye wherever one turns than to decide how seriously the poem is to be taken. The critics of Keats have given very different answers to this question, just as they have differed in their evaluation of the poem. Some have taken it as a serious philosophic work which must be expounded in detail if we are to understand Keats's thought: others have tended to dismiss it impatiently as the work of a poetic tyro.

Sidney Colvin and C. L. Finney both devote a great deal of space to *Endymion*, while Mr. E. C. Pettet, who does not deal with *Hyperion* at any length, gives nearly a quarter of his book to the earlier poem. At the other extreme, Garrod ignored *Endymion* altogether, remarking that 'if it were possible to say something about it without saying too much, it would have been done already'. One can readily understand these divergent points of view. Passages here and there seem to call out for symbolic interpretation; yet as soon as one undertakes such a task, irrelevancies and inconsistencies spring up on every side. It is as well to remember the poet's own avowal, in his draft for a preface: 'Before I began I had no inward feel of being able to finish; and as I proceeded my steps were all uncertain.' Yet *Endymion* is no mere Bottom's Dream, and to refuse to see more in it than the erotic fancies of a young man is to carry scepticism too far. We cannot brush aside all symbolic interpretation. The action describes the falling in love of Endymion with Cynthia, the moon goddess, and his pursuit of her. We know from 'I stood tip-toe' how deeply this myth appealed to Keats, and it is clear that he interpreted it as the pursuit of Beauty by the enamoured Soul. The resemblances between *Endymion* and *Alastor* are obvious, and Keats was probably influenced in some degree by Shelley. *Endymion* is 'A Poetic Romance', and like many Romances it is shot through with symbolic suggestions.

When Hunt tried to dissuade Keats from writing a long poem it was probably because he thought him too inexperienced to succeed rather than because he doubted the value of the long poem. If so, Hunt was both right and wrong. The publication of *Endymion* had a disastrous effect on the reputation of Keats: whereas his first volume was well received by his friends, and almost ignored by the reviewers, his second called forth some of the most bitter attacks in the history of periodical criticism. Yet Keats knew within himself that he must explore his own mind and his own poetic potentialities, and the way to do this was by writing a longer poem than any he had so far attempted. If he had not written *Endymion* his poetic progress would almost certainly have been less astonishingly swift. 'The whole thing must I think have appeared to you, who are a consequitive Man, as a thing almost of mere words', as he wrote to his publisher; 'but I assure you that when I wrote it, it was a regular stepping of the Imagination towards a Truth. My having

written that Argument will perhaps be of the greatest Service to me of any thing I ever did—It set before me at once the gradations of Happiness even like a kind of Pleasure Thermometer.' This might be applied to the whole poem, though Keats is writing about lines 777–81 of Book I:

> Wherein lies Happiness? In that which becks
> Our ready Minds to fellowship divine;
> A fellowship with essence, till we shine
> Full alchymized and free of space. Behold
> The clear Religion of heaven!

As we read these lines we are present at the birth of his characteristic philosophy of beauty. Up to now he has been attracted by beautiful things and moving thoughts without any conscious aim except that of delighting in their luxury. Now he is asking himself why he has become a collector of luxuries and trying to account for his strong sense that there is a profounder value in 'A thing of beauty' than might at first appear. What he is saying is that the deepest happiness for mankind lies in the attempt to get in touch with the highest reality—'essences'—and that this may be achieved through the apprehension of the beautiful. It was as he wrote *Endymion* that this belief began to formulate itself in his mind. The letters he wrote at the same time provide a commentary on it. Whatever the philosophical validity of this elusive belief, it is what supported Keats as he approached the task of writing his greatest poetry.

Almost all of this is contained in the one extraordinary volume, *Lamia, Isabella, The Eve of St. Agnes, and Other Poems*, which appeared in 1820. Each of the three tales tells a story of love. Each is drawn from a different source, set in a different period and place, and shows its lovers meeting with a different destiny. The hero of *Lamia* discovers that he has been deceived in the very nature of his love, and dies of sorrow: the hero of *Isabella* is murdered by the brothers of the lady he loves, but is loyally mourned by her until she dies of grief: while the hero of *The Eve of St. Agnes* escapes with his lady from the castle in which she has been living in the midst of his enemies. It is easy to think of this last poem as representing Keats's hopes in love, of *Isabella* as a sort of second best, and of *Lamia* as the portrayal of his deepest fears; but while this sort of autobiographical interpretation is attractive, it need not be taken very seriously. These

are the hopes and fears of any one who is in love, and they form the subject of most of the love-stories ever written.

By common consent, there is hardly a transition in the history of our literature more dramatic than that from *Endymion* to the volume of 1820; yet the transition from *Endymion* to the first two tales is less dramatic than that to the other poems. Although Keats himself, or his publisher, thought well enough of the Tales to put them at the beginning of the collection, the first two of them are not on a par with the remaining poems. We are told by Brown that *Lamia*, based on *The Anatomy of Melancholy* (Keats's favourite prose reading), was written 'after much studying of Dryden's versification'. This is interesting because it shows that Keats had come to agree with his critics that in rebelling against the Augustan modes of using the pentameter couplet he had gone too far in the direction of metrical licence and erratic syntax. In the opening lines we are fleetingly reminded of the Dryden of the Tales; while in one of the most impressive passages—the description of the banqueting room—Pope's *Homer* comes to mind; yet in most of the poem the verse is handled in a way much closer to Keats's own early manner than to Dryden's 'long majestic march, and energy divine'. The handling of the metre is not wholly satisfactory, while too many of the old amorous banalities remain—Keats is still capable of describing a kiss as 'the ruddy strife of hearts and lips' and assuring us that

> There is not such a treat among them all . . .
> As a real woman. (330–2)

The moral of the poem is as uncertain as the style: it is significant that Keats seems to have been uncertain how to bring it to an end. *Isabella or, The Pot of Basil* is based on a story in *The Decameron*, as are several of Dryden's Tales. Whereas Dryden chose stories that lent themselves to straightforward accounts of passion, however, Keats took one with potentialities for pathos, a story recommended to the attention of modern poets in one of Hazlitt's lectures. The heading of the tale in the edition which Keats probably used may also have attracted his attention:

> Wherein is plainly proved, that love cannot be rooted uppe, by any humane power or Providence; especially in such a soule, where it hath bene really apprehended.

Boccaccio tells the story for what it is worth as a tale. Keats

makes it four times as long, using *ottava rima* and embroidering the narrative with an elaborate rhetoric of pathos. A single line—

> The quiet glooms of such a piteous theme (152)

—sums up the atmosphere of the poem. The story unfolds in a leisurely manner, one sombre picture slowly succeeding another. Repetition is frequently used to emphasize the effect of pathos, as in stanza lv. Although good critics have thought highly of *Isabella*—Lamb devoted a large part of his review to it, and did not mention *Hyperion* at all—it now appears distasteful in theme and in parts poorly written. It is interesting to find that Keats himself was dissatisfied with it. 'There is too much inexperience of life, and simplicity of knowledge in it', he wrote in a letter. '. . . It is possible to write fine things which cannot be laugh'd at in any way. Isabella is what I should call were I a reviewer "A weak-sided Poem" with an amusing sober-sadness about it.'

The superiority of *The Eve of St. Agnes* to the other Tales is partly due to the fact that in it Keats has found the perfect metre for his theme. The story is based on a popular superstition and the atmosphere is vaguely medieval. It is not surprising, therefore, that Spenser was much in Keats's mind as he wrote it; for Spenser, like Chatterton, was always associated in his mind with any medieval subject. What had first appealed to Keats about Spenser, we may guess, was above all the music and the processional quality of his stanza, with the opportunities it gives for rich effects of vowel music and sensuous luxury. It is surprising that this is the only serious poem of his maturity in which he uses it. Whereas *ottava rima* does not seem the perfect metre for *Isabella*—its potentialities for epigram in the final couplet, which inspired Byron in *Don Juan*, are irrelevant to the purposes of Keats—it is impossible to imagine *The Eve of St. Agnes* in any other metre than the Spenserian stanza.

Another source of inspiration was Gothic architecture. The poem was written at Chichester, and it reminds us even more forcibly of Keats's love of Winchester. In the 'Specimen of an Induction' in his first volume he had asked:

> . . Then how shall I
> Revive the dying tones of minstrelsy,
> Which linger yet about lone Gothic arches?

Critics have often noticed the importance of the architectural background of the poem, and of the carving in the church described near the beginning. The description of 'the sculptur'd dead, on each side', who 'seem to freeze,

> Emprison'd in black, purgatorial rails',

contrasts brilliantly with the tale of youthful passion which is about to be told. We remember it when we come to the moment before the consummation of the lovers' desires:

> Upon his knees he sank, pale as smooth-sculptured stone.

No less brilliant is the description of 'The carved angels, ever eager-eyed' under the cornice,

> With hair blown back, and wings put cross-wise on their breasts.

We first see Porphyro 'Beside the portal doors, Buttress'd from moonlight', and when he enters he hides 'Behind a broad hall-pillar', much as Romeo must do. He follows Angela 'through a lowly arched way' into 'a little moonlight room,

> Pale, lattic'd, chill, and silent as a tomb'.

He is led to Madeline's room 'through many a dusky gallery'. No reader is likely to forget the casement[1] in the room in which she sleeps:

> A casement high and triple-arch'd there was,
> All garlanded with carven imag'ries
> Of fruits, and flowers, and bunches of knot-grass,
> And diamonded with panes of quaint device
> . . . . . . .
> Full on this casement shone the wintry moon,
> And threw warm gules on Madeline's fair breast,
> As down she knelt for heaven's grace and boon;
> Rose-bloom fell on her hands, together prest,
> And on her silver cross soft amethyst,
> And on her hair a glory, like a saint.

Just before the end of the tale one or two further touches of description of the castle give added vividness:

> The arras, rich with horseman, hawk, and hound,
> Flutter'd in the besieging wind's uproar;
> And the long carpets rose along the gusty floor.

[1] 'Casement' is a Gothic, Mrs. Radcliffe word: the heroine in *Northanger Abbey* is delighted to find that some of the windows are 'casements', though they are not as dark and gloomy as she could have wished.

We also hear of the wide stairs, the iron porch, and the heavy door through which the lovers escape into the night.

Colour-imagery, which is so brilliantly exemplified in this description of the casement, is less prominent than one might expect. At the beginning of the poem everything is colourless, as it is numb and cold. Colour really enters the poem with the wild thought that suddenly comes to Porphyro, 'like a full-blown rose, Flushing his brow' and making 'purple riot' in his heart. Colour, as we come to see, represents passion, and the arrival of the richest colours is heralded by the 'silver taper's light' which Madeline is carrying when she arrives at her room. Colour is used brilliantly in the description of Madeline and of the strange, rich meal which Porphyro heaps up beside her bed. But it is above all on sound that Keats depends to gain his effects. At the beginning only the muttering of the beadsman's prayer disturbs the unmoving silence. Then, with a powerful effect of contrast, we hear 'Music's golden tongue' through a door and have the incomparable image, which Browning must have envied, of music 'yearning like a God in pain'. Amidst the sounds of revelry and the whispers of the revellers (the poem is full of whispering, as it is of doors opening and closing)—Madeline is at first silent and preoccupied: we hear her sigh, and we hear her breathing. The feeble laugh of Angela, as she talks with Porphyro, is somehow macabre and shocking. When we return to Madeline silence takes over again in her room, 'silken, hush'd, and chaste'. Silence is part of the magic, and we hear nothing but the sound of her breathing and the rustling of her clothes as she prepares for sleep. For a moment a door opens and the sound of the music penetrates to the 'retired quiet' of her chamber. Silence returns, and the next thing we hear is Porphyro's whisper to Madeline, and the sudden tumult as he takes her lute and begins to play. She weeps, and begins to 'moan forth witless words with many a sigh'. As the lovers embrace 'the frost-wind blows

> Like Love's alarum pattering the sharp sleet
> Against the window-panes; St. Agnes' moon hath set'.

The lovers speak to one another, but as they make their escape silence descends once more:

> They glide, like phantoms, into the wide hall;
> Like phantoms, to the iron porch, they glide.

The bolts slide soundlessly, the chains 'lie silent on the footworn stones', and the last sound that we hear is that of the door as it groans on its hinges. Few poems are built so surely on a contrasting pattern of cold and warmth, colour and colourlessness, tumultuous sound and silence. This patterning echoes the contrast between the hostile world outside and the warmth and beauty within. The background of feud, which is reminiscent of *Romeo and Juliet*, also helps to give the tale its perfect frame and definition.

No poet is ever likely to write a finer description of young love in an unreal world of heart's desire, but some recent critics have accorded *The Eve of St. Agnes* praise which could only be appropriate to a poem of a much profounder nature. Professor Earl Wasserman, for example, considers the action symbolical: for him Porphyro's journey to Madeline's chamber represents the progress of the human soul as described in Keats's letter on life as a 'Mansion of Many Apartments'. It is impossible to believe that Keats had any such intention. Ten months after writing the poem, indeed, he wrote to John Taylor:

> The little dramatic skill I may as yet have however badly it might show in a Drama would I think be sufficient for a Poem—I wish to diffuse the colouring of St. Agnes eve throughout a Poem in which Character and Sentiment would be the figures to such drapery—Two or three such Poems . . . would be a famous gradus ad Parnassum altissimum—I mean they would nerve me up to the writing of a few fine Plays—my greatest ambition.

It is perfectly true that 'Character and Sentiment' are absent from *The Eve of St. Agnes*: one has only to remember *Troilus and Criseyde* to acknowledge the fact. It is surely sufficient praise for Keats's poem that it comes near perfection in its own kind.

If we remember *Endymion* as we approach the Odes in this volume of 1820 we shall be in a good position to understand them. In that poem Keats had begun to try to explain the unique value to mankind of the beautiful things which he had so often merely listed in his earliest poems. From the first line onwards Beauty is the theme:

> A thing of beauty is a joy for ever.

As he says a few lines later:

> Some shape of beauty moves away the pall
> From our dark spirits.

As examples, he gives a characteristically heterogeneous list of beautiful objects of contemplation: the sun and moon, trees, daffodils, 'the grandeur of the dooms We have imagined for the mighty dead' and 'all lovely tales'. He believes that 'these essences'

> Haunt us till they become a cheering light
> Unto our souls . . .
> They alway must be with us, or we die.

It is easy to see that the subjects of the first three Odes (in the order in which they appear in 1820, which is not that of composition) may be considered as examples of such 'essences': the song of a nightingale, a Grecian urn, and the goddess Psyche. A passage will be quoted shortly in which autumn is explicitly mentioned by Keats as a source of delight of this kind; while the subject of the remaining Ode, melancholy, may be regarded in much the same light. If we look back to the best-known of the hymns in *Endymion* which are the predecessors of the great Odes, the hymn to Pan, we find that the god is addressed in these words:

> Be still the unimaginable lodge
> For solitary thinkings; such as dodge
> Conception to the very bourne of heaven . . .
> Be still a symbol of immensity. (I. 293–9)

It is made clear that the poet has a special duty to such 'symbols', and the task laid on the shoulders of the enigmatic old man Glaucus in Book III represents this duty. He expounds

> The meanings of all motions, shapes, and sounds;
> . . Explores all forms and substances
> Straight homeward to their symbol-essences. (III. 698–700)

Only by doing so can he win immortality. This, we might say, is what Keats himself does with the nightingale's song and the subjects of the other Odes: he probes their meaning, their significance to man, and tries to discover what he here terms 'their symbol-essences'.

It is possible that the state immediately preceding the composition of the Odes was one of relaxation rather than of conscious effort. In one of his letters he describes the origin of the *Ode on Indolence*:

> This morning I am in a sort of temper indolent and supremely careless: I long after a stanza or two of Thompson's Castle of

indolence—My passions are all asleep. . . . In this state of effeminacy the fibres of the brain are relaxed in common with the rest of the body, and to such a happy degree that pleasure has no show of enticement and pain no unbearable frown. Neither Poetry, nor Ambition, nor Love have any alertness of countenance as they pass by me: they seem rather like three figures on a greek vase—a Man and two women—whom no one but myself could distinguish in their disguisement. This is the only happiness. . . .

(To George and Georgiana Keats, 19 March 1819.)

The *Ode on Indolence* seems to have been the last of the Odes to be written, except *To Autumn*, and it is so inferior to the rest that it might be the work of an imitator: Keats himself did not publish it, and probably never would have published it. Yet it may well be that the process of its gestation was similar to that of the great Odes. 'Contemplative indolence'—a phrase Keats heard Hazlitt use in relation to the letters of Gray—would probably fit the mood in which the Odes were written. They are reveries in which the contemplation of 'a thing of beauty' leads the poet into a train of reflections.

Critics who insist on the profundity of the thought in the Odes of Keats are doing his memory a doubtful service. It is true that he wished to make progress in philosophy: one reason for this was that he believed that an epic poet must be a philosopher. But alongside the passages in his letters where he talks of his philosophical ambitions we find others in which he expresses his fear that he is unsuited to such studies. He often realized that the truth which it was in his power to attain was not systematic philosophical truth but truth of 'sensation', truth of impression or feeling. The form of the Ode suited him both because it required less sustained physical effort than a long poem, and because it did not demand a full development of thought. In the famous passage about 'Negative Capability' he complains that Coleridge 'would let go by a fine isolated verisimilitude caught from the Penetralium of mystery, from being incapable of remaining content with half knowledge'. He continues: 'This pursued through Volumes would perhaps take us no further than this, that with a great poet the sense of Beauty overcomes every other consideration, or rather obliterates all consideration.' In some of the Odes the thought is very slight, while in others it is perplexed in a way that suggests confusion in the poet's own mind rather than philosophical profundity. The

value of these great poems lies in the fact that each of them gives us a 'fine verisimilitude', a splinter of the truth that has presented itself to Keats, though he may be quite unable to fit it into any coherent philosophical system.

The Odes are the sort of poetry that Hamlet might have written. One of the first two Odes that Keats ever wrote was addressed to Hope, and prays for relief from 'that fiend Despondence'. In 'Sleep and Poetry' and *Endymion* 'despondence' remains an enemy to be kept at bay. We know enough about the life of Keats to realize that there is no element of affectation in this. He once acknowledged that he had 'a horrid Morbidity of Temperament' which he considered 'the greatest Enemy and stumbling block I have to fear', while his brother George tells us that he was subject to 'many a bitter fit of hypochondriasm'. Although he says in one of his letters that he will not 'spoil [his] love of gloom by writing an Ode to darkness' it was inevitable that one of his Odes should be addressed to Melancholy, and although the result is not the finest of the Odes it is in a way the centre of the pattern. Except *To Autumn* every one of the Odes could be annotated from the *Anatomy of Melancholy*. Above all, the poet is obsessed by the transitoriness of love and beauty:

> She dwells with Beauty—Beauty that must die;
> And Joy, whose hand is ever at his lips
> Bidding adieu.

As Keats had said in the *Ode to a Nightingale*, this world is a place

> Where Beauty cannot keep her lustrous eyes,
> Or new Love pine at them beyond to-morrow.

It is because he is oppressed by this reflection that the poet searches for something beyond the transitory, some 'shape of beauty'. The attraction of the song of the nightingale and of the Grecian urn is that they are above the flux. The song has been heard 'In ancient days by emperor and clown': it is

> Perhaps the self-same song that found a path
> Through the sad heart of Ruth, when, sick for home,
> She stood in tears amid the alien corn;
> The same that oft-times hath
> Charm'd magic casements, opening on the foam
> Of perilous seas, in faery lands forlorn.

In the same way the love portrayed on the urn is independent of time on account of the very nature of art:

> She cannot fade, though thou hast not thy bliss,
> For ever wilt thou love, and she be fair!

Keats's obsession with time reaches its culmination in this poem, which has at its centre a series of tolling repetitions: 'Nor ever . . . Never, never . . . For ever . . . Nor ever . . . For ever . . . For ever . . . For ever . . . For ever . . . For ever . . .'

This obsession with Time is characteristic of the three central Odes, the Nightingale, the Grecian Urn, and Melancholy. It is not to be found in the last and most triumphant of them all, *To Autumn*. No melancholy throws its shadow over this poem of fruition and acceptance. Autumn had always been a season that had meant a great deal to Keats, as may be seen by tracing the earlier allusions in his poems; and it was always the achievement of autumn that appealed to him, rather than the fact that it heralds winter and death. Whereas Shelley, in the 'Ode to the West Wind', regards autumn as the forerunner of death, and rises to hope only by contemplating the resurgence of spring that lies beyond, Keats remains wholly in the present. This suits the characters of the two poems: Shelley's is one of the swiftest-moving in our literature, and is aptly cast in *terza rima*: Keats's poem is serenely poised and static, and is no less fittingly written in the elaborate galleon-like stanza-form which he had evolved for his Odes.

It is interesting to notice that autumn is given in a list of delights in one of Keats's early sonnets. He is using a string of images to illustrate the delightful way in which winter begins to give way to spring. Characteristically, he draws them from very different aspects of experience:

> Sweet Sappho's cheek—a sleeping infant's breath,—
> The gradual sand that through an hour-glass runs,—
> A woodland rivulet,—a Poet's death.

But here is the beginning of the list:

> The calmest thoughts come round us—as of leaves,
> Budding,—fruit ripening in stillness,—autumn suns
> Smiling at eve upon the quiet sheaves.

It is the most natural of transitions from this early sonnet to the letter in which Keats describes the origin of *To Autumn*:

> How beautiful the season is now—How fine the air. A temperate sharpness about it. Really, without joking, chaste weather—Dian skies—I never lik'd stubble fields so much as now—Aye better than the chilly green of the spring. Somehow a stubble plain looks warm—in the same way that some pictures look warm.

One of the secrets of the remarkable success of this poem is perhaps that the poet himself makes no appearance. One would have expected him to have made some reference to the parallel between the season and the corresponding period in a man's life. He does nothing of the kind. Nor does he explicitly contrast the recurrence and therefore, in a sense, the immortality of the season and its sights and occupations with the transitoriness of human life, as he does with the song of the nightingale. Like a painter he loses himself in the contemplation of what he is describing. Borrowing a word from Hopkins, we might say that he 'inscapes' the season. When he was writing the earliest of the Odes, the *Ode to Psyche*, he said that he hoped it would be in 'a more peaceable and healthy spirit' than anything else that he had composed. It is a paradox of genius that the Ode *To Autumn*, almost the last poem that he was ever to write, is written in precisely this spirit.

As several critics have pointed out, more light is thrown on the form of these remarkable poems by considering their relation to the sonnet than by exploring the work of earlier writers of the ode. 'I have been endeavouring to discover a better sonnet stanza than we have', Keats wrote immediately after transcribing the *Ode to Psyche*. 'The legitimate [Petrarchan] does not suit the language over-well from the pouncing rhymes—the other kind [the Shakespearian] appears too elegiac—and the couplet at the end of it has seldom a pleasing effect.' There follows a sonnet on the sonnet in which the poet emphasizes that it is necessary to 'weigh the stress

> Of every chord, and see what may be gain'd
> By ear industrious, and attention meet'.

This sonnet has the experimental rhyme-scheme *abc abd cabcdede*. Of the five other sonnets in the same letter, three are Shakespearian, one combines a Shakespearian octave with a sestet

rhyming *bcefef*, while the other rhymes *abab cdcd efeggf*. It is clear that the Shakespearian sonnet was one of the chief formative influences on the stanzaic form of the Odes. In an early poem—'Woman! when I behold thee flippant, vain'—we find Keats using one type of Petrarchan sonnet as a stanza; while the single stanza of the unfinished *Ode to May*, which was written a year before the *Ode to Psyche* and which is the true forerunner of the great Odes in its beauty of rhythm, has fourteen lines (of which four are shortened) rhyming *ababccdedefgfg*: that is to say it consists of the three quatrains of a Shakespearian sonnet, with a couplet following the first quatrain instead of the last. As Garrod pointed out, in its first form the first stanza of the *Ode to Psyche* consists of a Shakespearian octave followed by one of the permissible types of Petrarchan sestet, except that the twelfth line is a trimeter. In the final form of the poem each stanza begins with a Shakespearian octave, although there are trimeters in stanza ii, while stanza iii rhymes *cddc* instead of *cdcd* in lines 5–8.

After experimenting in this way Keats based what have been termed his three central Odes, as well as the inferior *Ode on Indolence*, on a stanza of ten lines rhyming *ababcdecde*. (The *Ode to a Nightingale* has a trimeter in the eighth line, three of the five stanzas of the *Ode on a Grecian Urn* have the rhyme-scheme slightly rearranged in the last six lines, while *To Autumn* has an eleventh line and a slightly varied rhyme-scheme). Essentially, the stanza consists of half of a Shakespearian octave followed by one of the commonest forms of the Petrarchan sestet. Keats disliked the couplets which may be found in both types of sonnet, and in the central Odes he manages to avoid couplets altogether, though there are four in the *Ode to Psyche* and one in each stanza of *To Autumn* as the concomitant of the eleventh line. Other influences may be found behind the stanza of the Odes: possibly that of Chatterton, whose 'Battle of Hastings' is in stanzas of ten lines: certainly that of Spenser, the rhythm of whose lines was always in Keats's mind (it is surprising that there is not a single Alexandrine in the Odes): and probably also that of some of the imitators of Spenser, notably Thomson in *The Castle of Indolence*. But all these influences are subordinate to that of the sonnet. In particular, only a man who knew Shakespeare's sonnets intimately could have evolved this stanza and handled its complicated rhymes

and rhythms with so certain a touch, succeeding so memorably in his search for a measure 'more interwoven and complete' than the conventional sonnet 'To fit the naked foot of poesy'.[1] This makes it interesting to notice the juxtaposition of the sonnet and the ode in the epistle to Charles Cowden Clarke:

> Who read for me the sonnet swelling loudly
> Up to its climax and then dying proudly?
> Who found for me the grandeur of the ode,
> Growing, like Atlas, stronger from its load? (60–63)

This is no doubt fortuitous, yet it is suggestive. When Keats turned to the writing of Odes he did not forget the secret of making a poem die proudly—what better description could there be of the end of the *Ode on Melancholy*?—

> His soul shall taste the sadness of her might,
> And be among her cloudy trophies hung.

In the description of the ode, the words 'grandeur' and 'load' are significant, and remind us of the advice Keats gave Shelley, ' "load every rift" of your subject with ore'. He loved richness in poetry, and the key words in the Odes—flowers, sweet, drowsy—are words that contribute to the effect of almost oppressive luxury. There are no poems in the language richer in sensuous imagery (even in imagery of taste, which is not common in poetry). This is what Keats himself once called 'distilled poesy'. Many of the remarks about poetry in the letters

[1] To demonstrate the close relationship between the Odes of Keats and the sonnet, here is the opening stanza of his *Ode to Sleep*:

> O soft embalmer of the still midnight,
> Shutting, with careful fingers and benign,
> Our gloom-pleas'd eyes, embower'd from the light,
> Enshaded in forgetfulness divine;
> O soothest Sleep! if so it please thee, close,
> In midst of this thine hymn, my willing eyes—
> Save me from curious conscience, that still lords:
> Or wait the amen, ere thy poppy throws
> Around my bed its lulling charities;
> Turn the key deftly in the oilèd wards.

This consists of the first six lines of the sonnet 'To Sleep', followed by lines 11, 7, 8, and 13. It is interesting to notice that it is not only the rhyme-scheme of the Odes that is close to that of many of the sonnets: the whole style is closely related. The syntax, diction, and imagery of these lines could hardly be distinguished from those of the Odes. This sonnet was written about the same time as the first of the major Odes, *Psyche*, and is given in the same letter.(To George and Georgiana Keats, 14 Feb.–3 May 1819, a.f.)

take on a new meaning when we consider them in relation to the Odes. 'Poetry should surprise by a fine excess,' he once wrote, for example; while in the same letter he goes on in these words: 'The rise, the progress, the setting of imagery should like the Sun come natural to him—shine over him and set soberly although in magnificence leaving him in the Luxury of twilight.'

The sudden illumination that such a sentence throws on the nature of poetry is characteristic of the letters of Keats, and it is not surprising that the publication of the first collection in 1848 had an important influence on the development of his reputation. Although the appearance of his letters to Fanny Brawne thirty years later was regretted by Matthew Arnold and most other admirers of his poetry, we notice that in 1880 Arnold repeatedly quotes from the main body of the letters in order to support his insistence that Keats 'had flint and iron in him . . ., had character'. Lecturing in Oxford at the beginning of the present century, Bradley was equally emphatic in his appeal to his audience to 'study the letters of Keats'. Today they are among the most famous letters in the language and it is even possible to imagine an anti-intentionalist critic making an appeal of a different sort. He might insist that we should base our estimate of Keats on the poems themselves: that there is danger in paying too much attention to the letters, with their hints about the poems that Keats intended to write, or would have liked to write. He might point to the misleading use occasionally made of the letters in Middleton Murry's brilliant *Keats and Shakespeare* and to Dr. Leavis's reliance on the letters to show that Keats is more of a poet after his own heart than the poems themselves might suggest. Yet although the danger is real, only a doctrinaire critic could argue in such a way. It would be as rational to argue that paintings must always be looked at with one eye closed as that the letters of Keats should be ignored by the reader who wishes to understand his poetry.

What distinguishes them from the letters of most other poets is that they do not only contain penetrating phrases and observations about poetry in general and his own poems in particular: they give us a peculiarly vivid impression of what it is like to be a poet:

As to the poetical Character itself, (I mean that sort of which, if I am any thing, I am a Member; that sort distinguished from the

wordsworthian or egotistical sublime; which is a thing per se and stands alone) it is not itself—it has no self—it is every thing and nothing—It has no character—it enjoys light and shade; it lives in gusto, be it foul or fair, high or low, rich or poor, mean or elevated —It has as much delight in conceiving an Iago as an Imogen. What shocks the virtuous philosopher, delights the camelion Poet... A Poet is the most unpoetical of any thing in existence.

(To Richard Woodhouse, 27 October 1818.)

It is clear that the act of writing the letters must have been of the greatest importance to Keats. Just as the composition of *The Prelude* helped Wordsworth to find himself, so that of his letters enabled Keats to discover his own poetic identity. As we read them we are not merely listening to a poet describing his own development: we are watching the process going on under our eyes.

Since Keats was exceptionally sensitive to the personalities of his correspondents—'I wish I knew always the humour my friends would be in at opening a letter of mine, to suit it to them [as] nearly as possible'—it is natural to inquire who they were. Most of the letters were written to men whose characters and abilities did not prevent him from enjoying his 'own unfettered scope'. On 8 October 1817 we find him writing to Bailey that he is 'quite disgusted with literary Men and will never know another except Wordsworth—no not even Byron', while in a later letter he complains that even with men like Wordsworth and Hunt conversation is too often 'not a search after knowlege, but an endeavour at effect'. He soon quarrelled with Hunt and Haydon: that he never broke with Hazlitt may be due to the fact that Hazlitt was usually so much more impressive in writing than in conversation. Keats felt at ease with this awkward man of genius as he could never have done with the aristocratic and charming Shelley. When he wrote a letter he wanted a good listener on paper: intelligent men of the second rank like John Hamilton Reynolds, Richard Woodhouse, and Benjamin Bailey provided him with the sort of sympathetic and understanding audience that he required, and we notice that passages of vital importance may be found in letters to any one of his small circle of close friends.

Yet it may be that more of them occur in the letters to his brother George than anywhere else, and one has only to glance through them to realize the significance to Keats of his brother's

departure to America. George had always played a very important part in the poet's life. As Keats wrote to Sarah Jeffrey at the end of May 1819:

> I have been always till now almost as careless of the world as a fly—my troubles were all of the Imagination—My Brother George always stood between me and any dealings with the world—Now I find I must buffet it—I must take my stand upon some vantage ground and begin to fight.

When so much has been said of the influence on Keats of Tom's illness and death it is surprising that the importance of George's departure should have attracted so little attention; yet in part of a letter to America written on 21 September 1819 we find him stating categorically: 'From the time you left me, our friends say I have altered completely—am not the same person.' Keats was developing very rapidly at this time, and one of the things that helped him to develop was the composition of these long journal-letters to George and Georgiana. To many passages in these letters one is tempted to apply his remark about a passage in *Endymion* that has already been quoted: 'My having written that Argument will perhaps be of the greatest service to me of any thing I ever did.'

Not the least interesting of the letters are those relating to *Hyperion*, to which we must now turn. The first thing to be understood if we are to have any chance of making sense of the poem is that it was intended to be an epic. Like most of his contemporaries, Keats was brought up to think of the epic as the greatest of the poetic kinds. Cowden Clarke, as he says in a verse-epistle,

> Shew'd me that epic was of all the king,
> Round, vast, and spanning all like Saturn's ring.
> (66–67)

His letters make it clear that he devoted a great deal of thought to the subject of epic poetry. 'No sooner am I alone', he wrote in October 1818, 'than shapes of epic greatness are stationed around me. . . . Then "Tragedy, with scepter'd pall, comes sweeping by".' In March of the following year he complains that he is in a bad mood for writing, 'not exactly on the road to an epic poem'. There is no need to wonder, with Garrod, whether 'this passion for grand-scale effects' was caught from Haydon: Haydon's profound enthusiasm for heroic painting

may well have had an influence on Keats: but there is, in any event, nothing surprising, or vulgar, in his desire to write an epic poem. This epic ambition helps to explain Keats's desire to master philosophy. He doubted whether he had the necessary powers; but he did not doubt that an epic poem required a secure philosophical foundation. It is no chance that a few weeks after the announcement that he intends to write a poem about Hyperion we find him speculating about the relation between poetry and philosophy and determining, in about a year's time, to seek Hazlitt's advice on 'the best metaphysical road'. While he had no use for directly didactic poetry—'poetry that has a palpable design upon us—and if we do not agree, seems to put its hand in its breeches pocket'—he realized that an epic poem does not merely tell a story: it embodies a whole interpretation of life. *Hyperion* was not simply to be a better-written *Endymion*: it was to belong to a different and much more important poetic kind.

It is because of this pre-occupation with the epic that Keats keeps returning to the relative merits of Milton and Wordsworth. In one letter he tells us that he has been reflecting on Wordsworth's genius, 'and as a help . . . how he differs from Milton. . . . Whether Wordsworth has in truth epic passion.' Unless we understand Keats's own ambitions this may seem rather an academic question, as may that of the precise 'difference' between Ariosto and Spenser, which we find mentioned in another letter. Spenser was important because he had gone a long way on the road to writing an epic: Milton was important because he was the one English poet who had completed a successful epic: Wordsworth was important because he was the only living poet who seemed possibly of epic calibre, as he had shown in *The Excursion*. The Italians Ariosto, Tasso, Boiardo, and above all Dante were important for ultimately the same reasons. Keats studied them for what they could teach him. His interest in epic poetry is similarly evident in his inferior *Ode to Apollo*, where Shakespeare is the only poet mentioned who did not write an epic. Keats wished to join the company of the

> Bards, that erst sublimely told
> Heroic deeds, and sang of fate.

Above all, Keats must have been interested in the philosophical standpoint of the epic poets and the nature of the high styles

which they had evolved. Milton had based *Paradise Lost* on Christian doctrine which Keats could not accept. Wordsworth had attempted to work out a private philosophy of which Keats disapproved—his disapproval eliciting some of the most perceptive comments on Wordsworth ever made. The phrase 'the wordsworthian or egotistical sublime' occurs in the same letter in which Keats remarks that he may well be reflecting on the characters of Saturn and Ops. It reminds us of the earlier letter in which he had asked:

> For the sake of a few fine imaginative or domestic passages, are we to be bullied into a certain Philosophy engendered in the whims of an Egotist—Every man has his speculations, but every man does not brood and peacock over them till he makes a false coinage and deceives himself—Many a man can travel to the very bourne of Heaven, and yet want confidence to put down his halfseeing.

Unable as he was to accept the Christian philosophy, and unwilling to erect a philosophical system of his own, Keats instinctively turned back to 'the beautiful mythology of Greece', with which he had already discovered an exceptional affinity. By doing so he made it inevitable that the teaching of his poem should be conveyed allegorically.

The discovery of a suitable style for epic poetry is perhaps the most difficult task that an English poet can set himself. It is made at once easier and more difficult by the fact that the man who has succeeded most brilliantly is Milton: easier, because there is the encouragement of his example: more difficult, because it is hardly possible to learn from Milton without falling into imitation. It was almost inevitable that it should have been of Milton that Keats was thinking most as he made his own bid to write an epic poem: no less inevitable that he should have been distressed by the fear of becoming a mere imitator.

The fragment called 'The Fall of Hyperion—A Dream' was first published by Monckton Milnes in 1856. At first he supposed it to be the first draft of *Hyperion*, but later he changed his mind, and although there is curiously little evidence about the relation of the two versions a close comparison of the texts makes it clear that 'The Fall' represents an attempt to rewrite the poem. It appears that Keats's reason for dissatisfaction was the feeling that he was being betrayed into insincerity by modelling himself on Milton: 'I have given up Hyperion [he wrote on

21 September 1819]—there were too many Miltonic inversions in it—Miltonic verse cannot be written but in an artful or rather artist's humour.' On the same day he wrote in another letter:

> I shall never become attach'd to a foreign idiom so as to put it into my writings. The Paradise lost though so fine in itself is a corruption of our Language—it should be kept as it is unique—a curiosity, a beautiful and grand Curiosity. The most remarkable Production of the world—A northern dialect accommodating itself to greek and latin inversions and intonations.

It seems possible that his dissatisfaction with his Miltonic style was connected with some doubts in his mind whether epic poetry was still possible. Haydon tells us that 'one day he was full of an epic poem; the next day epic poems were splendid impositions on the world'. In any event the 'sort of induction' that Keats wrote for the second version of the poem is almost a reversion to the manner of *Endymion* (though without rhyme) and is notable mainly for its final line—

> When this warm scribe my hand is in the grave.

The other 270 lines which now precede the revised former beginning of the poem, interesting as they are, are less splendidly impressive than the original opening. Keats presumably wrote them because he felt that some explanation of the action of the poem should be given before the reader is plunged *in medias res*. 'The Fall of Hyperion' should persuade anyone who believes that *Hyperion* is merely a narrative poem that such is not the intention (at least) of the revised form of the poem. Whereas the poet himself makes no appearance in the first *Hyperion*, so far as it goes, he is present (as the dreamer) throughout the second version. He finds himself in a beautiful garden and drinks a mysterious potion, as a result of which he swoons. He then finds himself in a vast building, at the end of which there is an immense flight of steps, with a priestess standing at the summit. A great deal of light is thrown on the interpretation of this by a letter which he had written to Reynolds in May 1818, comparing life to a 'large Mansion of Many Apartments'. The second apartment is the 'Chamber of Maiden-Thought': at first it is full of pleasant wonders, and we are tempted to remain in it for ever; but after a time our vision is

sharpened and we see more deeply 'into the heart and nature of Man', becoming convinced

> that the World is full of Misery and Heartbreak, Pain, Sickness and oppression—whereby This Chamber of Maiden Thought becomes gradually darken'd and at the same time on all sides of it many doors are set open—but all dark—all leading to dark passages—We see not the ballance of good and evil. We are in a Mist.

As he addresses the mysterious goddess Moneta, the dreamer is in such a mist:

> 'None can usurp this height,' returned that shade,
> 'But those to whom the miseries of the world
> Are misery, and will not let them rest.
> All else who find a haven in the world,
> Where they may thoughtless sleep away their days,
> If by a chance into this fane they come,
> Rot on the pavement where thou rotted'st half.'
> (i. 147–53)

Keats would not have published 'The Fall of Hyperion' as it stands: it is a draft, and a great deal is imperfectly worked out. But it seems clear that he is reverting to an old theme: the nature and value of poetry. The dreamer cries:

> Majestic shadow, tell me: sure not all
> Those melodies sung into the world's ear
> Are useless; sure a poet is a sage;
> A humanist, Physician to all men. (i. 187–90)

Moneta replies by insisting on the difference between true poets and mere dreamers:

> The poet and the dreamer are distinct,
> Diverse, sheer opposite, antipodes.
> The one pours out a balm upon the world,
> The other vexes it. (i. 199–202)

Although Keats intended to erase this passage, it is significant that he should be returning to one of his deepest preoccupations, the difference between romance (poetry of delight and escape) and the greatest poetry, which helps us to interpret the significance of human life itself: the difference between *The Faerie Queene* (as he read it) and *King Lear*. We are reminded of 'Sleep and Poetry', where he had prayed for ten years to devote himself

to poetry. There he had taken up his favourite image of poetry as a country of the mind:

> Then will I pass the countries that I see
> In long perspective, and continually
> Taste their pure fountains. First the realm I'll pass
> Of Flora, and old Pan: sleep in the grass,
> Feed upon apples red, and strawberries,
> And choose each pleasure that my fancy sees. (99–104)

But it is his duty to bid farewell to such joys:

> Yes, I must pass them for a nobler life,
> Where I may find the agonies, the strife
> Of human hearts. (123–5)

Instead of ten years, he was to be granted little more than three further years of active life. It is foolish to press a metaphor too far, but if we keep to the image of poetry as a territory we may say that in the *Poems* of 1817 we are still predominantly in the Realm of Flora and Old Pan, and that we stay there for most of *Endymion*, though in it there are glimpses of what lies beyond. The Odes, by their very nature, stand rather aside from the scope of the metaphor. It is in *Hyperion*, above all, that we reach the more serious of poetry's domains. No other poet has gone so far in so short a time. Perhaps it is useless to ask what Keats would have done if he had lived: to such a question there can be no answer: yet when it ceases to be asked, it will be because no one is any longer interested in English poetry.

# V

# CLARE AND THE MINOR POETS

THE most striking feature of this period is the contrast between the wealth of poetic talent and the shortage of satisfactory poems. Whereas in the early seventeenth century almost any educated man seems to have been able to produce one or two tolerable lyrics, two hundred years later we find men of unmistakable poetic ability who failed to produce a single good poem. It is as if the poetry were spilt between the poet and the poem that should have contained it. What makes Clare exceptional is that he was not merely a man with a gift for poetry, like Darley or John Hamilton Reynolds: he was a poet who produced one volume of poems—*The Shepherd's Calendar*—that ranks among the most delightful in our language, and who also wrote a handful of visionary lyrics that leave a resonance in the mind like that set up by Blake's *Songs of Innocence and Experience*.[1]

[1] John Clare (1793–1864) was born at Helpstone, the son of a Northamptonshire labourer. His father 'could read a little in a Bible, or testament, and was very fond of the superstitious tales that are hawked about a street for a penny', as Clare mentions in his memoir; but his mother was illiterate. His origins were thus more humble than those of Burns. He was at first 'of a waukly constitution' and although he was remarkably precocious his formal education was of the slightest. He soon revealed a 'furious' passion for reading, however, and he tells us that the Bible, popular ballads, chapbooks, and *Robinson Crusoe* were included in his early reading. The discovery of Thomson's *Seasons* about the age of thirteen was a landmark in his development. In his early years he worked at various country employments, scribbling verses on such pieces of paper as he could lay his hands on. In 1817 he finally succeeded in printing proposals for a volume of verse, and three years later the interest shown by Taylor and Hessey enabled him to fulfil his ambition. In 1820 he visited London for the first time, meeting Hazlitt, Lamb, De Quincey, and a number of the other Londoners. In the same year he married 'Patty' (Martha Turner). In 1832 he left Helpstone for Northborough and his wife gave birth to their seventh child. For some time he had suffered from delusions and other mental aberrations, and in 1837 he was removed to Dr. Allen's asylum at High Beech, Epping Forest, where he was kindly and intelligently treated and spent much of his time working in the fields. Four years later he escaped and was allowed to remain at home for five months, but at the end of 1841 he had to be taken to Northampton General Lunatic Asylum, where he spent the remainder of his life. He suffered from delusions—believing himself to be Byron or Napoleon—and longed for the girls whom he had known as a youth. The entry in the asylum records states that he died in 1864, 'After years addicted to Poetical prosing'.

The success of Clare's *Poems Descriptive of Rural Life and Scenery*, published in 1820, was partly due to the fact that there was an eager public for 'peasant poetry' at this time; yet it was not in the imitations of Burns that Clare revealed his promise, or in the poems influenced by Pomfret, Goldsmith, and Thomson, but in such pieces as 'Noon', 'Summer Morning', and 'Summer Evening': poems that reveal his gift for precise observation, his use of a countryman's words to gain exactness, and his skilled handling of tetrameter verse. Since several of the poems in this first volume deal with Clare's own life it is not surprising that the title-poem in his second collection, *The Village Minstrel* (1821), is autobiographical; but we notice at once that the descriptive parts of the poem are superior to the more personal passages, in which he is obviously writing for his patrons. The best things in the collection are such minor poems as 'Holywell', 'Cowper Green', 'Solitude', 'Rural Morning', and 'Rural Evening'. When Clare describes a blacksmith's shop, 'where ploughs and harrows lie', we are reminded of Crabbe, as we are when he describes sparrows leaving their nests 'In dust to flutter at the cool of eve'. Time and again he conveys the business and bustle of country life, the fact that something is always going on.

Although it was unsuccessful in its own day and its merit has even yet received scant acknowledgement, there is no doubt that *The Shepherd's Calendar* (1827) stands head and shoulders above Clare's earlier volumes. 'I hope my low station in life will not be set off as a foil against my verses', he wrote in the preface; but the only result of the fact that less attention was now paid to his origins was that less attention was paid to his poetry. The form of the principal series of poems in the volume was the result of a great deal of thought. Hessey had complained that Clare's poems contained 'too much . . . mere description' and not enough 'Sentiment and Feeling and human Interest'; and eventually his colleague John Taylor suggested that Clare should write two poems for each month of the year: a description and a narrative. Clare replied that he 'could soon daub pictures' but that he would find the narratives more difficult, and eventually he ran the descriptions together to form the title-poem and gave four Village Stories in a different section of the book. The structure of each month is simplicity itself: Clare does not even give a chronological description of the progress of

the day: he simply presents us with a series of pictures. He had a countryman's love of the evening, and the close of his January day is brilliantly managed:

> The shutter closed, the lamp alight,
> The faggot chopt and blazing bright—
> The shepherd now, from labour free,
> Dances his children on his knee;
> While, underneath his master's seat,
> The tired dog lies in slumbers sweet,
> Starting and whimpering in his sleep,
> Chasing still the straying sheep.

In 'February' we hear of the melting of the snow, of children hunting for pooty-shells, and prematurely building 'Their spring-time huts of sticks or straw', and then of the key-figures in Clare's village: the milkmaid, the shepherd, and the shepherds' dogs pursuing their sheep,

> While, following fast, a misty smoke
> Reeks from the moist grass as they run.

Each month has its characteristic sounds, as well as its sights: in July 'Scythes tinkle in each grassy dell' and the meadows are filled with the sound 'Of laughing maids and shouting boys': in September we hear the 'creaking noise of opening gate' and the 'clanking pumps': while there is a brilliant description of the strange silence that often falls about noon in midsummer, when 'day lies still as death'. Clare seldom turns aside from description to reflection in *The Shepherd's Calendar*, but when he does the result often reminds us vividly of the poets of the seventeenth century. Of children playing in a churchyard he writes:

> They think not, in their jovial cry,
> The time will come, when they shall lie
> As lowly and as still as they
> While other boys above them play,
> Heedless, as they are now, to know
> The unconscious dust that lies below.

On occasion he can write lines reminiscent of Marvell:

> But woodmen still on Spring intrude,
> And thin the shadow's solitude;
> With sharpen'd axes felling down
> The oak-trees budding into brown.

If we turn to Clare's poetry from that of other descriptive poets we are reminded of Corin's remark in *As You Like It*, 'Sir,

I am a true countryman.' It is not surprising that he was a severe critic of the pastoralizing of Shenstone or that he disliked the 'peasantry' of Darley's *Sylvia*. He also made a shrewd objection to the descriptions of natural scenery in Keats:

> When he speaks of woods, Dryads and Fauns and Satyrs are sure to follow, and the brook looks alone without her naiads to his mind.... With other inhabitants of great cities, he often described nature as she appeared to his fancies, and not as he would have described her had he witnessed the things he describes.

This gives us a hint of Clare's own secret. Even as a boy he was astonished by other people's lack of interest in the world of the eye. He had the psychology of a painter, and one notices how often he uses painter-like language in talking of poetry. He once decided to write a hundred sonnets 'as a set of pictures on the scenes . . . that appear in the different seasons'. He had every right to claim 'images . . . not noticed before' in many of his poems. It is not surprising that he numbered de Wint, Rippingille, and Hilton among his friends. His fragmentary essay on landscape throws a great deal of light on his poetry. The men and women in his poems remind us of the figures in a landscape painting: the true subject is the seasons as they pass, and the hours of the day: men and women figure only as playing their part in this unending natural process.

Clare was an expert naturalist. Even before he began to write poetry, he tells us, he 'noticd every thing as anxious' as he did later. He collected flowers, made a list of Northamptonshire birds, and studied the reproductive processes of plants. He once thought of calling his *Natural History of Helpstone* 'Biographies of Birds and Flowers'. His love of accuracy explains his characteristic use of unusual and provincial words in his poetry. If he felt that the usual word was imprecise, he did not hesitate to turn to 'the unwritten language of England'. He uses a great many unfamiliar epithets—in his early poetry, as in that of many poets, epithets are too common—but in his mature work it is his use of unusual verbs which is most striking, verbs which have a vivid exactness, visual or auditory, which would otherwise be unobtainable:

> The crow goes flopping on from wood to wood,
> The wild duck wherries to the distant flood,
> The starnels hurry o'er in merry crowds,
> And overhead whew by like hasty clouds.

In the same poem, 'The Flight of Birds', the pigeon 'suthers by on rapid wing' while the peewit 'whizzes' over the ploughman 'with many a whew and whirl and sudden scream'. In his desire to convey the precise nature of what he is describing Clare sometimes reminds us of Hopkins; yet his approach to truth is not that of a theologian but that of a countryman of genius who knows that most people keep their eyes and ears half shut. As we read these records of actuality we notice the delight that the poet is taking in the sequence of morning and evening, of spring and summer, his undulled pleasure in the perpetual bustle and purposeful activity of the countryside. No fewer than twenty-eight of his poems begin with the word 'Now'. A great many others begin with the words 'I love', while such words as 'joy', 'delight', 'merry', 'pleasure', 'glee', and 'mirth' occur on every page. It is when Clare is driven in on himself that he becomes a prey to melancholy. Uneducated as he was, he was a highly intelligent man, and he seems to have realized that to preserve his sanity it was essential for him to maintain his almost organic sense of unity with external nature. Far more than most descriptive poets, he is himself a part of the process that he describes: he is not a visitor to the country, but a part of it. Perhaps his awareness was increased by his observation of the way in which the enclosures were killing the beauty and the rhythm of country life.

Although his discovery of *The Seasons* marked an epoch in Clare's life, *The Shepherd's Calendar* has little in common with Thomson's poem. Thomson is a philosopher who takes the whole world and the whole of history for his subject: he is concerned with the universal causes of things. Clare writes as a countryman in one place at one time. In his inland poem he has nothing to do with the sublime: he is seldom the moralist and never the philosopher. He is Bewick to Thomson's Turner. Thomson's blank verse, with its diction, as Johnson said, 'in the highest degree florid and luxuriant', is the antithesis of Clare's simple metrical patterns and his pure English idiom.

Like 'The Cross Roads' in *The Village Minstrel*, the four tales in *The Shepherd's Calendar* owe a good deal to Crabbe. As in his descriptive poems Clare shows a countryman's knowledge of trees, flowers, and animals, so in these stories he describes the lives of country people without sentiment or humbug. In his view even Crabbe saw rural life from outside: 'Whats he know

of the distresses of the poor', he once wrote, 'musing over a snug coal fire in his parsonage box.' In 'The Sorrows of Love', which is a triumph in the informal style which is so difficult to manage, Clare 'keeps decorum' most skilfully, not indeed by limiting himself exclusively to such idioms as his narrator would use but by being careful to set passages in a colloquial style in key positions. At the end we are told how the old woman snuffed the candle,

> Then laid her knitting down, and shook her head,
> And stoop'd to stir the fire, and talk of bed.

The same volume includes a lyric which is, as Clare said himself, 'out of my way' ('Life, Death and Eternity') and a very remarkable poem, 'The Dream', which reveals an aspect of his genius that appears again in some of his asylum lyrics. It is a vision of the end of the universe:

> When years, in drowsy thousands counted by,
> Are hung on minutes with their destiny:
> When Time in terror drops his draining glass,
> And all things mortal, like to shadows, pass,
> As 'neath approaching tempests sinks the sun—
> When Time shall leave Eternity begun.

The combination of an apparent *naïveté* of expression with a penetrating prophetic vision is singularly impressive: Clare never revealed more clearly his gift for the incomparable image:

> Winds urged them onward, like to restless ships;
> And Light dim faded in its last eclipse;
> And Agitation turn'd a straining eye;
> And Hope stood watching like a bird to fly.

From the destruction of the world Clare makes something of a terrifying beauty:

> The colour'd flower, the green of field and tree,
> What they had been, for ever ceased to be:
> Clouds, raining fire, scorch'd up the hissing dews;
> Grass shrivell'd brown in miserable hues;
> Leaves fell to ashes in the air's hot breath,
> And all awaited universal Death.

It is natural to Clare to remember the fate of the brute creation,

the death of the cattle, the dogs that 'dropp'd, and dying lick'd their masters' feet', and the terrified birds that

> Beat through the evil air in vain for rest.

The supreme horror is the extinction of the light:

> The pallid moon hung fluttering on the sight,
> As startled bird whose wings are stretch'd for flight;
> And o'er the east a fearful light begun
> To show the sun rise—not the morning sun,
> But one in wild confusion, doom'd to rise
> And drop again in horror from the skies—
> To heaven's midway it reel'd, and changed to blood,
> Then dropp'd, and Light rush'd after like a flood.

For all its horror it is not a hysterical poem. The poignancy of the return to life in the last line is profoundly moving:

> I heard the cock crow, and I blest the sound.

It seems possible that Clare could have essayed more poems in this vein; but he shrank from the experience. 'I mustnt do no more terrible things yet', as he wrote in a letter, 'they stir me up to such a pitch that leaves a disrelish for my old accustomed wanderings after nature.'

After such a poem *The Rural Muse*, published in 1835, when Mrs. Emmerson had succeeded Taylor as Clare's adviser, comes as an anticlimax. Instead of concentrating on his true vein he seems here to be striving to show his capacity for variety and his competence in traditional poetic forms. Once again many of the poems are descriptive, but now they are too often turned to moral or personal applications of a highly conventional kind.

Literary influences are more obvious again, as in his earlier volumes: at least three of the poems had originally been written as imitations of seventeenth-century poetry, while we are often reminded of the muted music of Collins. 'Autumn' is in the unrhymed stanza of the 'Ode to Evening', as is the original version of 'Summer Images'. But adjectives in -y spring up on all sides like literary weeds:

> The pranking bat its flighty circlet makes

reads like a line from a parody of textbook 'Pre-Romanticism'. It is sickening to find a poet of Clare's stature using phrases

like 'silly sheep' and 'balmy trills'. There are also occasional reminiscences of Byron, a poet who meant less to Clare than did Wordsworth, although in his madness he came to think that he was himself the author of *Childe Harold* and *Don Juan*. In spite of the metrical variety of the volume it is interesting to notice that he avoids blank verse. Half of the poems (on the other hand) are sonnets, reminding us—in spite of an outburst in a letter against 'the short winded peevishness that hovers round this 14 line article in poetry'—that Clare was throughout his life a prolific sonneteer. As Taylor pointed out, he excelled in 'little things', and as we turn over his hundreds of sonnets we become aware that he was experimenting endlessly to find a verbal equivalent for the small woodcut so brilliantly practised by Bewick. Many of Clare's sonnets, indeed, are sketches or jottings rather than completed wholes, and they all have their interest for a critic who wishes to study his genius for recreating nature in words. In none of his poems is it more evident that description is his forte. 'The cat runs races with her tail' is a brilliant little genre-piece, while 'Farm Breakfast' is surely a poem of which Swift would have approved:

> Maids shout to breakfast in a merry strife,
> And the cat runs to hear the whetted knife.

From the end of 1836 until his death in 1864 Clare was never wholly sane, and no further collection of his verse was published in his lifetime. He was, however, treated with remarkable humanity, and over the years he wrote a great many poems, a few of them of the highest merit. The best of these are lyrics of a penetrating simplicity which neither requires nor permits of analysis, such as 'Song's Eternity', first published by Edmund Blunden and Alan Porter:

> Mighty songs that miss decay,
>   What are they?
> Crowds and cities pass away
>   Like a day.
> Books are out and books are read,
>   What are they?
> Years will lay them with the dead—
>   Sigh, sigh;
> Trifles unto nothing wed,
>   They die.

'Dying Child' appeared in J. L. Cherry's *Life and Remains of John Clare* in 1873:

He could not die when trees were green,
For he loved the time too well.

'*Now* is past' is one of the most remarkable of all these poems:

Wood strawberries faded from wood-sides,
Green leaves have all turned yellow;
No Adelaide walks the wood-rides,
True love has no bed-fellow.
*Now* is past.

One of the characteristic themes of these last poems is the poet's search for reality—his own reality and the reality of the past. In 'I am' he complains of the shipwreck of his life:

I AM: yet what I am none cares or knows,
My friends forsake me like a memory lost.

Sometimes, as in reading 'I lost the love of heaven above', we feel that Blake is the only possible parallel:

I snatched the sun's eternal ray,
And wrote till earth was but a name.

One of the most moving of these poems is the 'Invitation to Eternity', in which Clare's love-yearning fuses with his perpetual questionings about eternity:

Say, wilt thou go with me, sweet maid,
Say, maiden, wilt thou go with me
Through the valley-depths of shade,
Of night and dark obscurity;

. . .

Where stones will turn to flooding streams,
Where plains will rise like ocean's waves,
Where life will fade like visioned dreams,
And mountains darken into caves,
Say, maiden, wilt thou go with me
Through this sad non-identity,
Where parents live and are forgot,
And sisters live and know us not?

The questioning of life and death that we find in many of Clare's lyrics is the main subject of the poetry of Beddoes; but

in him it takes on a deeper and more macabre aspect. In background he was far removed from the poet of *The Shepherd's Calendar*. His father was a scientist of genius who had marked literary interests.[1] Although Dr. Beddoes died when his son was five it seems clear that the son's fascination with death was the direct result of the father's dissections and speculations about human anatomy and the human soul. The poet was a sort of Frankenstein, a sombre and impressive manifestation of the *Zeitgeist* who seems necessary to complete the literary scene in his age. He devoted many years of his own life to medicine, and claimed that 'the studies . . . of the dramatist & physician are closely, almost inseparably, allied; the application alone is different'.

The early work of Beddoes already exhibits the mixture of what his friends called 'mysticism' and grotesque humour that is one of his characteristics. We have only to read 'Alfarabi the World-Maker' to understand why Browning was so interested in Beddoes—intending to make him the subject of his first lecture, had he been elected Professor of Poetry at Oxford:

> But he was one not satisfied with man,
> As man has made himself: he thought this life
> Was something deeper than a jest, and sought
> Into its roots: himself was his best science.
> He touched the springs, the unheeded hieroglyphics
> Deciphered.

Like Shelley, whom he greatly admired, Beddoes nurtured his boyish imagination on Gothic romances, and the result of such reading is evident in the three 'tales of guilt and woe' which make up *The Improvisatore*, a work which Beddoes thought little of and later tried to suppress. It is in *The Brides' Tragedy*, so

[1] Thomas Lovell Beddoes (1803–49) was the son of Dr. Thomas Beddoes, the friend of Coleridge and Southey. His mother was a sister of Maria Edgeworth. He was educated at the Charterhouse and Pembroke College, Oxford. As a freshman there he published *The Improvisatore*. *The Brides' Tragedy* appeared in 1822. In 1825 he took his B.A. and began to work on *Death's Jest-Book*. Later he studied at Göttingen and Würzburg (where he took his M.D. in 1831). At Würzburg Beddoes took a prominent part in radical politics, being received into a club called the *Freie Reichsstadt*—an unusual distinction for a foreigner. Later he was obliged to flee to Berlin. There he studied at the university and continued to take a keen interest in politics. Although he paid occasional visits to England he spent the remainder of his life abroad, mainly in Switzerland, and wrote a good deal in German. His interest in German literature is discussed in Chapter XIV. In 1849 he committed suicide in Basle.

highly praised by Darley, that Beddoes first appears as a considerable writer. His subject is a murder commemorated in a popular ballad, and he handles it in a spirit that reminds us of Webster. As one reads this play it becomes difficult to agree with Professor Donner—the man who has done more than any other for the reputation of Beddoes—that the poet's obsession with death dates from the death of his mother. A passage in a letter written by his brother after the poet's death suggests that the bent of his mind had remained the same throughout his life: 'I was glad to find the Mandrake so much suppressed [in *Death's Jest-Book*]. It was a character in which my brother delighted long ago when a boy, and the idea I can imagine ever haunted his imagination.' *The Brides' Tragedy* was the work of a man who had thought a great deal about the nature of drama. Beddoes made some penetrating notes about the function of dramatic plot, as well as observations on the possibility of discriminating characters 'by appropriating to each . . . a peculiar style of versification; and metaphors drawn from certain circumstances of nature or art'. In the preface to *Death's Jest-Book* he was to follow the Schlegels and the Dutch critic Bilderdijk in maintaining that modern critics are unduly 'prejudiced . . . in favour of the literature of the South': he argues that there is an affinity 'between an old English Play and one of our ancient Cathedrals': 'it is not Shakspeare who is lawless, they are lawless who judge his British example by the precept of the Greeks'. Beddoes was more deeply read in the work of the Elizabethan dramatists than Darley or most of his other contemporaries: at one time he contemplated producing a volume of *Specimens* supplementary to Lamb's. Yet he found it difficult to decide how far the Elizabethans were eligible models. While he regretted that Shelley in *The Cenci* 'seemed to have the Greeks, instead of Shakespeare, as his model' (a surprising judgement), he wrote in another letter that 'just now the drama is a haunted ruin', concluding that 'we had better beget than revive'.

There can be no doubt that *Death's Jest-Book*, which Beddoes sometimes called *The Fool's Tragedy* and once described as an example 'of what might be called the florid Gothic in poetry', is more Elizabethan than classical in inspiration—and more German, perhaps, than either. Beddoes had little hope that it would be appreciated by reviewers 'who have learned the Odes of Horace by heart at Eton'. He was disconcerted when his

friends told him that he must not publish it without comprehensive revision. It is an interesting question whether his friends were right. If Beddoes had published this 'strange conglomerate' he would certainly have been attacked by the reviewers; yet publication is the only way in which a poet can escape from a poem, and as it turned out Beddoes was never to escape from *Death's Jest-Book*. There is a possible analogy with *Endymion*. If Keats had taken Hunt's advice and revised his poem, or left it unpublished, he would have been saved from severe and painful criticism; but he might not have developed as rapidly as he did to become the poet of *Hyperion* and the Odes. Beddoes was to struggle in the toils of his extraordinary poem for the rest of his life, practically everything that he wrote being apparently related to it in some way.

It would be difficult to find a better image for *Death's Jest-Book* than the image of a Gothic cathedral which Beddoes himself uses for the non-classical drama. It is 'intricate, vast, and gloomy, [intimating] the supernatural and . . . full of indistinct thoughts of immortality'. Like a cathedral it is the work of a 'wild fancy, sometimes light and joyous, sometimes fearfully hideous—often satirical, grotesque or ludicrous'. The grotesque and the ludicrous are particularly evident in the prose passages, which are an inherent part of the work and yet seldom successful. It is extraordinary to move from the laboured prose of the opening to the brilliance of the first lines of verse:

> The turning tide; the sea's wide leafless wind,
> Wherein no birds inhabit and few traffic,
> Making his cave within your sunny sails.

Sometimes a single line compels our admiration:

> When the thin harvests shed their withered grain.

As always, it is Time, Death, and Eternity that move Beddoes to the most memorable utterance:

> Can a man die? Ay, as the sun doth set:
> It is the earth that falls away from light. (II. ii. 39–40)

In a remarkable passage he refers to our remotest progenitors, 'who were

> Ere our grey ancestors wrote history;
> When these our ruined towers were in the rock;
> And our great forests, which do feed the sea

With storm-souled fleets, lay in an acorn's cup:
When all was seed that now is dust.' (II. iii. 532–7)

There is no difficulty in finding the 'mysticism' that distressed his friends in such lines as these—

. . . Deeply have I slept.
As one who doth go down unto the springs
Of his existence and there bathed, I come
Regenerate up into the world again (B text: I. ii. 64–67)

—a passage which might come from one of Shakespeare's last plays, as might the lines that follow:

'Tis nearly passed, for I begin to hear
Strange but sweet sounds, and the loud rocky dashing
Of waves, where time into Eternity
Falls over ruined worlds. (IV. iii. 107–110)

If the greatness of Shakespeare lay in isolated words and images, Beddoes too would rank as a great poet. But in fact *Death's Jest-Book* completely fails to become a coherent whole: there are few works which leave one in such uncertainty whether the author was a madman or a visionary. The intention is clearly to use 'Gothic' material as a means of exploring the problem of death and the whole significance of human life. Beddoes sets death before us with extraordinary vividness, in a manner that recalls both the medieval preacher and the modern dramatist:

As I was newly dead, and sat beside
My corpse, looking on it, as one who muses
Gazing upon a house he was burnt out of. (V. iv. 198–200)

While Beddoes acknowledged his own deficiency in humour, there are occasions when his characteristic *humour noir* appears to advantage, as in Mandrake's speech: 'After all being dead's not so uncomfortable when one's got into the knack of it.' The other great weakness of Beddoes, his inability (in Kelsall's words) to create 'characters quite different from his own', would be fatal to the work as an ordinary drama but seems hardly relevant to it as it stands. It is impossible to keep one's attention on the plot: what we listen for are the incomparable passages of meditation on life and death, the poet's own strivings towards 'a wished-for change of being'. It is as if one of the distempered

minds described by Burton were to step out of *The Anatomy of Melancholy* and write a play.

As a lyric poet Beddoes is seldom at his best. In reading some of his shorter poems one understands why he once described himself as 'essentially unpoetical'. 'Squats on a toad-stool under a tree' reminds one of Browning at his most uncompromising—and perhaps also of Hardy. Beddoes has a liking for rude mouthfuls of consonants and other unacceptable combinations of sounds:

> But the owl's brown eye's the sky's new blue.
> Heigho! Foolscap!

There is an element of the grotesque in him, something 'Gothic', unmelodious, unclassical. He turns as if by instinct from the classical orders of the Mediterranean to the wilder forms of the North. There is a revealing passage in one of his letters: 'I often very shrewdly suspect that I have no real poetical call. I w$^{d}$ write more songs if I could, but I can't manage rhyme well or easily; I very seldom get a glimpse of the right sort of idea in the right light for a song.' It is curious that a man with such a profound understanding of blank verse should have been so uncertain with the lighter metres. Although Beddoes told a friend that he had 'a decided and clear critical theory' about song-writing, his lyrics lack inevitability: in this respect he was the antithesis of Darley, who had a fine ear for lyric metres but suffered from a paucity of material. Beddoes once commented that if he could have 'rhyme[d] well and order[ed] complicated verse harmoniously' he would have written odes, and it seems possible that the weight and seriousness of the ode might have acted as an inspiration to him.

Yet it is not any aspect of his technique that is the most remarkable feature of the poetry of Beddoes: it is the extent to which Death dominates everything that he wrote. He often confessed to being 'haunted for ever' by the problem of death: he was the Muses' Sexton: by comparison with him, neither Donne nor Webster was 'much possessed by death'. In his unfinished play, *The Second Brother*, one of the characters points out that 'death is the one condition of our life', and it is the one subject of his poetry. For him man is 'a soul and skeleton in a flesh doublet'. He looks at men and women with the speculative eye of an undresser—only it is not the clothes that he strips off,

but the skin and flesh that cover the skeleton. He made notes on Dr. Dee, and his interest in magic and the occult occasionally reminds us of Yeats. His thoughts could not escape from the problems posed by the material and perishable nature of the human body:

> Art not sewn up with veins and pegged together
> With bony sticks and hinges?

—as one of his characters asks another. It is characteristic of him to have rewritten the story of Cupid and Psyche, turning the winged boy into a 'gaunt anatomy'. One of the last fragments of his writing describes him as wandering 'within the doubt-brakes of obscurest Thought'. If he had been as interested in life as he was in death he might have been a very great poet. As it is he remains the most tantalizing of all our writers: a man of genius who wrote nothing that is commonly remembered.

George Darley was an Irishman belonging to a gifted family who failed to win a Fellowship at Trinity College, Dublin, and spent his life as a freelance writer in London.[1] As his letters reveal, he had a good deal in common with Lamb. His very severe stutter, together with the terrible 'tertian headaches' from which he suffered, made him a 'Solitudinarian': much as he was attracted by 'fireside, tea-table, chit-chat, and petticoatism' he had the resolution to renounce the comforts of marriage. In the writing of mathematical textbooks he found something of the same steadying influence that Lamb found in his drudgery at the South Sea House. Throughout his career we notice a contrast between the unusual clarity of his critical insight and his apparent inability to profit from his own understanding. In a comment on *The Errors of Ecstasie*, for example, he pointed out that 'since the time of Rousseau, it has been the tendency of imaginative writers to embody their own history in their works', and in spite of his own disclaimer it is difficult not to identify the Mystic in this poem with Darley himself. His habit of using an exaggerated poetical diction is already evident when he talks

[1] George Darley (1795–1846) took his B.A. at T.C.D. in 1820. The following year he came to London, where he published *The Errors of Ecstasie* in 1822. He also became a contributor to the *London Magazine*. In the next few years he published several mathematical textbooks and *Sylvia*, which appeared in 1827. In 1830 he travelled on the Continent and studied painting and sculpture in France and Italy. From 1834 to his death he contributed to the *Athenaeum*, most often writing on fine art. *Nepenthe*, which he circulated among his friends in 1835, was a dismal failure. He was an excellent critic and letter-writer.

of the 'susurring' of the wind 'Puffing amid the flow'ry-finger'd groves'. As the work of a critic who understood the need for unity in drama *Sylvia; or, The May Queen* is a curiosity. It is serious and humorous by turns and seems to hover uneasily between Elizabethan masque and modern pantomime. One can imagine Lord Curryfin in *Gryll Grange* producing such a thing, if the ladies had pleaded for something less classical than an Aristophanic comedy.

The best parts of *Sylvia* are the lyrics, and Darley is always more at home in detached lyrics than in longer poems. His merits as a lyric poet are already foreshadowed in 'Love droop'd when Beauty fled the bow'r' in his first volume. In one of his letters we find him writing that 'the secret of true poetry' is to 'set beautiful thoughts to music'. 'Every true poet has a *song in his mind*', he wrote elsewhere, 'the notes of which, little as they precede his thoughts—so little as to seem simultaneous with them—do precede, suggest and inspire many of these, modify and beautify them. . . . Rhythm . . . is the poet's latent inspirer.' His success in catching the accents of our older poets is shown by the fact that Palgrave printed 'It is not beautie I demande' in *The Golden Treasury* as the work of an unknown Cavalier. It is not surprising that Tennyson was interested in Darley's work: 'To my dead Mistress' is very like Tennyson, while several of Darley's lyrics could have helped to inspire 'The Brook'. His lyrics often open splendidly, but unfortunately he had too often little to say, while his characteristic faults of diction are never far away. Few poets have in their language so little contact with the spoken idiom of their own day. He is too apt to avoid the obvious word even when it is the right word, and has an unfortunate habit of spoiling a fine line or stanza by suddenly using a word that is quite inappropriate, like a pianist striking the wrong key. In the unfinished *Nepenthe*, which was intended to illustrate 'the folly of discontent with the natural tone of human life', there are some gloriously ridiculous lines, such as 'With her flush bridegroom on the ooze' and 'Dingling beside me, as I glid'. The author of *Hudibras* would have enjoyed this poem, which is none the less nonsense for being the nonsense of a poet. It is curious that a man with a stutter should have produced such a work, unfinished and in an exceptionally unattractive format: as if he were resigned to the perpetual impossibility of communication.

On reading *Nepenthe* Miss Mitford advised Darley to turn to a subject uniting 'the imaginative and the real'. It is ironical that Darley should have needed such advice, for twelve years before he had begun to publish a series of 'Letters to the Dramatists of the Day' which contain shrewd and penetrating counsel and in which he censured his contemporaries for using 'a mode of language which is wholly inconsistent with dramatic effect' with the result that they produced 'not tragedies, but—Amoeban Poems, in five cantos each'. Yet Darley himself was driven to the inconsistency of writing closet dramas. In *Thomas à Becket* we find him faithful to his own view that the drama flourishes on bold effects rather than nuances, and the result is a play in which excellent use is made of contrast. The swift killing of Becket, followed almost at once by the silent enactment of the ceremony of a lustration in St. Benedict's Chapel, and then the procession of mourners past the bier of the dead Archbishop, shows real dramatic flair. Unfortunately *Ethelstan; or, The Battle of Brunanburh* in no way bears out this promise. It is interesting to notice that Darley was keenly interested in Saxon history and literature: in a letter with which Beddoes would have sympathized he tells a friend that he is turning back to the ruggedness of Old English poetry in reaction against the 'eternal cud of rose-leaves' of Barry Cornwall and other of his contemporaries. But the result of his choosing the Anglo-Saxon period for his play is that he has names like Gorm, Ellisif and Egil Skillagrym on his hands: 'torquetur Apollo, Nomine percussus'. The verse of *Ethelstan* is slightly influenced by that of Old English and presents what is presumably the first Sceop in the modern English drama.

By the time when he had acclaimed the work of Byron, Shelley, and Keats, Leigh Hunt was under no illusions about his own stature as a poet. Yet his poetry remains an interesting foil to that of his major contemporaries, while his prefaces and notes provide a shrewd commentary on the poetic scene in his time. It is characteristic of him to have written an essay on the subject 'Poetry and Cheerfulness', and his 1832 preface contains a significant protest against the fashion for melancholy, the snobbery of being miserable. Perhaps it was because there was a persistent, though shallow, vein of melancholy in his own temperament that Hunt deliberately cultivated his powers of enjoyment—a habit which made him the perfect mentor for the youthful Keats. Enjoyment is the spirit of most of Hunt's own

poetry: the antithesis of Beddoes, he is the least philosophical of poets and the furthest from tragedy. *Captain Sword and Captain Pen* (1835) is unique in his work in being a poem in which indignation led him to hammer out lines with a primitive urgency that is strangely compelling—

> The drums and the music say never a word.

Enjoyment, not indignation, is the usual inspiration of Hunt's poetry.

In his prematurely published *Juvenilia* (1801) we already see Hunt's accessibility to foreign influences (particularly that of Italian literature) and his love of painting. Something will be said in Chapter XIV of the important part Hunt played in introducing Italian literature into England, but here we may note that he turned to the Italians, as well as to Chaucer and Dryden, in his search for 'a freer spirit of versification'. He was particularly attracted by the double rhyming of Italian poetry. When he set out to 'correct' *Rimini* his first intention was to eliminate the double rhymes altogether, but he could not bring himself to go so far, and double rhymes are prominent in many of his poems. One reason for his love of Italy may have been that he had, as he believed, tropical blood in his veins, and his 'southern insight into the beauties of colour' is one of the outstanding features of his poetry. Edmund Blunden has described his poem 'To Hampstead', with its picture of 'The cold sky whitening through the wiry trees', as 'a sonnet in water colours', and Hunt often gives the impression of writing his poems on an easel. He peopled Hampstead Heath with gods and goddesses and nymphs. There are no more characteristic lines in his poetry than those describing the nymphs tying up their hair,

> Their white backs glistening through the myrtles green.

Too often, indeed, amorous description was the fatal Cleopatra for whom he lost the world, and was content to lose it. His descriptions of girls are the verbal equivalent of Etty's nudes. He had the imagination of a poet, and the fancy of a cit. At one moment he can write of 'The laughing queen that caught the world's great hands' and at another inform us that Francesca 'had stout notions on the marrying score' or describe

> The two divinest things this world has got,
> A lovely woman in a rural spot.

The reader of his poems may well echo the words of the Second Shepherd in *The Descent of Liberty* (1815):

> We have come, I think,
> Through nothing but sweet spots from first to last.

Hunt is fatally fond of such words as 'spot', 'gush', and 'balmy', and defends 'delicious' against Byron's view that it 'should be applied only to eatables'. He lacks the passion which can transform amorous feeling into poetry free from vulgarity. It is not surprising that Keats outgrew him, or that he was singled out to be the butt of an unscrupulous Right-wing journalistic stunt. Yet if there was an element of cheapness in his suburban epicureanism, there was an element of unmistakable nobility in the man himself.

It is remarkable that the poems of an even closer friend of Keats than Leigh Hunt, John Hamilton Reynolds, have never been collected. 'Let the man be who he will,' Clare wrote on reading *The Garden of Florence*, 'he's a poet & as far above many as white bread's before brown.'[1] His early work is of interest primarily because it reflects the main influences of the time. *Safie: An Eastern Tale* is a transparent imitation of Byron, to whom it is dedicated; while *The Eden of Imagination* is a sort of *Pleasures of the Imagination* in pentameter couplets that are more reminiscent of Campbell and Rogers than of Wordsworth. While such a phrase as 'usefulness, not luxury' marks the poem as decisively eighteenth-century, in other passages we see a new sensibility struggling to emerge from an outmoded idiom. Reynolds had a deep love of Wordsworth which survived that great poet's discouraging comments on *The Naiad*, a poem

[1] John Hamilton Reynolds (1794–1852) was the son of a schoolmaster who later taught at Christ's Hospital. He himself was educated at Shrewsbury and St. Paul's. For some years he worked in an insurance office, publishing *Safie* and *The Eden of Imagination* at the age of 19. In 1815 he began to contribute to the *Champion*. The following year he met Keats, with whom he became very friendly, and published *The Naiad*. At the end of 1816 Hunt hailed Shelley, Reynolds, and Keats as the coming poets of the day in an article in the *Examiner*. Reynolds published *The Fancy* in 1820 and *The Garden of Florence* in 1821, and began to contribute to the *London Magazine* in the latter year. By this time he had become a solicitor. Although he professed to bid farewell to the Muses before his marriage in 1822 he did not abandon poetry, collaborating with Hood in the *Odes and Addresses to Great People* in 1825. From this time onwards, however, he wrote mainly in prose, in the *Athenaeum* and other periodicals. In 1847 he was appointed an assistant clerk to the County Court in Newport in the Isle of Wight. During the last five years of his life he was bored and unhappy.

'founded on a beautiful Scotch ballad . . . procured from a young girl of Galloway, who delighted in preserving the romantic songs of her country' and written in the medley of metres which was fashionable at this time.

But it is by the poems contained in *The Garden of Florence* that Reynolds's reputation as a poet stands or falls. Although the volume was not published until 1821 the fact that most of the poems had been written some years before explains the valedictory air that hangs about it. As Reynolds writes to his fiancée in the dedicatory poem, he has decided to 'give up drawling verse for drawing leases'. 'The Romance of Youth' is the only canto that was completed of a projected poem in Spenserian stanzas on the poet's own development—that favourite theme of the time: it is interesting to notice that Keats refers to this poem in his letter about the Mansion of Many Apartments. Reynolds writes that 'the world of imagination is darkened by the shadow of the world of reality'. Unlike Keats he seems not to have conceived of a further world of poetry lying beyond the realm 'Of Flora and old Pan'. 'The Romance of Youth' is the work of a young poet who is still ambitious, and contains some good lines, such as the reference to the flowers of spring which

> Dance through all years in the eternal mind.

A short poem, in blank verse, 'Devon', shows higher promise than anything else that Reynolds was ever to write. It was no doubt inspired by *Tintern Abbey*, but contains some eloquent references to the sea

> That talks for ever to the quiet sands.

Reynolds reminds us of Keats in the passionate pleasure he takes in contemplating the sea in its every mood: he likes to watch it when it

> Tosses its hoar-hair on the raving wind,

but no less

> To see it gently playing on loose rocks,
> Lifting the idle sea-weed carelessly;
> Or hear it in some dreary cavern, muttering
> A solitary legend of old times.

The volume also contains a verse-epistle, three sonnets to Keats, and the sonnet in praise of dark eyes which inspired Keats to

write a reply. *The Garden of Florence* itself, like 'The Ladye of Provence', is a companion-piece to *Isabella*, the outcome of the design of the two friends to produce a volume of stories from Boccaccio. Each of the tales tells a tragic love-story with an element of the macabre about it, and each attains a measure of success. Lines 87–88 of *The Garden of Florence* remain memorable—

> Passion lays desolate the fields of sleep,
> And wakes a thousand eyes to watch and weep,

while 'The Ladye of Provence' tells a story that would have appealed to Browning in a loosely moving blank verse that might easily be his.

It was the 'sombre sadness of memory' in the poetry of Reynolds that appealed to Clare, but Reynolds had also a marked flair for parody and comic verse. In 1819, hearing that Wordsworth was about to publish a poem called *Peter Bell*, he wrote his brilliant parody under that title and succeeded in publishing it before Wordsworth's own poem appeared. If the preface parodies Wordsworth's complacency a trifle heavy-handedly, the poem itself is mischievously right:

> Not a brother owneth he,
> Peter Bell he hath no brother;
> His mother had no other son,
> No other son e'er call'd her mother;
> Peter Bell hath brother none.

The following year Reynolds published a curious volume, *The Fancy: A Selection from the Poetical Remains of the late Peter Corcoran.* It is tempting to suppose that Corcoran had been Reynolds himself, and that the account of his life given in the preface is meant as a humorous warning to his fiancée of what may happen to him if they become estranged. In the preface to one of the poems Reynolds refers to 'those literary deceptions for which this age has become too infamously celebrated', and the slightly indeterminate impression left by some of the lyrics in the volume may be due to the fact that they had originally been written seriously but were now meant to be laughed at. 'The Fields of Tothill' raises an interesting critical question. If it were not for the claim in the preface that its model is *Whistlecraft* we should have supposed it a parody of *Beppo*; and as such it would be a more successful achievement than simply as a comic poem in

its own right. Further evidence of Reynolds's ability as a comic poet is to be found in *Odes and Addresses to Great People*, in which he collaborated with Thomas Hood.

It is appropriate that one of the best of Reynolds's shorter pieces is a 'Farewell to the Muses'. As we read his work we have perpetually the impression of a man with a true poetic gift hesitating on the threshold of discovering his own poetic individuality. That he did not pursue his poetic career is greatly to our loss.

Reynolds's brother-in-law Thomas Hood published *The Plea of the Midsummer Fairies* in 1827.[1] His literary allegiances are indicated by the dedications to Lamb, Coleridge, and Reynolds himself. The allegorical title-poem contains some delightful description and manages to maintain contact with reality in a way in which Shelley's *Witch of Atlas*, for example, does not. Many of the conceits in 'Hero and Leander' remind us of Hood's interest in metaphor and simile, as do the 'elastic links' which in the lines 'To an Absentee' signally fail to rival Donne's compasses. Throughout the volume the influence of Keats, whose *Lamia* Hood had dramatized as a boy, is ubiquitous. Hood had the audacity to write an 'Ode: Autumn'—and the poetic skill to produce a reputable poem which is in no danger of ridicule. The other odes are less successful, but the sonnets contain some fine lines.

While these serious poems sold poorly, however, the *Odes and Addresses to Great People*, which had appeared two years before, were a resounding success. In their form the *Odes* represent the last indignity inflicted on the battered corpse of the eighteenth-century Pindaric. Coleridge praised the lack of sting in Hood's poems, and this lack of mordancy may be one reason why they do not survive as great satire survives: for all their technical expertise they remain brilliantly jocose journalism. As we read

[1] Thomas Hood (1799–1845) became a clerk about the age of thirteen, but in 1815 he was sent to Dundee on account of his delicate health. When he returned to London in 1817 he worked for some time with two firms of engravers, but in 1821 he was more suitably employed by Taylor and Hessey to help edit the *London Magazine*. He met the Londoners and collaborated with J. H. Reynolds (whose sister he had married in 1825) in *Odes and Addresses*. He was now a full-time writer and editor. At the end of 1834 he was beset by money difficulties, and he soon withdrew to the Continent so that he might earn enough to pay off his debts in full. He lived successively at Coblentz and Ostend. He returned to England in 1840 and edited Colburn's *New Monthly Magazine* for a time. Peel comforted him in his courageous last months by the award of a pension, which continued to be paid to his widow.

them we are often reminded of the eighteenth century, but more of its novelists than its poets. We are reminded how deeply Hood was influenced by Smollett by his Trunnion-like farewell to D. M. Moir. Having been apprenticed to an engraver early in his life, he remained a lifelong admirer of Hogarth; and we notice that such poems as the 'Ode to Mr. Malthus', the '*Friendly* Address to Mrs. Fry *in* Newgate', 'I'm going to Bombay', the under-ostler's 'Sonnet on Steam' and the ode to those in favour of the removal of Smithfield Market are illuminating documents on the history of his time. But although they resemble the paintings of Hogarth in this respect, they do not, like his pictures, remain works of art in their own right, so that Lamb's description of Hood as 'our half-Hogarth' is extremely apt.

Hood was a splendid human being, but we must not let our admiration for his courage blind us to the curious and unpleasant qualities that often appear in his verse. There is something sinister about his sense of humour: his pages are thronged with comic mourners and undertakers, and a corpse is always good for a horse-laugh. The nightmares of his imagination often burst out, like a skeleton falling from a cupboard. When this happens he puns his way out of the embarrassment. He began to pun as soon as he began to speak, and he died as he had lived. His puns are related to the interest in figurative language and in perceiving 'similarity in dissimilarity' that Wainewright noticed in his work. Each stanza of 'Faithless Sally Brown', for example, ends with a play on words, the last with the most famous of all:

> They went and told the sexton, and
> The sexton toll'd the bell.

One of the ways in which he uses puns may be regarded as a mode of Tieck's 'romantic irony': serious lines are followed, as Dryden said of Tassoni, by afterthoughts which 'turn them all into a pleasant ridicule'. So Hood tells us that he must 'die in harness like a Hero—or a horse'. As with Byron, we sense that the poet is on the defensive. The result is a juxtaposition of sentiment and humour rather than a fusion of passion and wit. To use Dryden's word, it is all rather 'boyish'. There is something pathological about Hood's punning: in his writings as in Cleveland's it becomes a nervous tic.

Three of his poems deserve particular mention. 'The Dream

of Eugene Aram, the Murderer' was based on an historical happening but owed its atmosphere to 'one of those unaccountable visions, which come upon us like frightful monsters . . . from the great black deeps of slumber'. 'The Last Man', a poem on a subject also attempted by Campbell, Beddoes, and (later) Mary Shelley, is even more impressive: something of the horror is due to the influence of *The Ancient Mariner*. 'The Song of the Shirt', which was inspired by a report in *The Times* and first published in *Punch* in 1843, is noteworthy for its celebrity in its own age. It 'ran through the land like wildfire . . . and . . . became the talk of the day'. The influence of such poems as 'The Lay of the Labourer' and 'The Bridge of Sighs', similarly inspired by actual cases mentioned in the Press, must have been very considerable. It is interesting to recall that Sir Robert Peel once told Hood that he had read almost everything that he had written: he praised 'the good sense and good feeling, which have taught you to infuse so much fun and merriment into writings correcting folly, and exposing absurdities'. Even so Hood sometimes felt that he had been deficient in charity, and in a remarkable letter to Peel written on his deathbed he protested against

> a literary movement in which I have had some share, a one-sided humanity, opposed to that Catholic Shaksperian sympathy, which felt with King as well as Peasant, and duly estimated the mortal temptations of both stations. . . . It should be the duty of our writers to draw [the different classes] nearer by kindly attraction, not to aggravate the existing repulsion, and place a wider moral gulf between Rich and Poor, with Hate on the one side and Fear on the other.

It is curious that Hood, of all men, should have reproached himself in this way. As he had once pointed out in a poem, he loved his neighbour 'far too well' to assail him with serious satire. Although such poems as 'My Tract' and the 'Ode to Rae Wilson, Esq.' are contributions to the chorus against cant which heralded the opening of the Victorian Age, Hood was too charitable to write satire with the sting and power of *Don Juan*. And so the force that might have directed a bullet towards the heart of the abuses of the time was used, time and again, to send up a series of puns as astonishing as a firework display, and as soon over.

There is all the difference in the world between the light verse of Hood and that of W. M. Praed.[1] With his fellow-Etonians John Hookham Frere and John Moultrie (remembered here for his brilliant *Lady Godiva*), Praed is one of a small group of men whose work forms a background to *Don Juan*. Like Byron these poets were naturally aristocratic and 'eighteenth-century' in their sympathies and chose to 'wander with pedestrian Muses' for reasons very different from those which led Wordsworth to advocate 'the real language of men'. As *The Etonian* (1820–1) reminds us—an extraordinary production, and surely the most gifted school magazine ever to appear—they were members of a 'circle of wit' who had the encouragement of knowing that what they wrote would be read with understanding. Praed was so precocious at Eton that his tutor considered that his 'scholarship' was already past its best when he reached the age of eighteen. His career there had been the opposite of Shelley's a few years before. Whereas Shelley completely failed to find an audience for his poetry at school (a failure which foreshadowed his later life), Praed found that his verses made him popular with his contemporaries as well as with the masters, and the boys at Eton were the prototype of the audience for which he was to write throughout his life. He was equally successful at Cambridge, where he became (in the words of Bulwer Lytton) 'to the University what Byron was to the world'. His attitude to contemporary poetry was not unlike that of Byron: he regarded *Endymion* as a Cockney effusion suitable for conversation at a dance, respected Wordsworth, but had a more instinctive admiration for Crabbe. He himself, we notice, could handle the pentameter couplet in the traditional manner, but he was more at home in short verse. It does not need the revealing rhyme of 'shoe-ties' and 'duties' in 'The Troubadour' to tell us that he was an admirer of *Hudibras*, to which these lines, for example, might easily be attributed:

> Resemblances begin to strike
> In things exceedingly unlike,
> All nouns, like statesmen, suit all places,
> And verbs, turned lawyers, hunt for cases.

[1] Winthrop Mackworth Praed (1802–39) had a brilliant career at Eton and at Trinity College, Cambridge, where he was elected a Fellow in 1827. Soon he became a barrister and entered Parliament. In 1834 he was appointed Secretary to the Board of Control under Peel. Most of his poems appeared in periodicals and annuals.

If he seldom reminds us of Pope, he often reminds us of Swift. The opening of 'Arrivals at a Watering-Place' is modelled on the 'Lines on the Death of Dr. Swift', and it is tempting to suppose that it was partly from Swift that Praed learned how to write idiomatic English in verse, and how to use a single, perfectly placed word, in the full assurance that his audience will take the point—as when he tells us the whole truth about one aspect of young love in the line

Some *hopes* of dying broken-hearted.

Yet to turn to Praed after reading Swift is to be struck by an absence of passion. Swift's weapon is a razor, Praed's a pair of exquisite scissors. For a parallel it is better to turn to another Augustan, Matthew Prior: 'To Elizabeth Winthrop' is precisely in Prior's manner, while 'An Everyday Character' echoes Prior's fine epitaph on 'Saunt'ring Jack and Idle Joan'. Like most of the Augustans, Praed is essentially an urban writer. He has no more than a gentlemanly feeling for the Picturesque: now that he is no longer young, he tells us—and he died at the age of 37—his imagination 'never wanders beyond Grosvenor-square'. It is fitting that he should have been an admirer of Matthew Green, for with Praed (as with his Augustan predecessors) the Spleen is an enemy to be kept at bay. His is the sober melancholy of the eighteenth-century Horatian, which has more in common with Gray's 'leucocholy' than with the ultimate depth of despair that was known to Swift. In this, as in other respects, he seems to have changed very little as he grew older, for at Eton his 'half-melancholy . . . veiled by levity' was noticed by the publisher Charles Knight. Praed comes nearest to 'speaking out' in this matter in one of his most unusual poems, 'Time's Song'.

Within his self-imposed limitations Praed has an extraordinary sureness of touch. It is remarkable how many of the English poets with the most unfailing sense of their native idiom have been sound or brilliant as classical scholars, and here Praed may be classed with men as different as George Herbert, Dryden, and Prior. It may have been his classical training that saved him from the Elizabethanizing that was the origin of so much of the worst writing in the period, as well as of some of the best. Whereas Darley is so enamoured of what he believes to be Elizabethan English that he often loses contact with English

altogether, Praed never violates the genius of the language. Light-hearted as his Tales are, for example, they are in a real sense better written than those of either Scott or Byron, and as we read them we come to see that his scrupulous regard for the grain of English was made possible by his remarkable command of metrical technique. Since he never put a foot wrong, he was never obliged to put a word wrong.

Praed's entry into political life in 1830 made it natural that he should try his hand at political verse, and some of the resulting poems are models of their kind; yet none of them transcends its occasion and challenges the description of major poetry, as does *Absalom and Achitophel*. Nor does it seem likely that he would have become a considerable political satirist if he had lived longer. He could write an excellent love lyric, when he chose, as he demonstrates in 'Oh fly with me! 'tis passion's hour'; but just as he instinctively turned away when he found himself on the verge of the language of passion, so he forbore from using the lash of satire. Almost the only occasion on which he employs mordant satire occurs in a suppressed stanza of his poem on George IV:

> He was the world's first gentleman,
> And made the appellation hideous.

Perhaps Praed was too 'well adjusted' (whatever we mean by the phrase) to be a major satirist; or perhaps Eton was, after all, too much of a forcing-house. As we study Praed we are reminded of Coleridge's view that as a boy the Younger Pitt acquired 'a premature and unnatural dexterity in the combination of words, which must of necessity have diverted his attention from present objects, obscured his impressions, and deadened his genuine feelings'. Although Praed was a very generous and likeable man, it would not be wholly untrue to apply to him what Coleridge went on to say of Pitt, that he was 'a plant sown and reared in a hot-house, for whom the very air that surrounded him, had been regulated . . . to whom the light of nature had penetrated only through glasses and covers'. When Praed was little more than a boy he wrote like a man of full maturity. It seems possible that some constraint of personal development was the price that he had to pay for his astonishing precocity.

From his early childhood onwards Coleridge's eldest son

Hartley was treated as a genius.[1] His father addressed him in 'Frost at Midnight' and 'The Nightingale', Wordsworth wrote a poem to him at the age of six, while Hazlitt twice painted his portrait. As we read of 'Ejuxria', the imaginary land of his childhood, and of the philosophical romance that he dictated to his mother, we are reminded of the Brontës. As a child he was a metaphysician, as a man he was to remain a child. Diminutive, brilliant in conversation, excluded from marriage and the domesticities for which he longed, he remained throughout his life a spiritual exile. He had a fine mind, as we can see in his letter to H. N. Coleridge analysing the genius of his father (8 May 1836); yet his yearnings were always for the past, and he was happy only in a household including a baby or a small girl. One of his sonnets opens aptly with the words

> Long time a child, and still a child.

A resigned sense of unworthiness, as in 'Poietes Apoietes', is the typical note in his most personal poems. Everywhere we find that combination of tenderness and sweetness that he himself singled out as characteristic of Wordsworth's later poetry. His fifth sonnet,

> What was't awaken'd first the untried ear
> Of that sole man that was all human kind?

has a quality of wondering innocence that reminds one of Edwin Muir a century later. 'Death-Bed Reflections of Michelangelo' is unusually powerful, while 'An Old Man's Wish' is in no way inferior to the better-known 'She is not fair to outward view'. It is not surprising that his second volume, to consist of poems in 'a higher strain', never appeared; yet it must be acknowledged that the fragmentary *Prometheus* shows him on the threshold of more powerful verse than one would have expected. The description of the storm is admirably done, and there are other memorable lines:

> For he shall hear us in the vocal gloom
> Of green Dodona's leafy wilderness.

[1] Hartley Coleridge (1796–1849) was the eldest son of S. T. C. He was educated at Ambleside School under the supervision of Southey, and then went to Merton College, Oxford. When a Probationer Fellow of Oriel he was dismissed for intemperance. He tried to earn a living first by journalism in London and then by teaching in Ambleside. In 1837–8 he was a master at Sedbergh School.

Yet it remains true that his characteristic occupation was writing a sonnet on his own inadequacy or addressing a lyric to a girl of eight. The poems published after his death reveal his ability to write an occasional memorable line: it would be difficult to find a more apt description of the Sublime than the line ''Tis the Eternal struggling out of Time' or to better the simile 'Like Patience slow subsiding to Despair'. But for the most part these later poems merely confirm the impression of a muted, limited accomplishment already made by his earlier work. Time, memory, and regret are the recurring notes in the resigned music of his verse, which forms a sad, ironic postscript to the work of his great father.

When he was an old man Bryan Waller Procter, who wrote under the name of 'Barry Cornwall', claimed to have known 'far more literary men than any other person' of the time.[1] He was at school with Byron, and lived to salute the mature work of Browning. Although Byron treated his poetry with unusual forbearance, Procter wrote in what might almost be regarded as the standard manner of his time: he often reminds us of Leigh Hunt, though he lacks his tendency to amorous banality and also his flashes of near-genius. He was influenced by both Wordsworth and Byron, shared in the contemporary passion for the Elizabethans, loved Greek mythology and Italian literature, and often reminds us of the interest in painting which was characteristic of so many of the poets of the age. As he acknowledges in his *Autobiographical Fragment*, he lacked both genius and ambition and wrote merely because he enjoyed writing. For him poetry represented an escape from the humdrum practicalities of the law, but one has only to contrast him with Keats to see how limited was his notion of escape. Whereas Keats adventured beyond the Realm of Flora and Old Pan, Procter remained in it, and experienced it much less fully. It is not surprising that Keats found that Procter's poems 'teased' him: 'They are composed of Amiability, the Seasons, the Leaves, the Moon &c. upon which he rings . . . triple bob majors.'

[1] Bryan Waller Procter (1787–1874) practised as a solicitor in London and eventually became a prosperous conveyancer. He began to contribute to the *Literary Gazette* in 1815 and became the friend of Leigh Hunt and Lamb and later of Dickens. He became a barrister and was from 1832 to 1861 a metropolitan commissioner in lunacy. He lived to the age of 87. The poetess Adelaide Anne Procter was his eldest child.

The greater part of Procter's first volume consisted of Dramatic Scenes of the sort that owed their popularity at this time to the depressing condition of the theatre. Lamb thought very highly of these scenes, but for us it is difficult not to ask what end is achieved by writing scenes from dramas which were never intended to be completed and which would have been singularly pointless if they had been. Procter seems to have chosen all the wrong stories from Boccaccio: there is something rather silly about his broken hearts and noble renunciations. He completely lacked the flair that Browning shows in his dramatic monologues for choosing a single moment in the life of a man by which the whole of his existence may be laid bare. The protagonist of *Marcian Colonna* (1820) is slightly more of a character than those of most of Procter's Dramatic Scenes, yet it remains true that this presentation of the ill-starred hero of the period fails to seize on the reader's imagination. Something relaxed and unimpressive about his handling of metre also appears in *A Sicilian Story* (1820) in which, as he so often does, he uses neither couplets nor stanzas but loosely organized verse paragraphs which rhyme in a rather random manner. In the title-poem he retells the story that Keats had used in *Isabella*, but substitutes 'the heart for the head of the lover'. The main interest of the Tales in which he uses *ottava rima* is that they demonstrate that the idiom of *Beppo* and *Don Juan* is not as easily attained as one might suppose. As we read these Tales we do not get the impression that what the poet is writing falls naturally into verse: the peculiar charm of the metre. Too often he is forced to use an awkward turn of expression. 'The man whose critical gall is not stirred up by such *ottava rimas* as Barry Cornwall's', as Shelley wrote to Peacock, 'may safely be conjectured to possess no gall at all. The world is pale with the sickness of such stuff.' Procter's one dramatic attempt, *Mirandola*, ran for sixteen nights, with Macready and Miss Foote in the main parts; but although there is some interest in the relationship between the father and son, on the whole it is a tragedy of situation rather than of character. The play is full of Elizabethan reminiscences, the verse being simple and Fletcherian (very different from the bombast of Maturin), with passages marked which are not designed for the stage. It is interesting to notice that the prologue denies that 'large Theatres the Drama mar'. In *The Flood of Thessaly* (1823) there are

passages in which the blank verse shows considerable power—

> . . The great Eagle still
> In his home brooded, inaccessible,
> Or, when the gloomy morning seemed to break,
> Floated in silence o'er the shoreless seas

—yet it is clear that Procter has chosen a theme beyond his imaginative reach, and we can only be glad that he did not attempt to develop it further. It is revealing to compare the vision of felicity with which the poem closes with the serene and towering eloquence of the comparable passage in *Prometheus Unbound.*

There is something unfinished and inconclusive about many of Procter's short poems, as there is about his Dramatic Scenes. He was much given to writing fragments and sets of stanzas that have no completeness in themselves. He can write agreeably and 'poetically', but he is always sounding the same note:

> Like the low voice of Syrinx, when she ran
> Into the forests from Arcadian Pan:
> Or sad Oenone's when she pined away
> For Paris.

It is not enough to be enamoured of Greek mythology: it is necessary to do something with it, and of this Procter was incapable. His Muse is blameless and bookish, spoilt perhaps, as Byron feared, 'by green tea, and the praises of Pentonville and Paradise Row'. One reason for his surprising popularity in his own day was no doubt the absence of disturbing features in his verse. In one of his prefaces he pointed out that he had avoided both 'politics and polemics', but with these disquieting subjects a great deal of life seems to be excluded. In his language we notice the absence of the nerve and sinew of English: in his poetry as a whole we notice the absence of human life. Too often Procter is not a poet but merely a poetical person. *English Songs and other Smaller Poems* (1832) were an attempt to make good what he regarded as a serious deficiency in our literature. Unfortunately they lack the qualities that prevent a song from ever being forgotten. Having had their day they now rest in peace.

'Barry Cornwall' occasionally reminds us of Peacock, a man with a much more vigorous mind who was known to a small circle of readers as a poet before he wrote the satiric tales discussed in Chapter VII. Peacock's literary career falls into two parts. In the pivotal year of 1818 he ceased to be a gentleman of leisure, entered the India House, produced his last published volume of verse, and scored a decided success with *Nightmare Abbey*. He was soon to write 'The Four Ages of Poetry', in which he asserted that 'A poet in our times is a semi-barbarian in a civilized community':

> He lives in the days that are past. His ideas, thoughts, feelings, associations, are all with barbarous manners, obsolete customs, and exploded superstitions. The march of his intellect is like that of a crab, backward. The brighter the light diffused around him by the progress of reason, the thicker is the darkness of antiquated barbarism, in which he buries himself like a mole, to throw up the barren hillocks of his Cimmerian labours.

His own early poetry might be the work of a respectable minor poet of the eighteenth century. *Palmyra* is a sort of Pindaric Ode in which the poet meditates on the fact that 'Time and change have absolute dominion over every thing terrestrial but virtue and the mind'. The 1806 version is explicitly Christian in its conclusion, but in the improved text of 1812 we notice that Peacock has already moved away from revealed religion. 'To a Young Lady, Netting', might be the work of Waller, and it would be easy to assign others of these early poems to writers of the previous epochs. We notice a considerable variety of stanzas and metrical forms: it is tempting to speculate that the anapaests of 'Fiolfar' may have given Browning a hint for 'How they brought the good news from Ghent to Aix'. *The Genius of the Thames*, in which Peacock mentions Denham, Pope, and Thomson, is a loco-descriptive poem which contains some agreeable passages:

> As now the purple heather blows,
> Where once impervious forests rose;
> So perish from the burthened ground
> The monuments of human toil:
> Where cities shone, where castles frowned,
> The careless ploughman turns the soil.

It is only once or twice that we feel that the poem is becoming a little ridiculous in its backward-looking:

> O'er Nuneham Courtnay's flowery glades
> Soft breezes wave their fragrant wings,
> And still, amid the haunted shades,
> The tragic harp of Mason rings.

It needed a retrospective ear to catch the reedy music of *Elfrida* in the year of *Childe Harold's Pilgrimage*. *The Philosophy of Melancholy*, which also appeared in 1812, is a didactic poem which occasionally and faintly reminds us of Pope or *The Vanity of Human Wishes* but which remains of interest primarily as a document of the vogue for melancholy at this time. Peacock's statement in the analysis of the second part that 'in art, as in nature, those pleasures, in which melancholy mingles, are more powerful, and more permanent, than those which have their origin in lighter sensations', is of particular interest as the assertion of the man who was soon to be telling Shelley that he was determined to 'make a stand' against 'the encroachments of black bile'. But the most ambitious of Peacock's poems is *Rhododaphne*, which Shelley described as 'the transfused essence of Lucian, Petronius and Apuleius', and which describes how Anthemion is stolen from his lover Calliroë by the enchantress Rhododaphne until the latter is killed by Uranian Love and the lovers are reunited. This poem, with its characteristically donnish preface and notes, throws light on the attraction which Greek mythology held for so many writers of the time. Like Keats in *Endymion*, Peacock wishes to touch again 'the beautiful mythology of Greece',

> And from the songs that charmed their latest ear,
> A yet ungathered wreath, with fingers bold,
> I weave, of bleeding love and magic mysteries drear.

*Rhododaphne* is full of the century's nostalgia for a Greek world that never existed except in the realm of poetry:

> In ocean's caves no Nereid dwells:
> No Oread walks the mountain-dells:
> The streams no sedge-crowned Genii roll
> From bounteous urn: great Pan is dead:
> The life, the intellectual soul
> Of vale, and grove, and stream, has fled
> For ever with the creed sublime
> That nursed the Muse of earlier time.

Although the poem is full of pleasant passages there is hardly one that insists on being quoted. The quality that is almost everywhere absent may be illustrated by a single quotation from near the end of Canto III:

> Till full from Athos' distant height
> The sun poured down his golden beams
> Scattering the mists like morning dreams,
> And rocks and lakes and isles and streams
> Burst, like creation, into light.

The imaginative power of the last line is extremely rare in Peacock. At first one is tempted to say that his verse is too poetical, yet on reflection we realize that it would be a more accurate account of the matter to say that it is not in fact poetical enough. What we miss is the sense of urgency that comes from a poet's having something real to say, and the imaginative vitality which (if he is a true poet) will accompany it. One has only to examine his diction to see that it is not the kind of language a man uses when he is writing imaginatively. Except for his habit of introducing an occasional learned word—'hypæthric' and 'primogenial' both occur in the first eight lines of *Rhododaphne*—we notice that the diction is highly conventional. It is too easy to guess which epithet will accompany any given noun. This combines with the lack of reality in the story to make the reader indifferent about what is to happen next. In the first note to *The Genius of the Thames* Peacock had remarked that

> The tutelary spirits, that formerly animated the scenes of nature, still continue to adorn the visions of poetry; though they are now felt only as the creatures of imagination, and no longer possess that influence of real existence, which must have imparted many enviable sensations to the mind of the ancient polytheist.

The trouble with Peacock's mythological beings, as with those in most of the writers of the time, is that they have no reality even as 'creatures of the imagination'. As he was soon to point out himself, 'we know . . . that there are no Dryads in Hyde-park nor Naiads in the Regent's-canal', and since mythology was his main source of poetic inspiration he did well to turn from verse to prose, from Anthemion and Carilloë and Rhododaphne to Scythrop and Marionetta and Stella. Yet before we leave his poetry something must be said of one fine forgotten poem and of the songs which are a characteristic ingredient of

his satiric tales. Unfortunately only the first half of 'Newark Abbey: August, 1842, with a Reminiscence of August, 1807' can be quoted here, but that may be enough to draw attention to a poem that seems to have escaped the attention of critics and anthologists:

I gaze, where Autumn's sunbeam falls
Along these gray and lonely walls,
Till in its light absorbed appears
The lapse of five-and-thirty years.

If change there be, I trace it not
In all this consecrated spot:
No new imprint of Ruin's march
On roofless wall and frameless arch:
The hills, the woods, the fields, the stream,
Are basking in the self-same beam:
The fall, that turns the unseen mill,
As then it murmured, murmurs still:
It seems, as if in one were cast
The present and the imaged past,
Spanning, as with a bridge sublime,
That awful lapse of human time,
That gulph, unfathomably spread
Between the living and the dead.

Peacock drew attention to the fourteen poems in *The Misfortunes of Elphin* by printing a list of them at the beginning of the book, and it comes as something of a surprise to find that the tales contain between fifty and sixty pieces of verse, apart from the Aristophanic comedy in *Gryll Grange*. There is a remarkable variety in these lyrics, from the defiant vigour of the drinking songs to the meditative note of 'The Sun-Dial' in *Melincourt*, from Clarinda's 'In the days of old' in *Crotchet Castle* to the admirable 'Song of the Four Winds' in *The Misfortunes of Elphin*. Yet it is inevitable that we should remember best the parody of Byron and Byronism in *Nightmare Abbey*:

There is a fever of the spirit,
  The brand of Cain's unresting doom,
Which in the lone dark souls that bear it
  Glows like the lamp in Tullia's tomb:
Unlike that lamp, its subtle fire
  Burns, blasts, consumes its cell, the heart,
Till, one by one, hope, joy, desire,
  Like dreams of shadowy smoke depart.

'Admirable', as Mr. Glowry comments. 'Let us all be unhappy together.'

Moore once pointed out that two of his principal incentives to writing had been an instinctive 'turn for rhyme and song', encouraged by the 'gay and sociable circle' in which he had been brought up, and the profound feelings aroused in him, as an Irishman and a lover of liberty, 'by the mighty change . . . working in the political aspect of Europe' in his youth and 'the stirring influence it had begun to exercise on the spirit and hopes of Ireland'.[1] If we add to these his perpetual need of money—he was a professional writer for most of his life, and a highly successful one—we have the main motives that led him to write. His early version of the *Odes of Anacreon* (1800) was followed by *The Poetical Works of the late Thomas Little* (Moore was a diminutive man), a collection of amorous poems which vary from the tolerable to the sort of love poetry that would make a cat wring its hands. A review of *Epistles, Odes, and Other Poems* (1806) in the *Edinburgh Review* made Moore's work a centre of controversy. Jeffrey's strictures on 'the languid, loving girl of Hayti' and her companions are of the sort that a Moderator of the Church of Scotland might pass on the *Folies-Bergère*, but it must be admitted that there is something rather distasteful in the mixture of licence and sentimentality which we find in these poems: they are vulgar in a characteristically Regency way. The publication of the *Irish Melodies* between 1808 and 1834 finally established Moore's reputation. He once wrote that his poetical talent was rooted in 'a strong and inborn feeling for music' so that it was an appropriate task for him to supply words to accompany 'a collection of the best Original Irish Melodies': words 'containing, as frequently as possible, allusions to the manners and history of the country'. The music—most of

[1] Thomas Moore (1779–1852) studied at Trinity College, Dublin, and entered the Middle Temple in 1799. After a remarkable social and literary success on his first arrival in London, he had a short period as Admiralty Registrar in Bermuda, and then returned to England by way of the United States. His *Irish Melodies* established him as the national poet of Ireland. He also took to satirical verse and became the friend of Byron and Leigh Hunt. When his deputy in Bermuda defaulted he became liable for £6,000 and took refuge abroad, visiting Italy with Lord John Russell. At Venice Byron presented him with his Memoirs. In 1822 the debt to the Admiralty was paid, and Moore returned to England. After Byron's death Moore consented to the destruction of the Memoirs, wrote a biography of Byron, and edited his writings. He remained a celebrity for the rest of his life, receiving a literary pension in 1835 and a Civil List pension as well fifteen years later.

which he knew to belong to the eighteenth century—was the *raison d'être* of the whole design, and the songs lose immensely if they are considered in isolation. Moore apologizes, for example, for 'occasional breaches of the laws of rhythm, which the task of adapting words to airs demands of a poet', in a sentence which might serve as a reminder to critics of Sir Thomas Wyatt. His main themes are love and patriotism, and he is often at his best when he laments the passing of the old days, as in 'The harp that once through Tara's halls' and 'Weep on, weep on, your hour is past'. The mystical and other-worldly quality of the Gaelic imagination was foreign to Moore's temperament, as it was, on the whole, to that of his age. His subject is the Irish character in society. The political spirit of the songs is always liberal; yet it is hard to agree with those of Moore's enemies who believed that their tendency was 'mischievous'. Too sentimental to be mischievous, they are rather songs of the sort that a sophisticated imperialism might connive at as a harmless safety-valve for national aspirations. A note to the *Irish Melodies* oddly confirms this view by pointing out that a publication 'of this nature' could never be intended for the lower classes, 'that gross and inflammable region of society', and claiming that the book could only be found 'upon the pianofortes of the rich and the educated,—of those who can afford to have their national zeal a little stimulated, without exciting much dread of the excesses into which it may hurry them'. The most severe comment was made by Beddoes, who wrote that Moore's 'song style is the best *false* one I know and glitters like broken glass—he calls us and will show us a beautiful prospect in heav'n or earth, gives us a tube to look thro', which looks like a telescope and is a kaleidoscope'. If we deny the *Irish Melodies* and Moore's other songs any trace of greatness it is not merely because they betray the lack of true imagination but also because in them we look in vain for the economy and purity of diction characteristic of great songs.

Someone has said that literary history deals with good books that no one read when they were first published, and bad books that no one should have read. There can be no doubt into which category *Lalla Rookh* falls. As has been mentioned in Chapter I, Longmans agreed to pay £3,000 for a poem 'upon some Oriental subject, and of those Quarto dimensions which Scott . . . had rendered the regular poetical standard'. The resultant poem

consists of four romances told to the beautiful Lalla Rookh as her splendid bridal procession makes its way from Delhi to Cashmere. The task of criticizing the stories may be left to Fadladeen, Great Nazir of the Haram, who comments on each story much in the manner of the *Edinburgh Review*:

> The chief personages of the story were, if he rightly understood them, an ill-favoured gentleman, with a veil over his face; —a young lady, whose reason went and came, according as it suited the poet's convenience to be sensible or otherwise; —and a youth in one of those hideous Bucharian bonnets, who took the aforesaid gentleman in a veil for a Divinity . . . From such materials . . . what can be expected? . . . With respect to the style, it was worthy of the matter.

Fortunately for Moore and his publisher the public by no means agreed with Fadladeen, and twenty editions, as well as numerous translations, had made their appearance by 1840.

Moore's feeling of buoyancy at the success of *Lalla Rookh* helped to inspire the light-hearted satire of *The Fudge Family in Paris*. His 'natural turn . . . for the lighter skirmishing of satire' had been apparent while he was still a boy in Dublin, when he became a member of a club one of whose objects 'was to burlesque, good-humouredly, the forms and pomps of royalty'. In 1808 he went on to publish *Corruption and Intolerance*, attempts (as he acknowledges) at 'the stately, Juvenalian style of satire'; but in spite of the occasional eloquence of these poems, and of the qualified success of *The Sceptic* (1809), which is more familiar and argumentative, it was in a less formal type of satire that he found his most natural expression. *Intercepted Letters* (1813) led on to *The Fudge Family in Paris* (1818), a series of letters in verse suggested by Anstey's *Bath Guide*. The serious intention behind the poem is most evident in the letters of the enthusiastic young Phelim Connor, but the best passages are the anapaestic epistles in which the young Fudges reveal their mindlessness, and the pompous letters to Castlereagh by the time-serving Mr. Fudge. In *The Fudges in England* (1835) Moore directs his satire against an unscrupulous Irish priest turned Protestant evangelist and against some of the literary absurdities of the time. The charming Miss Fanny begins by contributing poems to the Annuals and finally produces 'A Romaunt, in twelve Cantos, entitled "Woe Woe!" ' Her 'Irregular Ode' and her 'Stanzas to my Shadow; or, Why?—What?—How?' are excellent

parodies of the modish poetry of the age. The lighter satirical poems of Moore are the verbal equivalents of the cartoons of Gillray and his contemporaries, and there is no better way of reminding ourselves of the atmosphere of the time than by dipping into these witty pieces of political improvisation.

There is no need to say much of the other minor and minimus poets of the period, though several of them were much more widely read than most of their betters. The most remarkable features of the *Poems* (1808) of Felicia Dorothea Browne (later Mrs. Hemans) are the precocity of the author (they were written between the ages of eight and thirteen) and the length of the list of subscribers, which begins with the Prince of Wales and includes a thousand names.[1] In 1812 she published *The Domestic Affections*, while from 1816 another volume appeared almost every year until her death in 1835. In her work we find what may be loosely termed the new sensibility chastened and rendered thoroughly respectable: 'Turning from the dark and degraded, whether in subject or sentiment,' as D. M. Moir put it in his *Lectures on Poetical Literature*, 'she seeks out those verdant oases in the desert of human life, on which the affections may most pleasantly rest.' She took the pulse of her time, and helped to prevent it from quickening. Elaborate poems on the deaths of the Princess Charlotte and of the King himself put her loyalty beyond question, while in *Modern Greece* (1817) she had succeeded in the remarkable undertaking of producing a sort of respectable *Childe Harold's Pilgrimage*. The general level of her work is high, but unfortunately it almost always stops short of memorable poetry. Many of her better things, such as the line 'Blend with the plaintive murmur of the deep', might be the work of a poetical committee. For her, we feel, poetry was a feminine accomplishment more difficult than piano-playing and embroidery but no less respectable. She has a definite affinity with Scott in her fluency, her love of the picturesque, and her refusal to affront conventional morality. To descend a little lower, she might be described as a female Campbell—or Campbell might be described as a male Mrs. Hemans. What we miss in her work is

[1] Mrs. Hemans (1793–1835) was born Felicia Dorothea Browne. Her marriage with Captain Alfred Hemans at the age of 19 was unhappy and she separated from him six years later. The 'Egeria' of Maria Jane Jewsbury's *Three Histories*, she lived much at Dublin and early became a well-known literary figure and an acquaintance of Scott and Wordsworth. Her writings were extremely popular, not least in America.

poetic individuality. We read her, we commend, and we forget. In her precocity Letitia Elizabeth Landon rivalled Mrs. Hemans, but in temperament she was very different, and it is impossible not to be attracted and moved by the career of this headstrong and gifted young woman, so piquant and kitten-like in what Rossetti called the 'funnily-drawn plate' by Maclise, with her talked-of exploits, her friendships with Bulwer Lytton and Lady Blessington, her flights from the amorous Maginn, and her mysterious death in Africa.[1] William Jerdan was her first sponsor, and she began to contribute to the *Literary Gazette* when she was only thirteen. Her first volume of any note was *The Improvisatrice* (1824); while from *The Golden Violet* (1827), which contains a verbal portrait of Bulwer's Rosina, she is said to have made £1,000. The 'snub-nosed Brompton Sappho', as Disraeli called her, was as impulsive in her writing as in her life, and the best of her work has the merits of brilliant improvisation—so reminding us in some respects of the work of Byron. In the preface to *The Venetian Bracelet* (1828) she provides a spirited defence of a woman's right to take love as the subject of her poetry. Some of her best lyrics are in simple measures like the ballad-stanza:

I hear them speak of love, the deep,
The true, and mock the name;
Mock at all high and early truth,
And I too do the same.

At times we feel that her technique is not quite adequate to the intensity of her feeling—an unusual thing with a woman poet. At her best she writes with a simplicity that reminds us, at least, of the simplicity of great poetry:

I cannot bear to think of this,—
Oh, leave me to my weeping;
A few tears for that grave my heart,
Where hope in death is sleeping.

[1] The first volume of poems by 'L. E. L.' (1802–38) was published when she was 19. She contributed a great deal to periodicals and popular annuals and edited *The Drawing Room Scrapbook* from 1832. One of her best novels is *Ethel Churchill*, 1837. *Traits and Trials of Early Life* includes some passages no doubt founded on her own experience. Her first engagement (possibly to John Forster, the biographer of Dickens) was suddenly broken off and in 1838 she married George Maclean, governor of Cape Coast Castle in Africa. A few weeks after her arrival there she died mysteriously, apparently from an accidental overdose of prussic acid.

In the course of a distinguished career Henry Hart Milman was Dean of St. Paul's and Professor of Poetry at Oxford.[1] While he was still at Eton he wrote excellent verse, and 'The Belvidere Apollo' is one of the few Oxford Prize Poems that bear re-reading. He wrote *Fazio* when he was an undergraduate in an 'attempt to revive our old national drama with greater simplicity of plot'. It was written 'with some view to the stage', but Milman comments that it must be a good thing for a play to be printed before it is performed because it is 'impossible, on the present scale of our Theatres, for more than a certain proportion of those present to see or hear'. In an intellectual way he seems to have understood the nature of drama; but the important scenes are almost too obvious to be moving, while the morality of the piece is pervertedly severe, involving, as it does, a wife's informing against her husband, vindicating his name after his death, and then dying herself. *Samor, Lord of the Bright City* (1818), which was begun at Eton, is a remarkable achievement for so young a man, and remains of interest because of Milman's contention that English still lacks 'the perfect model of *narrative* blank verse'. Unlike most of Milton's eighteenth-century imitators, Milman realizes that Milton's verse is not 'for common use'; nor, he argues, can the styles of Crowe's *Lewesdon Hill*, Akenside's *Pleasures of the Imagination*, or *The Excursion* provide what is required, a metre which, 'sustaining a long poem above the level of prose, adapts itself with natural and unforced numbers to the infinite variety of thought, feeling, character, situation, interest, and even style, which must animate any long narrative poem which aspires to live'. *Samor* was followed by three of the dramas on religious subjects which form an imaginative accompaniment to Milman's laborious and creditable work as a Church historian. There was a vogue at this time for heroic poems on Biblical subjects which might all have been illustrated, like Atherstone's *Fall of Nineveh*, by John Martin. Designed to support the cause of 'virtue and religion', these works may be regarded as a sort of literary equivalent of

[1] Henry Hart Milman (1791–1868) went from Eton to Brasenose College, Oxford. He won the Newdigate Prize and the Chancellor's Essay Prize, becoming a Fellow of Brasenose in 1814 and publishing *Fazio* in 1815. He became incumbent of St. Mary's, Reading, four years later. In 1827 he was Bampton Lecturer. From 1821 to 1831 he was Professor of Poetry at Oxford. In 1849 he became Dean of St. Paul's. In the later part of his life he was better known as a divine and church historian than as a poet.

the Oratorio, and it is not surprising that they failed to compete with the sonorous uplift of such a celebration as the Crystal Palace Handel Festival. Milman once confessed to 'a latitudinarian love for poetry', adding that much as he loved Hebrew poetry, Greek, Latin, Italian, Spanish, German, and English, he could yet 'reserve some admiration for the exotic and barbarous ... but still occasionally beautiful and even sublime conceptions of the East'. He was led into such studies (as he tells us with engaging frankness) by running out of subjects for his professorial lectures, when he took the unusual course of widening his field of knowledge. In his volume of translations from the Sanskrit, *Nala and Damayanti* (1835), he carried on the work of Sir William Jones.

Although most of Keble's work belongs to the next volume, the publication of *The Christian Year* in 1827 must be recorded here. In preferring him to George Herbert, Oliver Elton does something monstrous: to read even the best of Keble after a poem like 'The Flower', 'The Collar' or 'Love' is to turn from the work of a great religious poet to that of a well-bred and talented versifier. It is instructive to compare the variety of Herbert's metrical patterns and the rich complexity of his poetic techniques with the limitations of Keble's technical range. Keble puts the Christian life, with all its complications and its struggles, into the pint-pot of his simple measures. But, of course, it is hardly fair to compare Keble's work with great poetry. His poems are religious or devotional exercises rather than poems of religious experience: their affinity is with the 'La Corona' sonnets of Donne, not with the great sonnets that succeeded them.

The name of Charles Wells should be borne in mind by those who are interested in this period, because it acts as a sobering reminder.[1] In an age when many young men of brilliant promise died young he, who was not the least promising of them, lived on into old age without in any way fulfilling the promise of his youth. A friend of Keats, who was only five years his senior, he died in 1879, the year which saw the publication of

[1] Charles Jeremiah Wells (1800–79) was educated at Edmonton, where he met Keats early in his life. He offended Keats by playing a practical joke on his brother Tom, but remained a friend of Hazlitt and Leigh Hunt. From 1820 to 1830 he was a solicitor in London: then he withdrew to the country. Ten years later he taught English for a while in Brittany. In 1874 he destroyed his manuscripts. He died at Marseilles.

Henry James's *Daisy Miller*. He published *Joseph and his Brethren* (1824) in his early twenties; but although he wrote a good deal more throughout his life it is only as the author of that long dramatic poem that he is ever remembered. While the praises of Rossetti and Swinburne now seem exaggerated, Wells shows considerable power in the handling of his story and in the way in which he writes blank verse. He is not only so steeped in the work of the Elizabethans that he can produce at will a passage that might come from a contemporary of Shakespeare's: he is also under the influence of the later work of Milton, and occasional lines in his strange drama have an air of austere distinction that reminds us irresistibly of *Paradise Regained*.

While there is room for disagreement about the merits of *Joseph and his Brethren*, the worthlessness of Bernard Barton's work is no longer in dispute.[1] Yet he also serves as a reminder—a reminder of the fact that the English, who have produced the greatest poetical literature in the world, have a deep instinctive preference for the third-rate. In an age in which *The Excursion*, the poems of Shelley and Keats, and Clare's *Shepherd's Calendar* lingered unsold in the booksellers' shops, Bernard Barton enjoyed a very considerable celebrity. The names of the Queen Dowager (12 copies), Prince Albert, and the Archbishop of Canterbury head the list of subscribers to his *Poems and Letters*, while the Society of Friends were so proud of their poet that they raised a large subscription to allow him more leisure. One of the paradoxes about him is that a man who had read so much good literature, and discussed it with Charles Lamb, should have caught so little by infection. The explanation seems to be that he was rather stupid, and very idle. 'How thankful I am that I have written what good-natured critics call poetry!', he once exclaimed. As a poet he always remained an 'Amateur', as the title of one of his collections acknowledged, and an amateur in the least honourable sense

[1] Bernard Barton (1784–1849) was the son of a Quaker manufacturer. At the age of 14 he was apprenticed to a shopkeeper and eight years later he married his employer's daughter. He worked as a tutor in Liverpool for a year, meeting the Roscoe circle, and then became a clerk in a bank at Woodridge, where he remained for the rest of his life. By 1812 he was corresponding with Southey, and ten years later his remonstrance to Lamb on the tone of his references to Quakers led to a lifelong friendship. In 1824 J. J. Gurney and other Friends raised £1,200 for his benefit. In 1845 he dedicated *Household Verses* to Queen Victoria, and soon Peel secured him a pension. Edward FitzGerald married his daughter and wrote a Memoir to accompany his literary remains.

of the word. He was far too lazy to make any determined effort to learn his art, and never completely conquered his Quaker scruples about the language of poetry: was the critic right who reproached him with using the profane word 'November' to describe the eleventh month? He scrupulously observes that the hardships of old age

> Might move the very hearts of stones,
> If stones had hearts to heed them

—a chastening qualification. He has no feeling for language, and displays a positive preference for the anti-poetical—as we see in such a phrase as 'however that may be'. In his work the worst of Wordsworth—'The Daddy', as he called him—was watered down until it could be consumed by the humblest domestic circle. Talking of a patriarch he wishes that we

> From the same hidden fount could inly quaff:
> We trust in outward aids too much by half!

It is a pity that he did not write his projected autobiography: it would have been a capital curiosity. When the Scots have made so much of McGonagall, it is curious that the English should have allowed Bernard Barton to remain unhonoured.

Like the popularity of Barton's poetry, that of the Annuals that proliferated in the 1820's and 1830's is a fact to be reckoned with by the historian of taste. The idea came from Germany, and in 1823 Rudolph Ackerman[1] produced his *Forget-me-Not*, the first of many volumes 'expressly designed to serve as tokens of remembrance, friendship, or affection'. Alaric Watts, himself a minor poet, soon followed with his *Literary Souvenir*, Samuel Carter with *The Amulet* (intended specifically for the amusement of 'serious persons'), and Messrs. Smith and Elder with *Friendship's Offering* in 1827. One of the best of the numerous other Annuals was *The Anniversary*, edited by the talented Allan Cunningham.

[1] Rudolph Ackerman (1764–1834) was born in Saxony and educated at Schneeberg. After a period in Paris he moved to London and in 1795 he opened a printshop in the Strand. The establishment of lithography as a fine art in this country is due to him. In 1817 he set up a press and engaged Prout and other eminent artists. He did a great deal to relieve the sufferers from the distress in Germany after the battle of Leipzig, and also employed many Spanish *émigrés*. From 1813 his Wednesday Literary Evenings were well known. He produced *The Repository of Arts, Literature, Fashions, Manufactures, etc.* from 1809 to 1828, Rowlandson supplying many of the plates.

A great deal of thought was given to the appearance of the Annuals, which were as carefully got up as boxes of chocolates. *The Literary Souvenir*, for example, was a small octavo 'bound in pale green, pink, or violet boards, ornamented by an engraved design by Corbould', and with the edges of the leaves tastefully gilded. No expense was spared to ensure that these books would form a fitting ornament to grace the boudoir or the sofa-table. Ackerman was a print-seller, and from the first engravings were an important feature of the Annuals. While some of the illustrations are of a surpassing silliness, others are the work of highly competent artists and must have played their part in introducing the visual arts to people little acquainted with them. The fact that the Annuals were intended for women—for one's wife, one's fiancée, or one's maiden aunt—dictated the nature of the literary contents, no less than their appearance. 'L. E. L. will be ready for you on Monday with some beautiful verses,' his publisher once wrote to Alaric Watts, 'but don't give us more poetry than prose. Poetry is beyond many of the purchasers of this description of book.' But on the whole there was no objection to poetry, and when one first looks into these volumes it is exciting to see the great names of the period as well as interesting minor names. While there are still discoveries to be made, however—some of Clare's poems in Annuals appear to have been overlooked—most of the contributions by considerable poets turn out to be reprints of their least important pieces. What was most in demand was poetry that exhibited that happy blend of 'sentiment purified by taste' which Bowles was thought to have introduced. The aim (to quote from *The Fudges in England*) was a volume

> Where all such ingredients—the flowery, the sweet,
> And the gently narcotic—are mix'd *per* receipt,
> With a hand so judicious, we've no hesitation
> To say that—'bove all, for the young generation—
> 'Tis an elegant, soothing, and safe preparation.

A due caution had to be exercised even with the cover. 'The design for the covers', Watts wrote to his publishers, 'instead of being naked women, should be something emblematic of the contents—Poetry, the Arts, etc; in short, polite literature.'

Whether the vogue for Annuals was a good thing for literature is most uncertain. At first sight it might seem so, since publishers often paid the contributors well. 'The world . . . seems

mad about "Forget me Nots" and Christmas boxes,' Scott wrote in 1828; 'here has been Heath the artist offering me £800 per ann: to take charge of such a concern.' The publisher of *The Keepsake* claimed to have spent no less than eleven thousand guineas on a single issue. But most of the serious writers of the time looked askance at the new commodity, even if they were prepared to contribute. Southey, who knew the literary market, complained that 'these Annuals have grievously hurt the sale of all such books as used to be bought as presents. In this way'—he adds—'my poems have suffered greatly—to the diminution, I doubt not, of half their sale.' Wordsworth told Rogers that he thought that *The Pleasures of Memory* had 'suffered in the common blight', adding that 'the ornamented annuals, those greedy receptacles of trash, those Bladders upon which the Boys of Poetry try to swim, are the cause'. For the literary historian these faded volumes retain some interest: partly because the occasional exceptional volume contains a good deal of significant work (such as *The Keepsake* for 1829, which contains two of Scott's finest short stories, as well as contributions by Wordsworth, Coleridge, Southey, Lockhart, and Shelley): and partly because it is useful to see the work of major writers surrounded by the forgotten literature of their period. To glance through the Annuals, for example, is to be reminded that the 'Ode on a Grecian Urn' was the product of a period in which many poems were written on individual paintings and works of sculpture. Yet while a comprehensive index to the Annuals would be of use, an excursion among them soon becomes fatiguing. Their epitaph may be found in *Middlemarch*, whose author was not the sort of woman for whom they were intended. Lydgate laughs scornfully at a volume of *The Keepsake* and wonders which 'will turn out to be the silliest—the engraving or the writing', so disconcerting young Plymdale, who points out that 'there are a great many celebrated people writing in "The Keepsake" ' and adds that this is the first time that he has 'heard it called silly'. It was in fact by no means the first time that it had been called silly. When Allan Cunningham told Southey that he hoped to make *The Anniversary* 'reflect the Literature of the Age' Southey replied that 'the best you can make of these things, is picturebooks for grown Children'.

Satire and parody are almost wholly lacking in the Annuals, and the absence of the latter is particularly to be regretted in

a period in which the prevalence of new poetic fashions gave the parodist a splendid opportunity. The fact that the major poets of the time expressed themselves so idiosyncratically made it natural that this mode of criticism by imitation should have reached a high level. Not that the best parodies were written by those hostile to the new modes of expression: most successful parodies have always been written by admirers of the writers parodied, and the parodists of this era were no exception. The authors of *Rejected Addresses*, for example, were themselves writers of some ability, and it has sometimes been maintained that one or two of the poems in the collection are imitations rather than parodies. Scott was convinced that one of the pieces was his own work, although he could not remember when he had written it. The occasion of the volume was the competition held to find an address to be spoken at the opening of the new Drury Lane Theatre. James and Horace Smith sat down and wrote a collection of bogus entries, and the fact that the volume was published within six weeks shows that they were so familiar with the styles of their contemporaries that they had no need to get them up for the occasion.[1] The rapidity of the undertaking helps to explain the unevenness of the pieces: it is surprising that writers who had parodied Wordsworth so brilliantly should have been so much less successful with Byron and Coleridge. But by confining themselves to 'writers whose style and habit of thought, being . . . marked and peculiar, was . . . capable of exaggeration and distortion' they succeeded far more often than they failed. Thomas Campbell, who felt aggrieved that he had been passed over by the Smith brothers, is also missing from James Hogg's *Poetic Mirror* (1816), a curious volume with a curious history. As Hogg tells us in his autobiography, he took it into his head to beg a poem from each of the principal English poets, collect them in a volume, and so make his fortune. For one reason or another most of the poets failed to oblige, however, and Hogg decided that he himself 'could write a better poem than any that had been sent or would be sent to me, and

[1] James and Horatio Smith (1775–1839 and 1779–1849) were the sons of a solicitor. James succeeded his father as solicitor to the Board of Ordnance in 1812. Among other things he produced farces and books of words for the comedian Charles Mathews. Horatio (who called himself 'Horace') was introduced to the literary world by Richard Cumberland the dramatist. The brothers became famous overnight on the publication of *Rejected Addresses* in 1812. Horatio produced numerous novels and assisted Campbell for a while with the *New Monthly Magazine*.

this so completely in the style of each poet, that it should not be known but for his own production'. The status of the volume is a little difficult to determine, and the reviewers were in some doubt. In a sense it is a piece of literary forgery as much as a volume of parodies: at times Hogg seems intent simply on imitating, though in other cases—such as the alleged passages from *The Recluse* and the Coleridgean 'Isabelle'—he is clearly at the satirist's work:

> Why I should dread I cannot tell;
> There is a spirit; I know it well!
> I see it in yon falling beam—
> Is it a vision, or a dream?
> It is no dream, full well I know,
> I have a woful deed to do!

Hogg himself was parodied—not to mention his own poem or parody in *The Poetic Mirror*—in a volume entitled *Warreniana*, published in 1824, the work of William Frederick Deacon. This collection of poems in praise of Warren's Patent Blacking is supposed to be edited by Gifford, the graceless pomposity of whose style is mirrored in the preface and other supplementary matter. It is a volume of considerable interest to the literary historian, and deserves better than to be neglected: some of the parodies are excellently done (those of Barry Cornwall and Moore, for example), while the Coleridge—'The Dream, A Psychological Curiosity'—is in parts quite admirable. Keats, Gessner, Spenser, Ambrose Philips, Leigh Hunt, Lamb, and Hogg are introduced as figures in a pastoral masque supposed to be the work of Charles Wells.

Although most of the poets of the period wrote at least one drama or 'dramatic poem' it was seldom with an eye to the theatre, and a brief account of the acting drama during what William Archer called its winter solstice must be sufficient. Conditions could hardly have been less propitious. The two licensed theatres, Covent Garden and Drury Lane, were of enormous size, and there can be no doubt that this made them unsuitable for the development of a serious drama. As Scott pointed out in 1819:

> Show and machinery have . . . usurped the place of tragic poetry; and the author is compelled to address himself to the eyes, not to the understanding or feelings of the spectators. . . . We have enlarged our theatres [he goes on], so as to destroy the effect of acting, without carrying to any perfection that of pantomime and dumb show.

An occasional critic, such as Bulwer Lytton, suggested that 'the astonishing richness and copiousness of modern stage illusion opens to the poet a mighty field, which his predecessors could not enter', and insisted that the dramatists should take advantage of these new possibilities instead of rejecting them; but unfortunately the typical audience of the time was perfectly happy with elaborate scenic effects alone, and did not care whether they subserved a true dramatic purpose. '*Venice Preserved* will scarcely draw a decent house', as Gerald Griffin complained to his brother; 'while such a piece of unmeaning absurdity as the Cataract of the Ganges has filled Drury Lane every night those three weeks past. The scenery and decorations, field of battle, burning forest, and Cataract of real water, afforded a succession of splendour. . . . A lady on horseback riding up a cataract is quite a bold stroke, but these things are quite the rage now' (*Life of G. Griffin*, p. 94). The general level of the audiences was low. The Court gave no lead in matters of taste, while a considerable proportion of the population was inspired by religion to 'see no plays'. The theatres were noisy and full of prostitutes, and it could never have been said of the Regency theatre that 'vice itself lost half its evil, by losing all its grossness'.

Altogether the fate of the aspiring dramatist was unenviable, as Griffin pointed out in a letter written in May 1824:

> Of all the walks in literature, it certainly is at present the most heart-rending. . . . The managers only seek to fill their houses, and don't care a curse for all the dramatists that ever lived. There is a rage for fire, and water, and horses got abroad. . . . Literary men see the trouble which attends [dramatic writing], the bending and cringing to performers—the chicanery of managers . . . and content themselves with the quiet fame of a 'closet writer'.

The monopoly enjoyed by the two large theatres rendered dramatic experiment almost impossible, while the growing rewards available to a successful novelist made the profits of an unlikely success in the drama seem of little account.

Another enemy of the dramatist was the censor. Although the Methodist John Larpent seems to have been guilty of larceny, or something very like it, throughout his career, while his successor George Colman had himself been the author of a number of licentious plays, each insisted on a stupid decency and piety

in the productions of others. The most vexatious and crippling aspect of the censorship was the prohibition of any serious treatment of religious or political controversy; for these were the crucial topics of the day, and the natural field for the dramatist. At the beginning of the century which immediately succeeded the French Revolution Larpent seems to have been opposed to any play dealing with rebellion. Bulwer Lytton as usual puts his finger on the point: with the Greeks (he insists) 'the theatre . . . was political':

> We banish the Political from the stage, and we therefore deprive the stage of the most vivid of its actual sources of interest. At present the English, instead of finding politics on the stage, find their stage in politics. . . . A censor is not required to keep immorality from the stage, but to prevent political allusions. . . . I doubt if the drama will become thoroughly popular until it is permitted to embody the most popular emotions. In these times the public mind is absorbed in politics, and yet the stage, which should represent the times, especially banishes appeals to the most general feelings. The national theatre . . . is like . . . *Hamlet* 'with the part of Hamlet left out by the particular desire'—of the nobility! (*England and the English*, Book IV, chap. v.)

In feeling his way towards religious and political themes and seeking inspiration from Alfieri, 'The Poet of Liberty', Byron was guided by a sure instinct; but his drama of liberty was destined to be played out on the stage of the world.

Byron was also unusual, though not alone, in his belief that great drama could not be written 'by following the old English dramatists, who are full of gross faults' and his insistence that Shakespeare is 'the *worst* of models, though the most extraordinary of writers'. The fact that the epidemic enthusiasm for the work of the Elizabethan and Jacobean dramatists was essentially an enthusiasm for their plays as poetry, and not as drama, also exerted an unfortunate influence on the dramatic attempts of the time. Having hardly any opportunities of seeing the plays satisfactorily performed, the lovers of the old dramatists naturally looked on their productions as books. It was a natural step for Charles Lamb to discuss whether *King Lear* could really be acted at all. In the theatre as he knew it, one might well agree that it could not. But the split between the theatre and the serious drama which is so oddly illustrated by the remark of Landor's brother, who had written a play called *The Count Arezzi*—'No one knows less of the theatre than I do'—

was profoundly unhealthy and led writers into a complete misunderstanding of the nature of a play. George Darley, writing in the *London Magazine*, made the point with admirable clarity. '*Action* is the essence of drama', he wrote, and he complained that 'our modern tragic writers are perpetually endeavouring to make drama poetical, instead of poetry dramatical.' With equal penetration he once wrote in a letter that 'Experience confirms me more and more in the opinion that a poetic whole is far greater than all its parts unconnected; to build it up well, forms the true basis of fame'. Unfortunately Darley's own plays demonstrate that it was one thing to see what had to be done, and another to do it. As we read his plays and the other un-acted dramas of the time we find almost everywhere a subordination of the whole to the part, of the thing said to the way in which it is said. The influence of Shakespeare and his contemporaries is ubiquitous; and whatever its effect on the plays as poetry, on the plays as drama it had almost everywhere a disastrous effect. The language of most of the plays of the time is neither nineteenth-century English, nor Elizabethan: the characters are neither the contemporaries of their creators, nor of Shakespeare: the ways in which they seem to think and express themselves are uncontemporary without being historical. They are close relations of the padded and bemuffed figures of historical romance. Not that all of the dramatists followed the Elizabethans: the influence of the German drama is also easy to trace in this period: but unfortunately it was the influence of bad plays rather than of good, and the result was too often the sort of 'insult and defiance to Aristotle's definition of tragedy' which Hazlitt discussed in the last of his *Lectures on the Age of Elizabeth*.

That the times were unpropitious for dramatists is startlingly demonstrated by the fact that the most successful serious dramatists, in this age of literary genius, were three forgotten Irishmen, R. L. Sheil, Robert Maturin, and Sheridan Knowles. Sheil was a Dubliner famous for his political oratory, and it was in Dublin that *Adelaide; or, the Emigrants* was first produced in 1814.[1] It is

[1] Richard Lalor Sheil (1791–1851) was educated at Stoneyhurst and Trinity College, Dublin. In 1814 he became a barrister at Lincoln's Inn. Soon he was well known as a playwright. Having protested against O'Connell's refusal of concessions to Protestants who supported Catholic emancipation he later joined him in agitation, and took a prominent part in political affairs. In 1827 he was indicted for libel, but Canning did not proceed with the indictment. He first became a Member

easier to see why the play failed in London than why it succeeded in Dublin. Perhaps Hazlitt was right in conjecturing that 'it would infallibly have been damned' on its first appearance if there had been one good passage in it; 'but it was all of a piece; one absurdity justified another'. Even its highly reactionary politics failed to carry it to success. 'Kotzebue and Fletcher seem to struggle over its silly corpse', as Professor Allardyce Nicoll observes with unaccustomed petulance. *The Apostate* and *Bellamira* are a distinct improvement, but it was with *Evadne; or, The Statue* (1819), a free adaptation of Shirley's *The Traitor*, that Sheil produced his most interesting play. The heroine is a considerable creation, 'truly feminine and noble' (as Leigh Hunt pointed out) without being a faultless monster.

If Maturin's *Bertram* retains more interest than any of Sheil's plays it is because it remains a document of the taste of the Byronic period.[1] Its atmosphere may be conveyed by one of its stage-directions:

The Rocks—the Sea—a Storm—The Convent illuminated in the back ground—the Bell tolls at intervals—a groupe of Monks on the rocks with torches—a Vessel in distress in the Offing.

The verse has a certain larger-than-life eloquence, verging on bombast; but the chief feature of interest is the character of the protagonist, a 'man of many woes'. After talking with him the Prior soliloquizes:

> Wild admiration thrills me to behold
> An evil strength, so above earthly pitch—
> Descending angels only could reclaim thee.

*Bertram* exemplifies the interest in the Outlaw which is characteristic of this period, and must have been influenced in some degree by Schiller. Salvator Rosa would have been the man to illustrate it. Scott and Byron were instrumental in having the play produced at Drury Lane: at first, we are told, Kean was worried by the thought that the part of the heroine was more

of Parliament in 1831, and proved an effective speaker. In 1838–41 he was Vice-President of the Board of Trade, and in 1844 acted as counsel for John O'Connell. He died soon after his appointment as Minister at Florence.

[1] Charles Robert Maturin (1782–1824) became a curate after taking his degree at Trinity College, Dublin, but soon set up a school. After six years he abandoned teaching, but persevered with his literary work. *Bertram* was a great success when it was produced at Drury Lane in 1816. Maturin also wrote a number of novels, which were extremely popular. His writings had a considerable influence in France.

important than Bertram's own, but on reflecting that there was no Mrs. Siddons 'to play Imogine and eclipse me' he went ahead with the play, which held the stage for twenty-two nights and ran through seven editions within a year, so earning its author £1,000. Kean found it 'a relief' to act in *Bertram* 'after such characters as Richard and Othello' because it was 'all sound and fury signifying nothing'. According to Scott, Maturin at one time intended to have 'our old friend Satan . . . brought on the stage bodily', but was persuaded to exorcize him. It is not necessary to attribute Coleridge's onslaught on *Bertram* in *Biographia Literaria* to jealousy on the part of the author of *Remorse*. He particularly objects to the unnatural surprise produced 'by representing the qualities of liberality, refined feeling, and a nice sense of honor . . . in persons and in classes where experience teaches us least to expect them; and by rewarding with all the sympathies which are the due of virtue, those criminals whom law, reason and religion have excommunicated from our esteem'. Although *Bertram* has some merit as a stage piece, everything about it is exaggerated and overwrought. All is for effect. At bottom it is a lie about human life, so that it is easy to understand Coleridge's indignation that such a drama should be looked to for 'the redemption of the British stage'. Maturin's second tragedy, *Manuel*, was described by Byron as 'the absurd work of a clever man'. The plot is more complicated than that of its predecessor, and there are some dramatic scenes; but it failed to hit the taste of the times as *Bertram* had done. In *Fredolfo* Maturin outdid himself in violence and horror, before returning to the writing of prose romance and producing *Melmoth the Wanderer*. Romance suited him better than the drama, for none of his writings evinces any genuine interest in human life as it really is.

There could be no more forcible illustration of the insignificance of the acting drama of the time than Hazlitt's statement that *Virginius*, by Sheridan Knowles,[1] was 'the best acting tragedy that has been produced upon the modern stage'. Such merit as his plays possess seems due to the fact that he had been

[1] James Sheridan Knowles (1784–1862) was the son of a lexicographer. After trying his hand as soldier, physician, actor, and schoolmaster, he had *Caius Gracchus* produced at Belfast in 1815. He visited America in 1834 and continued to act until 1843. Apart from his plays he published poems, adaptations, novels, and lectures on oratory.

an actor himself, and so understood the taste of his audience. *Virginius* (1820) has as its background the struggle between a tyrant and the liberty-loving forces in Rome, and the title-role of a Roman who kills his daughter to save her from being ravished gave Macready an admirable opportunity. The verse is respectable, but it never rises to eloquence and seems to have little contact with the spoken idiom of the day. *The Hunchback* (1832) is a toothless satire attacking some of the milder follies of the time. It is easy to believe that Fanny Kemble was enchanting as Julia, but in print the part seems no great matter. The morality of the play is almost absurdly innocent. The verse of an earlier play, *The Beggar's Daughter* (1828), has a boyish vigour appropriate to the story, which deals with wreckers on the Cornish coast and a hero who turns up to rescue the heroine at the moment at which she is being compelled to marry the villainous Black Norris. *The Wife* (1833) is a little more serious: in the prologue we are told what to expect:

> A touch of nature's work—an awkward start
> Or ebullition of an Irish heart.

Although some of the verse is tolerable, however, the passages of 'Elizabethan' prose are not. Knowles himself played the blameless St. Pierre, but his 'principal reliance', as he tells us, was upon the part of Mariana, which was played by Ellen Tree. Knowles was always at his best in delineating the characters of virtuous women. 'The only way in which Mr. Knowles personifies our age', R. H. Horne wrote in *A New Spirit of the Age*, 'is in his truly domestic feeling':

> The age is domestic, and so is he. Comfort—not passionate imaginings,—is the aim of every body, and he seeks to aid and gratify this love of comfort. All his dramas are domestic, and strange to say, those that should be most classic . . . are the most imbued with this spirit. . . . [In *Virginius*] we have Roman tunics, but a modern English heart,—the scene is the Forum, but the sentiments those of the 'Bedford Arms'.

It is appropriate that he should have abandoned poetry to become a Methodist preacher.

So striking was the inferiority of the acting drama that critics were tempted to suppose that there was something peculiarly undramatic about the age. Darley once suggested that the drama

was unlikely to revive because 'subjective composition' was the natural tendency of the time. 'Can we restrain the tendency?', he asked, 'or *should* we, if we could? Though fatal to the drama, it may be vital to something else as desirable.' Suggestive as Darley's remark is, however, we must remember that prose fiction, which is not one of the more 'subjective' modes of composition, prospered throughout our period and was soon to flourish as it had never flourished before. All that we can say is that for a variety of reasons, one of which was the bad state of the theatres, the novel was now consolidating its place as the dominant literary form. In 1844 we find R. H. Horne recognizing this and pointing out that the true drama of the age 'is to be found more living and real in the pages of . . . Dickens, Mrs. Gore, and Mrs. Trollope, than in the play-house pieces'. In the middle of the previous century Fielding had acknowledged the superior dignity of poetry by designing *Tom Jones* as 'a comic epic poem in prose'. In the heyday of the Victorian Age Browning was to turn to the novel for guidance in the composition of *The Ring and the Book*.

# VI

# THE WAVERLEY ROMANCES

THE last chapter of *Waverley* is called 'A Postscript, which should have been a Preface', and in fact it might have served as a preface to the whole series of the Waverley Romances, for the paragraphs in which Scott outlines the great changes which had come to Scotland in recent times describe the inspiration of the finest of these books.[1] 'There is no European nation', he remarks, 'which, within the course of half a century, or little more, has undergone so complete a change as this kingdom of Scotland. . . . The present people of Scotland [are] a class of beings as different from their grandfathers, as the existing English are from those of Queen Elizabeth's time.' He was fascinated by the contrast between the Highlands and the

[1] Walter Scott (1771–1832) was the son of a Writer to the Signet in Edinburgh. His father was an unworldly man of strict Calvinist views who was given to the study of theology and the history of Scots law. His mother was the daughter of a gifted Professor of Medicine. Scott liked to trace his family tree back to more adventurous forebears, to his great-grandfather, a Jacobite 'well-known in Teviotdale by the name of Beardie', and to other semi-legendary figures in the history of the Scottish Border. As a boy he was extremely lame, and he used to listen for hours to the stories of the past told him by his uncle, Thomas Scott, and a number of other elderly people with retentive memories and time on their hands. He early became a great reader and a great lover of traditional Scottish songs, particularly songs about Border raids and the Jacobite risings. When his health improved (though he never lost his limp) he became an enthusiastic walker and rider, and he used to ride about collecting traditional songs and tales. This led to the *Minstrelsy of the Scottish Border*, 1802–3, and thence naturally enough to his own poems, *The Lay of the Last Minstrel*, *Marmion*, and *The Lady of the Lake* (poems discussed in the previous volume of this *History*). The publication of *Waverley* marks Scott's turning from romance in verse to romance in prose, partly because he felt that Byron was outpacing him.

He had been educated at the Edinburgh Royal High School and at Edinburgh University, and in 1799 had been appointed sheriff-depute of Selkirkshire. In 1804 he took up residence with his wife (whom he had married in 1797) at Ashestiel on the Tweed, near Selkirk. In 1806 he became Clerk to the Court of Session. In 1820 he was created baronet. In 1811 he bought Abbotsford, which he extended and filled with antiquarian curiosities for the rest of his life. His undoing was his connexion with the printing firm of Ballantyne. The crash came in 1826, and from then until his death he worked heroically to pay off as much as possible of the immense debt. The sale of his copyrights after his death effected this object. He was a man of remarkable charm and generosity, though he hated innovation. He did not publicly acknowledge the authorship of *Waverley* and its successors until 1827.

Lowlands in his father's lifetime. 'So little was the condition of the Highlands known at that late period', he wrote of 1745, 'that the character and appearance of their population, while thus sallying forth as military adventurers, conveyed to the south-country Lowlanders as much surprise as if an invasion of African Negroes, or Esquimaux Indians, had issued forth.' Here was a rich vein to be worked. 'The ancient traditions and high spirit of a people, who, living in a civilized age and country, retained so strong a tincture of manners belonging to an early period of society, must afford a subject favourable for romance.' Scott's aim was to amuse and excite the *Aufklärung* of Edinburgh with an account of the manners and habits of the old Scotland, and particularly of the Highlands. Nor did he limit himself to Scottish readers. Emulating Maria Edgeworth, he hoped that he might write something that would introduce the natives of Scotland to English readers 'in a more favourable light than they had been placed hitherto, and [so] tend to procure sympathy for their virtues and indulgence for their foibles'.

For such a purpose Scott was born at the right time. In his boyhood it was not difficult to find men who had taken part in these events: by the time *Waverley* was published in 1814 very few of them were left. He was proud of the authenticity of his descriptions, and in the notes to the collected editions he frequently cites his authorities. The visit of Waverley to Rob Roy, for instance, is based on an adventure which befell 'the late Mr. Abercromby of Tullibody' and Scott mentions that he heard it 'many years since . . . from the mouth of the venerable gentleman who was concerned in it'. In another note he refers to his description of 'the Highland manual exercise' with pistol and dirk, insisting that he himself had seen it 'gone through by men who had learned it in their youth'. Waverley's journey into Scotland is an allegory of Scott's own imaginative development. When Rose Bradwardine told Waverley a story of Highland feuds, he 'could not help starting at a story which bore so much resemblance to one of his own day-dreams. Here was a girl . . . who had witnessed with her own eyes such a scene as he had used to conjure up in his imagination, as only occurring in ancient times. . . . He might have said with Malvolio, "I do not now fool myself, to let imagination jade me!" I am actually in the land of military and romantic adventures. . . . ' But it was no Rose Bradwardine who roused the young Scott with stories of

adventure: it was men and women in their sixties and seventies. Having nourished his boyish imagination with stories of imaginary romance, he had the good fortune to fall in with those who could satisfy the yearning that remained in him for stories at once improbable and true. To Scott himself, as to Waverley, 'it seemed like a dream . . . that these deeds of violence should be familiar to men's minds . . . as falling within the common order of things . . . without his having crossed the seas, and while he was yet in the otherwise well-ordered island of Great Britain'. This true dream was his imaginative inspiration until the end of his life.

As Scott admits, everything in *Waverley* is contrived with a view to the description of the old Scottish way of life. Waverley's journeyings do not constitute an adequate plot, being contrived merely to provide an excuse for 'some descriptions of scenery and manners, to which the reality [gives] an interest'. Nothing much happens until half the book is over. Such chapter-headings as 'A Horse-Quarter in Scotland', 'A Scottish Manor-House Sixty Years Since' and 'A Creagh [cattle-raid] and its consequences' make Scott's purpose evident enough. When we are told that Waverley's curiosity has been aroused by hearing 'many curious particulars concerning the manners, customs, and habits' of the patriarchal race of the Highland clans we are not surprised that he should inquire 'whether it was possible to make with safety an excursion into the neighbouring Highlands'. Since Waverley travels on behalf of the reader, to enable us to see what he sees, things are made easy for him, and we soon find Evan Dhu inviting him to study the headquarters of his cattle-thieves at first hand. When Waverley's Tour comes to an end and he returns to the Lowlands, geography may be said to give way to history as a background for the story. Through a series of improbable events he blunders into the '45, meets the Chevalier, attends the Jacobite ball at Holyrood, sees the Gathering of the Clans and the battle of Preston, and has many other adventures before he is united to his Rose Bradwardine. Before he returns—like Waverley himself—to every-day life, the reader has learned a good deal about some of the most striking features of Scotland and Scottish history.

Scott is no more seriously concerned with characterization than with constructing a careful plot. Waverley himself, the first of a long line of essentially similar heroes, is precisely

adapted to the role he has to play: an Englishman who has never been in Scotland before, he is intelligent enough to take a keen interest in what he sees, fond enough of the picturesque to go in quest of it, ingenuous enough to blunder farther than he intends, courageous enough to dislike the idea of flight, quixotic enough to be attracted by the cause of the Pretender, amorous enough to become emotionally concerned with two Scottish families. He is not impressive enough to become important in the Jacobite movement as quickly as he does—but that is one of Scott's romance conventions. We notice that most of the people whom he meets have been deliberately chosen for their typical quality. Baron Bradwardine, for example, is 'the very model of the old Scottish cavalier, with all his excellencies and peculiarities . . . a character . . . which is fast disappearing'. Davie Gellatley, the 'natural', gives Scott an opportunity for effects of pathos as well as the introduction of antiquarian lore, notably in his scraps of song. Flora's enthusiasm for 'Celtic poetry' serves the same purpose: she sings her own translation of a Gaelic song, and assures Waverley that if the ancient Highland poems 'are ever translated into any of the languages of civilized Europe' they will not fail 'to produce a deep and general sensation'.

Each of the characters in this book is the first of a long line, and Waverley's journey is the prototype of the journey in space and time which thousands of readers were to take, in the following years, at the guidance of his creator. Like Waverley, they were to gaze in awe at the picturesque scenery of the Highlands, to admire the 'rude sweetness of the Celtic minstrelsy', and to wonder at the wild loyalties of the clans. Most of the elements which may be found in the first, most powerful group of the Waverley Romances are present in this path-finding book: seldom has a writer given so clear and so attractive a sample of what was to come.

In the preface to *The Antiquary* Scott pointed out that the first three of his romances were 'intended to illustrate the manners of Scotland at three different periods. *Waverley* embraced the age of our fathers, *Guy Mannering* that of our own youth, and the *Antiquary* refers to the last ten years of the eighteenth century.' Behind this difference of period a remarkable similarity of pattern may be discerned—a similarity which extends to most aspects of *Old Mortality* and to several of the later books. The hero of each book is a young stranger, usually

of mysterious origins, who is visiting Scotland for what is actually or virtually the first time. Sometimes he turns out to be a long-lost son and heir. He becomes involved in a complicated series of events, which may be connected with historical occurrences. In spite of his youth and inexperience he rapidly becomes a person of great importance: in *Rob Roy*, for example, which exhibits most of the characteristics of this Common Form, it is suggested to the astonished hero that unless he pays his father's debts the failure of his business will precipitate the 1715 rebellion. Perhaps the most explicit statement of this peculiarity in the career of a Scott hero is to be found in a later book, *The Abbot*, where a youth of no importance whatever suddenly finds himself, as page to the imprisoned Mary Queen of Scots, in a position of vital significance:

> Yesterday he was of neither mark nor likelihood, a vagrant boy, the attendant on a relative, of whose sane judgement he himself had not the highest opinion; but now he had become, he knew not why, or wherefore, or to what extent, the custodier . . . of some important state secret, in the safe keeping of which the Regent himself was concerned. . . . He felt like one who looks on a romantic landscape, of which he sees the features for the first time, and then obscured with mist and driving tempest.

Equally characteristic of his situation is the fact that throughout he is passive rather than active: he does not initiate action but remains the sport of circumstances. 'I have been treated . . . as one who lacked the common attributes of free-will and human reason, or was at least deemed unfit to exercise them', complains the hero of the same book. 'A land of enchantment have I been led into, and spells have been cast around me—every one has met me in disguise—every one has spoken to me in parables—I have been like one who walks in a weary and bewildering dream.' His characteristic situation is following a mysterious guide to an unknown destination, as Frank Osbaldistone follows Rob Roy. In *The Fortunes of Nigel* the hero reproaches himself with having allowed himself to become 'a mere victim of those events, which I have never even attempted to influence—a thing never acting, but perpetually acted upon—protected by one friend, deceived by another'. A love story serves to lend some continuity to the plot. The heroine is usually a blameless but colourless girl. Often she is a loyal daughter comforting an aged and

foolish father who has fallen on evil days: in this situation union with the hero may be expected to bring an unexpected access of wealth which enables all to be set to rights. Romance elements abound: secret passages, villainous foreigners (Scott practically never portrays a foreigner in a favourable or a fair light), wicked upstarts (often attorneys), a family divided by Jacobitism or some other political difference, recognition-scenes, gipsies and smugglers and outcasts of various sorts, hidden priests, battles and chases and sieges and every possible aspect of the exciting and the picturesque. These are the same elements that may be found in *Waverley* itself, though later they are often more skilfully mixed; and it remains true of the later books, as it is of the first, that Scott was 'more solicitous to describe manners minutely, than to arrange in any case an artificial and combined narrative'.

This is manifestly true of *Guy Mannering* (1815), in which emphasis is laid throughout on the contrast between the old order in Scotland and the new: the feudal landlord is contrasted with the villainous Glossin, who is an example of the 'new men'. Scott's intention of describing Scots manners at a certain time and place is particularly clear in the passages dealing with Dandy Dinmont. 'The present store-farmers of the south of Scotland are a much more refined race than their fathers', Scott comments, 'and the manners I am now to describe have either altogether disappeared, or are greatly modified'; while in a note he refers to farmers whose hospitality he had known as a boy, 'in his rambles through that wild country, at a time when it was totally inaccessible' except to a traveller on foot or horesback. Harry Bertram's sojourn with Dandy Dinmont makes possible a description of the Scots manner of hunting and fishing, and also allows the introduction of a compliment to the 'blunt honesty, personal strength, and hardihood' of these men, and to their generosity and hospitality. While it is impossible to regret the creation of such a character, the hero's interruption of his journey to see Julia Mannering is not very credible; and while Scott is more careful than he would have been in *Waverley* to give Dandy Dinmont some part in the plot, the true reason for his introduction remains too evident. The same is true of Paulus Pleydell the advocate, introduced as he is primarily to enable Scott to describe a characteristic trait of Scottish manners.

Of the many differences between *Guy Mannering* and *Waverley* three are outstanding. First, the later book does not contain actual personages who figure in the history of Scotland, nor are important events in the political history of the country introduced: it is an 'historical' romance in a different sense from the part of *Waverley* dealing with the '45. Secondly, it is clear that Scott was determined to avoid the most glaring weakness of the earlier book, its casual plot. In this second book we are hurried into the midst of a complicated action. The fact that the hero, 'a young English gentleman' who has not been in Scotland since his early childhood, turns out to be the heir to a Scottish estate, also helps to give the story some semblance of unity. And, thirdly (which is most important), *Guy Mannering* contains characters whose interest and vitality completely transcend anything in *Waverley*. There is nothing in the earlier book to compare with Dominie Sampson, Dandy Dinmont or—finest of all—Meg Merrilies. Each of the three belongs to a humble social class, while Meg stands outside the ordinary structure of Scottish society altogether. Scott had always been fascinated by the gipsies, these 'Pariahs of Scotland', who lived 'like wild Indians among European settlers' and had therefore to be judged 'rather by their own customs, habits, and opinions, than as if they had been members of the civilized part of the community'. He was attracted by their picturesqueness, their rugged characters, and above all by their freedom from the ordinary restraints of society.

Scott seems to have resolved that the greatest character in the book should play an integral part in the plot. Right away we notice that Meg acts as an incomparably impressive chorus. In one of the greatest speeches in Scott she prophesies that disaster will overtake the house of Ellangowan:

> Ride your ways . . . ride your ways, Laird of Ellangowan—ride your ways, Godfrey Bertram!—This day have ye quenched seven smoking hearths—see if the fire in your ain parlour burn the blyther for that. Ye have riven the thack of seven cottar houses—look if your ain roof-tree stand the faster.—Ye may stable your stirks in the shealings at Derncleugh—see that the hare does not couch on the hearth-stane at Ellangowan.

Meg's conservatism, which is Scott's own, is peculiarly appropriate in a choric character. Harlot and thief as she is, she acknowledges loyalties to which Hatteraick, Glossin, and indeed

the younger gipsies are strangers. She is a great praiser of times gone by: 'The times are sair altered since I was a kinchen-mort. Men were men then, and fought other in the open field, and there was nae milling in the darkmans. And the gentry had kind hearts, and would have given baith lap and pannel to ony puir gypsy. . . . But ye are a' altered from the gude auld rules. . . . Yes, ye are a' altered.'[1] Yet Meg is not only a chorus: she is also the linchpin of the whole action. From the first she is convinced that Harry Bertram is still alive, and she infects others with her conviction, being always 'the unknown friend working on his behalf'. At each crisis in the action she appears as mysteriously as if she were a creature from another world. She is the first to recognize Bertram, and it is her announcement that finally confirms his identity in public: this done, she dies content. Her actions have played a vital part in bringing the restoration about, while her prophecies give the book as a whole something of poetic grandeur.

The basic pattern of *The Antiquary* (1816) is similar to that of the previous books. The hero is a young man of mysterious origins who comes to Scotland for virtually the first time and is swiftly involved in a complicated intrigue. Other romance elements are prominent: there is a visitor of unknown identity, an exciting rescue from the sea, a haunted room, a duel, a guilt-ridden earl, a villainous foreigner, a scene in a church at midnight, and a final dramatic recognition scene; while a history of past violence and wrong lies behind the events of the plot. Except in isolated scenes, however, it is impossible to feel that Scott is taking these romance elements seriously; the love interest is slight; the hero disappears during a considerable part of the action; while no attempt is made to render the villain Dousterswivel credible. From the brilliant opening scene onwards it becomes evident that the dominant spirit of the book, unlike that of its predecessors, is the spirit of comedy. So it is when the greatest of the characters is introduced:

'Yes, my dear friend [the Antiquary is remarking], from this stance it is probable,—nay, it is nearly certain, that Julius Agricola beheld what our Beaumont has so admirably described!—From this very Praetorium—'

A voice from behind interrupted his ecstatic description—'Praetorian here, Praetorian there, I mind the bigging o't.'

[1] kinchen-mort, girl; milling in the darkmans, murder by night; lap and pannel, liquor and food.

From this point onwards Edie Ochiltree steals the book. In some respects he is comparable with Meg Merrilies in *Guy Mannering*: the Antiquary describes him as 'one of the last specimens of the old-fashioned Scottish mendicant, who kept his rounds within a particular space, and was the news-carrier, the minstrel, and sometimes the historian of the district, . . . [a] rascal [who] knows more old ballads and traditions than any other man in this and the four next parishes'. Edie advances high claims for himself:

> What wad a' the country about do for want o' auld Edie Ochiltree, that brings news and country cracks frae ae farm-steading to anither, and gingerbread to the lasses, and helps the lads to mend their fiddles, and the gudewives to clout their pans, . . . and kens mair auld sangs and tales than a' the barony besides, and gars ilka body laugh wherever he comes?—troth . . . I canna lay down my vocation; it would be a public loss.

The blend of comedy and romance that is characteristic of *The Antiquary* is suggested by the fact that Edie's second appearance is as dramatic as his first has been amusing: it is he who saves Sir Arthur and his daughter from the sea. Like Meg Merrilies he knows everything that is going on, and turns up at critical times. He knows of Lovel's feelings for Miss Wardour earlier than anyone else, and takes his part. He tries to stop Lovel's duel with Captain M'Intyre and enables him to escape afterwards. By identifying a horn that Dousterswivel claims to have discovered and making a fool of him by 'haunting' the church he carries on the process of Dousterswivel's undoing. In acting as intermediary between Elspeth of the Craigburnfoot and the Earl, Edie also plays an important part in another aspect of the plot. Throughout he is Lovel's friend and Miss Wardour's defender, and it is appropriate that he is the bearer of the 'budget of good news' which begins the happy ending of the whole book.

In *Old Mortality* Scott continued his exploration of Scottish history. The germ of the story was his desire to show Claverhouse in a favourable light. When a friend pointed out that Claverhouse—of whom Scott had a portrait in his study—would make a fine 'hero of a . . . romance' and Scott replied that this would necessitate portraying the Covenanters much less favourably than most historians had done, his friend

suggested that he might employ the method of *The Lay of the Last Minstrel*: if the story were presented as being told by 'Old Mortality', then the required bias might be attributed to him. As it turned out, most of Scott's material did not come from this picturesque old man: as Lockhart remarks, Scott was now for the first time relying on written sources for his background. And in fact—very characteristically—Scott does not follow out the original dramatic idea: he forgets about 'Old Mortality' almost from the start. But he keeps stoutly to his intention of exhibiting Claverhouse as 'every inch a soldier and a gentleman'. While Claverhouse's cruelty is acknowledged, the plot is so manipulated as to throw the emphasis on his better qualities. The height of gentility is reached when (as Morton was sent into exile) 'Claverhouse shook him by the hand, and wished him good fortune, and a happy return to Scotland in quieter times'. Scott's desire to show Claverhouse in his later role as a zealous supporter of James II after the Revolution of 1688 is responsible for the clumsy structure of the book. The climax of the love plot, and the end invented for Burley, are among the weakest things he had yet done. Although he is often successful in catching the Scriptural turn of phrase of the Covenanters—Mause Headrigg's speeches are masterly, and Cuddie is excellent on a comic level—his portrayal of them is far from satisfactory: the result is not only biased history, it also detracts from the artistic value of the book. When Morton sides with the Covenanters for a while (so complicating the action and giving Scott an opportunity of describing them at close quarters) we are at a loss to understand why he should. If Scott had been more interested in the questions at issue between the two sides, *Old Mortality* might have been a major work: as it is it remains simply an admirable example of the historical romance. In spite of its many merits we notice that there is no great character in the book, and we are left with the impression that Scott has caught at some of the more picturesque aspects of a striking period without making any attempt to go deeper.

By this time an attentive reader must have felt that he knew pretty well what to expect in a new book 'By the Author of Waverley'; but in fact the greatest of the series, *The Heart of Mid-Lothian* (1818), differs greatly from its predecessors. The usual love-plot is thrown aside, and with it the usual hero. Scott had

already shown his mastery in the portrayal of Scots of a humble social class: now for the first time he makes such a character central. Jeanie Deans, who differs radically from the conventional heroine of romance, is not even allowed a love story of any importance: since it is essential that she should be a lonely figure her lover is made a very subsidiary character: there is no hero to draw our attention away from the heroine. The unity of the main part of the book—and in this it has no rival in Scott's work—springs directly from the all-importance of Jeanie Deans: this is the only one of his stories which is primarily concerned with one particular human being. The theme of Scots character, or at a deeper level of the passions of mankind, is here brought to the foreground: in this serious book there is no element of the Guide to Scotland. The effect is the more powerful because the central theme—that of a Quest for Mercy—is so simple and archetypal: its fine simplicity 'carries' the complications of the Robertson–Staunton plot. Scott's remark, in the preface to *Waverley*, that he would willingly consider the inculcation of moral lessons the main aim of his work, sounds less absurd of *The Heart of Mid-Lothian* than of most of the other books: it owes its supremacy to the fact that its action turns on a serious theme, that of a moral choice.

Scott said that he wrote it to show 'the possibility of rendering a fictitious personage interesting by mere dignity of mind and rectitude of principle, assisted by unpretending good sense and temper, without any of the beauty, grace, talent, accomplishment, and wit, to which a heroine of romance is supposed to have a prescriptive right'. It is remarkable to find a writer who had seemed so incapable of differentiating his heroines creating a woman who seems as certainly not to have been 'born to be an heroine' as Catherine Morland herself. Jeanie has no exceptional beauty to make up for her lack of birth. 'Her personal attractions were of no uncommon description. She was short, and rather too stoutly made for her size, had grey eyes, light-coloured hair, a round good-humoured face, much tanned with the sun [as well as freckled], and her only peculiar charm was an air of inexpressible serenity, which a good conscience, kind feelings, and the regular discharge of all her duties, spread over her features.' She is not clever, and she has no sense of the picturesque. Integrity, loyalty, and common sense are her characteristics: Jane Austen would have approved of her. Although

she is nervous when the Duke takes her off on a mysterious journey, and in the circumstances 'a romantic heroine might have suspected and dreaded the power of her own charms', Scott comments that 'Jeanie was too wise to let such a silly thought intrude on her mind'. Her imagination not being 'the most powerful of her faculties', her very dreams are sensible—'a wild farm in Northumberland, well stocked with milk-cows, yeald beasts, and sheep'. On the other hand, since she is 'no heroine of romance', worldly affluence has its attractions for her: she looks with curiosity at the domains of Dumbiedikes, of which she might so easily have become mistress.

What happens in the course of the action is that Jeanie's 'dignity of mind and rectitude of principle' are exhibited by her behaviour in a most testing situation. She is placed in precisely the circumstances in which, for a woman with her strong family feelings, the temptation is strongest: she is tempted to commit perjury not for herself but for a sister whom she believes to be innocent of the crime with which she is charged. Since her lover is unable to come to her aid she is 'compelled to trust for guidance to her own unassisted sense of what was right or wrong'. Her determination is simple: to save her sister from execution she will sacrifice 'all but truth and conscience'. She 'can promise nothing which is unlawful for a Christian'. The temptation is pressed home again and again. First, an anonymous stranger tempts her to forswear herself, but she replies: 'I wad ware the best blood in my body to keep her skaithless . . . but I canna change right into wrang, or make that true which is false.' Secondly, and more severely, she is subjected to the 'fearfu' temptation' of what she understands her father to be suggesting: 'Can this be? Can these be his words that I have heard, or has the Enemy taken his voice and features to give weight unto the counsel which causeth to perish?—A sister's life, and a father pointing out how to save it!—O God deliver me!' Thirdly, Jeanie has to submit to the ordeal of facing her sister in prison, and listening to the reproaches of the villainous Ratcliffe, for once compassionate: 'I must needs say that it's d—d hard, when three words of your mouth would give the girl the chance . . . that you make such scrupling.' But the greatest temptation of all occurs in the court, when her sister stretches out her hand and cries 'O Jeanie, Jeanie, save me, save me!', and the advocate for the defence puts to her the leading question whether her

sister had not told her that she was with child: when Jeanie stands firm her father falls in a faint. Throughout this lonely battle, which is reminiscent of Bunyan in its stark simplicity, Jeanie displays 'that superiority, which a deep and firm mind assures to its possessor, under the most trying circumstances'. It is a Wordsworthian theme.

If Scott had stopped with *The Heart of Mid-Lothian*, his reputation would stand higher today than it does. Although his historical range increases as the series progresses, the relentless operation of the law of diminishing returns becomes more and more evident. Driven by his need of money, and realizing that the opinion of the best critics mattered less than the apparently inexhaustible appetite of 'the great variety of readers', Scott did not give himself time to reflect or take fresh bearings. Such variations as he introduced serve only to emphasize the underlying sameness. The fact that the remaining romances must be considered as a group, instead of individually, matters the less because few of them have any serious claim to be regarded as unified wholes. It is their ingredients that demand attention.

No aspect of Scott's repetitiousness is more striking than the persistence of the Common Form already noticed in four of the first five books. Vestiges of this may be seen in most of the other Waverley Romances, while most of its characteristics may be found in *Rob Roy* (1818), *The Abbot* (1820), *The Fortunes of Nigel* (1822), *St. Ronan's Well* (1824), and *Redgauntlet* (1824). Although variations occur, the common element in these books is most striking. Surprisingly enough, it is in the best of Scott's books (*The Heart of Mid-Lothian* apart) that the Common Form is most in evidence. In *The Abbot*, where he tells us that he 'paid attention to such principles of composition, as I conceived were best suited to the historical novel', he reached back to it. Roland is one of Waverley's progeny; the suddenness with which he becomes a person of importance parallels Waverley's meteoric rise as a soldier and foreshadows that of Nigel Olifaunt, who hears (a few days after his arrival in London) that 'the King, and the Prince, and the Duke, have been by the lugs' about him. The attraction which the Common Form exercised on Scott is curiously illustrated in *St. Ronan's Well*. In the preface to this book we are given to expect 'a little drama of modern life' and are particularly assured that Scott is aiming at 'avoiding

worn-out characters and positions'. As the story progresses, however, the people at the Well are reduced more and more to the status of a chorus commenting on the main action, and that centres in the adventures of a young man of the kind familiar to readers of the earlier romances.

The adventures of such a young man formed a suitable framework for a series of scenes describing the life of a given place and period, and in these later romances, as in the earlier, 'manners' were Scott's true subject. The reader is a tourist in history. Frank Osbaldistone exists to enable Scott to describe Rob Roy and give an account of events which happened—or could have happened—just before the outbreak of the '15. Roland in *The Abbot* exists to give Scott an opportunity of describing Edinburgh in the sixteenth century and the situation of Mary Queen of Scots. *The Fortunes of Nigel* actually originated in a series of letters 'giving a picture of manners in town and country during the early part of the reign of James I'. Although he accepted the advice of his friends to lay that plan aside in favour of an historical romance, Scott admits in the preface that the incidents are 'few and meagre'—a fact further acknowledged in the motto of the book, a quotation from the *Anti-Jacobin*'s Knife-grinder:

> Story? Lord bless you! I have none to tell, Sir.

Like Captain Booth in Fielding's *Amelia*, Nigel is given a weak character so that the reader may visit the sanctuary of Whitefriars and learn something of 'Alsatian' cant and manners. He also sees *Richard II* at the Fortune Playhouse, while such features of the London of the time as the state of the Strand and Charing Cross are also described, as well as the nature of a Jacobean 'ordinary' and the social status of pages. As Lockhart remarks, the book is a 'commentary on the old English drama—hardly a single picturesque point of manners touched by Ben Jonson and his contemporaries but has been dovetailed into this story'. In the same way the hero of *Peveril of the Peak* (which unhealthily resembles its immediate predecessor) exists mainly to enable Scott to describe English life at the Restoration; while the fact that he spends some time in the Isle of Man gives him an opportunity of describing the interesting customs of the island and the superstitions in which it is 'perhaps richer than even Ireland, Wales, or the Highlands of Scotland'. The London

scene is described with an antiquary's enthusiasm, while the Popish Plot is prominently introduced.

Adolphus[1] pointed out that each of the Waverley Romances is an essay on a period of history, and this is just as true of those in which the Common Form is less in evidence. In *The Monastery* Scott set out to describe the period of the Reformation. 'The general plan', he tells us, 'was, to conjoin two characters in that bustling and contentious age, who . . . should, with the same sincerity and purity of intention, dedicate themselves' to the two sides. This being so, the scene between Henry Warden the Reformer and Father Eustace the Sub-Prior should have been the climax of the book: in fact its weakness makes it clear that the spiritual conflict which lay behind the Reformation had little reality for Scott. To atone for this he made too much of two subordinate characters, the supernatural White Lady of Avenel and Sir Piercie Shafton the Euphuist. It is difficult to say which of them is the more resounding failure. The contrast between this, the poorest of the books before the final decline, and *Kenilworth* (1821), the most successful of those in which Scott is not on his home ground, is extremely instructive. In *Kenilworth* it is evident that Scott has set out to describe Elizabethan England: we are given an account of the struggle between Leicester and Sussex, Raleigh and Blount appear, while there are frequent references to Shakespeare and Spenser. Drawing on the tracts collected by John Nichols in *The Progresses, and Public Processions, of Queen Elizabeth*, Scott gives a detailed picture of Elizabeth's progresses and in particular of the entertainments at Kenilworth. All this might have served as the background to a tale of the Armada, as Constable had suggested; but fortunately while Scott accepted the idea of an Elizabethan tale he rejected the Armada in favour of the story of Amy Robsart and Cumnor Hall, which had seized his imagination when he read it as a boy in the ballad version of Mickle. Although there are no great characters in the book the simple

[1] John Leycester Adolphus (1795–1862) was the son of the historian John Adolphus. He was educated at Merchant Taylors' and St. John's College, Oxford. In 1821 he published *Letters to Richard Heber, Esq.*, in which he argued forcibly that *Waverley* and its successors were the work of the same author as *The Lay of the Last Minstrel* and Scott's other poems. Scott was impressed by the *Letters*, which contain some illuminating criticism, and Adolphus paid several visits to Abbotsford. In 1822 he was called to the bar of the Inner Temple, and later he became judge of the Marylebone County Court.

romance of Amy's plight inspired a work which is an almost unqualified success, within the severe limitations of the historical romance.

A characteristic feature of these middle books is Scott's royal portrait-gallery. The Chevalier had made a brief appearance in *Waverley*, and Queen Caroline in *The Heart of Mid-Lothian*, but it was in *The Abbot* that such a portrait first became an important part of the story. By introducing Mary Queen of Scots, Scott was playing the trump-card of romance, and although she cannot be reckoned one of his greatest characters she is the most successful of his royal personages. Elizabeth in *Kenilworth* is adequate, but hardly more, while little can be said for the portrayal of James VI and I in *The Fortunes of Nigel* or that of Charles II in *Peveril of the Peak* and *Woodstock* (1826). A more significant feature of the Waverley Romances is Scott's interest in civil wars. A great many of his stories are set in a period of civil war, and the civil war *par excellence* was of course the rebellion of 1745. It was Scott's considered opinion that 'the Jacobite enthusiasm of the eighteenth century, particularly during the rebellion of 1745, afforded a theme, perhaps the finest that could be selected, for fictitious composition, founded upon real or probable incident'. In a letter to Byron he suggested that 'any success I may have had in hitting off the Stuarts is, I am afraid, owing to a little old Jacobite leaven which I sucked in with the numerous traditionary tales that amused my infancy'. At times he himself reminds us of the old soldier he describes in the introduction to *A Legend of Montrose*, a man who 'it is true ... had his inconsistencies. He was a steady jacobite, his father and his four uncles having been out in the forty-five; but he was a no less steady adherent of King George ... so that you were in equal danger to displease him, in terming Prince Charles, the Pretender, or by saying any thing derogatory to the dignity of King George.' Yet only a superficial reader could suppose that Scott was really on the side of the Pretender, and he had every reason to ridicule the suggestion, as he did when he dedicated the whole series to George IV. His real feelings are indicated by the passage in which he remarks that 'the Highlanders, who formed the principal strength of Charles Edward's army, were an ancient and high-spirited race, peculiar in their habits of war and of peace, brave to romance, and exhibiting a character turning upon points more adapted to poetry than to the prose of

real life'. This contrast between poetry and 'the prose of real life' is revealing, and reminds us that Scott was an admirer of Henry Mackenzie, 'The Man of Feeling' in his books but a hard-headed man of business the rest of the time. In the Jacobites Scott found the modern equivalent of the spirit of chivalry which he had admired as a boy in the pages of Froissart. It was for reasons imaginative rather than political tha. he loved to look back to those brave men 'who did nothing in hate, but all in honour'. As he explains at the end of *Waverley*, he found the Jacobites a perfect subject because 'averse [as they were] to intermingle with the English, or adopt their customs, [they] long continued to pride themselves upon maintaining ancient Scottish manners and customs'. In the introduction to *Redgauntlet* he laments their passing:

> The progress of time, which has withdrawn all of them from the field, has removed . . . a peculiar and striking feature of ancient manners. Their love of past times, their tales of bloody battles fought against romantic odds, were all dear to the imagination, and their little idolatry of locks of hair, pictures, rings, ribbons, and other memorials of the time in which they still seemed to live, was an interesting enthusiasm; and although their political principles, had they existed in the relation of fathers, might have rendered them dangerous . . . yet, as we now recollect them, there could not be on the earth supposed to exist persons better qualified to sustain the capacity of innocuous and respectable grandsires.

'An interesting enthusiasm'—the last word clearly retaining its full eighteenth-century force. One is reminded a little of Addison's treatment of the old Tory, Sir Roger de Coverley. There was no real need for Scott to apologize to 'those readers who take up novels merely for amusement' for 'plaguing them so long with old-fashioned politics, and Whig and Tory, and Hanoverians and Jacobites'. It is precisely on those aspects of 'old-fashioned politics' that are calculated to appeal to such readers that he concentrates. He dwells on the picturesque aspects of things and draws contrasts in black and white which have proved a lasting source of historical misunderstanding. In dealing with the English civil war he was no less guilty of over-simplification: the romance of royalty appealed to him irresistibly, and in writing of the Parliamentarians he was dealing

with people whom he understood far less well than he did the Covenanters. Whereas his intimate knowledge of the idiom of the Covenanters brought with it an instinctive feeling for the grain of their minds, for the style of the Parliamentarians he was content to rely on tracts and pamphlets and on such biased history as he found in the comic and satirical writers of the Restoration: he heads too many chapters with quotations from *Hudibras* for us to expect from him an impartial account of the matter.

In the *Lives of the Novelists* and elsewhere Scott wrote more about the practice of fiction than any of his predecessors. This was not because he was passionately interested in prose fiction as a form or had any high opinion of its social or moral function. On the contrary he repeatedly acknowledged that he was 'far from thinking that the novelist or romance-writer stands high in the ranks of literature'. In *Waverley* and its successors he regarded himself as writing 'for general amusement' and he often emphasized that he was 'no great believer in the moral utility to be derived from fictitious compositions'. Many of the remarks in the introductory epistle to *The Fortunes of Nigel* constitute a disclaimer of the high status recently claimed for the novel in the fifth chapter of *Northanger Abbey*. Although he is not consistent in the matter it is noticeable that he more often refers to his own books as 'romances' than 'novels'; it is because the distinction is an important one that the word 'romance' has been used throughout the present chapter.

His cavalier attitude to prose fiction helps to explain his carelessness about unity. In his anonymous review of *Tales of my Landlord* he pointed out that 'his stories are so slightly constructed as to remind us of the showman's thread with which he draws up his pictures and presents them successively to the eye of the spectator'. While he was usually prepared to admit the supremacy of the plotting of *Tom Jones* (to the deeper unity of *Emma* he does not refer), he maintained that such men as Le Sage and Smollett had emancipated fiction from such rigours: 'these great masters have been satisfied if they amused the reader upon the road; though the conclusion only arrived because the tale must have an end'. Convenience apart, the high praise which he always accords Smollett suggests that a looser form of construction than Fielding's made a strong appeal to Scott:

Believe me . . . I have repeatedly laid down my future work to scale, divided it into volumes and chapters, and endeavoured to

construct a story which I meant should evolve itself gradually and strikingly, maintain suspense, and stimulate curiosity; and which, finally, should terminate in a striking catastrophe. But I think there is a demon who seats himself on the feather of my pen when I begin to write, and leads it astray from the purpose. Characters expand under my hand; incidents are multiplied; the story lingers, while the materials increase; my regular mansion turns out a Gothic anomaly.... When I light on such a character as Bailie Jarvie, or Dalgetty, my imagination brightens, and my conception becomes clearer at every step which I take in his company, although it leads me many a weary mile from the regular road, and forces me to leap hedge and ditch to get back into the route again. If I resist the temptation, as you advise me, my thoughts become prosy, flat, and dull . . . I am no more the same author I was in my better mood, than the dog in a wheel . . . is like the same dog merrily chasing his own tail. (Introductory Epistle to *The Fortunes of Nigel.*)

In his self-reviewal Scott had compared his own characterization to that of Shakespeare, and in such a passage as this the account which he gives of his own imagination at work is strikingly similar to that attributed to Shakespeare by the critics of the period. Blending with the element of apology there is an element of scepticism whether the more 'correct' procedure has as much to recommend it as its advocates imagine. There were (in fact) two reasons for Scott's writing fast: one was that he was in a hurry to make money, but the other was that he did not really believe in the importance of unity in a work of fiction. It is significant that in a passage in his Journal he refers to 'the interest of a well-contrived story' as merely 'one way to give novelty' to a book. When his interlocutor in the Introductory Epistle from which a quotation has just been given taunts him with believing that the end of a plot is merely 'to bring in fine things', he replies: 'Grant that it were so, and that I should write with sense and spirit a few scenes unlaboured and loosely put together, but which had sufficient interest in them . . . to furnish harmless amusement'—would that be so very culpable? Perhaps the truth is that when the object of a writer of fiction is merely to amuse, and not to present his readers with an interpretation or criticism of life, then the case for careful construction and unity is greatly weakened, so that Scott was largely right, on his own terms. *The Heart of Mid-Lothian* is the one great novel of the series partly because in it Scott does not merely entertain us (whatever his original intention may have

been): the book has the deep unity of theme which is the condition of its profounder effect. The last volume always excepted, it is the only one of the Waverley series that passes Aristotle's test of unity: nothing can be added or taken away without impairing it as a whole.

There is a passage in Lockhart which makes it clear that Scott began many of his books without more than a general idea of how they would end. Discussing *Rob Roy*, 'Constable said the name of the real hero would be the best possible name for the book. "Nay", answered Scott, "never let me have to write up to a name. You well know I have generally adopted a title that told nothing." ' Most of his titles are more or less misnomers, *Old Mortality* being the extreme instance. As he wrote he often changed the whole direction of the story. In the introduction to *Redgauntlet* he acknowledges that 'various circumstances in the composition induced the author to alter its purport considerably, as it passed through his hands'. In the introduction to *The Abbot* he mentions that *The Monastery* 'was designed, at first, to have contained some supernatural agency, arising out of the fact, that Melrose had been the place of deposit of the great Robert Bruce's heart', so that as the book stands the discovery of the heart, which forms the main part of the introductory epistle, 'is a mystery unnecessarily introduced'. In the introduction to *The Fortunes of Nigel* the reader is given to understand that the hero is George Heriot, while the book is called after Nigel Olifaunt and near the end it is King James who is called 'our principal personage'. It is tempting to suppose that *A Legend of Montrose* (1819) was originally intended to end tragically (as it manifestly should), and that when Scott came to write the preface for the collected Edition he had forgotten that in fact it does not. We know that *Peveril of the Peak* was extended to four volumes because Scott felt that he was making a success of the Court scenes; while any suggestion that his habit of changing the shape of a book during its composition was of late development is refuted by the acknowledgement in the introduction to *Guy Mannering* that the whole plan and theme of the book were changed 'in the course of printing', with the result that 'the early sheets [which] retain . . . the vestiges of the original tenor of the story . . . now hang upon it as an unnecessary and unnatural incumbrance'—and the title is a flagrant misnomer. Other examples could be cited, but

perhaps it will be sufficient to mention the padding-out of *The Heart of Mid-Lothian*, so strangely noticed by Scott's remark in his Journal that 'a rogue' has written to say 'that he approves of the first three volumes . . . but totally condemns the fourth. . . . However, an author should be reasonably well pleased when three fourths of his work are acceptable to the reader.'

An uncertainty of focus resulting from this method of composition may be noticed in many of Scott's books, and it is responsible for the failure of three in particular. In *The Bride of Lammermoor*, which has been highly praised by several critics, it is evident that Scott is writing with his eye on *Macbeth*: a sense of doom hangs over the action, and the conclusion is starkly tragic. But by using Caleb Balderstone not only as a choric character but also as comic relief Scott destroys the unity of the book: although Balderstone is one of his finest comic creations his presence prevents everything in the tale from being in key. A similar uncertainty of purpose is reflected in the undefined status of the witch-like old women. The same is true of *A Legend of Montrose*, which shares the faults of its predecessor but few of its virtues. In spite of the happy ending it is essentially a tragic tale; yet Scott 'endeavoured to enliven' it by the introduction of Captain Dalgetty, who, with his horse Gustavus and his chatter of Marischal College, Aberdeen, goes far to turn the book from tragedy to farce. A fatal lack of homogeneity may also be seen in *St. Ronan's Well*, which is an interesting book to the critic of Scott. Expecting a story 'upon a plan different from any other that the author has ever written', the reader finds himself presented with yet another variation on the Common Form—and then when the end comes in sight and he expects the romance elements to combine to produce the familiar happy ending, melodrama takes over and the book ends in a storm of ghosts and Mrs. Radcliffe. The reason for this is known. When Laidlaw suggested that he should write a contemporary story Scott remembered 'a tale of dark domestic guilt which had recently come under his notice as Sheriff' and decided to make use of it. 'I have thoughts of making the tale tragic, having "a humour to be cruel" ', he wrote to Ballantyne. 'It may go off.' It did not, and the result is indeed (in spite of incidental excellences, such as Meg Dods) 'a pitiful tragedy, filled with the most lamentable mirth'. A better example could

hardly be found of Scott's besetting fault—the neglect of 'keeping' or consistency of atmosphere and tone.

Almost from the start the problem of ending a story irritated and bored him. In 'The Life of Mrs. Radcliffe' he refers feelingly to 'the torment of romance-writers, those necessary evils, the concluding chapters'. For the most part he remained the slave of the conventional happy ending, yet he found it more and more difficult to describe it with a good grace. As early as *Guy Mannering* he escapes by throwing a good deal of the description into the form of a dialogue between Colonel Mannering and Mr. Pleydell. At the end of *Old Mortality* he remarks that he had intended to leave the conclusion to the reader's imagination, 'a practice, which might be found convenient to both readers and compilers'; but instead he personifies the more conventional members of his 'reading public' and introduces subsequent events in the course of a dialogue between the author and Miss Martha Buskbody, whose demands are as stereotyped and as exacting as those of a modern reader of detective stories. In *Redgauntlet* we find a similar device: a letter from an imaginary antiquary gives the few facts of subsequent history which he has been able to discover. At the end of *The Fortunes of Nigel* Scott remarks with obvious relief that since 'the fashion of such narratives as the present changes like other earthly things', a circumstantial description of the final wedding is no longer necessary: 'a change which saves an author the trouble of attempting in vain to give a new colour to the commonplace description of such matters'.

Scott's boredom as he wrote the concluding chapters of his books sprang from his boredom with the conventional shape of story which he had taken over from his predecessors. For all the originality of the matter which he brought into the range of prose fiction, his view of the nature of the form itself was unoriginal and conventional. As the series progressed he often became worried and anxious for novelty, and when this happened he chose a new period or a new setting for his story. After stories mainly set in Scotland in the eighteenth century (his true field) he wrote a succession of books mainly set in the late sixteenth and early seventeenth centuries and dealing with a variety of places. Occasionally it is clear that he has set out in a given book to avoid the repetition of some particular feature of the previous books: Di Vernon differs superficially from his earlier heroines,

as Jeanie Deans differs essentially. But the relative insignificance of most of the differences between his books is underlined by the fact that when he refers to a 'different method' in *The Bride of Lammermoor* and *A Legend of Montrose* he means primarily that there is less dialogue than usual in these books, and more action. It was almost wholly the possibility of a change of subject-matter that presented itself to him: except in *The Heart of Mid-Lothian* it does not seem to have occurred to him that to write a book on a serious and unifying theme would be a novelty of a more important kind. Little interested as he was in the technique of fiction, he did not explore the possibilities of varying the point of view from which the story is told. It is a pity that he did not carry further the experiment in the epistolary novel represented by the first third of *Redgauntlet*, as this might have taught him the secret of dramatizing a story. As the prefatory matter to so many of the books bears witness, he enjoyed the creation of imaginary *personae*; but he was too impatient to sustain the pretence, and the prolonged process of revision which lies behind Jane Austen's novels was for him out of the question.

In his study of Pope, Professor Geoffrey Tillotson has used Correctness as a focal point: the Picturesque might similarly be used as the central concept in a study of the Waverley Romances. We have only to glance into the writings of William Gilpin to see how closely many of the scenes which Scott describes conform to the canons of the Picturesque. His favourite terrain—the Border country and the Highlands of Scotland—provided him with a rich storehouse of picturesque scenery, and when he moved to less familiar ground his choice was always largely dictated by the picturesque potentialities of the country. 'The site was singularly picturesque', he observes at the beginning of *St. Ronan's Well*, and the remark might stand as a comment on the great majority of his settings. Wordsworth was critical about this, complaining of 'the laborious manner in which everything is placed before your eyes for the production of picturesque effect' and insisting that 'the reader, in good narration, feels that pictures rise up before his sight, and pass away from it unostentatiously, succeeding each other. But when they are fixed upon an easel for the express purpose of being admired, the judicious are apt to take offence, and even to turn sulky at the exhibitor's officiousness.' Yet there is no

doubt that the exhibition of the most beautiful aspects of our scenery was one of Scott's objects, and it seems more reasonable to agree with Goethe that 'the beauty of the three British kingdoms' is one of the sources of the charm of his work.

As a boy Waverley is described sitting in a 'large and sombre library . . . exercis[ing] for hours that internal sorcery, by which past or imaginary events are presented in action, as it were, to the eye of the muser'. It was by this habit that Scott's own creative imagination was nourished, and to the end it remained very much a visualizing imagination. There is a description of a painting near the end of the first chapter of *The Bride of Lammermoor* which may well have been the germ from which the whole story grew, and it seems likely that Scott often conceived of an episode or even of a whole book in visual terms. The fact that he is composing in this way is often emphasized by the mention of a painter's name. As Adolphus pointed out, Scott was particularly fond of effects of chiaroscuro, and when he uses this device Rembrandt is the painter whom he most often mentions, as in Chapter XXXII of *The Antiquary*:

> The window, which had been shut, in order that a gloomy twilight might add to the solemnity of the funeral meeting, was opened as she commanded, and threw a sudden and strong light through the smoky and misty atmosphere of the stifling cabin. Falling in a stream upon the chimney, the rays illuminated, in the way that Rembrandt would have chosen, the features of the unfortunate nobleman, and those of the old sybil.

Most frequently of all it is his friend David Wilkie whom Scott invokes, as he does in the previous chapter of the same book and in the description of the reunion of Jeanie Deans and her father in *The Heart of Mid-Lothian*. The affinity between Fielding and Hogarth has often been remarked: that between Scott and David Wilkie is no less striking and no less significant.

Scott's quest for the picturesque is as evident in his choice of characters as in his local descriptions. His finest characters are usually men and women of striking appearance. Nothing could be more picturesque than the appearance of Meg Merrilies, for example, 'a female figure, dressed in a long cloak, [who] sate on a stone by this miserable couch; her elbows . . . upon her knees, and her face, averted from the light of an iron lamp beside her . . ., bent upon that of the dying person'. Edie

Ochiltree is no less striking. There is a fine passage in *The Antiquary* in which he is contrasted with the Earl, and this reminds us of another device which is thoroughly characteristic of Scott:

> The contrast . . . was very striking. The hale cheek, firm step, erect stature and undaunted presence and bearing of the old mendicant, indicated patience and content in the extremity of age, and in the lowest condition to which humanity can sink; while the sunken eye, pallid cheek, and tottering form of the nobleman . . . showed how little wealth, power, and even the advantages of youth, have to do with that which gives repose to the mind, and firmness to the frame.

Gilpin insisted that contrast was an essential element in the Picturesque, and one has only to read Scott's prefaces to see how often he refers to contrasts of various kinds. In the preface to *Peveril of the Peak* he explicitly mentions that once he has found a suitable subject he 'invests it with such shades of character, as will best suit with each other' and there can be no doubt that the desire for striking contrasts lay very near the heart of his imagination. At the end of the first chapter of *Waverley* he points out that 'some favourable opportunities of contrast' have been afforded him 'by the state of society in the northern part of the island at the period of my history', while in the introduction to *The Fortunes of Nigel* the importance to him of contrast and the Picturesque are particularly evident:

> The most romantic region of every country is that where the mountains unite themselves with the plains or lowlands. . . . The most picturesque period of history is that when the ancient rough and wild manners of a barbarous age are just becoming innovated upon, and contrasted, by the illumination of increased or revived learning, and the instructions of renewed or reformed religion. The strong contrast produced by the opposition of ancient manners to those which are gradually subduing them, affords the lights and shadows necessary to give effect to a fictitious narrative; and while such a period entitles the author to introduce incidents of a marvellous and improbable character, as arising out of the turbulent independence and ferocity, belonging to old habits of violence, . . . yet . . . the characters and sentiments of many of the actors may . . . be described with great variety of shading and delineation, which belongs to the newer and more improved period.

It is clear why Scotland in the eighteenth century provided

so rich a field for Scott. Rob Roy was in a sense the perfect character for him, 'playing such pranks in the beginning of the 18th century, as are usually ascribed to Robin Hood in the middle ages,—and that within forty miles of Glasgow, a great commercial city, the seat of a learned university'. It delighted Scott to reflect that 'a character like his, blending the wild virtues, the subtle policy, and unrestrained license of an American Indian, was flourishing in Scotland during the Augustan age of Queen Anne and George I. . . . It is this strong contrast betwixt the civilized and cultivated mode of life on the one side of the Highland line, and the wild and lawless adventures . . . [of] one who dwelt on the opposite side . . . which creates the interest attached to his name.' It is clear that the contrast between different characters and different modes of life attracted Scott as an eligible source of interest and a convenient structural device: that is one reason for his liking for civil wars. The deliberateness with which he used it is brought out by the fact that the first chapter of *Quentin Durward* is actually entitled 'The Contrast': there are many other chapters throughout the series that might bear the same heading.

Important as the concept of the Picturesque was to Scott, however, it does not cover what seemed to him the chief technical innovation in the Waverley Romances: he considered that they were more dramatic than the work of his predecessors, and by that he meant that they made more use of dialogue. In the first chapter of *The Bride of Lammermoor* an imaginary critic complains that his characters 'make too much use of the *gob box*; they *patter* too much. . . . There is nothing in whole pages but mere chat and dialogue'—so giving Scott an opportunity of vindicating his practice. 'The ancient philosopher', he replies, 'was wont to say, "Speak, that I may know thee"; and how is it possible for an author to introduce his *personæ dramatis* to his readers in a more interesting and effectual manner, than by the dialogue in which each is represented as supporting his own appropriate character?' This claim to originality in the matter of dialogue comes as something of a surprise today, yet there is no doubt of the importance of dialogue in most of Scott's books. Not that his dialogue is always successful. The ineptitude of many of his conversations between lovers is notorious. When a girl addresses her admirer with the words: 'Rise, Master Peveril . . . Rise! If you retain this unbecoming posture any

longer, I will leave the room, and you will never see me more' it is hardly surprising that he is 'overawed', and such language is too common in the mouths of Scott's heroines, highly endowed as they are 'with that exquisite delicacy which is imprinted on the female heart, to give warning of the slightest approach to impropriety'. It is also noticeable that in soliloquy—which he considered more dramatic than the direct description of a character's thoughts—Scott was often unsuccessful; perhaps because the thoughts of his great characters are so clear from their actions and conversations that it is mainly such characters as his young heroes who are obliged to soliloquize. It is in the dialogue of the Scots-speaking characters that his greatest passages are to be found. The advertisement to *The Antiquary*, in which he is referring particularly to that work and to *Guy Mannering*, makes it clear that Scott was aware of this:

> I have . . . sought my principal personages in the class of society who are the last to feel the influence of that general polish which assimilates to each other the manners of different nations. Among the same class I have placed some of the scenes, in which I have endeavoured to illustrate the operation of the higher and more violent passions; both because the lower orders are less restrained by the habit of suppressing their feelings, and because I agree with my friend Wordsworth, that they seldom fail to express them in the strongest and most powerful language. This is, I think, peculiarly the case with the peasantry of my own country, a class with whom I have long been familiar. The antique force and simplicity of their language, often tinctured with the Oriental eloquence of Scripture, in the mouths of those of an elevated understanding, give pathos to their grief, and dignity to their resentment.

It is difficult to realize the daring of Scott's innovation. For a long period before his time the Scots language had habitually been used in literature for the purposes of low comedy and farce. He had to contend with 'stock responses' which were the result of prejudice and ignorance. How clearly he knew what he was doing is evident from his own review, in which he draws attention to 'the singular skill and felicity with which, in conveying the genuine sentiments of the Scottish peasant in the genuine language of his native land, the author has avoided that appearance of grossness and vulgarity by which the success of every similar attempt has hitherto been defeated'. In his work, as he goes on to claim, 'the Scottish peasant speaks the

language of his native country, his *national* language, not the *patois* of an individual district; and in listening to it we not only do not experience even the slightest feeling of disgust or aversion, but our bosoms are responsive to every sentiment of sublimity, or awe, or terror which the author may be disposed to excite'. It has been given to few men to effect so great a revolution of taste in the response of readers to a language. This is the root of Scott's greatness. It is by their speeches that he creates every one of his most successful characters. When stress is laid on the fact that Scott is usually more concerned to describe Scottish life and manners than to create books which are artistic wholes the manner of his description must be remembered. It is not in the narrative or scenic passages that he most perfectly depicts Scots manners, but in those in which his characters are speaking. His painting of the countryside is nothing beside his re-creation of the men and women who inhabit the countryside and make up the nation. It is true that in describing the mountains and lochs of Scotland he extended the scenic possibilities of prose fiction, but in creating his greatest characters he did something much more important. What remains in one's mind, after the period trappings and even the natural descriptions have faded, is the voice of Meg Merrilies prophesying the downfall of the house of Ellangowan, the voice of Jeanie Deans pleading for her sister's life before the Queen.

# VII

# PEACOCK

If it is doubtful whether *Waverley* should be called a novel, it is certain that *Gryll Grange* should not. Peacock's works of prose fiction are best considered as satiric tales. In his essay on 'French Comic Romances' he distinguishes between two types of comic tale: that in which the characters are individuals and the events such as happen in real life, and that 'in which the characters are abstractions or embodied classifications, and the implied or embodied opinions [are] the main matter of the work'. As it happens the two types are illustrated by two books that appeared in the year 1818, *Northanger Abbey* and *Nightmare Abbey*. They have a good deal in common. In each an author whose attitude is conservative and 'eighteenth-century' satirizes the excesses of modern literature as exemplified in the work of Mrs. Radcliffe and the 'German' drama of the day. In each life in an Abbey turns out to be much like life anywhere else. When Mr. Glowry in *Nightmare Abbey* tells Scythrop that his behaviour might 'do very well in a German tragedy . . . but it will not do in Lincolnshire' we are reminded of Catherine Morland's discovery that it is not in the work of Mrs. Radcliffe and her followers that 'human nature, at least in the midland counties of England, was to be looked for'. In Jane Austen's book a young woman discovers the difference between life in books and life in fact: in Peacock's a young man makes the same discovery. But there is a great difference between the two. In *Northanger Abbey* the characters are individuals, whereas in *Nightmare Abbey* the characters are abstractions and it is their opinions which form 'the main matter of the work'. Unlike Jane Austen, Peacock is more interested in ideas than in people: his concern is not with what his characters do, but with what they say. He is the great satiric commentator on the age which we are considering, the Aristophanes of the period of which Hazlitt wrote, at the beginning of his essay on Coleridge: 'The present is an age of talkers, and not of doers; and the reason is, that the world is growing old'.[1]

[1] Thomas Love Peacock (1785–1866) was the son of a London merchant. As a young man he found business uncongenial, and worked without enthusiasm. In

The nature of Peacock's purpose accounts for the peculiar design of his books. *Headlong Hall* (1816), *Melincourt* (1817), *Crotchet Castle* (1831), and *Gryll Grange* (1860) are strikingly similar in pattern, while the other tales retain a family resemblance. The pattern may already be observed in the two farces which Peacock seems to have written about the years 1811–13, *The Dilettanti* and *The Three Doctors*. *Headlong Hall* represents Peacock's first attempt to use the formula for the purposes of prose fiction. The scene is set in a mansion in Wales, the characters being the members of Squire Headlong's Christmas house party. There is a tenuous love story, but the main interest of the book centres in the conversation of the philosophers and dilettanti. These 'humours', representing popular opinions of the day, include Mr. Foster the perfectibilian, Mr. Escot the deteriorationist, and Mr. Jenkison the statu-quo-ite, as well as Mr. Milestone the landscape-designer, Mr. Cranium the craniologist, and Miss Poppyseed the novelist. It is sometimes said that these characters are caricatures of actual people, but in fact it is only opinions that Peacock is concerned with: Mr. Foster serves as a mouthpiece for some of Shelley's youthful ideas, Mr. Escot's views are a caricature of Lord Monboddo's, while Miss Poppyseed is an intellectual caricature of Mrs. Opie. As in the later books, the other characters include a comfort-loving cleric (Dr. Gaster, a coarser figure than his successors) and a couple of eligible young ladies. *Headlong Hall* is in fact Peacock's prospectus, as *Waverley* is Scott's. The discussion of the true meaning of Progress which opens in the first chapter does not come to an end until we reach the last chapter of the last book, *Gryll Grange*; while we have to go no farther than the second chapter to find the characters seated at table and embarked on the learned and philosophical discussion of food and drink which forms the seasoning of all Peacock's work.

1812 he met Shelley. They soon became close friends, and throughout his life Peacock was to look back with an amused delight to the conversations that they had enjoyed at Marlow. In 1819 he entered the service of the East India Company, and the following year he married a Welsh girl, Jane Gryffydh. For many years Peacock was the East India Company's chief examiner. His brief essay, 'The Four Ages of Poetry', published in *Ollier's Literary Miscellany* in 1820, provoked Shelley's brilliant *Defence*. He repeatedly refused to write a biography of Shelley, but in 1858 and 1860 he published reminiscences in *Fraser's Magazine* to set right some matters unfairly represented by Trelawny, Hogg, and Charles S. Middleton. He was particularly anxious to defend the memory of Shelley's first wife, Harriet Westbrook. His comments on Shelley are both witty and understanding.

In *Melincourt* we again find a number of 'humours' representing (as Peacock acknowledged) the 'opinions and public characters' of men of the time. Mr. Feathernest's opinions are intended to represent Southey's, Mr. Derrydown's satirize those of Scott, Mr. Mystic's those of Coleridge, while Mr. Fax acts as spokesman for the Malthusians. One character, Sir Oran Hautton, is a new departure. In *Headlong Hall* Peacock had contented himself with mocking the opinions of Monboddo in the course of the dialogue: now he presents us with an oran-outang with 'an air of high fashion', a startling pair of whiskers, and great skill as an accompanist on a French horn. As well as a satire on Monboddo's interpretation of history, however, Sir Oran acts as an 'irresistible exposure of the universality and omnipotence of corruption', since he is bought a seat in Parliament and it is made clear that he has all the qualifications necessary for success in 'high life'.

In spite of the farcical element introduced by Sir Oran, *Melincourt* is a more serious work than *Headlong Hall*. In one of his letters about this time Shelley described Peacock as 'an enemy to every shape of tyranny and superstitious imposture', and this precisely describes the author of the book. Written in the period of reaction that followed Waterloo, *Melincourt* is a passionate protest against the 'loyalist' excesses and persecutions of the time. We are told that when Feathernest was asked to explain the spirit of the age of chivalry

> it burst upon him like the spectre of his youthful integrity, and he mumbled a half-intelligible reply, about truth and liberty—disinterested benevolence—self-oblivion—heroic devotion to love and honour—protection of the feeble, and subversion of tyranny. (Chap. viii.)

'All the ingredients of a rank Jacobin!', Lord Anophel bursts out. The same sort of satire becomes evident when Sir Telegraph promises to reform his own manner of life

> when ecclesiastical dignitaries imitate the temperance and humility of the founder of that religion by which they feed and flourish: when the man in place acts on the principles which he professed while he was out: . . . when poets are not to be hired for the maintenance of any opinion . . . when universities are not a hundred years in knowledge behind all the rest of the world. (Chap. xxiv.)

Peacock's anti-clericalism is particularly evident in this book, where it is associated with the attacks on *The Legitimate Review* (*The Quarterly*) which reach their climax in Chapter XXXIX. In this, transparently disguised, Wordsworth and Croker join Southey, Canning, and Gifford in chanting 'The church is in danger! the church is in danger!' whenever an embarrassing question is posed. There is an admirable scene in which Mr. Forrester asks to see the learned Mr. Portpipe's library:

The reverend gentleman hummed awhile with great gravity and deliberation: then slowly rising from his large arm-chair, he walked across the room to the further corner, where throwing open the door of a little closet, he said with extreme complacency, 'There is my library'. (Chap. xxxvi.)

It is Mr. Portpipe who defends paper money,

'and for this very orthodox reason, that the system of paper-money is inseparably interwoven with the present order of things, and the present order of things I have made up my mind to stick by precisely as long as it lasts'.
'*And no longer?*' said Mr. Fax.
'I am no fool, Sir,' said the divine. (Chap. xxx.)

Unlike *Headlong Hall*, however, *Melincourt* contains several sympathetic characters who contrast strongly with the time-servers and hypocrites who abound at Mainchance Villa. The heroine Anthelia, who has been brought up among 'the majestic forms and wild energies of Nature', is determined to marry no man who is not imbued with 'the spirit of the age of chivalry'. With Mr. Forester—and indeed Sir Oran, who is not a sophisticated beast—she stands in piquant opposition to the scheming suitors, the mercenary Mrs. Pinmoney, and the turncoats Feathernest, Mystic, and Derrydown. An uncritical belief in progress is satirized by the remarks of an old farmer whose freehold farm has been in his family for seven hundred years, Malthusianism by the conversation of a rustic lover and his sweetheart.

Brett-Smith conjectured that *Melincourt* originally ended with the Anti-Saccharine Fête, but that the publisher had asked Peacock to lengthen it; and it is difficult not to feel that the book as it stands is too long. It is not that the later chapters are inferior, but merely that the reader has had enough. The author

is very much in earnest. A year after the publication of the book we find Peacock writing to Hogg:

> I have been considering the question of marriage and divorce, and have read everything I can get on the subject . . . I shall write when I have leisure a dialogue on the subject, to get a clearer view of my own notions.

Coming from such a master of comic dialogue, this remark is of great interest. Yet Peacock's finest dialogue does not give us the impression that he is thinking things out as he writes: we rather feel that he has reached his own conclusions before beginning to write and is now making comedy from the percussion of ideas. In *Melincourt*, on the other hand, Peacock seems to be earnestly in pursuit of the truth, with more passion and less tolerance than usual. The conversation is not his most entertaining, while less is said about food and drink than in other of his books. He was too angry at the political situation, and was seeing too much of Shelley, to give his genius for comedy a free rein.

*Nightmare Abbey* has something in common with its predecessors. Once again we have a house party, an epicurean cleric (though Mr. Larynx is not prominent), and a number of visitors who are essentially 'humours'. The views of Mr. Flosky the Kantian satirize those of Coleridge: the views of Mr. Toobad, 'the manichaean Millenarian', satirize those of J. F. Newton: while those of Mr. Cypress satirize Byron. But unlike *Headlong Hall* and *Melincourt*, *Nightmare Abbey* has a proper plot, with unforeseen events and a reversal of fortune. This concerns Scythrop, the son of the host. Scythrop's opinions caricature those of Shelley at a certain point in his life; while his position, suspended between two girls as Mahomet's coffin is suspended between heaven and earth, reminds us of Shelley's position between Mary and Harriet. The scene in which Scythrop is confronted by them both comes straight from the world of stage comedy, as does the dénouement, in which each of the girls marries another man, leaving Scythrop alone and forlorn. As in *Melincourt*, rather less of the satire occurs in the form of dialogue than in most of Peacock's books: description and narrative are more prominent than usual. But the distinguishing feature of the book is its atmosphere of ironically described gloom. Melancholy is in fact the subject of the book, which is more unified in its satire than Peacock's other tales. The host is a

melancholy man, and accordingly there is little talk of food and drink (so that Mr. Larynx never gets a chance), while the action does not end with the customary Christmas revels. There are only three songs, and the best of these is the melancholy one (already quoted) which parodies Byron:

> There is a fever of the spirit,
> The brand of Cain's unresting doom.

Peacock told Hogg in a letter that he had been 'amusing myself with the darkness and misanthropy of modern literature, from the lantern jaws of which I shall endeavour to elicit a laugh'. 'I think it necessary', he wrote in another letter, 'to "make a stand" against the "encroachments" of black bile.' This satire on melancholy inspires the characterization of Scythrop and Mr. Flosky, and particularly that of Cypress: because his own affairs are in confusion the latter argues that human life 'is not in the harmony of things; it is an all-blasting upas'. Mr. Hilary acts as the author's own mouthpiece:

> I am one of those who cannot see the good that is to result from all this mystifying and blue-devilling of society. The contrast it presents to the cheerful and solid wisdom of antiquity is too forcible not to strike any one who has the least knowledge of classical literature. To represent vice and misery as the necessary accompaniments of genius, is as mischievous as it is false, and the feeling is as unclassical as the language in which it is usually expressed. (Chap. xi.)

Throughout the book *avant-garde* attitudes are satirized in conservative terms. The values of the fashionable but absurd 'German' drama are ridiculed in a mode that owes a great deal to eighteenth-century English comedy. The pretentious is satirized from the point of view of ordinary common sense. Scythrop, 'like a shuttle-cock between two battle-dores, changing its direction as rapidly as the oscillations of a pendulum, receiving many a hard knock on the cork of a sensitive heart, and flying from point to point on the feathers of a super-sublimated head', is in a situation which recalls that of a hypocritical rake in Goldsmith or Sheridan—for all his good intentions and his metaphysical theorizings. The final comic correction is administered by his father:

> 'And the next time, have but one string to your bow.'
> 'Very good advice, sir', said Scythrop.

In *Maid Marian* (1822) and *The Misfortunes of Elphin* (1829) Peacock is again searching for a satiric medium with more of a plot than his first two discussion-books: but instead of using a contemporary setting he now turns to the historical romance. The story of Robin Hood has always lent itself to modern application, and in *Maid Marian* (which is set in the twelfth century) Peacock makes it 'the vehicle of much oblique satire on all the oppressions that are done under the sun'. He was able to draw heavily on Ritson's collection of Robin Hood ballads not only for his material but also for some of his modern parallels, since Ritson was an uncompromising Jacobin. Throughout the book such phrases as 'social order' and 'distributive justice' are mischievously used, while Richard Coeur-de-Lion is presented as the complete anti-Jacobin. As the action progresses, however, Peacock's interest in his story and its idyllic background begins to get the upper hand of his satiric intention, and the result is a disconcerting juxtaposition of romance and satire. For those interested in the medieval enthusiasm of this period (a disillusioning study) the book has considerable interest; but otherwise, in spite of one or two agreeable scenes, it is far from successful. *The Misfortunes of Elphin* is liable to many of the same criticisms. It is possible that Peacock played with the idea of attempting to do for Wales something of what Scott had done for Scotland. The book is set in the sixth century, and his enthusiasm for Wales and its history is everywhere apparent. There are some fine descriptive passages, as well as fourteen songs, most of which are translations or adaptations of traditional bardic poetry. 'The Song of the Four Winds' is admirable. But once again Peacock's satiric intention conflicts with his antiquarian enthusiasm. Just as we are becoming interested in Wales and its legendary past we are pulled up by a reminder that at this happy period 'the science of political economy was sleeping in the womb of time', or by a comment that as yet mankind 'could neither poison the air with gas, nor the water with its dregs'. There are amusing things in the book, such as the celebrated curse of Seithenyn the mighty drinker, but as a whole it is unsatisfactory and reinforces the judgement that for Peacock the historical romance was a false direction.

In *Crotchet Castle* Peacock reverted to the model of his earlier books. Once again we find ourselves amongst a house party consisting of people with strong views on everything under the

sun, while a love story, set for the most part in Wales, serves as a sub-plot. Unamiable as he is, Mr. MacCrotchet shares Squire Headlong's passion for discussion. He hopes before he dies to hear the outcome of such debates as those concerning 'the sentimental against the rational, the intuitive against the inductive . . . , the intense against the tranquil, the romantic against the classical'. Dr. Folliott the cleric is a great advance on Dr. Gaster, being learned as well as gastronomical; while Lady Clarinda and Miss Touchandgo are more interesting than the ladies in *Headlong Hall*. The 'humours' include Mr. Mac Quedy the political philosopher, Mr. Skionar the Kantian, Mr. Trillo the musician, Mr. Fitzchrome the painter, and Mr. Chainmail, whose passion for the twelfth century anticipates the Greek enthusiasm of Mr. Falconer in *Gryll Grange*. There is also an unnecessarily long train of minor 'humours'.

Like most of Peacock's books, *Crotchet Castle* belongs to a particular point in time. We have only to glance into the Reviews of the period to realize that the main discussions in the book deal with disputes of the day. Peacock's principal theme is announced when Dr. Folliott bursts into the breakfast room and declares that he is 'out of all patience with this march of mind'. One of his main targets is Brougham and the Society for the Diffusion of Useful Knowledge. He inveighs against 'such science as the learned friend deals in: every thing for every body, science for all, schools for all, rhetoric for all, law for all, physic for all, words for all, and sense for none'. (Chap. II.) While Peacock must not be supposed to share all his views, there can be no doubting the intention of the peroration on political economy in Chapter X, any more than that of Mr. MacCrotchet's onslaught on the sin of the times in Chapter VII: 'Where the Greeks had modesty, we have cant; where they had poetry, we have cant; where they had patriotism, we have cant; where they had any thing that exalts, delights, or adorns humanity, we have nothing but cant, cant, cant.' In a sense the debate between Dr. Folliott and his host is a continuation of that between Mr. Escot and Mr. Foster, but the tone is now more urgent and less academic. The perplexities of the time hang heavily over this book, which appeared in the year before the Reform Act. Mr. MacCrotchet and his son, who has to flee to America, are examples of unscrupulous tradesmen becoming 'highly respectable gentlemen' at the expense of those whom they have defrauded. Sir Simon

Steeltrap, Member for Crouching Curtown, and Lord of the United Manors of Spring-gun and Treadmill, is no less a sign of the times. Dr. Folliott is actually set on by a pair of (highly stylized) desperadoes, one of whom is killed—so providing his companion with a commodity to sell to the anatomists. The Christmas revels with which, as we expect, the book concludes are dramatically interrupted by a mob shouting 'Captain Swing': 'the march of mind with a witness', as Dr. Folliott comments. The 'rabble rout'—as Peacock calls it, borrowing his phrase from *Hudibras*—has to be put to flight before the celebrations can follow their proper course, 'according to good customs long departed'. Although Peacock exerts himself to provide alternatives to the diseases of the time—whether the idyllic background of the Welsh mountains and a simple country life, or the 'images of old England' recommended by Dr. Folliott: 'old hospitality, old wine, old ale'—and sees to it that the values of Old England triumph in the end, *Crotchet Castle* lacks the sense of freedom from the pressures of everyday reality which is so remarkable in its successor.

In *Gryll Grange*, Peacock's last book by almost thirty years, the familiar formula is used once again, and the result is a masterpiece. Mr. Gryll is a much more delightful host than the dubious Mr. MacCrotchet: while he shares his love of conversation and his hospitable habits he is himself the personification of Dr. Folliott's 'Old England'. Dr. Opimian has a great deal in common with Dr. Folliott, but he is more tolerant and more intelligent, and he is hardly ever ridiculous. Mr. Falconer, with his tower and his seven damsels, is an inspired variation on Scythrop; while his passion for the Greeks forms an excuse for the ubiquitous classical conversation which is characteristic of this quintessentially Peacockian book. Lord Curryfin, an amiable Zimri, is much more interesting than his predecessor Lord Bossnowl in *Crotchet Castle*. Most of the other characters stand in recognizable descent from characters in the earlier books, though one notices that many of the minor 'humours' have been dropped: superfluous mouthpieces who 'will none of 'em be missed'. The principal additions are Miss Ilex, a charming old maid who is a marked improvement on Miss Evergreen in *Melincourt*, and Harry Hedgerow and his brothers-in-love, who form (with the damsels whom they woo) a chorus from the world of light opera.

The motto of the book comes from *Hudibras*—

> Opinion governs all mankind,
> Like the blind leading of the blind

—and in it we find one of Peacock's recurrent themes, the divergence between appearance and reality, between things as they are and things as they seem to be, consummately expressed. As Mr. Gryll comments, 'we live in a world of misnomers':

> A gang of swindling bankers is a respectable old firm . . . men who sell their votes to the highest bidder . . . are a free and independent constituency . . . a man who successively betrays everybody that trusts him, and abandons every principle he ever professed, is a great statesman, and a Conservative forsooth, *à nil conservando*. . . . A change for the worse is reform. (Chap. i.)

Brougham turns up again, only to be treated like Punch's wife: while we are presented with some memorable observations on lectures, as well as a fine specimen of that 'bore of all bores, an educationist': 'His subject had no beginning, middle, or end. It was education. Never was such a journey through the desert of mind: the Great Sahara of intellect. The very recollection makes me thirsty.' (Chap. XIX.) We notice that almost every feature of the contemporary scene of which Peacock disapproves is now presented as one of the hydra-heads of the monster Progress. This is particularly true of science. 'The day would fail', Dr. Opimian observes, 'if I should attempt to enumerate the evils which science has inflicted on mankind. I almost think it is the ultimate destiny of science to exterminate the human race.' Although it touches on many debates of the time, however, *Gryll Grange* dates much less than its predecessor. As we read it we are reminded of its author's alleged injunction to Trelawny: 'Don't talk to me about anything that has happened for the last two thousand years.'

The house party is now set in Wales again, and the proceedings close with a Twelfth Night ball and a number of marriages. The air of the whole book is festive. In *Crotchet Castle* we regret the fact that Peacock so often allows his characters to escape out-of-doors: here *Gryll Grange* is irreproachable. In this book 'those ornamental varieties of the human species who live to be amused for the benefit of social order'—as he describes the upper middle class in his 'Essay on Fashionable Literature'—do not

waste their time. Events are untoward, because they interrupt the conversation and the dining. From the opening lines onwards the dinner-table itself is in fact the centre of the 'action' (if such a word is in order): to it everything under the sun must be brought for judgement. The conversation is better than ever: more classical, more witty, and more quotable. Peacock must have begun the book about the time when he was completing his *Memoir of Shelley*, and it is clear that as he worked at it his mind was harking back to the early days of 'The Athenians' (as he and his friends had called themselves): not least perhaps to the time which Hogg had described, forty years before, as 'that winter at Bishopsgate, which was a mere Atticism'. The talk that had then passed between Shelley, Hogg and the rest was to remain one of Peacock's sources of inspiration throughout his life: it never produced more mellow fruit than *Gryll Grange*, which is compact of conversation recollected in tranquillity.

While the dialogue reaches a pitch of excellence higher than Peacock had attained before, we also notice that the love story and the peaceful background of the tale help to give the book its unique atmosphere. As we read it we enter an imaginative world, free from the anxieties and frustrations of everyday life. Nothing is less in demand than verisimilitude. The equable loves of Mr. Falconer and Miss Gryll belong to a world of fantasy: these favourites of fortune have nothing to do but to make up their minds. This is a realm in which when two men love the same lady the result is 'rivalry... without animosity'. No characters in literature are safer from the dangers of the outside world: when lightning kills their horses the only result is to bring them under the roof of an eligible bachelor at whose table they are soon seated at dinner. It is an 'enchanted palace' that Mr. Falconer inhabits: with its books and its wine and the seven charming sisters who administer to him, the Tower is a gesture of defiance at mundane reality. If the book has any 'moral', it is concerned with a wisely sceptical Epicureanism. Many years before, Peacock had remarked on the singularity of the fact that 'the popular conception of the sensualist refers his parentage to precisely that philosopher who had the most temperate doctrines and practice', insisting that Epicurus recommended temperance in all things. Mr. Gryll and Mr. Falconer are both professed Epicureans, and although the philosopher might have had difficulty in recognizing them as his disciples, they are

at least far removed from the adolescent philanderers of Moore's *Epicurean*. The conclusion of *Gryll Grange* is essentially that of a less deeply pessimistic *Candide*. We are explicitly assured that Lord Curryfin is now a wiser man than he had been when he thought that he could set the world to rights by waving his wand, and there is no suggestion that Mr. Falconer and his bride are going to set about reforming mankind. Tranquillity is the rational goal.

# VIII

# JOHN GALT AND THE MINOR WRITERS OF PROSE FICTION

As Miss Tompkins has pointed out in her admirable study, *The Popular Novel in England, 1770–1800*, 'during the years that follow the death of Smollett . . . the two chief facts about the novel are its popularity as a form of entertainment and its inferiority as a form of art'. In the first two decades of the new century the achievements of Maria Edgeworth, Jane Austen, and Sir Walter Scott greatly increased the prestige of prose fiction. A note which Jeffrey prefixed to his reviews of novels when he reprinted them sums up what had happened:

> As I perceive I have . . . made a sort of apology for seeking to direct the attention of my readers to things so insignificant as *Novels*, it may be worth while to inform the present generation that, *in my youth*, writings of this sort were rated very low. . . . For certainly a greater mass of trash and rubbish never disgraced the press of any country, than the ordinary Novels that filled and supported our circulating libraries, down nearly to the time of Miss Edgeworth's first appearance.

By 1844, the date of Jeffrey's collected *Contributions to the Edinburgh Review*, the position was very different. Nearly twenty years earlier, indeed, Plumer Ward was able to point out, in the preface to *De Vere; or, The Man of Independence*, that 'that species of literary composition called the Novel has been carried to so consummate a pitch of perfection during the last twenty or thirty years, that, in its power of delineating, exciting, or soothing the human heart, it almost rivals the Drama itself'. The comparison with drama, or epic, was often made. Bulwer Lytton, for example, pointed out that 'many who, in a healthful condition of our stage, would be dramatists, become novelists'. The new prestige of prose fiction was accompanied by a new interest in its origins, so that the appearance of John Dunlop's *History of Fiction* in the same year as *Waverley* is singularly appropriate.

If this were a comprehensive study of prose fiction in the period it would be necessary to classify the books into their main

types, including books dealing with contemporary life (particularly fashionable life), books dealing with some particular region (such as Scotland or Ireland), historical romances, tales of horror, directly didactic stories, and works of prose fiction inspired by theories and ideas. But since our concern is with what survives as literature it is possible to follow the simpler plan of beginning with books written by Scots and then passing on to a briefer consideration of books by English and Irish writers.

It is a striking fact that a number of the ablest writers of prose fiction at this time were Scots, notably John Galt, Susan Ferrier, Lockhart, and James Hogg. In different ways it is probably true to say that each of them owed something to Scott, even if it was merely the fact that books with a Scottish setting were in great demand. When Galt mentioned his *Annals of the Parish* to Constable in 1813 the latter replied that 'Scottish novels would not do'. *Waverley* changed all that. Yet none of these writers is in any important sense an imitator of Scott, and each must be considered separately.

In his *Autobiography* John Galt complains that his books 'have been all considered as novels' although the best of them are deficient in the sort of plot that is expected of a novel.[1] He describes his first work of prose fiction, the unsuccessful and unfinished *Majolo* (1816), as 'anything but a novel', and explains that it is 'a treatise, illustrated by incidents, on sympathies and antipathies, and that class of curious, undescribed feelings which all men obey, but which few are willing to acknowledge'. *The Majolo* is characteristic of Galt in that it shows him more concerned to demonstrate some truths about human life than to tell a story for its own sake. In *The Earthquake* (1820), which he described as his 'first legitimate novel', the plot is not the strong point, although we already see Galt's keen interest in national manners, and he prided himself on the truth-to-life of the behaviour of his Sicilian characters. But it was with Scottish

[1] John Galt (1779–1839) came to London in 1804, after working in the Customs House and in a business firm in Greenock. He went into business, and published a number of pieces in prose and verse. While on a commercial trip to the Continent, on which he visited Constantinople and Greece, he travelled from Gibraltar to Malta in the same ship as Byron. In 1826–9 he visited Canada as secretary to a company formed for the purchase of Crown land, and there he founded the town of Guelph. He was often short of money, and in 1829 he was imprisoned for debt. William IV sent him £200. Although he was paralysed in his last years he continued to compose as long as he was able to dictate.

characters that he was destined to excel, as *The Ayrshire Legatees* (1821) was at once to demonstrate. Galt tells us that he always enjoyed showing visitors to London 'the lions' (or sights), adding that 'the zest of this kind of recreation was in proportion to the eccentricity of the characters'. The result was this description of Dr. Zachariah Pringle's visit to London to see about a legacy, a book in which the humours of the Scottish character, and of the Lowland Scots tongue, are skilfully exploited. The greater part of it consists of letters home by the various members of the family, a device no doubt suggested by *Humphry Clinker* and perhaps also by Lockhart's *Peter's Letters to his Kinsfolk.* Since 1820 was an eventful year, what with the death of George III and the scandal about Queen Caroline, the Pringles have plenty to write about; but Galt is as much concerned with light-hearted satire on his travellers themselves as with London and its ways. A further element of comedy is provided by the reactions of the 'douce folks' in Garnock as they read these remarkable letters from the centre of fashionable dissipation.

Galt did not consider *The Ayrshire Legatees* a novel. In his *Autobiography* he classifies it with those of his books which are 'more properly characterised . . . as theoretical histories, than either as novels or romances'. The other books of this kind are the *Annals of the Parish* (1821), *The Provost* (1822), and probably *The Member* and *The Radical* (both 1832), and Galt's intention in such works may be gathered from his remark that 'fables are often a better way of illustrating general truths than abstract reasoning'. These are Galt's finest works, his unique contribution to prose fiction, and it is now time to give them some consideration.

The *Annals of the Parish* was the first of all these books to be conceived. When he was still very young it was his ambition to produce something 'that would be for Scotland what the Vicar of Wakefield is for England'. At one time he thought of writing the book, which he wished to be 'a kind of treatise on the history of society in the West of Scotland during the reign of George the Third', in the form of a register kept by a village schoolmaster; but when he finally began to write he reverted to his original idea of using the minister as his narrator. One of the most delightful things about the *Annals*, indeed, is the way in which the self-importance of the old minister betrays itself as he tells

his story: 'In the same year, and on the same day of the same month, that his Sacred Majesty King George . . . came to his crown and kingdom, I was placed and settled as the minister of Dalmailing.' When the news of the accession of George III reached the parish 'about a week thereafter' Mr. Balwhidder's parishioners saw the hand of Providence in the coincidence—and rightly so, the old man continues, for many years later 'in the same season that his Most Excellent Majesty . . . was set by as a precious vessel which had received a crack or a flaw . . . I was obliged, by reason of age and the growing infirmities of my recollection . . . to accept of Mr. Amos to be my helper'. His enumeration of the principal events of each year throws an amusing light on the character of the minister himself as well as on local values:

> The An. Dom. one thousand seven hundred and sixty, was remarkable for three things in the parish of Dalmailing. First and foremost, there was my placing; then, the coming of Mrs. Malcolm with her five children to settle among us; and next, my marriage upon my own cousin, Miss Betty Lanshaw.

In 1763 'the king granted peace to the French, and Charlie Malcolm . . . came home to see his mother'. In 1772 Mr. Balwhidder thought of writing to *The Scots Magazine* about the arrival of the first Muscovy duck ever seen in the parish and its narrow escape from choking—just as, in his temporary depression at the death of his first wife, he was 'seized with the notion of writing a book'. Unfortunately he could not decide between 'an orthodox poem, like *Paradise Lost* by John Milton', and 'a connect treatise on the efficacy of Free Grace', which he was inclined to think might prove 'more taking'.

Although in the *Annals* Galt gives us a fine foretaste of his skill in the ironical portrayal of character it is not to this book that we look for the most concentrated example of his art. As the *Annals* progress interest tends to shift from Mr. Balwhidder to his flock, and in particular to the changes which are affecting their lives. The very word by which Dalmailing is described changes, during these years, from 'clachan' to 'town'. We notice that while some of the changes described would certainly have been noted by a real-life Mr. Balwhidder—the new popularity of tea (from November 1762 he refrains from preaching against it as a wicked luxury), the increasing consumption of jam and

jelly, the wider practice of vaccination, the advent of the first stage coach and of the first actors in the town—others are Galt's own observations and reflections, set down without regard for the limitations of the narrator's understanding. During this period 'the taciturn regularity of ancient affairs' disappears. As a result of the American War, the French Revolution (a leitmotiv throughout the book), and the war with France, newspapers begin to make their appearance in the parish. A bookseller's shop is opened—not in the clachan itself, but in the little manufacturing town that has sprung up close by—by an emigrant who has returned from America with views that shock the worthy minister. 'Mankind read more', he notes, 'and the spirit of reflection and reasoning was more awake than at any time within my remembrance.' Galt was a born sociologist, and throughout the book he emphasizes the way in which political and economic developments have changed the traditional manner of life. Mr. Balwhidder particularly deplores 'the sad division of my people into government-men and Jacobins', which became complete about the year 1794. The opening of a Dissenting meeting-house is a sad blow to the ageing minister. Society is splitting up into different factions. Galt holds the scales between the old and the new much more evenly than his narrator would have done, however. He admits that 'the progress of book-learning and education has been wonderful' during recent years and acknowledges that this has been accompanied by 'a greater liberality than the world knew before', even while he deplores unwelcome 'signs of decay in the wonted simplicity of our country ways'. 'With wealth come wants . . .', as he sums the matter up, 'and it's hard to tell wherein the benefit of improvement in a country parish consists.'

Although the *Annals of the Parish* is the one book of Galt's that is generally remembered it is *The Provost*, designed as a companion-study, that should be regarded as his masterpiece. Like the *Annals*, *The Provost* is written in the first person; but whereas the earlier book is mainly about the parish, this is about the Provost. Social history is now less important than self-revelation. It is an exercise in sustained irony that has few rivals in the language. The key is struck in the opening paragraph:

It must be allowed in the world that a man who has thrice reached the highest station of life in his line has a good right to set forth the particulars of the discretion and prudence by which he

lifted himself so far above the ordinaries of his day and generation... I have, therefore, well weighed the importance it may be of to posterity to know by what means I have thrice been made an instrument to represent the supreme power and authority of Majesty in the royal burgh of Gudetown, and how I deported myself in that honour and dignity. . . .

While nothing could be more quintessentially Scots than the self-righteousness with which Mr. Pawkie describes his triumphant progress through life—unless it be the irony with which Galt allows his hero to describe his own career—the reader gradually becomes aware that Mr. Pawkie has a good deal in common with heroes on a larger stage. The way in which Galt comments that only 'the editors . . . of the autobiographic memoirs of other great men' will be able to appreciate his labours reminds us for a moment of Fielding's *Jonathan Wild the Great*, while it is with a sense of appropriateness that we discover that Galt was a great admirer of Machiavelli. When he first read *The Prince*, he tells us, he considered it merely 'an odious collection of state maxims'; but then he decided that it should be regarded as a satire, and re-read it with great delight. As he tells us in his *Literary Life* this 'set him a-cogitating', and the immediate result was a treatise on the Art of Rising in the World, a piece of 'grave irony' which began to appear in the *New Monthly Magazine*. This treatise was regarded as so mordant that he felt obliged to cease publishing it: it is to be hoped that the manuscript of the unpublished part may still be in existence. *The Provost* is an example of this same art—an art that many men have understood without reading 'the politic Florentine'. Mr. Pawkie understands as well as any Prince that 'to rule without being felt... is the great mystery of policy', and he also realizes that those anxious for power must steer their course according to the spirit of their time: 'By this time I had learnt that there was a wakerife [vigilant] common-sense abroad among the opinions of men; and that the secret of the new way of ruling the world was to follow, not to control, the evident dictates of the popular voice.' He prides himself on having 'lived to partake of the purer spirit which the great mutations of the age' have brought about, although we notice that he retains a marked gift for turning everything to his personal profit. Mr. Pawkie is indeed too great a realist to 'think it any shame to a public man to serve his own interests by those of the community, when he

can righteously do so'. He has his own reasons for regretting that 'such an ettering [putrefying] sore and king's-evil as a newspaper' is threatened 'in our heretofore . . . truly royal and loyal burgh; especially as it was given out that the calamity, (for I can call it no less), was to be conducted on Liberal principles, meaning, of course, in the most afflicting and vexatious manner towards his majesty's ministers'. In spite of all innovations, however, Mr. Pawkie keeps the reins of power in his own hands right to the end. When he retires he not only sees to it that he is presented with a piece of silver, but also composes the speech that is to be delivered in his honour.

Three other books written in the first person deserve consideration before we pass on to Galt's other works of fiction. He insisted that *Ringan Gilhaize* (1823) is not a novel in the usual sense, although it is not a 'philosophical sketch' like the *Annals*. Galt resented the unfair treatment of the Covenanters in *Old Mortality* and wished to present a very different interpretation of the events of that time. It is interesting to notice that whereas Scott did not in fact tell his story as if from the mouth of the old man who gives his tale its name, Galt (the great master of this art of literary ventriloquism) did keep to his plan of giving events as described by 'a covenanter of the olden time relating the adventures of his grandfather, who lived during the Reformation'. There is, therefore, a technical expertise or sophistication about *Ringan Gilhaize* which is seldom to be found in Scott—what Galt calls 'a transfusion of character'. He was disappointed by the reception of the book, since some critics treated it as if it were simply true history, while others regarded it as setting forth the writer's own views, without acknowledging the art that enabled him to recreate the character of the covenanting narrator. In fact it is an impressive book, though one feels that the powers displayed in it are out of proportion to the delight afforded by the result. *The Member* succeeds admirably, although it too was misunderstood by contemporary readers. Galt tells us that in it he 'tried to embody all that could, in my opinion, be urged against the tories of my own way of thinking' and insists that 'Mr. Jobbry is not made to make any acknowledgment unbecoming an honest man of the world, nor such as a fair partizan may not avow . . . I have represented him as neither saying nor doing aught that, I think, as the world wags, he may not unblushingly have done, nor which, in my heart,

I do not approve.' It is not surprising, then, that *The Member* is often misunderstood: it must be almost unique as a satire directed against the satirist's own point of view. The fictitious dedication, which is the work of Lockhart, catches the spirit of the book admirably:

> If the Reform Bill passes, which an offended Providence seems, I fear, but too likely to permit, [the result will] be a general convulsion . . . fatal to the established institutions of a once happy and contented country. If, indeed, my dear and worthy friend, the present horrid measure be carried into full effect, it is but too plain that the axe will have been laid to the root of the British Oak. . . . A melancholy vista discloses itself to all rational understandings;—a church in tatters; a peerage humbled and degraded—no doubt, soon to be entirely got rid of; that poor, deluded man, the well-meaning William IV., probably packed off to Hanover; the three per cents down to two, at the very best of it.

Mr. Jobbry, a 'nabob' who has retired from India with a comfortable fortune, thanks to his principle of always keeping his eye on 'the main chance', becomes a Member of Parliament, so giving Galt the opportunity for satire on electioneering and the parliamentary politics of the day. By a pleasing irony Mr. Jobbry, who admits that it is sometimes necessary to 'act upon . . . the double-dealing principle', becomes a member of a committee to investigate charges of 'the most abominable bribery'. He deplores the fact that 'The French Revolution has done a deal of damage to all those establishments which time and law had taken so much pains to construct' and is particularly opposed to 'the new-fangled doctrines of the Utilitarians'. The irony is very delicately managed, for all the world as if Galt were trying to discover for himself whether it is really true that ridicule is the test of truth. Sir John Bulky's son wishes to stand for Parliament, for example, but his father has no intention of encouraging him:

> I am not sure he is just the man fit for them; for though he is a young man of good parts, he has got too many philosophical crotchets about the rules and principles of government, to be what in my old-fashioned notions I think a useful English legislator. He's honest and he's firm, but honesty and firmness are not enough; there is a kind of consideration that folly is entitled to, that honesty and firmness will not grant.

In *The Radical* Galt's object was 'to show that many of those

institutes, which we regard as essentials in society, owe their origin to the sacrifices required to be made by man, to partake of its securities'. The result is a more straightforward book than *The Member*. As he describes his life Nathan Butt portrays himself as the constant victim of oppression. 'It has from time immemorial been the artful aim of all education to obscure the sense of natural right', he observes with the self-righteous complacency of his type. 'To education, therefore, I am inclined, with Mr. Owen, to ascribe all . . . vice and distress.' At an early age his 'innate perception of natural right' leads him to steal apples. When his father whips him he asks indignantly: 'Who ever heard that, in a state of nature, where all is beneficent and beautiful, the cruel hyæna, which so well deserves the epithet, inflicts coercive manipulations upon the young?' But it is only as he grows up that the fullness of enlightenment is granted to him. 'Although I had now turned my fifteenth year', he tells us at one point, 'I was not at all aware of the state of society'; but acquaintance with the writings of such writers as Rousseau, Owen, and Godwin soon changes this state of affairs, and Butt continues his triumphal career by becoming the leader of a local discussion society and getting a girl into trouble. At the end of the book, by a pleasing irony, he is bullied by his wife into having their child christened in church.

'We wish Mr. Galt would do nothing but write imaginary autobiographies', wrote a reviewer in the *Athenaeum*, commenting on *The Member*. The same skill is to be found in one of his least-known works, 'The Betheral; or, the Autobiography of James Howkings', which was published in his *Literary Life and Miscellanies* (1834). No earlier writer can be compared to Galt in this field: Defoe often wrote in the first person, but his books contain little of the irony which is the presiding spirit in Galt's subtle studies, and which makes a more fitful appearance in his other works of prose fiction, to which we must now turn.

Although *Sir Andrew Wylie* (1822) has often been admired, and contains some excellent scenes, as a whole it is a vulgarization of the Scottish theme so brilliantly exemplified in the *Annals* and *The Provost*. Galt tells us in his *Autobiography* that his intention had been to describe 'the rise and progress of a Scotchman in London', and the result is a success-story banal enough to be made into a bad film. When Galt is drawing on his own observation of Scots life, it is true, there are some vivid portrayals,

as in the conversation between Martha and Mr. Tannyhill about Andrew's future. We are told that Andrew had 'a happy vernacular phraseology which he retained through life and which those who had a true relish of character . . . enjoyed as something as rare and original as the more elegant endowment of genius', and many of Wylie's speeches are excellent. Like his hero, Galt himself was fascinated by 'the knacky conversation of old and original characters . . . it signified not . . . whether . . . douce or daft: it was enough that their talk was cast in queer phrases, and their minds ran among the odds and ends of things'. Yet the major failure of the book is the portrayal of Wylie's character. It is essential to the story that he should be extremely attractive, but in fact this mixture of James Boswell and Andrew Carnegie is a jaunty mannikin who would have infuriated everyone he met. Nothing could be less convincing than his success with the English aristocrats—unless it be their speech, which is very badly handled. And unfortunately, though the opening suggests that the book will contain some measure of satire on the 'great genius' whose career is about to be described, irony is almost wholly absent. *The Entail* (1823), which tells the story of an obsession, is a much more interesting book. The one object of Claud Walkinshaw's life is to recover the family estates, which have been lost by imprudence. He is a potentially tragic figure, driven further and further from the ways of common sense and common kindliness by his master-passion. Several of the scenes in which his half-witted son appears—notably the one in which, prostrated by grief at the death of his infant daughter, Claud steals another child and proclaims that it has somehow turned into his own 'little Betty Bodle'— are genuinely powerful. As the book goes on, however, Galt becomes more and more interested in Claud's widow, 'the Leddy'; yet though she is a considerable creation, with her Scots malapropisms and her characteristic mixture of meanness and generosity, in making so much of her Galt is departing from the true theme of the book, a sombre satire on greed and 'interest' which ought to have a tragic conclusion. As it stands *The Entail* is not a masterpiece, yet vestiges of the masterpiece that it might have been are to be found here and there. From time to time the lucid fidelity of Galt's portrayal of an obsession and its effects reminds the reader of Thomas Hardy. It is not surprising that Byron admired this history of a family.

*The Last of the Lairds* (1826), which deals with a subject that had been long in Galt's mind, is intended to 'delineate a set of persons, of his own rank, that such an obsolete character as a West Country Laird was likely, about twenty years ago, to have had for acquaintance and neighbours'. It is foreshadowed at the end of *Sir Andrew Wylie,* where we are told that an old lady has found a volume in her brother's handwriting containing 'a most full account of all manner of particularities anent the decay of the ancient families of the West Country'. D. M. Moir persuaded Galt that he would gain more than he would lose by abandoning the autobiographical form, but the fact that the autobiographical splinters of the book as we have it are the best parts suggests that the change of plan was a mistake. Galt himself finally came to this conclusion, and to the end of his life he cherished the desire of producing another book to represent 'the autobiography of one of the last race of lairds'.

*The Last of the Lairds* is in fact a reminder of three of the outstanding facts about Galt. One is that his rare gifts were not sufficiently appreciated during his own lifetime. He did not mix very much with other literary men, those who did give him advice (such as Moir and William Blackwood) were often mistaken, and he was too often considered a mere imitator of Sir Walter Scott. The second is that he was an exceptionally perceptive observer of the changes in the pattern of society which were going on in the Lowlands of Scotland in his day. This combined with his remarkable command of the spoken Scots idiom to enable him to recreate one section of society—and so one aspect of human life—with exceptional fidelity. 'Tell our friend Mr. North not to touch one of the Scotticisms', as we find him writing on one occasion. The third fact is that the imaginary autobiography was the medium which enabled him to approach greatness. He told Blackwood that if there was any merit in any of his sketches, it was 'in the truth of the metaphysical anatomy of the characters', and it was by his curious mastery of ironic autobiography that he was able to reach this truth and convey it to his readers.

Susan Ferrier has been called the Scots Jane Austen and although the title is something of a satire on the Scots her correspondence with a friend on the subject of *Marriage* (1818) makes it clear that her attitude to the novel had a good deal in common

with that of her great contemporary.[1] 'You say there are just two styles for which you have any taste', Susan Ferrier wrote to Miss Clavering, who had suggested that they should collaborate on a novel, 'viz. the horrible and the astonishing! . . . In truth it would be as easy to compound a new element out of fire and water, as that we two should jointly write a book!' It appears that Miss Clavering had had the temerity to suggest 'a Hottentot heroine and a wild man of the woods', or even a story about men in the moon, but such subjects had no attractions for her friend. 'I *will not* enter into any of your raw head and bloody bone schemes', Susan Ferrier replied in February 1810. 'I would not even *read* a Book that had a spectre in it, and as for committing a mysterious and most foul murder, I declare I'd rather take a dose of asafœtida.' It would be difficult to find anywhere a clearer confrontation of novelist and romance-writer than we find in these letters:

> You may laugh at the idea of its being at all necessary for the writer of a romance to be versed in the history, natural and political, the modes, manners, customs, &c. of the country where its wild and wanton freaks are to be played, but I consider it as most essentially so, as nothing disgusts an ordinary reader more than a discovery of the ignorance of the author, who is pretending to amuse and instruct him. (*Memoir and Correspondence of Susan Ferrier*, ed. John A. Doyle, p. 86.)

As Jane Austen asked a friend to inquire whether there were hedge-rows in Northamptonshire, so Susan Ferrier instructed her publisher to find out for her whether a midshipman could become a lieutenant in less than six years. We also notice that she was as certain as Jane Austen that a novel should instruct as well as amuse:

> I don't think . . . that 'tis absolutely necessary that the good boys and girls should be rewarded, and the naughty ones punished. Yet . . . where there is much tribulation, 'tis fitter it should be the *consequence*, rather than the *cause* of misconduct or frailty. . . . The only good purpose of a book is to inculcate morality. (*Memoir*, p. 75.)

[1] Susan Edmonstone Ferrier (1782–1854) was the daughter of an Edinburgh Writer to the Signet. Her father was a colleague of Sir Walter Scott, being a principal clerk of session, so that Susan Ferrier grew up in a literary society. Several of the characters in *Marriage* were associated by its readers with real people. She led a quiet life, keeping house for her father after the death of her mother in 1797. Scott described her as 'simple, full of humour, and exceedingly ready at repartee, and all this without the least affectation of the blue-stocking'.

The purpose of *Marriage* was to be 'to warn all young ladies against runaway matches' and part of the scheme was to describe 'the sudden transition of a high-bred English beauty, who thinks she can sacrifice all for love, to an uncomfortable solitary Highland dwelling among tall red-haired sisters and grim-faced aunts'. As the book developed, however, Susan Ferrier took the matter further. *Marriage* is based on the contrasting fates of a pair of twins who have been brought up in very different ways. Their mother, having herself been unhappy as the result of a runaway match, believes that a 'prudent' marriage is all that is necessary to secure a woman's happiness. The theme of the book is the harm caused by unwise marriages, prudent or imprudent, and the importance of a girl's early upbringing in helping her to make a wise choice of a husband. It was because of her own blindness that Lady Juliana

> looked no farther than to her union with Henry Douglas for the foundation of all her unhappiness—it never once occurred to her, that her marriage was only the *consequence* of something previously wrong; she saw not the headstrong passions that had impelled her to please herself—no matter at what price. She . . . considered herself as having fallen a victim to love; and could she only save her daughter from a similar error, she might yet by her means retrieve her fallen fortune. (ch. xxviii.)

Adelaide, whom Lady Juliana brings up in a foolish and unfeeling manner, is forced into a worldly marriage with an elderly Duke, and within a year she elopes with a worthless lover. But the greater part of the book is concerned with the fortunes of Mary, who has been brought up in Scotland. Mary feels bound to reject the ambitious match that her mother wishes to force on her, and in the end she marries the man she loves and returns to Scotland. Mary has a good deal in common with Elinor Dashwood in *Sense and Sensibility*, and fortunately she is contrasted with her cousin Lady Emily, who is also virtuous but less invariably admirable and whose first appearance comes as something of a relief. There are some amusing scenes in the book, and some telling phrases, as when we are told of Mary's Scottish aunts that 'their walk lay amongst thread and pickles; their sphere extended from the garret to the pantry', or when a blue-stocking insists proudly that 'nothing but conversation

was spoke in her house'. But pride of place must be granted to Miss Grizzy's observation that 'Reading does young people much harm. It puts things into their heads that never would have been there, but for books.' While there is a great deal of comedy and shrewd observation in the book, however, it takes the form of description and explicit comment rather than that of dramatic portrayal. Susan Ferrier has more in common with Fanny Burney than with Jane Austen, and it is significant that she was fond of the art of caricature: 'If you see any comical carikitury,' she wrote to a friend in Edinburgh, 'as a certain burring Dowager terms a caricature, will you get it franked and send me?' Artistic delicacy was a quality with which Susan Ferrier was too little concerned.

*Marriage* was a great success. Scott paid its author a resounding compliment at the end of *A Legend of Montrose*, and Susan Ferrier was able to secure £1,000 for her second book. The subject of *The Inheritance* (1824) is again the importance of a young woman's choosing the right husband. When Gertrude and her supposed mother have suddenly to leave the South of France for Scotland (the sudden shock of the transition is once again amusingly portrayed) two admirers of Gertrude soon make their appearance. But the contrast between the worldly Delmour and the admirable Lyndsay becomes evident far too quickly, so that the elaborate exhibition of their characters in action is quite unnecessary. It is a relief when at last Gertrude confesses that she has been 'blinded by romantic passion' for Delmour, although her marriage to Lyndsay is a little too passionless to be satisfactory. The plot is complicated and improbable, and yet only an obtuse reader could fail to realize, by the middle of the first volume, that Gertrude is not the daughter of Mrs. St. Clair, and therefore not the heiress for whom she has been taken. Gertrude's supposed father, the vulgar and villainous American, Lewiston, is stagey and unconvincing; while several of the most important events in the story, such as the death of the Earl and the scene in which Lewiston claims to be Gertrude's father, are unprepared for and curiously offhand. The most interesting characters are Gertrude's uncle, Adam Ramsay—a Scots type well observed—and Miss Pratt, the gossiping, inquisitive, self-centred and (in some degree) intelligent old maid whose arrival at Rossville Castle in a hearse during a snowstorm is the most entertaining moment in the

book. And once again there are excellent snatches of dialogue, as when Major Waddell attempts to explain to the blunt old Adam Ramsay that it is 'not customary to call ladies of a certain rank *wives* now'. But the whole thing goes on far too long. One is left longing for the brevity of a de Maupassant. The same is true of *Destiny* (1831), in which evangelical earnestness has all but killed Susan Ferrier's insight into character, and in which the comic scenes—such as those dealing with M'Dow, the gluttonous and rapacious 'Moderate' minister—tend to be unnecessarily crude.

'What a disgusting mind and imagination the author of "Matthew Wald" must possess', a friend wrote to Susan Ferrier in 1824, in a letter containing high praise of *The Inheritance*. She was not the only reader to find at least two of Lockhart's works of fiction arresting and disquieting, although the first of them, *Valerius, A Roman Story* (1821), could shock no one. Written in the first person, it describes how the son of a Roman settler in Britain travels to Rome during the reign of Hadrian to see about a lawsuit. In its romance-plot and in the author's obvious intention of describing a given place at a given time the book follows the general pattern of many of the *Waverley* romances; but though the plotting is more careful than Scott's, and the style much more deliberate (partly to suggest translation from a Latin original), there is a complete absence of the great passages that we would expect at least in the earlier of Scott's books. Valerius meets a number of persecuted Christians, and himself becomes a convert, but there is little vivid characterization and nothing penetrating about the influence of Christianity on the human character. It is an agreeable, slightly donnish sort of book that one can imagine being given as a prize in a school of the most old-fashioned kind. It was when Lockhart came to deal with the life that he knew at first-hand, life in the Lowlands of Scotland, the life of the country manse and the lawyer's office, that his gifts were revealed. *Adam Blair* (1822) and *Matthew Wald* (1824) leave us with the impression of unusual power seeking an outlet. In spite of their Scottish settings they remind us hardly at all of the work of Lockhart's father-in-law: they are more sombre than most of Scott's books and deal less with action than with the workings of the human mind. The motto of *Some Passages in the Life of Mr. Adam Blair* is from St. Paul: 'Let him that thinketh he standeth take heed lest he fall.' While

he is mourning the death of his wife, to whom he has been devoted, the upright Adam Blair is visited by Charlotte Campbell, whom he has known before his marriage. For some time she lives with him innocently as his house-keeper; but then her evil husband takes her away, Blair pursues them, and he and Charlotte yield to the temptation of passion. The dreams of anguish and remorse that succeed each other in Blair's mind are reminiscent of some of De Quincey's opium visions. There is a starkly powerful scene in which Blair, now recovering from his delirium, sees a boat containing Charlotte's coffin crossing a loch on its way to the graveyard. The description of the meeting of the Presbytery to consider the misconduct of their minister is equally fine. Blair confesses and is unfrocked, but at the end of the book he is reinstated. This might be considered as simply a concession to the conventional demand for a 'happy ending', but taken in conjunction with the final quotation against spiritual pride it may also be interpreted as evidence that Lockhart was concerned to emphasize the dangers of self-righteousness. Like Hogg's *Confessions of a Justified Sinner*, *Adam Blair* is an attempt to deal with a serious moral issue: as Henry James pointed out, it invites comparison with *The Scarlet Letter*. That it was bitterly attacked on its first appearance, and was said to be fit for 'the same shelf with "Faublas", and another book unmentionable', is hardly surprising. *The History of Matthew Wald* has a good deal in common with its predecessor. Written in the first person, it describes the life of a young man who loves his cousin Katherine, with whom he has been brought up. Some of the adventures that follow his running away from the home of his foster-parents are described to us: at one point he stumbles on the truth about a murder, and it is characteristic of Lockhart to emphasize the spiritual pride which lies behind the murderer's confession. Meanwhile Wald, who has been obliged to become a private tutor, falls in love with the step-daughter of the family with whom he is staying, and marries her. She becomes a Methodist, so giving Lockhart an opportunity of discussing the effects of Methodism on the mind. In a hectic scene Wald's wife dies of shock, having seen him embracing Katherine, who has reappeared. From this point onwards the action dissolves into a storm of melodrama, rather as if it were the work of a Scots Webster writing in prose. Like *Adam Blair*, *Matthew Wald* is a powerful, sombre book, the sort of thing one

can imagine the Brontës reading with approval. By way of contrast, *Reginald Dalton* (1823) is a reminder of the conventional streak in Lockhart. Whereas he explored some of the darker places of the human mind in the two books just mentioned, in this he wrote a contemporary romance of the most predictable kind. The ingredients are of the usual sort: the familiar type of hero; a heroine of mysterious foreign parentage living with a kindly old priest; unmitigated villains; the hero's father—a bookish parson who has been cheated of his rightful inheritance; satirical interludes, in which Lockhart draws on his undergraduate memories of Oxford (a tutor, the head of a college, a blue-stocking); debts, a duel and jail for the hero—all serving as a prelude to a happy ending. It is an inferior book, and proved very popular.

*The Private Memoirs and Confessions of a Justified Sinner* (1824) is so remarkable a work that it has sometimes been suggested that Hogg must have received help from another member of the *Blackwood's* group; and while it is dangerous logic to argue that because one book by an author seems to a critic better than all his others it cannot be his own work—as Johnson suggested with Swift and *A Tale of a Tub*—it is true that the interest in the windings of human motivation that we find in *A Justified Sinner* often reminds us of Lockhart.[1] The first third of the book describes how Robert Wringhim Colwan comes under the influence of a mysterious stranger and behaves in an extraordinary manner, harassing and finally murdering his half-brother and apparently committing a number of other horrifying crimes. The remainder of the book is a memoir by Colwan himself supposed to have been discovered when his grave is opened more than a century after his suicide. This memoir, which its supposed author describes as 'a religious parable such as the *Pilgrim's Progress*', is written throughout in a tone of extreme self-righteousness but in fact describes how its writer came completely under the sway of the Devil. He believes that the supernatural powers of the mysterious stranger must derive

[1] James Hogg (1770–1835), the Ettrick Shepherd, attracted attention by his verse and contributed material for Scott's *Minstrelsy of the Scottish Border*. His poems are discussed in the previous volume of this *History*. He became known to Wordsworth, Byron, Southey, and others, and settled at Altrive Lake in 1817. The same year he was part-author of the notorious 'Chaldee Manuscript', and he contributed a good deal to *Blackwood's* for the remainder of his life. He figures prominently in the *Noctes Ambrosianae*.

from 'on high'; and yet the contemplation of his own life fills him with weariness and repulsion:

> Thus was I sojourning in the midst of a chaos of confusion. I looked back on my by-past life with pain, as one looks back on a perilous journey, in which he has attained his end, without gaining any advantage either to himself or others; and I looked forward, as on a darksome waste, full of repulsive and terrific shapes, pitfalls, and precipices, to which there was no definite bourn, and from which I turned with disgust. . . . My principal feeling . . . was an insatiable longing for something that I cannot describe or denominate properly, unless I say it was for *utter oblivion* that I longed.

He describes the crimes that he has committed—he has murdered his half-brother, is prepared to murder the man whom he wrongly believes to be his father, murders his supposed mother, and murders a girl whom he has seduced, as well as an innocent preacher. The author of the book has deliberately left a good deal uncertain. The 'editor' of the Memoir suggests at the end that most, if not all, of the crimes described were delusions of Colwan's mind. 'In short', as he sums up,

> we must either conceive him, not only the greatest fool, but the greatest wretch, on whom was ever stamped the form of humanity; or, that he was a religious maniac, who wrote and wrote about a deluded creature, till he arrived at that height of madness that he believed himself the very object whom he had been all along describing.

There can be no doubt that the book is to be regarded as a satire of the most sombre sort on certain of the tenets of the fanatical Covenanters, so that the late (and unauthorized) title, *Confessions of a Fanatic*, is perfectly accurate. We notice that the Devil particularly detests any questioning of two of the most cherished beliefs of the Covenanters—the belief in Predestination, and the consequent notion that God's Elect may do as they please, 'good works' being of no account—and it is by insisting on these with the remorseless logic of a crazed theologian that he drives Colwan along the road to perdition. Colwan feels no love for his own mother, usually keeps himself at a distance from women, and takes no part in the innocent pleasures of the human race. The book is a study of the perversions of conscience which can be the consequence of a twisted faith fanatically held, an unflinching investigation of the secret places of a mind turned away from the sun of ordinary human affections.

Although *The Confessions* have occasionally been over-praised, it is not surprising that André Gide should have been impressed by so disturbing an indictment of religious 'melancholy'.

One further book by a Scottish writer can only be briefly mentioned. D. M. Moir's *Life of Mansie Waugh, Tailor in Dalkeith* (1828) is an imaginary autobiography written for 'the welfare of the human race and the improvement of society' and fittingly dedicated to John Galt.[1] The narrator is a kindly man, not without shrewdness, who sees life from the point of view of a tailor in Dalkeith: that is to say, he is as observant of the details of people's dress as Richardson's Pamela herself; while it is his secret conviction that ancient Troy, 'for all that has been said and sung about it, would be found . . . not worth half a thought when compared with the New Town of Edinburgh'—and that Dalkeith is in many ways preferable to Edinburgh. The sententiousness and complacency of the narrator are in Galt's manner, though a little more crudely done.

When we turn from Scots writers to English we are at once confronted by *Frankenstein* (1818), probably the only minor work of fiction of this period which is still widely read. When Shelley and his wife were neighbours of Byron's in Switzerland during the wet summer of 1816 Byron suggested that each of them should write a ghost story. Mary Shelley realized from the first that what was required was above all a good story, a tale 'which would speak to the mysterious fears of our nature, and awaken thrilling horror—one to make the reader dread to look round, to curdle the blood, and quicken the beatings of the heart'.[2] She could not find the perfect germ for her story until one day she heard Shelley and Byron discussing an experiment in which Erasmus Darwin was supposed to have created life

[1] David Macbeth Moir (1798–1851) was a doctor in Musselburgh. He soon became a regular writer of prose and verse in *Blackwood's* and other periodicals, usually signing himself Δ or Delta. He was a friend of De Quincey, with whom he no doubt discussed the nature and effects of opium. Apart from his literary works he published *Outlines of the Ancient History of Medicine*.

[2] Mary Wollstonecraft Shelley (1797–1851) was the daughter of William Godwin and Mary Wollstonecraft, the author of the *Vindication of the Rights of Women*. She was brought up by her stepmother with her own children, the Clairmonts. She went to the Continent with Shelley in July 1814 and married him when his first wife, Harriet Westbrook, committed suicide in December 1816. She remained in Italy after Shelley's death and saw a great deal of Byron, Leigh Hunt, and Trelawny. She returned to England in 1823, travelling on the Continent again in 1840–3. Apart from her fiction, she edited Shelley's poems and published a good deal in periodicals.

from inanimate matter. *Frankenstein* was the result of their talk of galvanism and corpses, and although it is not in fact a ghost story it certainly appeals to 'the mysterious fears of our nature'. The outline of the plot is well known. By creating a monster Frankenstein makes his own life a misery. Having murdered Frankenstein's little brother (a murder for which an innocent girl is executed), the monster pursues his creator to Chamonix. It explains to Frankenstein the progress of its intellect, and its frustrated yearning for love. Its appearance is so hideous that in spite of its original amiability everyone has always fled from it in horror. 'Everywhere I see bliss from which I alone am irrevocably excluded', it complains. 'I was benevolent and good; misery made me a fiend. Make me happy, and I shall again be virtuous.' Frankenstein is on the point of creating a mate for the monster when he feels an upsurge of remorse and destroys the new creature that he has been making. In its rage the monster devotes itself to revenge, killing Frankenstein's bride on the night of his wedding. Frankenstein's father dies broken-hearted, while he himself, assailed by calamities, sinks into madness. Recovering from his insanity he pursues the monster across the world in the hope of destroying it. This the monster encourages, as a form of revenge. In the end Frankenstein dies on a ship which has picked him up from the sea in the remote North. The monster laments over the body of his creator, explains its misery to the master of the ship, and departs across the sea to seek its own annihilation.

*Frankenstein* is a remarkable book to have been written by a girl of nineteen. Crude as it is in many ways, and full of gross improbabilities and fustian dialogue, it has the kind of theme that holds its reader's attention and leads different critics to produce rival interpretations. For it is not only an exciting story: it is also a philosophical romance. The way in which the monster describes the progress of his mind, his reading of Plutarch, Volney, and *The Sorrows of Werther*, and the development of his views on Man, Society, and Social Love, reminds us that Mary Shelley was the daughter of the author of *Social Justice* as well as the wife of the poet of *Alastor*. There is also an explicit parallel between Frankenstein and his monster and God and Satan; while a psychological interpretation of the tale would equally be possible. Yet it would be more effective if it were shorter, and this is much more obviously true of *Valperga, or the*

*Life and Adventures of Castruccio, Prince of Lucca* (1823), which is of a length to defeat all patience. The story is set in medieval Italy, and traces the deterioration of the character of the central figure, who begins as a generous youth and ends as a machiavellian tyrant, with 'a majestic figure and a countenance beautiful but sad, and tarnished by the expression of pride that animated it'. In *The Last Man* (1826) Mary Shelley seems to have been anxious to find a seminal idea as 'archetypal' as that of *Frankenstein*. Taking up a theme which fascinated a number of other writers of the time—Campbell, Beddoes, and Hood among them—she sets her story in the twenty-first century. The personal and political complications of the first part of the book are confusing, but when the plague strikes Europe the narrative improves and there are some powerful imaginative scenes. The dénouement, in which Verney is left alone in the world, is admirably conceived, although the execution does not quite match the conception. All that need be said of Mary Shelley's later fictions is that *Perkin Warbeck* is an historical romance, that *Lodore* is partly based on the relations of Shelley and Harriet, and that *Falkner*, in which the hero is modelled on Trelawny, appears to be an attempt to exculpate Shelley from any blame for the suicide of his first wife.

Lack of space forbids more than a mention of Thomas Hope's *Anastasius, or Memoirs of a Greek* (1819), a book which was at first attributed to Byron and which may possibly have influenced some of the later cantos of *Don Juan*; but something must be said of an analogous work, *Hajji Baba* (1824). Its author, James Morier, was born at Smyrna. His father was Consul-General of the Levant Company at Constantinople, while several other members of the family also had connexions with the Middle East. Morier himself returned to Constantinople after his schooling at Harrow, and in 1807 he entered the diplomatic service. In 1812 he published his *Journey through Persia, Armenia, and Asia Minor*, and six years later his *Second Journey through Persia*, a much more interesting book which is obviously the work of a man who knows Persian and is unusually at home with the Persian people. By this time Morier had already retired, and in an age in which novels were so much in demand and there was so keen an interest in the East it is not surprising that he should have decided to exploit his exceptional knowledge of a little-known country. The result was *The Adventures of*

*Hajji Baba of Ispahan*, the first of a number of works of fiction and the only one by which Morier is now remembered. His model, as he freely acknowledges, was *Gil Blas*: his aim was simply to produce a picaresque romance set in Persia and giving an entertaining account of life in that country. The nature of the book may be further defined by comparison with two of the best-known works of English fiction with Oriental settings. Whereas in *Rasselas* Johnson is concerned with the enforcement of important truths about human life in general, and chooses an Eastern setting for his narrative merely for the sake of vagueness and generality, Morier wishes to entertain his readers by emphasizing those aspects of life in Persia which differ most remarkably from the way of life familiar to his readers. *Rasselas* could be set almost anywhere, *Hajji Baba* nowhere but in Persia. Morier's aim is equally remote from Beckford's. The inspiration of *Vathek* was the *Arabian Nights*: that of *Hajji Baba* the real people of Persia. The one is the reverie of a young voluptuary, the other the record of long and sympathetic observation by a middle-aged man of the world who has 'done the state some service'. At the end of *Vathek* we are told how the central character, 'who for the sake of empty pomp and forbidden power had sullied himself with a thousand crimes, became a prey to grief without end and remorse without mitigation'. Hajji Baba, who tells his own story, ends on a very different note:

> I will not tire the reader with a description of the numerous details of my preparatives for the expedition. He would sicken and I should blush at my vanity. It is sufficient to say that I travelled to Ispahan with all the parade of a man of consequence; and that I entered my native city with feelings that none but a Persian, bred and born in the cravings of ambition, can understand. I found myself at the summit of . . . perfect human bliss. . . . Hajji Baba, the barber's son, entered his native place, as Mirza Hajji Baba, the Shah's deputy. Need I say more?

When we turn from Beckford's book to Morier's we turn from the world of melodrama to that of everyday Persian life, from a world of ghouls, djinns, and magic carpets to one of flattery, place-seeking, quack doctors, and petty thieving. Those who knew the old Persia best have been the most emphatic in insisting on the veracity of Morier's account. One eminent

Orientalist, E. G. Browne, was so struck by Morier's book that he questioned whether anyone who had not read it could be described as a man of cultivation 'in the full meaning of the term'. While this is absurd as a literary judgement it is impressive as a testimony to Morier's faithfulness as a recorder of Persian life.

It is a sure instinct that leads a writer whose inspiration is the urge to exploit a new milieu to revert to the picaresque tradition, and Hajji Baba is a true *picaro*, vain, resourceful, and unprincipled. No one could less resemble Johnson's Prince of Abissinia. What he is after is not the truth, but money, power, and pleasure. He has the resilience of a tennis ball: the harder he is struck downwards the higher he bounces back. In Chapter XXXIII he reflects on his own character:

> The first impulse of my nature was not cruelty, that I knew: I was neither fierce nor brave, that I also knew: I therefore marvelled greatly how of a sudden I had become such an unsainted lion. The fact is, the example of others always had the strongest influence over my mind and actions; and I now lived in such an atmosphere of violence and cruelty, I heard of nothing but of slitting noses, cutting off ears, putting out eyes, blowing up in mortars, chopping men in two, and baking them in ovens, that, in truth, I am persuaded, with a proper example before me, I could almost have impaled my own father.

In fact we hear little or nothing of some of the cruelties here mentioned, and when the others occur they are not so vividly described as to make a deep impression on the reader. *Hajji Baba* is an interesting example of the adaptation of the conventions of the picaresque romance to the taste and susceptibilities of the reading public of the 1820's.

One of the most striking features of the popular literature of this period was the vogue for 'Fashionable Novels' attacked by Hazlitt in his essay on 'The Dandy School':

> It was formerly understood to be the business of literature [he wrote] to enlarge the bounds of knowledge and feeling; to direct the mind's eye beyond the present moment and the present object . . . to make books the faithful witnesses and interpreters of nature and the human heart. Of late . . . it has taken a narrower and more superficial tone. . . . Instead of transporting you to faery-land or into

the *middle ages*, you take a turn down Bond Street or go through the mazes of the dance at Almack's. . . . Far from extending your sympathies, they are narrowed to a single point, the admiration of the folly, caprice, insolence, and affectation of a certain class;—so that with the exception of people who ride in their carriages, you are taught to look down upon the rest of the species with indifference, abhorrence, or contempt.

Before we glance at Thomas Hook, however, who was an authentic specimen of the *genus* 'Fashionable Novelist', it will be convenient to consider the work of Thomas Henry Lister, a minor novelist of real ability who has too often been loosely classified with men greatly his inferiors.[1] As we read Lister's novels we do not feel that we are peering in through the conservatory window. The important thing about his books is not that they deal with fashionable life, but that they are genuine novels. 'Do tell me your favourite novels', says a foolish character in *Granby*:

'I hope you like nothing of Miss Edgeworth's or Miss Austen's. They are full of common-place people, that one recognises at once. You cannot think how I was disappointed in Northanger Abbey, and Castle Rack-rent, for the titles did really promise something. Have you a taste for romance? . . . I am glad of it. . . . Dear Mrs. Radcliffe's were lovely things—but they are so old!'

Although there are elements of the romance in each of Lister's own novels, he is concerned for the most part with real people, and his action is illuminated by the clear light of common sense. As we read *Granby* (1826) we are repeatedly reminded of Jane Austen, both in large matters and in small—as when he refuses to describe a conversation between two women when no man is present, or shows the change in the attitude of the Jermyns to Granby when they discover that he is not as wealthy a man as they have supposed. In *Herbert Lacy* (1828) we are again reminded of Jane Austen: by the terms in which a proposal of marriage is turned down, for example: by the style of a lady's letter ('she was distinguished for her emphatic and judicious system of *dashing*'): and by the description of the hero, who was 'rather proud of the sturdiness of his

[1] Thomas Henry Lister (1800–42) was educated at Westminster and Trinity College, Cambridge. In 1834 and 1835 he served as commissioner to inquire into the state of religious instruction in Ireland and Scotland. In 1836 he became the first Registrar-General of England and Wales.

principles, in not being dazzled by the outward charms of the grand-daughter of an iron-monger'. There are also some admirable renderings of fashionable conversation:

> And as for the Lacys, they, you know, are as old as the flood, and very well connected too. Sir William Lacy's mother was Lady Mary Loftus, aunt of the mad Lord Loftus, whose wife ran away with Sir Clement Packworth, the brother of the man who shot Lord Cheadle, husband of the naughty Lady Cheadle, whose brother was that Colonel Blake, who won so much from poor George Templeton . . ., whose sister made that unhappy low connection which we were lamenting the other day. . . .

The satire is admirably managed, and we notice that Lister is not content with describing the manners and morals of his chosen section of society: he criticizes the fashionable world, though he does so without rancour. He is skilled in the art of distinguishing between appearance and reality in human affairs, and excels in tracing the complications of a man's character to their root in his early life. Yet at times we feel as if we were listening to a lecture on psychology, and we notice that Lister is not nearly as good as Jane Austen at the dramatic portrayal of a character's development. In his earlier books Lister pays homage to Jane Austen by borrowing the names of some of her characters (Morton, Bingley, and even Maria Dashwood): in his last novel, *Arlington* (1832), he uses amateur theatricals in a country house to expose the characters of some of his principal personages in a manner that recalls *Mansfield Park*: while Julia Crawford, who is prepared to fall in with Beauchamp's plan that she should become his mistress by first marrying Arlington, is like a less intelligent cousin of Mary Crawford's. As usual, there are some melodramatic incidents in the plot: indeed the book opens like a detective story, with the discovery of the body of Lord Arlington, shot by an unknown hand. But although the mystery is not cleared up until the beginning of the third volume Lister's true concern is once again with the manners and morals of upper-class society, and the book contains some finely caught conversation and some shrewd observations on human character. It is characteristic of Lister to insist that Arlington's own character 'was not one of those which accommodate themselves to the antithetical mode of description. There were no striking contrasts, no startling incongruities, no well balanced portions of good and bad qualities,

none of those improbable co-existences which make up a character so striking upon paper, and so nearly impossible to be found.' The worldling Denbigh, the Iago of the plot, is a considerable creation. In his criticism of the times in which he lived, both in this book and in its predecessors, Lister reveals himself as a very shrewd observer, avoiding equally a facile optimism and a reactionary pessimism. He is anti-Old-Boy, anti-reactionary, and above all anti-cant. Although the third volume of this last book contains a good deal of intelligent discussion that seems irrelevant to the plot, it remains true that Lister is a man who deserves to be remembered: he is notable equally as one of the very few early and intelligent imitators of Jane Austen and as one of the most able men to turn his attention to the novel in this period.

In *Arlington* a young man who is dancing with an unsophisticated girl, 'lately out', discovers

> that one of the subjects about which she was most anxious, was the internal construction of that unknown world of Fashion, which she had contemplated from a distance, and judged of, chiefly through the medium of books, written by some of the Mendez Pintoes of modern fiction, who, like their prototype, profess to describe regions which they have never trodden.

The essential characteristic of the Fashionable Novelists was that their aim was to describe fashionable life for the benefit of readers outside it, or on the fringes; and the most typical writer of this class was Theodore Hook.[1] The first series of his *Sayings and Doings*, which contained four tales, appeared in 1824, and it proved so successful that Hook produced nearly a score of other stories in the years that followed. Hook excels in the art of making people outside feel that at last they are learning the truth about people inside. Although it is a favourite trick of his to make a couple of his characters join in deploring the inaccurate account of fashionable life given by the gossip-columnists, the picture that he himself presents is essentially of the same

[1] Theodore Edward Hook (1788–1841) was the son of the organist at Vauxhall Gardens, who was a prolific composer and song-writer. As a boy at Harrow he wrote words for his father's comic operas and melodramas. He early became a friend of the Prince of Wales and was celebrated for his practical jokes and his gifts as an improviser. In 1813 he was sent to Mauritius as accountant-general, but after four years he was dismissed (perhaps unfairly) for deficiencies in the accounts. In 1820 he had begun to edit the Tory newspaper *John Bull*. He was a talented, disreputable man who wrote a great deal and served as the model for Lucian Gay in Disraeli's *Coningsby* and Mr. Wagg in *Pendennis*.

sort. He flatters his readers by making them feel superior to the common herd, while in fact he plays on the most vulgar attitudes and prejudices—as when he informs us that a true Dandy 'is a man who, dressing exceedingly well, without anything particularly *outré* about him, is well-informed, particularly *au fait* of what is going on, accomplished, unaffected, gay, and agreeable; whose appointments, whether of person or equipage, are resplendently fresh'—and so on. As Myron F. Brightfield has pointed out, the plot of Hook's *Merton* (1824) is similar in many ways to that of *Granby*; but one has only to make the comparison to see the difference in intention and value between the two books. Lister is seriously concerned with human nature and with moral values, while Hook's aim is simply to write an entertaining tale calculated to appeal to the socially aspiring. His claim to give a true picture of human life cannot be taken seriously: his books are essentially romances: in spite of the ubiquitous descriptions in his work of the material paraphernalia of upper-class life it is a mistake to use the word 'realism' of books like *Merton* and *Fathers and Sons*. His tales have little structural unity, and while he does occasionally seem serious (in some degree) in the morals that he preaches, they are never more than a secondary concern. There is a curious unreality about many parts of his books: although he did in fact move in fashionable society himself, his upper-class dialogue is often astonishingly stilted. On occasion, it is true, he may catch the slang of a couple of young Regency bucks; but his real flair is for homely comedy or farce, while we also notice that he is sometimes excellent in his descriptions of unpleasant people. In general it must be admitted that his books have little literary merit; but for the social historian they remain a mine of information, while it is at least possible that Bulwer Lytton, whose *Pelham* will be dealt with in the next volume of this *History*, was right in attributing an unexpected influence to the fashionable novelists as a class: 'Few writers', he wrote in *England and the English*,

> ever produced so great an effect on the political spirit of their generation as some of these novelists, who, without any other merit, unconsciously exposed the falsehood, the hypocrisy, the arrogant and vulgar insolence of patrician life. Read by all classes, in every town, in every village, these works . . . could not but engender a mingled

indignation and disgust at the parade of frivolity, the ridiculous disdain of truth, nature, and mankind, the self-consequence and absurdity, which, falsely or truly, [they] exhibited as a picture of aristocratic society. The Utilitarians railed against them, and [yet] they were effecting with unspeakable rapidity the very purposes the Utilitarians desired. (Book IV, chap. ii.)

It would be difficult to find a greater contrast to Theodore Hook than Plumer Ward, whose first work of fiction, *Tremaine, or the Man of Refinement* (1825), appeared when he was sixty.[1] Ward's idea of the novel (when he admitted to writing novels: at times he protested against the name) was that, like History, it was 'Philosophy teaching by examples'. In the preface he acknowledges that he may be asked why he has 'recorded the series of retired scenes, and sometimes abstruse conversations, which compose the following narrative', and answers that it is because he hopes to be able to do some good. He is particularly concerned about the manners and morals of the middle class, fearing that the spread of luxury 'has undermined our independence, and left our virtue defenceless':

> All would be Statesmen, Philosophers, or people of fashion. All, too, run to London. The woods and fields are unpeopled; the plain mansions and plain manners of our fathers deserted and changed; every thing is swallowed up by a devouring dissipation; and the simplicities of life are only to be found in books.

Not that Ward would counsel everyone to seek refuge in the country. One of the aims of his book, indeed, was to counter 'the very dangerous mistakes about solitude' for which he blamed Zimmermann, Byron, and 'the Swiss mountebank, Rousseau'. The trouble about *Tremaine*, which is a sort of literary equivalent of a vegetable marrow, is that it is extremely dull. After the first volume it becomes simply a very slow-moving love story, the only obstacle to the hero's happiness being that he has some doubts about Christianity. Practically the whole of the last volume is devoted to theological arguments in which

[1] Robert Plumer Ward (1765–1846) took his middle name in 1828. He was educated at Westminster and Christ Church, Oxford, and then travelled on the Continent. In 1790 he became a member of the Inner Temple. He wrote a great deal on legal and political questions, and was a strong supporter of Pitt. He was for many years a Member of Parliament, being at various times Under-Secretary for Foreign Affairs, a commissioner of the Admiralty, and clerk of the Ordnance.

his future father-in-law refutes the heresies by which Tremaine is tempted. Near the end Ward assures the reader that he dreads another argument 'for you as well as for myself' and the reader, for his part, is likely to become as 'silent and abstracted' as the hero of the book. If one of Ward's ancestors was Henry Mackenzie, another was Polonius. Few novels contain such long and tedious arguments: there is not even the element of drama that might result from a genuine confrontation of ideas. For a Fellow of Magdalen, Tremaine is remarkably deficient in dialectic power, and we can readily understand why one of his colleagues calls him 'little more than an illustrious mope'. What began as a novel to illustrate certain truths about Solitude and Society dwindles into a sentimental love story and drags to its conclusion as an exercise in Christian apologetics. 'Variety and incident are equally wanting', as the author disarmingly confesses: 'the Editor had almost said interest, but that his own feelings forbade'. The most dramatic thing that happens throughout these three volumes of the 'history of heart' is that the heroine scalds her pretty fingers when she spills a pot of tea, so giving Tremaine a chance to display his devoted gallantry. Little need be said of Ward's other books, *De Vere, or The Man of Independence* (1827) and *De Clifford, or The Constant Man* (1841). *De Vere* is a story of ambition and independence, set in the eighteenth century. *De Clifford*, which appeared when its author was over eighty, must have seemed laughably old-fashioned to readers of *Jane Eyre* and *Wuthering Heights*. Defending the 'many didactic digressions and episodes' in the book, Ward says that he cannot see how 'a novel which has for its object something more than the mere pictures of a magic-lanthorn, and aims at a knowledge of the springs of human nature, as well as amusement, can possibly realize that object without *partaking* of the didactic character'. Its theme is 'the impressions made by men and manners on a very young and unsophisticated mind, just starting into life, beginning even from his boyish days': a theme not wholly foreign to the interests of two writers as different from each other as Jane Austen and Dickens, but in this case totally unproductive of life or drama. When he reaches Volume IV the reader may well share the astonishment of the narrator on reflecting that he has only reached his hero's twenty-fifth year, in spite of the fact that he has not experienced any 'particular adventures'. The most that can be claimed for Ward today is

a certain faded charm—although it must also be acknowledged that he influenced both Bulwer Lytton and Disraeli.

When he sent a copy of *Brambletye House* (1826) to Sir Walter Scott, Horace Smith, whose talent for the imitation of poetic styles had already been evident in the *Rejected Addresses*, confessed that his new book was merely 'a humble imitation of that style which [Scott] had so successfully introduced'. In fact *Brambletye House* appeared a few weeks before *Woodstock*, in which Scott himself tells a story of the Civil Wars; but there is no need to suspect direct influence: once the idea of the historical romance has become current, history is bound to be searched for periods rich in stirring events. It is not surprising to find, therefore, that Scott was reading Harrison Ainsworth's first book, *Sir John Chiverton*, which is set in the days of chivalry, at the same time as *Brambletye House*. The similarities between Horace Smith's romance and *Woodstock* are very striking: each is an adventure story, written to entertain and without any regard for probability or truth of characterization. In each the idea of the Cavaliers and Roundheads has something of *1066 and All That* about it, although Smith is a little less unfair to the Roundheads than Scott. Each abounds in sieges, scenes of flight and pursuit, disguises, and Wardour Street dialogue. The period of the Civil Wars as it is portrayed in these two books stands to historical time as the Forest of Arden in *As You Like It* stands to geographical place. Neither book invites, or deserves, serious criticism. Scott himself was obviously puzzled by the success of his imitators. In his *Journal* he differentiates between himself and them by saying that his own knowledge of history is greater, so that he does not need to get it up for a particular book and is thereby saved from the danger of dragging in details 'by head and shoulders'. To the modern reader the curious thing is to find the man of genius and the man of talent reduced to roughly equal terms. Encouraged by the success of his first romance, which 'hit the public taste' and went through several editions in the year of publication, Horace Smith produced *The Tor Hill*, which deals with the period of the Reformation, and went on to write a dozen more historical romances. In *The New Forest* he showed himself particularly aware of the importance of picturesque scenery as an element in the Scott-ish romance. Many scenes in this book are 'tinted with the rich harmonious hues that a painter loves', and everywhere we find 'dark vistas,

athwart whose distant gloom the deer [are] occasionally seen to bound'. In the history of taste Smith's romances retain an interest which they have otherwise lost, and to the admirer of Scott it is interesting to compare *Waverley* and its successors with the romances of Mrs. Radcliffe, on the one hand, and with those of Horace Smith on the other. There is no better way of bringing out the greatness, and the originality, of Scott's earlier books, and in particular of *The Heart of Mid-Lothian*.

Each of the three Irish writers with whom this survey must end was also indebted to Scott in one way or another. The help which he gave Robert Maturin in having *Bertram* brought on the stage has already been mentioned in Chapter V, and he was similarly well disposed to Maturin's prose romances. Yet in spite of Scott's commendation we cannot linger over *The Fatal Revenge*, *The Wild Irish Boy*, or *The Milesian Chief*: if Maturin is remembered at all it is as the author of *Melmoth the Wanderer* (1820), a book which was praised by Thackeray, by Rossetti, and by Baudelaire, and which Balzac paid a double-edged compliment by writing a satirical sequel, *Melmoth Réconcilié à l'Église*. In the preface Maturin tells us that the idea of the romance came from the following passage in one of his own sermons:

> At this moment is there one of us present, however we may have departed from the Lord, disobeyed his will, and disregarded his word—is there one of us who would, at this moment, accept all that man could bestow, or earth afford, to resign the hope of his salvation? —No, there is not one—not such a fool on earth, were the enemy of mankind to traverse it with the offer!

It is tempting to speculate about how such a subject would have been handled by the author of *The Confessions of a Justified Sinner*: Maturin handles it in a manner that makes it clear that he is not completely in earnest, and for an impression of the result we may turn to the notice published in the *Edinburgh Review* for July 1821:

> It was said . . . of Dr. Darwin's Botanic Garden—that it was the sacrifice of Genius in the Temple of False Taste; and the remark may be applied to the work before us, with the qualifying clause, that in this instance the Genius is less obvious, and the false taste more glaring. . . . The imagination of the author runs riot, even beyond the usual license of romance . . . His hero is a modern Faustus, who has bartered his soul with the powers of darkness for

protracted life, and unlimited worldly enjoyment;—his heroine, a species of insular goddess, a virgin Calypso of the Indian ocean, who, amid flowers and foliage, lives upon figs and tamarinds; associates with peacocks, loxias and monkeys; is worshipped by the occasional visitants of her island; finds her way to Spain, where she is married to the aforesaid hero by the hand of a dead hermit, the ghost of a murdered domestic being the witness of their nuptials; and finally dies in the dungeons of the Inquisition at Madrid!—To complete this phantasmagoric exhibition, we are presented with sybils and misers; parricides; maniacs in abundance; monks with scourges pursuing a naked youth streaming with blood; subterranean Jews surrounded by the skeletons of their wives and children; lovers blasted by lightning; Irish hags, Spanish grandees, shipwrecks, caverns, Donna Claras and Donna Isidoras,—all opposed to each other in glaring and violent contrast, and all their adventures narrated with the same undeviating display of turgid, vehement, and painfully elaborated language.

Exaggerated as this censure is, it is all in a sense true—yet beside the point, as if Dr. Leavis were to write a critique of *Ben Hur*. As we read *Melmoth* we sense that Maturin knew he was writing nonsense—and enjoyed it. The occasions on which the Wanderer visits those of his fellow creatures who have sunk to the depths of human misery, in the hope of persuading them to take over the terrible privilege of unending life, provide some powerful melodramatic scenes. The Indian girl Immalee captured the imagination of those of Maturin's contemporaries who were less censorious than the northern reviewers. The conclusion of the third volume may serve to give those who have not read the book some idea of its atmosphere:

Through the furze that clothed this rock, almost to its summit, there was a kind of tract as if a person had dragged, or been dragged,... through it—a downtrodden track, over which no footsteps but those of one impelled by force had ever passed. Melmoth and Monçada gained at last the summit of the rock. The ocean was underneath—the wide, waste, engulphing ocean! On a crag beneath them, something hung as floating to the blast. Melmoth clambered down and caught it. It was the handkerchief which the Wanderer had worn about his neck the preceding night—that was the last trace of the Wanderer!

Melmoth and Monçada exchanged looks of silent and unutterable horror, and returned slowly home.

*Melmoth* contradicts the usual rule that easy writing makes hard

reading: we cannot doubt that it was easily written, yet in spite of the confusing plot and the sometimes careless syntax the book is remarkably easy to read, if one abandons one's mind to it. It is the sort of reading that the young Brontës delighted in. In the preface Maturin acknowledges that he has been charged with 'too much attempt at the revivification of the horrors of Radcliffe-Romance': what can be said for him is that he galvanized the corpse in such a way as to produce something that is almost impressive. 'With all his faults', as Edith Birkhead put it, 'Maturin was the greatest as well as the last of the Goths.' In the history of literature *Melmoth* counts for little: in the history of taste it remains a landmark.

John Banim, a Catholic from Kilkenny, was a man who had little in common with Maturin. His tedious tragedy, *Damon and Pythias*, was successfully produced at Dublin in 1821, under the ægis of Sheil; but it was the appearance of the first series of his *Tales by the O'Hara Family* four years later that revealed his genuine talent. Encouraged by the example of Maria Edgeworth and of Scott, he wished to help bring about 'the formation of a good and affectionate feeling' between his native country and England. His merits and faults are well revealed in 'Crohoore', which is set in an Ireland very different from that presented by Maria Edgeworth. In this tale and elsewhere, as Thomas Flanagan has written in his pioneering study, *The Irish Novelists, 1800–1850*, Banim

> was faced with the task of writing about a bloody and violent land, in which justice was measured out by hanging judges and packed juries, and exacted by the loaded whips of squireens and the brandings and mutilations of secret societies. But there no longer existed in English fiction conventions by which such a society could be represented. In default, he accepted the conventions of the shilling shocker.

The best of his tales is 'The Nowlans'. At first he intended to write a *roman à thèse* about an evangelical movement known as the New Reformation and supported by English people who were dangerously ignorant of Irish life and character, but fortunately he changed the direction of the book and the finest passages are those which have least relevance to the original theme. His study of a Catholic priest who falls in love and breaks his vows by marrying is admirably done, as is the

account of the Protestant family with whom he and his wife find lodgings:

> No charity was in the house, nor in a heart in the house. In the face of all professed beggars the street door was slammed without a word, but with a scowl calculated to wither the heart of the wretched suitor; and with respect to such as strove to hide the profession under barrel-organs, flutes, flageolets, hurdy-gurdies, or the big drum and pandean pipes, their tune was, indeed, listened to but never requited. . . . But nothing irked him so much as the ostentatious triumph over starvation, the provoking assumption of comfort, nay, elegance, as it were, and the audacious independence which resulted from the whole economy.

The description of the girls of the household—who 'gave no idea of flesh and blood. They never looked as if they were warm, or soft to the touch. One would as soon think of flirting with them, as with the old wooden effigies to be found in the niches of cathedrals'—might have won the approval of James Joyce. Banim's historical romances are of less account, though *The Boyne Water* shows an intelligent application of Scott's technique of contrast and picturesque description to the different opportunities provided by Irish history and character.

In 1823 Banim behaved with characteristic kindliness to a young compatriot who arrived in London full of literary ambition. Gerald Griffin was the more gifted man of the two, and he disapproved strongly of the way in which Irish life had been presented in the *Tales by the O'Hara Family*. His aim, as he tells us in the preface to *Holland-Tide* (1827), was to produce something true to life and 'illustrative of manners and scenery precisely as they stand in the South of Ireland', and the book consists of a series of tales told to that end. In the same year Griffin published his *Tales of the Munster Festivals*, and then with *The Collegians* in 1829 (which constituted the second series of the *Tales*) he produced the work by which he is still remembered. The germ of the story was a murder which had recently attracted attention; but Griffin transformed his material by setting his tale in the period of his father's youth, the 1770's, and using it as a means of exploring the structure and the dilemmas of Irish life at that time. The charming yet ultimately ruthless Hardress Cregan seduces Eily O'Connor, deserts her, and has her murdered. Although the girl, a rope-maker's daughter, is not very

vividly drawn, her seducer becomes an admirable symbol for one of the most characteristic aspects of Irish life. As Flanagan has commented, Cregan

> is invested with a kind of kingliness, but beneath his graces and powers lie the terror and the ruthlessness of a child. He has come to manhood in a society in which religion has decayed into social ritual—'the genteel religion'—and law into an extension of social privilege. What matters is *code*, that emptiest of moral patterns, which had become synonymous with honor. It had carried him successfully through balls and drinking bouts, duels and hunts. But, for the moral choice which lies at the novel's core, it has left him stripped of every weapon save the knife in the hand of Danny the Lord.

It is a revealing comment on the difficulty of writing serious fiction at this time that Griffin was persuaded to change his intended ending: instead of being hanged Cregan is sentenced to transportation, and dies on the voyage. Yet the conclusion, in which he looks for the last time at his native place, is admirably managed:

> He turned, with an aching heart, from the contemplation of the landscape, and his eye encountered a spectacle more accordant to his present feelings. The row of houses which lined the quay on which the party halted, consisted for the most part of coffin-makers' shops, a gloomy trade, although, to judge by the reckless faces of the workmen, it would appear that 'custom had made it with them a property of easiness'.
>
> Only one of those dismal houses of traffic was open at this early hour, and the light which burned in the interior showed that the proprietor was called to the exercise of his craft at this unseasonable time by some sudden and pressing call. The profession of the man was not indicated, as in more wealthy and populous cities, by a sculptured lid, or gilded and gaudy hatchment, suspended at a window-pane. A pile of the unfinished shells, formed for all ages from childhood to maturity, were thrust out at the open window, to attract the eye of the relatives of the newly-dead.

# IX

## HAZLITT

'ESSAY on the Principles of Human Action, sm. 8vo.—The Eloquence of the Brit. Senate, 2v. 8vo. 1808.—A new and improved Engl. Grammar, 18mo. 1810.' Such is the entry under Hazlitt's name in *A Biographical Dictionary of the Living Authors*, published in 1816, and it may serve as a reminder that the man we remember as a great critic and essayist came rather late to both these arts.[1] It was not until the year after the appearance of the *Dictionary* that he published his first volume of criticism and his first collection of essays. Before that time he was generally known only as a writer on philosophical and political topics and a contributor to the *Examiner*. If he had been less deeply interested in philosophy and politics he would have been a less penetrating critic of the writers of his time. And since his political views accompanied him everywhere—as John Scott pointed out—like a large dog, something must be said about them at the outset.

His father had supported the cause of American independence and was a friend of Dr. Price, the preacher of a celebrated sermon in praise of the French Revolution. Hazlitt's own first publication was a letter to a newspaper defending another friend of his father's, Dr. Priestley, who was the presiding genius at Hackney College until he was compelled to emigrate in 1794. While he himself was still studying there Hazlitt planned a *Project for a New Theory of Civil and Criminal Legislation*

[1] William Hazlitt (1778–1830) was the son of a Unitarian minister who had become an acquaintance of Benjamin Franklin's during the latter's visit to England. Although he himself was educated for the ministry he felt an aversion from such a life and left Hackney College about 1795. He heard Coleridge's last sermon, and visited him at Stowey in 1798. He was one of the earliest admirers of Wordsworth's poetry, but in 1803 Wordsworth and his circle broke with him on account of a moral lapse on Hazlitt's part. At this point he was studying painting, and in 1804 he painted his well-known portrait of Lamb as a Venetian Senator. Four years later he married Sarah Stoddart, obtaining a divorce in 1822. In 1824, after the infatuation described in *Liber Amoris*, he married a Mrs. Bridgwater, but she soon left him, probably in 1827. He lived by writing and lecturing. Throughout his life Lamb remained his constant friend.

which he took up again towards the end of his life. When he surveyed his own life in 1827 he saw clearly that the event which had done most to form it had been the French Revolution, which broke out when he was a boy of ten. 'I set out in life with the French Revolution', as he wrote in his essay 'On the Feeling of Immortality in Youth', 'and that event had considerable influence on my early feelings. . . . It was the dawn of a new era. . . . Little did I dream . . . that long before my eyes should close, that dawn would be overcast, and set once more in the night of despotism.' Whereas most English sympathizers with the revolutionaries lived to change their opinions, Hazlitt remained constant, by and large, to his early loyalties. He was a disapproving auditor of the lecture in which James Mackintosh, the author of *Vindiciæ Gallicæ*, made his recantation, and viewed with distrust the shifting opinions of Wordsworth, Coleridge, and Southey. He was a brilliant man, yet (as he was later to admit) he was in a sense 'no politician'. As his contributions to the *Morning Chronicle* and the *Examiner* make clear, his approach to politics was at once highly theoretical and highly emotional. He was a child of the Enlightenment, and the infamous thing that he hated was compounded of 'the Pope, the Inquisition, the Bourbons, and the doctrine of Divine Right'. For him Napoleon was simply the man who had set his foot on the neck of kings. After Waterloo, we are told, Hazlitt 'seemed prostrated in mind and body': he hated tyranny and loved freedom, and in the years that followed it seemed to him that tyranny was triumphing throughout Europe. He could not understand how a people who had executed one king and banished another could talk as Southey and the Tories were talking of the Divine Right of Kings. He once described himself as a Jacobin or Old Whig: his landmarks were Locke's *Treatise on Government* and the Glorious Revolution of 1688. The mystical Toryism of Coleridge repelled him because he felt that the clouds of eloquence concealed a lack of clarity and a lack of honesty. He wrote against Malthus, whose *Essay on the Principle of Population* was enjoying a great vogue amongst the conservatives, because he was appalled by the doctrine that it is idle to attempt to improve the condition of mankind. Intellectually, it is true, he came to believe that 'all things move, not in progress, but in a ceaseless round; our strength lies in our weakness; our virtues are built on our vices; our faculties are as limited as our being; nor can

we lift man above his nature more than above the earth he treads': yet emotionally he was always to remain true to 'that bright dream of our youth'. When he collected his *Political Essays* in 1819 it was characteristic of him to dedicate them defiantly to John Hunt, 'the tried, steady, zealous, and conscientious advocate of the liberty of his country, and the rights of mankind'. Near the end of his life he was to write his *Life of Napoleon* and to rejoice in the final overthrow of the Bourbons.

The *Memoirs of the late Thomas Holcroft*, finished in 1810 though not published until 1816, represent the transition from Hazlitt's political period to that of his essays and literary criticism. Dramatist, novelist, and radical, Holcroft had associated with Thelwall and Horne Tooke and the members of the Society for Constitutional Information and had been indicted in connexion with the trial of 1794. Hazlitt was asked to build a book on the autobiography which Holcroft had left unfinished; what he did was to follow the model of Mason's *Memoirs of Gray*, piecing together letters, diaries, and the reminiscences of his subject's other friends. The result is a biography that throws a good deal of light on a critical period in our intellectual history. In 1817 it was followed by *The Round Table* and *Characters of Shakespear's Plays*, which mark the opening of Hazlitt's major period. It will be convenient to concentrate first on his critical writings, and then to consider his work as an essayist.

Although *Characters of Shakespear's Plays* remains one of Hazlitt's best-known books, it does not represent his criticism at its best. The volume is dedicated to Charles Lamb, and throughout it Hazlitt remains a follower of Lamb's. He makes little attempt to divine the principal theme of each play; nor does he write with reference to dramatic production. By concentrating on the characters rather than the plays themselves he too often ignores the whole in favour of the part. He does not, indeed, analyse any of the characters in detail—as Maurice Morgann and others had begun to do in the previous century. What he does is to quote liberally from each play and discuss it in general terms. If the result sometimes reminds us of a collection of *Beauties of Shakespeare*, we must in justice remember that Hazlitt was reacting against the eighteenth century's tendency to condemn Shakespeare for violating rules which have in fact no relevance to his plays. Hazlitt has entered Shakespeare's universe, and is content to take it on its own terms. When he

was reviewing Schlegel's *Lectures on Dramatic Literature* he had suggested that German scholars are apt to write 'not because they are full of a subject, but because they think it is a subject upon which . . . something striking may be written'. Hazlitt was full of his subject, and wrote with enthusiasm. The result is a book that contains some brilliant passages, and which has helped to introduce a great many readers to the greatest of all our poets.

The treatment of Shakespeare in *Lectures on the English Poets* (1818), the first of the three series of lectures in which Hazlitt covered the central tract of our literary history, is in many ways superior to anything in the previous volume. Although he often opposes views which he believes to be mistaken, yet the *Lectures* as a whole do not show such a revolt from the criticism of the previous century as some might expect. Half of the space is devoted to the eighteenth century: Pope's poetry is nobly praised (as is Swift's), and while Hazlitt thinks more highly of Collins than did Johnson, he follows Johnson in praising Gray's *Elegy* while censuring the 'kind of methodical borrowed phrenzy' of the odes. He agrees with the common reader in a high estimation of Thomson, and opposes the fashionable 'cant . . . about genius'. Keats was one of a number among his audience who were annoyed by his treatment of Chatterton. Apart from Shakespeare, Spenser is the only Elizabethan discussed, while Donne and his followers are virtually ignored. But it is when he comes to the living poets that Hazlitt is most interesting. After conventional praise of 'the female writers of the present day' he moves in to an attack on the very popular Rogers and Campbell, in whose work 'the decomposition of prose is substituted for the composition of poetry'. Moore is let off more lightly, while Byron and Scott receive treatment which is severe but not unfair. It is when he reaches Wordsworth that we feel that Hazlitt's interest is most deeply aroused. He has delayed dealing with him as long as he can, and we sense an embarrassment that is due to the tension between his personal feelings and his critical appreciation. To survey Hazlitt's criticisms of Wordsworth, here and elsewhere, is to watch a great critic rising superior to political disagreements and personal resentment. He praises him highly, insisting that the most successful of his poems 'open a finer and deeper vein of thought and feeling than any poet in modern times has done, or attempted';

and although he believes that Wordsworth 'cannot form a whole . . . has not the constructive faculty . . . is totally deficient in all the machinery of poetry', he also insists that 'he has produced a deeper impression, and on a smaller circle, than any other of his contemporaries'. Having spoken out magnanimously in this way for a man whose 'powers have been mistaken by the age', Hazlitt permits himself to conclude the lecture with a semi-satirical account of 'that which has been denominated the Lake school of poetry', whose origins he traces to the French Revolution and the influence of translations from German literature:

> All was to be natural and new. Nothing that was established was to be tolerated. All the common-place figures of poetry, tropes, allegories, personifications, with the whole heathen mythology, were instantly discarded. . . . Rhyme was looked upon as a relic of the feudal system, and regular metre was abolished along with regular government.

As we read this critique we are reminded of Johnson on 'the metaphysical poets':

> The paradox they set out with was, that all things are by nature equally fit subjects for poetry; or that . . . the meanest and most unpromising are the best. . . . They claimed kindred only with the commonest of the people: peasants, pedlars, and village-barbers. . . . They were for bringing poetry back to its primitive simplicity and state of nature.

Although Southey and Coleridge are mentioned at the end, it is of Wordsworth that Hazlitt is thinking most of the time. The contrast between Wordsworth and Shakespeare that is implied throughout is the origin of Keats's phrase 'the egotistical sublime': we notice that when Hazlitt is discussing Wordsworth the word 'egotism' is never far away.

The contents of *The English Comic Writers* (1819) include a surprisingly wide range of authors: Elizabethan, Restoration and eighteenth-century dramatists, poets of the early seventeenth century, and essayists and novelists of the eighteenth century: while a lecture on Hogarth is thrown in for good measure. Taken together, Lectures II, IV and VIII constitute a fairly comprehensive account of English comedy from the Elizabethan period to the end of the eighteenth century. The

comparison of Shakespeare and Jonson is well managed: in spite of his admission that he 'cannot much relish Ben Jonson' Hazlitt contrasts his type of comedy with Shakespeare's very justly. On Wycherley, Congreve, Vanbrugh, and Farquhar he writes perceptively and *con amore*, while his account of Jeremy Collier, 'this sour, non-juring critic', may be read as a spirited defence of comedy.

When he reaches Donne and his followers in the third lecture, Hazlitt contents himself for the most part with quoting from Johnson; but when he comes to *Hudibras*, 'the greatest single production of wit of this period, I might say of this country', his enthusiasm is kindled and the result is the most brilliant discussion of the poem in English criticism.

It is when he is dealing with prose writers, and particularly with novelists, that Hazlitt is at his best in this volume. His account of the essayists of the early eighteenth century is admirable, and has a particular interest because it is the criticism of a later master of the form. He is excellent on the *Tatler* and the *Spectator*, decidedly preferring the former, and though he is severe on the *Rambler* and its author—*Rasselas* is described as 'the most melancholy and debilitating moral speculation that ever was put forth'—there is something fine about his description of Johnson's prejudices:

> His were not time-serving, heartless, hypocritical prejudices; but deep, inwoven, not to be rooted out but with life and hope, which he found from old habit necessary to his own peace of mind, and thought so to the peace of mankind. I do not hate, but love him for them.

When he reaches the novelists of the eighteenth century Hazlitt rises to his opportunity. As he himself points out, 'this is a department of criticism which deserves more attention than has been usually bestowed upon it'. Almost a century after the publication of *Pamela* there was still no authoritative discussion of the major novelists by a competent critic. It is true that Dunlop's *History of Prose Fiction* had appeared in 1814, but when he reviewed it Hazlitt pointed out its deficiency in the 'spirit of philosophic enquiry' and in 'critical acuteness'. He himself begins with a brief discussion of the nature of the novel, and says something about *Don Quixote* and other Spanish novels which may be regarded as naturalized British subjects.

Then he comes to Fielding. Although he devotes only a few pages to the author of *Tom Jones*, no one had written so ably about him before; and his comparison of Fielding and Smollett may serve to show his genuine understanding of both men:

> What then is it that gives the superiority to Fielding? It is the superior insight into the springs of human character, and the constant developement of that character through every change of circumstance. Smollett . . . seldom probes to the quick, or penetrates beyond the surface. . . . We read *Roderick Random* as an entertaining story . . . but we regard *Tom Jones* as a real history. . . . Smollett excels most as the lively caricaturist: Fielding as the exact painter and profound metaphysician.

The account of Richardson (one of the last writers one might have expected to find in this volume) is in no way inferior to that of Fielding. 'There is an artificial reality about his works', Hazlitt remarks, 'which is no where else to be met with. They have the romantic air of a pure fiction, with the literal minuteness of a common diary. The author had the strongest matter-of-fact imagination that ever existed.' 'If the business of life consisted in letter-writing'—Hazlitt says later in the lecture—'and was carried on by the post (like a Spanish game at chess), human nature would be what Richardson represents it.' Sterne is more briefly dealt with—Uncle Toby being described as 'one of the finest compliments ever paid to human nature'—and we hear something of Fanny Burney, Mrs. Radcliffe, Godwin, and Sir Walter Scott. The absence of Jane Austen from the gallery of novelists is regrettable, though hardly surprising; but even this gap cannot conceal the fact that Hazlitt here proves himself far and away the best critic of the English novelists up to his time.

Having had his say on Shakespeare and most of our main writers since the Restoration, Hazlitt chose *The Dramatic Literature of the Age of Elizabeth* for his next series of published lectures (1820). Here he is often dealing with writers whom he knew less well, and his primary intention is to introduce unfamiliar books to his audience:

> What I have undertaken to do . . . is merely to read over a set of authors with the audience, as I would do with a friend, to point out a favourite passage, to explain an objection; or if a remark or

a theory occurs, to state it in illustration of the subject, but neither to tire him nor puzzle myself with pedantic rules and pragmatical *formulas* of criticism that can do no good to any body.... In a word, I have endeavoured to feel what was good, and to 'give a reason for the faith that was in me'.

Accordingly he takes us on a conducted tour of such writers as Lyly, Marlowe, Heywood, Middleton, Rowley, Marston, Chapman, Dekker, and many others, quoting liberally 'to make these old writers . . . vouchers for their own pretensions'. For better or for worse one finds the germs of many historical commonplaces in this book, such as the misleading view that 'a rage for French rules and French models' did untold harm to our literature after the Restoration. As we read these lectures we are often reminded of Charles Lamb, as we are when Hazlitt quotes Johnson's remark that such writers 'were sought after because they were scarce, and would not have been scarce had they been much esteemed' and counters by saying that this is 'neither true history nor sound criticism'. Like Lamb, Hazlitt is here in search of good passages rather than good plays; but occasionally he breaks away from mere appreciation, as when he differs from Lamb about a passage in Ford's *Broken Heart* or censures the 'craving after striking effect' and the artificiality of Beaumont and Fletcher.

In the sixth and seventh lectures Hazlitt leaves the drama altogether and says something of the poetry of Drummond of Hawthornden, Herrick, and Marvell—'To his Coy Mistress' being given *in toto*. He then discusses four prose writers: Sidney, Bacon, Sir Thomas Browne, and Jeremy Taylor. The account of Bacon is in his best manner, and deserves to stand beside that 'perpetual model of encomiastick criticism' (as Johnson called it), Dryden's character of Shakespeare. It is more brilliant and pointed than the essay on Bacon's philosophy in the *Literary Remains*, yet like it could only have been written by a critic who took Bacon's thought seriously. In the eighth lecture Hazlitt returns to the drama, alluding to Lamb, Sheil, and 'Barry Cornwall' as modern writers 'who have imbibed the spirit and imitated the language of our elder dramatists' and then attempting to distinguish four schools of tragedy: the classical, the Gothic or romantic, 'the French or commonplace rhetorical style', and 'the German or paradoxical style'. Hazlitt makes some excellent points, and it is hardly his fault that his

categories sometimes proved more influential than they deserved. His account of the 'German' species of tragedy, in which the characters are 'mouth-pieces... of certain extravagant speculative opinions', is surprisingly severe. 'It embodies', he says, '. . . the extreme opinions which are floating in our time, and which have struck their roots deep and wide below the surface of the public mind.'

It is fortunate that Hazlitt did not content himself with the fragmentary treatment of his contemporaries in his earlier books. In 1825 he published *The Spirit of the Age*, which represents him at the summit of his powers as a critic. If the first condition of good criticism is that the critic must be passionately interested in the work which he is considering, then Hazlitt was ideally fitted to criticize the writers dealt with in this brilliant volume. Some, like Godwin and Coleridge, had been the masters of his youth: others had been his associates in writing: while others, like Gifford and Southey, had been and remained his enemies and detractors. In dealing with such men Hazlitt was at once writing his spiritual autobiography and holding up a mirror to the age. There is not a slack page from the beginning to the end, not a sentence which suggests boredom or indifference. Whether he is dealing with the economic theories of Malthus or the metaphysics of Coleridge, Hazlitt writes with passion and conviction. It follows that we are not to expect an academic impartiality: he is writing as the supporter of some of his subjects and the bitter opponent of others. Yet he writes also as a critic whose flair for good writing is so unfailing that he is incapable of denying it wherever he meets it. As he says in the fifth of his *Lectures on the Age of Elizabeth*: 'Anger may sharpen our insight into men's defects; but nothing should make us blind to their excellences.'

The critical method is unusual. It is not the individual book or poem that is the unit of consideration, but the writer himself. Yet we are not given a great deal of biographical information. It is true that the appearance of the writer is often described—and when this is done we notice that Hazlitt has a painter's eye for detail and picturesque effect. But we are never given description for description's sake. At times one is reminded of the Prologue to *The Canterbury Tales*: external details are used as pointers to character—and particularly to the character of an author's writings. We come to see that

Hazlitt does not concern himself with an author apart from his writings: he sees in him the man who wrote his books, and even details of personal description turn out to be relevant. 'Mr. Bentham', we are told, '. . . turns wooden utensils in a lathe for exercise, and fancies he can turn men in the same manner.'

What Hazlitt has done is to invent a new kind of 'character' writing. Drawing on his knowledge of the 'characters' which may be found in the literature of the seventeenth and eighteenth centuries he has evolved a new species of literary character in which the subject is neither the author as an individual nor his writings regarded in themselves, but the author as an author, in his works, and as a representative of the *Zeitgeist*. The enormous penultimate sentence of the chapter on Scott is an inspired variation of Pope's 'Atticus', and it was clearly from the writers of the previous century that Hazlitt learned how to use antithesis with such telling effect as he does when he says of Cobbett that 'his principle is repulsion, his nature contradiction: he is made up of mere antipathies, an Ishmaelite indeed without a fellow'. There is nothing affected about the style: it forms the fitting expression of a brilliantly analytic critic who has long reflected on the subjects about which he is writing. At times he carries conciseness to its logical limits, and the result is a strong element of wit—wit which is always used for a purpose, as when Hazlitt remarks that Bentham's writings 'have been translated into French—they ought to be translated into English'. Yet some of his most telling passages are written in a more relaxed style, like the second sentence of the chapter on Gifford:

> The low-bred, self-taught man, the pedant, and the dependant on the great contribute to form the Editor of the *Quarterly Review*. He is admirably qualified for this situation, which he has held for some years, by a happy combination of defects, natural and acquired; and in the event of his death, it will be difficult to provide him a suitable successor.

That is murder committed with words—though in the case of Gifford most courts would accept a plea of manslaughter.

Perhaps the wit of *The Spirit of the Age* has led some readers to underestimate its value as criticism. If so it is they who have been the losers. It is true that in this book certain of the critic's tasks are not attempted, certain of his techniques left unemployed: the formal *critique* is avoided, while theoretical

problems are set to one side. The grammar and groundwork of criticism are taken for granted, not because they are too difficult but because they have now been relegated to the background: we are being presented with findings, the conclusions of a lifetime's reflection. It is as if Hazlitt had written a book on each of these men, but presented us only with the final chapter, the summing-up of it all.

When we survey Hazlitt's criticism as a whole we are bound to be impressed by its wide range. In the drama he deals (though often very sketchily) with most of the principal landmarks from *Gammer Gurton's Needle* onwards. In the field of poetry he writes illuminatingly on Chaucer, Spenser, and most of our later poets, although he devotes comparatively little attention to Donne and his followers. In prose he not only deals excellently with the essayists and novelists of the eighteenth century: he also provides perceptive treatments, sometimes in unexpected places, of the Authorized Version (*The Age of Elizabeth*, I), Bunyan (*English Poets*, I), Sidney's *Arcadia*, Bacon, Sir Thomas Browne and Jeremy Taylor (*The Age of Elizabeth*, VI–VII). When it is remembered that there was no comprehensive History of English Literature in his day, or for more than half a century later, the twofold importance of Hazlitt's work becomes apparent. He is not only a major critic, a worthy successor to Dryden and Johnson, as surely excelling Coleridge in the practice of criticism as he is excelled by him in discussion of critical theory: he is also a key figure in literary historiography. Starting, virtually, where Warton had left off, he deals with most of the principal writers of the seventeenth and eighteenth centuries, as well as with those of his own age. The result is that his critical writings, which contain hardly a single date, have been one of the principal source-books on which literary historians have always relied.

He could scarcely have been born at a better time. As a contemporary of Wordsworth and Coleridge, he shared their early hopes for the future of mankind, so that there was no danger of his failing to understand the aspirations of his own generation. Political estrangement, on the other hand, ensured that he would not fall into uncritical enthusiasm of their work, and as a result his criticism has a sharp edge. His sympathy with the new currents in literature also put him in a favourable position for reviewing the history of English literature as a whole

from the standpoint of the new age. Although he was not greatly interested in medieval literature, he shared the new enthusiasm for the Elizabethans for which the way had been prepared by scholars like Farmer and Malone. His attitude to eighteenth-century literature is particularly interesting: his emphases and judgements differ a good deal from Johnson's, yet he is free from the tendency of many of his contemporaries to make up for exaggerated praise by exaggerated censure. He complains that 'it is mortifying to hear [Wordsworth] speak of Pope and Dryden whom, because they have been supposed to have all the possible excellences of poetry, he will allow to have none'. He once accused Lamb of reading nothing after the *Spectator*: no one could make the same charge against himself. It is clear that he relished the opportunity of revaluing Augustan literature from a new vantage ground, being stimulated by the rich deposits of anecdote and historical material which were being published during his lifetime. By avoiding the merely partisan and acknowledging merit wherever he found it he became, in effect, the first critical historian of our literature, the first man to sketch out a picture of English literary history in which the rules of perspective are decently observed.

It is now time to consider his work as an essayist. Most of the essays collected in *The Round Table* were originally published in the *Examiner*. Leigh Hunt had proposed a series of papers in the manner of the *Tatler* and the *Spectator*, undertaking as his own share 'the characteristic or dramatic part of the work'; but in the event Hazlitt wrote most of the essays. Although other influences may also be noticed, the main model is undoubtedly the eighteenth-century essay. Like the essayists of the eighteenth century Hazlitt devotes a proportion of his space to literary criticism—'Lycidas', Milton's Versification, *John Buncle*—and like them he deals with such general topics as 'The Love of Life', 'Patriotism', and 'Religious Hypocrisy'. Even in these early essays, however, he is less didactic than Addison and Steele: the opening sentence of the first essay—'It is our intention . . . to expose certain vulgar errors'—does not represent the general tone of the collection. And in other ways he differs from his famous predecessors: he does not concern himself with manners in the narrower sense: humour is not one of his main ingredients: while he never gives the impression of writing for 'the fair sex'.

In *The Round Table* we see Hazlitt developing his characteristic type of essay from eighteenth-century models: in *Table-Talk* (1821–2) and *The Plain Speaker* (1826), and such uncollected essays as 'My First Acquaintance with Poets', we find it fully evolved. Most of these essays are three or four times as long as their predecessors. In them (to quote from the admirable discussion of essay-writing in *The English Comic Writers*) the writer applies

the talents and resources of the mind to all that mixed mass of human affairs, which, though not included under the head of any regular art, science, or profession, falls under the cognizance of the writer, and 'comes home to the business and bosoms of men'. . . . [He] makes familiar with the world of men and women, records their actions, assigns their motives, exhibits their whims, characterises their pursuits in all their singular and endless variety, ridicules their absurdities, exposes their inconsistencies.

The essay 'is in morals and manners what the experimental is in natural philosophy, as opposed to the dogmatical method'. Today the essay is dying, and the reason is that we have an exaggerated faith in 'specialists': it flourishes in periods in which there is a belief in wisdom, and in the wise man. The task of the essayist is to collect the fruit of his experience, reflect on it, and set it out for our consideration. 'I endeavour to recollect all I have ever observed or thought upon a subject', Hazlitt remarks, 'and to express it as nearly as I can.' His grandson tells us that he would use every scrap of paper that came to hand for 'heads of contemplated essays on "Men and Manners"'—and sometimes resorted to writing down his ideas 'over the mantelpiece in lead-pencil'. Today we are more likely to find the fruits of this type of reflection in a novel than in an essay. If we turn from a psychologist's account of jealousy or frustration with a feeling of dissatisfaction, we may find in *A Passage to India* or *Elders and Betters* a profounder commentary on the matter. Hazlitt's method, however, is not dramatic: his aim is rather to combine the advantages of a set inquiry into a given topic with those of an informal discussion with his friends. As he wrote in the 'Advertisement' to the Paris edition of *Table-Talk*, explaining the title:

I had remarked that when I had written or thought upon a particular topic, and afterwards had occasion to speak of it with a friend, the conversation generally took a much wider range, and branched off

into a number of indirect and collateral questions, which were not strictly connected with the original view of the subject, but which often threw a curious and striking light upon it, or upon human life in general. It therefore occurred to me as possible to combine the advantages of . . . the *literary* and *conversational*; or after stating and enforcing some leading idea, to follow it up by such observations and reflections as would probably suggest themselves in discussing the same question in company with others. This seemed to me to promise a greater variety and richness, and perhaps a greater sincerity, than could be attained by a more precise and scholastic method. The same consideration had an influence on the familiarity and conversational idiom of the style which I have used.

In spite of the informality of the method, the inquiries which Hazlitt pursues are essentially serious. Although he is not 'precise and scholastic', he includes within his scope 'subtle distinctions and trains of thought'. The underlying subject of all his writings is the subject of the most abstruse of his books, *An Essay on the Principles of Human Action*: for all their eloquence and charm, his essays are the work of a man trained in philosophical speculation. His first course of lectures dealt with English Philosophy, and everywhere he writes as the pupil of Bacon, of Locke, and of Hume. Few men have better understood the tyranny that words exercise over our lives and thoughts. 'The history of politics, of religion, of literature, of morals, and of private life', as he once wrote, 'is too often little more than the history of nicknames.' The essays 'On Vulgarity and Affectation' and 'On Means and Ends' are examples of his admirable anxiety to define with the greatest possible clarity. As in his style he is the heir of much that is best in the prose writers of the seventeenth and eighteenth centuries, so in his thought he is the heir of the Age of Reason. He moves amongst abstract ideas with an ease and familiarity that contrast oddly with Lamb. Lamb wrote on chimney-sweeps, the South-Sea House, weddings, and whist: Hazlitt wrote 'On Reason and Imagination', 'On Egotism', 'On the Past and Future'. His essays are more serious than Lamb's, or serious in a different sense. Interested as he is in the essay as a form, he is more interested in the truth which he is pursuing. He was a man of letters in the comprehensive sense in which Johnson and Coleridge were men of letters.

Yet Hazlitt was no friend to the 'theoretical *mania*'. Unlike

the philosopher or the theoretical psychologist, the essayist limits himself to illustrating the workings of the human mind as they have fallen under his own observation. And since the only mind of which we have direct experience is our own, the essayist is bound in some degree to be personal and autobiographical. 'My object is to paint the varieties of human nature', as Hazlitt acknowledges in his essay 'On Means and Ends', 'and . . . I can have it best from myself.' It is ironical that he so often accuses Wordsworth of 'egotism', for in this respect there is an affinity between the two men. Earlier epic poets had written about the actions of mythical heroes: Wordsworth, taking 'the mind of man' as his subject, is inevitably autobiographical. Hazlitt stands to earlier essayists rather as Wordsworth stands to earlier epic poets. Rousseau is not the least important of his ancestors. Such essays as 'My First Acquaintance with Poets', 'The Conversation of Authors', and 'On the Pleasure of Painting' are in fact chapters of autobiography. In the fine essay 'On the Feeling of Immortality in Youth' Hazlitt tells us that he has 'turned for consolation to the past, gathering up the fragments of my early recollections, and putting them into a form that might live'. It is possible that he was thinking of writing an autobiography—and quite conceivable that, if he had, the result would have been the greatest in the language. It would not only have been a masterpiece in itself, but also a testament on behalf of all those who 'set out in life with the French Revolution', only to find their extravagant hopes disappearing like the morning mist.

If part of Hazlitt's autobiography had dealt with his fortunes in love, it might have contained the least successful chapters. It is strange that his most sustained piece of autobiography should be as weak a production as the *Liber Amoris* (1823). This description of his infatuation with the daughter of his landlord is a classic example of the folly of a literary man in love. It is pathetic to see a man of Hazlitt's great powers going through 'a sort of purgatory' on account of a lodging-house jilt. We are reminded of his pitiful vulnerability: as Keats realized, he thought that no one valued him. He was 'a very child in love'—and he knew it. While it is not surprising that he should have written an account of the affair to get it out of his system, it is remarkable that a man with such critical powers should have published the result. Those whom the gods wish to drive mad,

they first deprive of their sense of humour. *Liber Amoris* reads like a version of *Shamela* narrated by 'the young Squire': it is astonishing to reflect that it was written at almost the same time as *Table-Talk*.

Such essays as 'The Indian Jugglers' and 'On Living to One's Self' in that collection seem so naturally written that we are in danger of overlooking the pains that Hazlitt devoted to the perfection of his style. He refers to himself as a prose-writer with the pride of a professional. To him the writing of prose was as serious a matter—as challenging a problem—as the writing of verse. This is made clear when he discusses 'The Prose-Style of Poets'. The prose of poets lacks 'momentum' and 'elasticity', since they are in the habit of relying on metre to gain such effects. It also tends to draw attention to itself. 'The poetical prose-writer stops to describe an object, if he admires it', whereas 'the genuine prose-writer only alludes to . . . it in passing, and with reference to his subject'. The prose-writer's aim should be 'truth, force of illustration, weight of argument': his tone should be that of 'lively, sensible conversation'. Hazlitt's strictures on Coleridge help to illustrate his meaning. Coleridge

> has an incessant craving . . . to exalt every idea into a metaphor, to expand every sentiment into a lengthened mystery, voluminous and vast, confused and cloudy. . . . The simple truth does not satisfy him—no direct proposition fills up the moulds of his understanding. . . . To read one of his disquisitions is like hearing the variations to a piece of music without the score.

The criticism of Lamb in the essay 'On Familiar Style' is more appreciative, but it too helps to throw light on Hazlitt's own intention in his prose style:

> A sprinkling of archaisms is not amiss; but a tissue of obsolete expressions is more fit *for keep than wear*. I do not say I would not use any phrase that had been brought into fashion before the middle or the end of the last century; but I should be shy of using any that had not been employed by any approved author during the whole of that time. . . . Mr. Lamb is the only imitator of old English style I can read with pleasure. . . . There is an inward unction, a marrowy vein both in the thought and feeling . . . that carries off any quaintness or awkwardness arising from an antiquated style and dress. The matter is completely his own, though the manner is assumed.

It is interesting to note that Hazlitt's favourite, among the

*Essays of Elia*, was 'Mrs. Battle's Opinions on Whist', which he found 'the most free from obsolete allusions and turns of expression'. His own aim is the 'familiar style' described in this way:

It is not easy to write a familiar style. Many people mistake a familiar for a vulgar style, and suppose that to write without affectation is to write at random. On the contrary, there is nothing that requires more precision, and, if I may so say, purity of expression, than the style I am speaking of. It utterly rejects not only all unmeaning pomp, but all low, cant phrases, and loose, unconnected, *slipshod* allusions. It is not to take the first word that offers, but the best word in common use; it is not to throw words together in any combinations we please, but to follow and avail ourselves of the true idiom of the language. To write a genuine familiar or truly English style, is to write as any one would speak in common conversation, who had a thorough command and choice of words, or who could discourse with ease, force, and perspicuity, setting aside all pedantic and oratorical flourishes.

Although a familiar style is Hazlitt's most usual aim, he varied his style (like any writer worth his salt) according to the demands of the subject and the occasion. As he says of Burke, he 'rises with the lofty, descends with the mean. . . . It is all the same to him, so that he loses no particle of the exact, characteristic, extreme impression of the thing he writes about. . . .' Most of 'The Fight', for example, is deliberately written in a low, almost vulgar style, as suits the subject:

*Where there's a will, there's a way.*—I said so to myself, as I walked down Chancery lane, about half-past six o'clock on Monday the 10th of December, to inquire at Jack Randall's where the fight the next day was to be . . . I was determined to see this fight, come what would, and see it I did, in great style.

One of the editors of the *New Monthly Magazine* thought the essay too 'vulgar', but fortunately the other had the perception to see in it a masterly 'picture of manners'. If we wish to do justice to Hazlitt's range of styles we must remember 'The Fight' as well as the essay 'On the Feeling of Immortality in Youth': we must contrast the dry, precise manner of his philosophical essays with the moving eloquence of his excursions into autobiography, the epigrammatic rhetoric of *The Spirit of the Age* with the devastating directness of the *Letter to William Gifford, Esq.*: 'Sir,—You have an ugly trick of saying what is

not true of any one you do not like; and it will be the object of this letter to cure you of it.' Sometimes he reminds us of the 'character-writers' of the seventeenth century, sometimes of Locke, sometimes of Burke. Even within a single essay there may be a marked contrast of style, as there is between the matter-of-fact opening and the lyrical climax of 'On My First Acquaintance with Poets'. What we find everywhere is an absence of padding, a concern with sense. 'Every word should be a blow: every thought should instantly grapple with its fellow.' One of the marks of his style is the sparing use of conjunctions—a habit of which some of his editors disapproved. In his essay 'On Editors' he complains that some of them 'have a passion for sticking in the word *however* at every opportunity, in order to impede the march of the style. . . . An Editor abhors an ellipsis. If you fling your thoughts into continued passages, they set to work to cut them up into short paragraphs.' The editors would no doubt have replied that although Hazlitt might know more about prose, they knew more about 'the reading public'. Though he is the clearest of writers, when read with attention, a lazy reader will soon lose the thread of his argument. At times he piles up statements with an apparent lack of any evolution in the thought. Yet the absence of conjunctions in positions where we might expect them gives an immediacy to his prose that is reminiscent of good conversation—as we may verify by taking one of his essays and adding the half-dozen possible conjunctions to the opening paragraph. He did not wish the effect of his prose to be weakened by the intrusion of these officious little sign-posts.

Although Hazlitt's way of writing prose is in a sense highly personal, he is not (as has already been noted) an eccentric like Lamb. Whereas Lamb is all idiosyncrasy, dressed only for the society of his friends, Hazlitt goes with ease in any company. He learned most from the prose-writers of the eighteenth century, with whom Lamb had at best an imperfect sympathy. He is not concerned to build up a *persona*, lovable, unusual, odd. He does not go out of his way to avoid the plain, right word. Lamb is like a games-player who excels at one or two strokes: Hazlitt knows every stroke, and plays each as the situation demands. Lamb sometimes parodies himself and is the worst of models. Hazlitt is an admirable model. One of his few faults is that he makes rather too much use of quotation.

# X

# LAMB

LAMB's early letters to Coleridge reflect a personality very different from that of Elia.[1] The first of them reveals that he has recently recovered from a fit of insanity. 'I am got somewhat rational now', Lamb writes, 'and don't bite any one. But mad I was.' In Coleridge's letters Lamb finds the qualities of Rousseau's *Confessions*, 'the same frankness, the same openness of heart, the same disclosure of all the most hidden and delicate affections of the mind', and the tone of his own letters is correspondingly intimate. This 'faithful journal of all that passes within me' is highly un-Elian. It is astonishing to find Lamb, of all men, opening a letter with the words 'My brother, my Friend', and saying in another that he is 'heartily sick of the every-day scenes of life'. His literary taste at this point differs from that of his maturity as much as his manner of writing. 'Coleridge', another letter begins, 'I love you for dedicating your poetry to Bowles.' In *Rosamund Gray*, a tale of unfortunate love that borders on *simplesse*, one character lends another *Julia de Roubigné*, and this novel that so delighted Shelley is not the only sign in Lamb's early writings of the influence of Henry Mackenzie and the Sentimental Movement. When we first

[1] Charles Lamb (1775–1834) was the son of poor parents, his father being servant and general factotum to Samuel Salt in the Temple. He was educated at Christ's Hospital, where he became friendly with Coleridge. In 1790 he began work as a clerk: in 1791 he entered the employment of the South-Sea Company, and in the following year he transferred to the East India Company, for whom he worked until he retired. In 1795–6 he had a brief attack of insanity. After the tragedy of September 1796 he undertook to act as Mary's guardian, so preserving her from permanent confinement in an institution. From this time onwards he wrote little verse but a good deal of prose. In 1800 he and his sister moved from Pentonville to London, which he loved. Although he was of no importance in the world of affairs his friends included Wordsworth, Hazlitt, De Quincey, and other men of note. In 1806 his farce *Mr H.* was damned at Drury Lane, and he himself took part in the demonstration against it. *Tales from Shakespear*, in which he and Mary collaborated, appeared in 1807. His refusal to leave his sister prejudiced his chances of marrying: his charming and diffident proposal of marriage to the actress Fanny Kelly may be found among his letters. In 1825 he sent his last contribution to the *London Magazine* and retired from the East India House. Retirement did not suit him, although he continued to do some literary work. He was a man whom everyone loved.

Mary Lamb was born in 1764 and died in 1847.

meet Lamb he is as much a Man of Feeling as Mackenzie himself had been in his youth.

In September 1796 Lamb's sister went mad and killed their mother. He behaved with the greatest possible fortitude and loyalty, and made a resolution that the whole course of his life must be changed. 'Many a vagary my imagination played with me', he had written of his own fit of insanity, and from this time onwards we find in him a distrust of the unbridled workings of the imagination that recalls Samuel Johnson. Although he rejected his brother's view that Coleridge with his 'damned silly sensibility and melancholy' was responsible for his own fit of madness, it is clear that he associated Coleridge with an epoch in his life to which he must put an end. He burnt many of his poems and literary jottings, including a love-journal, and resolved to destroy Coleridge's letters. 'Mention nothing of poetry', he wrote to him. 'I have destroyed every vestige of past vanities of that kind.' Soon a new independence appears in his letters. When he wrote, early in 1798, that he owed Coleridge 'much under God', there was something valedictory about it, an anticipation of the dedication of his poems twenty years later. His character was changing, under the pressure of circumstance. His habit of smoking and drinking rather heavily dates from this time, while his attitude to life and literature underwent a profound change. 'With me "the former things are passed away" ', as he wrote to Coleridge, 'and I have something more to do than to feel.' He no longer likes to be called 'gentle-hearted'. 'My *sentiment* is long since vanished', as he wrote in August 1800. 'I hope my *virtues* have done *sucking*.' We find him remarking on another occasion that the word 'sentiment' in this sense 'came in with Sterne, and was a child he had by Affectation'.

To the end of Lamb's life an evening with Coleridge would set him up for weeks. Yet he came to see that his escape from Coleridge had been essential: otherwise he might have continued to be towed along in his wake, unable to discover his own identity. He was in fact exceptionally sensitive to the characters of other people, and this helps to explain his qualities as a letter-writer. Obscure as he was in his daily life, in terms of friendship he was an exceptionally fortunate man. Procter tells us that Wordsworth, Coleridge, Leigh Hunt, Hazlitt, and Haydon were among the people he met at the Lambs': Southey,

Manning, and Hood were also frequent visitors. Lamb lived with his equals: in an age of genius he corresponded with half the men of genius. He found inspiration in the variety of his friends. When he wrote to Manning, the Cambridge mathematician, for example, he was able to criticize Wordsworth's humourless egotism with a freedom which was out of the question in a letter to Coleridge. In many ways Manning was Lamb's spiritual Antipodes, and it is noticeable that the letters to him show an unusual acuteness and satirical edge. On the other hand, Lamb often reacted against the tastes of his correspondent. The praise of London which is one of the germs of 'The Londoner', and therefore one of the anticipations of Elia, occurs in a letter to Wordsworth. Bernard Barton, who was singularly lacking in wit and irony, drew from Lamb some of his most entertaining letters. Lamb came to be conscious of his own need of friends of different types. 'So many parts of me have been numbed', he wrote to Wordsworth on hearing of the death of a friend in March 1822:

> Every departure destroys a class of sympathies. . . . One never hears any thing, but the image of the particular person occurs with whom alone almost you would care to share the intelligence. . . . Common natures do not suffice me . . . I want individuals. I am made up of queer points and I want so many answering needles.

All in all, they are remarkable letters. It is true that we need not look to them for the news of the day. Lamb did not set out, as Horace Walpole had done, to be the historian of his age. He would have regarded it as a waste of time. Many of the great themes are not to be found in his letters, or figure there only slightly. After the first few letters, religion is seldom touched on. Philosophy makes no appearance: 'Nothing puzzles me more than time and space', as he wrote to Manning, 'and yet nothing puzzles me less, for I never think about them.' Politics are hardly mentioned. Instead we hear about Lamb's friends, his determination to give up smoking, his liking for roast pork, his boredom at the East India House, and above all books—his own books, his friends' books: books he has been reading, and books he has been buying: new books and old books. Most of his criticism is to be found in his letters: it takes the form of marginalia, records of reaction, brief comments delicately phrased but hardly ever argued or discussed. Like the other

contents of the letters, the criticism they contain is informal. The paragraphs never have the air of being composed. They seem to consist of vivid phrases following one another almost at haphazard. There is no evolution of argument: seldom indeed an argument to evolve. They are unmethodical letters, fanciful, ironical, courageous, punning, mischievous, aptly phrased, human.

Written in snatches, as he sat on his high stool, Lamb's letters were his way of escaping from the daunting sobriety of receipt-book and ledger. 'I fancy I succeed best in epistles of mere fun', as he wrote to Fanny Kelly; 'puns & *that* nonsense.' He would amuse himself by pretending to begin in the middle of a letter, or by writing alternate lines in inks of different colours. His hoaxing letters began in 1800, and it is not surprising that the more literal-minded of his correspondents were sometimes at a loss. 'Take my trifling *as trifling*', he told Manning. Some of the most amusing of the letters were written in deep unhappiness. The postscript of one of them, 'I write in misery', might serve for many. On one occasion he tells Manning that he has been suffering from melancholia, but that the arrival of a present of brawn has done much to cheer him. The praise of this delicacy leads him into an Elian passage fifteen years before Elia made his bow. It is a letter which throws a great deal of light on Lamb's character and reminds us that it is seldom the happiest of men who take *Vive la bagatelle* for their motto.

It is a striking fact that many of our finest letter-writers have been men and women who have been frustrated, people with marked literary gifts who have seldom or never found any other literary form which perfectly suited them. It has been true of Gray and Horace Walpole and Cowper; and of many women, such as Lady Mary Wortley Montagu and Jane Welsh Carlyle. It is no less true of Lamb, who found in the letter a medium of expression that suited him as did no other form which he attempted in early life. His essays are best regarded as developments from his familiar letters. It is in the letters written a year or two after Lamb's emergence from the shadow of Coleridge that we find the first traces of Elia, although twenty years were to pass before circumstances were favourable to his coming to maturity.

It is now time to acknowledge chronology and return to the

opening of Lamb's career. Like many writers destined for excellence in other forms, he began with verse. By 1802, when he was 27, the only prose he had published was *Rosamund Gray* and a brief imitation of Burton; but he had also printed some thirty poems and a poetic tragedy. It is fitting that the poem given first in the collected editions seems to have been a joint composition with Coleridge, for he (with Bowles and Charlotte Smith) is the dominating influence in all Lamb's early verse. One of these early pieces remains Lamb's best-known poem, 'The Old Familiar Faces'. The original version began with a stanza later omitted:

> Where are they gone, the old familiar faces?
> I had a mother, but she died, and left me,
> Died prematurely in a day of horrors—
> All, all are gone, the old familiar faces.

The unusual movement of the verse reminds us of Lamb's discussions of classical metrics with Coleridge, Southey, and other friends. The basic line is a hypermetrical iambic pentameter—the nostalgic effect owing a great deal to the final falling syllable—but dactylic suggestions counterpoint the rhythm, and the fifth line ('Drinking late, sitting late, with my bosom cronies') is almost a pure Sapphic. There is a piquant contrast between a syntax which is almost that of prose and an occasional stiffness of expression. It is hard to say how far the effect of the poem is due to metrical sophistication, and how far to a felicitous awkwardness. As we read Lamb's later poems we find that the stricter metres suited him best. He was at his worst in blank verse: at his best (often) in 'short verse' (iambic tetrameters) handled in the manner of the seventeenth century. 'Angel Help' might be the work of a lesser Crashaw, while the lines 'On an Infant Dying as soon as it was Born' remain his finest poetic achievement. He always protested against the notion that wit and feeling were incompatible, pointing out how Fuller's 'conceits are oftentimes deeply steeped in human feeling and passion' and protesting against critics who supposed that Donne's wit was a sign of lack of passion; and in this poem, and in one or two others, we find a union of wit and delicacy of feeling which was unusual at this time. The lines 'In My Own Album' are admirably turned, while the translations from Vincent Bourne—a poet after his own

heart, as local and urban as he was classical—show high technical accomplishment. The 'Farewell to Tobacco' is an admirable imprecation, written in a metre learnt from George Wither: since smoking helped Lamb to refrain from stuttering there is a mischievous decorum in his choice of 'stammering verse' for his valediction to tobacco. Many of his most successful poems recall our older poets. Mary 'thinks it a little too old-fashioned in the manner, too much like what they wrote a century back', he acknowledged of one of his poems. 'But I cannot write in the modern style, if I try ever so hard.'

Although the action of *John Woodvil* (1802) is supposed to take place after the Restoration, no play has ever been more obviously Elizabethan in inspiration. From Southey onwards, every critic has been provoked by the 'exquisite silliness' of the plot. In a revealing sentence Lamb wrote in a letter that he hoped to be able to 'edge in' a particular passage 'somewhere in my play', and it is clear that what he wanted was an excuse for putting together a number of speeches. Though it may be doubted whether any whole scene could be mistaken for the work of an Elizabethan, the authentic tone is often caught admirably in individual speeches and lines:

> Better the dead were gather'd to the dead,
> Than death and life in disproportion meet.

To read *John Woodvil* after *Otho the Great* shows the difference between the Elizabethanising of a major poet and that of a very minor one. Though it was written in a hurry and on a mistaken plan, *Otho* often succeeds in using the language with an Elizabethan vigour: *John Woodvil* imitates the mannerisms of the Elizabethans, not their spirit.

The fact that it was not the plays of the Elizabethans regarded as wholes that appealed to Lamb, but their poetry, is abundantly demonstrated in his *Specimens of English Dramatic Poets who Lived about the Time of Shakespear* (1808). As Lamb points out in a letter, 'Specimens' were proliferating at this time. The expanded edition of Ellis's *Early English Poets* came out in 1803 and his *Early English Metrical Romances* in 1805, to be followed by Southey's *Later English Poets* and George Burnett's *English Prose-Writers* (with which Lamb assisted) in 1807. Although Lamb remarks that 'Specimens' is a new term for

what used to be called 'Beauties', he does at least try to give whole scenes rather than detached speeches. He chose 'not so much passages of wit and humour . . . as scenes of passion . . . tragic rather than . . . comic poetry', and simply reprinted from accessible texts, omitting passages at will. He did not avoid writers who were tolerably known already, like Beaumont and Fletcher; but he also included many minor dramatists who bear out his assertion that more than a third of the plays represented could only be found in exceptionally good libraries. He was proud of this book. In his laconic 'Autobiographical Sketch' one of the few claims he makes for himself is that he was 'the first to draw . . . attention to the old English Dramatists'. It is difficult to adjust this claim precisely. Throughout the eighteenth century there had been a fair number of readers whose knowledge of the Elizabethan dramatists was by no means confined to Dodsley's collection, while separate editions of several of the dramatists had appeared. Malone, who died in 1812, knew much more about the Elizabethan drama than did Lamb. But Lamb's purpose was quite different from Malone's, and it was probably a help to him that he believed himself to be more of an explorer than he was. His aim was to recommend these plays to lovers of poetry, much as one would recommend a volume of new verse. While Swinburne's statement that Lamb was wholly responsible for the 'resurrection' of these writers is absurdly exaggerated, his claim to a very important part in the movement cannot be gainsaid: it is supported by those who must have known best, his friends and fellow-workers Coleridge, Hazlitt and Southey.

Many modern readers must have turned to the *Specimens* expecting to find full critiques of the authors represented. They will have been disappointed, for this volume presents us with the same paradox as the rest of Lamb's criticism. In the sense that the *Selections* are admirably made, they show Lamb to be an excellent critic of the Elizabethan drama; but the explicit criticism which they contain would not fill more than fifteen pages. While it is true that these *aperçus* have a value out of proportion to their bulk, we do not find in them any analysis of the dramatic structure of the plays or any detailed consideration of their characters or language. What we are given is a sentence or two in which Lamb characterizes the authors who interest him most and tries to convey to the reader his own appreciation

of their peculiar savour. As the *Monthly* reviewer noted disapprovingly, the style of the notes is often 'formally abrupt and elaborately quaint', and readers today may well be put off by a note beginning with the words: 'Kit Marlowe, as old Isaak Walton assures us'; yet those who reject all criticism in an idiom uncongenial to them will miss a great many penetrating remarks.

At no time did Lamb write much formal criticism. His essay 'On the Tragedies of Shakspeare' is his most elaborate piece of criticism, and it must be acknowledged that it remains an extremist document. It demonstrates that the aspects of Shakespeare which seemed most important to Lamb were those which had least to do with the drama—not merely with the drama in the conditions of Lamb's own time, but with any drama at any time. He tells us that 'the Characters of Shakspeare are . . . the objects of meditation rather than of interest or curiosity as to their actions'; and it is the characters (so regarded), and the poetry, that appeal to him. He does not object to the plays being acted, but he regards the stage as an inferior medium for them—though one which must be used for the sake of the unreading part of the population. His statement that *Hamlet* 'is made another thing by being acted' begs the whole question. Lamb's argument is not that Shakespeare's plays should be read as well as seen, but that if they are read it does not matter whether they are seen at all. They are 'essentially . . . different' from all other plays. The essay 'On the Artificial Comedy of the Last Century' is also celebrated, and also an example of special pleading: that 'On the Genius and Character of Hogarth' is admirable, and reminds us of the very high reputation this essentially eighteenth-century artist retained in the early part of the succeeding century. Unfortunately the only elaborate review that Lamb ever wrote was cut about by Gifford, but even as it stands it speaks out finely for 'the boldness and originality' of Wordsworth's genius.

It is to the letters that we must go to fill out our picture of Lamb's critical views. At first they show him as a disciple of Coleridge, almost ludicrously anxious to follow his lead. 'My second thoughts entirely coincide with your comments', he wrote on one occasion, '. . . and I can only wonder at my childish judgment. . . . Your full and satisfactory account of personifications . . . will be a guide to my future taste.' He thanked

Coleridge for introducing him to Quarles and Wither, and as his own taste developed his knowledge of seventeenth-century poetry became very extensive. He knew the more elaborate of the prose writers almost as well as the poets—particularly the work of such men as Sir Thomas Browne, Izaak Walton, Thomas Fuller and (in the sixteenth century) Richard Hooker. He found Burton highly congenial. As his own taste developed he realized that writers in close touch with the world of everyday made a special appeal to him: 'Burns was the god of my idolatry, as Bowles of yours', he once wrote to Coleridge. He was fond of the eighteenth-century novelists, and has some admirable comments on Defoe. His dislikes were the obverse of his likes: 'masques, and Arcadian pastorals, with their train of abstractions, unimpassioned deities, passionate mortals, Claius, and Medorus, and Amintas, and Amarillis'. It is not suprising that he objected to the poetry of Shelley as 'too ideal' and containing an 'efflorescence . . . not natural'. The imaginations of these two men represent the extremities of the human mind. What is perhaps more surprising is that Lamb was one of the first critics to comment perceptively on Blake, whom he termed 'one of the most extraordinary persons of the age'.

The limitations of Lamb's taste are considerable. It is not merely that he was 'a little exclusive and national in his tastes', as Hazlitt noted. Within the field of English literature he lacked the discriminating catholicity of Hazlitt himself. Reviewing for the *Athenaeum* he stipulated for 'no natural history or useful learning', and in fact his interests were limited to what used to be called the *belles lettres*. If he mentions Hooker or Sir Thomas Browne, it is for their style and their air of antiquity, not for what they say. In general it is the part that appeals to him in a work of literature, rather than the whole. 'I can vehemently applaud, or perversely stickle, at parts', he wrote to Godwin, 'but I cannot grasp at a whole.' He never discusses the structure of a play or poem. Even the plot of a novel did not greatly interest him. 'I naturally take little interest in story', he wrote to another friend, 'the manner and not the end is the interest.' In this matter he is a 'literary man' in a very limiting sense: he rarely indulges in analysis, and shrinks from argument. If one comes to him from Coleridge his lack of interest in abstract questions and in the terminology of criticism becomes very striking. That anyone should be able to 'fill 3 volumes up with an

Essay on the Drama'—no doubt he was thinking of the Schlegels —astonished him. 'I am sure a very few sheets would hold all I have to say on the subject.' These severe limitations must be mentioned because absurdly high claims have often been made for him. Bradley called him the greatest critic of his century. No one would have been more embarrassed by such a remark than Lamb himself. He prided himself on his discrimination, and his intimate knowledge of certain old books; but he had no desire for the critical *cathedra*.

The essays for which Lamb is chiefly remembered are the work of a man in his middle forties. His earlier journalism is of little account. 'The Londoner', which was published in the *Morning Post*, was intended to be the first of a number of essays by a man with 'an almost insurmountable aversion from solitude and rural scenes', and it is possible that Manning's suggestion that a volume of essays in this manner would be successful helped to inspire Elia nine years later. Meanwhile Lamb contributed to the *Reflector* and the *Examiner* and wrote a revealing essay on 'Christ's Hospital and the Character of the Christ's Hospital Boys' in the *Gentleman's Magazine*. Although this essay is intended to be an informative contribution to a public debate, it becomes more and more personal in tone as it goes on, until in the end Lamb is writing from the heart and addressing his contemporaries at the school. In the descriptions of scenes which, 'seen through the mist of distance, come sweetly softened to the memory', we are more than half-way to Elia's avowedly personal essay on the same subject.

But it was in the *London Magazine* of the 1820's that the *Essays of Elia* made their appearance. Everything about this periodical appealed to Lamb, and above all the sense that he was among friends who understood and appreciated him. For him, at least, the editorial dinners must have meant a good deal. Until the first freshness of the thing wore off, his old yearning to belong once again to a 'body corporate', as he had done at school, must in some measure have been satisfied.

The close relationship between Lamb's essays and his letters has already been mentioned. Some of the essays even derive from particular letters. The germ of 'Amicus Redivivus', for example, is a description of George Dyer walking into the river—when he writes about Dyer Lamb is always Elia: Manning gave Lamb the idea for his 'Dissertation upon Roast Pig',

which is first handled in a letter: while several letters dealing with Coleridge's retentive habits as a borrower of books are the inspiration of 'The Two Races of Men'. This makes the tone of the *Essays* less surprising. If we compare Lamb with a typical eighteenth-century essayist, we find that the latter is primarily concerned to improve his reader's mind: if he sets out to amuse, it is only that his instruction may be the more effective. In Lamb, on the other hand, the didactic intention of 'Modern Gallantry' is most exceptional. The subjects of his essays—'All Fools' Day', 'Mackery End, in Hertfordshire', 'Witches, and other Night-Fears'—may be contrasted with those of the *Rambler*: 'Happiness not Local', 'Passion not to be Eradicated', 'The Arts by which Bad Men are Reconciled to Themselves'. Lamb specifically abjures 'the airy stilts of abstraction' and the proud claim to a philosophic impartiality. He is the least philosophic of essayists, as he is the most human, 'a bundle of prejudices . . . the veriest thrall to sympathies, apathies, antipathies', in knowledge 'a whole Encyclopædia behind the rest of the world'. The schoolmaster who tried to talk with him about the provision for the poor in the present and the past had to abandon the attempt, 'finding me rather dimly impressed with some glimmering notions from old poetic associations, than strongly fortified with any speculations reducible to calculation on the subject'. In his essays, as in his letters, Lamb deliberately avoids whatever is urgent and disturbing: religion, sex, politics, suffering. The former acolyte of the metaphysical Coleridge and lifelong friend of the political Hazlitt chose such subjects as 'Old China' and 'Valentine's Day' for his own lucubrations. He dwells on the small, reassuring aspects of life. 'I wished it might have lasted for ever', he writes of the last game of whist that he played with Bridget, 'though we gained nothing, and lost nothing, though it was a mere shade of play: I would be content to go on in that idle folly for ever'.

Anyone who reads the *Essays* as direct autobiography will be seriously misled. Lamb was fond of lying, and loved to appropriate experiences which had befallen his friends. 'My biography, parentage, place of birth, is a strange mistake', he wrote to Moxon, after reading the proof (as it seems) of an account of his own life, 'part founded on some nonsense I wrote about Elia, and was true of him, the real Elia.' Defending his 'Character of

the late Elia' against the charge of egotism, Lamb emphasizes that what Elia 'tells us, as of himself, was often true only (historically) of another'. 'If it be egotism to imply and twine with his own identity the griefs and affections of another', as he goes on to say, then novelists and dramatists stand equally chargeable. In a revealing phrase he once calls the first person 'his favourite figure' of speech. Yet although Lamb was helped (as many writers have been) by the partial anonymity of a *nom de plume*, the main fact about Elia is that he stands for Lamb himself. It was a matter of dressing up, but the costume he chose—like the black clothes that he was in the habit of wearing—suited him very well. A descendant of 'The Londoner', Elia is the 'picture of my humours' that had been in Lamb's mind when he wrote that essay.

In nothing is Lamb more characteristic of his age than in the way in which he seeks inspiration in his past life, and particularly in his memories of childhood. His early surroundings must have encouraged his tendency to look backwards: the Temple, Christ's Hospital, and the East India House, as well as the old house in which his aunt lived. Few men have acknowledged more explicitly the importance of their childhood. 'Nothing that I have been engaged in since seems of any value or importance', he wrote, 'compared to the colours which imagination gave to everything then.' It was partly that he was afraid that the new world of railroad, factory, and political economists would rob the imagination of its food. 'While childhood, and while dreams, reducing childhood, shall be left', he reflects in a revealing passage, 'imagination shall not have spread her holy wings totally to fly the earth.' 'He was too much of the boy-man', he writes of himself elsewhere. 'The impressions of infancy had burnt into him, and he resented the impertinence of manhood. These were weaknesses; but such as they were, they are a key to explicate some of his writings.' They are a key—we may add—to a great deal in the literature of the nineteenth century. In the eighteenth century men wrote about the present: in the nineteenth they wrote about the past. Lamb is therefore a most significant figure. Many of the most characteristic of his essays deal with experiences that were half a lifetime away when he set out to describe them. They are personal memories 'recollected in tranquillity', and recollected in such a manner that whatever had been disturbing in the original experiences had

been alembicated off. It is appropriate that the *Essays* begin with 'The South-Sea House', with its description of men who were of no importance in their own day and who are now no more substantial than dreams: 'their importance is from the past'. Time is a felt presence throughout the *Essays*, the perpetual theme of Elia's soliloquies. What is to be—he confesses—means nothing to him: 'I am . . . shy of novelties; new books, new faces, new years,—from some mental twist which makes it difficult in me to face the prospective.' His essays are vistas revealed by an imagination playing round the experiences of a lifetime.

Although it is often simple, and on occasion penetratingly so, the style of Elia is never plain. His essays are much more highly wrought than those of Addison or Steele. His concern is not merely to say something with clarity and force: he wishes to evoke a mood or present a paradox in a highly personal way. His style is designed to create and sustain his *persona*, and as Elia is wayward and old-fashioned the style in which he writes is full of echoes and archaisms, ellipses and nuances, periphrases and calculated familiarities. Sometimes the result is close to self-parody, as in the passage beginning with the words 'This is *Saloop*—the precocious herb-woman's darling' in 'The Praise of Chimney-Sweepers'. The archaisms are essential to the style, yet at times they are overdone, and we sense this particularly if we read a number of the essays one after the other. In the same way the allusions are on occasion excessive, as in 'All Fools' Day', while the use of periphrasis can become tedious. But the triumphs infinitely outweigh the incomplete successes and the very few failures. It is a frankly literary style: Montaigne lies behind it, and Burton and Sir Thomas Browne. It reminds us that Lamb loved the prose of the seventeenth century more than that of the eighteenth. In particular we are often reminded of the character-writers, as we are when we read his descriptions of A Poor Relation, A Scotchman (in 'Imperfect Sympathies'), or A Beggar.

Yet it was an eighteenth-century novelist that Lamb echoed when he wrote 'The Character of the Late Elia'. His habit of thinking of himself as a Shakespearian Fool makes it the less surprising that Yorick lies behind this passage: no writer did more to help Lamb to his characteristic style than the author of *Tristram Shandy*. Parts of 'All Fools' Day' are precisely in

Sterne's manner, while nothing could be closer to *A Sentimental Journey* than the description of a poor girl tempted in 'Barbara S—': 'In these thoughts she reached the second landing-place—the second, I mean, from the top—for there was still another left to traverse. Now virtue support Barbara!' On another occasion Elia calls on 'the pen of Yorick' to describe one of his relations, saying that no other would be capable of 'those fine Shandian lights and shades, which make up his story'. Apart from a close literary kinship (if Lamb had imitated Burton, Sterne had pillaged him), there was a strong temperamental affinity between the two men. While Sterne drew perpetual inspiration from the 'association of ideas', Lamb seems to be the first writer to describe himself as 'introspective'. It is interesting to notice that Sterne begins to be mentioned in Lamb's letters just before the turn of the century, at the time when Elia's character was in the making. It is fortunate that Lamb went beyond Henry Mackenzie and the other imitators of Sterne to Yorick himself, a master of the processes of the human heart from whom he learned a great deal.

The *persona* of Elia is less prominent in the *Last Essays*, most of which are distinctly inferior to their predecessors. Lamb was beginning to run out of subjects: 'Where shall I get another subject', we find him writing soon after the beginning of the second series—'or who shall deliver me from the body of this death?' He was discouraged by the poor sale of the first series, when it appeared as a book, and depressed by Southey's attack on his religious opinions; while a third important reason for his falling-off was the decline in the *London Magazine* itself. The only masterpiece among the later of the *Last Essays* is 'The Superannuated Man', in which he was writing on a theme which his imagination had been contemplating throughout many laborious years: it stands as a fitting epilogue to an incomparable series of essays which have always, as their deepest and truest theme, the character of Elia himself.

# XI

# DE QUINCEY

THERE have been few stranger literary careers.[1] By the age of seventeen De Quincey had decided that his life was to be that of a thinker and a man of letters, and he had jotted down an ambitious list of works that he intended to write: by his late twenties he was even more firmly resolved to become 'the intellectual benefactor' of his species, to accomplish 'a great revolution in the intellectual condition of the world' which would include in its scope a complete reform of education, philosophy, and mathematics. But since, 'like all persons . . . in possession of *original* knowledge', he was unwilling to 'sell' his wisdom 'for money', he seems to have published virtually nothing, except a long note on Sir John Moore prefixed to Wordsworth's *Convention of Cintra*, until he was thirty-three. He then became editor of a provincial journal of small circulation and less importance, the *Westmorland Gazette*. By this time he seems also to have decided to contribute to the Reviews, for in August 1820 we find William Blackwood reproaching him with a 'long bygone engagement to the Magazine'. The following year his *Confessions of an English Opium-Eater* were published in the *London Magazine* and he became a celebrity overnight.

From the first, the structure of the *Confessions* gave him

[1] Thomas De Quincey (1785–1859) was the son of a Manchester merchant of literary interests. After eighteen months he ran away from Manchester Grammar School, to which he had been sent at the age of fifteen, and wandered about in Wales before going to London. There he led a Bohemian life and met the young prostitute, Ann, described in his *Confessions*. At Worcester College, Oxford, he led the life of a recluse and continued to increase his unusual stock of erudition. He left in a panic just before completing his examinations. At this time he had begun to take opium, as well as turning to the study of German literature. He was an early admirer of Wordsworth, Coleridge, and Southey, and lived for some time in the Lake District in order to be near them. Gradually he became estranged from the Wordsworths, and in 1817 he married Margaret Simpson. In 1818–19 he edited the *Westmorland Gazette*. The publication of his *Confessions* made him famous. For the remainder of his life he lived the life of a literary displaced person, moving between one set of rooms and another, in Bath, London, and Edinburgh. He never cured himself of the habit of opium-eating.

trouble. He was not aiming at autobiography: 'not the opium-eater, but the opium, is the true hero of the tale', as he tells us—though we note that 'hero' must be taken in a morally neutral sense, since the professed object of the book is to warn its readers of the dangers of opium. He also wished to describe the 'Pleasures of Opium' as well as its 'Pains'—to give an account of some of the astonishing dreams and visions that he had experienced. For this reason he tells us something about his early life, before he became an opium-eater, both to increase our interest in him as a person and to provide us with 'a key to some parts of that tremendous scenery which afterwards peopled the dreams of the opium-eater'.

Few readers can ever have been bored by the *Confessions*, in their first form. De Quincey is an Ancient Mariner who holds us captive with his eye—and we have no desire to escape. He is fascinated by his own experiences, and we are fascinated by what he tells us. The power of opium over the human mind is a profoundly interesting subject, and the interest is greatly enhanced by the fact that the opium-eater was a man of exceptional intelligence and imagination. De Quincey was deeply interested in the processes and resources of the mind, and planned to write a great work *De emendatione humani intellectus*. The introspective penetration which he displays is the less surprising. What we would not have expected is his journalistic astuteness. In a manner that reminds us for a moment of Defoe he makes it clear that we are to hear of forbidden and disreputable things, but only for our own good: it is an 'interesting record', but it should also be found 'in a considerable degree, useful and instructive'. No other motive could have led him to break through that 'delicate and honourable reserve' which distinguishes Englishmen from all Frenchmen and many Germans. He feels that it is his duty to warn us that opium-eaters have become 'very numerous': this is particularly true amongst men 'distinguished for talents, or of eminent station', as he goes on to demonstrate with a burst of dashes most of which are easy to fill in. At the other end of the social scale the work-people in the factories of Manchester are also becoming thralls to opium. As we read the *Confessions* we can therefore congratulate ourselves on taking an interest in a matter of grave public concern. All previous writers on the subject have been liars, and their readers dupes; but we are being told the truth. And just as

De Quincey refuses to accept any blame for his opium-eating, so he insists on the innocence of his association with the outcasts and prostitutes whom he met during his period adrift in London. He is an adept at flattering his readers with the sense of being liberal and broad-minded: 'Courteous, and, I hope, indulgent reader (for all *my* readers must be indulgent ones, or else, I fear, I shall shock them too much to count on their courtesy).' In fact we are not told anything that is remarkably shocking—or so one might suppose, until one studies the revisions De Quincey felt obliged to make in 1856. What is particularly reassuring about the book, for the timid reader, is its air of being the work of a retired sea-captain, let us say: an adventurous man who has seen some odd things in his time, and associated with some odd people, yet who has retired to live in respectability with his wife in the old country. 'These troubles are past', he writes, addressing his wife (whom he calls his Electra); 'and thou wilt read these records of a period so dolorous to us both as the legend of some hideous dream that can return no more.' It is all reassuringly domestic. The adventurer is home again, and in the evening he has agreed to tell us something of his experiences. The result is a story of exploration and adventure, of a search and a loss, and above all of a memorable escape.

The Third Part of the *Confessions* promised in the *London Magazine* in 1821 never appeared, and the following year De Quincey allowed the two parts to be republished as a small book, with the addition of an appendix on the medical aspects of opium in which he reveals that his cure has not been completed after all. Although this was the book which made him famous, there was from the first something tentative and unfinished about it, and he wondered for years whether he should rewrite it. The opportunity came at the end of his life, with the publication of a collected edition of his work. He decided to double the length of the *Confessions*, so that they would fill one volume. The 'crowning grace' of the book was to be a succession of the 'dreams and noonday visions' which had come to him over the years, accounts of some of which he had already written. When he began the revision, however, he found that he had mislaid most of these descriptions, with the exception of the one entitled 'The Daughter of Lebanon'. While this was set at the end of the revised *Confessions* as a specimen of the material from which the culmination of the work was to have been

constructed, De Quincey was now faced with the problem of expanding his book in some other way. This he did principally by greatly lengthening the account of his early life, by adding numerous digressions, and by rewriting the whole book in a more elaborate (and frequently verbose) style of prose.

In 1856 the account of De Quincey's early life is four times as long as it had been in 1822. This has an important effect on the proportions of the book. More than two-thirds of the narrative have passed before opium makes its appearance. In 1822 the 'Preliminary Confessions' really are preliminary: in 1856 De Quincey has moved in the direction of ordinary autobiography. In self-defence he insists that his 'opium miseries' were connected with his early sufferings in London 'by natural links of affiliation':

> The early series of sufferings was the parent of the later. Otherwise, these Confessions would break up into two disconnected sections: first, a record of boyish calamities; secondly, a record (totally independent) of sufferings consequent upon excesses in opium. And the two sections would have no link whatever to connect them, except the slight one of having both happened to the same person. (iii. 412.)

Interesting as many of the new incidents are, and valuable to the biographer, the *Confessions* of 1856 form a less unified work than those of 1822. And when we consider the long digressions which are characteristic of the revised text (such as the dog-fight with Coleridge at the very beginning) it becomes impossible to accept De Quincey's claim that he did not eke out the volume 'by any wiredrawing process'. Much of the new material is padding.

Reviewing his life at the age of 70, De Quincey naturally found himself seeing many episodes in a different light from that of his *London Magazine* days. He is much less severe, for example, in his judgements of people. But what is of more immediate interest is the fact that his attitude to opium itself has changed. Even in 1822 there are inconsistencies in his remarks about opium: although he professedly sets out to warn us against it, there are passages which would bear a rather different interpretation. In 1856 the earlier reference to 'the *moral* of my narrative' is cut altogether, and De Quincey's concern is to emphasize the medical value of opium as an anodyne and,

more particularly, its mysterious powers 'over the grander and more shadowy world of dreams':

> All passages, written at an earlier period under cloudy and uncorrected views of the evil agencies presumable in opium, stand retracted; although, shrinking from the labour of altering an error diffused so widely under my own early misconceptions of the truth, I have suffered them to remain as they were. (iii. 429.)

The superiority of the 1822 text is particularly evident when we consider its style. Although there are some elaborate passages in 1822, they occur only where they are appropriate, and in general the style is relatively simple and direct: in 1856 the style is more involved, 'literary', and artificial. To take two or three isolated examples, 'sometimes' becomes 'oftentimes', 'up' becomes 'astir', 'to which' becomes 'whither', 'no ways' becomes 'nowise'. Words and turns of phrase which might be regarded as colloquial or vulgar are softened or replaced by circumlocutions: unnecessary qualifications are frequently added. The revisions throw a great deal of light on the development (and in some respects the deterioration) of De Quincey's mind: they also illuminate changes in English taste during his lifetime. When he revised his *Confessions* Queen Victoria had been on the throne for almost twenty years: many things which had been openly discussed in the twenties were now considered indelicate. The influence of the new standards of propriety is particularly evident in the passages dealing with London prostitutes—passages which had never been at all objectionable. It must be stressed that some of the revisions are for the better: an outstanding example is the last dream in the main part of the book, which De Quincey revised like a master. It is clear, however, that he had lost the ability to write plainly, and as a result the 1856 text often seems flabby and debilitated in comparison with that of 1822. In their later form the *Confessions* remain a very interesting book; but the *Confessions* of 1822 may be regarded as a minor masterpiece. Perhaps the very scantiness of detail and inadequacy of the motivation contribute to the power of the early version. In 1856 De Quincey is relatively intelligible—and therefore exasperating: in 1822 we accept him as a mysterious, enigmatic figure, a Werther moved by sorrows beyond our comprehension.

For thirty-five years after the first publication of his

*Confessions* 'The English Opium-Eater' was one of the most prolific contributors to the periodical press. Except for a couple of prose romances (*Walladmor* and *Klosterheim* (1825, 1832), the former a professed 'translation from the German' of a supposed original by Scott) nothing that De Quincey wrote ever made its first appearance as a book. Although his original intention may have been to make money by writing articles, so earning leisure in which to concentrate on longer works, he seems soon to have realized that periodical writing was destined to be his profession. He therefore tried to put the best of himself into his articles, looking forward to the day when he could revise them and republish them in a collected form. We must now consider the contents of the edition which he collected near the end of his life. No strict chronology can be observed: it will be convenient to begin with his autobiographical writings, moving on to his literary criticism and ending with the *Suspiria de Profundis*.

As he wrote the *Autobiographic Sketches* (which Masson less accurately terms his *Autobiography*) De Quincey's capital difficulty was that the most dramatic part of his life had already been described. One of the results of this is that some of the *Sketches* appear to have little autobiographical significance. The chapter on Oxford is a defence of a University to which he himself never acknowledged any debt. The chapters on Ireland (which have been revised, unlike that on Oxford) simply deal with recent political history, and throw little light on their author. A similar charge might be brought against 'German Studies and Kant in Particular'; but in reading this last chapter we must remember the sort of autobiographical sketches he is attempting. His subject is not events in themselves but the effects of these events on his own mind and the meaning they have come to assume for him since. It is not for nothing that he keeps echoing and quoting from *The Prelude*: these *Sketches*, too, aim at tracing the development of a creative mind. What determines the space given to a topic is not its interest to readers but its importance to the writer. The persecution which he suffered at the hands of his brother is dwelt on, for example, at tedious length. We begin to feel that we are moving in a world in which the usual proportions of things have become obsolete: large objects are invisible, or can be distinguished with difficulty: small things assume a nightmare bulk. Unfortunately, for a great deal of the time De Quincey is not successful

in leading the reader to share his point of view, and the result is an effect of simple distortion. In some of the most remarkable passages, however, De Quincey's secret voice becomes audible: it is as if we were overhearing the monologue of a man under an anaesthetic retracing his own life and seeing in it the type and symbol of some profounder pattern. Yet there is also much that is of interest in the more objective parts of the *Sketches*. De Quincey was a keen observer of the changes that had taken place since his youth: changes in manners, in dress, in communications, in public opinion, in reading habits, in language, and in many other aspects of 'the shifting scenery and moving forces of the age'.

The most interesting of the papers called by Masson the *London Reminiscences* describe De Quincey's association with the brilliant group of writers who contributed to the *London Magazine* in its hey-day. He had been one of the few original purchasers of *John Woodvil*, and he gives us our only picture of Lamb at his office desk, perched on a high stool. Elsewhere he is sometimes unfair to Lamb as a prose writer, but here he sums up his merits admirably, concluding that 'of the peculiar powers which he possessed he has left to the world as exquisite a specimen as this planet is likely to exhibit'. There are also some penetrating comments on Clare, of whom De Quincey remarks: 'I very much doubt if there could be found in his poems a single commonplace image, or a description made up of hackneyed elements.' We also hear of Sir Humphry Davy, Godwin, Mrs. Grant of Laggan, Allan Cunningham, Edward Irving and the remarkable traveller John Stewart, whom he describes as 'the most interesting by far of all my friends' and the most naturally eloquent man he had ever met.

In the *Lake Reminiscences* (usually called *Recollections of the Lake Poets*) De Quincey sets out to cater for the growing interest in 'three men upon whom posterity . . . will look back with interest as profound as, perhaps, belongs to any other names of our era'. While he is most unreliable on facts, he is often a penetrating commentator, as in his denial of the existence of a 'Lake School':

> The critics . . . supposed them to have assembled under common views in literature—particularly with regard to the true functions of poetry, and the true theory of poetic diction. . . . They went on to *find* in their writings all the agreements and common characteristics which their blunder had presumed.

Inaccurate as they are, the articles on Coleridge are of considerable value. As De Quincey himself admits, through the ruin of his own mind he 'looked into and read the latter states of Coleridge. His chaos I comprehended by the darkness of my own [mind], and both were the work of laudanum.' He interprets Coleridge's love of abstractions as a form of escapism, but insists on defending him against the charge of purposeless digression. Unfortunately his own weakness in this respect is nowhere more evident. The section on Wordsworth also contains some penetrating criticism—De Quincey had the advantage of knowing *The Prelude* long before most critics—although it too suffers from unnecessary digressions, such as the long account of 'the bad Lord Lonsdale'.

Apart from the *Confessions*, De Quincey's literary criticism is the most important part of his work. Unlike Coleridge and Lamb, he was not concerned to recommend forgotten writers. His reading was wide, but in English literature at least he wrote only on the most eminent writers. On the minor Elizabethan dramatists he has nothing to say, while in the seventeenth century Milton is his only important theme, in the eighteenth Pope. On Shakespeare he wrote only once, but the result is important. It is characteristic that it was the Ratcliffe Highway murders which prompted the essay 'On the Knocking at the Gate in *Macbeth*': De Quincey writes as the author of 'Murder Considered as One of the Fine Arts'. The reasons he gives for the profound effect made by the knocking are, first, that Shakespeare wants to make the audience temporarily sympathize with Macbeth rather than Duncan, and, secondly, that the knocking is a sign that 'the pulses of life are beginning to beat again. . . . The re-establishment of the goings-on of the world . . . first makes us profoundly sensible of the awful parenthesis that had suspended them.' This penetrating piece of psychological criticism is introduced by a significant remark:

> My understanding could furnish no reason why the knocking at the gate . . . should produce any effect. . . . My understanding said positively that it could *not* produce any effect. But I knew better; I felt that it did; and I waited and clung to the problem until further knowledge should enable me to solve it.

No one has been more conscious of the dependence of literary criticism on psychology than De Quincey; as he once wrote,

'literary or *aesthetic* questions [must be brought] under the light of philosophic principles . . . problems of "taste" [must be] expanded to problems of human nature'. When he wrote on Milton, whose work he knew intimately, he also had recourse to psychology; but it is with his remarks on Milton's style that we are particularly concerned. He was clearly aware of an affinity with Milton in his love of pomp and elaboration. For critics who are disposed to censure Milton rashly he has a warning: 'You might as well tax Mozart with harshness in the divinest passages of *Don Giovanni* as Milton with any . . . offence against metrical science. Be assured it is yourself that do not read with understanding.' To Milton's language he paid the minutest attention, vehemently defending his 'exotic idioms'. Influenced perhaps by Capel Lofft, he points out the importance of Milton's characteristic spelling, and rclates it to the fact that italics were not used in his day for emphasis. On Pope De Quincey is less at home, although he has one or two admirable points to make. He begins well, in his review of Roscoe's edition, by denying that Pope is merely a satiric poet; and then proceeds to his famous distinction between literature of knowledge and literature of power. He opposes, admirably, the misconception that Pope 'belonged to what is idly called the *French* School of our literature' and the view that 'he was specially distinguished from preceding poets by *correctness*'. In fact, as he points out, there are occasional faults in Pope's use of language which have been condoned, but never justified, by his critics. As he develops the point elsewhere: 'Not for superior correctness, but for qualities the very same as belong to his most distinguished brethren, is Pope to be considered a great poet.' Unfortunately he does not illustrate these remarks but allows himself to be led into a fruitless discussion of the moral justification of satire.

De Quincey acknowledged that his discovery of the *Lyrical Ballads* had been 'the greatest event in the unfolding of [his] own mind', and it was on this collection that he wrote the nearest approximation to a formal critique in his work. He points out the blighting effect that Wordsworth's theory of diction has had on his reputation and emphasizes that it conflicts with the whole history of our poetry:

> If the leading classics of the English literature are . . . loyal to the canons of sound taste,—then you cut away the *locus standi* for yourself

as a reformer. . . . If they also are faulty, you undertake an *onus* of hostility so vast that you will be found fighting against [the] stars.

He shrewdly points out that Wordsworth is far from empirical, having been content with the same 'old original illustrations, —two, three, or perhaps three-and-a-quarter' throughout his whole life. An affinity between his own mind and the poet's enables him to write penetratingly on the nature of his imagination: 'He does not willingly deal with a passion in its direct aspect, or presenting an unmodified contour, but in forms more complex and oblique, and when passing under the shadow of some secondary passion.' The essay ends with the suggestion that 'meditative poetry is perhaps that province of literature which will ultimately maintain most power amongst the generations which are coming', and the claim that Wordsworth stands higher in this province than any other poet since Shakespeare.

On the younger poets De Quincey has little to say. It would have struck him as absurd to class Byron, Shelley, and Keats with Wordsworth and Coleridge. He hardly ever refers to Byron, indeed, though he had read him: he thought very highly of *Hyperion*, after being appalled by 'the most shocking abuse of [our] mother-tongue' in *Endymion*: while he was most attracted by Shelley, whose classical learning and visionary imagination answered to characteristics of his own. He was shocked, on the other hand, by Shelley's hostility to Christianity, and described him—in a phrase which Arnold may have remembered—as 'an angel touched by lunacy'. Nor did De Quincey write much on the novel. His remarks on prose style have a particular interest, and betray, as one might have expected, a remarkable lack of objectivity. In Swift he finds 'not . . . a graceful artlessness, but . . . a coarse inartificiality': no doubt he can write well enough on a straightforward subject (so can Dampier and Defoe); but what would happen if more were required?—

Suppose . . . that the Dean had been required to write a pendant for Sir Walter Raleigh's immortal apostrophe to Death, or to many passages . . . in . . . 'Religio Medici' and . . . 'Urn Burial', or to Jeremy Taylor's inaugural sections of his 'Holy Living and Dying'. . . . What would have happened? (xi. 18.)

What would have happened—we may be pardoned for asking —if De Quincey had been required to write a 'pendant' for

*Robinson Crusoe* or *Gulliver's Travels*? What interested him was 'impassioned prose' of the most elaborate and musical kind: when he is discussing writers of other types of prose he is completely unreliable. On one occasion he states that 'Lamb had no sense of the rhythmical in prose composition', while some of his comments on Hazlitt—such as the absurd remark that 'Hazlitt had read nothing'—can only have been inspired by jealousy. Some of his observations are penetrating:

> No man can be eloquent whose thoughts are abrupt, insulated, capricious, and . . . non-sequacious. . . . The main condition [of eloquence] lies in the *key* of the evolution, in the *law* of the succession. . . . Now Hazlitt's brilliancy is seen chiefly in separate splinterings of phrase or image. . . . A flash, a solitary flash, and all is gone. (v. 231.)

What De Quincey fails to notice, however, is that this style, which is not to be found everywhere in Hazlitt's work, was deliberately evolved to meet the demands of some of the types of writing on which he was engaged.

De Quincey wrote several essays on general literary topics which are interesting both for their central arguments and for their remarks on particular writers. The essay on Rhetoric contains a roll-call of his masters, including Burton, Milton (the only writer he ever censured for being 'too sequacious and processional'), Sir Thomas Browne, and Burke, 'the supreme writer of this century, the man of the largest and finest understanding'. De Quincey suggests that 'The Rhetorical Poets' would be a better title for Donne and his followers than 'The Metaphysical Poets', and terms Donne himself (whom he elsewhere describes as 'a man yet unappreciated') 'the first very eminent rhetorician in the English Literature'. 'Few writers have shown a more extraordinary compass of powers . . .; for he combined . . . the last sublimation of dialectical subtlety and address with the most impassioned majesty.' (x. 101.) The essay on Style is the work of a man who has thought long and deeply on the subject:

> The more . . . any exercise of mind is . . . *subjective* . . . the more . . . does the style . . . cease to be a mere separable ornament . . . [Mr Wordsworth once remarked] that it is in the highest degree unphilosophic to call language or diction 'the *dress* of thoughts'. . . . He would call it 'the *incarnation* of thoughts'. . . . If language were merely

a dress, then you could separate the two . . . [whereas in fact] an image . . . often enters into a thought as a constituent part. (x. 229–30.)

The *Letters to a Young Man Whose Education has been Neglected* are full of interesting things, such as the remark that 'no complex or very important truth was ever yet transferred in full development from one mind to another. . . . It must arise by an act of genesis within the [learner's] understanding itself.' The exclusive study of languages is deplored, as leading to 'the dry rot of the human mind', and De Quincey quotes with approval the advice that we should 'dare to be ignorant of many things'.

It seems likely that most of the seminal ideas from which De Quincey's criticism sprang had been planted by his twentieth year. Much his greatest debts were to Wordsworth and Coleridge, and he refers almost reverently to the time when 'Mr. Wordsworth . . . unveiled the great philosophic distinction between the powers of *fancy* and *imagination*'. In spite of his scorn for the Schlegels and his objection to the habit of 'yielding an extraordinary precedence to German critics' (to whom in fact Coleridge owed a great deal) he himself was very much one of the 'new critics' of his day. Many of the merits of his criticism—as well as many of its faults—are due to his determination to penetrate far below the surface. He objected to what seemed to him the lack of a metaphysical and psychological basis in the criticism of Dr. Johnson, and went so far as to claim that 'in the sense of absolute and philosophic criticism, we have little or none; for, before *that* can exist, we must have a good psychology, whereas, at present, we have none at all' (xi. 294). If we compare the two men we find that the criticism of Johnson is that of a man talking in society while the criticism of De Quincey is that of a philosopher speculating in solitude.

As one reads De Quincey's inferior work one concludes that he was uniquely unqualified for periodical journalism. His faults—prolixity, irrelevance, the passion for displaying his classical learning in and out of season—unfitted him for the role; while his merits—width of knowledge, subtlety of mind, and the determination to go deeply into everything—were hardly more helpful. One is equally astonished at the forbearance of his readers and the forbearance of his editors. The letters that passed between him and his publishers make extraordinary reading. On one occasion, stung by a reproachful

letter from Hessey, he described himself as 'the most benignest man that perhaps has appeared since the time of St. John'. He seldom wrote what he was asked to write, and hardly ever produced his material on time. When Lockhart invited him to contribute a book on the Lake District to a series called 'The Family Library', he replied by saying that he was 'not an Ornithologist, nor an Ichthyologist . . . no Botanist, no Mineralogist', and by doubting whether anyone less than a Humboldt or a Davy would suffice. He concluded by offering, as an alternative, 'a digest, at most in three... volumes, of the "Corpus Historiæ Byzantinæ"; that is, a continuous narrative . . . of the fortunes of the Lower Empire from Constantine to its destruction'. The result, he thought, could hardly fail to be 'a readable—a popular book'. The severity of Leslie Stephen, in his able essay on De Quincey, must be attributed partly to his own experience as an editor.

While nothing can counterbalance the fact that without the necessity of contributing to periodicals De Quincey might never have written anything, many of his characteristic faults must be attributed to this mode of publication. He did not often write on subjects that completely failed to interest him, but he was often obliged to begin before he had digested his materials. His extraordinary feats of digression—aggravated by his Shandian explanations that what seem to be irrelevancies are in fact supremely logical—must in part be attributed to this; while the tasteless facetiousness which spoils so much of his work is largely due to the same cause. In a perverse way his pedantry was enhanced by the knowledge that he had 'the unlearned equally with the learned amongst [his] readers'. This fact seems to have encouraged his besetting sin of starting with the Greeks. In the essay on Style, for example, the dissertation on Greek history and literature grows out of all proportion to its true place in the logic of the subject; while there is an extraordinary postscript in which he apologizes for forgetting to mention 'the Roman Recitations in the Porticos of Baths, &c.' There is something ominous in the announcement in the third part:

> Perhaps, the unlearned reader... will thank us for here giving him, in a very few words, such an account of the Grecian Literature in its periods of manifestation, and in the relations existing between these periods, that he shall not easily forget them. (x. 203.)

One is reminded of Chaucer's Eagle in *The Hous of Fame*:

> . . Lo, so I can
> Lewedly to a lewed man
> Speke, and shewe him swyche skiles,
> That he may shake hem by the biles.

It is the authentic voice of a bore.

The clue to a great deal in De Quincey is that he was a solitary. He once claimed that he had 'passed more of [his] life in absolute and unmitigated solitude, voluntarily, and for intellectual purposes, than any person of [his] age', and in the *Autobiographic Sketches* he traces the habit back to his unhappiness in childhood. How habituated he was to solitary thinking appears in his use of the word 'reverie' where most men would use 'reflection': he tells us, for example, that he once planned to write 'some reveries' on Greek literature. So much solitude is not good for a prose writer, in his more ordinary tasks, and many of De Quincey's faults were aggravated by the solitary life he led. At times it seems as if he is living in an Einsteinian universe in which our usual measuring-rods of importance no longer hold good. When he describes his childish aspirations and fears about his imaginary state of Gombroon, for example, the reader feels as if he were looking through an immensely powerful magnifying glass. Here there is a dramatic relevance, but De Quincey's habit of portraying things in the dimensions in which they present themselves to his private vision is not confined to his autobiographical writings. His sense of proportion is not that of other men. Yet it must be remembered that his finest writing is the fruit of his solitude no less than his inferior work; and it matters a thousand times more. 'Solitude', he once wrote, '. . . is . . . the mightiest of agencies; for solitude is essential to man.' (i. 48.) It is in the *Suspiria* that the climax of his thought on this subject is to be found: 'No man ever will unfold the capacities of his own intellect who does not at least checker his life with solitude. How much solitude, so much power.' It was in solitude that the visions came to him which he strove to express in 'impassioned prose'.

It was also as a result of the introspective musings of a solitary that his lifelong interest in psychology was born. He was of necessity a hypochondriac, and his Diary opens with the statement that 'the intimate connection . . . [between the] body and

the mind, has never (to my knowledge) been sufficiently enlarged on in theory or insisted on in practice'. Observation of the ways of his own body and mind led him to the general interest in psychology which may be found running through most of his work. His interest in 'pariahs', for example, was intellectual as well as emotional, psychological as well as sympathetic. His literary criticism, as has been pointed out, aspired to a psychological foundation. His interest in murder was not wholly that of a sensationalist: in reading police reports, he wrote, 'I stand aghast at the revelations . . . of human life and the human heart—at its colossal guilt, and its colossal misery.' Such reflections led him to the suggestion that

> It is not without probability that in the world of dreams every one of us ratifies for himself the original transgression. In dreams . . . each several child of our mysterious race completes for himself the treason of the aboriginal fall. (xiii. 304.)

His own sufferings and visionary dreams were the starting-point of most of his psychological speculations. He gives a detailed description of the extraordinary effect on him of the death of an infant daughter of Wordsworth's, for example, 'as having a permanent interest in the psychological history of human nature'. 'You will think this which I am going to say too near, too holy, for recital', he wrote in a fragment intended for the *Suspiria*. 'But not so. The deeper a woe touches me in heart, so much the more am I urged to recite it.' He lived on into an age that was hostile to most forms of confessional writing: it is possible, though not likely, that that is why he has nothing to say about sex. Yet he belongs, though in a lesser degree than Rousseau or Gide, to the company of the explorers of the human mind. It is not for nothing that Baudelaire was fascinated by him. And he went further, and deeper, than the majority of introspective writers; for in the *Suspiria* the attempt to trace the workings of his own mind becomes one with the striving to fathom the whole significance of human life.

*Suspiria de Profundis* was the title De Quincey gave to the sequel to his *Confessions*, dealing principally with his dreams. Four instalments, making up about a third of the work as he envisaged it, appeared in *Blackwood's* in 1845. By that date, or within a few years afterwards, he seems to have written much more; for in a passage already quoted from the preface to the

revised *Confessions* of 1856 he tells us that the 'crowning grace' of the book was to have been 'a succession of some twenty or twenty-five dreams and noon-day visions, which had arisen under the latter stages of opium influence'—but that most of these have been lost. Of the dreams which had not been lost, 'The Daughter of Lebanon' was printed at the end of the *Confessions* because of its connexion with the story of Ann; while others were reprinted under various headings in other volumes of the collected edition. In 1891 some further material was published by Alexander H. Japp, with a key to the *Suspiria* as a whole; so that we now possess about half of the work, though not in its final form. Since even what he had completed of the *Suspiria* seemed to De Quincey 'very greatly superior' to the *Confessions* themselves, we ignore them at our peril, and it remains possible to make out at least the main lines of the design.

The theme of the *Suspiria* as a whole is that pain and grief are essential to the development of the soul. This truth becomes apparent only to exceptional people, and even to them only when the original experience has sloughed off its 'accidents' and assumed a universal and perhaps symbolical form in the mind in a reverie years afterwards. The introductory passage on dreaming makes it evident what De Quincey is trying to do, and why he regards it as of the first importance. A man with an exceptional power of dreaming, he has come to realize that dreams are of a far profounder significance than is commonly understood, being 'the one great tube through which man communicates with the shadowy'. As he explains later, his power of dreaming is selective, interpretative, and therefore creative: 'far less like a lake reflecting the heavens than like the pencil of some mighty artist—Da Vinci or Michael Angelo—that cannot copy . . . but comments in freedom, while reflecting in fidelity'. One is reminded of both Plato and Wordsworth:

> The dreaming organ, in connexion with the heart, the eye, and the ear, composes the magnificent apparatus which forces the infinite into the chambers of a human brain, and throws dark reflections from eternities below all life upon the mirrors of that mysterious *camera obscura*—the sleeping mind. (xiii. 335.)

His aim is to take the reader into the *penetralia* of his mind, so

revealing truths of the greatest moment to the life and immortality of man.

In the first of the *Suspiria* we are taken back at one point to De Quincey's infancy. His earliest recollections are connected with death, and culminate in the loss of his sister when he was seven. Already the main themes of these meditations appear: the power of death, the quest for reunion with a girl who has died, the problem of the nature of time, the significance of solitude, the value of suffering. In accordance with his belief that 'experiences of deep suffering or joy first obtain their entire fulness of expression when they are reverberated from dreams', there follow two reveries on his sister's death, one dating from his Oxford years, the other occurring in old age, 'on this dovelike morning of Pentecost'. Sometimes the seminal event and its re-creation in reverie are disconcertingly juxtaposed. It is the same difficulty that had faced him in the *Confessions* themselves: although his real subject may be the effect of early experiences on his mind, without a narrative of these experiences the reader will fail to understand the reverie. 'The English Mail-Coach' illustrates the problem. A coaching accident witnessed in his youth had been 'carried, . . . raised and idealised, into my dreams', so becoming of great importance to him. The conclusion, in which we are presented with the final significance of the experience, is impressive in the highest degree. It is a 'Dream Fugue', culminating in music which celebrates a great victory:

> Then was completed the passion of the mighty fugue. The golden tubes of the organ, which as yet had but muttered at intervals—gleaming amongst clouds and surges of incense—threw up, as from fountains unfathomable, columns of heart-shattering music. Choir and anti-choir were filling fast with unknown voices. Thou also, Dying Trumpeter, with thy love that was victorious, and thy anguish that was finishing, didst enter the tumult; trumpet and echo—farewell love, and farewell anguish—rang through the dreadful *sanctus*.
> (xiii. 326.)

There is no more eloquent passage in English prose, but the success of 'The Mail-Coach' as a whole is another matter. In their length and at times their tone the opening sections are out of all keeping with what follows; while in the concluding passages, remarkable as they are, the figure of Ann associates somewhat incongruously with the Battle of Waterloo. De Quincey added

a note explaining the logic of the construction: but his claim that 'the Dream is a law to itself; . . . as well quarrel with a rainbow', merely raises the question whether many passages in the *Suspiria* do not have a higher value for the psychologist than for the literary critic.

Only the more important of the remaining *Suspiria* call for notice. The theme of 'The Palimpsest of the Human Brain', where once again the introduction is too long for what follows, is that nothing is ever finally erased from the memory. In 'Vision of Life' an analogy from music explains the connexion of grief and joy: 'The rapture of life . . . does not arise, unless as perfect music arises, . . . by the confluence of the mighty and terrific discords with the subtile concords. . . .' (xiii. 350.) Suffering is 'the price of a more searching vision'. The same theme is found in 'Levana and our Ladies of Sorrow', which as De Quincey points out prefigures the course of the whole work. The Destinies that have presided at his birth hold it as their 'commission . . . from God . . . to plague his heart until [they have] unfolded the capacities of his spirit'. In 'The Dark Interpreter' the 'root of dark uses . . . in moral convulsions' is again expounded. Perhaps the most brilliant illustration of all may be found among the notes for further *Suspiria*, where De Quincey explains that under the influence of suffering 'the mighty machinery of the brain' is exalted, 'and the Infinities appear, before which the tranquillity of man unsettles, the gracious forms of life depart, and the ghostly enters'. When 'The Daughter of Lebanon' is seen as part of the *Suspiria* its significance becomes clear. In it the Christian undertones which can just be caught elsewhere become clearly audible; in the end the help of 'one learned in the afflictions of man', an 'evangelist' (presumably St. Luke), enables the Outcast to save her life by losing it, and the quest for love and mercy which is as central in the *Suspiria* as it had been throughout its author's life comes to a triumphant close.

It is in the *Suspiria*, which he himself considered 'the *ne plus ultra* . . . which I can ever hope to attain', that the explanation and justification of De Quincey's views on prose style are to be found. They are the primary example of what he calls 'impassioned prose', a category in which he stresses the almost complete barrenness of earlier literature. Perhaps he felt that prose should extend its imaginative range, as poetry had been doing. He seems to have been groping towards the idea of 'impassioned

prose' all his life, as he mused on the splendour of the visions that had come to him in reverie. Music accompanied his most moving dreams, and it is always in musical terms that he thought of his problem: 'A single word in a wrong key, ruins the whole music.' Nothing could be more revealing than the title of the last section of 'The Mail-Coach': 'Dream Fugue: Founded on the Preceding Theme.' Poets have sometimes looked to music for help in the problem of organizing their material: here, in a work which has certain affinities with Eliot's *Four Quartets*, a writer of prose has attempted the same thing. Completed, the *Suspiria* might have suggested a majestic fugue: as they stand the analogy is rather with an unfinished set of themes and variations.

As we contrast De Quincey's potentialities with his achievement we are constantly reminded of Coleridge, that other 'man of infinite title-pages'. The two had a great deal in common. Each was interested in an exceptionally wide range of subjects: psychology, philology, logic, German metaphysics, theology, universal history—to name only a few. Each of them was a great reader of travel books, each depreciated French literature as if in compensation for setting so high a value on German, each was something of a John Bull, each was keenly interested in the faculty of dreaming and in the workings of the human mind, each was chronically behindhand with the world and its editors, each was the despair of his friends, each was on occasion sentimental, humourless, and sadly lacking in a sense of proportion.

No doubt De Quincey modelled himself to some extent on the older man, having the same ambition of becoming a '*Polyhistor*, or catholic student'. Yet when we read his comparison of Coleridge and Leibnitz in the *Letters to a Young Man* we realize that De Quincey had attempted rather to follow the thinker whom he regarded as Coleridge's own model. Whereas Coleridge had been 'too self-indulgent, and almost a voluptuary in his studies', Leibnitz had 'sacrificed to the austerer muses [and] submitted to . . . regular study [and] discipline of thought'. When De Quincey tells us that 'the German had been a discursive reader, —the Englishman a desultory reader' it is clear in which category he would have placed himself.

Yet De Quincey and Coleridge had something in common which differentiates them decisively from Leibnitz: they were both opium-eaters. The result of this may be seen in almost

everything either of them wrote. For this reason (as has already been pointed out) De Quincey is often an excellent commentator on the greater man. What he once wrote about a piece of his own writing is equally applicable to much of the work of Coleridge: 'In parts and fractions eternal creations are carried on, but the nexus is wanting, the life and the central principle which should bind together all the parts at the centre, with all its radiations to the circumference, are wanting.' 'Opium-eaters . . . never finish anything', as he sums up in his essay on 'Coleridge and Opium-Eating'. Yet he insists that opium gives as well as taking away: 'It defeats the *steady* habit of exertion; but it creates spasms of irregular exertion. It ruins the natural power of life; but it develops preternatural paroxysms of intermitting power.' It is possible that De Quincey would have been a happier man without opium, but unlikely that he would have been a greater writer; for, as he himself pointed out, 'it is in the faculty of mental vision, it is in the increased power of dealing with the shadowy and the dark, that the characteristic virtue of opium lies'.

# XII

# MISCELLANEOUS PROSE

THE paradox that confronts us as we consider the literature of this period, the fact that it is so much easier to name the major writers than the major works which they produced, is in no department of literature more striking than in that of miscellaneous prose. 'It is a great literary age', as Bulwer Lytton remarked, '—we have great literary men—but where are their works?'—and he answered his own question by pointing out that 'We must seek them not in detached and avowed and standard publications, but in periodical miscellanies. It is in these journals that the most eminent of our recent men of letters have chiefly obtained their renown.' As we consider the work of the writers discussed in this chapter we shall find that the greater part of it first appeared in periodicals of different types, and that even if it was republished in book form it often retains the marks of its origin.

If the importance of a writer were to be gauged by his demonstrable influence on his contemporaries, Cobbett[1] would have no rival in our period except Jeremy Bentham. To us as we look back he seems less a man than a phenomenon. It is impossible to think of the development of England at the beginning of the nineteenth century without thinking of Cobbett. He was an astonishingly prolific writer, and since he was born into an age of autobiography his writings are full of information about himself. As the son of unpretentious parents he received little formal education and spent most of his boyhood at the usual country tasks. During these early years he not only learned all that there was to be learnt about the country and its ways, however: he was also a great reader, and so came on the new ideas that were fermenting in Europe. We hear of him joining a circulating library at Chatham and reading the 'greatest part' of its con-

[1] William Cobbett (?1763–1835) was the son of a farmer and innkeeper at Farnham in Surrey. In 1784 he enlisted as a soldier. Between 1785 and 1791 he served in Nova Scotia and New Brunswick, but the following year he first took refuge in France and then in Philadelphia. Between 1805 and 1820 he farmed in Hampshire. In 1820 he wrote strongly in support of Queen Caroline. In 1826 he tried to enter Parliament: in 1832 he was successful, becoming M.P. for Oldham.

tents through more than once, and he early formed an admiration for Swift that was to have its effect on his own prose style. After an unhappy period as a clerk he joined the army, and soon we find him writing an official report on the condition of Nova Scotia and New Brunswick and building up a case against a corrupt group of officers. On his discharge he instigated a court martial against these men, but fearing that he was in greater danger than the accused he fled with his wife to France and then to the United States. His literary career probably began a few months after his arrival in America, and his first writings reveal him as a strong anti-Democrat, anti-Radical, and anti-Jacobin. Having quarrelled with his publisher he set up in Philadelphia as a bookseller and publisher for himself, soon writing *The Life and Adventures of Peter Porcupine* (1796), with its characteristic motto: 'Now you lying varlets, you shall see how a plain tale shall put you down.' Defiantly adopting the nickname that he had been given he sets out to describe his own career, and does so with the complacency of a self-made man. He makes no secret of his views, and pulls no punches. Every reader may hear that Cobbett dislikes Priestley, dislikes Franklin, enjoys life in France, and is extremely critical of what he has seen in America. His *Works*, as published in 1801, exhibit 'A Faithful Picture of the United States of America; of their Governments, Laws, Politics, and Resources; of the Character of their Presidents, Governors . . . and Military Men; and of the Customs, Manners, Morals, Religion, Virtues and Vices of the People . . .'. Before the publication of these twelve volumes, however, Cobbett thought it prudent to return to England, where he was flatteringly received by Pitt and other anti-Jacobin leaders. He insisted on retaining his independence, tried to run a newspaper of his own, and then in 1802 started the weekly *Political Register*, which continued to appear until after his death and constituted his main channel of communication with the public. He began as a supporter of William Windham and the Tories, but by 1809 the tendency of the *Register* is predominantly Radical and an article on military flogging published that year led to Cobbett's imprisonment. In 1816, worried by declining circulation, he produced a cheap version of the *Register* at 2*d*., so raising the circulation to between 40,000 and 50,000 copies a week and appealing direct to the working classes. The first of the 'Six Acts' of 1820 drastically cut his

circulation. In 1830–2 he reprinted some of the most important articles from the *Register* in his *Two-Penny Trash.*

The *Rural Rides*, which Cobbett himself reprinted as a book and which remain his best-known work, made their first appearance in the *Political Register* in 1821 and the following years. Already a celebrated person, Cobbett set out to see for himself the condition of the agricultural community in the period of distress which had followed Waterloo. He went on horseback, for a very characteristic reason:

> My object was, not to see inns and turnpike-roads, but to see the *country*; to see the farmers at home, and to see the labourers in the fields; and to do this you must go either on foot or on horseback. With a gig you cannot get about amongst bye-lanes and across fields, through bridle-ways and hunting-gates.

Wherever he went he noticed the quality of the soil, the state of the crops, and all those indications of fertility or poverty to which the townsman is blind. Cobbett knows about trees and birds, and is as interested in cloud-formations as Constable himself. He notices whether the girls are handsome and neatly dressed, not only because he is of an amorous disposition, but also because he regards them as one of the fruits of the land. He is the most abstemious of travellers, preferring milk even to small ale and making a point of being in bed by 8 p.m. It is as characteristic that he should tell us about this as it is that he should give the money so saved to the deserving poor.

But Cobbett did not only wish to see for himself. He wished to persuade the farmers that they were ill-advised to support the Corn Laws and would be better occupied in trying to have the burden of taxation lightened. His love of giving advice comes out even in small matters: when he sees a woman plaiting straw he gives her instructions and wishes to send her a copy of his *Cottage Economy* with its 'Essay on Straw Plat'. If he comes on a well-kept farm, it is sure to be because the farmer has been following Cobbett's instructions. We notice that the country people were as eager to hear Cobbett as he was to be heard, and that it was to substantial farmers and not to the discontented mob that he liked to address himself. 'I made a speech last evening to from 130 to 150', he wrote on 13 April 1830, 'almost all farmers, and most men of apparent wealth to a certain extent. I have seldom been better pleased with my audience. It is not the

clapping and huzzaing that I value so much as the *silent attention*, the *earnest look* at me from *all eyes* at once, and then . . . the *look and nod at each other*, as if the parties were saying, "Think of that!" ' Cobbett tells us that he has adopted this 'haranguing system' (later in the *Rides* he sometimes uses the word 'lectures') because he has been kept out of Parliament. In fact he could not have been nearly as effective in Parliament as he was out of it—as he discovered when he was carried into the Commons by the mounting wave of Reform. Through his writings and his endless public speeches Cobbett became a focus for reforming opinion, receiving letters from correspondents in all quarters. 'Since my return home', he writes near the end of one of the *Rides*, '. . . I have received letters from the east, from the north, and from the west. All tell me that . . . the crops are free from blight. . . . Before Christmas, we shall have the wheat down to what will be a fair average price in future.'

In agricultural affairs Cobbett was an expert and appears to be reasonably objective. In other matters it is clear that he finds what he sets out to find. His prejudices are deep-rooted and luxuriant. It is as certain that he will not find a man with a clean shirt in a rotten borough as that he will have no good to say of a watering place. He holds to the full rigours of the view that primary producers are the sole sources of wealth and does not hesitate to draw the conclusion that everyone else is a parasite: hence the disgust with which he regards such a place as Cheltenham, 'a nasty, ill-looking place, half clown and half cockney, . . . the residence of an assemblage of tax-eaters, . . . vermin [who] shift about between London, Cheltenham, Bath, Bognor, Brighton, Tunbridge . . . and other spots in England, while some of them get over to France and Italy'. He has the self-educated man's love of generalizations and the demagogue's habit of rousing one section of the population against another. He hates Jews, Irishmen, Quakers, clergymen, and many other categories of mankind. He would like to see some ferocious Old Testament curse falling on London, 'The Great Wen', overwhelming it in a night. He hates 'Scotch FEELOSOFERS', the *Edinburgh Review*, and Scotsmen in general, whom he regards as a 'greedy band of *invaders* . . . [who] . . . never . . . work themselves and . . . are everlastingly publishing essays, the object of which is to keep the Irish out of England!' At times he seems to approve of no one but farmers and their labourers, shoe-makers

(towards whom he displays a curious tenderness), and occasional good landlords of the old-fashioned kind.

Although he had a powerful mind Cobbett was an extraordinarily simple man, and he liked to think that reality was correspondingly simple. He had the moralist's vision of a happy community in which each man should play his part and receive his due reward, and failing to find it in the present he created it in the past. With a certain naïve felicity he chooses the moment of approaching Oxford to salute the Golden Age, 'when men lived on the simple fruits of the earth and slaked their thirst at the pure and limpid brook! when the trees shed their leaves to form a couch for their repose, and cast their bark to furnish them with a canopy!' Although he himself calls this a Quixote-like speech, it was this belief in a Golden Age that sustained Cobbett throughout his life, and like many men since he chose to locate his Golden Age in the Middle Ages. He took part of the truth and made so much of it that it became a lie. His view is summed up in the title of his *History of the Protestant 'Reformation': . . . Showing how that event has impoverished and degraded the main body of the People* (1824–6). It is easy to sympathize with him in his indignation at the complacency of many of his contemporaries about Progress:

> Talk of *vassals*! Talk of *villains*! Talk of *serfs*! [Were] there any of these . . . so debased, so absolutely slaves, as the poor creatures who, in the 'enlightened' north, are compelled to work fourteen hours in a day, in a heat of eighty-four degrees; and who are liable to punishment for looking out at a window of the factory!

Yet when Cobbett begins to compare contemporary Britain with 'this once happy and moral England' one need not be very learned or very cynical to sense that the contrast is overdrawn. His attitude to feudalism reminds one of that of the Webbs to the Soviet system: he is delighted by the theory, and heedless of the practice. He has nothing but contempt for the cant of those who deplore 'the *superstition* and *dark ignorance* that induced people to found monasteries', and it is true that such a system might have done a great deal of good in Cobbett's own day, if it had worked as it had been supposed to work. Cobbett saw what was wrong with contemporary Protestant England and assumed that all was well before. It is an attitude to the Reformation that was popular a decade or two ago and produced (as its strangest bloom) Mr. Eliot's remarkable hypothesis of the 'dissociation of

sensibility'. Like Scott's Meg Merrilies Cobbett was an inveterate *laudator temporis acti*. He was deeply moved by the beauty of our old churches and cathedrals and impressed by the piety of the ages in which they were built: 'I could not look up at the spire and the whole of the church at Salisbury without feeling that I lived in degenerate times. Such a thing never could be made *now*. We *feel* that, as we look at the building.' After showing his little son a cathedral Cobbett told him that 'that building was made when there were no poor wretches in England called *paupers* . . .; when every labouring man was clothed in good woollen cloth'. They then arrive at an inn, where they find an Italian translation of Cobbett's *History of the Protestant 'Reformation'* awaiting them. For sheer *naïveté* it would be hard to match Cobbett's comment—'There, Doctor Black. Write *you* a book that shall be translated into *any* foreign language.'

His own attitude to religion is a little in doubt. When he talks of the clergy it is the holders of rich livings in the South that he usually has in mind, and such clergymen he regards as 'tax-eaters', the natural associates of the 'Jews and Jobbers' who throng the watering-places. He deplores the reactionary politics of the average High Churchman, as expressed by the *Quarterly Review*. Yet we also find him writing that he knows 'of no more meritorious and ill-used men than the working clergy' (a reminder that he was a man who tried to be fair), and discover him one evening taking the service himself at St. Ives 'on a carpenter's bench in a wheelwright's shop'. He always insisted that he was a Christian, giving the very characteristic reason that he liked 'any religion, that tends to make men innocent and benevolent and happy, by taking the best possible means of furnishing them with plenty to eat and drink and wear'. He shows no interest in the dogmas or the supernatural part of the Christian faith.

His other writings, or such of them as one may reasonably be expected to read, reinforce the impression made by the *Rural Rides*: they do not modify it. *A Year's Residence in America*, reprinted from the *Political Register* in 1818–19, is one of the most interesting. Cobbett's *Grammar of the English Language* (1818) has rightly been said to be 'as entertaining as a story-book': it displays his flair for popular instruction and the same care for the purity of the English language (oddly combined with a contempt for the classics) which appears in the *Rural Rides*, where

he is always ready to interrupt his political argument to discuss the meaning and derivation of such a word as 'hanger' or 'Tommy'. Many thousands of people learned to write from the *Grammar*, just as thousands learned even more practical matters from Cobbett's *Cottage Economy* (1821–2), which deals with such subjects as the brewing of beer, bread-making, and the nurture of cows, pigs, ewes, goats, poultry, and rabbits. *Cobbett's Poor Man's Friend* (1826–7), for which he himself had a particular fondness, is a political pamphlet in which he contrasts the supposed prosperity of the working classes before the Reformation with their condition in his own time. *Advice to Young Men and (incidentally) to Young Women, in the Middle and Higher Ranks of Life* (1829–30) reminds us both of Defoe and of Richardson: it consists of letters 'addressed to a Youth, a Bachelor, a Lover, a Husband, a Father, and a Citizen, or Subject'. This book is egotistical, occasionally comical, but almost always sensible. Only a very wise man, or a very superior person, could read it through without coming on one or two pieces of advice that he would do well to follow.

If the definition of a good style is a manner of using words precisely suited to the writer's purpose, then Cobbett has an excellent style. As Hazlitt pointed out, he uses 'plain, broad, downright English': he is clear, forceful, and free from affectation. He makes much use of italics and exclamation-marks, and returns repeatedly to his favourite topics. His tone and manner were admirably suited to his original audience, and he had every justification for shouting. But we are not the audience for which he wrote, and as we read him we are driven to the conclusion that his purely literary merits have sometimes been exaggerated. Read in bulk, his writings become a little tedious. We admire the extraordinary machine at work, and we acknowledge how effective it proved; but after a while it is a relief to get away from the noise. There is little variety of subject or attitude. There are no nuances or half-tones. Everything is on one plane, without shading or perspective. There is no deep understanding of human nature. There are pleasant descriptions of the countryside, but they are never great prose. Although it is easy to make an agreeable volume of selections from Cobbett's work, it does not matter very much which passages one selects. He is seldom memorable: as Hazlitt pointed out, 'there is not a single *bon-mot*, a single sentence in Cobbett that

has ever been quoted again'. Perhaps the most eloquent passage in his writings occurs when he is describing the sight that he hated most and that was most characteristic of his time:

> It was dark before we reached Sheffield; so that we saw the iron furnaces in all the horrible splendour of their everlasting blaze. Nothing can be conceived more grand or more terrific than the yellow waves of fire that incessantly issue from the top of these furnaces, some of which are close by the way-side. (31 January 1830.)

As a rule he has little to say about the towns through which he passes: if he approves of it he will comment that a village or town is 'clean' and 'nice' (a word that he over-works), and that will be all. He sees everything, in fact, from his own meridian. Because he was not at school, he thanks God for it. When he passes through Oxford he reflects that he and his writings will have infinitely more effect than those of all the drones in the colleges. He uses Shakespeare (as G. D. H. Cole pointed out) as a stick for beating the potato crop, and has little interest in the things of the imagination. To him Dr. Johnson was simply a 'dastardly old pensioner', a judgement he would certainly have withdrawn if he had ever met him. He was a sort of portent, God's Judgement on the men who were writing Latin verses while the ricks were burning. For him Man was not 'a being darkly wise, and rudely great', but something much more simple. He was right to protest against the cant of talking about the souls of the poor when their bodies were starving, and the things which he admired—such as strength of character, honesty, and hard work—are truly admirable. But life is more complicated than Cobbett was capable of seeing. Once a man is provided for, Cobbett has no further interest in him except as a potential audience for his harangues and pamphlets.

If we wish to understand Leigh Hunt's work as an essayist and critic it will be as well to begin with a few facts about his numerous periodicals.[1] He started the *Examiner* with his brother

[1] James Henry Leigh Hunt (1784–1859) was educated at Christ's Hospital and was so precocious that his father published a volume of his poetry when he was only 17. Soon he was writing dramatic criticisms for the *News*, which was edited by his brother John. During his spell in prison, which permanently damaged his health, his visitors included Byron, Lamb, and Bentham. It was Hunt who brought about the meeting between Keats and Shelley. He lived on into the heart of the Victorian Age and produced a great many books and periodicals.

John in 1808 and continued to be the principal contributor until 1821. Its contents were 'Politics, Domestic Economy and Theatricals', while its motto proclaimed that 'Party is the madness of many for the gain of a few'. It supported the abolition of the slave trade, Catholic emancipation and the reform of the criminal law, had its doubts about the war with France, criticized the Prince of Wales, and soon stated with all possible emphasis that 'A REFORM IN PARLIAMENT WILL PURIFY THE WHOLE CONSTITUTION'. By 1812 Bentham calculated that the *Examiner* was selling between 7,000 and 8,000 copies. Its promoters were frequently threatened with libel actions. In 1811 they were unsuccessfully prosecuted for an article on the subject of military flogging, and in 1813 each of the brothers was fined £500 and sentenced to two years' imprisonment for one of their numerous attacks on the Prince of Wales. Although the two men were well treated in their separate prisons, and the *Examiner* was able to continue publication, Leigh Hunt was naturally regarded as a martyr to the cause of liberty, and in his *Poems* of 1817 we find Keats addressing him as 'Libertas'. After this the political influence of the *Examiner* declined, while its literary importance increased. This is not surprising: apart from the danger and difficulty of writing freely on politics at this point, Leigh Hunt's attitude to politics was from the first paradoxical. Although he was a passionate supporter of certain great causes, he was not a political animal: he was uninterested in ways and means, parties and cabals, arguments and indirect persuasions. 'Though I was a politician (so to speak)', as he puts it in a revealing passage in his *Autobiography*, 'I had scarcely a political work in my library. Spensers and Arabian Tales filled up the shelves.' The *Examiner*'s most important work was its perceptive and untiring advocacy of the new poets, and particularly of Shelley and Keats.

In the prospectus of the *Reflector*, a quarterly magazine that had appeared in 1810–11, we find Hunt speculating about the relation between politics and literature:

> Politics, in times like these, should naturally take the lead in periodical discussion, because they have an importance and interest almost unexampled in history, and because *they are now, in their turn, exhibiting their re-action upon literature, as literature in the preceding age exhibited its action upon them.*

'The Feast of the Poets', which appeared in the fourth issue, sums up Hunt's early critical views, while Lamb's essays on Hogarth and on the plays of Shakespeare 'considered with reference to their fitness for stage representation' are also to be found in the *Reflector*. A good deal of attention is devoted to painting and sculpture because (we are told) whereas the drama in England 'is in its second infancy, with all the vices of a frivolous dotage', the fine arts 'are in their first infancy and must be handled more tenderly'. In the *Indicator*, which appeared every Wednesday from 13 October 1819 to 21 March 1821, and which Edmund Blunden has aptly described as 'the literary supplement' of the *Examiner*, Leigh Hunt felt at liberty to take a holiday from politics, and the result is undoubtedly his most successful and characteristic piece of writing. 'They tell me I am at my best at this work', as he acknowledged, and from the first the *Indicator* sold well and won high praise from such judges as Hazlitt and Lamb. Once again Hunt prints and praises the work of the new poets ('La Belle Dame sans Merci' first appeared in the *Indicator*) and draws the attention of English readers to foreign literature.

The idea for the *Liberal* (1822–3), an intended quarterly of which only four issues appeared, seems to have been Byron's, and Shelley was not alone in doubting whether such an alliance between 'the wren and the eagle' would last for long. As Hazlitt tells us, 'the Tories were shocked that Lord Byron should grace the popular side' while 'the Whigs were shocked that he should share his confidence and counsels with any one who did not unite the double recommendations of birth and genius—like themselves!' The object of this work was 'not political, except inasmuch as all writing now-a-days must involve something to that effect'; the contributors intended to contribute their 'liberalities in the shape of Poetry, Essays, Tales, Translations, and other amenities'. The 'amenities' in fact opened with Byron's *Vision of Judgment*, not noticeably softened in its effect by the instruction on the Errata leaf: 'Instead of "a *worse* king never left a realm undone", read "a *weaker* king ne'er left a realm undone".' Italian literature was to be given particular prominence in these volumes of 'Verse and Prose from the South', as well as German and Spanish. In spite of the brilliance of individual contributions, however, the *Liberal* lacks unity, and the outcry which it occasioned was out of all proportion to

the size of its circulation. 'Never since I have been a publisher did I ever observe such a universal outcry . . .', Murray wrote to Byron: 'It is dreadful to think of yr. association with such outcasts from society.' The publisher was fined £100 for publishing a 'gross, impious and slanderous' libel on George III.

Some of Leigh Hunt's best essays are to be found in a weekly called the *Companion* which ran for the first seven months of 1828 and consists (as he says in his *Autobiography*) 'partly of criticisms on theatres, authors, and public events, and partly of a series of essays in the manner of the *Indicator*', but the new periodical 'did not address itself to any existing influence' and so failed to pay its way. We cannot pursue Hunt through his later periodicals, such as the *Tatler* (1830–2), which came out daily, *Leigh Hunt's London Journal* (1834–5), or *Leigh Hunt's Journal; A Miscellany for the Cultivation of the Memorable, the Progressive, and the Beautiful*, which appeared in 1850–1. Nor is there time to trace his contributions to periodicals edited by other men, from the *New Monthly Magazine* to *Household Words*. It will be more to the point to attempt a brief general characterization of his work as a critic and essayist. At Christ's Hospital Boyer was never tired of recommending the *Spectator* as the 'standard of prose writing' and the essayists of the eighteenth century were Leigh Hunt's masters. Hunt tells us that his own first essays were called 'The Traveller' and were the work of 'Mr. Town, *junior*, Critic and Censor-general'. Yet he instinctively rebelled against Boyer's 'exaction of moral observations on a given subject', preferring Goldsmith to Addison and deriving 'an entirely fresh and delightful sense of the merits of essay-writing' from the *Connoisseur*, by George Colman and Bonnell Thornton, which he discovered for himself. Whereas the eighteenth-century essayist is usually concerned to point a moral, Hunt's aim is to communicate enjoyment. Capable as he is of severity when oppression is in question (when he always remembers Voltaire, for him the great 'destroyer of the strongholds of superstition'), he is not really a moralist at all, except in the sense that he advocates a sort of innocent Epicureanism. His inborn tendency 'to reap pleasure from every object in creation' is the motive force of his essays. In his *Autobiography* he explains why he called one of the shorter-lived of his periodicals the *Seer*: 'The *Seer* does not mean a prophet . . ., but an observer of ordinary things about him, gifted by his admiration of nature

with the power of discerning what everybody else may discern by a cultivation of the like secret of satisfaction.' The same attitude inspired his literary criticism. Hunt wrote almost exclusively of what he enjoyed, and few men have had a more catholic capacity for enjoyment. He was the most important of Keats's early guides to 'the realms of gold' and continued to play this role for many other readers until the middle of the century. To the end of his life he retained an uncommon flair for recognizing excellence of new kinds even when it was accompanied by obvious defects. Whereas Croker lived to be as wrong about Tennyson as he had been about Keats, Hunt was as perceptive and as generous about the one as he had been about the other. It is true that he sometimes over-praised young poets who came to nothing, true also that he seldom wrote adverse criticism; yet if a critic is to be judged by the number of times he is right about his contemporaries then Hunt has no rival in the history of English criticism. Even so one hesitates to call him a great critic. He was more often right about his contemporaries than Hazlitt, far more often right than Jeffrey; yet he was a less intelligent man than either. His strength lay in his sensibility, in his accessibility to fresh literary experience, rather than in his intellect or his ability to reason about literature. Perhaps this very fact helped him to be fair to writers, like Scott and Wordsworth, whose views about politics and about life in general he was very far from sharing.

It should be mentioned that Hunt had first attracted attention as a dramatic critic. The notices that he wrote for the *News* at the beginning of his career were published as *Critical Essays on the Performers of the London Theatres* in 1807. They are a remarkable achievement for a critic of twenty, and exhibit a pugnacity for which we look in vain in his later criticism. Soon, we are told, his 'judgment was universally sought and received as infallible by all actors and lovers of the drama'. Unlike many of his contemporaries in literature Hunt was also a musical man, and his occasional criticism of music is always intelligent and sympathetic. His writings on the visual arts are of more importance, however, particularly because of the part that he played in opening Keats's eyes to the beauty of painting and sculpture. As he explained in the *Reflector*, his aim was to estimate art 'in no other way than by the general standard of poetry, music, and other works of genius; that is to say, by its

invention, its harmonious agreement, and its nature'. His object was to introduce the visual arts to 'persons of cultivated minds who would easily blend a love of painting and sculpture with that of the other liberal arts'. Like Haydon he hoped that English painting was on the threshold of a great renaissance. In his unjustly neglected book, *Imagination and Fancy* (1844), he draws some particularly interesting parallels between painting and poetry.

Although Hunt sometimes collected his essays into volumes, they remain essays rather than books, and it is better to read an individual essay than one of his books as a whole. Yet neither as an essayist nor as a critic does he reach the highest class. In spite of the part that politics played in his own life it was, as has been suggested, only in a special and limited sense that he was interested in politics; while in philosophy he was hardly interested at all. Compared with those of Coleridge, Hazlitt, or De Quincey his occasional writings are apt to seem slight and 'belletristic': what he has to say about literature, for example, excellent as it is, lacks the cross-fertilization that might have sprung from a deep and informed concern with other aspects of life. He remains a dilettante, a connoisseur, with something of the superficiality that the term implies. It is interesting to find him describing Coleridge 'eternally probing the depths of his own mind, and trying what he could make of them beyond the ordinary pale of logic and philosophy', and commenting: 'It is impossible to say what new worlds may be laid open, some day or other, by this apparently hopeless process.' Such a prophetic remark underlines Hunt's own limitations. He is content to remain on the surface of consciousness. Although he was courageous in facing political oppression, in his writing he tends to turn away from the darker sides of experience. His prose, fluent and agreeable as it is, is never concise, pointed, pregnant with meaning and reflection—as Hazlitt's so often is. It is difficult not to describe his style as 'chatty', and that is a word that cannot justly be used of the work of any of the great critics and essayists. Leigh Hunt is a delightful companion, but after a while we become tired of him, as Keats did.

When we turn from Leigh Hunt to Jeffrey we turn to a man who was less concerned with 'appreciation': Jeffrey took it for granted that his function was to evaluate, and to do so with severity: 'Iudex damnatur cum nocens absolvitur.' Although

the claim of Jeffrey's early biographer[1] that he was 'the greatest of British critics' now seems absurd, his criticism retains a higher value than it is usually allowed. The clue to all his work is his background: three universities and the Speculative Society produced a keen young lawyer with a quick mind and an advocate's ability to get up his brief. Although he became a judge, in literature he remained always an advocate. He was a versatile man, and he made no attempt to limit himself to subjects of which he had a detailed knowledge. The explanation of many of the articles in the *Edinburgh Review* that surprise or irritate us today is that they were the work of non-specialists writing at a time when specialization was already destined to win the day. In less than thirty years Jeffrey contributed some two hundred essays on subjects as various as philosophy, history, biography, jurisprudence, criminology, travel, and what we should now call sociology, as well as on literature itself. He was a product of the Northern *Aufklärung*, a man of the same race as David Hume and Adam Smith, though he was much less gifted; and he shared their view that literature should be regarded simply as one of the agents of human happiness. Since he was anxious 'to combine Ethical precepts with Literary Criticism' he naturally made 'the Moral tendencies of the works under consideration a leading subject of discussion'. His attitude to literature was as different as possible from that of Charles Lamb. He was no collector of books: in an age of bibliomania he was blind to the charms of a folio. After his death, as Nichol Smith pointed out, 'his cellar, which contained well over three hundred dozens . . ., was distributed by the auctioneer; but his library was divided quietly among his friends'. Unfortunately his lack of sympathy with literary antiquarianism led him to pay too little attention to the facts of literary history: he preferred wide views based on *a priori* assumptions. And, of course, he was out of sympathy with many of the ideas that stimulated the younger writers of his own day. Although his life spanned practically the

[1] Francis Jeffrey (1773–1850), later Lord Jeffrey, was educated at Edinburgh High School and the Universities of Glasgow, Edinburgh and Oxford. When he first became an advocate in 1794 he obtained little business, on account of his Whig opinions. At the Speculative Society he met Scott and others. In 1806 Moore challenged him to a duel, as a result of a review of his poems in the *Edinburgh Review*, but the two men were arrested before they could fight. Soon Jeffrey prospered, visited America, and took an active part in politics. He became Dean of the Faculty of Advocates, Lord Advocate, and then a Judge of the Court of Session. In 1831 he became a Member of Parliament. He knew Wordsworth and was a friend of Dickens.

same period as Wordsworth's, his critical views developed very little from first to last. One reason for this was probably that the mind grows in solitude, though it is sharpened in society; perhaps Jeffrey was too seldom alone. His essays, in any event, are interesting, vivacious, stimulating; but they are never really penetrating or seminal. They stimulate the surface of the mind but do not give us the feeling that we have been profoundly enlightened.

As a critic of his contemporaries Jeffrey was highly erratic. In 1829 he proclaimed, though with professed regret, that Southey, Keats, Shelley, Wordsworth, Crabbe, and Moore were all declining in reputation, while 'the blazing star of Byron himself is receding from its place of pride'. Who then remained? Rogers and Campbell. Even if it is conceded that Jeffrey was here concerned with the course of literary fashion rather than with absolute poetic values it is evident that he was no spotter of winners. Yet a great deal remains to be set on the other side of the account. He praised Scott's poetry eloquently, and wrote excellent reviews of *Waverley* and a number of its successors. On Crabbe he wrote with great insight and understanding. In spite of being attacked in *English Bards and Scotch Reviewers* he was one of the first and most emphatic acclaimers of *Childe Harold's Pilgrimage*, and although he disapproved of the moral tendency of much of *Don Juan* he was in no doubt about the genius there displayed. He began his review of *Endymion* and Keats's volume of 1820 by saying that he has been 'exceedingly struck with the genius they display, and the spirit of poetry which breathes through all their extravagance' and went on to speak out boldly in praise of the young poet: 'We are very much inclined . . . to add, that we do not know any book which we would sooner employ as a test to ascertain whether any one had in him a native relish for poetry, and a genuine sensibility to its intrinsic charm.' Jeffrey had the highest regard for Dickens, although unfortunately he did not write on him. But instead of illustrating the merits of Jeffrey's other criticism it may be of greater interest to devote the little space that remains to a brief consideration of his criticism of Wordsworth, both because it has been too unreservedly condemned and because it is in itself of some importance in the history of our literature.

To be fair to Jeffrey we must remember that Wordsworth's reputation as a great poet rests most securely on one long poem

and a number of shorter poems which make up only a small proportion of his total writings: *The Prelude*, 'Tintern Abbey', and certain of the other poems written between 1798 and 1808. Unfortunately Jeffrey did not have *The Prelude* before him, and he did have the preface to the second edition of the *Lyrical Ballads*. As has been suggested in Chapter I, there can be little doubt that the publication of the preface was a mistake which did a great deal of harm to Wordsworth's reputation. Jeffrey himself tells us that on their first appearance the *Lyrical Ballads* were 'unquestionably popular', adding that he considered their popularity well merited. The *Edinburgh Review* was founded in 1802, and Jeffrey's first hostile criticism of the Lake poets was a review of Southey's unreadable *Thalaba* in the first number: he used this as an occasion for writing about 'a *sect* of poets, that has established itself . . . within these ten or twelve years'. It is clear that Jeffrey was remembering Johnson's onslaught on 'the metaphysical poets': Wordsworth lies behind Southey, as Donne lies behind Cowley. There was an element of the 'stunt' about the article: it was a piece of brilliant journalism written as a *tour de force* to draw attention to a provocative new periodical for which no one anticipated a long life. But Jeffrey's attack, which was carried on in later articles and which enjoyed a wider influence than it deserved, was not merely a journalistic stunt. Since there was so much that was challenging and puzzling about Wordsworth's work, it was natural that critics should have looked round for guidance about his intentions, and inevitable that they should have regarded his preface as 'a kind of manifesto'. Unfortunately the preface is a misleading introduction to Wordsworth's poetry as a whole, as well as containing many statements which are completely incompatible with the known history of English poetry. Jeffrey was aware of the inconsistencies in Wordsworth's arguments and outraged by a document which seemed to him a heresy against the true doctrine of poetry. As we read his strictures on Wordsworth's theory about the language of poetry we are reading a critic in the main stream of Renaissance and neo-classical criticism, writing at a time when the doctrine was becoming slightly too rigid, as he deals with a revolutionary theory which is both unhistorical and self-contradictory. It is natural, though regrettable, that Jeffrey should have paid too much attention to the poems in which Wordsworth seemed to him to follow his

theory, and too little to those in which he gloriously departs from it.

The preface seems always to have come between Jeffrey and an open-minded reading of Wordsworth. He failed to appreciate the importance of the *Poems* of 1807. He also did less than justice to *The Excursion*, though too many readers remember only the opening words of his review—'This will never do.' If we read on we find that Jeffrey tells us that he admires some passages of the poem so much that he is 'half inclined to rescind the severe sentence' that he has passed: but he cannot. 'His former poems were intended to recommend [his] system . . . by their individual merit; —but this, we suspect, must be recommended by the system—and can only expect to succeed where it has been previously established.' Before we condemn Jeffrey we should recall that while the publication of *The Excursion* seemed an event of profound significance to Hazlitt, Keats, and a few of the other more penetrating critics of the day, the poem has never proved popular: today it may be doubted whether one reader in ten of *The Prelude* has read through *The Excursion*. It is to Jeffrey's credit that he at least gave full enough extracts to enable readers interested in Wordsworth to assess its quality for themselves.

In 1844 Jeffrey summed up his opinion of Wordsworth. He understands, he tells us, that many readers who admire the same passages as he himself does in the *Lyrical Ballads* and *The Excursion* may be more tolerant than he of the inferior passages: with such critics he is not in serious disagreement. But he is told that 'almost all those who seek to exalt Mr. Wordsworth as the founder of a new school of poetry, consider . . . as by far his best and most characteristic productions' *The White Doe of Rylstone*, *Peter Bell*, 'Martha Rae', and the 'Sonnets upon the Punishment of Death': with such a view he can never agree. This is perfectly reasonable. The real charge against Jeffrey remains that of failing to recognize the significance of Wordsworth as an intellectual and spiritual force. Yet it must be acknowledged that there are still Wordsworthians who remind one of James Joyce's claim that his readers must devote the whole of their lives to the study of his works. If fully to appreciate Wordsworth we must abandon our minds to his philosophy and forbid our normal critical responses to function, then there will be many who prefer to remain outside with Jeffrey. If Wordsworth

is to be appreciated and criticized like any other poet, then we must acknowledge that Jeffrey's attitude to him was at least perfectly defensible.

It is appropriate that Jeffrey should have dedicated his essays to Sydney Smith,[1] for although it was Jeffrey who made the *Edinburgh Review* a force to be reckoned with in the history of the early nineteenth century it was Sydney Smith who had been its 'original projector'. From the moment when he entered the Church, 'in obedience to the wishes of his father', Sydney Smith had proved himself an anomaly and a challenge to those in authority, and it is not surprising that some should have denounced his assumption of Orders as an act of hypocrisy. Yet the charge was unjust, and as we read through the letters to Jeffrey which form a running commentary on the early years of the *Edinburgh Review* we are struck by Smith's anxiety about its sceptical tendency. 'I certainly . . . do protest against your increasing and unprofitable scepticism', he wrote as early as the Spring of 1804:

> I exhort you to restrain the violent tendency of your nature for analysis, and to cultivate synthetical propensities. What's the use of virtue? What's the use of wealth? What's the use of honor? . . . The whole effort of your mind is to destroy. Because others build slightly and eagerly, you employ yourself in kicking down their houses, and contract a sort of aversion for the more honorable useful and difficult task of building well yourself.

Soon he is parodying Jeffrey's mode of reviewing: 'Damn the solar system! bad light—planets too distant—pestered with comets—feeble contrivance;—could make a better with great ease.' He complained with reason that Jeffrey was giving the *Review* a character 'which makes it perilous for a clergyman . . . to be concerned in it', and it is hardly surprising that his own contributions became less frequent and then stopped altogether. Yet his own mind had something in common with Jeffrey's, and it is possible to imagine him sympathizing with the spirit of

[1] Sydney Smith (1771–1845) was educated at Winchester and New College, Oxford, where he was elected Fellow in 1791. He took Orders, became tutor to Michael Hicks Beach, and helped to start the *Edinburgh Review* during his period of residence in Edinburgh. In 1803 he moved to London, where he soon became a familiar figure in the Holland House circle and a favourite lecturer on moral philosophy at the Royal Institution. In 1808 he settled down near his living of Foston, outside York. Twenty years later he was made a prebendary at Bristol and then a canon-residentiary at St. Paul's in London. He was witty, generous, and honest.

Jeffrey's gibe about 'obscure truths—if such things exist'. When he complained about the review of *The Excursion* it was not because he admired the poem but simply because 'the subject is . . . so very uninteresting'. It would hardly be an exaggeration to say that the dimension in which Wordsworth's greatest poetry has its being is one of which Sydney Smith was wholly unaware. He once described himself as a man without secrets, a man in a house made of glass. That is one reason why this most intelligent and entertaining of correspondents never quite reaches the ranks of the great letter-writers. Another reason was perhaps that he lacked the sense of frustration. He found an outlet for his talents in a crowded social life which was the more intense and the more enjoyable because it formed a series of brilliant interludes between the periods of pastoral duty. It is not from a player on the human scene so confident and so fulfilled that the half-lights and nuances of a great letter-writer are to be expected.

When we turn to his essays we find that he is most eloquent when he is protesting: when he is dealing with such subjects as Chimney Sweepers, Game Laws, Botany Bay, Poor Laws, Ireland, and Prisons. Satirists are most often conservative, but throughout his life Sydney Smith used his wit on the side of progress: not to ridicule new ideas, but rather to demonstrate the absurdity of traditional prejudices. The best-remembered of his writings are the *Letters of Peter Plymley*, published in 1807–8. By giving the imaginary author a brother Abraham who 'lives in the country' and is 'a bit of a goose' he provides himself with an ideal vantage-point from which to deploy his brilliant rhetoric:

> In the first place, my sweet Abraham, the Pope is not landed—nor are there any curates sent out after him—nor has he been hid at St. Alban's by the Dowager Lady Spencer—nor dined privately at Holland House—nor been seen near Dropmore. If these fears exist (which I do not believe), they exist only in the mind of the Chancellor of the Exchequer; they emanate from his zeal for the Protestant interest; and, though they reflect the highest honour upon the delicate irritability of his faith, must certainly be considered as more ambiguous proofs of the sanity and vigour of his understanding.

He argues vigorously that England cannot afford to alienate the Catholics of Ireland:

> You speak of danger to the Establishment: I request to know when

the Establishment was ever so much in danger as when Hoche was in Bantry Bay, and whether all the books of Bossuet, or the arts of the Jesuits, were half so terrible? Mr. Perceval and his parsons forgot all this, in their horror lest twelve or fourteen old women may be converted to holy water, and Catholic nonsense. They never see that, while they are saving these venerable ladies from perdition, Ireland may be lost, England broken down, and the Protestant Church, with all its deans, prebendaries, Percevals and Rennels, be swept into the vortex of oblivion.

Although Sydney Smith had himself no sympathy with Catholicism he had the penetration and honesty to point out that the popular feeling against Catholicism 'is not all religion; it is, in great part, the narrow and exclusive spirit which delights to keep the common blessings of sun, and air, and freedom from other human beings'. The spirit which informs *The Letters of Peter Plymley* is not the *saeva indignatio* of the Juvenalian satirist but rather the *indignatio liberalis* of a clear head and a generous heart.

William Gifford, the editor of the *Quarterly*, was a very different kind of person from the clever young men who had started the *Edinburgh Review*.[1] Whereas Jeffrey was still in his twenties when the *Edinburgh* first appeared, Gifford was in his fifties when the *Quarterly* began publication. In capacity he was greatly Jeffrey's inferior. Whereas Jeffrey was a critic with a touch of the satirist about him, Gifford was a satirist with a touch of the critic. He was much less intelligent than Jeffrey, and had much less sense of responsibility. In the brief autobiography prefixed to his translation of Juvenal and Persius he describes his humble beginnings: how he was orphaned at the age of eleven, then befriended by a series of patrons and so enabled to study at Oxford and to see something of Europe as tutor to Lord Grosvenor's son. His translations and *The Baviad* and *Maeviad*, two satires on the 'Della Cruscan' poetasters, have little merit and do not concern us here. What does concern us is to notice that his early struggles seem to have left him with a permanent desire for revenge against the world. In 1797 he became editor

[1] William Gifford (1756–1826) was born at Ashburton in Devonshire. Generous patrons sent him to Exeter College, Oxford, and later he attracted the attention of Lord Grosvenor. He was one of Murray's circle of trusted advisers, and read *Emma* before it was accepted for publication. Byron professed to have a high opinion of his judgement. Like many ungenerous men he was capable of great loyalty towards those who had befriended him.

of the *Anti-Jacobin*, supplying much of the abuse while Canning and Hookham Frere supplied the wit. When Scott refused the editorship of the *Quarterly* and Gifford was appointed instead, he may be said to have resumed his Anti-Jacobin role. He seems only to have written eight complete papers himself, but he revised and rewrote the papers of his contributors, and the letters of the time are loud with complaints about the activities of 'the prose-gelder'. Lamb was furious about Gifford's treatment of his review of *The Excursion*: 'More than a third of the substance is cut away', he wrote to Wordsworth, 'and that not all from one place . . ., so as to make utter nonsense. Every warm expression is changed for a nasty cold one.' Gifford regarded it as his duty to abbreviate the work of his contributors and to enliven and season it with political and personal abuse. He clearly enjoyed the unrivalled power which his position gave him and demonstrated conclusively that anonymous reviewing, conducted on his plan, is an intolerable imposition on the public. In private life he appears to have been an amiable man, passionately grateful to those who had helped him on his way; but he was an important figure in public life, and those who knew him only in that capacity had every reason for detesting him. The truth is that he rose to a position of authority for which he was intellectually and morally quite unsuited. In his most forbearing *Autobiography* Leigh Hunt tells us that Gifford was the only man he had ever attacked without subsequent regret. Hazlitt's 'character' of Gifford in *The Spirit of the Age* is as severe as Pope, and Gifford deserved it.

While Gifford was editor of the *Quarterly* a much abler man, John Wilson Croker, was one of his most constant contributors.[1] Although Croker's political career does not concern us it is important to remember that he was (as Gifford pointed out) 'the only link' joining the *Quarterly* with 'the Ministers', and it is on account of this link that the *Review* is so often a reliable guide to Government policy. Although he wrote in 1834 that he 'never was a friend to making the *Review* a political engine' most of his

[1] John Wilson Croker (1780–1857) studied at Trinity College, Dublin, and at Lincoln's Inn. In 1807 he became Member of Parliament for Downpatrick. As Secretary to the Admiralty he exposed defalcations. He was a friend of Canning and of Peel, but he offended the future William IV while the latter was Duke of Clarence. In 1830 he introduced the term 'Conservative'. He resigned from Parliament in 1832 but continued to support Peel until Peel adhered to Cobden's policy in 1845.

reviews have at least political undertones, while after 1832 we are told that 'practically *every* political article' was from his pen. He understood very clearly the value of official propaganda and saw no reason for keeping politics out of anything. He was an expert on French affairs, and it is a misfortune that he did not write a full study of the French Revolution, a task for which he was fitted both by the number of survivors that he knew personally and by his extensive collection of revolutionary pamphlets. Although he was far from impartial, his approach to the Revolution was more empirical than that of many of his contemporaries. So far from regarding revolutions as 'systematic and salutary movements, uniformly accomplishing the ends of justice with great fairness' he believed them to be terrible cataclysms in which the worst part of mankind gained the upper hand and tore down all that was civilized and valuable. His attitude to 'the mob' was similar to that of Samuel Butler and Dryden a century and a half before. He regarded France and America as England's natural enemies, Russia as her predestined ally. In home affairs he was equally uncompromising: if Reform became a reality, he prophesied, 'Anarchy, with all its horrors and miseries will ensue'. Although he was an Anglo-Irish Protestant he was theoretically in favour of Catholic emancipation; but when it came to a vote he was against it. He had a profound admiration for Burke but never learned the lesson of so much of Burke's greatest writing, that circumstances are the heart of every political problem. Like that of many of Burke's admirers, Croker's attitude to him reminds us of Rymer's attitude to Aristotle: he erected into dogma a body of observation and reasoning which was meant to be taken in quite a different spirit.

Few men of his day knew so much about the eighteenth century as Croker. He did a great deal of work on the *Grenville Papers* and wrote more than fifty reviews of biographies and memoirs covering the period 1775–1825. As we glance at his work for a projected edition of Pope we are reminded that most of the men of this period who were prepared to study the eighteenth century in a scholarly way were essentially conservatives: as were many of those who were prepared to study the Victorian period before about 1930. Croker's aim was to have been to 'endeavour to put the reader of 1831 back into the place of the reader of 1731', and the truth is that he would have been well

pleased to be put back to 1731 himself. A great deal of Croker's material went to enrich the Elwin-Courthope edition of Pope half a century later. His edition of Boswell's *Johnson* will be mentioned in Chapter XIV. His scholarly tenacity, like that of an academic bloodhound, may be seen at its best in his demonstration that Fanny Burney was twenty-five when *Evelina* appeared, and not seventeen. Annotation and the more limited tasks of scholarship were those at which he excelled. In a revealing passage he once envied Scott 'the *bold facility* with which he seized a subject and by the first glance determined all its properties'. As Croker pointed out, Scott 'was perpetually wrong in his details, but always right, luminous, and I had almost said exact, in his general view—but I am not of that power. I do nothing at all approaching to well but what I understand *in its details*. Would I could.' Croker could not have written Scott's *Lives* of Dryden and Swift, although he could have pointed out the errors they contain. If Scott had been a Whig Croker would not have praised him so generously; yet his enormous review of Macaulay's *History*, severe as it is, is much fairer than Macaulay's review of Croker's *Boswell*. Croker was a born scholar, and like many born scholars he lacked imagination.

As a critic he was much less respectable than as a scholar. As he himself pointed out, 'Party is much the strongest passion of an Englishman's mind. Friendship, love, even avarice give way before it'—and he was thoroughly at home in a *Review* where it was taken for granted that a writer's known or supposed political sympathies should help to determine the critic's attitude to his work. An article on the French novel, published in 1836, amusingly illustrates his inability to keep politics out of literary criticism. Than Rousseau (he tells us) 'a baser, meaner, filthier, scoundrel never polluted society', and he had no hesitation in finding evidence of the same pollution in the work of Dumas, Hugo, Balzac, and George Sand. Croker's criticism of the new poets of his own day has always been notorious for its political bias. His attitude to Leigh Hunt was bitterly hostile, though the fact that Leigh Hunt revised *The Story of Rimini* in the light of his review shows that many of Croker's strictures were just. Croker similarly regarded Shelley as a man with a 'disgraceful and flagitious history'. His, again, is the unenviable notoriety of having attacked *Endymion*, although he did refrain from

attacking Keats personally. He was in the habit of asking Murray to send him 'fools' for review. 'The public', he once wrote, 'is so fastidious and indeed so *blasé* that its appetite requires a great deal of the *piquant*.' So Keats was fricassee'd to enliven a dull number. It is not, unfortunately, surprising that Croker should have picked on a young and unknown writer: on the contrary it was characteristic—although he was also prepared to attack the old and celebrated. He was a confirmed snob, and his attitude to a 'gentleman' like Byron, even when he disapproved strongly of the tendency of his work, was always different from his attitude to a Cockney like Keats.

While Myron F. Brightfield's biography is a useful contribution to literary history, it is difficult to go as far as he does in rehabilitating Croker's character. Croker's political views were undoubtedly sincere, but he supported them with a violence which it is impossible to admire. Very few men put themselves in a position to be admonished by Lockhart on this point, but it was he who advised Croker, in 1849, that 'violence nowadays does not answer as well as it did thirty years ago'. Bagehot once said that Sydney Smith lacked 'fangs' for detailed historical research: Croker had fangs, but unfortunately he did not reserve them for that purpose. Like many unimaginative men, he was cruel: the evidence of the portrait painted by William Owen confirms that of his writings. He was a Churchman rather than a Christian: he would not have understood Christian charity unless a gentleman was in question, while it is easy to imagine what his attitude would have been to the Founder of Christianity. It is not surprising that he was much hated. 'Rigby' in *Coningsby* is a caricature, but a caricature of Croker.

John Wilson, who wrote as 'Christopher North', was the most extraordinary product of the anonymous journalism of the time.[1] The strikingly handsome son of a wealthy Paisley family, he spent several years at Glasgow University and Magdalen College, Oxford, and then lived for some time at Elleray and became an associate of the Wordsworth circle. Wordsworth rightly pointed out that Wilson's poems were merely 'an attenuation' of his own, and today they are devoid of interest; but the

[1] John Wilson (1785–1854) was an outstanding athlete, and made a famous leap over the Cherwell. He contributed to Coleridge's *Friend*. In 1815 he was called to the Scottish Bar. He became a Professor at Edinburgh University in 1820. He was a vain man with something unreal at his heart.

remarkable thing about Wilson was that he was storing up materials with which to attack the Lakists at the very time during which he was their sentimental disciple. The foundation of *Blackwood's Magazine* gave him his opportunity: he was the most important single contributor, and practically all his prose writings first made their appearance anonymously in the pages of 'Maga'. The systematic mystification in which the contributors indulged and their habit of collaboration make it difficult to identify individual contributions, but it is clear that Wilson collaborated with Hogg and Lockhart in writing the 'Translation from an Ancient Chaldee Manuscript' and wrote some of the attacks on the 'Cockney School' (of which Lockhart was the principal author), while he seems also to have been the writer of the deplorable attack on *Biographia Literaria*, which even Lockhart regarded with distaste. One of Wilson's oddest and most unamiable habits was his practice of praising and censuring the same writer at the same time. At one moment he stands out as one of the first reviewers to appreciate the genius of Wordsworth, at the next he rounds on him for 'ludicrously' over-rating his own powers, and calls *The Excursion* 'the worst poem of any character in the English language'. At times it is difficult to believe that Wilson was wholly sane. After attacking him on numerous occasions he had the assurance to ask Wordsworth for a testimonial; and although Wordsworth complied with this request we again find Wilson planning to attack him in the *Quarterly*, after his death, as 'a fat ugly cur'. His motives are hard to understand, but much must be laid to the account of vanity and envy. He was pathologically touchy, incapable of tolerating any criticism of his own writings or character; and for all his physical prowess he was an abject moral coward. Although he was capable of generosity, as we see in his treatment of De Quincey, he had an innate love of hurting people, even if they had been kind to him. 'Though averse to being cut up myself', he once wrote, without a trace of irony, 'I like to abuse my friends.' But the thought that he himself might be exposed filled him with horror. In the words of one of the characters in his *City of the Plague* (1816),

> The violent
> Are weaker than the mild, and abject fear
> Dwells in the heart of passion.

Nowhere can Scottish sentimentality of the most objection-

able kind be studied so remorselessly as in Wilson's *Lights and Shadows of Scottish Life* (1822), which contains stories supposed to describe the simple realities in the life of the Scottish peasantry. To describe the book as the work of 'a female Wordsworth', as one critic has done, is equally unfair to Wordsworth and to women. Wilson was outraged when Henry Mackenzie (who was an expert on sentiment and sentimentality) compared the book with the work of Gessner, but Mackenzie was right. The same sentimental falseness is to be found in *The Trials of Margaret Lyndsay* (1823) and *The Foresters* (1825). Wordsworth said that he had never come on 'more mawkish stuff' than the latter book. Yet in the history of taste it is a significant document.

But it was as the main author of *Noctes Ambrosianae* that 'Christopher North' was principally celebrated. Lockhart inaugurated the series in *Blackwood's* in 1822; but its origin may be found in the imaginary dialogues which began to appear three years earlier and which contain a mixture of fact and fiction that reminds us of Lockhart's *Peter's Letters*. Although only one of the characters, James Hogg, retains his real name, most of the speakers are based to a considerable extent on real individuals, while 'Ambrose's Tavern' had a real existence under another name. The subjects of the first dialogue give an idea of the whole: 'Apparitions—Miss Foote—The Shepherd on pastoral plays—Scott's poetry—Buchanan Lodge—The Shepherd on poultry... Tickler reappears.' The popularity of the series, which ran until 1835, reminds us of the popularity of some inferior radio or television serial today: the quality of the material is low, and it is difficult now to read more than a few pages with any enjoyment. The popularity of the *Noctes* in America is not difficult to explain: they appealed to the nostalgia of exiled Scots. The series is an example of that coarsening and cheapening of Scotland and its way of life which still proves so popular with tourists. It is easy to see why this sort of dialogue suited Wilson: he was able to attribute some sentimental outburst to the Shepherd and then make Christopher North interrupt with a sarcastic comment: rather as Byron so often turns on himself with a witty couplet at the end of an octave stanza. Throughout the series Wilson was in the position that he relished: that of the man to whom all the credit is due, but who stands safe from censure or imputed responsibility. It is interesting to notice that

after his election to the Chair of Moral Philosophy in the University of Edinburgh (one of the most discreditable academic appointments ever made) Wilson wrote more, not less, in *Blackwood's*; and this in spite of the fact that he found himself pitifully unfitted to write the lectures which were required of him. In the history of literature there are few more abject spectacles than that of Professor John Wilson begging his obscure friend Alexander Blair to write his lectures for him, and so save him from ignominy: for years the letters went on, and Blair, Wilson's Jamesian phantom, seems hardly ever to have let him down. At times Wilson (as Professor) seems to have been little more than a ventriloquist's dummy; but he had a fine appearance, and his students were deeply impressed. So long as he could not be brought to book for what he wrote, on the other hand, his pen moved rapidly and with pleasure, and many of his articles bear signs of the talent that his contemporaries attributed to him—though none gives any hint of the genius that they believed him to possess. There is an unreality about 'Christopher North' that makes him uninteresting in one way and fascinating in another. Carlyle saw through him better than most, as one would expect. He remains a tempting subject for psycho-analytical inquiry.

It is refreshing to turn from a man as unreal as 'Christopher North' to a woman as real as Mary Russell Mitford.[1] When the sketches which make up *Our Village* began to appear in the *Lady's Magazine* Miss Mitford was already known as an authoress: she had published several volumes of verse, in which Coleridge had taken an interest, and she was on the point of pro-

[1] Mary Russell Mitford (1787–1855) was born at Alresford in Hampshire. She was the only child of George Mitford, a man with a mania for speculation, gambling, and the game of whist. Although he was described by someone who knew him well as 'a detestable old humbug' he never lost the affection of his wife and daughter. At the age of ten Mary Mitford chose him a ticket in a lottery which won him £20,000, and with the proceeds he built a house in Reading. Her first publication, *Poems*, appeared in 1810. By 1820 her father's extravagance made it necessary for her to turn to literature as a source of income. The family removed to a cottage at Three Mile Cross, a village between Reading and Basingstoke, where they lived for the next thirty years. Her tragedy, *Julian*, was performed at Covent Garden in 1823 with Macready in the title-role: *Foscari* and *Rienzi* were even more successful. Meanwhile *Our Village* made its author a celebrity. Her mother died in 1830, but her father lived on until 1842, and in spite of her very considerable earnings Miss Mitford knew no respite from financial troubles. Although *Belford Regis* (1835) contains some agreeable sketches, the effects of strain are beginning to be apparent. After her father's death his remaining debts were paid off by a public subscription. In 1851 Miss Mitford removed to the village of Swallowfield, where she died.

ducing three or four poetic tragedies. Yet posterity has agreed with Elizabeth Barrett in holding that Miss Mitford 'stands higher as the authoress of *Our Village* than of *Rienzi*, and writes prose better than poetry, and transcends rather in Dutch minuteness and high finishing, than in Italian ideality and passion'. Her aim was to write a collection of 'essays and characters and stories, chiefly of country life, in the manner of the "Sketch Book", but without sentimentality or pathos—two things which I abhor'. While Washington Irving's book no doubt helped to give her the idea it is to her own delightful letters that a modern reader is likely to turn when he is searching for a background to *Our Village*. She describes the pleasure which letter-writing gave her in an article 'On Letters and Letter-Writers' in the *New Monthly Magazine* for 1821:

> How delightful it is to sit down and prattle to a dear friend just as carelessly as if we were seated in real talk, with our feet on the fender, by that glimmering fire-light when talk comes freest; sure that every half-word will be understood, that every trifle will interest, and every story amuse. . . . How delightful it is to pour out all one's thoughts and fancies with such a certainty of indulgence and sympathy.

The fact that she mentions Walpole, Voltaire, Shaftesbury, Hume, Johnson, Richardson, and half a dozen others within four pages makes it clear that she was a great reader of the collections of letters which had become numerous since the later eighteenth century. It is interesting to notice her objection to Gray's letters: 'Gray's letters are very clever, very poetical, very picturesque, but they want the good-nature, the constitutional kindliness: respect and admire him we must, and we do; but to love a man dead or alive it is necessary that he should know how to love too.' In the letters of Mme de Sévigné and of Cowper she found that 'tenderness and sweetness', that 'spirit of indulgence and of love to [our] kind' which she missed in Gray, and these are qualities everywhere apparent in her own letters.

As she herself pointed out, a great many of the poems in her first collection were 'addresses to private friends', and throughout her life the fact that she had friends with whom she could share her experiences meant a great deal to her. Before *Our Village* began to appear she corresponded with Sir William Elford, Haydon, and Talfourd (who acted as her literary adviser),

and soon she was also exchanging letters with Lamb, R. H. Horne, Ruskin, Elizabeth Barrett, and Landor. Although her life was one long battle to keep her impossible father from bankruptcy we notice that her letters contain remarkably few complaints. It was simply that writing about her own life and the daily events of the village helped her to find a point of stability in the perpetual uncertainty and insecurity caused by her father's extravagance. She was far from a self-regarding correspondent: on the contrary she was a woman who delighted in giving pleasure, and her letters were written with that object in view. In many ways she reminds us of Lamb, whose *Essays* were also the product of his talent as a correspondent; yet unlike him she was not concerned to create a *persona*, to project a literary personality. Her style is much simpler than his. It is without the archaisms and mannerisms that are so evident in Lamb, a good, fluent, unselfconscious epistolary style, always her servant and never her master. It is so unobtrusive that we tend to underestimate the skill with which it is deployed, and it is as well to remember her remark to Talfourd, 'what looks like ease in my style is labour'.

In her very first sketch Miss Mitford gives us an admirable account of her own scope and interests, a reminder—if reminder is needed—that she was completely aware of what she was doing. 'Even in books', she wrote,

> I like a confined locality, and so do the critics when they talk of the unities. . . . Nothing is so delightful as to sit down in a country village in one of Miss Austen's delicious novels, quite sure before we leave it to become intimate with every spot and every person it contains; or to ramble with Mr. White over his own parish of Selborne, and form a friendship with the fields and coppices, as well as with the birds, mice, and squirrels, who inhabit them.

So she gives us her double theme, 'country scenery and country manners' (as she puts it in the preface), 'as they exist in a small village in the south of England'. It seems an obvious subject to choose, yet a moment's reflection reminds one that it would have been inconceivable a century before; and in spite of all the imitations since the thing has hardly been so well done again.

As we read these sketches we notice that Miss Mitford writes as a countrywoman. If she is concerned with outdoor life or

scenery she begins by describing the season of the year and the state of the weather: 'April 18th.—Sad wintery weather; a north-east wind; a sun that puts out one's eyes, without affording the slightest warmth; dryness that chaps lips and hands like a frost in December; rain that comes chilling and arrowy like hail in January; nature at a dead pause.' The third essay gives an admirable description of the effects of frost on the landscape:

There had been just snow enough to cover the earth and all its colours with one sheet of pure and uniform white, and just time enough since the snow had fallen to allow the hedges to be freed of their fleecy load, and clothed with a delicate coating of rime. The atmosphere was deliciously calm; soft, even mild, in spite of the thermometer; no perceptible air, but a stillness that might almost be felt: the sky, rather grey than blue, throwing out in bold relief the snow-covered roofs of our village, and the rimy trees that rise above them, and the sun shining dimly as through a veil, giving a pale fair light, like the moon, only brighter. There was a silence, too, that might become the moon, as we stood at our little gate looking up the quiet street; a sabbath-like pause of work and play, rare on a work-day; nothing was audible but the pleasant hum of frost, that low monotonous sound, which is perhaps the nearest approach that life and nature can make to absolute silence.

At times her descriptions of landscape remind us vividly of painting. 'What a pretty picture they would make', she remarks of a child and a dog in the first essay:

What a pretty foreground they do make to the real landscape! The road winding down the hill with a slight bend, like that in the High-street at Oxford; a waggon slowly ascending, and a horseman passing it at a full trot; . . . half-way down, just at the turn, the red cottage of the lieutenant, covered with vines, the very image of comfort and content; farther down, on the opposite side, the small white building of the little mason; then the limes and the rope-walk; then the village street, peeping through the trees, whose clustering tops hide all but the chimneys, and various roofs of the houses, and here and there some angle of a wall: farther on, the elegant town of B—, with its fine old church-towers and spires; the whole view shut in by a range of chalky hills; and over every part of the picture, trees so profusely scattered, that it appears like a woodland scene, with glades and villages intermixed.

In another early essay she describes 'a deep, woody, green lane such as Hobbema or Ruysdael might have painted' and it is clear that her power of visualizing had been strengthened by a characteristic enjoyment of prints and paintings. In her own sketches the Village—as she puts it—sits for its picture, and she often refers to herself in similar terms, as when she replies to Sir William Elford's question about the authenticity of her descriptions:

> 'Are the characters and descriptions true?' Yes! yes! yes! As true as is well possible. You, as a great landscape painter, know that in painting a favourite scene you do a little embellish, and can't help it; you avail yourself of happy accidents of atmosphere, and if anything be ugly you strike it out, or if anything be wanting, you put it in. But still the picture is a likeness.

Some of her descriptions of people are strongly reminiscent of portraiture and caricature. Her description of 'the insides' in the coach, for example, in 'Walks in the Country: The Hard Summer':

> How well I remember the fat gentleman without his coat, who was wiping his forehead, heaving up his wig, and certainly uttering that English ejaculation, which, to our national reproach, is the phrase of our language best known on the continent. And that poor boy, red-hot, all in a flame, whose mamma, having divested her own person of all superfluous apparel, was trying to relieve his sufferings by the removal of his neck-kerchief—an operation which he resisted with all his might. How perfectly I remember him, as well as the pale girl who sate opposite, fanning herself with her bonnet into an absolute fever! They vanished after a while in their own dust; but I have them all before my eyes at this moment, a companion-picture to Hogarth's Afternoon, a standing lesson to the grumblers at cold summers.

As such a passage demonstrates, Miss Mitford was as good with 'country manners' as with 'country scenery'. Yet her longest narrative, *Atherton*, bears out her own opinion that she had not been born to write novels. 'I have begun two', she once wrote, 'and got on very well as long as I stuck to landscape and portrait painting; but when I was obliged to make my pictures walk out of their frames and speak for themselves, when I came to the action, I was foundered.' In *Our Village* she gives us little dialogue, but she excels at describing characters

in a manner that sometimes reminds us of the essayists of the eighteenth century:

> Of these the most notable was my friend Tom Cordery, who presented in his own person no unfit emblem of the district in which he lived—the gentlest of savages, the wildest of civilised men. He was by calling rat-catcher, hare-finder, and broom-maker; a triad of trades which he had substituted for the one grand profession of poaching, which he followed in his younger days with unrivalled talent and success, and would, undoubtedly, have pursued till his death, had not the bursting of an overloaded gun unluckily shot off his left hand. As it was, he still contrived to mingle a little of his old unlawful occupation with his honest callings; was a reference of high authority amongst the young aspirants, an adviser of undoubted honour and secrecy—suspected, and more than suspected, of being one 'who, though he played no more, o'erlooked the cards'.

Equally fine is 'The Talking Lady':

> The manner of her speech has little remarkable. It is rather old-fashioned and provincial, but perfectly lady-like, low and gentle, and not seeming so fast as it is; like the great pedestrians she clears her ground easily, and never seems to use any exertion; yet 'I would my horse had the speed of her tongue, and so good a continuer'. She will talk you sixteen hours a day for twenty days together, and not deduct one poor five minutes for halts and baiting time. Talking, sheer talking, is meat and drink and sleep to her. She likes nothing else.

She is capable of a damaging wit, as when she observes of 'An Old Bachelor' who has been a Fellow of a College in his day that he 'spoke so little, that people really fell into the mistake of imagining that he thought'. But understanding and enjoyment are her native element, not censure: she takes a delight in the human scene that recalls Charles Lamb, as when she describes the curate's landlord and landlady:

> Never were better or kinder people than his host and hostess: and there is a reflection of clerical importance about them, since their connection with the Church, which is quite edifying—a decorum, a gravity, a solemn politeness. Oh, to see the worthy wheeler carry the gown after his lodger on a Sunday, nicely pinned up in his wife's best handkerchief—or to hear him rebuke a squalling child or a squabbling woman! The curate is nothing to him. He is fit to be perpetual churchwarden.

What she says of 'Lucy' is equally true of herself: 'She was

a very charitable reporter too; threw her own sunshine into the shady places, and would hope and doubt as long as either was possible.' In her steady and deliberate emphasis on the agreeable aspects of life she reminds us above all of Leigh Hunt. She shared his genius for enjoyment, and was determined to set her face against the vogue of melancholy. It is not surprising that she knew and relished Matthew Green's delightful poem, *The Spleen*, which she quotes from in 'The Cowslip-Ball'.

Landor's long life[1]—he was born nine years before the death of Dr. Johnson and died in the year that saw the publication of Browning's *Dramatis Personæ*—makes it necessary for his work to be divided between this and the previous volume, and our concern is exclusively with his prose, and particularly the *Imaginary Conversations*. He seems first to have experimented with the dialogue form about 1802, when he appears to have written a dialogue between Burke and Lord Grenville and another between Henry IV and Arnold Savage. Both of these early dialogues must have dealt with politics. Some twenty years later we find Landor discussing the use of dialogue in his letters to Southey, who was at work on *Sir Thomas More: or, Colloquies on the Progress and Prospects of Society*. Southey acknowledges that his model has been Boethius and that his dialogues are 'consecutive' —merely a formal device to enable him to express his views on the condition of England—but takes it for granted that Landor will aim at a 'dramatic variety' foreign to his own intentions. At times there is no doubt that Landor took the view that his own dialogues were essentially dramatic. On one occasion he told Browning that he was 'more of a dramatist in prose than in poetry'. *Count Julian* had failed to reach the stage. Would it then be a true account of what happened to say that Landor was a man with a natural bent for the drama who found the times

[1] Walter Savage Landor (1775–1864) was educated at Rugby and at Trinity College, Oxford, from which he was rusticated in 1794. After three years at Tenby and Swansea he visited Paris, moved about between Bath, Bristol, and Wells, and fought as a volunteer in Spain. In 1808 he had bought Llanthony Abbey in Monmouthshire, and three years later he married Julia Thuillier. After a quarrel with the authorities at Llanthony he travelled abroad. In 1818 he was ordered to leave Como on account of an insult in one of his Latin poems. He spent most of the next 17 years in Italy. In 1835 he quarrelled with his wife and left Italy. From 1837 to 1858 he lived at Bath: then he returned to Florence. Browning admired him greatly. He was a passionate man of an abnormally irritable temper: it would be difficult to find any writer whose works had to be published by so many different publishers.

unpropitious and therefore took to writing 'imaginary conversations' instead of plays?

Some of the *Conversations* do reveal a certain dramatic sense. In 'Lord Bacon and Richard Hooker', in which the latter consoles the former for his fall from power, the way in which Bacon's supposed lack of wisdom and self-knowledge peeps out on every page is extremely dramatic—not least the exclamation with which he curses his servant for offering Hooker 'the beverage I reserve for myself'. The same is true of 'Leofric and Godiva'. In 'Leonora di Este and Father Panigarola' Leonora's passionate desire to hear that she is still the beloved of Tasso, although she is under sentence of death, is conveyed with an extraordinary economy of means and with a psychological insight that sets us speculating about Browning's debt to Landor. Yet these are three of the shortest of the *Conversations*, and they are hardly representative. Wordsworth criticized the dialogue between Landor himself and the Abbé Delille shrewdly when he said that 'the observations are invariably just . . .; but they are fitter for illustrative notes than the body of a Dialogue, which ought always to have some little spice of dramatic effect'. In the end there were some hundred and fifty *Imaginary Conversations*, and it is natural that some of them should be more dramatic than others; but as we read through them we find more and more often that dramatic effect is far to seek because Landor is less concerned with creating vivid men and women than with expressing his own views on human affairs. In his dialogue with Middleton Landor makes Magliabechi suggest 'that Cicero had asserted things incredible to himself, merely for the sake of argument, and had probably written them before he had fixed in his mind the personages to whom they should be attributed in his dialogues'; and this was no doubt true of Landor's own practice. R. H. Super has pointed out (for example) that 'Washington and Franklin' began life as an essay on the Irish problem; when he revised it Landor broke it up into speeches which he had no hesitation in shifting from one speaker to another. From boyhood onwards he had a strong desire to comment on life, often in the most passionate terms; yet he found any kind of systematic exposition, or sustained logical argument, extremely difficult to present. The dialogue therefore offered itself as a mode of expression well suited to his unusual temperament.

From the first politics are the most constant subject of the

*Conversations*. He set out most of his political views in 1812, in his *Commentary on Memoirs of Mr. Fox*. It was a characteristic production. 'From the manner, from the force, from the vehemence, I concluded it must be yours', Southey wrote, 'even before I fell upon the passage respecting Spain which proves that it was yours.' The book was so controversial that Landor was obliged to suppress it, but it remains of interest because it sums up so many of the views that are to be found throughout the *Imaginary Conversations*. Landor believed that if Fox's policy were pursued it would prove 'most fatal to our interests and glory': the book is dedicated to the President of the United States and deplores the war towards which Canning's policy seemed to Landor to be leading. The arrangement of the *Commentary* is characteristically unsystematic: Landor simply takes one passage after another from Trotter's *Memoirs* and uses it as a text for the expression of his own views. One of the more convincing and eloquent passages is that in which he contrasts the sentence of death that may be passed on a poor woman for a trivial theft with the lenient treatment of Viscount Melville. Once or twice Landor digresses to discuss literary matters: 'it is soothing to take the last view of politics from among the works of the imagination', as he comments towards the end of the text, '. . . [and] escape in this manner from the mazes of politics and the discord of party'; but in the postscript he is back in the thick of the political battle. The whole work makes it clear that passion was the main motive behind Landor's political views. If politics is the art of the practicable, he was as unfitted for politics as any man has ever been. He can be eloquent and moving on generalities, but he is incapable of consistency and has a fatal tendency to see complicated issues in terms of black and white. His insistence on the importance to statesmen of a knowledge of history contrasts markedly with his own lack of political understanding. He read history in an oddly Plutarchian way, as the lives of great men, and had no interest in the functioning of political institutions. At one time he intended to collaborate with Southey on a large-scale historical work. Later he thought of writing a History of England since 1775, the year of his own birth and of the outbreak of the War of American Independence. Undramatic as it is, the conversation between Washington and Franklin is one of the clearest statements of his own political views. In the years following Waterloo he was a passionate opponent of the Holy

Alliance and a passionate supporter of the nations that were striving for independence. He regarded Canning's attitude to the freedom-seeking nations as culpably half-hearted and returned his own Spanish title and decoration in protest against the behaviour of the King of Spain. England's treatment of Ireland was a subject to which he reverted time and time again. He supported Catholic emancipation, while frequently satirizing the superstitious element in the religious practices of the Catholic Church. We notice that a number of his *Conversations* include confessors, notably the highly satiric dialogue between Louis XIV and Father La Chaise. Landor hated all wielders of power: it is appropriate that one of the first of all the *Imaginary Conversations* should have portrayed Arnold Savage, whom he liked to regard as an ancestor of his own, warning Henry IV of the limits of kingly power. The dialogue between Cromwell and Walter Noble is of interest because it is at once a study of character and a serious discussion of the ethics of regicide. Here and elsewhere we notice that Landor's classical education made him a republican, though we may suspect that it was the idea of a republic that appealed to him, rather than the reality. He loved liberty, and despised the people.

As Wordsworth pointed out, the classical dialogues are among the best of the *Imaginary Conversations*. In one of them Cicero and his brother, who have for many years supported different sides in the civil war, meet on the day before the orator's death and talk of the fate of Rome and of the great issues of human existence. It is a dialogue at once sombre and serene, slow-moving yet impressive in an unusual way. The conversation between Aeschines and Phocion is less impressive, although in Phocion (the just man who despises the fickle mob) Landor found an excellent *persona* for his own character as he liked to imagine it. Nothing could be more maladroit than the way in which Aeschines suddenly asks: 'What is your opinion on the right and expediency of making wills?', so providing Phocion with an opportunity of delivering a discourse on the subject. Landor liked to regard Epicurus as his master, and his own favourite *Conversation* was the one in which he portrays the philosopher talking with two girl-disciples, Leontion and Ternissa. In it he touches on a number of his favourite topics: the praise of solitude, the fact that death is not to be feared, and in general the art of living a serene and happy life. It is charmingly done, and

just a trifle absurd: Peacock, one feels, would have handled the ending with more tact. In general it is difficult to believe in Landor's Greeks and Romans. He was a passionate admirer of the classics, and he reflected a good deal on the characters of the great men and women who were for him the makers of history; yet it is evident that his Epicurus and Aristotle are monuments of nineteenth-century classicism rather than convincing re-creations of the men who lived so many centuries ago. It may be doubted whether Landor possessed a truly historical imagination. Although what they teach is not always what is taught by schoolmasters, his Greeks and Romans remind us constantly of the classroom and the school debating club. It is ink that circulates in their veins, not blood. At times it is as if an image in Madame Tussaud's were to raise its arm and begin an oration to its neighbour. 'In such a profusion of viands, and so savoury,' Caesar remarks to Lucullus, 'I perceive no odour.' Lucullus replies: 'A flue conducts heat through the compartments of the obelisks; and if you look up, you may observe that those gilt roses, between the astragals in the cornice, are prominent from it half a span.' This is the Roman House for Sixth Forms.

*Pericles and Aspasia* (1836) began as an *Imaginary Conversation* but grew to the length of an independent book. It opens with a description of Aspasia's first meeting with Pericles at a performance of the *Prometheus Bound* of Aeschylus and ends with the death of Pericles during the plague at Athens. It is difficult to know how to classify the book: although it consists of letters it has few of the characteristics of an epistolary novel (or indeed of a novel of any kind), and in spite of eloquent passages it remains as a whole remarkably uninteresting. The *Citation and Examination of William Shakspeare* (1834) was an earlier dialogue that similarly grew to the dimensions of an independent book. In this curious work Landor has Shakespeare brought before Sir Thomas Lucy on a charge of stealing a deer. Sir Thomas condescends to the unlettered young man, not least on the subject of poetry, on which he regards himself as an authority. The humour is distinctly laboured: it is the sort of funny book that one might order with a clear conscience in the British Museum. If we compare Landor's dialogues with those in Peacock's satiric tales we notice how Peacock's wit acts as a preservative. Landor can be witty, but only sporadically: the comic view of life was not natural to him. He was too passionate, and too deficient in

a sense of proportion, to take naturally to comic writing. The nature of the third of his long conversation-books, *The Pentameron* (1837), is best indicated by its sub-title: 'Interviews of Messer Giovanni Boccaccio and Messer Francesco Petrarca, when said Messer Giovanni lay infirm at Viletta . . . after which they saw not each other on our side of Paradise: shewing how they discoursed upon that famous Theologian Messer Dante Alighieri, and sundry other matters.' By choosing Petrarch as his main speaker Landor gives himself dramatic justification for some severe judgements on Dante, whom he considered a great poet only in his finest passages. Written towards the end of Landor's prolonged sojourn at Fiesole, *The Pentameron* may be regarded as an appropriate thank-offering for one of the calmer periods in a stormy life.

Landor has often been acclaimed as a master of English prose style. In a limited sense he is. Almost everything that he ever wrote is either a copy of verses or a prose composition. His prose demands high marks from the examiner; but unfortunately it refuses to come alive. A dozen critics have noticed that it has the air of a distinguished translation from some great classical original. He was the kind of classicist who lacks the instinctive feeling for conversational and colloquial English that is so evident in the verse of the equally classical Praed. It is not just that his dialogue is mannered and stylized: so is Peacock's, which has a vivacity that is not to be found in Landor. Landor would have been the better for the discipline of writing for the theatre or for broadcasting. But he was a wealthy man with few responsibilities, and this emphasized his natural disregard of his audience. He admired Pindar for his 'proud complacency and scornful strength'. 'If I could resemble him in nothing else', he once wrote, 'I was resolved to be as compendious and as exclusive.' There is truth in Byron's gibe that he was 'a gentleman who cultivated the private celebrity of writing Latin verses'. His life was one long angry monologue. Unfortunately he lacked the intellectual power to be a profound commentator on human life. It would be a solecism to compare him with Plato, whom he wilfully underestimated; but if one thinks for a moment of Johnson or of Burke, Landor's limitations become almost embarrassingly evident. He had a gift for stating his own convictions with eloquence and passion, but he shrank from close argument and seldom condescended to examine the premisses on which

his opinions were based. He is the King Lear of English literary history, and in nothing does he resemble Lear more markedly than in his profound lack of self-knowledge. There is a startling lack of a sense of reality about a man who could talk, as Landor did, of chastising an attorney in a forthcoming Latin poem. There is more wisdom in any one of Hazlitt's essays than in a dozen of the *Imaginary Conversations*.

# XIII

# HISTORY, BIOGRAPHY, AND AUTOBIOGRAPHY

ALTHOUGH no historical work comparable with Gibbon's *Decline and Fall of the Roman Empire* or Macaulay's *History of England from the Accession of James II* was published in this period, the work of Hallam and his contemporaries deserves attention both because it illustrates some of the motives that led men to study history in the earlier part of the century and because the books they wrote, combining with the immense influence of the romances of Sir Walter Scott, provided the great Victorians with the material from which they derived their sense of the past. Henry Hallam, the father of Tennyson's friend, tells us that the aim of his *View of the State of Europe during the Middle Ages* (1818) is to give 'a comprehensive survey of the chief circumstances that can interest a philosophical enquirer'.[1] His intention is to avoid mere annals and to concentrate on events 'essentially concatenated with others, or illustrative of important conclusions'. He is more concerned with 'modes of government and constitutional laws' than with battles and the minutiae of political history, and has no hesitation in passing rapidly over periods which seem to him of little importance: 'Many considerable portions of time, especially before the twelfth century, may justly be deemed so barren of events . . . that a single sentence or paragraph is often sufficient.' The book consists of a series of dissertations, instead of a narrative, and is noteworthy for such chapters as those 'On the State of Society in Europe' and 'On the Feudal System, especially in France'. Hallam insists on the importance of understanding feudalism because of its bearing on the English constitution, and because 'one of the parties which at present divide [France] professes to appeal to the original principles of its monarchy, as they subsisted before the subversion of that polity'. It is characteristic of Hallam that

[1] Henry Hallam (1777–1859) was educated at Eton and Christ Church. He became a barrister, and was appointed a commissioner of stamps. He was an occasional contributor to the *Edinburgh Review*.

when he published a *Supplemental Volume* thirty years later he refused to make it necessary for readers to buy a revision of the work as a whole: no less characteristic that he had not in many instances 'seen ground for materially altering [his] views'. Once a phrenologist said that Hallam was a musician, Macaulay 'a landscape painter or historical painter'. It was an apt mistake. Although the two men shared many of their political views, their attitude to history is quite different. Hallam is not concerned with the trappings of history, nor does he attempt to put himself in the place of the men of the past: he is interested in attitudes and themes rather than in human beings: his view of historical truth is essentially abstract. His work lacks the extraordinary vividness of Macaulay's. As Mignet put it, 'il a plutôt l'intelligence que le sentiment du passé'. His legal training fitted him admirably for his *Constitutional History of England* (1827). He begins in the reign of Henry VII and stops at the end of that of George II, but in spite of his 'unwillingness to excite the prejudices of modern politics' his political views colour his whole reading of history and greatly increase its interest for us today. He is excellent on the terms Whig and Tory in the early eighteenth century, insisting that they 'have become equivocal, and do by no means, at all periods and on all occasions, present the same sense'. It is magnificent, though it is not Namier. Appearing as it did four years before the Reform Bill, his book ended, suitably enough, with a discussion of the 'extraordinary traffic' in seats in the House of Commons in the later eighteenth century. Unlike his first book, his *Constitutional History* was carefully revised, and it long remained a work of the first importance. 'It became and has remained a text-book in the Universities,' as Gooch wrote half a century ago, 'was quoted as an oracle in Parliament, and was studied as a guide by the youthful Victoria and her Consort. . . . It was inwardly digested by the friends of constitutional liberty all over the world.' Southey described it as 'Hallam's essence of Whig vinegar'. Like his second book, Hallam's third derives from his first. His *Introduction to the Literature of Europe in the Fifteenth, Sixteenth, and Seventeenth Centuries* (1837–9) deals with literature in the widest sense. On imaginative literature he is often illuminating, but frequently ill-informed and perverse. He is commonly much more interesting on poets and men of letters who are of importance in the history of ideas—men like Hooker and Milton. In dealing with the history of

philosophy he is lucid and persuasive, though hardly incisive. One can only admire the learning and the courage that carry him on through the literature of theology, mathematics, classical scholarship, physical science, and the rest. Whereas his previous book had been adversely reviewed in the *Quarterly*, his last work was praised to excess. As Hallam himself noted, such praise is apt to set one against him, but his *Introduction to the Literature of Europe* remains a remarkable achievement, as well as a remarkable attempt.

The views of John Lingard were as different from those of Hallam as one man's can be from another's.[1] His first important publication had been *The Antiquities of the Anglo-Saxon Church* (1806), and throughout his *History of England* (of which the first three volumes deal with the period before Henry VIII) his main aim is to show that the Reformation had been the fundamental disaster in English history. Lingard was a priest, and seems to be the first Roman Catholic to have written a full-scale History of England. His learning was very considerable, for his day, and the *Edinburgh Review* conceded that 'the fabric he has raised against the Reformation is reared by no vulgar hand'. His treatment of the early medieval period is superior to anything in preceding writers, and justifies his claim to have gone to the fountain-head of original sources. The attacks of the fanatical Catholic Bishop Milner show that Lingard was far from an extremist. Perhaps it would be fair to say that he is as impartial as any man can be whose general interpretation of history is determined before he begins his research. His religious bias becomes more obvious in his later volumes. He is opposed to 'the philosophy of history': as far as he is concerned what the Church proclaims as right, is right: what happened, happened. As a reviewer complained, 'he has no generous sympathy in the cause of freedom'. To the caricatures which had so long passed for likenesses of the leaders of the Roman Catholic Church he opposes caricatures of their opponents. His indignation is reserved for the wrongs done to his Church: the wrongs done by it are first minimized and then dispassionately chronicled. He is concerned to identify the Anglo-Saxon Church with the Roman Catholic,

[1] John Lingard (1771–1851) studied at the English College at Douay and was ordained and appointed vice-president of Crookhall College, near Durham, at the age of 24. He visited Rome in 1817 and 1825. He played a considerable part in the jurisdiction of the Roman Catholic Church in this country. In 1821 he was honoured by the Pope. His *History of England* went through five editions by the middle of the century.

and exaggerates the civilizing influence of the introduction of Christianity into Britain. His attitude to Calvinism is quite unfair, while his portrayal of the Puritans is reminiscent of *Hudibras*. Lessons learned from Hume and Gibbon are used to the disparagement of Protestantism. He has a strong bias against the Scots and the Welsh. 'Candour', in the fine eighteenth-century sense, is completely lacking. Yet he revised his work with care, and defended himself vigorously—though without ever giving the impression of having an open mind. He remains important for his genuine interest in medieval England, for his early and strong opposition to the Whig interpretation of history which dominated his century, and for the influence which his idealization of the Middle Ages exerted on many writers of his own time and the subsequent age. It is curious what an important part one exaggerated view of the Middle Ages and another have played in the history of later thought and feeling. Myth is more powerful than truth and does more to shape the course of human history. The influence of Lingard may be detected in the Oxford Movement and in many other currents of thought in the nineteenth century. His interpretation of the Middle Ages supplied nourishment to men whose views differed from his own as widely as did those of Cobbett and William Morris. The inspiration which the men of the eighteenth century had derived from the Noble Savage was often to be found by their successors in an idealized portrayal of the Middle Ages.

There is no room for more than a reference to Napier's *History of the War in the Peninsula* or Milman's *History of the Jews*, *History of Christianity*, and *History of Latin Christianity*. Patrick Fraser Tytler's *History of Scotland* is not without merit, yet one can only regret that Scott did not undertake the task himself, instead of suggesting it to one of his younger friends. James Mill's *History of British India* (1817) shows a much greater stretch of mind than Fraser Tytler was capable of, whether or not the result is better history.[1] Mill's aim was to give India 'a good sys-

[1] James Mill (1773–1836) was educated at the University of Edinburgh and licensed to preach in 1798. Four years later he moved to London and engaged in journalism, meeting Bentham in 1808 and soon losing his interest in theology. He was prominent in the movement that led to the foundation of University College, London. In 1819 he entered the India House. He was a friend of Ricardo's, encouraging him to publish his revolutionary views on political economy. Although he was not the editor of the *Westminster Review*, he was one of the principal contributors. The manner in which he educated his son is described in the *Autobiography of John Stuart Mill*.

tem of judicial procedure' and a judicial establishment capable of carrying it out, and this was to be done on Benthamite lines: as Bentham said, 'Mill will be the living executive—I shall be the dead legislative of British India'. Mill's immense volumes are an example of History harnessed for the purposes of practical reform. It is characteristic of Mill that he should have been able to argue that his never having been in India was in some ways an advantage: it is not merely that he is determined to avoid stirring narrative and picturesque description: it does not occur to him that the atmosphere of a country can be relevant to an historian or even to a reformer. This is history 'seraphically free From taint of personality'. The historian must understand 'the laws of human nature', but these are rather abstractly considered: he must also study 'the principles of human society' and 'the practical play of the machinery of government'. Mill seems to set himself deliberately to damp the kind of interest in Hindu civilization that the writings of Sir William Jones and others had encouraged, and the result is a sort of intellectual steam-roller which crushes flat the whole complex structure of traditional Indian society, as well as the flagrant abuses of the Company and its agents. The book is written entirely without charm and sometimes without clarity, and greatly as one is impressed by the vigour of Mill's intellect, one becomes more and more convinced, as one reads on, that human nature and human history are too subtle and complex to be treated in this manner. Macaulay's exaggerated praise of the book as the greatest historical work since Gibbon prompted Maine's no less exaggerated censure when he claimed that Mill's inaccuracy was equalled only by his bad faith.

On the whole it was not a period of distinguished historical writing; nor was it a period in which historical works sold very widely. Except for the work of Sir Francis Palgrave, whose style is intolerable but who advanced some important hypotheses about Anglo-Saxon England, the Record Commission had accomplished little, and Harris Nicolas was justified in the aggressive tone of the *Observations on the State of Historical Literature* which he addressed to the Home Secretary in 1830. 'The History of England', he wrote at the beginning of his book,

> is not merely imperfect and erroneous, but . . . discreditable to a country which boasts of intellectual pre-eminence over surrounding

nations. . . . If proof be demanded, it will be found in this incontrovertible fact, that whenever a contemporary document is discovered, and its contents are compared with our best historians, their narratives either receive elucidation which gives a new colouring to the transaction, or, as frequently happens, their representations are proved to be false.

One reason for this, as he goes on to explain in a chapter on the 'Want of Encouragement of Science and Literature', was that 'no remuneration whatever is to be derived from the publication of a standard Historical book, by which is meant works containing letters or other historical evidence, or treating of any particular event in English History'. It is difficult even to find a publisher for a work embodying original research. Perhaps Nicolas is looking on the gloomy side of things, but he is a witness of verity, and it is curious to realize that this was the position when Macaulay was on the threshold of his life's work—a History for which he succeeded in securing as large a circulation as that of a best-selling novel.

When we turn from history to biography we are at once confronted by Lockhart's *Memoirs of the Life of Sir Walter Scott, Bart.*, one of the few biographies that deserve the compliment of comparison with Boswell's *Life of Samuel Johnson.*[1] There are obvious parallels between the two men. Like Boswell, Lockhart was an aspiring Scots advocate whose father was unsympathetic to his literary ambitions. Like Boswell, he had already made something of a name for himself in literature before he met the most famous writer of his day, a man a generation older than himself. Scott took an immediate liking to the younger man, as Johnson did to Boswell, and hoped to draw out the best in him and save him from his own bad habits—in Lockhart's case, a marked tendency to cruel personal satire. Like Johnson, Scott came to rely on the younger man to a considerable extent—and perhaps it would have been better if he had relied on him more. In marrying the great man's daughter Lockhart may seem merely to have done the one thing that was impossible for Bos-

[1] John Gibson Lockhart (1794–1854) was educated at the University of Glasgow and at Balliol College, Oxford. He became an advocate in 1816 and began to play a leading part in *Blackwood's Magazine* the following year. In 1818 he met Scott, and two years later married his daughter Sophia. He was editor of the *Quarterly Review* from 1825 to 1853.

well, but which would logically have completed the pattern of his devotion. The great difference was that Lockhart was no hero-worshipper and seems to have had no intention of becoming Scott's biographer. He lacked the warm enthusiasm of Boswell's temperament—he regarded Boswell as a fool who happened to write a great book—and there is nothing to suggest that he intended to write Scott's life until he received the request contained in his will. The first definite reference to the *Life* in Lang's biography of Lockhart occurs in a letter to Robert Cadell written in 1835, while Lockhart was editing Scott's writings. 'Perhaps I may promise a volume of my own reminiscences of our intercourse and fireside talk', he remarks. 'I never thought of being a Boswell, but I have a fair memory, and to me he no doubt spoke more freely and fully on various affairs than to any other who now survives.' This is very different from Boswell, who tells us that he had a biography 'constantly in view' during the whole of the twenty years that he knew Johnson, and who was certainly collecting materials at intervals throughout the greater part of that period with a 'labour and anxious attention' which has been the admiration of his readers ever since.

Yet Lockhart produced a very remarkable book, and the first of its merits is its fullness. He distinguishes the different stages of Scott's career and shows how one evolved from another. He quotes the critic who said that the *Border Minstrelsy* contained 'the elements of a hundred historical romances' and emphasizes that the poems and prose romances which followed them owe a great deal to the researches lying behind these early volumes. Throughout his *Life*, indeed, we see the lame child becoming a boy, the boy becoming a young man with a passion for riding and picturesque excursions, the young man becoming a ballad-collector, the ballad-collector becoming an original writer, and so on to the end. He knew from Scott's own conversation that his imaginative inspiration was essentially local, springing from particular scenes and places and their history in the past, and he keeps reminding us of this essential part of the story. Lockhart was admirably qualified to be Scott's biographer by his close understanding of the milieu in which he grew up. He understands the bleak asceticism of the religion of Scott's father, and the influence that this had on his son's development. He understands the important difference in social status between an

advocate and a Writer to the Signet. He understands the amount of work involved in being a Principal Clerk of Session, so saving us from the sort of misconception into which Wordsworthian students have often fallen through supposing his Distributorship of Stamps a mere sinecure. Lockhart knew more than most people about the way in which Scott organized his daily life, and so made time to undertake such a prodigious amount of writing. He is most illuminating on Scott's passionate Toryism. Although Scott had been drawn to the younger man partly because there were not many thorough-going Tories among the men of letters in Edinburgh, Lockhart soon found that Scott tended to the 'purple' in a way with which he had not much sympathy; and he most interestingly relates this to Scott's resentment at 'the implied suspicion of his having accepted something like a personal obligation at the hands of adverse politicians' when his appointment as Clerk was ratified by a Whig Ministry. Having lived for considerable periods in London, Lockhart knew that Scott had always breathed 'the hot atmosphere of a very narrow scene' as far as politics were concerned. One of the most interesting things in the book is his exposition of the difference between the type of conversation admired in Edinburgh—'the talk of a society to which lawyers and lecturers had, for at least a hundred years, given the tone'—and the less combative form of conversation admired and practised in the south (the latter being much more congenial to Scott himself). Everywhere Lockhart provides illuminating details, such as the information that Scott had little ear for music, little sense of smell, and no delicacy of taste in matters of food and wine.

Lockhart makes it clear that he does not wish 'to Boswellize Scott' and says that his aim is to make him, as far as possible, 'his own historiographer'. There was no shortage of materials: Scott was a highly autobiographical writer, and although Lockhart seems not to have come on his fragmentary Autobiography until the *Life* was nearly completed, he had at his disposal the prefaces to the collected edition of *The Waverley Novels*, as well as thousands of Scott's letters, his unpublished Journal, and such things as the 'Essay on Imitations of the Ballad'. To this we must add the letter-books in which Scott kept the letters which he received, the earlier biographical accounts of Scott, and the reminiscences and memoranda sent to Lockhart by a great many of Scott's friends. When we come to consider the use Lock-

hart made of his materials, however, we find him not very scrupulous. In dealing with Scott's letters, for example, he does not hesitate to improve the English, omit passages without notice, conflate two different letters, or misdate. While this exasperated Grierson, it may be argued that few biographers scrupled to behave in this way until very recently. But Lockhart's inaccuracy goes farther. He did not have Boswell's passionate belief in the importance of every fact connected with his subject. He would not have run half across London to verify a date—or even half across Edinburgh. It is difficult to imagine Boswell writing the words: 'To this excursion he probably devoted the few weeks of an autumnal vacation—whether in 1786 or 1787, it is of no great consequence to ascertain': in fact it was an excursion which was of some importance to Scott's imaginative development. Lockhart's attitude may be that of common sense, but Boswell's is that of the dedicated biographer. Boswell would not have misdated the publication of *The Vanity of Human Wishes* by a month, as Lockhart does with *The Heart of Mid-Lothian*. Lockhart's unfairness to the Ballantynes may be regarded as more serious, at least from a moral point of view. As the author of a *Refutation* of Lockhart's 'Mistatements and Calumnies' pointed out in 1838, we find in his 'sketch of John Ballantyne's early history . . . a laboured particularity, and seeming accuracy of specification, calculated to impose upon the reader, and to induce a belief that it must have been drawn up from detailed, as well as authentic information. But a more erroneous notion could not possibly be entertained.' It is not for nothing that Lockhart admired Defoe, with his talent for 'lying like truth'. The biographer of Scott has no right over the reputations of lesser men with whom he was associated, but in his handling of the Ballantyne episode Lockhart shows himself an advocate of the unscrupulous sort—and an advocate with as little respect for his judges as for his opponents. As a young contributor to *Blackwood's* he had been famous for his stunts and his lies, and the habit of disrespect for the truth never left him, as may be seen in *Peter's Letters*. It is impossible to read his reply to the pamphlet just quoted, which he called *The Ballantyne-Humbug Handled*, without noticing that the tone is as far from impartiality as the title, with its reminiscence of the polemics of the seventeenth century. He shows a contemptuous disdain for the low fellows who were in fact among Scott's close associates.

Cadell congratulated him on the 'Rembrandt portraits' of the Ballantynes, which made him weep for joy (and also, perhaps, with relief); but in fact they bear less resemblance to Rembrandt portraits than to the highly coloured caricatures that Lockhart loved to produce. His natural turn was for satire, and he was quite capable of satirizing where he also admired. Yet he holds himself in check: only very seldom indeed does he allow himself such a remark as the one that Scott's days with the militia 'must have been more nobly spirit-stirring than even the best specimens of the fox-chase'. The difference between his view of things and Scott's is nowhere more evident than in his description of George IV's extraordinary visit to Edinburgh. We often catch him regarding Scott with the detached amusement of an adult watching a child at play, and are reminded of a phrase which he once used of some blue-stocking ladies, 'their great romance, *alias* absurd innocence'. Scott once told Lockhart that it was the writings of Cervantes which had inspired him to write tales, but it must have been of the creation rather than the creator that Lockhart was most often reminded as he studied the Great Unknown. Don Quixote, as he once wrote, 'is the symbol of Imagination, continually struggling and contrasted with Reality—he represents... the eternal discrepancy between the aspirations and the occupations of man, the omnipotence and the vanity of human dreams'.

The satire deployed against some of the minor characters in the *Life* may be regarded as compensation for the obligation to refrain from satirizing Scott himself. When the author of the *Refutation* described the *Life* as '*a romance of real life*—a picture of which the principal figure must be considerably flattered, and EVERY THING ELSE SACRIFICED TO ITS PROMINENCE AND EFFECT' he was exaggerating, yet his statement contains a part of the truth. Lockhart does not always gloss over what he calls 'the few darker points in his life and character'. The publishing troubles that brought about Scott's downfall may be compared (in a fine expression which Scott himself applied to Melville) to what we see 'when Providence . . . industriously turns the tapestry, to let us see the ragged ends of the worsted which compose its most beautiful figures'—the pattern *behind* the carpet. Yet we do sometimes detect some degree of romance or make-believe in the *Life*. One reason for this is that Lockhart was naturally eager to make use of the element of autobiography in Scott's

fiction; but Alan Fairford in *Redgauntlet* (for example) is a portrait of the young Scott as he thought of himself in later life, and it is hazardous to lean on romances for biographical information. Another reason is Lockhart's love of a set piece: his descriptions of picturesque scenes, or of Scott entertaining his friends at Abbotsford, sometimes give a definite impression of stage management. It is clear that the details are being composed with an eye rather to their general effect than to their exact accuracy. Lockhart also likes to make things as dramatic as possible. The year 1814 was indeed one of phenomenal activity, yet one is bound to share Grierson's doubts whether Scott could have done quite so much in it as Lockhart claims. What may be the culminating example of Lockhart's story-telling remains regrettably uncertain: the description of Scott on his death-bed telling Lockhart to 'be a good man—be virtuous—be religious'. It is just possible that this is true, but the probabilities seem to be against it.

Lockhart's merits stand out clearly when his biography is contrasted with Moore's *Life of Byron*. Behind this *Life* we catch sight of the tantalizing shadow of the Memoirs which Byron wrote between 1818 and 1821, and which contained (as he told Murray) 'many opinions, and some fun, with a detailed account of my marriage and its consequences, as true as a party concerned can make such accounts'. Byron gave the Memoirs to Moore and he (with Byron's full approval) allowed many friends to read them before selling them to Murray; but when the news arrived from Missolonghi there was an anxious meeting in Murray's parlour and those who wished to destroy the Memoirs (including the publisher himself) prevailed over Moore, and the manuscript was burnt in the grate. Later Murray commissioned Moore to write a *Life of Byron* as a counterblast to Leigh Hunt's *Lord Byron and Some of his Contemporaries*.

There is little in Moore's *Letters and Journals of Lord Byron: with Notices of his Life* (to give the work its full title) which obviously derives from the Memoirs, and such merit as the book has is largely due to Byron's own brilliance as a correspondent. It is clear that Byron intended his letters to be published: as Moore remarks, in the letters to John Murray Byron 'was shooting his shafts far beyond Albemarle Street'. Moore deserves credit for checking his own tendency to 'Asiatico-Hibernian eloquence' in favour of Byron's 'simple English diction', and

parts of his book are still of interest. Lockhart, who was soon to be describing the early life of another lame boy, commented that 'never was anything so drearily satisfactory to the imagination as the whole picture of the lame boy's start in life'. Occasionally Moore makes a shrewd comment, as when he remarks that Byron 'makes so boyishly much' of his Venetian *amourettes*. The fact that a great deal had to be omitted makes the picture a little misleading as a whole, however: as Croker pointed out, if the full story had been told it would have been clear that Byron 'sneered at all man and womankind in turn', and his sneers at his wife and mother would have been put into some sort of perspective. In general it may be said that Moore understands the poet of the Tales and of *Childe Harold* better than the man who wrote *Don Juan*. His tendency is to show Byron (in a prophetic phrase of the poet's own) as 'an *amiable*, ill-used gentleman'.

The phrase comes from the *Conversations of Lord Byron with the Countess of Blessington*, first published in the *New Monthly Magazine*, a record which remains of capital importance for anyone interested in the poet. Of the early biographies the only one which deserves attention, apart from Moore's, is Galt's *Life*. When the two men met at Gibraltar Byron came under the scrutiny of a man nine years his senior with a novelist's understanding of character. Galt considered Moore's picture 'too radiant and conciliatory', and he himself gives us a more critical study of the poet's character. He is particularly interesting on 'the Aberdonian epoch', and emphasizes that 'the dark colouring of his mind was plainly imbibed in a mountainous region, from sombre heaths, and in the midst of rudeness and grandeur'. As a consequence Byron 'had no taste for more cheerful images . . . only loneness and the solemnity of mountains'. He concentrates on Byron's 'intellectual features' rather than on the material suitable for a gossip-column. He regards the importance which Byron attached to his lameness as 'unmanly and excessive', but is under no misapprehensions about the influence it exerted on his character. Galt understood the working of a poet's imagination: he is excellent on the qualities that make a poet, and holds to the Johnsonian view that poets 'differ in no respect from other men of high endowment, but in the single circumstance of the objects to which their taste is attracted'. He cannot always restrain his satirical bent, and refers to Byron on shipboard

as 'a mystery in a winding-sheet, crowned with a halo'. He considered Byron's character as a complex structure built on a base that was not very hard to understand.

The early accounts of Shelley show little biographical skill. The most illuminating part of Hogg's *Life*, published in 1858, consists of the articles that he had contributed to the *New Monthly Magazine* a quarter of a century earlier. His book is rambling and egotistical and his attempts at wit do not always succeed. Medwin's *Memoir of Shelley* had first appeared in 1833, to be followed by a fuller biography fourteen years later. Medwin was a dishonest man, and he is unreliable with facts and dates; yet his book has the merit of preserving, in however inaccurate a form, a good deal of which we should otherwise have been ignorant. The element of romancing and inaccuracy in these accounts of Shelley, so characteristic of this period and so perplexing to those who wish to discover the truth about its great men, is even more pronounced in Edward John Trelawny's *Recollections of the Last Days of Shelley and Byron*, which was published in 1858. Something will be said of this later in the chapter: meanwhile we notice that it shared with the biographies of Shelley by Hogg and C. S. Middleton the distinction of calling forth Peacock's *Memoirs of Shelley*, printed in *Fraser's Magazine* between 1858 and 1862. Peacock did not like literary gossip: his aim in writing was to correct the inaccuracies of the earlier writers and to do justice to Harriet Westbrook. He had known Shelley intimately, and makes it clear both that he regards him as a man of genius, in many ways morally admirable, and also that he realizes that Shelley was unreliable in matters of fact, subject to delusions, and on occasion extremely comic. Peacock had always been Shelley's temperamental antithesis. He managed to convert Shelley to Italian opera, but not to comedy: he tells us that Shelley often talked of 'the withering and perverting spirit of comedy'. After the untruths, half-truths, idolatry, and salacity of so much that had been written on Shelley, Peacock comes like a breath of honest air: he is obviously reliable and fair minded, and his satiric genius does not seriously distort the picture. There have been few saner summings-up.

No feature of the literature of the early nineteenth century is more striking than the prominence of the element of auto-

biography. At no earlier time would a poet have written a poem as long as *The Prelude* on the growth of his own mind. In a very different way, Byron is even more 'egotistical' than Wordsworth: every reviewer noticed that each of his heroes was just a new presentation of himself, and a hostile critic might be pardoned for quoting Boileau:

> Souvent, sans y penser, un écrivain qui s'aime
> Forme tous ses héros semblables à soi-même.

In many of the poems of Shelley (as has been suggested earlier) autobiography and 'wish-fulfilment' lie equally near the surface. Similar tendencies are no less obvious in the prose of the time. Lamb's letters and essays may well be regarded as so many chapters of autobiography, while Hazlitt is never better than when he is writing of his own experiences—whether or not he actually played with the idea of composing an autobiography. When we turn from a consideration of the autobiographical element in poetry and the essay to the subject of autobiography itself, we find that Scott was the first of our considerable poets (with the solitary exception of Lord Herbert of Cherbury, who did not consider his poetry an important claim to notice) to embark on an autobiography. In 1808, six years before *Waverley*, he wrote a most interesting account of his own early life, giving as his excuse the fact that 'the present age has discovered a desire, or rather a rage, for literary anecdote and private history'. This evidence is the more impressive because it comes from a man whom no one has ever considered self-centred. A decade later Byron wrote his Memoirs. The tendency to autobiography was ubiquitous. In this period we no longer feel tempted to conjecture that writers with the desire to write about themselves belong to some particular psychological category—as we are with Pepys and Boswell, for example, in the seventeenth and eighteenth centuries. It is clear that there has been a great shift in man's way of looking at himself. A new importance was now attached to the uniqueness of each man, as the product of heredity and environment.

While it is disappointing that no autobiography was written of the stature of Rousseau's *Confessions*, Coleridge's *Biographia Literaria* and De Quincey's *Confessions of an English Opium-Eater* are only the most remarkable among a host of autobiographies of the most varied kinds. Men as varied as Clare, Galt, Hogg,

Gifford, Moore, Hood, Brydges, Hobhouse, and Leigh Hunt wrote autobiographies. For those of the writers of our period who lived well into the Victorian Age, particularly, it was to become very much of a 'financial sacrifice' to refrain from some form of autobiography. And there were soon to appear other names which are only remembered because their owners wrote accounts of their own lives—men like Samuel Bamford the Radical and Alexander Somerville the Working Man, whose autobiographies are invaluable quarries for the social historian. D. M. Moir satirized the fashion admirably when at the beginning of *The Life of Mansie Wauch, Tailor in Dalkeith*, he made his narrator observe that 'of late years . . . all notable characters, whatsoever line of life they may have pursued . . . have made a trade of committing to paper all the surprising occurrences and remarkable events that chanced to happen to them . . . during their journey through life—that such as come after them might take warning and be benefited'. People were beginning to realize that they might be interesting because they were 'typical' of something or other, even if they were not famous or exceptionally gifted. John Galt's finest works of fiction were inspired by the new vogue. There was an urge to explore the social structure, to survey mankind not only from China to Peru, but also from Windsor and Holland House to Pimlico and Manchester. It is interesting to notice that it was at this time that the word 'autobiography' first became current. It seems first to be used in English in the *Monthly Review* for December 1797 (xxiv. 375).[1] Reviewing Isaac D'Israeli's *Miscellanies* the writer uses the word '*Self-biography*', commenting: 'We are doubtful whether the . . . word be legitimate: it is not very usual in English to employ hybrid words partly Saxon and partly Greek: yet *autobiography* would have seemed pedantic.' In his *Specimens of English Prose-Writers* (1807) George Burnett claims that in English '*Autobiography* was begun by lord Herbert of Cherbury; and continued by various religious enthusiasts, who commenced the practice of keeping diaries'; while in his edition of Spence's *Anecdotes* in 1820 S. W. Singer points out that 'a complete though brief Auto-Biography of Pope may be collected' from the book. Evidence of the growing interest in autobiography as a form is provided by the series of the best autobiographies of the past published by Leigh Hunt and Cowden Clarke in the 1820's.

[1] I am indebted to Mr. James Ogden for this reference.

One of the first memoirs to be called an *Autobiography* was John Galt's, published in 1833; but the word had already been used in the titles of a number of novels, including Galt's own *Member* and *Radical* and Benjamin Disraeli's *Contarini Fleming: A Psychological Autobiography*. Galt concedes that 'it is certainly not a very gentlemanly occupation to write one's own life', yet in 1835 we find Sir Samuel Egerton Brydges publishing his *Autobiography*—and he was a man who was no more likely to doubt whether his actions were gentlemanly than whether they were of interest to the world. Of course there were opponents of the new fashion: one of them, at least at first, appears to have been Isaac D'Israeli, for in the *Quarterly Review* for May 1809 we find him expressing the fear that 'an epidemical rage for auto-biography' may break out, 'more wide in its influence and more pernicious in its tendency than the strange madness of the Abderites, so accurately described by Lucian'. 'England expects every driveller to do his Memorabilia', as another writer in the same *Review* complained in January 1827: 'thanks to "the march of intellect" we are already rich in the autobiography of pickpockets'. But the *Quarterly* was, as so often, protesting in vain: the literature of the century was to be profoundly influenced by what Colley Cibber had called 'the great pleasure of writing about one's self all day'. One aspect of the influence of this fact on literary criticism may be noticed in the title of a book published by Charles Armitage Brown, the friend of Keats, in 1838: *Shakespeare's Autobiographical Poems. Being his Sonnets clearly Developed: with his Character drawn chiefly from his Works.*

Leigh Hunt's own *Autobiography* was not published until 1850, but much of it had already appeared in 1828 in *Lord Byron and Some of his Contemporaries; with Recollections of the Author's Life.* Wishing to extricate himself from debt, Hunt seems to have planned a book of memoirs, but to have been persuaded by Colburn to feature Byron on his title-page. The whole of the first volume and part of the second are devoted to Byron, Shelley, Keats, Lamb, Coleridge, and other friends and acquaintances of Hunt's, and it was the long essay on Byron that sold the book and did the damage. Although Hunt is not wholly fair, there is little need to be indignant on Byron's behalf at this time of day. The contemporary press had changed its tone dramatically after Byron's death, and had begun to make much of him, to such a degree that Hunt felt moved to expostulate.

Having been the beneficiary of both men, he could not forbear from contrasting the instinctive gentleness and gentlemanliness of Shelley with the histrionic virtues and vices of Byron. Hunt was always at his best defending the under-dog, and his essay on Shelley is greatly superior to that on Byron. He is stimulated by the need to oppose the pious libels of established prejudice:

For his Christianity, in the proper sense of the word, he went to the gospel of St. James, and to the sermon on the Mount by Christ himself, for whose truly divine spirit he entertained the greatest reverence. There was nothing which embittered his reviewers against him more than the knowledge of this fact, and his refusal to identify their superstitions and worldly use of the Christian doctrines with the just idea of a great Reformer and advocate of the many; one, whom they would have been the first to cry out against, had he appeared now. (2nd ed., 1828, i. 323–4.)

Nothing could be finer than the passage in which he contrasts the behaviour of the 'licentious' Shelley with the conduct of the conventional man of pleasure tolerated by Regency society. He is equally illuminating on his poetry, the work, as he understands, of a reformer who failed to find an audience. There is a paradoxical truth in his remark that 'a great deal of Mr. Shelley's poetry ought to have been written in prose', while he admirably points out that some of his poems 'look rather like store-houses of imagery, than imagery put into proper action', adding that his images 'are too much in their elementary state, as if just about to be used, and moving in their first chaos'. On the poetry of Keats, which he understood intimately, Hunt is even better. A particular merit of these essays is to be found in the brief flashes of description which remind us that Hunt had a painter's eye. 'His forehead is prodigious', he remarks of Coleridge, '—a great piece of placid marble; and his fine eyes, in which all the activity of his mind seems to concentrate, move under it with a sprightly ease, as if it were pastime to them to carry all that thought.'

The *Autobiography* of 1850 is a better book. A man in his middle sixties, Hunt now looks back on the men of genius whom it has been his fate to outlive, and comments on the improvements which he has lived to see in the general state of the country and of mankind. It would be false as well as cheap to attribute his serener view to his pension and his relative prosperity.

He had always been a natural optimist. He can now analyse his own character more dispassionately, and tells us that he is 'quick to enjoy every object in creation, everything in nature and in art, every sight, every sound, every book, picture, and flower, and at the same time really qualified to do nothing, but either to preach the enjoyment of those objects . . . or to suffer with mingled cheerfulness and poverty the consequences of advocating some theory on the side of human progress'. He writes interestingly on Carlyle, his own antithesis: both were men of ardent and generous minds, but the one turned everything to gall, the other to honey. No less interesting is the contrast that Hunt draws between his own temperament and that of another greater man when he says that 'Scott saw the good of mankind in a Tory or retrospective point of view. I saw it from a Whig, a Radical, or prospective one.' He is excellent on the changes that he has lived to see. Railroads are changing the face of Britain. The Court has become 'at once correct and unbigoted . . ., and all classes are now beginning to permit the wisdom of every species of abuse to be doubted'. He is not shy about using the word 'progress' (or 'progression'). He makes no bones about his desire for Christianity (or 'Christianism') without Hell and without what he regards as superstitious accretions. It is the love in Christianity that seems to him its essence: he has no place for complete condemnation. He has not 'a single enemy' among the living or the dead. He does not withdraw all that he had said about Byron's faults, but he concentrates on the reasons for them. Perhaps the only man whom he can hardly pardon is Gifford, the man without genius but with the power 'to trample on Keats and Shelley'. In general the book has an elegiac glow, just melting into sentimentality. Dickens, whose Skimpole has done so much to perpetuate a caricature of Hunt, but who had helped him in other ways, is referred to generously. Yet unfortunately the book is not the masterpiece that it might have been, so raising Hunt from the rank of those whom we remember for their association with greater men to that of the men we remember for one great book. It is loosely put together, and lacks unity of purpose and direction rather as do De Quincey's *Autobiographic Sketches*. The reminiscences of the theatre are interesting in themselves, but they have little to do with autobiography.

Another friend of Byron and Shelley who published an

autobiography was Edward Trelawny, whose *Adventures of a Younger Son* appeared in 1831. If he had had his way he would have called the book *The Life of a Man*, and Thackeray might have had less reason to complain that no one had dared to tell the truth since Fielding. Yet 'truth' is perhaps hardly the word: whether the book as it stands is more of an autobiography or a romance is an open question. What would a writer of historical romance do, if he wished to write a book about this period? He would take for his hero a man belonging to an old and famous family, a man interested in poets and poetry and passionately in favour of liberal political views. He would be irresistible to women, and might be described by one of his lovers in some such terms as these: 'A kind of half Arab Englishman—whose life has been as changeful as that of Anastatius & who recounts the adventures of his youth as eloquently and well as the imagined Greek—he is clever'—she might go on '—for his moral qualities I am yet in the dark [:] he is a strange web which I am endeavouring to unravel. . . . He is six feet high—raven black hair which curls thickly & shortly like a Moors. . . . He excites me to think and if any evil shade the intercourse that time will unveil. . . .' Our hero would run away to sea as a boy: serve for a time on a privateer: become the friend of Shelley and reach Viareggio in time to light his funeral pyre: swim with Byron in the waters of the Mediterranean, and arrive quickly at Missolonghi on receiving the news of his death. Not being wholly a gentleman (no picaresque hero can afford to be that), he would raise the covering of the body to examine the crippled foot which had been responsible for so much in the poet's life. He would throw himself passionately into the fight for Greek independence, survive an attempt at murder in the Cave of Odysseus, marry the beautiful young daughter of an Arab pirate, and become the passionate admirer of Mary Shelley. He would appear as a speaker in one of Landor's *Imaginary Conversations*, and survive to a great age, picturesque and formidable to the end, the subject of a painting by Millais and of a poem by Swinburne. All of this—or practically all—is in fact true of Trelawny. Although we now know that certain of the adventures described in his book are fictitious—he did not desert from the Navy, for example, to serve on a French privateer—and while it is likely that he often exaggerates the importance of his own role in incidents at which he may have been merely a spectator,

a great deal of the book is essentially true. Trelawny is a reminder of the fact that nature sometimes imitates art. It is of a piece with the rest of his extraordinary life that he should have 'followed the fortunes of those invincible spirits who wandered, exiled outcasts, over the world, and lent [his] feeble aid to unveil the frauds contained in worn-out legends which have so long deluded mankind'. All Dumas had to do to increase his reputation as a writer of romance was to put Trelawny's autobiography into French.

The question of the reliability of *Recollections of the last Days of Shelley and Byron* is more important. Unfortunately Trelawny was incapable of telling the unadorned truth: instead he rushed about, Quixote-like, trying to adjust the balance of opinion so that it should be fair to both his former friends. His protective instincts were aroused by Shelley, and the attacks which followed his death brought Trelawny out strongly in his favour. The remaining two-thirds of his book, which deal with Byron, are less successful. They are just as inaccurate in detail, while the tendency of others to romanticize Byron after his death seems to have confirmed Trelawny in his early reaction against him. It is partly that Trelawny and Byron had too much in common; and partly that, while it was a privilege to have been befriended by Shelley, to have been befriended by Byron was apt to be felt as an irksome obligation. When he revised his *Recollections* near the end of his life Trelawny further shifted the balance in favour of Shelley and against Byron—while his attitude to Mary Shelley became less friendly. He was not born to be a reliable witness, but his books remain of value for their vividness and for the picturesque details which they provide.

Benjamin Robert Haydon was another remarkable man much associated with the writers of his time who wrote an account of his own life.[1] His *Autobiography* proper covers the years 1786–1820, while his Journals continue until his death in 1846. It has been common to laugh at Haydon, and there is something absurd about a man who seriously contemplated putting up

1 Benjamin Robert Haydon (1786–1846) came to London in 1804 to study painting. His great aim in life was the revival of 'historical painting' in England and he was profoundly influenced by the Elgin Marbles. He had a number of distinguished pupils, and mixed much with literary men: Wordsworth and Keats both addressed sonnets to him. *The Judgement of Solomon* and *The Raising of Lazarus* were among his most celebrated paintings. He committed suicide in despair after the failure of an exhibition.

a brass plate in his own honour and was capable of the reflection—'What a race the young Haydons would have been with the blood of Michael Angelo mingled with mine!' Yet he was a painter of real talent—not least in comic draughtsmanship—and if his talent had amounted to genius his absurdity might have passed unnoticed. He was highly intelligent, full of ideas, and had an infinite capacity for taking pains. When Keats met him in 1816 Haydon seemed well on the way to fame: it would have taken a shrewd prophet to have foretold that it was the painter who was destined to be remembered as the friend of the poet. Like many good judges, Keats deeply admired Haydon's paintings, as may be seen in the fragment called the 'Castle Builder', where he describes his ideal study:

> My pictures all Salvator's, save a few
> Of Titian's portraiture, and one, tho' new,
> Of Haydon's in its fresh magnificence.

It was in his studio that there took place the dinner at which Wordsworth, Keats, and Lamb were all present. Haydon describes it admirably:

> On December 28th the immortal dinner came off in my painting-room, with Jerusalem towering up behind us as a background. Wordsworth was in fine cue, and we had a glorious set-to—on Homer, Shakespeare, Milton and Virgil. Lamb got exceedingly merry and exquisitely witty; and his fun in the midst of Wordsworth's solemn intonations of oratory was like the sarcasm and wit of the fool in the intervals of Lear's passion.

This was the occasion on which Lamb and Keats agreed that Newton 'had destroyed all the poetry of the rainbow by reducing it to the prismatic colours' and proposed the surprising toast—'Newton's health, and confusion to mathematics'—the night on which Lamb addressed Wordsworth as 'you old lake poet, you rascally poet' and upbraided him for calling Voltaire dull. Haydon was keenly interested in literature. His taste, which typifies the enlightened opinion of his time, is summed up in his wish to be buried with Shakespeare placed on his heart, Homer in his right hand, Ariosto in his left, Dante under his head, Tasso at his feet, Keats also in a position of honour, and Corneille, that 'heartless tirade maker', in the reverse. It was he who gave Keats the best possible advice: 'Go on, dont

despair, collect incidents, study characters, read Shakespeare and trust in Providence.' His long campaign to have the Elgin Marbles purchased for the nation was successful, though its success may have owed more to others than to him. His passionate desire to revive English painting cannot be laughed at. Three months before his twenty-first birthday he had knelt down, brush in hand, and prayed that he might be permitted 'to create a new era in art, and to rouse the people and patrons to a just estimate of the moral value of historical painting'. 'My great object', he wrote to Keats, 'is the public encouragement of historical painting and the glory of England, in high Art, to ensure these I would lay my head on the block this instant.' Though he was not a genius, he thought he was, and his unquestioning adoption of the Life of Genius helped Keats to aim at the heights. His journals are full of vivid descriptions which (unlike so many of Trelawny's) carry instant conviction, such as his description of Wordsworth looking at a group of Cupid and Psyche kissing and exclaiming 'The Dev-ils!' He describes the Duke of Sussex's voice as 'loud, royal and asthmatic'. He was not a mere Gulley Jimson, but a true genius *manqué*. Everything about him was on a huge scale, appropriate to his conceptions of 'heroic painting'. His ambition was limitless, his paintings so large that it is now hardly possible to find them hanging in any gallery, while he wrote his own life in twenty-seven volumes in Folio. There is a sad appropriateness in the self-dramatization of his suicide, with the final quotation from *King Lear*.

It would be pleasant to say something of many other autobiographies of the time, such as Clare's *Sketches* of his own life or Thomas Bewick's *Memoir*, which contrasts as markedly with Haydon's as does his art as an engraver; but we must be content with a final glance at the autobiography of Sir Samuel Egerton Brydges, or to give it its full title, *The Autobiography, Times, Opinions, and Contemporaries of Sir Egerton Brydges, Bart., K.J. (Per legem terrae) Baron Chandos of Sudeley, etc.*[1] The title-page is further adorned with a device representing a medieval knight on his

[1] Sir Samuel Egerton Brydges (1762–1837) sacrificed his chances of a degree at Cambridge by 'giving himself up to English poetry'. He was called to the Bar, but never practised. In 1792 he bought Denton Court in Kent, where he did a great deal of literary work. About 1789 he persuaded his elder brother to put forward his claim to the barony of Chandos: the failure of the claim in 1803, after no fewer than 26 hearings, helped to sour the remainder of his life. Meanwhile he had moved

charger in full cry after the Infidel and by a characteristically inaccurate quotation from Shelley, while facing it we find a portrait of the author with his eyes 'in a fine frenzy rolling'. Much is to be expected of a man who tells us at the beginning that circumstances have conspired to 'torpify' his faculties. Wordsworth once pointed out that Brydges 'thinks laxly, and uses words inconsiderately'; and this is as true of his prose as of his verse. He had no feeling for words at all, and remains of interest as a fine specimen of certain of the critical views of the time carried to the point of absurdity. He believed that 'genuine and undisguised opinions... are often more valuable than arguments', and is as rich in the former as he is deficient in the latter. All that was necessary (he thought) was to be a genius, and write. Jane Austen read his novel, *Arthur Fitz-Albini*, and commented that 'there is very little story, and what there is told in a strange, unconnected way': it is pleasant to reflect that Sir Egerton may have been one of the models for Sir Walter Elliot of Kellynch-hall. Chronological arrangement is far to seek in his *Autobiography*, certain obsessive themes recurring everywhere—such as his insane pride of family. 'The peerage I claim', he remarks at one point,

> only mounts up to the year 1554, but historic evidence will establish that my male stock is baronial from the Conquest; ascending, as I will satisfy any general jurist and European genealogist, to Johannes de Burgo (Monoculus) founder also of the House of De Burgh, and ten other branches of ancient peerage . . . from all the chief of which I am also descended in the female line. This John De Burgo is said . . . to have been of the House of Charlemagne. . . . (ii. 422.)

While Sir Egerton Brydges had the satisfaction of seeing his *Autobiography* handsomely published (at his own expense) during his lifetime, many other writers of memoirs (like Haydon) left their work to be published by their literary executors. One of these, Henry Crabb Robinson, who lived until 1867, left diaries and reading-lists which are invaluable for the student of the literary history of this period. The *Recollections* of Byron's friend, Hobhouse, are also of some interest, though less relevant to literary history. Like Scott, Thomas Moore began an *Auto-*

to Lee Priory, near Canterbury. A compositor and a pressman had started a new press there, and Brydges supplied them with scarce old books which they reprinted for collectors in limited editions. From 1818 until his death he lived mainly abroad, particularly in Geneva, continuing his work as a littérateur and bibliographer.

*biography*, but he only reached his nineteenth year: after his death, however, eight volumes of his journals and other personal writings were published by Lord John Russell. The impulse to record one's own life was now widespread, though few men had the bravado or the honesty to begin their Memoirs, like the Ettrick Shepherd, with the words 'I like to write about myself: in fact, there are few things which I like better'.

# XIV

# INTEREST IN FOREIGN LITERATURE AND IN EARLIER ENGLISH LITERATURE

De Quincey once suggested that all literatures 'tend to superannuation' unless they are 'crossed by some other of different breed', and it seems likely that one of the reasons for the variety and vigour of English literature at the beginning of the nineteenth century was the exceptional amount of cross-fertilization at that time between our literature and the literatures of other countries. But before we turn to the relations between England and Italy and Germany we must first acknowledge the continuing influence of classical literature. It is true that some observers believed that knowledge of the classics was declining. In his 'Essay on Fashionable Literature' (1818), for example, Peacock complained that 'classical literature seems sinking into . . . repose'. It is his contention that while a few years before 'the favorite journals of the day . . . were seldom without a classical . . . article for the grace of keeping up appearances . . . now we have volume after volume . . . almost without any thing to remind us that such things were'. Yet although the influence of Latin literature was much less strong than it had been a century before, it remains true that most writers and readers were far more familiar with Virgil and Horace than we are today, thanks to the educational conservatism of the schools at which a high proportion of the future writers were still educated. 'Lily's' Latin Grammar, which had first appeared before Spenser was born, was to remain in use at Eton (with only slight modifications) until past the middle of the century. In the 1840's a master at Eton unwittingly produced a fine *reductio ad absurdum* of the argument for a classical education. 'If you do not take more pains, how can you ever expect to write good longs and shorts? If you do not write good longs and shorts, how can you ever be a man of taste? If you are not a man of taste, how can you ever be of use in the world?' Yet without embarking on the endless controversy about the best form of education, it

may confidently be asserted that there are worse trainings for a man of letters than a classical education, and it is worth noticing that most of the poets of our period were prepared to turn a passage of Latin into English verse, as Hobhouse did in his *Imitations and Translations from the Ancient and Modern Classics* (1809), a volume that is remembered because it contains some of Byron's early pieces. Although it was unusual by this time to produce an 'Imitation' of a Latin poet like Byron's *Hints from Horace*, the less direct influence of Latin poetry is not hard to discover. Shelley was influenced by Lucretius, while a recent scholar has reminded us of the influence exerted on Wordsworth by the Latin prose writers.

Yet it is clear that Latin literature no longer provided the imaginative stimulus to poets that it had provided in the age of Pope. Although Keats is said to have made a complete prose translation of the *Aeneid* while he was still a boy, it is evident from his letters that he was far more interested in Homer than in Virgil. The important new fact is the increasing influence of Greek literature in this period. In their decided preference of Greek literature over Latin the Schlegels were men of the new era. We are told that in his old age Dr. Samuel Parr, who died in 1825, would often remark 'with exulting pleasure' on the improvement in Greek scholarship since his youth, and it cannot be doubted that by influencing the pattern of education the work of Porson and his disciples helped to form the imagination of the new generation. Coleridge, De Quincey, Shelley, Landor and Praed were all widely read in Greek literature, while Peacock's passion for the Greeks was that of a man educationally 'under-privileged' living at a time when the more intellectual members of society believed wholeheartedly in Greek. And, of course, politics lent immediacy and urgency to a study that might otherwise have confined its influence to universities and schools. 'We are all Greeks', as Shelley wrote in the preface to *Hellas*. 'Our laws, our literature, our religion, our arts have their root in Greece.'

Neither the continuing interest in Latin nor the growing interest in Greek produced many translations of the highest quality. Admirable versions of most of the major classical writers had appeared during the previous century, and although these now seemed old-fashioned, classical literature did not challenge the translator as did more recent poetry and prose

from the Continent which had yet to make its first appearance in English. One has only to mention Gifford's translations of Juvenal and Persius, Wrangham's *Bucolics* and his *Lyrics of Horace*, Symmons's *Aeneid*, and Hawkins's *Claudian*, to make it clear that there is not much that is of literary interest. Moore's versions of Anacreon have at best an historical importance: Cary's *Pindar* and his *Birds* of Aristophanes have some value, though they cannot stand comparison with his *Dante*: while Hookham Frere's translations from Aristophanes still retain considerable merit. It is hardly surprising that those who were most deeply interested in literature began to turn back to the translators of the Elizabethan age and the early seventeenth century, so participating in that exploration of the English literary heritage which is one of the most striking features of the period. To remember Keats's sonnet 'On first looking into Chapman's Homer' is at once to be reminded of these fine old translations, and to be set on one's guard against the donnish fallacy that only those who can read the classics in the original can derive inspiration from them. Few critics have ever written anything more foolish than Lockhart wrote about Keats. Looking back with complacency on his own Balliol education he makes one of the speakers in *Peter's Letters to his Kinsfolk* utter the dangerous half-truth that there is 'no such thing as a translation', and in the same spirit we find him demanding, in *Blackwood's Magazine*, why Keats chose to write on the legends of Greece when he was ignorant of the language of the Greeks.

Yet it was not only to translations that Keats was indebted. He probably owed more to the visual arts than to any translations whatsoever, and if we wish to understand the imaginative interest in Greek mythology at this point we must remember the increased interest that men were taking in sculpture and in the paintings of Titian, Poussin, and Claude. It will be sufficient to quote from Hazlitt's description of his first visit to the Louvre:

> There [Art] had gathered together all her pomp, and there was her shrine, and there her votaries came and worshipped as in a temple .... Where the triumphs of human liberty had been, there were the triumphs of human genius. For there, in the Louvre, were the precious monuments of art;—There 'stood the statue that enchants the world'; there was the *Apollo*, the *Laocoon*, the *Dying Gladiator*, the

*Head of the Antinous*, *Diana* with her *Fawn*, the *Muses* and the *Graces* in a ring, and all the glories of the antique world:—

> There was old Proteus coming from the sea,
> And wreathed Triton blew his winding horn.

And apart from the Louvre and the growing vogue of Italian travel, great paintings were finding their way to England in increasing numbers, as we are reminded by W. Buchanan's *Memoirs of Painting, with a Chronological History of The Importation of Pictures by the Great Masters into England since the French Revolution* (1824). The arrival of the Elgin Marbles in England stimulated the imaginations of men like Keats and Haydon, while a great many fine paintings on classical subjects were available to interested members of the public even before the Angerstein Collection became the nucleus of the National Gallery in 1824.

It is not surprising that admirers of the paintings of Titian should have been keenly interested in Italy and its literature, and it may fairly be claimed that the 1820's represent the climax of English interest in Italian literature. The desire to visit Italy was stimulated by the fact that the country had been inaccessible to most travellers since the outbreak of the war with France. 'The opening of the long-cherished interior of Europe has produced a vast exportation of English tourists', as a writer in the *Annual Register* for 1814 commented rather sourly, 'who, whatever returns they may bring of amusement or instruction, will certainly not improve the balance of trade.' Whatever happened to the balance of trade, we may reply, the English imagination was greatly enriched. As Leigh Hunt pointed out in his Epistle to Byron 'on his departure for Italy and Greece',

> . . . All the four great Masters of our Song,
> Stars that shine out amidst a starry throng,
> Have turned to Italy for added light,
> As earth is kissed by the sweet moon at night.

This is certainly true of three of the 'great Masters of our Song' in the early nineteenth century, and as well as Byron, Shelley, and Keats there were a host of minor writers who owed a heavy debt to Italy. Nothing could be more characteristic of the period than the longing of Keats for 'skies Italian'. England is a beautiful country, he writes in his sonnet 'Happy is England', and England's 'artless daughters' are beautiful girls,

Yet do I often warmly burn to see
Beauties of deeper glance, and hear their singing,
And float with them about the summer waters.

Although Keats was to be a dying man when he reached the shores of Italy, much of the finest poetry of Byron and Shelley was written there.

English enthusiasm for Italy and Italian was encouraged by the fact that the language is so much easier to learn than German. Men who had been well grounded in Latin at school found it easy to pick up a reading knowledge of Italian, while for young ladies Italian came to be regarded as an eligible substitute for the classical languages. In *Gryll Grange* Morgana is delighted to be complimented on her Italian, but when she has to confess that she also knows Latin she adds that this may be the reason why she is still a spinster.

When we glance at the translations of Dante and other Italian writers which appeared in the early part of the century we find that they are often designed for readers who know a little Italian but cannot get far without assistance. When Cary published his translation of the *Inferno* in 1805–6 he gave the Italian on one page and the English opposite, and it is remarkable that this was the first time that the Italian text of Dante had been printed in England. At first Cary's work attracted little notice, and in 1814 he was obliged to publish his complete translation at his own expense. It was due to Coleridge, who praised the 'severity and *learned Simplicity*' of Cary's diction and the manner in which he had achieved 'the variety of Milton without any mere Miltonisms', that Taylor and Hessey published the edition that made Cary famous. The influence of Dante on English poets of the period is easy to trace. The 'minute volumes' of Cary's *Dante* were the only books that Keats took with him on his Northern tour: he seems to have read them closely, since in one of his letters he describes a dream inspired by the fifth canto of the *Inferno*, and it is clear that Dante sometimes presented himself to him as an alternative model to Milton. Like Keats, Byron was particularly delighted by the episode of Paolo and Francesca, though his translation of the passage has little to commend it. There were times when Byron reacted against Dante's theology, but numerous references in his letters make it clear how much the Italian poet meant to him and it is hardly surprising that he should have used him in *The Prophecy of Dante* to lend authority to his vision of

'liberty and the resurrection of Italy'. Yet Shelley understood Dante far better. Whereas the *terza rima* of *The Prophecy of Dante* is at best a curiosity, in the 'Ode to the West Wind' Shelley adapted the metre more brilliantly than any other English poet has ever done: the versification is very different from Dante's own, yet the poem as a whole is truly Dantesque in its speed and in the sombre urgency of its prophecy. It is not surprising that Shelley preferred the *Paradiso* to the other parts of the *Divina Commedia*: this 'perpetual hymn of everlasting love' (as he described it) is an analogue to the vision of paradise which is a recurrent element in his own longer poems. *Epipsychidion* is prefaced by a translation of two lines from the *Vita Nuova*—

> My Song, I fear that thou wilt find but few
> Who fitly shall conceive thy reasoning

—and it is in this poem, and in *Prometheus Unbound* and 'The Triumph of Life', that the influence of Dante on Shelley is to be seen at its profoundest. When we turn from Shelley to Wordsworth we find a poet who owed far less to Italian models. Although Wordsworth praised Cary's translation as 'a great national work' he seems at times to have had difficulty in making up his mind about Dante's stature as a poet. In 1824 we find him wondering whether the fashion has not gone too far:

> Let me know what you think of Dante [he wrote to Landor]—it has become lately—owing a good deal, I believe, to the example of Schlegel—the fashion to extol him above measure. I have not read him for many years; his style I used to think admirable for conciseness and vigour, without abruptness; but I own that his fictions often struck me as offensively grotesque and fantastic, and I felt the Poem tedious from various causes.

Wherever we turn at this time we find Dante's merits under discussion. Hazlitt, who refers to him as often as he does to any foreign writer, writes admirably about him in his review of Sismondi and tells us that Dante is the only one of the Italian poets that he would greatly like to have seen. As one might expect, Leigh Hunt was less at home with Dante than with many other Italian writers—perhaps he was not a big enough man to see him from a suitable elevation—yet he took from him the subject of his most un-Dantesque *Story of Rimini*. Landor was a passionate admirer of Dante, while Hallam wrote eloquently on him in his *Europe during the Middle Ages*.

Little can be said of the fortunes of Petrarch, Ariosto, and

Tasso at this time. Interest in Petrarch was stimulated by the work of Mrs. Dobson, Alexander Fraser Tytler, and Ugo Foscolo, but in general his influence is more obvious in the work of minor and minimus poets than in that of their betters—though it seems certain that a passage in the *Trionfi* gave Shelley a hint for the Platonic symbolism of light and shadow at the end of *Adonais*. Ariosto was readily available in Hoole's translation, the form in which he first became known to Southey and Scott. It is clear that Southey owed a good deal to Ariosto, while Scott told Edward Cheney that he himself 'had formerly made it a practice to read through the "Orlando" of Boiardo, and the "Orlando" of Ariosto, once every year'. It is as characteristic of Scott to have found Dante 'too obscure and difficult' as to have written an essay as a student in which he 'weighed Homer against Ariosto, and pronounced him wanting'. It was Hoole's notes that first revealed to Scott that 'the Italian language contained a fund of romantic lore'. It must be counted a misfortune that W. S. Rose's version of the *Orlando Furioso* in *ottava rima*, which appeared between 1823 and 1831 and won deserved praise from Foscolo, failed to supplant Hoole's less lively version. Tasso was also well known. Hoole's translation of the *Gerusalemme Liberata* reached its eighth edition in 1802, while a more spirited version became available with the reprinting of Fairfax's translation in 1817. John Black's *Life of Tasso* had appeared in 1810. Byron and Shelley were both keenly interested in Tasso. Byron went out of his way to visit Ferrara rather than Mantua, commenting (in a way that would have shocked the Augustans) that he 'would rather see the cell where they caged Tasso' than the birthplace of 'that harmonious plagiary and miserable flatterer whose cursed hexameters' had been drilled into him at Harrow: a not uncommon reaction to a sound classical education. Shelley similarly regarded Tasso as a brother in persecution, and we find him visiting his prison and sending Peacock a piece of wood from the door. Finding in him one of the *personae* that he was always looking for, Shelley read Tasso eagerly, investigated the merits of the various biographies, and planned to write a tragedy on his madness. By 1825, when J. H. Wiffen's translation of the *Gerusalemme* into Spenserian stanzas gave Foscolo an excuse for a long essay in the *Westminster Review*, Tasso's reputation was very firmly established.

It is an odd fact that the Italian poet whose influence on the

style of English poetry at this time is most readily demonstrable is Luigi Pulci. Hookham Frere told Foscolo in a letter that when he chanced on some stanzas by Pulci in Ginguené's *History of Literature* it occurred to him that Pulci's 'ingenious and humorous assumption of the vulgar character and vernacular phrase [of] rude popular attempts at poetry among his countrymen [was] capable of being transferred, *mutatis mutandis*, to the English nation and the present times'. Although he soon looked into Pulci for himself, Byron seldom made any secret of the fact that *Beppo* was inspired by Frere's *Whistlecraft*, and it has been argued in Chapter II that in discovering the new idiom Byron discovered a new aspect of his own personality and so became a great satiric poet. There can be no doubt that *Whistlecraft* did a good deal to draw the attention of English readers to Italian informal satire. Ugo Foscolo, whose arrival in England in 1816 is a fact of importance in the literary relations between the two countries, reviewed *Whistlecraft* in the *Quarterly Review* for April 1819, along with W. S. Rose's free translation of Casti's *Animali Parlanti*, *The Court and Parliament of Beasts*. His review, which was headed 'Narrative and Romantic Poems of the Italians', helped further to disseminate knowledge of Italian poetry in England. J. H. Merivale's *Orlando in Roncesvalles*, a poem in five cantos based on Pulci's *Morgante Maggiore*, had appeared in 1814, while in 1822 Lord Glenbervie published his inert translation of the first canto of Forteguerri's *Ricciardetto*. It is a striking fact that this interest in the Italian medley poets was almost exclusively an aristocratic affair: the easy transition from sentiment to cynicism characteristic of Pulci and Casti made a direct appeal to the temperament of the sophisticated Regency upper class.

As a sort of postscript to this section we may glance at Leigh Hunt, whose influence on Keats and on many others lends importance to his lifelong passion for Italian literature. For him Italy was 'the soil in which every species of modern poetry seems to have originally sprung up'. When he was in prison he bought a set of the *Parnaso Italiano*, and for the rest of his life Italian poetry was never to be out of his thoughts for long. While his feelings about Dante were mixed—he once called him a 'great semi-barbarian' who produced 'a kind of sublime nightmare'—he was very much at home with Ariosto, 'whose fine ear and animal spirits gave so exquisite a tone to all he said'. In

his 'Book of Beginnings' he quotes and then translates passages from Ariosto, Berni, and Forteguerri. These and other poets are again laid under tribute in his *Stories from the Italian Poets.* Hunt's attempt to restore to the pentameter couplet a freedom of movement which it had often been denied in the previous century owed a great deal to the inspiration of these and other Italian models. Although Keats soon outgrew Hunt, including 'Italian tales' with the other things that Hunt had spoilt by making too much of them, it was probably from Hunt that he had first caught his interest in Italian poetry and his desire to use the couplet with an un-Augustan freedom. When Hazlitt, who succeeded Hunt as Keats's guide in all matters of taste, recommended that a modern writer should translate some of the more serious tales of Boccaccio, Keats and his friend John Hamilton Reynolds soon set their hands to the task. The results were *Isabella,* 'The Garden of Florence', and 'The Ladye of Provence'.

We may note in passing that the *Decamerone* was not the only prose work in Italian to attract attention at this time. Dunlop's pioneering *History of Prose Fiction* emphasized the importance of the Italian story-tellers, while Thomas Roscoe's *Italian Novelists* (1825) contains translations from Boccaccio, Sacchetti, Ser Giovanni Fiorentino, Massuccio Salernitano, Cinthio, Bandello, and many others. Roscoe produced a translation of Benvenuto Cellini's *Memoirs* in 1822, while Manzoni's *The Betrothed* was added to Bentley's 'Standard Novels' twelve years later. It is the less surprising that the periodicals paid a good deal of attention to Italian prose literature, as well as to Italian poetry: Stendhal was among the writers in the *London Magazine* who wrote on Italian literature in the later 1820's.

If Italy was the Land of the Imagination at this time, Germany was the Land of the Intellect. In his *Autobiographic Sketches* De Quincey devotes a chapter to 'German Studies and Kant in particular' and compares his own discovery of German literature to the first appearance of America 'to an ardent and sympathising spirit': he describes it as

> rising, at once, like an exhalation, with all its shadowy forests, its endless savannas, and its pomp of solitary waters. . . . As a past literature [he goes on], as a literature of inheritance and tradition, the German was nothing. . . . But . . . its prospects, and the scale of its present development, were in the amplest style of American grandeur. . . . Not the tropics, not the ocean, not life itself, is such a type of

variety, of infinite forms, or of creative power, as the German literature in its recent motions (say for the last twenty years), gathering, like the Danube, a fresh volume of power at every stage of its advance. . . . It seemed, in those days, an El Dorado as true and undeceiving as it was evidently inexhaustible.

Edinburgh was the centre from which interest spread. It was as a result of Henry Mackenzie's lecture on the German Drama in 1788 that Scott and a few of his friends began to study German under a Dr. Willich, who played a humble part in introducing Kant to English readers. But Scott never mastered the grammar of the language, so that his German remained a hit-and-miss affair. Very few people knew German well—a fact worth remembering when sweeping assertions are made about the influence of German literature in England at this time. An amusing anthology might be compiled about the unsuccessful and often half-hearted attempts which men of letters made to learn German. When Wordsworth and Coleridge met Klopstock in Hamburg in September 1798 Wordsworth could converse with 'the German Milton' only in French, while Coleridge (for once in his life) was reduced to silence. Although Coleridge later acquired what might be described as a fluent cribbing knowledge of German, he was never able to speak the language correctly. Wordsworth regretted his own lack of German when he was a young man, but later in life he seems to have thought little about the matter. Although Shelley was a fine linguist his knowledge of German was comparatively slight. Keats did not even mention German as one of the languages that he hoped to learn. Landor knew no German. Byron could swear in it. Only a minority of writers—including Beddoes, Darley, De Quincey, Lockhart, and, of course, Carlyle—knew German at all well.

At the time of Waterloo very few people in England knew much about German literature. To the average reader, indeed, 'German' literature suggested only two things: sensational Gothic romances and wildly unclassical dramas. Of the former some were translations, while others—such as most of the 'horrid novels' which Catherine Morland borrows from the circulating library in *Northanger Abbey*—were the work of English hacks. Their aim was simply to produce a delicious *frisson* or thrill. As literature they were worthless; yet it was not only feather-headed young women who took pleasure in them, and their

interest for us is due to the fact that they provided imaginative stimulus to such major writers as Byron, Shelley and the Brontës. The 'German' plays which vied with these books in popularity and shared with them the attentions of innumerable satirists were more often of genuinely Teutonic origin. At the end of his *Lectures on the Age of Elizabeth* Hazlitt gives an amusing account of these plays, and emphasizes that it was as a concomitant or aftermath of the French Revolution that 'the loud trampling of the German Pegasus' was first heard on the English stage. Such dramas embody 'the extreme opinions which are floating in our time, and which have struck their roots deep and wide below the surface of the public mind'. Their writers are interested above all in gaining effect, and they seek this 'by going all the lengths not only of instinctive feeling, but of speculative opinion, and startling the hearer by overturning all the established maxims of society, and setting at nought all the received rules of composition':

> The poets and philosophers of Germany . . . the Goethes, the Lessings, the Schillers, the Kotzebues, felt a sudden and irresistible impulse by a convulsive effort to tear aside this factitious drapery of society. . . . These Titans of our days . . . have made the only incorrigible Jacobins, and their school of poetry is the only real school of Radical Reform.

Schiller's *Robbers* was the first German play that Hazlitt ever read, and it made an ineffaceable impression on him. It is interesting to notice that he thought more highly of *Don Carlos* than of *Wallenstein* (in Coleridge's translation) and retained a marked interest in Kotzebue, while finding little to appeal to him in the plays of Goethe (whose name was still usually pronounced 'Go-eth'). In general we notice that anyone interested in literature at this time was likely to own a few plays translated from the German—perhaps even the six volumes of *The German Theatre, translated by Benjamin Thompson*. By the beginning of the century, when Thompson's collection appeared, all Schiller's available plays seem to have been translated into English. Other books accessible in translation included Gessner's tearful *Death of Abel*, of which no fewer than twenty English editions had appeared by the end of the eighteenth century, Klopstock's *Messiah*, Wieland's *Agathon* and *Oberon*, Lessing's *Nathan*, and that strange but influential book, 'Zimmerman on

Solitude', which even the most predatory of Lamb's friends were content to leave unmolested on his shelves. *The Sorrows of Werther* had first been translated, through French, in 1779, and throughout the following century Werther was to remain one of the most famous characters in literature. Apart from the unsatisfactory rendering of Leveson Gower, on the other hand, the first complete translation of Part I of *Faust* did not make its appearance until 1833: it was the work of A. Hayward, who tells us that he was encouraged to produce this prose version by hearing that Lamb 'had derived more pleasure from the meagre Latin versions of the Greek tragedians, than from any other versions of them he was acquainted with'. John Anster's verse translation followed two years later. The fact that most of the English critics who referred to *Faust* before the thirties were basing their comments on scraps of translation and fragments of knowledge makes it the less surprising that a critic as gifted as Hazlitt should have preferred *Werther*.

'Whatever may be thought of the Germans as Poets', Wordsworth wrote in 1822, 'there is no doubt of their being the best Critics in Europe.' One of the books that did most to introduce German criticism into England was August Wilhelm Schlegel's *Lectures on Dramatic Art and Literature*, translated by John Black in 1815 with a preface drawing attention to 'the boldness of his attacks on rules which are considered as sacred by the French critics' and suggesting that 'it will be no disadvantage to him, in our eyes, that he has been unsparing in his attack on the literature of our enemies'. In spite of his denials, Coleridge owed a good deal to Schlegel, who was soon thought by many to be the greatest critic that Shakespeare had yet found. Hazlitt's long review is a fine tribute to a critic whose method differed radically from his own. But perhaps the most influential book of all, in stimulating English interest in Germany, was *De L'Allemagne*, by Mme de Staël, which appeared in French in 1810 and in English in 1813. This study, which must have been one of the models for Bulwer Lytton's *England and the English*, deals in turn with 'Germany, and the Manners of the Germans', 'Literature and the Arts' (the longest section), 'Philosophy and Morals', and 'Religion and Enthusiasm'. The importance of Mme de Staël's book may serve as a reminder that most knowledge of German literature and thought at this time was still second-hand. Even translations 'From the German' were more often in fact from

the French, as was to be the case with translations 'From the Russian' a century later.

Of the men who interpreted Germany to Englishmen at this time three deserve particular mention. First in time and importance was William Taylor of Norwich, whose *Historic Survey of German Poetry* appeared near the end of his life in 1830.[1] He had become interested in German literature during his travels there in 1781–2. Eight years later he made his famous translation of Bürger's *Lenore*, which circulated in manuscript before its publication in the *Monthly Magazine* in 1796 and which was destined to play an important part in guiding the development of Walter Scott. Taylor's translations of *Nathan the Wise* and Goethe's *Iphigenia* were privately printed in 1791 and 1793. In the latter year he became a contributor to the *Monthly Review*, to which (and to other periodicals) he contributed nearly 2,000 articles on German literature during the next thirty years. The books that he reviewed included Goethe's *Dichtung und Wahrheit* and Schlegel's *Lectures on Dramatic Art and Literature*. George Borrow was one of the many young men who became interested in German as a result of Taylor's advocacy. Unfortunately the *Historic Survey*, which is largely patched together from his articles and which contains a great many errors, was already out of date when it appeared, and Carlyle treated it with great severity. ' "The fine literature of Germany", no doubt, he has "imported" ', he commented in his review, 'yet only with the eyes of 1780 does he read it.' Following Bouterwek, Taylor regarded Novalis, Tieck, and Fouqué as 'shooting stars' and made no mention of H. von Kleist, Friedrich Schlegel, or E. T. A. Hoffmann. By this time it was a patent absurdity that so large a proportion of a general work should be devoted to Klopstock. Yet it was in no small degree due to Taylor himself that a more critical attitude to German literature existed in England by 1830, and the fact that his *Survey* contains a great many

[1] William Taylor (1765–1836) was the son of a well-to-do manufacturer who sent him abroad to study languages and the ways of commerce. In 1790 he visited France and attended the debates in the National Assembly. The following year he persuaded his father to retire and wind up the firm, and he himself was enabled to devote the remainder of his life to literature. He was a friend of Southey's. In his articles he made a number of suggestions for projects which were later to be realized, forecasting steam navigation, pointing out the feasibility of a Panama Canal, and recommending that Britain should establish colonies in Africa, 'the only quarter of the world' where British commerce had 'struck no root'.

translations, competently done, helps to give it a value greater than Carlyle was disposed to acknowledge.

Henry Crabb Robinson, the friend of Wordsworth, Coleridge, Lamb, and Carlyle, whose *Diaries* throw so much light on the literary history of the period, also did a good deal to make German literature better known.[1] In 1800 he went to Germany for the first time because, as he told his brother, he 'understood it to be a country in which there was a rising literature' and he was 'surfeited' but not 'nourished' by 'the cream of English literature'. He met Goethe, Schiller, Herder, Schelling, and Wieland, and spent two or three years studying at Jena, then one of the most active intellectual centres in Europe. Although he published translations and numerous articles on German literature it was above all by his enthusiastic conversation that he promoted the cause of German culture in England. Not the least of his services was his insistence on the supremacy of Goethe. 'It has been my rare good fortune to have seen a large proportion of the greatest minds of our age', he once wrote, 'in the fields of poetry and speculative philosophy . . ., but none that I have ever known came near him.' Another minor writer excited by the 'inexhaustible mine of the richest ore' to be found in German was R. P. Gillies, the friend of Scott, whose *Memoirs of a Literary Veteran* (1851) contain an amusing account of his 'vain quest after German books and German professors' in Edinburgh about the year 1817, and his eventual discovery of a Frenchman called Pierard who told him that he had '*von* German book—le voilà! mais il faut avouer,—dere are some sentences vich I do *not* understand!'[2] Gillies tells us that De Quincey was 'the first friend . . . who could profess to have a command over the German language and who consequently was able (*ex cathedrâ*) to corroborate my notions of the great stores that were contained therein'. When another friend put at his disposal a good collection of modern German literature he com-

1 Henry Crabb Robinson (1775–1867) was articled as an attorney at Colchester and became a clerk in London in 1796. In 1813 he became a barrister at the Middle Temple. He was one of the earliest members of the Athenæum and an active supporter of London University. He wrote for *The Times* on foreign affairs.

2 Robert Pearce Gillies (1788–1858) studied under Dugald Stewart and Playfair at the University of Edinburgh and was admitted advocate in 1813. He lost most of his money by a rash speculation and supported himself by his writing. In middle life he moved to London, where he was constantly being arrested for debt. For seven years he was obliged to live in Boulogne. His *Memoirs* contain reminiscences of Sir Walter Scott, Jeffrey, De Quincey, and John Galt.

ments that 'the discovery of Aladdin's lamp could not have been more elating'. Of his numerous translations perhaps the most important were those published in *Blackwood's* between 1819 and 1827 under the title 'Horæ Germanicæ' ('Horæ Danicæ' were also the work of Gillies). These consisted of translations of the most striking passages of many German plays, and Gillies tells us that he had often made a complete translation, although he did not print it. Later he looked back and wondered why he had not made a more determined effort to publish complete translations, commenting:

> Feeling that when I translated any one of them, fifty more equally interesting were awaiting the same process, I looked upon the printed fragments only as stepping-stones into the deeper mines of German literature. Or to improve the metaphor, they were like a bridge across the dark waters hitherto thought impassable, leading a way into the stupendous cavern, with its glittering stalactites, and its various treasures guarded by Teutonic genii, who would be propitiated by one who came before them humbly, but courageously. However, I set most store, as I do now, by the prose works [of] Germany, of which I had once a valuable collection to be used, when time served; but which . . . have drifted out of my grasp for ever. (*Memoirs*, ii. 265–6.)

It is unnecessary to provide further evidence of the fact that many writers of the time were convinced that German literature contained unexplored wealth, or to insist further on the important part played by such periodicals as *Blackwood's*, the *London Magazine*, the *Athenaeum*, and the *Foreign Quarterly Review* in introducing German literature to English readers. It will be more useful to consider very briefly how far certain of the authors of the day were influenced in their own work by the contemporary excitement about Germany.

Scott was interested above all by the ballads and the popular element in German literature, which presented itself to him as an alternative to Latin, for which he had little feeling. In his twenties he once sat up late into the night to translate Bürger's *Lenore*, while he also 'balladized one or two other poems of Bürger'. The result was *The Chase, and William and Helen: two ballads from the German*, a pamphlet the excessive rarity of which demonstrates its lack of success, in spite of favourable notice from one reviewer. Scott's translation of *Götz von Berlichingen*,

Goethe's 'knights-in-armour' drama, is an inaccurate piece of work. M. G. Lewis published Scott's imitation of Goethe's 'Der Untreue Knabe' in his *Tales of Wonder* in 1801, while Scott's version of *The Erl-King* dates from the same period. The harper's song in *Wilhelm Meister* may well have influenced the opening of *The Lay of the Last Minstrel*, while two of the least successful of Scott's characters were avowedly the result of his German reading: the White Lady in *The Monastery* is an adaptation of de la Motte Fouqué's Undine, and Fenella in *Peveril of the Peak* owes something to the fine sketch of Mignon in *Wilhelm Meister*. In general the German influence on Scott is most evident in the poems and in the least successful of his prose romances. In spite of his veneration for Goethe, whom he once rather oddly described to Lockhart as 'my old master', he was more at home with writers who innovated less. It is not surprising that most of the 300 German books in his library dealt with antiquities and folk-lore. As he had discovered when he became a member of the Speculative Society, Scott was no more a metaphysician than he was a revolutionary. He had no sympathy with the Jacobinism of the intellect: he turned away from the dark places of the human mind, and while the supernatural attracted him he felt obliged to explain it away. His interest in German literature declined as he grew older, though he wrote an essay on Hoffmann and sometimes talked about German writers with Lockhart.

Byron was younger than Scott had been when he suffered from Gessner's *Death of Abel*, but it seems to have been *De L'Allemagne* that really aroused his interest in German literature. As a boy he had been very much struck by *Der Geisterseher*, while in 1814 he fell under the spell of Schiller's *Robbers*. Of all German books it was *Faust* that was destined to influence Byron's own work most obviously. In 1816 he heard Lewis translating longish passages, and the result may be seen in *Manfred* and in *Cain*. Byron himself described *The Deformed Transformed* as 'a *Faustish* kind of drama', and Shelley rightly replied that it was a bad imitation. When Goethe reviewed *Manfred* enthusiastically in *Kunst und Alterthum* in 1820, so helping to establish Byron's European reputation, Byron responded by dedicating *Werner* to him. In one of two earlier but unpublished dedications to Goethe he had already described him as 'the first of existing writers, who has created the literature of his own country, and

illustrated that of Europe'. Yet while Byron was greatly impressed by German literature we must remember that knowledge of it came to him almost entirely at second hand. 'I have read . . . much less of Goethe, and Schiller, and Wieland, than I could wish', as he once confessed. 'I only know them through the medium of English, French, and Italian translations.' As one considers the influence of German literature on Byron's own writings one finds, as with Scott, that it is least evident in his finest work.

Unlike Keats, who knew next to nothing of German literature, Shelley frequently refers to German poets and philosophers, though he never fulfilled his intention of reading Kant. At first it was the most sensational type of German—and 'German'—literature that appealed to him, as may be seen from his absurd prose fictions, *Zastrozzi* and *St. Irvyne*. In 1815 he began to study the language, though he never came to know it well. As one would have expected, he was keenly interested in *Werther*: indeed he began to sketch out a different version of the story. Peacock tells us that *The Robbers* and *Faust* were among the works which 'took deepest root in his mind, and had the strongest influence on the formation of his character'. Shelley himself tells us that he read *Faust* 'over and over again . . . always with sensations which no other composition excites', and comments:

> The pleasure of sympathising with emotions known only to few, although they derive their sole charm from despair, and the scorn of the narrow good we can attain in our present state, seems more than to ease the pain which belongs to them. . . . Perhaps . . . we admirers of *Faust* are on the right road to Paradise. (Letter to John Osborn, 10. iv. 22.)

Of his translations from *Faust* the opening choruses of the Prologue in Heaven are particularly fine. Shelley once asked the Gisbornes whether they could detect the influence of *Faust* on his own poetry, and in fact several of his poems seem to owe something to Goethe's masterpiece: the influence of *Faust* can probably be detected in both *Alastor* and *Adonais*, while it is beyond doubt in *Hellas*.

Yet of all the poets of the time it was Beddoes who had the deepest affinity with Germany. He spent a considerable part of his life in Germany and wrote a good deal in German, both in verse and in prose. His remark that modern critics of the

drama are by education 'prejudiced . . . in favour of the literature of the South' has already been quoted. He himself had little interest in Italian literature, displayed 'an aversion to the manner and the character of the French', and turned instinctively for inspiration to 'Britain-grafted, flourishing Germany'. Believing as he did that German literature 'touches the heaven of the Greek in many places' he could never understand why his contemporaries would not study the German language. 'What an idle generation you are,' as he wrote to 'Barry Cornwall', 'why don't you learn German?' His letters are full of perceptive criticisms of German literature. He said that he had learned more from Wieland and Tieck than from any other German writers, and it was his view that Tieck—whose concept of 'romantic irony' particularly appealed to him and whose works he once thought of trying to introduce to English readers —deserved to be 'much more relished than Goethe'. He also thought very highly of Schiller, maintaining that 'most of our . . . dramatic writers would gain much by the study of the historic conduct of Schiller, & some of his predecessors . . . & a modified imitation of it'. Towards the end of his life he translated part of the *Philosophic Letters.* It is thoroughly appropriate that he seems to have written part of *Death's Jest-Book* while he was studying at Göttingen— a fact that would have delighted the authors of the *Anti-Jacobin.* His deep affinity with Germany may be seen in the genuinely metaphysical temper of his mind, in the remarkable masculine power of his blank verse, and perhaps also in a certain lack of psychological balance and in the strange harshness of many of his lyrics. Professor Donner has admirably illustrated his life and work with a number of woodcuts by John Stephan of Calcar: there are paintings and engravings by Dürer that would be hardly less appropriate.

Yet it is when one turns from poetry to philosophy and criticism that one finds the clearest evidence of German influence at this time. Coleridge belongs to the preceding volume in this series, and Carlyle to the volume that follows; but something must be said here of De Quincey's lifelong interest in German literature, since he was one of the principal channels by which knowledge of German philosophy reached England. As early as 1803 his diary records the purchase of a copy of *The Ghost Seer* for 4*d*., but it was from his friend De Haren that he obtained his 'first lessons in German' and his 'first acquaintance with German

literature'. It was on account of De Haren and the 'small portable library which filled one of his trunks' that De Quincey arrived in Oxford with a keen interest in German literature—an interest which was confirmed by his reading as an undergraduate and no doubt by conversation with Schwartzburg, who was almost the only friend he made during his period at the University. Soon we find him studying 'German metaphysics in the writings of Kant, Fichte, Schelling, etc.' He must also have made some translations about this time, since in his first published essay on German literature, which appeared in the *London Magazine* for December 1821, he makes use of a version of his own. Some of De Quincey's comments on Richter (the subject of the article) remind us of the author himself, and this is even more noticeable when De Quincey writes on Herder two years later. He describes Herder as 'the German Coleridge',

> having the same all-grasping erudition, the same spirit of universal research, the same disfiguring superficiality and inaccuracy, the same indeterminateness of object, the same obscure and fanatical mysticism (*schwärmerey*), the same plethoric fulness of thought, the same fine sense of the beautiful, and (I think) the same incapacity for dealing with simple and austere grandeur.

De Quincey also began a series of articles in *Blackwood's* entitled 'A Gallery of the German Prose Classics', the first author he dealt with being Lessing, and the second Kant. Although he wrote elsewhere on Schiller and on *Wilhelm Meister* De Quincey was more deeply interested in the German thinkers than in the poets, and when Carlyle described him as 'a man of very considerable genius, and . . . a German, a Kantist', he laid his finger on the deepest and most constant of his German preoccupations. Throughout his life it was his ambition to make known the name of Kant 'in a country where the structure and tendency of society impress upon the whole activities of the nation a direction almost exclusively practical'. When he talked to his friends in that 'most musical and impressive of voices', it was very often of Kant. 'In a few minutes'—R. P. Gillies tells us—'he could escape at will . . . to the soul's immortality, to Plato, and Kant, and Schelling, and Fichte.' In the important chapter on 'German Studies' in his *Autobiographic Sketches*, from which a quotation has already been given, De Quincey describes the newly discovered literature of Germany as an El Dorado and 'the

new or transcendental philosophy of Immanuel Kant' as 'the very tree of knowledge' standing in the centre. When De Quincey was most doubtful about the validity of Kant's philosophy (we are told) he was apt to become melancholy, assailed by a 'gloom of something like misanthropy'.

Although De Quincey always intended to try his hand as a writer of fiction, in the event he wrote only one long work of fiction, though he translated another. He translated *Walladmor*, a book by a German hack-writer which purported to be a German version of a book by Scott: as De Quincey became aware of the book's absurdities he handled his original with a great deal of freedom. *Klosterheim* appears to be original, though it would not be surprising if a German prototype were one day to turn up. It is a Gothic romance set in a town in Swabia during the Thirty Years' War. De Quincey also wrote a handful of short stories, several of them German in origin or by natural affinity. 'The Love Charm' is a translation from Tieck, while 'Mr. Snackenberger' and 'The King of Hayti' are free adaptations of German originals. Their ingredients are mystery, terror, a grotesque sense of humour, and a strong vein of sentiment verging on sentimentality. In general De Quincey's fictitious writings show little of the true novelist's interest in human character. Writing rather as the author of 'Murder considered as one of the Fine Arts', he reminds us often of Edgar Allan Poe. If he had been alive today he would have been a great reader of the more macabre and intellectual type of detective story.

Hazlitt was far from sharing De Quincey's enthusiasm for the Germans. 'He has not read Plato in his youth', De Quincey wrote in a footnote to the 1822 version of the *Confessions*, '(which most likely was only his misfortune); but neither has he read Kant in his manhood (which is his fault).' As a young man Hazlitt admired the Jacobin German drama of the time, and as early as 1796 we find him discussing German literature with his friend Joseph Fawcett; but although he wrote about German authors here and there we miss the spontaneous enthusiasm with which he wrote about Boccaccio and Ariosto. Kant must have reminded him too forcibly of the rigidity of his own upbringing, while his innate preference for lucidity of expression led him to look with distrust on the work of so abstruse a thinker (known to him only, it is probable, through Willich and Mme de Staël).

'As for the great German oracle Kant', he wrote in his review of *Biographia Literaria*, 'we must take the liberty to say, that his system appears to us the most wilful and monstrous absurdity that ever was invented.' He seems hardly ever to refer to Herder or to Schelling except when he describes Coleridge as a man 'who wandered into Germany and lost himself in the labyrinths of the Hartz Forest and of the Kantean philosophy, and amongst the cabalistic names of Fichtè and Schelling and Lessing, and God knows who'. The names of Kotzebue (an early weakness), Schiller, A. W. Schlegel and Goethe almost exhaust the list of the German writers of whom Hazlitt approved.

With Carlyle we reach a new chapter in the history of German literature in England. For us it will be sufficient to recall that three of his first four books were his translation of *Wilhelm Meister's Apprenticeship* (1824), his *Life of Schiller* (1825), and his four volumes of translations from *German Romance* (1827). It is wholly appropriate that Goethe should have served as a referee when Carlyle applied for the Chair of Moral Philosophy at St. Andrews, writing that he had 'observed with pleasure Mr. Carlyle's profound study of [German] literature'. It is no less appropriate that Goethe's testimonial should have arrived too late. Carlyle was not elected. We may remember the warning voice of Jeffrey: 'England *never will* admire your German divinities.'

While the influence of German literature in England at this time has frequently been discussed, that of French has received little attention. Yet in spite of the exaggerated contempt for the writers of France expressed by De Quincey and a few of his contemporaries, French influence was more important than might at first appear. In his *Passages of a Working Life* Charles Knight tells us that when he set up as a publisher in 1824 'translations from the French were in far greater demand than at present [1864], when an acquaintance with modern languages is much more general'. Although knowledge of French was shaky, many readers were prepared to take an interest in the literature of France, and particularly in the work of French prose writers. The same love of 'romantic research' that led Scott to study Italian as a young man induced him to improve his French, in order that he might explore the older French literature and extend his acquaintance with 'Tressan's romances, the Bibliothèque Bleue, and Bibliothèque des Romans'; while

a man as different from Scott as Hazlitt more than once echoed Gray's exclamation—'Be mine to read eternal new romances of Marivaux and Crébillon!' As one might expect, the poets of the seventeenth century were not generally popular—to put in a word for Boileau was usually just a back-handed way of attacking the Lakers and the Cockneys—while not the least agreeable thing about Schlegel's lectures was that they seemed to justify the innate British tendency to be bored by Racine and the classical dramatists. The first signs of an interest in the older French poets and the first English reactions to the moderns are of greater historical interest. In the *London Magazine* Cary published a series of articles on 'The Early French Poets', illustrated by quotations, which included such men as Marot, du Bellay, Ronsard, and Villon: poets not greatly regarded in France itself at the time. Cary also wrote on two recent poets, Béranger and Lamartine, though his praise was tepid. Stendhal (also in the *London Magazine*) was even less enthusiastic, dismissing Victor Hugo as the writer of odes which 'positively do not contain the smallest particle of an idea'. It was a few years later that informed interest in the new French literature began to manifest itself, as may be seen from a letter from Letitia Elizabeth Landon to William Jerdan in 1834:

> A most delightful series of articles might be written on French literature. *We* know nothing of it; and it would require an immense deal of softening and adaptation to suit it to English taste. . . . It is full of novelty, vivid conceptions, and . . . genius, but what we should call blasphemous and indelicate to the last degree.

It must have been of the recent novelists and poets that L. E. L. was thinking, for the work of Rousseau and the writers of the *Encyclopédie*, which many Englishmen did find 'blasphemous and indelicate to the last degree', was already well known. Rousseau's writings had proved influential in England by the end of the eighteenth century: *La Nouvelle Héloïse* and *Émile* were widely read, though few readers were as clear as Hazlitt about the superiority of the *Confessions* to Rousseau's other writings. 'The best of all his works is the *Confessions*', he wrote in the *Round Table*, 'though it is that which has been least read, because it contains the fewest set paradoxes or general opinions.' In general we notice that the writers of the French Enlightenment are frequently referred to in the literature of this period, and

that the tone of the references serves as a convenient index to the political sympathies of the writer. When Mr. Crotchet mentions the name of Diderot in chapter vii of *Crotchet Castle*, for example, the Rev. Dr. Folliott asks him who Diderot was:

'Who was he, sir?' [Mr. Crotchet echoes.] 'The sublime philosopher, the father of the encyclopædia, of all the encyclopædias that have ever been printed.'

The Rev. Dr. Folliott. 'Bless me, sir, a terrible progeny! they belong to the tribe of *Incubi*.'

Mr. Crotchet. 'The great philosopher, Diderot—'

The Rev. Dr. Folliott. 'Sir, Diderot is not a man after my heart. Keep to the Greeks, if you please.'

It is not surprising that the notes to *Queen Mab*, a poem which owes a considerable debt to Volney's *Ruins*, contain quotations from Rousseau, Laplace, Cabanis, Bailly, d'Holbach, Condorcet, and Cuvier. Nor is it surprising that the Reviews devote a good deal of attention to these French writers. In *Peter's Letters to his Kinsfolk* Lockhart describes 'the Scotch philosophers of the present day' as 'the legitimate offspring of the sceptical philosophers of the last age', and he would certainly have included Rousseau and Diderot among their ancestors. While *Blackwood's* attacked Playfair as 'the d'Alembert of the Northern Encyclopaedists', one notices that the *philosophes* were usually treated with respect by writers in the *Edinburgh Review*. Altogether a surprising number of books from France or about France received attention in the Reviews, and the discussions that resulted became part of the great political and constitutional debate that went on throughout the nineteenth century.

A number of Englishmen were also becoming interested in Spanish history and literature at this time. When the political situation in South America drew attention to Spain in 1809 an anonymous writer expressed the hope that the time had come when Spanish would obtain 'as many readers and admirers . . . as French or German'. Between 1810 and 1814 there was apparently a sufficient number of exiles and other readers of Spanish in London to justify Southey's friend Blanco White in producing a periodical called *El Español*. The growing interest in Spanish literature, which was the subject of an article in the *London Magazine* in 1820, was further stimulated by the arrival of a large number of émigrés in 1823. In August of that year

J. H. Wiffen tells us that he has 'had much conversation on the Spanish muses' with a number of the deputies of the late Cortes at a party at Sir John Bowring's. Southey had a fine collection of Spanish and Portuguese books, while his letters make it clear that he was keenly interested in many Spanish and Portuguese authors, notably Camoens (whose sonnets he at one time considered superior to *The Lusiad*). When he set out to write a description of English life and manners in 1807 he chose the pseudonym of a supposed Spanish visitor, Don Manuel Alvarez Espriella. Hookham Frere was another man who knew a good deal about Spanish literature: he had served as ambassador in both Lisbon and Madrid, and his translations from *El Cid* were described by Coleridge as 'incomparable'. Scott also took an interest in Spanish literature, while Lockhart made translations of a number of ballads for a new edition of Motteux's *Don Quixote* which appeared in 1822 and then went on to produce his volume of translations, *Ancient Spanish Ballads: Historical and Romantic* (1823). In the preface Lockhart complains of the neglect of these poems in Spain itself: while attention has been paid to very minor writers no critic of ability has studied 'those older and simpler poets who were contented with the native inspirations of Castilian pride. No Spanish Percy, or Ellis, or Ritson, has arisen.' He refers to Bouterwek's *History of Spanish and Portuguese Literature*, which was translated into English in the same year, and to the collection of Spanish ballads made by an Englishman called Depping and published at Leipzig in 1817. In 1840 Lockhart gave Borrow's *Bible in Spain* his blessing. Mrs. Hemans produced numerous translations from Camoens and other Portuguese and Spanish poets, while Thomas Campbell was also interested in the literature of Spain. Heber collected Spanish books. Richard Chenevix Trench, who contributed a number of papers on Spanish literature to the *Athenaeum* in 1828–9, had been one of 'The Apostles' at Cambridge, and it is worth remembering that Torrijos was connected with the Apostles, who made a point of supporting the cause of the Spanish exiles and studying the literature of their country. When Ferdinand VII, 'the tyrant of literature', died in 1836 and the exiles returned to Spain to launch a 'Romantic Movement' they left England a little less ignorant of their country and its literature than it had been, and took with them a considerable debt to Byron and his English contemporaries.

In 1820 there had appeared *Observations on the State of Religion and Literature in Spain*, by John (later Sir John) Bowring, and it seems appropriate to end this section with a salute to this extraordinary man.[1] A disciple of Jeremy Bentham's, he was the first editor of the *Westminster Review*, edited Bentham's *Works*, and left brief *Autobiographical Recollections* which contain glimpses of eminent contemporaries. Between 1820 and 1843 he favoured the world with translations from the poetry of Russia, Batavia, Spain, Servia, Poland, Hungary, and Bohemia.

Important as was the influence of foreign literature at this period, however, it was as nothing compared with the influence of earlier English literature. As Scott remarked in his preface to the poems of Patrick Carey, it was an age 'distinguished for research into poetical antiquities'. *Beowulf*, it is true, was first published abroad, by Thorkelin at Copenhagen in 1815, and until the publication of J. M. Kemble's edition in 1833 the event went almost unnoticed in England; yet a notable band of enthusiasts were now exploring the rich heritage of our older literature. The appearance of the first series of the *Retrospective Review* between 1820 and 1826 is not the least significant of the signs of the times. In the introduction Henry Southern makes his point of view clear:

> The British public are almost solely occupied by the productions which daily issue from the press; newspapers, reviews, pamphlets, magazines, the popular poetry, the fashionable romances, together with new voyages and travels, occupy the reading time, and fix the attention of the people.—The old and venerable literature of the country, which has . . . tended to make us what we are, is treated with distant reverence. . . . Their authors are apotheosized, but seldom worshipped.

Southern goes on to claim that 'no study is more interesting, and few more useful, than the history of literature,—which is, in fact, the history of the mind of man', and to explain that 'the design of this Review of past literature . . . is . . . to recal the public from an exclusive attention to new books, by making

[1] Sir John Bowring (1792–1872) belonged to an ancient Devonshire family. He early revealed a remarkable gift for languages which he developed as a result of extensive travels on commercial business. In 1831 he worked with Sir H. Parnell on a report which led to a radical change in the accounting methods of the Exchequer. He became a Member of Parliament in 1835 and helped to form the Anti-Corn-Law League. Later in his life he occupied important diplomatic posts in the Far East.

the merit of old ones the subject of critical discussion'. It is characteristic of the age that he should have wished to preserve 'the interesting form and manner of the present Reviews', though without their political bias and personal invective. Deploring 'the dearth of works on the history of literature in our own language'—a deficiency that was not to be remedied until near the end of the century—he emphasized that the reviewers would 'by a careful selection of particular extracts, not only endeavour to give an idea of the mode of thought and style of individual authors, but to furnish a collection of specimens of the greatest part of our writers, so as to exhibit a bird's-eye view of the rise and progress of our literature'. Roughly three-quarters of the articles in the first four volumes deal with English literature, while the others deal with foreign books available in translation (usually in old translations). Southern particularly mentions the lack of accounts of the English prose writers, and we notice that the *Review* contains rather more articles on prose than on poetry and the drama together. There are essays on Sir Thomas Browne, Bacon's *Novum Organum*, *Mandeville's Travels*, the *Arcadia*, Ascham's *Toxophilus*, the criticism of Rymer and Dennis (the latter, by T. N. Talfourd, containing an important digression on severity in contemporary criticism), Defoe's *Memoirs of a Cavalier*, Stubbes's *Anatomy of Abuses*, and a number of memoirs and historical works. Among the poets dealt with we notice George Herbert, Vaughan, Browne the pastoralist, Southwell, Davenant, Chamberlayne, and the forgotten Leonard Lawrence, author of *Arnalte and Lucenda*. There is a series of articles on the early English drama, while attention is also paid to Ben Jonson, Chapman, Davenport, and Lee. Some of the writers dealt with remain obscure to this day: occasionally there is still no other place in which extracts may be found. But unfortunately the critical level is very uneven, and we look in vain for the incisiveness of a Hazlitt. Obvious opportunities are missed, as when Herbert is briefly and condescendingly disposed of. Other articles are the work of able men, although their titles are sometimes unhelpful: Talfourd's essay on Robert Wallace's *Various Prospects of Mankind*, for example, contains an intelligent and spirited rebuttal of the pessimistic view that literature was declining which may be read as a reply to Peacock's 'Four Ages of Poetry': Byron, Moore, Campbell, and Crabbe are played down, while generous praise is given to Wordsworth, Coleridge,

Lamb, 'Barry Cornwall', and Leigh Hunt. Such an excursion into modern literature was exceptional, however, and we notice that the sixteenth and seventeenth centuries were the favourite hunting-ground of most of the reviewers.

While the more obscure of the books discussed in the *Retrospective Review* go unmentioned in the *Edinburgh* and the *Quarterly*, reprints of others drew them to the attention of the less antiquarian reviewers. In his autobiography Charles Knight tells us that early in the century 'no publisher had . . . thought it worth while to reprint Drayton, or Wither, or Herrick, or Herbert': between 1815 and 1836—it is interesting to notice—complete or selected editions of the last three poets all made their appearance. A single publisher, C. Whittingham of Chiswick, produced reprints of Bartholomew Griffin's *Fidessa, Hero and Leander*, the poems of Thomas Lodge, and Chalkhill's *Thealma and Clearchus*, in attractive little volumes that may well have caught the eye of Keats on the table of one of his friends. Soon Pickering was issuing the first volumes of his Aldine Poets. A number of meritorious editions of the older prose writers also appeared, such as Reginald Heber's edition of Jeremy Taylor in 1822. But of course we remember particularly the editions of the Elizabethan and Jacobean dramatists for which Lamb's *Specimens* helped to prepare the way. 'What news in the republic of letters?' we find Peacock asking a friend in 1809. 'Has Gifford undertaken to edit Beaumont and Fletcher? Or is any new edition of those dramatists in contemplation?' As Jeffrey wrote in the *Edinburgh Review* two years later, 'All true lovers of English poetry have been long in love with the dramatists of the time of Elizabeth and James; and must have been sensibly comforted by their late restoration to some degree of favour and notoriety.' It was not only critics of progressive tastes who shared in this enthusiasm for the Elizabethans. Gifford produced editions of Massinger, Jonson and Ford between 1805 and 1827. Weber, whose edition of Ford had preceded Gifford's, brought out an inaccurate edition of Beaumont and Fletcher in 1812. In 1830 a much better scholar, Alexander Dyce, edited Webster, while in 1833 he completed an edition of Shirley which Gifford had begun. Seven years later he edited Middleton. The unreliability of the texts of many of these editions was not important: what mattered was that they made available the works of our older dramatists and so provided inspiration

for many of the new poets. It is worth remembering that while no Englishman (perhaps) has ever been as passionately interested in Shakespeare as John Keats, he never refers to Malone's epoch-making edition, which had appeared in 1790 and was revised in 1821.

Collections and anthologies of our older literature continued to appear in this period: mention may be made of Campbell's *Specimens of the British Poets* (1819), in seven volumes, with its long but disappointing preface, and Allan Cunningham's *Songs of Scotland* (1825). But the most important work of this kind had been done earlier by such men as Percy, Ritson, Ellis, Scott, and Southey. As has already been mentioned, more attention was now paid to prose: George Burnett's *Specimens of English Prose-Writers* had appeared in 1807: the first edition of Dunlop's *History of Fiction* was published in 1814: while Scott's *Lives of the Novelists* (originally prefaces to the volumes of Ballantyne's *Novelists' Library*) came out between 1821 and 1824. Francis Cary had the excellent idea of continuing Johnson's *Lives of the Poets* in the *London Magazine*, but unfortunately he lacked the critical vigour to make a success of the undertaking. John Payne Collier produced his *Poetical Decameron* in 1820 and his *History of English Dramatic Poetry* eleven years later, while Allan Cunningham's *Biographical and Critical History of the British Literature of the last Fifty Years* made its appearance at Paris in 1824.

In this age of old books and new books, of antiquarian enthusiasm and fresh literary genius, Isaac D'Israeli stands in the background making notes. Like most men with literary aspirations, he set out with the ambition of becoming a creative writer; but finding that he was deficient in imaginative power he had the humility and the good sense to devote himself to the study of the lives and writings of men greater than himself. The result was a series of studies which include *Curiosities of Literature*, *Calamities of Authors*, *Quarrels of Authors*, and *Amenities of Literature*. Byron described him as 'the Bayle of literary speculation, who puts together more amusing information than anybody'. But he did not only collect and digest the materials of our literary history: he also produced one work, *The Literary Character*, which was something quite new in English. The best way to give an impression of the book will be to quote a few phrases from D'Israeli's own chapter-summaries:

Youth of genius.—Its first impulses may be illustrated by its subsequent actions. . . . Its melancholy.—Its reveries. Its love of solitude. An unsettled impulse, querulous till it finds its true occupation. . . . Of the irritability of genius.—Genius in society often in a state of suffering. . . . The habitudes of the man of genius distinct from those of the man of society. . . . The meditations of genius.—A work on the art of meditation not yet produced.

'I have a great respect for *Israeli* and his talents', Byron wrote to John Murray in 1819, 'and have read his works over and over and over repeatedly, and have been amused by them greatly, and instructed often.' As Byron read *The Literary Character*, he must have felt that he was looking into a mirror. His annotations, which encouraged D'Israeli to undertake an expanded version of the book, remain as evidence of the fact that the self-effacing recorder of the ways of genius helped the most celebrated man of genius of the age to know himself. As Byron was the perfect reader of *The Literary Character*, so D'Israeli would have been the perfect reader of Byron's Memoirs, and in 1822 we find Byron writing that he would be 'gratified' if D'Israeli had seen his manuscript, 'as you are curious in such things as relate to the human mind'. D'Israeli replied that Byron's 'Book of Life' had been 'locked up by Murray in an iron chest', but it is to be hoped that it did not always elude the eye of so penetrating a historian of the mind. In any event the friendship between these two men, the admirer of Pope who wrote *Childe Harold* and *Manfred*, and the scholar whose frustrated genius revealed itself in his brilliant and flamboyant son, remains one of the 'curiosities of literature' at this time.

D'Israeli once remarked that 'we have become a nation of book collectors', but little can be said here of the bibliophiles and bibliomaniacs who were so much a part of the literary scene. The Roxburghe sale was an event of real literary importance. 'At the death of this accomplished person', Scott wrote of the third Duke in the *Quarterly Review* for February 1831,

his noble collection . . . was at length brought to auction, attracting the greatest attention, and bringing the highest prices of any book sale that had ever been heard of in Britain. The number of noblemen and gentlemen . . . who assembled there from day to day, recorded the proceedings of each morning's sale, and lamented or boasted the event of the competition, was unexampled; and, in short, the concourse of attendants terminated in the formation of

a society of about thirty amateurs..., who agreed to constitute a club, which should have for its object of union the common love of rare and curious volumes.

The Roxburghe Club began its series of editions and reprints of rare and curious books and manuscripts in 1812, to be followed by the Bannatyne Club a decade later. Men like Richard Heber, Thomas Park and Sir Thomas Phillipps were a feature of the age: of any of them it might have been said (as was in fact said of Heber) that 'the cutting blast of Siberia or the fainting heat of a Maltese sirocco would not make him halt or divert his course in the pursuit of a favourite volume'. A number of bibliographical works gathered in the harvest of such accumulations. Sir Samuel Egerton Brydges published his *Censura Literaria*, *British Bibliographer*, *Restituta*, and other interesting though inaccurate volumes, as well as producing editions or reprints of a great many old books. Robert Watt's *Bibliotheca Britannica* (1824) and Lowndes's *Bibliographer's Manual* (1834, and subsequently revised) are still important reference books.

The analogous works of John Nichols and his son J. B. Nichols, *Literary Anecdotes of the Eighteenth Century* (1812–15) and *Illustrations of the Literary History of the Eighteenth Century* (1817–58), may serve as a reminder of a fact often forgotten: that a great number of books relating to that century, and to the later seventeenth century, first appeared in our period. The first edition of Aubrey's *Lives* appeared in 1813, while the diaries of Evelyn and Pepys were published in 1818 and 1825. The appearance of two editions of Spence's *Anecdotes of Pope* on the same day in 1820 is one of the oddities of literary history. Six volumes of Richardson's letters came out in 1804, while various volumes containing the incomparable letters of Cowper and Horace Walpole continued to make their appearance throughout the first part of the century. When Macaulay began work on his *History of England*, therefore, he had the stimulus of newly published authorities of the greatest interest—an advantage equally enjoyed by the numerous writers of historical romance during this period. It must also be remembered that important new editions of the work of eighteenth-century writers came out during the same years. Bowles's edition of Pope, which gave rise to so bitter and so inconclusive a controversy, had been published in 1806. Scott's editions of Dryden and Swift appeared in 1808 and 1814, each accompanied by a notable biography.

Croker's edition of Boswell's *Life of Johnson*, so savagely attacked by Macaulay yet so valuable that Birkbeck Hill was to be deeply indebted to it half a century later, came out in 1831. John Wilson's admirable biography of Defoe had appeared the previous year. The principal novels of the eighteenth century were frequently reprinted and familiar to most members of 'the reading public'. The importance of all these books cannot be overlooked by anyone who consults the Reviews. The average reader in the year 1820 was as likely to be reading a book written in the eighteenth century as a book by one of his contemporaries. While this often made things difficult for the newer writers, they benefited in a great many ways from the rich deposits of earlier literature which were available to them.

# XV

# THE LITERARY SCENE IN 1832

In France, the good people still divert themselves with disputing the several merits of the Classical School, and the Romantic. They have the two schools—*that* is certain—let us be permitted to question the excellence of the scholars in either. The English have not disputed on the matter, and the consequence is, that their writers have contrived to amalgamate the chief qualities of *both* schools. Thus, the style of Byron is at once classical and romantic. . . . And even a Shelley, whom some would style emphatically of the Romantic School, has formed himself on the model of the Classic. His genius is eminently Greek: he has become romantic, by being peculiarly classical. Thus while the two schools abroad have been declaring an union incompatible, we have united them quietly, without saying a word on the matter. Heaven only knows to what extremes of absurdity we should have gone in the spirit of emulation, if we had thought fit to set up a couple of parties, to prove which was best!

*England and the English*, Book IV, chap. IV.

In the year 1819 an Italian spy reported that Byron belonged to a secret society called the 'Società Romantica', that he was in the habit of writing 'poetry of this new school', and that he had composed 'certain rules, entitled "Statutes of the Joyous Company"'. Like the spy, foreign historians of our literature have long taken it for granted that Byron belonged to the Romantic Movement; and some of them have even attempted to formulate the 'certain rules' of the Company—though none of them seems to have called it Joyous. English literary historians have usually followed their lead, though with greater caution. Since the word 'romantic' has not been used in this book—except in one or two quotations—something must now be said to explain this abstention. I do not wish to argue that the word is useless, but merely that the idea that there was a Romantic Movement in England at this time is accompanied by certain dangers—above all the danger that it tempts us to over-simplify the complicated literary landscape of the age.

The idea of a Romantic School of poetry was born in Germany. As Byron pointed out in 1821, 'Schlegel and Madame de

Staël have endeavoured . . . to reduce poetry to *two* systems, classical and romantic'—adding prophetically, 'the effect is only beginning'. Later Goethe claimed that the idea originated in an argument between Schiller and himself:

> The idea of the distinction between classical and romantic poetry [he told Eckermann], which is now spread over the whole world, . . . came originally from Schiller and myself. I laid down the maxim of objective treatment in poetry, and would allow no other; but Schiller, who worked quite in the subjective way . . ., wrote the treatise upon *Naïve and Sentimental Poetry* [in defence of his view]. He proved to me that I myself, against my will, was romantic. . . . The Schlegels took up this idea, and carried it further, so that it has now been diffused over the whole world; and every one talks about classicism and romanticism—of which nobody thought fifty years ago.

But since, as Professor Wellek has pointed out, Schiller's terminology differs in intention from that of A. W. Schlegel (Shakespeare is 'naïve' to Schiller but 'romantic' to Schlegel), it is primarily with Schlegel and Mme de Staël that we are concerned.

In the lectures which he delivered in Berlin between 1801 and 1804 August Wilhelm Schlegel makes a good deal of the contrast between romantic and classical literature. He asserts that 'romantic poetry is indisputably much nearer to our mind and heart than classical' and attempts to sketch the rise of romantic literature, which he associates with Christian chivalry. Dante, Petrarch, and Boccaccio are the writers whom he regards as the founders of romantic literature. In the Vienna lectures of 1809–11, of which an English translation appeared in 1815, Schlegel had a good deal more to say about romantic literature. He associates the antithesis between romantic and classical with the antitheses between organic and mechanical and picturesque and plastic. He contrasts the literature of classical antiquity and of the French seventeenth century with the romantic drama of Shakespeare and Calderón, the poetry of finished perfection with that of *Sehnsucht* or yearning and desire.

Mme de Staël did a great deal to popularize the concept in her influential book *De L'Allemagne*. 'If we do not admit that the empire of literature has been divided between paganism and Christianity', she wrote, 'the north and the south, antiquity and the middle ages, chivalry and the institutions of Greece and

Rome, we shall never succeed in forming a philosophical judgment of ancient and modern taste.'

In Germany, Italy, and France there was a great deal of discussion about the terms 'classical' and 'romantic', and in each of these countries it came to be the accepted view that the early nineteenth century had seen the birth of some sort of Romantic Movement:

> I perceive that in Germany, as well as in Italy, there is a great struggle about what they call '*Classical*' and '*Romantic*', [Byron wrote from Ravenna on 14 October 1820]—terms which were not subjects of classification in England, at least when I left it four or five years ago. Some of the English Scribblers, it is true, abused Pope and Swift, but the reason was that they themselves did not know how to write either prose or verse; but nobody thought them worth making a sect of. Perhaps there may be something of the kind sprung up lately, but I have not heard much about it, and it would be such bad taste that I shall be very sorry to believe it.

Since the English are notoriously lazy about general ideas and problems of historiography it is perhaps the less surprising that there was an increasing tendency, as the century wore on, to assent to the view that English literature too had had its Romantic Movement. The idea was given currency partly by foreign scholars and *comparatistes* struck by the similarities between the English literature of the early nineteenth century and the literature of Germany (in particular), and partly by Englishmen impressed by the usefulness of the terms when they were applied to foreign literature.

The question remains whether there was really a Romantic Movement in England, or rather (to put it in a more realistic form) whether it is useful to think of the major English writers of the age as forming a Romantic Movement.

It may be as well to begin with a reminder that the commonest meaning of the word 'romantic' at this time was not the same as its commonest meaning today. In his well-known essay 'On the Application of the Epithet Romantic', published in 1805, John Foster complains that the word is most often used as a vague term of abuse and recommends that it should be used only in passages describing the dangerous ascendancy of the imagination over the judgement. Although Foster was not a major writer, this testimony that to him the word 'romantic' was still essen-

tially pejorative is of great interest. A survey of the uses of the word in a number of representative writers of the time is badly needed. Meanwhile it may be worth while to outline the ways in which it is used in Leigh Hunt's *Lord Byron and Some of his Contemporaries* (1828)—the first version of the autobiography of the critic who did more than any other to win recognition for the new poets.

The centre from which the different shades of meaning radiate is of course 'like something in a story'. On at least one occasion the modern reader is likely to hesitate over Hunt's meaning—when he describes an eccentric friend some of whose stories 'were a little romantic, and no less authentic'. When he insists that 'some of the most romantic sorrows' with which men are afflicted are really due to faulty diet, he reminds us of Johnson's remark that he has no sympathy with 'metaphysical' distresses. In the reference to the chivalrous Lord Dillon, who 'ought to have been eternally at the head of his brigade, charging on his war-horse, and meditating romantic stories', the word is more definitely favourable, as it is when Hunt describes Byron listening to music 'with an air of romantic regret' which was in fact largely affectation. The meaning is similar when we are told that when Byron had discovered 'that the romantic character was not necessary to fame' he shocked Shelley by asking him 'whether he did not feel . . . a greater respect for the rich man of the company, than for any other?' Similarly Hunt tells us that his jailers 'were more like the romantic jailers drawn in some of our modern plays, than real Horsemonger-lane palpabilities'. Approaching the shores of Spain, Hunt felt that he was 'crossing a real line, over which knights and lovers had passed. And so they have, both real and fabulous; the former not less romantic, the latter scarcely less real.' The sight of the flag of an unfriendly country is 'less romantic' than that of 'the coast of Provence . . ., the land of the Troubadours'. It is important to notice that when Hunt, more than once, refers to the 'classical and romantic' associations of Italy and the Mediterranean, he has no idea of any opposition between the two: he simply means that these parts of the world remind us of books and of ancient times. His use of the word 'romance' corresponds to his use of 'romantic'. On one occasion he finds 'a greater degree of romance' in Gibbon than he would have expected: on another he remarks that Don Quixote might have

attacked a mysterious statue that he saw near Lyons, 'and not been thought mad: so much has romance done for us'. We notice that most or all of these passages could have been written a century before; and when we turn to the *Autobiography* of 1850 we find that practically all of them are retained, while on the few occasions on which the word 'romantic' makes a new appearance its meaning remains unchanged. The only omission of interest occurs in the sentence 'Here commences the (classical) ground of Italian romance', where Hunt must have realized that some readers might feel an incompatibility between the two words. The most striking fact is that in neither form of a book which is so largely concerned with the men who are now termed the 'Romantic Poets' does Hunt ever use the word 'romantic' with reference to the poetry that they wrote.

A careful study of the meanings of the word 'romantic' in the poetry and prose of a number of the major writers of the period might produce some interesting results. Hazlitt, for example, seems less often to use the word pejoratively than most of his contemporaries. But it is quite clear that most writers of the time commonly used the word in what we regard as being its eighteenth-century sense and did not usually think of it as denoting a particular kind of literature. It is equally clear that Wordsworth, Byron, Shelley, and Keats did not regard themselves as writing 'romantic' poems and would not—in fact—have been particularly flattered if they had been told that that was what they were doing. They did not regard themselves as constituting a Romantic Movement. Did they regard themselves as part of a Movement at all?

In the strict sense a Movement consists of a number of writers who share certain views on literature (views which may be expressed in some sort of manifesto) and who are conscious of moving in roughly the same direction. To determine whether these writers conceived of themselves as forming a Movement it will therefore be necessary to summarize their views on the poetry of each other.

Except for Coleridge, for whose powers he had the highest admiration, Wordsworth was a severe and unsympathetic critic of his contemporaries. Since he had a high sense of the didactic function of poetry it is not surprising that he was shocked by Byron: 'Though cordially admitting his lordship's extraordinary power, and his claims as a man of genius'—R. P. Gillies tells

us—Wordsworth 'firmly believed that his application of that power was reprehensible, perverted, and vicious.' Wordsworth noticed that a good deal in *Childe Harold* III was inspired by his own poetry but had no doubt that it was 'spoiled in the transmission'. In general he 'admitted the power of Byron in describing the workings of human passion, but denied that he knew anything of the beauties of Nature'. He considered *Don Juan* 'infamous' and told John Scott that Byron would probably end his career in a madhouse. Although he disapproved of Shelley's opinions on many subjects, Wordsworth thought him superior to Byron in poetic genius. According to Trelawny (an unreliable witness), Wordsworth said in 1819 that he thought nothing of Shelley as a poet, but later admitted that he was 'the greatest master of harmonious verse in our modern literature'. He also expressed the view that he was a poet who appealed mainly to the young because his work was too remote from 'the humanities'. Wordsworth regarded Keats as another poet who had not lived to fulfil his promise, complaining that he tended —like the young Tennyson—to be 'overluscious'. It is very clear that he had no sense of being the leader of a Movement of which these other poets were members. He was conscious of a great debt to Coleridge, but otherwise—in spite of the fame which came to him as he grew older—his creative career was essentially a lonely one.

If Wordsworth was coldly detached about contemporary poetry, Byron was positively hostile. Although his opinions fluctuated to some extent he never wavered in his passionate admiration for Pope or in his pessimistic view of the condition of poetry in his own lifetime:

> That this is the age of the decline of English poetry will be doubted by few who have calmly considered the subject. That there are men of genius among the present poets makes little against the fact, because it has been well said, that 'next to him who forms the taste of his country, the greatest genius is he who corrupts it'. (*Letters and Journals*, iv. 485.)

He had no doubt that the conservative writers of the age would outlive the revolutionaries. In the dedication to *Don Juan* he attacks Southey, Wordsworth, and Coleridge and assures them that

> Scott, Rogers, Campbell, Moore, and Crabbe, will try
> 'Gainst you the question with posterity

Although his early hostility to Wordsworth was modified later, in 1820 we still find him describing Wordsworth as 'essentially a bad writer'. He had no patience with what he regarded as Wordsworth's perverse views about the subjects and diction appropriate to poetry. Byron also disagreed 'essentially' with Shelley on the merits of Keats, whom he regarded at first simply as a follower of Leigh Hunt's. Some of the cruellest and most uncomprehending remarks about Keats ever made are to be found in Byron's letters, though he later revised his opinion to some extent, acknowledging that *Hyperion* was 'as sublime as Æschylus' and that Keats's genius, 'malgré all the fantastic fopperies of his style, was undoubtedly of great promise'. One reason for his improved opinion of Keats may have been the report that Keats had been 'persuaded to reform . . . his style upon the more classical models of the language'. Of Shelley Byron thought more highly. He had an uncritically high opinion of *Queen Mab*, which Medwin described as one of his 'favourite *cribbing* books', considered that *The Revolt of Islam* 'had much poetry', and gave high praise to *Prometheus Unbound.* His most interesting remark about Shelley occurs in a letter written on 26 April 1821: 'You . . . know my high opinion of your own poetry,—because it is of *no* school. I read *Cenci*—but, besides that I think the *subject* essentially *un*dramatic, I am not an admirer of our old dramatists *as models*. . . . Your *Cenci*, however, was a work of power, and poetry.' It is interesting that Byron should have said that Shelley belonged to '*no* school', because he believed that many of his contemporaries did belong to a school. He was infuriated by the 'attorneys' clerks' and others who were 'smitten by being told that the new school were to revive the language of Queen Elizabeth, the true English; as every body in the reign of Queen Anne wrote no better than French, by a species of literary treason'. He himself had been by no means guiltless:

> I am convinced, the more I think of it, that . . . *all* of us—Scott, Southey, Wordsworth, Moore, Campbell I,—are . . . in the wrong, one as much as another; that we are upon a wrong revolutionary poetical system, or systems, not worth a damn in itself, and from which none but Rogers and Crabbe are free . . . I am the more confirmed in this by having lately gone over some of our classics, particularly *Pope*. . . . (*Letters and Journals*, iv. 169.)

It is not surprising that this passage delighted Gifford, but it is

a great pity that Byron did not explain what he meant by the 'wrong revolutionary poetical system, or systems', particularly in view of his earlier decided rejection of the terms 'classical' and 'romantic'. It is clear in any event that Byron believed that there was something wrong with most contemporary poetry and felt that he had contributed to this by writing too heedlessly and allowing himself to be too much influenced by his contemporaries.

Shelley was an abler critic than Byron and it is not surprising that the two men failed to agree about poetry:

> We talked a great deal of poetry and such matters last night [Shelley wrote on 7 August 1821]; and as usual differed, and I think more than ever. He affects to patronise a system of criticism fit for the production of mediocrity, and although all his fine poems and passages have been produced in defiance of this system, yet I recognise the pernicious effects of it in the 'Doge of Venice'; and it will cramp and limit his future efforts however great they may be, unless he gets rid of it.

Whereas Byron was hostile to the new poetry, Shelley admired it and regarded it as natural that the poets of the age should have something in common:

> I have avoided [he wrote in the preface to *The Revolt of Islam*] . . . the imitation of any contemporary style. But there must be a resemblance, which does not depend upon their own will, between all the writers of any particular age. They cannot escape from subjection to a common influence which arises out of an infinite combination of circumstances belonging to the times in which they live.

As examples Shelley cites the tragic poets of the age of Pericles, 'the Italian revivers of ancient learning', and Shakespeare and his contemporaries. He was exasperated by the charge that he himself was an imitator of Wordsworth: 'It may as well be said that Lord Byron imitates Wordsworth, or that Wordsworth imitates Lord Byron, both being great poets, and deriving from the new springs of thought and feeling, which the great events of our age have exposed to view, a similar tone of sentiment, imagery, and expression.' It is most unfortunate that Shelley never wrote the second and third parts of his *Defence of Poetry*, in which he proposed to apply his general principles 'to the present state of the cultivation of poetry' and to provide

'a defence of the attempt to idealise the modern forms of manners and opinions, and compel them into a subordination to the imaginative and creative faculty'. Even as it stands, however, the *Defence of Poetry* makes it clear that Shelley's sense of a unity in the poetry of the day was largely due to his passionate interest in political reform. He argues that 'the literature of England, an energetic development of which has ever preceded or accompanied a great and free development of the national will, has arisen as it were from a new birth', and goes on to claim that he and his contemporaries 'live among such philosophers and poets as surpass beyond comparison any who have appeared since the last national struggle for civil and religious liberty', adding that 'it is impossible to read the compositions of the most celebrated writers of the present day without being startled by the electric life which burns within their words'. His opinion of individual writers of the time corresponded with this general view. He venerated Wordsworth's genius as a poet, though he distrusted his views on the language of poetry and detested his politics. He thought very highly of much of the poetry of Byron, going so far as to claim that one of his volumes contained 'finer poetry than had appeared in England since the publication of *Paradise Regained*'. As one would expect, however, he disapproved of Byron's determination to 'follow the French tragedians and Alfieri, rather than those of England and Spain'. It is easier to sympathize with his low opinion of *The Doge of Venice* than with his high admiration for *Cain*, which he described as 'apocalyptic . . . a revelation not before communicated to man'. It is remarkable how justly he appreciated the genius displayed in *Don Juan*, a poem remote from his own poetic scope and aims. 'He has read to me one of the unpublished cantos of Don Juan', he wrote in August 1821, 'which is astonishingly fine. It sets him not only above, but far above, all the poets of the day—every word is stamped with immortality. . . . It fulfils, in a certain degree, what I have long preached of producing—something wholly new and relative to the age, and yet surpassingly beautiful.' The poetry of Keats he knew much less well: he realized that the early poems revealed promise rather than achievement, but he was profoundly impressed by *Hyperion*, 'an astonishing piece of writing, [which] gives me a conception of Keats which I confess I had not before'. It is disappointing to find that he makes no reference to the Odes.

As we are reminded by his famous advice to Shelley to 'be more of an artist', Keats lacked Shelley's ability to appreciate the work of poets working on quite different lines from himself. He had no sense of common purpose with Shelley, whom he regarded as being too much preoccupied with causes other than that of poetry itself, and once told Bailey that he had 'refused to visit' him in order that he might retain his 'own unfetterd scope'. In many ways the brief and astonishing career of Keats may be regarded as a study in increasing, though voluntary, loneliness. When he wrote the early sonnet 'Great spirits now on earth are sojourning' he felt himself to be the ally of Wordsworth, Leigh Hunt, and Haydon; but he was soon to become estranged from both Hunt and Haydon, and while his admiration for Wordsworth persisted (in spite of his hatred of his political views) it became increasingly clear to him that his own genius had little in common with that of the older poet and his 'egotistical sublime'. Coleridge does not seem to have attracted him deeply, if we may judge from his passage about Coleridge's lack of 'negative capability' and by the fact that he never made any attempt to go to any of his lectures. Byron was a poet for whom Keats had little admiration. 'Lord Byron cuts a figure'—he once wrote—'but he is not figurative': unlike Shakespeare and the truly great poets. 'There is this great difference between us', he wrote on another occasion. 'He describes what he sees—I describe what I imagine.—Mine is the hardest task.' He detested *Don Juan*, 'Lord Byron's last flash poem': he read it on his way to Italy, and exclaimed that it was 'a paltry originality, which consists in making solemn things gay, and gay things solemn'. When he wrote his greatest work, Keats was on his own as a writer.

It is clear, therefore, that these four 'romantic' poets were very much inclined to be individualists. Only one of them seems to have regarded himself as in any sense a part of a Movement of which he approved, and even he (Shelley) thought of this Movement as something vague and impersonal. Byron, who explicitly rejected the terms 'classical' and 'romantic', sometimes regarded himself as part of a Movement; but in his case it was a Movement of which he strongly disapproved, while his greatest work—*Don Juan* and *The Vision of Judgment*—has little in common with the poetry of Wordsworth, Shelley, and Keats. Neither Wordsworth nor Keats appears to have regarded

himself as belonging to a Movement. It is consistent with this that Shelley was the only one of the four who warmly admired the poetry of all three of the others—although even he highly admired only one of Keats's poems, *Hyperion.*

There is certainly nothing that can be regarded as a manifesto of the new poets. There has, indeed, only been one candidate for this position, the preface to the second edition of *Lyrical Ballads*. To the end of his life Wordsworth maintained that he wrote the preface 'solely to gratify Coleridge', and he soon had reason to regret it. In *Biographia Literaria* Coleridge himself had no difficulty in demonstrating that some of Wordsworth's tenets were historically untenable, others logically inconsistent. As has already been suggested, eloquent as many passages are, the preface is a most misleading introduction to Wordsworth's poems and there can be no doubt that it did his reputation a great deal of harm. It is hardly surprising that the other poets of the day made no attempt to follow its precepts. The effect of the preface was in fact to provide Coleridge with a perfect subject for dissection, to prejudice Byron against the greatest poet of the day, and to furnish the journalistic critics of the time with a big stick with which to belabour 'The Lake School'. There are few references to the preface in the writings of Shelley, hardly any in those of Keats. The only poet who appears to have tried to carry out Wordsworth's precepts on the language of poetry seems, ironically enough, to have been Leigh Hunt, and by common consent *The Story of Rimini* is neither a successful poem nor the sort of thing that Wordsworth had in mind when he wrote that the poet should use a selection of 'the real language of men'.

But of course historians often discover movements of which contemporaries were partly or wholly unaware. Granted that 'The Romantic Movement' is an historian's term, someone may ask, can it be denied that it stands very well for something that happened to English literature in the early nineteenth century? The answer to this question depends on the standpoint of the observer and the degree of precision in definition that he considers desirable.

It depends on the standpoint of the observer. The question whether Keats is a poet of the Romantic Movement is a little like the question whether an Englishman is a European: of course he is, if you look at him from far enough away. An

observer in any particular European country will be more aware of the differences between Englishmen, Frenchmen, and Greeks, for example, than of anything that they have in common. If he then moves to Australia he is more likely to notice that Englishmen share certain characteristics with other Europeans which are not necessarily to be found in Australians. It is the same with literary history. A man who has been reading the literature of the early nineteenth century for a period of years becomes more conscious of the differences between the writers of the time than of any qualities that they have in common. If he were then to concentrate on some other period—let us say the fourteenth century—he might soon find himself contrasting the poets he was reading with 'the romantics'. Although this would in a sense be inexact—it would still be more useful to compare Chaucer with Wordsworth, on the one hand, or with Keats, on the other, than to compare him with 'the romantics' in general—it would not be altogether wrong. It depends on the degree of generalization to which one aspires, or which one is prepared to tolerate. 'The Romantics' will always serve as a sort of accommodation address.

The trouble is that several bad companions tend to accompany the idea of a Romantic Movement in England. One of them is the tendency to value any given poet rather as he is 'romantic'—or characteristic of the European Romantic Movement as a whole—than according to the merit of his poetry. Byron is the obvious instance. Continental critics have always taken him more seriously than his compatriots, and it is not always his best poems that they consider most important. *Childe Harold* and *Manfred* often receive more attention than *Don Juan* and *The Vision of Judgment*. As has been argued in Chapter II, if Byron had not discovered his characteristic satiric mode he would not be considered a great poet at all by English critics today; yet continental critics would still have regarded him (like Ossian) as one of the central figures in the European Romantic Movement. There are far more references to Byron than to Keats in most French and German studies of 'English Romanticism'; yet Keats was the greater poet.

Another and greater danger is that 'romantic' is a word that always brings another with it for company. It is unavoidably linked with 'classical', and 'classical' is a term that cannot without ambiguity be applied to any period of English literature. In

France we may call the seventeenth century the 'classical' period without fear of misunderstanding: it was not only the period in which Greek and Latin models were kept most constantly in view, but also the greatest period of French literature. In England the epoch in which Greek and Latin models were most important was probably the century following the Restoration; but this was by no means the greatest period of our literature and if we call it 'classical' we are in danger not only of underestimating the importance of classical influence in other periods but also of encouraging the old fallacy that this was a time at which English poetry was somehow diverted from its true course and dominated by the influence of the French. As soon as we begin to talk about 'the classical' and 'the romantic' ages we are in danger of over-emphasizing the differences between the Augustans and their predecessors (for in many ways the Augustan age is best regarded as the last wave of the Renaissance) and of exaggerating the (very great) differences between the Augustans and the writers of the early nineteenth century until we create a false antithesis. There was, after all, some continuity. No one has ever admired Pope more passionately than did Byron: Boswell's *Life of Johnson* was the only book about which Byron and Leigh Hunt were in agreement: *The Vanity of Human Wishes* was one of Scott's favourite poems: Keats studied Dryden in order to learn how to improve on the verse of *Endymion*: *Rasselas* was the source of Shelley's description of poets as 'the unacknowledged legislators of the world'. Every one of the great writers of the early nineteenth century owed something to the literature of the previous century, and several of them—like Scott and Wordsworth himself—owed a great deal.

A further danger of this schematization is that critics are tempted to suppose that 'the romantics' had a definite and largely shared aesthetic which distinguishes them sharply from 'the classicists' and other earlier writers. Like the inventors of the term 'The Lake School', such critics are in danger of supposing that the writers in question had 'common views in literature—particularly with regard to the true functions of poetry, and the true theory of poetic diction. Under this original blunder'—to repeat the quotation from De Quincey—'laughable it is to mention that they [go on] to *find* in their writings all the agreements and common characteristics which their blunder [has]

presumed' (*Collected Writings*, ed. Masson, ii. 172–3). Even Sir Maurice Bowra is not beyond reproach in this matter. 'If we wish to distinguish a single characteristic which differentiates the English Romantics from the poets of the eighteenth century,' he writes in *The Romantic Imagination*, 'it is to be found in the importance which they attached to the imagination and in the special view which they held of it.' But is it really true to say that 'on this, despite significant differences on points of detail, Blake, Coleridge, Wordsworth, Shelley, and Keats agree, and for each it sustains a deeply considered theory of poetry'? One notices that Byron, inevitably, is excluded; and one begins to wonder whether it is the case that a poet writes a certain kind of poetry because he possesses 'a deeply considered theory of poetry'. Did Keats write his great Odes because he had a certain theory of the imagination? Did he, for that matter, have a completely different kind of imagination from Shakespeare?

While *The Romantic Imagination* may raise these questions in our minds, *The Romantic Theory of Poetry* by Mrs. Dodds (A. E. Powell) illustrates the dangers of such reasoning far more vividly. Mrs. Dodds assures us that from the work of Blake, Coleridge, Wordsworth, De Quincey, Shelley, and Keats 'there emerges, in spite of individual differences, a coherent theory of the poet's function'. Following Croce she argues that 'the romantic artist . . . is one who values content more than form', whereas 'the classic cares first for form and scarcely knows what he forms until it emerges in the completed work'. We have only to try to apply such remarks to the Odes of Keats, on the one hand, and to the *Epistle to Arbuthnot*, on the other, to see how profoundly unhelpful they are. When the words 'classical' and 'romantic' are contrasted in this way they make nonsense of the true complexity of literary history and have a fatal tendency to drift semantically towards creative–positive–good and critical–negative–bad respectively. In *The Romantic Movement in English Poetry* Arthur Symons makes the revealing claim that 'the great poets of every age but the eighteenth have been romantic: what are Chaucer [and] Shakespeare . . . if not romantic?'

A critic who believes that all great poets are 'romantic' may at least be saved from one other danger that often accompanies too unquestioning a belief in the English Romantic Movement: the belief that there is a 'typically romantic' style in poetry or in prose. It is true that in this period, as in others, a critic who is

widely read can usually date a passage with more or less accuracy; but it is easy to deceive such a critic, and most writers who refer to a 'typically romantic style' appear to be claiming more than they would if they were to claim that they could usually date a passage of verse written in the early nineteenth century. Some believe that there is a 'characteristically romantic' use of versification, diction, imagery, or personification. Others seek to demonstrate an affinity between the style of the poetry or prose written at this time in different countries. This is as dangerous as it is attractive. As Chateaubriand once pointed out, 'ideas can be and are cosmopolitan, but not style, which has a soil, a sky, and a sun all its own'. That is why the idea of a Romantic Movement is so much more attractive to the historian of ideas than to the critic who is primarily interested in literature itself.

The truth is perhaps that the writing of literary history follows a dialectic course, and we have reached a point at which it may be useful for one critic to have written about the literature of the early nineteenth century in England without using the word 'romantic'. The task of the first literary historians was to draw large outline maps: that of their successors is to point out the faults of their maps as a preliminary to improving them. There is no harm in talking about a Romantic Movement in European literature as a whole, and not much in talking about a Romantic Movement in English literature itself, so long as we realize that we are using very general terms and that as soon as we say that something is 'typically romantic', discuss whether one poem is 'more romantic' than another, or give way to the temptation of using the term 'Romanticism' to explain everything that happened, the risk that we are saying less than we think is increasing alarmingly. The historians who have written most confidently of a Romantic Movement in England have always been men whose primary training has been in German or French literature, and they have shown a marked tendency to make Romanticism a bed of Procrustes on which to stretch the English literature of the time. Since their knowledge is horizontal rather than vertical, such scholars are always more keenly aware of the qualities that the English literature of the period shares with the literature of Germany or France than of the qualities in it that may be found in English literature of quite different periods. The reasons why something in any literature is as it is are more often

to be found in earlier literature, after all, than in contemporary literature from another country. And to me at least sources have always been more interesting than analogues.

But it is time to turn back from hypothesis to fact, from historiography to history; and it is a matter of history that there occurred in the mid-1820's a severe slump in publishing, and particularly in the publishing of poetry. As a result of the financial crisis of 1825–6 the whole structure of Ballantyne and Constable collapsed, and they were not the only publishers to go under in the storm. The entire book-trade was affected. It is symptomatic of the change in the spirit of the age that T. F. Dibdin, who had published *The Bibliomania or Book-Madness* in 1809, turned in 1832 to write *Bibliophobia. Remarks on the Present Languid and Depressed State of Literature and the Book Trade*, a curious work in which he looks back nostalgically to the happy days of publishing and book-collecting and reports John Murray's decided opinion that 'the taste for literature [is] ebbing'. Old books were no longer in demand as they had been fifteen or twenty years before, while publishing had become a hazardous and unrewarding profession. In February 1832 Carlyle told Macvey Napier that he had 'given up the notion' of hawking his *History of the French Revolution* round any further publishers. 'The bookselling trade', he wrote, 'seems on the edge of dissolution; the force of puffing can go no farther, yet bankruptcy clamours at every door: sad fate! to serve the Devil, and get no wages even from *him*!' While all imaginative literature was hit in some degree—Murray went so far as to sell the copyright in Jane Austen's novels—poetry suffered most of all. The boom which had once led Murray to 'wade through seven hundred . . . poems in a year' and Wordsworth to complain that 'poetry . . . overruns the country in all the shapes of the Plagues of Egypt' was now a thing of the past.

There is no lack of evidence of the waning interest in poetry at this time. Within a few weeks of Byron's death we find a writer in *Blackwood's* remarking that nowadays 'few write poetry . . . and nobody at all reads it. Our poets . . . have over-dosed us.' Although Wordsworth's reputation continued to rise among people seriously interested in poetry, it took Longmans four years to exhaust the five hundred copies of the collected edition which they published in 1820. There was a reaction even against Byron, while new poetry was not in demand. Publishers did not

dare to meddle with poetry: it is startling to find John Taylor, the friend and publisher of Keats, describing himself in 1830 as 'no publisher of poetry now'. As a writer commented in the *Edinburgh Review* on the appearance of Henry Taylor's *Philip van Artevelde* in 1834, it was 'a period of marked indifference to poetical productions'. In the same year a writer in the *New Monthly Magazine* complained that 'in the department of poetry we have had nothing for several years worth mentioning. A desultory effusion now and then finds its way into the periodical journals, as if to show that the fire of genius is not as yet wholly extinct amongst us. But no poem of any length or character has lately seen the light in this country.' The letters of the time are full of the complaints of unpublished poets: in 1837 Beddoes told an aspiring poet that his own poems remained in his desk, 'there being no vent for such things in a *market* more than glutted'.

It is appropriate that the most successful volume of verse to be published at this time should have been the *Corn-Law Rhymes* of Ebenezer Elliott. 'Strange as it may seem', Carlyle wrote in the *Edinburgh Review* for July 1832, '... here we have once more got sight of a Book calling itself Poetry, yet which actually is a kind of Book, and no empty pasteboard Case.' He emphasizes that the Corn-Law Rhymer is a self-taught man, and comments that 'for a generation that reads Cobbett's Prose, and Burns's Poetry, it need be no miracle that here also is a man who can handle both pen and hammer like a man'. The review throws a great deal of light on the condition of England in a memorable year:

Most persons, who have had eyes to look with, may have verified, in their own circle, the statement of this Sheffield Eye-witness, and 'from their own knowledge and observation fearlessly declare that the little master-manufacturer', that the working man generally, 'is in a much worse condition than he was in twenty-five years ago'. Unhappily, the fact is too plain.... In this state of things, every new man is a new misfortune.... It is as if from that Gehenna of Manufacturing Radicalism, from amid its loud roaring and cursing, whereby nothing became feasible, nothing knowable, except this only, that misery and malady existed there, we heard now some manful tone of reason and determination, wherein alone can there be profit, or promise of deliverance. In this Corn-Law Rhymer we seem to trace something of the antique spirit; a spirit which had long become invisible among our working as among other classes;

which here, perhaps almost for the first time, reveals itself in an altogether modern political vesture. . . . It appears to us as if in this humble chant of the *Village Patriarch* might be traced rudiments of a truly great idea. . . . Rudiments of an Epic, we say; and of the true Epic of our Time,—were the genius but arrived that could sing it! Not 'Arms and the Man'; 'Tools and the Man', that were now our Epic.

Yet while the work of the Corn-Law Rhymer is of great interest to the social historian it is of little account as poetry, and Carlyle acknowledged this when he urged Elliott (as he was soon to be urging Tennyson) to leave verse and rhyme for prose and work. England was entering an age of prose, and Thomas Hood was only one of a number of promising poets who did in fact turn away from serious poetry to other forms of composition in order to make a living. A few years later R. H. Horne was to sell the first edition of his epic, *Orion*, at a farthing; and about the same time we find an adaptable authoress, Eliza Acton, being told by Longman that there is no point in sending him poetry. 'Nobody wants poetry now', he wrote. 'Bring me a cookery book, and we might come to terms.' Such was the origin of a highly successful volume entitled *Modern Cookery*.

Nothing could better epitomize the practical temper of the new age than a laconic remark in Knight's *Passages of a Working Life*. 'Coleridge died in 1834. I went to live at Highgate the year after.' This was the age of Harriet Martineau, with her hearing-aid and her *Illustrations of Political Economy*. 'Every time has its genius,' as Bulwer Lytton observed, 'the genius of this time is wholly anti-poetic':

When Byron passed away, the feeling he had represented craved utterance no more. With a sigh we turned to the actual and practical career of life: we awoke from the morbid, the passionate, the dreaming. . . . And this with the more intenseness, because, the death of a great poet invariably produces an indifference to the art itself. . . . Hence that strong attachment to the Practical, which became so visible a little time after the death of Byron, and which continues . . . to characterize the temper of the time. Insensibly acted upon by the doctrine of the Utilitarians, we desired to see Utility in every branch of intellectual labour. (*England and the English*, Book IV, chap. ii.)

There were many reasons for the waning interest in imaginative literature, but probably the most important was the political crisis. As Dibdin put it in *Bibliophobia*, 'the wished for *Reform in*

*Parliament*, like Aaron's serpent, has swallowed up every other interest and pursuit'.

Nowhere are such signs of the time to be seen more clearly than in the *Westminster Review*, founded in 1824 and already mentioned in Chapter I. Before a little more is said of this most important periodical a brief account must be given of Jeremy Bentham himself, since he was a man who exerted a profound influence on his own age and the age that was to follow.[1] By 1815 he was already 67, but he lived on in robust health until the year of the Reform Act. Although his first book, the *Fragment on Government*, had appeared as early as 1776, and by 1792 he was so highly thought of in France that the National Assembly made him an honorary 'French Citizen', his fame in England grew much more slowly. By our period, however, he had gathered round himself a small but brilliant circle who were destined to carry his influence into almost every department of the national life.

Bentham was by training a lawyer and the *Fragment on Government* is a closely reasoned attack on Blackstone's eulogy of the British Constitution. The book was characteristic of Bentham: as John Stuart Mill pointed out in an admirable essay, Bentham's 'peculiar province' was 'the field of practical abuses'. It was his task 'to carry the warfare against absurdity into things practical'. From the law he moved to government itself, always with the same purpose. In Mill's words, 'he has swept away the accumulated cobwebs of centuries—he has untied knots which the efforts of the ablest thinkers, age after age, had only drawn tighter; and it is no exaggeration to say of him that over a great part of the field he was the first to shed the light of reason'.

Although Bentham's initial stimulus was usually the illogicality or absurdity of the existing state of affairs, he was by no means a purely destructive thinker. He always tried to propose a sound alternative to the unsound principle that he rejected. In order to do this he would begin by surveying the particular problem as comprehensively as he could—in relation, that is, to the whole problem of the right conduct of human life. And this

[1] Jeremy Bentham (1748–1832) was educated at Westminster and Queen's College, Oxford. He took his B.A. at the age of 16, and summed up the effects of an English university education as 'Mendacity and insincerity'. He went on to study the law, but made little attempt to succeed as a barrister, turning his mind to the physical sciences and to speculations on politics and jurisprudence. His principal writings are listed in the Bibliography.

great problem he regarded, characteristically, as essentially a practical problem. His primary aim was clarity: he hated the vague, the general, the indefinite. His object was to introduce some sort of scientific method into the study of man's behaviour in society, though in pursuing it he may be said to have paid too little attention both to history and to psychology. It is characteristic of him to have drawn up a 'Table of the Springs of Action': no less characteristic that (as Mill pointed out) the table 'overlooks the existence of about half of the whole number of mental feelings which human beings are capable of, including all those of which the direct objects are states of their own mind'. By Bentham 'Man is conceived . . . as a being susceptible of pleasures and pains, and governed in all his conduct partly by the different modifications of self-interest, and the passions commonly classed as selfish, partly by sympathies, or occasionally antipathies, towards other beings'. And here Bentham's conception of human nature stops. If ethics or psychology had been his main concern such limitations would have been fatal; but fortunately he concerned himself primarily with the practical aspects of human life. He is an outstanding example of the fact that those who have influenced human affairs most decisively have often been men who have seen one side of the truth with unusual clarity, while remaining unusually blind to the other. Through his disciples James Mill, John Stuart Mill, Ricardo, Sir Samuel Romilly, Henry Brougham, and John Bowring, Bentham exerted a great and beneficial influence on the development of English society and its institutions throughout the nineteenth century. That is why John Stuart Mill bracketed him with Coleridge as one of 'the two great seminal minds of England in their age'. These two men, he wrote,

> have never been read by the multitude. . . . Their readers have been few: but they have been the teachers of the teachers; there is hardly to be found in England an individual of any importance in the world of mind, who (whatever opinions he may have afterwards adopted) did not first learn to think from one of these two. . . . There is already scarcely a publication of any consequence addressed to the educated classes, which, if these persons had not existed, would not have been different from what it is.[1]

[1] Bentham was also responsible for some additions to the English vocabulary. Apart from 'utilitarian' itself, he seems to have been the first man to use the words 'international', 'codify', and 'minimize'.

It was largely through the *Westminster Review* that Bentham's opinions were drawn to the attention of those outside the circle of his immediate disciples and so made available to help meet the problems of the Victorian Age. The classic account of the establishment of the *Review* is to be found in John Stuart Mill's *Autobiography*. As he there points out,

> the need of a Radical organ to make head against the Edinburgh and Quarterly (then in the period of their greatest reputation and influence), had been a topic of conversation between [James Mill] and Mr. Bentham many years earlier...; but the idea had never assumed any practical shape. In 1823, however, Mr. Bentham determined to establish the Review at his own cost.

The prospectus made it clear that it was the intention of the proprietors to make the *Review* 'the representative of the true interests of the majority, and the firm and invariable advocate of those principles which tend to increase the sum of human happiness, and to ameliorate the condition of mankind'. The contributors to the *Review* did not speak with one voice, but they taught one lesson: they were all believers in the doctrine of 'the greatest happiness of the greatest number'. James Mill had recently provided an admirable summary of Bentham's views in a supplement to the *Encyclopaedia Britannica*: the *Review* carried on the work of dissemination. Like the early contributors to the *Edinburgh*, we notice, most of the writers in the *Westminster* were young men. Bentham himself seldom contributed, and while James Mill and Francis Place were both in their fifties Bowring was in his early thirties and most of his contributors were younger—John Stuart Mill being only seventeen.

For so serious a periodical the *Westminster* sold remarkably well. Of the first number, which contained nearly 300 pages and cost 6*s*., some three thousand copies were sold; and since (as Bowring pointed out) most of its readers were to be found 'among the non-opulent and democratic classes, whose access to books is principally by associations of various sorts, the number of its readers was very great'. It was therefore a large and receptive audience that attended to the *Westminster*'s exposure of prejudice and its warfare against the 'Establishment' of the day: the aristocracy, the clergy, the law, and the Tory and Whig parties as represented by the *Quarterly* and the *Edinburgh*. Among the most characteristic contributions to the first number they found

an attack on aristocratic education, a severe criticism of fashionable poetry (as exemplified by Tom Moore), two defences of the democratic system of the United States (the *Westminster* was highly favourable to most things American, except slavery), and the trenchant article on the two official Reviews already referred to in Chapter I. As G. L. Nesbitt has pointed out in his book *Benthamite Reviewing*, during its first few years the *Westminster* concentrated on weakening the power of the two main political factions and strengthening that of the educated middle class, while insisting on the need for a number of specific reforms in government and society.

As might be expected, the diminishing prestige of imaginative literature at this time is particularly evident in the pages of the *Westminster*. Bentham allowed his dislike of things which cannot be precisely defined to prejudice him against poetry, so betraying a misunderstanding of the true nature of language which is not uncommon among philosophers. We are even told that he 'could not bear to hear pronounced in his presence' the phrases '*good* and *bad taste*'. He explained the difference between poetry and prose by saying that '*prose* is where all the lines but the last go on to the margin—*poetry* is where some of them fall short of it'—and while this was a joke it was the joke of a man who once stated that 'All poetry is misrepresentation.' When he decided that half the space in the *Review* was to be 'consecrated to politics and morals, the other half left to literary insignificancies' the latter provision was simply designed as a sop to those who did not understand, as he did himself, that, 'quantity of pleasure being equal, push-pin is as good as poetry'. He disliked the very word 'literature': as a reviewer wrote in an early issue, literature 'is a cant word of the age; and to be literary, to be a littérateur, . . . a bel esprit, or a blue stocking is the disease of the age. The world is to be stormed by poetry and to be occupied by reviews and albums.' It is as if Peacock's prophecy in 'The Four Ages of Poetry' had now come to pass:

> Mathematicians, astronomers, chemists, moralists, metaphysicians, historians, politicians, and political economists . . . have built into the upper air of intelligence a pyramid, from the summit of which they see the modern Parnassus far beneath them, and, knowing how small a place it occupies in the comprehensiveness of their prospect, smile at the little ambition and the circumscribed perceptions with

which the drivellers and mountebanks upon it are contending for the poetical palm and the critical chair.

About the same time Peacock had written to Shelley that 'there is no longer a poetical audience among the higher class of minds; . . . moral, political, and physical science have entirely withdrawn from poetry the attention of all whose attention is worth having; . . . the poetical reading public [is] composed of the mere dregs of the intellectual community'. In 1820 that had been a pessimistic view: by the late 1820's it approximated to the simple truth. England was entering on what one survivor from an earlier age, Leigh Hunt, described as 'this formidable mechanical epoch, that was to take all the *dulce* out of the *utile*', an age in which there was much to do and in which many of the leading minds felt for literature that impatience with theory and disinterested speculation that is characteristic of such periods. Bentham and his followers often failed to remember how much visionaries and poets had done to prepare the public to desire a better order of society. Poetic justice is a conception with which Bentham would have had little patience, yet there is poetic justice in the fact that it was in the poetry of Wordsworth that his brilliant disciple John Stuart Mill was to find relief from his dejection in the autumn of 1828:

I now began to find meaning in the things which I had read or heard about the importance of poetry and art as instruments of human culture [he wrote in his *Autobiography*]. . . . What made Wordsworth's poems a medicine for my state of mind, was that they expressed, not mere outward beauty, but states of feeling, and of thought coloured by feeling, under the excitement of beauty. They seemed to be the very culture of the feelings, which I was in quest of. . . . From them I seemed to learn what would be the perennial sources of happiness, when all the greater evils of life shall have been removed.

The effects of the practical temper of the new age and of the crisis in the book trade may be seen in the fashion for cheaper books. About the year 1831 John Murray complained to Dibdin that nowadays 'men wished to get for *five*, what they knew they could not formerly obtain for *fifteen*, shillings. The love of quartos was well nigh extinct. . . . There was no resisting the tide of fashion. . . . The dwarf had vanquished the giant.' In this revolu-

tion Cobbett and other left-wing writers had led the way. In 1819 Charles Knight had pointed out that as a result of the increase of literacy there had been an 'excessive spread of cheap publications almost exclusively directed to the united object of inspiring hatred of the Government and contempt of the Religious Institutions of the country'. Such works were often published in parts 'at a price accessible even to the unhappy mechanics who labour sixteen hours a-day for less than a shilling'. The promoters of the Christian Knowledge Society were timid and ineffectual opponents of such publications: they 'meddled not with dangerous Science or more dangerous History', while 'Poetry and all works of Imagination they eschewed'. And so Knight himself began his long campaign to bring knowledge within the reach of the working classes with his periodical *The Plain Englishman.*[1] At first, as he acknowledges, 'the very notion of cheap books stank in the nostrils' of publishers:

> For a new work which involved the purchase of copyright, it was the established rule that the wealthy few, to whom price was not a consideration, were alone to be depended upon for the remuneration of the author and the first profit of the publisher. The proud quarto, with a rivulet of text meandering through a wide plain of margin, was the 'decus et tutamen' of the Row and of Albemarle Street. (*Passages of a Working Life*, i. 276.)

Soon other publishers were obliged to compete in this new field. Lockhart describes a conversation between Scott and Constable in 1825 in which the publisher complained that even middle-class families were too apt to be 'contented with a review or a magazine, or at best with a paltry subscription to some circulating library' and announced his new idea of producing 'a three-shilling or half-crown volume every month' which should sell in unprecedented numbers. The preface to the resulting series, *Constable's Miscellany*, is an interesting document:

> The change that has gradually taken place during the last thirty or forty years in the numbers and circumstances of the reading public,

[1] Charles Knight (1791–1873) was the son and for a time the apprentice of a bookseller at Windsor. Having gained experience as a newspaper reporter for the *Globe* and the *British Press*, he started the *Windsor and Eton Express* with his father in 1812. He was a friend of Praed and of many other men of letters of the time. His main publications are listed in the Bibliography.

and the unlimited desire of knowledge that now pervades every class of society, have suggested the present undertaking. Previously to the commencement of the late war, the buyers of books consisted principally of the richer classes—of those who were brought up to some of the learned professions, or who had received a liberal education. The saving of a few shillings on the price of a volume was not an object of much importance. . . . But now . . . a change in the mode of publishing seems to be called for. The strong desire entertained by most of those who are engaged in the various details of agriculture, manufactures, and commerce, for the acquisition of useful knowledge, and the culture of their minds, is strikingly evinced by the establishment of subscription libraries and scientific institutions, even in the most inconsiderable towns and villages.

The intention was to intersperse original books among reprints of standard works, always avoiding both 'party politics' and anything contrary to 'the principles of religion and morality'. Although the progress of the series was soon interrupted by Constable's financial ruin it performed a notable service and led the way, as Lockhart remarked, 'in one of the greatest revolutions that literary history will ever have to record'. Publishers began to vie with one another in cheap books, as they were already doing in Reviews and Magazines. The same day in April 1829 saw the appearance of the first volume of Murray's *Family Library* and Knight's *Library of Entertaining Knowledge*; but Knight hastened to assure his formidable competitor that they had 'plenty of sea-room and need never run foul of each other', adding that it was his belief that 'in a very few years, scarcely any other description of books will be published'. Another venture of Murray's, the *Cabinet Cyclopædia*, also deserves mention. In his *Bibliomania* Dibdin describes his discovery that 'a whole army of Lilliputians, headed by Dr. Lardner, was making glorious progress in the Republic of Literature. *Science*, *History*, and *Art*, each and all contributed to render such progress instrumental to the best interests of the body politic.' In 1830 the newly formed firm of Colburn and Bentley projected no fewer than four series of inexpensive books: the *National Library of General Knowledge*, the *Novelist's Library*, the *Library of Voyages and Travels*, and the *Juvenile Library*. 'Many are the hands which are feeding and stuffing that great lubberly brat, the Public', as the *Athenaeum* complained. Some publishers, like Constable and Murray, concentrated on middle-class readers, while others were

more concerned with working men. The *Library of Useful Knowledge*, published by Knight for the Society for the Diffusion of Useful Knowledge, was intended above all for working-class readers. It consisted of fortnightly parts of thirty-two pages and cost sixpence a part. The subjects of the books in this series were almost exclusively practical and at first the scheme worked well, nearly 30,000 copies of some of the early parts being sold. Christopher Thomson, who published his *Autobiography of an Artisan* in 1847, was the sort of person Knight had in mind: Thomson tells us how he went without sugar in his tea in order to buy Knight's *Penny Magazine*, which began to appear in 1832. Chambers's *Edinburgh Journal* started earlier in the same year. As Knight rightly claimed, such publications 'were making readers. They were raising up a new class, and a much larger class than previously existed, to be the purchasers of books, [and so] changing the whole form of social life.' Booksellers had to become reconciled to 'the terrible era of cheapness which commenced in 1827'. In Knight's words, 'Books, which at the beginning of the century had been a luxury, had now become a necessity.'

Yet an important reservation must be made. Although the vogue for cheap books is a major fact to be reckoned with in the history of the nineteenth century, it does not follow that they made their publishers' fortunes. Knight and his fellow-enthusiasts took a sanguine view of the reading public, and in particular of the working man. As Professor Royal A. Gettmann has recently pointed out, while 'a significant number of them did read the serious factual books prepared for them by publishers and educational organisations . . . there were some who refused to be marshalled and who preferred inflammatory political pamphlets'. And apart from these there were others, more numerous, 'who craved even more amusement than they found, for example, in *Insect Architecture*, one of the titles in the Library of Entertaining Knowledge which Charles Knight founded when the series on Useful Knowledge failed to capture as many readers as was hoped. In the late 1830's this last group had a decided preference for faded imitations of the novel of fashionable life.' Although it was a utilitarian age the imagination of the public continued to demand some sustenance, so that Bentley's *Standard Novels* were a great success while his *National* and *Juvenile Libraries* were hopeless failures.

Henry Brougham, who played an important part in the

Society for the Diffusion of Useful Knowledge, was no less active in promoting the Mechanics' Institutes which were to be so much a part of the Victorian scene.[1] The idea was provided by Dr. George Birkbeck, who organized science classes for Glasgow artisans at the beginning of the century. The London Mechanics' Institution was founded in 1824, and within twenty-five years there were more than seven hundred similar institutions with more than a hundred thousand members between them. Although the main emphasis was intended to be on the teaching of the more practical aspects of science it was also hoped that the institutes, with their libraries, would serve as general centres of knowledge and enlightenment. As an enthusiastic pamphleteer put it in 1825, 'the spectacle of hundreds of industrious individuals, who have finished the labours of the day, congregating together in a spacious apartment, listening with mute admiration to the sublime truths of philosophy, is worthy of a great and enlightened people'. Yet by no means everyone shared the feelings of the pamphleteer. 'God bless my soul, sir!', exclaims the Reverend Doctor Folliott at the beginning of the second chapter of *Crotchet Castle*, 'I am out of all patience with this march of mind. Here has my house been nearly burned down, by my cook taking it into her head to study hydrostatics, in a sixpenny tract, published by the Steam Intellect Society, and written by a learned friend who is for doing all the world's business as well as his own, and is equally well qualified to handle every branch of human knowledge.' The 'learned friend' is

[1] Henry Peter Brougham, Baron Brougham and Vaux (1778–1868), was educated at the High School and the University of Edinburgh. As a young advocate he was one of the original contributors to the *Edinburgh Review*. He then moved to London, was called to the Bar, and in 1810 became a Member of Parliament. He quickly attracted attention by his eloquent and untiring advocacy of the abolition of slavery and by his speeches and writings on popular education, a sound commercial policy, and the question of the abuse of charitable funds by the public schools and universities. Queen Caroline appointed him her Attorney General: at her trial in 1820 it fell to him to defend her. In 1826 he formed the Society for the Diffusion of Useful Knowledge, and soon he was playing a leading part in establishing the University of London. Having urged the Government to resist the dictation of the Holy Alliance in Europe, and done a great deal to reform the common law procedure, he was elevated to the peerage on becoming Lord Chancellor in 1830. In 1831 he made a celebrated speech on the second reading of the Reform Bill. Three years later he lost office on the dismissal of Melbourne's government. He sat constantly in the supreme Court of Appeal and on the Judicial Committee of the Privy Council. He was a man of extraordinary energy. He was often attacked and satirized, but it is easier to laugh at a man like Brougham than to be a man like Brougham.

Brougham, the Steam Intellect Society is the Useful Knowledge Society, and the objections of Doctor Folliott are those of the majority of the Tories and the orthodox churchmen of the time. They did not believe that a smattering of scientific knowledge would make the working classes more pious, and they did not see what good it could do to encourage them to meddle with matters above their station. Nor did they like the idea that the institutes should branch out and deal with subjects other than science. In 1825 a clergyman told the members of the newly formed Mechanics' Institution in Aberdeen that 'Belles Lettres, Political Economy, and even History, were dangerous studies'. It was not only the Tories who were critical: there are many sarcastic passages in Cobbett's *Political Register* about the 'brilliant enterprise to make us '*a*' *enlightened*' and fill us with '*antellect*', brought, ready bottled up, from the north of the Tweed'. 'The "*expansion* of the *mind*" is very well', Cobbett wrote on another occasion, 'but, really, the thing which presses most, at this time, is the getting of something to *expand the body* a little more: a little more *bread*, *bacon*, and *beer*.' Another reason for Cobbett's hostility to the institutes was his realization that they would inevitably fall under the domination of the middle classes. This happened almost from the first. Most working men were too deficient in elementary education to make much of the books and lectures—you cannot study engineering if you have never been taught to count—and they were far too tired to start learning at the end of the day. It is not surprising that they were mainly interested in matters bearing directly on their own standard of living. 'Take at random any score of working-men', as one contemporary wrote, 'and it will almost invariably be found that they would sooner attend a political meeting, to demand what they consider their 'rights', than a scientific lecture; that they would rather read a party newspaper than a calm historical narrative; and that they would sooner invest money in a benefit club or building society than in a mechanics' institute.' As the Victorian Age wore on, however, the influence of the Mechanics' Institutes did begin to make itself felt fairly widely, encouraging the habit of reading and debating and so lending weight to the growing demand for public libraries.

'There have been periods when the country heard with dismay that the soldier was abroad', Brougham told the Commons in 1828. 'That is not the case now. . . . There is another person

abroad—a less important person, in the eyes of some an insignificant person, whose labours have tended to produce this state of things—the schoolmaster is abroad, and I trust to the schoolmaster armed with his primer more than I do to the soldier in full military array for upholding and extending the liberties of the country.' The schoolmaster was one of the influences that helped to bring about the Reform Act and determine the way in which England was to develop as the nineteenth century went on. Another was the invention of a cheaper method of printing, which greatly increased the power of the press. In *Arlington* in 1832 T. H. Lister comments that 'the activity of the press' at the beginning of the century had been 'but as that of the dray-horse to the racer' compared with its activity and 'unexampled expedition' in more recent years. The increasing speed of travel, inconsiderable as it must seem to us today, also played its part in modifying the pattern of English life. It is curious to find Lister remarking elsewhere on the 'macadamization' of the roads and complaining that road travel is no longer adventurous enough to provide a novelist with rich materials:

> Farewell those golden days when an hundred miles' journey was an era in the life of him who undertook it; when the making of a will was the proper preface to a journey to London. . . . Then, it was chiefly at the outset of a journey that [the novelist] plunged with [his hero] into the thickest medley of conflicting events—an inn became the hot-bed of incident—and fear and laughter dogged the wheels. . . . Witness the rambles of a Jones; the slow, but varied and eventful progress of a Roderick Random in the stage-waggon; and the fortunes of the day that exposed an Andrews to the tender mercies of a couple of footpads. . . . But the age of highwaymen is past . . . and the glories of the road are extinguished for ever. (*Granby*, 1826, i. 231–2.)

Within a decade Dickens was to demonstrate that the imaginative possibilities of the English Road were by no means exhausted. Yet it was railways that were the true portent of the new era, and as it approached England itself was beginning to gather speed, ready to thunder into the Victorian Age, with its shining rails, its dark cuttings, its smoke-filled tunnels, and its ugly, sprawling cities—with tantalizing glimpses from the windows of an old England that was rapidly being destroyed.

Everything was changing. As we move into the Railway Age we are bound to notice the growing addiction to an exag-

gerated propriety of language. Lockhart tells us that a great-aunt of Scott's once asked him to lend her a copy of Aphra Behn, whose novels she had greatly enjoyed as a girl. When next they met she gave him back the book and advised him to burn it, adding: 'Is it not a very odd thing that I, an old woman of eighty and upwards, sitting alone, feel myself ashamed to read a book which, sixty years ago, I have heard read aloud for the amusement of large circles, consisting of the first and most creditable society in London?' This appears to have taken place about the turn of the century, and Lockhart comments that it 'was owing to the gradual improvement of the national taste and delicacy'. A later example is mentioned in Leigh Hunt's *Autobiography*, when he explains why one of the poems in his *Poetical Works* of 1832 bears a curious title, 'The Gentle Armour':

> It originated in curious notions of delicacy. The poem is founded on one of the French *fabliaux*, *Les Trois Chevaliers et la Chemise*. . . . The late Mr. Way, who first introduced the story to the British public, and who was as respectable and conventional a gentleman . . . as could be desired, had no hesitation, some years ago, in rendering the French title of the poem by its (then) corresponding English words, *The Three Knights and the Smock*; but so rapid are the changes that take place in people's notions of what is decorous, that not only has the word 'smock' (of which it was impossible to see the indelicacy, till people were determined to find it) been displaced since that time by the word 'shift'; but even that harmless expression for the act of changing one garment for another, has been set aside in favour of the French word 'chemise'; and at length not even this word, it seems, is to be mentioned, nor the garment itself alluded to, by any decent writer! . . . The title was [therefore] altered . . .; and in a subsequent edition of the Works, the poem itself was withdrawn.

Particularly revealing examples of this shift of sensibility may be found in books written early in the century and later revised. In the 1822 version of *Confessions of an English Opium-Eater*, for example, De Quincey refers straightforwardly to women who 'subsist upon the wages of prostitution', whereas in 1856 he refers to them as 'the outcasts and pariahs of our female population'. If we compare the passages in detail we are likely to be struck by the shrillness of the one written at the middle of the century: De Quincey is by now thoroughly embarrassed by the necessity of

mentioning prostitutes at all. The reasons for the change were complex, but from one point of view what happened was that standards of gentility originally associated with the middle or lower-middle classes came to be shared by the upper classes themselves. This development had some curious results. Paradoxically enough, as Humphry House pointed out, the new standards of 'delicacy' were often a hindrance to the very men who were most set on reform, so that the more distressing consequences of Nancy's occupation in *Oliver Twist* could not be referred to, while a writer in *The Times* rebuked a Parliamentary committee for its 'indecency' in asking a woman factory worker how often she had had a miscarriage.

It is not surprising that the approach of the Victorian Age was greeted by an outburst of satire on cant. 'The cant which is the crying sin of this double-dealing and false-speaking time' is one of the most constant objects of Byron's satire, and it has been argued in Chapter II that *Don Juan* may be read as a sustained satire on cant. 'The truth is', Byron wrote in his letter to Murray 'On the Rev. W. L. Bowles' Strictures on Pope', 'that in these days the grand "*primum mobile*" of England is *cant*; cant political, cant poetical, cant religious, cant moral; but always *cant*, multiplied through all the varieties of life.' 'Luz is an excellent joke', Beddoes wrote from Germany in 1829, 'but tell me if I do not write too irreligiously for Cantland.' Lamb and Hood were never tired of attacking cant, the latter using his gifts as an etcher to this end as well as his gifts as a writer. In Hood's 'Progress of Cant', as Lamb pointed out in the *New Monthly Magazine*, 'all the projected improvements of the age' are depicted as so many different species of cant, as 'priests, anti-priests, architects, politicians, reformers, flaming loyalty men, high and low, rich and poor, one with another, all go on "progressing"'. Peacock's tales are full of satire on the characteristic failing of the time. As Mr. Crotchet points out in a passage already quoted, 'where the Greeks had modesty, we have cant; where they had poetry, we have cant; where they had patriotism, we have cant; where they had any thing that exalts, delights, or adorns humanity, we have nothing but cant, cant, cant'. In 1831 England stood on the threshold of what Grote was to call 'The Age of Steam and Cant'.

The following year, that of the Reform Act, is as good a terminal date as any for a volume of literary history. Keats,

Shelley, and Byron were dead, as was Hazlitt. Coleridge and Lamb had only two more years to live. And while Wordsworth lived on, with Southey, De Quincey, Peacock, and Leigh Hunt, they were by now unmistakably figures from a former age. In 1832, as Scott lay on his deathbed, we find Lockhart wondering whether to produce a special, 'entirely biographical' issue of the *Quarterly Review*. So many men had died: 'we have just lost Cuvier, Goethe, Mackintosh, Crabbe and Bentham', as Lockhart wrote to Milman. One age had ended, and another was beginning—for several of the men whom we think of as the great Victorians were now hard at work. Carlyle, Macaulay, and Disraeli were already well known. Dickens was working as a journalist. Lyell's *Principles of Geology* began to appear in 1830, while at the end of the following year Darwin set out in the *Beagle* on the voyage that was to have such memorable results. In 1832 Tennyson was 23, Browning 20. In five years a young Queen would mount the throne, and the Victorian Age would have begun.

# CHRONOLOGICAL TABLES

NOTE: In compiling the list of plays I have leaned heavily on Professor Allardyce Nicoll's *History of Early Nineteenth Century Drama, 1800–1850*, rev. ed. 1955. I have given a few examples of the dramatizations of Scott's romances as a reminder of their great popularity at this time.

No indication of anonymity is given in these lists.

| *Date* | *Public Events* | *Literary History (including translations)* | *Verse* |
|---|---|---|---|
| 1815 | Napoleon's return from Elba. Battle of Waterloo. Restoration of Louis XVIII. Napoleon exiled to St. Helena. | Anthony Trollope b.<br>Byron marries.<br>Ackermann's *University of Cambridge.*<br>Béranger, *Chansons.*<br>F. Schlegel, *Geschichte der alten und neuen Literatur.*<br>*Beowulf* pub. at Copenhagen, ed. Thorkelin.<br>A. W. Schlegel's *Lectures on Dramatic Art and Literature,* trans. J. Black.<br>Cowper, *Poems,* ed. J. Johnson.<br>Charles Lloyd trans. *The Tragedies of Alfieri.* | Byron, *Hebrew Melodies.*<br>Hogg, *The Pilgrims of the Sun.*<br>Hunt, *The Descent of Liberty.*<br>Milman, *Fazio.*<br>Scott, *The Lord of the Isles*; *The Field of Waterloo.*<br>Wordsworth, *The White Doe of Rylstone*; *Poems,* 2 vols. |
| 1816 | Depression and discontent. Spa Fields Riot. Prosecution of Hone. | R. B. Sheridan d.<br>Harriet Westbrook commits suicide.<br>Shelley marries Mary Godwin.<br>Charlotte Brontë b.<br>Byron leaves England for the last time.<br>Coleridge settles at Highgate.<br>Elgin Marbles become accessible to the general public.<br>Benjamin Constant, *Adolphe.*<br>Goethe, *Italienische Reise* (1816–17). Jacob and Wilhelm Grimm, *Deutsche Sagen* (concl. 1818).<br>Goethe, ed. *Über Kunst und Alterthum* (1816–32).<br>Cowper, *Memoir of Early Life, Written by Himself.*<br>Gifford, ed. Ben Jonson.<br>Gray, *The Works,* ed. J. Mitford.<br>Johnson, *A Diary of a Journey into North Wales in 1774,* ed. R. Duppa.<br>W. S. Rose, *The Court and Parliament of Beasts freely translated from Casti.*<br>Ugo Foscolo arrives in England. | Byron, *The Siege of Corinth* [with] *Parisina*; *The Prisoner of Chillon*; *Childe Harold's Pilgrimage,* Canto III.<br>Coleridge, *Christabel* [with] *Kubla Khan, a Vision* [and] *The Pains of Sleep.*<br>Hogg, *The Poetic Mirror*; *Mador of the Moor.*<br>Mrs. Hemans, *The Restoration of the Works of Art to Italy.*<br>Hunt, *The Story of Rimini.*<br>Moore, *Sacred Songs,* i.<br>J. H. Reynolds, *The Naiad.*<br>Shelley, *Alastor.*<br>Southey, *The Poet's Pilgrimage to Waterloo*; *The Lay of the Laureate.*<br>J. Wilson ('Christopher North'), *The City of the Plague.*<br>Wordsworth, *Thanksgiving Ode, January 18, 1816.* |
| 1817 | Death of the Princess Charlotte. Monroe President of U.S.A. | Jane Austen d.<br>Mme de Staël d.<br>Thoreau b.<br>G. H. Lewes b. | Byron, *The Lament of Tasso*; *Manfred.*<br>Coleridge, *Sibylline Leaves*; *Zapolya.* |

| *Prose* | *Drama (date of acting)* |
| --- | --- |
| Sir John Malcolm, *The History of Persia.* Malthus, *An Inquiry into Rent.* Jane Porter, *The Pastor's Fire-Side.* Scott, *Guy Mannering.* Dugald Stewart, *A General View of the Progress of Philosophy* (Supplement to *Encyclopaedia Britannica,* pt. i, 1815; pt. ii, 1821.) | Sheridan Knowles, *Caius Gracchus.* Isaac Pocock, *The Magpie, or the Maid?* |
| Jane Austen, *Emma.* Bentham, *Chrestomathia.* Coleridge, *The Statesman's Manual.* Galt, *The Majolo*; *Life and Studies of Benjamin West*, i (ii, 1820). Hazlitt, *Memoirs of Thomas Holcroft.* Hunt, 'Young Poets', in the *Examiner.* Lady Caroline Lamb, *Glenarvon.* Peacock, *Headlong Hall.* Scott, *The Antiquary*; *Tales of my Landlord* (*The Black Dwarf* and *Old Mortality*); *Paul's Letters to his Kinsfolk.* Wordsworth, *A Letter to A Friend of Robert Burns.* | Maturin, *Bertram.*<br>Milman, *Fazio* (as *The Italian Wife*).<br>Benjamin Thompson, *Oberon's Oath.*<br>John Tobin, *The Faro Table.*<br>T. J. Dibdin, *What Next?*<br>Scott and D. Terry, *Guy Mannering* (adaptation). |
| E. S. Barrett, *Six Weeks at Long's.* Coleridge, *Biographia Literaria.* T. F. Dibdin, *The Bibliographical Decameron.* N. Drake, *Shakespeare and his Times.* Maria Edgeworth, *Harrington* | Joanna Baillie, *The Election.*<br>George Colman the younger, *The Actor of All Work.*<br>Maturin, *Manuel.* |

| *Date* | *Public Events* | *Literary History (including translations)* | *Verse* |
|---|---|---|---|
| 1817 (*cont.*) | | Tom Taylor b. Branwell Brontë b. Benjamin Jowett b. *Blackwood's Edinburgh Magazine* started. The *Literary Gazette* started by William Jerdan. *The Scotsman* started. Grillparzer, *Die Ahnfrau.* Chesterfield, *Letters to Arthur Charles Stanhope. Theological and Miscellaneous Works of Joseph Priestley*, ed. J. T. Rutt (1817–32.) *Letters from Mrs. Carter to Mrs. Montagu*, ed. M. Pennington. | Frere, *The Monks and the Giants*, i–ii (iii–iv, 1818). Mrs. Hemans, *Modern Greece.* Keats, *Poems.* Moore, *Lalla Rookh.* Scott, *Harold the Dauntless.* Southey, *Wat Tyler* (maliciously pub. by his enemies). Wolcot ('Peter Pindar'), *Epistle to the Emperor of China.* C. Wolfe, 'The Burial of Sir John Moore' (first pub. in *The Newry Telegraph*, 19 April 1817). |
| 1818 | General Election. Conference of Aix-la-Chapelle. European Alliance. Karl Marx b. | M. G. Lewis d. Emily Brontë b. J. A. Froude b. J. M. Neale b. Shelley's final departure from England. Attacks on Keats. Evelyn, *Memoirs*, ed. W. Bray. Horace Walpole, *Letters to George Montagu, William Cole and Others.* Grillparzer, *Sappho.* | Barton, *Poems by an Amateur.* Byron, *Childe Harold's Pilgrimage*, Canto iv; *Beppo.* T. Doubleday, *Sixty-five Sonnets.* Mrs. Hemans, *Translations from Camoens.* Hunt, *Foliage.* Keats, *Endymion.* Milman, *Samor.* Moore, *National Airs*, i (compl. 1827); *The Fudge Family in Paris.* Peacock, *Rhododaphne.* Shelley, *The Revolt of Islam.* Sotheby, *Farewell to Italy.* |
| 1819 | The Peterloo 'Massacre'. The Six Acts. Murder of Kotzebue. Birth of Queen Victoria. | John Wolcot ('Peter Pindar') d. Charles Kingsley b. John Ruskin b. J. R. Lowell b. A. H. Clough b. Mary Ann Evans ('George Eliot') b. Herman Melville b. Walt Whitman b. Campbell, *Specimens of the British Poets.* Hogg, ed. *The Jacobite Relics of Scotland*, i (ii, 1821). Hugo and his brother found *Le Conservateur littéraire.* | Byron, *Mazeppa*; *Don Juan*, i–ii. Crabbe, *Tales of the Hall.* Barron Field, *The First Fruits of Australian Poetry.* (priv. prtd.) Mrs. Hemans, *Tales and Historic Scenes*; *Wallace's Invocation to Bruce.* Hunt, *Hero and Leander, and Bacchus and Ariadne*; *Poetical Works.* Charles Lloyd, *Nugae Canorae.* H. Luttrell, *Lines Written at Ampthill Park.* Macaulay, *Pompeii.* |

| *Prose* | *Drama (date of acting)* |
| --- | --- |
| [with] *Ormond*. Godwin, *Mandeville*. Hazlitt, *Characters of Shakespear's Plays*; *The Round Table*. Hogg, *Dramatic Tales*. James Mill, *The History of British India*. John Nichols, *Illustrations of the Literary History of the Eighteenth Century* (concl. 1858). Robert Owen, *Report to the Committee on the Poor Law*. Peacock, *Melincourt*. Ricardo, *Principles of Political Economy and Taxation*. Shelley, *A Proposal for Putting Reform to the Vote*; *History of a Six Weeks' Tour* (with Mary Shelley). Southey, *A Letter to William Smith, Esq., M.P.*; ed. Malory, *The Byrth, Lyf, and Actes of Kyng Arthur*. | Pocock, *Robinson Crusoe*.<br>R. L. Sheil, *The Apostate*. |
| Lucy Aikin, *Memoirs of the Court of Queen Elizabeth*. Jane Austen, *Northanger Abbey and Persuasion* (with memoir). Cobbett, *A Year's Residence in the United States of America*; *A Grammar of the English Language*. Coleridge, *On Method* (in *Encyclopaedia Metropolitana*). Pierce Egan, *Boxiana* (1818–24). Susan Ferrier, *Marriage*. Hallam, *View of the State of Europe during the Middle Ages*. Hazlitt, *Lectures on the English Poets*; *A View of the English Stage*. Hogg, *The Brownie of Bodsbeck*. Hunt, *The Literary Pocket-Book* (1818–22). Lamb, *The Works*. Maturin, *Women, or Pour et Contre*. Lady Morgan, *Florence Macarthy*. Mrs. Opie, *New Tales*. Peacock, *Nightmare Abbey*. Scott, *Rob Roy*; *Tales of my Landlord, Second Series* (*The Heart of Mid-Lothian*). Mary Shelley, *Frankenstein*. Mary Sherwood, *The History of the Fairchild Family* (1818–47). | T. J. Dibdin, *The Invisible Witness* (based on Pixérécourt's *La chapelle du bois, ou le témoin invisible*).<br>W. T. Moncrieff, *Rochester, or King Charles the Second's Merry Days*.<br>J. R. Planché, *Amoroso, King of Little Britain*.<br>Pocock, *The Antiquary* (based on Scott).<br>R. L. Sheil, *Bellamira*.<br>[Scott] *Rob Roy*: numerous stage-adaptations from this year onwards. |
| Bentham, *Radical Reform Bill*. Mary Brunton, *Emmeline*, with Memoir by A. Brunton. Hazlitt, *Lectures on the English Comic Writers*; *Political Essays*; *A Letter to William Gifford, Esq.* Hunt, *The Indicator* (1819–21); Hone, *The Political House that Jack Built*. Thomas Hope, *Anastasius*. Washington Irving, *The Sketch Book* (New York, 1819–20). Lingard, *A History of England* (concl. 1830). Lockhart *Peter's Letters to his Kinsfolk*. H. Matthews, *The Diary of an Invalid*. J. W. Polidori, *The Vampire*. Scott, *Tales of my Landlord, Third Series* (*The Bride of Lammermoor* and *A Legend of Montrose*). | Charles Bucke, *The Italians*.<br>Holcroft, *The Marriage of Figaro*.<br>Maturin, *Fredolfo*.<br>T. Morton, *A Roland for an Oliver*.<br>[Scott], *The Heart of Mid-Lothian* (at least five versions).<br>Sheil, *Evadne, or the Statue* (based on *The Traitor*, by Shirley).<br>Horace Twiss, *The Carib Chief*. |

| *Date* | *Public Events* | *Literary History (including translations)* | *Verse* |
|---|---|---|---|
| 1819 (*cont.*) | | Chénier, *Œuvres choisies*, ed. H. de Latouche.<br>Goethe, *West-östlicher Divan*.<br>Hoffmann, *Die Serapionsbrüder* (1819–21).<br>Schopenhauer, *Die Welt als Wille und Vorstellung*.<br>*The Poems of Allan Ramsay*, ed. W. Tennant.<br>*Poetical Remains of John Leyden*, ed. J. Morton. | James Montgomery, *The Poetical Works*; *Greenland*.<br>B. W. Procter ('Barry Cornwall'), *Dramatic Scenes*.<br>J. H. Reynolds, *Peter Bell*; *Benjamin, the Waggoner*.<br>Rogers, *Human Life*.<br>Shelley, *Rosalind and Helen*.<br>Wordsworth, *Peter Bell*; *The Waggoner*. |
| 1820 | Death of George III. Accession of George IV. Trial of Queen Caroline. Dissolution of Parliament. Cato Street Conspiracy. Royalist reaction in Europe. Revolution in Spain and Portugal. | William Hayley d.<br>Anne Brontë b.<br>Herbert Spencer b.<br>Jean Ingelow b.<br>*London Magazine* started.<br>*Retrospective Review* started.<br>*John Bull* started.<br>*The Etonian* (1820–1).<br>Lamartine, *Méditations poétiques*.<br>Joseph Spence, *Anecdotes*, ed. Malone and ed. S. W. Singer (two separate eds.)<br>*Private Correspondence of Horace Walpole*.<br>Tasso's *Amyntas*, trans. by Hunt.<br>Hegel, *Grundlegung einer Philosophie des Rechts*.<br>Grillparzer, *Das goldene Vliess*. | Robert Anderson, *Poetical Works*.<br>Sir J. Bowring, *Specimens of the Russian Poets*.<br>Elizabeth Barrett [Browning], *The Battle of Marathon*.<br>B. Barton, *Poems*.<br>Clare, *Poems Descriptive of Rural Life and Scenery*.<br>Combe, *The Second Tour of Dr. Syntax*.<br>George Croly, *The Angel of the World*.<br>Mrs. Hemans, *The Sceptic*; *Stanzas to the Memory of the late King*.<br>J. A. Heraud, *The Legend of St. Loy*.<br>Keats, *Lamia, Isabella, The Eve of St. Agnes, and Other Poems*.<br>Landor, *Idyllia Heroica Decem*.<br>Henry Luttrell, *Advice to Julia*.<br>E. G. E. Lytton (Bulwer Lytton), *Ismael*.<br>Milman, *The Fall of Jerusalem*.<br>B. W. Procter ('Barry Cornwall'), *A Sicilian Story*; *Marcian Colonna*.<br>J. H. Reynolds, *The Fancy*.<br>Scott, *Miscellaneous Poems*.<br>Shelley, *The Cenci*; *Prometheus Unbound*; *Oedipus Tyrannus*.<br>J. H. Wiffen, *Julia Alpinula*.<br>Wordsworth, *The River Duddon*; *Memorials of a Tour on the Continent*. |

*Prose*

R. H. Barham, *Baldwin, or a Miser's Heir.* Thomas Brown, *Lectures on the Philosophy of the Human Mind.* J. P. Collier, *The Poetical Decameron.* M. Edgeworth, *Memoirs of R. L. Edgeworth.* John Foster, *An Essay on the Evils of Popular Ignorance.* Galt, *The Earthquake.* Godwin, *Of Population, An Answer to Mr. Malthus.* Hazlitt, *Lectures on the Dramatic Literature of the Age of Elizabeth.* Hogg, *Winter Evening Tales.* Lamb, *Essays of Elia* (in *London Magazine*, 1820–2). Lloyd, *Isabel.* Malthus, *Principles of Political Economy.* Maturin, *Melmoth the Wanderer.* Mrs. Opie, *Tales of the Heart.* Peacock, *The Four Ages of Poetry* (in *Ollier's Literary Miscellany*). Scott, *Ivanhoe*; *The Monastery*; *The Abbot.* Southey, *The Life of Wesley, and the Rise and Progress of Methodism.*

*Drama (date of acting)*

Charles Dibdin, Jr., *Shakespeare Versus Harlequin.*
C. Farley, *The Battle of Bothwell Brig* (based on *Old Mortality*).
T. E. Hook, *Oil and Vinegar*; *Exchange no Robbery.*
Sheridan Knowles, *Virginius.*
W. T. Moncrieff, *The Lear of Private Life.*
Pocock and D. Terry, *The Antiquary* (based on Scott).
[Scott], *Ivanhoe* (at least seven versions for the stage).
R. L. Sheil, *Montoni, or The Phantom.*

| *Date* | *Public Events* | *Literary History (including translations)* | *Verse* |
|---|---|---|---|
| 1821 | Death of Napoleon. Death of Queen Caroline. Measures for Catholic relief. *Cordon sanitaire.* Greek War of Liberation begins. Monroe President of U.S.A., second term. | Keats d.<br>Hester Lynch Piozzi (Mrs. Thrale) d.<br>John Scott killed in duel by John Christie, deputizing for Lockhart.<br>H. T. Buckle b.<br>G. J. Whyte-Melville b.<br>Malone's ed. of Shakespeare, ed. J. Boswell, Jr.<br>*Memoirs* of James, Earl of Waldegrave, pub.<br>*Manchester Guardian* started.<br>Flaubert b.<br>Baudelaire b.<br>Goethe, *Wilhelm Meisters Wanderjahre* (1821–9).<br>H. von Kleist, *Der Prinz von Homburg.*<br>Hogg, *Jacobite Relics*, ii.<br>*The Lyrics of Horace*, trans. F. Wrangham. | Joanna Baillie, *Metrical Legends.*<br>Beddoes, *The Improvisatore.*<br>Byron, *Marino Faliero*; *The Prophecy of Dante*; *Sardanapalus*; *The Two Foscari*; *Cain*; *Don Juan*, iii–v.<br>Clare, *The Village Minstrel.*<br>Combe, *The Third Tour of Dr. Syntax.*<br>Mrs. Hemans, *Dartmoor.*<br>L. E. Landon, *The Fate of Adelaide.*<br>Charles Lloyd, *Desultory Thoughts in London*; *Poetical Essays.*<br>Moore, *Irish Melodies* (first authorized ed. of words alone).<br>Newman, *St. Bartholomew's Eve* (with J. W. Bowden).<br>B. W. Procter ('Barry Cornwall'), *Mirandola, A Tragedy.*<br>J. H. Reynolds, *The Garden of Florence.*<br>Shelley, *Epipsychidion*; *Adonais.*<br>H. Smith, *Amarynthus, the Nympholept.*<br>Southey, *A Vision of Judgement.* |
| 1822 | Suicide of Castlereagh. Canning Foreign Secretary. Peel Home Secretary. Independence of Brazil. | Shelley d.<br>E. T. A. Hoffmann d.<br>Matthew Arnold b.<br>Sir Henry Maine b.<br>Thomas Hughes b.<br>Sir Francis Galton b.<br>? Boucicault b.<br>Hunt starts *The Liberal* (1822–3).<br>The *Sunday Times* starts.<br>Walpole, *Memoires of the Last Ten Years of George II*, ed. Lord Holland.<br>Edmond Goncourt b.<br>Hugo, *Odes et poésies diverses.*<br>Stendhal, *De l'amour.*<br>*Memoirs of Benvenuto Cellini*, trans. T. Roscoe.<br>Bannatyne Club founded.<br>Heine, *Gedichte.*<br>Jeremy Taylor, *The Whole* | Beddoes, *The Brides' Tragedy.*<br>Bloomfield, *May Day with the Muses.*<br>Bowles, *The Grave of the Last Saxon.*<br>Byron, *The Vision of Judgment* (in *The Liberal*).<br>Allan Cunningham, *Sir Marmaduke Maxwell.*<br>Darley, *The Errors of Ecstasie.*<br>Sir Aubrey De Vere, *Julian the Apostate.*<br>Mrs. Hemans, *Welsh Melodies.*<br>Charles Lloyd, *The Duke D'Ormond.*<br>Henry Luttrell, *Letters to Julia* (3rd ed., rev. and enlarged).<br>Milman, *The Martyr of* |

| Prose | Drama (*date of acting*) |
|---|---|
| J. L. Adolphus, *Letters to Richard Heber* (on the *Waverley Novels*). Byron, *A Letter on W. L. Bowles' Strictures on Pope*. Cobbett, *The American Gardener*; *Cottage Economy*. J. Fenimore Cooper, *The Spy*. De Quincey, *Confessions of an English Opium-Eater* (in the *London Magazine*). T. F. Dibdin, *A Bibliographical Tour in France and Germany*. Pierce Egan, *Life in London*. Galt, *The Ayrshire Legatees* (in book form); *The Annals of the Parish*. Hazlitt, *Table Talk* (1821–2). Hunt, *The Months*. Lockhart, *Valerius, A Roman Story*. James Mill, *Elements of Political Economy*. Sir W. E. Parry, *Journal of a Voyage for the Discovery of a N.-W. Passage* (1821–4). Scott, *Kenilworth*; *Lives of the Novelists* (prefaces to Ballantyne's *Novelist's Library*, 1821–4). | J. Banim, *Damon and Pythias* (altered for the stage by R. L. Sheil). Alfred Bunn, *Kenilworth* (a rehandling of T. J. Dibdin's dramatization). Byron, *Marino Faliero, Doge of Venice*. B. W. Procter ('Barry Cornwall'), *Mirandola*. W. T. Moncrieff, *Tom and Jerry* (adapted from P. Egan's *Life in London*). James Haynes, *Conscience, or The Bridal Night*. Douglas Jerrold, *More Frightened than Hurt* (originally called *The Duellists*); *The Chieftain's Oath*; *The Gipsy of Derncleuch* (partly based on *Guy Mannering*). [Scott], *Kenilworth* (at least six versions). |
| Lucy Aikin, *Memoirs of the Court of James I*. Bentham, *The Influence of Natural Religion upon Temporal Happiness*. Allan Cunningham, *Traditional Tales of the English and Scottish Peasantry*. Kenelm Digby, *The Broad Stone of Honour*. De Quincey, *Confessions of an English Opium-Eater* (as a book). Galt, *Sir Andrew Wylie*; *The Provost*; *The Gathering of the West*. Hogg, *The Three Perils of Man*. Washington Irving, *Bracebridge Hall*. Lady Caroline Lamb, *Graham Hamilton*. Lockhart, *Adam Blair*. Nares, *Glossary*. Peacock, *Maid Marian*. Francis Place, *Illustrations and Proofs of the Principle of Population*. Scott, *The Pirate*; *The Fortunes of Nigel*; *Peveril of the Peak*. C. J. Wells, *Stories after Nature*. John Wilson ('Christopher North'), *Lights and Shadows of Scottish Life*. Wilson, Hogg, Lockhart, and Maginn, *Noctes Ambrosianae* (in *Blackwood's Magazine*, 1822–35). Wordsworth, *A Description of the Scenery of the Lakes* (3rd ed., first separate ed.) | George Colman the younger, *The Law of Java*. E. Fitzball, *The Fortunes of Nigel* (from Scott). [Scott], *Waverley* (anon. dramatization); *The Pirate* (at least three dramatic versions). R. L. Sheil, *The Huguenot*. |

| Date | Public Events | Literary History (including translations) | Verse |
| --- | --- | --- | --- |
| 1822 (*cont.*) | | *Works*, ed. Reginald Heber. | *Antioch*; *Belshazzar*.<br>Procter, *The Poetical Works of Barry Cornwall.*<br>Rogers, *Italy*, i.<br>Scott, *Halidon Hill.*<br>Shelley, *Hellas, A Lyrical Drama.*<br>A. Watts, *Poetical Sketches.*<br>Wordsworth, *Ecclesiastical Sketches.*<br>Crabbe, *The Poetical Works.* |
| 1823 | Agricultural discontent. War between France and Spain. Monroe Doctrine. | Ann Radcliffe d.<br>Coventry Patmore b.<br>E. A. Freeman b.<br>Charlotte Mary Yonge b.<br>Spanish émigrés arrive in London.<br>Max Müller b.<br>Renan b.<br>Stendhal, *Racine et Shakspeare.*<br>*La Muse française*, 1823–4.<br>Knight's *Quarterly Magazine* begun.<br>*The Lancet* begins.<br>Lamartine, *Nouvelles Méditations.*<br>W. S. Rose, trans. Ariosto's *Orlando furioso*, 1823–31.<br>Bouterwek's *History of Spanish and Portugese Literature*, trans. Thomasina Ross.<br>Lockhart, trans. *Ancient Spanish Ballads.*<br>*Tales* of J. L. C. and W. C. Grimm, trans. E. Taylor, 1823, 1826. | Bowles, *Ellen Gray.*<br>Sir John Bowring, *Matins and Vespers.*<br>Byron, *The Age of Bronze*; *The Island*; *Werner*; *Don Juan*, vi–xiv.<br>Joseph Cottle, *Dartmoor.*<br>Sir Aubrey De Vere, *The Duke of Mercia.*<br>Mrs. Hemans, *The Siege of Valencia* [with] *The Last Constantine.*<br>Hunt, *Ultra-Crepidarius.*<br>Charles Lloyd, *Poems.*<br>Bulwer Lytton, *Delmour and other Poems.*<br>Moore, *The Loves of the Angels*; *Fables for the Holy Alliance.*<br>Praed, *Australasia.*<br>B. W. Procter ('Barry Cornwall'), *The Flood of Thessaly* [with] *The Girl of Provence.*<br>Shelley, *Poetical Pieces.* |
| 1824 | Conference at St. Petersburg, 1824–5. | Byron d.<br>Wilkie Collins b.<br>George Macdonald b.<br>Sydney Dobell b.<br>F. T. Palgrave b.<br>William Allingham b.<br>Opening of National Gallery.<br>*Westminster Review* started.<br>Foundation of London Mechanics' Institution.<br>A. Watts, first volume of *The Literary Souvenir.* | Barton, *Poetic Vigils.*<br>Robert Bloomfield, *The Remains.*<br>Byron, *Don Juan*, xv–xvi; *The Deformed Transformed.*<br>Campbell, *Theodric and Other Poems*; *Miscellaneous Poems.*<br>Josiah Conder, *The Star in the East.*<br>L. E. Landon, *The Improvisatrice.*<br>R. E. Landor, *The Count* |

*Prose* | *Drama (date of acting)*

Joseph Bosworth, *The Elements of Anglo-Saxon Grammar*. Fenimore Cooper, *The Pioneers*; *The Pirate*. De Quincey, *Letters to a Young Man whose Education has been Neglected* (in *London Magazine*). I. d'Israeli, *Curiosities of Literature* (expanded ed.). Sir John Franklin, *Narrative of a Journey to the Polar Sea*. Galt, *The Entail*; *Ringan Gilhaize*; *The Spaewife*. Hazlitt, *Liber Amoris*; *Characteristics*. Hogg, *The Three Perils of Woman*. Lady Caroline Lamb, *Ada Reis, A Tale*. Lamb, *Essays of Elia* (as a book). Lockhart, *Reginald Dalton*. Scott, *Quentin Durward*. Mary Shelley, *Valperga*. Southey, *History of the Peninsular War* (concl. 1832). John Wilson ('Christopher North'), *The Trials of Margaret Lyndsay*.

E. Fitzball, *Peveril of the Peak* (from Scott).
Mrs. Hemans, *The Vespers of Palermo*.
T. E. Hook, *A Day at an Inn* (based on his own *Killing No Murder*).
Douglas Jerrold, *The Island* (based on Byron's poem); *Dolly and the Rat*; *The Smoked Miser*.
H. M. Milner, *Frankenstein* (based on Mary Shelley's romance: several other stage versions).
M. R. Mitford, *Julian*.

Bentham, *Book of Fallacies*. Cobbett, *A History of the Protestant 'Reformation'* (1824–6). R. C. Dallas, *Recollections of Lord Byron*. Susan Ferrier, *The Inheritance*. Galt, *Rothelan*. Godwin, *History of the Commonwealth of England*. Hazlitt, *Sketches of the Principal Picture-Galleries*. Hogg, *The Private Memoirs and Confessions of a Justified Sinner*. Landor, *Imaginary Conversations*, i–ii. Lockhart, *The History of Matthew Wald*. Medwin, *Journal of the Conversations of Lord Byron at Pisa*. M. R. Mitford, *Our Village* (1824–32). James Morier, *The Adventures of Hajji Baba of Ispahan*. W. E. Parry, *Journal of a Second*

George Croly, *Pride shall have a Fall*.
J. F. Kind, *Der Freischütz* (at least five adaptations this year).
W. T. Moncrieff, *Zoroaster*.
Planché, *A Woman never Vext*.
[Scott], *Redgauntlet* (adaptation).
Sir Martin Archer Shee, *Alasco*.

| *Date* | *Public Events* | *Literary History (including translations)* | *Verse* |
|---|---|---|---|
| 1824 (*cont.*) | | Robert Watt, *Bibliotheca Britannica.*<br>J. H. Wiffen, trans. Tasso's *Jerusalem Delivered,* 1824–5.<br>W. Roscoe's ed. of *The Works of Pope.*<br>Carlyle, trans. Goethe's *Wilhelm Meister's Apprenticeship.*<br>H. F. Cary, trans. *The Birds of Aristophanes.*<br>Heyday of 'The Apostles' at Cambridge begins. | *Arezzi.*<br>J. Montgomery, ed. *The Chimney-sweeper's Friend.*<br>Moore, *Sacred Songs,* ii.<br>Shelley, *Posthumous Poems.*<br>Charles Wells, *Joseph and his Brethren.* |
| 1825 | Speculative frenzy. Financial panic. George IV opposes further measures for Catholic Emancipation. Death of Tsar Alexander I. John Quincy Adams President of U.S.A. | Anna Barbauld d.<br>Samuel Parr d.<br>H. Fuseli d.<br>T. H. Huxley b.<br>William Stubbs b.<br>R. D. Blackmore b.<br>Richter d.<br>Lamartine, *Le Dernier Chant du pèlerinage d'Harold.*<br>Grillparzer, *König Ottokar.*<br>A. Cunningham ed. *The Songs of Scotland, Ancient and Modern.*<br>Milton, *De Doctrina Christiana.*<br>*Memoirs of Samuel Pepys,* ed. Braybrooke.<br>Manzoni, *I Promessi Sposi,* 1825–6.<br>Walpole, *Letters to Lord Hertford and Henry Zouch,* ed. Croker. | Mrs. Hemans, *The Forest Sanctuary*; *Lays of Many Lands.*<br>Hogg, *Queen Hynde.*<br>Hood and J. H. Reynolds, *Odes and Addresses to Great People.*<br>L. E. Landon, *The Troubadour.*<br>Bulwer Lytton, *Sculpture.*<br>William Sotheby, *Poems* (enlarged ed.)<br>Southey, *A Tale of Paraguay.*<br>Charles Wolfe, *The Burial of Sir John Moore, with Other Poems.*<br>Thomas Wade, *Tasso, and the Sisters.* |
| 1826 | End of Liverpool's ministry. England sends troops to Portugal. Election brings Catholic Emancipation and Corn Laws into prominence. | William Gifford d.<br>Reginald Heber d.<br>Walter Bagehot b.<br>Hone's *Every-Day Book* (1826–7).<br>Hugo, *Odes et ballades.*<br>de Vigny, *Poèmes antiques et modernes*; *Cinq-Mars.*<br>Chateaubriand, *Les Aventures du dernier Abencérage.*<br>Eichendorff, *Aus dem Leben eines Taugenichts.*<br>Heine, *Die Harzreise.*<br>John Burke's *Dictionary of the Peerage and Baronetage* first appears. | Barton, *Devotional Verses.*<br>Elizabeth Barrett [Browning], *An Essay on Mind; with Other Poems.*<br>Hood, *Whims and Oddities,* i (ii, 1827: verse and prose).<br>Milman, *Anne Boleyn.*<br>J. Montgomery, *The Pelican Island.*<br>Wordsworth, *The Poetical Works,* Paris ed.<br>Moore, *Evenings in Greece, First Evening* (ii, 1832). |

| *Prose* | *Drama (date of acting)* |
| --- | --- |
| *Voyage, 1821–3*. Scott, *St. Ronan's Well*; *Redgauntlet*. Southey, *The Book of the Church*. William Thompson, *An Inquiry into the Principles of the Distribution of Wealth.* | |
| Banim, *Tales by the O'Hara Family*, i (ii, 1826). Bentham, *The Rationale of Reward* (first English ed.). Brougham, *Practical Observations upon the Education of the People.* Carlyle, *The Life of Schiller.* Coleridge, *Aids to Reflection.* T. C. Croker, *Fairy Legends and Traditions of the South of Ireland*, 1825–8. De Quincey, *Walladmor.* Galt, *The Omen.* R. G. Gleig, *The Subaltern.* Hazlitt, *Table-Talk*; *The Spirit of the Age.* Macaulay, essay on Milton (in *Edinburgh Review*). J. R. McCulloch, *Principles of Political Economy.* James Mill, *Essays on Government, etc.* (privately printed). Moore, *Memoirs of Sheridan.* Mrs. Opie, *Tales of the Pemberton Family.* W. S. Rose, *Thoughts and Recollections.* Scott, *Tales of the Crusaders* (*The Betrothed* and *The Talisman*). H. Smith, *Gaieties and Gravities.* Plumer Ward, *Tremaine.* Charles Waterton, *Wanderings in South America.* John Wilson, *The Foresters.* | Fitzball, *The Pilot* (from Fenimore Cooper).<br>Douglas Jerrold, *The Living Skeleton*; *London Characters: Puff! Puff! Puff!*<br>Sheridan Knowles, *The Fatal Dowry* (adapted from Massinger); *William Tell.*<br>Harriet Lee, *The Three Strangers.*<br>J. R. Planché, *Success, or A Hit if you like it.*<br>J. Poole, *Tribulation* (from *Un moment d'imprudence*).<br>George Soane and Daniel Terry, *Faustus.* |
| Anna Bray, *De Foix.* A. Cunningham, *Paul Jones.* Fenimore Cooper, *The Last of the Mohicans.* Darley, *The Labours of Idleness.* Disraeli, *Vivian Grey*, i–ii (iii–v, 1827). Galt, *The Last of the Lairds.* Hazlitt, *The Plain Speaker*; *Notes of a Journey through France and Italy.* Anna Jameson, *Diary of an Ennuyée.* Lister, *Granby.* W. E. Parry, *Journal of a Third Voyage.* P. G. Patmore, *Rejected Articles.* Jane and Anna Porter, *Tales round a Winter Hearth.* Scott, *Woodstock.* Mary Shelley, *The Last Man.* H. Smith, *Brambletye House*; *The Tor Hill.* Southey, *Vindiciae Ecclesiae Anglicanae.* Whately, *Elements of Logic.* | J. B. Buckstone, *Luke the Labourer.*<br>George Macfarren, *Malvina.*<br>M. R. Mitford, *Foscari.*<br>Douglas Jerrold, *Popular Felons.*<br>Pocock, *Woodstock* (from Scott). |

| *Date* | *Public Events* | *Literary History (including translations)* | *Verse* |
|---|---|---|---|
| 1827 | Death of Canning. Battle of Navarino. University of London (University College) founded. Thomas Arnold becomes Headmaster of Rugby. | Blake d.<br>Helen Maria Williams d.<br>Ugo Foscolo d.<br>'Cuthbert Bede' (Edward Bradley) b.<br>Scott acknowledges authorship of the *Waverley Novels*.<br>*Constable's Miscellany* started.<br>W. J. Thoms, *Early Prose Romances* (1827–8).<br>Gifford's ed. of Ford.<br>Burke, *Epistolary Correspondence with Dr. French Laurence*.<br>Sir Kenelm Digby (d. 1665), *Private Memoirs*, ed. Sir N. H. Nicolas.<br>Hone's *Table Book* (1827–8).<br>Hugo, preface to *Cromwell*.<br>Heine, *Das Buch der Lieder*.<br>Carlyle, *German Romance: Specimens of its chief Authors*. | Barton, *A Widow's Tale*.<br>R. Bloomfield, *The Poems*.<br>Clare, *The Shepherd's Calendar*.<br>Darley, *Sylvia*.<br>Reginald Heber, *Hymns*.<br>Hood, *The Plea of the Midsummer Fairies*.<br>Keble, *The Christian Year*.<br>L. E. Landon, *The Golden Violet*.<br>H. Luttrell, *Crockford-House*.<br>Bulwer Lytton, *O'Neill, or the Rebel*.<br>Mitford, *Dramatic Scenes*.<br>Poe, *Tamerlane*.<br>Pollok, *The Course of Time*.<br>Tennyson (with C. Tennyson), *Poems by Two Brothers*.<br>Wordsworth, *The Poetical Works*, 5 vols. |
| 1828 | Wellington Premier. Repeal of the Test and Corporation Acts. George IV opposed to Catholic Relief. Russia goes to war with Turkey. The Greek Question. | Dugald Stewart d.<br>Meredith b.<br>D. G. Rossetti b.<br>Mrs. Oliphant b.<br>Taine b.<br>The *Athenaeum* started.<br>The *Spectator* started.<br>A. Watts, *The Poetical Album* (2nd series, 1829).<br>Balzac, *Physiologie du mariage*.<br>de Musset, *L'Anglais mangeur d'opium* (a very free trans.).<br>Sainte-Beuve, *Tableau historique et critique de la poésie française et du théâtre français au XVIe siècle*.<br>Manzoni, *I Promessi Sposi*, trans. English by C. Swan. | Barton, *A New Year's Eve*.<br>S. L. Blanchard, *Lyric Offerings*.<br>Bowles, *Days Departed*.<br>Mrs. Hemans, *Records of Woman*.<br>L. E. Landon, *The Venetian Bracelet*.<br>R. E. Landor, *The Impious Feast*.<br>Robert Montgomery, *The Omnipresence of the Deity*.<br>Moore, *Odes upon Cash, Corn, Catholics, and other Matters*.<br>Rogers, *Italy*, ii.<br>Coleridge, *The Poetical Works*, 3 vols.<br>J. H. Merivale, *Poems Original and Translated*, i (ii, 1838). |

*Prose*

Bentham, *The Rationale of Evidence*, ed. J. S. Mill. Fenimore Cooper, *The Prairie*. W. Crowe, *A Treatise on English Versification*. De Quincey, 'On Murder considered as One of the Fine Arts' (in *Blackwood's Magazine*). Pierce Egan, *Anecdotes of the Turf*. Hallam, *Constitutional History*. J. C. and A. W. Hare, *Guesses at Truth*, i. Hood, *National Tales*. Bulwer Lytton, *Falkland*. Sir John Malcolm, *Sketches of Persia*. Moore, *The Epicurean*. Scott, *Chronicles of the Canongate* (*The Highland Widow, The Two Drovers, The Surgeon's Daughter*); *Life of Napoleon*; *Miscellaneous Prose Works*; ed. *The Bannatyne Miscellany*. H. Smith, *Reuben Apsley*. Plumer Ward, *De Vere*. Lady Charlotte Bury, *Flirtation*.

*Drama (date of acting)*

E. Fitzball, *The Flying Dutchman, or The Phantom Ship*.
Douglas Jerrold, *Paul Pry*.
Pocock, *Alfred the Great*.
Charles de Vœux, *William Tell* (from Schiller).

Carlyle, essay on Burns (in *Edinburgh Review*). George Combe, *The Constitution of Man*. Fenimore Cooper, *The Red Rover*. Croly, *Salathiel, A Story of the Past, the Present, and the Future*. A. Cunningham, *Sir Michael Scott*. B. Disraeli, *The Voyage of Captain Popanilla*. I. d'Israeli, *The Life and Reign of Charles I*, (1828–31). N. Drake, *Memorials of Shakespeare*. Pierce Egan, *Finish to the Adventures of Tom, Jerry and Logic*. Sir John Franklin, *Narrative of a Second Expedition to the Polar Sea*. Hazlitt, *Life of Napoleon*, i–ii (iii–iv, 1830). Reginald Heber, *A Journey through India*. Hunt, *Lord Byron and Some of his Contemporaries*; *The Companion*. Landor, *Imaginary Conversations*, iii. Washington Irving, *History of Christopher Columbus*. T. H. Lister, *Herbert Lacy*. Lockhart, *Life of Robert Burns*. Bulwer Lytton, *Pelham*. D. M. Moir, *Mansie Wauch*. Morier, *Hajji Baba in England*. Napier, *History of the War in the Peninsula* (concl. 1840). Sir W. E. Parry, *Narrative of an Attempt to reach the North Pole*. Scott, *Tales of a Grandfather*, i; *Chronicles of the Canongate, Second Series* (*The Fair Maid of Perth*); 'My Aunt Margaret's Mirror', 'The Tapestried Chamber', 'Death of the Laird's Jock' (all in *The Keepsake*); *Religious Discourses. By a Layman*. J. T. Smith, *Nollekens and his Times*. D. Stewart, *The Philosophy*

Douglas Jerrold, *The Statue Lover*; *Descart, the French Buccaneer*; *The Tower of Lochlain*; *Wives by Advertisement, or Courting in the Newspapers*; *Ambrose Gwinett*; *Two Eyes between Two*; *Fifteen Years of a Drunkard's Life!*
Sheridan Knowles, *The Beggar's Daughter of Bethnal Green*.
M. R. Lacy, *The Two Friends* (adapted from Scribe's *Rodolphe*).
M. R. Mitford, *Rienzi*.
Planché, *Paris and London*.
Thomas Wade, *Woman's Love*.

| *Date* | *Public Events* | *Literary History (including translations)* | *Verse* |
|---|---|---|---|
| 1829 | Wellington and Peel support Catholic Relief. Catholic Emancipation. Duel between Wellington and Winchilsea. Huskisson killed by a railway train. Exclusion of O'Connell from Parliament. Jackson President of U.S.A. | Alexander Smith b.<br>S. R. Gardiner b.<br>T. W. Robertson b.<br>Knight's *Library of Entertaining Knowledge* started.<br>Murray's *Family Library* started.<br>Lady Anne Fanshawe, *Memoirs*, ed. Sir N. H. Nicolas.<br>Balzac, *Les Chouans*.<br>Hugo, *Les Orientales*.<br>Dumas père, *Henri III et sa cour*.<br>de Vigny, *Othello* (adaptation).<br>Mérimée, *Chronique du règne de Charles IX*.<br>Sainte-Beuve, *Vie de Joseph Delorme*.<br>*La Revue des Deux Mondes* founded. | *The Poetical Works of Coleridge, Shelley and Keats*, unauthorized Paris ed.<br>E. Elliott, *The Village Patriarch*.<br>Hood, 'The Dream of Eugene Aram' (in *The Gem*); *The Epping Hunt*.<br>Poe, *Al Aaraaf, Tamerlane and other Poems*.<br>Southey, *All for Love*, and *The Pilgrim to Compostella*.<br>Tennyson, *Timbuctoo*. |
| 1830 | Reform agitation. Death of George IV and accession of William IV. Fall of Wellington's Ministry. Grey accepts office. Regency Bill. Manchester and Liverpool Railway. July Revolution in France. Louis Philippe recognized. Greece independent. France conquers Algiers. | Hazlitt d.<br>Christina Rossetti b.<br>Henry Kingsley b.<br>J. Goncourt b.<br>*Fraser's Magazine* started.<br>Lardner's *Cabinet Cyclopaedia* and *Cabinet Library* started.<br>Hood's *Comic Annual*, 1830–42.<br>T. Forster ed. *Letters of Locke, Algernon Sidney and Shaftesbury*.<br>Southey ed. *The Pilgrim's Progress*.<br>Gautier, *Poésies*.<br>Comte, *Cours de philosophie positive* (1830–42).<br>Hugo, *Hernani*.<br>Lamartine, *Les harmonies poétiques et religieuses*. | Coleridge, *The Devil's Walk* (with Southey: first pub. 1799).<br>Croly, *Poetical Works*.<br>Mrs. Hemans, *Songs of the Affections*.<br>Heraud, *The Descent into Hell*.<br>Lamb, *Album Verses*.<br>Robert Montgomery, *Satan*.<br>Rogers, *Italy*, illustrated by J. M. W. Turner and T. Stothard.<br>Tennyson, *Poems, chiefly Lyrical*. |
| | First Reform Bill. Dissolution of Parliament. General Election. Second Reform Bill rejected | H. Mackenzie d.<br>W. Roscoe d.<br>Hegel d.<br>'Mark Rutherford' (W. | E. Elliott, *Corn-Law Rhymes*.<br>Hogg, *Songs*.<br>Campbell, *Poland*. |

| *Prose* | *Drama (date of acting)* |
|---|---|
| *of the Active and Moral Powers of Man.* Patrick Fraser Tytler, *History of Scotland* (concl. 1843). William Taylor, *Historic Survey of German Poetry* (concl. 1830). Whateley, *Elements of Rhetoric.* | |
| T. Arnold, *Sermons*, i. Carlyle, 'Signs of the Times' (in *Edinburgh Review*). A. Cunningham, *Lives of British Painters* (concl. 1833). Darley, *The New Sketch Book.* Reginald Heber, *Sermons.* Hogg, *The Shepherd's Calendar.* Hood, *The Epping Hunt.* Washington Irving, *The Conquest of Granada.* Jefferson, *Autobiography.* Landor, *Imaginary Conversations*, iv–v. Bulwer Lytton, *The Disowned*; *Devereux.* Marryat, *The Naval Officer, or Frank Mildmay.* James Mill, *Analysis of the Human Mind.* Milman, *History of the Jews.* Peacock, *The Misfortunes of Elphin.* Michael Scott, *Tom Cringle's Log* (in *Blackwood's Magazine*, 1829–33). Scott, *Anne of Geierstein*; *Tales of a Grandfather, Second Series.* Southey, *Sir Thomas More: The Progress and Prospects of Society.* Isaac Taylor, *The Natural History of Enthusiasm.* | A. V. Campbell, *The Forest Oracle.*<br>Douglas Jerrold, *Vidocq! The French Police Spy*; *Bampfylde Moore Carew*; *John Overy, the Miser*; *Law and Lions!*; *Black Eyed Susan, or All in the Downs*; *The Flying Dutchman*; *The Lonely Man of Shiraz*; *Thomas à Becket*; *The Witch-Finder.*<br>T. H. Lister, *Epicharis.*<br>Scott, *The House of Aspen.*<br>C. A. Somerset, *Shakespeare's Early Days.* |
| Bentham, *The Rationale of Punishment*; *Constitutional Code for all Nations.* Byron, *Letters and Journals*, with *Life* by Moore. Carleton, *Traits and Stories of the Irish Peasantry, First Series.* Cobbett, *Rural Rides*, i; *Advice to Young Men.* Coleridge, *On the Constitution of the Church and State.* Frere, *Fables for Five-Years-Old.* Galt, *Lawrie Todd*; *Life of Lord Byron.* Godwin, *Cloudesley.* Hazlitt, *Conversations of James Northcote.* Hook, *Maxwell.* Hunt, *The Tatler*, 1830–2. G. P. R. James, *De L'Orme.* Keightley, *History of the War of Independence in Greece.* Lyell, *Principles of Geology* (concl. 1833). Bulwer Lytton, *Paul Clifford.* Macaulay, essay on Robert Montgomery (in *Edinburgh Review*). Mackintosh, *History of England*, i. Maginn, *Gallery of Illustrious Literary Characters* (in *Fraser's Magazine*, 1830–8). Marryat, *The King's Own.* Moore, *Life of Byron* (as above). Nicolas, *Observations on the State of Historical Literature.* Scott, *Letters on Demonology and Witchcraft*; *Essays on Ballad Poetry*; *Tales of a Grandfather, Third Series.* Mary Shelley, *Perkin Warbeck.* W. Wilson, *Memoirs of Daniel De Foe.* | T. H. Bayly, *Perfection or The Lady of Munster.*<br>Byron, *Werner.*<br>Douglas Jerrold, *Sally in our Alley*; *Gervaise Skinner*; *The Mutiny at the Nore*; *The Press-Gang*; *The Devil's Ducat.*<br>J. Kerr, *The Wandering Boys* (adapted from Pixérécourt's *Le Pèlerin blanc*).<br>W. T. Moncrieff, *Shakespeare's Festival.*<br>Scott, *Auchindrane, or The Ayrshire Tragedy.*<br>Thomas Wade, *The Phrenologists*; *The Jew of Aragon.* |
| Sir D. Brewster, *Treatise on Optics.* J. P. Collier, *The History of English Dramatic Poetry and Annals of the Stage.* B. Disraeli, *The Young Duke.* S. Ferrier, *Destiny.* Galt, | Mrs. Gore, *The School for Coquettes*; *Lords and Commons.*<br>Douglas Jerrold, *Martha Willis, the Servant Maid, or Service in London*; *The Bride of* |

| *Date* | *Public Events* | *Literary History (including translations)* | *Verse* |
|---|---|---|---|
| 1831 (*cont.*) | by the Lords. Riots. Final Reform Bill introduced. Leopold becomes King of the Belgians. War between Belgium and Holland. Faraday's electromagnetic current. | Hale White) b.<br>E. R. Bulwer Lytton, Earl Lytton ('Owen Meredith') b.<br>C. S. Calverley b.<br>First meeting of the British Association.<br>Croker ed. Boswell's *Life of Johnson.*<br>J. Boaden ed. *Private Correspondence of David Garrick*, 1831–2.<br>Hugo, *Les Feuilles d'automne.*<br>Dumas père, *Antony.*<br>Grillparzer, *Des Meeres und der Liebe Wellen.*<br>Sotheby trans. *The Iliad.*<br>Balzac, *La Peau de chagrin.*<br>Stendhal, *Le Rouge et le Noir.*<br>Bentley's Standard Novels started. | Moore, *The Summer Fête.*<br>Poe, *Poems.*<br>C. Whitehead, *The Solitary.*<br>Whittier, *Legends of New England.* |
| 1832 | Grey resigns. Wellington fails to form a ministry. Grey recalled. Reform Act becomes law. Cholera epidemic. General election. Jackson's second term as President of U.S.A. | Goethe d.<br>Sir Walter Scott d.<br>Crabbe d.<br>Jeremy Bentham d.<br>Sir James Mackintosh d.<br>C. L. Dodgson ('Lewis Carroll') b.<br>Sir Leslie Stephen b.<br>T. Watts-Dunton b.<br>Sir Edwin Arnold b.<br>Chambers's *Edinburgh Journal* started.<br>*Tait's Edinburgh Magazine* started.<br>*The British Magazine* started.<br>Caedmon ed. and trans. by Benjamin Thorpe.<br>de Vigny, *Stello* (as a book).<br>Dumas père, *La Tour de Nesle.*<br>Gautier, *Albertus ou l'âme et le péché.*<br>Goethe, *Faust*, ii.<br>Knight's *Penny Magazine* started.<br>Sainte-Beuve, *Critiques et portraits littéraires*, i. | Byron, *Works*, ed. Moore, 1832–5.<br>Hunt, *Poetical Works.*<br>R. Montgomery, *The Messiah.*<br>B. W. Procter ('Barry Cornwall'), *English Songs.*<br>Shelley, *The Masque of Anarchy.*<br>Tennyson, *Poems* ('1833'). |

| *Prose* | *Drama (date of acting)* |
|---|---|
| *Bogle Corbet*; *Lives of the Players*. Godwin, *Thoughts on Man*. Mrs. Gore, *Mothers and Daughters*. Grote, *Parliamentary Reform*. Charles Knight, *The Working Man's Companion*. L. E. Landon, *Romance and Reality*. Lover, *Legends and Stories of Ireland*, 1831–4. Macaulay, essay on Boswell (rev. of Croker's ed. in *Edinburgh Review*). Moore, *Life of Lord Edward Fitzgerald*. Peacock, *Crotchet Castle*. Jane Porter, *Sir Edward Seaward's Narrative of his Shipwreck*. Trelawny, *The Adventures of a Younger Son*. Watts, *Scenes of Life and Shades of Character*. | *Ludgate*.<br>Sheridan Knowles, *Alfred the Great, or The Patriot King*.<br>M. R. Mitford, *Inez de Castro*.<br>J. R. Planché, *Olympic Revels*.<br>C. M. Westmacott, *Nettlewig Hall*.<br>Lord Francis Leveson-Gower, *Hernani, or The Honour of a Castilian* (adapted from Hugo.) |
| John Austin, *The Province of Jurisprudence determined*. Frances Burney, *Memoirs of Dr. Burney*. R. Chambers, *Biographical Dictionary of Eminent Scotsmen*. (concl. 1835). De Quincey, *Klosterheim*. Dibdin, *Bibliophobia*. Disraeli, *Contarini Fleming*. Genest, *Account of the English Stage*. Hogg, *Altrive Tales*; *A Queer Book*. Hunt, *Sir Ralph Esher*; *Christianism* (privately printed). Galt, *The Member*; *The Radical*. Washington Irving, *The Alhambra*. G. P. R. James, *Henry Masterton*. Anna Jameson, *Characteristics of Women*. T. H. Lister, *Arlington*. Bulwer Lytton, *Eugene Aram*. Harriet Martineau, *Illustrations of Political Economy* (concl. 1834). Marryat, *Newton Forster*. Scott, *Tales of my Landlord, Fourth Series* (*Count Robert of Paris*, *Castle Dangerous*). Earl Stanhope, *History of the War of the Succession in Spain*. Frances Trollope, *The Refugee in America*; *Domestic Manners of the Americans*. S. Warren, *Passages from the Diary of a late Physician* (pirated American edition the previous year: concl. 1838: originally pub. in *Blackwood's Magazine*, 1830–7). Southey, *Essays, Moral and Political*. | T. H. Bayly, *My Eleventh Day*; *Der Alchymist*; *Cupid*.<br>Lord Francis Leveson-Gower, *Catherine of Cleves* (adapted from *Henri III*, by Dumas).<br>Douglas Jerrold, *The Broken Heart*; *The Rent Day*; *The Golden Calf*; *The Factory Girl*.<br>Frances Anne Kemble (Mrs. Butler), *Francis the First*.<br>Sheridan Knowles, *The Hunchback*; *The Vision of the Bard* (in honour of Scott).<br>T. E. Wilks, *The Wolf and the Lamb*.<br>*Eugene Aram* (several stage versions). |

# BIBLIOGRAPHY

THIS bibliography is arranged in six sections:

I. General Bibliographies and Works of Reference.

II. General Collections and Anthologies.

III. General Literary History and Criticism (Early Studies; Histories and Surveys; Studies of Romanticism).

IV. Special Literary Studies and Literary Forms (The Language; Newspapers, Reviews, and Magazines; Prose Fiction; Literary Criticism; The Drama; History, Biography, and Autobiography; Interest in Foreign Literature and in Earlier English Literature; Travel; Annuals, and the Reading Public; The Profession of Letters and the Publishing Trade).

V. The Background of Literature (Political and Social History, and Political Thought; Contemporary Autobiographies, Memoirs, and Letters; Religion and Moral Attitudes; Science and Technology; Education; Architecture, Painting, and Music).

VI. Individual Authors.

**Since this bibliography is selective a good deal that is of interest has had to be omitted. Those seeking further guidance are referred to Section I below.**

A great many of the novels and other books of the time first appeared anonymously: as a rule no mention is made of this in the Bibliography. Short titles are usually given—the words 'and Other Poems' (for example) being often omitted.

ABBREVIATIONS:

*CBEL* *Cambridge Bibliography of English Literature.*
*DNB* *Dictionary of National Biography.*
*EC* *Essays in Criticism.*
*EHR* *English Historical Review.*
*ELH* *English Literary History.*

*ERP* *The English Romantic Poets: A Review of Research*, ed. T. M. Raysor, rev. ed., New York, 1956.
*ERPE* *The English Romantic Poets and Essayists: A Review of Research and Criticism*, ed. C. W. and L. H. Houtchens, New York, 1957.
*ESEA* *Essays and Studies by Members of the English Association* (entitled *English Studies* in 1948 and 1949).
*HLB* *Huntington Library Bulletin.*
*HLQ* *Huntington Library Quarterly.*
*JEGP* *Journal of English and Germanic Philology.*
*JHI* *Journal of the History of Ideas.*
*K.-Sh.B.* *Bulletin of the Keats–Shelley Memorial Association.*
*K.-Sh.J.* *The Keats–Shelley Journal* (New York).
*MLN* *Modern Language Notes.*
*MLQ* *Modern Language Quarterly.*
*MLR* *Modern Language Review.*
*MP* *Modern Philology.*
*NQ* *Notes and Queries.*
*PMLA* *Publications of the Modern Language Association of America.*
*PQ* *Philological Quarterly.*
*RES* *Review of English Studies.*
*SP* *Studies in Philology.*
*SR* *Studies in Romanticism* (Boston).
*TLS* *Times Literary Supplement.*
*UTQ* *University of Toronto Quarterly.*

The place of publication is usually given if it is other than London, Edinburgh, Oxford, Cambridge, or (for French books) Paris.

## I. GENERAL BIBLIOGRAPHIES AND WORKS OF REFERENCE

The best guide is, of course, the *Cambridge Bibliography of English Literature*, ed. F. W. Bateson, of which vol. iii (1940) covers the nineteenth century. This is supplemented in vol. v, ed. G. Watson (1957). The *Concise Cambridge Bibliography*, 1958, gives some later books. The Oxford *Annals of English Literature, 1475–1950*, 2nd ed., 1961, list the main books published each year. The *Oxford Companion to English Literature*, ed. Sir Paul Harvey, 3rd ed., 1946, gives brief details of some of the principal writers and their books.

Valuable lists of new books throughout the period may be found in a book-trade periodical, Bent's *Monthly Literary Advertiser*. From 1826 this attempted a complete list of new books once a year. The *Monthly Review* also published lists of new books, while the *Quarterly* similarly gave the titles of many new publications. Reference may also be made to *The English Catalogue of Books . . . 1801–36*, ed. R. A. Peddie and Q. Waddington, 1914, although it is not wholly reliable and the fact that it is one huge consolidated list detracts from its usefulness.

Help may also be found in the *British Museum General Catalogue of Printed Books* (in progress) and *The Bibliographer's Manual*, by W. T. Lowndes, rev. ed., 6 vols. in eleven, 1857–64.

Halkett and Laing's *Dictionary of Anonymous and Pseudonymous English Literature*, rev. by J. Kennedy and others, 7 vols., 1926–34, suppl. vols. 1956 and 1962, is a valuable guide, though inevitably very incomplete.

There is a useful *Guide to Archives and Manuscripts in the United States*, ed. P. M. Hamer, New Haven, 1961, the first attempt at a really comprehensive survey of MS. material in the United States. It is inevitably incomplete: no details are given of the papers in the Berg collection at the New York Public Library, for example, while the Byron material in the Pierpont Morgan Library is not mentioned.

The *Dictionary of National Biography* is particularly valuable for writers of the nineteenth century, although there are of course errors and natural reticences.

The best bibliographies of recent work on this period are to be found in two books published at New York by the Modern

Language Association of America: *The English Romantic Poets: A Review of Research*, ed. T. M. Raysor, 1950 (2nd ed., 1956), covers the Romantic Movement, Wordsworth, Coleridge, Byron, Shelley, and Keats: while *The English Romantic Poets and Essayists: A Review of Research and Criticism*, ed. Carolyn W. and L. H. Houtchens, 1957, deals with Blake, Lamb, Hazlitt, Scott, Southey, Campbell, Moore, Landor, Hunt, and De Quincey. Each book consists of signed articles in which the relevant scholarship is discussed and evaluated. 'The Romantic Movement: A Selective and Critical Bibliography' appeared in *ELH* from 1937 to 1949 and now appears in *PQ*. *The Year's Work in English Studies* is an annual volume published by the English Association; while there is also an *Annual Bibliography of English Language and Literature* which is published by the Modern Humanities Research Association. *PMLA* publishes a list of books and articles on this period once a year, though its list of 'Research in Progress' has been abandoned.

A critical bibliography of writings on the Romantic Movement may be found in the 2nd ed. of E. Bernbaum's *Guide through the Romantic Movement*, 1949. L. Leary's *Contemporary Literary Scholarship: A Critical Review*, New York, 1958, has 30 pp. on the Romantic Movement, with brief discussions of the work listed.

For bibliographies of the novel and other literary forms see Section IV below.

## II. GENERAL COLLECTIONS AND ANTHOLOGIES

### 1. Prose

There are innumerable anthologies which give selections from Hazlitt and Lamb and the other essayists. Among the fullest are W. Peacock, *English Prose*, vols. iii–iv (World's Classics, 1921), and E. Bernbaum, *Anthology of Romanticism and Guide through the Romantic Movement*, 5 vols., New York, 1929–30. See also H. Craik, *English Prose Selections*, vol. v, 1896; F. W. Roe, *Nineteenth Century English Prose*, New York, 1923; C. H. Grabo, *Romantic Prose of the Early Nineteenth Century*, New York, 1927; R. W. King, *England from Wordsworth to Dickens*, [1929]; G. Sampson, *Nineteenth Century Essays*, Cambridge, 1929; E. H. Lacon Watson, *Contemporary Comments: Writers of the Early*

*Nineteenth Century as they appeared to each other*, 1931; O. J. Campbell, J. F. A. Pyre, and B. Weaver, *Poetry and Criticism of the Romantic Movement*, New York, 1932; C. F. Macintyre and M. Ewing, *English Prose of the Romantic Period*, 1938; G. Grigson, *The Romantics*, 1943; and *Prose of the Romantic Period, 1780–1830*, ed. R. Wright, 1956 (*The Pelican Book of English Prose*, ed. K. Allott, vol. iv).

F. A. Mumby's *Letters of Literary Men: The Nineteenth Century*, 1906, is a useful collection. *A Cabinet of Gems*, ed. B. A. Booth, Berkeley, 1938, is a collection of short stories from the *Annuals*. For collections of critical essays see IV. 4 below.

## 2. Poetry

There is an interesting early anthology, published in Paris: *The Living Poets of England*, 2 vols., 1827, which in fact includes selections from Byron, Shelley, and Keats, as well as many minor poets of the period, and contains biographical and critical introductions, including an essay on 'Wordsworth and the Lake-School of Poetry'. *The Poetical Album*, ed. A. A. Watts, 2 vols., 1828–9, contains much interesting minor verse.

The fullest selections are those in A. H. Miles and others, *The Poets and the Poetry of the Century*, which first appeared in 10 vols. in 1891–7 and was revised in 12 vols. in 1905–7. Selections may also be found in Bernbaum and in Campbell, Pyre, and Weaver, as above; in T. H. Ward and others, *The English Poets*, vol. iv, 1880; in the *Oxford Book of English Verse of the Romantic Period, 1798–1837*, ed. H. S. Milford, 1935 (first issued as the *Oxford Book of Regency Verse*, 1928); in *Blake to Poe* (vol. iv of *Poets of the English Language*, ed. W. H. Auden and N. H. Pearson), 1951; and in *English Romantic Poetry*, ed. H. Bloom, New York, 1961.

Palgrave's *Golden Treasury*, which first appeared in 1861 and has frequently been revised, occupies a special place in the history of taste. His *Treasury of Sacred Song*, 1889, and *The Golden Treasury, Second Series*, 1897, may also be consulted. Other anthologies include *The English Parnassus*, ed. W. Macneile Dixon and H. J. C. Grierson, 1909, which contains longer poems by Byron, Shelley, and Keats; J. D[over] Wilson, *The Poetry of the Age of Wordsworth*, 1927; O. J. Campbell, J. F. A. Pyre, and B. Weaver, *Poetry and Criticism of the Romantic Move-*

*ment*, 1932 (as above); J. Hayward, *Nineteenth-Century Poetry: An Anthology*, 1932; S. Spender, *A Choice of English Romantic Poetry*, New York, 1947; *Pope to Keats* and *Hood to Hardy*, both ed. D. K. Roberts, 1949 (vols. iii–iv of *The Centuries' Poetry*, Penguin Books); and J. Heath-Stubbs and D. Wright, *The Forsaken Garden: An Anthology of Poetry, 1824–1909*, 1950. *Fifteen Poets*, by H. S. Bennett, C. S. Lewis, and others, 1941, contains selections from Byron, Shelley, and Keats, with brief prefaces.

For Scottish poetry see *The Scottish Songs*, ed. R. Chambers, 2 vols., 1829–32; *The Modern Scottish Minstrel*, ed. C. Rogers, 6 vols., 1856–7; and *Modern Scottish Poets*, ed. D. H. Edwards, 16 vols., Brechin, 1880–97.

## III. GENERAL LITERARY HISTORY AND CRITICISM

So much has been written on this period, in England and America and elsewhere, that it seems necessary to be exceptionally selective in this section. This list is accordingly confined to (*a*) a few Early Studies; (*b*) Histories and Surveys; and (*c*) Studies of Romanticism which are of particular relevance to the period.

(*a*) Book IV of Bulwer Lytton's *England and the English*, 2 vols., 1833, gives a 'View of the Intellectual Spirit of the Time' which includes penetrating remarks on the state of literature. A good deal of biographical and other information may be found in *The Living Poets*, mentioned above on p. 462. Two early surveys are Allan Cunningham's *Biographical and Critical History of the British Literature of the Last Fifty Years*, Paris, 1834, and D. M. Moir's *Sketches of the Poetical Literature of the Past Half-Century, in Six Lectures*, Edinburgh, 1851. Mrs. [Margaret] Oliphant's *The Literary History of England in the End of the Eighteenth and Beginning of the Nineteenth Century*, 3 vols., 1882 (new issue), remains of real interest.

*The Poets and their Critics*, vol. ii, ed. H. Sykes Davies, 1962, gives outstanding passages of criticism of the poets from Blake to Browning.

(*b*) Two of the best surveys are those by Oliver Elton in *A Survey of English Literature, 1780–1830*, 2 vols., 1912, and by S. C. Chew in *The Nineteenth Century and After, 1789–1939*,

part iv of *A Literary History of England*, ed. A. C. Baugh, New York, 1948 (Eng. ed., 1950). The period is also intelligently treated in *A History of English Literature*, by P. Legouis and L. Cazamian, rev. ed. (Eng. trans.) 1948, and in D. Daiches's *Critical History of English Literature*, vol. ii, 1960. Vol. iv of George Brandes's *Main Currents in Nineteenth Century Literature, Naturalism in England* (Eng. trans. 1905), is still worth consulting, as is vol. vi (1910) of W. J. Courthope's *History of English Poetry*. Helene Richter's *Geschichte der englischen Romantik*, 2 vols., Halle, 1911–16, is now of less interest. Vol. xii is the relevant volume of the *Cambridge History of English Literature* (*The Nineteenth Century I*, 1914, 2nd ed., 1932). *The Age of Wordsworth*, by C. H. Herford, 1897, is a sensible old-fashioned survey. *Currents and Eddies in the English Romantic Generation*, by F. E. Pierce, New Haven, 1918, deals interestingly with minor writers and the literary *milieux* of Bristol, Edinburgh, London, and the Lakes. (On Bristol see also C. A. Weber, *Bristols Bedeutung für die englische Romantik und die deutsch-englischen Beziehungen*, Halle, 1935.)

Mention must also be made of *Literary Anecdotes of the Nineteenth Century: Contributions towards a Literary History of the Period*, ed. W. Robertson Nicoll and Thomas J[ames] Wise (*verb. sap.*), 2 vols., 1895–6, which contains information about Shelley, Keats, Charles Wells, the Landor–Blessington papers, and other topics; and *Little Memoirs of the Nineteenth Century*, by 'George Paston', 1902, which contains essays on Haydon, Lady Morgan, N. P. Willis, Lady Hester Stanhope, William and Mary Howitt, and Prince Pückler-Muskau in England.

Vol. iii of G. Saintsbury's *History of English Prosody, From Blake to Mr. Swinburne*, 1910, includes this period, as do chapters ix and x of his *History of English Prose Rhythm*, 1912.

Good brief surveys include *Augustans and Romantics, 1689–1830*, by H. V. D. Dyson and J. Butt, rev. ed. 1950 (*Introductions to English Literature*, ed. B. Dobrée, vol. iii: with useful brief bibliographies); and *The Romantic Poets*, by G. Hough, 1953. Vol. 5 of the *Pelican Guide to English Literature*, ed. B. Ford (*From Blake to Byron*, 1957), can only be described as disappointing.

(*c*) In his *Guide through the Romantic Movement*, 2nd ed., 1948, Bernbaum discusses twenty-eight of the hundreds of meanings of the words 'romanticism'. For the earlier period there is an elaborate and admirable study by F. Baldensperger, ' "Romantique", ses analogues et ses équivalents: tableau synoptique de

1650 à 1810' in *Harvard Studies and Notes in Philology and Literature*, xix (1937). One of the most learned and patient discussions is the two-part article by R. Wellek in *Comparative Literature*, vol. i, nos. 1–2, 1949: Part i of 'The Concept of "Romanticism" in Literary History' is entitled 'The Term "Romantic" and its Derivatives', and Part ii 'The Unity of European Romanticism'. In vol. ii of his *History of Modern Criticism, 1750–1950* (*The Romantic Age*, 1955) Wellek gives it as his view that 'In England, as opposed to the Continent, there was no "romantic" movement, if we limit the meaning of such a term to a conscious program and consider the precise name as crucial' (p. 110). A. O. Lovejoy's well-known essay, 'On the Discrimination of Romanticisms' is reprinted from *PMLA* xxxix (1924) in his *Essays in the History of Ideas*, New York, 1948 (a volume which also contains several other essays relevant to the concept 'romanticism'), and in *English Romantic Poets: Modern Essays in Criticism*, ed. M. H. Abrams, New York, 1960. For a criticism of Lovejoy's approach see B. Phillips, 'Logical Positivism and the Function of Reason', in *Philosophy*, 1948. Praz discusses the word as 'an approximate term' in *The Romantic Agony* (mentioned below). H. J. C. Grierson's 'Classical and Romantic', reprinted in his *The Background of English Literature*, 1925, is still of some interest, while L. P. Smith's *Four Words* (1924, as a pamphlet: reprinted as 'Four Romantic Words' in *Words and Idioms: Studies in the English Language*, 1925) remains one of the most suggestive approaches to the whole period: the words are 'romantic', 'originality', 'creative', and 'genius'. The meaning of 'romantic' and 'romanticism' are also intelligently discussed in M. H. Abrams, *The Mirror and the Lamp: Romantic Theory and the Critical Tradition*, New York, 1953, and W. K. Wimsatt, Jr., and Cleanth Brooks, *Literary Criticism: A Short History*, 1957. Other discussions are mentioned in *ERP*, pp. 24–27, and in articles listed by R. Wellek and A. Warren on pp. 381–2 of their *Theory of Literature*, 1949.

The so-called 'pre-romantic movement' is outside our scope. *Le mouvement romantique*, by P. van Tieghem, 2nd ed., Paris, 1923, is an annotated collection of statements about literature by the leading writers of England, Germany, Italy, and France. The same writer's *Le romantisme dans la littérature européenne*, 1948, is a wide survey. See also his articles, 'La place du romantisme anglais dans le romantisme européen', *Lettres* v–vi, 1946. The

very brief treatment of English literature by H. N. Fairchild in 'Romanticism: A Symposium' (*PMLA*, vol. lv, No. 1, March 1940) is of little value.

One of the most stimulating books on the romantic period is still Irving Babbitt's *Rousseau and Romanticism*, 1919: Babbitt has, of course, far more references to Byron and Shelley than to Keats. The value of his book lies in his learning, wit, and detachment. *The Romantic Comedy*, by D. G. James, 1948, throws a great deal of light on Shelley and Keats. Sir Maurice Bowra's *The Romantic Imagination*, 1950, is a notably lucid exposition from a point of view different from that adopted in this study. A. Gérard's *L'Idée romantique de la poésie en Angleterre*, 1955, is another intelligent study.

Mario Praz is the author of two stimulating books. *The Romantic Agony*, Eng. trans. 1933 (Italian ed., *La carne, la morte, e il diavolo nella letteratura romantica*, Milan and Rome, 1930), is a study of the erotic sensibility of the nineteenth century, demonstrating how the decadents may be regarded as the descendants of the writers of the earlier part of the century. In *The Hero in Eclipse in Victorian Fiction* (Eng. trans. 1956), Praz argues that in the work of Coleridge, Wordsworth, Scott, Lamb, De Quincey, Peacock and later writers 'romanticism turns bourgeois'. F. Brie's *Exotismus der Sinne, eine Studie zur Psychologie der Romantik*, Heidelberg, 1920, is a briefer study on lines partly similar to those of *The Romantic Agony*.

*The Romantic Movement in English Poetry*, by Arthur Symons, 1909, has the merit of dealing individually and often perceptively with a great many major and minor writers. *A History of English Romanticism in the Nineteenth Century*, by H. A. Beers, 1902, is mainly concerned with the revival of medievalism and is now of little value. *Nature in English Literature*, by E. Blunden, 1929, and *The Concept of Nature in Nineteenth-Century English Poetry*, by J. W. Beach, New York, 1936, may also be consulted. *The Visionary Company*, by H. Bloom, New York, 1961, gives a highly individual reading of certain of the principal poems.

Three stimulating books are *The Poet's Defence*, by J. Bronowski, 1939, which deals with attitudes to the imagination in our period and in the present century; *Romanticism and the Modern Ego*, by J. Barzun, Boston, 1943 (rev. as *Classic, Romantic, and Modern*, 1962); and *The Misinterpretation of Man*, 1949, by P. Roubiczek, an attack on European romanticism. *The Decline and*

*Fall of the Romantic Ideal*, by F. L. Lucas, 1936, is a series of related essays. *Le Romantisme anglais*, 1946, is a special issue of *Les Lettres* containing essays by L. Cazamian, Middleton Murry, P. van Tieghem, and others; *JHI* ii, 1941, contains a symposium on Romanticism by A. O. Lovejoy and others. *Romanticism: Points of View*, ed. R. F. Gleckner and G. E. Enscoe, New Jersey, 1963, is a collection of essays from Pater onwards.

There are several collections of essays on the period mainly by American scholars. *The Major English Romantic Poets: A Symposium in Reappraisal*, was edited by C. D. Thorpe and others and published in Southern Illinois in 1957. *English Romantic Poets: Modern Essays in Criticism*, ed. M. H. Abrams, 1960 (Galaxy paperback), contains Lovejoy's essay mentioned on p. 465 above, 'The Structure of Romantic Nature Imagery', by W. K. Wimsatt, and 'The Correspondent Breeze: A Romantic Metaphor', by Abrams himself, as well as essays on individual authors mentioned elsewhere (some of them reprinted from the previously mentioned collection). A forthcoming volume, ed. J. E. Jordan, Northrop Frye, and J. V. Logan, will contain essays on many of the major writers of the period.

D. Bush's *Mythology and the Romantic Tradition in English Poetry*, Cambridge, Mass., 1937, is a learned and valuable survey which devotes more than a hundred pages to our period. A. C. Bradley's 'The Long Poem in the Age of Wordsworth', in his *Oxford Lectures on Poetry*, 1909, is still illuminating. K. Kroeber's *Romantic Narrative Art*, Madison, Wisconsin, 1960, discusses the poetry of Byron and others. The scope of D. Perkins, *The Quest for Permanence: The Symbolism of Wordsworth, Shelley and Keats*, Cambridge, Mass., 1959, is sufficiently indicated by its title. Ilse Gugler's study, *Das Problem der fragmentarischen Dichtung in der englischen Romantik* (*Schweizer Anglistische Arbeiten*, xv, Bern, 1944), should also be mentioned. In *The Romantic Assertion*, 1958, R. A. Foakes discusses modern approaches to nineteenth-century poetry and offers his readings of *The Eve of St. Agnes* and *Adonais*. *The Lost Travellers*, by B. Blackstone, 1962, is a study of Blake, Byron, and other major writers of the period in relation to the common theme of travel which he finds running through their work.

T. S. Eliot has not written much about the writers of this period, although there is a brief discussion of Shelley and Keats in *The Use of Poetry and the Use of Criticism*, 1933. In *The Star-Lit*

*Dome: Studies in the Poetry of Vision*, 1941, G. Wilson Knight has written characteristically and often penetratingly on Keats and Shelley.

Two articles by R. H. Fogle discuss critical approaches: 'Romantic Bards and Metaphysical Reviewers', *ELH* xii, 1945, and 'A Recent Attack upon Romanticism', *College English*, ix, 1948.

## IV. SPECIAL LITERARY STUDIES AND LITERARY FORMS

This section comprises: (1) The Language; (2) Newspapers, Reviews, and Magazines; (3) Prose Fiction; (4) Literary Criticism; (5) The Drama; (6) History, Biography, and Autobiography; (7) Interest in Foreign Literature and in Earlier English Literature; (8) Travel; (9) Annuals, and the Reading Public; and (10) The Profession of Letters and the Publishing Trade.

### 1. The Language

The development of the English language in the eighteenth and nineteenth centuries has been very much neglected. The best general *History of the English Language*, that by A. C. Baugh, New York, 1935, 2nd edn. 1959, has naturally little to say about our period. A number of brief studies of eighteenth-century usage are of background relevance: see (for example) two notes by R. W. Babcock, 'Benevolence, Sensibility and Sentiment in Some Eighteenth-Century Periodicals', *MLN* lxii, 1947, and 'A Note on Genius, Imagination and Enthusiasm in Some Late Eighteenth-Century Periodicals', *NQ* cxcii, 1947; and Caroline Thompson's 'Sensibility', *Psyche*, xv, 1935. An example of one of the kinds of study that is wanted is R. W. Chapman's appendix on 'Miss Austen's English' in his edition of *Sense and Sensibility*, 1923 (3rd edn. 1933). Also see Index VII to his edition of *Jane Austen's Letters*, 2nd ed., 1932. Cobbett's *Grammar* and other writings provide a great deal of information. Reference may also be made to the essay by L. P. Smith mentioned above on p. 465, and to Baldensperger's study of the meanings of the word 'romantique' up to 1810 (pp. 464–5 above). Uno Philipson's *Political Slang, 1750–1850* (Lund Studies in English,

9, 1941), should also be mentioned. The language of Dickens, which lies beyond our limits, has recently been studied by Professor Randolph Quirk in *Charles Dickens and Appropriate Language* (Durham, 1959), and in 'Some Observations on the Language of Dickens', *A Review of English Literature*, ii, 1961.

The emergence of key terms in political and social thinking deserves further study, as does the development of the terminology of literary criticism. Changes in linguistic habits also throw light on the increasing squeamishness of the time, and on changes in people's feelings about social class. The Reviews are full of material, while revisions in books republished many years after their first appearance sometimes provide unusually precise evidence. See (for example) 'De Quincey Revises his *Confessions*', by I. Jack, *PMLA* lxxii, 1957.

## 2. Newspapers, Reviews, and Magazines

For guidance on where to find runs of periodicals and other general information see the American *Union List of Serials in Libraries of the United States and Canada*, ed. W. Gregory, 2nd ed., New York, 1943 (Supplements 1945 and 1953), the *British Union-Catalogue of Periodicals: A Record of the Periodicals of the World, from the Seventeenth Century to the Present Day in British Libraries*, ed. J. D. Stewart, M. E. Hammond, and E. Saenger, 4 vols., 1955–8 (and *Supplement to 1960*, ed. J. D. Stewart and others, 1962); and the *Index and Finding List of Serials published in the British Isles, 1789–1832*, ed. W. S. Ward, Lexington, 1953.

'*The Times*' *Centenary Handlist of English and Welsh Newspapers, Magazines and Reviews* [by J. G. Muddiman], 1920, is still of use, though not invariably accurate.

### (*a*) *Newspapers*

The scope of Stanley Morison's *The English Newspaper: Some Account of the Physical Development of Journals Printed in London between 1622 & the Present Day*, 1932, is accurately defined by the sub-title. The book includes numerous illustrations of newspapers. There is no good up-to-date history of English journalism. H. R. Fox Bourne's *English Newspapers*, 2 vols., 1887, is still the best general book; but see also F. Knight Hunt, *The*

*Fourth Estate: Contributions towards A History of Newspapers, and of the Liberty of the Press*, 2 vols., 1850, and W. H. Wickwar, *The Struggle for the Freedom of the Press, 1819–1832*, 1928. A. Aspinall is the author of an important book, *Politics and the Press, c. 1780–1850*, 1949, and of a number of articles, notably 'Statistical Accounts of the London Newspapers, 1800–36', *EHR* lxv, 1950 (on advertisement duty returns); 'The Circulation of Newspapers in the Early Nineteenth Century', *RES* xxii, 1946; and 'The Social Status of Journalists at the Beginning of the Nineteenth Century', *RES* xxi, 1945. E. E. Kellett's chapter in *Early Victorian England, 1830–1865*, ed. G. M. Young, 2 vols., 1934, touches on the end of our period. D. Read's *Press and People, 1790–1850*, 1961, gives information about the circulation of newspapers in Leeds, Manchester and Sheffield.

Vol. i of *The History of The Times, 'The Thunderer' in the Making, 1785–1841*, 1935 (anonymous), throws important light on the period, as does D. Hudson's briefer *Thomas Barnes of 'The Times'*, 1943.

For further books and articles see *CBEL* iii, 779, and v, 678. Reference should also be made to Barnes, Hone, Jerdan, Hook, Knight, and others in the individual entries below. See also *Babylon the Great*, referred to on p. 485 below.

(*b*) *Reviews and Magazines*

*The Wellesley Index to Victorian Periodicals*, ed. W. E. Houghton and others, will list all known authors in some thirty quarterlies and monthlies from 1824 to 1900. It will also include the *Edinburgh Review* from its foundation, but not the early years of *Blackwood's* or the *Quarterly*, as indexes for these already exist (see below).

W. A. Copinger's *On the Authorship of the First Hundred Numbers of the 'Edinburgh Review'*, privately printed, Manchester, 1895, goes up to January 1830. More recent information may be found in important articles by E. Schneider and others in *MP* xlii–xliii, 1945–6, and *MLN* lxi, 1946; by L. G. Johnson and C. Blagden in *The Library*, 5th series, vii, 1952; by F. W. Fetter in the *Journal of Political Economy*, lxi, 1953; and by P. L. Carver, *RES* iv, 1928. *The Quarterly Review under Gifford: Identification of Contributors, 1809–1824*, by H. and H. C. Shine, Chapel Hill, 1949, is authoritative and contains a list of memoirs, &c., throwing light on problems of authorship. For the contributors on

literary subjects under Lockhart's editorship see M. F. Brightfield in *PMLA* lix, 1944. For the contributors to *Blackwood's* see A. L. Strout, *A Bibliography of Articles in Blackwood's Magazine, 1817–1825*, 1959.

A great deal of information will be found in volumes of letters, memoirs, &c., listed under individual authors below. Scott's letters are particularly important, as are Southey's (see particularly *The Life and Correspondence*, ed. C. C. Southey, 6 vols., 1849–50, and *Selections from the Letters*, ed. J. W. Warter, 4 vols., 1856).

The best survey of Reviews and Magazines in the period is Walter Graham's valuable study, *English Literary Periodicals*, New York, 1930.

Of the mass of contemporary comment one may refer to Edward Copleston's brilliant parody, *Advice to a Young Reviewer, with a Specimen of the Art*, 1807, and the comments in Bulwer Lytton's *England and the English*, 2 vols., 1833, and in Lockhart's anonymous *John Bull's Letter to Lord Byron*, 1821. Peacock refers to the Reviews in his 'Essay on Fashionable Literature' (in vol. viii of the Halliford Edition) and elsewhere in his writings.

A great deal of information about the *Edinburgh*, the *Quarterly*, and *Blackwood's* may be found in (respectively) T. Constable, *Archibald Constable and his Literary Correspondents*, 3 vols., 1873; S. Smiles, *A Publisher and his Friends: Memoir and Correspondence of the late John Murray*, 2 vols., 1891; and Mrs. [Margaret] Oliphant, *Annals of a Publishing House: William Blackwood and his Sons*, 2 vols., 1897 (vol. iii, by Mrs. Gerald Porter, 1898, deals with a later period). See also under the names of individual contributors below.

The *Memoirs and Correspondence of Francis Horner, M.P.*, ed. L. Horner, 2 vols., 1843, throw light on the early years of the *Edinburgh Review*, while *Selections from the Correspondence of Macvey Napier*, ed. M. Napier, 1877 (privately printed), are important for the slightly later period. For the *Monthly Review* see J. W. Robberds, *A Memoir of William Taylor*, 2 vols., 1843. For the *Westminster* see the *Autobiography* of John Stuart Mill, 1873 (*The Early Draft* . . . was ed. by J. Stillinger, Urbana, Illinois, 1961), as well as entries under Bentham, Bowring, and James Mill, below. Colburn's *New Monthly Magazine* has received little attention from scholars: information may, however, be found

in many contemporary memoirs, notably the *Life and Letters of Thomas Campbell*, by W. Beattie, 3 vols., 1849.

The following monographs are of importance: J. Clive, *Scotch Reviewers*, 1957; W. Graham, *Tory Criticism in the Quarterly Review, 1809–1853*, Columbia, 1921; *Leigh Hunt's 'Examiner' Examined*, by E. Blunden, 1928; *The London Magazine, 1820–29*, by Josephine Bauer, Copenhagen, 1953 (*Anglistica*, ed. T. Dahl and others, vol. i: see also E. Blunden, *Keats's Publisher: A Memoir of John Taylor (1781–1864)*, 1936); and *Rebellious Fraser's*, by Miriam M. H. Thrall, New York, 1934. *Benthamite Reviewing*, by G. L. Nesbitt, New York, 1934, deals with the *Westminster Review* from 1824 to 1836. *The Dissidence of Dissent*, by F. E. Mineka, North Carolina, 1944, deals with *The Monthly Repository* from 1806 to 1838 and includes a chapter on religious periodicals between 1700 and 1825. *The Athenaeum: A Mirror of Victorian Culture*, by L. A. Marchand, Chapel Hill, North Carolina, 1941, is an admirable study. (See also the Memoir of C. W. Dilke prefixed to *The Papers of a Critic*, 2 vols., 1875.)

Special mention should be made of *Selected Journalism from the English Reviews by Stendhal*, ed. G. Strickland, 1959. In the 1820's Stendhal contributed (from Paris) to the *London Magazine*, the *New Monthly Magazine*, and the *Athenaeum*. *Shelley–Leigh Hunt: How Friendship Made History*, ed. R. Brimley Johnson, 1928, is a valuable collection of reviews and leaders from the *Examiner*, with letters between the Shelleys and Leigh Hunt.

Two important essays with the same title, 'The First Edinburgh Reviewers', by Leslie Stephen and Walter Bagehot, respectively, may be found in *Hours in a Library*, 3rd series, 1879, and *Literary Studies*, ed. R. H. Hutton, vol. i, 1895. See also 'Memorials of a Man of Letters' in J. Morley's *Studies in Literature*, 1891. *Cobwebs of Criticism*, by T. Hall Caine, 1883, is an indignant 'Review of the First Reviewers of the "Lake", "Satanic", and "Cockney" Schools'.

*The Criticism of Poetry in British Periodicals, 1798–1820*, by W. S. Ward (Duke University dissertation, 1943: microcards, University of Kentucky, 1955), is a statistical survey based on 831 periodicals. R. D. Mayo's *The English Novel in the Magazines, 1740–1815*, Illinois, 1962, stops on the threshold of our period. Recent articles include R. G. Cox, 'The Great Reviews', *Scrutiny*, vi, 1937; J. J. Welker, 'The Position of the Quarterlies on Some Classical Dogmas', *SP* xxxvii, 1940; V. Lloréns, 'Colaboraciones

de emigrados españoles en revistas inglesas (1824–34)', *Hispanic Review*, xix, 1951; W. Graham, 'Robert Southey as Tory Reviewer', *PQ* ii, 1923, and 'Some Infamous Tory Reviews', *SP* xxii, 1925; W. S. Ward, 'Some Aspects of the Conservative Attitude toward Poetry: 1798–1820', *PMLA*, lx, 1945; and G. Carnall, 'The *Monthly Magazine*', *RES*, new series, v, 1954. '*The Edinburgh Review' and Romantic Poetry (1802–29)*, by T. Crawford, Auckland, New Zealand, 1955, is a brief treatment in the compass of 42 pages.

*Selections from the Edinburgh Review*, ed. M. Cross, 4 vols., 1833, is a collection of 'the best articles' with a preliminary dissertation and explanatory notes. For other books containing selections from the Reviews see p. 475 below. See also Jeffrey, Brougham, Croker and others under Individual Authors.

## 3. Prose Fiction

*XIX Century Fiction: A Bibliographical Record*, by Michael Sadleir, 2 vols., 1951, is a mine of accurate information, although it is limited to books in his own collection. *The Minerva Press, 1790–1820*, by Dorothy Blakey, published by the Bibliographical Society in 1939, is also of value for our period. The chapters on 'Printing and Publishing at the Minerva, 1773–1859', 'Forgotten Favourites, 1790–1820', and (particularly) 'The Circulating Library' are of interest and importance. A. Block's *The English Novel, 1740–1850. A Catalogue including Prose Romances, Short Stories, and Translations of Foreign Fiction*, 1939 (2nd ed., 1961), is also of use, though it is not invariably reliable. There is also *A General Analytical Bibliography of the Regional Novelists of the British Isles, 1800–1950*, by L. Leclaire, Clermont-Ferrand, 1953. *A Gothic Bibliography*, by Montague Summers [1941], includes some novels of the nineteenth century.

Some account of the fiction of the period is given in histories of the novel. The fullest, that by E. A. Baker, 10 vols., 1924–1939, is in many ways unsatisfactory. *The Popular Novel in England, 1770–1800*, by J. M. S. Tompkins, 1932, provides an amusing and reliable background. *The Tale of Terror: A Study of the Gothic Romance*, by Edith Birkhead, 1921, is a dependable survey which includes the early nineteenth century. See also *The Gothic Flame*, by D. P. Varma, 1957. *The Gothic Quest: A History of the Gothic Novel*, by Montague Summers [1938], is unreliable but

full of curious information. Eino Railo, *The Haunted Castle*, English trans. 1927, deals with certain 'elements of English Romanticism' mainly in eighteenth-century fiction. P. Yvon, *Le Gothique et la Renaissance Gothique en Angleterre, 1750–1880*, Caen & Paris, 1931, covers the period 1750–1880. *Le Roman Social en Angleterre (1830–1850)*, by L. Cazamian, 2 vols., 1903 (2nd ed., 1934) deals very briefly with 'le roman à thèse avant 1830'. Kathleen Tillotson's learned and illuminating *Novels of the Eighteen-Forties*, 1954, contains a great deal of relevant information. G. Lukács's important study was translated into English in 1961 as *The Historical Novel*. For *The Hero in Eclipse in Victorian Fiction*, by M. Praz, see p. 466 above. We may also consult *Horace Walpole and the English Novel: A Study of the Influence of 'The Castle of Otranto', 1764–1820*, by K. K. Mehrotra, 1934, and *The English Novel in the Magazines* (p. 472 above).

On the fashionable novelists see M. W. Rosa, *The Silver-Fork School: Novels of Fashion preceding 'Vanity Fair'*, New York, 1936, and M. F. Brightfield, *Theodore Hook and his Novels*, Cambridge, Mass., 1928. T. Flanagan's *The Irish Novelists, 1800–1850*, New York 1959, is cited in the text.

Although Bulwer Lytton falls outside our scope reference must be made to two books relating to him by a scholar who knew this period as few have ever known it: Michael Sadleir's *Edward and Rosina*, 1931 (reissued as *Bulwer and his Wife: a Panorama, 1803–1836*, 1933), and *Blessington–d'Orsay: A Masquerade*, 1933 (revised ed., 1947). Both studies throw a great deal of light on the literary and social scene.

There are important articles on Gothic fiction by R. D. Mayo in *MLR* xxxvii, 1942, *MLN* lviii, 1943, and *PMLA* lxv, 1950. See also W. F. Gallaway, 'The Conservative Attitude toward Fiction, 1770–1830', *PMLA* lv, 1940; *Early Opposition to the English Novel: The Popular Reaction from 1760 to 1830*, by T. T. Taylor, New York, 1943; and B. A. Booth, 'Form and Technique in the Novel', in *The Reinterpretation of Victorian Literature*, ed. J. E. Baker, Princeton, 1950.

## 4. Literary Criticism

There is no collection of critical essays of this period comparable with those of Gregory Smith, Spingarn, and Elledge. A good collection with a wide scope is *Literary Criticism: Pope to Croce*, ed. G. W. Allen and H. H. Clark, New York, 1941 (re-

printed 1962). See also *Critical Essays of the Early Nineteenth Century*, ed. R. M. Alden, New York, 1921. Some criticism of the period is to be found in other collections, such as *Criticism: The Major Texts*, ed. W. J. Bate, New York, 1952. There is also a volume of *English Critical Essays: Nineteenth Century*, ed. E. D. Jones, in the World's Classics series (1916). For *The Poets and Their Critics*, ii, see p. 463 above.

There are several collections of reviews of the period. As one would expect, they tend to overlap. These include *Early Reviews of Great Writers (1786–1832)*, ed. E. Stevenson (The Scott Library [1890]); *Early Reviews of English Poets*, ed. J. L. Haney, Philadelphia, 1904; *Famous Reviews*, ed. R. Brimley Johnson, 1914 (the fullest selection); and *Contemporary Reviews of Romantic Poetry*, ed. J. Wain, 1953. Jeffrey and many other reviewers collected much of their work. See under Individual Authors.

The criticism of the time is discussed in vol. iii of G. Saintsbury's *A History of Criticism and Literary Taste in Europe*, 1904. For our period this is now largely superseded by vol. ii of R. Wellek's *A History of Modern Criticism: 1750–1950* (*The Romantic Age*, 1955). W. J. Bate's *From Classic to Romantic: Premises of Taste in Eighteenth-Century England*, Harvard, 1946, is a penetrating examination of critical development in the previous century. W. K. Wimsatt and Cleanth Brooks, *Literary Criticism: A Short History*, 1957, has intelligent discussions, while *The Mirror and the Lamp: Romantic Theory and the Critical Tradition*, by M. H. Abrams, New York, 1953, is outstanding. See also A. E. Powell's *The Romantic Theory of Poetry: An examination in the light of Croce's Æsthetic*, 1926; and *English Poetic Theory, 1825–65*, by A. H. Warren, Princeton, 1950. There are brief considerations of some of the critics of the period in W. J. Bate's *Prefaces to Criticism* (paperback 1959, reprinted from *Criticism: The Major Texts*, above) and G. Watson, *The Literary Critics*, 1962 (Penguin). *Dryden & Pope in the Early Nineteenth Century*, by U. Amarasinghe, 1962 is a study in the history of taste.

## 5. The Drama

The best general account of the drama of the time is *A History of Early Nineteenth Century Drama, 1800–1850*, by Allardyce Nicoll, 2 vols., 1930, rev. ed., one vol., 1955. The second section consists of a Hand-List of Plays. John Genest's *Some Account of*

*the English Stage from 1660 to 1830*, 10 vols., Bath, 1832 (anon.), includes our period. R. W. Lowe's *A Bibliographical Account of English Theatrical Literature*, 1888, is also useful. Background is supplied by *The Reminiscences of Thomas Dibdin*, 2 vols., 1827. For *The Life of Edmund Kean*, by 'Barry Cornwall', 2 vols., 1835, and other biographies of actors the reader is referred to Nicoll. Quotations from the *Life of Gerald Griffin*, 1843, have been given in the text of this *History*. The first chapter of *Thomas Lovell Beddoes*, by H. W. Donner, 1935, gives a clear account of 'Tragedy in the Early Nineteenth Century'. A little information may be gleaned from *Early Victorian Drama (1830–1870)*, by E. Reynolds, 1936, and *The Burlesque Tradition in the English Theatre after 1660*, by V. C. Clinton-Baddeley, 1952. *The Old Drama and the New. An Essay in Re-Valuation*, by William Archer, 1923, is brief and devastating on the early nineteenth century. W. M. Merchant's *Shakespeare and the Artist*, 1959, throws a great deal of light on stage production. In 'English Tragedy: 1819–1823', *PQ* xli (1962) C. J. Stratman discusses some of the bibliographical problems connected with tragedy in this period. For the most intelligent comments on the state of the drama see the letters of Byron and Beddoes and Darley's 'Letters to the Dramatists of the Day'. Hazlitt and Hunt were the best dramatic critics of the time. Also see below under Knowles, Maturin, Sheil, and Horace and James Smith.

## 6. History, Biography, and Autobiography

Such general Histories of History as H. E. Barnes, *A History of Historical Writing*, Oklahoma, 1937, and J. W. Thompson and B. J. Holm, *A History of Historical Writing*, 2 vols., New York, 1942, have naturally little to say about the (comparatively minor) historians of our period. G. P. Gooch's *History and Historians in the Nineteenth Century*, 1913, has brief treatments of one or two of our men, while T. P. Peardon's *The Transition in English Historical Writing, 1760–1830*, New York, 1933, is of obvious relevance. The reviews of historical works in the *Edinburgh* and *Quarterly* often throw a great deal of light on the interrelations between historical attitudes and the political actualities of the time.

See also under the names of individual historians.

This is not the place to list general studies of biography, though reference may be made to W. H. Dunn, *English Biography*, New York, 1916; A. Maurois, *Aspects of Biography* (Eng. trans. 1929); E. Johnson, *One Mighty Torrent: The Drama of Biography*, New York, 1937 (new ed., New York, 1957); H. Nicolson, *The Development of English Biography*, 1927; and J. A. Garraty, *The Nature of Biography*, New York, 1957. In *Biography as an Art: Selected Criticism, 1560–1960*, 1962, James L. Clifford includes extracts from several writers of this period, including the author of 'the first full-scale book on biography', James Field Stanfield, who published *An Essay on the Study and Composition of Biography* at Sunderland in 1813. Clifford gives a useful list of twentieth-century writings on biography. As he mentions, J. L. Adolphus published a prize essay, on biography, at Oxford in 1818. There is an illuminating article by F. R. Hart, 'Boswell and the Romantics: A Chapter in the History of Biographical Theory', in *ELH* xxvii, 1960.

I. D'Israeli discusses 'self-biography' at several points in his writings, while the Reviews frequently complain about the spate of memoirs and autobiographies. There is a useful list by W. Matthews, *British Autobiographies. An Annotated Bibliography*, Berkeley, *c.* 1957, which comes up to 1950. Most of the general books, such as W. Shumaker's *English Autobiography: Its Emergence, Materials, and Form*, Berkeley, 1954, and R. Pascal's *Design and Truth in Autobiography*, 1960, have no special bearing on our period. Leslie Stephen's essay in *Hours in a Library*, 3rd series, 1879, remains of interest. The present writer has not seen Zaidée Eudora Greene's privately printed *Nineteenth Century Autobiography*, Ithaca, New York, 1933, an abstract of a dissertation.

## 7. Interest in Foreign Literature and in Earlier English Literature

The first place to look is in the Reviews and Magazines. Of particular importance are the *Foreign Quarterly Review* (1827–46) and the *Retrospective Review* (1820–8). The list of modern writings below is confined mainly to book-length studies.

For classical literature there is a bibliography of *English Translations from the Greek*, by F. M. K. Foster, New York, 1918. M. L. Clarke's *Greek Studies in England, 1700–1830*, 1945, contains

a list of translations in an appendix. J. E. Sandys deals with this period in vol. iii of his *History of Classical Scholarship*, 1908.

See also the section on Education on pp. 494–5 below.

For Philhellenism in this period one may refer to T. Spencer's *Fair Greece Sad Relic: Literary Philhellenism from Shakespeare to Byron*, 1954 (with bibliography); to *The Broken Column: A Study in Romantic Hellenism*, by H. Levin, Cambridge, Mass., 1932; and to *British and American Philhellenes during the War of Greek Independence, 1821–1833*, by D. Dakin, Thessalonika, 1955. See also an article by Virginia Penn, 'Philhellenism in England (1821–1827)', in the *Slavonic Review*, xiv, 1935–6.

A good deal has been written on the Italian influence on English literature at this time. R. Marshall's *Italy in English Literature, 1755–1815*, New York, 1934, leads up to our period. C. P. Brand's *Italy and the English Romantics: The Italianate Fashion in Early Nineteenth-Century England*, 1957, deals fully with the years covered in the present volume. H. W. Rudman's *Italian Nationalism and English Letters: Figures of the Risorgimento and Victorian Men of Letters*, 1940, begins *c.* 1830. All three books have useful bibliographies. P. Toynbee's *Dante in English Literature from Chaucer to Cary*, 2 vols., 1909, is a useful collection of passages with an introduction and notes. H. G. Wright's *Boccaccio in England from Chaucer to Tennyson*, 1957, also contains a great deal that is relevant to our period. There is an important article by R. W. King, 'Italian Influence in English Scholarship', *MLR* xxi, 1926. Reference may also be made to M. C. W. Wicks, *The Italian Exiles in London 1816–1848*, Manchester 1937.

On Foscolo, a central figure, see F. Viglione, *Ugo Foscolo in Inghilterra*, Catania, 1910; and E. R. Vincent, *Ugo Foscolo: An Italian in Regency England*, 1953, and *Byron, Hobhouse and Foscolo: New Documents in the History of a Collaboration*, 1949. Foscolo's *Essays on Petrarch* were privately printed in 1820 and 1821 and finally published in 1823. F. May has written a number of studies of the history and publication of these *Essays*, notably in the *University of Leeds Review*, viii, 1962, in *The Library* (forthcoming), and in *Italian Studies presented to E. R. Vincent*, 1962. See also his 'Milman and Foscolo', *TLS*, 29 June 1962.

Material relevant to Italian influence may be found under many of the Individual Authors below.

Early works worth mentioning, in addition to those named in the text, include the edition of Boiardo's *Orlando Innamorato*

and Ariosto's *Orlando Furioso*, by A. Panizzi, 9 vols., 1830–4 (including an essay on the romantic narrative poetry of the Italians); H. Stebbing's *Lives of the Italian Poets*, 3 vols., 1831; C. Herbert's *Italy and Italian Literature*, 1835; and *Lives of the Most Eminent Literary and Scientific Men of Italy, Spain and Portugal*, 2 vols., 1835.

So much has been written on German influence at this time that only a few of the principal contributions can be mentioned. B. Q. Morgan's *Critical Bibliography of German Literature in English Translation*, 2nd ed., Stanford, 1938, is still of use, though inevitably incomplete; F. W. Stokoe's *German Influence in the English Romantic Period, 1788–1818*, 1926, concentrates on Henry Mackenzie, William Taylor, Crabb Robinson, Scott, Coleridge, Shelley, and Byron and makes virtually no reference to Beddoes. V. Stockley's *German Literature as Known in England, 1750–1830*, 1929, is pedestrian but occasionally useful. H. Shine's introduction to *Carlyle's Unfinished History of German Literature*, Kentucky, 1953, describes the impact of German literature in England up to 1830. There are several important German studies, notably W. F. Schirmer's *Der Einfluß der deutschen Literatur auf die englische im 19. Jahrhundert*, Halle, 1947. See also E. Margraf, *Der Einfluß der deutschen Literatur auf die englische am Ende des 18. und im ersten Drittel des 19. Jahrhunderts*, Leipzig, 1901; and H. Oppel, 'Englische und deutsche Romantik: Gemeinsamkeit und Unterschiede', *Die Neueren Sprachen*, 1956.

R. Wellek deals interestingly with English–German relations in his *History of Modern Criticism*, mentioned above on p. 475. See also his important *Immanuel Kant in England (1793–1838)*, Princeton, 1931. There is a useful book by B. Q. Morgan and A. R. Hohlfeld, *German Literature in British Magazines, 1750–1860*, Madison, Wisconsin, 1949. The influence of English literature on German is outside our scope, but reference may be made to L. M. Price's *English > German Literary Influences: Bibliography and Survey*, Berkeley, 1919–20, 1953.

On Goethe see E. Oswald's bibliography, *Goethe in England and America*, 2nd ed., 1909; J.-M. Carré, *Goethe en Angleterre*, 2 parts, 1920; F. Strich and others, *Goethe and World Literature*, trans. C. A. M. Sym, 1949; W. H. Bruford, 'Goethe's Reputation in England', in *Essays on Goethe*, ed. W. Rose, 1949; L. Baumann, *Die englischen Übersetzungen von Goethes Faust*, Halle, 1907; S. P. Atkins, *The Testament of Werther in Poetry and*

*Drama*, Cambridge, Mass., 1949; W. F. Hauhart, *The Reception of Goethe's Faust in England in the first half of the Nineteenth Century*, New York, 1909; and E. M. Butler, *The Fortunes of Faust*, 1952. For E. M. Butler's *Byron and Goethe*, see p. 514 below.

R. Pick's *Schiller in England* (Institute of Germanic Languages and Literatures) is a bibliography of publications 'by, of or about Schiller in English books and periodicals from 1787 to 1960'. It has a useful introduction.

See also C. A. Weber, *Bristols Bedeutung für die englische Romantik und die deutsch-englischen Beziehungen*, Halle, 1935; Sir Leslie Stephen, 'The Importation of German', in *Studies of a Biographer*, vol. ii, 1898; and A. C. Bradley, *English Poetry and German Philosophy in the Age of Wordsworth*, 1909, reprinted in *A Miscellany*, 1929.

Information in the text of this *History*, pp. 383–95, is not repeated here. Coleridge belongs to the previous volume, Carlyle to vol. xi. A good deal of information bearing on German influence may also be found under Individual Authors below.

French influence at this time has received little attention. F. Baldensperger, *Le mouvement des idées dans l'émigration française*, 2 vols., 1924, may be consulted. M. E. Elkington, *Les relations de société entre l'Angleterre et la France, 1814–30*, 1929, is also of interest. Books on the influence of the French Revolution in England are mentioned below on p. 488. There is a study by E. Partridge, *The French Romantics' Knowledge of English Literature*, Paris, 1924. M. Moraud's *Le Romantisme français en Angleterre*, 1933, is mainly concerned with the Victorian period. For Stendhal's contributions to English periodicals see p. 472 above. See also *Stendhal et l'Angleterre*, by D. Gunnell, 1909.

Southey is one of the central figures in the story of English interest in Spain and its literature. Reference may be made here to his correspondence, and to his *Letters Written During a Short Residence in Spain and Portugal*, Bristol 1797. Other material is mentioned under Individual Authors: see particularly Bowring, Mrs. Hemans, Lockhart, and Wiffen. See also *Lives of the Most Eminent Literary and Scientific Men of Italy, Spain and Portugal*, 2 vols., 1835. *The Life of the Rev. Joseph Blanco White written by Himself*, ed. J. H. Thom, 3 vols., 1845, is an important document. See also Blanco White's *Letters from Spain*, by 'Don

Leucadio Boblado, 1822; and A. Anaya, *An Essay on Spanish Literature*, 1818.

More detailed information may be found in V. L. Castillo's *Liberales y Románticos*, Mexico, 1954, and an important article by N. Glendinning, 'Spanish Books in England: 1800–1850', in *Transactions of the Cambridge Bibliographical Society*, III. i, 1960. V. Lloréns has an article on 'Colaboraciones de emigrados españoles en revistas inglesas (1824–34)', *Hispanic Review*, xix, 1951.

For Scandinavia see F. E. Farley's *Scandinavian Influence on the English Romantic Movement*, 1903.

For interest in earlier English literature in the period the *Retrospective Review* is of primary importance, as are the letters of Coleridge, Southey, and Lamb. See below under Brydges, Cary, Dibdin, D'Israeli, Dunlop, Gifford, Hazlitt, and Jeffrey. Vol. 3 (1954) of *Phillipps Studies*, by A. N. L. Munby, describes the growth of the library of Sir Thomas Phillipps up to the year 1840. *The Heber Letters, 1783–1832*, ed. R. H. Cholmondeley, 1950, throw light on the activities of another great book-collector. J. P. Collier edited *A Catalogue of Heber's Collection of Early English Poetry* in 1834.

## 8. Travel

A list of some of the principal travel books of the nineteenth century may be found in *CBEL* iii. 988–93. J. N. L. Baker's *History of Geographical Discovery and Exploration*, 1931, includes this period. J. R. Hale discusses some aspects of Italian travel in his introduction to *The Italian Journal of Samuel Rogers*, 1956; while T. Spencer considers English travellers in Greece in *Fair Greece Sad Relic*, 1954. See also Wallace C. Brown, 'The Popularity of English Travel Books about the Near East, 1775–1825', *PQ*, xv, 1936; 'Byron and English Interest in the Near East', *SP* xxxiv, 1937; and 'English Travel Books, 1775–1825', *PQ* xvi, 1937.

Some descriptions of the English scene by foreign visitors are mentioned below on p. 485.

## 9. Annuals, and the Reading Public

On the Annuals see *Literary Annuals and Gift Books: A Bibliography with a Descriptive Introduction*, by F. W. Faxon, Boston, 1912. Unfortunately the Index to the Annuals by Andrew

Boyle remained unpublished at his death. A. Bose wrote on 'The Verse of the English "Annuals"' in *RES*, N.S., iv, 1953 (repr. in his *Chroniclers of Life*, Orient Longmans, 1962). Information may also be found in Knight's *Passages of a Working Life*, vol. ii (1864), pp. 53–54, and in many memoirs and collections of letters: see (for example) *Alaric Watts: A Narrative of his Life*, by A. A. Watts, 2 vols., 1884, and *The Literary Life and Correspondence of the Countess of Blessington*, ed. R. R. Madden, 3 vols., 1855. Numerous references to the Annuals may be found in the two books by Sadleir mentioned on p. 474. There are two modern volumes of selections: *The Annual: Being a Selection from the Forget-Me-Nots, Keepsakes, and Other Annuals*, ed. Dorothy Wellesley, with an introduction by V. Sackville-West, London, n.d.; and *A Cabinet of Gems*, ed. B. A. Booth, Berkeley, 1938, a collection of short stories from *The Keepsake* and its competitors.

On the Reading Public R. D. Altick's excellent study, *The English Common Reader: A Social History of the Mass Reading Public, 1800–1900*, Chicago, 1957, may be supplemented by R. K. Webb's *The British Working Class Reader, 1790–1848: Literacy and Social Tension*, 1955. On the 'dainty delicacy' of the time one may consult M. J. Quinlan, *Victorian Prelude*, New York, 1941, and *Pamela's Daughters*, by R. P. Utter and Gwendolyn B. Needham, 1937. O. Maurer's article, 'My Squeamish Public', in *Studies in Bibliography*, Charlottesville, Virginia, 1958, like other articles on the subject elsewhere, is concerned with the Victorian period. The development of squeamishness earlier in the century calls for further investigation.

## 10. The Profession of Letters and the Publishing Trade

There is no need to repeat the names of the primary sources referred to in the first and last chapters of this book. The only account of writing as a career at this time, *The Profession of Letters: A Study of the Relation of Author to Patron, Publisher, and Public, 1780–1832*, 1928, by A. S. Collins, needs to be revised or superseded.

A standard work on the book trade is F. A. Mumby's *Publishing and Bookselling: A History from the Earliest Times to the Present Day*, 4th ed., 1956, which contains a useful bibliography. G. Pollard dealt briefly with this period in his unpublished Sandars Lectures for 1959, 'The English Market for Printed

Books'. I am indebted to Dr. A. N. L. Munby for an opportunity of reading these lectures in typescript. It is to be hoped that Mr. Pollard will soon produce a book on the subject.

A great deal of information is to be found in the histories of the publishing houses of Constable, Murray, and Blackwood listed above on p. 471. To these we may add E. Blunden's admirable study, *Keats's Publisher: A Memoir of John Taylor (1781–1864)*, 1936; R. A. Gettmann's *A Victorian Publisher: A Study of the Bentley Papers*, 1960; *The Publishing Firm of Cadell & Davies: Select Correspondence and Accounts, 1793–1836*, ed. T. Besterman, 1938, a valuable collection of material with a helpful introduction; *Edward Moxon, Publisher of Poets*, by H. G. Merriam, New York, 1939; *The House of Collins*, by D. Keir, 1952, which is sketchy on our period; and a very brief study, *The House of Longman, 1724–1924*, 1925, by H. Cox and J. E. Chandler (privately printed).

An important book, frequently cited in the text, is *Passages of a Working Life*, by Charles Knight, 3 vols., 1864–5. See also *Reminiscences of Literary London*, by T. Rees and J. Britton, 1853 (privately printed, rev. ed., New York, 1896), 1896. The bibliographies by Sadleir and Dorothy Blakey listed above on p. 473 contain a great deal of information. There is also an interesting article by G. Barber, 'Galignani's and the Publication of English Books in France from 1800 to 1852', in *The Library*, 1961.

## V. The Background of Literature

This section comprises: (1) Political and Social History, and Political Thought; (2) Contemporary Autobiographies, Memoirs, and Letters; (3) Religion and Moral Attitudes; (4) Science and Technology; (5) Education; and (6) Architecture, Painting, and Music.

### 1. Political and Social History, and Political Thought

Useful bibliographical guidance may be found in *Reaction and Revolution 1814–1832*, by F. B. Artz, New York, 1934, rev. ed. 1945 (a vol. in the series *The Rise of Modern Europe*, ed. W. L. Langer). Artz's book may be supplemented by G. Weill, *L'éveil des nationalités et le mouvement libéral, 1815–48*, 1930 (in the series *Peuples et civilisations*, vol. xv). Another valuable work is

A. Stern's *Geschichte Europas seit den Verträgen von 1815 bis zum Frankfurter Frieden von 1871*, new ed., 10 vols., Stuttgart, 1913–28. E. J. Hobsbawm's study, *The Age of Revolution: Europe 1789–1848*, 1962, covers this period, as will vol. ix of the *New Cambridge Modern History*.

The *Annual Register* gives an account of the main events of each year. Documents may be found in *English Historical Documents, 1783–1832*, ed. A. Aspinall and E. A. Smith, 1959, and in two smaller collections: *Britain and Europe: Pitt to Churchill, 1793–1940*, ed. J. Joll, 1950, and *The English Radical Tradition, 1763–1914*, ed. S. MacCoby, 1952 (both in *The British Political Tradition Series*, ed. A. Bullock and F. W. Deakin).

Much the best account of English history at this time is still Élie Halévy's *Histoire du peuple anglais au XIX*[e] *siècle*, which appeared in French between 1912 and 1932. The relevant volumes of the English translation are *England in 1815*, 1924, *The Liberal Awakening 1815–1830*, 1926, and *The Triumph of Reform 1830–1841*, 1927 (revised editions, 1949–50).

*The History of England (1801–1837)*, by G. C. Brodrick and J. K. Fotheringham, new impression, 1911 (vol. xi of *The Political History of England*, ed. W. Hunt and R. L. Poole), is still useful on account of its lucid narrative and the annalistic arrangement of the Table of Contents. An authoritative and up-to-date book is *The Age of Reform, 1815–1870*, by Sir Llewellyn Woodward, 2nd ed., 1962 (vol. xiii of the *Oxford History of England*).

Other books of interest to the student of literature include: *British History in the Nineteenth Century (1782–1901)*, by G. M. Trevelyan, 1922; the same author's *English Social History . . . Chaucer to Queen Victoria*, 1942 (in the illustrated edition our period is covered in vol. iv, 1952); *The Age of Improvement*, by A. Briggs, 1959 (vol. viii in *A History of England*, ed. W. N. Medlicott: covers the years 1780–1867); *The First Four Georges*, by J. H. Plumb, 1956; *The Age of Elegance, 1812–1822*, by Sir Arthur Bryant, 1950; R. J. White, *From Waterloo to Peterloo*, 1957, an agreeable sketch of social transition; O. MacDonagh, *A Pattern of Government Growth*, 1961; F. O. Darvall, *Popular Disturbances and Public Order in Regency England*, 1934; and G. Kitson Clark, *The Making of Victorian England*, 1962.

A small but interesting category of writings includes real and supposed travel books by visitors to England about this time.

Southey's *Letters from England* ('By Don Manuel Alvarez Espriella') were published in 1807; while in *Peter's Letters to his Kinsfolk*, 3 vols., 1819, Lockhart mixed fiction with fact to give a striking picture of Edinburgh. Genuine travel-books include Louis Simond's anonymous *Journal of a Tour and Residence in Great Britain, during the Years 1810 and 1811, by a French Traveller*, 2 vols., 1815; A. Pichot's anonymous *Voyage historique et littéraire en Angleterre et en Écosse*, 3 vols., 1825 (Eng. trans., 2 vols., the same year); *Erik Gustaf Geijer: Impressions of England, 1809–1810: Compiled from his Letters and Diaries* by Anton Blanck, translated from the Swedish, 1932; and Prince Pückler-Muskau's *Tour in England*, 4 vols., 1832 (selections ed. E. M. Butler as *A Regency Visitor*, 1957).

Satirical accounts of Edinburgh and London are given in two books published anonymously by Robert Mudie in 1825: *The Modern Athens: A Dissection and Demonstration of Men and Things in the Scotch Capital. By a Modern Greek*; and *Babylon the Great: A Dissection and Demonstration of Men and Things in the British Capital*, 2 vols. (vol. ii contains seven chapters on the Press).

Of particular importance are the studies by J. L. and Barbara Hammond: *The Skilled Labourer, 1760–1832*, 1919; *The Town Labourer, 1760–1832*, 1917; *The Village Labourer, 1760–1832*, 1911; and *The Rise of Modern Industry*, 1925. Their *The Age of the Chartists, 1832–1854*, 1930, like other books on Chartism, also throws light on our period, as does *The Bleak Age*, 2nd ed., 1947, which is based on it. See also *A History of the English Agricultural Labourer*, by W. Hasbach, 2nd impr., 1909 (German ed., 1894), and two shorter studies by J. L. Hammond, 'The Industrial Revolution and Discontent', *Economic History*, ii, no. 2, and *The Growth of Common Enjoyment*, 1933.

Dorothy George's *England in Transition*, 1931 (rev. ed., Penguin Books, 1953), helps to explain how England in 1815 came to be what it was. *Early Victorian England, 1830–1865*, ed. G. M. Young, 2 vols., 1934, throws a great deal of light on what had happened by 1832, as does his *Victorian England: Portrait of an Age*, 1936. *Culture and Society 1780–1950*, by Raymond Williams, 1958, is 'an account and an interpretation of our responses in thought and feeling to changes in English Society'. On the Reform Bill one may consult G. M. Trevelyan, *Lord Grey of the Reform Bill*, 2nd ed., 1929; H. W. C. Davis, *The Age of Grey and Peel*, 1929; J. R. M. Butler, *The Passing of the Great*

*Reform Bill*, 1914; and G. Milner, *The Threshold of the Victorian Age*, 1934.

Of the numerous modern studies of the statesmen of the period very few can be mentioned here: *William Huskisson and Liberal Reform*, by A. Brady, 1928; *The Patriot King* (William IV), by G. E. Thompson, 1932; *The Divorce Case of Queen Caroline*, by W. D. Bowman, 1930 (a popular account); *The Rise of Castlereagh*, by H. M. Hyde, 1933; *The Foreign Policy of Castlereagh, 1815–1822*, by C. K. Webster, 2nd ed., 1934; *The Foreign Policy of Canning, 1822–1827*, by H. W. V. Temperley, 1925; *The Monroe Doctrine, 1823–6*, by D. Perkins, Cambridge, Mass., 1927; *Mr. Secretary Peel*, by N. Gash (1961); *Lord Liverpool and Liberal Toryism, 1820–7*, by W. R. Brock, 1941; *Lord Brougham and the Whig Party*, by A. Aspinall, Manchester, 1927; and *Radical Jack: The Life of John George Lambton, first Earl of Durham*, by L. Cooper, 1959. In *Sketches in Nineteenth Century Biography*, 1930, K. Feiling deals incisively and wittily with Pitt, Liverpool, Canning, Croker, Southey and Wordsworth, Coleridge, Newman, Bulwer Lytton, and others.

Apart from the work of the Hammonds, already mentioned, there are the following important studies of the working classes, trade unionism, and allied subjects: *Some Working Class Movements of the Nineteenth Century*, by R. F. Wearmouth, 1948; *The Early English Trade Unions: Documents*, ed. A. Aspinall, 1949; *Agricultural Depression and Farm Relief in England, 1813–52*, by L. P. Adams, 1932; Sidney and Beatrice Webb, *The History of Trade Unionism*, rev. ed., 1920; *A Short History of the British Working Class Movement, 1789–1947*, by G. D. H. Cole, rev. ed., 1948; the same author's *Attempts at General Union . . ., 1818–1834*, 1953; *A History of Factory Legislation*, by B. L. Hutchins and A. Harrison, 3rd ed., 1926; and 'The Combination Laws Reconsidered', by M. D. George, *Economic Journal* (Economic Series i, 1927).

*The Life of Francis Place, 1771–1854*, by G. Wallas, rev. ed., 1918, throws a great deal of light on the first half of the nineteenth century.

The first volume of J. H. Clapham's *Economic History of Modern Britain: The Early Railway Age, 1820–1850*, 1926, 2nd ed., 1930, is an authoritative work. There is an excellent survey of writings on the Industrial Revolution by T. S. Ashton in the *Economic History Review* for Oct. 1934 (vol. v, no. 1), which may

be supplemented by J. U. Nef's article in the *Journal of Economic History* for 1943 and by 'Progress and Poverty in Britain, 1750–1850: A Reappraisal', by A. J. Taylor, in *History*, vol. xlv, no. 153 (February 1960). *The Industrial Revolution in the Eighteenth Century*, by P. Mantoux (Fr. ed., 1906), rev. ed. trans. into English 1928, remains an admirable study. T. S. Ashton's *The Industrial Revolution, 1760–1830*, 1948 (Home University Library) is a good brief survey. See also *The Industrial Revolution and the World of To-day*, by L. W. White and E. W. Shanahan, 1932; *English Apprenticeship and Child Labour*, by O. J. Dunlop, 1912; *Health, Wealth, and Population in the Early Days of the Industrial Revolution*, by M. C. Buer, 1926; 'The Population Problem during the Industrial Revolution', by T. H. Marshall, in *Economic History*, vol. i, no. 4 (a powerful criticism of G. Talbot Griffith's *Population Problems of the Age of Malthus*, 1926); W. W. Rostow, *British Economy of the Nineteenth Century*, 1948; *The Malthusian Controversy*, by K. Smith, 1951; E. C. K. Gonner, *Common Land and Inclosure*, 1912; L. C. A. Knowles, *The Industrial and Commercial Revolutions in Great Britain during the Nineteenth Century*, rev. ed., 1924; C. R. Fay, *Life and Labour in the Nineteenth Century*, 1920; and Sir John Clapham, *The Bank of England*, 1944. A great deal of information may be found in the recent histories of Birmingham, Brighton, and Manchester by C. Gill, E. W. Gilbert, and A. Redford respectively.

Special mention must be made of *The Works and Correspondence of David Ricardo*, ed. P. Sraffa with M. H. Dobb, 10 vols., 1951–5, an important collection admirably edited.

A further group of books on particular topics sufficiently indicated by their titles may be listed here: D. G. Barnes, *A History of the English Corn Laws, 1660–1846*, 1930; C. R. Fay, *The Corn Laws and Social England*, 1932; D. R. Gwynn, *The Struggle for Catholic Emancipation, 1750–1829*, 1928; R. Coupland, *The British Anti-Slavery Movement*, 1933; C. W. Crawley, *The Question of Greek Independence: A Study of British Policy in the Near East, 1821–1833*, 1930; C. H. Philips, *The East India Company, 1784–1834*, Manchester, 1940; K. Feiling, *The Second Tory Party: 1714–1832*, 1938; *Britain and the Independence of Latin America, 1812–30: Select Documents*, ed. C. K. Webster, 2 vols., 1938; F. A. Bruton, *Three Accounts of Peterloo by Eyewitnesses*, Manchester, 1921; W. W. Kaufmann, *British Policy and the Independence of Latin America, 1804–28*, New Haven, 1951; D. M. Young, *The Colonial Office in the Early*

*Nineteenth Century*, 1961; A. S. Turberville, *The House of Lords in the Age of Reform, 1784–1837*, 1958; *Lectures on the Relation between Law & Public Opinion in England during the Nineteenth Century*, by A. V. Dicey, 1905 (rev. ed., 1962); and the *History of the Athenæum* [Club], *1824–1925*, by Humphry Ward, 1926. C. W. Cunnington's *English Women's Clothing in the Nineteenth Century*, 1956, also throws light on the period, as does a study he has written with Phillis Cunnington, *Handbook of English Costume in the Nineteenth Century*, 1959. *English Political Caricature, 1793–1832: A Study of Opinion and Propaganda*, by M. Dorothy George, 1959, throws an amusing light on the social life of the time, and includes a useful Index of Artists. Vols. vii–xi of the same author's *Catalogue of Political and Personal Satires*, 1942–54, cover the corresponding period. The studies by Michael Sadleir mentioned on p. 474 above are of interest to the social historian.

Two books by E. W. Bovill, *The England of Nimrod and Surtees, 1815–1854* (1959), and *English Country Life, 1780–1830* (1962), give an agreeable picture of life outside the towns.

A great deal has been written on the influence of the French Revolution on English literature. Mention may be made of *The French Revolution and English Literature*, by E. Dowden, 1897; *The French Revolution and the English Poets*, by A. E. Hancock, New York, 1899; *La révolution française et les poètes anglais (1789–1809)*, by C. Cestre, 1906; *The French Revolution and the English Novel*, by Allene Gregory, New York 1915.

C. E. Vaughan's *Studies in the History of Political Philosophy*, ed. A. G. Little, 2 vols., Manchester, 1925, contains material relevant to the early nineteenth century. C. C. Brinton's *English Political Thought in the Nineteenth Century*, 1933, suffers from over-simplification, as does his earlier *The Political Ideas of the English Romanticists*, 1926. On Socialist thought see H. L. Beales, *The Early English Socialists*, 1933; H. W. Laidler, *A History of Socialist Thought*, 1927; S. MacCoby, *English Radicalism, 1786–1832*, 1955; and G. D. H. Cole's *History of Socialist Thought*, i, 1953.

A whole library of books has been devoted to the Utilitarians. The *Autobiography* of John Stuart Mill, 1873, remains of primary importance: there have been various editions, while J. Stillinger published *The Early Draft of John Stuart Mill's 'Autobiography'* in 1961 (Urbana, Illinois). The outstanding secondary books are *The English Utilitarians*, by Leslie Stephen, 3 vols., 1900; and *La formation du radicalisme philosophique*, by Élie Halévy, Paris, 1901–4,

Eng. trans. as *The Growth of Philosophic Radicalism*, 1928. See also *Mill's Utilitarianism reprinted with a study of the English Utilitarians*, by J. Plamenatz, 1949. A briefer account is that of W. L. Davidson: *Political Thought in England: The Utilitarians from Bentham to Mill*, 1915 (Home University Library). E. Stokes, *The English Utilitarians and India*, 1959, is of great interest.

The importance of writers dealt with in other volumes hardly needs to be stressed, but one or two secondary books should perhaps be mentioned here: A. V. Dicey, *The Statesmanship of Wordsworth*, 1917; *Robert Southey and his Age: The Development of a Conservative Mind*, by G. Carnall, 1960; R. K. Webb, *Harriet Martineau: A Radical Victorian*, 1960; *Political Thought of S. T. Coleridge*, ed. R. J. White, 1938; and *Coleridge: Critic of Society*, by J. Colmer, 1959.

There are several collections of political pamphlets which include this period: see, for example, *From the French Revolution to the Nineteen-Thirties*, ed. R. Reynolds, 1951 (*British Pamphleteers*, ii), and *Political Tracts of Wordsworth, Coleridge and Shelley*, ed. R. J. White, Cambridge, 1953.

For Scottish history see G. S. Pryde, *Scotland from 1603 to the Present Day*, 1962; Agnes Mure Mackenzie, *Scotland in Modern Times, 1720–1939*, 1941; L. J. Saunders, *Scottish Democracy, 1815–40: the Social and Intellectual Background*, 1950; and G. E. Davie, *The Democratic Intellect* (p. 495 below).

Three interesting books on Ireland are D. Gwynn, *Daniel O'Connell, the Irish Liberator*, rev. ed., Cork, 1947; J. E. Pomfret, *The Struggle for Land in Ireland, 1800–1923*, Princeton, 1930; and W. F. Adams, *Ireland and Irish Emigration to the New World, from 1815 to the Famine*, New Haven, 1932.

For Welsh history see D. Williams, *A History of Modern Wales, 1485–1939*, 1950.

## 2. Contemporary Autobiographies, Memoirs, and Letters

Material relating to Wordsworth, Coleridge, Southey, Jane Austen, Campbell, and Rogers, on the one hand, and to Harriet Martineau, Macaulay, Carlyle, Dickens, and Bulwer Lytton on the other, must be sought in other volumes. Fuller lists of letters, diaries, and autobiographies may be found in *CBEL* iii. 14–17 and 149–55, and v. 522 and 546–7.

For the details of 'who's in, who's out' at Court we may consult *The Greville Memoirs*, by Charles Greville, Clerk to the Privy Council. The first part, which covers our period, appeared in 3 vols., ed. H. Reeve, in 1874. The most recent edition of the *Memoirs* as a whole is that of Lytton Strachey and R. Fulford, 8 vols., 1938. There is a volume of selections edited by C. Lloyd, 1948. Other memoirs throwing light on the life of the Court and aristocracy include the third series of the *Despatches, Correspondence, and Memoranda of the Duke of Wellington*, ed. by his son, 8 vols., 1867–80. The *Memoirs and Correspondence* of Castlereagh were edited by C. W. Stewart in 12 vols. in 1848–53. *The Early Correspondence of Lord John Russell*, ed. R. Russell, 2 vols., 1913, covers the years 1805–40. See also Lady Charlotte Bury's *Diary Illustrative of the Times of George IV*, 2 vols., 1838 (ed. A. F. Steuart, 2 vols., 1908); *The Public and Private Life of John Scott* (*Earl of Eldon*), by H. Twiss, 3 vols., 1844 (but also the anonymous *Life, political and official, of John, Earl of Eldon*, 1827, which is sometimes more illuminating); *Life and Correspondence of Henry Addington* (*Lord Sidmouth*), ed. G. Pellew, 3 vols., 1847; *Memoirs of the Life of Sir Samuel Romilly, Written by Himself*, ed. by his sons, 3 vols., 1840; *The Creevey Papers*, ed. Sir H. Maxwell, 2 vols., 1903, and *Creevey's Life and Times*, ed. J. Gore, 1934; *The Jerningham Letters* (*1780–1843*), ed. E. Castle, 2 vols., 1896; and *The Life of Henry John Temple, Viscount Palmerston*, ed. Sir H. Lytton Bulwer and A. E. M. Ashley, 5 vols., 1871–6 (revised and abridged, 2 vols., 1879).

For the Holland House circle, which was of great importance to literature at this time, see Sydney Smith under Individual Authors and also *The Holland House Circle*, by L. Sanders, 1908; *Holland House*, by Princess Marie Liechtenstein, 2 vols., 1874 (a Victorian conducted tour, with anecdotes); *The 'Pope' of Holland House*, ed. Lady Seymour, 1906; *The Home of the Hollands 1605–1820* and *Chronicles of Holland House 1820–1900*, both by the Earl of Ilchester and both published in 1937; *Lord Melbourne's Papers*, ed. L. C. Sanders, 1889; *Lady Bessborough and her Family Circle*, ed. Earl of Bessborough and A. Aspinall, 1940; *The Journal of the Hon. Henry Edward Fox* [later Lord Holland] *1818–1830*, ed. the Earl of Ilchester, 1923; *Elizabeth, Lady Holland to her Son* (letters, 1821–45), ed. the Earl of Ilchester, 1946; C. and F. Brookfield, *Mrs. Brookfield and her Circle*, 1905; and two books by Lord David Cecil, *The Young Melbourne*, 1939, and *Lord M.*, 1954.

Other contemporary records include *Three Early Nineteenth Century Diaries* (by Sir D. Le Marchant, E. J. Littleton, and Lord Ellenborough), ed. A. Aspinall, 1952; *The Correspondence of Charles Arbuthnot*, ed. A. Aspinall (Camden Society, 3rd series, lxv, 1941); *The Journal of Harriet Arbuthnot* [*née* Fane], *1820–1832*, ed. F. Bamford and the Duke of Wellington, 2 vols., 1950; *The Heber Letters, 1783–1832*, ed. R. H. Cholmondeley, 1950; *The Remains of Henry Angelo*, 2 vols., 1830 (reprinted, 2 vols., 1904); *Reminiscences of the University, Town and County of Cambridge from the Year 1780*, by Henry Gunning, 2 vols., 1854–5; the autobiographies of Samuel Roberts (1849), Ann Taylor (later Gilbert, 1874), and Eliza Fletcher (1875); and the scandalous *Memoirs* of Harriette Wilson, 1825 (ed. J. Laver, 1929).

Books by men near the bottom of the social scale include *Passages in the Life of a Radical*, by S. Bamford, 2 vols., 1844 (ed. H. Dunckley, 2 vols., 1893); *The Autobiography of an Artisan*, by Christopher Thomson, 1847; *The Autobiography of a Working Man* [by Alexander Somerville], 1848 (abridged ed. by J. Carswell, 1951); *The Life of Robert Owen, Written by Himself*, 1857; *The Life and Struggles of William Lovett*, 1876 (ed. R. H. Tawney, 2 vols., 1920); and *Memoirs of a Working Man* [by T. Carter], ed. C. Knight, 1845 (followed by a *Continuation* in 1850).

Charles Knight's *Passages of a Working Life*, 3 vols., 1864–5, has already been mentioned elsewhere. Other memoirs by people more or less closely connected with literature include P. G. Patmore's important book, *My Friends and Acquaintances*, 3 vols., 1855; Lady Morgan's *Memoirs: Autobiography, Diaries and Correspondence*, ed. W. H. Dixon, 2 vols., 1862; *The Life and Correspondence of John Foster*, ed. J. E. Ryland, 2 vols., 1846; *Recollections of Literary Characters and Celebrated Places*, by Mrs. Thomson ('Grace Wharton'), 2 vols., 1854; *Fifty Years' Recollections, Literary and Personal*, 3 vols., 1858, and *Past Celebrities Whom I Have Known*, 2 vols., 1866, by C. Redding; *Letters of Sir James Stephen*, ed. by his daughter, 1906 (Gloucester, priv. prtd.); *Autobiographical Recollections*, by C. R. Leslie, ed. T. Taylor, Boston, 1860; *A Book of Memories*, 1871, and *Retrospect of a Long Life*, 2 vols., 1883, by S. C. Hall; *Memoir of the Rev. Francis Hodgson* (the friend of Byron), ed. J. T. Hodgson, 2 vols., 1878; *Reminiscences of Thomas John Dibdin*, 2 vols., 1827; *Records of my Life*, by John Taylor (1757–1832), 2 vols., 1832; *Memoirs of Lady Hester Lucy Stanhope*, ed. C. L. Meryon, 1845; *Remains of Richard Hurrell Froude*, 4 vols.,

ed. J. Keble, J. H. Newman, and J. B. Mozley, 1838–9; *Diary of Henry Hobhouse, 1820–1827*, ed. A. Aspinall, 1947; *Harriet Martineau's Autobiography*, ed. Maria Weston Chapman, 3 vols., 1877; *The Life of Joseph Blanco White, Written by Himself*, ed. J. H. Thom, 3 vols., 1845; *Extracts of the Journals and Correspondence of Miss* [Mary] *Berry, . . . 1783–1852*, ed. Lady T. Lewis, 3 vols., 1865; and, of course, the *Diary and Letters of Madame d'Arblay* (*née* Burney), ed. C. Barrett, rev. A. Dobson, 6 vols., 1904–5.

Memoirs from Scotland include *Memorials of his Time*, by Henry Thomas, Lord Cockburn, Edinburgh, 1856; *Memoir and Correspondence of Mrs. Grant of Laggan*, ed. J. P. Grant, 3 vols., 1844; *Letters from and to Charles Kirkpatrick Sharpe*, ed. A. Allardyce, with a Memoir by W. K. R. Bedford, 2 vols., 1888; *Reminiscences of Scottish Life and Character*, by E. B. Ramsay, 1858; and *Parties and Pleasures: The Diaries of Helen Graham, 1823–26*, ed. J. Irvine, 1957.

Three of the Americans who left a record of their impressions of England at this time were Washington Irving, whose *Life and Letters* was ed. by P. M. Irving in 4 vols. in 1862–4 (New York); G. Ticknor, whose *Life, Letters, and Journals*, 2 vols., 1876 (2nd ed.), contain useful information about publishing and other matters; and N. P. Willis, whose *Pencillings by the Way*, 3 vols., 1836 (rev. ed. 1852) and *Famous Persons and Famous Places*, New York, 1854, are also of interest (on Willis see 'G. Paston', *Little Memoirs of the Nineteenth Century*, 1902).

## 3. Religion and Moral Attitudes

The standard history of the Church at this time is F. Warre Cornish's *The English Church in the Nineteenth Century*, two parts, 1910; J. H. Overton's *The English Church in the Nineteenth Century, 1800–1833*, 1894, is important for the old High Church party; S. C. Carpenter's *Church and People, 1789–1889*, 1933, is a good popular outline. We may also consult *The Church in an Age of Revolution, 1789 to the Present Day*, by A. R. Vidler, 1961, and *The Development of English Theology in the Nineteenth Century, 1800–1860*, by V. F. Storr. Vol. iii of *Worship and Theology in England*, by Horton Davies, 1962, covers the period 'From Watts and Wesley to Maurice, 1690–1850'. G. S. R. Kitson Clark's *The English Inheritance*, 1950, considers the general influence of religion in nineteenth-century England. W. L. Mathieson's *English Church*

*Reform, 1815–1840*, 1923, covers an important topic (see also the same writer's *Church and Reform in Scotland, 1797–1843*). Thomas Arnold's *Principles of Church Reform*, 1833 (reprinted in his *Miscellaneous Works*, 1845), has recently been reprinted again (1962). Book III of Bulwer Lytton's *England and the English*, 1833, considers 'the general influences of morality and religion in England'. In 'The Whigs and the Church Establishment in the Age of Grey and Holland', *History*, vol. xlv, no. 154 (June 1960), G. F. A. Best discusses the Tory claim that the Whigs were hostile to the Church of England. There is a useful bibliographical article by Canon C. Smyth in the *Cambridge Historical Journal*, vol. vii, 1943 ('The Evangelical Movement in Perspective'). J. P. Whitney's *Bibliography of Church History* (Historical Association Leaflet lv, 1923) is useful so far as it goes. Father Hugh's *Nineteenth Century Pamphlets at Pusey House* (Faith Press, Oxford), lists 18,500 pamphlets of religious interest.

On Methodism we may consult R. F. Wearmouth, *Methodism and the History of Working Class Movements of England, 1800–1850*, 1937; M. L. Edwards, *After Wesley: A Study of the Influence of Methodism, 1791–1849*, 1943; J. F. Hurst, *The History of Methodism*, 3 vols., 1901; W. J. Townsend and others, *A New History of Methodism*, 2 vols., 1909; W. J. Warner, *The Wesleyan Movement in the Industrial Revolution*, 1930; and F. C. Gill, *The Romantic Movement and Methodism*, 1937.

Ford K. Brown's *Fathers of the Victorians: The Age of Wilberforce*, 1961, deals interestingly with the Evangelicals; see also L. E. Binns [Elliott-Binns], *The Evangelical Movement in the English Church*, 1928; J. Venn, *Annals of a Clerical Family*, 1904; E. Stock, *A History of the Church Missionary Society*, 3 vols., 1899; R. G. Cowherd, *The Politics of English Dissent*, 1959; and F. E. Mineka, *The Dissidence of Dissent: 'The Monthly Repository', 1806–1838*, Chapel Hill, 1944 (a useful study). Olive Brose's *Church and Parliament*, 1959, should also be mentioned.

There is no need to emphasize the historical importance of *The Letters and Diaries of John Henry Newman*, ed. by C. S. Dessain (in progress), of which the first volumes will be relevant to our period.

Many books bear on the history of the Quakers at this time. See, for example, *Mary Howitt: An Autobiography*, ed. Margaret Howitt, 2 vols., 1889; Amice Lee, *Laurels and Rosemary: The Life of William and Mary Howitt*, 1955; *Memoir of Elizabeth Fry*,

*ed. by two of her daughters*, 2 vols., 1847; *A Quaker Journal* (by William Lucas), ed. G. E. Bryant and G. P. Baker, 2 vols., 1834; and Bernard Barton under Individual Authors.

Basil Willey's *Nineteenth Century Studies*, 1949, concentrates on the thought of the Victorian Age, but also throws light on the earlier age. The most ambitious attempt to deal with the religious views of the poets of the period is vol. iii of Hoxie N. Fairchild's *Religious Trends in English Poetry* (*Romantic Faith*), New York, 1949.

### 4. Science and Technology

There is a good general *History of Science*, by J. D. Dampier, 3rd ed., New York, 1942. One may also consult F. Albèrgamo, *La critica della scienza nel novecento*, Florence, 1941, and *A Short History of Science in the Nineteenth Century*, by C. Singer, 1941. *The Edge of Objectivity*, by C. C. Gillispie, Princeton 1960, is an outstanding history of scientific thought which throws light on our period. There are two useful books on chemistry: *The Chemical Industry during the Nineteenth Century*, by L. F. Haber, 1958, and *The Chemical Revolution*, by A. and N. L. Clow, 1952.

There is a *History of Technology*, ed. C. Singer, E. J. Holmyard, A. R. Hall, and T. I. Williams. Vol. 4 covers the early nineteenth century. A. P. Usher's *History of Mechanical Inventions*, 1929, may also be consulted, as may *Kulturgeschichte der Technik*, by F. Feldhaus, 2 vols., Berlin, 1928–30. H. J. Habakkuk's *American and British Technology in the Nineteenth Century*, 1962, deals with difficult economic and historical problems and rewards the reader who is prepared to follow rigorous reasoning. Two studies by Samuel Smiles are still of interest: *Lives of the Engineers*, 3 vols., 1861–2, and *Industrial Biography: Iron Workers and Tool Makers*, 1863. Other writings on technology are listed in the article by T. S. Ashton referred to on p. 486 above.

E. Nordenskiöld's *History of Biology*, New York 1928, is still the best general account of the subject. A good deal has recently been written on the history of the concept of evolution. L. Eiseley's book, *Darwin's Century: Evolution and the Men Who Discovered It*, 1960, is an excellent survey of evolutionary biology in the nineteenth century. *Forerunners of Darwin, 1745–1859*, ed. B. Glass and others, 1959, contains essays by members of the Johns Hopkins History of Ideas Club.

## 5. Education

J. W. Adamson's *English Education, 1789–1902*, 1930, is sound in itself and useful for its bibliography. See also S. J. Curtis, *History of Education in Great Britain*, rev. ed. 1957; E. H. Reisner, *Nationalism and Education since 1789*, New York, 1922; and R. L. Archer, *Secondary Education in the Nineteenth Century*, 1921 (useful bibliographies). In general, histories of universities and schools cannot be included here, but exception must be made for A. P. Stanley's *Life and Correspondence of Thomas Arnold*, 2 vols., 1844; G. A. T. Allen, *Christ's Hospital*, 1937; E. Blunden, *Christ's Hospital: A Retrospect* [1923]; Sir C. E. Mallet, *A History of the University of Oxford*, vol. 3, 1927; D. A. Winstanley, *Early Victorian Cambridge*, 1940; Sir G. C. Faber, *Jowett*, 1957; and H. H. Bellot, *University College, London, 1826–1926*, 1929. T. Kelly's *History of Adult Education in Great Britain*, Liverpool, 1962, may also be consulted.

For classical studies see J. E. Sandys, *A History of Classical Scholarship*, vol. iii, 1908, and M. L. Clarke, *Greek Studies in England 1700–1830*, Cambridge, 1945. *The Democratic Intellect*, by G. E. Davie, 1961, throws light on the different educational traditions of Scotland and England.

## 6. Architecture, Painting, and Music

On the architecture of the period one may consult *Architecture in Britain, 1530 to 1830*, by (Sir) John Summerson, 1953 (a volume in the *Pelican History of Art*, ed. N. Pevsner). It has a brief bibliography of books relevant to our period. See also *The Regency Style, 1800 to 1830*, by D. Pilcher, 1947; *The Romantic Theories of Architecture of the Nineteenth Century in Germany, England and France*, by R. Bradbury, New York, 1934; *British Architects and Craftsmen: A Survey of Taste, Design, and Style . . . 1600–1830*, by S. Sitwell, 1945.

Modern books on the history of painting include *English Art, 1800–1870*, by T. S. R. Boase, 1959 (vol. x of the *Oxford History of English Art*), with its useful bibliography, and two books by W. T. Whitley, *Art in England 1800–1820*, 1928, and *Art in England 1821–1837*, 1930. *The Gothic Revival*, by (Sir) Kenneth Clark, 1923 (2nd ed., 1950), and *The Picturesque*, by C. Hussey, 1927, are also of some relevance. For M. Dorothy George's *English Political Caricature, 1793–1832* see p. 488 above.

On literature and the visual arts see S. A. Larrabee, *English Bards and Grecian Marbles: The Relationship between Sculpture and Poetry, Especially in the Romantic Period*, New York, 1943; C. B. Tinker, *Painter and Poet*, Princeton, 1939 (Blake, Wilson, Turner, Constable, and others); and E. Blunden, *Romantic Poetry and the Fine Arts* (British Academy Lecture, 1942). *Shakespeare and the Artist*, by W. M. Merchant, 1959, is of particular interest.

The following biographies are outstanding: *Nollekens and his Times: Comprehending Memoirs of Several Artists*, by J. T. Smith, 2 vols., 1828 (ed. Sir E. Gosse, 1894; ed. W. Whitten, 2 vols., 1920; ed. G. W. Stonier, 1949; abridged ed. in World's Classics, 1929); C. R. Leslie, *Memoirs of the Life of John Constable, R.A.*, 1843 (ed. and enlarged by A. Shirley, 1937; ed. J. Mayne, 1951); *Autobiographical Recollections of the Life of C. R. Leslie*, ed. T. Taylor, 1860; *Samuel Palmer's Valley of Vision*, by G. Grigson, 1960. And see below under Ackermann, Bewick, Haydon, Hazlitt, Hunt, Wainewright, and others.

Haydon's *Journals* (listed under Individual Authors) are of particular importance to the student of literature. *The Farington Diary*, ed. J. Greig, 8 vols., 1922–8, throws a great deal of light on the history of art during these years. Fifteen typed volumes of the *Correspondence and Other Memorials of John Constable, R.A.*, compiled by Mr. R. B. Beckett, may be consulted in the Reference Library of the Victoria and Albert Museum. Each volume has a separate index. Mr. Beckett has published *John Constable and the Fishers*, 1952, and *John Constable's Correspondence*, 1962 (mainly family letters to Constable).

E. Walker's *History of Music in England*, 2nd ed., 1924, gives an account of music at this time. The chapter on music in vol. ii of *Early Victorian England*, by E. Dent, begins at 1830. For reference we have the *Oxford Companion to Music*, ed. P. A. Scholes, 9th ed., 1955, and Grove's *Dictionary of Music and Musicians*, 5th ed., ed. E. Blom, 1954.

## VI. INDIVIDUAL AUTHORS

RUDOLPH ACKERMAN(N), 1764–1834.

As a publisher Ackermann was responsible for the appearance of a great many works, most of them illustrated, highly characteristic of the period. *The Microcosm of London* came out

in 3 vols. in 1808–11. The most interesting of all his publications, *Ackermann's Repository of Arts, Literature, Commerce, Manufactures, Fashions and Politics*, was published in three series from January 1809 to December 1828. The work contains 1,500 colour plates and is without a rival as a guide to the external appearance of Regency life. Many contributions were afterwards reprinted in other forms. Ackermann's *Poetical Magazine*, in which Combe's 'Dr. Syntax's Tour in search of the Picturesque' first appeared, came out between 1809 and 1811. Ackermann's other publications include *The History of . . . Westminster* [Abbey], 2 vols., 1812; *A History of the University of Oxford*, 2 vols., 1814; *A History of the University of Cambridge*, 2 vols., 1815; and *The Colleges of Winchester, Eton, Westminster, &c.*, 1816. From 1823 onwards he published *The Forget-Me-Not* and so set the fashion for Annuals. He also produced a number of notable 'Picturesque Tours'. Rowlandson and Pugin were two of his principal collaborators.

A brief account of Ackermann's career may be found in the *DNB*. See also *NQ*, fourth series, iv, pp. 109, 129; fifth series, vol. ix, p. 346 and vol. x, p. 18; *Didaskalia* (Frankfurt-am-Main), no. 103, 13 April 1864; *Gentleman's Magazine*, 1834, i. 560; and the *Annual Biography* for 1835.

JOHN LEYCESTER ADOLPHUS, 1795–1862.

Adolphus is remembered for his *Letters to Richard Heber, Esq. containing Critical Remarks on the Series of Novels beginning with 'Waverley', and an Attempt to ascertain their Author*, which he published anonymously in 1821. There was a second edition the following year. In 1814 he published an Oxford Prize Poem on 'Niobe', and in 1818 a prize essay on *Biography*. In later life his principal publication was a work entitled *Letters from Spain in 1856 and 1857*, 1858.

Scott admired Adolphus's detective work, and the two men became friends. Adolphus contributed reminiscences to Lockhart's *Memoirs of . . . Scott*. Information about Adolphus may be found in contemporary memoirs, in the *DNB*, and in an article by W. F. Gray, 'An Early Critic of Scott', in the *Sir Walter Scott Quarterly*, 1927.

JOHN BANIM, 1798–1842, AND MICHAEL BANIM, 1796–1874.

The following works by the Banim brothers are listed by Sadleir: *The Celt's Paradise: in four Duans*, by John Banim, 1821; *Damon and Pythias: a Tragedy*, 1821; *A Letter to the Committee . . .*

[concerning a] *National Testimonial*, by John Banim, 1822; *Revelations of the Dead-Alive*, 1824 (a satirical tale reissued in 1845 as *London and its Eccentricities in the Year 2023: or Revelations of the Dead Alive*); *Tales by the O'Hara Family*, 3 vols., 1825; *Tales by the O'Hara Family: Second Series*, 3 vols., 1826; *The Boyne Water: a Tale*, 3 vols., 1826; *The Anglo-Irish of the Nineteenth Century: a Novel*, 3 vols., 1828; *The Croppy: a Tale of 1798*, 3 vols., 1828; *The Denounced*, 3 vols., 1830; *The Chaunt of the Cholera: Songs for Ireland*, 1831; *The Smuggler: a Tale*, 3 vols., 1831; *The Ghost Hunter and his Family*, 1833; *The Mayor of Wind-Gap and Canvassing*, 3 vols., 1835; *The Bit o' Writin' and other Tales*, 3 vols., 1838; *Father Connell*, 3 vols., 1842; *The Town of the Cascades*, by Michael Banim, 2 vols., 1864.

The pseudonym 'The O'Hara Family' was sometimes used by one or other of the brothers and sometimes by the two when collaborating.

See D. Griffin, *The Life of Gerald Griffin*, 1843; R. H. Horne, *A New Spirit of the Age*, vol. ii, 1844; 'John Banim', *Irish Quarterly Review*, iv–vi, 1854–6; P. J. Murray, *The Life of John Banim*, 1857; A. Steger, *John Banim, ein Nachahmer Walter Scotts*, Erlangen, 1935; and T. Flanagan, *The Irish Novelists, 1800–1850*, New York, 1959.

BERNARD BARTON, 1784–1849.

Barton's principal publications were *Metrical Effusions* (1812); *The Triumph of the Orwell*, Woodbridge [1817]; *The Convict's Appeal* (1818); *Poems by an Amateur* (1818); *A Day in Autumn, A Poem* (1820); *Poems* (1820: reprinted with additions, 1821, 1822, 1825); *Napoleon, and other Poems* (1822); *Verses on the Death of P. B. Shelley* (1822); *Minor Poems* (1824); *Poetic Vigils* (1824); *Devotional Verses* (1826); *A Missionary's Memorial* (1826); *A Widow's Tale* (1827); *A New Year's Eve* (1828); *Household Verses* (1845); *A Memorial of J. J. Gurney*, 1847; and 4 vols. published at Woodbridge: *Sea-Weeds, gathered at Aldborough* [1846] (privately printed); *Birthday Verses at Sixty-Four* (1848); *Ichabod!* (1848); and *On the Signs of the Times* (1848). He also contributed material to *Bible Letters for Children* [by Lucy Barton], 1831, and other collections.

*Selections from the Poems and Letters of Bernard Barton* were edited by his daughter L. Barton in 1849 and 1853 (with a memoir by E. FitzGerald).

E. V. Lucas published *Bernard Barton and his Friends* in 1893.

See also 'Unpublished Letters from Edward FitzGerald to Bernard Barton', *Scribner's Magazine*, lxxii, 1922; A. M. Terhune, *The Life of Edward FitzGerald* (New Haven, 1947); and C. R. Woodring, 'Letters from Bernard Barton to Robert Southey', *Harvard Library Bulletin*, iv, 1950.

THOMAS LOVELL BEDDOES, 1803–49.

Beddoes published two volumes of verse: *The Improvisatore* (1821), and *The Brides' Tragedy* (1822). *Death's Jest-Book or The Fool's Tragedy* was published anonymously after his death, in 1850. Vol. ii of *The Poems posthumous and collected*, 2 vols., 1851, includes *Death's Jest-Book*, 1850: there was also a 1-vol. edition without *Death's Jest-Book*, but with a Memoir by T. F. Kelsall, in 1851. The *Poetical Works* were edited by Sir E. Gosse in 2 vols. in 1890. This and the original Muses' Library edition (by R. Colles, 1907), and Sir E. Gosse's *Complete Works* (2 vols., 1928), were rendered obsolete by *The Works*, ed. H. W. Donner, 1935 (which also includes the letters and supersedes Gosse's edition of *The Letters*, 1894). Donner has also produced a new Muses' Library edition (*Plays and Poems*, 1950), which includes the first version of *Death's Jest-Book*: written the standard biography, *Thomas Lovell Beddoes: The Making of a Poet* (1935): and collected letters relating to Beddoes in *The Browning Box* (1935). F. L. Lucas's *Thomas Lovell Beddoes: An Anthology* (1932) has an introduction reprinted in *Studies French and English* (1934). See also R. H. Snow, *Thomas Lovell Beddoes. Eccentric and Poet* (New York, 1928), and C. A. Weber (p. 464 above). There are articles by C. C. Abbott ('The Parents of Beddoes', *Durham University Journal*, xxxiv, 1941–2); H. K. Johnson ('Beddoes: a Psychiatric Study', *Psychiatric Quarterly*, 1943); H. Gregory ('On the Gothic Imagination . . . and the Survival of Beddoes', in *The Shield of Achilles*, New York, 1944); J. Heath-Stubbs (in *The Darkling Plain*, 1950); L. Forster ('Beddoes's Views on German Literature', *English Studies*, xxx, 1949); and A. C. Todd ('Beddoes and his Guardian', *TLS*, 10 Oct. 1952). Donner's 'Echoes of Beddoesian Rambles', *Studia Neophilologica*, vol. xxxiii, no. 2, 1961, is an important article which contains more letters and fresh information. See also A. C. Todd's article on the poet's mother, in *Studia Neophilologica*, vol. xxix, 1957.

JEREMY BENTHAM, 1748–1832.

Bentham's principal individual works include: *A Fragment on*

*Government*, 1776 (ed. F. C. Montague, 1891: ed. W. Harrison (with *An Introduction to the Principles of Morals and Legislation*), 1948); *A View of the Hard-Labour-Bill*, 1778; *Defence of Usury*, 1787; *An Introduction to the Principles of Morals and Legislation*, 1789, 2 vols., 'corrected', 1823 (reprinted, Oxford, 1879); *Panopticon; or, The Inspection House*, 1791; *A Protest against Law Taxes*, 1795; 'Poor Laws and Pauper Management' (in Arthur Young's *Annals*, Sept. 1797 and later); *A Plea for the Constitution*, 1803; *Scotch Reform*, 1808; *Panopticon versus New South Wales*, 1812; *Chrestomathia*, 1816; *'Swear not at all'*, 1817; *A Table of the Springs of Action* (printed 1815, first published 1817); 'Catechism of Parliamentary Reform', *The Pamphleteer*, January 1817; *Papers upon Codification and Public Instruction*, 1817; *Church of Englandism and its Catechism examined*, 1818; 'Radical Reform Bill, with Explanations', *The Pamphleteer*, December 1819; *Elements of the Art of Packing as applied to Special Juries*, 1821; *Three Tracts relating to Spanish and Portuguese Affairs*, 1821; *On the Liberty of the Press*, 1821; *Analysis of the Influence of Natural Religion on the Temporal Happiness of Mankind*, by 'Philip Beauchamp', 1822; *Not Paul, but Jesus*, by 'Gamaliel Smith', 1823; *Codification Proposals*, 1822; *Book of Fallacies*, 1824; *The Rationale of Reward*, 1825; *The Rationale of Evidence* [ed. J. S. Mill], 5 vols., 1827; *The Rationale of Punishment*, 1830 (this and the *Rationale of Reward* were translated from the French version of E. Dumont, with some reference to Bentham's early MSS.); *Constitutional Code for the use of all Nations*, vol. i, 1830 (no more published separately); *Official Aptitude maximised—Expense minimised*, 1830 (a collection of papers); and *Deontology; or, the Science of Morality*, ed. Sir J. Bowring, 2 vols., 1834. *The Theory of Legislation* (first published in English in the translation by R. Hildreth in 1876) was edited by C. K. Ogden in 1931. C. W. Everett, ed. *A Comment on the Commentaries* in 1928 and *The Limits of Jurisprudence Defined* in 1945 (New York). The *Handbook of Political Fallacies* was ed. by H. A. Larrabee, Baltimore, 1952. Like several other works, this latter had appeared in French, compiled by E. Dumont from Bentham's manuscripts.

Bentham's *Works* were edited by Sir John Bowring in 11 vols. in 1838–43, the last 2 vols. containing a Life and Index. W. Stark edited *Bentham's Economic Writings: [A] Critical Edition Based on his Printed Works and Unprinted Manuscripts*, in 3 vols. in 1952–4. A complete edition of his writings, making use of the voluminous manuscripts, is under way at University College, London.

*Jeremy Bentham 1748–1792*, by Mary Mack, is the first part of a comprehensive new study (1962). The best guide to Bentham's thought is in many ways E. Halévy's *The Growth of Philosophic Radicalism*, English translation, 1928 (French ed., 3 vols., 1901–4). Earlier books partly or wholly on Bentham include *Dissertations and Discussions*, i, by J. S. Mill, 1859; *Geschichte und Litteratur der Staatswissenschaften*, iii, by R. von Mohl, Erlangen, 1858; *The English Utilitarians*, by Leslie Stephen, 3 vols., 1900; *Études de Droit international*, by E. Nys, 1901; *Miscellaneous Essays and Addresses*, by H. Sidgwick, 1904; *Jeremy Bentham*, by C. M. Atkinson, 1905; *Lectures on the Relation between Law & Public Opinion in England . . .*, by A. V. Dicey, 1905 (rev. ed., 1962); *The Philosophical Radicals*, by A. S. Pringle Pattison, 1907; *Political Thought in England: The Utilitarians from Bentham to Mill*, by W. C. Davidson, 1915; *Bentham's Theory of Fictions*, by C. K. Ogden, 1932; *Jeremy Bentham*, by J. L. Stocks, Manchester, 1933 (a lecture); *The Education of Bentham*, by C. W. Everett, New York, 1931; *Bentham and the Ethics of Today, with Bentham Manuscripts Hitherto Unpublished*, by D. Baumgardt, Princeton, 1952; *Machiavelli to Bentham*, by W. T. Jones (*Masters of Political Thought*, ed. E. M. Sait, vol. ii, 1947); *Bentham and the Law: A Symposium*, ed. G. W. Keeton and G. Schwartzenberger, 1948; and *The Province and Function of Law*, by J. Stone, Sydney, 1950. For one example of Bentham's tremendous influence abroad one may consult V. A. Belaunde's *Bolivar and the Political Thought of the Spanish American Revolution*, Baltimore, 1938.

Of the many articles on Bentham very few can be mentioned: see, for example, C. S. Kenny in the *Law Quarterly Review*, xi, 1895; G. Wallas in the *Political Science Quarterly*, March 1923, and the *Contemporary Review*, March 1926; 'Bentham's Place in English Legal History', by Sir W. Holdsworth, *California Law Review*, xxviii, 1940; 'Benthamism in England and America', by P. A. Palmer, *American Political Science Review*, xxxv, 1941; 'Bentham as an Economist', by W. Stark, *Economic Journal*, li and lvi, 1941 and 1946; 'Bentham's "Censorial" Method', by D. Baumgardt, *JHI* vi, 1945; 'A Bentham Collection', by A. Muirhead, *The Library*, 5th series, i, 1946; 'The "Proof" of Utility in Bentham and Mill', by E. W. Hall, *Ethics*, lx, 1949; 'Bentham's Ideal Republic', by P. T. Peardon, *Canadian Journal of Economics*, xvii, 1951; and 'Utilitarianism: A System of Political Tolerance', by S. R. Letwin, *Cambridge Journal*, vi, 1953.

*Mill on Bentham and Coleridge*, ed. F. R. Leavis, 1950, reprints these two important essays from the *Dissertations and Discussions*.

C. W. Everett contributed a useful bibliography of books by and about Bentham (now, inevitably, somewhat out of date) to the English translation of Halévy's *Growth of Philosophic Radicalism*.

Also see above, pp. 488–9.

THOMAS BEWICK, 1753–1828.

*A Memoir of Thomas Bewick, Written by Himself*, appeared in 1862. There are subsequent editions by A. Dobson, Newcastle, 1887; Selwyn Image, 1924; M. Weekley, 1961 (with omissions, but a valuable introduction); and E. Blunden, 1961 (a photo-lithographic reproduction of the 1924 edition with a new introduction). There is no full edition from the manuscript in the British Museum, Add. MSS. 41481. In 1885–7 A. Dobson edited the Memorial Edition of the *Works*, in 5 vols.

T. Landseer's *Life and Letters of William Bewick* appeared in 2 vols. in 1871, to be followed by D. C. Thomson's *Life and Works* in 1882, A. Dobson's *Thomas Bewick and his Pupils* in 1884 (revised edition, 1889) and R. Robinson's *Life and Times* in 1887 (Newcastle). M. Weekley published his *Thomas Bewick* in 1953. As early as 1866 T. Hugo published *The Bewick Collector: A Descriptive Catalogue of the Works of Thomas and John Bewick* (Supplement, 1868). We now have *Thomas Bewick. A Bibliography Raisonné*, by S. Roscoe, 1953.

SAMUEL LAMAN BLANCHARD, 1804–45.

Blanchard published *Lyric Offerings* in 1828 and edited the *Life and Literary Remains* of L. E. L[andon] in 2 vols. in 1841. His essays were collected as *Sketches from Life* and edited with a memoir by Sir E. Bulwer Lytton in 3 vols. in 1846. His prose sketches, *Corporation Characters*, came out in 1855. His *Poetical Works* were edited, with a memoir, by B. Jerrold in 1876. His Memoir of Harrison Ainsworth is to be found in the 14-vol. edition of the latter's *Works* published in 1850–1. He contributed to *The Examiner* and many other periodicals. Among periodicals which he edited at one time or another were the *Monthly Magazine*, *The True Sun*, *The Constitutional and Public Ledger*, *The Court Journal*, *The Courier*, and *George Cruickshank's Omnibus*. See W. M. Thackeray, 'A Brother of the Press . . . the Chances of the

Literary Profession', *Fraser's Magazine*, xxxiii, 1846 (reprinted in Thackeray's *Works*, ed. A. T. Ritchie, xiii, 1899). Selections are given in Miles, iii, with an essay by A. H. Japp.

BLESSINGTON, MARGUERITE, COUNTESS OF (*NÉE* POWER), 1789–1849.

She wrote a number of novels: *The Repealers*, 3 vols., 1833 (as *Grace Cassidy*, 3 vols., 1834); *The Confessions of an Elderly Gentleman*, 1836; *The Victims of Society*, 3 vols., 1837; *The Confessions of an Elderly Lady*, 1838; *The Governess*, 2 vols., 1839; *The Lottery of Life*, 3 vols., 1842; *Meredith*, 3 vols., 1843; *Strathern; or Life at Home and Abroad*, 4 vols., 1845; *Memoirs of a Femme de Chambre*, 3 vols., 1846; *Marmaduke Herbert, or the Fatal Error*, 3 vols., 1847; and *Country Quarters*, 3 vols., 1850 (with a Memoir by Miss Power). As well as editing and contributing largely to *The Book of Beauty*, *The Keepsake* and other gift-books, the Countess also published *The Magic Lantern, or Sketches of Scenes in the Metropolis*, 1822; *Sketches and Fragments*, 1822 [a doubtful attribution]; *Conversations of Lord Byron with the Countess of Blessington*, 1834 (first published in the *New Monthly Magazine*, July 1832–December 1833); *The Honeymoon, and Other Tales*, 2 vols., Philadelphia, 1837; *The Idler in Italy*, 2 vols., 1839 (2nd ed., with new third volume, also 1839); *Desultory Thoughts and Reflections*, 1839; *The Belle of a Season* (a poem), 1840; and *The Idler in France*, 2 vols., 1841. *The Works of Lady Blessington*, published in 2 vols. at Philadelphia in 1838, contain some material which Lady Blessington did not herself collect, and some which is probably not her work.

The second of the two editions of *The Literary Life and Correspondence of the Countess of Blessington*, edited by R. R. Madden in 3 vols. in 1855, is the less inaccurate, but A. Morrison's *The Blessington Papers*, 1895, is much more reliable. See also W. Maginn, *A Gallery of Illustrious Literary Characters*, ed. W. Bates [1873]; M. Sadleir, *Blessington–D'Orsay*, rev. ed., 1947 (valuable); and M. W. Rosa, *The Silver-Fork School: Novels of Fashion preceding Vanity Fair*, New York, 1936. On her *Conversations* with Byron see (among others) Doris Langley Moore, *The Late Lord Byron*, 1961.

SIR JOHN BOWRING, 1792–1872.

Bowring's voluminous writings include a number of volumes of translations: *Specimens of the Russian Poets*, 1820 (enlarged

into two parts, 1821–3); *Batavian Anthology; or, Specimens of the Dutch Poets* (1824, with H. S. Van Dyk); *Ancient Poetry and Romances of Spain* (1824); *Servian Popular Poetry* (1827); *Specimens of the Polish Poets* (1827); *Poetry of the Magyars* (1830); *Cheskian* [Czech] *Anthology* (1832); *Manuscript of the Queen's Court. A Collection of Old Bohemian Lyrico-Epic Songs* (Prague, 1843); *Ode to the Deity: Translated from the Russian of Derzhavin* [Brighton, 1861]; and *Translations from A. Petöfi, the Magyar Poet* (1866).

In original verse Bowring also published *Matins and Vespers* (1823, revised and enlarged 1824 and 1841); and *Hymns* (1825). *A Memorial Volume of Sacred Poetry*, with a Memoir, was edited by Lady Bowring in 1873.

In prose Bowring published *Observations on the State of Religion and Literature in Spain*, 1820; *Peter Schlemihl: from the German* (1824); a *Sketch of the Language and Literature of Holland* (Amsterdam, 1829); and *Minor Morals for Young People*, 3 parts, 1834–9. His *Autobiographical Recollections* were edited by L. B. Bowring in 1877.

Bowring was editor of the *Westminster Review* from 1824 to 1836 and edited Bentham's *Collected Works*, 1838–43.

On Bowring see 'The Oratory of Sir John Bowring', *Fraser's Magazine*, xxxiv, 1846; L. Moor, *Bowring, Cobden and China: A Memoir*, 1857; G. L. Nesbitt, *Benthamite Reviewing*, New York, 1934; A. C. Wardle, *Benjamin Bowring and his Descendants*, 1938; M. Sova, 'Sir John Bowring and the Slavs', *Slavonic Review*, xxi, 1943; and D. F. S. Scott, *Some English Correspondents of Goethe*, 1949.

HENRY PETER BROUGHAM (BARON BROUGHAM AND VAUX), 1778–1868.

His main publications include *An Inquiry into the Colonial Policy of the European Powers*, 2 vols., 1803; *An Inquiry into the State of the Nation*, 1806; *A Letter to Sir Samuel Romilly upon the Abuse of Charities*, 1818 (first published in *The Pamphleteer*); *Practical Observations upon the Education of the People*, 1825; *Thoughts upon the Aristocracy of England. By Isaac Tomkins, Gent.*, 1835; '*We Can't Afford It!*' (Part 2 of the preceding), 1835; *A Discourse of Natural Theology*, Brussels, 1835; *Select Cases decided by Lord Brougham in the Court of Chancery, 1833 and 1834*, vol. i, ed. C. P. Cooper, 1835; *Speeches upon Questions relating to Public Rights, etc.*, 4 vols., 1838 (several had been published separately); *Historical Sketches of Statesmen in the Time of George III*, 3 series, 1839–43, 6 vols., 1845;

*Political Philosophy* (Society for the Diffusion of Useful Knowledge), 3 vols., 1842–3; *Albert Lunel: or the Château of Languedoc*, 3 vols., 1844 (a novel); *Lives of Men of Letters and Science, in the Time of George III*, 2 vols., 1845–6; *A Letter to Lord Denman . . .*, 1850; *History of England and France under the House of Lancaster*, 1852; *Contributions to the Edinburgh Review*, 3 vols., 1856; and *Tracts, Mathematical and Physical*, 1860. His *Works* were collected in 11 vols. in 1855–61, 2nd ed., 1872–3. New's biography lists his very numerous and important contributions to the *Edinburgh Review.*

As New pointed out, a complete bibliography of writings relating to Brougham would be 'gigantic, hopeless, and useless'. There are two important modern studies, *Lord Brougham and the Whig Party*, by A. Aspinall, Manchester, 1927, and C. W. New's *Life of Henry Brougham to 1830*, 1961. *The Life and Times of Henry, Lord Brougham, Written by Himself* had appeared in 3 vols. in 1871 (see A. Aspinall, *English Historical Review*, lix, 1944). We may also consult *Lord Brougham's Law Reforms*, by Sir J. E. Eardley-Wilmot, 1860; *The Work of Lord Brougham for Education in England*, by A. M. Gilbert, Chambersburg, 1922; and 'Wordsworth versus Brougham (1818, 1820, 1826)' and 'Thomas Clarkson as Champion of Brougham in 1818', by A. L. Strout, *NQ*, 4 and 28 May 1938. G. T. Garratt's *Lord Brougham*, 1935, is of no scholarly value. Mrs. Hawes's biography, published in 1957, is brief but accurate.

CHARLES BROWN, 1787–1842.

Charles Brown, who changed his name to Charles Armitage Brown long after the death of Keats, had a comic opera, *Narensky; or, The Road to Yaroslaf*, produced at Drury Lane in January 1814, and published the same year. His book, *Shakespeare's Autobiographical Poems*, a study of the sonnets, appeared in 1838. He contributed to *The Examiner*, *The Liberal*, the *New Monthly Magazine*, and other periodicals. M. Buxton Forman collected *Some Letters & Miscellanea of Charles Brown* in 1937. Brown's unpublished *Life of John Keats* was edited by D. H. Bodurtha and W. B. Pope in 1937. Up-to-date information about him may be found in *The Keats Circle: Letters and Papers*, ed. H. E. Rollins, 2 vols., Harvard, 1948 (which includes a brief Memoir by his son); an article by H. E. Rollins in the *Harvard Library Bulletin*, iv, 1950; and *The Letters of John Keats*, ed. H. E. Rollins, 2 vols., 1958.

THOMAS BROWN, 1778–1820.

Professor Thomas Brown, M.D., a philosopher of importance in his day, published *Observations on the Zoonomia of Erasmus Darwin*, 1798; *Observations on . . . the Doctrine of Mr. Hume . . .*, 1805 (enlarged in third edition in 1818 as *Inquiry into the Relation of Cause and Effect*); and *Lectures on the Philosophy of the Human Mind*, 4 vols., 1820.

Brown also published a well-known satirical poem, *The Paradise of Coquettes* (with an interesting preface), in 1814. His *Collected Poems*, 1820, includes poems from several volumes, published between 1814 and 1819.

There is an *Account of the Life and Writings*, by the Rev. D. Welsh, 1825, of which an abridged version is prefixed to later editions of Brown's *Lectures*. See also A. L. Jones, 'A Note on Dr. Thomas Brown's Contribution to Aesthetics', *Studies in the History of Ideas*, vol. i, New York, 1918.

SIR SAMUEL EGERTON BRYDGES, 1762–1837.

Books published by Brydges include *Sonnets and Other Poems*, 1785 (expanded in later editions); *Mary de Clifford: a Story*, 1792; *Verses on the Late Unanimous Resolutions to Support the Constitution*, 1794; *Arthur Fitz Albini: A Novel*, 2 vols., 1798; *Le Forester, A Novel*, 3 vols., 1802; *The Sylvan Wanderer . . . Essays*, 4 parts, Lee Priory, 1813–21 (privately printed); *The Ruminator: . . . A Series of . . . Essays*, 2 vols., 1813; *Occasional Poems, written in the year MDCCCXI*, Lee Priory, 1814 (privately printed); *Select Poems*, Lee Priory, 1814 (privately printed); *Bertram, a Poetical Tale*, Lee Priory, 1814 (privately printed); *Desultoria: or Comments . . . on Books and Men*, Lee Priory, 1815 (privately printed); *Lord Brokenhurst*, Geneva, 1819 (reprinted, like the next entry, in *Tragic Tales*, 1820); *Coningsby*, Paris, 1819; *Sir Ralph Willoughby*, Florence, 1820; *The Hall of Hellingsby*, 3 vols., 1821; *Odo, Count of Lingen: a poetical tale in six cantos*, Geneva, 1824; *Gnomica, Detached Thoughts . . .*, Geneva, 1824; *Letters on the Character and Poetical Genius of Lord Byron*, 1824; *An Impartial Portrait of Lord Byron*, Paris, 1825; *Recollections of Foreign Travel on Life, Literature, and Self-knowledge*, 2 vols., 1825; *Modern Aristocracy or the Bard's Reception*, Geneva, 1831 (a poem on Byron); *The Lake of Geneva, A Poem*, 2 vols., Geneva, 1832; *Imaginative Biography*, 2 vols., 1834; *The Autobiography, Times, Opinions, and*

*Contemporaries of Sir Egerton Brydges*, 2 vols., 1834; *Moral Axioms in Single Couplets: for the use of the young*, 1837; *Human Fate, and An Address to the Poets Wordsworth & Southey: Poems*, Great Totham, 1846 (privately printed).

His bibliographical and antiquarian publications include *The Topographer*, 4 vols., 1789–91 (with L. S. Shaw); *Topographical Miscellanies*, 1792; *Censura Literaria*, 10 vols., 1805–9, 10 vols., 1815 (articles rearranged according to chronology); *The British Bibliographer*, 4 vols., 1810–14; *Restituta; or Titles, Extracts, and Characters of Old Books*, 4 vols., 1814–16; *Excerpta Tudoriana*, 2 vols., Lee Priory, 1814–18 (privately printed); *Archaica: Containing A Reprint of Scarce Old English Tracts*, 2 vols., 1815 (privately printed); *Res Literariae: Bibliographical and Critical*, 3 nos., Naples, Rome, Geneva, 1821–2.

A much fuller list of Brydges's publications may be found in *The Literary Career of Sir Samuel Egerton Brydges*, by Mary Katherine Woodworth, 1935. A few *addenda* are noted in *TLS*, 16 November 1935, p. 744.

GEORGE GORDON BYRON, BARON BYRON, 1788–1824.

*Fugitive Pieces* were privately printed at Newark in [1806]. Like a number of Byron's later volumes, this was anonymous. A facsimile was edited by H. Buxton Forman in 1886, another by M. Kessel in 1933 (New York). There are twelve new pieces in *Poems on Various Occasions*, Newark, 1807, also anonymous and privately printed; *Hours of Idleness* was published at Newark in 1807, and contained twelve further new pieces.

*Poems Original and Translated. Second Edition*, Newark, 1808, contains only five new pieces. Nine poems by Byron were published in *Imitations and Translations from the Ancient and Modern Classics*, by J. C. Hobhouse, 1809. *English Bards, and Scotch Reviewers, A Satire*, came out in [1809], incorporating a good deal of an unpublished poem, *The British Bards* [Newark, 1808], of which there is a proof copy in the British Museum: there were considerable additions and revisions in the 2nd and 5th editions of *English Bards*, 1809 and 1816; (there is a facsimile edition of a copy with Byron's MS. notes, ed. J. Murray for the Roxburghe Club, 1936); *Hints from Horace* was not published in full during Byron's lifetime, but an 1811 proof exists in the British Museum.

The first two cantos of *Childe Harold's Pilgrimage, A Romaunt*, came out in 1812: Canto III in 1816: and Canto IV in 1818. The four cantos were published together in 2 vols. in 1819. *Euthanasia* was first published in the 2nd edition of *Childe Harold*, I–II, 1812.

The following volumes appeared in the next few years: *The Curse of Minerva*, 1812 (privately printed), 'Philadelphia', 1815, and later editions; *Waltz: An Apostrophic Hymn*, 'By Horace Hornem, Esq.', 1813; *The Giaour, A Fragment of a Turkish Tale*, 1813 (later editions had various additions); *The Bride of Abydos, A Turkish Tale*, 1813; *The Corsair, A Tale*, 1814; *Ode to Napoleon Buonaparte*, 1814; *Lara, A Tale* (with *Jacqueline, A Tale* [by Samuel Rogers]), 1814, 4th ed., 1814 (first separate and acknowledged edition); *Hebrew Melodies*, 2 parts, 1815; *The Siege of Corinth, A Poem* [with] *Parisina, A Poem*, 1816; *Poems*, 1816; *The Prisoner of Chillon, and other Poems*, 1816; *Monody on the Death of the Right Honourable R. B. Sheridan*, 1816; *The Lament of Tasso*, 1817; *Manfred. A Dramatic Poem*, 1817; *Beppo. A Venetian Story*, 1818 (4th ed. with additional stanzas, 1818); *Mazeppa. A Poem*, 1819.

The first two cantos of *Don Juan* appeared in 1819; Cantos III–V in 1821; Cantos VI–VIII, Cantos IX–XI, and Cantos XII–XIV all in 1823; Cantos XV–XVI in 1824; and the Dedication in 1833. There were editions of Cantos I–V in 1822, V–XI in 1823, and I–XVI in 1826, in two volumes.

*Marino Faliero, Doge of Venice* was published with *The Prophecy of Dante. A Poem* in 1821; *Sardanapalus, A Tragedy, The Two Foscari, A Tragedy*, [and] *Cain, A Mystery* in 1821; there is an 1821 proof of *Heaven and Earth*, but it was first published in *The Liberal*, no. 2, 1823; *The Vision of Judgment* first appeared in *The Liberal*, no. 1, 1822; *The Age of Bronze; or, Carmen Seculare et Annus haud Mirabilis* appeared in 1823, as did *The Island, or, Christian and his Comrades* and *Werner: A Tragedy. The Deformed Transformed* was published in 1824.

Several minor pieces are omitted from this list, but mention should also be made of the so-called 'Poems on his Domestic Circumstances', two poems first printed at Bristol by Barry and Son in 1816.

The standard collected edition of the poems is still vols. i–vii of *The Works*, ed. E. H. Coleridge, 1898–1904. The basis of his text is the 6-vol. *Works* published by Murray in 1831. Murray

had published earlier editions in 1815 (4 vols.), 1818–20 (8 vols.), 1825 (8 vols.), and at other times, and there were numerous unauthorized collections. The fullest edition of *Don Juan* is now that edited by T. G. Steffan and W. W. Pratt, 4 vols., 1957: vol. i contains a detailed study of the composition of the poem.

There is a 3-vol. edition of Byron's *Poems* in Everyman's Library, ed. G. Pocock, 1949. There are innumerable volumes of selections, including those with the prefaces of Swinburne and Matthew Arnold, 1866 and 1881. Mention may also be made of *Poems*, ed. H. J. C. Grierson, 1923; *The Best of Byron*, ed. R. A. Rice, New York, 1933; *Selected Poems*, ed. L. A. Marchand ('Modern Library'); *Don Juan and Other Satiric Poems*, ed. L. I. Bredvold, New York, 1935; *Childe Harold's Pilgrimage and Other Romantic Poems*, ed. S. C. Chew, 1936; *Satirical and Critical Poems*, ed. Joan Bennett, 1937; and *Selections* (poetry and prose), ed. P. Quennell, 1950 (Nonesuch edition).

In prose Byron published a 'Letter to the Editor of "My Grandmother's Review"', in the *Liberal*, no. 1, 1822; and *A Letter to* [John Murray] *on the Rev. W. L. Bowles' Strictures on . . . Pope*, 1821. Several other prose pieces were printed after his death, some of them existing in earlier 'proofs'.

Unpublished verse has been printed by T. G. Steffan in 'An Early Byron MS. in the Pierpont Morgan Library', *Texas Studies in English*, xxvii, 1948, and by W. Pafford in 'An Unpublished Poem', *K.-Sh.J.* i, 1952.

The *Correspondence of Lord Byron with a Friend* was edited by A. R. C. Dallas in [1824], but suppressed before publication. It appeared in 3 vols. in Paris in 1825. His *Letters and Journals* first appeared in Moore's biography in 2 vols. in 1830. Other letters were published at various times. At the moment the standard edition of the letters remains that by R. E. Prothero, 6 vols., 1898–1901 (which complements E. H. Coleridge's ed. of the poems); but see also *Astarte* (mentioned below); *Poems and Letters of Lord Byron*, ed. W. N. C. Carlton, Chicago, 1912 (privately printed); and (more important) *Lord Byron's Correspondence, chiefly with Lady Melbourne, Mr. Hobhouse, the Hon. Douglas Kinnaird, and P. B. Shelley*, ed. John Murray, 2 vols., 1922. Other letters may be found in *The Last Attachment*, by Iris Origo, 1949; *Byron: A Self-Portrait. Letters and Diaries, 1798 to 1824*, ed. P. Quennell, 2 vols., 1950; and 'Byron and Count Alborghetti', by L. A. Marchand, *PMLA* lxiv, 1949. Readers of Russian may refer to

'Avtografy Bayrona v SSSR', by M. P. Alekseev, in *Literaturnoe Nasledstvo*, lviii, 1952.

There are several volumes of selected letters, including one in Everyman's Library, ed. R. G. Howarth, 1936.

For the writings of J. C. Hobhouse relevant to Byron see under Hobhouse. Only a few of the other early biographical accounts can be mentioned here: *Journal of the Conversations of Lord Byron at Pisa*, by Thomas Medwin, 1824; *Recollections of the Life of Lord Byron* (1808–1814), by R. C. Dallas, 1824; Leigh Hunt, *Lord Byron and Some of his Contemporaries*, 1828 (2-vol. ed. same year) and *Autobiography*, 3 vols., 1850; *Letters and Journals of Lord Byron, with Notices of his Life*, by Thomas Moore, 2 vols., 1830; *The Life of Lord Byron*, by John Galt, 1830; *Conversations of Lord Byron with the Countess of Blessington*, 1834 (first published in *New Monthly Magazine*, July 1832–December 1833); E. J. Trelawny, *Recollections of the Last Days of Shelley and Byron*, 1858, revised as *Records of Shelley, Byron, and the Author* (see Trelawny); and *My Recollections of Lord Byron and those of Eye-witnesses of his Life*, by the Countess Guiccioli, translated by H. E. H. Jerningham, 2 vols., 1869. Much information is to be found in the *Memoirs* of Thomas Moore, in *A Publisher and his Friends* (see p. 471 above), and in many other memoirs and accounts of the period. There are discussions of these and other early biographical accounts in S. C. Chew's *Byron in England: His Fame and After-Fame*, 1924, L. A. Marchand's *Byron*, 3 vols., 1957, and Doris Langley Moore's *The Late Lord Byron*, 1961.

Of later biographies, Karl Elze's *Lord Byron*, Berlin, 1870 (English translation, with additions, 1872), John Nichol's volume in the English Men of Letters series, 1880, and J. C. Jeaffreson's *The Real Lord Byron*, 1883, are now of slight importance. *Astarte, A Fragment of Truth concerning . . . Lord Byron*, by the Earl of Lovelace (privately printed, 1905: better edition by Lady Lovelace, 1921), which concerns Byron's relations with Augusta Leigh, is still of interest. See further Harold Nicolson, *Byron: The Last Journey*, 1924 (rev. ed., 1940); *Byron*, by Ethel Colburn Mayne, 2 vols., 1912 (rev. ed., 1 vol., 1924), for many years the main biography (see also her *Life and Letters of . . . Lady Noel Byron*, 1929); J. Drinkwater, *The Pilgrim of Eternity: Byron—A Conflict*, 1925; Helene Richter, *Lord Byron: Persönlichkeit und Werk*, Halle, 1929; and Charles du Bos, *Byron et le besoin de la fatalité*, 1929 (translated by Ethel Colburn Mayne [1932]), a

speculative psychological study which is of greater value than A. Maurois's biography, as is M. Castelain's *Byron*, Paris, 1931. Peter Quennell has produced *Byron. The Years of Fame*, 1935, and *Byron in Italy*, 1941, as well as editing some letters to Byron (with 'George Paston') in '*To Lord Byron*': *Feminine Profiles*, 1939. W. A. Borst's *Lord Byron's First Pilgrimage*, New Haven, 1948, provides a useful background for *Childe Harold*, I–II. *Byron, Shelley, Hunt, and* '*The Liberal*', by W. H. Marshall, Philadelphia, 1960, is also of interest. C. L. Cline's *Byron, Shelley and their Pisan Circle*, 1952, provided a little new information, as did F. L. Jones by editing the *Journal of Edward E. Williams* in 1951. *The Last Attachment* (Byron and Teresa Guiccioli), by Iris Origo, 1949, is an important study. In general the truth is the last thing that one looks for in the work of Byron's biographers, but a remarkable amount of it is to be found in L. A. Marchand's *Byron: A Biography*, 3 vols., 1957, which should long remain the standard Life. See also *Lord Byron's Wife*, by M. Elwin, 1962.

A most useful book is *His Very Self and Voice*, ed. E. J. Lovell, 1954, a collection of Byron's conversation. His conversations with Medwin and the Countess of Blessington are reserved for a second volume. Some new light on Byron's early poetic career is contained in W. W. Pratt's *Byron at Southwell: The Making of a Poet*, Austin, Texas, 1948. Some letters may be found in *Shelley and his Circle* (p. 615 below).

G. Wilson Knight has written at length on Byron in *The Burning Oracle*, 1939, where he is also concerned with Spenser, Milton, and Pope; in 'Byron's Dramatic Prose' (Byron Foundation Lecture, Nottingham, 1953); in *Lord Byron: Christian Virtues*, 1952, a work on 'a man in whom poetry has become incarnate . . . our greatest poet in the widest sense of the term since Shakespeare' (reviewed by R. W. King in *RES*, new series, v, 1954); and in the highly conjectural *Lord Byron's Marriage: The Evidence of Asterisks*, 1957 (on which see A. Rutherford's review in *EC* viii, 1958). See also Wilson Knight's *Byron and Hamlet*, Manchester, 1963.

The Reviews of Byron's own day contained much intelligent comment, as did certain of the early biographical studies. A few early reviews are reprinted in the volumes of selections mentioned on p. 475 above. Lockhart's anonymous *John Bull's Letter to Lord Byron*, 1821, was reprinted by A. L. Strout in 1947. S. C. Chew's *Byron in England: His Fame and After-Fame*, 1924, deals with early reactions to Byron.

Sir Egerton Brydges's *Letters on the Character and Poetical Genius of Lord Byron*, 1824, remain a curiosity. Macaulay's essay on Byron is reprinted from the *Edinburgh Review*, June 1831, in *Critical and Miscellaneous Essays*, vol. i, 1843. Ruskin's interesting remarks on Byron are most readily found in *Ruskin as Literary Critic, Selections*, ed. A. H. R. Ball, 1928, or by means of the index to the Cook–Wedderburn edition. Swinburne's 'Wordsworth and Byron', *Nineteenth Century*, April–May 1884, is reprinted in his *Miscellanies*, 1886. Arnold's important essay may be found in *Essays in Criticism*, 2nd series, 1888 (it first appeared in 1881 as a preface to his volume of selections).

Turning to recent criticism, we find a balanced and intelligent treatment in *Byron: A Critical Study*, by A. Rutherford, 1961. W. W. Robson's *Byron as Poet* (British Academy, 1957) is a penetrating critique stimulated by the essays of F. R. Leavis and T. S. Eliot mentioned below. *Lord Byron: un tempérament littéraire*, by R. Escarpit, 2 vols., 1955–7, is a valuable and thorough study in which biography is subordinated to criticism. Most modern critics, including those just mentioned, pay particular attention to Byron's satires. Their work is usefully supplemented by the important study of the composition of the poem in vol. i of the 1957 Variorum edition of *Don Juan* mentioned above (1957); by *Byron's Don Juan: A Critical Study*, by Elizabeth French Boyd, 1945 (reprinted 1958); by *The Style of Don Juan*, by G. M. Ridenour, New Haven, 1960; and by the introduction to R. D. Waller's edition of Hookham Frere's *The Monks and the Giants*, Manchester, 1926. Important sidelights on Byron may also be found in *The Romantic Agony*, by M. Praz, translated by A. Davidson, 1933 (Italian edition, *La carne, la morte ed il diavolo nella letteratura romantica*, Milan, 1930); and in *Rousseau and Romanticism*, by Irving Babbitt, Boston and New York, 1919. See also *Byron the Poet*, by M. K. Joseph, 1964.

Other books which deserve attention include *Lord Byron as a Satirist in Verse*, by C. M. Fuess, New York, 1912; *The Dramas of Lord Byron*, by S. C. Chew, Göttingen, 1915; *Byron the Poet* (essays by Haldane, Grierson, and others), ed. W. A. Briscoe, 1924; *Byron: Romantic Paradox*, by W. J. Calvert, North Carolina, 1935 (reprinted, New York, 1962); *Byron as Skeptic and Believer*, by E. M. Marjarum, Princeton, 1938 (reprinted 1962); *Byron: The Record of a Quest: Studies in a Poet's Concept and Treatment of Nature*, by E. J. Lovell, Austin, Texas, 1949; *The Byronic*

*Hero: Types and Prototypes*, by P. L. Thorslev, Minnesota, 1962; and *The Structure of Byron's Major Poems*, by W. H. Marshall, Philadelphia, 1963. Bertrand Russell devotes a chapter of his *History of Western Philosophy* to Byron (1946: see also Russell's article in *JHI* i, 1940). *Fair Greece Sad Relic: Literary Philhellenism from Shakespeare to Byron*, by T. Spencer, 1954, throws a good deal of light on Byron. *Byron and the Spoiler's Art*, by P. West, 1960, is fitfully illuminating. *The Death of Tragedy*, by G. Steiner, 1961, has a brief discussion of Byron's tragedies in their European setting. One of the best of the various discussions of the Don Juan story is *La Légende de Don Juan*, by G. Gendarme de Bevotte, Paris, 1906.

A number of essays first published separately were included by their authors in collections of essays. These include 'Byron, 1824–1924', by H. W. Garrod (in *The Profession of Poetry and other Lectures*, 1929); 'Byron and the Comic Spirit', by G. R. Elliott (in *The Cycle of Modern Poetry*, Princeton, 1929: reprinted from *PMLA* xxxix, 1924); 'Byron', by W. P. Ker (in *Collected Essays*, ed. C. Whibley, i, 1925); 'Byron and English Society', by H. J. C. Grierson (in *The Background of English Literature*, 1925: see also his British Academy lecture, 'Lord Byron: Arnold and Swinburne', 1921); and 'Byron', by E. de Selincourt (in *Wordsworthian and other Studies*, 1947). 'Byron's Satire' in *Revaluation*, by F. R. Leavis, 1936, has been influential, as has 'Byron', by T. S. Eliot, in *From Anne to Victoria*, ed. B. Dobrée, 1937 (reprinted in Eliot's *On Poetry and Poets*, 1957, and in *English Romantic Poets*, ed. M. H. Abrams, mentioned on p. 467 above).

Lectures and articles of importance include *Ruskin (and others) on Byron*, by R. W. Chambers (English Association, 1925); 'Coleridge and Byron', by E. L. Griggs, *PMLA* xlv, 1930; 'Byron and English Interest in the Near East', by W. C. Brown, *SP* xxxiv, 1937 (cf. 'Byron and the East: Literary Sources of the Turkish Tales', by H. S. L. Wiener, in *Nineteenth-Century Studies in Honor of C. S. Northup*, ed. H. Davis and others, Ithaca, New York, 1940); 'Byron and the Colloquial Tradition in English Poetry', by R. Bottrall, *The Criterion*, xviii, 1939 (reprinted in Abrams's collection, as above); five articles by D. V. Erdman—'Byron's Stage Fright: the History of his Ambition and Fear of Writing for the Stage', *ELH* vi, 1939; 'Lord Byron and the Genteel Reformers', *PMLA* lvi, 1941; 'Lord Byron as Rinaldo',

*PMLA* lvii, 1942; 'Byron and Revolt in England', *Science and Society*, xi, 1947; and 'Byron and "the New Force of the People"', *K.-Sh.J.* xi, 1962; two articles by E. D. H. Johnson—'Don Juan in England', *ELH* xi, 1944, and 'A Political Interpretation of Byron's *Marino Faliero*', *MLQ* 1942; 'The Poetry of Byron', by Sir Harold Nicolson (English Association, 1943); 'Byron's "Hours of Idleness" and other than Scotch Reviewers', by W. S. Ward, *MLN* lix, 1944; 'Byron and the Ballad', by A. P. Hudson, *SP* xlii, 1945; 'Manfred's Remorse and Dramatic Tradition', by B. Evans, *PMLA* lxii, 1947; 'Byron's "Observations on an Article in *Blackwood's Magazine*"', by P. B. Daghlian, *RES* xxiii, 1947; 'The Colloquial Mode of Byron', by M. Bewley, *Scrutiny*, xvi, 1949; 'Byron's *Hebrew Melodies*', by J. Slater, *SP* xlix, 1952; 'Lord Byron's Fiery Convert of Revenge', by C. Lefevre, *SP* xlix, 1952; 'The Devil a Bit of Our Beppo', by T. G. Steffan, *PQ* xxxii, 1953; 'Traduzioni e citazioni di Byron dai classici italiani', by A. Guidi, *Annali Triestini*, xxiii, Trieste, 1953; and two articles by A. Rutherford—'An Early MS. of *English Bards and Scotch Reviewers*', *K.-Sh.B.* vii, 1956, and 'The Influence of Hobhouse on *Childe Harold's Pilgrimage*, Canto IV', *RES*, N.S., xii, 1961.

The following are among the best of the Nottingham Byron Foundation lectures: *Byron's Lyrics*, by L. C. Martin (1948); *Byron and Switzerland*, by H. Straumann (1948–9); *Byron and Shelley*, by D. G. James (1951); *Byron's Dramatic Prose*, by G. Wilson Knight (1953: already mentioned); *Two Exiles: Lord Byron and D. H. Lawrence*, by G. Hough (1956: reprinted in *Image and Experience*, 1960); *Byron and Italy*, by G. Melchiori (1958); *Byron and the Greek Tradition*, by T. J. B. Spencer (1959); and *Byron's Dramas*, by B. Dobrée (1962).

Although the best considerations of Byron's criticism are usually to be found in studies of his poetry, mention may also be made of two old-fashioned studies, H. Hartmann, *Lord Byrons Stellung zu den Klassizisten seiner Zeit*, 1932, and J. J. Van Rennes, *Bowles, Byron, and the Pope-Controversy*, 1927. U. Amarasinghe's book is also relevant (p. 475, above).

So much has been written on Byron's influence in Europe and elsewhere that only very few titles can be mentioned here: *Byron and Goethe: Analysis of a Passion*, by E. M. Butler, 1956, is primarily concerned with 'the extraordinary effect of Byron's personality and life on the mind and heart of Goethe'. It was

inspired by J. G. Robertson's *Goethe and Byron* (English Goethe Society, 1925), which superseded Brandl's earlier study. Two studies with a more general scope are *Die Aufnahme Lord Byrons in Deutschland und sein Einfluß auf den jungen Heine*, Berne, 1905, by W. Ochsenbein, and *Lord Byron in Deutschland*, by G. Dobosal, Zwickau, 1911. His influence on Italy has often been studied: there were two pioneering studies by G. Muoni, *La Fama del Byron e il Byronismo in Italia*, Milan, 1903, and *La Leggenda del Byron in Italia*, Milan, 1907. M. Praz's *La Fortuna di Byron in Inghilterra*, Florence, 1925, has some useful illustrations. For France, E. Estève's *Byron et le romantisme français: Essai sur la fortune et l'influence de l'œuvre de Byron en France de 1812 à 1850*, 1907, remains of great value. Studies of his influence in other countries are listed in the standard bibliographies. Escarpit's bibliography is particularly helpful.

Further bibliographical aid may be sought in *CBEL*; in E. H. Coleridge's edition; in *ERP*; in *The Roe–Byron Collection, Newstead Abbey*, Nottingham, 1937; in *A Descriptive Catalogue of . . . Manuscripts and First Editions . . . at the University of Texas*, ed. R. H. Griffith and H. M. Jones, Austin, Texas, 1924; and in *Byron and his Circle: A Catalogue of Manuscripts in the University of Texas Library*, by W. W. Pratt, Austin, Texas, 1948. (See also T. G. Steffan's contribution to *Texas Studies in English*, 1946, and comments in *SP* xliii, 1946, and *MLQ* viii, 1947.)

Henry Francis Cary, 1772–1844.

Cary published *An Irregular Ode to General Elliott*, Birmingham [1788]; *Sonnets and Odes* (1788); and an *Ode to General Kosciusko* (1797). *The Inferno of Dante Alighieri . . ., With a Translation in English Blank Verse, Notes, and a Life of the Author*, appeared in 2 vols. in 1805–6. His complete translation, *The Vision; or Hell, Purgatory, and Paradise, of Dante Alighieri* was published at his own expense in 3 vols. in 1814 and republished in a much superior format by Taylor and Hessey in 3 vols. in 1819. It was illustrated by Gustave Doré in 1866, and has been often reprinted. Cary's other productions were *The Birds of Aristophanes. Translated*, 1824; *Pindar in English Verse*, 1833; *Lives of English Poets, from Johnson to Kirke White*, 1846 (reprinted from *The London Magazine*, August 1821–December 1824); and *The Early French Poets: Notices and Translations*, 1846 (also reprinted from

*The London Magazine*, November 1821–April 1824: ed. T. E. Welby, without the French texts, 1923).

Cary's son, Henry, published his *Memoir of the Rev. Henry Francis Cary . . . with his Literary Journal and Letters* in 2 vols. in 1847. In 1925 R. W. King produced *The Translator of Dante*, an interesting and reliable study. See also articles in the *Edinburgh Review*, xxix, February 1818 (by Ugo Foscolo and others), and the *Quarterly Review*, li, March 1834 (by H. N. Coleridge); P. Toynbee, *Dante in English Literature from Chaucer to Cary*, 2 vols., 1909; P. Toynbee, 'The Centenary of Cary's Dante', *MLR* vii, 1912; A. Farinelli, 'Dante in Inghilterra', in *Dante in Spagna, Francia, &c.*, Turin, 1922; V. Cenami, *La Divina Commedia nelle traduzioni di Longfellow e di Cary*, Lucca, 1933; and S. Roscoe, 'Cary: "Dante"', *Book Collector*, ii, 1953. In the *TLS* for 3 May 1934 J. L. Lowes wrote briefly on '"La Belle Dame sans Merci" and Dante', and on 19 August 1944 W. M. Parker wrote on the centenary of Cary's death.

JOHN CLARE, 1793–1864.

Clare published four collections of poetry: *Poems Descriptive of Rural Life and Scenery* (1820, 4th ed., 1821); *The Village Minstrel and other Poems*, 2 vols. (1821); *The Shepherd's Calendar; with Village Stories, and other Poems* (1827); and *The Rural Muse, Poems* (1835). Throughout his life he contributed numerous poems to periodicals and annuals, some of them still uncollected. The *Life and Remains*, by J. L. Cherry, appeared in 1873. N. Gale published *Poems by John Clare* at Rugby in 1901, and another volume of selections was produced by Arthur Symons in 1908. More important were *John Clare: Poems Chiefly from Manuscript*, ed. E. Blunden and A. Porter, 1920, and *Madrigals and Chronicles*, ed. E. Blunden, 1924. In 1935 J. W. Tibble produced much the fullest edition of Clare, *The Poems*, in 2 vols., although even this omits many of the poems which Clare himself published and is unsatisfactory in other respects. Geoffrey Grigson's *Poems of John Clare's Madness* (1949) prints some poems from the manuscript for the first time and has a notable introduction. Grigson also edited *Selected Poems* (Muses' Library, 1950). J. Reeves edited a volume of selections in 1954. *Sketches in the Life of John Clare Written by Himself*, ed. E. Blunden, appeared in 1931. J. W. and Anne Tibble edited *The Prose of John Clare* (1951) and *The Letters* (1951).

The first biography was F. Martin's *Life of John Clare* (1865). In 1932 J. W. and Anne Tibble produced *John Clare: A Life*, superseded by their own briefer *John Clare: His Life and Poetry* (1956). J. Wilson's *Green Shadows: The Life of Clare* (1951) is of little independent value. There is still no satisfactory biography.

See also *Four Letters from the Rev. W. Allen, to the Rt. Hon. Lord Radstock . . . on the Poems of John Clare* (1824); De Quincey, *London Reminiscences* (*Collected Writings*, ed. Masson, vol. iii, 1890); *The John Clare Centenary Exhibition Catalogue* [ed. C. Dack and J. W. Bodger], Peterborough, 1893; J. Middleton Murry, 'The Poetry of John Clare', in *Countries of the Mind*, first series, 1922 (revised edition, 1931); J. Heath-Stubbs, 'Clare and the Peasant Tradition', in *The Darkling Plain*, 1950; 'Some Unpublished Poetical Manuscripts of John Clare', by A. J. V. Chapple, *Yale University Library Gazette*, vol. 31 (July 1956); E. Robinson and G. Summerfield, 'John Clare: An Interpretation of Certain Asylum Letters', *RES*, new series, vol. xiii, May 1962; and I. Jack, 'The Sanity of John Clare', in a collection of essays on this period to be edited by J. E. Jordan, Northrop Frye, and J. V. Logan.

William Cobbett, ? 1763–1835.

Cobbett wrote, translated, edited, and published so much, often anonymously, that the bibliography of his writings is extremely complicated. Much guidance is provided by M. L. Pearl's *William Cobbett: A Bibliographical Account of his Life and Times*, 1953, although Pearl is not invariably to be relied on. Here only a few of Cobbett's principal writings can be listed, with drastically abbreviated titles: *Observations on the Emigration of Dr. Joseph Priestley*, Philadelphia, 1794; *A Bone to Gnaw for the Democrats*, 2 parts, Philadelphia, 1795; *A Kick for a Bite*, Philadelphia, 1795; *Le Tuteur Anglais, ou Grammaire . . . de la Langue Anglaise*, Philadelphia, 1795; *A Little Plain English addressed to the People of the United States*, Philadelphia, 1795; *A New Year's Gift to the Democrats*, Philadelphia, 1796; *The Bloody Buoy* (an account of atrocities in France), Philadelphia, 1796; *The Political Censor or Monthly Review of . . . Political Occurrences, Relative to the United States of America*, Philadelphia, 1796–7 (the first number was entitled *A Prospect from the Congress Gallery*: several articles were reprinted separately); *The Life and Adventures of*

*Peter Porcupine*, Philadelphia, 1796; *Porcupine's Gazette*, 4 March 1797–13 January 1800 (edited by Cobbett and mainly published in Philadelphia: much material was reprinted in pamphlet form); *The Democratic Judge*, Philadelphia, 1798 (London, 1798, as *The Republican Judge*: this work is Cobbett's account of his trial for an alleged libel against the King of Spain); *Detection of a Conspiracy . . .* [against] *. . . the United States of America*, Philadelphia, 1798; *The Trial of Republicanism*, Philadelphia, 1799; *The Rush-Light*, 6 numbers, 1800 (the first 5 published at New York, and the 6th at London: the London edition was entitled *The American Rush-Light*); *The Porcupine*, 1800–1 (a daily newspaper); *A Collection of Facts and Observations, relative to the Peace with Bonaparte*, 1801 (mostly reprinted from *The Porcupine*); *Letters to the Right Honourable Lord Hawkesbury, and . . . Henry Addington . . .*, 1802; *Cobbett's Political Register*, 1802–35 (a weekly periodical, after the first two numbers, of which the title varied slightly from time to time. From 12 September 1810 to 22 June 1811 it appeared twice a week). Cobbett and others reprinted a great deal from this work, including most of the following titles: *Letters on the Late War between the United States and Great Britain*, 1815; *Paper against Gold*, 2 vols., 1815; *To the Journeymen and Labourers of England, Wales, Scotland and Ireland*, 1816; *Cobbett's New Year's Gift to Old George Rose*, Nottingham, 1817; *A Year's Residence in the United States of America*, 3 parts, New York, 1818–19; *A Grammar of the English Language*, New York, 1818; *Cobbett's Evening Post*, 29 January–1 April 1820 (a daily paper edited by Cobbett); *Cobbett's Parliamentary Register* (a periodical edited by Cobbett from 6 May to December 1820); *Cobbett's Sermons*, 12 monthly parts, 1821–2 (the first 3 were entitled *Cobbett's Monthly Religious Tracts*); *The American Gardener*, 1821; *Cottage Economy*, 1822 (first published in seven monthly parts, 1821–2); *A French Grammar*, 1824; *A History of the Protestant 'Reformation', in England and Ireland* (first published in parts 1824–6: another part was published in 1827); *Big O. and Sir Glory; or, 'Leisure to Laugh'. A Comedy*, 1825; *Cobbett's Poor Man's Friend*, 1826 (first published in parts, some additional parts appearing after 1826); *The Woodlands; or, A Treatise On the preparing of ground for planting*, '1825' (actually 1828: first published in parts); *The English Gardener*, 1828 (a revised form of *The American Gardener*); *A Treatise on Cobbett's Corn*, 1828; and *The Emigrant's Guide*, 1829.

The first collection of *Rural Rides*, reprinted from the *Political Register*, 1821–6, appeared in 1830. Later editions contained further *Rides*. Later publications included: *Advice to Young Men and (incidentally) to Young Women*, '1829' (actually 1830: first issued in parts); *Eleven Lectures on the French and Belgian Revolutions, and English Boroughmongering*, 1830 (first published in parts); *History of the Regency and Reign of King George the Fourth*, 1830 (first published in parts); *Cobbett's Two-Penny Trash; or, Politics for the Poor*, 2 vols., 1831–2 (partly reprinted from the *Political Register*, and first published in parts); *A Spelling Book*, 1831; *Cobbett's Manchester Lectures, in Support of . . . Reform*, 1832; *A Geographical Dictionary of England and Wales*, 1832; *Cobbett's Tour in Scotland: and in the Four Northern Counties of England: in the Autumn of the Year 1832*, '1832' (actually 1833); *Cobbett's Legacy to Labourers*, '1834' (actually 1835); and *Cobbett's Legacy to Parsons*, 1835. Mention must also be made of *Cobbett's Parliamentary Debates*, 1804–12, which Cobbett sold to the printer, T. C. Hansard, in the latter year, and which became known as *Hansard's Parliamentary Debates* from 1818. A companion series, *Cobbett's Parliamentary History*, also passed out of Cobbett's hands in 1812, having begun in 1806.

The first collection calling itself *The Works of Peter Porcupine* appeared as early as 1795, in Philadelphia. There were other collections, of which the most notable was *Porcupine's Works*, collected by Cobbett himself, 12 vols., 1801. *Selections from Cobbett's Political Works* were edited with notes by J. M. Cobbett and J. P. Cobbett, in 4 vols. in 1835. *The Last of the Saxons*, ed. E. P. Hood, 1854, is a volume of selections.

There are several later editions of the *Rural Rides*, including those edited by J. P. Cobbett (1853), P. Cobbett (2 vols., 1885), and J. H. Lobban, 1908. The 1957 reprint of the Everyman Edition, in 2 vols., has a brief preface by A. Briggs. The best edition, that of G. D. H. and M. Cole, 3 vols., 1930, includes the *Tour in Scotland* and *Letters from Ireland*. S. E. Buckley edited an abridged version of the *Rural Rides* in 1948. G. D. H. Cole edited *The Life . . . of Peter Porcupine* in 1927, and other works have been reprinted as follows: *A Year's Residence in the United States* . . ., ed. J. Freeman, 1923; *A Grammar of the English Language*, ed. J. P. Cobbett, 1866, ed. A. Ayres, New York, 1888, ed. H. L. Stephen, 1906; *Cobbett's Cottage Economy*, reprinted 1916, ed. G. K. Chesterton, 1926; *A History of the Protestant 'Reformation'*,

ed. F. A. Gasquet, 1896; *Advice to Young Men*, ed. H. Morley, 1887, ed. P. Snowden, 1926, ed. E. E. Fisk, 1930; *Cobbett's Legacy to Labourers*, ed. J. M. Cobbett, 1872; *Cobbett's Legacy to Parsons*, ed. W. Cobbett, jun., 1869; and *A History of the Last Hundred Days of English Freedom*, ed. J. L. Hammond, 1921 (extracted from the *Political Register*, 1817). In 1937 G. D. H. Cole edited *Letters from William Cobbett to Edward Thornton . . . 1797 to 1800*. *The Progress of a Plough-Boy to a Seat in Parliament*, ed. W. Reitzel, 1933, is a useful collection of autobiographical passages from Cobbett's writings, revised in 1947 as *The Autobiography of Cobbett*. See also *Cobbett: Selections*, ed A. M. D. Hughes, 1923, and *The Opinions of Cobbett*, by G. D. H. and M. Cole, 1944.

Throughout his life Cobbett was a centre of controversy: many of the resulting pamphlets are mentioned in Pearl's bibliography. J. M. Cobbett wrote an obituary in the *Political Register*, lxxxviii, 1835. The best modern *Life* is that by G. D. H. Cole, 1927. There were earlier biographies by R. Huish (2 vols., 1836: inaccurate), E. Smith (2 vols., 1879), E. I. Carlyle (1904), T. Smith (1906), and 'Lewis Melville' (L. S. Benjamin, 2 vols., 1913). There are later books by G. K. Chesterton (1925), M. Bowen (*Peter Porcupine*, 1935), and W. B. Pemberton (1949, Penguin). On the date of his birth see A. Booth, *TLS*, 16 February, 1962.

Hazlitt wrote on Cobbett in *Table-Talk*, i, 1821, the essay being transferred to the 2nd ed. of *The Spirit of the Age*. There are also essays or chapters in the following books: *Galleries of Literary Portraits*, ii, by G. Gilfillan, 1857; *Political Characters*, ii, by Sir H. L. Bulwer, 1868; *Historical Gleanings*, by J. E. T. Rogers, 1869; *Horae Sabbaticae*, iii, by Sir J. F. Stephen, 1892; *English Portraits and Essays*, by J. Freeman, 1924; *Pioneers of Reform. Cobbett, Owen, Place*, by D. C. Johnson, 1925; *Collected Essays*, i, by G. Saintsbury, 1925; and *Votive Tablets*, by E. Blunden, 1931. The comparative scarcity of articles in learned periodicals emphasizes the need for a more scholarly approach to Cobbett's life and work. L. Woolf wrote on 'An Englishman' in the *Nation*, 25 August, 1923; E. Sellers on 'Cobbett on Choosing a Wife' in the *Contemporary Review*, cxxxiii, 1928; J. Beresford on 'Cobbett and the Reverend Beresford' in the *TLS*, 29 January 1931; H. H. Bellot on the sources of the *Parliamentary History* in the *Bulletin of the Institute of Historical Research*, x, 1932–3; and W. Reitzel on 'Cobbett and Philadelphia Journalism, 1794–1800', in the *Pennsylvania Magazine*, lix, 1935. Also see Raymond

Williams, *Culture and Society 1780–1950*, 1958. On the date of Cobbett's birth see a letter by A. Booth, *TLS*, 16 February 1962.

HARTLEY COLERIDGE, 1796–1849.

Hartley Coleridge published *Poems. Vol. i* (all published) in Leeds in 1833 (a book reissued as *Poems, Songs and Sonnets*); *Biographia Borealis; or Lives of Distinguished Northerns*, Leeds, 1833 (3 vols., 1852, as *Lives of Northern Worthies; Lives of Illustrious Worthies of Yorkshire* is part of the same work re-issued at Hull in 1835 with a new title-page); and *The Dramatic Works of Massinger and Ford, with an Introduction by Hartley Coleridge*, 1840.

His brother, Derwent Coleridge, edited his *Poems*, with a Memoir in 2 vols. in 1851 and his *Essays and Marginalia*, also in 2 vols., in the same year. R. Colles produced *The Complete Poetical Works* in 1908 (n.d., Muses' Library). J. Drinkwater edited his *Essays on Parties in Poetry and on the Character of Hamlet* (from the *Essays and Marginalia*) in 1925. G. E. and E. L. Griggs edited his *Letters* in 1937, while E. L. Griggs also produced *New Poems, including a Selection from his Published Poetry* in 1942. The standard books are those by E. L. Griggs (*Hartley Coleridge: His Life and Work*, 1929) and H. Hartman (*Hartley Coleridge, Poet's Son and Poet*, 1931). There are useful studies of Hartley Coleridge in R. H. Horne, *A New Spirit of the Age*, vol. i, 1844; W. Bagehot, *Literary Studies*, vol. i. 1879; A. M. Turner, 'Wordsworth and Hartley Coleridge', *JEGP* xxii, 1923; M. J. Pomeroy, *The Poetry of Hartley Coleridge*, Washington, 1927; S. T. Williams, 'Hartley Coleridge as a Critic of Literature', *Southern Atlantic Quarterly*, xxiii, 1924; four articles by E. L. Griggs, 'Coleridge and his Son', *SP* xxvii, 1930; 'Hartley Coleridge on his Father', *PMLA* xlvi, 1931; 'Hartley Coleridge's Unpublished Correspondence', *London Mercury*, xxiv, 1931; and 'Four Letters of Hartley Coleridge', *HLQ* ix, 1946; E. Blunden, 'Coleridge the Less' (in *Votive Tablets*, 1931); and J. D. Rea, 'Hartley Coleridge and Wordsworth's Lucy', *SP* xxviii, 1931. One of his numerous unprinted poems was published in the *TLS* by A. S. Whitefield, 15 March 1947.

WILLIAM COMBE, 1741–1823.

A great many of Combe's volumes of verse belong to the later eighteenth century. Here we are concerned only with *Dr. Syntax* and his later publications. *The Tour of Dr. Syntax in Search of the Picturesque* was first published in Ackermann's

*Poetical Magazine* in 1809 as 'The Schoolmaster's Tour'. It appeared as a volume in 1812 and other editions followed quickly. *The Second Tour of Dr. Syntax. In Search of Consolation* came out in 1820 (having first been issued in monthly parts). *The Third Tour of Dr. Syntax in Search of a Wife* appeared in 1821. Each of the three had coloured plates by Rowlandson. *The Three Tours of Dr. Syntax* were collected in 3 vols. in 1826, and there were several later editions.

In verse Combe also published *Six Poems. Illustrative of Engravings by H.R.H. the Princess Elizabeth*, 1813; *Poetical Sketches of Scarborough*, 1813; *The English Dance of Death from the Designs of Thomas Rowlandson with Metrical Illustrations*, 2 vols., 1815; *The Dance of Life*, 1816–17; and *The History of Johnny Quae Genus the Little Foundling of the late Dr. Syntax*, 1822 (first issued in monthly parts). The verse-portions of *The Forget-me-not* for 1823 are by Combe, who also published numerous books in prose, most of them in the eighteenth century.

On Combe see H. W. Hamilton, *William Combe*, Ithaca, 1935; H. Fluchère, 'Sterne et Combe', *Revue Anglo-américaine*, viii, 1931; L. P. Curtis, 'Forged Letters of Laurence Sterne', *PMLA* l (50), 1935; F. Montgomery, 'Alexander Mackenzie's Literary Assistant', *Canadian Historical Review*, xviii, 1937; and the same writer's note on 'The Birth and Parentage of Combe', *NQ*, 12 April 1941; and 'William Combe', *TLS*, 19 July 1941. The article in the *DNB* is still helpful. A great deal of Combe's work was done for Rudolph Ackermann.

John Wilson Croker, 1780–1857.

Croker's poems include: *Familiar Epistles . . . on the Present State of the Irish Stage*, Dublin, 1804; *An Intercepted Letter from J— T—, . . . at Canton*, Dublin, 1804; and *The Battles of Talavera*, Dublin, 1809 (often reprinted, in 1812 with *Other Poems*).

Croker's most important writings were in the *Quarterly Review*. M. F. Brightfield's biography lists more than 250 contributions. Several of his articles were reprinted, often in revised form: for example, his *Robespierre*, 1835, his *History of the Guillotine*, 1853, and his *Essays on the Early Period of the French Revolution*, 1857. He also published two children's books and a number of important speeches and writings on political questions. More relevant to us is his editing of Boswell's *Life of Samuel Johnson*, 5 vols., 1831, a labour of love to which subsequent editors have

been indebted. He also edited a number of historical memoirs. His *Correspondence with the Rt. Hon. Lord John Russell on Some Passages of Moore's Diary* appeared in 1854. *An Essay towards a new edition of Pope's works* was privately printed in 1871, the year that the first volume of the Elwin–Courthope edition appeared, with its acknowledgement on the title-page that the 'new materials' had been 'collected in part by the late Rt. Hon. John Wilson Croker'.

*The Croker Papers: The Correspondence and Diaries* were edited with a memoir by L. J. Jennings in 3 vols. in 1884 (revised edition, 1885). Macaulay's severe (and unfair) review of the *Boswell* was reprinted in his *Critical and Historical Essays*, 3 vols., 1843. There is an article on Croker in the *Quarterly Review* for October 1884, and an incisive little portrait by K. Feiling in *Sketches in Nineteenth Century Biography*, 1930. The standard modern study is M. F. Brightfield's *John Wilson Croker*, 1940. Notes on Croker and Tennyson appeared in the *TLS* for 30 November 1946, 14 and 21 December 1946, and 18 January 1947, and a communication on 'Croker's Pettifoggery' on 25 August 1950.

ALLAN CUNNINGHAM, 1784–1842.

Cunningham wrote romances and poems as well as editing Burns and collecting Scottish songs and stories. The date of *The Magic Bridle* may be *c.* 1812; *Songs, chiefly in the Rural Language of Scotland* appeared in 1813; *Sir Marmaduke Maxwell, A Dramatic Poem* (with other poems and songs) in 1822; *Traditional Tales of the English and Scottish Peasantry* in 2 vols. in 1822 (all but one Tale had previously appeared in the *London Magazine*: the book was edited by H. Morley, without the interesting preface, 1887); and *The Songs of Scotland, Ancient and Modern* in 4 vols. in 1825. Cunningham also wrote two romances, *Paul Jones* and *Sir Michael Scott*, each in 3 vols., in 1826 and 1828; *Lives of the Most Emiment British Painters, Sculptors and Architects*, 6 vols., 1829–33 (selections were edited by W. Sharp in 1886); *The Maid of Elvar, A Poem in Twelve Parts*, 1833; *The Cabinet Gallery of Pictures . . . with Biographical and Critical Descriptions*, 2 vols., 1833–4; *Biographical and Critical History of the British Literature of the Last Fifty Years* (Paris, 1834: first published in the *Athenaeum*); *Lord Roldan, A Romance*, 3 vols., 1836; and *The Life of Sir David Wilkie* [ed. P. Cunningham], 3 vols., 1843. In 1841

Cunningham edited Thomson's *Seasons* and *Castle of Indolence. Poems and Songs*, ed. P. Cunningham, appeared in 1847.

Mention should also be made of Cunningham's work on Burns. In 1826 he contributed 'Last Moments of Robert Burns' to *The Curious Book* (Edinburgh). In 1834 there appeared *The Works of Robert Burns* with a biography by Cunningham in the first of the eight volumes.

Cunningham was one of the *London Magazine* group: many of his contributions were subsequently reprinted in his separate publications. He also edited *The Anniversary* for some years and contributed to *The Club Book*, edited by Andrew Picken, 3 vols., 1831, and many other periodicals.

A *Life of Allan Cunningham, with Selections from his Works and Correspondence* was published by David Hogg at Dumfries in 1875. Reminiscences of him may be found in De Quincey's *London Reminiscences* (*Collected Writings*, ed. Masson, vol. iii, 1890), and in the work of other members of the London group. See also G. Gilfillan, *Galleries of Literary Portraits*, vol. i, 1856; S. C. Hall, 'Allan Cunningham', *Art Journal*, xviii, 1866; *TLS*, 31 October 1942; and L. A. Marchand, *The Athenaeum: A Mirror of Victorian Culture*, Chapel Hill, 1941.

GEORGE DARLEY, 1795–1846.

Darley published two volumes of verse and two verse-plays: *The Errors of Ecstasie* (1822); *Sylvia; or, The May Queen* (1827); *Thomas à Becket* (1840) and *Ethelstan; or, The Battle of Brunanburh* (1841). *Nepenthe* was privately printed in 1835. He also published *The Labours of Idleness, or, Seven Nights' Entertainments* ('By Guy Penseval'), 1826; a number of mathematical textbooks; *The New Sketch Book* ('by G. Crayon, Jun.', 2 vols., 1829); and *The Works of Beaumont and Fletcher*, with an introduction, 2 vols., 1840. A volume of selections, *Poems*, was published at Liverpool in [1889] for private circulation and contains the first printing of 'Lenimina Laborum'. R. A. Streatfeild produced *Selections* in 1904, and R. Colles, *The Complete Poetical Works* in 1908 (n.d. Muses' Library edition). Professor C. C. Abbott is preparing a new edition for the Muses' Library. There is a reprint of *Sylvia*, ed. J. H. Ingram, 1892, and one of *Nepenthe*, ed. R. A. Streatfeild, 1897.

Darley contributed to a number of annuals and periodicals, including the *London Magazine* (which contains his 'Letters to the Dramatists of the Day', by 'John Lacy'), the *Athenaeum*, and

*Bentley's Miscellany* (1844). The standard biography is *The Life and Letters*, by C. C. Abbott, 1928, which contains a fuller bibliography. See also E. Blunden (in *Votive Tablets*, 1931); R. Bridges (in *Collected Essays*, v, 1931 (written 1906)); L. Wolff ('George Darley, poète et critique d'art', *Revue Anglo-américaine*, Feb. 1931); C. C. Abbott ('The Letters of Darley', *Durham University Journal*, xxxiii, 1940); J. Heath-Stubbs in *The Darkling Plain*, 1950; and 'Uncollected Authors, No. 28' by C. Woolf, in *The Book Collector*, Summer 1961. For the dating of the memorial *Poems* as [1889] instead of [1890] see the notice of Woolf's article in the *TLS*.

Thomas De Quincey, 1785–1859.

The greater part of De Quincey's writings first appeared in periodicals. The only books that he published were *Confessions of an English Opium-Eater*, 1822 (reprinted from the *London Magazine*, September and October 1821, with an appendix added: for the 1856 text see below); *Walladmor. A Novel. Freely translated from the English of Sir Walter Scott, and now freely translated from the German into English*, 2 vols., 1825 (De Quincey made a very free rendering indeed of this German forgery); *Klosterheim, or the Masque*, 1832; and *The Logic of Political Economy*, 1844.

He also contributed to the following books: *Juvenile Library*, i, 1800 (trans. of Horace, Ode 22, Lib. 1); *Concerning the Relations of Great Britain, Spain and Portugal . . .*, 1809 (Wordsworth's 'Tract on the Convention of Cintra': contains an appendix by De Quincey on the letters of Sir J. Moore); *Popular Tales and Romances of the Northern Nations*, 3 vols., 1823 (De Quincey contributed 'The Fatal Marksman', trans. from the German of J. A. Apel); *The Gallery of Portraits*, ed. A. T. Malkin, 7 vols., 1832–7 (De Quincey contributed a Life of Milton to vol. i); *Encyclopaedia Britannica*, 7th ed., 1827–42 (De Quincey wrote on Goethe, Pope, Schiller, and Shakespeare).

There is no absolutely complete edition of De Quincey's writings, and there may never be. But numerous attempts have been made to collect his contributions to the *London Magazine*, *Blackwood's Magazine*, *Tait's Magazine*, *Hogg's Instructor*, and the numerous other periodicals for which he wrote. The American publishers Ticknor and Fields published *De Quincey's Writings* in 24 vols. at Boston in 1851–9. *Selections Grave and Gav from . . . Thomas De Quincey*, published by James Hogg (not the Ettrick

Shepherd) in 14 vols. in 1853–60 is a collected edition of his writings revised by De Quincey himself. The later and much longer text of the *Confessions* first appeared as vol. v of this edition. Of later attempts at collected editions much the most important is that edited by David Masson in 14 vols. (1889–90). Although it is unsatisfactory in many ways, this is still regarded as the standard edition. It contains prefaces, notes, and an index.

Other writings of De Quincey's have been reprinted in *The Uncollected Writings*, ed. James Hogg, 2 vols., 1890; *The Posthumous Works*, ed. A. H. Japp, 2 vols., 1891–3; *A Diary of Thomas De Quincey, 1803*, edited, with manuscript facsimile, by H. A. Eaton, [1927]; and *Niels Klim, being an Incomplete Translation, by Thomas De Quincey, from the Danish*, ed. S. Musgrove (Auckland, N.Z., 1953).

Many letters may be found in Japp's biography (below), in *De Quincey Memorials. Being Letters and other Records*, ed. A. H. Japp, 2 vols., 1891; in *De Quincey at Work: As Seen in One Hundred and Thirty . . . Letters*, ed. W. H. Bonner, Buffalo, 1936; in 'Some Unpublished Letters of Thomas De Quincey', by E. H. Moore, *RES* ix, 1933; and in *De Quincey to Wordsworth: A Biography of a Relationship*, by J. E. Jordan, Berkeley and Los Angeles, 1962, which contains De Quincey's letters to the Wordsworth family.

The bibliography by J. E. Jordan in *ERPE* gives further information about De Quincey manuscripts and scattered writings reprinted in various places.

The original text of the *Confessions* has been reprinted on several occasions: ed. R. Garnett, 1885 (with 'Notes of Conversations with Thomas De Quincey', by R. Woodhouse); ed. G. Saintsbury, 1928; ed. E. Sackville-West, 1950; and ed. M. Elwin, 1956 (both versions, with a useful introduction and the *Blackwood's* text of the *Suspiria*). The 1856 text has been frequently reprinted. The Everyman's Library edition has an Introduction by J. E. Jordan.

There are various volumes of selections. *De Quincey's Literary Criticism*, ed. H[elen] Darbishire, 1909, is of particular interest. *Recollections of the Lake Poets* were edited by E. Sackville-West in 1948 and by J. E. Jordan in 1961 (Everyman's Library, as *Reminiscences of the English Lake Poets*).

It is impossible to mention all the books of the period which contain information about De Quincey: they include books by, and about, Wordsworth, Carlyle, John Wilson, Crabb

Robinson, R. P. Gillies, and Charles Knight. James Hogg's *De Quincey and his Friends: Personal Recollections, Souvenirs and Anecdotes*, 1895, is a useful collection. The first full biography, which is still of interest, is *Thomas De Quincey: His Life and Writings. With Unpublished Correspondence*, by A. H. Japp, 2 vols., 1877 (rev. ed., 1 vol., 1890). D. Masson's volume in the English Men of Letters series, 1881, leans heavily on Japp. Of more recent biographies and book-length studies the best are: *A Flame in Sunlight*, by E. Sackville West, 1936; *Thomas De Quincey*, by H. A. Eaton, 1936; and *De Quincey to Wordsworth*, by J. E. Jordan, as mentioned above.

Other books wholly or partly about De Quincey include *De Quincey*, by H. S. Salt, 1904 (see also his *Literary Sketches*, 1888); *De Quincey's Editorship of the Westmorland Gazette, with Selections . . .*, by C. Pollitt, 1890; *Thomas De Quincey. A Study*, by R. Hitchcock, 1899; *Thomas De Quincey's Relation to German Literature and Philosophy*, by W. A. Dunn, Strasburg, 1900; *The Prose Poetry of Thomas De Quincey*, by L. Cooper, Leipzig, 1902; *Étude médico-psychologique sur Thomas De Quincey*, by P. Guerrier, Lyons, 1907 (a book which contains information about French translations, and about nineteenth-century studies of opium); *Rydal*, by M. L. Armitt, 1916; *Immanuel Kant in England (1793–1838)*, by R. Wellek, Princeton, 1931; *Baudelaire and De Quincey*, by G. T. Clapton, 1931; *The Milk of Paradise. The Effect of Opium Visions on . . . De Quincey, Crabbe, Francis Thompson, and Coleridge*, by M. H. Abrams, Cambridge, Mass., 1934; *Grands névropathes*, by A. Cabanès, 1935; *Geschichtliches und religiöses Denken bei De Quincey*, by E. T. Sehrt (*Neue Deutsche Forschungen* CIII, Berlin, 1936); *Thomas De Quincey's Theory of Literature*, by S. K. Proctor, Ann Arbor, 1943 (with an appendix on De Quincey scholarship by C. D. Thorpe); *Thomas De Quincey, Literary Critic*, by J. E. Jordan, Berkeley, 1952; and *Rhythm in the Prose of Thomas De Quincey*, by S. Kobayashi, 1956.

The French have always been interested in De Quincey. In 1828 de Musset produced a fictionalized version of the *Confessions*, *L'anglais mangeur d'opium*, while in 1860 Baudelaire wrote penetratingly about De Quincey in *Les paradis artificiels, opium et haschisch*, including passages of translation.

The following include some of the more important essays and articles: 'Life and Writings of Thomas De Quincey', by H. W. S., *Fraser's Magazine*, 1860–1; review of *Selections, Grave and Gay*,

[by T. E. Kebbel], *Quarterly Review*, cx, 1861; 'De Quincey', by Sir Leslie Stephen, in *Hours in a Library*, i, 1874; *Studies in Prose and Verse*, by A. Symons, 1904; 'De Quincey's Love of Music', by H. A. Eaton, *JEGP*, 1914; 'De Quincey as Literary Critic', by J. H. Fowler, 1922 (Eng. Assoc.); 'The Syntax of De Quincey', by 'Vernon Lee' (Violet Page), in *The Handling of Words*, 1923; *The Romantic Theory of Poetry*, by A. E. Powell, 1926; 'Impassioned Prose', *TLS*, 16 September 1926; 'De Quincey's Autobiography', in *The Common Reader*, 2nd series, by Virginia Woolf, 1932; 'The Musical Structure of De Quincey's *Dream-Fugue*', by C. S. Brown, *Musical Quarterly*, 1938; ' "Libellous Attack" on De Quincey', by K. Forward, *PMLA* lii, 1937, and 'De Quincey's "Cessio Bonorum" ', by the same scholar, *PMLA* liv, 1939; 'De Quincey's Status in the History of Ideas', by R. Wellek, *PQ* xxiii, 1944; 'De Quincey's Use of Americanisms', by R. E. Hollinger, *American Speech*, 1948; '*Walladmor*: A Pseudo-Translation of Scott', by L. H. C. Thomas, *MLR*, xlvi, 1951; 'De Quincey on Wordsworth's Theory of Diction', by J. E. Jordan, *PMLA* lxviii, 1953; the same writer's earlier 'De Quincey's Dramaturgic Criticisms', *ELH* xviii, 1951; 'De Quincey and the Ending of *Moby-Dick*', by F. S. Rockwell, *Nineteenth-Century Fiction*, 1954; 'Some Unpublished Works of De Quincey', by R. H. Byrns, *PMLA* lxxi, 1956; and 'De Quincey Revises his *Confessions*', by I. Jack, *PMLA* lxxii, 1957.

See also 'How De Quincey Worked', by E. Dowden, *Saturday Review*, lxxix, 1895; 'The Letters of De Quincey to Wordsworth, 1803–7', by H. A. Eaton, *ELH* iii, 1936; 'The Depreciation of De Quincey', by H. S. Salt, *National Review*, cxliii, 1928; 'Coleridge, De Quincey, and Nineteenth-Century Editing', by E. L. Griggs, *MLN* xlvii, 1932; 'The Woes of Thomas De Quincey', by C. O. Parsons, *RES* x, 1934; 'Thomas De Quincey, mystique et symboliste', by G.-A. Astre, *La revue hebdomadaire*, 23 October 1937, and the same writer's essay on Balzac and De Quincey, *Revue de la littérature comparée*, December 1935; 'Is Thomas De Quincey Author of *The Love-Charm?*', by H. K. Galinsky, *MLN* lii, 1937; 'Wordsworth and De Quincey in Westmorland Politics, 1818', by J. E. Wells, *PMLA* lv, 1940, and 'De Quincey and *The Prelude* in 1839', by the same writer, *PQ* xx, 1941; 'Some De Quincey Manuscripts', by C. E. Jones, *ELH* viii, 1941; 'De Quincey, Symptomatologist', *PMLA* lx, 1945, by C. H. Hendricks; and 'Berlioz, Musset

and De Quincey', by J.-G. Prud'homme, *Musical Quarterly*, xxxii, 1946.

Bibliographical information may be found in an appendix to Masson's edition, in *Thomas De Quincey: A Bibliography based upon the De Quincey Collection in the Moss Side Library*, by J. A. Green, 1908 (supplemented by W. E. A. Axon in 'The Canon of De Quincey's Writings . . .', *Transactions of the Royal Society of Literature*, 1914), in the *CBEL*, and in J. E. Jordan's excellent contribution to *ERPE*.

THOMAS FROGNALL DIBDIN, 1776–1847.

Dibdin's main publications include: *Poems*, 1797; *An Introduction to the Knowledge of Rare and Valuable Editions of the Greek and Latin Classics*, Gloucester, 1802 (revised and enlarged editions, 1804, 1808 (2 vols.) and 1827 (2 vols., 'greatly enlarged')); *The Director. A Weekly Literary Journal*, 2 vols., 1807; *Specimen Bibliothecae Britannicae*, 1808; *The Bibliomania; or Book-Madness*, 1809, 1811 (enlarged edition), 1842 (fuller edition), 1876; *Typographical Antiquities; or the History of Printing in England*, 4 vols., 1810–19 (based on the work of Ames and Herbert); *Bibliotheca Spenceriana: A Descriptive Catalogue of* [rare and early books] *in the Library of Earl Spencer*, 4 vols., 1814–15 (supplemented in *Ædes Althorpianæ* [with a] *Supplement to the Bibliotheca Spenceriana*, 1822, and the *Catalogue of the Books . . . of the Duke de Cassano Serra*, 1823); *The Bibliographical Decameron*, 3 vols., 1817; *Sermons Doctrinal and Practical*, 2 vols., 1820; *A Bibliographical, Antiquarian and Picturesque Tour in France and Germany*, 3 vols., 1821 (another edition, with omissions and additions, 3 vols., 1829); *The Museum*, 27 April 1822–14 February 1824 (from 1823, *The Literary Museum*); *The Library Companion: or, The Young Man's Guide, and The Old Man's Comfort, in the Choice of a Library, Vol. I* (all published), 1824 (2nd ed., 1825); *The Sunday Library: A Selection of Sermons from Eminent Divines*, 6 vols., 1831; *Bibliophobia: Remarks on the Present Languid . . . State of Literature and the Book Trade*, 1832; *Reminiscences of a Literary Life*, 2 vols., 1836; *Roxburghe Revels . . . including Answers to the Attack on the Memory of Joseph Haslewood*, privately printed, 1837; *A Bibliographical Antiquarian and Picturesque Tour in the Northern Counties of England and in Scotland*, 2 vols., 1838 (also in 3 vols., another format); and *Cranmer* (a novel), 3 vols., 1839. *Bibliography, A Poem*, 1812, was privately printed. Dibdin also edited numerous books and pamphlets for

the Roxburghe Club. Information about him may be found in the *DNB* and in *The Bibliographer's Manual*, by W. T. Lowndes, rev. ed., vol. ii, part i, 1858.

Isaac D'Israeli, 1766–1848.

His main publications were *A Defence of Poetry* [and] *Specimens of a New Version of Telemachus*, 1790; *Curiosities of Literature*, 3 vols., 1791, 1793, 1817 (a Second Series, in 3 vols., appeared in 1823: the 9th edition, in 6 vols., included both Series); *Eighty-Nine Fugitive Fables*, 1792; *A Dissertation on Anecdotes*, 1793; *Domestic Anecdotes of the French Nation*, 1794; *An Essay on the Literary Character*, 1795 (enlarged and revised editions in 1818, 1822, and 1828); *Miscellanies; Or, Literary Recreations*, 1796 (*Literary Miscellanies*, 2nd edition, with 2nd edition of *A Dissertation on Anecdotes*, 1801); *Vaurien*, 2 vols., 1797 (a novel); *Romances*, 1799 (revised editions, 1801 and 1807); *Narrative Poems*, 1803; *Flim-Flams!*, 3 vols., 1805 (a novel); *An Apology for Flim-Flams*, 1806; *Despotism*, 2 vols., 1811 (a novel); *Calamities of Authors*, 2 vols., 1812; *Quarrels of Authors*, 3 vols., 1814; *An Inquiry into the Character of James I*, 1816; *Psyche*, [? 1823]; *Commentaries on the Life and Reign of Charles I*, 5 vols., 1828–31 (revised edition, 2 vols., 1851); *Eliot, Hampden, and Pym*, 1832; *The Genius of Judaism*, 1833; *The Illustrator Illustrated*, 1838; and *Amenities of Literature*, 2 vols., 1841. *A Letter from I. D'Israeli to C. P. Cooper* was privately printed in 1857.

A partial collection of his writings on literary history appeared as *Miscellanies of Literature* in one huge volume in 1840. *The Works*, edited by his son, first appeared in 7 vols. in 1859, including *Curiosities*, *Amenities*, *The Literary Character*, *Literary Miscellanies*, *James I*, *Calamities*, and *Quarrels*. His 'Unpublished Notes on the Romantic Poets' were published by C. L. Cline in *Texas Studies in English* in 1941.

There are numerous references to Isaac D'Israeli in the literature of his age. Benjamin Disraeli wrote a memoir of his father for the 1849 edition of the *Curiosities* which was also prefixed to *The Works*. Information may also be found in the *DNB*, in Monypenny and Buckle's *Life of Benjamin Disraeli*, 2 vols., 1929 (rev. ed.), and in other works on the statesman. Sarah Kopstein's German study, *Isaac D'Israeli*, Jerusalem, 1939, does not add very much. There is a good unpublished thesis by James Ogden (Oxford, 1961), now being rewritten as a book.

Recent information has been provided by C. L. Cline in 'The Correspondence of Robert Southey and D'Israeli', *RES* xvii, 1941; by G. K. Anderson in 'D'Israeli's "Amenities of Literature": A Centennial Review', *PQ* xxii, 1943; and by W. S. Samuel in 'D'Israeli: First Published Writings', *NQ*, 30 April 1949.

JOHN COLIN DUNLOP, d. 1842.

Dunlop published *The History of Fiction . . . from the Earliest Greek Romances to the Novels of the Present Age* in 3 vols. in 1814. There was a revised edition, also in 3 vols., two years later, and the work was translated into German in 1851. There is also an edition revised and edited by H. Wilson, 2 vols., 1888. Dunlop's *History of Roman Literature from its Earliest Period to the Augustan Age* appeared in 3 vols. in 1823–8: his *Memoirs of Spain . . . from 1621 to 1700* in 2 vols. in 1834: and his *Selections from the Latin Anthology, Translated into English Verse* in 1838.

EBENEZER ELLIOTT, 1781–1849.

Elliott's (mostly indifferent) earlier poetry includes *The Vernal Walk*, 1801; *Night*, 1818; *Love*, 1823; and *The Village Patriarch*, 1829. His *Corn-Law Rhymes* appeared in 1831 and went through several editions. *The Splendid Village; Corn-Law Rhymes; and Other Poems* appeared in 3 vols. in 1833–5, and his *Poetical Works* in 1840 and then in 3 vols. in 1844. In 1876 they were edited by E. Elliott, in 2 vols. *More Verse and Prose by the Corn-Law Rhymer* was published in 2 vols. in 1850.

*The Life, Poetry, and Letters of Ebenezer Elliott*, ed. John Watkins, 1850, includes a brief autobiographical sketch. See also the *Edinburgh Review*, lv, 1832 (reprinted in *Critical and Miscellaneous Essays of Thomas Carlyle*, 1839); *Blackwood's Magazine*, xxxv, 1834 (repr. in *The Works of John Wilson*, vi, 1856); 'J. Searle' (G. S. Phillips), *The Life of Ebenezer Elliott*, 1850; J. W. King, *Ebenezer Elliott, A Sketch*, Sheffield, 1854; W. Odom, *Two Sheffield Poets: James Montgomery and Ebenezer Elliott*, [1929]; G. L. Phillips, 'Elliott's "The Giaour" ', *RES* xv, 1939; E. R. Seary, 'Robert Southey and Ebenezer Elliott', *RES* xv, 1939; A. A. Eaglestone, E. R. Seary, and G. L. Phillips, *Ebenezer Elliott: A Commemorative Brochure with Bibliography*, Sheffield, 1949; J. B. Hobman, 'Ebenezer Elliott, Corn Law Rhymer', *Contemporary Review*, clxxvi, 1949; 'Corn-law Rhymer', *TLS*, 2 December 1949; and

A. Briggs, 'Ebenezer Elliott, the Corn Law Rhymer', *Cambridge Journal*, iii, 1950.

SUSAN EDMONSTONE FERRIER, 1782–1854.

She published three novels, *Marriage*, 3 vols., 1818; *The Inheritance*, 3 vols., 1824; and *Destiny, or, The Chief's Daughter*, 3 vols., 1831. Her novels were republished in 6 vols. in 1882 and in 6 vols. in 1894, ed. R. B. Johnson. They were edited with an introduction by Lady Margaret Sackville in 4 vols. in 1928 as *The Works*, vol. iv being a reissue of the Ferrier–Doyle *Memoir*. There are editions of *Marriage* and *The Inheritance* with biographical prefaces by A. Goodrich-Freer and critical notices by Walter, Earl of Iddesleigh (each in 2 vols.), 1902, 1903.

The *Memoir and Correspondence of Susan Ferrier . . . by her Grand-nephew John Ferrier*, ed. J. A. Doyle, 1898, is the only book. See also 'Noctes Ambrosianae', lviii [by J. G. Lockhart], in *Blackwood's Magazine*, xxx, 1831; *Edinburgh Review*, lxxiv, 1842; 'Miss Ferrier's Novels', *Temple Bar*, liv, 1878; C. J. Hamilton, *Women Writers, their Works and Ways*, Series 1, 1892; Sir G. Douglas, *The Blackwood Group* [1897]; R. B. Johnson, *The Women Novelists* [1918]; and A. Birrell, *More Obiter Dicta*, 1924.

JOHN HOOKHAM FRERE, 1769–1846.

Frere contributed to *The Microcosm*, Eton, 1786–7, and *The Anti-Jacobin*, 1797–8. He also produced the following books: *Prospectus and Specimen of an Intended National Work, by William and Robert Whistlecraft . . . relating to King Arthur and his Round Table*, cantos i–ii, 1817, cantos iii–iv, 1818: as *The Monks and the Giants*, 1818 (ed. R. D. Waller, with a useful introduction on Frere's Italian models, Manchester, 1926); *Fables for Five-Years-Old*, Malta, 1830; *The Frogs*, 1839 (privately printed); *A Metrical Version of the Acharnians, the Knights and the Birds*, 1840 (each play having been privately printed for Frere in Malta the previous year); *Theognis restitutus*, Malta, 1842 (privately printed); and *Psalms, &c.*, [? 1848]—verse paraphrases. His Etonian metrical version of the 'Ode on Athelstan's Victory' was printed in the 2nd edition of Ellis's *Specimens of the Early English Poets*, vol. i, 1801, and three of his passages of translation from the 'Poem of the Cid' were printed as an appendix to Southey's *Chronicle of the Cid*, 1808. Although he was one of the original projectors of the *Quarterly Review* his only certain

contribution was the review of Mitchell's translation of Aristophanes in July 1820.

His *Works . . . in Verse and Prose*, with a Memoir by Sir Bartle Frere, appeared in 2 vols. in 1872 and in a revised 3-vol. edition in 1874. See also G. Festing, *John Hookham Frere and his Friends*, 1899, and A. von Eichler, *John Hookham Frere: Sein Leben und seine Werke . . .*, Vienna, 1905.

JOHN GALT, 1779–1839.

Galt published the following principal books: *The Battle of Largs. A Gothic Poem*, 1804; *Voyages and Travels in the Years 1809, 1810 and 1811*, 1812; *The Life and Administration of Cardinal Wolsey*, 1812; *The Tragedies of Maddalen, Agamemnon, Lady Macbeth, Antonia and Clytemnestra*, 1812; *Letters from the Levant*, 1813; *The Majolo*, 2 vols., 1816; *The Crusade* (a poem), 1816; *The Life and Studies of Benjamin West*, Part i, 1816; *The Appeal: A Tragedy*, 1818 (with a prologue by Lockhart and an epilogue by Scott); *The Wandering Jew*, 1820 ('By the Rev. T. Clark'); *The Life, Studies and Works of Benjamin West*, Parts i–ii, 1820; *All the Voyages round the World* ('By Samuel Prior', 1820); *A Tour of Europe and Asia*, 2 vols., 1820 ('By the Rev. T. Clark'); *The Earthquake*, 3 vols., 1820; *George the Third, his Court and Family*, 2 vols., 1820; *Glenfell, or Macdonalds and Campbells*, 1820; *Pictures, Historical and Biographical, drawn from . . . History*, 2 vols., 1821; *The Ayrshire Legatees*, 1821 (*Blackwood's*, Oct. 1820–March 1821); *Annals of the Parish*, 1821; *Sir Andrew Wylie, of That Ilk*, 3 vols., 1822; *The Provost*, 1822; *The Steam-Boat* (*Blackwood's*, 1821), 1822; *The Gathering of the West*, 1823; *The Entail*, 3 vols., 1823; *Ringan Gilhaize*, 3 vols., 1823; *The Spaewife*, 3 vols., 1823; *Rothelan*, 3 vols., 1824 (with three other tales appended in vol. iii); *The Bachelor's Wife . . ., Extracts, with Cursory Observations*, 1824 (an anthology, with dramatized comments); *The Omen*, '1825' (probably 1826); *The Last of the Lairds*, 1826; *Lawrie Todd*, 3 vols., 1830; *Southennan*, 3 vols., 1830; *The Life of Lord Byron*, 1830; *The Lives of the Players*, 2 vols., 1831; *Bogle Corbet*, 3 vols., [1831]; *The Member*, 1832; *The Radical*, 1832 (the two books were also published together the next year as *The Reform*); *Stanley Buxton*, 3 vols., 1832; *The Canadas as they . . . commend themselves to . . . Emigrants . . . from . . . Documents furnished by John Galt* (by Andrew Picken), 1832; *Eben Erskine*, 3 vols., 1833; *Poems*, 1833; *The Stolen Child*, 1833 ('The Library of Romance',

published by Smith, Elder, vol. iv); *The Autobiography of John Galt*, 2 vols., 1833; *Stories of the Study*, 3 vols., 1833; *The Ouranologos, or the Celestial Volume*, 1833 (illustrated by John Martin); *The Literary Life, and Miscellanies, of John Galt*, 3 vols., 1834; *Efforts, By an Invalid*, Greenock, 1835; *A Contribution to the Greenock Calamity Fund*, Greenock, 1835 (poems); and *The Demon of Destiny and Other Poems*, Greenock, 1839. In 1831 he had contributed five tales to *The Club Book*, ed. Andrew Picken (3 vols.)

A fuller list of his writings, including those in periodicals and other collections, may be found in *John Galt*, by Jennie W. Aberdein, 1936. See also the list in the *Autobiography*, and H. Lumsden, 'The Bibliography of John Galt', *Records of Glasgow Bibliographical Society*, ix, 1931, and B. A. Booth, 'A Bibliography of John Galt', *Bulletin of Bibliography*, xvi, 1936.

For discussions of the authorship of 'The Canadian Boat Song' see Lockhart below.

*The Works*, ed. D. S. Meldrum and W. Roughead, 10 vols., 1936, include only the principal novels. Several of the novels have been reprinted more than once, particularly the *Annals of the Parish* (the 1908 reprint has a preface by G. Gordon reprinted in *The Lives of Authors*, 1950). W. Roughead edited *The Howdie and Other Tales* in 1923 and *A Rich Man and Other Stories* in 1925. There are recent editions of *The Life of Benjamin West*, ed. N. Wright, Gainesville, Florida, 1960, and of *The Gathering of the West*, ed. B. A. Booth, Baltimore, 1939.

For early criticism see *Edinburgh Review*, xxxix, Oct. 1823, (reprinted in Jeffrey's *Contributions*, 4 vols., 1844); and A. Cunningham, *Biographical and Critical History of the British Literature of the Last Fifty Years*, Paris, 1834.

There is a valuable Memoir by 'Δ' (D. M. Moir) in *The Annals of the Parish and The Ayrshire Legatees*, n.d. [1841] ('Blackwood's Standard Novels'). There are modern studies by R. K. Gordon (*John Galt*, Toronto, 1920); Jennie W. Aberdein (as above); and E. Frykman (*John Galt's Scottish Stories, 1820–1823*, Uppsala, 1959). F. H. Lyell's *Study of the Novels of John Galt* is an unpublished Princeton dissertation (1942): there is a mimeographed copy in Edinburgh University Library.

*John Galt's Dramas: A Brief Review*, by G. H. Needler, Toronto, 1945, is a pamphlet containing an expanded form of an article first published in *UTQ*, January 1942. See also 'John Galt', by G. Kitchin, in *Edinburgh Essays on Scots Literature*, ed. H. J. C.

Grierson, 1933; W. M. Parker, 'New Galt Letters', *TLS*, 6 June 1942; B. A. Booth, 'Galt's Lives of the Admirals', *NQ*, 29 October 1938; M. Q. Innis, 'A Galt Centenary', *Dalhousie Review*, xix, 1940; and V. S. Pritchett, 'A Scottish Documentary', in *The Living Novel*, 1946.

WILLIAM GIFFORD, 1756–1826.

Gifford's main claim to remembrance is that he was editor of the *Quarterly Review* from 1809 to 1824 (having edited the *Anti-Jacobin* in 1797–8). But he also wrote the following: *The Baviad. A Paraphrastic Imitation of . . . Persius*, 1791; *The Mæviad*, 1795 (the two were printed together in 1797 and frequently reprinted); *An Epistle to Peter Pindar*, 1800 (revised in subsequent printings and later reprinted with the preceding satires); *The Satires of Decimus Junius Juvenalis Translated*, 1802 (preceded by a brief autobiography, reprinted separately in 1827); *An Examination of the Strictures of the Critical Reviewers on the translation of Juvenal*, 1803 (Supplement, 1804); and *The Satires of . . . Persius Translated*, 1821 (first published in *The Satires of D. J. Juvenalis, and of A. Persius Flaccus, Translated into English Verse*, 2 vols., 1817).

Gifford edited *The Plays of Philip Massinger*, 4 vols., 1805; *The Works of Ben Jonson*, 9 vols., 1816; and *The Dramatic Works of John Ford*, 2 vols., 1827. Alexander Dyce completed his edition of *The . . . Works . . . of James Shirley* in 6 vols. in 1833.

Much information about Gifford is to be found in the works relating to the *Quarterly Review* mentioned above on pp. 470–3.

Outstanding early attacks on Gifford are Hazlitt's *A Letter to William Gifford*, 1819, and the essay in *The Spirit of the Age*, 1825. Leigh Hunt published *Ultra-Crepidarius; a Satire on William Gifford*, in 1823. There are two books about Gifford: J. Longaker's *The Della Cruscans and William Gifford*, Philadelphia, 1924, and R. B. Clark's *William Gifford: Tory Satirist, Critic, and Editor*, New York, 1930.

ROBERT PEARCE GILLIES, 1788–1858.

Gillies's writings include *Wallace, a Fragment*, 1813; *Childe Alarique: A Poet's Reverie*, 1814; *Confessions of Sir H. Longueville* (a novel), 1814; *Oswald; A Metrical Tale: Illustrative of a Poetical Character: In Four Cantos*, 1814 (privately printed; not published), 1817; *Rinaldo the Visionary, a Desultory Poem*, 1816; *Illustrations of*

*a Poetical Character, in six tales, with other Poems*, 2nd ed., 1816; *Müllners's Guilt, or the Anniversary*, 1819 (privately printed); *German Stories, selected . . . by R. P. Gillies*, 3 vols., 1826; *The Seventh Day*, 1826; *Tales of a Voyager to the Arctic Ocean*, 6 vols., 2 series, 1826 and 1829; *Thurlston Tales*, 3 vols., 1835; *Recollections of Sir Walter Scott, Bart.*, 1837; *Palmario*, 1839; and *Memoirs of a Literary Veteran*, 3 vols., 1851. In 1814 he edited the *Essayes of a Prentise in the Divine Art of Poesie* by King James VI and I. He was associated with the founding of the *Foreign Quarterly Review* in 1827, contributed voluminously to *Blackwood's* and other periodicals, and is a figure of importance in the introduction of German literature into England. In 1876 R. H. Stoddard edited selections from his Memoirs, with a biography, for the 'Bric à Brac' series, New York. There are numerous references to Gillies in Lockhart and other writers of the period. See in particular J. G. Robertson, 'Gillies and Goethe', *MLR* iv, 1908, and R. Girardin, *R. P. Gillies and the Propagation of German Literature in England*, Berlin, 1916. A little information is to be found in the books by F. W. Stokoe and V. Stockley mentioned above on pp. 479–80.

George Robert Gleig, 1796–1888.

Gleig published the following works of fiction: *The Subaltern*, 1825 (first published in *Blackwood's*: revised and corrected edition, 1872); *Tales of a Voyage to the Arctic Ocean*, 3 vols., 1826; *The Chelsea Pensioners*, 3 vols., 1829; *The Country Curate*, 2 vols., 1830; *Allan Breck*, 3 vols., 1834; *The Chronicles of Waltham*, 3 vols., 1835; *The Hussar*, 2 vols., 1837; *The Light Dragoon*, 2 vols., 1844; and *With the Harrises Seventy Years Ago*, 1889. He also edited *Katherine Randolph, or Self-Devotion*, 1847.

His historical, religious, and miscellaneous writings, most of which appeared in the Victorian Age, are listed in *CBEL* and *DNB*. He published *Essays, Biographical, Historical and Miscellaneous: Contributed chiefly to the Edinburgh and Quarterly Reviews* in 2 vols. in 1858. He had also contributed to *Fraser's Magazine* and other periodicals.

The fullest account of Gleig is that in the *DNB*.

Gerald Griffin, 1803–40.

In fiction Griffin published *Holland Tide, or Munster Popular Tales*, 1827; *Tales of the Munster Festivals*, 3 vols., 1827; *The*

*Collegians*, 3 vols., 1829 (ed. P. Colum, 1918); *The Rivals* [with] *Tracy's Ambition*, 3 vols., 1829; *The Christian Physiologist: Tales Illustrative of the Five Senses*, 1830 (Dublin, 1854, as *The Offering of Friendship*); *The Invasion*, 4 vols., 1832; *Tales of my Neighbourhood*, 3 vols., 1835; and *The Duke of Monmouth*, 3 vols., 1836. After his death there appeared *Talis Qualis, or Tales of the Jury Room*, 3 vols., 1842. He also wrote *Gisippus . . . A Play*, published in 1842. There is an 8-vol. edition of *The Life and Works*, 1842–3, vol. i being a *Life* by his brother. This contains the best of his prose fiction and his poems. His *Poetical Works* appeared separately in 1851 and were reprinted with *Gisippus* at Dublin in 1926.

See Ethel Mannin, *Two Studies in Integrity: Gerald Griffin and the Rev. Francis Mahony*, 1954, and the more scholarly treatment in T. Flanagan, *The Irish Novelists, 1800–1850*, New York, 1959.

Henry Hallam, 1777–1859.

Hallam published his *View of the State of Europe during the Middle Ages* in 2 vols. in 1818. *Supplemental Notes* appeared in 1848 and were incorporated in the edition of 1853 and later editions. *The Constitutional History of England from . . . Henry VII to . . . George II* came out in 2 vols. in 1827. In 1833 Sir R. H. Inglis and Hallam published their *Survey of the Principal Repositories of the Public Records*. The *Introduction to the Literature of Europe, in the Fifteenth, Sixteenth, and Seventeenth Centuries* appeared in 4 vols. between 1837 and 1839. There were numerous editions of Hallam's three main books. In 1834 he edited the privately printed *Remains In Verse and Prose of Arthur Henry Hallam*, with a Memoir. He also contributed to the *Edinburgh Review*, and wrote a brief account of his friend Lord Webb Seymour, published in an Appendix to the first volume of the *Memoirs . . . of Francis Horner*, 1843.

There is still no full biography or historiographical study of Hallam. Southey reviewed his *Constitutional History* in the *Quarterly Review*, xxxvii, 1828, Macaulay in the *Edinburgh Review*, xlviii, 1828. C. Wordsworth published *King Charles the First, the Author of Icôn Basilikè, in Reply to Mr. Hallam*, in 1828. See also J. C. Hare's 'Reply to Mr Hallam's Remarks on Luther' in his *In Vindication of Luther*, 1855 (2nd ed.), and F.-A. 'Hallam', in *Éloges historiques*, 1864. See also the books on historiography mentioned on p. 476 above.

BENJAMIN ROBERT HAYDON, 1786–1846.

Among other things Haydon published *The Judgment of Connoisseurs upon Works of Art compared with that of Professional Men, in Reference more particularly to the Elgin Marbles*, 1816; *New Churches . . .* [and] *the Encouragement of Painting*, 1818; *Some Enquiry into the Causes which have obstructed . . . Historical Painting . . . in England*, 1829; *On Academies of Art* (*more particularly the Royal Academy*), *and their Pernicious Effect on the Genius of Europe: Lecture xiii*, 1839; *Thoughts on . . . Fresco and Oil Painting . . .* [for] *the Houses of Parliament*, 1842; and *Lectures on Painting and Design*, 2 vols., 1844–6. Haydon was for some time virtual editor of James Elmes's *Annals of the Fine Arts*, 1817–20. His *Correspondence and Table-Talk* were edited by F. W. Haydon in 2 vols. in 1876.

*The Life of Benjamin Robert Haydon, from his Autobiography and Journals*, ed. Tom Taylor, appeared in 3 vols. in 1853: the same year there was another 3-vol. edition with an additional appendix and an index. There is also an edition with an introduction by Aldous Huxley (2 vols., 1926): an edition by A. P. D. Penrose, 1927: and one by E. Blunden (World's Classics, 1927). W. B. Pope's edition of *The Diary*, 5 vols., Cambridge, Massachusetts, 1960–3, is definitive.

The only books about Haydon are 'G. Paston', *B. R. Haydon and his Friends*, 1905; E. George, *The Life and Death of Benjamin Robert Haydon*, 1948; and C. Olney, *Benjamin Robert Haydon*, Georgia, 1952. Four early articles are to be found in *Fraser's Magazine*, xxxvi, 1847 and xlviii, 1853, the *Edinburgh Review*, xcviii, 1853, and the *Quarterly Review*, xciii, 1853 (the last three all dealing with his *Autobiography*). See also *Temple Bar*, xciv, 1891; H. B. Forman, 'Keats and Haydon', *Athenaeum*, 21 May 1904; F. W. Sargant, 'Benjamin Haydon, Fore-runner', *Nineteenth Century*, xciii, 1923; Virginia Woolf, 'Genius: Haydon', in *The Moment and Other Essays*, 1947 (reprinted from the *New Republic*, xlix, 1926); F. R. Walker, 'The Diary of a Defeated Painter', *The Independent*, cxviii, 1927; E. Blunden, 'Haydon outside his Autobiography', *Nation*, 7 April 1928; and 'Haydon's Tragedy', *TLS*, 22 June and 6 July 1946. *Letters from Elizabeth Barrett to B. R. Haydon* were edited by M. H. Shackford at New York in 1939.

WILLIAM HAZLITT, 1778–1830.

Hazlitt's principal publications were: *An Essay on the Prin-*

*ciples of Human Action*, 1805; *Free Thoughts on Public Affairs: or Advice to a Patriot*, 1806; *An Abridgment of The Light of Nature Pursued*, by Abraham Tucker, 1807; *The Eloquence of the British Senate . . . With Notes*, 2 vols., 1807; *A Reply to the Essay on Population, by the Rev. T. R. Malthus*, 1807 (Letters i–iii first published in Cobbett's *Political Register*, 14 March–23 May, 1807); *A New and Improved Grammar of the English Tongue*, 1810; *Memoirs of the late Thomas Holcroft*, 3 vols., 1816 (ed. E. Colby, 2 vols., 1925); *The Round Table: A Collection of Essays*, 2 vols., 1817 (includes 12 essays by Leigh Hunt: most of Hazlitt's essays had first appeared in the *Examiner*); *Characters of Shakespear's Plays*, 1817; *A View of the English Stage*, 1818 (originally published in various periodicals); *Lectures on the English Poets*, 1818; *A Letter to William Gifford, Esq.*, 1819 (first draft in the *Examiner*, 15 June 1818); *Lectures on the English Comic Writers*, 1819; *Political Essays, with Sketches of Public Characters*, 1819 (mainly reprinted from periodicals); *Lectures chiefly on the Dramatic Literature of the Age of Elizabeth*, 1820; *Table Talk; or, Original Essays*, 2 vols., 1821–2 (some of these essays were reprinted from the *London Magazine* and the *New Monthly Magazine*), ed. W. Hazlitt, jun., 2 vols., 1845–6 (includes two other essays); *Liber Amoris; or, the New Pygmalion*, 1823 (ed. R. Le Gallienne and W. C. Hazlitt, 1894); privately printed: contains additional matter: ed. C. Morgan, with Hazlitt's *Dramatic Criticisms*, 1948); *Characteristics: in the Manner of Rochefoucault's Maxims*, 1823; *Sketches of the Principal Picture Galleries in England*, 1824 (originally published in the *London Magazine*, 1822–3, and in *The Round Table*); *Select British Poets . . . with critical remarks*, 1824 (1825, omitting copyright material, as *Select Poets of Great Britain*); *The Spirit of the Age: or Contemporary Portraits*, 1825 (the second edition, which appeared in the same year, contains some additional material, while the 2-vol. Paris edition of 1825 omits Moore and adds Canning and Knowles. Parts of the volume were reprinted from the *London Magazine* and the *New Monthly Magazine*); *Table-Talk: or, Original Essays*, 2 vols., Paris, 1825 (a selection from *Table Talk*, 1821–2, and from the next book mentioned, made by Hazlitt himself); *The Plain Speaker: Opinions on Books, Men, and Things*, 2 vols., 1826 (mainly reprinted from the *London Magazine* and the *New Monthly Magazine*); *Notes of a Journey through France and Italy*, 1826; *The Life of Napoleon Buonaparte*, 4 vols., 1828–30; *Conversations of James Northcote, Esq., R.A.*,

1830 (reprinted from *New Monthly Magazine* and other periodicals: ed. F. Swinnerton, 1949).

After his death there appeared *Literary Remains of the late William Hazlitt. With a notice of his life, by his son, and thoughts on his genius and writings, by E. L. Bulwer . . . and Mr. Sergeant Talfourd*, 2 vols., 1836 (the *Remains* being mainly reprinted from periodicals); *Painting* [by B. R. Haydon] *and the Fine Arts* [by Hazlitt], 1838 (reprinted from the *Encyclopaedia Britannica*, 7th ed., Supplement, vol. i, 1816); *Sketches and Essays. Now first collected by his son*, 1839 (reprinted from various periodicals: reprinted in 1852 as *Men and Manners*); *Criticisms on Art: and Sketches of the Picture Galleries of England*, edited by his son, 2 series, 1843–4; *Winterslow*, 1850; *Memoirs of William Hazlitt. With Portions of his Correspondence*, ed. W. C. Hazlitt, 2 vols., 1867; *Lamb and Hazlitt. Further Letters*, ed. W. C. Hazlitt, 1900; *A Reply to Z.*, ed. C. Whibley, 1923 (an unpublished retort to an article in *Blackwood's Magazine*, August 1818); *New Writings of William Hazlitt*, ed. P. P. Howe, 2 series, 1925 and 1927 (reprinted from various periodicals); and *Hazlitt in the Workshop: The Manuscript of 'The Fight'*, ed. S. C. Wilcox, Baltimore, 1943.

There are two collected editions: *The Collected Works*, ed. A. R. Waller and A. Glover with an introduction by W. E. Henley, 12 vols. and index, 1902–6: and the standard edition, *The Complete Works*, ed. P. P. Howe, 20 vols. and index, 1930–4 (a reissue of the previous edition with additional notes, *The Life of Napoleon*, and other new material). Between 1838 and 1851 Hazlitt's son edited 12 vols., which were part of a projected complete edition; and between 1869 and 1886 W. C. Hazlitt produced 7 vols. that were part of another projected collection.

There is a *Bibliography of William Hazlitt* by G. Keynes, 1931, which confines itself to books and leaves aside questions of attribution. Recent additions to the canon have been made by G. Carnall, *TLS*, 19 June 1953, and E. L. Brooks, *NQ*, 1954.

Of many volumes of selections one of the best and most comprehensive is *Selected Essays*, ed. G. Keynes, 1930. Others include *Hazlitt: Essays on Poetry*, ed. D. Nichol Smith, 1901; *Essays*, ed. C. Whibley, [1906]; *Hazlitt on English Literature*, ed. J. Zeitlin, New York, 1913 (with comprehensive introduction); *Hazlitt: Selected Essays*, ed. G. Sampson, 1917; *The Best of Hazlitt*, ed. P. P. Howe, 1923; and *The Essays: A Selection*, ed. C. M. Maclean, 1949. *Hazlitt Painted by Himself and Presented by Catherine*

*Macdonald Maclean*, 1948, is a first-person retelling of his life 'as closely as possible in his own words'. Unfortunately the editor has done a good deal of rewriting, so that the result is neither pure Hazlitt nor pure Miss Maclean. Additional letters were published by P. P. Howe in the *Athenaeum*, 8 and 15 August 1919, in the *London Mercury*, March 1923, May 1924, and August 1925, in the *TLS*, 21 March 1936, and in *PMLA* lxxvii (1962).

A great deal of biographical information is to be found in three works edited by W. C. Hazlitt: *Memoirs of William Hazlitt. With Portions of his Correspondence*, 2 vols., 1867 (already mentioned); *Four Generations of a Literary Family*, 2 vols., 1897; and *The Hazlitts: an Account of their Origin and Descent. With Autobiographical Particulars of William Hazlitt*, 2 vols., 1911–12 (privately printed). The standard biography is still *The Life of William Hazlitt*, by P. P. Howe, 1922, revised 1928, revised 1947.

Other studies are A. Birrell, *William Hazlitt*, 1902 ('English Men of Letters' series: badly dated); J. Douady, *Vie de William Hazlitt, l'Essayiste*, 1907; H. W. Stephenson, *William Hazlitt and Hackney College*, 1930 (a useful pamphlet); M. F. Brightfield, 'Scott, Hazlitt and Napoleon', *University of California Publications in English*, xiv, 1943; Catherine M. Maclean, *Born Under Saturn: A Biography of Hazlitt*, 1943; W. P. Albrecht, *William Halitt and the Malthusian Controversy*, Albuquerque, 1950; *William Hazlitt's Life of Napoleon: Its Sources and Characteristics*, by R. E. Robinson, Geneva and Paris, 1959 (a concise study of limited interest); and *William Hazlitt*, by H. Baker, Cambridge, Mass., 1962 (an important book on Hazlitt's life, his ideas, and his age).

A list of some of the early reviews and criticisms of Hazlitt may be found in *CBEL* iii, 643. P. G. Patmore's *My Friends and Acquaintances*, 3 vols., 1854, includes important reminiscences of Hazlitt. Briefer accounts may be found in B. W. Procter ('Barry Cornwall'), 'My Recollections of the late William Hazlitt', in the *New Monthly Magazine*, November 1830; G. Gilfillan, 'William Hazlitt' and 'Hazlitt and Hallam' *in Galleries of Literary Portraits*, vol. ii, 1850; the *Collected Writings of Thomas De Quincey*, ed. D. Masson, vols. ix and xi, 1890; and R. H. Stoddard, *Personal Recollections of Lamb, Hazlitt and Others*, 1903. There is an excellent critique of Hazlitt by Leslie Stephen in *Hours in a Library*, series 2, 1876.

Of the many articles and chapters in books devoted to Hazlitt mention may be made of: O. Elton, *A Survey of English Literature, 1780–1830*, vol. ii, 1912; G. Saintsbury, *Essays in English Literature (1780–1860)*, 1890; P. E. More, *Shelburne Essays*, series 2, New York, 1905; S. T. Irwin, 'Hazlitt and Lamb', *Quarterly Review*, cciv, 1906; three articles by P. P. Howe: 'Hazlitt and *Liber Amoris*', *Fortnightly Review*, cv, 1916: 'Hazlitt's Second Marriage', *Fortnightly Review*, cvi, 1916: and 'Hazlitt and *Blackwood's Magazine*', *Fortnightly Review*, cxii, 1919; R. S. Newdick, 'Coleridge on Hazlitt', *Texas Review*, ix, 1924; P. L. Carver, 'Hazlitt's Contributions to the *Edinburgh Review*', *RES* iv, 1928; C. Olney, 'William Hazlitt and Benjamin Robert Haydon', *NQ* 5 and 12 October 1935; A. L. Strout, 'Hunt, Hazlitt and *Maga.*', *ELH* iv, 1937; R. Vigneron, 'Stendhal et Hazlitt', *MP* xxxv, 1938; four articles by S. C. Wilcox: 'Hazlitt and Northcote', *ELH* vii, 1940: 'A Manuscript Addition to Hazlitt's Essay "On the Fear of Death" ', *MLN* lv, 1940: 'Hazlitt on Systematic in Contrast to Familiar Composition', *MLQ*, ii, 1941; and 'Hazlitt's Aphorisms', *MLQ* ix, 1948; R. M. Wardle, 'Outwitting Hazlitt', *MLN* lvii, 1942; R. Withington, 'Old Books and New', *South Atlantic Quarterly*, xliii, 1944; M. Goodwin, 'The Childhood of Hazlitt', *Nineteenth Century*, cxxxix, 1946; W. J. Sykes, 'Hazlitt's Place in Literature', *Queen's Quarterly*, liii, 1946; P. G. Gates, 'Bacon, Keats and Hazlitt', *South Atlantic Quarterly*, xlvi, 1947; C. D. Thorpe, 'Keats and Hazlitt: A Record of Personal Relationship and Critical Estimate', *PMLA* lxii, 1947; W. P. Albrecht, 'Hazlitt's Principles of Human Action and the Improvement of Society' in *If by your Art: Testament to Percival Hunt*, Pittsburgh, 1948; R. K. Gordon, 'Hazlitt on some of his Contemporaries', *Transactions of the Royal Society of Canada*, xlii, 1948; B. B. Cohen, 'Hazlitt: Bonapartist Critic of "The Excursion" ', *MLQ* x, 1949; J. C. Maxwell, 'Some Hazlitt Quotations', *NQ* 15 September 1951 (and see subsequently S. C. Wilcox, 10 May 1952 and D. S. Bland, 19 July 1952); and L. Haddakin, 'Keats's "Ode on a Grecian Urn" and Hazlitt's Lecture "On Poetry in General" ', *NQ* 29 March 1952. Letters in the *TLS* between February and June 1953 discussed the persons alluded to in the essay 'Of Persons One Would Wish to have Seen', H. Tyler and R. W. King being the principal correspondents.

Many of these books and articles deal in part with Hazlitt as a critic, but this is the particular theme of a number of other

writers. In *The Aesthetics of William Hazlitt*, Philadelphia, 1933 (2nd impr., 1952), Elisabeth W. Schneider is concerned with the theoretical basis of his criticism. The preface to J. Zeitlin's *Hazlitt on English Literature*, 1913 (already mentioned), contains a conscientious survey of Hazlitt's criticism. 'The Place of Hazlitt in English Criticism', by H. W. Garrod, in *The Profession of Poetry and Other Lectures*, 1929, is brief but intelligent. R. Wellek considers Hazlitt in vol. ii of his *History of Modern Criticism, 1750–1950*, 1955. See also R. W. Babcock, 'The Direct Influence of Late Eighteenth-Century Criticism on Hazlitt and Coleridge', *MLN* xlv, 1930; G. Schnöckelborg, *August Wilhelm Schlegels Einfluß auf William Hazlitt als Shakespeare-Kritiker*, 1931; J. M. Bullitt, 'Hazlitt and the Romantic Conception of the Imagination', *PQ* xxiv, 1945; C. I. Patterson, 'William Hazlitt as a Critic of Prose Fiction', *PMLA* lxviii, 1953; and G. D. Klingopulos, 'Hazlitt as Critic', *EC*, vi, 1956. A. Whitley has considered his theatrical criticism in 'Hazlitt and the Theatre', *University of Texas Studies in English*, 1955. Few writers have done justice to Hazlitt as a critic of the visual arts, though one may consult 'Hazlitt as a Critic of Art', by S. P. Chase, *PMLA* xxxix, 1924; 'Hazlitt as a Critic of Painting', by G. M. Sargeaunt, in *The Classical Spirit*, 1936; and 'Hazlitt's Criticism of Greek Sculpture', by S. A. Larrabee, *JHI* ii, 1941.

For work on other aspects of Hazlitt's life, such as the break with Wordsworth and the disputed authorship of the review of *Christabel* (almost certainly not by Hazlitt), the reader is referred to the relevant article in *ERPE*, as listed on p. 459 above. For the question of Hazlitt's influence on Keats, see under Keats.

## Reginald Heber, 1783–1826.

Heber's *Hymns, written and adapted to the Weekly Church Service of the Year* were published in 1827 [ed. A. Heber], and reached a tenth edition by 1834. Some of them had first been published in *The Christian Observer*, 1811–16. His Prize Poem, *Palestine*, had been published at Oxford in 1807 and had gone through several editions, being translated into Welsh and Latin. He also published (in verse) *Europe; Lines on the Present War*, 1809; and *Poems and Translations*, 1812. *Select Portions of Psalms and Hymns: With Some Compositions of a late Distinguished Prelate* appeared in 1827. His *Poetical Works* were published in 1841; and *Blue-Beard. A Serio-Comic Oriental Romance in One Act* in 1868.

His prose writings include *A Sense of Honour, a Prize Essay*, 1805; *Narrative of a Journey through . . . India, 1824–5* [ed. A. Heber], 2 vols., 1828 (and several later editions); *Sermons Preached in England* [ed. A. Heber], 1829; and *Sermons Preached in India* [ed. A. Heber], 1829. *The Personality and Office of the Christian Comforter* were Bampton Lectures published in 1816. He also published a number of other sermons, and edited the *Whole Works* of Jeremy Taylor, 15 vols., 1822 (revised edition by C. P. Eden, 10 vols., 1847–54). His *Life of . . . Jeremy Taylor, D.D., with a Critical Examination of his Writings*, was published separately in 2 vols. in 1824 and in 1 vol. in 1828. Taylor also contributed to the *Quarterly Review*. In 1830 his widow published *The Life and Unpublished Works*, in 2 vols.

On Heber see articles in the *Quarterly Review*, xxxv, 1827, xxxviii, 1828, and lxx, 1842, and in the *Edinburgh Review*, xlviii, 1828. Reference may also be made to *Some Account of the Life of Reginald Heber* (anon.), 1829; T. S. Smyth, *The Character and Religious Doctrines of Bishop Heber*, 1831; G. Bonner, *Memoir of Heber*, Cheltenham, 1833; T. Taylor, *Memoirs of Heber*, 3rd ed., 1836; and G. Smith, *Bishop Heber: Poet and Missionary*, 1895. His hymns are discussed in J. Julian's *Dictionary of Hymnology*, 1892. A number of his letters are printed in *The Heber Letters, 1783–1832*, ed. R. H. Cholmondeley, 1950.

## Felicia Dorothea Hemans (*née* Browne), 1793–1835.

*Poems* by Felicia Dorothea Browne were published at Liverpool in 1808. Her other publications were as follows: *England and Spain* (a poem), 1808; *The Domestic Affections, and Other Poems*, 1812; *The Restoration of the Works of Art to Italy, A Poem*, 1816; *Modern Greece*, 1817; *Translations from Camoens and Other Poets*, 1818; *Tales and Historic Scenes*, 1819; *Wallace's Invocation to Bruce, a Poem*, 1819; *The Sceptic*, 1820; *Stanzas to the Memory of the late King*, 1820; *Dartmoor, A Poem*, 1821; *Welsh Melodies*, 1822; *Vespers of Palermo*, 1823 (a tragedy in verse); *The Siege of Valencia, a Dramatic Poem* [and] *The Last Constantine, with Other Poems*, 1823; *The Forest Sanctuary, and Other Poems*, 1825 (2nd ed., including 'Casabianca', 1829); *Lays of Many Lands*, 1825; *Records of Woman, with Other Poems*, 1828; *Songs of the Affections, with Other Poems*, 1830; *Hymns on the Works of Nature for the Use of Children*, 1833; *Hymns for Childhood*, Dublin, 1834 (American

ed., 1827); *National Lyrics and Songs for Music*, Dublin, 1834; and *Scenes and Hymns of Life, with Other Religious Poems*, 1834.

Her *Poetical Remains*, with a Memoir by 'Δ' (D. M. Moir), were published in 1836. (There had been an American edition, edited by Professor Norton, in 1825.) Juvenile poems, *Early Blossoms*, appeared with a *Life* in 1840. Mrs. Hemans contributed to numerous periodicals, including *Blackwood's Magazine*, Colburn's *New Monthly Magazine*, and the *Edinburgh Monthly Magazine*. In 1839 her sister Mrs. Hughes edited *The Works*, in 7 vols., with a Memoir. There were various subsequent editions.

*A Short Sketch of the Life of Mrs. Hemans* appeared in 1835. H. F. Chorley's *Memorials of Mrs. Hemans*, 2 vols., 1836, is a fuller biography. W. Ledderbogen published *Felicia Hemans Lyrik* at Heidelberg in 1913, and E. Duméril, *Une femme poète au déclin du romantisme anglais: Felicia Hemans* at Toulouse in 1929.

See also Jeffrey's article in the *Edinburgh Review*, l (50), 1829; D. M. Moir, *Sketches of the Poetical Literature of the Past Half-Century*, 1851; Lady A. T. Ritchie, 'Felicia Felix', in *Blackstick Papers*, 1908; I. A. Williams, 'Wordsworth, Mrs. Hemans, and R. P. Graves', *London Mercury*, vi, 1922; W. K. Rupprecht, 'Felicia Hemans und die englischen Beziehungen zur deutschen Literatur', *Anglia*, xlviii, 1924; and W. R. Cunningham, 'Mrs. Hemans at Mount Rydal', *TLS*, 23 October 1943.

JOHN CAM HOBHOUSE (BARON BROUGHTON), 1786–1869.

Hobhouse began and ended his literary career in association with Byron. His *Imitations and Translations from the Ancient and Modern Classics*, 1809, contains nine poems by Byron. *A Journey through Albania and Other Provinces of Turkey*, 2 vols., 1813 (see Borst, below: rewritten as *Travels in Albania*, 2 vols., 1855), describes the journey that also produced *Childe Harold's Pilgrimage*. *The Substance of Some Letters Written by an Englishman Resident at Paris during the Last Reign of the Emperor Napoleon* was published in 2 vols. in 1816, the proofs having been submitted to Benjamin Constant. 'Voilà les libelles finis', Napoleon is said to have commented on reading the book, 'les bons livres vont commencer'. The *Quarterly* reviewer, on the other hand, read the volumes 'with equal displeasure and disgust'. In 1818 Hobhouse produced *Historical Illustrations of the Fourth Canto of Childe Harold*. He then wrote two articles in the *Westminster Review*

worth mentioning: 'Lord Byron's Residence in Greece', July 1824, and a review of 'Dallas's Recollections and Medwin's Conversations', January 1825. In 1859 he published *Italy; Remarks Made in Several Visits from 1816 to 1854*, 2 vols.; and in 1865 he printed privately *Recollections of a long Life*, in 5 vols. This was published in 6 vols. in 1909–11, vol. ii then including his 'Contemporary Account of the Separation of Lord and Lady Byron, also of the Destruction of Lord Byron's Memoirs', which had been privately printed in 1870.

There is a biography of Hobhouse, *My Friend H*, by M. Joyce, 1948. Contemporary reviews of his books provide a useful background. Much information about his early career is to be found in books on Byron, including *Lord Byron's First Pilgrimage*, by W. A. Borst, New Haven, 1948. See also E. R. Vincent's *Byron, Hobhouse and Foscolo*, 1949, and A. Rutherford's 'The Influence of Hobhouse on *Childe Harold's Pilgrimage*, Canto IV', *RES*, N.S., xii, 1961. Joyce's biography contains some information about the numerous manuscripts and about Hobhouse's other writings on politics, &c. According to the *New English Dictionary* Hobhouse invented the phrase 'His Majesty's Opposition', in 1826.

JAMES HOGG, 'THE ETTRICK SHEPHERD', 1770–1835.

His principal volumes of verse may be mentioned here, although most of them fall outside the scope of this study: *Scottish Pastorals, Poems, Songs*, &c., 1801; *The Mountain Bard; consisting of Ballads and Songs*, 1807 (enlarged in later editions); *The Forest Minstrel; a Selection of Songs* (by Hogg and others), 1810; *The Queen's Wake: a Legendary Poem*, 1813; *The Hunting of Badlewe, a Dramatic Tale*, 1814; *The Pilgrims of the Sun; a Poem*, 1815; *The Ettricke Garland; being Two Excellent New Songs*, 1815 (one of the songs is by Hogg, the other by Scott); *The Poetic Mirror, or The Living Bards of Britain*, 1816 (ed. T. E. Welby, 1929); *Mador of the Moor; a Poem*, 1816; *Dramatic Tales*, 2 vols., 1817; *The Royal Jubilee: A Scottish Mask*, 1822; *Queen Hynde*, 1825; *Select and Rare Scottish Melodies*, 1829; *Songs, Now First Collected*, 1831; *A Queer Book*, 1832.

His other principal writings include *The Shepherd's Guide: being a Practical Treatise on the Diseases of Sheep*, 1807; *The Spy: A Periodical Paper, of Literary Amusement and Instruction*, 1811 (mainly by Hogg); *The Long Pack: A Northumbrian Tale*, Newcastle, 1817; *The Brownie of Bodsbeck, and other Tales*, 2 vols.,

1818; *The Jacobite Relics of Scotland . . . Collected and illustrated by James Hogg*, 2 series, 1819, 1821; *Winter Evening Tales*, 2 vols., 1820; *The Three Perils of Man; or War, Women and Witchcraft: A Border Romance*, 3 vols., 1822; *The Three Perils of Woman, or Love, Leasing, and Jealousy: A Series of Domestic Scottish Tales*, 3 vols., 1823; *The Private Memoirs and Confessions of a Justified Sinner: written by himself*, 1824 (1828, as *The Suicide's Grave;* 1837, with omissions and alterations, as *The Confessions of a Fanatic*; ed. T. E. Welby, 1924; with an introduction by André Gide, 1947); *The Shepherd's Calendar*, 2 vols., 1829; *Altrive Tales*, 1832 (only 1 vol. published); *A Series of Lay Sermons*, 1834; *The Domestic Manners and Private Life of Sir Walter Scott*, Glasgow, 1834; *Tales of the Wars of Montrose*, 3 vols., 1835 (ed. J. E. H. Thomson, Stirling, 1909); *The Works of Robert Burns: Edited by the Ettrick Shepherd, and William Motherwell*, 5 vols., Glasgow, '1840' (1838–41: vol. v contains a Memoir of Burns by Hogg); *A Tour in the Highlands in 1803: A Series of Letters by James Hogg . . . to Sir Walter Scott*, Paisley, 1888. Hogg contributed to *The Club Book*, edited by Andrew Picken, 3 vols., 1831.

It should be mentioned that a great deal that was later reprinted in the books just mentioned had first appeared in *Blackwood's Magazine* and other periodicals. A complete edition of Hogg's writings would hardly be possible. The *Poetical Works* appeared in 4 vols. in 1822, and in 5 vols. in [1838–40] (published at Glasgow: with his Memoir or Autobiography in vol. v). *Tales and Sketches . . . Including . . . several Pieces not before printed* were published in 6 vols. in 1837, while *The Works*, ed. T. Thomson, 2 vols., 1865, includes both poems and tales and is the most complete edition, though the text is not always reliable. There are two selected eds. of his *Poems*, ed. Mrs. Garden, 1887, and ed. W. Wallace, 1903. See also *Works, Letters and Manuscripts*, ed. R. B. Adam, priv. prtd., Buffalo, 1930.

Bibliographical information is to be found in the books by Edith C. Batho and A. L. Strout mentioned below, and in 'Notes on the Bibliography of James Hogg', *The Library*, xvi, 1935, by Edith C. Batho, as well as F. E. Pierce's 'James Hogg', *Yale University Library Gazette*, v, 1931.

There are a number of books on Hogg: *Memorials of James Hogg*, edited by his daughter Mrs. Garden, published at Paisley in [1884] and twice reprinted; H. T. Stephenson's *The Ettrick Shepherd: a Biography*, Bloomington, 1922; *The Ettrick Shepherd*, by

Edith C. Batho, 1927 (an excellent study); *The Life and Letters of James Hogg, vol. i, 1770–1825*, by A. L. Strout, Lubbock, Texas, 1946; and *James Hogg: A Critical Study*, by L. Simpson, 1962. The Memoir in T. Thomson's edition of *The Works* is also of use.

Further information may be found in a series of notes and articles by A. L. Strout listed in *CBEL* and largely incorporated into his book ('Hogg's "Chaldee Manuscript"', *PMLA* lxv, 1950, is later, and deserves separate mention). D. Carswell, *Sir Walter: a Four-Part Study in Biography*, 1930, deals with Scott, Hogg, Lockhart, and Joanna Baillie. There are also two notes in the *TLS*: 'The Ettrick Shepherd: a Centenary Exhibition', 30 November 1935, and 'The Ettrick Shepherd', by D. Cook, 8 May 1937; as well as 'The Ettrick Shepherd: two Unnoted Articles', *NQ*, 2 September 1950.

WILLIAM HONE, 1780–1842.

A complete bibliography of Hone is never likely to be compiled, since he published on a large scale and many of his publications were necessarily anonymous. Bibliographical help may be found in the *DNB* and *CBEL*, F. W. Hackwood's *William Hone: His Life and Times*, 1912, in F. G. Stephens's *Memoir of G. Cruikshank*, 1891, in B. Jerrold's *Life of G. Cruikshank*, 1891, and in some of the articles mentioned below.

*The Every-Day Book: or Everlasting Calendar of Popular Amusements* appeared in 2 vols. in 1826–7; *The Table Book* in 1827–8; and *The Year Book of Daily Recreation and Information* in 1832. Mention may also be made here of *Ancient Mysteries Described*, 1823, and of *The Early Life and Conversion of William Hone by Himself: Edited by his Son*, 1841 (see also *Some Account of the Conversion of the late W. Hone, with . . . Extracts from his Correspondence*, 1853). A dozen of his most successful political pamphlets were reprinted as *Facetiae and Miscellanies with One Hundred and Twenty Engravings drawn by George Cruikshank* in 1827 (2nd ed.) Further information may be found in *The Three Trials of William Hone*, 1818 (ed. W. Tegg, 1876); and in H. M. Sikes, 'William Hone: Regency Patriot, Parodist, and *Pamphleteer*', *Newberry Library Bulletin*, vol. v, no. 8 (Chicago: The Library). A background to Hone is provided by *English Political Caricature, 1793–1832*, by M. Dorothy George, 1959.

THOMAS HOOD, 1799–1845.

*Odes and Addresses to Great People* appeared anonymously in

1825, the joint work of Hood and J. H. Reynolds. The two series of *Whims and Oddities: in Prose and Verse* were published in 1826–7. Hood then published *The Plea of the Midsummer Fairies, Hero and Leander, Lycus the Centaur, and other Poems*, 1827; *National Tales* (in prose), 2 vols., 1827; *The Epping Hunt* (illustrated by Cruikshank), 1829; *The Dream of Eugene Aram* (with designs by W. Harvey), 1831 (first published in *The Gem*, 1829); *Tylney Hall: A Novel*, 3 vols., 1834; *Hood's Own, or Laughter from Year to Year* (containing the *Literary Reminiscences*), 1839, 2nd series, with preface by his son, 1861; *Up the Rhine*, Frankfort, 1840 (mainly prose); *The Loves of Sally Brown and Ben the Carpenter* ([1840?]: a single quarto sheet); *Whimsicalities: A Periodical Gathering: With Illustrations by Leech*, 2 vols., 1844, 1870 (enlarged: verse and prose). *Fairy Land: By the late Thomas and Jane Hood, their Son and Daughter*, appeared in 1861. 'The Song of the Shirt' first appeared in the Christmas Number of *Punch*, 1843. 'Lamia; A Romance' was printed in vol. i of *The Autobiography of William Jerdan*, 4 vols., 1852–3.

Hood edited *The Gem*, vol. i, 1829; *The Comic Annual*, 11 vols., 1830–42 (he himself wrote most of the literary contributions: no volumes were issued for 1840–1); the *New Monthly Magazine and Humorist*, lxiii–lxviii, 1841–3; and *Hood's Magazine and Comic Miscellany*, i–iii, 1844–5. He assisted John Taylor to edit the *London Magazine*, iv–viii, July 1821–July 1823, and contributed a good deal. He also contributed to *Sporting*, ed. 'Nimrod' (C. J. Apperley), 1838.

*Poems*, 2 vols., 1846, and *Poems of Wit and Humour*, 1847, constitute the first collected edition of his poems. *The Poetical Works, with Some Account of the Author* appeared at Boston in 4 vols. in 1856. There have been numerous other editions of his poems, including *The Poetical Works*, ed. W. M. Rossetti, illustrated by G. Doré, 2 series [1871–5]; and a selection in the World's Classics series. The fullest edition is that published at Oxford in 1920, ed. W. Jerrold. There have been various volumes of selections, including one edited by C. Dyment, 1948.

*The Works . . . Comic and Serious, in Prose and Verse*, were edited with notes by his son, T. Hood, Jr., in 7 vols. in 1862. There is also a 10-vol. edition with illustrations, 1869–73 (11 vols., 1882–4).

*Memorials of Thomas Hood: Collected by his Daughter* [F. F. Broderip]: *With a Preface and Notes by his Son* appeared in 2 vols.

in 1860. In 1945 L. A. Marchand edited at New Brunswick a small volume of *Letters of Thomas Hood from the Dilke Papers in the British Museum.* There are also books by A. Elliot (*Hood in Scotland,* Dundee, 1885), E. Oswald (*Thomas Hood und die soziale Tendenzdichtung seiner Zeit,* Vienna and Leipzig, 1904), and W. Jerrold (*Thomas Hood: His Life and Times,* 1907, and *Thomas Hood & Charles Lamb, The Story of a Friendship*—with a reprint of the *Literary Reminiscences,* 1930). J. C. Reid published a new study in 1963.

See also R. H. Horne, *A New Spirit of the Age,* vol. ii, 1844; G. Gilfillan, *A Gallery of Literary Portraits,* vol. i, 1845; D. Masson, 'Thomas Hood', in *Macmillan's Magazine,* August 1860; W. M. Thackeray, 'On a Joke I once heard from the late Thomas Hood', in *Roundabout Papers,* 1863; J. Ashton, 'The True Story of Eugene Aram', in *Eighteenth Century Waifs,* 1887; W. E. Henley, *Views and Reviews,* 1890; H. C. Shelley, 'Thomas Hood's Homes and Friends', in *Literary By-paths in Old England,* 1909; P. E. More, 'The Wit of Thomas Hood', in *Shelburne Essays,* vii, New York, 1910; W. H. Hudson, 'Thomas Hood: the Man, the Wit, and the Poet', in *A Quiet Corner in a Library,* Chicago, 1915; 'The Exhibition of Hood MSS. at Bristol Reference Library', *Bookman,* lxiv, 1923; J. H. Swann, 'The Serious Poems of Thomas Hood', *Manchester Quarterly,* li, 1925; and E. Blunden, 'Hood's Literary Reminiscences', in *Votive Tablets,* 1931.

There have been notes and articles in the last thirty years as follows: T. O. Mabbott, 'Letters of Leigh Hunt, Thomas Hood, and Allan Cunningham', *NQ,* 23 May 1931; J. M. Turnbull, 'Reynolds, the Hoods, and Mary Lamb', *TLS,* 5 November 1931; J. Heath-Stubbs, 'Hood', *Time and Tide,* 28 April 1945; 'Hood: The Poet Behind the Jester's Mask', *TLS,* 5 May 1945; 'L.B.', 'Thomas Hood: A Centenary Note', *NQ,* 19 May 1945; D. Hudson, 'Hood and Praed', *TLS,* 19 May 1945; V. S. Pritchett, 'Our Half-Hogarth', in *The Living Novel,* 1946; A. Voss, 'Lowell, Hood and the Pun', *MLN* lxiii, 1948; A. Whitley, 'Hood and Dickens: Some New Letters', *HLQ* xiv, 1951, and 'Hood as a Dramatist', *SE* xxx, 1951; J. Hennig, 'The Literary Relations between Goethe and Hood', *MLQ* xii, 1951; and 'Hood: The Language of Poetry', *TLS,* 19 September 1952.

THEODORE EDWARD HOOK, 1788–1841.

Hook published a number of farces and other slight dramatic

pieces, including: *The Soldier's Return*, 1805; *Catch Him Who Can*, 1806; *The Invisible Girl*, 1806; *Tekeli; or, The Siege of Montgatz*, 1806; *The Fortress . . . from the French*, 1807; *Music Mad*, 1808; *Killing No Murder*, 1809 (2nd ed. the same year, with a preface and the scene censored by the Lord Chamberlain); *Safe and Sound*, 1809; *Darkness Visible*, 1811; *Trial by Jury*, 1811; and *Exchange No Robbery*, 1820.

He also wrote the following prose fictions: *The Man of Sorrow*, by 'Alfred Allendale', 3 vols., 1808 (reprinted as *Ned Musgrave*, 1842); *Sayings and Doings: A Series of Sketches from Life*, three series, 9 vols., 1824–8; *Maxwell*, 3 vols., 1830; *Love and Pride*, 3 vols., 1833 (1842, as *The Widow and the Marquess, or Love and Pride*); *The Parson's Daughter*, 3 vols., 1833, 1835 (revised and corrected); *Gilbert Gurney*, 3 vols., 1836; *Jack Brag*, 3 vols., 1837; *Gurney Married*, 3 vols., 1838; *Births, Deaths, and Marriages*, 3 vols., 1839 (1842, as *All in the Wrong; or, Births, Deaths, and Marriages*); *Precepts and Practice*, 3 vols., 1840; *Fathers and Sons*, 3 vols., 1842; and *Peregrine Bunce*, 3 vols., 1842. There have been various reprints and partial collections of his novels.

A fuller list of Hook's writings may be found in *CBEL* iii, 399–400, and in Myron F. Brightfield's useful study, *Theodore Hook and his Novels*, Cambridge, Mass., 1928. Hook wrote and edited a large number of books and did a great deal of journalism, editing and contributing to *John Bull* from 1820 to his death and the *New Monthly Magazine and Humorist*, vols. xlix–lxii. Some of his journalism was reprinted in *The Ramsbottom Letters*, 1872, and *The Choice Humorous Works . . . with a New Life of the Author . . .* [1873].

Lockhart produced *Theodore Hook: A Sketch* in 1852. Earlier accounts of Hook had appeared in the *New Monthly Magazine*, lxiii, 1841, and the *Quarterly Review*, May 1843 (by Lockhart). Other accounts may be found in R. H. Horne's *A New Spirit of the Age*, vol. ii, 1844; *Chambers's Journal*, v, 1846; the *New Monthly Magazine*, lxxx, 1847 ('A Graybeard's Gossip, no. 6'); and A. M. and S. C. Hall's 'Memories of Authors', in the *Atlantic Monthly*, xv, 1865. R. H. D. Barham produced a fuller account in *The Life and Remains*, 2 vols., 1849 (revised and corrected in 1853 and 1877).

See also W. Maginn's *A Gallery of Illustrious Literary Characters*, ed. W. Bates [1873]; F. G. Waugh, 'Unpublished Letters of Theodore Hook', *Gentleman's Magazine*, lvi, 1896; S. H. N.

St. Cyres, 'Theodore Hook', *Cornhill Magazine*, lxxxix, 1904; A. Repplier, 'The Laugh that Failed', *Atlantic Monthly*, clviii, 1936; and 'Hoaxer and Wit: Theodore Hook, 1788–1841', *TLS*, 23 August 1941.

LEIGH HUNT, 1784–1859.

Hunt published the following volumes of verse: *Juvenilia*, 1801; *The Feast of the Poets*, 1814 (first published in *The Reflector* for December 1811: significantly revised in this and later editions); *The Descent of Liberty, a Mask*, 1815; *The Story of Rimini*, 1816; *Foliage, or Poems Original and Translated*, 1818; *Hero and Leander, and, Bacchus and Ariadne*, 1819; *Amyntas . . . from the Italian of . . . Tasso*, 1820; *Ultra-Crepidarius; a Satire on William Gifford*, 1823; *Bacchus in Tuscany, a Dithyrambic Poem, from . . . Redi*, 1825; *Captain Sword and Captain Pen*, 1835, 1849 (with new preface); *A Legend of Florence: A Play*, 1840; *The Palfrey; A Love-Story of Old Times*, 1842; and *Stories in Verse: Now first collected*, 1855. He contributed the tales of the Squire and the Friar to *The Poems of Geoffrey Chaucer Modernized*, 1841 (ed. R. H. Horne).

The most nearly complete edition of Hunt's poems is H. S. Milford's *The Poetical Works*, 1923. His own editions of his *Poetical Works* in 1819 (3 vols.), 1832, and 1844, are in fact selected editions. His son, Thornton Hunt, produced a revised edition in 1860. In 1922 L. A. Brewer edited Hunt's *Ballads of Robin Hood*, Cedar Rapids, Iowa.

His main volumes in prose include *Critical Essays on the Performers of the London Theatres*, 1807; *An Attempt to Shew the Folly and Danger of Methodism*, 1809; *The Prince of Wales v. the Examiner*, 1813; *The Round Table: A Collection of Essays*, 2 vols., 1817 (a number of the essays are by Hunt); *The Months*, 1821; *Lord Byron and Some of his Contemporaries*, 1828 (two eds., one in 2 vols.); *Sir Ralph Esher*, 3 vols., 1832 (a novel); *Christianism, or Belief and Unbelief Reconciled*, 1832 (expanded and revised as *The Religion of the Heart*, 1853); *The Indicator, and the Companion*, 2 vols., 1834 (a selection from these periodicals); *The Seer*, 1840–1 (a similar selection); *Imagination and Fancy, with an essay in answer to the question 'What is Poetry?'*, 1844; *Wit and Humour, Selected from the English Poets, with an Illustrative Essay*, 1846; *Stories from the Italian Poets*, 2 vols., 1846; *Men, Women, and Books*, 2 vols., 1847; *A Jar of Honey from Mount Hybla*, 1848: *The Town: Its Memorable*

*Characters and Events*, 2 vols., 1848; *The Autobiography*, 3 vols., 1850 (a rewriting of *Lord Byron and Some of his Contemporaries*); *Table Talk*, 1851; *The Old Court Suburb, or Memorials of Kensington*, 2 vols., 1855 (enlarged ed. the same year); and *A Saunter through the West End*, 1861. Hunt contributed to many periodicals and gift-books throughout his life. No collected edition of his prose writings exists. In 1870 J. E. B[abson] collected some of his scattered essays as *A Day by the Fire*, and three years later he similarly collected *The Wishing-Cap Papers*, Boston, 1873. In 1891 there was an edition of his *Tales . . . with a . . . Memoir* by William Knight. In 1923 L. A. and E. T. Brewer collected some essays as *The Love of Books*, published at Cedar Rapids, Iowa.

There are editions of *The Autobiography*, by Thornton Hunt, '1860' (1859: 'revised'); by R. Ingpen, 2 vols., 1903; by E. Blunden, 1928 (World's Classics); and by J. E. Morpurgo, 1949 (with a useful key to corresponding passages in *Lord Byron and Some of his Contemporaries*). In 1959 S. N. Fogle published at Florida *Leigh Hunt's Autobiography: The Earliest Sketches*.

Hunt edited the following periodicals: *The Examiner, a Sunday Paper*, 1808–21 (although he ceased to be editor in 1821, Hunt continued to be an occasional contributor); *The Reflector, A Quarterly Magazine*, 1810–11 (reissued as *The Reflector, a Collection of Essays*, in 2 vols. in 1812); *The Literary Pocket-Book*, 1818–22 (an annual); *The Indicator*, 1819–21 (a weekly: reissued in 1 vol. in 1822); *The Liberal: Verse and Prose from the South*, 1822–3 (collected as 2 vols.); *The Literary Examiner*, 1823 (probably edited by John Hunt, although commonly attributed to Leigh Hunt); *The Companion*, 1828 (a weekly); *The Chat of the Week*, 1830 (also a weekly); *The Tatler: A Daily Journal of Literature and the Stage*, 1830–2; *Leigh Hunt's London Journal*, 1834–5 (a weekly); *The Monthly Repository*, 1837–8; and *Leigh Hunt's Journal*, 1850–1 (distinct from Leigh Hunt's *London Journal*, though also a weekly). Many of Hunt's numerous contributions to other periodicals are mentioned in the *CBEL* and in the bibliographies mentioned at the end of this entry.

Books edited by Leigh Hunt include *Classic Tales . . . with Critical Essays on the . . . Authors*, 5 vols., 1806–7; *The Masque of Anarchy, a Poem by . . . Shelley*, 1832; *The Dramatic Works of R. B. Sheridan*, 1840; *The Dramatic Works of Wycherley, Congreve, Vanbrugh and Farquhar*, 1840; *One Hundred Romances of Real Life*, 1843; *The Foster Brother*, 3 vols., 1845 (by Thornton Hunt:

introduction by Leigh Hunt); *Readings for Railways*, 1849 (series 2, 1853, with J. B. Syme); *A Book for a Corner*, 2 vols, 1849; *Beaumont and Fletcher . . . selected*, 1855; and *The Book of the Sonnet*, edited by Leigh Hunt and S. Adams Lee, 2 vols., Boston, 1867 (contains an essay on the sonnet by Leigh Hunt).

Hunt's *Dramatic Criticism, 1808–31*, was collected by L. H. and C. W. Houtchens in 1949, much of his uncollected *Literary Criticism* by the same scholars in 1956 (with a long essay on Hunt as a man of letters by C. D. Thorpe), and his *Political and Occasional Essays* in 1962. *Shelley—Leigh Hunt: How Friendship Made History*, ed. R. Brimley Johnson, 1928 (revised edition, 1929), is a useful book which reprints the reviews of Shelley's poems in the *Examiner*, as well as a great many political articles from the same periodical, with other relevant material. Selections are also to be found in *Leigh Hunt's 'Examiner' Examined*, by E. Blunden, 1928.

*The Correspondence of Leigh Hunt* was edited by his eldest son in 2 vols. in 1862. In 1874–5 S. R. Townshend Mayer published anonymously selections from Leigh Hunt's correspondence with B. R. Haydon, Charles Ollier, and Southwood Smith in the *St. James's Magazine*, while in 1876 he published 'Leigh Hunt and Lord Brougham: With Original Letters', in *Temple Bar*, xlvii. *Six Letters . . . to W. W. Story, 1850–6*, were printed in 1913. Vol. ii of L. A. Brewer's *My Leigh Hunt Library* contains *The Holograph Letters* (1938), many of which had been privately printed earlier by the same collector. Many of the letters in Brewer's collection are still unpublished. In 1934 A. N. L. Munby published *Letters to Leigh Hunt from his Son Vincent*. Other letters of Hunt's may be found in many different books and articles, and in *Shelley and his Circle* (p. 615 below).

Of the numerous volumes of selections only a few can be mentioned. Those consisting wholly of prose, often with good introductions, include *A Tale for a Chimney Corner*, ed. E. Ollier [1869]; *Essays*, ed. A. Symons, 1887 (enlarged ed., 1903); *Dramatic Essays*, ed. W. Archer and R. W. Lowe, 1894; *Essays and Sketches*, ed. R. B. Johnson [1907]; *Prefaces . . . mainly to his Periodicals*, ed. R. B. Johnson, 1927 (not limited to the prefaces); and *Essays*, ed. J. B. Priestley, 1929 (Everyman's Library). Others include both verse and prose, notably *Leigh Hunt as Poet and Essayist*, ed. C. Kent, 1889; *Essays, and Poems*, ed. R. B. Johnson, 2 vols., 1891; *Selections*, ed. J. H. Lobban,

1909; and *Leigh Hunt*, ed. E. Storer [1911]. In 1893 A. S. Cook published *An Answer to the Question 'What is Poetry?'* with notes and other relevant material.

Since Hunt knew many of the leading men of letters from the time of Byron to that of Dickens, information about him is to be found in a great many books of the period, as well as in later biographies. The best general study remains E. Blunden's *Leigh Hunt*, 1930, an admirable book in spite of a few minor inaccuracies. L. Landré's *Leigh Hunt . . . Contribution à l'histoire du Romantisme anglais*, 2 vols., 1935–6, is an excellent scholarly study. The author makes use of some of the manuscript material in America, and provides a full bibliography. The earlier biographies by W. C. Monkhouse (1893) and R. Brimley Johnson (1896) retain a slight value. Blunden's study, *Leigh Hunt's 'Examiner' Examined* and Brimley Johnson's *Shelley—Leigh Hunt: How Friendship Made History* (both 1928) have already been mentioned. There is a monograph, *The Political History of Leigh Hunt's Examiner*, by G. D. Stout, St. Louis, 1949. Two German studies are *Leigh Hunts Kritik der Entwicklung der englischen Literatur bis zum Ende des 18. Jahrhunderts*, by O. Moebus, Straßburg, 1916, and *Hunt und die italienische Literatur*, by E. Fisher, Freiburg, 1936.

There are numerous articles and other studies which throw light on Hunt's life and writings. Thornton Hunt wrote on his father in 'A Man of Letters of the Last Generation', *Cornhill Magazine*, 1860, and in the introduction to his edition of his father's *Autobiography*, '1860' (1859). J. D. Campbell published Hunt's 'Attempt . . . to Estimate his Own Character' in the *Athenaeum* for 25 March 1893. Several recent scholars have investigated the attacks of the reviewers on 'The Cockneys': see particularly P. M. Wheeler, 'The Great Quarterlies . . . and Leigh Hunt', *South Atlantic Quarterly*, 1930; G. D. Stout, 'The Cockney School', *TLS*, 7 February 1929; A. L. Strout, 'Hunt, Hazlitt, and *Maga*', *ELH* iv, 1937, and the same writer's article in *Studia Neophilologica*, 1953–4. Other articles of primarily biographical importance include Monica C. Grobel, 'Leigh Hunt and "The Town"', *MLR*, xxvi, 1931 (Hunt, Charles Knight, and the Useful Knowledge Society); and J. P. Brawner, 'Leigh Hunt and his wife Marianne', *W. Virginia Univ. Stud.*, 1937. Sylva Norman's book on the reputation of Shelley, *Flight of the Skylark*, 1954, deals with Hunt's relations with Mary Shelley from 1822. H. E. Rollins deals usefully with Hunt and Keats in

*The Keats Circle*, 2 vols., 1948. J. R. MacGillivray discusses Hunt's importance in the introductory essay to his *Keats: A Bibliography and Reference Guide*, Toronto, 1949. On Hunt's role in *The Liberal* see W. H. Marshall, *Byron, Shelley, Hunt, and 'The Liberal'*, Philadelphia, 1960. Nettie S. Tillett's 'Elia and "The Indicator" ', *South Atlantic Quarterly*, 1934, deals with Hunt's relations with Lamb. P. P. Howe's *Life of William Hazlitt*, 1922 (3rd ed., 1947), and R. W. Armour's *Barry Cornwall*, Boston, 1935, give good accounts of two other important friendships. For similar studies see D. Hudson, *Thomas Barnes of 'The Times'*, 1943; R. D. Altick, *The Cowden Clarkes*, 1948; and C. R. Woodring's *Victorian Samplers: William and Mary Howitt*, 1952. S. F. Fogle's 'Skimpole Once More', *Nineteenth-Century Fiction*, 1952, is a fair summary of the Dickens affair; but also see G. D. Stout, 'Leigh Hunt's Money Troubles: Some New Light', *Washington University Studies*, and K. J. Fielding, 'Skimpole and Leigh Hunt Again', *NQ*, 1955.

Saintsbury wrote on Hunt in *Essays in English Literature, 1780–1860*, 1890, as well as in his *History of English Prosody*, 1910, and his *History of Criticism*, vol. iii, 1904. Reference may also be made to 'Italian Influence on English Scholarship and Literature during the "Romantic Revival", Part iii', by R. W. King, *MLR*, xxi, 1926; 'Leigh Hunt e "The Examiner" (1808–1812)', by B. Cellini, in *Studi sul romanticismo inglese*, 1932; 'Leigh Hunt's Place in the Reform Movement, 1808–1810', by M. Roberts, *RES*, xi, 1935; *Mythology and the Romantic Tradition in English Poetry*, by D. Bush, Cambridge, Mass., 1937; 'Leigh Hunt and *The Rambler*', by W. W. Pratt, *Texas Studies in English*, 1938; *The Dissidence of Dissent*, by F. E. Mineka, Chapel Hill, 1944 (Hunt and the *Monthly Repository*); 'The *Spectator* Tradition and the Development of the Familiar Essay', by M. R. Watson, *ELH*, xii, 1946; 'Hunt's Review of Shelley's Posthumous Poems', by P. C. Gates, *Papers of the Bibliographical Society of America*, xlii, 1948; *English Poetic Theory, 1825–1865*, by A. H. Warren, 1950; *Dante's Fame Abroad, 1350–1850*, by W. P. Friederich, 1950; 'Leigh Hunt's Shakespeare: A "Romantic" Concept', by G. D. Stout, *Studies in Memory of F. M. Webster*, 1951; 'Hunt's *Horace*', by F. H. Ristine, *MLN* lxvi, 1951; 'Leigh Hunt, Moore and Byron', by Sylva Norman, *TLS*, 2 January 1953; 'A Leigh Hunt–Byron Letter', by P. C. Gates. *K.-Sh.J.* ii, 1953; and 'Leigh Hunt's Shakespearean Criticism', by J. Fleece, *Essays in Honor of W. C. Curry*, 1955.

For bibliographical information one may consult the *CBEL*, Landré, and the article in *ERPE*. Milford's edition of the poems has a useful bibliography. L. A. Brewer's *My Leigh Hunt Library: The First Editions*, Iowa, 1932, is also useful. Many of the books with annotations by Hunt now in the United States are listed in 'Leigh Hunt's Marginalia', by W. J. Burke, *Bulletin of the New York Public Library*, 1933.

JEFFREY, FRANCIS, LORD JEFFREY, 1773–1850.

Jeffrey wrote *Observations on Mr. Thelwall's Letter to the Editor of the Edinburgh Review*, 1804; *A Summary View of the Rights and Claims of the Roman Catholics of Ireland*, 1808 (reprinted from the *Edinburgh Review*); a Memoir published in *The Works of John Playfair* [ed. J. G. Playfair], 4 vols., 1822; *Combinations of Workmen: A Speech*, 1825; and *Corrected Report of the Speech of the Lord Advocate of Scotland upon . . . Reform of Parliament*, 1831.

Jeffrey contributed an 'Essay on Beauty' to the *Encyclopaedia Britannica Supplement*, 1824 (being a revised reprint from the *Edinburgh Review*) and also a 'Eulogium of James Watt' (reprinted from the *Encyclopaedia Britannica* in D. F. J. Arago's *Life of Watt*, 1839). His speeches as Rector of Glasgow University may be found in *Inaugural Addresses*, ed. J. B. Hay, Glasgow, 1839. He published a selection from his *Contributions to the Edinburgh Review* in 4 vols. in 1844 (3 vols., 1846, 1853). After his death there appeared two pamphlets, *Samuel Richardson* and *Jonathan Swift*, both 1853; and a story, *Peter and his Enemies*, 1859 ('2nd ed.').

In the 'New Universal Library' there is a selection, *Essays on English Poets and Poetry From the Edinburgh Review, by Francis Jeffrey*, n.d. In 1910 D. Nichol Smith edited selections from *Jeffrey's Literary Criticism*, with a list of his articles in the *Edinburgh Review*; and in 1934 J. Purves edited *The Letters of Francis Jeffrey to Ugo Foscolo*.

In 1852 Lord Cockburn published his *Life of Lord Jeffrey with a Selection from his Correspondence*, in 2 vols. (including a list of Jeffrey's articles in the *Edinburgh Review*), a biography which has not yet been superseded. There are four other books or pamphlets about Jeffrey: James Taylor, *Lord Jeffrey and Craigcrook*, 1892; R. Elsner, *Francis Jeffrey und seine kritischen Prinzipien*, Berlin, 1908; R. Noyes, *Wordsworth and Jeffrey in Controversy*,

Bloomington, 1941; and J. A. Greig, *Francis Jeffrey of the Edinburgh Review*, 1948 (an uncritical survey of his criticism).

Material may also be found in the following books and studies: G. Gilfillan, *A Gallery of Literary Portraits*, ii, 1850; T. Carlyle, 'Lord Jeffrey', in *Reminiscences*, ed. J. A. Froude, 2 vols., 1881 (a penetrating portrait; also see Carlyle's letters); L. E. Gates, *Three Studies in Literature*, New York, 1899 (still of value); M. Y. Hughes, 'The Humanism of Francis Jeffrey', *MLR* xvi, 1921; J. M. Beatty, 'Lord Jeffrey and Wordsworth', *PMLA* xxxviii, 1923; R. C. Bald, 'Francis Jeffrey as a Literary Critic', *Nineteenth Century*, xcvii, 1925; Leslie Stephen, *Hours in a Library*, ii, 1876; Sir G. O. Trevelyan, *The Life and Letters of Lord Macaulay*, 2 vols., 1876; M. H. Goldberg, 'Jeffrey: Mutilator of Carlyle's "Burns" ', *PMLA* lvi, 1941, and 'Carlyle, Pictet and Jeffrey', *MLQ* vii, 1946; R. Daniel, 'Jeffrey and Wordsworth: the Shape of Persecution', *Sewanee Review*, l (50), 1942; R. Derby, 'The Paradox of Jeffrey: Reason versus Sensibility', *MLQ* vii, 1946; and B. Guyer, 'Jeffrey's "Essay on Beauty" ', *HLQ* xiii, 1950, and 'The Philosophy of Jeffrey', *MLQ* xi, 1950. Jeffrey's criticism is sympathetically discussed by R. Wellek (see p. 475 above). See also *Edinburgh Review*, on p. 470–3 above.

William Jerdan, 1782–1869.

From 1817 to 1850 Jerdan edited the *Literary Gazette*, an influential periodical later eclipsed by the *Athenaeum*. Earlier he had edited a number of other journals, including the *Satirist* (which he edited from 1812 to 1814) and the *Sun*. His *Foreign Literary Gazette*, 1831, was short-lived. His other writings include *Six Weeks in Paris, by a late Visitant*, 3 vols., 1818 (2nd ed.); *Personal Narrative of a Journey overland from the Bank to Barnes*, 1829 (a skit on the vogue for travel books); *The National Portrait Gallery of the Nineteenth Century*, 5 annual vols., 1830–4; *Illustrations of the Plan of a National Association for the Encouragement and Protection of Authors and Men of Talent and Genius*, 1839; and a handbook for the South-Eastern Railway Company (*Manual No. 1. Main Line to the Coast and Continent*, 1854). His *Autobiography* appeared in 4 vols. in 1852–3, and was supplemented by *Men I have Known*, 1866. He contributed to many periodicals, including *Fraser's*, the *Gentleman's Magazine*, and *Notes and Queries* (as 'Bushey Heath'). In 1831 he contributed to *The Club Book*, ed. Andrew Picken, vol. ii. He edited the

Rutland Papers and the Perth Correspondence for the Camden Society.

There is a useful account of Jerdan's career, which is of interest as that of a typical man of letters of the day, in the *DNB*. Information about the *Literary Gazette* may also be found in *The Athenaeum: A Mirror of Victorian Culture*, by L. A. Marchand, Chapel Hill, 1941.

JOHN KEATS, 1795–1821.

Keats published three volumes: *Poems*, 1817; *Endymion: A Poetic Romance*, 1818; and *Lamia, Isabella, The Eve of St. Agnes, and Other Poems*, 1820. The first attempt at a collection of his poems is to be found in *The Poetical Works of Coleridge, Shelley, and Keats*, Paris, 1829. Neither this nor *The Poetical Works* of 1840 had any authority. In 1848 there appeared the *Life, Letters, and Literary Remains, of John Keats*, edited by Richard Monckton Milnes, in 2 vols. Vol. II contains unpublished poems. There is a reprint of Milnes's book, without the poems, in Everyman's Library, 1927. In 1856–7 Milnes (Lord Houghton) published *Another Version of Keats' 'Hyperion'*. Since this time some forty-two further short pieces have come to light.

In 1909 M. Robertson edited a facsimile of *Lamia*, &c. There are also Noel Douglas facsimiles of the volumes of 1817 and 1820 (both 1927). There is a facsimile of *Endymion* in two different forms, with and without an introduction by H. Clement Notcutt (1927). There are also American facsimiles of the volumes of 1817 and 1820, New York, 1934.

The standard modern edition of *The Poetical Works* is that of H. W. Garrod, 1939, revised 1958. The same text is given with a less elaborate apparatus in the Oxford Standard Authors edition, also ed. Garrod (new ed., 1956). Of innumerable other editions mention may be made of the edition of *The Poems* in Everyman's Library, ed. G. Bullett, 1944, and of the *Complete Poetry and Selected Prose*, ed. H. E. Briggs, New York, 1951. For explanatory notes one must refer to E. de Sélincourt's edition, 1905, revised 1907 and 1926. The Hampstead Edition of Keats's *Works*, ed. H. B. and M. Buxton Forman, 8 vols., 1938, is an amplification of H. B. Forman's *Complete Works*, 5 vols., Glasgow, 1900–1, and still contains a little material not readily available elsewhere.

The standard edition of the letters was for many years that

of M. Buxton Forman, 2 vols., 1931, 4th edition (1 vol.) 1952. This has now been superseded by *The Letters of John Keats 1814–1821*, ed. H. E. Rollins, 2 vols., 1958.

Only a few of the more recent of the numerous volumes of selections from the poems and the letters can be mentioned: *Keats: Poetry and Prose*, ed. H. Ellershaw, 1922; *Selected Poetry and Letters*, ed. R. H. Fogle, New York, 1951; *Selected Letters of John Keats*, ed. L. Trilling, New York, 1951, enlarged ed. 1955 (with a notable essay mentioned on p. 563 below); *Selected Letters and Poems of John Keats*, ed. J. H. Walsh, 1954; and *John Keats: Selected Poems and Letters*, ed. D. Bush, New York, 1959. There is also a volume of *Letters of John Keats*, ed. F. Page, in the World's Classics series, 1954.

*The Keats Circle: Letters and Papers, 1816–78*, ed. H. E. Rollins, 2 vols., Cambridge, Mass., 1948, contains a great deal of material about Keats, including reprints of a number of the writings mentioned in the next paragraph. *More Letters and Poems of the Keats Circle*, 1955, is a small supplement by the same editor. F. Edgcumbe edited *The Letters of Fanny Brawne to Fanny Keats*, 1937.

Charles (Armitage) Brown's unpublished *Life of John Keats* was edited by Dorothy H. Bodurtha and W. B. Pope in 1937. R. M. Milnes printed about eighty letters in the *Life, Letters, and Literary Remains* of 1848. Sir Sidney Colvin's *John Keats: His Life and Poetry, His Friends, Critics, and After-Fame*, 1917, revised 1925, still remains one of the best general books on Keats, in spite of all the material that has become available more recently. Colvin's briefer *Keats* in the English Men of Letters series, 1887, gave him the incentive to write the fuller work. Amy Lowell's *John Keats*, 2 vols., 1925, is enthusiastic but unreliable. C. L. Finney's *The Evolution of Keats's Poetry*, 2 vols., Cambridge, Mass., 1936, also deals with the life as well as the poetry and remains of considerable value. Dorothy Hewlett published *Adonais: A Life of John Keats* in 1937: a revised edition, *A Life of Keats*, appeared in 1949. B. Ifor Evans's *Keats*, 1934, is very brief but sensible. *John Keats: The Living Year*, 1954, by R. Gittings, is a brilliant foray into the field of biographical and interpretative conjecture. (See also *The Mask of Keats: A Study of Problems*, 1956, by the same writer.) The best biography is now *John Keats: The Making of a Poet*, by Aileen Ward, 1963.

Other material of biographical relevance may be found in

E. Blunden's useful compilation, *Shelley and Keats as they Struck their Contemporaries*, 1925, in the same writer's *Keats's Publisher*, 1936, and in Joanna Richardson's *Fanny Brawne*, 1952. In 1938 Sir William Hale White published *Keats as Doctor and Patient*; see also *John Keats's Anatomical Notebook*, ed. M. B. Forman, 1934.

Articles of biographical importance include 'John Keats and Benjamin Robert Haydon', by C. Olney, *PMLA* xlix, 1934; 'Keats and Wordsworth: A Study in Personal and Critical Impressions', by C. D. Thorpe, *PMLA* xlii, 1927; and 'Keats and Hazlitt: A Record of Personal Relationship and Critical Estimate', by the same writer, *PMLA* lxii, 1947 (on this topic see also *John Keats' Fancy*, by J. R. Caldwell, mentioned below).

The history of Keats's reputation is surveyed in the introduction to J. R. MacGillivray's *John Keats: A Bibliography and Reference Guide*, Toronto, 1949. See also 'Keats and the Periodicals of his Time', by G. L. Marsh and N. I. White, *MP* xxxii, 1934; *Keats and the Victorians . . . 1821–1895*, by G. H. Ford, New Haven, 1944; and *Keats' Reputation in America to 1848*, by H. E. Rollins, Cambridge, Mass., 1946. *Keats and the Bostonians*, by H. E. Rollins and S. M. Parrish, Cambridge, Mass., 1951, is concerned with collectors rather than the poet himself.

The books by J. Middleton Murry are both biographical and critical in their scope. The most remarkable remains *Keats and Shakespeare*, 1925, a brilliant example of interpretative criticism of the most hazardous kind. His evolving views may be followed in the various versions of his subsequent essays on Keats, *Studies in Keats*, 1930, 1939, 1949 (as *The Mystery of Keats*), 1955 (*Keats*).

Apart from the books by Colvin, Finney, and Middleton Murry already mentioned, the most helpful critical studies are those by Garrod (*Keats*, 1926, revised 1939), E. C. Pettet (*On the Poetry of Keats*, 1957), and W. J. Bate (*John Keats*, 1963). A few of the numerous other studies may also be mentioned. An early book still of some interest is *John Keats, A Study*, by Mrs. F. M. Owen, 1880. *The Mind of John Keats*, by C. D. Thorpe, New York, 1926, deals particularly with Keats's aesthetic ideas. *The Genius of Keats*, by A. W. Crawford, 1932, supports the view that Keats was a strenuously intellectual poet. *Keats's Shakespeare*, by Caroline F. E. Spurgeon, 1928 (2nd edition, 1929) is a close study of his marginalia on certain of Shakespeare's plays. W. J. Bate's *The Stylistic Development of John Keats*, 1945, may be read with *Keats's Craftsmanship*, by M. R. Ridley, 1933. Bate's *Negative*

*Capability: The Intuitive Approach in Keats*, Cambridge, Mass., 1939, is another intelligent study. *John Keats' Fancy*, by J. R. Caldwell, Ithaca, New York, 1945, incorporates a good deal of the material in his *Beauty is Truth . . .* (*University of California Publications in English*, 1940), and explores his relation to the associationist aestheticians of the eighteenth century. Two careful German studies are *Die Anschauungen von John Keats über Dichter und Dichtkunst*, Marburg, 1946 (Habilitationsschrift), by H. Viebrock, and *Zum magischen Realismus bei Keats und Novalis*, by G. Bonarius, Giessen, 1950. *Keats and the Daemon King*, by W. W. Beyer, 1946, makes a great deal of the influence of Wieland's *Oberon. The Prefigurative Imagination of John Keats*, by N. F. Ford, Stanford, 1951, deals with the 'Beauty-Truth Identification and its Implications'. *The Finer Tone: Keats's Major Poems*, by E. R. Wasserman, Baltimore, 1953, offers an ambitiously philosophical reading of certain of the major poems. L. J. Zillman's *Keats and the Sonnet Tradition in English*, Los Angeles 1939, throws more light on Keats than does G. Shuster's *The English Ode from Milton to Keats*, 1940. In *Keats and Mrs. Tighe*, New York, 1928, E. V. Weller made too much of interesting resemblances between the poems of Keats and Mrs. Tighe's once-famous *Psyche*, only to be demolished by D. Bush, in his 'Notes on Keats's Reading', *PMLA* l (50), 1935. *John Keats: A Reassessment*, ed. K. Muir, Liverpool, 1959, contains a collection of essays by various hands. *The Consecrated Urn*, by B. Blackstone, 1959, is an eccentric and occasionally illuminating attempt to present 'An Interpretation of Keats in Terms of Growth and Form'.

The following books contain important sections or chapters on Keats: *Mythology and the Romantic Tradition in English Poetry*, by D. Bush, Cambridge, Mass., 1937; *The Starlit Dome*, by G. Wilson Knight, 1941; *English Bards and Grecian Marbles*, by S. A. Larrabee, New York, 1943; the books by H. N. Fairchild mentioned above on p. 494; *The Romantic Comedy*, by D. G. James, 1948; *Major Adjectives in English Poetry from Wyatt to Auden*, by Josephine Miles, 1946; *The Imagery of Keats and Shelley: A Comparative Study*, by R. H. Fogle, Chapel Hill, 1949; and *The Quest for Permanence: The Symbolism of Wordsworth, Shelley and Keats*, by D. Perkins, Cambridge, Mass., 1959. Five important essays on Keats, by Bush, W. J. Bate, Cleanth Brooks, E. Wasserman, and R. H. Fogle, are to be found in the collection of essays edited by M. H. Abrams mentioned on p. 467 above.

Important essays and articles with a general bearing include: 'John Keats', by Matthew Arnold, *Essays in Criticism*, 2nd series, 1888 (reprinted from *The English Poets*, ed. T. H. Ward, iv, 1880); *A Critical Introduction to Keats*, by Robert Bridges, in his *Collected Essays*, iv, 1929 (first privately printed in 1895, and published in the Muses' Library *Keats*, 1896); 'The Letters of Keats', by Andrew Bradley, in his *Oxford Lectures on Poetry*, 1909; the same writer's 'Keats and "Philosophy"', *A Miscellany*, 1929; 'Keats', by E. de Sélincourt, 1921 (British Academy Lecture, reprinted in *The John Keats Memorial Volume*, ed. G. C. Williamson, 1921), a volume which contains other interesting essays; 'Keats's Epithets', by D. W. Rannie, *ESEA*, 1912; 'Keats', by F. R. Leavis, *Revaluation*, 1936; 'From Good to Bright: A Note in Poetic History', by Josephine Miles, *PMLA* lx, 1945; 'The Validity of the Poetic Vision: Keats and Spenser', by E. E. Stoll, *MLR* xl, 1945; 'Romanticism and Synaesthesia: . . . Sense Transfer in Keats and Byron', by S. De Ullmann, *PMLA* lx, 1945; 'Empathic Imagery in Keats and Shelley', by R. H. Fogle, *PMLA* lxi, 1946; 'A Reading of Keats', by Allen Tate, *The American Scholar*, xv, 1946; 'Of Beauty and Reality in Keats', by R. D. Havens, *ELH* xvii, 1950; 'Coleridge, Keats and the Modern Mind', by A. Gérard, *EC* i, 1951; 'Keats the Apollonian: The Time-and-Space Logic of his Poems as Paintings', by R. W. Stallman, *UTQ* xvi, 1947; 'The Poet as Hero: Keats in his Letters', by L. Trilling, in *The Opposing Self*, New York, 1950; 'Keats and William Browne', by Joan Grundy, *RES*, N.S., vi, 1955; and *Keats and Reality*, by John Bayley, 1962 (British Academy Lecture).

Only a few of the articles on individual poems can be mentioned here. On poems in the volume of 1817 one may consult 'Keats's Approach to the Chapman Sonnet', by B. Ifor Evans, *ESEA* xvi, 1930; 'Keats's Realms of Gold', by J. W. Beach, *PMLA* xlix, 1934; and 'The Realm of Flora in Keats and Poussin', by I. Jack, *TLS*, 10 April 1959. There are notable discussions of *Endymion* by L. Brown ('The Genesis, Growth, and Meaning of *Endymion*', *SP* xxx, 1933); N. F. Ford ('*Endymion*: a Neo-Platonic Allegory?', *ELH* xiv, 1947, and 'The Meaning of "Fellowship with Essence" in *Endymion*', *PMLA* lxii, 1947); J. D. Wigod ('The Meaning of *Endymion*', *PMLA* lxviii, 1953); G. O. Allen ('The Fall of Endymion: A Study in Keats's Intellectual Growth', *K.-Sh.J.* vi, 1957); and S. M. Sperry, 'The Allegory of *Endymion*', *SR* ii, 1962.

On the Tales in the 1820 volume see J. H. Roberts, 'The Significance of *Lamia*', *PMLA* l (50), 1935; H. G. Wright, 'Possible Indebtedness of Keats's *Isabella* to the *Decameron*', *RES*, N.S., ii, 1951; and the discussion between H. G. Wright and M. Whitely on the question whether *The Eve of St. Agnes* has a tragic ending (*MLR* xl and xlii, 1945 and 1947).

On the Odes in general, which are of course discussed in most of the critical studies of Keats, one may also consult H. M. McLuhan's 'Aesthetic Pattern in Keats's Odes', *UTQ* xii, 1943; the article by T. E. Connolly in *ELH* xvi, 1949; the essay by J. Holloway in the *Cambridge Journal*, v, 1952 (reprinted in *The Charted Mirror*, 1960); 'Keats's Odes and Letters: Recurrent Diction and Imagery', by D. Perkins, *K.-Sh.J.* ii, 1953; and 'Keats's Odes: Further Notes', by E. Blunden, *K.-Sh.J.* iii, 1954. The 'Grecian Urn' has been discussed by K. Burke in *A Grammar of Motives*, 1945; by Cleanth Brooks in *The Well Wrought Urn*, New York, 1947; by A. Whitley in *K.-Sh.B.* iii, 1952; and by C. Patterson in *ELH* xxi, 1954. On the 'Nightingale' we may consult R. H. Fogle in *MLQ* viii, 1947, and *PMLA* lxviii, 1953; A. Gérard in the *Yale Review*, 1944; and Janet Spens in *RES*, N.S., iii, July 1952. There are discussions of 'Autumn' by E. J. Lovell in *Texas Studies in English*, xxix, 1950; by R. A. Brower in *The Fields of Light*, 1951; and by B. C. Southam in *K.-Sh.J.* ix, 1960.

On 'Hyperion' there are important articles by Martha Hale Shackford, *SP*, xxii, 1925; Helen Darbishire, *RES* iii, 1927 ('Keats and Egypt'); D. Bush, *MLN* xlix, 1934 ('The Date of Keats's *Fall of Hyperion*'); J. R. Caldwell, *PMLA* li, 1936 ('The Meaning of *Hyperion*'); J. Livingston Lowes, *PMLA* li, 1936 ('Moneta's Temple'); K. Muir, *EC* ii, 1952 ('The Meaning of *Hyperion*', reprinted in his *John Keats: A Reassessment*, Liverpool, 1958); and S. M. Sperry ('Keats, Milton, and *The Fall of Hyperion*', *PMLA* lxxvii, 1962).

The lines to Fanny, 'What can I do to drive away', are discussed by H. E. Briggs in 'Keats, Robertson and "That Most Hateful Land" ', in *PMLA* lix, 1944. 'The Meaning of Keats's "Eve of St. Mark" ' is the subject of an article by W. E. Houghton, in *ELH* xiii, 1946. Gittings's dating of the 'Bright Star' sonnet is rejected by Aileen Ward in an article in *SP* lii, 1955.

Those wishing more complete information about the work that has been done on Keats may refer to the *CBEL*; to J. R. MacGillivray's *John Keats: A Bibliography and Reference Guide*,

Toronto, 1949; and to the chapter by C. D. Thorpe in *ERP*. The *K.-Sh.J.* contains annual bibliographies.

There is a *Concordance*, ed. D. L. Baldwin, J. W. Hebel, L. N. Broughton, and others, Washington, 1917. Also of use is *The Keats Letters, Papers, and Other Relics forming the Dilke Bequest in the Hampstead Public Library*, ed. G. C. Williamson, 1914. There are several articles on manuscript material, notably Mabel A. E. Steele, 'The Woodhouse Transcript of the Poems of Keats', *Harvard Library Bulletin*, iii, 1949, and her 'Three Early Manuscripts of Keats', *K.-Sh.J.* i, 1952; W. A. Coles, 'The Proof Sheets of Keats's "Lamia"', *Harvard Library Bulletin*, 1954; and H. E. Rollins, 'Unpublished Autograph Texts of Keats', *Harvard Library Bulletin*, vi, 1952. In 1905 E. de Sélincourt edited *Hyperion: A Facsimile of Keats's Autograph Manuscript with a Transliteration of the Manuscript of The Fall of Hyperion A Dream.*

CHARLES KNIGHT, 1791–1873.

Only a few of the productions of Knight's long and useful life can be recorded here. He wrote *Arminius, or The Deliverance of Germany. A Tragedy*, Windsor, 1814; *The Bridal of the Isles, A Mask*, 1817 (2nd ed.); *The Menageries*, 3 vols. (Society for the Diffusion of Useful Knowledge), 1829–40 (anon.); *The Working-Man's Companion: The Rights of Industry*, 2 parts (*Capital and Labour*, and *The Results of Machinery*), 1831 (anon.); *Trades' Unions and Strikes*, 1834 (anon.); *William Shakspere: A Biography*, 1842 (1850, as *Studies and Illustrations of the Writings of Shakspere*, vol. i); *William Caxton. A Biography*, 1844; *Studies and Illustrations of the Writings of Shakspere*, 3 vols., 1850; *The Struggles of a Book against Excessive Taxation* ([1850], 2nd ed.); *The Case of Authors as regards the Paper Duty*, 1851; *Once upon a Time*, 2 vols., 1854 (essays); *The Old Printer and the Modern Press*, 1854; *The Popular History of England*, 8 vols., 1856–62; *Passages of a Working Life*, 3 vols., 1864–5; *Shadows of the Old Booksellers*, 1865; and *Begg'd at Court: A Legend of Westminster* (novel), 1867.

Knight also contributed editorial information to an edition of Fairfax's translation of Tasso, Windsor, 2 vols., 1817. He edited *The Pictorial Edition of the Works of Shakspere*, 7 vols., [1839–]41, rev. ed., 5 vols. 1867; and wrote on 'Shakspere and his Writings', in *Knight's Store of Knowledge*, 1841. He contributed a great deal to *London*, a 6-vol. work which he edited in 1841–4 (rev. E. Walford, 6 vols. [1875–7]).

In 1823–4 he edited *Knight's Quarterly Magazine*, continued in 1825 as *The Quarterly Magazine, New Series*. In 1828–9 he was editor of the *London Magazine*. From 1832 he edited *The Penny Magazine of the Society for the Diffusion of Useful Knowledge*. He collaborated with Harriet Martineau in *The Land We Live In*, 1847.

In 1892 A. A. Clowes published *Charles Knight, A Sketch*, with a bibliography. Otherwise the main source of information remains Knight's *Passages of a Working Life*, though a good deal of information may also be found in *Harriet Martineau's Autobiography*, 3 vols., 1877; in *Recorder of Birmingham: A Memoir of Matthew Davenport Hill*, by his daughters, 1878; and in *The English Common Reader*, by R. D. Altick, Chicago, 1957. Many of the publications for which Knight was responsible are mentioned in Lowndes and the *DNB*.

JAMES SHERIDAN KNOWLES, 1784–1862.

Knowles's first play, *Leo; or, The Gypsy*, was performed at Waterford in 1810: see *The Life of Edmund Kean*, by B. W. Procter, 2 vols., 1835. His second, *Brian Boroihme; or, The Maid of Erin*, was performed in 1811 and first published in B. N. Webster's *The Acting National Drama*, vol. viii, in the 1840's. For his later plays only the date of separate publication is here given (Allardyce Nicoll also gives dates of performance): *Virginius*, Glasgow, 1820; *Caius Gracchus*, Glasgow, 1823; *The Fatal Dowry* (from Massinger), 1825; *William Tell*, 1825; *The Beggar's Daughter of Bethnal Green*, 1828; *Alfred the Great*, 1831; *The Hunchback*, 1832; *The Vision of the Bard*, 1832; *The Wife*, 1833; *The Daughter*, 1837; *The Bridal*, [1837] (from *The Maid's Tragedy*, by Beaumont and Fletcher); *The Love-Chase*, 1837; *Woman's Wit*, 1838; *The Maid of Mariendorpt*, 1838; *Love*, 1840; *John of Procida*, 1840; *Old Maids*, 1841; *The Rose of Arragon*, 1842; *The Secretary*, 1843; and *The Rock of Rome*, 1849. *True unto Death* was published in 1863.

Knowles published his *Dramatic Works* in 3 vols. in 1841–3. This collection includes fifteen plays. R. Shelton Mackenzie had provided a Memoir for a previous collection, published at Baltimore in 1835. In 1874 there was a privately printed edition of *Various Dramatic Works of James Sheridan Knowles*, in 2 vols.

Knowles also wrote: *The Welch Harper: A Ballad*, 1796; *Fugitive Pieces*, 1810; *The Elocutionist* (an anthology for reading

aloud), Belfast [? 1823]; *Fortescue: A Novel*, 3 vols., 1847 (first published serially, in *The Sunday Times*, 1846, and privately printed in the same year); *George Lovell: A Novel*, 3 vols., 1847; *The Rock of Rome, or the Arch Heresy*, 1849; *The Idol demolished by its own Priest: An Answer to Cardinal Wiseman's Lectures on Transubstantiation*, 1851; *The Gospel attributed to Matthew is the Record of the whole original Apostlehood*, 1855; 'Old Adventures', in *The Tale Book*, by Knowles and others, Königsberg, 1859; *Lectures on Dramatic Literature*, ed. S. W. Abbott and F. Harvey, 2 vols., 1873 (privately printed); and *Tales and Novelettes*, revised and edited by F. Harvey, 1874 (privately printed).

On Knowles see the last paragraph of Hazlitt's *The Spirit of the Age*, 1825; R. H. Horne's *A New Spirit of the Age*, vol. ii, 1844; *Blackwood's Magazine*, xciv, 1863; *The Life of James Sheridan Knowles*, by R. B. Knowles, revised and edited by F. Harvey, 1872 (privately printed: only twenty-five copies); W. Maginn, *A Gallery of Illustrious Literary Characters*, ed. W. Bates [1873]; L. Hasberg, *James Sheridan Knowles' Leben und dramatische Werke*, Lingen, 1883; W. Klapp, *Sheridan Knowles' Virginius und sein angebliches französisches Gegenstück*, Rostock, 1904; *The Diaries of W. C. Macready, 1833–1851*, ed. W. Toynbee, 2 vols., 1912; and L. H. Meeks, *Sheridan Knowles and the Theatre of his Time*, Bloomington, Indiana, 1933 (with bibliography).

CHARLES LAMB, 1775–1834 (AND MARY LAMB, 1764–1847).

A handful of poems by Lamb may be found in *Poems on Various Subjects*, by S. T. Coleridge, 1796; in a privately printed collection of sonnets, without a title, produced by Coleridge in the same year; and in *Poems on the Death of Priscilla Farmer*, by Charles Lloyd, 1796. Lamb helped James White with *Original Letters, &c. of Sir John Falstaff and his Friends*, 1796. The second edition of *Poems*, by S. T. Coleridge, Bristol, 1797, includes poems by Lamb on pp. 215–40. In 1798 Lamb published *A Tale of Rosamund Gray and Old Blind Margaret* at Birmingham, and *Blank Verse*, by Charles Lloyd and Charles Lamb. *John Woodvil* appeared in 1802. *Mr. H., or Beware a Bad Name* was published without authority in Philadelphia in 1813. Lamb contributed to *The Poetical Recreations of 'The Champion'*, 1822, published *Album Verses* in 1830, and *Satan in Search of a Wife* the following year.

*Specimens of English Dramatic Poets* first appeared in 1808. *Elia:*

*Essays which have appeared under that Signature in the London Magazine*, was published in 1823 (some copies being issued in 1822). *The Last Essays of Elia* came out in 1833, the two series being collected in 1835. The 1828 Philadelphia edition of the two series was unauthorized. The 1835 Paris edition, also unauthorized, included other prose of Lamb's. *Eliana: Being the Hitherto Uncollected Writings*, was edited by [J. E. Babson], Boston, 1864. *Recollections of Christ's Hospital*, published in the *Gentleman's Magazine* in 1813, was issued separately in 1835.

Lamb also published a number of books for children: *The King and Queen of Hearts*, 1805 (facsimile edition, ed. E. V. Lucas, 1902); *Tales from Shakespear*, 2 vols., 1807 (with Mary Lamb); *Mrs. Leicester's School*, 1807; *The Adventures of Ulysses*, 1808; *Poetry for Children*, 1809; *Prince Dorus*, 1811; and *Beauty and the Beast*, 1811.

Apart from the *London Magazine*, Lamb contributed to a great many journals, including the *Reflector*, the *Examiner*, the *Indicator*, the *New Monthly Magazine*, Hone's *Every-Day Book*, *Table-Book*, and *Year Book*, *Blackwood's Magazine*, Moxon's *Englishman's Magazine*, the *Athenaeum*, and several newspapers. He also helped G. Burnett with his *Specimens of English Prose-Writers*, 3 vols., 1807.

His letters were first published in 1837, in *Letters of Charles Lamb, with a Sketch of his Life*, ed. Sir T. N. Talfourd, 2 vols. In 1848 Talfourd published *Final Memorials of Charles Lamb* in 2 vols. Later editions have contained more letters, for example those of W. C. Hazlitt, 2 vols., 1886; A. Ainger, 2 vols., 1888; and W. Macdonald, 2 vols., 1903, and 2 vols., 1906 (Everyman's Library). E. V. Lucas first edited the *Letters* in 2 vols. in 1905. His 3-vol. edition of 1935, which includes the letters of Mary Lamb, is at present the standard edition (but see the comments of G. L. Barnett in *MLQ* ix, 1948, and *HLQ*, 1955, and those of P. F. Morgan in *NQ* for December 1956). There is a 2-vol. selection from the letters in Everyman's Library, ed. G. Pocock, 1945, and a selection in a 1-vol. edition by G. Woodcock, 1950.

Lamb published his *Works* in 2 vols. as early as 1818. An unauthorized edition of *The Poetical Works* of Rogers, Lamb, and others appeared at Paris in 1829. There was a 3-vol. edition of *The Prose Works* in 1835. Talfourd edited the *Works* (prose and

verse) in five parts in 1840. Later editions of the *Works* include those edited by R. H. Shepherd, 1874, A. Ainger, 1878–88 (7 vols., also *Life and Works*, 12 vols., 1899–1900), and W. Macdonald, 1903–4 (12 vols.) The standard edition is that in 7 vols., edited by E. V. Lucas in 1903–5 (reissued in 6 vols. in 1912 with a revised edition of the letters now in turn superseded by the edition mentioned in the previous paragraph, but without the *Dramatic Specimens*). In [1908] T. Hutchinson produced a convenient smaller edition in 2 vols. (1 vol., 1924), which contains useful bibliographical information.

There are numerous volumes of selections. Mention may be made of *The Best of Lamb*, ed. E. V. Lucas, 1914; *Charles Lamb: Prose and Poetry*, ed. George Gordon, 1921; *Lamb's Criticism*, ed. E. M. W. Tillyard, 1923; *Charles Lamb: Essays and Letters*, ed. J. M. French, New York, 1937; and *The Portable Lamb*, ed. J. M. Brown, New York, 1949. Of the many separate editions of the *Essays of Elia*, one of the most recent, which gives both series, is that edited by M. Elwin, 1952.

Since Lamb published so much anonymously in periodicals it is not surprising that many ascriptions should have been made. Some of these are mentioned in the *CBEL* iii, 633–4, while there is a brief discussion in *ERPE*, pp. 37–38.

The best biography is still *The Life of Charles Lamb*, by E. V. Lucas, 2 vols., 1905, revised edition, 1 vol., 1921. For earlier accounts we may go to the *New Monthly Magazine* for 1835 (Lamb's brief 'Autobiographical Sketch', written in 1827); Leigh Hunt's *Lord Byron and Some of his Contemporaries*, 2 vols., 1828, and his *Autobiography*, 1850; Sir T. N. Talfourd's *Letters of Charles Lamb, with a Sketch of his Life*, 2 vols., 1837 (on his reliability see R. S. Newdick, *The First Life and Letters of Charles Lamb—A Study of Talfourd as Editor and Biographer*, Ohio State University, 1935); P. G. Patmore, *My Friends and Acquaintances*, 3 vols., 1855; *Love's Last Labour Not Lost*, by George Daniel, 1863; *Charles Lamb: A Memoir*, by Barry Cornwall (B. W. Procter), 1866 (see also his *Autobiographical Fragment*, 1877); *Charles Lamb—His Friends, His Haunts, and His Books*, by Percy Fitzgerald, 1866; A. Ainger, *Charles Lamb*, 1882 (English Men of Letters); and *The Lambs: Their Lives, Their Friends, and Their Correspondence*, by W. C. Hazlitt, 1897.

There are a great many references to Lamb in the letters and memoirs of his contemporaries. See, for example, *Henry Crabb*

*Robinson on Books and Their Writers*, ed. Edith J. Morley, 3 vols., 1938. The comments of Hazlitt and De Quincey may be found scattered throughout their writings. There is a useful collection by E. Blunden, *Charles Lamb: His Life Recorded by his Contemporaries*, 1934, which complements S. M. Rich's *The Elian Miscellany*, 1931. There are also several volumes which throw particular light on Lamb and his friends: for example, *Lamb and Hazlitt*, by W. C. Hazlitt, 1900; *The Letters of Thomas Manning to Charles Lamb*, ed. G. A. Anderson, 1925; E. V. Lucas, *Charles Lamb and the Lloyds*, 1898; *Lamb's Friend the Census-Taker: Life and Letters of John Rickman*, by O. Williams, 1911; *Thomas Hood & Charles Lamb*, by W. Jerrold, 1930; E. C. Ross, *Charles Lamb and Emma Isola* (Charles Lamb Society Booklet, 1950); and 'Charles Lamb's "Companionship . . . in Almost Solitude"', *Princeton University Library Chronicle*, vi, 1945, by J. S. Finch (an article which gives details of MSS. at Princeton).

Also worth mentioning are F. V. Morley, *Lamb Before Elia*, 1932; J. Derocquigny's intelligent *Charles Lamb: sa vie et ses œuvres*, Lille, 1904; W. Jerrold's *Charles Lamb*, 1905, an introduction; and three contributions by E. Blunden: his British Council pamphlet (Writers and their Work, no. 56); *Charles Lamb and his Contemporaries*, 1933, his Clark Lectures; and 'Elia and Christ's Hospital', *ESEA* xxii, 1937. Two specialized studies are B. Lake's *Introduction to Charles Lamb . . . With a . . . Study of His Relation to Robert Burton*, Leipzig, 1903, and J. S. Iseman's *A Perfect Sympathy: Charles Lamb and Sir Thomas Browne*, Cambridge, Mass., 1937.

Carlyle's unfavourable view of Lamb is expressed in his *Reminiscences*, ed. J. A. Froude, 2 vols., 1881, and elsewhere. The following books also contain interesting discussions of Lamb: *Miscellanies*, by A. C. Swinburne, 1886; *Appreciations*, by Walter Pater, 1889; *Shelburne Essays*, 2nd and 4th series, by Paul Elmore More, 1905–6; *Determinations*, ed. F. R. Leavis, 1934 ('Our Debt to Lamb', a rather humourless essay on Lamb's influence by Denys Thompson); *Selected Essays*, by A. R. Orage, ed. H. Read and D. Saurat, 1935 ('The Danger of the Whimsical'); *The Liberal Imagination*, by L. Trilling, 1950 ('The Sanity of True Genius'); *A History of Modern Criticism: 1750–1950*, vol. ii, *The Romantic Age*, by R. Wellek, 1955; and *The Hero in Eclipse in Victorian Fiction*, by M. Praz, 1956.

Articles include 'The Equation of the Essay', by G. William-

son, *Sewanee Review*, 1927; 'Charles Lamb Sees London', by A. D. McKillop, *Rice Institute Pamphlet*, 1935; 'Lamb and Coleridge', by Edith C. Johnson, *American Scholar*, 1937; 'Charles Lamb, Marston, and Du Bartas', by M. P. Tilley, *MLN* liii, 1938; 'Antiquarian Interest in Elizabethan Drama Before Lamb', by R. D. Williams, *PMLA* liii, 1938 (for a fuller background see E. R. Wasserman's *Elizabethan Poetry in the Eighteenth Century*, 1947); 'A Chip from Elia's Workshop', by J. M. French, *SP* xxxvii, 1940; 'The Character in the Elia Essay', by V. Lang, *MLN* lvi, 1941; 'History of Ideas versus Reading of Poetry', by L. Spitzer, *Southern Review*, 1941 (a discussion of how to read 'The Old Familiar Faces'); 'Romantic Apologiae for Hamlet's Treatment of Ophelia', by A. P. Hudson, *ELH* ix, 1942; 'Lamb's Criticism of Restoration Comedy', by W. E. Houghton, *ELH* x, 1943; 'Dating Lamb's Contributions to the *Table Book*', by G. L. Barnett, *PMLA* lx, 1945; 'Lamb and the Elizabethans', by R. C. Bald, *Studies in Honor of A. H. R. Fairchild*, Columbia, Missouri, 1946; 'Yorick and Elia', by J. V. Logan, *Charles Lamb Society Bulletin*, lxxxv–lxxxvi, 1948; 'Lamb's Insight into the Nature of the Novel', by C. I. Patterson, *PMLA* xlvii, 1952; 'Lamb's Latinity', a correspondence in the *TLS* by P. Legouis, I. P. M. Chambers, and R. G. C. Levens, 10 and 24 June and 11 August 1952; 'Charles Lamb's Contribution to the Theory of Dramatic Illusion', by S. Barnet, *PMLA* xlix, 1954; 'The Mind of Elia', by B. Jessup, *JHI*, 1954; and 'Charles Lamb and the Tragic Malvolio', by S. Barnet, *PQ*, 1954.

Lamb's method of working is discussed with reference to the manuscripts in G. L. Barnett's unpublished study, 'The Evolution of Elia', a Princeton dissertation (1942) available on microfilm.

The best bibliographies are those in *CBEL* and *ERPE*, which may be supplemented by the annual bibliographies in *PQ*. J. C. Thomson's *Bibliography*, 1908, lists many of Lamb's contributions to periodicals. W. C. Hazlitt's *Mary and Charles Lamb: Poems, Letters, and Remains*, 1874, lists the books sold from Lamb's library. See also 'The Scribner Lamb Collection', by J. S. Finch, *Princeton University Library Chronicle*, vii, 1946.

There is a separate *Life of Mary Lamb*, by Anne Gilchrist, ed. J. H. Ingram, 1883, which has been rendered obsolete by E. C. Ross's *The Ordeal of Bridget Elia*, Norman, Oklahoma, 1940. See also 'The Tragedy of Mary Lamb', by W. R. Riddell,

*Transactions of the Royal Society of Canada*, 1928. Florence V. Barry sets the Lambs' writings for children in perspective in *A Century of Children's Books*, 1922.

LETITIA ELIZABETH LANDON (afterwards Maclean, 'L.E.L.'), 1802–38.

In verse 'L.E.L.' published *The Fate of Adelaide: A Swiss Romantic Tale; and other Poems*, 1821; *The Improvisatrice*, 1824; *The Troubadour, Catalogue of Pictures, and Historical Sketches*, 1825; *The Golden Violet, with its Tales of Romance and Chivalry*, 1827; *The Venetian Bracelet, The Lost Pleiad, A History of the Lyre, and other poems*, 1828; *The Vow of the Peacock*, 1835; *A Birthday Tribute, addressed to the Princess Alexandrina Victoria*, [1837]; *Flowers of Loveliness . . . with Poetical Illustrations by L.E.L.*, 1838; and *The Easter Gift: A Religious Offering*, [1838]. *The Zenana, and Minor Poems of L.E.L. With a Memoir by Emma Roberts* appeared in 1839. *The Miscellaneous Poetical Works* had appeared in 1835. There were various editions of *The Works*, the first appearing at Philadelphia in 2 vols. in 1838. *The Poetical Works* appeared in 4 vols. in 1839 and in 2 vols. in 1850 (with a Memoir). W. B. Scott produced an edition in [1873].

L.E.L. also wrote four three-volume novels: *Romance and Reality*, 1831; *Francesco Carrara*, 1834; *Ethel Churchill: or, The Two Brides*, 1837; and *Lady Anne Granard; or Keeping Up Appearances*, 1842. She 'edited' *The Heir-Presumptive*, by Lady Stepney, 3 vols., 1835, and *Duty and Inclination* (no author given), 1838.

Of her numerous other writings mention may also be made of *Traits and Trials of Early Life*, 1836 (tales, with some poems). She contributed to Jerdan's *Literary Gazette*, the *New Monthly Magazine*, and other periodicals. She edited *Fisher's Drawing Room Scrap Book: with Poetical Illustrations by L.E.L.* from 1832 to 1838, and *The Book of Beauty* for 1833.

S. L. Blanchard's *Life and Literary Remains of L.E.L.*, 2 vols., 1841, contains a good deal of unpublished writing. In 1841 S. S[heppard] published *Characteristics of the Genius and Writings of L.E.L.* In 1928 D. E. Enfield produced his *L.E.L.: A Mystery of the Thirties*. See also A. K. Elwood, *Memoirs of the Literary Ladies of England*, vol. ii, 1843; *A Book of Memories*, 1871, by S. C. Hall; 'Memories of Authors: Miss Landon', by S. C. and A. M. Hall, *Atlantic Monthly*, xv, 1865; J. Le Fèvre-Deumier,

*Célébrités anglaises*, Paris, 1895; W. Maginn, *A Gallery of Illustrious Literary Characters*, ed. W. Bates [1873]; the *Autobiography* of W. Jerdan, 4 vols., 1852–3; *Thirty Years' Musical Recollections*, by H. F. Chorley, 2 vols., 1862 (ed. E. Newman, 1926); *My Life and Recollections*, by Grantley Berkeley, 4 vols., 1864–6; *The Literary Life and Correspondence of the Countess of Blessington*, by R. R. Madden, 3 vols., 1855; and the letters of Mary Russell Mitford. Information may also be found in the two books by M. Sadleir mentioned on p. 474 above.

ROBERT EYRES LANDOR, 1781–1869.

R. E. Landor published *An Essay on the Character and Doctrines of Socrates*, 1802; *The Count Arezzi, A Tragedy*, 1824; *The Impious Feast: a Poem in Ten Books*, 1828; *The Earl of Brecon: a Tragedy*, 1841 (also contains two other tragedies, *Faith's Fraud* and *The Ferryman*); and two novels, *The Fawn of Sertorius*, 1846, and *The Fountain of Arethusa*, 2 vols., 1848.

The only book about Landor is *Robert Eyres Landor: Selections from his Poetry and Prose with an Introduction Biographical & Critical* by E. Partridge, 1927. Information about R. E. Landor is mainly to be found in accounts of his brother. In 'The Authorship of "Guy's Porridge Pot" and "The Dun Cow"', *The Library*, 5th series, v, 1950, R. H. Super disputes two of Partridge's attributions.

WALTER SAVAGE LANDOR, 1775–1864.

Landor's poems and plays are outside our scope, as are his minor and privately printed works. The most nearly complete edition of his writings is *The Complete Works*, ed. T. Earle Welby and S. Wheeler, 16 vols., 1927–36, although the editing of the prose writings (vols. i–xii, ed. Welby) is far from satisfactory. Landor himself had published his *Works* in 2 vols. in 1846, vol. i containing the prose. This he supplemented with *Last Fruit off an Old Tree* in 1853. In 1876 John Forster produced an edition in 8 vols., vol. i being a condensation of his 1869 biography. In 1891 C. G. Crump published an edition of the *Imaginary Conversations* in 6 vols., with some of the poems and longer prose works in four further volumes, 1891–3. This remains the best edition of Landor's prose.

*Imaginary Conversations of Literary Men and Statesmen* had

appeared in 3 vols. in 1824–8, vols. i and ii being 'corrected and enlarged' in 1826. A Second Series was published in 2 vols. in 1829. *The Pentameron and Pentalogia* followed in 1837, being reprinted in *Last Fruit off an Old Tree. Imaginary Conversations of Greeks and Romans* appeared in 1853. *Last Fruit off an Old Tree*, 1853, includes the *Imaginary Conversation of King Carlo-Alberto and The Duchess Belgioioso*, 1848, and eighteen further Conversations. *Savonarola e il Priore di San Marco* was published at Florence in 1860.

*The Citation and Examination of William Shakspeare* was published in 1834, *Pericles and Aspasia* in 1836 (in 2 vols.). Other prose works were as follows: *Three Letters, Written in Spain, to D. Francisco Riguelme*, 1809; *Commentary on* [J. B. Trotter's] *Memoirs of Mr. Fox*, 1812 (suppressed by Landor, ed. S. Wheeler, 1907); *Letters Addressed to Lord Liverpool . . . on the Preliminaries of Peace: By Calvus*, 1814 (suppressed by Landor); *Letters of a Conservative*, 1836; *Popery: British and Foreign*, 1851 (reprinted in *The Last Fruit off an Old Tree*, 1853); *Letters of an American, mainly on Russia and Revolution*, 1854; and a *Letter from W. S. Landor to R. W. Emerson*, Bath [1856] (reprinted in *Literary Anecdotes of the Nineteenth Century*, ed. W. Robertson Nicoll and Thomas J. Wise, vol. ii, 1896).

Four new *Imaginary Conversations* were printed from manuscript by M. F. Ashley-Montagu in the *Nineteenth Century* in 1930–1. The same scholar published further 'waifs' in *RES* viii, 1932, and the *Nineteenth Century* for 1939.

S. Wheeler edited *Letters and Other Unpublished Writings* in 1897 (an unreliable book), and *Letters of Walter Savage Landor Private and Public* two years later. H. C. Minchin published *Walter Savage Landor: Last Days, Letters and Conversations* in 1934. Many of Landor's letters had been published during his lifetime in *The Literary Life and Correspondence of the Countess of Blessington*, by R. R. Madden, 3 vols. The second of the two editions of 1855 is the better, but A. Morrison's *The Blessington Papers*, 1895, is much more reliable. Further letters from Landor to Lady Blessington may be found in *Literary Anecdotes of the Nineteenth Century* (above), vol. i, 1895. The article in *ERPE* records the publication of other letters in various books and journals.

There are selections by Sir S. Colvin, 1882 (Golden Treasury series); E. de Sélincourt, 1915 (World's Classics: prose only); H. Ellis, 1933 (Everyman's Library); and E. K. Chambers,

1946. There is also a selected edition of the *Imaginary Conversations*, chosen by T. Earle Welby and edited by F. A. Cavenagh and A. C. Ward, 1934.

John Forster's *Walter Savage Landor: A Biography*, 2 vols., 1869, was for a long time the authoritative Life. His 1-vol. edition of 1876 (reprinted 1895) is abbreviated, though occasionally corrected. Sir S. Colvin's volume in the English Men of Letters series appeared in 1881. The standard modern studies are *Savage Landor*, by M. Elwin, New York, 1941; *Walter Savage Landor: A Biography*, by R. H. Super, New York, 1954 (English ed., 1957); and *Landor: A Replevin*, by M. Elwin, 1958. There is an essay by George Rostrevor Hamilton ('Writers and their Work', no. 126, 1960).

Early accounts of Landor, sometimes based on information provided by himself, may be found in S. C. Hall's *Book of Gems*, 3rd series, 1838; the same writer's *Book of Memories*, 1871; *A New Spirit of the Age*, by R. H. Horne, vol. i, 1844; and *Homes and Haunts of the Most Eminent British Poets*, by W. Howitt, 1847 (the 1857 ed. has corrections by Landor). 'The Life and Opinions of Walter Savage Landor', by E. Spender, *London Quarterly Review*, 1865, utilized information given by Robert Landor (see R. H. Super's account of Robert Landor's marginal comments in *MLN* lii–liii, 1937–8). There are numerous references to Landor in the writings of Crabb Robinson, De Quincey and Browning. Emerson wrote about him in *English Traits*, 1856, while Boythorn in *Bleak House* is partly based on him.

We may also refer to E. Quillinan's 'Imaginary Conversation, between Mr. Walter Savage Landor and the Editor', *Blackwood's Magazine*, 1843; 'Last Days of Walter Savage Landor', by Kate Field, *Atlantic Monthly*, 1866; Dickens's review of Forster in *All the Year Round*, 24 July 1869; 'Reminiscences of Walter Savage Landor', by E. Lynn Linton, *Fraser's Magazine*, July 1870; *Monographs, Personal and Social*, by R. M. Milnes (Lord Houghton), 1873; 'Landor's Imaginary Conversations', by Leslie Stephen, in *Hours in a Library*, 2nd series, 1876 (an admirable, and severe, critique); 'Reminiscences of Walter Savage Landor', by R. Bulwer Lytton (Lady Lytton), *Tinsley's Magazine*, June 1883; Swinburne's *Miscellanies*, 1886; *Red-Letter Days of my Life*, by Mrs. A. Crosse, 1892; 'Landor', by Francis Thompson, *The Academy*, 27 February 1897; and 'The Llanthony Maze' in E. Betham's *A House of Letters*, 1905.

The discussion of 'The Rhetoric of Landor' in *The Handling of Words*, by 'Vernon Lee', 1923, forms an intelligent companion-study to Leslie Stephen's essay. In his *History of English Prose Rhythm*, 1912, Saintsbury had been more laudatory. The following are mostly articles in learned journals: 'The Classicism of Walter Savage Landor', by Elizabeth Nitchie, *Classical Journal*, 1918; 'Walter Savage Landor as a Critic of Literature', by S. T. Williams, *PMLA* xxxviii, 1923; 'Walter Savage Landor und seine "Imaginary Conversations" ', by H. M. Flasdieck, *Englische Studien*, 1924; 'The Spanish Adventure of Walter Savage Landor', by C. P. Hawkes, *Cornhill Magazine*, lxxiv, 1933; 'Three Unknown Portraits of Landor', by M. F. Ashley-Montagu, *Colophon*, ii, 1937; 'Landor's Political Purpose', by G. J. Becker, *SP* xxxv, 1938; 'Landor's Treatment of his Source Materials in the "Imaginary Conversations of Greeks and Romans" ', by Doris E. Peterson, unpublished dissertation at the University of Minnesota, 1942; the same writer's 'Note on a Probable Source of Landor's "Metellus and Marius" ', *SP* xxxix, 1942; 'A New Landorian Manuscript', by R. F. Metzdorf, *PMLA* lvi, 1941; 'Landor's Critique of *The Cenci*', by K. G. Pfeiffer, *SP* xxxix, 1942 (see also R. H. Super in *SP* xl, 1943); 'Landor and Ireland', by M. J. Craig, *Dublin Magazine*, 1943; 'Some New Letters of Landor', by J. B. Hubbell, *Virginia Magazine of History and Biography*, li, 1943; 'Some Notes on Landor', by Sir E. K. Chambers, *RES* xx, 1944; 'Landor's Prose', by E. de Sélincourt, *Wordsworthian and Other Studies*, 1947; and 'Leigh Hunt, Landor and Dickens', by M. Fitzgerald, *TLS*, 26 October 1951 (see also a letter from G. Artom Treves, 28 December 1951). The numerous articles by R. H. Super are not listed here, as most of the information that they contain is included in his biography.

In *Southey und Landor*, 1934, E. Erich regarded Landor as a Fascist. The book contains some new information. Giuliana Artom Treves's *Anglo-fiorentini di cento anni fa*, 1953 (English translation, *The Golden Ring*, 1956), also embodies some fresh research. H. W. Rudman's *Italian Nationalism and English Letters*, 1940, throws light on Landor's political activities.

There are a number of bibliographical aids. The catalogue of books and manuscripts bequeathed to the Victoria and Albert Museum by John Forster (1888–93) is still of use. The 1919 *Bibliography* by S. Wheeler and Thomas James Wise remains

indispensable. Wise's *A Landor Library*, 1928, supplements it. *The Publication of Landor's Works*, by R. H. Super (London: The Bibliographical Society, 1954 for 1946), is an admirable guide through the labyrinth, although (as the author points out) it does not include research after 1949. 'Landor's Unrecorded Contributions to Periodicals', *NQ*, 8 November 1952, by Super, is a useful supplement to the information in Wise and Wheeler. His article in *ERPE* surveys the field of Landor scholarship and provides more detailed bibliographical information.

John Lingard, 1771–1851.

His principal works include *The Antiquities of the Anglo-Saxon Church*, 2 vols., Newcastle-upon-Tyne, 1806 (entirely recast as *The History and Antiquities of the Anglo-Saxon Church* in 2 vols. in 1845); *A History of England from the First Invasion by the Romans to the Accession of Henry VIII*, 3 vols., 1819; 8 vols. (to 1688), 1819–30; 13 vols., 1837, 1839 (revised); 10 vols., 1854–5 (further revised); *A Vindication of Certain Passages in the Fourth and Fifth Volumes of the History of England*, 1826; and *A Collection of Tracts, on . . . the Civil and Religious Principles of Catholics*, 1826.

A full list of Lingard's works may be found in *The Life and Letters* by M. Haile and E. Bonney, [1911]. See also H. Phillpotts, *Letters to Charles Butler, with Remarks on . . . Dr. Lingard*, 1825; J. Fletcher, *John Lingard* (reprinted from *The Dublin Review*), Lingard Society, 1925; J. Lechmere, 'A Great Catholic Historian', *Ecclesiastical Review*, xciv, 1926; and C. Hollis in *Great Catholics*, ed. C. C. H. Williamson, 1938. The *DNB* mentions other writings relating to Lingard.

Thomas Henry Lister, 1800–42.

Lister published three novels, *Granby*, 3 vols., 1826 (1838, with a preface); *Herbert Lacy*, 3 vols., 1828; and *Arlington*, 3 vols., 1832. He also edited *Anne Grey*, 3 vols., 1834, an (anonymous) novel by his sister Lady Harriet Cradock. The other novels attributed to him in *CBEL* are authoritatively rejected by Sadleir (*XIX Century Fiction*, 1951, i, 212).

Lister also published *Epicharis: An Historical Tragedy*, 1829; *The Life and Administration of Edward, First Earl of Clarendon . . .*, 3 vols., 1837–8 (a valuable study); and *An Answer to the Misrepresentations . . . in an Article on the Life of Clarendon* (by Croker in the *Quarterly Review*), 1839.

Information about Lister may be found in the *DNB* and in *Bulwer and his Wife: a Panorama, 1803–1836*, by M. Sadleir, 1933.

JOHN GIBSON LOCKHART, 1794–1854.

Lockhart published *Peter's Letters to his Kinsfolk* anonymously in 3 vols. in 1819 (nominally 'Second Edition'), and then four novels: *Valerius. A Roman Story*, 3 vols., 1821 (rev. ed. 1842); *Some Passages in the Life of Mr. Adam Blair*, 1822 (ed. D. Craig, 1963); *Reginald Dalton*, 3 vols., 1823; and *The History of Matthew Wald*, 1824.

His principal other publications were *Ancient Spanish Ballads: Historical and Romantic, Translated*, 1823 (revised ed., 1841); *Janus, or the Edinburgh Literary Almanack*, 1826 (ed. by Lockhart); *Life of Robert Burns*, 1828 (reprinted several times, and reissued in Everyman's Library in 1907); *The History of Napoleon Buonaparte*, 1829 (reprinted several times, including Everyman's Library, 1906); *The History of the late War . . . For Children*, 1832; *Memoirs of the Life of Sir Walter Scott, Bart.*, 7 vols., 1837–8; 2nd ed., 10 vols., 1839 (followed by other reprints and several abridgements); *The Ballantyne-Humbug Handled*, 1839; and *Theodore Hook, A Sketch*, 1852 (first published in the *Quarterly Review*, May 1843). Lockhart edited the 12-volume edition of Scott's *Poetical Works*, 1833–4. A. L. Strout edited and attributed to Lockhart *John Bull's Letter to Lord Byron*, 1821, in 1947 (Norman, Oklahoma). Lockhart also translated F. Schlegel's *Lectures on Ancient and Modern Literature*, 1815; provided an essay on Cervantes, and notes, for a reprint of Motteux's *Don Quixote*, 5 vols., 1822; played a part in some of the earlier papers in the *Noctes Ambrosianæ* (see John Wilson below); and contributed regularly to *Blackwood's* and other periodicals, as well as editing the *Quarterly Review* from 1825 to 1853. M. C. Hildyard edited *Lockhart's Literary Criticism* in 1931 and included a list of his contributions to periodicals.

A. Lang's *Life and Letters of John Gibson Lockhart*, 2 vols., 1897, has not yet been wholly superseded, although Lang was denied access to some important material. A great deal of information about Lockhart is to be found in Scott's letters and in books about Scott, in S. Smiles, *A Publisher and his Friends*, 2 vols., 1891, and in articles on the *Quarterly Review*. The pamphlet which occasioned *The Ballantyne-Humbug Handled* was entitled, *Refutation of the Mistatements* [sic] *and Calumnies contained*

*in Mr. Lockhart's Life of Sir Walter Scott, Bart. respecting the Messrs. Ballantyne: By the Trustees and Son of the late Mr. James Ballantyne*, 1838. The same authors published their *Reply to Mr. Lockhart's Pamphlet* in 1839.

See also the *Quarterly Review*, October 1864 [by G. R. Gleig]; W. Maginn, *A Gallery of Illustrious Literary Characters*, ed. W. Bates, [1873]; *The Croker Papers*, L. J. Jennings, 3 vols., 1884; M. C. Hildyard, 'J. G. Lockhart', *Ccrnhill Magazine*, lxxii, 1932; F. Ewen, 'J. G. Lockhart, Propagandist of German Literature', *MLN* xlix, 1934; Elsie Swann, *Christopher North*, 1934; G. Macbeth, *John Gibson Lockhart: A Critical Study* (Urbana, 1935, with bibliography); and a long series of useful snippets of information and unpublished letters by A. L. Strout listed in *CBEL* (iii, 676 and v, 664).

See also W. M. Parker, 'Lockhart and Scott', *TLS*, 1 October 1938, and 'Lockhart's Obiter Dicta', *TLS*, 5 and 12 February 1944; C. L. Cline, 'D'Israeli and Lockhart', *MLN*, lvi, 1941; 'L.F.', 'Lockhart's Novels', *NQ*, 15 March and 5 April 1941; M. F. Brightfield, 'Lockhart's Quarterly Contributors', *PMLA* lix, 1944; C. O. Parsons, 'The Possible Origin of Lockhart's "Adam Blair" ', *NQ*, 17 November 1945; and Virginia Woolf, 'Lockhart's Criticism', in *The Moment and Other Essays*, 1947. M. Lochhead's *Lockhart*, 1954, contains a little new material.

There is a long-standing controversy on the authorship of 'The Lone Shieling', a lyric which appeared in *Blackwood's* in September 1829 with the description: 'Canadian Boat-song—(from the Gaelic).' This famous poem, which is neither a boat-song (in any usual sense) nor a translation from the Gaelic, has been attributed to Scott, 'Christopher North', Hogg, and others. In *The Lone Shieling*, Toronto, 1941, G. H. Needler argued at some length that it was written by D. M. Moir, inspired by Galt's work for the Canada Company. A full bibliography of the controversy cannot be included here, but Francis R. Hart argued well in the *TLS* for 27 February 1959 that the poem is the work of Lockhart. Mr. Hart is the author of an important unpublished study of Lockhart. He has written on the significance of the corrected proof sheets of Lockhart's *Scott* in *Studies in Bibliography*, vol. xiv (Charlottesville, Virginia).

HENRY LUTTRELL, ?1765–1851.

Henry Luttrell, who was a natural son of Lord Carhampton,

published *Lines written at Ampthill-Park, in the Autumn of 1818* in 1819. *Advice to Julia: A Letter in Rhyme*, a witty poem admired by Byron, appeared in 1820. *Letters to Julia, in Rhyme*, 3rd ed., 1822, includes *Lines written at Ampthill-Park* as well as a revised form of the main poem. *Crockford-House, a Rhapsody: In Two Cantos* [with] *A Rhymer in Rome*, appeared in 1827.

A. Dobson's 'A Forgotten Poet of Society' (*St. James's Magazine*, xxxiii, January 1878) is reprinted as 'Luttrell's Letters to Julia', in *A Paladin of Philanthropy*, 1899. See also A. Crosse, 'An Old Society Wit', *Temple Bar*, civ, 1895. Luttrell was a great wit and diner-out. There are numerous references to him in *The Greville Memoirs* (see p. 490 above), as well as in the letters and journals of Samuel Rogers (and see P. W. Clayden, *Rogers and his Contemporaries*, 2 vols., 1889), Moore, Sydney Smith, and other members of the Holland House circle.

WILLIAM MAGINN, 1793–1842.

Maginn's *Miscellaneous Writings* were edited by R. Shelton Mackenzie, 5 vols., New York, 1855–7. A 2-vol. collection, *Miscellanies: Prose and Verse*, ed. R. W. Montagu [Johnson], with a Memoir, appeared in 1885; *Ten Tales*, with a preface signed 'W. B.', appeared in 1933.

Throughout his life Maginn contributed to numerous periodicals, notably *Blackwood's* (he was one of the writers of the *Noctes Ambrosianæ*: see John Wilson below) and *Fraser's*. Apart from uncertain attributions (such as *The Red Barn: A Tale, Founded on Fact*, 1828), the following includes all his writings published in book form, mostly after his death: *Whitehall, or The Days of George IV*, [1827]; *Magazine Miscellanies*, [1840]; *John Manesty, the Liverpool Merchant*, 2 vols., 1844; *Maxims of Sir Morgan O'Doherty, Bart.*, 1849; *Homeric Ballads: with Translations and Notes*, 1850; *Shakespeare Papers: Pictures Grave and Gay*, 1859 (1860, adds an essay on *Hamlet*); and *A Gallery of Illustrious Literary Characters (1830–1838). Drawn by . . . Daniel Maclise . . . with Notices chiefly by . . . William Maginn*, ed. by W. Bates, [1873]. *A Story without a Tale*, first published in *Blackwood's Magazine*, April 1834, and reprinted in *Tales from Blackwood*, ii, was separately issued with a preface by G. Saintsbury in 1928 as no. 4 of the 'Baskerville Series'. Maginn contributed four tales to vol. i of T. Crofton Croker's *Fairy Legends and Traditions of the*

*South of Ireland* (3 vols., 1825–8). One or two other short stories and possible attributions are mentioned in the *CBEL*.

The list of Maginn's writings in Appendix IV of Michael Sadleir's *Bulwer and his Wife: A Panorama, 1803–1836*, 1933, should be checked against that in vol. i of the same writer's *XIX Century Fiction*. The fullest recent account of Maginn is that by Miriam M. H. Thrall in *Rebellious Fraser's*, New York, 1934. See also 'The Doctor', in *Fraser's Magazine*, January 1831 (by Lockhart: reprinted in *A Gallery of Illustrious Literary Characters*, ed. W. Bates, [1873]); E. V. Kenealy and D. M. Moir, 'William Maginn, LL.D.', *Dublin University Magazine*, xxiii, 1844; S. C. Hall, *A Book of Memories*, 1871; M. Elwin, *Victorian Wallflowers*, 1934; *TLS*, 22 August 1942 ('Tragedy of a Writer: Maginn'); and R. M. Wardle, 'Outwitting Hazlitt', *MLN* lvii, 1942.

Charles Robert Maturin, 1782–1824.

Maturin published the following works of prose fiction: *Fatal Revenge, or the Family of Montorio*, 3 vols., 1807; *The Wild Irish Boy*, 3 vols., 1808; *The Milesian Chief*, 4 vols., 1812; *Women, or Pour et Contre*, 3 vols., 1818; *Melmoth the Wanderer*, 4 vols., 1820; and *The Albigenses*, 4 vols., 1824.

Maturin also published three tragedies, *Bertram, or The Castle of St Aldobrand*, 1816; *Manuel*, 1817; and *Fredolfo*, 1819; and *Sermons*, 1819. 'Extracts from some Unpublished Scenes of Manuel' appeared in the *New Monthly Magazine*, xi, 1819, and *Six Sermons of the Errors of the Roman Catholic Church* at Dublin in 1824.

*Tales of Mystery*, ed. G. Saintsbury, 1891, contains selections from Maturin, as well as from Mrs. Radcliffe and M. G. Lewis.

Early essays may be found in the *Edinburgh Review*, July 1821 (a review of Melmoth, partly reprinted in *Famous Reviews*, ed. R. B. Johnson, 1914); 'The Writings of Maturin', *London Magazine*, iii, 1821; 'The Conversations of Maturin', *New Monthly Magazine*, xix, 1827. See also the 3-vol. reprint of *Melmoth* published in 1892, which contains a Memoir, a critical essay, and a bibliography; O. Elton, *A Survey of English Literature 1780–1830*, vol. i, 1912; 'Maturin and the Novel of Terror', *TLS*, 26 August 1920; Edith Birkhead, *The Tale of Terror*, 1921; N. Idman, *Charles Robert Maturin, his Life and Works*, Helsingfors, 1923; W. Scholten, *Charles Robert Maturin, the Terror-Novelist*, Amsterdam, 1933; and E. A. Baker, *The History of the*

*English Novel*, v, 1934. In his early years Balzac was much influenced by *Melmoth*, which was translated into French in 1821. In 1835 he published *Melmoth réconcilié*, one of the 'Études philosophiques' of his *Comédie humaine*. See G. T. Clapton, 'Balzac, Baudelaire and Maturin', *French Quarterly*, June and September 1930.

THOMAS MEDWIN, 1788–1869.

An early poem, *The Pindarries* (afterwards affixed to *The Angler in Wales*), seems to have been published *c.* 1815. *Sketches in Hindoostan with Other Poems* appeared in 1821. *Ahasuerus the Wanderer*, a dramatic legend in six parts, was published in London in 1823. His *Journal of the Conversations of Lord Byron . . . at Pisa* appeared in 1824. In 1832 he published a translation of the *Agamemnon* of Aeschylus. *The Shelley Papers*, containing the *Memoir of Percy Bysshe Shelley: By T. Medwin, Esq.*, were published in 1833. *The Angler in Wales, or Days and Nights of Sportsmen* came out in 2 vols. in 1834 (vol. ii contains a good deal relating to Byron). *Lady Singleton, or the World as It Is*, a novel in 3 vols., was published in 1842. Medwin's *Life of Shelley* was published in 2 vols. in 1847 (ed. H. B. Forman, 1913). Four of his contributions to *Bentley's Miscellany*—'Mascalbruni', 'The Contrabandista', 'Pasquale', and 'The Quarantine'—are reprinted in *Tales from Bentley*, 1859–60.

The reliability of the *Conversations of Lord Byron* is discussed in studies of Byron: for early treatments of the matter see *Blackwood's Magazine*, November 1824; the *Gentleman's Magazine*, November 1824; John Murray's privately printed *Notes on Capt. Medwin's Conversations of Lord Byron*, 1824 (reprinted in *The Works of Lord Byron*, Murray, 1829); and *Capt. Medwin Vindicated from the Calumnies of the Reviewers by Vindex*, 1825. Medwin's account of Shelley is examined by N. I. White and other writers on Shelley. There is a biographical study, *Captain Medwin: Friend of Byron and Shelley*, by E. J. Lovell, Austin, Texas, 1962.

JOHN HERMAN MERIVALE, 1779–1844.

*Poems Original and Translated, now first Collected*, appeared in 2 vols. in 1828–38, and 'corrected' in 1844. There may have been a separate edition of *The Minstrel, Book III: In Continuation of Dr. Beattie's Poem*, which is included in *Poems Original and*

*Translated.* Apart from contributions to the *Quarterly Review*, the *New Monthly Magazine* and the *Gentleman's Magazine*, and some writings on legal subjects, Merivale also published *Translations chiefly from the Greek Anthology, with Tales and Miscellaneous Poems*, 1806 (with R. Bland); *Collections from the Greek Anthology: By R. Bland and Others*, 1813; *Orlando in Roncesvalles, a Poem*, 1814 (based on the *Morgante Maggiore* of Pulci); *The Two first Cantos of Richardetto, from the Original of N. Fortiguerra*, 1820; and *The Minor Poems of Schiller, translated*, 1844 (partly reprinted from the *New Monthly Magazine*). In 1911 E. H. A. Koch edited *Leaves from the Diary of a Literary Amateur* (published at Hampstead). Merivale was a friend of Byron's, and his name crops up in memoirs of the time. See also *Blackwood's Magazine*, xxxiii–iv; the *Quarterly Review*, xlix, 1833 (H. N. Coleridge on his Greek translations); C. Merivale's article in *Transactions of the Devonshire Association*, 1884; and the article in the *DNB*. Merivale's translations are mentioned in the books on Italian influence by R. Marshall and C. P. Brand mentioned above on p. 478.

JAMES MILL, 1773–1836.

Mill's main publications were *The History of British India*, 3 vols., 1817; *Elements of Political Economy*, 1821; *Essays on Government, Jurisprudence, Liberty of the Press* [etc.] . . . *Reprinted from the Supplement to the Encyclopaedia Britannica* (privately printed, [1825]: other articles, those on 'Caste', 'Economists', and 'Beggars', were not reprinted: the *Essay on Government* was edited by E. Barker, 1937); *Analysis of the Phenomena of the Human Mind*, 2 vols., 1829 (ed. J. S. Mill, 2 vols., 1869); *A Fragment on Mackintosh*, 1835; and *The Principles of Toleration* (reprinted from the *Westminster Review*, July, 1829), 1837.

A. Bain published *James Mill: A Biography* in 1882, G. S. Bower's *Hartley and James Mill* having appeared the previous year. A great deal of information about Mill is to be found in the books on the Utilitarians listed above on pp. 488–9. His son's *Autobiography* is, of course, a primary source. See also *Benthamite Reviewing*, by G. L. Nesbitt, New York, 1934; *The Life of John Stuart Mill*, by M. St. J. Packe, 1954; *The English Utilitarians and India*, by E. Stokes, 1959; *Works and Correspondence of David Ricardo*, ed. P. Sraffa, vols. vi–ix, 1952 (Mill's letters to Ricardo); *Selections from the Correspondence of Macvey*

*Napier*, privately printed, 1877; D. Forbes, 'James Mill and India', *Cambridge Journal*, v, 1951; and W. J. Burston, 'James Mill on the Aims of Education', *Cambridge Journal*, vi, 1952.

HENRY HART MILMAN, 1791–1868.

In verse Milman published *Fazio. A Tragedy*, 1815 (1821, with *The Belvidere Apollo* [a Prize Poem, first published 1812], &c.); *Samor, Lord of the Bright City: An Heroic Poem*, 1818; *The Fall of Jerusalem: A Dramatic Poem*, 1820; *The Martyr of Antioch: A Dramatic Poem*, 1822; *Belshazzar: A Dramatic Poem*, 1822; and *Anne Boleyn: A Dramatic Poem*, 1826. The *Poetical Works of Milman, Bowles, Wilson, and Barry Cornwall* appeared in Paris in 1829. Milman's *Poetical Works* were collected in 3 vols. in 1839. Milman also translated *Nala and Damayanti and Other Poems . . . from the Sanscrit into English Verse*, 1835, and was responsible for the translation of the *Bacchae* in *The Agamemnon of Æschylus and the Bacchanals of Euripides, &c.*, translated, 1865 (1888, *Bacchae* only). He contributed a number of hymns to Reginald Heber's collection.

His principal writings in prose were *The History of the Jews*, 3 vols., 1829–30 (revised in later editions; 'Everyman's Library', 2 vols., 1909); *The History of Christianity, to the Abolition of Paganism in the Roman Empire*, 3 vols., 1840 (3 vols., 1863, revised); and the *History of Latin Christianity; including that of the Popes to Nicolas V*, 6 vols., 1854–5.

He also provided notes for Gibbon's *Decline and Fall*, 12 vols., 1838–9, and edited *The Life of Edward Gibbon, with Selections from his Correspondence*, 1839, and *The Works of Q. Horatius Flaccus illustrated . . . from the Remains of Ancient Art*, 1849 (with a Life by Milman).

His obituary of Macaulay, first published in *Proceedings of the Royal Society*, xi, 1862, appeared as a pamphlet in 1862 and was reprinted in vol. viii of Macaulay's *History* the same year. He contributed to the *Quarterly Review*, from which *Savonarola, Erasmus, and other Essays* were reprinted in 1870. His minor writings include *Annals of S. Paul's Cathedral*, 1868, sermons, and two prize essays.

There is a biography by A. Milman, *Henry Hart Milman: A Biographical Sketch*, 1900. C. Venatier's *Milman's Fall of Jerusalem*, Breslau, 1893, is a dissertation. See also A. P. Stanley, 'The Late Dean of St. Paul's', *Macmillan's Magazine*, January

1869; and C. H. E. Smyth, *Dean Milman*, 1949. In the *TLS*, 29 June 1962, F. May claims for Milman some translations from Petrarch in Foscolo's *Essays on Petrarch.*

MARY RUSSELL MITFORD, 1787–1855.

In verse she published *Poems*, 1810 (with additions, 1811); *Christina: The Maid of the South Seas. A Poem*, 1811; *Blanche of Castile*, 1812; *Watlington Hill*, 1812; *Narrative Poems on the Female Character*, vol. i, 1813 (the only volume); *Julian: A Tragedy*, 1823; *Foscari: A Tragedy*, 1826 (together as *Foscari and Julian*, 1827); *Dramatic Scenes, Sonnets, and Other Poems*, 1827; *Rienzi: A Tragedy*, 1828; *Mary, Queen of Scots: A Scene in English Verse*, 1831; *Charles the First: An Historical Tragedy*, 1834; and *Sadak and Kalasrade, or the Waters of Oblivion: A Romantic Opera*, 1835. Her *Dramatic Works* appeared in 2 vols. in 1854, with an interesting autobiographical introduction.

*Our Village: Sketches of Rural Character and Scenery* appeared in 5 vols. between 1824 and 1832. Some of the Sketches had been turned down by Campbell for the *New Monthly Magazine*, but many of them had been published in *The Lady's Magazine* and other 'respectable publications'. According to information supplied by Mr. S. H. Horrocks (of Reading Public Libraries) the most complete edition ever published after the original editions was the Bohn edition, which first appeared in 1848 and which 'lacks only two items from the original 5 vols.'. Most later 'editions' of *Our Village* consist in fact of selections. *Belford Regis: or Sketches of a Country Town* appeared in 3 vols. in 1835, and *Country Stories* in 1837. A collection, *Atherton and Other Tales*, appeared in 3 vols. in 1854. Miss Mitford also contributed a number of stories to *The Edinburgh Tales*, ed. C. I. Johnstone, 3 vols., 1845–6; to *Finden's Tableaux*, 1838, 1839, and 1841; and to numerous Annuals.

Miss Mitford edited *Stories of American Life by American Writers*, 3 vols., 1830; *Lights and Shadows of American Life*, 3 vols., 1832; and two series of *American Stories for Little Boys and Girls*, 1831–2.

*Recollections of a Literary Life; or Books, Places, and People* appeared in 3 vols. in 1852. Letters have been published in *The Life of Mary Russell Mitford . . . in a Selection from her Letters*, ed. A. G. L'Estrange, 3 vols., 1870 ('Second and Revised Edition'); *Letters of Mary Russell Mitford*, 2nd series, ed. H. Chorley, 2 vols., 1872; *The Friendships of Mary Russell Mitford in Letters from her*

*Literary Correspondents*, ed. A. G. L'Estrange, 2 vols., 1882; *Mary Russell Mitford: Correspondence with Charles Boner & John Ruskin*, ed. Elizabeth Lee, 1914; and R. M. Kettle, *Memoirs and Letters with Letters of Mary Russell Mitford to him during Ten Years*, 2 vols., 1871. In 1925 R. B. Johnson published a selection from her letters.

There are several books about her: W. J. Roberts, *Mary Russell Mitford: The Tragedy of a Blue Stocking*, 1913; Constance Hill, *Mary Russell Mitford and her Surroundings*, 1920; Marjorie Astin, *Mary Russell Mitford: her Circle and her Books*, 1930; and Vera Watson, *Mary Russell Mitford*, [1949]. There are early impressions by M. O. Oliphant, *Blackwood's Magazine*, June 1854 and March 1870 ('Miss Austen and Miss Mitford'); W. Maginn, *A Gallery of Illustrious Literary Characters*, ed. W. Bates, [1873]; and H. Martineau, *Biographical Sketches, 1852–1875*, 1877. Further information may be found in *The Literary Life of the Rev. William Harness*, by A. G. L'Estrange, 1871; *Memorials of Mrs. Hemans*, by H. F. Chorley, 2 vols., 1836; *Thirty Years' Musical Recollections*, 2 vols., 1862, by the same author; *Some Literary Recollections*, by J. Payn, 1884; and *Elizabeth Barrett to Miss Mitford*, ed. Betty Miller, 1954. More recent notes and essays include M. Kent, 'Mary Mitford's Letters', *Cornhill Magazine*, clix, 1936; 'R. H. Horne on Miss Mitford after Forty Years', *NQ*, 9 March 1946; V. G. Watson, *NQ*, 11 June 1949; and M. H. Dodds, 'Mary Russell Mitford and Jane Austen', *NQ*, 29 April 1950. See also J. Carter and G. Pollard, *An Enquiry into the Nature of Certain XIX Century Pamphlets*, 1934.

Reading Public Libraries published a brief catalogue of their centennial exhibition, *Mary Russell Mitford: 1787–1855*, compiled by Miss D. J. Phillips. This contains information about manuscripts and a list of the individual Tales. There is a useful article by W. A. Coles in *Studies in Bibliography, Published by the University of Virginia*, 1959: 'Magazine and other Contributions by Mary Russell Mitford and T. N. Talfourd.'

David Macbeth Moir ('*Δ*'), 1798–1851.

In 1816 Moir published *The Bombardment of Algiers, and Other Poems*, and in 1824 *The Legend of Geneviève: With other Tales and Poems*, (by 'Delta'). *The Life of Mansie Wauch*, first published in *Blackwood's*, appeared as a book in 1828 (the 1839 edition was revised, and illustrated by Cruikshank). *Domestic Verses: By Δ*, came out in 1843. *Sketches of the Poetical Literature of the Past Half-*

*Century, in Six Lectures*, were published in 1851. Moir's *Poetical Works* were edited with a Memoir by T. Aird in 2 vols. in 1852.

Moir also wrote the final chapters of Galt's *The Last of the Lairds*, 1826; contributed an interesting Memoir of Galt to the [1841] edition of *The Annals of the Parish and The Ayrshire Legatees*, ('Blackwood's Standard Novels'); wrote 'School Recollections' in *Friendship's Offering*, 1829, and 'The Bridal of Borthwick', in *The Club Book*, ed. Andrew Picken, 3 vols., 1831; and contributed the account of the Roman Antiquities of Inveresk in the *Statistical Account of Scotland*, 1845 (the account was published separately in 1860).

Moir began contributing to periodicals when he was about fourteen, and soon he was writing in the *Scots Magazine*. Throughout his life he wrote a great deal in periodicals, including Constable's *Edinburgh Magazine*, *Fraser's*, and the *Edinburgh Literary Gazette*. A list of nearly 400 of his contributions to *Blackwood's* is printed on pp. 128–30 of the *General Index* to the first fifty volumes, 1855. In 1826 he contributed to *Janus, or the Edinburgh Literary Almanack*, ed. Lockhart. He also wrote several medical books and a number of memoirs, including that of Mrs. Hemans in the 1848 edition of her poems. The view that he wrote 'The Canadian Boat Song', advanced by E. MacCurdy in *A Literary Enigma*, Stirling, 1935, was supported by G. H. Needler but rejected by F. R. Hart (see Lockhart above).

On Moir see W. Maginn's *Gallery of Illustrious Literary Characters*, ed. W. Bates, [1873]; *Blackwood's Magazine*, lxx, 1851; *Eclectic Review*, xcvi, 1852; G. Gilfillan, *A Gallery of Literary Portraits*, vol. ii, 1850; Sir G. Douglas, *The Blackwood Group* [1897]; and E. H. A. Robson, *A Preparation for a Study of Metropolitan Scots of the . . . Nineteenth Century as exemplified in 'Mansie Wauch'*, 1937.

Information about Moir may be found in the *DNB* and in books about Galt, De Quincey, and the *Blackwood's* group.

ROBERT MONTGOMERY, 1807–55.

Montgomery's main publications in verse include *The Stage-Coach*, 1827; *The Age Reviewed: A Satire*, 1827 (1828, rev. ed.); *The Omnipresence of the Deity*, 1828 (28 editions by 1855); *The Puffiad: A Satire*, 1828; *A Universal Prayer; Death; A Vision of Heaven; and a Vision of Hell*, 1828; *Satan*, 1830; *Oxford*, 1831 (4th ed., Oxford, 1835, adds recollections of Shelley); *The Messiah*,

1832; *Woman, the Angel of Life*, 1833; *Ellesmere Lake: Poems*, 1836; *Sacred Meditations in Verse*, 1842; *Luther*, 1842; *Scarborough: A Poetic Glance*, 1846; *The Christian Life: A Manual of Sacred Verse*, 1849; *The Hero's Funeral*, 1852; and *The Sanctuary: A Companion in Verse for the Prayer Book*, 1855. Montgomery's sermons and theological writings are not listed here.

The *Poetical Works* appeared in 6 vols. in 1839–40, and again in 1841–3. In 1853 there was an edition by J. Twycross. *Selections* were published in 1836, with an introduction. *The Poetical Works*, 3 vols., Glasgow, 1839, is a full selection. See also *Religion and Poetry*, ed. S. J. H., 1847; *Lyra Christiana*, 1851 (Montgomery's own selection); and *Christian Poetry*, ed. E. Farr, [1856].

Macaulay attacked *The Omnipresence of the Deity* in the *Edinburgh Review*, li, 1830, his essay being reprinted in his *Critical and Historical Essays*, 1843, &c. See also E. Clarkson, *Robert Montgomery and his Reviewers*, 1830; the same writer's *The Reviewers Reviewed*, [? 1830]; R. H. Horne, *A New Spirit of the Age*, vol. ii, 1844; W. Maginn, *A Gallery of Illustrious Literary Characters*, ed. W. Bates, [1873]; and *The London Quarterly and Holborn Review*, ed. J. Alan Kay, April 1954. There is a fuller list of Montgomery's writings in the *Gentleman's Magazine*, 1856, i, p. 312. Further information may be found in the *DNB*. An accurate bibliography of Montgomery would be very difficult to compile; for, as Lowndes observes, 'this author was extremely anxious to make his books appear very popular, and therefore constantly changed his title pages, and even cancelled or sold off almost as waste one edition for the sake of printing another'.

THOMAS MOORE, 1779–1852.

Moore's main publications in book form were *Odes of Anacreon, translated into English Verse*, 1800; *The Poetical Works of the late Thomas Little, Esq.*, 1801; *Oh Lady Fair: A Ballad*, 1802; *A Candid Appeal to Public Confidence*, 1803; *Sequel to Oh Lady Fair!*, 1804; *Songs and Glees*, 1804; *A Canadian Boat-Song, arranged for three Voices*, 1805; *Epistles, Odes, and other Poems*, 1806; *A Selection of Irish Melodies*, 10 parts and supplement [1808–34]; *Irish Melodies*, 1821 (first authorized edition of the words alone); *Corruption and Intolerance: Two Poems*, 1808; *The Sceptic: a Philosophical Satire*, 1809; *A Letter to the Roman Catholics of Dublin*, Dublin, 1810; *M. P.; or, The Blue Stocking: a Comic Opera*, 1811 (libretto and music by Moore); *A Melologue upon National*

*Music*, 1811 (reprinted with *Irish Melodies*); *Parody of a Celebrated Letter*, 1812 (privately printed); *Intercepted Letters; or, The Two-penny Postbag*, 1813; *Sacred Songs*, 2 parts, 1816–24; *Lines on the Death of* — [Sheridan], 1816; *Lalla Rookh; an Oriental Romance*, 1817; *National Airs*, 6 parts, 1818–27; *The Fudge Family in Paris*, 1818; *Melodies, Songs, and Sacred Songs*, 1818; *The World at Westminster*, 2 vols., 1818; *Tom Crib's Memorial to Congress*, 1819; *The Loves of the Angels*, 1823; *Fables for the Holy Alliance; Rhymes on the Road, &c., &c.*, 1823; *Memoirs of Captain Rock, the celebrated Irish Chieftain*, 1824; *Memoirs of . . . Sheridan*, 1825 (5th ed., 1827, with new preface); *Evenings in Greece*, 2 parts, 1826–32; *The Epicurean: A Tale*, 1827; *A Set of Glees*, 1827; *Odes upon Cash, Corn, Catholics, and other Matters*, 1828; *Legendary Ballads*, 1828; *Letters and Journals of Lord Byron; with Notices of his Life*, 2 vols., 1830; *The Life and Death of Lord Edward FitzGerald*, 2 vols., 1831; *The Summer Fête*, 1831; *Travels of an Irish Gentleman in Search of a Religion*, 2 vols., 1833; *Vocal Miscellany*, 2 nos., 1834–5; *The Fudges in England*, 1835; *History: Ireland* (in D. Lardner's *The Cabinet Cyclopaedia*, 4 vols., 1835–46); *Alciphron: a Poem*, 1839. In 1878 R. H. Shepherd edited *Prose and Verse . . . with Suppressed Passages from the Memoirs of Lord Byron*.

Throughout his life Moore contributed a great deal to numerous periodicals, including *The Times* and the *Edinburgh Review*.

*The Poetical Works of Thomas Moore, Collected by Himself* appeared in 10 vols. in 1840–1, superseding earlier unauthorized editions. Shepherd's *Prose and Verse*, mentioned above, contains some other poems. In 1910 A. D. Godley edited the Oxford edition, *The Poetical Works. Poetry of Thomas Moore*, ed. C. L. Falkiner, 1903, is a selection in the Golden Treasury series, with an interesting preface. In 1929 S. O'Fáolain edited another selection, *Lyrics and Satires from Tom Moore*, Dublin.

Moore's *Memoirs, Journal, and Correspondence* were edited by Lord John Russell in 8 vols. in 1853–6. *Tom Moore's Diary*, ed. J. B. Priestley, 1925, consists of selections from these volumes. Other letters by Moore are to be found in numerous books, notably in *Notes from the Letters of Thomas Moore to His Music Publisher, James Power*, ed. T. C. Croker, New York [? 1854], an inaccurate volume. A series of manuscript letters from Moore to Mary Shelley was sold at Sotheby's in 1962. Professor W. S. Dowden of the Rice Institute is now completing an edition of

Moore's letters. Much the best biography is H. M. Jones's *The Harp that Once —*, New York, 1937. Other general books of varying merit are G. Vallat's *Étude sur la vie et les œuvres de Thomas Moore*, 1886; Stephen Gwynn's *Thomas Moore*, 1905 (English Men of Letters); L. A. G. Strong's *The Minstrel Boy*, 1937; A. Stockmann, *Thomas Moore, der irische Freiheitssänger*, 1910; and W. F. Trench, *Tom Moore*, 1934 (a sensible brief study). A great deal of information is to be found in books by his contemporaries, such as *Conversations of Lord Byron with the Countess of Blessington*, 1834; Leigh Hunt's *Lord Byron and Some of his Contemporaries* (1828) and *Autobiography* (1850); N. P. Willis's *Pencillings by the Way*, 3 vols., 1835; W. Gardiner's *Music and Friends*, 1838–53; Lockhart's *Memoirs of Scott*, 1837–8; and Crabb Robinson's journals.

The *Irish Melodies* have often been discussed, notably in C. V. Stanford's *The Irish Melodies of Thomas Moore: The Original Airs Restored and Arranged for the Voice*, 1895; *The Minstrelsy of Ireland*, by A. Moffat, 1897; and D. J. O'Sullivan's 'The Bunting Collection of Irish Folk Music and Songs', ed. for the *Journal of the Irish Folk Song Society*, 1926–32.

A good deal has been written on Moore's influence abroad. See particularly A. B. Thomas, *Moore en France . . . 1819–1830*, 1911; F. Baldensperger, 'Thomas Moore et Alfred de Vigny', *MLR*, i, 1906; K. Campbell, *The Poems of Edgar Allan Poe*, 1917, and 'Poe's Reading', *University of Texas Studies in English*, 1925; H. H. Jordan, 'Poe's Debt to Thomas Moore', *PMLA* lxiii, 1948; and T. O. Mabbott, 'Poe's "The Sleeper" Again', *American Literature*, 1949.

Hazlitt often wrote about Moore, notably in *The Spirit of the Age*, 1825. Peacock's attack on *The Epicurean* was first published in the *Westminster Review*, viii, 1827, and is now in vol. ix (1926) of his *Works*, ed. H. F. B. Brett-Smith and C. E. Jones. Leigh Hunt wrote well on *M. P.; or, The Blue Stocking* (see his *Dramatic Criticism*, ed. L. H. and C. W. Houtchens, 1949).

Also worth noting are W. C. Brown, 'Thomas Moore and English Interest in the East', *SP* xxxiv, 1937; H. O. Brogan, 'Thomas Moore, Irish Satirist and Keeper of the English Conscience', *PQ* xxiv, 1945; W. F. P. Stockley, 'Moore's Satirical Verse', *Queen's Quarterly*, 1905, and his study in *Essays in Irish Biography*, Cork, 1933; J. Hennig, 'Thomas Moore and the Holy Alliance', *Irish Monthly*, 1946. The fullest discussion of his

*Letters and Journals of Lord Byron* is in Doris Langley Moore's *The Late Lord Byron*, 1961. H. H. Jordan's 'Byron and Moore', *MLQ* ix, 1948, is a useful study of Moore's influence on Byron. R. Birley discusses *Lalla Rookh* in *Sunk Without Trace*, 1962.

Apart from *CBEL*, the following present bibliographical assistance: M. J. MacManus, *A Bibliographical Hand-List of the First Editions of Thomas Moore*, Dublin, 1934; P. H. Muir, 'Thomas Moore's Irish Melodies, 1808–1834', *Colophon*, no. 15, 1933; and H. H. Jordan in *ERPE* (a useful account of scholarly work on Moore). In 'Thomas Moore and the Review of *Christabel*', *MP*, liii, 1956, Jordan argues against Moore's authorship, maintained by Elisabeth Schneider in *MLN* lxi, 1946. H. G. Wright has made another attribution in 'Thomas Moore as the Author of *Spirit of Boccaccio's Decameron*', *RES* xxiii, 1947.

MORGAN, LADY (SYDNEY OWENSON), 1776–1859.

Lady Morgan published the following works of prose fiction: *St. Clair, or the Heiress of Desmond*, 1803 (3rd edition, much revised, 2 vols., 1812); *The Novice of St. Dominick*, 4 vols., 1805; *The Wild Irish Girl: a National Tale*, 3 vols., 1806; *Woman, or Ida of Athens*, 4 vols., 1809; *The Missionary: an Indian Tale*, 3 vols., 1811; *O'Donnel: a National Tale*, 3 vols., 1814; *Florence Macarthy: an Irish Tale*, 4 vols., 1818; *The O'Briens and the O'Flahertys: a National Tale*, 4 vols., 1827; *The Princess, or The Beguine*, 3 vols., 1835; *Woman and her Master*, 2 vols., 1840.

Her other writings include *Poems*, Dublin, 1801; *The Lay of an Irish Harp, or Metrical Fragments*, 1807; *Patriotic Sketches of Ireland*, 2 vols., 1807; *France*, 1817; *France in 1829–30*, 2 vols., 1830; *Italy*, 2 vols., 1821 (slightly different edition, in 3 vols., the same year); *The Mohawks: a Satirical Poem* (with Sir Charles Morgan) 1822; *The Life and Times of Salvator Rosa*, 2 vols., 1824; *Absenteeism*, 1825; *The Book of the Boudoir*, 2 vols., 1829; *The Book without a Name* (with Sir Charles Morgan), 2 vols., 1841; and *An Odd Volume, extracted from an Autobiography*, 1859. Lady Morgan's *Memoirs: Autobiography, Diaries and Correspondence* [ed. by W. Hepworth Dixon] appeared in 2 vols. in 1862.

There is a modern study by L. Stevenson, *The Wild Irish Girl*, 1936. See also the characteristic attacks by Croker in the *Quarterly Review*, xvii (1817) and xxv (1821); *The Friends, Foes, and Adventures of Lady Morgan*, by W. J. Fitzpatrick, Dublin, 1859; 'Lady Morgan', by G. E. Jewsbury, *Cornhill Magazine*, vii,

1863; *English Women of Letters*, by J. Kavanagh, vol. ii, 1863; *A Gallery of Illustrious Literary Characters*, by W. Maginn, ed. W. Bates, [1873]; *Little Memoirs of the Nineteenth Century*, by 'George Paston', 1902; and *These were Muses*, by Mona Wilson, 1924.

JAMES JUSTINIAN MORIER, 1780–1849.

Morier wrote the following works of prose fiction: *The Adventures of Hajji Baba of Ispahan*, 3 vols., 1824 (2nd ed., 3 vols., 1824, with long preface: rev. eds. 1835 and 1863: numerous other editions and reprints including editions in 'Everyman's Library', 1914, and 'World's Classics', 1923); *The Adventures of Hajji Baba of Ispahan in England*, 2 vols., 1828 (rev. ed. 1835; 'World's Classics' ed. 1925); *Zohrab the Hostage*, 3 vols., 1832 (revised with notes, 1833); *Ayesha: The Maid of Kars*, 3 vols., 1834; *Abel Allnutt: a Novel*, 3 vols., 1837; *An Oriental Tale*, Brighton, 1839 (privately printed); *The Mirza*, 3 vols., 1841; *Misselmah: A Persian Tale*, Brighton, 1847; *Martin Toutrond: A Frenchman in London in 1831*, 1849 (two issues, one anonymous).

Morier also wrote a *Journey through Persia, Armenia and Asia Minor to Constantinople, 1808–9 . . .*, 1812; *Second Journey through Persia, Armenia and Asia Minor . . . 1810–16 . . .*, 1818; *The Adventures of Tom Spicer, who advertised for a Wife*, 1840 (privately printed); and contributed to *Literary Contributions by Various Authors in aid of . . . The Hospital . . . at Brompton*, 1846. He 'edited' *The Banished*, 3 vols., 1839 (from the German of Hauff), and *St. Roche: A Romance, from the German*, 3 vols., 1847.

Scott wrote an anonymous review of *Hajji Baba* in the *Quarterly Review*, xxxix, 1829. See also 'James Morier', *Fraser's Magazine*, vii, 1852; W. Maginn, *A Gallery of Illustrious Literary Characters*, ed. W. Bates, [1873]; F. W. Chandler, *The Literature of Roguery*, vol. ii, Boston and New York, 1907; K. J. Zeidler, *Beckford, Hope und Morier als Vertreter des orientalischen Romans*, Leipzig, 1909; 'The Sun and the Pen', *TLS*, 22 July 1949; and 'Orientals in Picaresque: A Chapter in the History of the Oriental Tale in England', by Fatma Moussa-Mahmoud, in *Cairo Studies in English*, ed. M. Wahba, Cairo, 1961–2.

JOHN MOULTRIE, 1799–1874.

In verse Moultrie published *Poems*, 1837; *The Dream of Life, and other Poems*, 1843; *Saint Mary, the Virgin and the Wife*, 1850; *The Black Fence, a Lay of Modern Rome*, 1850; *The Song of the*

*Rugby Church-Builders*, [1851]; *A Pentecostal Ode*, 1852; and *Altars, Hearths, and Graves*, 1854.

He also contributed to *The Etonian*, 1820–1, and to Knight's *Quarterly Magazine*, 1823–4. He compiled *Psalms and Hymns*, 1851, which contains a number of his own hymns, and edited *The Poetical Remains of W. S. Walker*, with a Memoir, 1852. He edited Gray's *Poetical Works*, Eton, 1847 (2nd ed.). He published a volume of *Sermons* in 1852.

His *Poems, with a Memoir by Prebendary [Derwent] Coleridge* appeared in 2 vols. in 1876.

J. Julian's *Dictionary of Hymnology*, 1892, contains information about Moultrie's hymns. Further sources of information are mentioned in the *DNB*. Praed, Macaulay, and Thomas Arnold were among his friends.

EDWARD MOXON, 1801–58.

Moxon published *The Prospect, and Other Poems*, 1826; *Christmas, A Poem*, 1829; *Sonnets*, 2 parts, 1830–5 (reprinted 1837, 1843, and 1871); and *Charles Lamb*, 1835 (privately printed). He published and edited *The Englishman's Magazine*, August–October, 1831.

Lamb's *Athenaeum* review of the sonnets (13 April 1833) is reprinted in his *Works*, ed. E. V. Lucas, i, 1903. Croker attacked the sonnets in the *Quarterly* in 1837 (vol. lix). Information about Moxon is to be found in books about Lamb (whose adopted daughter, Emma Isola, Moxon married), Wordsworth, Samuel Rogers, and other men of letters of the time. Crabb Robinson often refers to him. See also N. I. White, 'Literature and the Law of Libel', *SP* xxii, 1925 (an account of Moxon's trial for blasphemous libel in 1841: see *State Trials*, new series, iv, 693–722); E. G. Wilson, 'Edward Moxon and the First Two Editions of Milnes's Biography of Keats', *Harvard Library Bulletin*, v, 1951; and particularly H. G. Merriam, *Edward Moxon, Publisher of Poets*, New York, 1939.

SIR WILLIAM FRANCIS PATRICK NAPIER, 1785–1860.

The *History of the War in the Peninsula and in the South of France* appeared in 6 vols. in 1828–40, and in a revised edition in 6 vols. in 1851. Apart from other editions, there was an edition abridged by Napier himself and entitled *English Battles and Sieges in the Peninsula*, 1852. He also wrote *The Conquest of Scinde*,

*with some Introductory Passages in the Life of . . . Sir Charles Napier*, 2 vols., 1845; *History of Sir Charles Napier's Administration of Scinde, and Campaign in the Cutchee Hills*, 1851; *Defects, Civil and Military, of the Indian Government, by Sir Charles Napier*, 1853 (edited, with supplementary chapter, by Sir W. Napier); and *The Life and Opinions of General Sir C. J. Napier*, 4 vols., 1857. Napier was an untiring controversialist. Many of his pamphlets and other controversial writings, usually in defence of his own historical works, are listed in the *CBEL* and the *DNB*.

See Sir James Outram, *The Conquest of Scinde: A Commentary*, 1846; G. Buist, *Corrections of a Few of the Errors contained in Sir Wm. Napier's Life of Sir Charles Napier*, 1857; H. A. Bruce (Baron Aberdare), *Life of Sir William Napier*, 2 vols., 1864 (edited by Aberdare); the Hon. Sir J. W. Fortescue, *The Last Post*, 1934; 'General John Jacob's Notes on Sir William Napier . . .', ed. Sir P. R. Cadell, *Journal of Sind Historical Society*, iii, 1938; and M. G. T. Lambrick, *Sir Charles Napier and Sind*, 1952.

Sir Nicholas Harris Nicolas, 1799–1848.

*Observations on the State of Historical Literature* appeared in 1830. It is often bound up with Nicolas's *Refutation of Mr. Palgrave's 'Remarks in Reply to "Observations on the State of Historical Literature"'*, 1831, which contains an appendix relative to the dispute between the two men. Of Nicolas's other numerous and important historical and antiquarian publications only a few can be mentioned here: *Life of William Davison, Secretary of State . . . to Queen Elizabeth*, 1823; *The History of the Battle of Agincourt*, 1827; *History of the Orders of Knighthood of the British Empire*, 4 vols., 1841–2; *A History of the Royal Navy*, 2 vols., 1847 (uncompleted); and *Memoirs of the Life and Times of Sir Christopher Hatton*, 1847. Nicolas also edited *The Literary Remains of Lady Jane Grey*, 1825; *The Poetical Rhapsody of Francis Davison*, 2 vols., 1826; *Private Memoirs of Sir Kenelm Digby*, 1827; *The Letters of Joseph Ritson*, 2 vols., 1833 (with a Memoir of Ritson by Nicolas); *The Complete Angler of Izaak Walton and Charles Cotton*, 2 vols., 1836; and other works. He was responsible for a number of volumes in the Aldine series. With H. Southern, Nicolas was editor of *The Retrospective Review*, 2nd series, 1827–8. He also contributed frequently to the *Gentleman's Magazine*, *Archaeologia*, and other periodicals. A fuller account of his writings may be found in the *DNB*.

Peter George Patmore, 1786–1855.

Patmore published *Letters on England* ('By Victoire, Count de Soligny'), 1823; *British Galleries of Art*, 1824; *Mirror of the Months*, 1826 (a novel); *Rejected Articles*, 1826 (parodies which reached a 4th edition in 1844 under the title, *Imitations of Celebrated Authors*); *Sir Thomas Lawrence's Cabinet of Gems, with . . . Memorials by Peter George Patmore*, 1837; *Finden's Gallery of Beauty, or the Court of Queen Victoria*, ed. Patmore, [1841]; *Chatsworth, or the Romance of a Week*, 3 vols., 1844 [ed. by R. Plumer Ward]; *Marriage in May Fair: A Comedy*, 1854 (2nd ed.); and *My Friends and Acquaintances*, 3 vols., 1855.

Patmore edited the *New Monthly Magazine* from 1841 to 1853, and contributed largely to numerous periodicals. His 'Reminiscences of Charles Lamb, with Original Letters', appeared in the *Court Magazine*, March and December 1835. Hazlitt's *Liber Amoris* was partly based on letters to Patmore.

Information about Patmore may be found in many memoirs of the time, in biographies of his son, Coventry Patmore, and in *Portrait of my Family*, by D. Patmore, 1935.

Thomas Love Peacock, 1785–1866.

In verse Peacock published *The Monks of St. Mark*, 1804; *Palmyra, and other Poems*, 1806; *The Genius of the Thames*, 1810 (reissued in 1812 with *Palmyra, and other poems*); *The Philosophy of Melancholy*, 1812; *Sir Hornbook; or, Childe Launcelot's Expedition. A Grammatico-allegorical Ballad*, 1814; *Sir Proteus: A Satirical Ballad* (by 'P. M. O'Donovan, Esq.'), 1814; *The Round Table; or, King Arthur's Feast* [1817]; *Rhododaphne: or The Thessalian Spell*, 1818; and *Paper Money Lyrics, and Other Poems*, 1837 (privately printed). *A Bill for the Better Promotion of Oppression on the Sabbath Day* was privately printed in 1926.

Peacock's seven works of prose fiction appeared as follows: *Headlong Hall*, 1816; *Melincourt*, 3 vols., 1817, 1856 (with new preface); *Nightmare Abbey*, 1818; *Maid Marian*, 1822; *The Misfortunes of Elphin*, 1829; *Crotchet Castle*, 1831; and *Gryll Grange*, 1861 (first published serially in *Fraser's Magazine*, lxi and lxii, 1860).

In 1837 *Headlong Hall*, *Nightmare Abbey*, *Maid Marian*, and *Crotchet Castle* were republished as vol. 57 of 'Bentley's Standard Novels', with a new preface.

Peacock also wrote 'The Four Ages of Poetry', in *Ollier's Literary Miscellany*, no. 1 (only issue), 1820 (ed. H. F. B. Brett-Smith, 1921, with Shelley's *Defence* and Browning's *Essay on Shelley*); 'Memoirs of Percy Bysshe Shelley', in *Fraser's Magazine*, July 1858 and January 1860, with a supplementary notice in March 1862 (ed. H. F. B. Brett-Smith, 1909); and *Gl'Ingannati: the Deceived . . . and Aelia Laelia Crispis*, 1862.

Peacock's *Works* were edited by H. Cole in 3 vols. in 1875, with a preface by Lord Houghton and a biographical notice by his granddaughter, Edith Nicolls. This edition includes his principal contributions to periodicals. The *Novels, Calidore and Miscellanea* were edited by R. Garnett in 10 vols. in 1891: the *Novels and Rhododaphne* by G. Saintsbury in 5 vols. in 1895–7. An edition of the *Poems* appeared in [1906], edited by R. B. Johnson. *Plays published for the First Time* were edited by A. B. Young, 1910. Peacock's *Letters to Edward Hookham and Percy B. Shelley with Fragments of Unpublished MS.* were edited by R. Garnett, Boston, 1910. All these were superseded by the Halliford Edition, ed. H. F. B. Brett-Smith and C. E. Jones, 10 vols., 1924–34. Vol i is a dry but accurate biography. For further material see *Shelley and his Circle* (p. 615 below).

There is an excellent one-volume edition of *The Novels*, ed. D. Garnett, 1948. There are numerous reprints of the individual novels.

Selections were edited by H. F. B. Brett-Smith in 1928 and by B. R. Redman in 1947 (*The Pleasures of Peacock*, New York).

The best critical study is J.-J. Mayoux's *Un Épicurien anglais: Thomas Love Peacock*, 1933. J. B. Priestley's *Thomas Love Peacock* (English Men of Letters, 1927) is a good introduction. Of the numerous other books mention may be made of *The Life of T. L. Peacock*, by C. van Doren, 1911; A. M. Freeman, *T. L. Peacock: A Critical Study*, 1911; A. H. Able, *Meredith and Peacock: A Study in Literary Influence*, Philadelphia, 1933; and B. Cellini, *T. L. Peacock*, Rome, 1937.

Essays and articles worth mentioning are the article in the *Edinburgh Review*, lxviii, 1839 [by J. Spedding], and that in cxlii, 1875; J. Davies, 'Thomas Love Peacock', *Contemporary Review*, xxv, 1875; R. Buchanan, 'Thomas Love Peacock: A Personal Reminiscence', *New Quarterly Magazine*, iv, 1875; H. Paul, 'The Novels of Peacock', *Nineteenth Century*, liii, 1903 (reprinted in *Stray Leaves*, 1906); Sir H. Newbolt, 'Peacock,

Scott and Robin Hood', *Transactions of the R. Society of Literature*, iv, 1924; H. Wright, 'The Associations of Thomas Love Peacock with Wales', *ESEA* xii, 1926; A. Digeon, 'T. L. Peacock, Ami de Shelley', *Revue anglo-américaine*, February 1928; F. Dannenberg, 'Peacock in seinem Verhältnis zu Shelley', *Germanisch-Romanische Monatszeitschrift*, xx, 1932; H. F. B. Brett-Smith, 'The L'Estrange–Peacock Correspondence', *ESEA* xviii, 1933; H. R. Fedden, 'Peacock', in *The English Novelists*, ed. D. Verschoyle, 1936; F. J. Glasheen, 'Shelley and Peacock', *TLS*, 18 October 1941; R. Mason, 'Notes for an Estimate of Peacock', *Horizon*, ix, 1944; H. House, 'The Works of Peacock', *The Listener*, 8 December 1949; and F. L. Jones, 'Macaulay's Theory of Poetry in "Milton" ', *MLQ* xiii, 1952.

*The Critical Reputation of Thomas Love Peacock*, by B. Read (Boston, 1960, available on microfilm and as Xerox book), gives a survey of his reputation and a list of his writings and of criticism on him.

John William Polidori, 1795–1821.

Polidori wrote a Latin thesis on nightmare, 1815; 'On the Punishment of Death', *The Pamphleteer*, vol. viii, 1816; *An Essay upon the Source of Positive Pleasure*, 1818; *Ximenes, The Wreath, and Other Poems*, 1819; *The Vampyre: A Tale*, 1819 (first published in the *New Monthly Magazine*, April 1819: attributed to Byron); *Ernestus Berchtold, or the Modern Œdipus: A Tale*, 1819; and *The Fall of the Angels*, 1821.

Information about Polidori is to be found in books about Byron, Shelley, and the Rossettis (since one of his sisters became the mother of Dante Gabriel and Christina Rossetti), and in *NQ*, 3rd series, vols. vii, ix, and x.

Robert Pollok, 1798–1827.

Pollok's main publications were *Ralph Gemmel, a Tale* (prose), [? 1825]; *Helen of the Glen, a Tale for Youth* (prose) [? 1825]; *The Course of Time: a Poem in Ten Books*, 2 vols., 1827 (25 editions by 1867); and *Tales of the Covenanters* (prose), 1833 (ed. A. Thomson, 1895).

See D. Pollok's *Life of Robert Pollok*, 1843, and R. O. Masson's *Pollok and Aytoun*, [1898]. There are selections from his verse in Miles, x (xi).

WINTHROP MACKWORTH PRAED, 1802–39.

In English verse Praed published *Lillian, a Fairy Tale*, 1823; *Australasia*, 1823, and *Athens*, 1824 (both reprinted in *Cambridge Prize Poems*, 4th edn., 1828); *The Ascent of Elijah, A Poem*, 1831; *Intercepted Letters about the Infirmary Bazaar* (n.d., four four-page pamphlets in verse) and *Trash dedicated without Respect to J. Halse, Esq. M.P.*, Penzance, 1833. In 1832 he published his *Speech . . . on the Reform Bill.*

*The Poetical Works, now first collected by R. W. Griswold*, appeared at New York in 1844. *Lillian and Other Poems, now first collected*, by the same editor, appeared there in 1852. Another American edition of *The Poetical Works* was edited by W. A. Whitmore in 1859. At last an authorized edition, *The Poems, with a Memoir by Derwent Coleridge*, was published in 2 vols. in 1864. (In 1885 *Poems: Revised and Complete Edition* was published at New York in 2 vols.)

There were several volumes of Selections, including that of A. D. Godley, 1909, and *Selected Poems*, with an excellent introduction, by K. Allott, 1953 ('Muses' Library'). Praed's *Essays* were edited by Sir G. Young in 1887 (Morley's Universal Library).

In his lifetime Praed published mainly in periodicals. With W. Blunt he was the editor and chief contributor to *The Etonian*, 2 vols., 1820–1. He contributed largely to Knight's *Quarterly Magazine*, 1823–4, and to the *Brazen Head*, 1826 (four numbers only). His poems were often printed in the Annuals, and he also contributed to the *Albion*, 1830–2, the *Morning Post*, 1832–4, *The Times*, and other papers.

D. Hudson's *A Poet in Parliament: The Life of . . . Praed*, 1939, is a useful biography (with an appendix on 'The Editing of Praed's Poems'). See also G. Saintsbury, *Essays in English Literature, 1780–1860*, 1890; M. Kraupa, *W. M. Praed, sein Leben und seine Werke*, Vienna, 1910; 'Letters of Praed', *Etoniana*, 1 July 1941–28 December 1943 (67 letters); D. Hudson, 'W. M. Praed', *NQ*, 3 January 1942; and K. Allott, 'The Text of Praed's Poems', *NQ*, March 1953.

BRYAN WALLER PROCTER ('BARRY CORNWALL'), 1787–1874.

In verse Procter published *Dramatic Scenes and Other Poems*, 1819 (enlarged, and illustrated by Birket Foster, Tenniel, and others, 1857); *A Sicilian Story . . . and Other Poems*, 1820; *Marcian*

*Colonna, An Italian Tale with Three Dramatic Scenes . . .*, 1820; *Mirandola, A Tragedy*, 1821; *The Flood of Thessaly, the Girl of Provence, and Other Poems*, 1823; and *English Songs*, 1832 (new eds., 1844, 1851). His *Poetical Works* were collected in 3 vols. in 1822. *The Poetical Works of Milman, Barry Cornwall* [and others] appeared at Paris in 1829.

He also published *Effigies Poeticae, or the Portraits of the British Poets*, 1824; *The Life of Edmund Kean*, 2 vols., 1835; *The Works of Ben Jonson, with a Memoir*, 1838; *The Works of Shakespeare, with a Memoir and Essay on his Genius* (by Procter), 1843; *Essays and Tales in Prose*, 2 vols., Boston, 1853; *Selections from Robert Browning* [ed. B. W. Procter and J. Forster], 1863; and *Charles Lamb: a Memoir*, 1866 (reprinted in *Essays of Elia, with a Memoir of Lamb*, 1879). See also *Bryan Waller Procter: An Autobiographical Fragment*, ed. C. P[atmore], 1877.

Procter contributed to many periodicals, including the *Literary Gazette*, the *Edinburgh Review*, the *London Magazine*, the *New Monthly Magazine*, and the *Athenaeum*.

See J. T. Fields, *Old Acquaintance: Barry Cornwall and Some of his Friends*, Boston, 1876; F. Becker, *Bryan Waller Procter*, Vienna, 1912; and R. W. Armour, *Barry Cornwall: A Biography . . . with . . . hitherto unpublished letters*, Boston, 1935. Jeffrey noticed *A Sicilian Story* in the *Edinburgh Review*, xxxiii, 1820. Lamb reviewed *Marcian Colonna* in the *New Times*, 22 July 1820; while Darley attacked Procter in 'The Characteristic of the Present Age of Poetry', *London Magazine*, ix, 1824. H. Martineau has an essay on him in her *Biographical Sketches, 1852–75*, 1877. Recent notes and articles include F. Price, 'Barry Cornwall and Patmore on Child-Love', *NQ*, 14 August 1943; G. H. Ford, 'Keats and Procter: a Misdated Acquaintance', *MLN* lxvi, 1951; R. G. Townend, 'Barry Cornwall's Memoir of Charles Lamb', *Charles Lamb Society Bulletin*, March 1953; and E. L. Brooks, 'B. W. Procter and the Genesis of Carlyle's *Frederick the Great*', *Harvard Library Bulletin*, vii, 1953.

John Hamilton Reynolds, 1794–1852.

Reynolds published *Safie: An Eastern Tale*, 1814; *The Eden of Imagination*, 1814; *An Ode*, 1815; *The Naiad: a Tale*, 1816; *Peter Bell: A Lyrical Ballad*, 1819 (signed 'W. W.', a parody of Wordsworth's poem then on the point of publication); *Benjamin, the Waggoner . . . A Fragment*, 1819 (another parody); *The Fancy:*

*A Selection from the Poetical Remains of the late Peter Corcoran*, 1820; *The Garden of Florence, and Other Poems* (by 'John Hamilton'), 1821; *Odes and Addresses to Great People*, 1825 (in collaboration with Thomas Hood); *One, Two, Three, Four, Five: by Advertisement, a Musical Entertainment* (acted 1815: published anonymously in J. Cumberland's *British Theatre*, vol. xxxi, 1829); and *Confounded Foreigners: A Farce in One Act* [1838].

There is no collected edition of Reynolds's poems. J. Masefield edited a reprint of *The Fancy* in 1905. The only modern edition is *John Hamilton Reynolds:* [Selected] *Poetry and Prose, with an Introduction and Notes*, by G. L. Marsh, 1928.

Reynolds contributed to numerous periodicals, including the *Champion*, the *London Magazine*, the *Edinburgh Review*, the *Westminster Review*, the *Retrospective Review*, the *Athenaeum*, and the *New Monthly Magazine*. On this and other topics Marsh's introduction is supplemented by his important articles in *SP* xxv, 1928; *MP* xl, 1943; and *K.-Sh.J.* i, 1952. Some information may be found in *The Keats Circle*, ed. Rollins, 2 vols., 1948, and *The Letters of John Keats*, ed. Rollins, 2 vols., 1958. According to a note on p. 84 of vol. i of *The Letters* 'by far the best biography' of Reynolds is that in an unpublished Harvard dissertation by W. B. Pope (1932). Further views and information may be found in the memoirs of Reynolds's friends, and in C. W. Dilke's *Papers of a Critic*, 2 vols., 1875; Sir E. Gosse, *Gossip in a Library*, 1891; H. C. Shelley, *Literary By-Paths in Old England*, 1909; A. E. H. Swaen, 'Peter Bell', *Anglia*, xlvii, 1923; W. B. Gates, 'A Sporting Poet of the Regency', *Sewanee Review*, xxxv, 1927; J. M. Turnbull, 'Keats, Reynolds, and *The Champion*', *London Mercury*, xix, 1929; E. Blunden, 'Friends of Keats', in *Votive Tablets*, 1931; and W. B. Pope, 'J. H. Reynolds', *Wessex*, iii, 1935. See also P. Kaufman's article, 'The Reynolds–Hood Commonplace Book: A Fresh Appraisal', *K.-Sh.J.* x, 1961.

HENRY CRABB ROBINSON, 1775–1867.

In 1838 Robinson edited *Strictures* [by T. Clarkson] *on a Life of W. Wilberforce* and in 1840 he published his *Exposure of Misrepresentations contained in the Preface to the Correspondence of William Wilberforce*. Throughout his life he was a prolific contributor to *The Times* and to many other periodicals, often on Germany and German literature. But he is remembered because of his Diary. The *Diary, Reminiscences, and Correspondence* were first edited by

T. Sadler in 3 vols. in 1869. Sadler's edition of 1872, in 2 vols., also contains A. De Morgan's 'Recollections' of Robinson. In 1922 Edith J. Morley published at Manchester *Blake, Coleridge, Wordsworth, etc., being Selections from the Remains of Henry Crabb Robinson*, and in 1938 she edited *Henry Crabb Robinson on Books and their Writers*, an invaluable collection in 3 vols. Edith Morley also edited *The Correspondence of Henry Crabb Robinson with the Wordsworth Circle (1808–66)*, 2 vols., 1927, and *Crabb Robinson in Germany, 1800–5: Extracts from his Correspondence*, 1929.

The fullest account of Crabb Robinson is Edith J. Morley's *The Life and Times of Henry Crabb Robinson*, 1935. There is a good essay (reprinted in Edith J. Morley's biography) by W. Bagehot in *Literary Studies*, ii, 1879. See also H. G. Wright, 'Henry Crabb Robinson's "Essay on Blake"', *MLR* xxii, 1927; R. W. King, 'Crabb Robinson's Opinion of Shelley', *RES* iv, 1928; D. G. Larg, 'Mme de Staël et Henry Crabb Robinson', *Revue de la littérature comparée*, viii, 1928; 'Henry Crabb Robinson and Mme de Staël', by the same writer *RES* v, 1929; P. Norman, 'Henry Crabb Robinson and Goethe', 2 parts, *English Goethe Society*, 1930–1; B. J. Morse, 'Crabb Robinson and Goethe in England', *Englische Studien*, lxvii, 1932; J. M. Baker, *Henry Crabb Robinson of Bury, Jena, the 'Times' and Russell Square*, 1937; and M. E. Gilbert, 'Two Little-known References to Henry Crabb Robinson', *MLR* xxxiii, 1938. An *Index to the Henry Crabb Robinson Letters in Dr. Williams's Library*, compiled by Inez Elliott, supplements Edith Morley's edition.

WILLIAM STEWART ROSE, 1775–1843.

Rose's writings include *A Naval History of the late War*, vol. i (no more published), 1802; *Amadis de Gaul: Freely translated from the First Part of the French version*, 1803; *Partenopex de Blois: Freely translated*, 1807; *The Crusade of St Lewis, and King Edward the Martyr*, 1810 (ballads); *The Court and Parliament of Beasts freely translated from The Animali Parlanti of Giambattista Casti*, 1819 (anon. ed., 1816); *Letters from the North of Italy. Addressed to Henry Hallam, Esq.*, 2 vols., 1819; *The Orlando Innamorato: Translated into Prose*, 1823 (abridged); *The Orlando Furioso Translated into English Verse*, 8 vols., 1823–31 (2 vols., 1858, with a brief Memoir by C. Townsend); *Thoughts and Recollections*, 1825; and *Rhymes*, Brighton, 1837 (privately printed).

Rose became a linguist at Eton, contributing to *Musæ*

*Etonenses*. Later in life he became a friend of Scott's. There is a brief account of him in the *DNB*, apart from Townsend's Memoir mentioned above. C. R. Leslie's *Autobiographical Recollections*, 1860, give an account of his stay at Abbotsford.

FRANCIS BARRY ST. LEGER, 1799–1829.

As Sadleir remarks in *XIX Century Fiction: A Bibliographical Record*, 1951, St. Leger was 'a writer of great promise, whose mature work might well have been of importance'. He printed *Remorse and Other Poems* privately in 1821. *Some Account of the Life of the late Gilbert Earle, Esq. Written by Himself*, 1824 (fiction); *Mr. Blount's MSS.: Being Selections from the Papers of a Man of the World*, 2 vols., 1826; *Tales of Passion*, 3 vols., 1829; and (posthumously) *Stories from Froissart*, 3 vols., 1832. He collaborated with Charles Knight in editing a periodical called the *Brazen Head*, and himself edited an interesting quarterly periodical, *The Album*, 4 vols., 1822–3. On St. Leger see Charles Knight, *Passages of a Working Life*, 3 vols., 1864–5. He was a friend of Praed, who contributed to the *Album*.

JOHN SCOTT, 1783–1821.

At different times Scott edited a number of periodicals, including the *Morning Advertiser*, the *Day*, the *News* (a weekly), and the *Statesman* (an evening paper, 1809–14). He is remembered primarily as the editor of the *Champion, A Weekly Political and Literary Journal*, and the *London Magazine* (1820–1). He also wrote a poem, *The House of Mourning*, 1817, and two interesting travel books: *A Visit to Paris in 1814; being a Review of the Moral, Political, Intellectual, and Social Condition of the French Capital*, 1815, and *Paris Revisited, in 1815, by Way of Brussels: including A Walk over the Field of Battle at Waterloo*, 1816. He wrote the English letterpress for *Picturesque Views of Paris and its Environs: Drawings by Frederick Nash*, 1820–3. After his death there appeared *Sketches of Manners* [and] *Scenery in the French Provinces, Switzerland, and Italy*, 1821.

There is no Life of John Scott. Information must be sought in studies relating to the *London Magazine* (p. 472 above), and in letters and memoirs of the time. See, e.g., *My Friends and Acquaintances*, by P. G. Patmore, 1855, ii, 283–7; the letters of Sir Walter Scott; and Andrew Lang's *Life and Letters of John Gibson Lockhart*, 2 vols., 1897. There is a brief Memoir by Horace Smith in the *New Monthly Magazine*, lxxxi, 1847, 415–18.

SIR WALTER SCOTT, 1771–1832.

The poems and the *Minstrelsy of the Scottish Border* are outside the scope of this volume, which confines itself to the Waverley Romances and Scott's other work in prose. The dates of the main works of prose fiction are as follows: *Waverley, or 'Tis Sixty Years Since*, 3 vols., 1814; *Guy Mannering, or The Astrologer*, 3 vols., 1815; *The Antiquary*, 3 vols., 1816; *Tales of my Landlord*, 4 vols., 1816 (*The Black Dwarf* and *Old Mortality*); *Rob Roy*, 3 vols., 1818; *Tales of my Landlord: Second Series*, 4 vols., 1818 (*The Heart of Mid-Lothian*); *Tales of my Landlord: Third Series*, 4 vols., 1819 (*The Bride of Lammermoor* and *A Legend of Montrose*); *Ivanhoe: A Romance*, 3 vols., 1820; *The Monastery: A Romance*, 3 vols., 1820; *The Abbot*, 3 vols., 1820; *Kenilworth: A Romance*, 3 vols., 1821; *The Pirate*, 3 vols., 1822; *The Fortunes of Nigel*, 3 vols., 1822; *Peveril of the Peak*, 4 vols., 1822; *Quentin Durward*, 3 vols., 1823; *St. Ronan's Well*, 3 vols., 1824; *Redgauntlet: A Tale of the Eighteenth Century*, 3 vols., 1824; *Tales of the Crusaders*, 4 vols., 1825 (*The Betrothed* and *The Talisman*); *Woodstock: or, The Cavalier: A Tale of the Year Sixteen Hundred and Fifty-One*, 3 vols., 1826; *Chronicles of the Canongate*, 2 vols., 1827 (*The Highland Widow, The Two Drovers,* and *The Surgeon's Daughter*, with an introduction in which Scott acknowledges the authorship of *Waverley* and its successors); *Chronicles of the Canongate: Second Series*, 3 vols., 1828 (*St. Valentine's Day: Or, The Fair Maid of Perth*); *Anne of Geierstein: or The Maiden of the Mist*, 3 vols., 1829; and *Tales of my Landlord: Fourth and Last Series*, 4 vols., 1832 (*Count Robert of Paris* and *Castle Dangerous*).

Of his other separate works in prose the following are the most important: the introduction (1817) to *The Border Antiquities of England and Scotland*, 2 vols., 1814–17; *Paul's Letters to his Kinsfolk*, 1816; *Provincial Antiquities of Scotland*, 10 parts, 1819–26 (2 vols., 1826); Lives of the Novelists, prefixed to *Ballantyne's Novelist's Library*, 10 vols., 1821–4 (2 vols., Paris, 1825; ed. G. Saintsbury, Everyman's Library, 1910); *The Life of Napoleon Buonaparte, Emperor of the French: With a Preliminary View of the French Revolution*, 9 vols., 1827; *Religious Discourses: By a Layman*, 1828; *Tales of a Grandfather: Being Stories taken from Scottish History*, 9 vols., 1828–30; *History of Scotland*, 2 vols., 1829–30 (Lardner's *Cabinet Cyclopaedia*); *Letters on Demonology and Witchcraft*, 1830; and *Tales of a Grandfather: Being Stories taken from the History of France*, 3 vols., 1831. His essays on chivalry, romance, and the drama first appeared in the *Encyclopaedia*

*Britannica*, 1818–24, and were first republished in the *Miscellaneous Prose Works*, 1827.

Of the many works edited by Scott mention may be made of *Original Memoirs written during the Great Civil War*, 1806; *The Works of John Dryden ... with ... a Life of the Author*, 18 vols., 1808 (50 copies of Scott's fine *Life of Dryden* were printed separately for presentation: on this biography see *John Dryden: Some Biographical Facts and Problems*, by J. M. Osborn, New York, 1940); *Queenhoo-Hall, a Romance; and Ancient Times, a Drama, by the late Joseph Strutt*, 4 vols., 1808; *Memoirs of Capt. George Carleton, written by himself*, 1808; *Memoirs of Robert Cary ...*, 1808; *A Collection of Scarce and Valuable Tracts*, 13 vols., 1809–15 (known as the *Somers' Tracts*); *English Minstrelsy: Being a Selection of Fugitive Poetry ...*, 2 vols., 1810; *The Poetical Works of Anna Seward: With Extracts from her Literary Correspondence*, 3 vols., 1810; *Secret History of the Court of James the First*, 2 vols., 1811; *The Works of Jonathan Swift. ... With notes and a life of the Author*, 19 vols., 1814 (the *Memoirs of Swift* were published separately at Paris in 1826); *Memorie of the Somervilles*, 2 vols., 1815; and *Memorials of the Haliburtons*, 1820 (privately printed).

Scott began to produce a collected edition of the *Waverley Novels* in 1829. It was completed in 1833, in 48 vols. This edition, 'The Magnum', has long and interesting prefaces dealing with the sources and historical background of the books. The best of the innumerable subsequent editions is the Dryburgh Edition, 25 vols., 1892–4. There is still no scholarly edition, but the first volume of such an edition is due to appear shortly, under the editorship of Dr. J. C. Corson.

In 1827 Scott produced a 6-vol. collection of his *Miscellaneous Prose Works*. Lockhart collected *The Miscellaneous* [Prose] *Works* in 28 vols. in 1834–6. Two further volumes, containing the *Letters on Demonology and Witchcraft*, the *Religious Discourses*, and the *Memoir of George Bannatyne*, were added in 1871.

There is a good edition of *The Heart of Mid-Lothian*, ed. D. Daiches, New York, [1948]. Lord David Cecil has edited *Short Stories by Scott* in the World's Classics series, 1934. *Private Letters of the Seventeenth Century*, ed. D. Grant, 1947, are bogus letters by Scott himself which were the germ of *The Fortunes of Nigel*. (W. M. Parker had written on the matter in his article, 'The Origin of Scott's *Nigel*', *MLR*, xxxiv, 1939.)

Earlier collections of Scott's letters were rendered obsolete by

*The Letters of Sir Walter Scott*, ed. by H. J. C. Grierson, assisted by D. Cook, W. M. Parker, and others, 12 vols., 1932–7. It is a scandal that no index has been published. An index on cards, by Mr. W. M. Parker, may be consulted in the National Library of Scotland. The originals or copies of the many Scott letters which were rejected by Grierson or which have turned up since his edition are kept in the library. Articles relating to such letters are listed in the *CBEL* and in *ERPE*: no mention is made of them here. See also *The Correspondence of Sir Walter Scott and C. R. Maturin*, ed. F. E. Ratchford and W. H. McCarthy, Austin, Texas, 1937; and W. Partington's *The Private Letter-Books of Sir Walter Scott*, 1930, and his *Sir Walter's Post-Bag: More stories and sidelights from his unpublished Letter-Books*, 1932.

*The Journal of Sir Walter Scott* was edited by D. Douglas in 2 vols. in 1890 (1891, 1910, 1 vol.). There is a better text in 3 vols., by J. G. Tait, 1939–46 (1 vol., 1950), but Douglas's annotations remain valuable.

Of the numerous accounts of Scott that appeared before Lockhart's biography mention may be made of G. Allan's *Life . . . with Critical Notices of his Writings*, 5 parts, 1832–4 (the part dealing with Scott's early life is by William Weir); of J. Hogg's *Domestic Manners and Private Life of Sir Walter Scott*, Glasgow, 1834; and of the *Life* by Robert Chambers first published in *Chambers's Edinburgh Journal* in 1832 which formed the basis of his *Life* of 1871. Another early account was published in Toronto by G. H. Needler in 1953 and in this country by J. C. Corson in 1957 as *Reminiscences of Sir Walter Scott in Italy by Sir William Gell.*

Lockhart's *Memoirs of the Life of Sir Walter Scott, Bart.*, were published in 7 vols. in 1837–8 and in 10 vols. (slightly revised) in 1839. It includes Scott's brief autobiography in Chapter I. (See also *The Ballantyne-Humbug*, under Lockhart.) A. W. Pollard's edition, 5 vols., 1900, contains additional material from Lockhart's 2nd edition and from his abridged *Narrative* of 1848. The only major biographical study to appear since Lockhart's is Sir Herbert Grierson's *Sir Walter Scott, Bart., A New Life supplementary to, and corrective of, Lockhart's Biography*, 1938. A great deal of information about Scott may be found in memoirs and other books of the period, and in the histories of the publishing firms of Constable and John Murray listed above on p. 483. R. H. Hutton's volume in the English Men of Letters series (1878) is concise and reasonable. Other books and monographs

of biographical interest include *Sir Walter Scott's Friends*, by Florence MacCunn, 1909; *Sir Walter Scott's Congé*, by C. N. Johnston (Lord Sands), 3rd edition, 1931 (an account of Scott's unsuccessful love for Williamina Belsches); *Sir Walter: A Four-Part Study in Biography*, by D. Carswell, 1930; *Sir Walter Scott*, by John Buchan, 1932; *The Laird of Abbotsford*, by Una Pope-Hennessy, 1932; and *Sir Walter Scott's Journal and its Editors*, by J. G. Tait, 1938. Professor Edgar Johnson is at work on a full-scale study on the same lines as his fine biography of Dickens.

Essays and articles of primarily biographical interest include 'The Story of Scott's Ruin', by Sir Leslie Stephen, *Studies of a Biographer*, ii, 1898; 'The Early Literary Life of Sir Walter Scott', three articles by O. F. Emerson, *JEGP*, xxiii, 1924; 'Lockhart's Treatment of Scott's Letters', by D. Cook, *The Nineteenth Century*, September, 1927; *Lang, Lockhart and Biography*, by H. J. C. Grierson, 1934 (reprinted in *Essays and Addresses*, 1940); and 'James Hogg's Familiar Anecdotes of Sir Walter Scott', by A. L. Strout, *SP* xxxiii, 1936.

Much intelligent criticism of *Waverley* and its successors may be found in contemporary reviews. Some of these are reprinted in the books mentioned above on pp. 475, in Jeffrey's *Contributions to the Edinburgh Review*, 4 vols., 1844, and in *Essays on Fiction*, by Nassau Senior, 1864. *Letters to Richard Heber, Esq.*, in which J. L. Adolphus (anonymously) identified the author of the prose romances with the famous poet, contain some shrewd criticism in the course of their argument. Two early studies still of some interest are *Illustrations, Critical, Historical, Biographical, and Miscellaneous, of Novels by the Author of Waverley*, 3 vols., 1821–4, by R. Warner, and *Illustrations of the Author of Waverley: being Notices and Anecdotes of Real Characters, Scenes, and Incidents, supposed to be Described in his Works*, by Robert Chambers, 2nd ed., 1825. Hazlitt has a brilliant chapter in *The Spirit of the Age*, 1825. The severe views of Carlyle and Harriet Martineau may be found in Carlyle's *Critical and Miscellaneous Essays*, 4 vols., 1839, and Harriet Martineau's *Miscellanies*, 2 vols., [Boston], 1836.

The following books contain criticism or background information about Scott's writings: *The Influence of 'Gothic' Literature on Sir Walter Scott*, by W. Freye, 1902; *The Waverley Novels: An Appreciation*, by C. A. Young, Glasgow, 1907; *Sir Walter Scott as a Critic of Literature*, by Margaret Ball, New York, 1907; *The Scott Originals*, by W. S. Crockett, 1912; *Scott and Goethe:*

*German Influence on the Writings of Sir Walter Scott*, by W. Macintosh, 1925; *Sir Walter Scott's Novels on the Stage*, by H. A. White, New Haven, 1927; *Scott Centenary Articles*, by T. Seccombe, W. P. Ker, and others, 1932; *Sir Walter Scott Today: Some Retrospective Essays and Studies*, ed. Sir H. J. C. Grierson, 1932; *Religious Creeds and Philosophies* [of] *Characters in Scott's Works and Biography*, By K. Bos, Amsterdam, 1932; *The Waverley Novels and their Critics*, by J. T. Hillhouse, Minneapolis, 1936; *Scott and Scotland: The Predicament of the Scottish Writer*, by Edwin Muir, 1936; *Die romantische Landschaft bei Walter Scott*, by J. Möller, 1936; *Scott, Hazlitt and Napoleon*, by M. F. Brightfield (*University of California Publications in English*, Berkeley, 1943); and *Goethe and Scott*, by G. H. Needler, Toronto, 1950. *The Historical Novel*, by G. Lukács (Eng. trans., 1961) throws a great deal of light on Scott. See also *The Hero of the Waverley Novels*, by A. Welsh, New Haven, 1963.

*Sir Walter Scott Lectures 1940–1948*, with an introduction by W. L. Renwick, 1950, includes important lectures delivered at the University of Edinburgh by Grierson, Edwin Muir, G. M. Young, and S. C. Roberts. Subsequent lectures, by D. Nichol Smith, J. R. Sutherland, J. C. Corson, and Mary Lascelles may be found in the *Edinburgh University Journal*. Those by Dr. J. C. Corson constitute a useful survey of 'Scott Studies' (*EUJ*, autumn 1955 and summer 1956).

When we turn to essays and articles we encounter right away Sir Leslie Stephen's admirable study in *Hours in a Library*, i, 1874, and Walter Bagehot's essay in *Literary Studies*, ii, 1879 (first published in 1858, also reprinted in his *Estimations in Criticism*). Ruskin's interesting criticisms of Scott may be found in his *Works*, but most of them are usefully assembled in *Ruskin as Literary Critic*, ed. A. H. R. Ball, 1928. Mrs. Oliphant's chapter in her *Literary History of England in the End of the Eighteenth and Beginning of the Nineteenth Century*, 3 vols., 1882, is still worth reading. J. M. Collyer wrote interestingly on ' "The Catastrophe" in *St. Ronan's Well*' in the *Athenaeum* for 4 February 1893, referring to a cancelled sheet which reveals the original ending. Paul Elmer More's 'The Scotch Novels and Scotch History', in *Shelburne Essays*, iii, 1905, may serve as a bridge to more recent studies.

A number of essays and pamphlets attempt a general assessment of Scott as a writer of fiction. They include Lord David

Cecil's *Sir Walter Scott*, 1933, a long and interesting essay reprinted from the *Atlantic Monthly*, 1932; Edwin Muir's essays in *The English Novelists*, ed. D. Verschoyle, 1936, and *From Anne to Victoria*, ed. B. Dobrée, 1937; V. S. Pritchett's brief yet illuminating essay in *The Living Novel*, 1946; David Daiches's fine assessment, 'Scott's Achievement as a Novelist', reprinted from *Nineteenth-Century Fiction*, vi, 1951, in his *Literary Essays*, 1956; I. Jack's British Council pamphlet, 1958 ('Writers and their Work', no. 103); and an essay in C. S. Lewis's *They Asked for a Paper*, 1962.

The following essays and articles, usually on more limited topics, also deserve attention: three essays in vol. i of the *Collected Essays of W. P. Ker*, ed. C. Whibley, 2 vols., 1925; '*Ivanhoe* and its Literary Consequences', by G. H. Maynadier, *Essays in Memory of Barrett Wendell*, 1926; 'Sir Walter Scotts Beziehungen zu Deutschland', by J. Koch, *Germanische-romanische Monatsschrift*, 1927 (2 parts); 'Scott and Carlyle', by H. J. C. Grierson, *ESEA*, 1928 (reprinted in *Essays and Addresses*, 1940); 'Sir Walter Scott and the Sagas', by Edith Batho, *MLR* xxiv, 1929; 'The Chapter-Tags in the *Waverley Novels*', by T. B. Haber, *PMLA* xlv, 1930; 'Sir Walter Scott and *Emma*', by C. B. Hogan, *PMLA* xlv, 1930 (proves Scott's authorship of the review in the *Quarterly*); 'Witchcraft in the Novels of Sir Walter Scott', by M. C. Boatright, *Texas Studies*, xiii–xiv, 1933–4; and 'Scott's Theory and Practice concerning the Use of the Supernatural in Prose Fiction in Relation to the Chronology of the *Waverley Novels*', by the same author, *PMLA*, l (50), 1935; 'Character Names in the *Waverley Novels*', by C. O. Parsons, *PMLA* xlix, 1934; 'Sir Walter Scott und die Geschichte', by Max Korn, *Anglia* lxi, 1937; 'The *Waverley Novels*, or A Hundred Years After', by P. N. Landis, *PMLA* lii, 1937; 'Scott's Unpublished Translations of German Plays', by D. M. Mennie, *MLR* xxxiii, 1938; 'Sir Walter Scott and the Development of Historical Study', by D. Munroe, *Queen's Quarterly*, 1938; 'Critics of *The Bride of Lammermoor*', by E. Owen, *Dalhousie Review*, xviii, 1938; 'Shakespeare and Some Scenes in the *Waverley Novels*', by R. K. Gordon, *Queen's Quarterly*, 1938 (see also his contributions to *MLR*, 1942 (Scott and *Henry IV*) and to *Transactions of the Royal Society of Canada*, 1945 (Scott and Shakespeare's tragedies)); 'Scott and Shakespeare', by J. C. Smith, *ESEA* xxiv, 1938; 'Scott's *Letters on Demonology and Witchcraft:* Outside Contributors', by C. O. Parsons, *NQ*, 21 and 28 March and 5 December

1942; 'Scott's Antiquary', by R. W. Chapman, *RES* xix, 1943; 'The Original of the Black Dwarf', by C. O. Parsons, *SP* xl, 1943; 'The Power of Memory in Boswell and Scott', by F. A. Pottle, in *Essays on the Eighteenth Century Presented to David Nichol Smith*, 1945; 'The Chronology of the *Waverley Novels*: The Evidence of the Manuscripts', by R. D. Mayo, *PMLA* lxiii, 1948 (a refutation of the theory of Dame Una Pope-Hennessy, D. Carswell, and M. C. Boatright that some of the later novels were written before *Waverley*); '*Waverley* and the "Unified Design" ', by S. S. Gordon, *ELH* xviii, 1951; 'The Rationalism of Sir Walter Scott', by D. Forbes, *Cambridge Journal*, 1953; 'Sir Walter Scott's Contributions to the English Vocabulary', by P. Roberts, *PMLA* lxviii, 1953; 'Providence, Fate and the Historical Imagination in Scott's *Heart of Mid-Lothian*', by P. F. Fisher, *Nineteenth-Century Fiction*, x, 1955; 'Sir Walter Scott', in *The Hero in Eclipse in Victorian Fiction*, by M. Praz, 1956; and 'Scott's *Redgauntlet*', by D. Daiches, in *From Jane Austen to Joseph Conrad: Essays . . . In Memory of James T. Hillhouse*, ed. R. C. Rathburn and M. Steinmann, jun., 1958.

Bibliographical information may be found in the *CBEL* (which has numerous inaccuracies), in *ERPE*, and in *A Bibliography of Sir Walter Scott: A Classified and Annotated List of Books and Articles . . . 1797–1940*, by J. C. Corson, 1943. G. Worthington's *Bibliography of the Waverley Novels*, 1931, is strictly limited in its scope. Two useful books are M. F. A. Husband's *Dictionary of the Characters in the Waverley Novels*, 1910, and Allston Burr's *Sir Walter Scott: An Index Placing the Short Poems in His Novels and in His Long Poems and Dramas*, 1936. Gillian Dyson's useful census of the manuscripts and proof sheets of the *Waverley Novels* may be found in *Edinburgh Bibliographical Society Transactions*, vol. iv, part i (Session 1955–6), 1960. The catalogue of Scott's Library at Abbotsford, edited by J. G. Cochrane and published by the Bannatyne Club, appeared in 1838.

JOSEPH SEVERN, 1793–1879.

Severn published 'The Vicissitudes of Keats's Fame' in the *Atlantic Monthly*, xi, 1863. Specimens of his attempts at fiction may be found in W. Sharp's *Life and Letters of Joseph Severn*, 1892, the best (though unsatisfactory) biography. *Against Oblivion*, 1943, by the Countess of Birkenhead, is another study of Severn's life.

Some information may be found in *The Keats Circle*, ed. H. E. Rollins, 2 vols., 1948, and *The Letters of John Keats*, ed. H. E. Rollins, 2 vols., 1958.

RICHARD LALOR SHEIL, 1791–1851.

Sheil published four plays, one of them an adaptation. They were *Adelaide, or the Emigrants*, Dublin, 1814; *The Apostate*, 1817; *Bellamira, or the Fall of Tunis*, 1818; and *Evadne, or The Statue* (adapted from Shirley's *The Traitor*), 1819. He altered and prepared for the stage *Damon and Pythias*, by John Banim, 1821. In 1824 Sheil adapted Massinger's *Fatal Dowry* for Drury Lane. Two of his plays were unprinted: *Montoni, or the Phantom* (Covent Garden, 1820), and *The Huguenot* (Covent Garden, 1822). Sheil's *Speeches* were edited with a memoir by T. MacNevin, Dublin, 1845. He was joint author of *Sketches of the Irish Bar*, ed. R. S. Mackenzie, 2 vols., New York, 1854–6 (first published in the *New Monthly Magazine*. W. H. Curran was the other author. Sheil's contributions, with other papers, were reprinted in 1855 in 2 vols. as *Sketches, Legal and Political*. ed. M. W. Savage.)

See 'The Tragic Drama—The Apostate', [by Maturin and Gifford], *Quarterly Review*, xvii, 1817; 'Richard Lalor Sheil', *Fraser's Magazine*, xxxiii, 1846; and W. T. MacCullagh (later MacCullagh Torrens), *Memoirs of the Rt. Hon. Richard Lalor Sheil*, 1855.

MARY WOLLSTONECRAFT SHELLEY, NÉE GODWIN, 1797–1851.

Mary Shelley published six long works of prose fiction: *Frankenstein or the Modern Prometheus*, 1818 (many reprints); *Valperga or the Life and Adventures of Castruccio Prince of Lucca*, 3 vols., 1823; *The Last Man*, 3 vols., 1826 (reprinted 1954); *The Fortunes of Perkin Warbeck: A Romance*, 3 vols., 1830 (2 eds., the later 'revised, corrected, and illustrated with a new introduction by the author'); *Lodore*, 3 vols., 1835; and *Falkner: A Novel*, 3 vols., 1837. See also 'The Swiss Peasant' in *The Tale Book*, by C. A. Bowles, J. S. Knowles, M. W. Shelley, &c., Königsberg, 1859, and *Tales and Stories by Mary Wollstonecraft Shelley, now first collected with an Essay by R. Garnett*, 1891.

She also wrote a *History of a Six Weeks' Tour through a Part of France, Switzerland, Germany, and Holland*, 1817 (anon.: with P. B. Shelley); *Lives of the Most Eminent Literary and Scientific*

*Men of Italy, Spain and Portugal* (with others: in D. Lardner's *Cabinet Cyclopaedia*, 3 vols., 1835–7); *Lives of the Most Eminent Literary and Scientific Men of France* (with others: also in D. Lardner's *Cabinet Cyclopaedia*, 1838); and *Rambles in Germany and Italy . . ., 1840–3*, 2 vols., 1844. After her death there appeared 'The Choice: A Poem on Shelley's Death', ed. H. B. Forman, 1876 (privately printed); *Proserpine & Midas: Two unpublished Mythological Dramas*, ed. A. Koszul, 1922; and *Mathilda*, ed. E. Nitchie, North Carolina, 1959.

For her editions of the works of P. B. Shelley see next entry.

Some letters were published in *The Romance of Mary W. Shelley, John Howard Payne and Washington Irving*, Boston, 1907, and *Letters, mostly Unpublished*, ed. H. H. Harper, Boston, 1918. F. L. Jones produced a scholarly edition of *The Letters* in 2 vols. in 1944 and of the *Journal* in 1947 (both Norman, Oklahoma). E. Nitchie edited some further letters in the *K.-Sh.B.* iii, 1950. M. Spark and D. Stanford edited *My Best Mary: Selected Letters*, in 1953. Much relevant material may also be found in *Shelley and his Circle 1773–1822*, ed. K. N. Cameron, 8 vols., 1961– (in progress).

There are books on Mary Shelley by Helen Moore, Philadelphia, 1886; F. A. Marshall, 2 vols., 1889 (*Life and Letters*); L. M. Rossetti, 1890; M. Vohl (*Die Erzählungen der Mary Shelley und ihre Urbilder*, Heidelberg, 1912); R. Church, 1928; C. I. Dodd, 1933 (*Eagle-Feather*, a biography); R. Glynn Grylls, 1938; Muriel Spark, 1951 (*Child of Light: A Reassessment*); and Elizabeth M. S. Nitchie, Rutgers, 1953.

See also G. Gilfillan, *Galleries of Literary Portraits*, vol. i, 1856; T. J. Wise, *A Shelley Library*, 1924; F. L. Jones, 'Letters of Mary W. Shelley in the Bodleian Library', *Bodleian Quarterly Record*, viii, 1937; F. L. Jones, 'Mary Shelley and Claire Clairmont', *South Atlantic Quarterly*, xlii, 1943, and 'Unpublished Fragments by Shelley and Mary', *SP* xlv, 1948; B. A. Booth, ' "The Pole": A Story by Claire Clairmont?', *ELH* v, 1938; Sylva Norman, *On Shelley*, 1938; E. Nitchie, 'The Stage History of *Frankenstein*', *South Atlantic Quarterly*, xli, 1942, 'Mary Shelley's "Mathilda": An Unpublished Story and its Biographical Significance', *SP* xl, 1943, and 'Mary Shelley, Traveller', *K.-Sh.J.* ix, 1960; T. G. Ehrsam, 'Mary Shelley in her Letters', *MLQ* vii, 1946; 'Mary Shelley and G. H. Lewes', *TLS* 12 January 1946; M. Millhauser, 'The Noble Savage in . . . *Frankenstein*', *NQ* 15 June

1946; C. L. Cline, 'Two Mary Shelley Letters', *NQ* 28 October 1950; E. J. Lovell, 'Byron and the Byronic Hero in the Novels of Mary Shelley', *Texas Studies in English*, xxx, 1951, and 'Byron and Mary Shelley', *K.-Sh.J.* ii, 1953.

PERCY BYSSHE SHELLEY, 1792–1822.

Four *juvenilia* before *Queen Mab* may first be mentioned: *Original Poetry; By Victor and Cazire* (P. B. Shelley and Elizabeth Shelley), Worthing, 1810; *Posthumous Fragments of Margaret Nicholson*, ed. 'John Fitz-Victor', Oxford, 1810; *A Poetical Essay on the Existing State of Things: By a Gentleman of the University of Oxford*, 1811; and *The Devil's Walk; a Ballad* [1812: broadside]. *Queen Mab; a Philosophical Poem*, was published in 1813, and followed by: *Alastor; or, The Spirit of Solitude: and Other Poems*, 1816; *Laon and Cythna; or, The Revolution of The Golden City: A Vision of the Nineteenth Century: In The Stanza of Spenser*, 1818 (printed 1817: suppressed and reissued, in revised form, as *The Revolt of Islam*, 1818); *Rosalind and Helen, A Modern Eclogue; with Other Poems*, 1819; *The Cenci: A Tragedy, in five acts*, Italy, 1819; *Prometheus Unbound A Lyrical Drama in four acts With Other Poems*, 1820; *Oedipus Tyrannus; or, Swellfoot the Tyrant. . . . Translated from the Original Doric*, 1820; *Epipsychidion*, 1821; *Adonais An Elegy on the Death of John Keats*, Pisa, 1921; and *Hellas A Lyrical Drama*, 1822. After his death there appeared *Poetical Pieces*, 1823; *Posthumous Poems* [ed. M. W. Shelley], 1824; *The Masque of Anarchy*, with a Preface by Leigh Hunt, 1832; and *Relics of Shelley*, ed. R. Garnett, 1862.

There are facsimiles of *Alastor* (ed. B. Dobell, 1885); *Rosalind and Helen* (ed. H. B. Forman, 1888); *Epipsychidion* (ed. S. A. Brooke, A. C. Swinburne, and R. A. Potts, 1887); *Adonais* (type-facsimile edition, ed. T. J. Wise, 1886; photo-facsimile, 1927); and *The Masque of Anarchy* (facsimile of the MS., ed. H. B. Forman, 1887).

Mention should also be made of editions of *Original Poetry*, ed. R. Garnett, 1898; *Posthumous Fragments of Margaret Nicholson*, ed. H. B. Forman, 1877 (privately printed); *The Cenci*, ed. A. and H. B. Forman, 1886, ed. G. E. Woodberry, Boston, 1909; *Prometheus Unbound*, ed. G. L. Dickinson, 1898, ed. A. M. D. Hughes, 1910 (the poems of 1820: rev. ed., 1957), and ed. L. J. Zillman, Washington, 1959; *Adonais*, ed. W. M. Rossetti and A. O. Prickard, 1903; and *Hellas*, ed. T. J. Wise, 1886.

*The Daemon of the World* . . . (the second part being printed from the MS.) was privately printed by H. B. Forman, 1876; and *The Wandering Jew* was edited by B. Dobell, 1887. *Shelley's Skylark, A Facsimile of the Original MS., with a Note on Other MSS. of Shelley in Harvard College Library*, was published at Cambridge, Mass., in 1888.

The best text of 'The Triumph of Life' may be found in *Studia Neophilologica*, xxxii, 1960, ed. G. M. Matthews. See the same scholar's article in the *TLS*, 5 August 1960, 'The "Triumph of Life" Apocrypha'.

Shelley published the following prose works: *Zastrozzi, A Romance: By P. B. S.*, 1810; *St. Irvyne; or, The Rosicrucian: A Romance: By a Gentleman of the University of Oxford*, 1811; *The Necessity of Atheism*, Worthing [1811]; *An Address to the Irish People*, Dublin, 1812 (ed. T. J. Wise, 1890); *Proposals for an association of . . . philanthropists*, Dublin [1812]; *Declaration of Rights* [Dublin], 1812 (broadsheet: reprinted *Philobiblon Society Miscellany*, vol. xii, 1868–9); *A Letter to Lord Ellenborough* [1812]; *A Vindication of Natural Diet*, 1813 (reprinted 1884); *A Refutation of Deism, in a Dialogue*, 1814; *A Proposal for Putting Reform to the Vote throughout the Kingdom: By the Hermit of Marlow*, 1817 (facsimile of the MS., ed. H. B. Forman, 1887); *An Address to the People on the Death of the Princess Charlotte* [1817] (reprinted [1843?]); and *History of a Six Weeks' Tour*, 1817 (ed. C. I. Elton, 1894: written with Mary Shelley). 'A Defence of Poetry', part of a longer essay designed as a reply to Peacock's 'Four Ages of Poetry', was first published in *Essays, Letters from Abroad*, &c., 1840 (see below). It has been reprinted several times, notably in 'The Percy Reprints', No. 3 (with Peacock's essay), ed. H. F. B. Brett-Smith, 1921, in the edition of A. S. Cook, New York, 1890, and in *English Critical Essays: Nineteenth Century*, ed. E. D. Jones, 1916 (World's Classics: plain text). Other prose writings which appeared after Shelley's death include *Notes on Sculptures in Rome and Florence*, ed. H. B. Forman, 1879 (privately printed); *Review of Hogg's Memoirs of Prince Alexy Haimatoff*, &c., ed. E. Dowden and T. J. Wise, 1886; *A Philosophical View of Reform*, ed. T. W. Rolleston, 1920 (also privately printed by W. E. Peck, 1930, and reprinted, with 'A Defence of Poetry', in *Political Tracts of Wordsworth, Coleridge and Shelley*, ed. R. J. White, 1953); *On the Vegetarian System of Diet*, ed. R. Ingpen, 1929 (privately printed); and *Plato's Banquet translated from the*

*Shelley*, by E. Dowden, 2 vols., 1886 (rev. and condensed ed., 1896); *Percy Bysshe Shelley: Poet and Pioneer*, by H. S. Salt, 1896; *Life of Shelley*, by W. Sharp (with bibliography), 1887; *La Jeunesse de Shelley*, by A. Koszul, 1910; *Shelley in England: New Facts and Letters*, by R. Ingpen, 1917; *Ariel, ou la vie de Shelley*, by A. Maurois, 1923 (Eng. trans. 1924: of no scholarly value); *Shelley His Life and Work*, by W. E. Peck, 2 vols., 1927 (of little value); *Shelley*, by N. I. White, 2 vols., New York, 1940 ('corrected', 2 vols., London, 1947: an authoritative work, abbreviated as *Portrait of Shelley*, New York, 1945); and *Shelley A Life Story*, by E. Blunden, 1946. See also *Byron, Shelley, Hunt, and 'The Liberal'*, by W. H. Marshall, Philadelphia, 1960. There is a biography of *Harriet Shelley*, by L. S. Boas, 1961, discussed in correspondence in the *TLS*, February 1961.

*The Nascent Mind of Shelley*, by A. M. D. Hughes, 1947, is both biographical and interpretative and forms an admirable introduction to Shelley's life and work.

There are studies of Shelley's reputation by N. I. White (*The Unextinguished Hearth: Shelley and his Contemporary Critics*, Durham, N. Carolina, 1938); and by Sylva Norman (*Flight of the Skylark*, 1954). See also E. Blunden's *Shelley and Keats as they Struck their Contemporaries*, 1925. *The Shelley Legend*, by R. M. Smith and others, was published at New York in 1945. N. I. White, F. L. Jones and K. N. Cameron demolished it in *An Examination of The Shelley Legend*, Philadelphia, 1951.

The principal interpretative and critical studies include the following: *Shelley*, by G. Barnett Smith, 1877; *Shelley*, by Francis Thompson, 1909 (first published in the *Dublin Review*); *Shelley: An Essay*, by A. A. Jack, 1904; *Shelley, Godwin and their Circle*, by H. N. Brailsford, 1913; *Shelley and the Unromantics*, by O. W. Campbell, 1924; *Mad Shelley*, by J. R. Ullman, Princeton, 1930; *Desire and Restraint in Shelley*, by F. Stovall, Durham, N. Carolina, 1931; *Toward the Understanding of Shelley*, by B. Weaver, Ann Arbor, 1932; *The Pursuit of Death: A Study of Shelley's Poetry*, by B. P. Kurtz, New York, 1933; *Shelley*, by R. Bailey, 1934; *The Magic Plant: The Growth of Shelley's Thought*, by C. Grabo, Chapel Hill, 1936 (and see next paragraph); *Shelley's Major Poetry: The Fabric of a Vision*, by Carlos Baker, 1948; *The Young Shelley: Genesis of a Radical*, by K. N. Cameron, 1951; *Shelley's Idols of the Cave*, by P. H. Butter, 1954; *The Deep Truth: A Study of Shelley's Scepticism*, by C. E. Pulos, Lincoln, Nebraska, 1954; *Shelley*

*at Work*, by N. Rogers, 1956; *Shelley's Later Poetry: A Study of his Prophetic Imagination*, by M. Wilson, New York, 1959; *Shelley's Mythmaking*, by H. Bloom, New Haven, 1959; and *Shelley: Poète des Éléments*, by Hélène Lemaitre, 1962.

The following are more specialized in their scope: *Studien zu Shelleys Lyrik*, by H. Huscher, Leipzig, 1919; *Shelley: His Theory of Poetry*, by M. T. Solve, Chicago, 1928; three studies by C. Grabo, published at Chapel Hill—*A Newton among Poets: Shelley's Use of Science in Prometheus Unbound*, 1930, *Prometheus Unbound: An Interpretation*, 1935, and *The Meaning of 'The Witch of Atlas'*, 1935; *An Odyssey of the Soul: Shelley's Alastor*, by H. L. Hofman, New York, 1933; *A Classification of Shelley's Metres*, by J. B. Mayor, 1888; *An Analytical Study of Shelley's Versification*, by L. Probst (*University of Iowa Studies*, v. 1932); *Shelley et la France*, by H. Peyre, 1935; *Shelley's Religion*, by E. Barnard, Minneapolis, 1937; *Shelleys Geisterwelt*, by W. Clemen, Frankfurt, 1948; *The Platonism of Shelley*, by J. A. Notopoulos, Durham, North Carolina, 1949; *The Imagery of Keats and Shelley: A Comparative Study*, by R. H. Fogle, Chapel Hill, 1949; and *Il pensiero religioso di Shelley*, by B. Chiappelli, Rome, 1956. For *The Early Collected Editions*, by C. H. Taylor, see p. 621 below.

Important studies of Shelley may be found in the following books: *Shelley and Calderón and Other Essays*, by S. de Madariaga, 1920; *Mythology and the Romantic Tradition in English Poetry*, by D. Bush, Cambridge, Mass., 1937; *Revaluation*, by F. R. Leavis, 1936 (the most influential of all the attacks); *Rehabilitations and Other Essays*, by C. S. Lewis ('Shelley, Dryden, and Mr. Eliot'), 1939; *In Defence of Shelley and Other Essays*, by H. Read, 1936 (revised in *The True Voice of Feeling*, 1953); *The Starlit Dome*, by G. Wilson Knight, 1941; *English Bards and Grecian Marbles*, by S. A. Larrabee, New York, 1942; *English Poetry and its Contribution to the Knowledge of a Creative Principle*, by L. Vivante, 1950; *The Romantic Poets*, by G. Hough, 1953; *The Discipline of Letters*, by G. S. Gordon, 1946 ('Shelley and the Oppressors of Mankind', British Academy lecture, 1922); *Purity of Diction in English Verse*, by D. Davie, 1952 (the chapter on Shelley is reprinted in *English Romantic Poets: Modern Essays in Criticism*, ed. M. H. Abrams, New York, 1960); *Poets' Grammar*, by F. Berry, 1958 ('Shelley and the Future Tense'); and *The Quest for Permanence: The Symbolism of Wordsworth, Shelley and Keats*, by D. Perkins, Harvard, 1959. *The Subtler Language*, by

E. R. Wasserman, Baltimore 1959, contains three essays on Shelley.

Browning's *Essay on Shelley* was prefixed to an edition of *Letters of Shelley*, most of which were spurious, in 1852. It has been edited by W. T. Harden, 1888, R. Garnett, 1903, and H. F. B. Brett-Smith, 1921 (with essays by Peacock and Shelley). There is an intelligent essay by W. Bagehot in *Literary Studies*, i, 1879. Arnold's essay, which hardly shows him at his best, is in *Essays in Criticism*, 2nd series, 1888. Leslie Stephen has an essay on 'Godwin and Shelley' in *Hours in a Library*, iii, 1879. Yeats wrote on Shelley more than once: see particularly 'The Philosophy of Shelley's Poetry', in *Ideas of Good and Evil*, 1903. Bradley also wrote on Shelley several times: see 'Shelley's View of Poetry', in *Oxford Lectures on Poetry*, 1909, and three essays in his *A Miscellany*, 1929. 'The Case of Shelley', by F. A. Pottle was published in *PMLA* lxvii, 1952, and revised for *English Romantic Poets: Modern Essays in Criticism*, ed. M. H. Abrams, New York, 1960 (see also Pottle's essay in *MP*, February 1958, formally a review of the book by N. Rogers). C. Baker wrote on 'The Permanent Shelley' in the *Sewanee Review*, xlviii, 1940.

There are important articles as follows: 'The Early Reviews of Shelley', by G. L. Marsh, *MP* xxvii, 1929; 'Peterloo, Shelley, and Reform', by A. S. Walker, *PMLA* xl, 1925; 'Shelley and the Active Radicals of the Early Nineteenth Century', *South Atlantic Quarterly*, xxix, 1930, by N. I. White; and three articles by K. N. Cameron in *JEGP* xlii, 1943 ('Shelley, Cobbett, and the National Debt'), *Sewanee Review*, l (50), October 1942 ('The Social Philosophy of Shelley'), and *ELH* xii, 1945 ('Shelley and the Reformers'). For the influence of Bacon on Shelley see D. L. Clark in *PMLA* xlviii, 1933. On Shakespeare and Shelley see D. L. Clark in *PMLA* liv, 1939, B. Langston in *HLQ* xii, 1949, and F. L. Jones in *PMLA* lix, 1944. In 'Shelley's "Disinterested Love" and Aristotle', *PQ* xxxii, 1953, J. A. Notopoulos pursues his study of Shelley's thought. Also of interest are 'Hogg and *The Necessity of Atheism*', by F. L. Jones, *PMLA* lii, 1937; 'Shelley, Godwin, Hume, and the Doctrine of Necessity', by F. B. Evans, *SP* xxxvii, 1940; 'How Poetic is Shelley's Poetry?', by G. R. Elliott, *PMLA* xxxvii, 1922; the articles on Shelley and Spenser, and Shelley and Milton, by F. L. Jones, in *SP* xxxix, 1942, and xlix, 1952; 'Latter-Day Critics of Shelley', by W. Warren Beach, *Yale Review*, 1922;

'Shelley Once More', by C. B. Tinker, *Yale Review*, xxxi, 1941 (reprinted in *Essays in Retrospect*, New Haven, 1948); 'Structure and Prosodic Pattern in Shelley's Lyrics', by R. D. Havens, *PMLA* lxv, 1950; three articles by R. H. Fogle—'The Abstractness of Shelley', *PQ* xxiv, 1945, 'Empathic Imagery in Keats and Shelley', *PMLA* lxi, 1946, and 'Romantic Bards and Metaphysical Reviewers', *ELH* xii, 1945; 'Shelley's Eccentricities', by C. Grabo (*University of New Mexico Publications*, no. 5, Albuquerque, 1950); and 'Shelley and Calderón', by E. J. Gates, *PQ* xvi, 1937.

A few of the innumerable articles on individual poems may be singled out: 'Shelley's *Queen Mab* und Volney's "Les Ruines" ', by L. Kellner, was published in *Englische Studien*, xxii, in 1895. Many critics have considered the problems set by the interpretation of *Alastor*: see particularly 'Shelley's *Alastor*', by R. D. Havens, *PMLA* xlv, 1930; 'Wordsworth as the Prototype of the Poet in Shelley's *Alastor*', by P. Mueschke and E. L. Griggs, *PMLA* xlix, 1934; '*Rasselas* and *Alastor*: A Study in Transmutation', by K. N. Cameron, *SP* xl, 1943; 'The Inconsistency of Shelley's *Alastor*', by F. L. Jones, *ELH* xiii, 1946, and his 'The Vision Theme in Shelley's *Alastor* and Related Works', *SP* xliv, 1947; '*Alastor*: A Reinterpretation', by E. K. Gibson, *PMLA* lxii, 1947; '*Alastor*', by A. M. D. Hughes, *MLR* xliii, 1948; and '*Alastor*, or the Spirit of Solipsism', by A. Gerard, *PQ*, 1954.

On *The Revolt of Islam* see 'The Revision of *Laon and Cythna*', by F. L. Jones, *JEGP* xxxiii, 1933; 'A Major Source of *The Revolt of Islam*', by K. N. Cameron, *PMLA* lvi, 1941; 'Shelley's Use of Metempsychosis in *The Revolt of Islam*', by W. S. Dowden (*Rice Institute Pamphlets*, xxxviii, 1951); and 'Canto I of *The Revolt of Islam*', by F. L. Jones, *K.-Sh.J.* ix, 1960. R. D. Havens has written on *Julian and Maddalo* in *SP* xxvii, 1930, as have C. Baker ('Shelley's Ferrarese Maniac') in *English Institute Essays*, 1946, and J. E. Saveson in *K.-Sh.J.* x, 1961.

Apart from the discussions of *Prometheus Unbound* in book form and in the various editions, culminating in Zillman's, one may consult 'Shelley's *Prometheus Unbound*, or Every Man his Own Allegorist', by N. I. White, *PMLA* xl, 1925; 'The Political Symbolism of *Prometheus Unbound*', by K. N. Cameron, *PMLA* lviii, 1943; 'The Unbinding of Prometheus', by J. S. Thomson, *UTQ* xv, 1945; and 'Image and Imagelessness: A Limited Reading of *Prometheus Unbound*', by R. H. Fogle, *K.-Sh. J.* i, 1952. See also B. Weaver's study, Michigan, 1957. K. N. Cameron

and H. Frenz have written on 'The Stage History of Shelley's *The Cenci*', in *PMLA* lx, 1945. D. L. Clark has an article on 'Literary Sources of Shelley's *The Witch of Atlas*', in *PMLA* lvi, 1941, while J. E. Jordan has written on 'Wordsworth and *The Witch of Atlas*', in *ELH* ix, 1942. K. N. Cameron has studied 'The Planet-Tempest Passage in *Epipsychidion*', in *PMLA* lxviii, 1948. On *Adonais* one may consult 'Spenser and Shelley's *Adonais*', by T. P. Harrison (*Texas Studies in English*, 1933); *Shores of Darkness*, by E. B. Hungerford, New York, 1941; 'The Thematic Unity of *Adonais*' by M. R. Watson, *K.-Sh.J.* i, 1952; and '*Adonais*: Progressive Revelation as a Poetic Mode', by E. Wasserman, *ELH* xxi, 1954. *Hellas* and *Charles I* have been discussed by R. D. Havens in *SP* xliii, 1946.

Of the numerous studies of 'The Triumph of Life' we may mention that by M. Stawell in *ESEA*, v, 1914; that by Bradley in *A Miscellany*, 1929, mentioned above; that by W. Cherubini in *SP* xxxix, 1942 ('Shelley's Own Symposium . . .'); and that by P. H. Butter, *RES*, N.S., xiii, 1962. On the text see G. M. Matthews, as above on p. 613.

The most discussed of the shorter poems has been the 'Ode to the West Wind': see the articles by I. J. Kapstein, *PMLA* li, 1936; R. H. Fogle, *ELH* xv, 1948; and S. C. Wilcox, *SP* xlvii, 1950. See also the discussion by F. Berry in *Poets' Grammar*, already mentioned. Of the numerous discussions of 'To a Skylark' the following deserve particular mention: 'The Symbolism of Shelley's "To a Skylark"', by E. W. Marjarum, *PMLA* lii, 1937; 'The Sources, Symbolism and Unity of Shelley's "Skylark"', by S. C. Wilcox, *SP* xlvi, 1949; and 'Shelley and the Skylark', by N. Rogers, *TLS*, 24 July 1953.

I. J. Kapstein and C. H. Vivian have written on 'Mont Blanc', in *PMLA* lxii, 1947, and *K.-Sh.J.* iv, 1955; D. W. Thompson, J. G. Griffiths, and J. Parr on 'Ozymandias', in (respectively) *PQ* xvi, 1937, *MLR* xliii, 1948, and *MLR* xlvi, 1951. B. Weaver wrote 'Shelley Works out the Rhythm of *A Lament*', in *PMLA* xlvii, 1932. N. Rogers has considered the poem 'On the Medusa of Leonardo da Vinci' in 'Shelley and the Visual Arts', *K.-Sh.B.* xii, 1961. See also 'Two Notes on Shelley', by J. A. Notopoulos, *MLR* xlviii, 1953 (on *Adonais* and 'Ozymandias'). On the 'Lines Written Among the Euganean Hills' see D. H. Reiman in *PMLA* lxxvii, 1962.

K. N. Cameron wrote on 'A New Source for Shelley's *A*

*Defence of Poetry* [*Rasselas*]', in *SP* xxxviii, 1941 (and see also L. Verkoren's full study of the *Defence*, Amsterdam, 1937).

Two valuable aids are *A Lexical Concordance to the Poetical Works*, ed. F. S. Ellis, 1892, and *The Early Collected Editions of Shelley's Poems*, by C. H. Taylor, New Haven, 1959. Earlier works which retain some value are *The Shelley Library*, by H. B. Forman, 1886; *A Descriptive Catalogue of the First Editions of Shelley*, by R. S. Grannis, New York, 1923; *A Shelley Library*, by T. J. Wise, 1924; and *A Bibliography of Shelley's Letters*, by S. A. de Ricci, Paris, 1927 (privately printed). Since so much has been written on Shelley a particular warning must be given that this selective bibliography may be supplemented by *CBEL* iii and v, by the article by B. Weaver in *ERP*, and by the annual bibliographies in the *K.-Sh.J.*

Shelley's 'Esdaile Notebook', which contains some 2,000 lines of unpublished juvenile verse, is to be edited by Mr. N. Rogers, as a forerunner to his Oxford edition of *The Poetical Works.*

HORATIO (HORACE) SMITH, 1779–1849.

(For *Rejected Addresses* and *Horace in London* see next entry.)

In prose Smith published *A Family Story*, 3 vols., 1799; *The Runaway, or the Seat of Benevolence*, 4 vols., 1800; *Trevanion, or Matrimonial Errors*, 4 vols., 1801; *Horatio, or Memoirs of the Davenport Family*, 4 vols., 1807; *Gaieties and Gravities*, 3 vols., 1825 (prose and verse, mainly reprinted from the *London Magazine* and the *New Monthly Magazine*); *The Tor Hill*, 3 vols., 1826; *Brambletye House, or Cavaliers and Roundheads*, 3 vols., 1826; *Reuben Apsley*, 3 vols., 1827; *Zillah: A Tale of the Holy City*, 4 vols., 1828; *The New Forest: A Novel*, 3 vols., 1829; *Walter Colyton: A Tale of 1688*, 3 vols., 1830; *The Midsummer Medley for 1830: A Series of Comic Tales* (prose and verse), 2 vols., 1830; *Tales of the Early Ages*, 3 vols., 1832; *Gale Middleton: A Story of the Present Day*, 3 vols., 1833; *The Involuntary Prophet: A Tale of the Early Ages*, 1835; *Jane Lomax, or a Mother's Crime*, 3 vols., 1838; *The Moneyed Man, or the Lesson of a Life*, 3 vols., 1841; *Massaniello: A Historical Romance*, 3 vols., 1842; *Adam Brown, the Merchant*, 3 vols., 1843; *Arthur Arundel: A Tale of the English Revolution*, 3 vols., 1844; and *Love and Mesmerism*, 3 vols., 1845. Smith edited *Oliver Cromwell: An Historical Romance*, 3 vols., 1840.

He also wrote *First Impressions, or Trade in the West: A Comedy*, 1813; *Amarynthus the Nympholept: A Pastoral Drama . . . With other*

*Poems*, 1821; *Festivals, Games, and Amusements, Ancient and Modern*, 1831; and *The Tin Trumpet, or Heads and Tales for the Wise and Waggish. To which are added Poetical Selections by the late Paul Chatfield, M.D.* ('ed. Jefferson Saunders, Esq.'), 2 vols., 1836. He contributed to *Literary Contributions by Various Authors in aid of . . . The Hospital . . . at Brompton*, 1846. His *Poetical Works* appeared in 2 vols. in 1846. His edition of his brother's *Memoirs, &c.*, is mentioned below.

There is a book by A. H. Beavan, *James and Horace Smith*, 1899. See also P. G. Patmore, *My Friends and Acquaintances*, 3 vols., 1855.

JAMES SMITH, 1775–1839.

*Rejected Addresses: or The New Theatrum Poetarum*, the work of the two brothers, first appeared anonymously in 1812. The 2nd edition, 1812, was carefully revised. There are editions by P. Cunningham, 1851, E. Sargent, New York, 1871, P. Fitzgerald, 1890, A. D. Godley, 1904, and A. Boyle, 1929 (with a bibliography). *Horace in London: consisting of Imitations of the First Two Books of the Odes of Horace* appeared in 1813 (the translations are reprinted from *The Monthly Mirror*, and are mainly the work of James Smith). Horace Smith edited *Comic Miscellanies in Prose and Verse by the late James Smith*, in 2 vols. in 1840. James Smith had also contributed to various periodicals and written the text for Charles Mathews's comic entertainments, 'The Country Cousin', 'The Trip to France', and 'The Trip to America' (1820–2).

Apart from the books by Beavan and P. G. Patmore mentioned above, see the *Edinburgh Review*, xx, 1812 (Jeffrey on the *Rejected Addresses*); A. Hayward, *Biographical and Critical Essays*, vol. i, 1858; R. W. Lowe, 'The Real Rejected Addresses', *Blackwood's Magazine*, cliii, 1893; W. C. Jerrold, 'The Centenary of the *Rejected Addresses*', *Fortnightly Review*, xciv, 1912; E. Blunden, 'The Rejected Addresses', in *Votive Tablets*, 1931; and G. Kitchin, *A Survey of Burlesque and Parody in English*, 1931.

SYDNEY SMITH, 1771–1845.

Smith published *Six Sermons*, 1800 (enlarged edition, 2 vols., 1801); *Elementary Sketches of Moral Philosophy*, 1804, 1805, 1806 (lectures: privately printed), 1850 (public edition); *The Letters of Peter Plymley to* [his] *Brother Abraham who lives in the Country*, 1807–8; 1808 (collected edition), ed. H. Morley, 1886 (with *Selected*

*Essays*), ed. G. C. Heseltine, 1929 (with other writings); *A Sermon upon . . . Conduct . . . towards Catholics . . .*, 1807; *Extracts from the Edinburgh Review*, [1810?]; *The Lawyer that tempted Christ: A Sermon*, York, 1824 (privately printed); *Catholic Claims: A Speech*, 1825; *A Sermon on Religious Charity*, York, 1825; *A Letter to the Electors, upon the Catholic Question*, York, 1826; *Mr. Dyson's Speech to the Freeholders on Reform*, 1831; *Speech at the Taunton Reform Meeting*, 1831; *The New Reign: The Duties of Queen Victoria: A Sermon*, 1837; *A Letter to Archdeacon Singleton, on the Ecclesiastical Commission*, 1837; *A Letter to Lord John Russell on the Church Bills*, 1838; *Second Letter to Archdeacon Singleton . . .*, 1838; *Third Letter to Archdeacon Singleton*, 1839; *Ballot*, 1839; *Letters on American Debts*, 1844 (reprinted from the *Morning Chronicle*); and *A Fragment on the Irish Roman Catholic Church*, 1845.

After his death there appeared *Essays, 1802*–[1827], 2 vols., 1874–80 (reprinted from the *Edinburgh Review*); *Essays, Social and Political, 1802–1825*, 1874, 1877 (much fuller); and *Nine Letters*, ed. E. Cheney, *Philobiblon Society Miscellany*, vol. xv, 1877–84.

His *Works* appeared in 4 vols., 1839–40, and in subsequent editions. *Selections* appeared in 2 vols. in 1855. *Wit and Wisdom of the Rev. Sydney Smith*, ed. E. A. Duychuick, New York, 1858, contains extracts from his main writings. *The Wit and Wisdom*, 1860, is a different (English) volume of selections. E. Rhys, also edited *Selections* in 1892. See also *Bon-Mots of Sydney Smith and R. Brinsley Sheridan*, ed. W. Jerrold, 1893; *The Letters of Peter Plymley*, &c., ed. G. C. Heseltine, 1929 (as above); and W. H. Auden, *Selected Writings*, 1957.

*The Letters of Sydney Smith* were edited in 2 vols. in 1953, by Nowell C. Smith (but see *TLS*, 11 December 1953, and John Butt in *RES*, new series, vol. v, 1954).

The principal book is Lady Holland's *Memoir of the Reverend Sydney Smith . . . with a Selection from his Letters*, ed. Mrs. Austin, 2 vols., 1855 (with a list of his articles in the *Edinburgh Review*). There are other books by S. J. Reid (*A Sketch of the Life and Times of the Rev. Sydney Smith*, 1884); A. Chevrillon (*Sydney Smith et la renaissance des idées libérales en Angleterre au XIX^e^ siècle*, 1894); G. W. E. Russell (English Men of Letters Series, 1905); O. Saint Clair (*Sydney Smith: A Biographical Sketch*, 1913); O. Burdett (*The Rev. Smith, Sydney*, 1934); Hesketh Pearson (*The Smith of Smiths*, 1934); and G. Bullett (*Sydney Smith: a Biography and a Selection*, 1951).

See also R. H. Horne, *A New Spirit of the Age*, vol. i, 1844; G. Gilfillan, *Galleries of Literary Portraits*, vol. ii, 1856; R. A. Vaughan, *Essays and Remains*, 2 vols., 1858; W. Maginn, *A Gallery of Illustrious Literary Characters*, ed. W. Bates [1873]; R. M. Milnes (Lord Houghton), *Monographs*, 1873; Abraham Hayward, *Selected Essays*, vol. i, 1878; Sir H. C. Biron, 'A Victorian Prophet', *Fortnightly Review*, January 1921; S. T. Williams, 'The Literary Criticism of Sydney Smith', *MLN* xxxviii, 1923; J. Murphy, 'Some Plagiarisms of Sydney Smith', *RES* xiv, 1938; and 'The Smith of Smiths', *TLS*, 24 February 1945.

See also the entry for the *Edinburgh Review* on pp. 470–3 above.

HENRY SOUTHERN, 1799–1853.

Southern edited the *Retrospective Review*, series i, 1820–6, and series ii, 1827–8 (assisted by Sir N. H. Nicolas). From 1825 to 1828 he edited the *London Magazine*. He was also literary editor of the *Westminster Review* for its first three years or so, as well as contributing at various times to the *Atlas*, the *Spectator*, and the *Examiner*. Information about him may be found in Crabb Robinson, in G. L. Nesbitt's *Benthamite Reviewing*, New York, 1934, and in Josephine Bauer's study, *The London Magazine 1820–29*, Copenhagen, 1953 (*Anglistica*, vol. i).

JOHN TAYLOR, 1781–1864.

Taylor is important because of his work as a publisher and on account of the *London Magazine*, which he edited from 1821 to 1824 and to which he himself contributed. But he also wrote a great many books and pamphlets. A fairly full list may be found in E. Blunden, *Keats's Publisher: A Memoir of John Taylor*, 1936. No mention need be made here of most of his pamphlets on financial questions, but some of his other publications may be recorded: *A Discovery of the Author of the Letters of Junius*, 1813; *The Identity of Junius with a Distinguished Living Character Established*, 1816 (in the 2nd ed., 1818, Taylor argues for the authorship of Sir Philip Francis, having earlier suggested his father, Dr. Francis, possibly helped by his son); *A Supplement to Junius Identified, consisting of Facsimiles of Hand-Writing*, 1817; *What is the Power of the Greek Article, and How may it be expressed in the English Version of the New Testament?*, 1842; *The Case of the Industrious Classes Briefly Stated*, 1843; *Propositions Concerning the Cause and Remedy of the Present Distress*, 1843; *Emancipation of Industry*, 1844;

*The Gemini Letters*, 1844; *The Astronomy of an Ancient Carthaginian Tablet*, 1850; *Cinderella and her Glass Slipper: a Story of Ancient Astronomical Mythology*, 1850; *The Emphatic New Testament . . . With an Introductory Essay on Greek Emphasis by J. Taylor*, 1852–4; *The Revised Liturgy of 1689*, ed. J. Taylor, 1855; *The Great Pyramid; Why was it Built? and Who Built It?*, 1859; *The Battle of the Standards: The Ancient, of Four Thousand Years, Against the Modern, of the Last Fifty Years—The Less Perfect of the Two*, 1864; and *Light Shed on Scripture Truth by a more uniform Translation*, 1864. Taylor wrote the prefaces to Clare's *Poems Descriptive of Rural Life and Scenery*, 1820, and *The Village Minstrel*, 2 vols., 1821. A mass of papers relating to Taylor has been dispersed, but much remains in the British Museum. Commonplace books and manuscript poems by Taylor were sold at Sotheby's in 1961.

WILLIAM TAYLOR OF NORWICH, 1765–1836.

Taylor's *Historic Survey of German Poetry: Interspersed with Various Translations* appeared in 3 vols. in 1830, and was severely reviewed by Carlyle in the *Edinburgh Review* for March 1831. Throughout his life he was an astonishingly prolific contributor to periodicals, particularly the *Monthly Review* from 1793 to 1824. He produced the following separate translations: Lessing's *Nathan the Wise*, Norwich, 1791 (privately printed), 1805, 1886 (ed. H. Morley); Goethe's *Iphigenia in Tauris*, 1793 (privately printed), 1794; Wieland's *Dialogues of the Gods*, 1795; Bürger's *Ellenore*, 1796 (reprinted in revised form from the *Monthly Magazine*, March 1796); *Select Fairy Tales from the German of Wieland*, 1796; and *Tales of Yore*, 3 vols., 1810 (from French and German). He also published *A Letter concerning the Two First Chapters of Luke*, 1810; *English Synonyms Discriminated*, 1813; 'Some Biographic Particulars of the late Dr. Sayers' (prefixed to Frank Sayers's *Collective Works*, Norwich, 1823); and *A Memoir of the late Philip Meadows Martineau, Surgeon* (with F. Elwes), 1831.

There is a *Memoir* by J. W. Robberds, 2 vols., 1843, containing many letters and lists of his contribution to periodicals; and a study, by G. Herzfeld, *William Taylor of Norwich: Eine Studie über den Einfluß der neueren deutschen Literatur in England*, Halle, 1897. See also Section IV, 7 above.

EDWARD JOHN TRELAWNY, 1792–1881.

Trelawny published *The Adventures of a Younger Son*, 3 vols.,

1831 (ed. E. Garnett, 1890: ed. H. N. Brailsford, 1914: ed. E. C. Mayne, 1925, World's Classics), and *Recollections of the last Days of Shelley and Byron*, 1858 (1878, with additions, as *Records of Shelley, Byron and the Author*); ed. E. Dowden, 1906; ed. J. E. Morpurgo, 1952.

His *Letters* were edited by H. Buxton Forman in 1910. *The Relations of Percy Bysshe Shelley with his Two Wives, Harriet and Mary, and a Comment on the Character of Lady Byron*, and *The Relations of Lord Byron and Augusta Leigh* (4 letters), were both privately printed in 1920.

There are several books about Trelawny: R. Edgcumbe, *Edward Trelawny: A Biographical Sketch*, Plymouth, 1882; Joaquin Miller, *Trelawny with Shelley and Byron*, 1922; H. J. Massingham, *The Friend of Shelley: A Memoir of Edward John Trelawny*, 1930; M. Armstrong, *Trelawny: A Man's Life*, New York, 1940; and R. G. Grylls, *Trelawny*, 1950. See also R. Garnett, 'Shelley's Last Days', *Fortnightly Review*, xxix, 1878; Mathilde Blind, *Whitehall Review*, 10 January 1880 (a record of Trelawny's conversation); and W. M. Rossetti, 'Talks with Trelawny, 1879–1880', *Athenaeum*, 15 and 29 July and 5 August 1882. There is also a good deal about Trelawny in William Sharp's *The Life and Letters of Joseph Severn*, 1892. His (un)reliability as a witness is discussed in studies of Byron and Shelley and (with new evidence) in the *K.-Sh.J.* v, 1956, by Lady Anne Hill.

PATRICK FRASER TYTLER, 1791–1849.

Fraser Tytler published the *Life of James Crichton of Cluny, the Admirable Crichton*, 1819; *An Account of the Life and Writings of Sir Thomas Craig* (reprinted from *Blackwood's Magazine*), 1823; *The Life of John Wickliff*, 1826; a *History of Scotland*, 9 vols. (and index), 1828–43 (and later editions); *Lives of Scottish Worthies*, 3 vols., 1831–3; a *Historical View of the Progress of Discovery on the More Northern Coasts of America*, 1832; a *Life of Sir Walter Raleigh*, 1833; a *Life of King Henry the Eighth*, 1837; *England under the Reigns of Edward VI and Mary*, 2 vols., 1839; and 'Scotland' in the 7th (1839) and some later editions of the *Encyclopaedia Britannica*. This article was later enlarged and published separately. He contributed occasionally to *Blackwood's Magazine*. With Scott and others he was one of the founders of the Bannatyne Club, whose poet-laureate he became. In 1833 he and others edited for the club Hugh Mackay's *Memoirs . . . 1689–91*.

There is a Memoir by the Rev. J. W. Burgon, *The Portrait of a Christian Gentleman: A Memoir of Patrick Fraser Tytler*, 1859. The *DNB* mentions a few minor writings.

Thomas Griffiths Wainewright, 1794–1847.

Wainewright's *Essays and Criticisms* were edited by W. Carew Hazlitt in 1880, most of them having been published in the *London Magazine*. A list of his contributions is included in Jonathan Curling's *Janus Weathercock: The Life of Thomas Griffiths Wainewright*, 1938, the best study. Little is added by J. Lindsey's *Suburban Gentleman*, 1942, or R. Crossland's *Wainewright in Tasmania*, Melbourne, 1954. Some reminiscences may be found in B. W. Procter's *Autobiographical Fragment*, 1877, and in the writings of other members of the *London* group. (See also Josephine Bauer's *The London Magazine 1820–29*, Copenhagen, 1953.) Dickens, Bulwer Lytton, and Oscar Wilde were all fascinated by Wainewright: *For the Term of his Natural Life*, by Marcus Clarke, owes something to Wainewright's career, as do Dickens's *Hunted Down* and Lytton's *Lucretia, or The Children of Night*, 1846.

William Sidney Walker, 1795–1846.

Walker published *Gustavus Vasa, and other Poems*, 1813; *The Heroes of Waterloo: An Ode*, 1815; *Poems from the Danish*, 1815; and *The Appeal of Poland: An Ode*, 1816. He edited a *Corpus Poetarum Latinorum*, 1828, and Milton's *De Doctrina Christiana*, 1825 (nominally ed. by C. R. Sumner). The *Poetical Remains* were edited with a long Memoir by his friend J. Moultrie in 1852. See also *Shakespeare's Versification and its Apparent Irregularities Explained*, ed. W. N. Lettsom, 1854, and *A Critical Examination of the Text of Shakespeare*, ed. W. N. Lettsom, 3 vols., 1860. As a young man Walker had contributed to *The Etonian*, 1820–1, and later he wrote in Knight's *Quarterly Magazine* and the *Classical Journal*. He was a friend of Praed.

Robert (later Plumer) Ward, 1765–1846.

This tedious writer produced five works of fiction: *Tremaine, or the Man of Refinement*, 3 vols., 1825; *De Vere, or the Man of Independence*, 4 vols., 1827; *Illustrations of Human Life*, 3 vols., 1837; *Pictures of the World at Home and Abroad*, 3 vols., 1839; and *De Clifford, or the Constant Man*, 4 vols., 1841. He edited P. G. Patmore's

anonymous *Chatsworth, or the Romance of a Week*, 3 vols., 1844. His other prose works have little literary interest.

*Memoirs of . . . Robert Plumer Ward* with letters and unpublished remains were edited by E. Phipps in 2 vols. in 1850. See also P. G. Patmore's *My Friends and Acquaintances*, 3 vols., 1855, and 'Robert Plumer Ward', in *Bentley's Miscellany*, xxviii, 1850. As Michael Sadleir pointed out in *Bulwer and his Wife: a Panorama 1803–1836*, 1933, both Disraeli and Bulwer Lytton were influenced by Ward.

ALARIC ALEXANDER WATTS, 1797–1864.

As writer and editor, Watts was responsible for a great many productions. Of his own books mention may be made of *Poetical Sketches*, 1822 (privately printed); *Poetical Sketches: The Profession; The Broken Heart, etc.*, 1823; *Scenes of Life and Shades of Character*, 2 vols., 1831 (prose); and *Lyrics of the Heart*, 1851. In 1828–9 he produced a most interesting two-volume anthology of contemporary poetry, *The Poetical Album*, followed by *The Lyre* and *The Laurel* (reprinted together in 1867 as *The Laurel and the Lyre*).

He helped to edit the *New Monthly Magazine* from about 1815 to 1819, and the *Literary Souvenir* from 1825 to 1835. He wrote a good deal for the *Literary Gazette*. He also edited the *Leeds Intelligencer*, 1822–5; the *Manchester Courier*, 1825–6 (at first a weekly); the *Standard* (1827); and the *United Service Gazette* (1833–41). He was responsible for the *Cabinet of British Art*, 1835–8 (a sequel to the *Literary Souvenir*), and *Men of the Time*, 1856, which includes an article on Watts himself three times as long as that on Tennyson.

His son Alaric Alfred Watts published *Alaric Watts: A Narrative of his Life* in 2 vols. in 1884. See also Watts's own entertaining article, 'Some Passages in the Life of a Magazine Editor', in the *Literary Magnet*, 1826.

CHARLES JEREMIAH WELLS, 1800–79.

Wells published a volume of prose, *Stories after Nature*, in 1822 (ed. W. J. Linton, 1891), and *Joseph and his Brethren, a Scriptural Drama*, in '1824' (really December 1823: by 'H. L. Howard': ed. A. C. Swinburne, 1876, reprinted in 1908 in the World's Classics). He wrote two papers in *Fraser's Magazine* and contributed a tale, 'Claribel', to Linton's *Illuminated Magazine* for 1845. Swinburne's essay, first published in the *Fortnightly Review*

for February 1875, was just too late to prevent Wells from burning a great mass of his unpublished writings. 'A Dramatic Scene', ed. H. B. Forman, was printed in *Literary Anecdotes of the Nineteenth Century*, ed. W. Robertson Nicoll and Thomas J. Wise, vol. i, 1895.

Miles's *Poets and Poetry of the Century*, iii, contains a selection and a brief critique by H. B. Forman. See also Sir E. Gosse's obituary in the *Academy*, 1 March 1879, and the notice in the *DNB*.

JEREMIAH HOLMES WIFFEN, 1792–1836.

With T. Raffles and J. B. Brown, Wiffen published *Poems by Three Friends*, 1813. With his brother, Benjamin Barron Wiffen, he published *Elegiac Lines* in 1818. On his own he then published *Aonian Hours and other Poems*, 1819; *Julia Alpinula, with The Captive of Stamboul, and other Poems*, 1820; *Jerusalem Delivered: Book the Fourth*, 1821 (a specimen of his projected translation of Tasso, with a critique of earlier translations); *The Works of Garcilasso de la Vega, translated*, 1823; *Jerusalem Delivered. . . . Translated into English Spenserian Verse . . .*, 2 vols., 1824–5; *Verses on the Alameda at Ampthill Park*, 1827 (privately printed); *Historical Memoirs of the House of Russell*, 2 vols., 1833; *Appeal for the Injured African*, Newcastle upon Tyne, 1833 (verse); and *Verses Written at Woburn Abbey*, 1836 (privately printed).

He also published a number of reviews and other writings in prose. He wrote on 'The Character and Poetry of Lord Byron' in the *New Monthly Magazine* for May 1819.

*The Brothers Wiffen: Memoirs and Miscellanies*, ed. S. R. Pattison, 1880, includes a selection from their poems. The *Quarterly Review*, xxxiv, 1826, contains an interesting review of Wiffen's *Tasso*.

JOHN WILSON ('CHRISTOPHER NORTH'), 1785–1854.

In verse he published *A Recommendation of the Study of the Remains of Ancient . . . Architecture . . . A Prize Poem*, Oxford, 1807; *Lines Sacred to the Memory of the Rev. James Grahame*, 1811; *The Isle of Palms*, 1812; *The Magic Mirror*, 1812; and *The City of the Plague*, 1816. His *Poems* were published in 2 vols. in 1825, and there were subsequent editions.

His principal writings in prose include *Translation From an Ancient Chaldee Manuscript* (with Lockhart: reprinted from *Blackwood's Magazine*, October 1817); *Lights and Shadows of Scottish*

*Life* (by 'Arthur Austin'), 1822; *The Trials of Margaret Lyndsay*, 1823; *The Foresters*, 1825; *Tales*, 1865 (the last three books together); *Janus, or the Edinburgh Literary Almanack* (ed. by Lockhart: contains contributions by Wilson), 1826; *Some Illustrations of Mr. M'Culloch's Principles of Political Economy* (by 'Mordecai Mullion'), 1826; *The Recreations of Christopher North*, 3 vols., 1842; *The Noctes Ambrosianæ of 'Blackwood'*, ed. R. Skelton Mackenzie, 5 vols., New York, 1854, revised 1863 (fullest edition); 4 vols., 1864; selected edition, ed. J. Scott Moncrieff, n.d., New Universal Library (mainly the work of North, but with collaboration from Hogg, Lockhart, and others); *Specimens of the British Critics*, Philadelphia, 1846; and *Essays Critical and Imaginative*, 4 vols., 1866. *The Works of Professor Wilson*, in 12 vols., ed. Professor Ferrier, appeared between 1855 and 1858.

The fullest accounts are to be found in Mary Gordon's *Christopher North: A Memoir*, 2 vols., 1862, and Elsie Swann's *Christopher North*, 1934. See also J. G. Lockhart, *Peter's Letters to his Kinsfolk*, 3 vols., 1819; G. Gilfillan, *Galleries of Literary Portraits*, ii, 1856; J. Hannay, 'Professor Wilson', in *Characters and Criticisms*, 1865; W. Maginn, *A Gallery of Illustrious Literary Characters*, ed. W. Bates, [1873]; G. Saintsbury, *Essays in English Literature, 1780–1860*, ser. i, 1890; D. Masson, 'Christopher North', in *Memories of Two Cities*, 1911; H. von Struve, *John Wilson . . . als Kritiker*, Leipzig, 1922; M. Elwin, 'Christopher North', in *Victorian Wallflowers*, 1934; and a series of brief articles by A. L. Strout, as follows: *MP* xxxi, 1934; *ELH* ii, 1935; *MLN* li, 1935 (and *RES* xiii, 1937, pp. 46–63 and 177–89); *Shakespeare Jahrbuch*, lxxii, 1936; *RES* xiv, 1938; *NQ* 11 March 1939, 1 April 1939; *PMLA* lv, 1940; *NQ* 6 June and 1 August 1942. R. M. Wardle's 'The Authorship of the "Noctes Ambrosianæ"' (*MP* xlii, 1944–5) was supplemented by Strout in *The Library*, ser. v, vol. xii, no. 2 (June 1957). See also 'An Unknown Castigator of Christopher North', by N. S. Aurnor, in *If by Your Art: Testament to Percival Hunt*, Pittsburgh, 1948; and M. P. Alekseev's essay on *The City of the Plague* in *Iz istorii angliyskoy literatury*, Moscow and Leningrad, 1960. See also the section on *Blackwood's Magazine* on pp. 470–3 above.

FRANCIS WRANGHAM, 1769–1842.

*The Lyrics of Horace: being the First Four Books of his Odes*, translated by Wrangham, was published in 1821. (The previous

year Wrangham had published *Q. Horatius Flaccus: Carmina . . . Specimens of a version of Book III.*) His other work in verse (often Cambridge prize poems) includes *The Restoration of the Jews*, 1795; *The Destruction of Babylon*, 1795; *Poems* (privately printed 1795, but not published till *c.* 1802); *The Holy Land*, 1800; *The Raising of Jaïrus' Daughter*, 1804; *A Poem on the Restoration of Learning in the East*, 1805; *A Volunteer Song*, York, [? 1806] (11 pieces in verse); *The Sufferings of the Primitive Martyrs*, 1812; *Joseph Made Known to his Brethren*, 1812; *Death of Saul and Jonathan*, 1813; *Poetical Sketches of Scarborough* (by Wrangham and others), 1813; *Poems*, [? 1814] (privately printed); *Virgil's Bucolics*, Scarborough, 1815; *A Few Sonnets Attempted from Petrarch in Early Life*, Lee Priory, 1817; *Scarborough Castle*, Scarborough, 1823; *Psychae; or Songs on Butterflies, by T. H. Bayly, attempted in Latin Rhyme*, 1828; *Homerics*, 1834 (translation of *Odyssey* V, and *Iliad* III); *Epithalamia tria Mariana*, &c., Chester, 1837 (translations); and *A Few Epigrams: Attempted in Latin Translation*, Chester, 1842.

In 1792 he had published *Reform: A Farce Modernised from Aristophanes . . . By S. Foote Jr.* He produced several editions of Langhorne's *Plutarch*. *The British Plutarch, containing the Lives of the most Eminent Divines, &c.*, 6 vols., 1816, a revision by Wrangham of Thomas Mortimer's book, is a quite distinct work. For an account of Wrangham, with a detailed list of these and of other publications of religious interest, see Michael Sadleir, *Archdeacon Francis Wrangham 1769–1842*, Bibliographical Society, 1937 (Supplement no. 12).

# INDEX

Main entries are in bold figures. An asterisk indicates a biographical footnote. The index excludes the Bibliography, except in the case of a few minor writers who are not mentioned in the text, or mentioned only in passing.


Ackerman(n), Rudolph, 173*–4.
Acton, Eliza, 423.
Addison, Joseph, 201, 265, 271, 290, 322.
Adolphus, John Leycester, 199*, 208.
Aeschylus, 81, 86, 302, 348.
Ainsworth, William Harrison, 254.
Akenside, Mark, 170.
Albert, Prince, 172.
Aldine Poets, 401.
Alfieri, Vittorio, 61, 66, 179, 414.
*Amulet, The*, 173.
Anacreon, 165, 377.
Angerstein Collection, 378.
Anne, Queen, 210.
*Anniversary, The*, 173.
*Annual Register, The*, 378.
Annuals, 167–8, 169 n., **173–5**.
Anster, John, 386.
Anstey, Christopher, 167.
*Anti-Jacobin, The*, 13–14, 51, 63 and n., 332.
'Apostles, The', 398.
Apuleius, 162.
*Arabian Nights, The*, 246.
Archer, William, 177.
Archimedes, 78.
Ariosto, 53, 125, 371, 380–3, 394.
Aristophanes, 46, 145, 377.
Aristotle, 180, 204, 333, 348.
Arnold, Matthew, 4, 122, 301.
Ascham, Roger, 400.
Athenæum Club, 27.
*Athenaeum, The*, 24, 44, 144 n., 148 n., 233, 286, 389, 398, 430.
Atherstone, Edwin, 170.
Aubrey, John, 404.
Austen, Jane, 29, 34, 58, 112 n., 195, 202, 207, 213, 225, 235–8, 248–50, 253, 266, 331 n., 373, 384, 421.
Autobiography, 363–74.

Bacon, Francis, 12, 105, 267, 270, 273, 345, 400.
Bacon, Roger, 71.
Bailey, Benjamin, 123, 415.
Bailly, Sylvain, 397.
Baker, Carlos, 95.
Ballantyne, John, 185 n., 205, 359, 360, 421.
Ballantyne's *Novelist's Library*, 402.
Balzac, Honoré de, 255, 334.
Bamford, Samuel, 365.
Bandello, Matteo, 383.
Banim, John and Michael, **257–8**.
Bannatyne Club, 404.
Barrett, Elizabeth (Elizabeth Barrett Browning), 339, 340.
Barton, Bernard, 31–32, 36, 42, **172*–3**, 280.
Baudelaire, Charles, 255, 306.
Bayle, Pierre, 402.
Beattie, James, 55.
Beaumont and Fletcher, 267, 284, 401.
Beaumont, Sir George, 25.
Beaumont, Lady, 45.
Beckford, William, 246.
Beddoes, Thomas Lovell, 37, **138*–44**, 146, 153, 166, 245, 384, 391–2 (interest in German literature), 422, 436.
Bede, 71.
Behn, Aphra, 435.
Bentham, Jeremy, 16, 269, 312, 319 n., 354 n., 355, 399, **424*–8**, 437.
Bentley, Richard, 34, 430.
Bentley's 'Standard Novels', 383, 430–1.
Bent's *Monthly Literary Advertiser*, 38 n.
*Beowulf*, 399.
Béranger, Pierre-Jean, 396.
Bernard, Sir Thomas, 45.
Berni, Francesco, 383.
Bewick, Thomas, 134, 137, 372.
Bible, The, 270.
Bilderdijk, 140.
Biography, 356–63.
Birkbeck, Dr. George, 432.
Birkhead, Edith, 257.
Black, A. and C., 27.
Black, John, 381, 386.
Blackstone, Sir William, 424.
Blackwood, William, 19, 25, 28, **29*–30**, 235.
*Blackwood's Edinburgh Magazine*, 1, **17–22**, 37, 241 n., 292, 306, 336–8, 356 n., 359, 377, 389, 393, 397, 421.
Blair, Alexander, 338.
Blake, General, 12.
Blake, William, 130, 138, 286, 419.
Blanchard, Samuel Laman, 502.

Blessington, Marguerite, Countess of, 24, 34, 169, 362.
Blunden, Edmund, 137, 147, 321.
Boccaccio, 110, 159, 383 ;394, 407.
Boethius, 344.
Boiardo, 125, 381.
Boileau, 106, 364, 396.
Borrow, George, 387, 398.
Bossuet, 331.
Boswell, James, 234, 334, 356–8, 364, 405, 418.
Bourne, Vincent, 283.
Bouterwek, 387, 398.
Bowles, William Lisle, 51–52, 174, 278, 282, 286, 404, 436.
Bowra, Sir Maurice, 419.
Bowring, Sir John, 398, **399***, 425, 426.
Boyer, the Rev. James, 322.
Bradley, A. C., 122, 287.
Brawne, Fanny, 105 n., 122.
Brett-Smith, H. F. B., 216.
Brightfield, M. F., 251, 335.
Brontë, Charlotte, 58.
Brontës, the, 157, 241, 257, 385.
Brougham, Henry Peter, Baron Brougham and Vaux, 11, 39, 48, 220, 222, 425, **431*–4**.
Brown, Charles (Armitage), 22, 105 n., 107, 110, 366.
Brown, Thomas, 506.
Browne, E. G., 247.
Browne, Sir Thomas, 267, 270, 286, 290, 301–2, 400.
Browne, William, 106, 400.
Browning, Robert, 113, 139, 143, 150, 158, 159, 161, 184, 344 and n., 345, 437.
Bryant, Sir Arthur, 41.
Brydges, Sir Samuel Egerton, 33, 365–6, **372*–3**, 404.
Buchanan, W., 378.
Bunyan, John, 197, 241, 270.
Bürger, Gottfried August, 387 .389.
Burgo, Johannes de, 373.
Burke, Edmund, 15, 71, 276, 277, 302, 333, 344, 349.
Burnett, George, 283, 365, 402.
Burney, Fanny, 238, 266, 334.
Burns, Robert, 59, 106, 130 n., 131, 286, 422.
Burton, Robert, 99, 110, 117, 143, 282, 286, 290–1, 302.
Butler, Samuel (see also *Hudibras*), 67.
Byron, George Gordon, Lord Byron, 2 (reputation), 6–7, 19, 27 n., 28, 32, 35–36, 40, 42–43, 47, **49*–76**, 77 and n., 80, 123, 130 n., 137, 146, 148, 150, 152, 154, 156, 158–60, 162, 164, 165 n., 168–9, 176, 179, 181–2, 185 n., 200, 217–18, 226 n., 234, 241 n., 243 and n., 245, 252, 263, 301, 319 n., 321–2, 326, 331 n., 335, 337, 349, 361–4, 366–70 (and Leigh Hunt), 376, 378–82 (and Italian), 384–5, 390–1, 398, 400, 402–3, 406, 408–19 (and the 'Romantic Movement'), 421, 423, 436–7.

Cabanis, Georges, 397.
Cadell, Robert, 357.
Cadell, Thomas, 19, 25, 26.
Calderón, 407.
Camoens, 398.
Campbell, Thomas, 3, 23–24, 51, 55, 57, 148, 153, 168, 245, 263, 326, 398, 400, 402, 411–12.
'Canadian Boat-Song', 579.
*Candide* (Voltaire's), 224.
Canning, George, 8, 13–14, 33, 62, 63 n., 180 n., 216, 332 and n., 346, 347.
Cant, satirized in the 1820's, 436.
Carey, Patrick, 399.
Carlyle, Jane Welsh, 281.
Carlyle, Thomas, 8–9, 16, 27, 176 and n., 338, 368, 384, 387–8, 392, 393, 395, 421–3, 437.
Carnegie, Andrew, 234.
Caroline, Queen, 75, 200, 227, 312 n., 432 n.
Carter, Samuel, 173.
Cary, Henry Francis, 30, 377, **379**, 396, 402.
Casti, Giovanni Battista, 382.
Castlereagh, Robert Stewart, Viscount Castlereagh, 1, 65, 167.
*Cato* (Addison's), 67.
Cecil, William, Lord Burleigh, 71.
Cellini, Benvenuto, 383.
Cervantes, 360.
'Chaldee MS.', 18–20, 241 n., 336.
Chalkhill, John, 401.
Chamberlayne, William, 400.
*Chambers's Edinburgh Journal*, 431.
Chapman, George, 106, 107, 267, 377, 400.
Charlemagne, 373.
Charles II, 200.
Charlotte, the Princess, 168.
Chateaubriand, 420.
Chatterton, Thomas, 106, 111, 120, 263.
Chaucer, 69, 71, 106, 114, 147, 268, 270, 305, 417, 419.
Cheap books, 428–31.
Cheney, Edward, 381.
Cherry, J. L., 138.
Christianity and the writers of the time, 6–8.
Christie, John, 22.
Churchill, Charles, 51, 59.
Cibber, Colley, 65, 366.
Cicero, 345, 347.
*Cid, El*, 398.

Cinthio, Giraldi, 383.
Cintra, Convention of, 54.
Clairmont, Claire, 49 n.
Clare, John, 21, 22, 30, 40, 43, **130*–8**, 139, 148, 172, 174, 298, 364, 372.
Clarke, Charles Cowden, 105 n., 121, 124, 365.
'Classical' and 'Romantic', 406-21.
Claude Lorraine, 377.
Clavering, Miss, 236.
Cleveland, John, 152.
Cobbett, William, 43, 269, **312*–19**, 354, 422, 429, 433.
Cobden, Richard, 332 n.
Cockburn, Henry, 26.
'Cockney School of Poetry', 19–22, 396.
Colburn, Henry, 23–24, **30–31**, 34, 366, 430.
Cole, G. D. H., 319.
Coleridge, Hartley, 4, 21, **156*–8.**
Coleridge, Henry Nelson, 157.
Coleridge, Sir John Taylor, 36.
Coleridge, Samuel Taylor, 4–8 (reputation), 12, 27, 29, 31, 43, 45–47 (lectures), 51, 116, 139 n., 151, 153, 156, 175–7, 182, 213, 215, 217, 260–1, 264, 268, 270, 273, 275, 278, 282, 284–6 (and Lamb), 288, 292 n., 295, 299, 301, 303, 310–11, 324, 335 n., 336, 339, 364, 366–7, 376, 379, 384–6 (and German), 388, 392–3, 395, 398, 400, 410–11, 415–16, 419, 423, 425, 437.
Collier, Jeremy, 265.
Collier, John Payne, 402.
Collins, A. S., 33, 35.
Collins, William, 136, 263.
Colman, George, 178, 322.
Colquhoun, Patrick, 43.
Colvin, Sidney, 108.
Combe, William ('Dr. Syntax'), 521–2.
Compton-Burnett, Ivy, 272.
Condorcet, Antoine-Nicolas de, 105, 397, 429–30.
Congreve, William, 265.
Constable, Archibald, 10, 19, **24–27***, 33–37, 199, 204, 226, 421.
*Constable's Miscellany*, 429–30.
Copleston, Edward, 15.
Corbould, 174.
Corneille, Pierre, 371.
*Corn-Law Rhymes*, 422–3.
'Cornwall, Barry' (Bryan Waller Procter), 146, **158*–60**, 161, 177, 267, 279, 392, 401.
Cowley, Abraham, 327.
Cowper, William, 51, 71, 281, 339, 404.
Crabbe, George, 27, 44, 51, 131, 134–5, 154, 326, 400, 411–12, 437.
Cranmer, Thomas, 71.
Crashaw, Richard, 89–90, 282.
Crébillon *fils*, 396.
Croce, Benedetto, 419.
Croker, John Wilson, 14, 27, 33, 34, 216, 323, **332*–5**, 362, 405.
Cromwell, 5.
Crowe, William, 170.
Cumberland, Richard, 176 n.
Cunningham, Allan, 21, 40, 173, 175, 298, 402.
Cuvier, Georges, 397, 437.

d'Alembert, Jean le Rond, 397.
Dallas, R. C., 35, 54.
Dalyell, James Graham, 19.
Dampier, William, 301.
Dante, 88–89, 93, 125, 349, 371, 377, 379–82, 407.
Darley, George, 21, 37–38, 130, 133, 140, 143, **144*–6**, 155, 180, 183–4, 384.
Darwin, Charles, 437.
Darwin, Erasmus, 243, 255.
Davenant, Sir William, 400.
Davenport, Robert, 400.
Davy, Sir Humphry, 27, 298, 304.
Deacon, William Frederick, 177.
Dee, Dr., 144.
Defoe, Daniel, 130 n., 233, 286, 293, 301–2, 312, 359, 400, 405.
Dekker, Thomas, 267.
'Della Cruscans, The', 331.
Denham, Sir John, 161.
Dennis, John, 400.
Depping, 398.
De Quincey, Thomas, 5 6, 17–18, 21, 30, 37, 46, 130 n., 240, 243 n., 278 n., **292*–311**, 324, 336, 364, 368, 375, 376, 383–4, 388 and n., 392–4 (and German literature), 418–19, 435–7.
De Staël, Mme de, 29, 58, 101, 386, 390, 394, 406–7.
De Wint, Peter, 133.
d'Holbach, 105, 397.
Dibdin, Thomas Frognall, 28, 421, 423–4, 428, 430.
Dickens, Charles, 44, 158 n., 169 n., 184, 253, 325 n., 326, 368, 434, 436–7.
Diderot, Denis, 397.
Dillon, Lord, 409.
Disraeli, Benjamin, 169, 250 n., 254, 335, 366, 437.
D'Israeli, Isaac, 27, 366, **402–3.**
Dobson, Mrs. 381.
Dodsley, Robert, 284.
Donne, John, 90, 99, 143, 151, 171, 263, 265, 270, 282, 302, 327.
Donner, H. W., 140, 392.
*Don Quixote*, 265, 360.
Dowden, Edward, 78.
Doyle, John A., 236.

Drama, 59–62 (Byron), 81–88 (Shelley), 140–2 (Beddoes), 146 (Darley), **177–84**.
Drayton, Michael, 401.
Drummond, Sir William, 105.
Drummond, William of Hawthornden, 267.
Drury Lane, 49 n.
Dryden, John, 5, 59, 110, 147, 152, 155, 156, 267, 270, 271, 333, 334, 404, 418.
Du Bellay, Joachim, 396.
Dumas, Alexandre, 334, 370.
Dunlop, John Colin, 225, 265, 383, 402.
Dürer, Albrecht, 392.
Dyce, Alexander, 401.
Dyer, George, 287.

Eckermann, J. P., 407.
Edgeworth, Maria, 33, 139 n., 186, 225, 248, 257.
*Edinburgh Review, The*, **8–12**, 13–18 (and *Quarterly*), 26, 29, 36–37, 39, 40, 41, 44, 48, 50, 54, 56, 67, 167, 255–6, 315, 325–7 (and Jeffrey), 329–31, 351 n., 353, 397, 401, 422, 426, 432 n.
Eldon, Lord, 10.
Elford, Sir William, 339, 342.
Elgin Marbles, The, 370 n., 372.
'Eliot, George', 175.
Eliot, T. S., 5, 62, 92–93, 310, 316.
Elizabeth I, 185, 200.
Elliott, Ebenezer, 422–3.
Ellis, George, 13–14, 283, 398, 402.
Elton, Oliver, 171.
Elwin–Courthope edition of Pope, 334.
Emmerson, Mrs., 136.
*Encyclopaedia Britannica*, 27, 29 n., 426.
*Encyclopédie*, The, 20, 396–7.
Epicurus, 223, 347, 348.
Escarpit, Robert, 76.
*Español, El*, 397.
'Espriella, Don Manuel Alvarez', 398.
*Etonian, The*, 154.
Etty, William, 147.
Euripides, 86.
Evelyn, John, 404.
*Examiner, The*, 260, 261, 271, 287, 319–20.
Ezekiel, 302.

Fairfax, Edward, 381.
Farmer, Richard, 271.
Farquhar, George, 265.
Fashionable Novels, 247–52.
*Faust*, 60, 100, 391.
Fawcett, Joseph, 394.
Ferdinand VII, 398.
Ferrier, Susan, 29, 33, 40 226, **235*–9**.
Fichte, J. G., 393, 395.
Fielding, Henry, 66, 184, 198, 202, 208, 230, 266, 369, 434.
Finney, C. L., 108.
FitzGerald, Edward, 172 n.
Flanagan, Thomas, 257–9, 332.
Fletcher, John, 181.
Foote, Miss, 159.
Ford, John, 98, 267, 401.
*Foreign Quarterly Review, The*, 389.
*Forget-Me-Not, The*, 173.
Forster, E. M., 272.
Forster, John, 169 n.
Forteguerri, Niccolo, 382–3.
Foscolo, Ugo, 381–2.
Foster, John, 408.
Fouqué, F. de la Motte, 387, 390.
Fox, Charles James, 71, 346.
*Frankenstein*, **243–5** (*and see* Mary Shelley).
Franklin, Benjamin, 74, 260 n., 313, 346.
*Fraser's Magazine*, 24, 363.
French literature, 395–7.
Frere, John Hookham, 28, 29, 62*–63, 70, 150, 154, 377, 382, 398.
*Friendship's Offering*, 173.
Froissart, 201.
Fry, Mrs., 152.
Fuller, Thomas, 282, 286.

Galt, John, 18, 29, 40–41, **226*–35**, 243, 362, 365–6, 388 n.
*Gammer Gurton's Needle*, 270.
Garrod, H. W., 108, 120, 124.
*Gentleman's Magazine, The*, 17, 287.
George I, 210.
George II, 200, 352.
George III, 65, 70–75, 168, 227–8, 321–2.
George IV, 27, 156, 360.
German literature, 383–95 (*and see* particular writers).
Gessner, Salomon, 177, 337, 385, 390.
Gettmann, Royal A., 431.
Gibbon, Edward, 351, 354, 355, 409.
Gide, André, 243, 306.
Gifford, William, 8, 12–13, 27, 37, 51, 70–71, 177, 200, 216, 268, 269, 276–7, 285, **331*–2**, 365, 368, 377, 401.
Gillies, Robert Pearce, 388–9, 393, 410–12.
Gillray, James, 168.
Gilpin, William, 207, 209.
Ginguené, Pierre-Louis, 382.
Giovanni, Ser Giovanni Fiorentino, 383.
Gisbornes, the, 90, 391.
Gleig, George Robert, 34.
Glenbervie, Lord, 382.
Godwin, William, 33, 40, 77 n., 105, 233, 243–4, 266, 268, 286, 298.
Goethe, 50, 76, 385–8, 387, 388, 390–2, 395, 407, 437.

Goldsmith, Oliver, 131, 218, 322.
Gooch, G. P., 352.
Gore, Mrs. Catherine Grace Frances, 184.
Gower, Leveson, 386.
Goya, 93.
Grant, Mrs. (of Laggan), 298.
Gray, Thomas, 116, 155, 262, 263, 281, 339, 396.
Greek literature, 375–7.
Green, Matthew, 155, 344.
Grenville, Lord, 344.
*Grenville Papers, The*, 333.
Grierson, H. J. C., 359, 361.
Griffin, Bartholomew, 401.
Griffin, Gerald, 178, **258–9**.
Grosvenor, Lord, 331 and n.
Grote, George, 436.
Guiccioli, the Countess, 64, 70.

Halévy, Élie, 75.
Hallam, Henry, 40, **351–3***, 380.
*Hamlet*, 117.
Hammond, J. L. and Barbara, 41.
Hampden, John, 12.
Handel, 71.
Hardy, Thomas, 143, 234.
Haren, De, 392–3.
Hastings, Warren, 71.
Hawthorne, Nathaniel, 240.
Haydon, Benjamin Robert, 7, 123, 124, 127, 279, 324, 340, **370*–2**, 373, 378, 415.
Hayley, William, 40.
Hayward, A., 386.
Hazlitt, William, 4, 5, 7, 16, 19–20, 21, 24, 30, 31, 35, 37, 40, 46–47, 110, 116, 123, 125, 130 n., 157, 171 n., 180–2, 213, 247–8, **260*–77**, 278 n., 279, 284, 286, 288, 302, 318–19, 321, 323, 324, 328, 332, 350, 364, 377–8, 380, 383, 385–6, 394–5, 396, 400, 410, 437.
Heath, Charles, 175.
Heber, Reginald, 401.
Heber, Richard, 199 n., 398, 404.
Hemans, Mrs. (Felicia Dorothea Browne), **168*–9**, 398.
Henry IV, 344.
Henry VII, 352.
Herbert, George, 98, 155, 171, 400, 401.
Herbert, Lord Herbert of Cherbury, 365.
Herder, J. F., 388, 393, 395.
Herrick, Thomas, 267, 401.
Herschel, Sir John, 48.
Hessey, James Augustus, 304.
Heywood, Thomas, 267.
Hill, George Birkbeck, 405.
Hilton, William, 133.
Historical writing, **351–6**, 399–405 (literary historians).
Hobbema, Meindert, 342.
Hobhouse, John Cam, 28, 49 n., 53, 56, 365, 373, 376.
Hoche, Louis-Lazare, 331.
Hoffmann, E. T. A., 387, 390.
Hogarth, William, 71, 152, 208, 264, 285, 321, 342.
Hogg, James ('The Ettrick Shepherd'), 19, 29, 176, 177, 226, 240, **241–3***, 255, 336–7, 364, 374.
Hogg, Thomas Jefferson, 214 n., 217, 218, 223, 363.
Holcroft, Thomas, 262.
Holland House, 329 n., 330.
Holland, Lord, 25, 34–35.
Homer, 53, 371, 376, 377, 381.
Hone, William, 548.
Hood, Thomas, 21–22, 44–45, 148 n., **151*–3**, 154, 245, 280, 365, 423, 436.
Hook, Theodore, 24, 248, **250*–2**.
Hooker, Richard, 286, 345, 352.
Hoole, John, 381.
Hope, Thomas, 245.
Hopkins, Gerard Manley, 119, 134.
Horace, 68, 375, 376.
Horne, R. H., 25, 30, 183–4, 340, 423.
Horner, Francis, 9, 36.
House, Humphry, 436.
*Household Words*, 322.
*Hudibras*, 67, 145, 154, 202, 221, 222, 265, 331, 333, 354.
Hugo, Victor, 334, 396.
Humboldt, F. H. A. von, 304.
Hume, David, 105, 273, 325, 339, 354.
Hunt, James Henry Leigh, 3, 7, 19, 29, 32, 40, 77 n., 79, 81, 91, 97, 105 n., 106, 108, 123, 141, **146–8** (poems), 158 and n., 165 n., 171 n., 177, 181, 243 n., 271, 279, **319*–24** (prose), 332, 334, 344, 361, 365–8 (autobiography), 378, 380, 382–3 (interest in Italian literature), 401, 409–10, 412, 415, 416, 418, 428, 435, 437.
Hunt, John, 29, 70, 72, 262, 319 n., 320.

Institutions, 432–3.
Irving, Edward, 298.
Irving, Washington, 339.
Italian literature, 378–83 (*and see* particular Italian writers).

James I of Scotland, 49.
James II of England, 194.
James VI and I, 198, 200, 204.
James, Henry, 171, 240.
*Jane Eyre*, 58, 253.
Japp, A. H., 307.

Jeffrey, Francis, 3, 8, 9–12, 13, 16, 18, 29, 36, 37, 44, 165, 225, 323, **324*–9**, 331, 388 n., 395, 401.
Jeffrey, Sarah, 124.
Jerdan, William, 169, 396.
Jewsbury, Maria Jane, 168 n.
Jimson, Gulley, 372.
*John Bull*, 250 n.
*John Buncle*, 271.
Johnson, Samuel, 17, 45, 47, 134, 162, 241, 246–7, 263, 265, 267, 270, 271, 273, 279, 288, 303, 319, 327, 334, 339, 344, 349, 356–8, 402, 405, 409, 418.
Jones, Isabella, 105 n.
Jones, Sir William, 171, 355.
Jonson, Ben, 198, 265, 400, 401.
Joyce, James, 258, 328.
'Junius', 71, 74.
Juvenal, 167, 331, 377.

Kant, Immanuel, 383–4, 391, 393–5.
Kean, Edmund, 85, 181–2.
Keats, George and Georgiana, 116, 123–4.
Keats, John, 3, 4, 7, 19–21 (and *Blackwood's*), 22, 30, 36, 37, 40, 42, 47, 50, 76, 90–92, **105*–129**, 133, 141, 146, 148 and n., 149, 150, 151, 154, 158, 159, 162, 171 and n., 172, 177, 263, 264, 274, 283, 301, 319 n., 320, 321, 323, 324, 326, 328, 334–5, 366, 367–8, 370 n., 371–2, 376–9 (and Greek and Italian literature, and painting), 382–3, 384, 391, 401–2, 410–17 (and the 'Romantic Movement'), 419, 422, 436.
Keats, Tom, 124.
Keble, John, 4, 171.
*Keepsake, The*, 175.
Kelly, Fanny, 278 n., 281.
Kelsall, T. F., 37, 142.
Kemble, Fanny, 183.
Kemble, J. M., 399.
Kenrick, William, 45.
King, Edward, 91.
*King Lear*, 371–2.
Kipling, Rudyard, 69.
Kleist, H. von, 387.
Klopstock, F. G., 384–5, 387.
Knight, Charles, 1, 4–5, 17, 38–39, 42, 155, 395, 401, 423, **429*–31**.
Knowles, James Sheridan, 180, **182*–3**.
Kotzebue, A. von, 181, 385, 395.

Lackington, James, 38.
*Lady's Magazine, The*, 338.
'Lake Poets, The', 5, 51, 60, 264, 298, 327–8, 336, 396, 416, 418-19.
Lamartine, 396.
Lamb, Charles, 7–8, 21, 30, 31–32, 47, 111, 130 n., 140, 144, 151, 152, 158 n., 159, 172 and n., 177, 179, 183, 260 n., 262, 267, 271, 273, 275–7 (and Hazlitt), **278*–91**, 298, 299, 302, 319 n., 321, 325, 332, 340, 343, 364, 366, 371, 386, 388, 401, 436–7.
Lamb, Mary, 278 n., 279, 283.
Landon, Letitia Elizabeth, **169***, 174, 396.
Landor, Robert Eyres, 179.
Landor, Walter Savage, 12, 340, **344*–50**, 369, 376, 380, 384.
Lang, Andrew, 14, 357.
Laplace, Pierre-Simon, Marquis de, 105, 397.
Lardner, Dr., 430.
Larpent, John, 178–9.
Latin literature, 375–7.
Lawrence, Leonard, 400.
Leavis, Dr. F. R., 92–94, 122, 256.
Lectures, 45–48.
Lee, Nathaniel, 400.
Lee Priory Press, 373 n.
Leibnitz, 310.
Leonardo da Vinci, 307.
Le Sage, Alain-René, 202.
Lessing, 385, 393, 395.
Lewis, M. G., 390.
*Liberal, The*, 321–2.
'Lily's' Latin Grammar, 375.
Lind, Dr., 77 n., 96.
Lingard, John, **353–4***.
Lister, Thomas Henry, 40, **248*–50**, 251, 434.
*Literary Gazette, The*, 158 n., 169.
*Literary Souvenir, The*, 173–4.
Locke, John, 261, 273, 277.
Lockhart, John Gibson, 8, 10–11, 17–21 (and *Blackwood's*), 22, 26–27, 29, 33, 34, 37, 175, 194, 198, 204, 226, 227, 232, **239–41** (novels), 304, 335, 336, 337, **356*–61** (*Memoirs of Scott*), 377, 384, 390, 397, 398, 429–30, 435, 437.
Lodge, Thomas, 401.
Lofft, Capel, 300.
*London Magazine, The*, **21–23**, 30, 37, 40, 69, 144 n., 151 n., 278 n., 287, 291, 292, 294, 298, 389, 393, 396, 397, 402.
London University, 17, 388 n., 432 n.
Longman, Hurst, Rees, Orme and Brown, 31, 35, 166, 421, 423.
Lonsdale, Lord, 299.
Louvre, The, 377–8.
Lowndes, W. T., 404.
Lucian, 162, 366.
Lucretius, 78, 376.
Lucy, Sir Thomas, 348.
Luke, St., 309.
Luttrell, Henry, 579–80.
Lyell, Sir Charles, 437.
Lyly, John, 267.
Lytton, Bulwer, 2, 4, 24, 31, 154, 169, 178, 179, 225, 251–2, 254, 312, 386, 406, 423.

Macaulay, Thomas Babington, 10, 12, 16, 334, 351, 352, 355, 356, 404–5, 437.
*Macbeth*, 205.
McCulloch, John Ramsay, 10.
McGonagall, William, 173.
Machiavelli, 230.
Mackenzie, Henry, 201, 253, 278–9, 291, 337, 384.
Mackintosh, James, 261, 437.
Maclise, Daniel, 169.
Macready, William Charles, 159, 183, 338 n.
Magazines, 17–24 (*and see* the names of particular Magazines).
Maginn, William, 169.
Maine, Sir Henry James Sumner, 355.
Malone, Edmond, 271, 284, 402.
Malthus, Thomas Robert, 152, 215, 261, 268.
Mandeville, Sir John, 400.
Manning, Thomas, 280, 281, 287.
Manzoni, 383.
Marivaux, Pierre Carlet de Chamblain de, 396.
Marlowe, Christopher, 267, 285, 401.
Marot, Clément, 396.
Marston, John, 267.
Martin, John, 170.
Martineau, Harriet, 423.
Marvell, Andrew, 132, 267.
Mary, Queen of Scots, 189, 198, 200.
Mason, William, 162, 262.
Massinger, Philip, 401.
Masson, David, 298.
Massuccio Salernitano, 383.
Mathias, Thomas James, 51.
Maturin, Charles Robert, 159, **180*–2** (plays), **255–7** (*Melmoth*).
Maupassant, Guy de, 239.
Medwin, Thomas, 91, 363, 412.
Melbourne, Lord, 432 n.
Melville, Viscount, 346, 360.
Merivale, John Herman, 382.
Michelangelo, 307, 371.
Mickle, William Julius, 199.
Middleton, C. S., 214 n., 363.
Middleton, Thomas, 267, 401.
Mignet, François-Auguste, 352.
Milbanke, Annabella, 49 n.
Mill, James, 16, **354*–5**, 425–6.
Mill, John Stuart, 4, 6, 16, 17, 354 n., 424–6, 428.
Millais, Sir John Everett, 369.
Milman, Henry Hart, 36, **170–1***, 354, 437.
Milner, Bishop, 353.
Milnes, Richard Monckton, Baron Houghton, 126.
Milton, John, 12, 29, 76, 91, 125–7, 142, 228, 271, 299–300, 352, 371, 379, 414.
Mitford, Mary Russell, 24, 146, **338*–44**.
Moir, David Macbeth, ('Delta'), 29. 152, 168, 235, **243***, 365.
Monboddo, Lord, 214–15.
Montagu, Lady Mary Wortley, 281.
Montaigne, 290.
Montgomery, Robert, 42, Bibliography.
*Monthly Magazine, The*, 17, 387.
*Monthly Review, The*, 285, 365, 387.
Moore, Sir John, 292.
Moore, Thomas, 3, 25, 27–29, 31, 33–36 (earnings), 40, 42, 72, **165*–8**, 177, 224, 263, 325 n., 326, 361–2, 365, 373–4, 377, 400, 411–12, 427.
More, Hannah, 47.
Morgan, Lady ('Sydney Owenson'), 33, 34, 591–2..
Morgann, Maurice, 262.
Morier, James Justinian, **245–7**.
*Morning Chronicle, The*, 261.
*Morning Post, The*, 287.
Morris, William, 354.
Morritt, J. B. S., 56.
Motteux, Peter Anthony, 398.
Moultrie, John, 154, 592–3.
Moxon, Edward, 31, 288.
Mozart, 300.
Muir, Edwin, 157.
Murray, John, 12–13, 20, 24, **27*–29**, 32, 34–35, 37, 41, 42, 61, 63, 68, 70, 72, 76, 322, 331 n., 335, 361, 403, 421, 428, 430, 436.
Murry, J. Middleton, 122.

Napier, Macvey, 10, 12, 27, 421.
Napier, Sir William Francis Patrick, 29, 354.
Napoleon, 1, 23, 130 n., 261–2.
National Gallery, 378.
Nelson, 71.
Nesbitt, G. L., 427.
*New Monthly Magazine, The*, **23–24**, 37, 151 n., 230, 322, 362, 363, 422, 436.
*News of Literature, The*, 24–25.
Newton, Sir Isaac, 371.
Newton, J. F., 217.
Nichols, John, 199, 404.
Nicolas, Nicholas Harris, 355–6.
Nicoll, Allardyce, 181.
*Noctes Ambrosianæ*, 241 n., 337–8.
Novalis (F. von Hardenberg), 387.
Nugent, Lord, 12.

O'Connell, Daniel, 180 n.–181 n.
*Odyssey*, 53.
Ogden, James, 365 n.
Oliphant, Mrs. Margaret, 29.
Ollier, Charles and James, 31, 88.

O'Neill, Miss, 85.
Opie, Mrs. Amelia, 214.
Osborn, John, 391.
Ossian, 417.
Otway, Thomas, 178.
Owen, Robert, 79, 233.
Owen, William, 335.
'Owenson, Sydney' (Lady Morgan), 33, 34, 591–2.
Oxford Movement, 354.

Paine, Tom, 23.
Palgrave, Sir Francis, 355.
Palgrave, Francis Turner, 145.
Park, Thomas, 404.
Parnell, Sir Henry Brooke, 399 n.
Parr, Dr. Samuel, 376.
Pasha, Ali, 52.
Patmore, Peter George, 595.
Peacock, Thomas Love, 8, 15, 47–48, 77, 80, 85, 98, 104, 145, 159, **161–5** (poetry), **213*–24** (satiric tales), 348, 349, 363, 375, 376, 379, 391, 397, 400, 401, 427–8, 432–3, 436–7.
Peel, Sir Robert, 14, 44, 151 n., 153, 154 n., 172 n., 332 n.
Pepys, Samuel, 364, 404.
Perceval, Spencer, 71.
Percy, Thomas, 398, 402.
Pericles, 413.
Periodicals, *see* Reviews, Magazines, and the names of particular periodicals.
Persius, 331, 377.
Petrarch, 67, 106, 119–120, 349, 380–1, 407.
Petronius, 162.
Pettet, E. C., 108.
Philips, Ambrose, 177.
Phillipps, Sir Thomas, 404.
Phillips, Sir Richard, 23.
Philosophic Radicals, The, 232, 252, 423–8.
Pickering William, 401.
Pierard, 388.
Pindar, 349.
Pitt, Thomas (the Younger), 9, 71, 156, 252 n., 313.
Place, Francis, 426.
Plato, 81, 307, 349, 393, 394.
Playfair, John, 34, 388 n., 397.
Plutarch, 244.
Poe, Edgar Allan, 394.
Poetry Slump, 421–3.
Polidori, John William, 597.
Pollok, Robert, 597.
Pomfret, John, 131.
Pope, Alexander, 51, 52, 60, 65, 68, 110, 155, 161–2, 263, 269, 271, 299, 332, 333, 365, 376, 404, 408, 411–12, 418–19, 436.
Porson, Richard, 376.
Porter, Alan, 137.
Poussin, Nicolas, 377.
Powell, A. E., 419.
Praed, Winthrop Mackworth, **154*–6**, 349, 376, 429 n.
Pretender, The Young, 200.
Price, Richard, 7, 260.
Price of books, 39–41, 428–31.
Priestley, Dr. Joseph, 260, 313.
Prior, Matthew, 32, 68, 155.
Procter, Adelaide Anne, 158 n.
Procter, Bryan Waller, 146, **158*–60**, 161, 177, 267, 279, 392, 401.
Profession of letters, 31–38, 421–3.
Publishers, and the circulation and price of books, 24–31, 38–45, 426–31 (*and see* the names of particular Publishers).
Publishing Slump, 421–3.
Pulci, Luigi, 63, 72, 382.
*Punch*, 153.
Pye, Henry James, 5.

Quarles, Francis, 286.
*Quarterly Review, The*, 7, 8, 11, **12–16**, 17–18, 26–28, 36–37, 40–41, 43, 53, 55, 57, 65, 92, 216, 269, 317, 331–5, 336, 356 n., 366, 382, 401, 403–4, 426, 437.

Racine, 396.
Radcliffe, Ann, 112 n., 205–6, 213, 255, 257, 266.
Railway Age, The, 434–5.
Raleigh, Sir Walter, 301.
*Rasselas*, 94, 246–7.
'Reading Public, The', 43–45, 426–31.
*Reflector, The*, 287, 320–1, 323.
*Rehearsal, The*, 59.
Rembrandt, 208, 360.
*Retrospective Review, The*, 43–44, **399–401**.
Reviews, 8–17, 36–38, 397, 399, 426–7, 429 (*and see* under the names of particular Reviews).
Reynolds, John Hamilton, 21, 105 n., 123, 127, 130, **148*–51**, 383.
Ricardo, David, 354 n., 425.
Richard Coeur-de-Lion, 219.
Richardson, Samuel, 243, 265, 266, 318, 339, 404.
Richter, J. P. F. (Jean Paul), 393.
Rippingille, E. V., 133.
Ritson, Joseph, 219, 398, 402.
Robinson, Henry Crabb, 45, 46–47, 373, **388***.
Rogers, Samuel, 42, 51, 57, 148, 175, 263, 326, 411–12.
'Romantic' and 'Classical', 406–421.
Romilly, Sir Samuel, 425.
Ronsard, 396.
Roscoe, Thomas, 383.
Roscoe, William, 300.

Roscoes, the, 172 n.
Rose, William Stewart, 381–2.
Rossetti, Dante Gabriel, 172, 255.
Rousseau, 93, 144, 233, 252, 274, 278, 306, 334, 364, 396, 397.
Rowlandson, Thomas, 173 n., 243.
Rowley, William, 267.
Roxburghe Club, 403–4.
Royal Institution, The, 45–46.
Rundell, Mrs., 35.
Ruskin, John, 340.
Russell, Bertrand, 76.
Russell Institution, The, 46.
Russell, Lord John, 165 n., 374.
Rymer, Thomas, 333, 400.

Sacchetti, 383.
Sadleir, Michael, 30–31.
Salvator Rosa, 181, 371.
Sand, George, 334.
Saunders and Otley, 34.
Savage, Arnold, 344.
Schelling, F. W. J. von, 388, 393, 395.
Schiller, J. F. von, 385, 388, 390–1, 392, 393, 395, 407.
Schlegel, A. W., 61, 263, 287, 303, 376, 380, 386–7, 395, 396, 406–7.
Schlegel, F., 263, 376, 387.
Schwartzburg, 393.
Scott, John, 21–23, 260, 411.
Scott, Sir Walter, 2, 3, 5, 6, 8–16 (and *Edinburgh* and *Quarterly Reviews*), 26, 27, 31–37 (earnings), 40–43 (sales), 51, 56, 57, 58, 63 n., 156, 166, 168 and n., 175–7, 181–2, **185*–213**, 215, 219, 225, 226, 231, 235, 236 n., 238, 239, 241 n., 254–5, 257, 258, 263, 266, 269, 317, 323, 325 n., 326, 332, 334, 337, 351, 356–61, 364, 368, 373, 381, 384, 387, 388–90 (and German), 394, 395–6, 398, 399, 402, 403–4, 411–12, 418, 429, 435, 437.
Sedgwick, Adam, 48.
Severn, Joseph, 91, 105 n.
Sévigné, Mme de, 339.
Shaftesbury, Anthony Ashley Cooper, 3rd Earl of, 339.
Shakespeare, William, 45, 47, 61, 62, 71, 76, 87, 92, 106, 114, 119–20, 125, 128, 140, 142, 172, 179, 180, 198, 199, 203, 254, 262, 264–5, 267, 285, 290, 299, 301, 319, 348, 366, 371, 372, 407, 413, 415, 419.
*Shamela*, 275.
Sheil, Richard Lalor, **180–1***, 257, 267.
Shelley, Hellen, 96.
Shelley, Mary, 77 and n., 80–81, 85–86, 88, 93–94, 96, 98, 104, 153, **243*–5**, 369–70.
Shelley, Percy Bysshe, 7, 20, 22, 31, 36, 42–43, 49 n., 55–57 (and Byron), 63, 70, **77*–104**, 105–6, 108, 118, 121, 123, 139, 140, 146, 148 n., 151, 154, 159, 160, 162, 172, 175, 214 and n., 215, 217, 223, 243–5, 278, 286, 301, 319 n., 320, 321, 326, 334, 363, 364, 366–70 (accounts of), 373, 376, 378–81 (and Italian), 384–5, 390–1, 406, 409–19 (and the 'Romantic Movement'), 428, 436–7.
Shenstone, William, 133.
Sheridan, Richard Brinsley, 40, 218.
Shirley, James, 181, 401.
Siddons, Mrs. 182.
Sidney, Sir Philip, 2, 267, 270, 400.
'Silver Fork Novelists', 247–52.
Singer, Samuel Weller, 365.
Sismondi, 61, 380.
Smith, Adam, 325.
Smith and Elder, 173.
Smith, Charlotte, 282.
Smith, David Nichol, 325.
Smith, Horace and James, 24, 34, 40, 90, **176*** (verse), **254–5** (novels).
Smith, Sydney, 9–10, **329*–31**, 335.
Smollett, Tobias, 152, 202, 225, 266, 434.
Society for the Diffusion of Useful Knowledge, The, 431–3.
Somerville, Alexander, 365.
Sophocles, 86.
Sotheby, William, 45.
Southern, Henry, 43–44, 399.
Southey, Robert, 5, 6, 9, 14–16 (and *Quarterly*), 27, 29, 31–33 (earnings), 36–37 (earnings), 41, 51, 58, 65, 70–75 (and Byron), 77 and n., 139 n., 172 n., 175, 215–16, 241 n., 261, 264, 268, 279, 282, 283, 284, 291, 292 n., 326, 327, 344, 346, 352, 381, 387 n., 397, 398, 402, 411–12, 437.
Southwell, Robert, 400.
Spanish literature, 397–9.
*Spectator, The*, 265, 271, 322.
Speculative Society, 390.
Spence, Joseph, 365, 404.
Spenser, Edmund, 54, 71, 91, 106, 107, 111, 120, 128, 177, 199, 263, 270, 320, 375.
Spinoza, 105.
Squeamishness, verbal, 435–6.
Staël, Mme de, 29, 58, 101, 386, 390, 394, 406–7.
Stanley, Lord (Derby), 14.
Starke, Mrs. Mariana, 27 n.
Steele, Sir Richard, 271, 290.
Stendhal (Henri Beyle), 383, 396.
Stephan, John, of Calcar, 392.
Stephen, Sir Leslie, 304.
Sterne, Laurence, 66, 266, 290–1.
Stewart, Dugald, 34, 388 n.
Stewart, John, 298.
Stubbes, Philip, 400.

Super, R. H., 345.
Surrey Institution, The, 47.
Sussex, Duke of, 372.
Swift, Jonathan, 67, 137, 155, 241, 263, 301–2, 313, 334, 404, 408.
Swinburne, Algernon Charles, 172, 284, 369.
Symmons, Charles, 377.
Symons, Arthur, 419.

Talfourd, Thomas Noon, 24, 46–47, 340, 400.
Tasso, 125, 345, 371, 381.
Tassoni, 152.
*Tatler, The*, 265, 271.
Taylor, Sir Henry, 422.
Taylor and Hessey, 22, **30**, 40, 130 n., 131, 151 n., 379.
Taylor, Jeremy, 270, 301, 401.
Taylor, John, 114, 136, 137, 422.
Taylor, William, of Norwich, **387*–8.**
Tennyson, Alfred Lord, 42, 76, 92, 145, 323, 351, 411, 423, 437.
Thackeray, William Makepeace, 250 n., 255, 369.
Thelwall, John, 262.
Thompson, Benjamin, 385.
Thomson, Christopher, 431.
Thomson, James, 120, 130 n., 131, 134, 161, 263.
Thorkelin, G. J., 399.
Thornton, Bonnell, 322.
Ticknor, George, 27.
Tieck, J. L., 152, 387, 392, 394.
Tillotson, Geoffrey, 207.
*Times, The*, 41, 153, 388 n., 436.
Titian, 371, 377, 378.
Tompkins, Miss J. M. S., 225.
Tooke, Horne, 74, 262.
Torrijos, 398.
Tree, Ellen, 183.
Trelawny, Edward John, 77 n., 214 n., 222 n., 243 n., 345, 363, **369–70**, 372, 411.
Trench, Richard Chenevix, 398.
Tressan, 395.
Trollope, Mrs Frances, 34, 184.
Trotter, J. B., 346.
Turner, J. M. W., 134.
Tytler, Alexander Fraser, 381.
Tytler, Patrick Fraser, 354.

Utilitarians, The, 232, 252, 423–8.

Vanbrugh, Sir John, 265.
Vaughan, Henry, 400.
Vaux, J. H., 69.
Victoria, Queen, 172 n., 296, 352, 437.
Villon, 396.
Virgil, 371, 375, 376–7, 381.
Viviani, Emilia, 86–89, 103.
Volney, Constantin, Comte de, 94, 104, 244, 397.
Voltaire, 20, 78, 322, 339, 371.

Wainewright, Thomas Griffiths, 152.
*Wakefield, The Vicar of*, 227.
Walker, William Sidney, 627.
Wallace, Robert, 400.
Walpole, Horace, 280–1, 339, 404.
Walton, Izaac, 285–6.
Ward, Humphry, 27.
Ward, Robert Plumer, 225 **252*–4.**
Warton, Thomas (the younger), 270.
Washington, George, 71, 74, 346.
Wasserman, Earl, 114.
Waterloo, 1, 48, 215, 261, 308, 314, 346, 384.
Watt, Robert, 404.
Watts, Alaric Alexander, 173–4.
Way, Mr., 435.
Webb, Sidney and Beatrice, 316.
Weber, Henry William, 401.
Webster, John, 98, 140, 143, 240, 401.
Wellek, René, 407.
Wellington, Duke of, 1, 14.
Wells, Charles Jeremiah, **171*–2,** 177.
*Werther, The Sorrows of*, 244, 386, 391.
Wesley, John, 71.
Westbrook, Harriet, 77 n., 214 n., 243 n., 245, 363.
*Westminster Review, The*, **16–17,** 354 n., 381, 399, 424–8.
*Westmorland Gazette, The*, 292 and n.
*Whistlecraft*, 382.
White, Joseph Blanco, 397.
White, Newman Ivey, 89.
Whittingham, C., 401.
Wieland, C. M., 385, 388, 391, 392.
Wiffen, Jeremiah Holmes, 381, 398.
Wilkes, John, 71, 74.
Wilkie, David, 208.
William IV, 226 n., 232, 332 n.
Willich, A. F. M., 384, 394.
Wilson, John (biographer of Defoe), 405.
Wilson, John ('Christopher North'), 17–19, 29, 235, **335*–8.**
Windham, William, 313.
Wither, George, 283, 286, 401.
Wolcot, John ('Peter Pindar'), 25.
Wolfe, James, 71.
Wollstonecraft, Mary, 96, 243 n.
Woodhouse, Richard, 123.
Wordsworth, William, 2–6 (reputation), 12, 19, 22, 31, 36, 42, 51–52 (and Byron), 55–57 (and Byron), 68, 123, 125–6, 137, 148–9, 154, 157–8, 168 n. 170, 172–7, 207, 211, 216, 241 n.,

260 n., 261, 263–4, 270–1, 274, 278–80 (and Lamb), 285, 292 and n., 297–303 (and De Quincey), 306–7 (and De Quincey), 323, 325–30, 332, 335–7, 345, 347, 358, 363, 370 n., 371–3, 376, 380, 384, 386, 388, 400, 410–19 (his views on contemporary poets, and theirs on him), 421, 428, 437.
Wrangham, Francis, 377, 630–1.
Wyatt, Sir Thomas, 166.
Wycherley, William, 265.

Yeats, William Butler, 81, 89, 144.
Young, Thomas, 11.

'Z', in *Blackwood's*, 19.
Zimmerman(n), Johann Georg, 95, 252, 385.
'Zimri', 221.

DATE DUE

| | | | |
|---|---|---|---|
| | | | |
| | | | |
| | | | |
| | | | |
| | | | |
| | | | |
| | | | |
| | | | |
| | | | |
| | | | |
| | | | |
| | | | |
| | | | |
| | | | |
| | | | |
| | | | |

# About the Author

David Sosnowski has worked as a gag writer, fireworks salesman, telephone pollster, university writing instructor, and environmental protection specialist, while living in cities as varied as Washington, DC; Detroit, Michigan; and Fairbanks, Alaska. He is the author of three previous critically acclaimed novels, *Rapture*, *Vamped*, and, most recently, *Happy Doomsday*. For more about David, visit www.wingznfangz.com.

*How Life and Consciousness Are the Keys to Understanding the True Nature of the Universe*; Sebastian Seung for *Connectome: How the Brain's Wiring Makes Us Who We Are*; and Daniel C. Dennett for *From Bacteria to Bach and Back: The Evolution of Minds*. Reading each and every one of you was what can only be described as a consciousness-expanding experience, no drugs required.

early readers, Josie Kearns, Laura Voss Berry, and, in memoriam, the late Mark Schemanske, who was with me in spirit. For good old-fashioned moral support (and the occasional free meal) I'd like to thank my sisters and brother, Sue Dudek, Kathy Rodriguez, and Mike Sosnowski. And for their understanding of my unsavory writing habit (as well as their support for my decision to retire from among their ranks to pursue said habit more seriously), I'd like to thank my former coworkers at the United States Environmental Protection Agency. Who would have thought that working to protect the health of our fellow Americans would be such a thankless job, one which has become increasingly difficult for reasons beyond your control and, often, beyond reason or understanding? For the work you do every day on behalf of the planet—selflessly, thanklessly, and with perennial good humor and grace—I thank you all.

Last but not least, I want to thank all the helpers who didn't know they were helping by supplying me with inspiration and information as I researched the many different subjects dealt with in these pages, from World War II to computer hacking, from the basics of machine learning and neural nets to the physiology of dementia, hallucinations, and the philosophy of consciousness. For their wonderful and insightful works in these areas, I thank the following: Liza Mundy for *Code Girls: The Untold Story of the American Women Code Breakers of World War II*; Jon Erickson for *Hacking: The Art of Exploitation*; Mark Bowden for *Worm: The First Digital World War*; Bruce Schneier for *Click Here to Kill Everybody: Security and Survival in a Hyper-Connected World*; David Shenk for *The Forgetting: Alzheimer's: Portrait of an Epidemic*; Nicholas Carr for *The Shallows: What the Internet Is Doing to Our Brains*; James Barrat for *Our Final Invention: Artificial Intelligence and the End of the Human Era*; Lauren Slater for *Blue Dreams: The Science and the Story of the Drugs That Changed Our Minds*; Julian Jaynes for *The Origin of Consciousness in the Breakdown of the Bicameral Mind*; Robert Lanza (with Bob Berman) for *Biocentrism:*